Dedicated to my wife, Bettie Anne, in appreciation of her forbearance with a husband who spends most of his days behind a typewriter, wreathed in clouds of blue pipe smoke.

CONTENTS

PREFACE

The serious study of popular culture is a fairly recent phenomena; and while popular literature has long been considered second class, new insight into such, particularly escape literature, has provided additional sociological information about the people, their attitudes, and morals. Proper understanding of each generation and the problems and situations faced can best be mirrored through their contemporary reading pleasures. Magazines have played an important role in reflecting the immediate concerns, the economic problems, and life in general of the common man. Yet, the very class of literature which best portrays this has long been neglected by scholarly studies. Popular escape literature has been delegated as less than desirable and has been criticized and condemned. Mystery, detective, and espionage fiction have consistently provided a large share of the reading matter pursued by the masses. The major part of this has been through magazines, an affordable medium widely distributed worldwide. Depite this, there have been no comprehensive studies made of this type of magazine, and this work is an attempt to provide at least a beginning. There can be no claim made for completeness, although coverage of magazines published in the United States, England, and Canada is fairly complete. Magazines included here are of both the professional and amateur categories, and nonfiction magazines providing commentary, as well as magazines providing fiction are included.

In addition to those magazines consisting entirely of mystery, detective, and espionage fiction, some magazines that overlap into the fantasy, horror, and supernatural fields have been included, since there is sometimes only a thin distinction when categorizing stories with inexplicable elements. Magazines primarily oriented to the weird, horror, fantasy, and the supernatural have been included if some of the fiction can be defined as being in the crime category, however improbable it may be, or if they contain fiction by well-known mystery fiction authors. There has been no attempt to include all magazines of such orientation, since most do not qualify even under this broad concept, and they will be included in another volume in Greenwood Press's Historical Guides to the World's Periodicals and Newspapers.

General interest magazines and general short story magazines have been excluded, although they may have included some detective fiction. Many of the pulp-format short story magazines, such as *Argosy*, contained detective fiction, but not as the main thrust of these periodicals. Comic book publications devoted to mysteries have also been excluded. True crime magazines, many of which were hybrids relating true occurrences in highly fictionalized accounts, have not been included, although a checklist has been provided of both U.S. and Canadian true crime magazines in the appendixes. Titles of many of these magazines may be encountered in further reading, and the similarity to fiction magazine titles is likely to be confusing.

There are a host of magazines and newsletters published by Sherlock Holmes societies, but since the majority of these are available only to members of the scion group, these have been excluded. The Sherlock Holmes periodicals intended for general public circulation have, however, been included. A listing of the limited circulation magazines will be found in the appendix for reference.

Whereas fan and semiprofessional magazines have long been a staple of the science-fiction and fantasy field, the number devoted to the mystery genre has been relatively sparse. There is, however, in these a wealth of valuable information, including bibliographies and checklists, reviews and critical commentary, author biographies, and announcements of forthcoming books. Such magazines have been included. These entertaining periodicals are primarily nonfiction, but certain titles have included fiction on occasion. The few professionally published magazines covering this facet of the genre, as well as the more scholarly magazines, have also been included.

A broad view of the field must also consider the many series of boys' and girls' books (that is, The Hardy Boys series, the Nancy Drew series, for example) published primarily in the first half of the twentieth century. Accordingly, periodicals relating to the reading and collecting of these books have been included. A large percentage of these books were detective adventures, albeit on a juvenile level.

The principal portion of this work consists of individual profile studies of each magazine. Here the magazine is discussed in detail, providing background information, the circumstances of inception and cessation, and, in general, a narrative history of the magazine. For those magazines centering attention upon a particular hero detective or crime-fighter, the profile highlights the activities of the hero as related in the stories published. Each entry has a section giving pertinent bibliographical material for further research, location of files of the magazine in public institutions, when known, and sources of published indexes. A publication history section for each entry provides information as to title changes, commencement and termination dates, volume and issue data, number issued, editors and publishers information, price per issue, size, and whether currently published.

Magazines are treated alphabetically, with all change-of-titles included; profiles mentioning other magazines that are individually treated are cross-referenced with an asterisk following the first mention of such referenced titles.

The narrative profile section includes a comprehensive treatment of magazines published in the United States, Great Britain, and Canada. Immediately following this is a section on representative foreign magazines, with a general summary, checklist, and specific profiles.

A section on mystery book clubs of the U.S. and Britain provides a brief history of each club.

For those who are primarily interested in a specific type of magazine, there is a listing of magazines by category. There is also in the appendix a listing of the more important writers who commenced their careers with the pulp magazines, along with a list of the magazines in which their work is to be found.

A chronological listing of the commencement date of each magazine is included in the appendix, as well as a discussion and short description of other periodicals of interest to collectors.

Further reading may be gleaned from a selected bibliography.

There is a surprising lack of published material on the magazines and publishers of this type of popular literature. With but few exceptions, libraries lack collections although an increasing number of people have become interested in mystery and other escape literature. *The Union List of Serials* reveals almost a total lack of these magazines reported in library depositories.

In the United States, interest in mystery magazines, particularly in the pulp format, has remained strong among collectors, but in England there are few. The collecting of dime novels is eagerly pursued by a small group of collectors, hampered by the ever decreasing supply.

The amateur press has provided some information but it is usually confined to a specialized topic or magazine. Perhaps the bulk of knowledge of many of these periodicals is known only to a few scholars, students, and collectors, and this storehouse is rapidly diminishing as they pass from the scene.

Note should be made of the larger collections available for study among various libraries and universities. Any attempt to use these facilities should be preceded by an inquiry to determine the availability and rules for use. Most of the older magazines are on paper that has deteriorated, and thus research is strictly controlled.

Cleveland Public Library, Popular Library Department, Cleveland, Ohio (dime novels).
Harvard University Libraries, Cambridge, Massachusetts (pulp magazines).
Huntington Library, San Marino, California (dime novels).
Library of Congress, Washington, D.C. (dime novels, some pulp magazines).
New York Public Library, New York, New York (dime novels, some pulp magazines).
New York University Library, New York, New York (dime novels).
Northern Illinois University, Swen Franklin Parson Library (Johannsen collection of dime novels).
Oberlin College Library, Oberlin, Ohio (dime novels).

San Francisco Academy of Comic Art, San Francisco, California (perhaps largest overall collection of pulp magazines, dime novels, and related material).

San Francisco Public Library, Literature Department, San Francisco, California (pulp magazines).

State Historical Society Library, Madison, Wisconsin (pulp magazines).

University of Arkansas, Little Rock, Arkansas (Gerald J. McIntosh dime novel collection).

University of California Los Angeles, Los Angeles, California (large pulp magazine collection).

University of Minnesota, Minneapolis, Minnesota (George H. Hess dime novel colection).

University of Oregon, Eugene, Oregon (pulp magazines).

University of Wyoming, Laramie, Wyoming (Michael L. Cook Collection).

Yale University Libraries, New Haven, Connecticut (dime novels).

The intent of this work has been to gather together as much information as possible and to make it available in one source. It is hoped that this encyclopedia of mystery, detective, and espionage magazines will be of interest and assistance to both the layman, who reads for pleasure, and the serious scholar, in doing further research, as well as for collectors of this type of popular fiction, and that the nostalgic value will be of benefit to all.

ACKNOWLEDGMENTS

The author is most grateful to the distinguished roster of scholar-contributors whose work has been indispensable in the preparation of this book. Special thanks are due Robert Sampson, Will Murray, J. Randolph Cox, and Joseph Lewandowski for the excessive amount of time and interest given. Walter Albert is due special attention for translating French material. And special appreciation is expressed to Bob Adey, Iwan Hedman, Bjarne Nielsen, Graeme K. Flanagan, Nils Nordberg, and François Guerif for the wealth of information and assistance rendered.

Thanks and appreciation are also due the following for their interest, cooperation and assistance in various ways:

MIKE ASHLEY, Chatham, Kent, England.
W. RITCHIE BENEDICT, Calgary, Alberta, Canada.
MARIAN BABSON, Secretary, Crime Writers Association, London, England.
BILL BLACKBEARD, San Francisco Academy of Comic Art, San Francisco, California.
HILDA BOEHM, Librarian, University of California–Los Angeles, Los Angeles, California.
RICHARD E. CLEAR, The Dragon's Lair, Inc., Dayton, Ohio.
CAROLYN A. DAVIS, Manuscripts Librarian, The George Arents Research Library, Syracuse University, Syracuse, New York.
DEIDRE JOHNSON, University of Minnesota, Minneapolis, Minnesota.
WALKER MARTIN, Trenton, New Jersey.
HARALD MOGENSEN, Copenhagen, Denmark.
JOHN NIEMINSKI, Park Forest, Illinois.
BILL PRONZINI, San Francisco, California.
DANIEL RICHE, Paris, France.
LESTER ROBBINS, Tulsa, Oklahoma.
HENRY STEEGER, New York, New York

SYMBOLS AND TERMINOLOGY

An asterisk (*) is used to provide cross-references when an entry mentions a magazine that is discussed in another entry.

"Bimonthly" is used to indicate every other month; "biweekly" refers to every other week (or in some cases, twice a month).

INTRODUCTION

There was no need to read through several pages of description and background before coming to the action in the story. It started off with a bang (and sometimes two or three bangs, with the "bad guys" having the best of it); the interest never lagged until the final paragraph was reached. That the story was sensational cannot be disputed, and whether the writing lacked polish cannot be argued. Probably this was one of the reasons why dime novels appealed to so many—they were easily understood and followed; and, despite criticism, the stories always pointed to a moral. Right triumphed in the end. The wicked were punished. Virtue was rewarded. It is sometimes difficult to understand why there was so much objection from parents and educators since the dime novel stories were always models of decency, the criminal was always caught and punished, and the heroines were always perfect ladies.

Popular literature has seldom been the concern of the scholarly critic until it has long passed. Even today, the enjoyment obtained by millions in eagerly devouring the dime novels, pulps, and other popular literature is dismissed as inconsequential to formal historical studies of early literature. The "new" American literature, however, did present a drastic change. Commencing with the War of 1812, a few American authors dared to break with tradition and produce easily readable fiction. James Fenimore Cooper, with his bold, imaginative stories of the frontiersmen and Indians, set the stage for the future. Edgar Allan Poe, a displaced Southerner, gave a new meaning to the short story. The pompous, long-winded European novels became second choice to thousands of readers, and the new action adventures added thousands more who had never read for pure entertainment. While many of the writers of the era were still seeing the American scene through an Englishman's or a Frenchman's eyes, a few innovators were introducing a new style that would soon inundate the prospective reader. The uncouth and inferior new frontiers were not proper settings for the many writers who ignored them, but those who believed otherwise were producing stories that had never before been available. And once the public had experienced a taste for this type of fiction, the demand exceeded the supply.

The grandfather of the popular literature magazine as we know it today was actually the weekly story-paper of the 1830s. Although keeping up the tradition of editorials, occasional letters from readers, and small paragraphs concerned with current topics, the emphasis was on stories. Crowded onto the pages with small type, there seemed to be an effort to determine which could present the most on a page. Short stories ("novels") usually shared the space with a serialized story. While there was soon an over-abundant supply of material, the earliest publications thought nothing of pirating stories from other papers, particularly those printed in England. Editorials soon ceased to be political, and a cardinal rule seemed to insure that the reading public would not be antagonized.

In recognition of this new market, the first crude story-paper appeared in 1839, the *Brother Jonathan Weekly*, a mammoth-sized (22" X 32") news and story paper, crudely produced but aimed at the new mass audience. With a U.S. population of nearly twenty million, most of whom were literate, the publication found ready acceptance. The need to produce at a low cost—vital to the demand— was satisfied with the introduction of the steam rotary press. The railroads provided the wide distribution necessary, and even the postmasters were authorized to accept subscriptions. Other papers quickly followed—for the most part consisting of several short stories, chapters from serialized novels, and a few news items—in newspaper format. Although the very small, indistinct type would render them almost unreadable by today's standards, the story-papers filled a need and were an immediate success.

Competition was intense, and when on June 9, 1860, there appeared what is generally considered as the first "dime novel," the publishers little knew of the impact this would have on the industry. Ann S. Stephens, unknown today but one of the best-known writers of the period, penned *Maleska: The Indian Wife of the White Hunter*, published under the imprint of Irwin P. Beadle & Company in one booklet, complete, 128 pages, advertised as a "dollar book for a dime." It immediately became a best seller, and within a few months more than 65,000 copies had been sold. The stirring action, albeit often padded prose, all in one "book" for a dime, immediately attracted other publishers (as well as many would-be authors), and the flood of dime novels was upon the public in a seemingly never-to-end parade. Stories of pirates, detectives, soldiers, highwaymen, outlaws, bootblacks, and villains galore! The acceptance was phenomenal. By April 1864, Beadle's Dime Books alone had sold more than five million copies.

The name "Beadle" today is recognized as synonymous with "dime novel" and perhaps rightfully so. The firm commenced in 1851 as Beadle & Vanduzee, of Buffalo, New York, owned by Erastus F. Beadle and Benjamin C. Vanduzee. Irwin Beadle entered the firm two years later when Vanduzee dropped out, with the name being changed to Beadle & Brother. By 1856, Irwin was no longer a firm member, the partnerhsip interest being shared between Erastus F. Beadle and Robert Adams. The Beadle brothers were still associated, though, by sharing the same address, and in 1859 magazines were appearing under both imprints, Beadle & Adams, and Irwin P. Beadle. Irwin, in 1862, severed the relationship unamicably and formed a partnership with George Munro, publishing as Irwin P. Beadle & Co. With but several minor name changes, Beadle & Adams continued in operation until 1898, when assets were purchased by the M. J. Ivers & Company, and it was this successor that supposedly fed the old records of Beadle & Adams into the furnace to heat its warehouse. By 1898, the "Adams" referred to the two surviving brothers of Robert Adams, William and David.

The Beadles were responsible for well over three thousand novels, many reprinted a number of times, of adventure, western history, romance, detectives, Indians, pioneers, backwoodsmen, and pirates. Many were intended for adult consumption; others were aimed at the juvenile market. Survival depended on outwitting the rivals by starting new series, changing the name of the author and title, and reprinting favorites as often as the traffic would bear.

George Munro was in partnership with Irwin P. Beadle but became sole owner of that firm in 1864, changing the name to The George Munro & Co. They were responsible for more than three hundred ten-cent novels and well over three thousand other editions. Publishing dime novels, cheap story-papers, and inexpensive reprints of foreign novels, the output included the *Old Sleuth Library** series, which had many imitators. In 1888, Munro sued Beadle & Adams, asking that the court prohibit that firm from using the word *sleuth* in their titles, and this was done in 1890.

A similar firm was commenced in 1873 by Norman L. Munro and Frank Tousey, becoming known in the detective field particularly for the *Old Cap. Collier Library.**

One of the best-known early publishers, Street & Smith, commenced in 1855 and was active as late as 1960 with a gamut of publications ranging form dime novels, paperbound books, and magazines to even clothbound books. Horatio Alger, Jr., Theodore Dreiser, Gilbert Patten (Burt L. Standish), Ned Buntline (Edward Judson), Upton Sinclair, and Edward Stratemeyer were published here with their earliest works. The firm was formed by two newspapermen, Francis Scott Street and Francis Shubael Smith, while both were working for *The Sunday Dispatch*. Taking over the publication of that weekly newspaper was the first task of the new firm. Street died in 1883, and Smith's son, Ormond, purchased that share of the business. The same year, Ormond's brother, Gerald, joined the firm, and the two were actually responsible for the imaginative approach and varied types of publications that made Street & Smith known worldwide. Street & Smith are known for the Nick Carter periodicals, *Old Broadbrim Weekly*,* and a host of other dime novel series, as well as many of the early pulp detective magazines; *Detective Story Magazine* (Street & Smith),* changing to digest format, was publisehd as late as 1948.

Another of the principal publishers of the inexpensive popular literature during the latter part of the last century was Frank A. Tousey. Tousey, a partner of Norman L. Munro from 1873 to 1876, and with George G. Small from 1876 to 1879, founded Frank A. Tousey & Company in 1879. While especially remembered for his boys' story-papers and reprint series, he was also responsible for the *New York Detective Library,** *Secret Service: Old and Young King Brady, Detectives,** and the *Young Sleuth Library** weeklies, as well as for a number of later detective pulp magazines.

Many other publishers were active during this pioneer period of popular literature, publishing detective stories as a part of their attempt to meet the ever increasing demand. But the number of pure detective periodicals could in no way compare with the flood of stories about highwaymen and robbers, western fiction, and particularly Jesse James and Buffalo Bill.

A true-crime mystery, detailed in 1883 as "The Beautiful Victim of the Elm City Tragedy," furnished the starting point for detective dime novels, and its first paragraph was designed to attract immediately the attention and interest of the reader:

> New Haven, the beautiful City of Elms, was startled from its propriety and awakened to a sense of horror by a terrible announcement at half-past five o'clock on the morning of August 6th, 1881. Jennie E. Cramer, a comely young girl, was discovered in the water, face downward, DEAD![1]

This story introduced Old Cap. Collier, who was to become one of the most well-known detective characters in the mass of detective fiction that followed. Appearing first as a series character, his name was later used in over seven hundred full-length novels published in the dime-novel form, written by various authors who described his adventures in every imaginable scene and locale. The name of the hero was used as a pseudonym by the authors, the first identifiable being W. I. James, and this name itself may have been a house name for a group of writers.

The Old Cap. Collier stories were produced in a larger format (about 6″ × 10″) with a colored-paper cover, no interior illustrations, and were almost staid in appearance. Action, however, dominated the contents with fist-fights, knife and bludgeon attacks, explosives, poisonings, steel traps, and even several instances of being buried alive. The detective employed frequent disguises and was always a "shrewd thinker." Persons of other nationalities were exemplified with accented speech and mannerisms.

Other detective heroes were quickly summoned into existence, many by authors who made no fundamental changes in the type of story they had been writing but substituting a detective for some other hero. Here the detective continued to rescue heroines from abductors, violently subduing the bad guys, and often discovering that the victim was the long-lost daughter of the wicked landlord. There were no complicated plots or solutions. Emphasis was more on snatching the weapon from the villain than tracing clues, and when a clue was found, an explanation was given at length. Fast-moving stories were the rule rather than puzzles.

The popularity of one detective, the Old Sleuth, and his assistant, Badger, quickly developed into stories in which Badger himself was the principal character, and then his son, Young Badger, as well as Young Sleuth. These characters were appropriated by other authors, which resulted in lengthy court suits. City-life stories began to dominate, with the detective perfectly adapted to the bewildering ways of the city.

Sexton Blake, the "office-boy's Sherlock Holmes," appeared on the British scene by at least 1893 and was supposedly based on the character created by Arthur Conan Doyle in 1887. Despite having few of the characteristics of Holmes, Blake, a distinguished Victorian gentleman with a high-crowned bowler and carrying a heavy walking-stick, in partnerhsip with a French detective, joined the ranks of those whose exploits and adventures were eagerly awaited. Heroes, villains, and sweet maidens filled the pages of his remarkable adventures. In later years, Blake became "hawklike," and "incisive" and acquired a landlady to look after him while he concentrated on defeating the long line of villains that marched endlessly through his stories.

Sexton Blake was only one of the first of a long line of British detectives who became a major literary industry in the 1890s. By 1900, the Aldine Company alone had more than 250 detective titles in its catalogue, some of which were imports from the United States. Here one could read of the Lightning Detective, The Bound Boy Detective, New York Nell, The Demon Detective, The Jew Detective, The Shadower, and others, both male and female. There were combinations of family members as detectives, and specialist detectives such as the Science Detective, the Actress Detective, the Hansom Cab Detective, and the Post Office Detective. The mortaility rate was high, some characters lasting for no more than one or two novels. Others enjoyed long runs and were found in magazines of more than one title and publisher.

For approximately sixty years, the dime novels represented the low-cost fiction that the public demanded; but competition arose in the attempt to give the reader more for his nickel or dime, and the pulp magazine was born. As early as 1888 the thick *Argosy* appeared, an outgrowth of the juvenile story-paper *The Golden Argosy*, and in 1903, the *Popular Magazine* was born. *Blue Book* commenced in 1904 under the title of *The Monthly Story Magazine* and then *All-Story* in 1905. These were followed in rapid succession by a host of others. The thirty-two page dime novel had passed into history.

During the twenties, thirties, and forties, millions of readers of all ages barricaded themselves behind bathroom doors with the latest hair-raising adventures in their favorite pulp magazines. Condemned by parents and educators, ignored by critics, and deplored by scholars, the pulps were but a continuation of the action tales which first found acceptance in the early story-papers and dime novels. There were, according to *Playboy Magazine,* "those likable lurid novels for which whole forests were leveled and upon which a whole generation of American youth was hair-raised."[2]

With the rise in prosperity following World War I, and the decline during the depression, and with the introduction of the radio, automobile, and movies, much of the reading public demanded the more active popular literature. Better means of transportation brought people into more immediate contact with a wide variety of situations to which the reader could relate. Authors and publishers were quick to respond to changes, and such changes were quickly translated into story and magazine titles. With the rise in popularity of cowboy movies, sports heroes, trains, and aviation, these were mirrored in pulp magazines that specialized in that type of story. With the advent of Prohibition, a new wave of pulps was presented with stories of the gangsters, gun molls, and the FBI. The private eye was born during this period, and the masked avenger had his heyday. At the close of World War I, there had been less than twenty-four different pulp magazine titles; this was changed rapidly with the hope of garnering the reader's dimes and was soon developed into hundreds of titles.

During the depression period, the life of a pulp magazine was exceptionally precarious. The profit margin on one issue could be as low as fifty dollars and on many was "in the red." A publisher would print one issue of a title, then wait to see how it was accepted before a second issue was prepared. If the title did not do well, it was promptly discarded, either changed to a different title or dropped completely, and a new attack was made. Additional titles were added on whatever ideas the publisher formulated but always following, or trying to follow, the trend. Unsold issues were often redistributed. There was little job security for editors and others associated with the production.

For writers, however, the pulps were the life-blood of their vocation. Many writers had handsome incomes, even during the depth of the depression yars, and could command as much as five cents a word for their work. With the hundreds of titles on the newsstands, new writers could break into print with less than polished prose, and the number of magazines demanding stories presented more opportunity than ever before or since.

The pulp magazines contained probably some of the best and much of the worst fiction ever written. Some of the best writers were attracted and became well known, Edgar Rice Burroughs, Dashiell Hammett, Edgar Wallace, Erle Stanley Gardner, John D. MacDonald, August Derleth, and H. P. Lovecraft, for example. It is probable that many of these found the pulps fun to write for, with little supervision as to the kind of story and the opportunity to write fast, violent, albeit puritanical, tales. Sex may have been implied but was never explicit—with what else was going on, sex was not needed. And the pulps offered, as a rule, some of the highest pay scales available. Although the covers of many portrayed well-endowed females, the cover art itself was remarkable.

Throughout this thirty-year period, the pulps were indeed an accurate barometer of the social trends, the worries and pleasures, and the economic situation. Plot and characterization were not as important as the puzzle itself in the mysteries. Hard-boiled characters and detectives appeared but were secondary to the mystery solution. This seemed to change with *The Black Mask** under the direction of Joseph Shaw in the mid-1920s, and story emphasis began to show more plot and character as a means of developing the puzzle situation. Conflict among the characters became dominant.

Frank Gruber, one of the pioneer pulp authors and editors, maintained that to write a salable mystery story there should be a colorful hero, a theme in addition to the murder plot, a supervillain or one with many assistants, a colorful background, an unusual murder method, a motive, a clue for the alert reader, a trick when the hero wins against seemingly impossible odds, fast pace and movement, a smashing climax, and hero involvement emotionally—as he explained in his book, *The Pulp Jungle.*

Perhaps the popularity of the pulp's hero is understood when each seemed to follow the elements Gruber described as necessary for a salable story. Each hero was a mighty avenger, fearlessly devoted to defeating a heinous villain. Each was unique, having his own special methods and *modus operandi*, powers, weapons, and comrades. Each became an immortal symbol to thrill the hearts of the reader and make the pulse beat faster. The Shadow, Doc Savage, The Avenger, The Spider, Operator 5, Secret Agent X, and even Tarzan are remembered and well known today, although their pulp adventures are in the distant past.

Millions of these untrimmed, rough, wood-pulp paper magazines with vividly colored covers poured onto the newsstands with fierce display competition and prospered until the Second World War. With paper in short supply, and a new sophistication being demanded by readers, many of the pulp publishers and magazines became wartime casualties. A few survived into the 1950s, but the competition from paperbound books, comic magazines, and later television had dealt the deathknell to the traditional pulp magazine. Several publishers changed to offering the same magazine with a trimmed edge, but this met only short-lived success. The slick-paper magazines completed the blow.

An actual outgrowth of the pulp magazine, however, has been the digest-sized magazine, and while few of these were continuations of the pulp titles, the publishers recognized the need to change to fiction that reflected the times and brought forth new titles by the score. Few of these were successful. Notable exceptions have been *Ellery Queen's Mystery Magazine,* Alfred Hitchcock's Mystery Magazine,* The Saint Detective Magazine* Mike Shayne Mystery Magazine,** and, in England, *London Mystery Selection,* Edgar Wallace Mystery Magazine,* Bloodhound Detective Story Magazine,** and *MacKill's Mystery Magazine.**

''Fanzines'' are a particular, little-known kind of publication, the name being derived from the word *fan* (an admirer or devotee), and from the last syllable of *magazine*. As such, the word is a descriptive term, a magazine by and for fans of a particular subject. And although the term is somewhat disliked by many, it has gradually become a recognized term for amateur magazines devoted to a certain subject.

While the earliest fan magazines were devoted to the fantasy and science fiction field, in 1930, it was not until more than thirty years later that they appeared in the mystery field. The number of mystery fanzines has remained relatively small in comparison, having spawned less than thirty titles if one does not include the myriad publications of the various Sherlock Holmes societies. Fanzines are noncommercial, nonprofessional, small-circulation magazines produced, published, and edited by one or a few persons. However, professionalism can certainly be found in these, and the fan magazine serves the valuable need of providing communication and contact between the amateur and professional fields. Writers in the fan magazines are surprisingly outspoken and critical, yet their views are presented in a logical fashion and can be accepted or rejected with the reader the wiser for the experience. Within the mystery and detective amateur magazines will be found articles and comments by many of the established writers, plus a host of amateur authors who have a very knowledgeable grasp of their topics. Research is intense and thorough. Letters of comments, when included, provide valuable insight. There is always a wealth of bibliographical data.

Fanzines, in general, have been overlooked. Academic and general readers do not know of them. The same is true of most libraries, and the Library of Congress subject listings have no category for fanzines at all. Perhaps as a whole fan magazines are unconventional. This cannot be said for those in the mystery and detective field, however, as these meet or approach academic standards in most cases, and many have attained sizable circulation. Fanzines have made for themselves a significant place in the study, development, and enjoyment of popular fiction and are a vital part of it.

NOTES

1. Edmund Pearson, *Dime Novels* (Boston: Little, Brown & Co., 1929); the crime was committed in 1881 and used as the basis for an account appearing in *Old Cap. Collier Library,* no. 1 (1883), in a very melodramatic version.

2. Charles Beaumont, ''The Bloody Pulps,'' *Playboy,* September 1962, p. 66.

THE MAGAZINES IN PROFILE

A

ACCUSED DETECTIVE STORY MAGAZINE

Accused Detective Story Magazine was an attractively packaged, short-run, digest-size magazine oriented to the detective and crime-adventure type of fiction that developed out of the pulp magazines in the 1950s. Behind red-tinted, black-and-white covers picturing threatening situations were to be found many of the same authors who had produced similar stories for the late pulp magazines, although there was a noticeable improvement in quality, contemporary and with crisper dialogue. There were also many new authors who would become well known.

The first issue, dated January 1956, included Richard S. Prather's "Trouble Shooter," Richard Deming's "Stationary Target," Stephen Marlowe's "Terrorists," and Robert Turner's "Night Talk," as well as crime adventures by Hal Ellson, Jack Webb, Gil Brewer, Richard Marsten, John Jakes, and William Logan. Two true-crime episodes were related in "The Ghosts That Wanted Company" by Tom Beach and "Vitelli's Wife" by Thomas Boyd.

The bimonthly magazine appeared regularly for four issues. The second issue, March 1956, presented a story by Frank Kane featuring Johnny Liddell, a tough private eye, in "Insurance." Liddell was already well known to mystery fans, having appeared in three full-length mystery novels by Kane (*Green Light for Death, Slay Ride,* and *Red Hot Ice*) that were particularly good, as well as others. Hal Ellson appeared with a realistic and brutal tale involving Harlem teenagers in "The Kids." Jack Webb (a different person from that on the television series "Dragnet") and "The Mad Mantini" added a chilling story in the longest piece, and Gil Brewer offered a surprising and shocking story in "Home." Among other contributors were Bryce Walton, Richard Marsten, Fletcher Flora, and Tedd Thomey, all of whom had been appearing in other magazines of the period.

In May 1956, Johnny Liddell was again featured, in "The Killing" from the pen of Frank Kane, and Hal Ellson brought another of his powerful tales of the New York streets and Harlem teenagers in a suspenseful "Big Trouble." A violent carnival vignette provided fast action and intense activity in John Jakes's "The Siren and the Shrill." Eight short stories completed the issue, along with a true-crime story and "Criminal Capers," a regular column listing short paragraphs of unusual or humorous crime news.

The last issue brought a surprise—a new story by B. Traven, whose novel, *Treasure of the Sierra Madre*, won him critical and popular acclaim both as a book and a hard-hitting movie. Traven, with a reputation as a "mystery man" somewhere in Mexico, refused to disclose his true identity, and the story, "His Wife's Legs," came from a Mexican "go-between." Another noteworthy story in this issue was Jonathan Craig's "A Lady of Talent," featuring detectives Steve Manning and Walt Logan, a realistic tale supposedly based on true-to-life stories from the New York police department. And a Clancy Ross novelette, "Optical Illusion" by Richard Deming, made this a particularly fine issue. Ross, a light-hearted, but very tough, gambling-house owner and incidental detective, was a believable though different kind of character in an unusual setting. Robert Turner, Stephen Marlowe, Bryce Walton, and Hal Ellson, among others, contributed short stories.

With tough, fast-moving, and colorful fiction, this magazine should have survived, but no further issues appeared.

Information Sources

INDEX SOURCES: Cook, Michael L. *Monthly Murders*. Westport, Conn.: Greenwood Press, 1982.
LOCATION SOURCES: Private collectors.

Publication History

MAGAZINE TITLE: *Accused Detective Story Magazine*.
TITLE CHANGES: None.
VOLUME AND ISSUE DATA: Vol. 1, no. 1 (January 1956) through Vol. 1, no. 4 (July 1956); 4 issues.
PUBLISHER: Theodore Simms as Atlantis Publishing Co., Inc., 1 West 47th Street, New York 36, New York.
EDITOR: Theodore Simms; managing editor, William R. Thompson.
PRICE PER ISSUE: 35 cents.
SIZE AND PAGINATION: 5-1/4" X 7-5/8"; 128 pages.
CURRENT STATUS: Discontinued.

ACE DETECTIVE

For *Ace Detective,* said the editor, "Woman interest is important and necessary."[1] And through the pages of this short-run magazine, the young beauties move—competent, tender-hearted, loving, and saving the bound hero as often as he saves them.

The life of a detective was harsh in this mid-1936 magazine. On all sides hulked crime masters with concealed identities, smirking gangsters, wholesale murder plots, torture, terror, and fear. The stories brim with menace. But the girls and their smitten men will slip through them all unhurt, although you wonder just how, the odds being what they are.

Each issue of *Ace Detective* contained roughly four novelettes and three short stories. The leads were law officers all—FBI agents, patrolmen, headquarters detectives. Their adventures were recorded by a rather small group of writers whose names appeared frequently on mastheads of the Magazine Publishers Group: Norman Daniels, James Perley Hughes, Frederick C. Painton, Dale Clark, occasionally Steve Fisher, and often Emile C. Tepperman and Frederick C. Davis.

Ace Detective seems to have been a continuation of *Gold Seal Detective*,* although the relationship has not been confirmed.[2] All six issues of *Gold Seal Detective* (December 1935 through May 1936) were identified as volume 1. The first issue of *Ace Detective* seems to have been June 1936, volume 2, number 1. About five issues were released, the last one noted being dated December 1936.

Notes

1. Harriet A. Bradfield, "Markets for Your Stories, Articles and Novels," *Writer's Digest* (August 1936), p. 20.
2. Ibid., p. 20. "*Ace Detective* is the new title at Magazine Publishers...and seems to succeed *Gold Seal Detective*."

Information Sources

BIBLIOGRAPHY:
Bradfield, Harriet A. "Markets for Your Stories, Articles and Novels." *Writer's Digest*, Vol. 16, no. 9 (August 1936): 20.
INDEX SOURCES: None known.
LOCATION SOURCES: University of California–Los Angeles Library; private collectors.

Publication History

MAGAZINE TITLE: *Ace Detective*.
TITLE CHANGES: None; may have been the continuation of *Gold Seal Detective*.
VOLUME AND ISSUE DATE: Vol. 2, no. 1 (June 1936) through Vol. 3, no. 1 (December 1936); first two issues monthly basis, thereafter bimonthly; 5 issues.
PUBLISHER: Magazine Publishers, Inc., 29 Worthington Street, Springfield, Massachusetts.
EDITOR: May Lou Butler.
PRICE PER ISSUE: 10 cents.
SIZE AND PAGINATION: 6-7/8" X 9-3/4"; 128 pages.
CURRENT STATUS: Discontinued.
—*Robert Sampson*

ACE G-MAN STORIES

The enormous outpouring of gangster films, plays, books, and magazines during the late 1920s through early 1930s subsided gradually. As gangsters faded out, a new fad materialized—this one featuring G-Men, the new darlings of films, books, radio, and magazines. True, these G-Men of the mass media acted almost like gangsters. Their collars were cleaner. But their machine guns flamed as brightly, and they performed their wonderful deeds in that social vacuum, lacking laws, responsibility, or common sense, which is our complex world as interpreted by 1930s films and magazines.

About a year after moving pictures went G-Man mad, the pulp magazines seized on the trend. In 1935, *G-Men (G-Men Detective*)* was published, and by 1936 similar titles came pouring forth: *The Feds,* Federal Agent (Public Enemy*),* and *Ace G-Man Stories.*

Ace G-Man Stories was published by Popular Publications, not by Wyn's Magazine Publishers. The two publishers had some difficulty about the title, for Magazine Publishers put out a line of magazines called the "Ace Fiction Group," using the word *Ace* in titles such as *Ace Sports Monthly, Ace Detectives,** and *Ace Mystery.** Eventually the problem was settled, and *Ace G-Man Stories* was free to pursue its peculiar destiny.

The magazine was first offered for sale on March 25, 1936, the initial issue being dated May–June 1936. It would be a bimonthly (with one monthly issue in 1940) for all of its forty-one issues; there would be, in addition, a later Canadian series of at least twenty-one issues.

According to its editorial requirements, stories were desired with actual G-Man backgrounds—accurate descriptions of training, with solid accounts of how Hoover's boys investigated, used lab equipment, and penetrated complex criminal riddles. What the magazine published was far different. It featured the usual blood-soaked, pulp action-adventure, the lone hero's flaming guns against the deadly fiends.

> To crack a Federal bank robbery, solve a baffling murder mystery—and save his fiancée from a blood-hungry killer clique—Special Agent Walt Clark accepted a bid to an exclusive club for which the initiation fee was——certain death![1]

> G-Man Jaynes shot it out with the crime master of an entire continent.[2]

> It was a dead man's date which Special Agent Muldoon kept—to save from death a girl who was not afraid to denounce a savage gang of high-salaried corpse-makers.[3]

Occasional reference to FBI training leaked into a few stories. Often J. Edgar Hoover appeared, although not mentioned by name. It was always The Chief or The Director, described as a hard-bitten, cold-eyed man, but with great capacity for human warmth. From the stories you learn that The Chief ran the entire FBI from the top of his desk, unaided by the complex administrative organization required by the real world. In his single-handed struggle against gigantic crime, The Chief relied on numerous unorthodox agents. Very unorthodox, secret fellows!

There was, for example, The Ghost (a series written by Wyatt Blassingame). The Ghost was an ex-magician named Brian O'Reilly. After he killed a man during a counterespionage job, he is officially wanted for murder by the FBI— except that official records also show that he is dead. As The Ghost, a tall, lean, sleight-of-hand artist with a quick gun, he handled public enemies otherwise too well entrenched to touch. Apparently he received secret help from The Chief.

G-X, The Phantom Fed, was another remarkable agent, in a series by Harry Lee Fellinge. G-X, a disguise master, bummed around the country sniffing out trouble. You saw his symbol everywhere, a circle pierced by an arrow, with the letters "GX" beneath. This brought fear to the crime masters.

The Suicide Squad (Kerrigan, Murdoch, and Klaw) appeared from 1939 to 1943 in a series by Emile C. Tepperman. They were three feisty, slangy, aggressive, murderous agents who received assignments that could only lead to their immediate death. They accepted these jobs gladly, thirsting for excitement. The stories are savage, filled with battle, murder, fist fights, death, and traps, concluding in glorious terminal battles that left the streets waist-deep in corpses. What seem to be earlier versions of the Suicide Squad stories appear in 1937 issues of the magazine, the writer identified as "W. Wirt." It is probable this was a pseudonym for Tepperman.

In the 1940s, there was The Voice (by Edward S. Williams). This was a former G-Man pretending to be totally paralyzed so that he could sprint secretly around the country, fighting foreign agents, then revealing their black plots over the radio for all the world to hear.

These specialized G-Men began appearing about 1939, prior to which there was a multitude of stories with single-appearance agents. These battered away at crime, using tactics that would have shut off funding to the Bureau in real life. More than half the heroes bore Irish names; perhaps one in four was red-haired. Most of them found their lives were made complex by the appearance of a delicious girl (often as deadly as the hero, himself), who either required saving or was framed or blackmailed into helping the foul criminals. It was high, bright, violent fun. Guns flamed and bodies flopped and it was action all the way—unsubtle, crude stuff that never slowed and never, even accidentally, reflected the real world existing beyond pulp-paper pages.

Ace G-Man Stories customarily featured a novel, three novelettes, and two short stories (or, more accurately, a long story and five brief to medium short stories). From 1936 to 1940, the magazine included a department, "Turn on the Heat," which was a brief article about hero lawmen or a cry of outrage at the thought of crime. The editor also provided another similar short article, variously titled, which rhapsodized about this and that.

In 1939, a column, "Wanted by the F.B.I.," was added. This described wanted criminals and lasted into 1940, when it was discontinued together with "Turn on the Heat." Both were replaced by "Off the Record," another column on general crime topics.

While the departments came and went, the magazine's fiction contents remained stable. At the end, in 1943, the table of contents listed five short stories (identified as two novels and three novelettes).

Other than the writers heretofore mentioned, *Ace G-Man Stories* presented stories by Popular Publications regulars. Norvell Page appeared, plus Arthur Leo Zagat, Dale Clark, Paul Ernst, Day Keene, W. T. Ballard, and William R. Cox.

After the magazine was cancelled in the United States, the title continued in a Canadian edition. These issues have not been examined in detail, and it is not known when the Canadian version began. Issues noted are all identified as volume 9, issued bimonthly with sequential whole numbers. The Canadian edition continued through at least number 21 (November 1945). Although the title remained the same, stories about G-Men were rarities in these issues; private detectives appeared, and tough police and crooks. But the fiction contents in no way justified the title. The 1943 issues noted contain fiction by E. Hoffman Price, Harold de Polo, Frederick C. Davis, C. S. Montayne, and Frederick C. Painton. Later issues seem to have been published to clear out the inventory of stories not suitable in companion publications. Most 1944–1945 stories were by lesser-known authors.

Notes

1. Contents page, "Death's Private Club," by Arthur Leo Zagat, *Ace G-Man Stories*, Vol. 3, no. 1 (September–October 1937), p. 2.

2. Contents page, "Glory Comes in Coffins," by John B. Starr, *Ace G-Man Stories*, Vol. 5, no. 2 (March–April 1939), p. 2.

3. Contents page, "Special Agent for the Dead," by Anthony Clemens, *Ace G-Man Stories*, Vol. 6, no. 1 (September–October 1939), p. 2.

Information Sources

BIBLIOGRAPHY:
Hickman, Lynn. "The Pulp Collector." *The Pulp Era*, no. 75 (Spring 1971): 6–7.
Johnson, Tom. "The Phantom Fed." *Pulp*, Vol. 1, no. 10 (Winter 1978): 5–6.
INDEX SOURCES: Hickman, Lynn. "The Pulp Collector." *The Pulp Era*, no. 75 (Spring 1971): 6–7.
LOCATION SOURCES: University of California–Los Angeles Library (7 issues); private collectors.

Publication History

MAGAZINE TITLE: *Ace G-Man Stories*.
TITLE CHANGES: None.

VOLUME AND ISSUE DATA: Vol. 1, no. 1 (May–June 1936) through Vol. 11, no. 1
     (April 1943); 41 issues.
PUBLISHER: Popular Publications, Inc., 2256 Grove Street, Chicago, Illinois.
EDITORS: Henry Sperry (1936); Moran Tudury (1937–1939).
PRICE PER ISSUE: 10 cents.
SIZE AND PAGINATION: 6-7/8'' X 10'' (Vol. 1, no. 1–Vol. 6, no. 3); 6-7/8'' X 9-
     1/2'' (Vol. 6, no. 4–Vol. 11, no. 1); 112–114 pages.
CURRENT STATUS: Discontinued.

Canadian Edition

PUBLISHER: Popular Publications, Inc., 100 Adelaide Street, West, Toronto 1, Canada.
VOLUME AND ISSUE DATA: Vol. 9, no. 1 (July 1942) through Vol. 9, no. 21
     (November 1945); 21 issues.
—*Robert Sampson*

ACE G-MAN STORIES (Canadian)

See ACE G-MAN STORIES

ACE-HIGH DETECTIVE MAGAZINE

The Chinese fiend has wrapped this poor girl entirely up in a slow-burning fuse and has ignited it. Her lover has the choice of watching her shriek in agony or cutting her throat with a sword. That's the cover of the first issue of *Ace-High Detective Magazine*, illustrating the story ''The Creeping Doom'' by John Murray Reynolds. (The cover artist was Malvin Singer, with interior illustrations by Ralph Carlson.) The issue was dated August 1936.

The magazine promise, thus, was fiendish treatment of pitiful girls by men with distorted senses of humor—the sort of thing that made *Horror Stories** and *Terror Tales** (see *Horror Stories*) a success. But not so here. Although the story titles smacked of the diabolical, such as ''Skeleton Key,'' ''Brink of the Grave,'' and ''The Upside-Down Man,'' all suggested more weird menace than they provided.

What you did find in this magazine were mystery-adventure stories in which the hero lumbered into an odd situation and then was thumped by very tough citizens with guns until somebody got shot. Then the hero explained for half of a page, and it was all over. This was not first-class detective pulp fiction, albeit competent, run-of-the-mill prose. Frequent contributors were Norbert Davis, O. B. Myers, Leslie T. White, Fred MacIsaac, William Barrett, Carroll John Daly, Wyatt Blassingame, and other regular writers appearing in periodicals of Popular Publications.

The first issue contained three novelettes and five short stories. A department by Lawrence Treat gave you a chance to solve a crime by reproducing documents found on the body; from these you could solve the murder, and the puzzle was complex enough to work up into a short story.

But the magazine was never quite sure of itself. It was not hard-boiled, not quite weird menace, and not very good. After seven issues it was terminated. The final issue bore a bimonthly date. The Hardin-Hocutt "Checklist of Popular Publications Titles" indicates that it may have been transformed into *Strange Detective Mysteries*.*[1]

Note

1. Nils Hardin and George Hocutt, "A Checklist of Popular Publications Titles," *Xenophile,* no. 33 (July 1977), p. 21.

Information Sources

BIBLIOGRAPHY:
Hardin, Nils, and George Hocutt. "A Checklist of Popular Publications Titles, 1930–1955." *Xenophile,* no. 33 (July 1977): 21.
Hickman, Lynn. "The Pulp Collector." *The Pulp Era,* no. 75 (Spring 1971):7.
INDEX SOURCES: None known.
LOCATION SOURCES: University of California–Los Angeles Library; private collectors.

Publication History

MAGAZINE TITLE: *Ace-High Detective Magazine.*
TITLE CHANGES: None.
VOLUME AND ISSUE DATA: Vol. 1, no. 1 (August 1936) through Vol. 2, no. 3 (February–March 1937); 7 issues.
PUBLISHER: Popular Publications, Inc., 2256 Grove Street, Chicago, Illinois.
EDITOR: Kenneth White.
PRICE PER ISSUE: 10 cents.
SIZE AND PAGINATION: 6-7/8" X 9-3/4"; 128 pages.
CURRENT STATUS: Discontinued.
—*Robert Sampson*

ACE MYSTERY

Hooded fiends dip a girl into flame as her boy friend stares in horror (May 1936 cover).

A turbaned foreign beast carries off a shrieking girl, his hand clawed over her breast (July 1936 cover).

A decayed monster, half leper, half skeleton, clutches toward a cowering maiden (September 1936 cover).

Magazine covers in the extravagant terror-pulp style—the hapless girl, doom impending in weird ways, the gash-awful monster. These elements were offered by *Ace Mystery* for three issues, a curious mixture of sadistic fantasy, weird menace, and sexual apprehension.

Each issue contained eight or nine stories—being called two novelettes, six short stories, and a lead novel by Frederick C. Davis. The story titles reflected the magazine's tone: "Priestess of Pain," "The Devil's Nightmare," "Witch Girl," "The Singing Scourge," "Death Lovers." Among those writers represented were Hugh B. Cave, Maitland Scott (son of R.T.M. Scott), Paul Chadwick, G. T. Fleming-Roberts, Paul Ernst, and Robert C. Blackmon. Most of these also appeared consistently in the more successful Popular Publications' *Horror Stories,* Terror Tales,** (see *Horror Stories*), and *Dime Mystery Magazine,** in which the weird sex and sadism story came as close to an art form as it was likely to get.

But such success was denied *Ace Mystery*. The magazine was permeated by a strong *Weird Tales** reek, like the afterscent of a diabolical incense. Adjectives thundered and boomed through waddling paragraphs. The characters slobbered, lurched, reeled, clutched their burning faces. The effects were shoveled forth, terrors bizarre and, frequently, banal. Here sniggled the insane doctor, deep in his crypt of fetid lepers. Here the smiling young madman schemed for the fair young thing's body. And here characters, no more complex than a single-cell organism, were terrorized by papier mache dreadfuls.

Part of the fiction concentrated on girls who were confronted by horrific sexual menace after some weird event. Like it or not, those stories often worked effectively. But other stories, deeply bitten by *Weird Tales*, heaved ponderous horrors that lumbered, emitting blue light, to the chant of stereotyped fiends. The real abilities of Cave, Davis, and Blackmon to write tense, flowing narrative could not carry the burden, and the magazine was discontinued after the third issue. It tried hard and was not completely bad, but it was never able to decide just what it was, a fatal indecision.

Information Sources

BIBLIOGRAPHY:
Jones, Robert Kenneth. *The Shudder Pulps*. West Linn, Ore.: Fax Collector's Editions, 1975.
Wolheim, Donald A. "From Blue Swastika to the Ace of Spades." *The Pulp Era,* no. 68 (November 1967):4–9.
INDEX SOURCES: None known.
LOCATION SOURCES: University of California–Los Angeles Library (Vol. 1, no. 1, only); private collectors.

Publication History

MAGAZINE TITLE: *Ace Mystery*.
TITLE CHANGES: None.
VOLUME AND ISSUE DATA: Vol. 1, no. 1 (May 1936) through Vol. 1, no. 3 (September 1936), bimonthly; 3 issues.
PUBLISHER: Periodical House, Inc., 29 Worthington Street, Springfield, Massachusetts.
EDITOR: H. M. Widmer.
PRICE PER ISSUE: 10 cents.
SIZE AND PAGINATION: 6-3/8" X 9-1/2"; 128 pages.
CURRENT STATUS: Discontinued.
—*Robert Sampson*

AGE OF THE UNICORN, THE

The Age of the Unicorn began life as an advertising journal devoted to the fantastic, mysterious, weird, and imaginative fields of publication. The magazine was a short-lived effort on the part of Cook-McDowell Publications (founded by Michael L. Cook of Evansville, Indiana, and Sam McDowell of Hartford, Kentucky), a firm normally specializing in genealogical works. Cook, a devoted fan of all the fields represented in the journal (particularly the pulp magazines, Sherlock Holmes, and H. P. Lovecraft) and author of many books, became editor. McDowell concentrated on the actual production of the magazine.

The purpose of the journal was to be an advertising medium while including articles, checklists, and illustrations in the genre. Unlike most new literary magazines, the publishers adhered to a precise bimonthly schedule. "The birth of the journal," wrote Cook in his first editorial, "arose due to a void in the field, and although the one publication of similar nature now appears to be continuing, and another has announced commencement, there should be space for all."[1]

It was intended that the journal be known as *The Unicorn*, but that was changed by the editors' discovery of another periodical by that name, a miscellaneous journal published in Massachusetts, mainly for college and graduate-school students and faculty and published on an irregular basis. Although there seemed to be no conflict, the magazine's name was changed to *The Age of the Unicorn*.

The first issue, April 1979, included such articles as "An Index to *The Haunt of Horror*" by Dr. Roger C. Schlobin, "Why I Wrote the Bantan Novels" by Maurice B. Gardner, and "*The Spider* Checklist" by John Steinkuhl. The journal, in subsequent issues, carried reports on the Pulpcons, original artwork, occasional poetry, checklists, news, reviews, indexes to both current and discontinued magazines in the field, articles, and personal reminiscences by pulp writers. A special column beginning in the second issue was "Smokerings and Things," a review of books and magazines.

The magazine's first letter column began in the same issue and contained an enthusiastic response from Robert Bloch. "*The Unicorn* arrived today and I must compliment you on a fine job. Looks as though it will be a welcome and worthy addition to the bibliographic field."[2]

W. Paul Ganly, a friendly competitor (editor and publisher of *Fantasy Mongers**), was unable to continue his fine magazine due to personal reasons. In August 1979, with issue number 3, *Unicorn* assumed the fulfillment of subscriptions with a merger; nearly 80 percent of Ganly's subscribers were new to *Unicorn*, thus increasing circulation considerably.

The seventh issue, April 1980, began the second volume and included a cumulative index by Dana Martin Batory for the first volume. But the same issue brought a sad message from editor Cook.

The monster that made *The Age of the Unicorn* possible in the beginning, our primary business of publishing historical and genealogical books, has grown to a point where there can be no more time to devote to *The Unicorn*. It has been quite a time-consuming matter. I am sorry and saddened by this as it has always been a labor of love for me. And we felt there was a need for this publication; we hope that we have filled this need, at least for the past fourteen months.[3]

The decision to discontinue was a very late one, just prior to publication of the seventh issue.

The demise, however, was with a blaze of glory. A large number of particularly fine articles was on hand for future issues, and to avoid wasting these, Cook decided to prepare a special issue of the journal. This was a mammoth-sized issue, 146 pages, with no advertising and no regular columns. Just the cream of the crop of the articles on hand, more than three times the amount in a regular issue. Among these were "Fantastic Fighting Men of Fiction" by Tom Johnson, "Michael Avallone: Writer Extraordinaire" by Michael L. Cook, and "The War of the Worlds" by Dana Martin Batory. By this time, circulation had topped five hundred.

Arrangements were made with J. Grant Thiessen, publisher of *The Science Fiction Collector (Megavore*)* and proprietor of Pandora's Books Ltd., to continue the aims and purpose of the *Unicorn* by a merger with his journal, a major magazine of nonfiction with over 2,500 subscribers and a reputation for its bibliographic contributions. This was a fitting end for Cook and McDowell's magazine.

Notes

1. Editorial by Michael L. Cook, *The Age of the Unicorn*, Vol. 1, no. 1 (April 1979), p. 1.
2. Robert Bloch in "Letters" column, *The Age of the Unicorn*, Vol. 1, no. 2 (June 1979), p. 48.
3. Editorial by Michael L. Cook, *The Age of the Unicorn*, Vol. 2, no. 1 (April 1980), p. 1.

Information Sources

INDEX SOURCES: Batory, Dana Martin. "First Cumulative Index to *Unicorn*" (index for Vol. 1). *The Age of the Unicorn*, Vol. 2, no. 1 (April 1980): 32–40.
LOCATION SOURCES: Private collectors.

Publication History

MAGAZINE TITLE: *The Age of the Unicorn*.
TITLE CHANGES: None.
VOLUME AND ISSUE DATA: Vol. 1, no. 1 (April 1979) through Vol. 2, no. 2 (special issue 1980); 8 issues.
PUBLISHER: Cook-McDowell Publications, 3318 Wimberg Avenue, Evansville, Indiana 47712.
EDITOR: Michael L. Cook.
PRICE PER ISSUE: $1.50 (nos. 1–4); $2.50 (no. 7); $6.50 (no.8).
SIZE AND PAGINATION: 8-1/2'' X 11''; 54–146 pages.
CURRENT STATUS: Discontinued.
—*Dana Martin Batory*

ALDINE CELEBRATED DETECTIVE TALES, THE (British)

See DETECTIVE TALES (Aldine Publishing)

ALDINE DETECTIVE TALES (British)

See DETECTIVE TALES BRITISH (Aldine Publishing)

ALDINE MYSTERY NOVELS (British)

A series of twenty-eight small, thin periodicals, the *Aldine Mystery Novels* were much in the style of the American dime novel and the English "penny dreadfuls" that had continued to be popular ever since the Victorian Age. The Aldine Publishing Company had commenced in the late 1880s, under the guidance of Charles Perry Brown, and promptly became a new source of the fierce and bizarre reading entertainment that had captured the public's fancy. Its publishing pace was just as frantic as most of the stories it presented, with a profusion of "libraries" and "series" on a wide variety of subjects from highwaymen to horse racing. While at first specializing in reprints of American dime novels of the wild west heroes, it soon had a heavy interest in detective characters, and home-grown villains were portrayed in every conceivable type of situation. Dick Turpin, Spring-Heeled Jack, Claude Duval, and Jack Sheppard were among the favorites. The titles were just as imaginative, "The Silver Skeleton" or "Dick Turpin and the Queen of the Pirates," for example.

The individual detective and villain "penny dreadfuls" were supplanted, however, with more general titles of still wildly imaginative and improbable tales, and *Aldine Mystery Novels* was one of the last general titles attempted, commencing in 1925 and ending in 1928.

Information Sources

BIBLIOGRAPHY:
Daniel, C. W. "Aldine Papers." *Dime Novel Roundup*, Vol. 15, no. 174 (March 1947).
Lofts, W.O.G., and Derek J. Adley. *Old Boys Books, A Complete Catalogue*. London: privately printed, 1969.
Turner, E. S. *Boys Will Be Boys*. London: Michael Joseph, 1948.
INDEX SOURCES: None known.
LOCATION SOURCES: Private collectors only.

Publication History

MAGAZINE TITLE: *Aldine Mystery Novels*.
TITLE CHANGES: None.
VOLUME AND ISSUE DATA: 1925–1928; 28 issues.
PUBLISHER: Aldine Publishing Company, London.
EDITOR: Not known.

PRICE PER ISSUE: 4 pence.
SIZE AND PAGINATION: Not available.
CURRENT STATUS: Discontinued.

ALDINE THRILLERS (British)

The Aldine Publishing Company, by 1900, boasted of more than 250 detective titles, all "penny dreadfuls," the British equivalent to the American dime novel. While many of the brave and fearless (intrepid but often foolhardy) detectives were imported from the United States, there was a hardy crop of detectives of peculiar titles—the Demon Detective, the Jew Detective, the Girl-Boy Detective, Old Electricity, and the Lightning Detective, among others. These brought about a new era to what was advertised as juvenile periodicals but which were read, more often than not, by adults. The previous dull and uncolorful story-paper was dramatized with brightly colored covers and even more spectacular events within. Of pocket size, they appealed to many and were most successful. By the mid-1920s, however, the individual titles were all publishing history, and the more general titles had taken their place. Such was *Aldine Thrillers*.

The *Aldine Thrillers* was one of the last series published by the company and while late to do so, and undistinguished, was reminiscent of the old dime novels of the United States. It was published from 1930 to 1932, for twenty-eight issues, and perished with the company—a publisher that had survived some forty years.

Information Sources

BIBLIOGRAPHY:
Daniel, C. W. "Aldine Papers." *Dime Novel Roundup*, Vol. 15, no. 174 (March 1947).
Lofts, W.O.G., and Derek J. Adley. *Old Boys Books, A Complete Catalogue*. London: privately printed, 1969.
Turner, E.S. *Boys Will Be Boys*. London: Michael Joseph, 1948.
INDEX SOURCES: None known.
LOCATION SOURCES: Private collectors only.

Publication History

MAGAZINE TITLE: *Aldine Thrillers*.
TITLE CHANGES: None.
VOLUME AND ISSUE DATA: 1930–1932; 28 issues.
PUBLISHER: Aldine Publishing Company, London.
EDITOR: Not known.
PRICE PER ISSUE: 4 pence.
SIZE AND PAGINATION: 5-3/8'' X 7''; 32 pages.
CURRENT STATUS: Discontinued.

ALFRED HITCHCOCK'S MYSTERY MAGAZINE

Alfred Hitchcock's Mystery Magazine first appeared in December 1956. Although Hitchcock gave his name to its title, signed the brief editorial introductions to each issue, and appeared on its cover for over twenty-five years, the magazine was never really his in the sense of any direct or personal involvement. It did, however, owe its beginning, at least in part, to Hitchcock's successful television series.

For as long as the T.V. series lasted, all stories submitted to the magazine were considered as possible sources for adaptation to the small screen. Potential contributors were advised to watch the telecasts in order to become familiar with the kind of stories desired. The television shows, like his films, reflected Hitchcock in suspenseful, crafty, ironical stories, often leavened with a strong dose of grim humor and ending with an unexpected twist. For millions of film and television viewers, and for readers as well, such stories were Hitchcock's trademark. While every tale that appeared in the magazine did not follow these lines, the Hitchcock style was a strong influence. In this sense, then, one might well say that the magazine was his, at least in spirit.

For its first two decades, *Alfred Hitchcock's Mystery Magazine* (*AHMM*) was published by H.S.D. Publications, first from New York City and later from Florida. During these years, save for some fluctuations in page length, it was a notably stable publication. There was a brief period—from May 1957 through January 1958—when the format was changed from digest to a large, 8-1/2" X 11" size. That this was neither a successful nor popular variation seems obvious from the brevity of its duration.

Cover illustrations during this period were mostly uniform, usually featuring a picture of Alfred Hitchcock. In addition to the illustrated covers, each story featured a drawing—reflecting a story scene—on its title page, along with the familiar Hitchcock profile silhouette in outline in one corner of the drawing. This, of course, was a carry-over from Hitchcock's film work, for he had always appeared, however briefly, in one scene in each of his films.

AHMM's emphasis from its inception was on new stories as opposed to reprints. In addition to several of these in each issue, a novelette was frequently featured. Most were written by authors who had or would become well known for their work in the field of mystery fiction. While a significant number of authors were represented by only a single story, the majority of contributions came from those who repeatedly wrote for *AHMM* over a substantial period of time.

The magazine began as a monthly and continued as such, with only a single break, for nearly a quarter of a century. The one hiatus occurred in its first full year of publication—there was no issue for April 1957. This very probably resulted from the temporary change in format noted above. Its price was also fairly stable during these years. In January of 1964, it rose from thirty-five cents to fifty cents; to sixty cents in January 1970; and to seventy-five cents in July 1971, where it remained until July 1978.

Although the magazine was very stable in content and publication schedule during its first twenty years, the same was not always true of its finances. By early 1976, its publisher, Richard Decker, was prepared to discontinue the title.

Even though *AHMM* and *Ellery Queen's Mystery Magazine** were in a sense competing for the same market, the latter's publisher, Davis Publications, came to the rescue. Davis's president, Joel Davis, noting his firm's reluctance to see the death of yet another magazine in the field of mystery fiction, arranged for the purchase of *AHMM*. While some personnel changes would obviously be inevitable, Davis announced that neither the magazine's editorial policy nor its image would be changed.

To a large extent this was true. Although Eleanor Sullivan, managing editor of *Ellery Queen's* since September 1970, became *AHMM*'s new editor, there were few noticeable changes. One which was quite obvious was the way in which Hitchcock's likeness was portrayed on the covers. These became less sober, more humorous, albeit solidly within that strain of grim and grisly humor so long identified with Hitchcock himself. These portrayals actually harkened back to the way in which Hitchcock had depicted himself in many of the introductions to the television series of the late fifties. Some examples were Hitchcock as a barber, sharpening a dagger while a customer waited for a shave; as a nightshirted householder building a fire beneath Santa Claus's dangling boots; and as a burglar, picking the lock on the gate of Heaven!

The magazine's contents and interior layout remained largely unchanged for several years, although its publication schedule, like that of *Ellery Queen's*, was changed to thirteen issues per year beginning with the Januasry 1980 issue. The brief editorials were still "signed" by Alfred Hitchcock (through the June 1980 issue), an illustrative drawing continued to head each story (complete with the Hitchcock silhouette), and the short stories and occasional novelettes "in the Hitchcock tradition" continued. In August 1978, the price went to $1.00 and in March 1980 rose to the current price of $1.25.

The first significant change in content occurred in July 1979 with the debut of Peter Christian's film and television review column, "Crime on Screen," a most appropriate topic in a magazine named for the man whose films were synonymous with crime, mystery, and suspense. The column continues to this date. For the twenty-fifth anniversary issue in December 1980, *AHMM*'s usual three to four pages were replaced by a special thirty-two-page addition in the form of a "photoquiz" devoted to the films of Alfred Hitchcock.

A less successful and much shorter innovation was also announced in the July 1979 issue. This was to be a "letters column" for "questions or comments about specific stories we publish or about the mystery field in general...." The first letters appeared in the issue of January 30, 1980, and the last in the September 1980 issue. The October 1980 editorial announced that "... most of [our readers] would prefer the space we've given to the Letters column be used for stories."[1]

Other changes followed Hitchcock's death, which was announced in the July 1980 issue's editorial, now simply signed "The Editors." The April 1, 1981, issue was the first without some version of Hitchcock's face. This was also true of the April 29 and May issues. Reader protest brought about a return of Hitchcock's silhouette—as a part of the cover illustration—with the June 1981 issue. This has remained a part of each cover illustration since that date. Although the interior illustrations for each story have continued, the little Hitchcock outline silhouette last appeared in the February 1982 issue in this context.

In February 1982, Cathleen Jordan became editor, replacing Eleanor Sullivan (who continues as managing editor of *Ellery Queen's*), and the editorial in that issue announced some "Coming Attractions," including the possibility of a longer magazine but one with "at least as much fiction as at present" (a wording which implied the future addition of nonfiction features). Through May 1982, the issues have remained at 127–128 pages. The editorials, however, have become much longer and more personal in tone, containing more than the usual few words about the issue's contents. The editorial in the March 31, 1982, issue included a long review/discussion of *The Lord Peter Wimsey Cookbook*, and that in the May 1982 issue announced the intent to revive the questions-and-answers letter column.

Comparisons between *Alfred Hitchcock's* and *Ellery Queen's* through the years were inevitable and obviously increased after the former's acquisition by Davis Publications, publisher of the latter. Some similarity between the two was equally inevitable; both were, after all, in the same field. Size, price, frequency of publication, emphasis on new stories over older reprints, and a certain commonality of authors very probably derived in large part from market factors and reader reception. Any debate over the quality of stories presented by each is at least in part a matter of judgment and perception of both by readers and critics and as such is hardly susceptible to any sort of final decision. While *Alfred Hitchcock's* has been called "No. 2" to *Ellery Queen's* as "No. 1," this claim can be factually demonstrated only quantitatively in terms of circulation figures. Eleanor Sullivan has frequently asserted that, while the two magazines do exchange stories submitted, it is not true that *Alfred Hitchcock's* publishes only "second-run" material.

Both are "for profit" productions, and reader reception and response certainly account for the fact that the efforts of many popular writers in the field will appear in both. At the same time, Eleanor Sullivan also states that both magazines continue to publish the type of story for which each is best known. For *AHMM*, this means a continuing emphasis on plot, irony, and unexpected endings.

Authors such as James Holding, Lawrence Treat, Edward D. Hoch, Jack Ritchie, Henry Slesar, Talmage Powell, Bill Pronzini, and countless others have appeared in both *Ellery Queen's* and *Alfred Hitchcock's*. Powell, Treat, and Slesar have written for both since 1957. James Holding, who failed to appear in *Ellery Queen's* in only one year between 1960 and 1982, has appeared each year in *Alfred Hitchcock's* during the same period. Edward D. Hoch, who has not missed an issue of *Ellery Queen's* since January 1973, has appeared several times each year in *Alfred Hitchcock's* from 1962 through 1981 and has appeared once thus far in 1982. Countless other authors, both more and less prolific than these, have written for both magazines, before as well as after *AHMM*'s acquisition by Davis Publications.

In the years since its first issue appeared, *Alfred Hitchcock's Mystery Magazine* has published over 3,700 stories by over 900 authors. Of these, some 440 were one-time appearances, with approximately 500 authors accounting for the remaining 3,300 stories. Of the authors mentioned above, all save Bill Pronzini have also seen one or more of their stories appear in *The Saint Mystery Magazine (Saint Detective Magazine, The*)* as well. Such crossovers among different magazines in the same field are inevitable and of themselves neither support nor refute the statement that *Alfred Hitchcock's* continues to publish the type of story for which it is best known.

Alfred Hitchcock's Mystery Magazine is published in many countries outside the United States. One of the longest running of the foreign editions is the British. The first series was published from 1957 to 1958 (with the early issues corresponding in size to the U.S. 8-1/2" X 11" experiment) by Strato Publications Ltd. The second series began in 1967, published by Alex White & Co., Ltd.

Note

1. Editorial, *Alfred Hitchcock's Mystery Magazine*, Vol. 25, no. 10 (October 1, 1980), reverse front-cover page.

Information Sources

BIBLIOGRAPHY:
Taublieb, Paul. "Profile: Alfred Hitchcock's Mystery Magazine." *Mystery*, Vol. 2, no. 3 (May 1981):34–36.
INDEX SOURCES: Cook, Michael L. *Monthly Murders*. U.S. and British editions, Westport, Conn.: Greenwood Press, 1982.
LOCATION SOURCES: Private collectors.

Publication History

MAGAZINE TITLE: *Alfred Hitchcock's Mystery Magazine*.
TITLE CHANGES: None.
VOLUME AND ISSUE DATA: Vol. 1, no. 12 (first issue, number coinciding with month, December 1956) through Vol. 27, no. 5 (to date, May 1982); 308 issues.
PUBLISHERS: H.S.D. Publications, Inc., 545 Fifth Avenue, New York 17, New York, later 2441 Beach Court, Riviera Beach, Florida 33404, and 784 U.S. 1, Suite 6, North Palm Beach, Florida 33408; from 1976, Davis Publications, Inc., 380 Lexington Avenue, New York, New York 10017.
EDITORS: William Manners; G. F. Goster, Ernest M. Hutter, Eleanor Sullivan; Cathleen Jordan.
PRICE PER ISSUE: 35 cents (through December 1963); 50 cents (through December 1969); 60 cents (through June 1971); 75 cents (through July 1978); $1.00 (through February 1980); $1.25 (subsequent issues).
SIZE AND PAGINATION: 5-1/4" X 7-5/8" (except for May 1957 to January 1958, 8-1/2" X 11"); 128–160 pages.

CURRENT STATUS: Active.

British edition
MAGAZINE TITLE: *Alfred Hitchcock's Mystery Magazine*.
TITLE CHANGES: None.
VOLUME AND ISSUE DATA: First series: no. 1 (September 1957)
    through no. 11 (August 1958); 11 issues. Second series: Vol. 1,
    no. 1 (May 1967) through Vol. 1, no. 5 (September 1967); 5
    issues.
PUBLISHERS: First series: Strato Publications Ltd., 39 Upper Brook
    Street, London W.1, England. Second Series: Alex White & Co.,
    Ltd., Market Buildings, Guildford, Surrey, England.
EDITOR: Not known.
PRICE PER ISSUE: 1 shilling 6 pence (first series); 3 shillings 6 pence
    (second series).
SIZE AND PAGINATION: Average 5-1/4" X 7-1/2"; 112 pages.
CURRENT STATUS: Discontinued (British editions).
—David H. Doerrer

ALFRED HITCHCOCK'S MYSTERY MAGAZINE (British)

See ALFRED HITCHCOCK'S MYSTERY MAGAZINE

ALIBI

Alibi is presumed to have been a pulp magazine title that commenced publication in January 1934.[1] No other information is available.

Note

1. This title is included on the "Tentative Pulp Checklist" from the San Francisco Academy of Comic Art (unpublished manuscript, n.d.).

Information Sources

INDEX SOURCES: None known.
LOCATION SOURCES: None known.

Publication History

MAGAZINE TITLE: *Alibi*.
TITLE CHANGES: None known.
VOLUME AND ISSUE DATA: Vol. 1, no. 1 (January 1934); number of issues and
    extent unknown.
PUBLISHER: Not known.
EDITOR: Not known.
PRICE PER ISSUE: Not known.
SIZE AND PAGINATION: Not known.
CURRENT STATUS: Discontinued.

ALL DETECTIVE MAGAZINE

The *All Detective Magazine* is little known today, even among collectors, but it was most important to the detective field and is probably a precursor to the *Doctor Death** title.

Commencing in November 1932, from Dell Publishing Company, the magazine was pulp-size (7'' X 10'') but very thin; issues sold for five cents until about April 1933.

The archfiend, Doctor Death, is featured in the August 1934 (''Dr. Death''), September 1934 (''Cargo of Death'') and January 1935 (''13 Pearls'') issues. There is no question that this is the same character later honored with a magazine of his own; the hero is Nibs Holloway, and the author, a pseudonym, is Edward P. Norris.

Another surprise awaits readers of this obscure magazine. In ''Spawn of the Spider'' in the December 1933 issue, the principal character is the Spider, but here the Spider is the criminal! Frederick C. Painton was the author.

Among other hero characters are stories of the Scarlet Ace, an obscure crime fighter.

Cover artists included Norman Saunders, George Rozen, and Frank Tinsley, with J. Fleming Gould supplying interior illustrations. Authors read like a who's who in the pulps: Erle Stanley Gardner, Lester Dent, Paul Ernst, Norman A. Daniels, H. Bedford Jones, and Arthur J. Burks, as well as Frederick C. Painton and ''Edward P. Norris.''

With the last issue published in January 1935, and the *Doctor Death* character pulp commencing in February 1935, both from Dell Publishing Company, the connection is likely but not confirmed.

Information Sources

BIBLIOGRAPHY:
Myers, Dick. ''The Birth of (Dr.) Death.'' *Bronze Shadows,* no. 6 (September 1966):5.
INDEX SOURCES: None known.
LOCATION SOURCES: University of California–Los Angeles Library (nos. 1, 5, 12, 22 only); private collectors.

Publication History

MAGAZINE TITLE: *All Detective Magazine.*
TITLE CHANGES: None confirmed.
VOLUME AND ISSUE DATA: Vol. 1, no. 1 (November 1932) through Vol. 9, no. 27 (January 1935); 27 issues.
PUBLISHER: Dell Publishing Co., Inc., 149 Madison Avenue, New York, New York.
EDITOR: Not known.
PRICE PER ISSUE: 5 cents (through March 1933); 10 cents.
SIZE AND PAGINATION: 7'' X 10''; 64 pages.
CURRENT STATUS: Discontinued.

ALL FICTION DETECTIVE ANTHOLOGY

See ALL FICTION DETECTIVE STORIES

ALL FICTION DETECTIVE STORIES

All Fiction Detective Stories was one of a series of oversized, 160-page, 150,000-word reprint annuals published by Street & Smith during the 1940–1947 period. The first of these special magazines, *Detective Story Annual,** was issued in December 1940 with a 1941 date; a second issue followed in 1942. About six months after the 1942 *Detective Story Annual* was published, the first *All Fiction Detective Stories* was issued.

Except for title, the two magazines are essentially identical. The 1942 *All Fiction Detective Stories* contained five long stories ("book-length novels") and two novelettes drawn from *Detective Story Magazine** and *Clues.** Prominent writers were featured, including Ellery Queen, Frank Gruber, Steve Fisher, William C. Barrett, and Norbert Davis. The 1943 issue also featured well-known names such as Margaret Millar, Fredric Brown, and Brett Halliday (with a Mike Shayne novelette). Here were four novels, three novelettes, and two short stories.

In later issues, the magazine reprinted fiction only from Street & Smith's *Detective Story Magazine*. Ten stories were used in the 1945 issue, seven in the 1946. Writers included Roger Torrey and such Street & Smith regulars as Julius Long and Inez Sebastian. No issues of *All Fiction Detective Stories* have been noted after 1946. In 1948, however, the *All-Fiction Detective Anthology* was published; and this was identical, in all but the title, to earlier *All Fiction Detective Stories* issues.

Information Sources

BIBLIOGRAPHY:
Reynolds, Quentin. *The Fiction Factory*. New York: Random House, 1955.
INDEX SOURCES: None known.
LOCATION SOURCES: George Arents Research Library, Syracuse, New York University (1942–1943, 1945–1946, 1948); University of California–Los Angeles (1943); private collectors.

Publication History

MAGAZINE TITLE: *All Fiction Detective Stories*.
TITLE CHANGES: *All-Fiction Detective Anthology* (1948).
VOLUME AND ISSUE DATA: Six annuals issued, dated 1942 to 1946, and 1948; no volume numbers; 6 issues.
PUBLISHER: Street & Smith Publications, Inc., 79 Seventh Avenue, New York, New York.
EDITORS: Ronald Oliphant (1942–1943); Daisy Bacon (from 1944).
PRICE PER ISSUE: 25 cents.

SIZE AND PAGINATION: 8-1/2'' X 11''; 160 pages (1941–1945), 144 pages (1946),
    128 pages (1948).
CURRENT STATUS: Discontinued.
—*Robert Sampson*

ALL MYSTERY

The *All Mystery* magazine was Dell Publishing Company's first attempt to
participate in the digest-size mystery magazine market. Apparently it was not a
successful venture since but one issue was released.

Four "cover" illustrations highlighted the cast of well-known authors. The
front cover, in color, by Bob Stanley, illustrated the story "Murder Mixup" by
George Harmon Coxe; the back cover, in color, by Bob Abbett, depicted a scene
from "The Nameless Clue" by Helen McCloy. An inside front cover by John
Murray and an inside back cover by Jack Stevens, both in black and white,
illustrated "Rear Window" by William Irish and "One More Murder" by G.
T. Fleming-Roberts, respectively. Other authors of note included Vincent Starrett, Ray Bradbury, Steve Fisher, and Allan Vaughan Elston. A true-crime story,
"Belle of Indiana" by Stewart H. Holbrook, completed the contents.

Despite a well-produced product and best-selling authors, a second issue did
not appear.

Information Sources

INDEX SOURCES: Cook, Michael L. *Monthly Murders*. Westport, Conn.: Greenwood
    Press, 1982.
LOCATION SOURCES: Private collectors.

Publication History

MAGAZINE TITLE: *All Mystery*.
TITLE CHANGES: None.
VOLUME AND ISSUE DATA: October–December 1950 (no volume or issue desig-
    nation); 1 issue.
PUBLISHER: Dell Publishing Co., Inc., 162 Fifth Avenue, New York 16, New York
    (George T. Delacorte, Jr., president; Helen Meyer, vice-president; Albert P.
    Delacorte, vice-president).
EDITOR: Not known.
PRICE PER ISSUE: 25 cents.
SIZE AND PAGINATION: 5-1/2'' X 7-5/8''; 160 pages.
CURRENT STATUS: Discontinued.

ALL STAR DETECTIVE

A "Red Star" publication of Manvis Publications, *All Star Detective* commenced in October 1941 and apparently ended with but three issues published.
Featured were sadistic "stockings and torture" type of detective stories.

Information Sources

INDEX SOURCES: None known.
LOCATION SOURCES: University of California–Los Angeles Library (Vol. 1, no. 3, only); private collectors.

Publication History

MAGAZINE TITLE: *All Star Detective*.
TITLE CHANGES: None known.
VOLUME AND ISSUE DATA: Vol. 1, no. 1 (October 1941) through Vol. 1, no. 3 (May 1942); 3 issues known.
PUBLISHER: Manvis Publications, Inc., 4600 Diversey Avenue, with editorial offices at 330 West 42nd Street, New York, New York.
EDITOR: Not known.
PRICE PER ISSUE: Not known.
SIZE AND PAGINATION: Not known.
CURRENT STATUS: Discontinued.

ALL STAR DETECTIVE STORIES

The first issue of this Clayton Publications pulp magazine appeared in February 1928, and issues have been noted as late as April 1932, published on a quarterly basis. Another Clayton magazine of similar title, *All Star Adventure Fiction*, commenced in 1935.

Information Sources

INDEX SOURCES: None known.
LOCATION SOURCES: University of California–Los Angeles Library (1929–1931, 17 issues); private collectors.

Publication History

MAGAZINE TITLE: *All Star Detective Stories*.
TITLE CHANGE: None known.
VOLUME AND ISSUE DATA: Vol. 8, no. 1 (first issue, February 1928) through Vol. 16, no. 1. (April 1932); 33 issues.
PUBLISHER: Clayton Magazines, Inc., 155 E. 44th Street, New York City.
EDITOR: Not known.
PRICE PER ISSUE: Not known.
SIZE AND PAGINATION: Not known.
CURRENT STATUS: Discontinued.

ALL-STORY DETECTIVE

All-Story Detective first appeared in January 1949, the initial issue being dated February. The cover showed a pretty girl endangered by a thrown knife, and inside were high-action detective-adventure stories, tersely hard-boiled. John

MacDonald had the lead story, accompanied by other writers regularly appearing in other Popular Publications detective magazines.

But the magazine was born to hard luck. It appeared only a few months before Street & Smith terminated their pulp magazines and at a time when the pulp publishing business was entering its final illness. *All-Story Detective* was one of those polished professional products that Popular Publications put together so skillfully. Its writers were vigorous, its stories interesting. Nonetheless, it was interchangeable with any of the other Popular Publications detective titles. And there lay the problem. It was as good as, but no better than, the well-established titles such as *Dime Detective,* * *New Detective Magazine,* * and *Detective Tales* (Popular Publications).*

So *All-Story Detective* immediately faced a contracting readership, severe competition from even companion magazines, and the downside of the curve. It almost immediately became a bimonthly, struggled along until the November 1949 issue, and then was temporarily suspended.

After a short pause for redecoration, it was given a new title, *15 Story Detective,* and sent forth again, still a bimonthly, the initial issue dated February 1950. Volume and issue numbers were continued.

The actual differences between the two magazines were few. The new title added a few more pieces of short fiction and a few more departments, two of these being true-crime features that combined sketches and text. The fiction was provided by writers of proven popularity, among them Robert Turner, Frederick C. Davis, D. L. Champion, T. W. Ford, and Day Keene, all skilled in Popular Publications' narrative style. In other times, the revised magazine would have succeeded nicely, but times were wrong, and the magazine was cancelled with the July 1951 issue. There were at least three issues published of a British reprint edition.

Information Sources

INDEX SOURCES: None known.
LOCATION SOURCES: Private collectors.

Publication History

MAGAZINE TITLE: *All-Story Detective.*
TITLE CHANGES: *15 Story Detective* (with vol. 2, no. 3 [February 1950]).
VOLUME AND ISSUE DATA: Vol. 1, no. 1 (February 1949) through Vol. 4, no. 3 (July 1951); 6 issues as *All-Story Detective,* 9 issues as *15 Story Detective.*
PUBLISHER: Popular Publications, Inc., 1125 East Vaile Avenue, Kokomo, Indiana.
EDITOR: Not known.
PRICE PER ISSUE: 25 cents.
SIZE AND PAGINATION: 6-7/8'' X 9-3/8''; 114 pages.
CURRENT STATUS: Discontinued.
—*Robert Sampson*

ALL-STORY DETECTIVE (British)

See *ALL-STORY DETECTIVE*

AMAZING DETECTIVE MYSTERY STORIES (British)

This pulp magazine, of which one issue is known, possibly reprinted stories from the U.S. magazine, *Amazing Detective Tales (Scientific Detective Monthly*)*. No other information is available.

Information Sources

INDEX SOURCES: None known.
LOCATION SOURCES: Private collectors.

Publication History

MAGAZINE TITLE: *Amazing Detective Mystery Stories*.
TITLE CHANGES: None known.
VOLUME AND ISSUE DATA: Not available.
PUBLISHER: Not known.
EDITOR: Not known.
PRICE PER ISSUE: Not known.
SIZE AND PAGINATION: Not known.
CURRENT STATUS: Discontinued.

AMAZING DETECTIVE TALES

See *SCIENTIFIC DETECTIVE MONTHLY*

AMERICAN AGENT

In 1956, Lyle Kenyon Engel, later to be known for book packaging, induced a Texas millionaire to finance a string of magazines (and assorted show business ventures) which would provide entertainments that were "new" and "missing" from the general newsstand selections. One of the results was a trio of digest-size magazines called *American Agent, Tales of the Frightened,** and *Space Science Fiction*. The titles indicate what game was afoot: *American Agent,* with the subhead "The Magazine of the Secret Services," was just that—a magazine where one could find stories that had to do with agents, spies, and global shenanigans involving American and foreign powers. The format was a full-length novel backed by one or two short stories. This rule of thumb was handsomely served by John Jakes's "Operation Zero," which kicked off the first issue in Spring 1957. The second issue featured "Operation: Man on the Run" by John Kennedy. Two notes here are worthy of mention: years later, John Jakes converted "Operation Zero" into one of the many Nick Carter paperbacks for

Award Books, also engineered by Lyle Kenyon Engel. And the John Kennedy mentioned is not the late president of the United States.

American Agent was a fine idea for a magazine and opened up a good market for writers, and reader response and fan interest resulted in healthy sales. But Engel's entire project of magazine production was doomed by the American News Company strike which forced newsstand dealers to focus most of their attention on better-known magazines. Thus, *American Agent, Tales of the Frightened,* and *Space Science Fiction,* which had debuted simultaneously, all failed. Another casualty, after only two issues, was *Private Investigator Detective Magazine,** which featured an Ed Noon novel by Michael Avallone in each issue.

While Lyle Kenyon Engel was the guiding light behind these magazines, the actual editor was author Michael Avallone, who read, edited, and selected the stories, did all the copy work, blurbing, and the subheading material for all the issues. It was decided not to list Avallone on the editorial credit page since in many cases the magazines would run some of his own material either under his own byline or a pen name. Hence, Lyle Kenyon Engel was listed as editorial director. Illustrations, provided by Victor Olson, were superb for a digest-size magazine.

The loss of this magazine has not been filled; one might say, given the years 1956 and 1957, that James Bond via Ian Fleming only partially filled the vacuum.

Information Sources

INDEX SOURCES: Cook, Michael L. *Monthly Murders*. Westport, Conn.: Greenwood
    Press, 1982.
LOCATION SOURCES: Private collectors.

Publication History

MAGAZINE TITLE: *American Agent.*
TITLE CHANGES: None.
VOLUME AND ISSUE DATA: Vol. 2, no. 1 (April 1957) through Vol. 1, no. 2 (August
    1957); 2 issues.
PUBLISHER: Republic Features Syndicate, Inc., 39 West 55th Street, New York, New
    York.
EDITOR: Lyle Kenyon Engel.
PRICE PER ISSUE: 35 cents.
SIZE AND PAGINATION: 5-1/4'' X 7-1/2''; 128 pages.
CURRENT STATUS: Discontinued.
—*Michael Avallone*

ANGEL DETECTIVE, THE

The only issue of *The Angel Detective* appeared in 1941 near the beginning of the last decade of the pulps. The story exemplified all that was good, as well as all that was bad, in pulp writing.

At its best, pulp writing was characterized by rapid pacing, lots of action, smoothly flowing words, and intricate plotting. Little time or space was given to character development or to descriptive passages devoted to scenery, architecture, furnishings, or garb unless such an item directly impacted the action or the development of the plot.

To replace character development, the authors depended on characterization, gimmicks. accouterments, peculiarities of physique or physiognomy, and on superficial traits and quirks of personality. But the writers, editors, and copy-readers were literate and well versed in grammar, language usage, and style. Thus the perceptive (or receptive) reader received a grounding in correct spelling, punctuation, grammar, and syntax. There was no deliberate effort to restrict the vocabulary to the 2,500 basic English words. On the contrary, most pulp authors had extensive vocabularies and utilized them to the fullest.

Just about the only concession made to the reader by the pulp editor was a tendency to avoid compound sentences or long paragraphs. Even words and phrases from foreign languages were acceptable if they contributed to the atmosphere or fitted the action and if their meaning was somewhat implicit from the preceding or subsequent paragraphs.

In these respects, then, "The Angel and the Totem Pole Murders" is a typical pulp story. The basic plot premise involves the efforts of a young man to bring to some sort of justice the murderers of his father. For this purpose, Gabriel Wilde had left his native Alaska and had come to New York City accompanied by his friend, Totem, a Thlinget chief whose Eskimo name is described as unpronounceable.

In a meeting with three of the gangsters whom he had traced, Gabriel announced himself as "... the Angel... the Angel Gabriel... the Angel of Death." He carried "Belshazzar," an automatic pistol which he had designed and built, unusual in that its butt contained a design (an angel blowing a horn) that could be imprinted on surfaces.

Most pulp detective stories had little time for romance, but practically all had a small role reserved for a girlfriend, fiancée, or female assistant. This role was filled by two possible contenders, Sue Gordon, who operated a private detective agency, and Nina Hastings. The latter sought excitement by operating as the "Black Cat," a female Robin Hood. Another departure from the typical pulp practice was when Police Lieutenant Eric Lamont was depicted as competent, efficient, and "possessing a brain."

The action was fast-paced, the plot complications more believable than those of the majority of pulp yarns, and the resolution satisfactorily achieved. However, several loose ends were left dangling.

The story was billed as a book-length novel but started on page 8 and ended on page 50; taken in conjunction with the number of loose ends, this suggests that as originally planned the story was to have been longer, perhaps by at least 50 percent. Such a length would have allowed for a more complete utilization of the varied characters introduced, as well as a fuller development of the motivation for their actions.

In the last four paragraphs, the author left himself the option of recounting more adventures of The Angel, but the editor or publisher did not seem to share any optimism that the issue would be well-enough received to warrant any continuation. Contrary to normal publishing practice in this period, there is nowhere in the magazine any indication a second issue was even contemplated.

In addition to the lead story, there was one twenty-eight-page tale that was described as a feature-length novel, and three short stories.

Information Sources

INDEX SOURCES: Weinberg, Robert, and Lohr McKinstry. *The Hero Pulp Index.* Evergreen, Colo.: Opar Press, 1971.
LOCATION SOURCES: University of California–Los Angeles Library; private collectors.

Publication History

MAGAZINE TITLE: *The Angel Detective.*
TITLE CHANGES: None.
VOLUME AND ISSUE DATA: Vol. 1, no. 1 (July 1941); 1 issue.
PUBLISHER: Manvis Publications, Inc., 4600 Diversey Avenue, Chicago, Illinois, with editorial offices at 330 West 42nd Street, New York, New York.
EDITOR: Not known.
PRICE PER ISSUE: 10 cents.
SIZE AND PAGINATION: 7'' X 10''; 114 pages.
CURRENT STATUS: Discontinued.
—*Joseph Lewandowski*

ARMCHAIR DETECTIVE, THE

In September 1967, the field of crime fiction criticism was virtually non-existent. Mystery and detective novels were regularly reviewed in newspapers, and there would be an occasional book, such as Howard Haycraft's *The Art of the Mystery Story* or G. C. Ramsey's *Agatha Christie: Mistress of Mystery.* And, of course, there was *The Baker Street Journal** delving into more esoteric detail on Sherlock Holmes than most people wanted to know. But those books tended to be collections of essays and articles by mystery writers themselves, or adulatory biographies with little thoughtful criticism or placing of the author in the field. Then in October 1967, *The Armchair Detective* was born, giving a focus and forum for the readers to express their views and exchange knowledge.

Editor and originator Allen J. Hubin was the spark that ignited the explosion of mystery criticism that was waiting to be printed. From the beginning, *The Armchair Detective (TAD),* had the support and help of such well-known critics as Anthony Boucher, Howard Haycraft, and Ellery Queen but in such a way that they did not overpower the magazine. *TAD* established itself as a magazine of mystery readers and has remained so until today. The majority of articles and letters are written by amateurs, people who read crime fiction for enjoyment and want to pass on their opinions to others. For many years (until volume 9), *TAD* maintained even the appearance of an amateur publication. It was printed on closely typed pages containing a cornucopia of information, and it was assembled in the editor's home. When publication moved to The Mystery Library, Publishers Inc., in 1976, *TAD* took on a more professional look, with more advertisements, illustrations, and photos of authors and book jackets. The content may have become more academic for a while, but *TAD* remained a magazine of its readers, concentrating on quality and accuracy.

Trustworthiness and reliability have always been strong points of *The Armchair Detective*. In the second issue, Anthony Boucher wrote concerning several misleading or incorrect comments made in the first issue. Editor Hubin immediately established a policy of accuracy. At that time, Ordean Hagan's *Who Done It?* was not yet publsihed, nor, of course, Hubin's own *The Bibliography of Crime Fiction 1749–1975*. There was no source to verify easily or research specific author or title information. *TAD* filled that gap by printing corrections of commonly held misinformation and difficult-to-find bibliographic details. With the numerous reference works now available in the mystery field, it is somewhat surprising to see some of the things that were not known when *TAD* began. For example, the identity of Emma Lathen, and John Rhode's pseudonym of Miles Burton, were established here. Title changes of a book when reprinted in paperback, or crossing the Atlantic, were also given. Pseudonyms of many authors were revealed as general information for the first time.

Editor Allen Hubin's own contribution has been immense. In the early issues, his voice was very prominent. He frequently made remarks or answered letters in print, and his reviews of new books were scattered throughout each issue. His editorials gave direction and clarification of what he wanted *The Armchair Detective* to be. Over the years, his contributions diminished and then were seen only in his column of reviews. When publication was taken over by Publishers Inc., Managing Editor David Hellyer initiated a short commentary at the beginning of each issue called "The Uneasy Chair." Hubin is still listed as consulting editor but has apparently relinquished active control.

Through the years, *TAD* has developed a policy of printing extended, in-depth analyses of a particular author or subject. These usually are continued through several issues and often read like a master's or doctoral dissertation. In volumes 9, 10, and 11, several of these series ran at one time, giving the magazine a weighty atmosphere. Crime fiction was being studied very seriously—too seriously for many readers. The fun and enjoyment of mysteries was seemingly forgotten in the effort to criticize it on the level of "literature."

Those extended series are not to be ignored, however. They are valuable additions to detective fiction criticism. Some of the titles of these are: "The Problem of Moral Vision in Dashiell Hammett's Detective Novels" in volume 6, number 3 through volume 8, number 2; "Margery Allingham's Albert Campion: A Chronological Examination of the Novels in Which He Appears" in volume 9, number 1, through volume 12, number 4; "Dicks on Stage: Form and Formula in Detective Drama" in volume 11, number 3, through volume 13, number 3; "Paradox and Plot: The Fiction of Frederic Brown" in volume 9, number 4, through volume 10, number 4; and "The Police Procedural" in volume 10, number 2, through Volume 11, number 3. Each covers a significant portion of the detective fiction field. "Dicks on Stage" and "The Police Procedural" are particularly helpful in delineating the structure and regulations of their topics.

Later issues of *The Armchair Detective* have been more successful in maintaining a balance among the in-depth studies, informal reminiscences, and articles and reviews with bibliographic listings. Bibliographies and checklists have always been an important part of *TAD*. Hubin's own *Bibliography* has eliminated the need for some of the lists, but there are still invaluable treasures in listings of short stories by an author, such as that of John Lutz in volume 12, number 3; Bill Pronzini in volume 13, number 4; and John Buchan in volume 7, number 3.

Closely related to the checklist material is the "Bibliography of Secondary Sources" by Walter Albert. This yearly entry began in volume 7 and covered the year 1972. That first listing contained only thirty-seven entries. The series has continued through 1980 (in volume 14, number 4) and now contains almost four hundred entries broken down into four categories: (I) Bibliographic, Indices, Checklists; (II) History and Criticism; (III) Periodicals, Fan Organizations, Societies; (IV) Authors. This later, annotated bibliography is reflective of both the increase in the material available and Mr. Albert's expertise in locating and cataloging it.

Another checklist that first appeared in volume 2, number 1, and continues to the present is the "Checklist of Mystery, Detective and Suspense Fiction Published in the U.S." Each segment contains a three-month listing. The hardcover portion provides a form of supplement to Hubin's *Bibliography* since 1975 but does not note series characters. The paperback portion is not as complete, omitting some of the paperback originals published by some of the smaller houses.

The Armchair Detective has always made it a point to include more than material on mystery/suspense novels and short stories. The subtitle that appeared on the first volumes was "A Quarterly Journal Devoted to the Appreciation of Mystery, Detective and Suspense Fiction." In practice, *TAD* printed articles and reviews of films, television, plays, and radio shows, as well as book and magazine publications. It included material on all forms of the field—mystery, suspense, hard-boiled private eyes, crime, psychological studies, horror, and even a bit of true crime. No area or subsection of the genre was excluded. Now after fourteen years, few, if any, categories or interests have not been discussed to some extent in *TAD*'s pages.

In volume 14, the classification and attention to all areas took a more apparent format with the introduction of more regular columns. These included "*TAD* Goes to the Movies" by Tom Godfrey, "*TAD* on TV" by Richard Meyers, "The Radio Murder Hour" by Chris Steinbrunner, and "Minor Offenses" (about short stories) by H. Edward Hunsberger. In volume 11, number 3, John McAleer began his "Rex Stout Newsletter" for fans and fanatics of the Nero Wolfe Saga. Barzun and Taylor have also been supplementing their *Catalogue of Crime* since volume 9, number 2. These are not re-reviews but a continuation of their notes and comments in their published book.

Another regular feature beginning in volume 11, number 4, is "Classic Corner"—reprints of short story classics. This column is unusual in that it adds fiction to a journal of history, analysis, and criticism. The first stories were deserving of the "classic" label, but "obscure" or "unknown" would be more appropriate for the more recent offerings, such as "The Happy Land" by James M'Levy, "Nesho Naik, Dacoit" by Sir Edmund Cox, and "Garroted" by Frank Price. Otto Penzler chooses these stories and provides a brief commentary before each selection, but these are historical comments rather than analytical.

Much of the content of *TAD*, however, has not even yet been touched on in the above paragraphs. These are the reviews, articles, interviews, and letters. The reviews cover current and out-of-print works. Any subscriber is welcome to offer a review of any book. This has provided a rich backlog of material on older books for which it is difficult to locate criticism. Paperback originals that have been ignored in newspaper reviews also get their opportunity here.

Individual articles have covered virtually every facet of crime fiction. They range from studies of an author's total work to cover artwork; from biographies of detectives to essays on the use of a particular theme by an author or group of authors; from the story of a publishing house that seemed to specialize in terrible books to an overview of books describing the academic or business scene. Interviews with authors have appeared regularly. These, coupled with articles by authors themselves, provide a counterpoint to the readers' view.

The "letters" section is one of the features that made *The Armchair Detective* so successful in the beginning. This was the mystery fiction reader's first chance to share information and discuss favorite books or topics with other fans. The major critical reference works were not yet published, so readers could turn only to each other for information. To a large extent, that need no longer exists, and the letters have certainly diminished in length and number. They still provide corrections and background material for some of the articles, but they no longer give the atmosphere of a close-knit group sharing a secret.

One item lacking in *TAD* is a periodic index. Steven A. Stilwell has compiled an excellent *Index to TAD* for volumes 1 through 10. But waiting ten years for the next index makes locating material difficult, if not impossible, at times. Disregarding that gap, *The Armchair Detective* has been instrumental in igniting and focusing detective fiction criticism and well deserves the excellent reputation it has achieved.

Information Sources

BIBLIOGRAPHY:

Breen, Jon L. "All You Need Is a Comfortable Chair, or Did You Hear the One About the Two Tadpolls?" *The Armchair Detective,* Vol. 6, no. 2 (February 1973):78–79.

Hellyer, David. "TAD: The First Decade" (interview with editor Allen J. Hubin). *The Armchair Detective*, Vol. 10, no. 2 (April 1977):142–45.

Hubin, Allen J. "The Past, Present and Hopeful Future of This Journal." *The Armchair Detective*, Vol. 1, no. 1 (October 1967):28.

Landrum, Larry N., Pat Browne, and Ray Browne, eds. *Dimensions of Detective Fiction*. Bowling Green, Ohio: Bowling Green University Popular Press, 1976.

INDEX SOURCES: Stilwell, Steven A. *The Armchair Detective Index, Volumes 1–10, 1967–1977*. New York: The Armchair Detective, 1979.

"Index to The Armchair Detective, Vols. 1–2," *The Armchair Detective*, Vol. 2, No. 4 (July 1969): 281–85; "Vols. 3–4," *The Armchair Detective*, Vol. 4, no. 4 (July 1971): 259–64; "Vols. 5–6," *The Armchair Detective*, Vol. 6, no. 4 (August 1973): 281–86; "Vols. 7–8," *The Armchair Detective*, Vol. 8, no. 4 (August 1957): 326–32.

LOCATION SOURCES: Private collectors.

Publication History

MAGAZINE TITLE: *The Armchair Detective*.

TITLE CHANGES: None.

VOLUME AND ISSUE DATA: Vol. 1, no. 1 (October 1967) through Vol. 14, no. 4 (Winter 1981); 56 issues to date.

PUBLISHERS: Allen J. Hubin, 3656 Midland Avenue, White Bear Lake, Minnesota 55110 (Vol. 1, no. 1, through Vol. 9, no. 2); Publishers Inc., 243 Twelfth Street, Del Mar, California 92014 (Vol. 9, no. 3, through Vol. 11, no. 4); The Mysterious Press, 129 West 56th Street, New York, New York 10019 (Vol. 12, no. 1, to present).

EDITORS: Allen J. Hubin (Vol. 1, no. 1, through Vol. 13, no. 4); Michael Seidman (commencing Vol. 14, no. 1).

PRICE PER ISSUE: currently $4.00.

SIZE AND PAGINATION: 8-1/2" X 11"; 86–104 pages.

CURRENT STATUS: Active.

—*Fred Dueren*

AUGUST DERLETH SOCIETY NEWSLETTER, THE

In the realm of mystery and detective fiction, August Derleth may be remembered for his Judge Peck mysteries. More likely, however, is the chance that students of the genre will continue to associate his name with the excellent Sherlock Holmes pastiches, the Solar Pons stories. These were originally published in hardcover editions by Mycroft and Moran of Sauk City, Wisconsin, and later reprinted in paperback editions by Pinnacle Books.

During the summer of 1977, Richard Fawcett, a school administrator from Uncasville, Connecticut, was browsing in a local book store. He came upon a book by August Derleth entitled *Walden West*. He had had some passing acquaintance with the works of August Derleth, having read one or two of the author's Arkham House collections of macabre stories, but he was totally unaware of Derleth's many literary accomplishments in other fields. Fawcett purchased *Walden West* out of curiosity, little realizing that he held in his hand what he has since described as "the heart beat of middle America preserved in amber." He was so impressed by the book that he wrote to Arkham House publishers inquiring into the possible existence of an August Derleth appreciation society. It soon became apparent that no such organization existed; and as Fawcett's knowledge of Derleth's literary achievements expanded, it became equally obvious that here was an all-too-little-known American author who had been responsible for the creation of a considerable number of works on a remarkable number of subjects during his lifetime. Determined to seek out other fans and associates of this remarkable man, and anxious to share his discovery with fellow members from the ranks of the uninitiated, Fawcett organized the August Derleth Society in October 1977.

The first issue of the *August Derleth Society Newsletter* was published in Fall 1977 and featured a number of letters written in support of the concept of founding the Society. Perhaps the least encouraging of these letters, and yet the most helpful, was one written by Robert Bloch stating: "It would seem to me that the basic difficulty you may encounter with your proposed society lies in the diversity of Derleth's writings.... The fantasy fans aren't generally interested in the Sac Prairie Saga—the regional-novel devotees don't necessarily care for the Solar Pons series—the Solar Pons devotees may take a dim view of Judge Peck—the Pons fans aren't necessarily interested in Derleth's poetry.... How does one appeal to such a various readership? Solve that and you'll have a success...."

Heeding Bloch's advice, the Society has been presented from the first as an organization that would try to have something for everyone in at least one issue of its newsletter each year. The *Newsletter,* then, attempts to feature a different aspect of Derleth's varied writing career with each issue. Solar Pons pastiches and other mystery fiction may be featured in one issue, while another is devoted to regional writings, historical fiction, or poetry. Once the cycle of Derleth's works has been addressed, the process commences once again. As a result of this policy, the Society has grown from a handful of faithful fans to an organization that presently boasts in excess of two hundred members sharing a variety of interests.

The Society meets once each year in Sac Prairie, Wisconsin, usually in the fall. It exists to educate the reading public to the remarkable literary achievements of August Derleth, to encourage and foster the study of his writings.

With over 150 published works in his lifetime, August Derleth was by any measure one of America's most prolific writers. Added to this is the fact that he wrote on a wide variety of subjects, never limiting his production to any single or related genre. In addition to his activities in the mystery field, Derleth was the author of numerous macabre stories. He was a regional novelist, author of historical fiction, poet, newspaper columnist, editor, anthologist, publisher and owner of Arkham House (one of the premier small-press publishing houses), an accomplished essayist, and compiler of numerous journals that masterfully blend the world of man and nature. Nor does this list entirely encompass his contributions to American letters. He was, as well, an accomplished writer of juvenile fiction.

Derleth appeared on numerous occasions in *Ellery Queen's Mystery Magazine,* * *Alfred Hitchcock's Mystery Magazine,* * and other major periodicals. His Judge Peck mysteries are (1934–1953):

Murder Stalks the Wakely Family
The Man on All Fours
Three Who Died
Sign of Fear
Sentence Deferred
The Narracong Riddle
The Seven Who Waited
Mischief in the Lane
No Future for Luana
Fell Purpose

And his pastiches of Solar Pons are published as (1945–1968):

In Re: Sherlock Holmes, The Adventures of Solar Pons
The Memoirs of Solar Pons
The Return of Solar Pons
The Reminiscences of Solar Pons
The Casebook of Solar Pons
The Chronicles of Solar Pons
Mr. Fairlie's Final Journey
A Praed Street Dossier

Information Sources

BIBLIOGRAPHY:
August Derleth Society. *The August Derleth Society*. Sauk City, Wisc., August Derleth Society, 1980.
Fawcett, Richard H. "Some Thoughts on the Future of the Newsletter." *The August Derleth Society Newsletter,* Vol. 2, no. 2 (1978):9.
INDEX SOURCES: None known.
LOCATION SOURCES: Private collectors.

Publication History

MAGAZINE TITLE: *The August Derleth Society Newsletter.*
TITLE CHANGES: None.
VOLUME AND ISSUE DATA: Vol. 1, no. 1 (October 1977) through Vol. 5, no. 2 (to date, January 1982); 17 issues.

PUBLISHER: Richard Fawcett, for August Derleth Society, 61 Teecomwas Drive, Un-
      casville, Connecticut 06382.
EDITOR: Richard Fawcett.
PRICE PER ISSUE: By subscription to Society members only at $5.00 year (Society
      Treasurer: George Marx, 20 East Delaware Place, Chicago, Illinois 60611).
SIZE AND PAGINATION: 8-1/2'' X 11''; 10 pages.
CURRENT STATUS: Active.
—*Richard Fawcett*

AVENGER, THE

The Avenger magazine was Street & Smith's last major attempt to dupicate
the success of their formative single-character pulps, *The Shadow Magazine**
and *Doc Savage.** Henry W. Ralston, business manager, and Editor John L.
Nanovic, who engineered the twin successes of these, created *The Avenger* in
1939 in response to the industry-wide expansion of pulp magazine titles that
year.

Ralston and Nanovic employed all their resources in an effort to make *The
Avenger* successful. They arrived at a character, Richard Henry Benson, who,
like Doc Savage, was based upon a soldier of fortune named Richard Henry
Savage. But Benson was an older character with a varied past and a cold,
mysterious demeanor, much like The Shadow. Ralston and Nanovic picked
veteran pulp writer Paul Ernst to write the series; Ernst agreed with some reluctance and only when he was promised assistance with his plots. The format
of the series was brainstormed in a session at which Lester Dent and Walter B.
Gibson, authors of *Doc Savage* and *The Shadow Magazine*, respectively, gave
Ernst the benefit of their many years' experience writing similar characters.

The character who emerged was a combination of Doc Savage, The Shadow,
Richard Henry Savage, and Ernst's 1936 *Detective Tales** (Popular Publications)* crime-fighter with the pliable face, The Wraith. The first novel, "Justice,
Inc.," is a remarkably grim effort in which retiring adventurer Richard Henry
Benson, on an airline flight with his wife and daughter, returns to his seat to
find them both missing, and the remaining passengers confound the mystery by
swearing Benson had boarded the plane alone. Benson's search for his wife and
daughter prove frustratingly fruitless, and the strain puts him in a hospital. When
he regains consciousness, Benson finds his hair has turned white; his facial
muscles have frozen into an emotionless mask which he finds he can reshape
by hand. This enables him to become a master of disguise. The features, combined with his cold, colorless eyes, give him a terrible aspect, and he goes in
search of the criminals who were responsible for his family's fate. He is joined
by two other crime-scarred aides, chemist Fergus MacMurdie, and Algernon
Heathcote Smith, a giant electrical engineer who answers to the name of Smitty.
Both characters are firmly in the Doc Savage tradition, and both share many
outlandish physical and temperamental characteristics.

In the second novel, "The Yellow Hoard," Benson acquires a source of operating capital also in the Doc Savage tradition—the lost gold of the Aztecs—and a female aide, a tiny blonde named Nellie Gray.

The final additions to the group, known as Justice, Inc., were the black husband-and-wife team of Josh and Rosabel Newton. Josh and Rosabel became regular characters, and their appearance was unusual for the time period. Indications are that Smitty was perhaps intended to be a black character; early spot illustrations give him a distinctly ethnic look, one deliberately altered in later issues. Josh and Rosabel were introduced in the third novel, "The Sky Walker," a story of a man who seemingly walked through the sky and destroyed buildings. It is one of the best in the series.

Although *The Avenger* was marketed as a Doc Savage imitation in many respects (Ernst wrote them under the same Kenneth Robeson house name, and the series was advertised as by the creator of Doc Savage; early editorials even referred to The Avenger as the "Man of Steel"), the overall thrust was that of a Shadow variant. Early covers by H. Winfield Scott usually depicted a scene over which the ghostly face of The Avenger loomed.

This approach evidently did not translate into sales, however; for after the first year, the magazine dropped to bimonthly frequency. Behind the scenes, Nanovic and Ralston instituted swift changes, hoping to salvage the magazine. Publication of three novels was held back ("House of Death," "Nevlo," and "Death in Slow Motion"), and rushed into print was "Murder on Wheels," in which Benson's frozen face was cured by exposure to an electrical ray. His white hair grows back black. After this issue, The Avenger becomes younger and begins to wear black clothes instead of the gray outfits that matched his cold demeanor. Added to the cast is Cole Wilson, a young mechanical engineer. The covers by Scott, Graves Gladney, and others drop the looming face as a motif and often show the new, younger Avenger in action.

Whether this deliberate, youthful slanting improved sales is not known. The magazine continued bimonthly another two years, during which the three previously withheld novels were released with minor revisions. After the September 1942 issue, the magazine was discontinued; the character was continued in *Clues Detective Stories (Clues*)* until 1943, when paper shortages caused by the war forced that magazine's suspension. The *Clues* stories were novelettes written by Emile C. Tepperman under the Kenneth Robeson byline. Only five of these novelettes appeared in *Clues Detective*; a sixth was in the August 1944 issue of *The Shadow* under Tepperman's own name. A short-lived Avenger radio series ran in New York City briefly in 1941 but little resembled the pulp series.

The Avenger novels were competent and the characters sound, but the series never really achieved the appeal of either the Doc Savage or The Shadow stories. While the supporting cast was good, the problem may have rested with the character of Richard Henry Benson. Introduced as a cold, relentless, and unemotional crime fighter, he lacked the mystery of the equally remote Shadow and did not possess the warmth and human appeal of Doc Savage. Even after the second accident made him more human and real, he remained austere and distant from the other members of Justice, Inc. This made it difficult for readers to empathize with Benson, a situation not helped by Paul Ernst's evident lack of personal involvement with his characters. Once the Justice, Inc., team was established in their Greenwich Village headquarters (a fortress disguised as a warehouse), Ernst never bothered to explore their characters or backgrounds further.

However, Ernst did an exemplary job with the novels. They are well plotted and conscientiously realized. The plots often followed the Shadow pattern more than the Doc Savage, with the exception of the old Doc Savage device wherein The Avenger's enemies invariably fall into traps of their own making.

Of the twenty-four novels, the first three—"Justice, Inc.," "The Yellow Hoard," and "The Sky Walker"—are excellent. After these, the story lengths drop, which contributed to their lack of power. Several novels are quite good, however, among them "The Frosted Death," "The Flame Breathers," "The River of Ice," and "Nevlo." The pivotal "Murder on Wheels" is of interest. Some, like "The Devil's Horns" and "Stockholders in Death," are typically in The Shadow tradition and are less than dynamic. Others, like "The Smiling Dogs" and "The Green Killer," reflect the adventurous quality found in the Doc Savage tales. Overall, Ernst attempted to duplicate Lester Dent's style but met with only modest success. For a writer who was a frequent contributor to the science-fiction and horror pulps, the science fiction element was quite muted and understated. The Avenger fought superstrong killers in "The Happy Killers," mind-controlled devices in "Tuned for Murder" and "The Hate Master," and artificial blackouts in "Nevlo." The final Avenger novel, "Midnight Murder," is minor, and the novelettes are even more so.

The backup features in the magazine are equally minor. Writers such as Norman A. Daniels, Edwin V. Burkholder, Harold A. Davis, and others contributed short crime stories. Ed Bodin did a column on numerology, which seemed singularly inappropriate.

In 1974, Warner Paperback Library hired Ron Goulart to continue their Avenger series in mass-market paperbacks after they had reprinted all of the original novels. Goulart did twelve novels, beginning with "The Man from Atlantis." Deliberately writing in the style of Lester Dent, Goulart's novels succeeded in being humorous and lively, and he introduced a recurring villain, The Iron Skull. However, these stories were extremely short and somewhat self-conscious. Goulart was unable to empathize with the character of Richard Henry Benson; he downplayed the Avenger and accented Cole Wilson, whom he found to be more interesting. In the final analysis, the limitations built into the series were too much for Goulart—or any writer—to overcome completely.

Information Sources

BIBLIOGRAPHY:
Banks, Jeff R. "Goulart's Version of The Avenger: New Wine, Old Bottles, and Something Extra." *The Armchair Detective*, Vol. 9, no. 2 (February 1976):122–24.

Carr, Wooda Nicholas. "Adieu to The Avenger." *Xenophile*, no. 11 (March 1975):123.
———. "Checklist, The Avenger." *The Mystery Reader's Newsletter,* Vol. 3, no. 6 (August 1970):16.
———. "The Avenger." *The Mystery Reader's Newsletter,* Vol. 3, no 6 (August 1970):13–16.
———. "The Avenger's Aides." *Pulp*, no. 5 (Winter 1973):6–11.
Jones, Robert Kenneth. "The Avenger's First Appearance." *Bronze Shadows,* no. 8 (January 1967):17–19.
———. "The Great Escape Artist." *Bronze Shadows,* no. 9 (March 1967):19–21.
Laidlaw, Bill. "A Recurring Little Villain." *Doc Savage Quarterly,* no. 5 (April 1981):9–11.
———. "The Red Baron, The Avenger, and Doc Savage." *Doc Savage Quarterly,* no. 3 (October 1980):4–7.
Reynolds, Quentin. *The Fiction Factory.* New York: Random House, 1955.
INDEX SOURCES: Weinberg, Robert, and Lohr McKinstry. *The Hero Pulp Index.* Evergreen, Colo.: Opar Press, 1971.
LOCATION SOURCES: University of California–Los Angeles Library (Vol. 1, no. 1, only); George Arents Research Library, Syracuse (New York) University (1939–1942), various issues; Spanish edition *El Vengador* 1942–1946); private collectors.

Publication History

MAGAZINE TITLE: *The Avenger.*
TITLE CHANGES: None.
VOLUME AND ISSUE DATA: Vol. 1, no. 1 (September 1939) through Vol. 4, no. 6 (September 1942); 24 issues.
PUBLISHER: Street & Smith Publications, Inc., 79 Seventh Avenue, New York, New York, later 122 East 42nd Street, New York 17, New York.
EDITOR: John L. Nanovic.
PRICE PER ISSUE: 10 cents; 1940, 15 cents.
SIZE AND PAGINATION: 6-7/8" X 9- 3/8"; 128 pages.
CURRENT STATUS: Discontinued.

Spanish edition

El Vengador, published at least from May 1942 through June 1946, monthly; reprints from U.S. edition.
—*Will Murray*

AVENGER, THE (Spanish)

See AVENGER, THE

AVON DETECTIVE MYSTERIES

Appearing as a sister volume to *Rex Stout Mystery Magazine (Rex Stout's Mystery Monthly*),* *Avon Detective Mysteries* hit the stands in March 1947.

Basically a reprint magazine, each issue featured an original story, with the last issue having two not previously printed—one being a story written by Fredric Brown ("Miss Darkness").

The editorial policy was somewhat loose. According to the first issue's cover, "All is demanded is that each story must carry the reader from the first word to the last with no letdown in interest. Every story must be extremely readable and exciting. There will be no attempt to classify stories as pulp, slick, hard-boiled, etc."[1] The stories ran the course from suspense by Starrett, Woolrich, and others; humorous crime such as Frank Gruber's "Oliver Quade, The Human Encyclopedia" and Percival Wilde's "P. Moran"; and occult represented by Sax Rohmer's Morris Klaw, The Dream Detective. The women detectives also put in an appearance with Mignon Eberhart's Susan Dare and Agatha Christie's immortal Miss Marple.

Though the magazine featured colorful, painted covers, unlike most of the mystery digests of that time, they were not enough. *Avon Detective Mysteries* came to an end in six months with its third issue.

Note

1. Editorial announcement (Herbert Williams), *Avon Detective Mysteries*, no. 1 (March 1947), reverse front cover.

Information Sources

INDEX SOURCES: Cook, Michael L. *Monthly Murders*. Westport, Conn.: Greenwood Press, 1982.
LOCATION SOURCES: Private collectors.

Publication History

MAGAZINE TITLE: *Avon Detective Mysteries*.
TITLE CHANGES: None.
VOLUME AND ISSUE DATA: No. 1 (March 1947) through no. 3 (July 1947); 3 issues.
PUBLISHER: Avon Book Co., 119 West 57th Street, New York, New York.
EDITOR: Herbert Williams.
PRICE PER ISSUE: 25 cents.
SIZE AND PAGINATION: 5-1/4" X 7-5/8"; 160 pages.
CURRENT STATUS: Discontinued.
—*Paul Palmer*

AVON MURDER MYSTERY MONTHLY

Whether this publication should be considered as a magazine or a paperback book is in the eye of the beholder. *Avon Murder Mystery Monthly* was published monthly, as the title implies, in a digest-sized format, on pulp paper. It contained a full-length novel or a long novelette in each issue, behind pulplike covers that were decorated with a skull emblem prominently displayed. Commencing in 1942, there were at least forty-seven published.

It would be remiss to not at least consider it as a magazine since there was a magnificent list of stories and authors included, as well as a variety of offerings.

Lovers of British detection had titles by Christie, Sayers and Allingham, while devotees of American detection had Anthony Abbot and Rex Stout. Addicts of the hard-boiled genre could have a field day with Chandler, Gruber, and Raoul Whitfield, not to mention W. R. Burnett and James M. Cain. And if you momentarily tired of the American hard-boiled school, you could always tackle its British cousin in the person of Peter Cheyney. Edgar Wallace and Leslie Charteris for the London thriller, Simenon for European atmosphere, Woolrich for nail-biting suspense—an incredibly diverse feast, with literally something for everyone. It's easy to forgive the editors their unaccountable delusion that the fantasies of A. Merritt were murder mysteries.[1]

Note

1. Francis M. Nevins, Jr., "Remembering Avon Murder Mystery Monthly," *Mystery*File*, no. 7 (May 1975), pp. 3–4. (The fantasy novels of Abraham Merritt published were *Seven Footsteps to Satan, Burn Witch Burn!, Creep Shadow Creep, The Moon Pool, Dwellers in the Mirage, The Face in the Abyss, The Ship of Ishtar,* and *The Metal Monster*; all other novels published are undeniably mystery or detective.)

Information Sources

BIBLIOGRAPHY:
Nevins, Francis M., Jr. "Remembering Avon Murder Mystery Monthly." *Mystery*File*, no. 7 (May 1975): 3–4.
INDEX SOURCES: Nevins, Francis M., Jr. "Remembering Avon Murder Mystery Monthly." *Mystery*File*, no. 7, (May 1975): 3–4.
LOCATION SOURCES: Private collectors.

Publication History

MAGAZINE TITLE: *Avon Murder Mystery Monthly*.
TITLE CHANGES: None.
VOLUME AND ISSUE DATA: No. 1 (1942) through at least no. 47, (1947); 47 issues.
PUBLISHER: Avon Book Co., 119 West 57th Street, New York, New York.
EDITOR: Not known.
PRICE PER ISSUE: 25 cents.
SIZE AND PAGINATION: 5-1/4" X 7-5/8"; 125–150 pages.
CURRENT STATUS: Discontinued.

B

BAFFLING DETECTIVE MYSTERIES

A one-issue title, *Baffling Detective Mysteries* was published in March 1943 by Baffling Mysteries, Inc. Note should be taken of a periodical by a similar name, *Baffling Detective Fact Cases,* in the true-crime field.

Information Sources

INDEX SOURCES: None known.
LOCATION SOURCES: University of California–Los Angeles Library; private collectors.

Publication History

MAGAZINE TITLE: *Baffling Detective Mysteries.*
TITLE CHANGES: None.
VOLUME AND ISSUE DATA: Vol. 1, no. 1 (March 1943); 1 issue.
PUBLISHER: Baffling Mysteries, Inc., New York City.
EDITOR: Not known.
PRICE PER ISSUE: Not known.
SIZE AND PAGINATION: Not known.
CURRENT STATUS: Discontinued.

BAKER STREET JOURNAL, THE

"I publish a magazine you will enjoy reading,"[1] Ben Abramson wrote to one of his younger customers in 1948, and truer words were never uttered. The magazine was *The Baker Street Journal*, and its pages have served for many years as a magnificent introduction to the arcane world inhabited by the Baker Street Irregulars and a multitude of admirers of the world's greatest detective, Sherlock Holmes.

Founded in 1934 by Christopher Morley, the Baker Street Irregulars meet annually in New York to celebrate Sherlock Holmes's birthday and to carry on their own "grand game" of pseudo scholarship based on investigation of and debate about the many inconsistencies and peculiarities found in the sixty published accounts of Sherlock Holmes's cases. It has always been an enthusiastic pursuit and has resulted over the years in a flood of articles, poems, pastiches, parodies, queries, challenges, and reviews of Sherlockian material.

Edgar W. Smith edited a collection of the best of that material, published in 1944 by Simon and Schuster as *Profile by Gaslight: An Irregular Reader about the Private Life of Sherlock Holmes*. And there was more than enough left unpublished to fill another collection, *A Baker Street Four-Wheeler*, also edited by Smith and published by his own private press, The Pamphlet House, in 1944.

The appearance of the two collections naturally encouraged other authors, and the first issue of *The Baker Street Journal* appeared in January 1946, edited by Smith and "dedicated to the proposition that there is still infinitely much to be said about the scene in Baker Street, and that it is of the first importance to safeguard the meritorious offerings laid upon our common shrine from that swift oblivion to which, by a heedless and unheeding world, they might otherwise be condemned."[2]

The magazine was published by Ben Abramson, proprietor of the legendary Argus Book Shop, and its pages were filled with contributions from the greatest Sherlockians of that era: Vincent Starrett, Anthony Boucher, Jay Finley Christ, August Derleth, Robert Keith Leavitt, Bliss Austin, H. W. Bell, Frederic Dannay, Julian Wolff, and a long list of other players of the game. Their enthusiasm and wit were thoroughly seductive, and their leadership attracted a legion of followers.

Unfortunately, Ben Abramson's enthusiasm exceeded his financial resources, and he was able to publish only thirteen issues of his "Irregular Quarterly of Sherlockiana," leaving his subscribers waiting forlornly for what is still described as "the missing three-quarters."

But there was only a brief hiatus, and Edgar W. Smith began publishing a "new series" of *The Baker Street Journal* in January 1951, mimeographed rather than typeset, forty pages per issue rather than 132 pages, and without illustrations, but continuing in the high quality of its contents. The Baker Street Irregulars (BSIs) "stood upon the terrace" for Smith in 1960, and Julian Wolff inherited the editorial duties as well as the office of commissionaire of the BSIs. Fordham University Press took over the task of publishing the magazine, now expanded to sixty-four pages an issue, typeset and illustrated, in 1975.

And *The Baker Street Journal* remains today as the voice of the Baker Street Irregulars and a window on the fascinating world of Sherlock Holmes. Paid circulation borders on two thousand copies, and the magazine still fulfills the motto devised many years ago by Christopher Morley: "Never has so much been written by so many for so few."[3]

Notes

1. Unpublished private correspondence, 1948.
2. Edgar W. Smith, editorial, *The Baker Street Journal,* Vol. 1 (Old Series), no. 1 (January 1946), p. 5.
3. The original use of the quote is in question. It was quoted by Edgar W. Smith in *The Baker Street Journal,* Vol. 3 (Old Series), no. 1 (January 1948), p. 3, but there may be an earlier use. This quotation has become a byword for Sherlockian scholars worldwide.

Information Sources

INDEX SOURCES: None known.
LOCATION SOURCES: Private collectors.

Publication History

MAGAZINE TITLE: *The Baker Street Journal.*
TITLE CHANGES: None.
VOLUME AND ISSUE DATA: Old Series: Vol. 1, no. 1 (January 1946) through Vol. 4, no. 1 (January 1949); 13 issues. New Series: Vol. 1, no. 1 (January 1951) through Vol. 31, no. 4 (to date, December 1981); 124 issues. Christmas annuals, separate (1956–1960).
PUBLISHERS: Ben Abramson, 3 West 46th Street, New York 19, New York (Old Series entire); The Baker Street Irregulars, 51 East 10th Street, New York 3, New York (New Series, Vol. 1, no. 1 [January 1951] through Vol. 4, no. 1 [January 1954], 13 issues); 221B Baker Street, Morristown, New Jersey (Vol. 4, no. 2 [April 1954] through Vol. 14, no. 3 [September 1964], 42 issues); 33 Riverside Drive, New York 23, New York (Vol. 14, no. 4 [December 1964] through Vol. 23, no. 4 [December 1974], 41 issues); Fordham University Press, University Box L, Bronx, New York 10458 (Vol. 25, no. 1 [March 1975 to present]).
EDITORS: Edgar W. Smith (Old Series, Vol. 1, no. 1, through New Series, Vol. 10, no. 4 [October 1960], 53 issues); Julian Wolff (Vol. 11, no. 1 [March 1961] through Vol. 27, no. 2 [June 1977], 66 issues); John M. Linsenmeyer (Vol. 27, no. 3 [September 1977 to present]).
PRICE PER ISSUE: By annual subscription, $3.00 to $12.50. Current: $12.50 per year; quarterly.
SIZE AND PAGINATION: 5-1/2" X 8-1/2"; 6" X 9"; 40–132 pages.
CURRENT STATUS: Active.
—*Peter Blau*

BAKER STREET MISCELLANEA

The Sherlock Holmes craze of the mid-seventies gave rise to many Holmesian literary efforts, most of which fell by the wayside—with one notable exception.

"With the first issue of *Baker Street Miscellanea,*" wrote coeditor John Nieminski, "the proprietors of The Sciolist Press add their modest rivulet to the steady stream. We know not the motivations of other contributors to the Holmes Boom of 1974/75. Ours are stated simply: an abiding interest in the great detective and his life and works; a desire to share our enthusiasm through the medium of a self-wrought amateur publication which, hopefully, will open yet another channel for speculation and creative expression for ourselves and others; and not the least, the making of a few new friends along the way.

"The aim of BSM is as modest as its initial format: the offering at quarterly intervals of brief articles, essays, commentary and what-have-you on any and all aspects of the Baker Street *mise–en–scène*—a periodic unpretentious mini-anthology, the best of the new spiced with a goodly dollop of the old, the rare and the little known, each issue a diverting mixture of odds and ends which complement rather than duplicate the more substantial fare of senior publications in the field."[1]

Partial contents of the first issue included part one of William D. Goodrich's twenty-four-part series, "The Sherlock Holmes Reference Guide," a major revision, updating, and expansion of Professor Jay Finley Christ's "An Irregular Guide to Sherlock Holmes of Baker Street" (1947). Also appearing was "Misadventures of Sheerluck Gnomes," a parody by T. P. Stafford originally published on March 8, 1898, and never before reprinted. It became the first of many reprints of little-known Sherlockian parodies and pastiches. The first issue also introduced the "Data! Give Us Data!" column, a miscellaneous collection of editorial comments on the magazine's contents and authors. One unusual feature about this issue was the printer's error that resulted in an overreduced type size.

Effective with issue number 4 of December 1975, *Baker Street Miscellanea* obtained the sponsorship of The Advisory Committee on Popular Culture, Northeastern Illinois University, Chicago, a sponsorship the journal enjoyed until the fall of 1980, when the English department of the same university took over.

"This most desirable and most welcome arrangement," wrote Nieminski, "negotiated by Dr. Elly Liebow, Chairman of NIU's Department of English...increases our optimism for the continuing growth and development of *Baker Street Miscellanea*. Not only are certain mundane financial considerations attending publication thereby rendered less pressing, but we hope to be able to take advantage of the Committee's resources and expertise to expand our readership and subscription rolls and improve both the form and substance of the product we offer."[2]

Issue number 4 also heralded the appearance of a new feature, "Has Anything Escaped Me?," being a review of other publications in the Holmesian genre.

Jon L. Lellenberg, of the Baker Street Irregulars,[3] joined the *Baker Street Miscellanea (BSM)* as contributing editor with issue number 9, March 1977. This issue also carried the journal's first photographic cover, featuring a calorie-laden version of Sherlock Holmes sculpted in butter by the noted chef and Sherlockian, Frederick H. Sonnenschmidt, who along with Julia C. Rosenblatt authored *Dining with Sherlock Holmes*.

Pollock was replaced by Ann Byerly, a music student at the Westtown School in Pennsylvania and winner of the *BSM*'s first Fortescue Prize, with issue number 15, September 1978. Pollock relocated to Brazil in October to begin a two-year assignment combining teaching and anthropological field work.

In issue number 19, September 1979, Goodrich's continuing series was joined by D. A. Redmond's "Sherlockian Sourcenotes," a scholarly attempt at tracing down the names "invented" by Sir Arthur Conan Doyle.

To mark the anniversary of its first five years, it was planned to include with volume 6, number 1, a supplementary author/title index to the first twenty numbers, along with a special "Data!" section on the members of the editorial staff. However, for some reason, it failed to appear.

During its short history, *BSM* has run several noteworthy articles. Issue number 10, June 1977, contained "The Higham Biography: A Familial Observation," by Doyle's daughter, Dame Jean Conan Doyle. This piece was a commentary on *The Adventures of Conan Doyle* by Charles Higham, drawing upon her personal knowledge of a number of matters treated by Higham. Noted science-fictionist Philip Jose Farmer had his "Sherlock Holmes and Tarzan" published in issue number 11, September 1977, which examined the similar appeal of Tarzan and Holmes. Issue number 14, June 1978, was a special all-Doyle issue numbering forty-four pages.

Circulation has risen steadily over the last seven years and now numbers some 430. The journal has featured riddles, puzzles, limericks, articles, reprints, poetry, artwork, and news and reviews. It is very reminiscent of the old *Baker Street Journal** in style and content and is, in many ways, superior to the new version of the latter publication.

Notes

1. Editorial comment, *Baker Street Miscellanea*, Vol. 1, no. 1 (April 1975), inside rear cover.
2. Editorial comment, *Baker Street Miscellanea*, Vol. 1, no 4 (December 1975), reverse front cover.
3. See Sean M. Wright, *Mystery* (Mystery Magazine, Inc.), Vol. 2, no. 2, pp. 24–25.

Information Sources:

INDEX SOURCES: None known.
LOCATION SOURCES: Private collectors.

Publication History

MAGAZINE TITLE: *Baker Street Miscellanea*.
TITLE CHANGES: None.
VOLUME AND ISSUE DATA: Vol. 1, no. 1 (April 1975) through Vol. 7, no. 2 (to date, Summer 1981); 26 issues.
PUBLISHER: Sciolist Press, P.O. Box 2579, Chicago, Illinois 60690.
EDITORS: William D. Goodrich, John Nieminski, and Donald K. Pollock, Jr. (Vol. 1, no. 1, through Vol. 2, no. 4); with Vol. 4, no. 3, Pollock replaced by Ann Byerly. Jon L. Lellenberg, contributing editor, commencing with Vol. 3, no. 1.
PRICE PER ISSUE: By subscription only; Vol. 1 through Vol. 4, $4.00 per year; Vol. 5 to date, $5.00 per year.
SIZE AND PAGINATION: 5-1/2" X 8-1/2"; 28–40 pages.
CURRENT STATUS: Active.
—*Dana Martin Batory*

BATTLE ACES

See G-8 AND HIS BATTLE ACES

BATTLE BIRDS

See DUSTY AYRES AND HIS BATTLE BIRDS

BEST DETECTIVE

Best Detective, a pulp magazine, commenced in December 1947, published by Exclusive Detective Stories, Inc., and should not be confused with the magazine published by Street & Smith (*Best Detective Magazine,** 1929–1937). No other information is available.

Information Sources

INDEX SOURCES: None known.
LOCATION SOURCES: University of California–Los Angeles Library (Vol. 1, no. 1); private collectors.

Publication History

MAGAZINE TITLE: *Best Detective*
TITLE CHANGES: None known.
VOLUME AND ISSUE DATA: Vol. 1, no. 1 (December 1947); number of issues and extent unknown.
PUBLISHER: Exclusive Detective Stories, Inc., New York, New York.
EDITOR: Not known.
PRICE PER ISSUE: Not known.
SIZE AND PAGINATION: Not known.
CURRENT STATUS: Discontinued.

BEST DETECTIVE MAGAZINE

Best Detective Magazine was a staid, undistinguished periodical, conservative and somewhat dull. Its covers were sober. Its interiors were unillustrated, its fiction archaic reprints, its authors old hat.

Through the volcanic bellowing of the 1930s pulps, *Best Detective Magazine* plodded sedately along. It survived while more brilliant titles blazed to ash. Continuing for almost eight years, it published ninety-five issues, nearly one thousand stories, from late 1929 through late 1937.

Best Detective Magazine was a reprint vehicle for the enormous bulk of material formerly published in Street & Smith's *Detective Story Magazine.** It is remotely possible that a few stories were drawn from other Street & Smith publications, although none have been specifically identified.[1]

The first issue established the format and tone. For twenty cents, you received 160 pages of sedately obsolete detective and mystery fiction. The only ads puffed

Street & Smith magazines. From front to back cover, *Best Detective Magazine* was unillustrated, except for a pair of small sketches of pistols, nightsticks, flashlight, and handcuffs that decorated the table of contents.

Early issues of the magazine contained a lead novelette, a serial part, eight to ten short stories, and a department, "The Jury Box." This latter feature was written in the style of a judge addressing a jury, a ponderous conceit continued to the last issue.

Initially, *Best Detective Magazine* stressed writers. On the front cover, their signatures appeared, or at least their names in script. Inside glowed luminous names of the day: Sax Rohmer with a five-part serial, "The Yellow Claw"; Arthur B. Reeves with a 1918 Craig Kennedy story; Johnston McCulley with a Thubway Tham adventure (Tham was a lisping pickpocket, very cute, and of proven audience appeal—he would appear monthly through the July 1936 issue).

Another series was Howard Fielding's "Tales of the Chemist Club" from the 1916 *Detective Story Magazine*. This series, running for nine consecutive issues, consisted of unconnected tales narrated by members of the club, a narrative-framing device fairly obsolete even in 1916.

Other short fiction was supplied by writers then appearing in slick-paper magazines and books, among them Stephen Vincent Benet, Herbert Asbury, Carolyn Wells, Arthur Train, Octavius Roy Cohen, and Richard Marsh. Most of the writers were *Detective Story Magazine* regulars, including Hugh Keller, Oscar Schisgall, Roy W. Hinds, and Anna Alice Chapin.

Filler paragraphs were used, commencing with the January 1930 issue, to wipe out any space remaining at a story's end. These paragraphs, gigantically termed "Articles," were listed on the contents page, giving the unwary reader the illusion that the magazine brimmed with material.

A second serial, "The Butler's Ruby," in three parts, began in the February 1930 issue, but this would be the final serial. The June 1930 cover cried loudly that there are "No Continued Stories in This Issue."

If the readership did not care for serials, it did like series characters. With the June 1930 issue, a distinct shift takes place, as writers are subordinated to series detectives and criminals. Particularly criminals. Huge numbers of crook stories were available, for *Detective Story Magazine* had long specialized in fiction about criminal masterminds, con men, safecrackers, thieves, and tricky women.

To begin this feast of crime, the June issue reprinted the original Black Star novelette, "Rogue for a Day" (March 5, 1916), signed John Mack Stone, a Johnston McCulley pseudonym. Black Star was a hooded mastermind whose armies of criminals robbed largely without bloodshed. A second master criminal, White Rook (1918), appeared in the July 1930 issue. Other short fiction told of the exploits of Simon Trapp, a dishonest pawnbroker; the confidence man, Clackworthy; and, from 1925, the adroit safecracker, Sanderson, who was pursued by a millionaire's vengeance and a mean detective.

That superior Chinese fiend, murderer, and social nuisance, Mr. Chang (by A. E. Apple), began irregular appearance in the November 30 issue; the stories were of the 1924–1926 vintage.

Rather less emphasis was given to the many detective series that filled the magazine. The rather precious "Exploits of Garnett Bell, Detective" (1916), by Cecil Bullard, appeared as a four-story series commencing in August 1930. This was followed by the historically important "Balbane, Conjurer Detective" series from 1921–1922. Written by Lewen Hewitt, Balbane was one of the earliest magician-detectives. Sixty years later, the stories have aged well, proving that magic and good sense are equally imperishable.

The December 1930 issue revived the cigar-smoking, razor-tongued psychiatrist, Dr. Bentiron, a giant among doctor-detectives. He had been featured in *Detective Story Magazine* from 1919 through 1921, with later scattered appearances. The author, Ernest M. Poate, was himself a physician.

At least one other Craig Kennedy story was published (April 1931). So were many of the stories from the most saccharin detective series in modern history, Ruth Aughiltree's Old Windmills (1925), featuring the dearest, little, old, cute country fellow (and ex-convict) who detects countrified crimes.

While the series characters enlivened the magazine's interior, drastic steps were taken to freshen the drab exterior. In 1931, the covers were transformed into jewels. White type gleamed against a rich blue background. From the center of the cover shone a small, 5" X 6" painting, dramatic with red tints and shadow effects. From the illustration, terrified women or grim-faced men peered out. Later, the painting expanded to fill three-quarters of the cover; below the magazine's title block, people stared in horror or gripped each other sternly.

Change had not finished its work with *Best Detective Magazine*. Beginning with the May 1931 issue, the number of pages was reduced from 160 to 144. Soon afterward, series of articles were added. The first of these carried the glittering title of "Women in Crime" (by Edward H. Smith) and ran from July 1931 through February 1932. It was followed by "Crime As a Business" (1932–1933). Subsequent series, mainly by Smith, offered "Mysteries of the Missing" (1933–1934), "Mysteries of the District Attorney's Office" (1934–1935), and "Great Escapes" (1935–1936). In July 1936 began a series titled "Inside History of Famous Crimes (The Body in the Box)," by George Munson; it was a promising beginning that unaccountably ended with that first article. After that, only single articles appeared until the final issue of the magazine.

In September 1935, the price was reduced from twenty cents to ten cents, and its pages were cut back to 128. By this date, the magazine contained five pages of ads in addition to the usual advertising material on the covers. The text was occasionally interrupted by a quarter-page ad announcing the virtues of Star razor blades or Black Hawk whiskey.

And still once more the cover format was altered most oddly. The illustration narrowed to a 2-1/4-inch-wide strip that ran top to bottom the right side of the cover. The art was generalized and often symbolic. The remaining two-thirds of the cover, in blue or red, was densely strewn with story titles and writers' names.

Short stories wre reduced to four in the August 1936 issue, and the novelettes increased to two. These included several of *Detective Story Magazine*'s more popular series characters, including Dr. Bentiron, Sanderson, and the Crimson Clown—this last, a cheerful Johnston McCulley thief, with red clown suit and gas gun who robbed only respectable crooks. One lengthy Crimson Clown story was reprinted in the September 1936 issue; originally it had been published in 1926.

By November 1936, the short stories were again increased to eight. Thereafter, the contents stabilized at one novelette and eleven short stories, until the final issues of the magazine. Then two or three novelettes were used, plus seven to nine short stories.

All this changing of the contents suggested that sales languished. It was late in the 1930s now. Fiction styles had changed and changed again; and quaint old mysteries, like a diet of olives, appealed to an ever-shrinking audience. And more change loomed. Since 1936, a new magazine had been discussed betwen Street & Smith Vice-President Henry W. Ralston, Editor John Nanovic, and writer Walter Gibson— a magazine that would feature several continuing characters in novelettes of their own.

It was decided to discontinue *Best Detective Magazine* in its 1937 format, to change the editorial policy and the title at one blow, but to retain the volume and issue number sequence. At the last moment, minds were changed again, and the printer's plates identifying *Crime Busters** as volume 16, number 6, were scrapped.[2] The new magazine began from the beginning, volume 1, number 1: and *Best Detective Magazine,* that amiable relic from the past, vanished in silence with no public rites.

Notes

1. In his book, *The Fiction Factory* (see Bibliography), Quentin Reynolds remarks that *Best Detective Magazine* "contained the best detective stories from all of the other Street & Smith magazines..." (p. 203). That may have been the original intention, but in practice *Detective Story Magazine* contributed 98% of the fiction and probably more.

2. Will Murray's article (see Bibliography) on Street & Smith's *Crime Busters* points out that the September 1937 issue of *Best Detective Magazine* contained six pages extracted from two short stories which would appear in *Crime Busters* the following month. The stories were Lester Dent's "Talking Toad" and Theodore Tinsley's "White Elephant." Information about the decision not to continue *Best Detective Magazine*'s volume and issue number sequence was secured by Will Murray from the original Street & Smith files.

Information Sources

BIBLIOGRAPHY:
Murray, Will. "Street & Smith's Crime Busters."*Xenophile,* no. 38 (March–April 1978):132.
Reynolds, Quentin. *The Fiction Factory.* New York: Random House, 1955.
INDEX SOURCES: None known.

LOCATION SOURCES: Private collectors only.

Publication History

MAGAZINE TITLE: *Best Detective Magazine.*
TITLE CHANGES: None.
VOLUME AND ISSUE DATA: Vol. 1, no. 1 (November 1929) through Vol. 16, no.
    5 (September 1937); 95 issues.
PUBLISHER: Street & Smith Corporation, 79–89 Seventh Avenue, New York, New
    York.
EDITOR: Frank E. Blackwell.
PRICE PER ISSUE: 20 cents (through August 1935); 10 cents.
SIZE AND PAGINATION: 7'' X 10''; 128–160 pages.
CURRENT STATUS: Discontinued.
—*Robert Sampson*

BESTSELLER MYSTERY MAGAZINE

With the July 1958 issue, Mercury Press, Inc., changed the long-running
"Bestseller Mystery" series of digest-sized, paperbound, full-length and condensed novels to a magazine basis. *Bestseller Mystery Magazine* featured a
complete novel (novelette) plus several short stories. Although the "whole issue"
numbering was continued as no. 210, the "new" magazine utilized a volume
1, number 1, designation. The complete novels, actually long "short stories,"
in accordance with the trend of the times, were primarily mystery rather than
detective and were usually by well-known mystery writers. The shorter pieces
followed the same pattern.

Among the more notable stories were "The Black Path of Fear" by Cornell
Woolrich and "The Well-Liked Victim" by Craig Rice (both in the July 1958
issue), "Wish You Were Dead" by Helen McCloy and "The Fast Fix" by
Robert Bloch (both in November 1958 issue), "The Intruders" by Evan Hunter
(March 1959), "Memory Man" by Norman A. Daniels (September 1960), and
"Murder in Eden" by Arthur W. Upfield (April 1961).

Violence was not the key to the stories published by this magazine. Apparently,
the same criteria for selecting stories were used here as were utilized for another
Mercury Press publication, *Ellery Queen's Mystery Magazine,** and the puzzle
plot, rather than pictorially bloody episodes, was evident.

When a companion magazine, *Mercury Mystery Magazine (Mercury Mystery-
Book Magazine**), ceased publication in April 1959, *Bestseller* stated on its
masthead that it now included the former.

The magazine was discontinued in April 1961, without prior announcement.

Information Sources

INDEX SOURCES: Cook, Michael L. *Monthly Murders.* Westport, Conn.: Greenwood
    Press, 1982.

Meyerson, Jeff. "Bestseller Mystery Checklist." *The Poisoned Pen,* Vol. 1, no. 5 (September 1978):33–34.
Tinsman, Jim. "Bestseller Mysteries, Checklist Addendum." *The Poisoned Pen,* Vol. 1, no. 6 (November 1978):27, and Vol. 2, no. 1 (January–February 1979):31.
LOCATION SOURCES: Private collectors.

Publication History

MAGAZINE TITLE: *Bestseller Mystery Magazine.*
TITLE CHANGES: None (however, *Bestseller* stated, "Including *Mercury Mystery Magazine,*" with May 1959 issue).
VOLUME AND ISSUE DATA: Vol. 1, no. 1 (July 1958; whole no. 210 through Vol. 3, no. 2 (April 1961; whole no. 226; 17 issues.
PUBLISHERS: Mercury Press, Inc., 527 Madison Avenue, New York 22, New York; Joseph W. Ferman, Publisher.
EDITOR: Joseph W. Ferman.
PRICE PER ISSUE: 35 cents.
SIZE AND PAGINATION: 5-3/8'' X 7-5/8''; 130 pages.
CURRENT STATUS: Discontinued.

BIG-BOOK DETECTIVE MAGAZINE

Big-Book Detective Magazine, a companion to *Big-Book Western Magazine* (1933–1953), was published by Fictioneers, Inc., a subsidiary of Popular Publications, Inc., for eight issues. A Canadian edition, carrying the same volume and issue numbers as the U.S. edition, was published by Popular Publications, Inc., of Toronto. The magazine commenced with the December 1941 issue and was discontinued with the February 1943 issue.

Information Sources

BIBLIOGRAPHY:
Hardin, Nils, and George Hocutt. "A Checklist of Popular Publications Titles 1930–1955." *Xenophile,* no. 33 (July 1977): 21–24.
INDEX SOURCES: None known.
LOCATION SOURCES: Private collectors.

Publication History

MAGAZINE TITLE: *Big-Book Detective Magazine.*
TITLE CHANGES: None.
VOLUME AND ISSUE DATA: Vol. 1, no. 1 (December 1941) through Vol. 2, no. 4 (February 1943); 8 issues.
PUBLISHER: Fictioneers, Inc., a subsidiary of Popular Publications, Inc., 2256 Grove Street, Chicago, Illinois, with editorial offices at 205 East 42nd Street, New York 17, New York.
EDITOR: Not known.
PRICE PER ISSUE: Not known.
SIZE AND PAGINATION: Not known.
CURRENT STATUS: Discontinued.

BIG-BOOK DETECTIVE MAGAZINE (Canadian)

See BIG-BOOK DETECTIVE MAGAZINE

BIZARRE! MYSTERY MAGAZINE

Despite the title of this magazine and the editors' promise for fiction of "the supernatural, the weird, the wild, the fantastic," the contents presented primarily stories of murder mystery and suspense. Supernatural elements, as well as some humor, shaded a number of the stories, but the mystery fan is not disappointed with the fare.

The first issue included the short novels "One Drop of Blood" by Cornell Woolrich and "The Horror at Red Hook" by H. P Lovecraft, both reprints, as well as twelve short stories. Henry Slesar, Romain Gary, Arthur Porges, Avram Davidson, and Robert Edmond Alter were among the authors represented. The second issue featured the short novel "Planet of the Apes" by Pierre Boulle, and the third issue showcased "The Lady Says Die" by Mickey Spillane. These issues also included stories by Robert Bloch, August Derleth, Fletcher Flora, and John Jakes, among others.

There were no extra features in any of the "blood-chilling" issues. The majority of the contents were original stories, and numerous illustrations added to the presentation.

Information Sources

INDEX SOURCES: Cook, Michael L. *Monthly Murders*. Westport, Conn.: Greenwood Press, 1982.
LOCATION SOURCES: Private collectors.

Publication History

MAGAZINE TITLE: *Bizarre! Mystery Magazine*.
TITLE CHANGES: None.
VOLUME AND ISSUE DATA: Vol. 1, no. 1 (October 1965) through Vol. 1, No. 3 (January 1966); 3 issues.
PUBLISHER: Pamar Enterprises, Inc. (Gerald Levine), 10 Perry Street, Concord, New Hampshire, with editorial offices at 122 East 42nd Street, New York, New York 10017.
EDITOR: John Pie; assistant editor, Sean Kelly.
PRICE PER ISSUE: 50 cents.
SIZE AND PAGINATION: 5-3/8" X 7-3/8"; 144 pages.
CURRENT STATUS: Discontinued.

BLACK ACES

Black Aces, the 1932 Big Shot of the magazine world, hits the deadline with a big array of 100-proof fiction. Here's the real McCoy in up-to-the-minute action. Stories of Broadway and the Loop, the Blue Chip boys, the muscle men, the bright lights.[1]

That was how *Black Aces* saw itself. Subtitled "Lone Wolf Stories of Action," *Black Aces* never quite managed to live up to these editorial promises. It was a short-lived *Black Mask** imitation, published from January through July 1932. Its covers, by George Cutts, nicely reproduced the *Black Mask* cover style, showing men in action against a blank white background. As far as art was concerned, you had to look closely to detect a difference.

Inside the magazine, the difference was more apparent. The Edgar Cooper interior illustrations were close to the *Mask*'s style, but the prose was usually not. Although several *Black Mask* writers contributed—Tinsley and Bruce among others—the *Black Aces* fiction was synthetically tough. If the words were hard-boiled, they didn't ring with the *Black Mask* music. In the classic *Black Mask* fiction, from the mid-1920s to the mid-1930s, the reader was required to deduce character attitudes from meager descriptive clues. What was left unsaid spoke loudly; but in the *Black Aces* fiction, it was all spelled out. The characters talked too much, and the authors persistently explained the meaning of it all. The result was not hard-boiled prose but a near imitation.

Customarily, *Black Aces* used six stories per issue. Perhaps two of these were adventure stories, rough doings on the Pacific rim or other lawless places where a man was on his own. The remaining fiction kept close to the city scene. This was populated by gamblers, gunmen, newspaper hawks, crooked lawyers, and various law enforcement types of dubious ethics. Familiar figures all, most of them were self-consciously hard-nosed, as if they had not quite learned their lines.

The magazine featured several series characters. Among them was the thick-skinned police detective, Nick Rongetti (by George Bruce). Theodore Tinsley did several stories about Amusement, Inc., a band of ex-marines, headed by Major Jim Tattersall Lacy, which fought crime as a series of military engagements, complete with rifles and bayonets (the ghost of early Bulldog Drummond hovers behind the series). The Tinsley work, in particular, is spare, hard-driving, and often coldly objective, but he was the exception.

Other writers, such as Franklin H. Martin and John Wilstock, produced pastiches of the hard-boiled story. Their characters were mean without being tough. They existed to perform in an exciting action story, but they held no private beliefs and they stood for nothing. *Black Aces* was the difference between a clever imitation and the real thing.

Note

1. Straight to the Bullseye, *Black Aces*, Vol. 1, no. 4 (April 1932), p. 124.

Information Sources

INDEX SOURCES: None known.

LOCATION SOURCES: University of California–Los Angeles Library (Vol. 1, no. 1 only); private collectors.

Publication History

MAGAZINE TITLE: *Black Aces.*
TITLE CHANGES: None.
VOLUME AND ISSUE DATA: Vol. 1, no. 1 (January 1932) through Vol. 1, no. 7 (July 1932); 7 issues.
PUBLISHER: Fiction House, Inc., 220 East 42nd Street, New York, New York.
EDITOR: Not known.
PRICE PER ISSUE: 20 cents.
SIZE AND PAGINATION: 6-7/8" X 9-3/4"; 128 pages.
CURRENT STATUS: Discontinued.
—Robert Sampson

BLACK BAT DETECTIVE MYSTERIES

Although the title of this magazine would tend to link it with the more famous Black Bat, crime fighter, featured in the *Black Book Detective Magazine,** the Black Bat hero here is not the same. The Black Bat of this magazine was not a costumed hero, but a very tall and very thin individual who worked closely with a Police Lieutenant Hines. The very promising titles of the novels (such as "The Body in the Taxi," "The Hollywood Murders," and "The Maniac Murders") are followed by somewhat disappointing, undistinguished, contemporary stories.

Here the stories were written by Murray Leinster. Each issue also contained several short stories in addition to the Black Bat novelette.

Information Sources

INDEX SOURCES: None known.
LOCATION SOURCES: Private collectors only.

Publication History

MAGAZINE TITLE: *Black Bat Detective Mysteries.*
TITLE CHANGES: None.
VOLUME AND ISSUE DATA: Vol. 1, no. 1 (October 1933) through Vol. 1, no. 6 (April 1934), 6 issues.
PUBLISHER: The Berryman Press, Inc., 103 Park Avenue, New York, New York.
EDITOR: Perry Waxman.
PRICE PER ISSUE: 20 cents.
SIZE AND PAGINATION: 6-3/4" X 9-1/2"; number of pages, not known.
CURRENT STATUS: Discontinued.

BLACK BOOK DETECTIVE MAGAZINE

The *Black Book Detective Magazine,* a "Thrilling Publication" under the editorial direction of Leo Margulies, first appeared on the newsstands with the

June 1933 issue. The crime-adventure stories were packed with action, and, like other contemporary detective pulps, were replete with scantily clad girls.

By 1939, the roaring heyday of the pulps had passed, and many were on their final journey into literary history. The real stalwarts remaining were those that featured the single-character, distinctive hero, such as The Shadow, the Phantom Detective, Doc Savage, and G–8. Then, in July 1939, *Black Book Detective Magazine* (volume 9, number 2) published a story titled "Brand of the Black Bat," a "complete book-length novel of a mysterious nemesis of crime" who called himself The Black Bat; and whether intentional or not, the magazine had found its reason for a longer life. About ninety issues of the magazine were published, of which some fifty-five had Black Bat stories. One more story, "The Lady of Death," was announced but never appeared on the newsstands.

The magazine had a rather erratic history until its demise in the winter of 1953. It was bimonthly through May 1943, then quarterly until Fall 1946; it followed a bimonthly schedule through May 1949, then was a quarterly once more until its end.

In addition to the lead novel, there were usually two "gripping stories," plus a department titled "Off the Record." Covers of the magazine were, for the most part, well done; one artist identified was Rudolph Belarski, no stranger to pulpdom. Interior illustrations were in keeping with the story theme. Two sketches of the Black Bat were used, each different, but both showing the hood covering the lower portion of his eyes and ending along the bridge of the nose.

One particularly outstanding cover was the September 1939 issue, "Murder Calls the Bat." The scene depicted is undoubtedly the best Black Bat painting of the series. However, artist Rudolph Belarski, deliberately or otherwise, made a mistake. In the story, a mad doctor was about to stab one of the Black Bat's assistants, Silk Kirby, just as the hero came through the doorway. Belarski instead depicted a female, Carol Baldwin, stretched out.

Two of the Black Bat novels had identical titles, "The Murder Prophet," published in September 1942 and June 1943; but the stories were, fortunately, entirely different.

Several writers had a hand in penning the stories under the house name of G. Wayman Jones, including Stewart Sterling and Norman A. Daniels. Daniels probably did the bulk of the work. Pulpologist and collector Alan Grossman, in talking to Daniels, learned that the hero was originally titled The Tiger because of the acid scars under his eyes. Daniels also remarked that the Black Bat preceded Batman, the first novel having been sold to the magazine on December 6, 1938. For this story, a total of 45,000 words, Daniels received $250.00.

As was the case with both the Phantom Detective and Secret Agent X, identity-crisis situations eventually came up in each adventure. For example, in "The Nazi Spy Murders" (November 1942), the Black Bat was fighting with the mastercrook on a cliff above the ocean. He removed his hood just before disposing of the villain. In "The Black Bat's Summons" (July 1941), underworld thugs had given Silk Kirby a dose of truth serum. He revealed the true identity of the Black Bat; but Silk was rescued in short order, and all of the crooks were exterminated by the Black Bat.

The Black Bat was in reality Tony Quinn, a young district attorney, tall, rugged, strong, accomplished. He would indeed have been handsome except for deep, ugly scars burned into the flesh around his eyes. These marked the acid burns that once destroyed his eyes. With his promising career cut short, Quinn, now blind, set about developing his other senses. At the same time, his physical development became superlative. Then, a pretty, blue-eyed blond, Carol Baldwin, appeared. (In "The Black Bat's Summons," July 1941, her name was Carol Hastings.) It seemed that her father, a police sergeant, had fallen to the guns of snarling mobsters and had willed his eyes to Quinn. A doctor operated on Quinn. When the bandages were removed, Quinn could see—and with a sight more profound than that of any other man. His singular characteristic, if not supernatural, seemed close to it—he could see in the dark. Thus the Black Bat was born, a weird form: tall, well built, with a shining black hood and winglike cape. His identification mark, usually left on a dead villain's forehead, was the emblem of a tiny black bat. Soon his name became the most dreaded word on the criminal scene.

Quinn lived on New York's West Side, his house set among stately mansions in one of the most exclusive sections. It was surrounded by trees and shrubs. An iron gate barred outsiders. Within the house, and just off the main study where Quinn spent most of his time, was a concealed laboratory—the workshop of the Black Bat.

The Black Bat was aided by Police Commissioner Jerome Warner, despite his suspicions about the ex-district attorney now engaged in private law practice. "I'm going to be very frank," Warner told him. "As District Attorney you had a shrewd mind. Certain people believe you are the Black Bat. For my part I'm on the fence between doubt and theory."[1] Also present was Captain McGrath, who also suspected Quinn's secret identity. Usually twice in a story he sought to prove this, flashing matches in Quinn's face (his pupils never contracted) or offering his hand in a friendly manner to acknowledge they were both on the side of law and order. When proven wrong, he would leave, muttering around his cigar. On numerous occasions McGrath, backed by other police, succeeded in trapping the Black Bat. Then, when disclosure was eminent, the captain would turn away. McGrath was one of the more vivid and true-to-life characters in the series, a person you might meet anytime.

In addition to Carol Baldwin, only two other individuals knew the true identity of the Black Bat. One was Silk Kirby, a former confidence man who broke into Quinn's home one night, and stayed, becoming Quinn's valet and confidant. The other was Butch O'Leary, the usual bundle of muscle. O'Leary, short on intelligence but long on loyalty, had joined Quinn as a companion and was always nearby when needed.

The Black Bat novels were fast-moving, exciting, and held your interest. Quinn was a true American, fighting for justice in the only way he knew how.

His .45-caliber automatics spoke a message of death to the underworld in a way the criminals could fully understand, and virtue always triumphed.

The *Black Book Detective Magazine* was a companion magazine to others, such as *Texas Rangers, The Masked Rider, The Lone Eagle,* and *G-Men Detective** published by the same company.

A British reprint edition of the U.S. Spring 1946, Fall 1946, and February 1947 issues was published by Pemberton's of Manchester, Ltd. These bore no dates nor volume/issue designations.

Note

1. *Black Book Detective Magazine,* Vol. 1, no. 1 (June 1933), p. 4.

Information Sources:

INDEX SOURCES: None known.
LOCATION SOURCES: University of California–Los Angeles Library (1934–1953, 7 issues); private collectors.

Publication History

MAGAZINE TITLE: *Black Book Detective Magazine*
TITLE CHANGES: None.
VOLUME AND ISSUE DATA: Vol. 1, no. 1 (June 1933) through Vol. 29, no. 3 (Winter 1953); about 90 issues.
PUBLISHER: Better Publications, Inc., 4600 Diversey Avenue, Chicago, Illinois, with editorial offices at 22 West 48th Street, New York New York; Ned L. Pines, president.
EDITOR: Leo Margulies.
PRICE PER ISSUE: 10 cents.
SIZE AND PAGINATION: 6-7/8'' X 9-3/4''; 128 pages.
CURRENT STATUS: Discontinued.
—*Lester Belcher*

BLACK BOX MYSTERY MAGAZINE (Canadian)

The Bakka Book Stores, Ltd., of Toronto, published seven issues of a combination magazine-catalog which included considerable mystery and related items along with science fiction and weird and fantasy articles. Also included were commentary, puzzles, quizzes, some fiction, and some bibliographical material.

The last issue, number 7, in 1977, was titled *Black Box Mystery Magazine,* with the comment that "we've graduated from being a mere section of the *Bakka Magazine* to a complete 80 pages long magazine/catalogue devoted entirely to mystery and suspense."[1] This promising beginning, however, was marred when no further issues appeared.

Note

1. Editorial, *Black Box Mystery Magazine*, no. 7 (Fall 1977), p. 1.

Information Sources

INDEX SOURCES: None known.
LOCATION SOURCES: Private collectors.

Publication History

MAGAZINE TITLE: *Black Box Mystery Magazine.*
TITLE CHANGES: None.
VOLUME AND ISSUE DATA: No. 7 (Fall 1977; only issue).
PUBLISHER: Bakka Book Stores, Ltd., 282–86 Queen Street West, Toronto, Ontario,
    Canada M5V 2A1.
EDITOR: Kathleen Kuklinski.
PRICE PER ISSUE: $1.50.
SIZE AND PAGINATION: 8-1/2" X 11"; 80 pages.
CURRENT STATUS: Discontinued.

BLACK CAT MYSTERY MAGAZINE (Canadian)

Originally started as a bimonthly and envisioned as an eventual monthly, the first three issues of this publication appeared under the title of *Black Cat Mystery Magazine* and were dated March 1981, July–August 1981, and Halloween 1981. With volume 1, number 4, however, plans were changed, and the magazine became a quarterly under the new title of *Black Cat Mystery Quarterly*. The cover price was increased from $1.75 (United States and Canada) to $2.50, and the contents were expanded so that four quarterly issues would equal the originally intended six bimonthlies. The reason, as cited by Publisher-Editor Faith Clare-Joynt, was "the enormous increase in postal rates."[1] It was the misfortune of *Black Cat* to start publication just at the time of the lengthy Canadian postal strike in 1981, so the price increase explanation was more than justified. Beginning with volume 1, number 4, subscription rates for four quarterly issues in the United States and Canada were eight dollars, in Britain five pounds for airmail (four pounds surface), and overseas ten dollars. The *Black Cat Mystery Quarterly* title which appears on the cover starting with volume 1, number 4, may be tentative since elsewhere in the issue it is still referred to as the *Black Cat Mystery Magazine*.

Volume 1, number 1, was basically a collection of stories, many of which were reprints by such authors as Sir Arthur Conan Doyle, Ambrose Bierce, and Edgar Allan Poe. Also included was the first installment of a three-part serial entitled "The Demon Dentist of Dundas Street," by Felicity Cameron. Beginning with volume 1, number 2, there was added a continuing feature on astrology, by astrological consultant David J. Knight, entitled "Knight Under the Stars." Also beginning with volume 1, number 2, were brief biographical sketches on the various authors whose work was included, writers such as Hal Charles (a pseudonym for Hal Sweet and Charlie Blythe), Richard Ciciarelli, Edward D. Hoch, Bill Crider, and Joe R. Lansdale. After the initial issue, most of the fiction is original, with a limited number of reprints.

The editorial policy from the outset requested material in good taste, with no explicit sex or bad language. "Stories should build suspense and not have a predictable ending. Crime stories should emphasize that 'crime does not pay.' Stories may be humorous or spine-chilling. Length up to 3,000 words. Longer stories occasionally accepted. Rates—3¢ to 5¢ depending upon rights purchased."[2] Also acceptable are serials up to three installments, poems of a mystery/occult nature, puzzles, and reader-participation stories having follow-up solutions in the next issue. Subscribers were also promised membership in the Black Cat Mystery Circle, entitling them to gifts from time to time.

There is no uniformity in the physical size of the first four issues, volume 1, number 1, being slightly larger than the others, which, themselves, are also uneven. The largest to date measures 5-1/2" X 8-1/4". Covers are in single, solid colors with black-cat-in-black-circle cover logo on all, front and rear.

The magazine doubled its print order with the fourth issue and was planning to be on display in 1982 at major book fairs in Europe, the United States, and Canada. Paid advertising is accepted.

Notes

1. Notice accompanying *Black Cat Mystery Quarterly*, volume 1, number 3 (Winter 1981–1982).
2. Letter of invitation sent to prospective authors and subscribers from the publisher.

Information Sources

INDEX SOURCES: None known.
LOCATION SOURCES: Private collectors.

Publication History

MAGAZINE TITLE: *Black Cat Mystery Magazine*.
TITLE CHANGES: *Black Cat Mystery Quarterly* (with the fourth issue).
VOLUME AND ISSUE DATA: Vol. 1, no. 1 (March 1981) through Vol. 1, no. 4 (to date, Winter 1981–1982); 4 issues.
PUBLISHER: March Chase Publishing, 45 Southport Street, Suite 712, Toronto, Ontario, Canada M6S 3N5.
EDITOR: Faith Clare-Joynt.
PRICE PER ISSUE: $1.75; $2.50 (from Vol. 1, no. 4).
SIZE AND PAGINATION: Average 5" X 8"; 71–96 pages.
CURRENT STATUS: Inactive.
—*James R. McCahery*

BLACK CAT MYSTERY QUARTERLY (Canadian)

See BLACK CAT MYSTERY MAGAZINE

BLACK HOOD DETECTIVE

See HOODED DETECTIVE

BLACK MASK, THE

The Black Mask made a modest and unassuming debut in April 1920 and ceased publication in July 1951 after 340 issues, having made its reputation as the finest detective pulp magazine ever published. Copies today are cherished by collectors and librarians, and a complete set is a rarity of rarities.

Volume 1, number 1, was priced at twenty cents, contained a dozen stories, had 128 pages, and was subtitled "An Illustrated Magazine of Detective Mystery, Adventure, Romance, and Spiritualism" (the sub was consistently tinkered with), which covered just about everything in the field. It was far removed from the hard-boiled, tough-guy item it became in later years. Pro-Distributors was the New York City publisher. *Mask's* logo was a dueling pistol crossed with a dirk, surmounted by a black domino mask. Few readers today would recognize any author on the title page, with the exception of Vincent Starrett. *Mask* was a monthly, with F. M. Osborne as editor.

Osborne remained in the editor's chair until September 1922. The following month, George W. Sutton, Jr., assumed the reigns; in turn, he was replaced by Philip C. Cody with the April 1, 1924, issue. Cody was succeeded by the famous Joseph T. Shaw, whose name as editor first appeared on the November 1926 masthead (volume 9, number 9).

Shaw's tenure was exactly ten years (until November 1936), and under him the magazine achieved the very peak of popularity and influence in the detective pulp field. Indeed, *Black Mask* was Shaw, and vice versa.

He left his desk after a policy-salary dispute—he was fired!—and in came Fanny Ellsworth, to my knowledge the only woman ever to edit a detective pulp. She was competent in her tasks and worked there until April 1940. The June issue carried Kenneth S. White as editor and continued to do so through, apparently, November 1948. The last issues were supervised, if not edited per se, by Henry Steeger, president and secretary. *Black Mask* had endured a little over thirty-one years, a very long time in the pulp business.

In May 1920, Osborne ran a bragging announcement: "[Our] plan...is novel, and yet very simple. What we propose to do is to publish in every issue the best stories obtainable in America....No effort or expense will be spared....[It] will be illustrated by the best artists we can find....We will offer more...in one magazine than is now offered in any five."[1]

He increased the number of stories to fourteen and topped that in subsequent numbers. The tales were (by our standards) embarrassingly overwritten, too mysterious, occultish, or just plain silly. They were often—too often—set in far-away, "romantic" places, such as the South Seas or in some Poe-like American locale. Their titles hankered after the mysterious, too, and relentlessly used the definite article, for example, "The Man Who Was Two" or "The Man Who Was Seven."[2]

Osborne's stable of writers included such unknowns as J. Frederic Thorne, Harold Ward (with at least three other pseudonyms), Hamilton Craigie, J. C. Kofoed, John Baer, Lloyd Lonergan, J. J. Stagg; on the other hand, he also printed the well-known names of Murray Leinster, J. S. Fletcher, Herman Petersen, Frederick C. Davis, and Vincent Starrett. But, generally, quality was not a strong point, and quite a few of the authors were amateurs moonlighting in fiction.

In fall 1922, Osborne was out; Sutton was in, with H. C. North as his associate. *Mask* had been struggling, and Sutton set to work. He had some advice for readers in his first editorial foray:

> Each story is designed to leave you with a definite, powerful impression. . . . BUT IN ORDER to get this effect and enjoy it to the fullest you must not read these stories the way you probably read most other fiction tales. If you skip quickly over the pages you will miss the background and details. . . . If you read the first paragraphs and then jump to the end . . . you will cheat yourself. . . . You cheat your own pleasure by reading them the wrong end first.[3]

In this same issue, Sutton introduced Carroll John Daly with a story, "Dolly," that was to cause some stir. And he brought on Robert E. Sherwood, not yet a playwright, to inaugurate a movie column to go along with the mystery-book review column. Sherwood did not last; he was too witty, too sophisticated. He was more at home in *Life* where he had a weekly film column.

Sutton had other gimmicks, and they seem to have worked—for example, a series called "My Underworld" by ex-automobile bandit Joe Taylor, partly autobiographical fact (perhaps), part fiction (November 1922 onward); a series of ghostly tales called "Daytime Stories" (also November 1922), which Sutton said "should not be read at night"; a similar series, "Cemetery Tales," commenced in early 1923; and "The Manhunters," supposedly factual crimes, composed by Charles Somerville (February 1923 to May 1926).

The big moment in *Mask*'s early days, unknown to Sutton, was the advent of Peter Collinson, a.k.a. Dashiell Hammett, with "The Road Home" (December 1922). By the end of 1923, Collinson/Hammett had appeared eight times, twice as a duet in the same issues. The first Continental Op story, "Arson Plus" (October 1, 1923), was under Hammett's pseudonym. What began as a professional relationship became an *affaire de coeur*. No other words can delineate *Mask*'s esteem over the years. Sutton published his letters, trumpeted his stories in advance. He told his fans in November 1924: "In our recent voting contest for favorite *Black Mask* authors, Dashiell Hammett received thousands of votes because of. . . the adventures of his San Francisco detective. . . one of the most convincing and realistic characters in all detective fiction." Little wonder he could say, "We wouldn't consider an issue complete without one of Mr. Hammett's stories in it."[4]

On June 1, 1923, *Black Mask* produced what it considered its supreme achievement to date, the Ku Klux Klan issue. Sutton immodestly opined that it would prove to be "the most interesting and sensational number of any American magazine this year." *Mask* claimed absolute neutrality toward the Klan, but it had difficulty hiding its tacit support and encouragement. Argument to the contrary is illogical for a pulp that more than once was out-and-out racist and ethnically biased.

The most significant piece in the issue was Carroll John Daly's "Knights of the Open Palm," featuring and introducing Race Williams, Private Investigator, derived from an earlier Daly creation, Three-Gun Terry Mack, P.I.; Williams became the most popular character of them all, out-rivaling even The Op. Daly knew he had a good thing going, and he relentlessly hauled up Race Williams capers from his well of imagination as if his typewriter was a windlass. Race's final appearance was in November 1934 in *Black Mask*—his fifty-third appearance.

Sutton—who had brought along such writers and their "heroes" as Eustace Hale Ball (The Scarlet Fox), Ray Cummings (T. McGuirk), and J. Paul Suter—bowed out on March 15, 1924, to pursue what he called in a farewell letter his "automobile and motorboat" interests.[5] He had done a good job, not the least of which was to present Erle Stanley Gardner, then known as Charles Green, in the December 15, 1923, issue.

Under Philip C. Cody, the magazine steadily progressed. Cody, who has never really received the credit due him for editorial achievements, encouraged Gardner and published the first stories starring Ed Jenkins, The Phantom Crook, who was to reach the popular stature of The Op and Race Williams before too long. Suter's Reverend McGregor-Daunt was another popular character. The good minister's debut was in November 1924, the authors of which had been voted for by *Mask* readers that previous summer in a poll conducted by Cody. He kept in constant touch. In March 1926, he announced that "the rapid increase in the sale of *The Black Mask*...has induced us to increase our print order by 50 percent—at one shot."[6] It was in this issue that Raoul F. Whitfield first appeared along with Frederick L. Nebel and Katherine Brocklebank with her most unusual heroine, Tex of the Border Service.

Cody was first-rate, make no mistake about that. His fiction recruiting drives had nabbed Tom Curry, who was to become well known for his Macnamara and DeVrite stories, and Nels Leroy Jorgensen, who was to gain an even better reputation because of Black (Stuart) Burton, the square-shooting gambler from the Southwest (debut, August 1925). His thirty-second appearance was in September 1938.

The time had come for Captain Joseph Thompson Shaw, veteran of World War I, and in he came, November 1926. As editor, he not only brought fame to the magazine and himself but also sharpened and honed to a fine cutting edge the "hard, brittle style" of tough-guy fiction, the magazine's hallmark. He nurtured and brought to full bloom many, many hard-boiled writers; he was their father figure if not, in fact, their father. He took *Black Mask* into the apogee of its fortune. As editor, he literally worshipped Hammett, thereby provoking Gardner to accuse him of demanding that everyone write like Dash. (Shaw had little to fear on that score from Erle Stanley Gardner.)

But let us face facts. Shaw inherited from his predecessors; indeed, he was more an heir than a successor. In place in the pulp heavens in November 1926 were The Stars; in place was the action story he loudly professed to love; in place was the western genre, which he did not abandon entirely until about 1932. "Cap" Shaw had the talent and the sense of a superb editor, but he did not do it alone. Nor did he veer more than a fraction from the policies of Sutton and Cody during his ten-year rule. Names and faces changed with passing time but not editorial policy. His forte was scenting out talent and class.

"We will offer more," Osborne had promised back in 1920. Shaw abided by that. His suite of writers and their series figures is a veritable who's who in detective writing: Carl L. Martin (Lon Havens); William Donald Bray (Hardsley); Horace McCoy (Jerry Frost); Earl W. and Marion Scott (Craleigh and Kirby); Eugene Cunningham (Cleve Corby); Ramon Decolta, better known as Raoul F. Whitfield (Jo Gar); Stewart Stirling (Hi Gear); Ed Lybeck (Harrigan); Paul Cain (Gerry Kells); Norbert Davis; Theodore A. Tinsley (Tracy); Roger Torrey (Prentice, Killeen, Marge and McCarthy, *et al.*); H. H. Stinson (O'Hara); John Lawrence; Thomas Walsh; W. T. Ballard (Bill Lennox and Drake); Raymond Chandler (Carmady and Mallory, among others); Dwight V. Babcock (Beek and G-Man Thompson); James Duncan (Ivor Small); George Harmon Coxe (Flashgun Casey); Hugh B. Cave; John K. Butler (Rod Case); Edward S. Williams; Lester Dent (Sail); and do not forget Hammett and the serializations of "Red Harvest," "The Maltese Falcon," "The Glass Key," and "The Dain Curse"; and Whitfield and the serializations of "Death in a Bowl" and "Green Ice."

An astonishing group—many more could be added—and Cap Shaw, never one to hide his light under a bushel, always made sure that as many readers as possible knew of these writers' doings both in and away from the pages of the magazine. They were his "outfit" and he was their "captain" in the battle of the "rough paper" (to use his term) magazines. In an editorial titled "Plain Talk—And to Heck with Modesty," April 1932, he wrote:

> *Black Mask* is unique among fiction magazines, appealing to a wide group of readers ranging from those who like action fiction for action alone, where it is real and convincing, to the most discriminating readers in the professional classes—clergymen, bankers, lawyers, doctors, the heads of large businesses, and the like. While it is commonly classed as a detective fiction magazine, it has, with the help of its writers, created a new type of detective story which is now being recognized and acclaimed by book critics as inaugurating a new era in fiction dealing with crime and crime combatting.[7]

He was absolutely right, and he most certainly had had a hand in the "new era." But he was disingenuous, to say the least, when he took too much credit in his retrospective introduction to *The Hard-Boiled Omnibus* (1946). Erle Stanley Gardner rapped him but good for that bit of overstepping. Or was it overreaching?

But to other matters. One mark of an editor worth his keep is his attention to format, for example, to interior and exterior illustrations. Here Shaw excelled with what Mr. David A. Orr (Louisville, Kentucky) has called "white covers," those vividly colored paintings against a white (gesso?) background by Jes Wilhelm Schlaikjer (trained at the Ecole des Beaux-Arts, Lyon, France; and at the Art Institute, Chicago) and by John Drew, better than anything executed by artists for *Dime Detective,* Detective Fiction Weekly,** and their ilk. Inside, Arthur Rodman Bowker provided his quasi-realistic headings, often signed in what appeared to be modified Chinese ideograms, and the decorated capital letters used to mark breaks in the prose.

Fanny Ellsworth moved into the editorial office with the December 1936 issue. Having had several years of experience as editor of *Ranch Romances,* she guided the *Black Mask* on an even keel for the next three and one-half years with her retinue of new fictioneers: Cornell Woolrich, Donald Wandrei, Baynard H. Kendrick (Miles Standish Rice, The Hungry One), Wyatt Blassingame (The Bishop), Dale Clark (O'Hanna), Frank Gruber (Oliver Quade, The Human Encyclopedia), Steve Fisher, Stewart Sterling, and Peter Paige. Not a bad lineup, all things considered; not a bad editor, by any standards. The problem was that the magazine was marking time.

And evidently there was financial difficulty during her editorship. The May 1938 number was skipped, the first time such had occurred. Then in 1940, ownership changed hands and editors, resulting in another missed issue, May 1940. Kenneth S. White, who lasted over eight years, had the tricky assignment of leading the pulp through World War II and the postwar years when, at first, paper was scarce and, later, when television began to sound the bell for the last round for the pulps and many other periodicals.

Skilled writers made their debut during White's tenure: Cleve F. Adams (Canavan), D. L. Champion (Rex Sackler), Robert Reeves (Cellini Smith), C. P. Donnel, Jr. (Doc Rennie), William Rough (Slabbe), Merle Constiner (Luther McGavock), Julius Long (Corbett), William Campbell Gault (Mortimer Jones), Robert C. Dennis (Carmody), and John D. MacDonald (pre-Travis McGee). They were all in the *Mask* mode and tradition. Readers should recognize that the Sackler, Smith, McGavock, and Jones sagas were some of the better fiction in all the pulps.

White was confident of his first-line troops and said so. He pointed a finger at the January 1941 issue, which had five series characters: "If any one thing can be said to be the main factor in *Black Mask*'s success down through the years it is unquestionably the great parade of series characters who have marched through its pages bringing readers back issue after issue to renew old friendships and make new ones they know will be continuing."[8]

Naturally enough, World War II provided new settings for the genre's stories; and such was something of a shame, for the espionage, defense-plant and military intelligence stories were downright bad and today are unreadable. But *Mask* was doing its bit for the war effort. May 1943 saw the magazine become bimonthly, and wartime restrictions forced White to use the cheapest quality of paper.

When he bade adieu in late 1948, the magazine was in a downward spiral and never rose to success again. Reprints began to appear, finally dominating contents. At the end it was digest-sized, a shadow of its former glory, a run-of-the-mill product. The last issue was dated July 1951. Demise came quietly, without an obituary, a whimper, obsequies, or an epitaph.

There were at least ninety-one issues published also in a British reprint series, from 1940 through 1953.

Notes

1. Editorial, *Black Mask*, Vol. 1, no. 2 (May 1920).
2. It was not until Joseph T. Shaw's tenure as editor that *Black Mask* became known for its "hard-boiled" detective fiction.
3. Editorial, *Black Mask*, Vol. 5, no. 7 (October 1922).
4. Editorial, *Black Mask*, Vol. 7, no. 9 (November 1924).
5. Editorial, *Black Mask*, Vol. 6, no. 24 (March 15, 1924).
6. Editorial, *Black Mask*, Vol. 9, no. 1 (March 1926).
7. Editorial, *Black Mask*, Vol. 15, no. 2 (April 1932).
8. Editorial, *Black Mask*, Vol. 24, no. 2 (January 1941).

Information Sources

BIBLIOGRAPHY:
Goodstone, Tony, ed. *The Pulps*. New York: Bonanza Books, 1970.
Goulart, Ron. *Cheap Thrills: An Informal History of the Pulp Magazines*. New Rochelle, N.Y.: Arlington House, 1972.
Hagemann, E. R. "Annotated Raoul Whitfield Checklist." *The Armchair Detective*, Vol. 13, no. 3 (Summer 1980):183–84.
Kemble, Stewart. "Gardner and Black Mask—Incomplete?" *The Pulp Era*, no. 73 (December 1969):4–5.
Lewis, Dave. "The Backbone of Black Mask." *Clues: A Journal of Detection,* Vol. 2, no. 2 (Fall/Winter 1981):117–127.
Murray, Will. "Lester Dent, The Last of Joe Shaw's Black Mask Boys." *Clues: A Journal of Detection,* Vol. 2, no. 2 (Fall/Winter 1981):128–134.
Nevins, Francis M., Jr. *The Mystery Writer's Art*. Bowling Green, Ohio: Bowling Green University Popular Press, 1970.
Nolan, William F. "The Black Mask Boys Go Legit." *The Armchair Detective,* Vol. 13, no. 1 (Winter 1980):23–24.
INDEX SOURCES: Hagemann, E. R. *A Comprehensive Index to Black Mask 1920–1951*. Bowling Green, Ohio: Bowling Green University Popular Press, 1982.

LOCATION SOURCES: University of California–Los Angeles Library (1921–1951, 185 issues); private collectors.

Publication History

MAGAZINE TITLE: *The Black Mask*

TITLE CHANGES: *Black Mask* (May 1927, Vol. 10, no. 3), *Black Mask Detective*, (September 1950, Vol. 35, no. 1), *Black Mask Detective Magazine* (July 1951, Vol. 36, no. 2).

VOLUME AND ISSUE DATA: Vol. 1, no. 1 (April 1920) through Vol. 36, no. 2 (July 1951); 340 issues.

PUBLISHERS: Pro-Distributors, Inc., 25 West 45th Street, New York, New York, until 1940; then Popular Publications, Inc., 2256 Grove Street, Chicago, Illinois, with editorial offices at 205 East 42nd Street, New York 17, New York.

EDITORS: F. M. Osborne (April 1920–September 1922); George W. Sutton, Jr. (October 1922–March 1924); Philip C. Cody (April 1924–October 1926); Joseph T. Shaw (November 1926–November 1936); Fanny Ellsworth (December 1936–April 1940); Kenneth S. White (June 1940–November 1948); none indicated for period January 1949–July 1951.

PRICE PER ISSUE: 20 cents; 15 cents; 20 cents; 15 cents; 25 cents.

SIZE AND PAGINATION: 6-3/4" X 9-3/4"; in 1940s 6-1/2" X 9"; last issues digest-sized; 126–130 pages.

CURRENT STATUS: Discontinued.

—*E. R. Hagemann*

BLACK MASK DETECTIVE

See BLACK MASK, THE

BLACK MASK DETECTIVE MAGAZINE

See BLACK MASK, THE

BLOODHOUND DETECTIVE STORY MAGAZINE (British)

Anyone who liked the rough and violent crime adventure of *Manhunt** (a U.S. publication) was sure to like the British equivalent, *Bloodhound Detective Story Magazine*. The covers were reprinted from *Manhunt*, and the contents, hard-boiled throughout, were unashamedly *Manhunt*. There was little need, then, to include in the fourth issue the statement (repeated in all later issues) that "This magazine is a British edition of *Manhunt*."[1] Oddly enough, there had been an equally brief publication of a British edition of *Manhunt*, by that same U.S. name, seven years earlier.

There were several minor differences. The Boardman Company (*Bloodhound*'s publisher) had been publishing a series of paperbound mystery books which each carried the symbol of a head of a bloodhound in caricature, wearing a deerstalker's hat and smoking a large bent pipe (a la Sherlock Holmes). This same symbol appeared on the cover of each *Bloodhound Detective Story Magazine*. A chatty editorial by Tom Boardman introduced each issue.

And there was not exact adherence in reprinting issues of *Manhunt* as a whole. The first issue of *Bloodhound* in May 1961, for example, printed all the stories that had appeared in *Manhunt*, vol. 1, no. 1 (January 1953), except "I'll Make the Arrest" by Charles Beckman, Jr. This story appeared in the second issue of *Bloodhound*. In its place in the first issue of *Bloodhound* was "The Imaginary Blonde" by John Ross Macdonald, a story that did not appear in the U.S. *Manhunt* until its second issue. This *Bloodhound* policy prevailed, with stories not in the same order and not necessarily included in the same issue of *Manhunt* that was being reprinted.

The story line was, of course, of top quality, American hard-boiled, contemporary crime fiction. Jonathan Craig, John Evans, John Ross Macdonald, Mickey Spillane, Evan Hunter (under various pseudonyms), Craig Rice, Leslie Charteris, William Irish (Cornell Woolrich), and othes were ably represented. They are all here, cheek by hard-bitten jowl.

While the covers of *Bloodhound* were reprinted from *Manhunt*, the interior artwork was all provided by British artist Denis McLoughlin, a man who was responsible for the artwork in many of the favorite comics of British boyhood. He brought to *Bloodhound* the same flair for capturing action scenes. One major difference in this artwork from that used in the U.S. *Manhunt* was the lack of a single color that highlighted the U.S. illustrations. All were in black and white, pen-and-ink sketches, and the color was not missed.

The British mystery-buying public seems eager for reprints of U.S. mystery magazines but does not seem to support them for long. Perhaps a steady diet is too much. *Bloodhound* survived for only fourteen issues, from May 1961, on a monthly basis, to July 1962. No issue was published in June of the last year. While it lasted, *Bloodhound Detective Story Magazine* seemed to be a popular seller and is today a sought-after item by collectors.

Note

1. Copyright notice, *Bloodhound Detective Story Magazine,* Vol. 1, no. 4 (August 1961), p. 1.

Information Sources

INDEX SOURCES: Cook, Michael L. *Monthly Murders*. Westport, Conn.: Greenwood Press, 1982.
LOCATION SOURCES: Private collectors.

Publication History

MAGAZINE TITLE: *Bloodhound Detective Story Magazine*.
TITLE CHANGES: None.
VOLUME AND ISSUE DATA: Vol. 1, no. 1 (May 1961) through Vol 2, no. 14 (July 1962); 14 issues (monthly, except no issue for June 1962).
PUBLISHER: T. V. Boardman & Company, Ltd., 16 Maddox Street, London W.1, England.

EDITOR: Tom Boardman, Jr. (no editor stated for final issue).
PRICE PER ISSUE: 2 shillings 6 pence.
SIZE AND PAGINATION: 5'' X 7-1/4''; 128 pages.
CURRENT STATUS: Discontinued.
—*Robert Adey*

BLUE STEEL MAGAZINE

Only two issues of this cops-and-gangsters magazine were published, in March and June 1932.

The title connoted the blue-steel revolver that had gained notoriety. Another Popular Publications title, *Gang World,** was to be discontinued as it was not doing well on the newsstands.

> You are quite right in assuming that we made a sudden change from *Gang World*. We noticed that the circulation was not doing so well, so we took an issue of *Gang World* already in the works and decided to try *Blue Steel*, which obviously came from the word pistol. At first we thought it only as a one-shot but then decided to go ahead further, but the results after awhile were not sufficiently good enough to justify regular publication. Then *Gang World* picked up a bit and we continued with that. All the confusion came about because everything was done at the last minute and in a rush.[1]

This was typical, of course, of pulp magazine publishing. If one title or subject did not sell, it was quickly changed or dropped and another tried in its place.

The first issue of *Blue Steel*, thus, was a retitling of an already-prepared issue of *Gang World*. A statement within reveals it is the October 1931 issue of that latter magazine, but there was also an October 1931 issue (as well as a March 1932 issue) published of *Gang World*.

Note

1. Henry Steeger (president and editor, Popular Publications), in "An Interview with Henry Steeger," by Nils Hardin, *Xenophile*,no. 33 (July 1977), p. 3.

Information Sources

BIBLIOGRAPHY:
Hardin, Nils. "An Interview with Henry Steeger." *Xenophile*, no. 33 (July 1977):3–18.
Hardin, Nils, and George Hocutt. "A Checklist of Popular Publications Titles 1930–1955." *Xenophile*, no. 33 (July 1977):21–24.
INDEX SOURCES: None known.
LOCATION SOURCES: Private collectors.

Publication History

MAGAZINE TITLE: *Blue Steel Magazine*.
TITLE CHANGES: None.

VOLUME AND ISSUE DATA: Vol. 1, no. 2 (first issue, March 1932) through Vol. 1,
     no. 3 (June 1932); 2 issues.
PUBLISHER: Popular Publications, Inc., 2256 Grove Street, Chicago, Illinois.
EDITOR: Henry Steeger.
PRICE PER ISSUE: 10 cents.
SIZE AND PAGINATION: 6'' X 9''; 128 pages.
CURRENT STATUS: Discontinued.

BOB BROOKS LIBRARY

Considered as an imitation of the popular *Nick Carter Library** which had
begun two years earlier in 1891, the *Bob Brooks Library* series never attracted
a large readership and ceased publication after twenty-seven issues.

Bob Brooks, chief of detectives, received his orders from Superintendent
Byrnes but never was confined to working in only one city. A list of the titles
in this rare series indicates settings as far away as Chicago, as localized as
Halsted Street or Sing Sing, and as contemporarily topical as the World's Fair.
Bank robbers, train robbers, missing cashiers, famous outlaws were all part of
the world of Bob Brooks, who was advertised as "the greatest of living detectives" and whose *Library* was "the favorite five-cent Library of detective
adventure."

The pseudonymous author, "the author of 'Bob Brooks,' " used an abundance
of dialogue, with one-sentence paragraphs, to tell stories in which the villains
were more prominent and more interesting than the detective. The stories were
padded, not without incident, but seldom did the detective really do anything;
seldom did anything happen to him; seldom, if ever, was he in jeopardy. His
boy assistant, Mum, spoke in a kind of street dialect filled with "dese" and
"dose" and sentences like "how der yer spell T'rough?". The girl assistant,
Kit, was of the same mold.

Brooks was described in the final issue as "a young fellow, full of fun and
life, and with slightly wavy hair, without a sign of a gray hair," belying the
impression given in the earlier episodes of a much older man. The portrait of
Brooks on the cover shows a stern man with a handle-bar mustache. His assistant
in the later stories was named Eddie Hart and spoke as correct English as that
of his chief, with whom he had a number of conversations filled with attempts
at humor. A business card used by Brooks read: "B. B. Phoolum, President
C.A.C.C.Ry.," which meant "Catch as Catch Can Railway."

There may have been an attempt to present a more realistic style of story or,
at least, a more adult style. At one point, Brooks plied a suspect with drink to
make him talk, and characters were more likely to use the word "damn" or
refer to unmarried mothers. A survey of the story titles indicates a certain lack
of focus or a consistent formula. Toward the end, there were stories about Jack
Sheppard, Billy the Kid, and the James gang. Perhaps this was part of the reason
there seemed to be no market for the adventures of Bob Brooks. The final issue

asked readers to "keep your eye open for No. 28. Don't fail to buy No. 28 and read it." That request was as exciting as the series had ever been.

Information Sources

BIBLIOGRAPHY:

Bragin, Charles. *Dime Novels Bibliography 1860–1928*. Brooklyn, N.Y.: privately printed, 1938.

LeBlanc, Edward T. "Dime Novel Sketches No. 89: Bob Brooks Library." *Dime Novel Roundup*, no. 416 (May 15, 1967):45.

INDEX SOURCES: None known.

LOCATION SOURCES: George H. Hess Collection, University of Minnesota, Minneapolis (incomplete run); private collectors.

Publication History

MAGAZINE TITLE: *Bob Brooks Library*.

TITLE CHANGES: None.

VOLUME AND ISSUE DATA: No. 1 (February 15, 1893) through no. 27 (January 1894) (*Dime Novel Roundup* indicates August 16, 1893, but copy examined has 1894 date); weekly to no. 12, then quarterly; 27 issues.

PUBLISHERS: Lou H. Ostendorff, Jr., 14 Ann Street, New York, New York; A. E. Ostendorff, 14 & 16 Ann Street, New York, New York.

EDITOR: Not known.

PRICE PER ISSUE: 5 cents.

SIZE AND PAGINATION: 8-1/2" X 11-3/4"; 16 pages.

CURRENT STATUS: Discontinued.

—*J. Randolph Cox*

BONDAGE

Among the various fanzines concerned with mystery and detective fiction are several which are devoted to the works of a single author or a single character. One of the newer of these is *Bondage*, the semiannual publication of the James Bond 007 Fan Club. While certainly of some interest to the reader of mystery and detective fiction, and more so to those with a particular interest in espionage fiction, *Bondage*'s primary clientele are the fans of Ian Fleming's creation, James Bond.

Consequently, the magazine carries considerable advertising for various items of "fan fare," available from either the Club itself or from other vendors. These include 007 pins, posters from the James Bond films, photographs, photograph books, tee-shirts, games, and even toys.

In addition, however, there are articles, interviews, and news notes. Recent issues, which have featured full-color covers and black-and-white interior illustrations (mostly photographs and occasional drawings), have emphasized the James Bond films. Thus they have included a number of interviews with various people involved in the films' making—directors, script writers, designers, special effects and stunt directors. Recent issues have also carried interviews with the two actors who have portrayed James Bond in all but one of the major films, Sean Connery and Roger Moore, and an occasional article by Ian Fleming.

The latest issue examined (number 11) included an interview with author John Gardner, who is continuing the Bond saga; an article on the 007 Night Spot (a late-night club which flourished in the London Hilton Hotel from the 1960s until the winter of 1978); and an article by Stephen Jay Rubin on the making of his book, *The James Bond Films: A Behind the Scenes History,* which is particularly noteworthy for its large number of previously unpublished photographs. The main feature of this *Bondage* issue was a series of interviews by Editor Richard Schenkman with many of those involved in the latest Bond film, "For Your Eyes Only." These included Topol, Julian Glover, Sheena Easton, Maurice Binder, Robin Young, Cubby Broccoli, and Roger Moore.

Bondage is supplemented by the Club's newsletter (available only to members), *Bondage Quarterly.*

Information Sources

INDEX SOURCES: None known.
LOCATION SOURCES: Private collectors.

Publication History

MAGAZINE TITLE: *Bondage.*
TITLE CHANGES: None.
VOLUME AND ISSUE DATA: No. 1 (undated) through no. 11 (undated, to date); 11 issues.
PUBLISHER: The James Bond 007 Fan Club, P.O. Box 414, Bronxville, New York 10708.
EDITOR: Richard Schenkman.
PRICE PER ISSUE: By membership only, annual membership $8.00 ($9.00 first-class mail); $10.00 Europe; $12.00 Far East.
SIZE AND PAGINATION: 8-1/2" X 11"; average of 25 pages.
CURRENT STATUS: Active.
—*David H. Doerrer*

BONDAGE QUARTERLY

See BONDAGE

BRONZE SHADOWS

Fred Cook's *Bronze Shadows* has the distinction of being the first fanzine to concern itself almost exclusively with the character pulp magazines. (Lynn Hickman's *The Pulp Era,* which predated *Bronze Shadows,* began as a fanzine for *Argosy* collectors.) It was within the pages of *Bronze Shadows* that pulp fandom, as it is known today, first began to form.

First appearing in 1965, *Bronze Shadows* was inspired by the 1964 reissuing by Bantam Books of the Doc Savage novels; it derived its title from Doc Savage and The Shadow. For fifteen issues, until 1968, its pages were crowded with amiable commentary, articles, and information.

Its contributors were largely, if not exclusively, old-time readers who had been weaned on the pulps in the 1930s and 1940s; and as a consequence, *Bronze Shadows* was more preoccupied with nostalgic flights of remembrance than in hard assessment or research, although it was by no means lacking in the latter. Here, pulp fandom took its first stumbling steps independent of the science fiction or Edgar Rice Burroughs type of special interest groups which had previously existed, and out of its pages emerged a hard-core group of enthusiasts who by and large maintained their interest even after the magazine had succumbed.

Contributors included Nick Carr, Bob Jones, Al Grossman, Dick Meyers, and Herman S. McGregor. McGregor's running essay, "A Critical Analysis of the Doc Savage Novels," was one of the highlights. Bob Jones serialized much of the early form of his outstanding book, *The Shudder Pulps*. And there were many informative articles dealing with various pulp authors, including reminiscences by John D. MacDonald and Paul Orban.

If *Bronze Shadows* tended to founder at times over the question of author identity behind the innumerable house name novels featuring Doc Savage, The Spider, and others, it certainly was willing to speculate and compare notes in an effort to arrive at answers. In the course of this activity, the first complete indexes to various series, along with tentative author information, were formulated. More ambitious plans, including the publication of booklets on various pulp characters, were contemplated but never published. It remained for younger, less nostalgic, fans to pick up where *Bronze Shadows* left off and guild upon its sure foundation.

Information Sources

INDEX SOURCES: None known.
LOCATION SOURCES: Private collectors.

Publication History

MAGAZINE TITLE: *Bronze Shadows*.
TITLE CHANGES: None.
VOLUME AND ISSUE DATA: No. 1 (October 1965) through no. 15 (November 1968); 15 issues.
PUBLISHER: Fred Cook, present address 501 Farr Avenue, Wadsworth, Ohio 44881.
EDITOR: Fred Cook.
PRICE PER ISSUE: Not stated.
SIZE AND PAGINATION: 8-1/2" X 11"; 6–24 pages.
CURRENT STATUS: Discontinued.
—*Will Murray*

BULLSEYE, THE

See BULL'S EYE, THE (British)

BULL'S EYE, THE (British)

The first series of *The Bull's Eye* detective magazine commenced with the February 23, 1898, issue; and for ninety-four weekly issues (until December 11, 1899), the public was regaled with novels based primarily on the "Annals of Scotland Yard." The "penny bloods" were published by the Aldine Publishing Company and sold for a halfpence per copy.

A second series was instituted on January 24, 1931, by the Amalgamated Press, Ltd., and was successful for 183 issues, being replaced by *Film Picture Stories*.

Information Sources

BIBLIOGRAPHY:

Cummings, Ralph F. "The English Novels of Today." *Dime Novel Roundup*, Vol. 2, no. 21 (July–August 1933).

Lofts, W.O.G., and Derek J. Adley. *Old Boys Books, A Complete Catalogue*. London: privately printed, 1969.

Rogers, Denis R. "The Early Publications of the Aldine Publishing Company." *Dime Novel Roundup*, Vol. 47, no. 4 (August 1978).

INDEX SOURCES: None known.

LOCATION SOURCES: Private collectors only.

Publication History

MAGAZINE TITLE: *The Bull's Eye*.

TITLE CHANGES: *The Bullseye* (Second Series).

VOLUME AND ISSUE DATA: First Series: no. 1 (February 28, 1898) through no. 94 (December 11, 1899); 94 issues. Second Series: January 24, 1931, through July 21, 1934; 183 issues.

PUBLISHER: First Series: Aldine Publishing Company; Second Series: Amalgamated Press, Ltd., London.

EDITOR: Not known.

PRICE PER ISSUE: 1/2 pence (First Series); 2 pence (Second Series).

SIZE AND PAGINATION: Not known.

CURRENT STATUS: Discontinued.

BULL'S EYE DETECTIVE

Bull's Eye Detective was published by Love Romance Publishing Company (Fiction House) and was a companion magazine to their *Bull's-Eye Western Stories*. The first issue was dated Fall 1938, and the latest issue found was that of Fall 1939. The Spring 1939 issue featured one of the most violent of all pulp covers.

Information Sources

INDEX SOURCES: None known.
LOCATION SOURCES: University of California–Los Angeles Library (1938–1939), 2 issues); private collectors.

Publication History

MAGAZINE TITLE: *Bull's Eye Detective*.
TITLE CHANGES: None.
VOLUME AND ISSUE DATA: Vol. 1, no. 1 (Fall 1938) through at least Vol. 1, no. 3 (Fall 1939); 3 issues.
PUBLISHER: Love Romance Publishing Company, 461 Eighth Avenue, New York, New York.
EDITOR: Not known.
PRICE PER ISSUE: Not known.
SIZE AND PAGINATION: Not known.
CURRENT STATUS: Discontinued.

BURNT GUMSHOE

See FATAL KISS

C

CAPTAIN COMBAT

Each of the three issues of this 1940 pulp magazine contained a Captain Combat novel, two short stories, and two editorial departments. The novels were all attributed to Barry Barton, while the six short stories were credited to five different authors. However, the publisher's records indicate that all the novels, stories, and departments were the work of Robert J. Hogan, one of the most prolific pulp authors of the 1930s.

The novels certainly exhibit his style—rapid pacing and furious action, with few words wasted on description. Readers of the G–8 stories will recognize the plots; only the characters and dates were changed. Even though the stories give evidence of hasty writing, they are still as gripping and exciting today as the year they first appeared, over four decades ago.

The hero, William Combat, had been born in the American Hospital in Paris on Armistice Day in 1918, the son of an American soldier killed in action. He spoke several languages fluently and was an aeronautical expert. While operating under the cover of being an English aircraft manufacturer's official representative, he was also an unofficial spy.

The first novel included the inevitable "incredible secret weapon," as did the second novel (a compound consisting of two powders to be sprayed on targets, combining to burst into flames and melt everything); the third novel emphasized a highly placed double-agent but did include a powerful explosive which could blow a battleship out of the water.

Taken as a whole, the stories were fun to read but had no "message." They were not concerned with moral uplift. All they promised was a brief respite from the problems of the day.

Information Sources

BIBLIOGRAPHY:
Hickman, Lynn. "Checklist." *The Pulp Era,* no. 75 (Spring 1971):7.
INDEX SOURCES: Weinberg, Robert, and Lohr McKinstry. *The Hero Pulp Index.* Evergreen, Colo.: Opar Press, 1971.
LOCATION SOURCES: Private collectors only.

Publication History

MAGAZINE TITLE: *Captain Combat.*
TITLE CHANGES: None.
VOLUME AND ISSUE DATA: Vol. 1, no. 1 (April 1940) through Vol. 1, no. 3 (August 1940); 3 issues.
PUBLISHER: Fictioneers, Inc., a subsidiary of Popular Publications, Inc., 2256 Grove Street, Chicago, Illinois, with editorial offices at 210 East 42nd Street, New York, New York.
EDITOR: Robert J. Hogan.
PRICE PER ISSUE: 10 cents.
SIZE AND PAGINATION: 9-3/4" X 7"; 112 pages.
CURRENT STATUS: Discontinued.
—*Joseph Lewandowski*

CAPTAIN HAZZARD

Captain Hazzard magazine (1938) was the only other character pulp magazine published by A. A. Wyn's Magazine Publishers, a firm responsible for *Secret Agent X.** While *Secret Agent X* borrowed its concept from *The Shadow Magazine* and *Doc Savage** in about equal shares, *Captain Hazzard* has the distinction of being the only magazine to attempt to duplicate the enormous success of *Doc Savage* alone.

Captain Hazzard was a young adventurer, blind from birth, who studied mental disciplines—including yoga, psychology, hypnotism, and telepathy—until he was proficient in them all. Regaining his sight, he launched a career as an adventurer/scientist, collecting a group of assistants who shared his telepathic ability. His assistants included an ex-cowhand, Jake Cole; a mathematician, Washington MacGowen; pilot G. Crandall; and Martin Lacey. Known as "America's Ace Adventurer," Hazzard (whose first name is not given) worked out of Long Island and flew a rocket-powered aircraft, the Silver Bullet.

In the first Captain Hazzard novel, "Python Men of Lost City," Hazzard and his entourage are called to Guatemala to fight an evil villain called the Phoenix, who has harnessed a volcano in his plans to dominate the world. He also controls a deadly curtain of electrical force with which he disposes of his enemies, and he commands a group of native Central American Indians called Python Men. This opening novel is a pale, spiritless effort—duplicating many of the trappings and none of the escapist spirit of Doc Savage. Hazzard, unlike Doc Savage, is physically unimposing, and his assistants are no more colorful.

"Python Men of Lost City" was ostensibly written by Chester Hawks, in reality a house name disguising Paul Chadwick (the originating author of the Secret Agent X series). Chadwick's moody, claustrophobic style was well suited to the clandestine exploits of Secret Agent X but not easily adapted to Captain Hazzard's globe-girdling adventures. That fact, and the apparently slap-dash character concept, seems to have killed the series almost as soon as it appeared. The second issue of the magazine was never published. The novel intended for that issue was rewritten as a Secret Agent X story and appeared thus in September 1938 as the "Curse of the Crimson Horde."

Information Sources

INDEX SOURCES: Weinberg, Robert, and Lohr McKinstry. *The Hero Pulp Index.* Evergreen, Colo.: Opar Press, 1971.
LOCATION SOURCES: Private collectors only.

Publication History

MAGAZINE TITLE: *Captain Hazzard.*
TITLE CHANGES: None.
VOLUME AND ISSUE DATA: May 1938; 1 issue.
PUBLISHER: Magazine Publishers, Inc. (A. A. Wyn), 29 Worthington Street, Springfield, Massachusetts, with editorial offices at 67 West 46th Street, New York, New York.
EDITOR: Rose Wyn.
PRICE PER ISSUE: 10 cents.
SIZE AND PAGINATION: 6" X 9"; 128 pages.
CURRENT STATUS: Discontinued.
—*Will Murray*

CAPTAIN SATAN

Imagine, if you will, a mixture of Doc Savage, The Saint, and The Spider. Throw in a touch of Raffles, season with a dash of Arsene Lupin and a pinch (a very tiny pinch) of Ellery Queen, and you have the essential ingredients for the pulp hero who bowed in as Captain Satan, King of Adventure, in the spring of 1938.

The inky blackness of Pier Four was split by a fugitive ray of light, then was plunged into darkness again so quickly that it was as if a giant lightning bug had flown along the dank, dark place, lighted once, then gone on.
    A low whistle sounded from the darkness, and in its wake came a blinding flash of light which stayed on this time.

There was a gasp when the strong beam outlined clearly a group of men standing close to one corner—a gasp that was evoked by the silhouetted figure of a rampant satan, thrown on the wall above them. . . .

Captain Satan remained standing.

His tight-fitting black coat was buttoned over a black sweater, showing the perfect symmetry and powerful muscles of the man. Black trousers and rubber-soled black shoes completed a garb that would blend with the unlighted night outside the wharf.

But it was Captain Satan's face that attracted all eyes there.

Square without being heavy, with a strong well-rounded chin, ears ample and flat against the head—a head that was cropped as close as a convict's. Stern gray eyes were framed in a face that was brown as an Indian's. The nose was straight.

Satan moved, his sloping shoulders and large biceps speaking of the tremendous power of this man. But it was the sort of power that could be effectively concealed had he chosen to wear looser fitting clothes.

His straight, strong mouth was clamped tight for a moment while he let his eyes range over his men.[1]

Though there were but five issues of this magazine, and it apparently served as a temporary replacement for another Popular Publications title, *Strange Detective Mysteries*,* it gave a new dimension to the character pulp field, for it eschewed many of the stock props and standard ploys of the born-in-the-early-thirties hero pulps. It made a conscious effort to lean toward the lightness of style and deftness of writing typical of Charteris, Chandler, and Hammett, without the hard-boiled approach of the *Black Mask** stories. Its major fault was in making its pitch at too juvenile a level; this proved fatal.

Who was Captain Satan? Author William O'Sullivan identified him as Cary Adair, a wealthy man-about-town: a faultlessly dressed coupon-cutter and loafer—and a hunter. He had gray eyes, dark hair, and clean-cut features, with a strong chin, chiseled nose, and slanting forehead. His rangy frame and broad shoulders were part of a powerfully muscled body whose deceptive bulk rode lightly on muscular columns of legs. He had long, tapering fingers, and a smoothly rugged face that had been tanned by the winds of seven seas.

At the opening of the series, he was living in a penthouse atop one of New York's business skyscrapers. Sharing the apartment with him was his man-servant, Jeremy Watkyns, a tall, gaunt, gangling man with abnormally long, thin, sensitive hands and bean-pole legs.

A frequent visitor to the penthouse was Jo Desher, chief of the FBI, who had met Adair some ten years earlier. Before that, Desher and Satan had encountered each other on three occasions, on two of which Satan had saved Desher's life—once, in Samoa, when Desher was running down a slave-traffic gang (slavery in Samoa in the late twenties?) and again when an international jewel-smuggling gang had him cornered.

On all three occasions, Satan, according to Desher, "...beat us to the punch, we found our quarry stripped of whatever worldly goods they had possessed. And smashed as well."

The FBI chief continued, "He's an amazing man. Strong as an ox, cunning, daring.... When he's on the job, he lets us know. Lets both sides know, as a matter of fact. Whenever he strikes, he leaves behind him a mark. It's a silhouetted figure of Satan—horned head and pointed tail—with a pitchfork raised to attack."[2]

On the question of Satan's age, Desher remarked, "You could be anywhere between—thirty years old and fifty. Fifty-five even!" He continued, "You know more history—and from a personal angle—than any man I ever knew. It takes time to get an intimate knowledge of the Boxer Rebellion in China, of the Boer War—of the Spanish War—the World War; the history of Europe and the set-up in Soviet Russia; the...."[3]

In the third novel, though, Adair admitted to having been in Germany "twenty years ago."

Desher was described as having a stubby, powerful frame, with meaty shoulders and pudgy hands. There was a gleaming, honest light in the brown eyes in his dark, round face. He had a hearty, booming voice full of vigor and energy, smoked venomous-looking cigars, and was most definitely not a baseball fan. In retrospect, it is easy to see that the characterization of Desher was one of the weak points of the series, for no FBI chief could be as unaware of Adair's double status as described in the stories. Yet when the stories appeared, the idea of the FBI being so nonplussed seemed rather cute. Perhaps the repeated hammering of the pulp authors on the theme of the police official as unimaginative and lacking in intelligence had had more effect than realized.

An intriguing aspect of the Captain Satan yarns was that they presented the members of Satan's crew as being subject to human failings, like treachery, double-dealing, and double-crossing. Also, they are mortal and can be killed—and some of them are. Satan is not presented as an all-knowing, all-powerful superbeing always able to save his aides by a combination of cunning, boldness, and strategy.

This may not seem remarkable now, but in 1938 it was rather revolutionary. No instance comes to mind of any aide of The Shadow or The Spider who became a traitor. It just was not done. To be sure, there were instances of aides who died, but they were few.

There were a total of fifteen men (this was in the days before ERA and Women's Lib) who appeared as members of the Satanic crew in the five published novels. Five of these fifteen died during the course of the stories. In addition, there was mention of two others, Dutch and Paddy, former members who died before the start of the first recorded caper.

Each member of the crew was known to the others only by a nickname and, for special identification, had emergency call letters: Slim's, for example, from the first and last letters of his nickname, was "ess-emm" or "S-M."

In each novel, as it developed, Satan summarized the basic plot line. In the first novel, for example, when he called the crew together to announce they were once again entering the lists against crime, he filled them in as follows:

"...We're after the biggest game of our lives, men. But if we slip, it won't be funny, it won't be any game. It'll be our lives!...We're gunning for the United States government....Our quarry suspects us, seems to know that we're in the field. And the government knows that we're in, too. Both the G-Men and the gang we're pointing for will be on the watch for us.

"...The government is being raided by a gang, I don't know who, with a view to wrecking it....We'll crush them and take whatever they have. Share and share alike when we do on all but my portion. I'll take the usual one-third cut....

"I'm very much afraid that a mob has gotten to the government already....If it has, then I'll smash the Big Wigs in Washington—if I must—to get at the man behind this thing...."[4]

Forty pages, and some extremely fancy footwork later, he had gained sufficient information to be able to amplify these statements considerably.

"And here's the plot," he continued. "Gold has already been transferred from the Treasury to the Atlas Bank. I'm positive that Manganni plans to get that gold. How? By planting doubles in important places in the government, by having those doubles order certain shifts in their departments that will stagger the nation.

"...After the financial crash that follows, after the national scandals...the people's lack of faith in their own government would lead to revolution!"[5]

This quintet of pulp-hero novels was marred more than most such short-lived series by evidence of hasty writing—inconsistencies and coincidences abound. In spite of minor flaws, the stories make fascinating reading, for they are lovely examples of the fine art practiced by the best of the pulp masters.

The general development of the stories is highly reminiscent of The Spider novels of 1937–1939, being characterized by the swift pacing and rapidly unfolding action that Norvell Page put into those. The one major element missing from the Captain Satan tales is the frustration that The Spider habitually met at every step until the denouement. Captain Satan was not even plagued by the unfortunate turn of events that seemed so often to mar the brilliantly conceived strategies of The Shadow.

Maybe it was all these little touches that made the stories so appealing back in 1938. Though the years have robbed them of some of their appeal, they are still an enjoyable (and preferable) way to spend an evening when you are disgruntled over the number of commercials on television.

Notes

1. *Captain Satan*, Vol. 1, no. 3 (March 1938), pp. 22–25.
2. Ibid., p. 18.
3. Ibid., p. 11.
4. Ibid., pp. 26–27.
5. Ibid., pp. 67–68.

Information Sources

BIBLIOGRAPHY:
Grennell, Dean A. "Captain Satan." *The Pulp Era*, no. 72 (September 1969): 15–17.
———. "How Are the Fallen Mighty Departments." *Xenophile,* no. 42 (September–October 1979): 9–10.
Hardin, Nils. "An Interview with Henry Steeger." *Xenophile*, no. 33 (July 1977): 3–18.
———, and George Hocutt. "A Checklist of Popular Publications Titles 1930–1955." *Xenophile,* no. 33 (July 1977): 21–24.
Hickman, Lynn. "Checklist." *The Pulp Era*, no. 75 (Spring 1971): 11.
Weinberg, Robert. "A Minor Mystery Finally Resolved." *Pulp*, no. 2 (Spring 1971): 31–33.
INDEX SOURCES: Weinberg, Robert, and Lohr McKinstry. *The Hero Pulp Index.* Evergreen, Colo.: Opar Press, 1971.
LOCATION SOURCES: University of California–Los Angeles Library (Vol. 2, no. 1, only); private collectors.

Publication History

MAGAZINE TITLE: *Captain Satan.*
TITLE CHANGES: None.
VOLUME AND ISSUE DATA: Vol. 1, no. 3 (first issue, March 1938) through Vol. 2, no. 3 (July 1938); 5 issues.
PUBLISHER: Popular Publications, Inc., 2256 Grove Street, Chicago, Illinois, with editorial offices at 205 East 42nd Street, New York, New York.
EDITOR: Not known.
PRICE PER ISSUE: 10 cents.
SIZE AND PAGINATION: 7" X 10"; 96 pages.
CURRENT STATUS: Discontinued.
—Joseph Lewandowski

CAPTAIN ZERO

At midnight, his fingertips go translucent. Slowly the flesh fades out, leaving the detailed bone. Then that, too, grays and melts. His face blurs to a dissolving mist. The revealed skull grows transparent, exposing the gray brain. This vanishes. The armless, headless, legless torso floats suspended above the floor, ridiculously clothed in close-fitting woolen underwear. On the floor, woolen socks with rawhide soles gape upright.

After a time, even the clothing vanishes.

Only two flecks of light remain, the glimmer of contact lenses before unseen eyes.

Lee Allyn has become Captain Zero. Each night. Every night. Midnight to dawn.

"It's an affliction—not an asset," Allyn points out. An invisible man has many problems. He can't open doors, drive automobiles without causing havoc, can't eat or smoke, can't walk on soft, dusty, or sticky surfaces. His breathing must be controlled, lest someone hear. And he must somehow conceal his clothing after the change, yet have it available when he changes back. It's all a pain in the neck.

This iconoclastic twist to the invisible man theme gives a pleasing sting to the adventures of Captain Zero. This 1940–1950 magazine was the final new, single-character publication to feature a mystery figure battling for justice—an idea exploited by the pulps since the 1931 *The Shadow Magazine.** The series was written by G. T. Fleming-Roberts, who published extensively in the detective-action magazines during the mid-1930s and 1940s. He also contributed single-character novels for *G-Men Detective,** *Secret Agent X*, probably *The Phantom Detective,** *Black Hood Detective (Hooded Detective*)*, and *The Green Ghost Detective (Ghost, Super-Detective, The*)*.

In *Captain Zero*, Fleming-Roberts turned the conventional mystery hero on its head. His hero, Lee Allyn, was not a superhuman figure battling through novels of romanticized violence: he was, instead, a generally average man who disliked his special powers and moved unwillingly through a boil of realistic action.

The novels are *Black Mask** in tone, in spite of their scientific-fantasy premise. They are peopled with fallible characters having emotions and understandable motives, and humor often softens the atmosphere of scowling menace.

As a concession to pulp formula, a secret criminal genius gnaws at the heart of each story. His identity is concealed by scarfs and hat brims; his soul is ice, his brain a computer, and his avarice boundless as the sky. He is served by a ruthlessly aggressive and clever woman and a small batch of gangsters. These are very tough people, with no more sentiment than a stone wedge. All are feral as a hungry cat, but each shows some flash of human vulnerability.

Against this human steel, Lee Allyn seems decidedly fragile. He is about twenty-nine years old, a small, thin, blond man with pale eyes and a lean jaw. He is hardly hero material. We are told that he has only an average brain and is often forgetful and prone to error. Still, he has a quick feel for motive and deduces like mad under pressure.

Furthermore, Allyn is constantly pressed for money. He lives in a rather shabby boardinghouse; his presence there is barely tolerated because of his dog, Blackie, a seeing-eye Newfoundland (mostly) who does useful things during the stories.

Since Allyn customarily spends most nights awake, he is chronically short of sleep. During the day, he takes extended naps—most often in the *World*'s city room. This is to the intense annoyance of City Editor Fairish, a red-headed pepper pot with an eye for young women. Only the indulgence of Fleming-Roberts keeps Allyn from being kicked awake and into the unemployed lines.

As the central series character, Allyn is provided with an elaborate background history. For about twelve years, from the age of sixteen, he was totally blind. We aren't told why. After his father's death, the boy sold his inheritance, a fruit store, and invested in an eye operation. This restored partial sight. It also left him able to see moderately well in the dark and to move briskly about unlighted places (the characteristics parallel those of The Black Bat in *Black Book Detective Magazine**). With corrective glasses, Allyn can see fairly well, although his eyesight is too poor for military service.

Wishing to contribute to the war effort, he offered himself for medical research at the Lockridge Research Foundation near Chicago. There he was injected with radioactive arsenic, among other substances. These fermented in his system, periodically generating the unspecified radioactive rays which cause his invisibility.

Wisely telling no one of this unfortunate side-effect, Allyn left the Foundation and begged a job as a reporter on the Pendleville *World*.

As the series opens, Allyn has lived with the dubious joys of invisibility for three and one-half months. He has confided his problem to Steve Rice, publisher of the *World*. Recognizing a tool to fight corruption in Pendleville, Rice names the invisible Allyn "Captain Zero." "How's that a name for a nothingness?"

Rice is soon murdered, and Captain Zero's identity is quickly learned by Ed Cavanaugh, a big, rugged, competent police detective, later chief of police. Cavanaugh and Allyn form an alliance and become wary friends—and rivals for the hand of our heroine, Doro Kelly.

Twenty-five-year-old Miss Kelly is Irish, black-haired, small, vivid, and aggressively intelligent. Her nose is tip-tilted and lightly dusted with freckles, and her eyes vary from turquoise to green depending on her mood. A reporter for five years, she sports a breezy, hard-boiled air. Her heart alternates between Allyn, for whom she feels faintly sorry, and Cavanaugh; but her adoration is reserved for Captain Zero.

Although kissed, hugged, and carried about by Zero, Doro has never connected him with Allyn. With a difference in voices (Zero's being deep, resonant, and firm), Zero is more sure of himself than Allyn and reacts more quickly. Zero is also uncommonly observant and takes a keener pleasure in physical violence. He is the perfect alter ego.

These, then, are the main actors, and this is the situation.

The three published Captain Zero novels are complex and pound along with hair-raising incidents. "City of Deadly Sleep" (November 1949) describes how Zero cleans Pendleville. The town is being plundered by a criminal genius who is directing a complicated blackmail scheme. At the same time, he is maneuvering a pair of insubordinate lieutenants to eliminate each other. A lost briefcase, full of revealing documents, releases a tornado of murder, and the invisible Zero is hunted as a killer—while Lee Allyn sits in a jail cell. It is a busy story, full of twists and high suspense.

In "The Mark of Zero" (January 1950), a criminal conspiracy, headed by The Black Hat, blasts away at law and order. The Big Plan is to take control of the country (afterward, the world) by substituting look-alikes for key government officials. Lee Allyn gets banged on the head, beat up, and almost shot—par for the course. But at the end, Doro and the country are saved by Captain Zero's amazing markmanship during a free-wheeling gun fight.

"The Golden Murder Syndicate" (March 1950) features serial murder of members of the Bachelor's Club. Through violent pages, Zero detects a confidence game involving spurious stock certificates. The Man in Black is using gangster guns to steal these and is setting one part of his organization against the other, while behaving dreadfully. A Geiger counter threatens Zero's existence; and Doro, captured still again, is drugged and kidnapped (but not for long).

These novels range from 58,000 to 60,000 words. They are brilliantly illustrated by an unidentified artist, whose crisp, stylish figures are caught in moments of brisk action. It is clean, bright, satisfying work, vividly done.

The magazine covers are less satisfying. All three feature tough-types firing an automatic past the shoulder of a captive girl. The January 1950 cover is by Rafael DeSoto and was reprinted on the 1974 *Black Mask* reissue. On all covers, Captain Zero is represented by a ghostlike, floating robe and hood. Its eyes glare. Strange electric threads sizzle from its grasp. Awful.

The magazine contents were rather sparse. In the November 1949 issue, the long novel was accompanied by one short story and a fact article. Two short stories were used in January 1950. In the March issue there was only one short story, plus a filler department of amusing real-crime anecdotes. All issues also included a "Mystery Department," written by the editor and titled "The Zero Hour." Each was dedicated to the exploits of a "faceless, anonymous champion of justice" and was claimed to be true. Since each was written as a short story, there is room for doubt.

Captain Zero was cancelled without notice—and apparently without warning to Fleming-Roberts, who had just completed the fourth novel of the series. Never published, that manuscript is now owned by a private collector. Appropriately enough, the painting of the second cover, also owned by a private collector, shows no trace at all of a ghostlike figure.

Information Sources

INDEX SOURCES: Weinberg, Robert, and Lohr McKinstry. *The Hero Pulp Index*. Evergreen, Colo.: Opar Press, 1971.

LOCATION SOURCES: University of California–Los Angeles Library (Vol. 1, no. 1, only); private collectors.

Publication History

MAGAZINE TITLE: *Captain Zero*.

TITLE CHANGES: None.

VOLUME AND ISSUE DATA: Vol 1, no. 1 (November 1949) through Vol. 1, no. 3 (March 1950); 3 issues.

PUBLISHER: Recreational Reading, Inc. (subsidiary of Popular Publications, Inc.), 205
    East 42nd Street, New York, New York.
EDITOR: Not known.
PRICE PER ISSUE: 25 cents.
SIZE AND PAGINATION: 7'' X 10''; 130 pages.
CURRENT STATUS: Discontinued.
—*Robert Sampson*

CASH GORMAN

See WIZARD, THE

CASTLE DRACULA QUARTERLY

An amateur journal, the *Castle Dracula Quarterly* was well illustrated and of
quality, devoted to Count Dracula and particularly to the movie versions with
Bela Lugosi. The first and only issue showed great promise; but for reasons not
known, no further issues were published. One should note in the same field the
British publication, *The Dracula Journals.**

Information Sources

INDEX SOURCES: None known.
LOCATION SOURCES: Private collectors.

Publication History

MAGAZINE TITLE: *Castle Dracula Quarterly.*
TITLE CHANGES: None.
VOLUME AND ISSUE DATA: Vol. 1, no. 1 (1978); 1 issue.
PUBLISHER: Gordon R. Guy, Box 423, Glastonbury, Connecticut.
EDITOR: Gordon R. Guy.
PRICE PER ISSUE: $1.00.
SIZE AND PAGINATION: 5-1/2'' X 8-1/2''; 44 pages.
CURRENT STATUS: Discontinued.

CELEBRATED DETECTIVE TALES (British)

See DETECTIVE TALES (Aldine Publishing)

CHARLIE CHAN MYSTERY MAGAZINE

The sixth and final Earl Derr Biggers novel recounting the adventures of Charlie
Chan, detective sergeant and later inspector of the Honolulu Police Department,
was published in 1932 (*Keeper of the Keys*). The author, who died the following
year, never chose to write a Chan short story or novelette, preferring instead to
expand good plot ideas into the longer form. All six Charlie Chan novels,

however, did appear in serialized form in *The Saturday Evening Post* before being published in book form.

In November 1973, Publisher Leo Margulies saw fit to revive the ever-popular Hawaiian sleuth in a quarterly from Renown Books, aptly entitled *Charlie Chan Mystery Magazine*. Each of the three subsequent issues of this short-lived digest contained a "short novel" featuring Charlie Chan and presumably written by one Robert Hart Davis, actually a house name. At least one of these, "The Temple of the Golden Horde" (volume 1, number 3; incorrectly printed as "The Temple of the Golden Death" on the title page), was actually written by talented and prolific author Dennis Lynds, who that same year (1974) was responsible for the full-length Charlie Chan novel from Bantam entitled *Charlie Chan Returns*. A second story, "The Pawns of Death," has been suggested as the work of Bill Pronzini and Jeff Wallmann. The author or authors of the two earlier titles under the house name remain a mystery.

In addition to the "short novel," each issue also contained one or more novelette and five or six short stories by such well-known writers as Bill Pronzini, Lawrence Treat, Hal Ellson, John Lutz, Henry Slesar, Edward D. Hoch, James Holding, Al Nussbaum, and Gary Brandner.

There were two other "short novels" written for the magazine but never used. One, "The City of Brotherly Death" (author unknown), was announced as scheduled for volume 1, number 3, but never appeared, and it was later rewritten as a Mike Shayne story and published in the May 1975 issue of *Mike Shayne Mystery Magazine*.* The other, by Gary Brandner, "Death on the Strip," was scheduled for volume 1, number 5, and later appeared as a two-part story in the December 1979 and January 1980 issues of *Mike Shayne Mystery Magazine* with the deletion, of course, of the Chan character. Also scheduled for volume 1, number 5, was a Mongo Frederickson novelette, "Tiger in the Snow," by George C. Chesbro.

Why the digest folded after only four issues is, itself, a mystery, especially in view of the fact that volume 1, number 4, initiated a subscription plan ("8 issues—for only $6"). Until volume 1, number 3, there had not even been an editor, only an editorial director in the person of Cylvia Kleinman. Thom Montgomery joined her as editor for the last two issues. All four covers were by Bill Edwards.

Information Sources

BIBLIOGRAPHY:

Breen, Jon L. "Who Killed Charlie Chan." *The Armchair Detective*, Vol. 7, no. 2 (February 1974):100.

Edwards, John. "The Story of Dennis Lynds." *The Age of the Unicorn*, Vol. 1, no. 4 (October 1979):21–26.

INDEX SOURCES: Cook, Michael L. *Monthly Murders*. Westport, Conn.: Greenwood Press, 1982.

LOCATION SOURCES: Private collectors.

Publication History

MAGAZINE TITLE: *Charlie Chan Mystery Magazine*.
TITLE CHANGES: None.
VOLUME AND ISSUE DATA: Vol. 1, no. 1 (November 1973) through Vol. 1, no. 4 (August 1974); 4 issues.
PUBLISHER: Leo Margulies as Renown Books, Inc., 8230 Beverly Boulevard, Los Angeles, California 90048.
EDITOR: Thom Montgomery (Vol. 1, nos. 3, 4); editorial director, Cylvia Kleinman (all issues).
PRICE PER ISSUE: 75 cents.
SIZE AND PAGINATION: 5-1/4" X 7-1/2"; 128–160 pages.
CURRENT STATUS: Discontinued.
—*James R. McCahery*

CHASE

Chase was launched in 1964 by Health Knowledge, Inc., and for at least its first two issues was a digest of considerable promise. Those issues featured many contributors who were then, or later, important figures in the field. So many were from the West Coast that the magazine might well have been titled "Southern California Mystery Stories." The third issue was, alas, another matter.

In the first issue, Editor Jack Matcha had the longest story, "The Girl from Havana," a short novel. Where is the anti-Castro Cuban beauty, a medical student and bathing beauty contestant, who disappeared mysteriously on her morning walk at Long Beach, without money and wearing only a bikini and robe? In Mexico, seeking political asylum? In Cuba, kidnapped by Castro's secret police? Public relations man Ballard seeks her among California's neon-lit dives and oil fields in an interesting but flawed work.

"A Hearse of Another Color," a short story by (then) rising star William F. Nolan, ascended above a conventional unfaithful-wife murder story by skillful writing and an unusual ending that let the reader identify the killer. Dorothy B. Hughes provided a distinguished reprint with "The Black and White Blues," a crime short story about a white girl and a black musician on a steamy Southern night. Dell Shannon had a short story, gimmicky but believable, suggesting that sheer marital boredom is reason enough to kill. Robert Bloch's *Ellery Queen's Mystery Magazine** reprint, "The Man Who Looked Like Napoleon," featured one of his trademarks—the insane killer. An article about Mickey Spillane, then in his best-selling glory, was featured on the cover, with Spillane's name in big type and the rest of the title in smaller letters: "Mickey Spillane's Sex and Sadism Pay Off," by Shelley Lowenkopf.

The second issue, stapled instead of squarebound and glued, kept up the pattern. An article featured on the cover was "The Fabulous World of Ian Fleming," in which the famous British spy writer is interviewed by William F.

Nolan while touring the gangster spots of Chicago. (Fleming's name is now the same size as the rest of the title.) George Clayton Johnson had an icily effective short-short, "The Cold at the End of the Pier"; Stuart Palmer, and old pro, brought back Detective Howard Rook in a case involving a missing rich wife and a broke husband in the hills above Hollywood, later expanded into book form with the same title, "Rook's Gambit." Under a pen name of F. E. Edwards, Nolan gave us the first case of private eye Bart Challis in "Strippers Have to Die," a short later expanded into the first Challis novel, *Death Is for Losers*, with a memorable first line: "I work out of the armpit of L.A." There were two good shorts about juvenile delinquency, "Death Drag" by "Frank Anmar" (Nolan again), about a car race in Beverly Hills at night, and Henry Farrell's "The Do-Gooder" about an older man with his own way of dealing with the problem. In Shelley Lowenkopf's coldly funny short, "Let Me Kill You, Sweetheart," the new breed of Mafia man, armed with briefcase and computer, clashes with his older boss's guns-and-goons methods. Old pro Day Keene was here with a pulp reprint, plus two average novelettes by Robert Turner and Allan Moran rounded out the issue.

The stories seemed to be picked for literary quality alone, and Editor Matcha and Managing Editor Charles E. Fritch succeeded. The atmosphere was Chandler's Southern California, the tone halfway between a milder *Manhunt** and a rougher *Ellery Queen's Mystery Magazine*. A good part of the contents was anthologized, collected, or expanded into novels.

But with the third and last issue, all this changed. There was a new editor, Robert W. Lowndes; the West Coast writers for the first two issues were gone; the big-name writers were fewer and, when present, were represented with inferior stories. There were no articles.

Ed Lacy had a surprise-ending short story about a man who married a mentally ill woman to learn the location of hidden loot from a mail truck robbery; Fletcher Flora's "The Appointed Agent" had a strong central concept about a marriage between a rich atheist and a fanatically religious woman that ended in a bathtub killing, but the story was poorly written. John Holbrook Vance (Jack Vance) had a short story that was hard to believe about an astronomer apparently killed by an exploding meteorite. The best story was a reprinted novelette, "Day of the Wizard" by Edward D. Hoch, involving stage magicians, a pretty girl, and a search for an Americn bomber lost years earlier in the Egyptian desert. The story features one of Hoch's most memorable characters, Simon Ark, reputed to be a two-thousand-year-old Coptic priest, in whose life good and evil were so equally matched that God himself could not decide whether Ark belonged in Heaven or Hell—and left him to walk the earth again until he performed some great feat that tilted the balance.

Lowndes has long been justly admired for his ability to work wonders with almost nonexistent budgets, and he turned out a capable issue here. Nevertheless, there is a distinct drop in literary quality, and the total effect is much like that of a typical issue of another Lowndes detective magazine, *Double-Action Detective Stories.* *

Why did *Chase* fail? Possibly, hurried buyers, seeing Spillane's name in big print on the cover, may have been turned off by finding not the expected story by Spillane himself, but an article about him instead. There may have been complaints—note that the name of the next famous writer featured on the cover is the same size as the rest of the article about him. By sheer accident, the magazine may have gotten off to a bad start.

But there are more important reasons. The two-color pictureless covers, the appearance every four months instead of the listed three suggest the same problems that plagued the rest of this publisher's line: inadequate financing and poor distribution. And there was the increased competition from television and the paperbacks.

Judging from its first two issues, at least, *Chase* was a promising magazine that deserved a better fate.

Information Sources

INDEX SOURCES: Cook, Michael L. *Monthly Murders*. Westport, Conn.: Greenwood Press, 1982.
LOCATION SOURCES: Private collectors only.

Publication History

MAGAZINE TITLE: *Chase*.
TITLE CHANGES: None.
VOLUME AND ISSUE DATA: Vol. 1, no. 1 (January 1964) through Vol. 1, no. 3 (September 1964); 3 issues.
PUBLISHER: Health Knowledge, Inc., 119 Fifth Avenue, New York 3, New York.
EDITORS: Jack Matcha (issue nos. 1 and 2); Robert A. W. Lowndes (issue no. 3).
PRICE PER ISSUE: 35 cents.
SIZE AND PAGINATION: 5-1/4'' X 7-1/4''; 130 pages.
CURRENT STATUS: Discontinued.
—*Frank D. McSherry, Jr.*

CHING CHING YARNS (British)

Ching Ching, a Pekinese boy who spoke in a pidgin dialect, was an early version of the Hardy Boys; but while just as popular, especially to the younger readers, he was constantly involved in dangerous and tangled situations that would try even the most experienced hero.

There were several series of Ching Ching stories, some as early as 1881, and the tales published in *Ching Ching Yarns* are possibly all reprints.

The creator was F. Harcourt Burrage, a popular English writer of boys' stories who published at least thirty-five numbers of a boys' paper called *Ching Ching's Own* in 1888; he portrayed the wily and cunning youth as one of infinite resources and inextinguishable cheerfulness. One memorable experience had Ching Ching tackling a secret society in South America that was somehow master of the Nihilists in Russia, the Socialists in Germany, and the Communists in France!

At least eight issues of *Ching Ching Yarns* were published by T. Harrison Roberts.

Information Sources

BIBLIOGRAPHY:
Lofts, W.O.G., and Derek J. Adley. *Old Boys Books, A Complete Catalogue*. London: privately printed, 1969.
Cummings, Ralph F. "Newsy News" [column]. *Dime Novel Roundup*, Vol. 10, no. 119 (August 1942).
Turner, E. S. *Boys Will Be Boys*. London: Michael Joseph, 1948.
INDEX SOURCES: None known.
LOCATION SOURCES: Private collectors only.

Publishing History

MAGAZINE TITLE: *Ching Ching Yarns*.
TITLE CHANGES: None.
VOLUME AND ISSUE DATA: 1893; 8 issues.
PUBLISHER: T. Harrison Roberts, London.
EDITOR: Not known.
PRICE PER ISSUE: Not known.
SIZE AND PAGINATION: Not known.
CURRENT STATUS: Discontinued.

C.I.D. LIBRARY (British)

Two series of the *C.I.D. Library*—a small, "pocket size," paperback periodical—were published during 1933 by Target Publishing Company, Ltd. (twelve issues in the "First Series," twenty issues in the "Second Series"). No other information is available.

Information Sources

BIBLIOGRAPHY:
Lofts, W.O.G., and Derek J. Adley. *Old Boys Books, A Complete Catalogue*. London: privately published, 1969.
INDEX SOURCES: None known.
LOCATION SOURCES: Private collectors.

Publication History

MAGAZINE TITLE: *C.I.D. Library*.
TITLE CHANGES: None.
VOLUME AND ISSUE DATA: First Series: no. 1 (1933) through no. 12 (1933); 12 issues. Second Series: no. 1 (1933) through no. 20 (1933); 20 issues.
PUBLISHER: Target Publishing Company, Ltd., London.
EDITOR: Not known.

PRICE PER ISSUE: Not known.
SIZE AND PAGINATION: 5-3/8'' X 7''; 64(?) pages.
CURRENT STATUS: Discontinued.

CLOAK AND DAGGER

The first five issues of *Cloak and Dagger* were one-sheet, 8-1/2'' X 11'', Xeroxed newsletters on new and forthcoming films, T.V. shows, and books, with an occasional review. In issue number 3, Editor Jim Huang announced his intention of changing to a twelve-page digest-size journal, effective with the January issue, and asked for submissions of articles, short fiction, and book reviews. The rate for fiction would be one cent to two cents a word, while reviewers using personal copies for review would receive one-half cent to two cents, with a limit of four hundred words.

Issue number 6 (February 17, 1978) was the first of the digest-sized issues and was printed on lavender stock (8-1/2'' X 11'', folded in the middle), creating an unstapled twelve-page fanzine. It was not until the tenth issue that pages were stapled. The cover piece was on plays and films, and the issue also contained reviews by Editor Huang, Mary Groff, Jane Bakerman, Amnon Kabatchnik, and Bonnie Pollard, and an editorial by Huang. In this, he expressed his disappointment at the paucity of news, his small budget, and his gratitude that at least one publisher (Doubleday) regularly sent review copies of books.

Issue numbers 7 and 8 appeared in April and May 1978; issue numbers 9 to 12 were published bimonthly from July 1978 through January 1979; double-issue numbers 13–14 appeared in July 1979; and the last two issues (nos. 15 and 16) appeared in August and September 1980.

Cloak's first fiction, a story by Jon Breen (''The Pun Detective and the Great Seal Mystery''), was published in issue number 7. News and letters also appeared, as well as an editorial by Huang on what he saw as an antipathy between science-fiction and mystery fans and the ''too stagnant form'' of mystery fiction where, claimed Huang, there had not been any major changes since the 1940s.

In issue number 8, the results of a mail survey of subscribers were announced. There was a response of ''13 out of 63 subscribers,'' a sampling Huang described as ''statistically significant.''[1] The following information was tablulated: mean age—36.6; percent of male to female—2 to 1; favorite authors—Christie (seven votes), Queen, Carr/Dickson (four votes each), and Hammett, Lathen, Stout, Freeman (two votes each); other magazines in the field read by the respondents—*Ellery Queen's Mystery Magazine,** The Armchair Detective,** The Mystery Fancier,** The Poisoned Pen,** and *The Mystery Nook.** Readers were of various opinions about the features, and the result was that Huang decided on no change in policy. There was a majority (eight to five) opinion against the publication of fiction; but since Huang was concerned about the scarcity of outlets for fan fiction, he intended to continue publishing it. The other feature in issue number

8 was an article by Andy Jaysnovitch on T.V. detectives and the collecting of T.V. films, and the remainder of the issue was filled out with reviews and notes.

In issue number 10 appeared fiction by G. Arthur Rahman and James A. McKraken (a collaboration), an article by Mary Groff on reference works, and reviews, notes and letters.

The next two issues saw appearance of part II of the reference works article by Groff and a list of other fanzines, reviews, notes, and Jaysnovitch again on T.V. films. Editor Huang apologized for the typeface (his "wonderful" new typewriter was broken, again) and for the fluctuating schedule resulting in issues not delivered.

After a six-month interval, a double issue was published (with no apologies), which included fiction by B. F. Watkinson, plus reviews, notes, and a column by Jaysnovitch.

With the lead editorial of issue number 15 (July 1980), Huang announced the revival of the magazine out of his frustration that mystery fandom was dead; *Cloak* was to be a "mystery news zine." He reported a subscriber list of seventy-nine, reiterated the difficulty he had in getting review copies, and promised alternating columns by Stuart Kaminsky on films and the ubiquitous Jaysnovitch on T.V. This issue also had reviews, notes, and an index of issue numbers 1 through 13/14.

The final issue to appear (September 1980) had articles on fans and fandom by David Rose and B. F. Watkinson, views, notes, Kaminsky's column, letters, and an optimistic forecast by Huang characterizing this issue as the "best yet." It is ironic that the most enthusiastic of the editorials graced the last issue.

It is not difficult to understand why *Cloak and Dagger* ceased publication. The frustrations common to all publishers of amateur magazines were frankly described by Huang in his chatty editorials: lack of interest from publishers, a devoted but tiny readership, the relative passivity of mystery readers—the "armchair solipsists" as one wag has called them—and the editorial fatigue that sets in under the attempt to maintain both a regular schedule and the personal goals of the editor/publisher. However, on a small budget and with limited editorial support (Managing Editor Jack Gendelman disappeared from the masthead after issue number 9), *Cloak and Dagger* was a useful publication that attempted to fill a genuine need for a general interest newsletter that still exists.

Note

1. Jim Huang, Editorial, *Cloak and Dagger*, number 8 (May 26, 1978), p. 2.

Information Sources

INDEX SOURCES: "Index to Issues Nos. 1 to 13/14." *Cloak and Dagger*, no. 15 (August 10, 1980):10–15.

LOCATION SOURCES: Private collectors.

Publication History

MAGAZINE TITLE: *Cloak and Dagger*.

TITLE CHANGES: None.
VOLUME AND ISSUE DATA: No. 1 (1977) through no. 16 (September 30, 1980); 15
    issues (one issue numbered 13/14).
PUBLISHER: Jim Huang, 55 North Virginia Court, Englewood Cliffs, New Jersey 07362.
EDITOR: Jim Huang; Managing Editor (nos. 1–9), Jack Gendelman.
PRICE PER ISSUE: 15 cents (nos. 1–5); 35 cents (nos. 6–16).
SIZE AND PAGINATION: 8-1/2'' X 11'' (nos. 1–5); 5-1/2'' X 8-1/2'' (nos. 6–16); 1–
    16 pages.
CURRENT STATUS: Discontinued.
—*Walter Albert*

CLOAK AND PISTOL

With a distinguished first issue, professionally produced, typeset in two columns per page with justified margins, printed via offset press on quality paper,
and no advertising, thus appeared the first issue of *Cloak and Pistol*, a "pulpzine."
The front and back covers were artwork by the well-known artist Frank Hamilton,
and interior illustrations were produced by Marty Powell. The magazine was
also profuse with illustrations reproduced from the pages of the old pulps.

The forty pages of material contained four articles: one each on The Shadow
and Secret Agent X, one on Farmer's Holmesian pastiche,[1] and one on vignettes
used in *The Phantom Detective*.*

Note

1. Philip José Farmer, *The Adventure of the Peerless Peer,* as told by "John H. Watson, M.D."
(Boulder, Colorado: The Aspen Press). This relates that in 1916 Holmes and Watson are sent on a
secret mission to Cairo via two airplanes to track down Von Bork, a German agent. On the way
they become prisoners aboard a German zeppelin flying to Tanganyika to relieve the harassed German
forces there. During their adventures they encounter Lord Greystroke, otherwise known as Tarzan
of the Apes.

Information Sources

INDEX SOURCES: None known.
LOCATION SOURCES: Private collectors.

Publication History

MAGAZINE TITLE: *Cloak and Pistol*.
TITLE CHANGES: None.
VOLUME AND ISSUE DATA: Vol. 1, no. 1 (to date, Fall 1981); 1 issue.
PUBLISHER: Joseph Lewandowski, 26502 Calle San Francisco, San Juan Capistrano,
    California 92675.
EDITOR: Joseph Lewandowski.
PRICE PER ISSUE: $4.25.
SIZE AND PAGINATION: 8-1/2'' X 11''; 40 pages.
CURRENT STATUS: Active.
—*Joseph Lewandowski*

CLUES

For seventeen years and 216 issues, *Clues* offered fiction for the times. Were inspired amateur investigators desired? *Clues* had them. Did you wish crook stories, gangster stories, ex-con stories? *Clues* published those, too, just as it offered stories of violent people, murder, and lunatic series characters.

Clues offered them all. Perhaps it was never quite a first-rate magazine. But it was always a sound, second-rate, always-reliable, solid citizen not given to flights of novelty. To the end of its days, however, it was always your third choice of magazines to buy.

The magazine was first issued late in 1926. By then *Flynn's Weekly,** a magazine of detective fiction, had been attracting attention on the stands for about two years, almost the same length of time that *The Black Mask** had been hard-boiled and tough.

Clues was certainly not tough. If anything, it was vaguely literary, and vaguely spurious, in the manner of *Detective Story Magazine* (Street & Smith).* Through the pages of *Clues* ranged a leisurely stream of characters not quite in focus—police detectives speaking in square sentences, improbable gangsters and ex-cons, mysterious Orientals. The magazine's tone was set by such writers as Carolyn Wells, Lemuel De Bra, and Garret Smith. Their work had appeared in the early morning of magazine mystery fiction, in the distinguished, if obsolete, style of *Detective Story Magazine* and *Popular Magazine*. These writers were supplemented by a host of others whose names and work have long since plunged from sight as completely as lead shot spilled into a lake.

Much of the fiction here read as if it had been starched, but among the angular rigidities flowed stories by H. Bedford Jones, Erle Stanley Gardner, and George Worts. Their stories hustled, full of eagerness and bizarre gimmicks.

Most of the other fiction offered improbable gray prose about detectives and crooks, peppered with a slang that seemed invented for each issue. *Clues* was fascinated by slang and such examples of criminal argot as came its way, as were most pulp detective magazines of the time. For a number of early issues, there even appeared lists of "crook's slang" to charm the reader. The words, for a wonder, were authentic, being provided by a convict serving time in the Missouri penitentiary. That was one of the few points at which the magazine touched real life.

However those early issues strike us now, in the mid-1920s they pleased the readership—so much so that the magazine began publishing twice a month beginning with the February 10, 1926, issue. Issues were identified as "first" and "second" of a given month. Actual magazine dates, either the 10th or 25th of each month, were given only in small type at the bottom of the contents page. Pages were numbered sequentially within each volume of four issues.

As the 1930s opened, *Clues, A Magazine of Detective Stories* (one of the subheads used during the magazine's history), contained 160 pages and was illustrated by many artists in many styles. For twenty cents you received a novel, a serial part, about six short stories, and five features. Type was small and the lines set closely together. The features included two true-crime articles; a letters column, "Following Clues"; and a pair of puzzle departments, both offering prizes to astute readers.

Series abounded. During mid-1930, Edgar Wallace published a group of articles on famous English criminals. Then Oscar Schisgall told the adventures of that extraordinary criminologist, Barron Ixell, at whose feet fawned the police of the world. And C. M. Rockwell wrote about The Blue Ghost, an international crook who might be foiled but never caught.

Over the next several years, many more series characters entered the magazine. These included such forgotten masters as Hammerlock Wilson, the Fighting Dick (by Earl W. Scott); Martin Eagan, a police detective bright with "intrepidity and acumen" (by Tom Curry); and John J. Jaffray, a wonderful private investigator (by Harry Lynch) who appeared for years. Several characters transferred to *Clues* from *All Star Detective Stories*,* a companion pulp magazine which failed after several years and was absorbed by *Clues* with the latter's July 1932 issue, which by that date was a monthly. It had been so since June 1931, suggesting the unseen presence of business woes.

The "Master Authors Number," August 1932, gave a good cross-section of the magazine's most popular writers. You found, among them, Johnston McCulley, Schisgall, Gardner, Milo Ray Phelps, Thomas Topham, and other similar luminaries. The fiction was leaner now, and more crisp, the action less deductive, the openings less verbose. T. T. Flynn and J. Allan Dunn published action stories which contrasted oddly with the more bland 1920s style of all those Madeleine Sharps Buchanan serials. It did seem that the magazine was slowly learning the *Black Mask** lesson.

This slow invigoration of style was interrupted after the April 1933 issue. Abruptly, the magazine ceased publication for six months. Without warning, the publisher, Clayton Magazines, Inc., had plunged into bankruptcy. Its list of titles was offered for sale. From these, Street & Smith Publications selected *Cowboy Stories, Astounding Stories,* and *Clues.* With a new title, *Clues Detective Stories,* and retaining its former editor, Orlin Tremaine, the magazine resumed publication with the October 1933 issue. The volume and issue numbers were continued.

As a Street & Smith publication, *Clues* received a general facelift. Larger type was used and shorter stories. Larger illustrations appeared inside, many spreading across two pages. The covers grew bright and busy, showing leaping men and squealing women. Familiar Clayton artists and writers were replaced by familiar Street & Smith personnel. Only a few writers survived the transition, among them Johnston McCulley and Harry Lynch. They were joined by Paul Ernst, George Harmon Coxe, Cleve Adams, Steve Fisher, and Richard Sale.

Contents of the new magazine included a novel, two novelettes, four short stories, and (during 1935) a long-lived prize contest in which you could win one hundred dollars by solving "The Perfect Crime." No departments were used until 1938. The stories vibrated with action and a distinctly tough tone. New series characters appeared, among them Donald Wandrei's Ivy Frost, a professor with a taste for violence. Arthur J. Burks introduced crime fighter Eddie Kelly, a blind ex-prize fighter. Nick Carter returned in a single story, July 1936 ("Murder in a Black Frame," by Harrison Keith, who was apparently Philip Clark). And Cleve Adams presented Violet McDade, a grossly overweight woman who owned a private detective agency and waddled ruthlessly through stories that mixed humor and danger.

Fiction was published during 1937–1938 by an increasing number of unfamiliar writers, but each issue was salted with familiar names as well. Christopher Booth, John Jay Chichester, and Paul Ellsworth Triem were featured—all had published scores of stories in *Detective Story Magazine* and *Best Detective Magazine*,* two other Street & Smith publications. During 1937, Johnston McCulley revived Thubway Tham, the lovable, lisping pickpocket, another familiar face.

At the same time, the contents of the magazine were again adjusted. Now it offered three long stories (variously identified as novels and novelettes), four or five short stories, and five to eight features. The features were mainly filler material, usually presented with a light touch, few over two hundred words long. For two years, 1937–1939, more formal departments were also presented—a letters column, "The Line-Up," and a collection of fact-crime paragraphs titled "The Law and the Lawless." In late 1939, however, these features were dropped, leaving only the department, "The Story Trail," to enthuse about the current issue and rave about the next one.

From mid-1939, *Clues* was edited by John Nanovic, the guiding force behind *The Shadow Magazine,** *Doc Savage,** and *Crime Busters.** To *Clues*, Nanovic brought an array of writers now identified with many of the top single-character magazines. These included Emile Tepperman (*The Spider,** *Operator 5**), Theodore Tinsley (*The Shadow*), Norman A. Daniels (*The Phantom Detective,** The Black Bat in *Black Book Detective Magazine**), Paul Ernst (*The Avenger**), and William G. Bogart, Harold Davis, and Alan Hathway—all involved with the 1940s *Doc Savage*. Most of these writers also appeared in *Crime Busters* and *Detective Story Magazine*. They provided a sound, dependable product in the desired upbeat tempo, mixing suspense, humor, and violent action in equal doses.

But in spite of these improvements, the introduction of trimmed pages, and a generally glossy appearance, the magazine wavered. After the April 1940 issue, the regular pulse of the monthly schedule faltered, and there were no issues until the July 1940 issue. It was now a bimonthly, containing a novel, two novelettes, and two short stories. Illustrations by Edd Cartier and Greig Flessel were used, and covers were by Modest Stein.

Subsequent issues contained much interesting material, the bimonthly period being a bright sequence in the history of the magazine. These issues are notable for a short Race Williams series by Carroll John Daly (beginning August 1940) and for the appearance of a novel by Theodore Tinsley titled "Satan's Signature"

(November 1941). This was a rejected Shadow novel, revised and shortened, with the Shadow's part changed to that of Walt Kenny, a tough detective.

At this point, something seemed to happen to *Clues* with every issue. The pages of the January 1942 issue grew by a quarter of an inch. Columns widened slightly and added four more lines of type. The cover announced "20 Per Cent More Reading Material." In September 1942, the page count jumped to 162 pages, and the magazine offered two of everything—two novels, two novelettes, two short stories, and two features.

One of these short stories featured Richard Henry Benson, The Avenger. By a remarkable coincidence, the final issue of Benson's magazine, *The Avenger*, was dated September 1942. Thereafter, his adventures, greatly shrunken, moved to *Clues*. There, they were written by Emile Tepperman rather than Paul Ernst (who had done the novels), although they remained signed by the house name, Kenneth Robeson. Five Avenger short stories were published in *Clues* during 1942–1943.

At the same time that the Avenger was transferred, a new puzzle department was added to the magazine. Tinsley, Tepperman, G. T. Fleming-Roberts, and Frederick Brown contributed fiction. And William Timmins painted some oddly conceived covers. But this was not enough. Crisis faced the Street & Smith pulp magazines. Just ahead loomed the era of the digest-size magazines. Weaker magazines were being weeded out.

After the May 1943 issue, there was a hiatus until August. Then, both Street & Smith's *Mystery (Crime Busters*)* and *Clues Detective* were cancelled.

Information Sources

BIBLIOGRAPHY:
Cox, J. Randolph. Bibliographic Listing Supplement. *Dime Novel Roundup,* Vol. 49, no. 2 (April 1980).
Murray, Will. *Duende History of the Shadow Magazine.* Greenwood, Mass.: Odyssey Publications, 1980.
Rogers, Alva. *A Requiem for Astounding.* Chicago: Advent Publishers, 1964.
INDEX SOURCES: None known.
LOCATION SOURCES: University of California–Los Angeles Library (166 issues, 1926–1939); private collectors.

Publication History

MAGAZINE TITLE: *Clues* (with various subtitles, that is, *Clues: A Magazine of Detective Stories; Clues: All Star Detective Stories).*
TITLE CHANGES: *Clues Detective Stories* (commencing with Vol. 30, no. 5 [October 1933]).
VOLUME AND ISSUE DATA: Vol. 1, no. 1 (September 1926) through Vol. 47, no. 2 (August 1943); 216 issues.
PUBLISHERS: Clues, Inc., 799 Broadway, New York, New York (1927) and 80 Lafayette Street, New York, New York (1930); The Clayton Magazines, Inc., 155 East 44th Street, New York, New York (May 25, 1931–April 1933); Street &

Smith Publications, Inc., 79 Seventh Avenue, New York, New York (1935–1943).

EDITORS: Harold Hersey (1926–1929); Carl Happel (1930–1932); F. Orlin Tremaine (1933–1936); Anthony Rud (1936–1939); Hazlett Kessler (1939); John Nanovic (1939–1943).

PRICE PER ISSUE: 20 cents (1926–1933); 15 cents (1933–1934); 10 cents (1934–1942); 15 cents (1942–1943).

SIZE AND PAGINATION: Various, average 7" X 9-1/4"; 114–160 pages.

CURRENT STATUS: Discontinued.

—*Robert Sampson*

CLUES: A JOURNAL OF DETECTION

Under the guidance of Pat Browne, founding editor, *Clues: A Journal of Detection* "is dedicated to detection in the widest sense of the word and as evidenced in all the media and in all aspects of culture,"[1] according to its published editorial policy. *Clues* is a scholarly journal; submissions are read and adjudicated by a board of editorial advisers composed of faculty members from several universities, all experts in crime fiction criticism. Partially as a result of the recent surge of academic attention to many aspects of popular culture (a movement extensively fostered by Ray and Pat Browne of Bowling Green State University's Popular Culture Center and by the Popular Culture Association), the appearance of *Clues* on the publishing scene in 1980 is an important indication that crime writing is now viewed as serious fiction, worthy of careful, critical attention. Because of *Clues'* wide scope and in an attempt to tap several sources and areas of expertise, future plans call for "In-Depth" sections about special-interest topics (the detective pulps, for example), some of these sections to be guest-edited.

Volume 1, number 1 (Spring 1980) introduced the "In-Depth" pattern with a section focusing on the work of John D. MacDonald (see also *JDM Bibliophile**). These articles were originally presented as papers at a 1978 conference on the works of John D. MacDonald and crime fiction, sponsored by the University of South Florida and the Popular Culture Assocation. At the conference, MacDonald spoke about each of the papers treating his work; in *Clues*, also, MacDonald responds to each article ("I take advantage of the opportunity to make more thoughtful comment than was possible from the small stage of that meeting place"[2]), his commentaries serving as introduction to the section.

Another useful *Clues* feature is the book review section begun in volume 1, number 2. Each column (by various hands) offers introduction to and evaluation of some half-dozen new titles, and works of both fiction and criticism are considered. The reviews are generally informed and thorough; the section is a valuable addition.

Although *Clues'* format is scholarly (essays are footnoted in standard form, thus clearly identifying both primary and secondary sources), the articles are of considerable interest to general readers and especially to fans of detective fiction.

As a rule, the contributors' writing styles are enjoyable, clear, and direct. Almost all articles indicate extensive reading and knowledge of both the immediate subject and the general field; and despite the objectivity for which most contributors strive, readers can readily perceive the underlying appreciation of their subject-author or authors as well as their appreciation of (sometimes passion for) the field.

To date, *Clues* has been faithful in its attempt to cover the broad scope described in its editorial policy. Works representing several nations (England, the United States, Sweden, and India) have been discussed; almost all categories within the genre—hard-boiled, classical, procedural, spy—have been examined, and articles have dealt with theme, characterization, setting, symbolism, and style. Contributors have analyzed the work of little known authors (Kay Cleaver Strahan, volume 2, number 1) and relatively new writers (Robert B. Parker, Tony Hillerman, volume 2, number 1) as well as, of course, some of the "giants" (Christie, volume 1, number 1; Hammett, volume 1, number 2; Keating and Ross Macdonald, volume 2, number 1). Crime writers whose work has been given less critical attention than it deserves (A. B. Guthrie, volume 1, number 2; Edgar Box, actually Gore Vidal, volume 2, number 1) are also evaluated, and—as in the case of Guthrie, Isaac Asimov, Alfred Bester, Stanislaw Lem, and John LeCarre (volume 1, number 2)—authors who combine mystery with the western, science fiction, or the spy story are discussed.

Though still a very young journal, *Clues* has established a solid reputation for competently fulfilling a genuine need. Dealing with print, film, and television media, the journal appeals to both fans and scholars. It points out the serious purpose of some crime fiction, as well as the fun and excitement of the puzzle, demonstrating the similarities and the differences between popular and "high" culture as exemplified by the genre.

Notes

1. Description of editorial policy, *Clues, A Journal of Detection*, Vol. 1, no. 1 (Spring 1980), reverse front cover.

2. John D. MacDonald in "Introduction and Comment," *Clues: A Journal of Detection*, Vol. 1, no. 1 (Spring 1980), p. 63.

Information Sources

INDEX SOURCES: None known.
LOCATION SOURCES: Bowling Green State University Library, Bowling Green, Ohio; private collectors.

Publication History

MAGAZINE TITLE: *Clues: A Journal of Detection*.
TITLE CHANGES: None.
VOLUME AND ISSUE DATA: Vol. 1, no. 1 (Spring 1980) through Vol. 2, no. 1 (to date, Spring/Summer 1981); 3 issues.

PUBLISHER: Bowling Green University Popular Press, Bowling Green University, Bowling Green, Ohio 43403.
EDITOR: Pat Browne.
PRICE PER ISSUE: $5.00.
SIZE AND PAGINATION: 6'' X 9''; 134–140 pages.
CURRENT STATUS: Active.
—*Jane S. Bakerman*

CLUES: ALL STAR DETECTIVE STORIES

See CLUES

CLUES: A MAGAZINE OF DETECTIVE STORIES

See CLUES

CLUES (MYSTERY WRITERS OF AMERICA)

See THIRD DEGREE, THE

CLUES DETECTIVE STORIES

See CLUES

COMPLETE DETECTIVE

Complete Detective was published by Western Fiction Publishing Company, with the first issue designated as May 1938. It existed for at least two issues.

Information Sources

INDEX SOURCES: None known.
LOCATION SOURCES: University of California–Los Angeles Library (2 issues); private collectors.

Publication History

MAGAZINE TITLE: *Complete Detective.*
TITLE CHANGES: None.
VOLUME AND ISSUE DATA: Vol. 1, no. 1 (May 1938); one other issue noted, with no volume or number designated, and with month shown as February but no year date.
PUBLISHER: Western Fiction Publishing Co., Inc., 4600 Diversey Avenue, Chicago, Illinois, with editorial offices at RKO Building, New York, New York.
EDITOR: Not known.
PRICE PER ISSUE: 15 cents.
SIZE AND PAGINATION: 7'' X 10''; 112 pages.
CURRENT STATUS: Discontinued.

COMPLETE DETECTIVE NOVEL MAGAZINE

Featuring four complete detective novels, this monthly magazine first appeared with the June 1928 issue; later issues contained a long novel (varying from 20,000 to 75,000 words) plus several short articles on true crime and filler material. *Complete Detective Novel Magazine* ceased publication with the January/February 1935 issue. Seventy-six issues were published. Lee Ellmaker, president of Novel Mfg. Corporation (later as Teck Publications, Inc.), of New York, was publisher; the editor was R. A. Mackinnon.

Information Sources

BIBLIOGRAPHY:
"Literary Market Tips." *The Author & Journalist* 13 (July 1928):22.
INDEX SOURCES: None known.
LOCATION SOURCES: University of California–Los Angeles Library (2 issues, 1928); private collectors.

Publication History

MAGAZINE TITLE: *Complete Detective Novel Magazine.*
TITLE CHANGES: None.
VOLUME AND ISSUE DATA: Vol. 1, no. 1 (June 1928) through January-February 1935; 76 issues.
PUBLISHER: Novel Mfg. Corp./Teck Publications, Inc., New York, New York.
EDITOR: R. A. Mackinnon.
PRICE PER ISSUE: Not known.
SIZE AND PAGINATION: Not known.
CURRENT STATUS: Discontinued.
—*Robert Sampson*

COMPLETE GANG NOVEL MAGAZINE

Complete Gang Novel Magazine made its appearance with the March 1931 issue, published by Complete Gang Novel Co. (a Harold Hersey company) and edited by W. M. Clayton, to capitalize on the fleeting trend then in existence for rousing gangster stories. Although the lawmen always came out for the good in the end, it was not the same for the magazine, and it had a short life. The exact number of issues published is not known.

Information Sources

BIBLIOGRAPHY:
Hersey, Harold. *Pulpwood Editor*. New York: Frederick A. Stokes Co., 1937.
INDEX SOURCES: None known.
LOCATION SOURCES: Private collectors.

Publication History

MAGAZINE TITLE: *Complete Gang Novel Magazine.*
TITLE CHANGES: None.
VOLUME AND ISSUE DATA: Vol. 1, no. 1 (March 1931); number of issues not known.
PUBLISHER: Complete Gang Novel Co. (Hersey Magazines), New York, New York.
EDITOR: W. M. Clayton.
PRICE PER ISSUE: Not known.
SIZE AND PAGINATION: Not known.
CURRENT STATUS: Discontinued.

COMPLETE MYSTERY NOVELETTES

Complete Mystery Novelettes debuted with the December 1931 issue. Issues have been noted as late as April 1933, but like most of the Clayton magazines, this one had a relatively short life. While featuring the word "mystery" in the title, the stories were predominantly cops-and-robbers crime adventures with blazing guns and often organized crime playing featured roles.

Information Sources

INDEX SOURCES: None known.
LOCATION SOURCES: University of California–Los Angeles Library (Vol. 1, no. 1, only); private collectors.

Publication History

MAGAZINE TITLE: *Complete Mystery Novelettes.*
TITLE CHANGES: None.
VOLUME AND ISSUE DATA: Vol. 1, no. 1 (December 1931) through at least April 1933; number of issues unknown.
PUBLISHER: The Clayton Magazines, Inc., 155 East 44th Street, New York, New York.
EDITOR: W. M. Clayton.
PRICE PER ISSUE: Not known.
SIZE AND PAGINATION: Not known.
CURRENT STATUS: Discontinued.

COMPLETE UNDERWORLD NOVELETTES

Although typical of the period, *Complete Underworld Novelettes,* a quarterly, featured some of the better-known authors, such as W. T Ballard, J. Warrenton Burke, and Ace Williams. It was edited by Tom Wood, who was also publisher under the name Carwood Publishing Co. The first issue was dated Spring 1932; the latest issue noted was dated October 1934.

Information Sources

INDEX SOURCES: None known.
LOCATION SOURCES: Private collectors only.

Publication History

MAGAZINE TITLE: *Complete Underworld Novelettes.*
TITLE CHANGES: None.
VOLUME AND ISSUE DATA: Vol. 1, no. 1 (Spring 1932) through at least October 1934; 10(?) issues.
PUBLISHER: Carwood Publishing Co., 29 Worthington Street, Springfield, Massachusetts, with editorial offices at Suite 301, 22 West 48th Street, New York, New York.
EDITOR: Tom Wood.
PRICE PER ISSUE: Not known.
SIZE AND PAGINATION: Not known.
CURRENT STATUS: Discontinued.

CONFLICT

The introductory and only issue of this magazine, dated Fall 1953, was subtitled "Stories of Suspense" but actually provided a standard fare of murder and detective mystery short stories, all new, by some of the more prominent mystery authors. The feature article, however, was an expose-type, nonfiction piece titled "Hollywood Confidential—Shocking 'Sinside' Story!" by Jack Lait and Lee Mortimer. This, one of a series of "Confidential" articles and books by the pair of veteran newsmen, explored the moral and ethical breakdown of Hollywood, it was claimed.

Among the authors included were William P. McGivern, Roy Huggins, and Charlotte Armstrong. Although with a most attractive cover, and a good lineup of stories, the debuting issue failed to find favor, and the title was discontinued.

Information Sources

INDEX SOURCES: Cook, Michael L. *Monthly Murders*. Westport, Conn.: Greenwood Press, 1982.
LOCATION SOURCES: Private collectors.

Publication History

MAGAZINE TITLE: *Conflict.*
TITLE CHANGES: None.
VOLUME AND ISSUE DATA: Vol. 1, no. 1 (Fall 1953); 1 issue.
PUBLISHER: Ziff Davis Publishing Co., 64 East Lake Street, Chicago, Illinois, with editorial offices at 366 Madison Avenue, New York 17, New York.
EDITOR: Howard Browne; managing editor, Paul W. Fairman; assistant editor, Michael Kegan.
PRICE PER ISSUE: 35 cents.
SIZE AND PAGINATION: 5-1/2" X 7-5/8"; 162 pages.
CURRENT STATUS: Discontinued.

CONFLICT: TALES OF FIGHTING ADVENTURERS

At least one issue of *Conflict: Tales of Fighting Adventurers* was published, dated Summer 1933, by Centaur Publications, Inc. It promised stories of "Detective—Adventure—Western" as a subtitle and included two book-length novels and a number of short stories in its generous 256 pages.

Information Sources

INDEX SOURCES: None known.
LOCATION SOURCES: University of California–Los Angeles Library (Vol. 1, no. 1); private collectors.

Publication History

MAGAZINE TITLE: *Conflict: Tales of Fighting Adventurers*.
TITLE CHANGES: None.
VOLUME AND ISSUE DATA: Vol. 1, no. 1 (Summer 1933); no other issues known.
PUBLISHER: Centaur Publications, Inc., New York, New York.
EDITOR: Not known.
PRICE PER ISSUE: Not known.
SIZE AND PAGINATION: 7" X 10"; 256 pages.
CURRENT STATUS: Discontinued.

COURTROOM STORIES

The first issue of *Courtroom Stories*, dated August/September 1931, featured "The Trial of Oscar Wilde." Other pieces included lawyer-gangster situations, styled for the reading public who were at the time enthralled with the romanticized gangsters. The magazine was edited by Harold B. Hersey and published by his own company, The Good Story Magazine Company. It is not known whether there were additional issues.

Information Sources

BIBLIOGRAPHY:
Hersey, Harold B. *Pulpwood Editor*. New York: Frederick A. Stokes Co., 1937.
INDEX SOURCES: None known.
LOCATION SOURCES: Private collectors.

Publication History

MAGAZINE TITLE: *Courtroom Stories*.
TITLE CHANGES: None.
VOLUME AND ISSUE DATA: Vol. 1, no. 1 (August/September 1931); 1 issue known.
PUBLISHER: The Good Story Magazine Co., Inc., New York, New York.
EDITOR: Harold B. Hersey.
PRICE PER ISSUE: Not known.
SIZE AND PAGINATION: Not known.
CURRENT STATUS: Discontinued.

COVEN 13

This magazine was borderline to the mystery field but did include some stories by mystery fiction authors. While labeled "The Supernatural—Witchcraft—Horror" on each cover, the fiction here presented was with a definite intention to provide fare for adult readers. The editor proclaimed in the second issue that there would be no "ridiculous, freaked-out monster mummy to gurgle tana leaves and drag itself along at 1/8 of a mile per hour, through the fuzz-patroled, well-lighted suburbs of an American city; and no fruity King Kong will grace our pages to threaten the peace and quiet of our populace...."[1] While hoping, however, to reverse the material trend of macabre fiction, the magazine did hope to emulate the old *Weird Tales** magazine with a sophisticated literary level. The editor suggested that many of the stories would deal with the occult, the supernatural, and phenomena usually opposed by established religion.

Correspondence from readers was invited, and commencing with the second issue, letters were published. A column, "Bell, Book and Tarot," by Jean Cirrito, provided nonfictional comments on various aspects of the occult.

The first issue contained a serialized story, "Let There be Magick," by James R. Keaveny, and this was concluded with an eighty-four-page section in the fourth issue, two installments at one time: "since our distributor has suggested that we stick with a bimonthly for another three issues, our Coven (the staff and myself) deemed it only proper to conclude our serial in this issue."[2] Perhaps the intent to discontinue the magazine had already made itself known since this was the final issue of the magazine. A continuation of the title was carried over to another magazine by another publisher (*Witchcraft & Sorcery**).

Notes

1. Editorial comment, *Coven 13*, Vol. 1, no. 2 (November 1969), reverse front cover.
2. Editorial, *Coven 13*, Vol. 1, no. 2 (March 1970), p. 3.

Information Sources

INDEX SOURCES: Cook, Michael L. *Monthly Murders*. Westport, Conn.: Greenwood Press, 1982.
LOCATION SOURCES: Private collectors.

Publication History

MAGAZINE TITLE: *Coven 13*.
TITLE CHANGES: None.
VOLUME AND ISSUE DATA: Vol. 1, no. 1 (September 1969) through Vol. 1, no. 2 (March 1970); 4 issues.
PUBLISHER: Arthur H. Landis as Camelot Publishing Co., 2412 West 7th Street, Suite 302, Los Angeles, California 90057.
EDITOR: Arthur H. Landis.
PRICE PER ISSUE: 60 cents.
SIZE AND PAGINATION: 5-1/4" X 7-3/8"; 146 pages.
CURRENT STATUS: Discontinued.

CRACK DETECTIVE

Crack Detective. Crack Detective Stories. Famous Detective. Crack Detective and Mystery Stories. These many titles represent one magazine, one face, which began with a January 1940 date and continued, through turbulence and troubles, title changes, and variations of editorial concept, for seventeen years. It finally terminated in 1957, making it one of the very last of the detective pulp magazines, an interesting survivor from the past.

It began as the ten-cent *Crack Detective.* This was a thin bimonthly that featured fairly good stories by such established writers as Norman Daniels and Robert C. Blackmon. But it also published pieces by Robert Turner and Thomas Thursday, representatives of a somewhat later style of writing, who were re-working the old pulp action-story format to fill it with human emotion and the feel of real situations.

In September 1943, *Crack Detective* became *Crack Detective Stories,* a fifteen-cent publication of ninety-eight pages—a page count which included both sides of the front cover. It offered a novel, sometimes two novelettes, and four to six short stories. The fiction quality varied wildly. Perhaps this was due to Editor Robert Lowndes's habit of publishing stories that he personally enjoyed, rather than stories selected to appeal to a wide variety of tastes. Many issues contained Frank Kane's novelettes about Johnny Liddell—crisp, hard-action, private detective adventures. Other stories, less crisp, less hotly active, told of dangerous action when crime touched the lives of average people. Many stories concealed a snap in the final paragraphs, a moment of rueful irony, a satiric twist, or an obvious moral. It was often interesting fiction, but it was almost always lesser fiction, lacking the bite or specialized polish that would sell to more major markets.

To this judgment, as any other, exceptions can be found. Certainly, Alan Ritner Anderson's series about J. Fenimore Yost, a wild, drunken lawyer, in a madly veering group of stories, darkly comic, was particularly satisfactory. But just when you began to look forward to more Yost stories, the magazine changed character completely. This was in 1948.

Perhaps the 1948 change was foreshadowed in the 1946–1947 shuffling of departments and articles. These had come and gone. "According to the Book," which was about the law, if loosely, appeared regularly; "Law and Disorder," a collection of humorous anecdotes, came and went, together with an assortment of fact articles. Some of these were wildly inappropriate, such as the single illustrated page of "Great Heroes of the Navy" which somehow slipped in. Occasionally these features were cited on the contents page; at other times, they simply appeared at the end of a story to fill in the dreaded blank space.

Then, in 1948, departments, features, and short stories were severely slashed back. The magazine was radically changed. Now it contained a single, very long novel that filled almost the entire issue. The novel, announced as a "First Magazine Publication," was a quick-moving, contemporary mystery adventure with much action and a strong woman interest. Typical titles were "Dig Another Grave" by Don Cameron; "Death Be My Destiny" by John Roeburt; and "Bullets for Ballots" by Clarence Mullen. The novel swallowed up so much room that only an occasional article or short story managed to find space. By 1949, however, the novel's length had been reduced, and the short fiction increased to two or three stories plus the usual fact articles.

At this point, as if strong medicine was required, the magazine title was changed. The November 1949 issue became *Famous Detective*. But if the title had changed, almost nothing else about the magazine did. A full-length novel was still featured, the November selection being "Devil on Two Sticks" by Wade Miller, a hard-bitten story about a syndicate hit man. A single article accompanied this effective story.

For perhaps a year, *Famous Detective* continued in this format. It does not seem to have been particularly successful, for, in mid-1950, the magazine became a quarterly of about 130 pages, published in February, May, August, and November. It would remain a quarterly until mid-1954.

By 1952 the single-novel approach had been scrapped, and the magazine reverted to a more conventional mix of long and short fiction, true articles, and departments. The continuing "Spotlight on Crime" told "True Stories of Fascinating Crimes." Miscellaneous filler material closed all cracks. Somewhat later, Thomas Thursday wrote a fact-article series, and J. J. Mathews provided a Quiz-Story that let the reader be the detective.

At this point, a few—a very few—famous detectives did appear. The most prominent of these was Professor Henry Poggioli, who had appeared in the 1920s *Adventure* and was then appearing in *Ellery Queen's Mystery Magazine.** Poggioli was featured at least twice in *Famous Detective*: "Death Deals Diamonds" (November 1952) and "Figures Don't Die" (February 1953). These were hardly author T. S. Stribling's best efforts, but the dialogue flashed and the stories contained nicely bizarre patches.

A second famous detective, Satan Hall, was featured in Carroll John Daly's "Avenging Angel" (February 1954). Big, hard-handed, green-eyed Satan Hall had been popular in *Detective Fiction Weekly** fifteen years earlier, although his popularity had waned over the years.

A scattering of other series characters also appeared. These included Kewpie Donovan and tough Archie McCann, whose adventures were also appearing in the companion magazine, *Smashing Detective.** However, it is not the series characters that catch your eye in these early 1950s issues; what you see are the science fiction writers who have contributed detective-action yarns.

Robert Lowndes was also editor for the Columbia Publications' science fiction magazines *Future, Science Fiction Quarterly,* and the later *Future Combined with Science Fiction..* Contributors to these magazines began appearing on the pages of *Famous Detective*: Judith Merril, Philip St. John, Algis Budrys, Rog Phillips, William Tenn, Sam Merwin, Basil Wells, and Bryce Walton. Most of their stories were of crime or cops and robbers, but occasionally science fiction and mystery interreacted to produce a story about telekinetic robbery or how a chiseller with extrasensory perception was swindled.

In 1954, *Famous Detective* reverted to bimonthly publication, its pages cut back to ninety-eight. It was now a twenty-five-cent magazine, with an occasional Norman Saunders cover and a surprising variety of fiction. The fiction focused as often on mystery problems as on hair-raising action. Frequently the prose was tough, slangy, heated by human emotion. The writers included Day Keene, Rex Vickers, Arthur J. Burks, and Norman Daniels.

In the December 1955 issue, Edward D. Hoch introduced a major series character, Simon Ark, whose first appearance was in "The Village of the Dead." Ark was a highly ambiguous figure, apparently a deathless wanderer through time, searching for a confrontation with the ultimate evil, Satan himself. The stories, as ambiguous as the hero, were dense with occult and supernatural events. Or so it seemed. The entire population of a small village leaps over a cliff to their death ("The Village of the Dead," December 1955); a witch's curse ravages a girls' school ("The Witch Is Dead," April 1956); Satan worshipers rampage through London ("The Vicar of Hell," August 1956); packs of wolves slaughter through a Polish village ("The Wolves of Werclaw," October 1956). All stories have rational explanations. But they could have happened either way, and the irrational solution is at least as probable as the rational one.

But Simon Ark had arrived too late. *Famous Detective* had reached the end with its final issue, October 1956. It was replaced without warning by *Crack Detective and Mystery Stories*. This magazine was an exact duplicate of *Famous Detective* and would last but four issues. The new title would publish a few more Simon Ark adventures; it would hold its head high before an indifferent universe, become a quarterly, and be discontinued with the July 1957 issue, volume 17, no. 1.

There was at least one British reprint issued under the title *Crack Detective Stories* and five issues as *Famous Detective*.

Information Sources

BIBLIOGRAPHY:
Lowndes, Robert A. "The Columbia Pulps." *The Pulp Era,* no. 67 (May/June 1967): 5–20.
Rock, James A. *Who Goes There*. Bloomington, Ind.: James A. Rock & Co., 1967.
INDEX SOURCES: None known.
LOCATION SOURCES: University of California–Los Angeles Library *(Crack Detective Stories,* 1948–1949, 2 issues; *Famous Detective Stories*, 1953–1956, 3 issues); private collectors.

Publication History

MAGAZINE TITLE: *Crack Detective*.
TITLE CHANGES: *Crack Detective Stories* (with vol. 4, no. 5 [September 1943] through Vol. 10, no. 4 [September 1949]); *Famous Detective* (with Vol. 10, no. 5 [November 1949] through Vol. 16, no. 3 [October 1956]); *Crack Detective and*

Mystery Stories (with Vol. 16, no. 4 [December 1956] through Vol. 17, no. 1 [July 1957]).
VOLUME AND ISSUE DATA: Vol. 1, no. 1 (January 1940) through Vol. 17, no. 1 (July 1957) (note title changes); 97 issues.
PUBLISHER: Columbia Publications, Inc., 1 Appleton Street, Holyoke, Massachusetts.
EDITOR: Robert A. W. Lowndes; associate editors, 1955–1957, Marie Antoinette Park and Cliff Campbell.
PRICE PER ISSUE: 10 cents; 15 cents; 25 cents.
SIZE AND PAGINATION: Average 7'' X 10''; 98–130 pages.
CURRENT STATUS: Discontinued.
—*Robert Sampson*

CRACK DETECTIVE AND MYSTERY STORIES

See CRACK DETECTIVE

CRACK DETECTIVE STORIES (British)

See CRACK DETECTIVE

CRACK DETECTIVE STORIES (U.S.)

See CRACK DETECTIVE

CRAIG RICE CRIME CASEBOOK

See DETECTIVE FILES

CRAIG RICE CRIME DIGEST

In the mid-1940s, Craig Rice (Georgiana Ann Randolph) was at the peak of her fame as a writer of comic mysteries about hard-drinking, screwball characters. She had published a dozen novels as Craig Rice and seven under other names. Two of her books had been filmed, and, in January 1946, she made the cover of *Time* magazine. This was a rare honor, as she was the first crime writer, and one of the very few women, to appear there.

In the fall of 1946, Anson Bond Publications decided to try to exploit her fame by launching a *Craig Rice Crime Digest*. Each bimonthly issue would contain "three current best-sellers digested in the author's own words for smooth, speedy reading of your favorite mystery writers." However, the books actually used were anything but current, and the magazine lasted for only two issues. The lead novel of the first issue (dated August–sSeptember 1946) was Carter Dickson's "The White Priory Murders," first published in 1934 and which had already been reprinted in paperback by Pocket Books in 1942. In fact, not one of the stories in the two issues of the *Digest* was less than two years old; most were older. These included "The Sister of Cain" by Mary Colins, "The Sunday Pigeon Murders" by Rice, "Don't Catch Me" by Richard Powell, "O as in Omen" by Lawrence Treat, and "Bury the Hatchet" by Manning Long.

Each novel was severely abridged, and this was touted as a "really new treatment of crime stories. Here the plot will unfold in a hurry and offer a challenge to the mystery fan to keep pace with the clues as they are rapidly uncovered. Here the plot is laid bare, without an abundance of adjectives and embellishments."[1] Each novel was cut to 18,000 words, which is bare indeed. By comparison, novels reprinted separately by the same company were cut only to 62,000 words.

Actually, the entire appearance of the *Craig Rice Crime Digest* was of a cut-rate, shoddy production. The cover is a bare drawing of a tombstone with the story titles lettered on it. There are no interior illustrations, no columns, and no features aside from single-page introductions by Rice for each story. There is no advertising except ads for other Bond publications. Both issues are labeled on the cover with volume numbers but dated only on the inside.

Bonded Publications was an imprint of Anson Bond Publications, started in 1946 after Anson Bond had split from Leslie Charteris in a former partnership (Bond-Charteris Enterprises) producing a line of digest-size paperback books. This line had included a single issue *Craig Rice Mystery Digest**, which served as a market test for the *Craig Rice Crime Digest*. The January 28, 1946, issue of *Time* magazine reported that Bond had sold out his interest in Bond-Charteris to Rudy Vallee for $100,000. Bond-Charteris then became Saint Enterprises, Inc.

Note

1. Editorial, *Craig Rice Crime Digest,* Vol. 2 (October/November 1946), p. 2.

Information Sources

BIBLIOGRAPHY:
Masliah, Michael. Letter. In *The Armchair Detective,* Vol. 12, no. 4 (Fall 1979):354.
INDEX SOURCES: Cook, Michael L. *Monthly Murders.* Westport, Conn.: Greenwood Press, 1982.
LOCATION SOURCES: Private collectors.

Publication History

MAGAZINE TITLE: *Craig Rice Crime Digest.*
TITLE CHANGES: None.
VOLUME AND ISSUE DATA: Vol. 1 (August/September 1946) through Vol. 2 (October/November 1946); 2 issues.
PUBLISHER: Anson Bond Publications, 913 La Cienega Boulevard, Hollywood, California.
EDITOR: Craig Rice.
PRICE PER ISSUE: 25 cents.

SIZE AND PAGINATION: 5-1/4'' X 7-1/2''; 120 pages.
CURRENT STATUS: Discontinued.
—*Brian KenKnight*

CRAIG RICE MYSTERY DIGEST

The *Craig Rice Mystery Digest* was confined to a single issue published in 1945 by Bond-Charteris Enterprises, a joint venture of Leslie Charteris and Anson Bond. Like *The Saint's Choice** anthology series that Charteris edited, the *Craig Rice Mystery Digest* falls into the gray area somewhere between book and magazine. Both series were numbered and undated. The *Craig Rice Mystery Digest* contained four abridged novels: "Prelude to War" by Charteris, "The Big Midget Murders" by Craig Rice, "The Bamboo Blonde" by Dorothy B. Hughes, and "Cold Steel" by Alice Tilton. In effect, it served as a trial balloon for the *Craig Rice Crime Digest** which was to be launched the next year.

Information Sources

BIBLIOGRAPHY:
Masliah, Michael. Letter. In *The Armchair Detective,* Vol.12, no. 4 (Fall 1979):354.
INDEX SOURCES: Cook, Michael L. *Monthly Murders.* Westport, Conn.: Greenwood Press, 1982.
LOCATION SOURCES: Private collectors.

Publication History

MAGAZINE TITLE: *Craig Rice Mystery Digest*.
TITLE CHANGES: None.
VOLUME AND ISSUE DATA: Labeled as a "Bonded Collection," no. 12 (1945); 1 issue.
PUBLISHER: Bond-Charteris Enterprises, 314 North Robertson Boulevard, Hollywood, California.
EDITOR: Craig Rice.
PRICE PER ISSUE: 25 cents.
SIZE AND PAGINATION: 5'' X 7-1/2''; 144 pages.
CURRENT STATUS: Discontinued.
—*Brian KenKnight*

CREASEY MYSTERY MAGAZINE, THE (British)

See JOHN CREASEY MYSTERY MAGAZINE (British)

CRIME AND JUSTICE DETECTIVE STORY MAGAZINE

Whether the mystery/detective reading public actually demanded a "rawer" type of fiction, or whether several publishers just thought so, is not known. But approximately from 1956 to 1962, such stories did appear with some frequency and they did sell, but not well. With but three notable exceptions (*Guilty Detective Story Magazine,* * *Hunted Detective Story Magazine,* * and *Trapped Detective Story Magazine*, magazines publishing this type of coarseness existed for a lifespan of only a few issues.

Students of the genre should recognize the type of fiction as presented by this group of magazines as an anachronism, enlivened by a fillip of sex and set in contemporary surroundings. It is very similar to that published in the last of the pulp magazines, and much of it, indeed, is written by the same authors. G. T. Fleming-Roberts, Robert Turner, Day Keene, Philip Perlmutter, Francis C. Battle, Robert G. Baird, and others continued to produce but under a more daring formula and definitely more crude in manners and taste. It was what was contemporary, or, at least, it was what some readers thought was contemporary. Street-tough gangs and street-wise hoods involved innocent and not-so-innocent citizens in a constant turmoil for power and money. And a healthy dollop of sex was thrown in to maintain interest.

The first issue of *Crime and Justice Detective Story Magazine* appears to have been designed to take whatever advantage there was in the fact that a similar magazine by another publisher, *Justice* * had ceased with its January 1956 issue. *Crime and Justice Detective Story Magazine* commenced with a September 1956 date, and its logo emphasized only the word *Justice* with a very similar appearance to the magazine of that name. Subsequent issues gave equal emphasis, however, to the complete title.

Crime and Justice Detective Story Magazine had less prurient sex than did most of its contemporaries, preferring instead an emphasis on gangsters, and was probably closer to pulp fiction than any other digest-size magazine. The first issue commenced with a novelette by Day Keene, "I'll Die for You," in which a gangster kills his boss, a former racketeer and loan shark who is now wheelchair-confined, and takes up an identity in a small religious sect village in the Catskills, with resulting difficulties. Robert C. Dennis's "Philadelphia Fix" details an episode of a gangster boss in prison arranging the murder of several who are "outside." G. T. Fleming-Roberts contributed a story in his usual style, "The Dead Man Said No," involving a killer; and there were fast-action, gun-smoking tales by David Crewe, Robert Sidney Bowen, Robert Turner, and Jim Harmon. This set the stage for what was to follow in succeeding issues. Here were to be found murder thrillers rather than a mystery puzzle.

The four issues published were solid fiction, with no features, columns, or editorials, and no advertising except on the back cover.

Information Sources

INDEX SOURCES: Cook, Michael L. *Monthly Murders*. Westport, Conn.: Greenwood Press, 1982.
LOCATION SOURCES: Private collectors.

Publication History

MAGAZINE TITLE: *Crime and Justice Detective Story Magazine*.

TITLE CHANGES: None.
VOLUME AND ISSUE DATA: No. 1 (September 1956) through no. 4 (March 1957); 4 issues.
PUBLISHER: Everett M. Arnold as Arnold Magazines, Inc., 1 Appleton Street, Holyoke, Massachusetts, with editorial offices at 303 Lexington Avenue, New York 16, New York; associate publisher, Marilyn Mayes.
EDITOR: Alfred Grenet.
PRICE PER ISSUE: 35 cents.
SIZE AND PAGINATION: 5-3/8" X 7-1/4"; 128–130 pages.
CURRENT STATUS: Discontinued.

CRIME BUSTERS

Crime Busters is an extremely rare and unusual Street & Smith magazine. It was edited by John L. Nanovic, who handled the firm's single-character novels, but the magazine was originally conceived by Walter B. Gibson, author of The Shadow stories. Gibson, aware of Nanovic's desire to duplicate the success of *Doc Savage** and *The Shadow Magazine,** and knowing the difficulties in doing so, suggested a magazine to be called "The Big Three," which could feature three single-character novels per issue. These could then be spun off into magazines of their own if successful and replaced with new, experimental characters.

However, when the magazine debuted with the November 1937 issue, it was called *Crime Busters* and featured eight stories, not three. Originally, the magazine was to be a continuation in numbering from the firm's *Best Detective,** but at the last minute the magazine was replated as volume 1, number 1.

Crime Busters was an unusual experiment. Editor Nanovic, drawing upon his stable of authors (as well as some of the more famous of his competition), invited them to create characters of their own. These would be tried out in the new magazine and would be continued (or not) based upon a regular readers' poll, the results of which were to be printed periodically. In effect, the magazine would be edited by the readers. In practice, this led to a rather chaotic situation, with characters and authors appearing with peculiar infrequency.

The first issue contained three strong series. Lester Dent's Gadget Man stories began with "The Talking Toad." It featured a hot-headed inventor forced against his will to solve crimes by a strange individual who communicated with him through a radio in the shape of a toad. Theodore Tinsley's Carrie Cashin was equally whacky. She was a tough private detective whose male partner pretended to be in charge of the agency. As a twist, Carrie was more intelligent than her partner. "White Elephant" was the first of the Carrie Cashin tales. Walter B. Gibson, writing as Maxwell Grant, began the adventures of a traveling magician who fought crime wherever he found it. "Norgil" was the first of the Norgil the Magician stories.

Norwell W. Page, author of the rival *The Spider** novels, offered "Death's Ruby," the first of the Dick Barrett and Miss Fay stories. It, like most of the first issue's lineup, would be short-lived. James Perley Hughes's Hollywood trouble-shooter, Charles Q. Logan, originated in *Detective Fiction Weekly** and failed to find success in *Crime Busters,* as did Steve Fisher's judo expert, The Spinner.

In the first year of the magazine, any number of authors tried their hand at one or more stories featuring a series character. Laurence Donovan made several attempts, but his stories about two postal inspectors (Bimbo and Howdy), a railroad detective (Boxcar Reilly), and a crime fighter called The Wasp all left readers cold. Likewise, Harold A. Davis's Stevie the Greek died quickly. On the other hand, Alan Hathway's character, The Keyhole, about a newspaper columnist, was successful enough to continue intermittently. Norvell Page's Dick Barrett stories gave way to his more successful escapades of Angus St. Cloud, "the Death Angel," an effete ex-boxer whose tailcoats and Oxford accent belied his fatal fists.

Some of the early characters had made their first appearance in then-defunct magazines. Tinsley's *The Whisperer** character, Bulldog Black, appeared in the second issue of *Crime Busters.* From the same magazine came Frank Gruber's Jim Strong, Rackets Man. He lasted longer than in his original home. From *The Feds,** Steve Fisher's Naval Intelligence investigator, Big Red Brennan, was continued, but only briefly.

Characters that had failed in their own magazines were also given a chance. These included one story each featuring The Whisperer, The Skipper, and Nick Carter. Of these, the Nick Carter story (bylined Nick Carter but actually the work of William G. Bogart) was a movie tie-in. The others were simultaneously appearing in the back pages of other publications, although *The Whisperer* magazine was revived not long after.

After the first year, the regular series characters were firmly established. These included Norgil, Carrie Cashin, Jim Strong, and the Gadget Man, as well as two newer series characters, Robert C. Blackmon's medical-doctor-turned-detective, Doc Trouble, and Lester Dent's Ed Stone. Stone was an ex-boxer who, in "Ring Around a Rosy," inherited a Chinese valet named One. This valet tricked Stone into solving a crime in each story. Dent wrote the Stone tales under the house name of Kenneth Robeson; the series was a simple variation on the Gadget Man stories and just as good, but for some reason the readers seemed to like only the six stories Dent wrote under his own name.

With the June 1939 issue, the magazine began to feature lead novelettes; John L. Nanovic's crime articles, written as Henry Lysing, were dropped. The lead novelettes were by authors such as Norvell W. Page, Emile C. Tepperman, Norman A. Daniels, Paul Ernst, and Joseph T. Shaw (former *Black Mask** editor) writing as Mark Harper. Under that pseudonym, Shaw also did a series about Detective Cass Manning. The lead novelettes were unrelated to other series and signalled a new direction in the magazine, away from series characters.

At about the same time, *Crime Busters'* appearance was changed. In a daring departure, covers were from photographs of posed scenes. This, unfortunately, gave *Crime Busters* the look of a confession magazine. However, these were gradually phased out in favor of action covers by artists Graves Gladney, Dan Osher, Modest Stein, and others. Throughout the run, the interior illustrations— by Paul Orban, Edd Cartier, Earl Mayan, and others—were typical of the pulps of the period.

Despite its hard-hitting title, the magazine carried an inordinate number of humorous and off-beat series, some of which were the best stories.

With the November 1939 issue, *Crime Busters* was retitled, as *Mystery*, and most of the humorous characters were dropped. The Gadget Man ceased with "The Green Birds" in the next issue; Norgil ended his career in "Tank-town Tour" in the November 1940 issue; and The Death Angel bowed out in March 1941 with "The Demon-Mask Murders." Carrie Cashin, however, continued until "The Unusual Mr. Smith" in November 1942.

Several minor characters started their careers in *Mystery*: W. T. Ballard's racetrack detective, Red Drake; Norman A. Daniels's Dynamite Dolan; and Ned O'Doherty's Cy English. The bulk of the *Mystery* issues, however, contained crime stories not very much different from the fiction Nanovic was then running in *Clues Detective Stories (Clues*)*. Several new contributors appeared, including Fredric Brown, William Campbell Gault, Schuyler G. Edsall (writing as Gary Barton), and various writers under the house names of Jack Storm and Clifford Goodrich. When *Mystery* ceased publication with the May 1943 issue, the only remaining series character was Ballard's Red Drake. Doc Trouble had managed to hold on to almost the end.

Although *Crime Busters* and *Mystery* were two different names for the same magazine, in a strict sense they were two different entities: the funny, screwball *Crime Busters* and the undistinguished *Mystery*. The later version, of course, was the more commercial and therefore more viable in the markets of its day, but unquestionably it is *Crime Busters*, with its all-star crew of authors and characters, which remains in the minds of nostalgic collectors. In the final analysis, *Crime Busters* was a wonderful experiment which ended too soon and was replaced by a weaker version of itself.

Information Sources

BIBLIOGRAPHY:
Murray, Will. "Street & Smith's Crime Busters." *Xenophile*, no. 38 (March/April 1978):132–34.
Reynolds, Quentin. *The Fiction Factory*. New York: Random House, 1955.
INDEX SOURCES: Murray, Will. "The Crime Busters/Mystery Magazine Index." *Xenophile*, no. 38 (March/April 1978):134–37.
LOCATION SOURCES: University of California–Los Angeles Library (1937–1939, including Vol. 1, no. 1, 6 issues); private collectors.

Publication History

MAGAZINE TITLE: *Crime Busters*.
TITLE CHANGES: *Mystery* (with November 1939 issue).

VOLUME AND ISSUE DATA: Vol. 1, no. 1 (November 1937) through Vol. 9, no. 2
       (May 1943); 50 issues (24 issues as *Crime Busters*).
PUBLISHER: Street & Smith Publications, Inc., 79 Seventh Avenue, New York, New
       York, later 122 East 42nd Street, New York, New York.
EDITOR: John L. Nanovic.
PRICE PER ISSUE: 10 cents; 1940, 15 cents.
SIZE AND PAGINATION: Average 7" X 9-1/2"; 128 pages.
CURRENT STATUS: Discontinued.
—*Will Murray*

CRIME DETECTIVE (British)

At least one issue of *Crime Detective*, a pulp magazine, was published by
Hamilton & Company. No other information is available.

Information Sources

INDEX SOURCES: None known.
LOCATION SOURCES: Private collectors.

Publication History

MAGAZINE TITLE: *Crime Detective*.
TITLE CHANGES: None.
VOLUME AND ISSUE DATA: Not known.
PUBLISHER: Hamilton & Company, Glasglow, Scotland.
EDITOR: Not known.
PRICE PER ISSUE: Not known.
SIZE AND PAGINATION: Not known.
CURRENT STATUS: Discontinued.

CRIME DIGEST

A magazine offering condensed versions of some of the "best-selling books
in the crime, espionage, suspense, murder and mayhem"[1] categories was introduced with the October/November 1981 issue by Davis Publications, Inc. The
magazine was promised as a bimonthly, and to date, two issues have appeared
on schedule.

The editor commented, "What we'll be doing in *Crime Digest* is giving our
readers a taste of the best excerpts and condensations, all in the author's own
words, of major and bestselling books—in an easily affordable, convenient
package."[2]

The two first issues would seem to indicate that the editors are hedging their
bets, however, in that both issues have contained at least one mainstream fiction
book, and the second issue a nonfiction excerpt which would appeal to the true-
crime buffs. The first isssue included "The Devil's Alternative" by Frederick
Forsyth, "Mind over Murder" by William X. Kienzle, and "Masterstroke" by
Marilyn Sharp. The second issue featured "The Glitter Dome" by Joseph Wam-

baugh; an espionage story reviving James Bond, "License Renewed," by John Gardner; "Chiefs" by Stuart Woods; and the story of Jean Harris and the Scarsdale Diet Doctor, Herman Tarnower, in "Love Gone Wrong" by Duncan Spencer.

Both issues included book reviews, and the second issue added a film review column, "Real Criminals" by Chris Steinbrunner.

A similar magazine was launched simultaneously in the science fiction field by the same publisher, *Science Fiction Digest*.

Notes

1. Editorial announcement by Elana Lore, *Crime Digest,* Vol. 1, no. 1 (October/November 1981), p. 3.

2. Ibid.

Information Sources

INDEX SOURCES: None known.
LOCATION SOURCES: Private collectors.

Publication History

MAGAZINE TITLE: *Crime Digest*.
TITLE CHANGES: None.
VOLUME AND ISSUE DATA: Vol. 1, no. 1 (October/November 1981) through Vol. 1, no. 2, (to date, December 1981/January 1982); 2 issues.
PUBLISHER: Davis Publications, Inc., 380 Lexington Avenue, New York, New York 10007.
EDITOR: Elana Lore.
PRICE PER ISSUE: $1.50.
SIZE AND PAGINATION: 5-1/4" X 7-5/8"; 192 pages.
CURRENT STATUS: Active.

CRIME INVESTIGATOR (British)

At least one issue of *Crime Investigator*, a pulp magazine, was published by Hamilton & Company. No other information is available.

Information Sources

INDEX SOURCES: None known.
LOCATION SOURCES: Private collectors.

Publication History

MAGAZINE TITLE: *Crime Investigator*.
TITLE CHANGES: None known.
VOLUME AND ISSUE DATA: Not known.
PUBLISHER: Hamilton & Company, Glasgow, Scotland.
EDITOR: Not known.
PRICE PER ISSUE: Not known.

SIZE AND PAGINATION: Not known.
CURRENT STATUS: Discontinued.

CRIME MYSTERIES

An early horror-oriented crime pulp magazine with a decided macabre slant, *Crime Mysteries* was published by Dell Publishing Company. The first issue was dated August 19, 1927, and appeared weekly at first, terminating with the December 1927 issue.

Information Sources

INDEX SOURCES: None known.
LOCATION SOURCES: University of California-Los Angeles Library (Vol. 1, no. 1, only); private collectors.

Publication History

MAGAZINE TITLE: *Crime Mysteries*.
TITLE CHANGES: None.
VOLUME AND ISSUE DATA: Vol. 1, no. 1 (August 19, 1927) through December 1927.
PUBLISHER: Dell Publishing Co., Inc., 149 Madison Avenue, New York, New York.
EDITOR: Arthur Lawson(?).
PRICE PER ISSUE: 15 cents.
SIZE AND PAGINATION: 7″ × 10″; 128 pages.
CURRENT STATUS: Discontinued.

CRIME WRITER (BRITISH)

See: RED HERRINGS

CURRENT CRIME (BRITISH)

Current Crime, a nicely produced and very inexpensive magazine, commenced in 1973 and was primarily given to reviews of new books in the mystery and detective field. It was the only comprehensive review source for such books and covered the genre very well, usually providing a short, three- or four-line summary along with bibliographical data. From the fourteenth issue, most numbers also contained a full-page editorial, and there would occasionally also be a short article or short story by the editor, Nigel Morland.

Nigel Morland is a well-known name in British mystery circles. A prolific author in his own right, he also wrote under the pseudonyms of Mary Dane, John Donavan, Norman Forrest, Roger Garnett, Vincent McCall, and Neal Shepherd. At one time, he was editor of the *Edgar Wallace Mystery Magazine (British)** and was either editor or on the editorial staff of a number of other publications. He is the proprietor of The Book Guild and Mystery Book Club;

founding editor of *The Criminologist* (since 1966), *Forensic and Medico-Legal Photography* (1973), and *The International Journal of Forensic Dentistry*, as well as *Current Crime*. He was co-founder in 1953 of the Crime Writers Association.

Current Crime, while of immense value for its purpose, was nonetheless useless as a critical tool since virtually all the reviews were complimentary. However, since authors are less inclined to be critical of the work of others, perhaps rightly so, this can be excused. It was only in the last issue that a discernible change was apparent, a trend toward a critical review; but unfortunately, the magazine was then discontinued (due to a fire on the premises) with the December 1980 issue.

Information Sources

INDEX SOURCES: None known.
LOCATION SOURCES: Private collectors.

Publication History

MAGAZINE TITLE: *Current Crime.*
TITLE CHANGES: None.
VOLUME AND ISSUE DATA: No. 1 (September 1973) through no. 30 (December 1980); 30 issues.
PUBLISHER: Current Crime, P.O. Box 18, Bognor Regis, Sussex, PO22, 7AA, England.
EDITOR: Nigel Morland.
PRICE PER ISSUE: By annual subscription, 50 pence; was slated to increase to 60 pence in 1981.
SIZE AND PAGINATION: 5" × 8"; 8-25 pages.
CURRENT STATUS: Temporarily discontinued.
—*Robert Adey*

D

DAN DUNN DETECTIVE MAGAZINE

A one-issue title, September 1936, *Dan Dunn Detective Magazine* was edited by W. M. Clayton and tried to capitalize on the popularity of comic-strip characters by placing them in pulp stories. *Dan Dunn* was published by C.J.H. Publications, Inc., a Hersey company. There is a possibility that a November 1936 issue was also published.

Information Sources

INDEX SOURCES: None known.
LOCATION SOURCES: University of California–Los Angeles Library; private collectors.

Publication History

MAGAZINE TITLE: *Dan Dunn Detective Magazine*.
TITLE CHANGES: None.
VOLUME AND ISSUE DATA: Vol. 1, no. 1 (September 1936); 1 issue.
PUBLISHER: C.J.H. Publications, Inc., New York, New York.
EDITOR: W. M. Clayton.
PRICE PER ISSUE: Not known.
SIZE AND PAGINATION: Not known.
CURRENT STATUS: Discontinued.

DAN TURNER, HOLLYWOOD DETECTIVE

At first the magazine was pure Dan Turner. "Adventures of the Movie-Colony's Super-Sleuth—A Bookful of Novelettes and Short Stories," all by Robert Leslie Bellem. Each issue contained a long novelette and some seven shorter adventures. Most (or all) of these had originally been published in *Spicy*

*Detective** and were reprinted with title changes and minor rewriting. Nowhere in the magazine was there a hint that the contents had been published before.

For that matter, nowhere in the magazine is an indication that *Dan Turner, Hollywood Detective* was published on any periodic schedule. First issues began appearing during 1942 and were identified only as number 1, number 2, and on through number 5. With the January 1943 issue, more formal procedures appeared, and that issue was identified as volume 1, number 6. The initial issues were twenty-five cents, changed to fifteen cents with the sixth issue.

The covers featured scenes of wild disorder. Girls in filmy underwear faced guns or were carried about, kicking and squealing, by big, hard-looking men wearing panama hats and with jaws like cliffs. Interior illustrations concentrated on women drunk and women dead and numbers of women being slugged by their friends. Few of these women wore clothing enough to matter, and those who were dressed were afflicted with such frontal overdevelopment that they would have difficulty standing erect.

The illustrations quite accurately reflected the fiction. This was all first-person narrative by Dan Turner himself—a hard-boiled private detective with a surrealistic prose style, vividly slangy. Fueled by Vat 69 Scotch, cigarettes, and scalding kisses, he stomped heavy-footed through tangles of murder and violence among the Hollywood movie makers. It was ferocious fun.

The magazine went bimonthly in mid-1943 and, with the September issue, changed its title to *Hollywood Detective*. Other writers were introduced, drawn from the ranks of the regulars writing for the *Spicy* titles—Roger Torrey, E. Hoffmann Price, and Ray Cummings among them. Dan Turner continued to appear once or twice an issue in fiction and once an issue in an eight page, black-and-white comic book adventure. At the same time, the number of special features was increased from one or two to six or more. These were filler paragraphs or brief articles designed to use up blank space at the ends of stories.

The magazine was published with great irregularity. Although the table of contents indicated that it was usually a monthly, publication varied between bimonthly and quarterly during the late 1940s. During the war years, the number of pages was reduced to ninety-six. By mid-1949, it returned to 128 pages. At this time, it was published quarterly but briefly returned to monthly publication with the December 1949 issue.

As *Hollywood Detective* entered the 1950s, it offered two Dan Turner stories; five other short stories and novelettes by various pseudonyms; the department, ''Focus on Crime,'' which rambled on about crime and moving pictures; and two comic-book features. One of these was about Dan Turner, the other featured Queenie Starr.

But even Queenie's skills failed to revive the magazine. The October 1950 issue came forth as a pocket-size digest—and a tiny one at that, only 4-5/8 X 6-5/8 inches. The title had become *Hollywood Detective Magazine,* and across the top of the minute cover ran the words ''15¢ 100 THRILLING PAGES!''

(This was not quite true—to reach one hundred pages you had to count both sides of the front and back covers, and two of these were blank.)

Inside, you found seven stories. Three of these were about Dan Turner and were signed Bellem. The others, signed by other names, some palpably fake, appear to be by Bellem also. "Focus on Crime" appeared again. And the magazine offered two dollars for every letter published explaining the excellence of the new format. Unfortunately, the next issue never appeared. Four issues of a British reprint series were released, under the title *Hollywood Detective Magazine*.

Information Sources

BIBLIOGRAPHY:
Mertz, Stephen. "Robert Leslie Bellem: The Great Unknown." *Xenophile*, Vol. 2, no. 8 (February 1976):49–51.
INDEX SOURCES: None known.
LOCATION SOURCES: University of California–Los Angeles Library (1942–1950), 26 issues); private collectors.

Publication History

MAGAZINE TITLE: *Dan Turner, Hollywood Detective*.
TITLE CHANGES: *Hollywood Detective* (with Vol. 2, no. 5 [September 1943]); *Hollywood Detective Magazine* (last issue, Vol. 10, no. 5 [October 1950]).
VOLUME AND ISSUE DATA: No. 1 (undated, 1942) through Vol. 10, no. 5 (October 1950); 59 issues.
PUBLISHERS: Culture Publications, Inc., 900 Market Street, Wilmington, Delaware (nos. 1–5); Trojan Publishing Corporation, 2246 Grove Street, Chicago, Illinois, later 29 Worthington Street, Springfield, Massachusetts (last issue as Trojan Magazines, 125 East 46th Street, New York, New York).
EDITOR: Adolphe Barreaux (1949–1950).
PRICE PER ISSUE: 25 cents; 15 cents; 25 cents; 15 cents.
SIZE AND PAGINATION: Average 7" X 9-1/2", except for last issue, 4-5/8" X 6-5/8"; 96–130 pages.
CURRENT STATUS: Discontinued.
—*Robert Sampson*

DAPA-EM

See ELEMENTARY, MY DEAR APA

DELL MYSTERY NOVELS MAGAZINE

Right from the start, *Ellery Queen's Mystery Magazine** covered the mystery short story field so successfully that many other digests did not even try to compete. Instead, some sought for gaps in that coverage. *Manhunt** specialized in the hard-boiled, *Black Mask** type of story; *Mystery Book Magazine** printed full-length, quality novels.

Dell Mystery Novels worked the street between, running short, hard-boiled mystery novels and novelettes. Its first (and only) issue commenced with "A Bundle for the Coroner," a short novel by Brett Halliday featuring red-headed private eye Michael Shayne.

Lucy Hamilton, before she became Shayne's secretary, met the man her mother warned her against. Years later, handsome Jack Bristow shoves his way into her Miami apartment one night and collapses on the rug before Lucy realizes he is not drunk—he has been shot. Not knowing about the wounded man, Shayne innocently tells searching police there was no one in the apartment other than himself and Lucy—and he has to solve a shooting, a murder, and an eighty-grand robbery before he's arrested for these crimes himself. The story is a typical Halliday tale and, like its hero, is tough, fast, and competent.

However, the best story in the issue is the longest, William Campbell Gault's short novel, "But the Prophet Died." Sergeant Joe Parrish is assigned to the D.A.'s office to investigate a new Southern California cult, the Children of Proton. Is it religion or racket? And be careful, Joe—the cult is big, it's growing, it has a lot of influential people in it. Parrish has hardly started when he finds another reason to be careful—the Hollywood private eye who has been investigating the cult before him (and is half convinced it's genuine) is shot to death. Parrish sets to work in a Chandler-type case involving blackmail, crooked cops, a millionaire's pretty daughter, and the handsome, older cult leader she admires. Written in pre-Civil Rights time, the novel has a sympathetic portrait of an intelligent black woman. Though reflecting the fifties' fear of an atomic war, it isn't dated; the novel is tight, tense, and full of feeling.

Bruno Fischer ended the issue with a novelette, "The Quiet Woman," a tale of a woman who has a problem for private detective Ben Helm. Years ago, she killed her husband in self-defense; now there's a dead man in her house, killed in exactly the same way. Convinced she's being framed, Helm searches for the real killer among members of a little-theater group in an upstate New York town, in a low-keyed but realistic story.

Paperback-cover artist Robert Stanley's cover showing red-headed Mike Shayne in action, and Fred Segal's black-and-white interiors, are both competent. Indeed, perhaps that is the best way to describe the magazine: competent. It seems a pity that Dell, though listing this magazine on the contents page as a quarterly, apparently published only one issue.

Inforamtion Sources

INDEX SOURCES: Cook, Michael L. *Monthly Murders*. Westport, Conn.: Greenwood
        Press, 1982.
LOCATION SOURCES: Private collectors.

Publication History

MAGAZINE TITLE: *Dell Mystery Novels Magazine*.
TITLE CHANGES: None.

VOLUME AND ISSUE DATA: Vol. 1, no. 1 (January/March 1955); 1 issue.
PUBLISHER: Dell Publishing Company, Inc., 261 Fifth Avenue, New York 16, New
    York.
EDITOR: Don Ward.
PRICE PER ISSUE: 25 cents.
SIZE AND PAGINATION: 5-1/2'' X 7-1/2''; 128 pages.
CURRENT STATUS: Discontinued.
—*Frank D. McSherry, Jr.*

DETECTIVE (British)

Detective was a small (''pocket size'') thriller published by Gerald Swan twice
a month during 1949. No other information is available.

Information Sources

BIBLIOGRAPHY:
Lofts, W.O.G., and Derek J. Adley. *Old Boys Books, A Complete Catalogue*. London:
    privately printed, 1969.
INDEX SOURCES: None known.
LOCATION SOURCES: Private collectors.

Publication History

MAGAZINE TITLE: *Detective*.
TITLE CHANGES: None.
VOLUME AND ISSUE DATA: No. 1 (1949) through no. 24 (1949); 24 issues.
PUBLISHER: Gerald Swan, London.
EDITOR: Not known.
PRICE PER ISSUE: Not known.
SIZE AND PAGINATION: 5-3/8'' X 7''; 64 pages.
CURRENT STATUS: Discontinued.

DETECTIVE ACES (British)

See DRAGNET, THE

DETECTIVE ACTION STORIES

Detective Action Stories was one of the first four magazines (the others being
*Battle Aces, Gang World,** and *Western Rangers*) published in October 1930
by the then-new partnership of Henry Steeger and Harold Goldsmith that was
to become so well recognized as Popular Publications.

Henry Steeger was an editor with Dell Publishing Company during 1927–
1929, and Harold Goldsmith was managing Ace Publications at the time when
Steeger, anxious to get into the pulp publishing business on his own (despite
the depression), proposed the partnership for the new company. With their first-

hand knowledge of the pulp trends of the time, it was natural that their first titles would emphasize the air war heroes, detectives, and westerns.

Each invested $5,000 in the new company. "The main problem we faced was to get the necessary credit. We talked with John F. Cuneo, and Goldsmith had extended conferences with him, and finally we were given the necessary credit to proceed with the four titles."[1] On the basis of the initial investment, a line of credit of $125,000 was arranged.

"We used the same engraver that Goldsmith had used, namely Aetna; also Goldsmith hired an advertising manager on a part-time basis—Sam Perry—and we gave the distribution to the Eastern Distributing Company which was owned on a 50-50 basis by Paul Sampliner and Charles Dreyfus. After one year in business they went into bankruptcy and left us holding the bag for three issues. The printing, binding, typesetting and mailing were all handled by Cuneo. . . . I selected every single cover we ever published. . . . One of the editorial people from Dell chose to come along with us, Edith Symes, and she was our one assistant. . . . We divided our little one-room office into five compartments. Goldsmith and I each had an office, Edith Symes had one and Alex Portegal had one. Our secretary occupied the outside office and we had a very tiny reception area."[2]

Alexander Portegal served as art director for the interior art, and he designed the magazines.

Operating on a thin line financially, the new firm never had a large backlog of stories; only those that Steeger personally liked were contracted for the early issues. For each of the four magazines, an initial print run of 100,000 was ordered. *Battle Aces* sold nearly 80 percent and was the only magazine of the group to show a profit; the other three sold from 40 percent to 60 percent, with *Detective Action Stories* the one selling the smallest number.

Detective Action Stories was never a great financial success. It was discontinued in April 1932, although a second series ran from October 1936 to October 1937. While detective fiction was popular, there was competition not only from other publishers with well-established titles, but the public's interest was being weaned into two related fields, that of gangster and federal agent fiction, and a weird menace fiction that was beginning to sweep the country by 1933. In the fall of that year, "a wave of mysterious maladies struck many areas of the United States. Soon, it had reached epidemic proportions. As was typical in those days, the pulp magazines were the first public media to report the bizarre occurrences. The green death infected its victims with leprosy . . . the fungus death ate away the skin . . . the rotting death turned faces a sickening green as the afflicted aged a hundred years in a few minutes . . . the marble death, later analyzed as a solution of siliceous salts, hardened cell walls into a stony substance."[3]

Popular Publications, always quick to note and lead the public's reading tastes, countered with *Dime Mystery Magazine (Dime Mystery Book*)*, but the detective fiction suffered and was not to recover until the single-character pulp heroes made their debut.

As a result, *Detective Action Stories* published but a total of twenty-eight issues.

Notes

1. Henry Steeger, in "An Interview with Henry Steeger," by Nils Hardin, *Xenophile,* no. 33 (July 1977), p. 3.

2. Ibid., pp. 3–4.

3. Robert Kenneth Jones, *The Shudder Pulps*, (West Linn, Ore.: Fax Collector's Editions, 1975), p. 3.

Information Sources

BIBLIOGRAPHY:

Hardin, Nils. "An Interview with Henry Steeger." *Xenophile,* no. 33 (July 1977): 3–18.

————, and George Hocutt. "A Checklist of Popular Publications Titles 1930–1955." *Xenophile,* no. 33 (July 1977):21–24.

Jones, Robert Kenneth. *The Shudder Pulps*. West Linn, Ore.: Fax Collector's Editions, 1975.

INDEX SOURCES: None known.

LOCATION SOURCES: Private collectors only.

Publication History

MAGAZINE TITLE: *Detective Action Stories*.

TITLE CHANGES: None.

VOLUME AND ISSUE DATA: First Series: Vol. 1, no. 1 (October 1930) through Vol. 5, no. 3 (April 1932); Second Series: Vol. 5, no. 4 (October 1936) through Vol. 7, no. 4 (October/November 1937); 28 issues.

PUBLISHER: Popular Publications, Inc., 2256 Grove Street, Chicago, Illinois, with editorial offices at 205 East 42nd Street, New York, New York.

EDITOR: Henry Steeger.

PRICE PER ISSUE: 10 cents.

SIZE AND PAGINATION: 7" X 9"; 128 pages.

CURRENT STATUS: Discontinued.

DETECTIVE ADVENTURES

One issue of *Detective Adventures* was published in May 1935, by Lorelei Publishing Company of Chicago. No other information is available.

Information Sources

INDEX SOURCES: None known.

LOCATION SOURCES: Private collectors.

Publication History

MAGAZINE TITLE: *Detective Adventures*.

TITLE CHANGES: None known.

VOLUME AND ISSUE DATA: Vol. 1, no. 1 (May 1935); 1 issue.

PUBLISHER: Lorelei Publishing Company, Chicago, Illinois.
EDITOR: Not known.
PRICE PER ISSUE: Not known.
SIZE AND PAGINATION: Not known.
CURRENT STATUS: Discontinued.

DETECTIVE AND MURDER MYSTERIES (1935)

At least one issue of *Detective and Murder Mysteries* was published, in 1935, by Associated Authors, Inc. It should not be confused with the magazine of the same title published by Blue Ribbon Magazines, Inc., and Columbia Publications, Inc., commencing in 1939 (see *Detective and Murder Mysteries* [1939–1941]).

Information Sources

INDEX SOURCES: None known.
LOCATION SOURCES: Private collectors.

Publication History

MAGAZINE TITLE: *Detective and Murder Mysteries.*
TITLE CHANGES: None.
VOLUME AND ISSUE DATA: Vol. 1, no. 1 (1935); 1 issue.
PUBLISHER: Associated Authors, Inc., 1008 West York Street, Philadelphia, Pennsylvania.
EDITOR: Not known.
PRICE PER ISSUE: Not known.
SIZE AND PAGINATION: Not known.
CURRENT STATUS: Discontinued.

DETECTIVE AND MURDER MYSTERIES (1939–1941)

Of the same title as an earlier magazine published by Associated Authors, Inc. (see *Detective and Murder Mysteries* [1935]), this standard-sized pulp magazine first appeared in March 1939 featuring one of the early marijuana stories, and it is noted for its garish and weird covers often featuring torture and mayhem. The publisher was Blue Ribbon Magazines, Inc.

A second series commenced in February 1941, published by Columbia Publications, Inc.

Information Sources

INDEX SOURCES: None known.
LOCATION SOURCES: University of California–Los Angeles Library (Vol. 1, no. 1 [1939], Blue Ribbon Magazines, Inc.; Vol. 1, no. 1 [1941], Columbia Publications, Inc.); private collectors.

Publication History

MAGAZINE TITLE: *Detective and Murder Mysteries.*

TITLE CHANGES: None.
VOLUME AND ISSUE DATA: First Series: Vol. 1, no. 1 (March 1939); number of
     issues and extent unknown. Second Series: Vol. 1, no. 1 (February 1941); number
     of issues and extent unknown.
PUBLISHER: First Series: Blue Ribbon Magazines, Inc. Second Series: Columbia Pub-
     lications, Inc., 1 Appleton Street, Holyoke, Massachusetts.
EDITOR: Not known.
PRICE PER ISSUE: Not known.
SIZE AND PAGINATION: Not known.
CURRENT STATUS: Discontinued.

DETECTIVE BOOK MAGAZINE

One of the more creditable pulp magazines with a fairly long existence (1933–1950, nearly seventeen years), *Detective Book Magazine* featured and emphasized a complete, unabridged, book-length detective novel in each issue, accompanied by two or three short stories. The full-length novels were by the better-known authors who had or would become household words to the mystery fan. Included were "Murders in Volume 2" by Elizabeth Daly, "Search for a Scientist" by Charles L. Leonard, "The 3–13 Murders" by Thomas B. Black, "Call the Lady Indiscreet" by Paul Whelton, "One Cried Murder" by Jean Leslie, and "Green Hazard" by Manning Coles, among others.

These ran the gamut from the mad scientist in a moss-covered mansion to the private eye stalking down a dirty street and rather well followed the trend of the reading public since each lead novel was selected from contemporary best-sellers. The "spine-tingling short stories" portrayed an assortment of police, government agents, and private investigators, as well as the usual innocent citizens, tangling with the crime hierarchy from organized crime to petty crooks, all with some degree of violence: "The dick had to frame his girl's speed-crazy brother to nab the kidnap killers";[1] "He alone knew who the killer was—and he alone knew that tonight was the night to strike!"[2]

The covers were usually striking and geared for attention, with voluptuous, scantily clad females on many of the bright covers. The Fall 1942 issue ("The G-String Murder" by Gypsy Rose Lee) and the December 1949 issue ("The Triple Cross" by Joe Barry) used the same eye-riveting illustration of a blonde in a harem costume.

Many one-inch advertisements in the later issues offered to publish song poems, train you to be a mechanic, a baker, or a hypnotist, or even a magician, and to give you advice should you be lonesome, wanting a lover, or seeking power and money.

The magazine, however, ran its course; its size and rough pulp-paper interior could not compete with the smaller, more convenient, paperbound books that were then serving the same market. And perhaps there was more appeal for a book that looked like a book and not like a magazine.

Notes

1. William Campbell Gualt, "Hell on Wheels," *Detective Book Magazine,* Vol. 4, no. 1 (Fall 1942), p. 1.
2. H. R. Hunt, "Killer in the Night," *Detective Book Magazine,* Vol. 5, no. 4 (December–February 1946–1947), p. 1.

Information Sources

INDEX SOURCES: None known.
LOCATION SOURCES: University of California–Los Angeles Library (1941–1948), 4 issues only); private collectors.

Publication History

MAGAZINE TITLE: *Detective Book Magazine.*
TITLE CHANGES: None.
VOLUME AND ISSUE DATA: Vol. 1, no. 1 (Fall 1933) through Vol. 6, no. 3 (Spring 1950, last issue noted); 75 issues.
PUBLISHER: Fiction House, Inc., 461 Eighth Avenue, New York, New York, later 670 Fifth Avenue, New York, New York.
EDITORS: Larrabie Cunningham (1942); Malcolm Reiss (1947); Wallace T. Foote (1949–1950).
PRICE PER ISSUE: 20 cents.
SIZE AND PAGINATION: 7" X 9-7/8"; average 112 pages.
CURRENT STATUS: Discontinued.

DETECTIVE CLASSICS

Detective Classics was an obscure, early detective pulp magazine published by Fiction House, Inc., with its first issue appearing July 1929. No other information is available.

Information Sources

INDEX SOURCES: None known.
LOCATION SOURCES: Private collectors.

Publication History

MAGAZINE TITLE: *Detective Classics.*
TITLE CHANGES: None.
VOLUME AND ISSUE DATA: Vol. 1, no. 1 (July 1929); number of issues and extent unknown.
PUBLISHER: Fiction House, Inc., 461 Eighth Avenue, New York, New York.
EDITOR: Not known.
PRICE PER ISSUE: Not known.
SIZE AND PAGINATION: Not known.
CURRENT STATUS: Discontinued.

DETECTIVE DIGEST

The first, and possibly only, issue of *Detective Digest* was published in January 1937 by Ace Magazines, Inc. No other information is available.

Information Sources

INDEX SOURCES: None known.
LOCATION SOURCES: Private collectors.

Publication History

MAGAZINE TITLE: *Detective Digest*.
TITLE CHANGES: None known.
VOLUME AND ISSUE DATA: Vol. 1, no. 1 (January 1937); number of issues and extent unknown.
PUBLISHER: Ace Magazines, Inc., 29 Worthington Street, Springfield, Massachusetts.
EDITOR: Not known.
PRICE PER ISSUE: Not known.
SIZE AND PAGINATION: Not known.
CURRENT STATUS: Discontinued.

DETECTIVE DIME NOVELS

The success of The Black Bat in *Black Book Detective Magazine** (July 1939) and *The Avenger** (September 1939) had briefly revitalized the faltering single-character magazine field. During 1940, a flurry of new, brightly competent heroes swept the pulps—The Ghost, The Crimson Mask, Captain Future, Captain Combat, The Whisperer, and others.

During the first half of that year, at the height of the stampede, the Frank A. Munsey Company introduced no less than six series characters and four single-character magazines. First to appear was *Famous Spy Stories** (January 1940), reprinting adventures of Anthony Hamilton which had previously appeared in the 1935 *Detective Fiction Weekly.** Then *Double Detective** in April 1940 began featuring the Green Lama. Of the four single-character magazines introduced, the first was *Detective Dime Novels* (April 1940), followed by *Western Dime Novels* (May 1940), which featured the Silver Buck. The next month, two additional magazines were released: *Red Star Adventures* with Matalaa, The White Savage; and *Red Star Mystery,** which introduced The Scarlet Wizard, Don Diavolo. Both magazines were dated June 1940.

None of these magazines prospered. Of them all, only *Double Detective* and The Green Lama lasted for any significant time. One of the earliest to be terminated was *Red Star Detective,* which was a retitling of *Detective Dime Novels*.

It was a greater loss than it seemed at the time, for the lead character of *Detective Dime Novels/Red Star Detective* was Dr. Thaddeus Harker, one of the more pleasing pulp heroes. On the face of it, Doc Harker was a medicine show pitchman who traveled the country selling Chickasha Remedies from a most peculiarly outfitted trailer. Outside, the trailer was all gaudy paint; inside, the medicine show apparatus was tucked into a single cupboard, and the rest of the space was devoted to the technical laboratory equipment of a traveling criminologist. For that was Doc Harker's true vocation—a criminologist with a formidable reputation for cracking cases too tough for anyone else.

Like the trailer, Harker's external appearance was deceptive. He was a clean, thin, old man looking like the last of the southern colonels, with string tie, frock coat, white mustache and goatee. He affected the courtly manners of the Old South, had an eye for young girls, and an unquenchable fondness for bourbon. This he consumed often. He was as close-mouthed a hero as ever got on paper. He told nothing. What his fine-edged intelligence gleaned from any situation was revealed to no one—neither to the reader nor Harker's aides.

He had two aides: Hercules Jones, a 6'2" ex-wrestler and professional strongman, with muscles of battleship steel and wits as impenetrable. He understood nothing and spent his life in a fog of incomprehension that lifted only at the dinner table.

The second aide, Brenda Sloan, was a tall, tanned, young lady with shining black hair and the type of figure that is most customarily seen in pulp magazines. Hercules adored her, but she spent little time with him, more usually acting as Harker's undercover agent, gathering information and softening the way for Harker.

These three had a splendid time of it. Corpses dogged their paths, along with deadly peril and some first-class roughhouses. Brenda was endangered often but was too stunning to be permanently damaged. Hercules Jones was clobbered on the head a lot, but you can't hurt a human tank, and he had Doc Harker to think for him. It was a busy, interesting series, full of pleasing people, even if the story kept erupting into bloody explosions and gunfire.

The first *Detective Dime Novels* cover showed a stately Doc Harker holding up a lighted stick of dynamite while being menaced by two machine guns, three automatics, and a pistol. Inside was the novel, "Crime Nest," by Edwin Truett; the contents also included a novelette by Robert Leslie Bellem and three short stories. The second issue, June 1940, promptly changed the magazine's title— you wonder what they had been thinking about originally—to *Red Star Detective*. (This was a format title in use at that time, which resulted in such companion magazines as *Red Star Mystery, Red Star Adventures, Red Star Western, Red Star Love Revelations,* and *Red Star Secret Confessions*.) The second novel bore the curious title, "Woe to the Vanquished," and was followed in August 1940 by "South of the Border." Doc Harker slicked, manipulated, and outfoxed his enemies, a stinking black stogie in his teeth and deception in his heart. But all his wiles failed to save the magazine, which was terminated after the third issue.

Information Sources

BIBLIOGRAPHY:
Rogers, Denis R. "The Lovell Complex" (publishers' early history). *Dime Novel Roundup,* whole no. 527 (October 1977); 97–115.

INDEX SOURCES: None known.
LOCATION SOURCES: Private collectors.

Publication History

MAGAZINE TITLE: *Detective Dime Novels.*
TITLE CHANGES: *Red Star Detective* (with Vol. 1, no. 2 [June 1940]).
VOLUME AND ISSUE DATA: Vol. 1, no. 1 (April 1940) through Vol. 1, no. 3 (August 1940); 3 issues.
PUBLISHER: The Frank A. Munsey Company, 280 Broadway, New York, New York.
EDITOR: Not known.
PRICE PER ISSUE: 10 cents.
SIZE AND PAGINATION: 6-3/4'' X 9-5/8''; 112 pages.
CURRENT STATUS: Discontinued.
—*Robert Sampson*

DETECTIVE DRAGNET MAGAZINE

See DRAGNET, THE

DETECTIVE FICTION

See DETECTIVE FICTION WEEKLY

DETECTIVE FICTION WEEKLY

Detective Fiction Weekly offered a robust assortment of detectives and rogues. Many were from the typewriters of big-name (for the pulps) authors such as Erle Stanley Gardner, George Harmon Coxe, and Max Brand. But the magazine also nurtured a modest group of its own writers.

Begun as *Flynn's* by Frank A. Munsey in September 1924, it was one of that company's first specialized titles. Though it dropped "Flynn's" from the masthead in June 1928, it still carried a "formerly Flynn's" tag for many years. Inside it sported the motto, "The magazine with the detective shield on the cover." In 1943, the title was sold to Popular Publications and became a monthly titled *Flynn's Detective Fiction Magazine.* This title lasted twenty issues before being combined with *Dime Detective** and was revived for seven final issues in 1951.

Detective Fiction Weekly's most vital period was in the 1930s when it competed with the likes of *Dime Detective* and *The Black Mask.** All three titles relied heavily on series characters. *Detective Fiction Weekly* shared some writers (Gardner, Daly, Coxe, Brand) with the other two detective titles and also with its sister pulp, *Argosy.*

Detective Fiction Weekly's formula, little changed through many editors, was a 12,000- to 20,000-word novelette, a handful of short stories (series and non-series), a serial, a true-crime story, an illustrated crime, a cipher or puzzle, and a letters page.

A blurb for the magazine in the March 1932 *Writer's Digest* stated: "We buy a wide variety of stories, no types are barred, but trite plots are avoided and the impersonal superdetective is not liked. We make no effort to encourage promising beginners. We pay one and one-half cent a word and up for material accepted."

Series characters came and went with the magazine. Among the more popular, and durable, were Gardner's roguish Sidney Zoom and Patent Leather Kid; Carroll John Daly's devilish cop, Satan Hall; H. Bedford-Jones's jewel thief, Riley Dillon; Milo Ray Phelps's comic crook, Fluffy McGoff; H. H. Matteson's Aleutian detective, Hoh-Hoh Stevens; Judson Philips's Park Avenue Hunt Club; George Harmon Coxe's reporter, Daffy Dill; Richard Sale's photographer, Candid Jones; and Anthony Rud's weird detective, Jigger Masters.

The magazine also hosted occasional visits by well-known writers who had already popularized their characters elsewhere, such as "Sapper's" Bulldog Drummond or Frank L. Packard's Jimmy Dale. Max Brand's Spy series, featuring Anthony Hamilton, from the mid-1930s, was later reprinted in its own title, *Famous Spy Stories,* from Red Star (by the Munsey Company). The eight Spy stories and one eight-part serial also later formed three hardcover books.

Detective Fiction Weekly was innovative in giving women strong roles, both as secondary characters (Dinah Mason in Coxe's Dill, Trixie Meehan in T. T. Flynn's Mike Harris series) and as lead characters (reporter Katie Blayne, private eye Sarah Watson).

While some of the magazine's characters were fairly normal detectives, it was the eccentric heroes that set it apart. Typical were Gardner's off-beat Lester Leith, who delighted in outwitting his rather obtuse policeman-posing-as-a-butler sidekick, Scuttle; or Daly's not-quite-honest cop, Satan Hall, who had his own methods for achieving justice. There were overweight detectives, rural detectives, bumbling crooks, dangerous crooks—all characters just different enough to draw a steady readership.

It is difficult to list all of the magazine's editors; they were seldom listed in the magazine. In 1932, Howard V. Bloomfield was editor, according to *Writer's Digest.* In 1934, Duncan Norton-Taylor held the post. In November 1934, a publisher's statement in the magazine itself listed no editor but said Albert J. Gibney was managing editor. *Writer's Digest* in January 1937 said Henry McComas had left as editor and was succeeded by William Kostka. Kendall Foster Crossen served as editor in the early 1940s.

Despite the frequent changes, the magazine maintained a strong identity. Artistically, it favored bold blue and yellow covers. There were periods of variety, such as the series of watercolors by C. Calvert in the early 1930s. Some of the most attractive covers depicted in romantic detail the faces of its various series heroes. In sharp contrast were the occasional gruesome covers showing decapitated heads and grisly murders.

Detective Fiction Weekly maintained a strong personality in a crowded field, through a rigid weekly publication schedule, for two decades. It is greatly underrated today.

British reprints appear under the title *Detective Magazine*.

Information Sources

BIBLIOGRAPHY:
Drew, Bernard A. "Hoh Hoh to Satan, Detective Fiction Weekly's Nutty Series Heroes of the 1930's." *Clues: A Journal of Detection,* Vol. 2, no. 2 (Fall-Winter 1981), p. 88.
Jones, Robert Kenneth. *The Shudder Pulps.* West Linn, Ore.: Fax Collector's Editions, 1975.
INDEX SOURCES: None known.
LOCATION SOURCES: University of California–Los Angeles Library; private collectors.

Publication History

MAGAZINE TITLE: *Detective Fiction Weekly*.
TITLE CHANGES: Commenced as *Flynn's* (September 1924 to May 1926); *Flynn's Weekly* (May 1926 to June 1927); *Flynn's Weekly Detective Fiction* (June 1927 to June 1928); *Detective Fiction Weekly* (June 1928 to December 1942); *Flynn's Detective Fiction Magazine* (Popular Publications, January 1943 to August 1944); combined with *Dime Detective* (after August 1944); *Detective Fiction* (January 1951 to July 1951).
VOLUME AND ISSUE DATA: Vol. 1, no. 1 (September 1924) through Vol. 156, no. 3, July 1951; 468 issues.
PUBLISHERS: Red Star News Company (Frank A. Munsey), 280 Broadway, New York, New York: commencing January 1943, Popular Publications, Inc., 2256 Grove Street, Chicago, Ilinois.
EDITORS: Various (see text).
PRICE PER ISSUE: 10 cents to 25 cents.
SIZE AND PAGINATION: Average 7" X 10"; 144 pages.
CURRENT STATUS: Discontinued.
—Bernard A. Drew

DETECTIVE FILES

Only one issue of *Detective Files* has been reported, published in the summer of 1956 and labeled number 103. Whether preceding issues were published, or possibly exist in another format or genre, is not known.

This known issue, subtitled "The Craig Rice Crime Casebook," featured primarily short stories by Craig Rice. Included were "The Campfire Corpse," "Frankie and Johnnie, M.D.," "One Last Ride," "House for Rent," "Small Footprints," "The Perfect Couple," "Do Not Disturb," "Breaking Point," "The T.V. Killer," "Death in a Pick-Up Truck," "No Motive," "The Woman-

Hater,'' ''No One Answers,'' and ''Identity Unknown.'' Additional stories by other than Craig Rice were by James T. Bragg and Arthur Tyler.

Information Sources

INDEX SOURCES: Cook, Michael L. *Monthly Murders*. Westport, Conn.: Greenwood Press, 1982.
LOCATION SOURCES: Private collectors.

Publication History

MAGAZINE TITLE: *Detective Files: The Craig Rice Crime Casebook.*
TITLE CHANGES: None.
VOLUME AND ISSUE DATA: One issue known, no. 103 (Summer 1956).
PUBLISHER: Caravan Books, Inc., 1 West 47th Street, New York 36, New York.
EDITOR: Not known.
PRICE PER ISSUE: 35 cents.
SIZE AND PAGINATION: 5-1/4'' X 7-5/8''; 128 pages.
CURRENT STATUS: Discontinued.

DETECTIVE LIBRARY (1895) (British)

Richard Crompton published a short-lived periodical by this title in 1895, borrowing heavily from the American dime novels. There were five ''pocket-size'' issues of *Detective Library*. No other information is available. (See also *Detective Library* [1919–1920]).

Information Sources

BIBLIOGRAPHY:
Lofts, W.O.G., and Derek J. Adley. *Old Boys Books, A Complete Catalogue*. London: privately printed, 1969.
INDEX SOURCES: None known.
LOCATION SOURCES: Private collectors.

Publication History

MAGAZINE TITLE: *Detective Library.*
TITLE CHANGES: None.
VOLUME AND ISSUE DATA: No. 1 (1895) through no. 5 (1895); 5 issues.
PUBLISHER: Richard Crompton, London.
EDITOR: Not known.
PRICE PER ISSUE: Not known.
SIZE AND PAGINATION: 5-3/8'' X 7''; 32 pages.
CURRENT STATUS: Discontinued.

DETECTIVE LIBRARY (1919–1920) (British)

The Amalgamated Press, Ltd. (later Fleetway Publications and presently still in business as I.P.C. Magazine Division), like its American counterparts, had no compulsion against dropping titles that were not doing well and instituting one or a dozen new ones. As a result the publisher produced a profusion of periodicals that were supposedly aimed at the youth market but which satisfied the reading requirements of all ages.

The firm was founded in the 1880s by Alfred Harmsworth (who became Lord Northcliffe in 1905), a crusader against using the term "penny dreadful" to describe the thin, often pocket-sized magazines that were filled with tales of dread and daring. The late A. A. Milne, though, was presumptuous when he wrote: "It was Lord Northcliffe who killed the 'penny dreadful' by the simple process of producing a ha'penny dreadfuller."

The Amalgamated Press series of *Detective Libary*, the second British paper to bear that name (see *Detective Library* [1895]), was published from August 2, 1919, to July 10, 1920, for fifty thirty-two-page pocket-size issues. With a temporary lull in the taste for detectives, the magazine was changed to *Nugget Weekly*, which continued for another thirty-four issues, but as a "new" magazine. On March 5, 1921, this title was incorporated into another Amalgamated publication, *Marvel*, which was replaced April 22, 1922, by *Sport and Adventure*. By October 21, 1922, *Sport and Adventure* had given way to the third series of *Pluck*, and this, in turn, to *Triumph*. Thus, the effort to follow the public trends had dealt the death knoll to *Detective Library*.

Information Sources

BIBLIOGRAPHY:
Lofts, W.O.G., and Derek J. Adley. *Old Boys Books, A Complete Catalogue*. London: privately printed, 1969.
Turner, E. S. *Boys Will Be Boys*. London: Michael Joseph, 1948.
INDEX SOURCES: None known.
LOCATION SOURCES: Private collectors only.

Publication History

MAGAZINE TITLE: *Detective Library*.
TITLE CHANGES: None; replaced by *Nugget Weekly*.
VOLUME AND ISSUE DATA: No. 1 (August 2, 1919) through no. 50 (July 10, 1920); 50 issues.
PUBLISHER: Amalgamated Press, Ltd., London.
EDITOR: Not known.
PRICE PER ISSUE: Not known.
SIZE AND PAGINATION: 5-3/8" X 7"; 32 pages.
CURRENT STATUS: Discontinued.

DETECTIVE LIBRARY (U.S.)

See NEW YORK DETECTIVE LIBRARY

DETECTIVE LIBRARY, THE

A short-run pulp magazine, *The Detective Library* was first published in March 1932 by Clayton Magazines. No other information is available.

Information Sources

BIBLIOGRAPHY:
Clayton, W. M. "The Clayton Corral." *Dime Novel Roundup,* no. 15 (March 1932): 7; no. 16 (April 1932): 7–8; no. 17 (May 1932): 7–8; no. 18 (June 1932): 7–8; no. 19 (July/August 1932): 9–10.
INDEX SOURCES: None known.
LOCATION SOURCES: Private collectors.

Publication History

MAGAZINE TITLE: *The Detective Library.*
TITLE CHANGES: None known.
VOLUME AND ISSUE DATA: Vol. 1, no. 1 (March 1932); number of issues and extent unknown.
PUBLISHER: W. M. Clayton as The Clayton Magazines, Inc., 155 East 44th Street, New York, New York.
EDITOR: Not known.
PRICE PER ISSUE: Not known.
SIZE AND PAGINATION: Not known.
CURRENT STATUS: Discontinued.

DETECTIVE MAGAZINE (British)

See DETECTIVE FICTION WEEKLY

DETECTIVE MYSTERIES

Detective Mysteries, a pulp detective fiction magazine, was first published November 1938.[1] No other information is available.

Note

1. This title is included on the "Tentative Pulp Checklist" from the San Francisco Academy of Comic Art (unpublished manuscript, n.d.).

Information Sources

INDEX SOURCES: None known.
LOCATION SOURCES: Private collectors.

Publication History

MAGAZINE TITLE: *Detective Mysteries.*
TITLE CHANGES: None known.

VOLUME AND ISSUE DATA: Vol. 1, no. 1 (November 1938); number of issues and extent unknown.
PUBLISHER: Not known.
EDITOR: Not known.
PRICE PER ISSUE: Not known.
SIZE AND PAGINATION: Not known.
CURRENT STATUS: Discontinued.

DETECTIVE MYSTERY NOVEL MAGAZINE

Detective Mystery Novel Magazine, first published under the date of June 1928, was a "Thrilling" publication by Best Publications, Inc., of Ned L. Pines. It was very similar in both appearance and content to another of Pines's pulp magazines, *Detective Novels Magazine,** which commenced ten years later.

Action-filled paragraphs portrayed very contemporary fictional characters: gangsters, police, and private investigators, and the innocent citizen who believably became involved. The usual issue included one novel (in reality, a long novelette), several pieces of shorter fiction, and filler material. The same authors contributed material as did to other magazines of the Standard group, with Best Publications having changed to Standard Magazines, Inc., at the same address.

With gunfire on every page and enticing females in distress gracing the covers, the magazine continued to the Fall 1949 issue. At that time, the title was changed to *2 Detective Mystery Novels,** which survived another five issues.

Information Sources

INDEX SOURCES: None known.
LOCATION SOURCES: Private collectors.

Publication History

MAGAZINE TITLE: *Detective Mystery Novel Magazine.*
TITLE CHANGES: *2 Detective Mystery Novels* (with Winter 1950 issue; see separate entry).
VOLUME AND ISSUE DATA: Vol. 1, no. 1 (June 1928) through Vol. 29, no. 3 (Fall 1949, as titled); 87 issues.
PUBLISHER: Best Publications, Inc. (later as Standard Magazines, Inc.), 10 East 40th Street, New York, New York.
EDITOR: Not known.
PRICE PER ISSUE: 25 cents.
SIZE AND PAGINATION: 6-3/4" X 9-1/2"; 112–146 pages.
CURRENT STATUS: Discontinued.

DETECTIVE NOVEL MAGAZINE

See DETECTIVE NOVELS MAGAZINE

DETECTIVE NOVELS MAGAZINE

In its best-known form, *Detective Novels Magazine* offered two short novels and a small selection of short stories, plus a few features as fillers. Initially, it appeared with awesome irregularity. During its first year, 1938, it was published quarterly, bimonthly, and monthly: none came out on a predictable date. After these early variations, the magazine settled into the peaceful cycle of a bimonthly until it changed to a quarterly in 1948 and died soon afterward.

Indifferent to coming history, that first issue, January–February 1938, bustled forward eagerly. The cover showed a man and woman shooting away over a stair bannister at off-the-cover evil, while on the stairs above them glared a dead man. Inside were two active novels—"Port of Murdered Men" by Gerald Verner and "The Death Parade" by Barry Perowne (whose stories of the master thief, Raffles, were then appearing in other Standard Publications magazines).

Over the years, *Detective Novels Magazine* would feature long fiction by most of the writers appearing in Standard's magazine group. Sam Merwin, Jr., and J. Lane Linklater were frequently represented. But the writer most often published in *Detective Novels* was Norman Daniels, writing under various pseudonymns as well as his own name. Daniels seems to have been responsible for most of the novels about the two main series characters appearing—Jerry Wade (The Candid Camera Kid) and The Crimson Mask.

Jerry Wade arrived in June 1939 ("Murder by Pictures"). He was featured in twenty-three novels, the final one, "Murder of a Shutter Bug," dated June 1944. The name John L. Benton was signed to the series.

Wade was a short, slight, young man with glaring red hair and a glaring red temper. He traveled about, loaded down with cameras and equipment, photographing everything that moved. This allowed him to solve crime after crime, from plain murder to fancy espionage plots. The background story was that he came from New York, a simple country lad with a cheap camera, got an assignment as a joke, and managed to break a major crime case. He was helped by Christine Stuart, a reporter on the *New York Globe,* who felt sorry for him. She was a feisty, slangy, tough-minded blond. Pretty soon they fell in love but decided not to get married because their work was dangerous, and, besides, Christine wished to wait until she got tired of newspaper work. They roved all over the country together, and nobody lifted an eyebrow. In early stories, Jerry was a freelance photographer; later he was employed by a syndicate and had an office at the *Globe*. But he spent little time in the office, preferring to dodge bullets and escape death by a hair, issue after issue.

The Crimson Mask stories (by Frank Johnson) began August 1940 with "Enter the Crimson Mask." Fifteen novels were published from that date through April 1944, the last being "Traffic in Murder."

The Crimson Mask was the alter ego of Robert Clarke, Ph.G.—a pharmacist owning a drug store in a slum area. Unlike most drug stores, Clarke's business handled only drugs and medical supplies, and these he gave away lavishly to the poor. In the back room is the inevitable well-appointed laboratory, without which no concealed hero could function, and in the lab is the inevitable makeup table at which Clarke dons disguises.

Hunted by gangland, admired by the police, the Crimson Mask was created for vengeance. Clarke's father, a police sergeant, was shot in the back by a vile crook. As the sergeant lay dying, his face flushed with blood, he seemed to be wearing a crimson mask. Thus the symbol and thus the disguise. After considerable self-training, the Mask set forth to punish crime and criminals.

Like most avengers, Clarke was aided by a small group of friends, three of whom knew the Mask's identity. There is former police commissioner Theodore Warrick, friend of Clark's father, who uses his connections with the police department to help the Mask. A second friend, Dave Small, is an old college pal; short, pudgy, cheerful, he now assists at the pharmacy. And, finally, there is the woman—Sandra Grey, a tiny girl, a lovely blond, a crack shot, and as undefined a personality as was ever included in a series.

Collectively, these people battle gangsters, kidnappers, crime rings, and, because the times required it, one Nazi spy ring after another. The subject matter is exciting, but the stories move in a sort of monotone, full of borrowings from other series. For some reason, the Crimson Mask adventures never develop a really distinctive tone. Stories and characters alike are more than a little nondescript.

For a year, from August 1940 through August 1941, *Detective Novels Magazine* published only Jerry Wade and Crimson Mask stories. After August 1941, the novels began appearing in alternate issues. This continued until 1944 when both characters were terminated and the magazine changed both its editorial policy and its title.

That happened with the issue dated August 1944. The title altered to *Detective Novel Magazine*, featuring one novel, usually a novelette, and up to four short stories. The department, "The Bulletin Board," was continued, giving a forum for enthusiastic readers' letters and extensive summaries of the novel in the next issue. A large number of one-inch advertisements offered relief and pleasure from every known complaint and desire.

Over the next four years, the magazine published novels of considerable quality, including Q. Patrick's "Death for Dear Clara" (November 1947), Alice Tilton's "Dead Ernest" (January 1948), and Helen Reilly's "Man with the Painted Head" (Spring 1948). But improved quality was hardly sufficient to keep the magazine alive, and it terminated with the Summer 1949 issue (the last six issues having been quarterly).

Information Sources

BIBLIOGRAPHY:
Weinberg, Robert. "A Snappy Hero, Jerry Wade, with Checklist of Jerry Wade and The Crimson Mask Stories." *Pulp*, no. 2 (Spring 1971): 20–24.
INDEX SOURCES: Weinberg, Robert, and Lohr McKinstry. *The Hero Pulp Index.* Evergreen, Colo.: Opar Press, 1971.

LOCATION SOURCES: University of California–Los Angeles Library (Vol. 2, no. 2, and Vol. 19, no. 1, only); private collectors.

Publication History

MAGAZINE TITLE: *Detective Novels Magazine*.
TITLE CHANGES: *Detective Novel Magazine* (with Vol. 14, no. 1 [August 1944]).
VOLUME AND ISSUE DATA: Vol. 1, no. 1 (January/February 1938) through Vol. 23, no. 1 (Summer 1949); 67 issues.
PUBLISHER: Better Publications, Inc., 22 West 48th Street, New York, New York (1938–1940); 10 East 40th Street, New York, New York (1941–1949).
EDITOR: Not known.
PRICE PER ISSUE: 10 cents; 15 cents; 20 cents.
SIZE AND PAGINATION: 6-7/8'' X 9-5/8''; 86–146 pages.
CURRENT STATUS: Discontinued.
—*Robert Sampson*

DETECTIVE REPORTER

There is no confirmation that *Detective Reporter* was crime fiction in lieu of true-crime stories. At least one issue was published, the first, dated September 1937.[1] No other information is available.

Note

1. This title appears on the ''Tentative Pulp Checklist'' from the San Francisco Academy of Comic Art (unpublished manuscript, n.d.).

Information Sources

INDEX SOURCES: None known.
LOCATION SOURCES: Private collectors.

Publication History

MAGAZINE TITLE: *Detective Reporter*.
TITLE CHANGES: None known.
VOLUME AND ISSUE DATA: Vol. 1, no. 1 (September 1937); number of issues and extent unknown.
PUBLISHER: Not known.
EDITOR: Not known.
PRICE PER ISSUE: Not known.
SIZE AND PAGINATION: Not known.
CURRENT STATUS: Discontinued.

DETECTIVE ROMANCES

Detective Romances, a pulp magazine, commenced May 1936 and continued at least through November 1936. No other information is available.

Information Sources

INDEX SOURCES: None known.

LOCATION SOURCES: Private collectors.

Publication History

MAGAZINE TITLE: *Detective Romances.*
TITLE CHANGES: None known.
VOLUME AND ISSUE DATA: Vol. 1, no. 1 (May 1936) through at least November 1936; number of issues and extent unknown.
PUBLISHER: A. A. Wyn as Ace Magazines, Inc., 29 Worthington Street, Springfield, Massachusetts.
EDITOR: A. A. Wyn.
PRICE PER ISSUE: 10 cents.
SIZE AND PAGINATION: Not known.
CURRENT STATUS: Discontinued.

DETECTIVE SHORTS (British)

Four issues of *Detective Shorts,* a pocket-size, sixty-four page magazine, were published during 1945 and 1946 by Gerald Swan. No other information is available.

Information Sources

BIBLIOGRAPHY:
Lofts, W.O.G., and Derek J. Adley. *Old Boys Books, A Complete Catalogue.* London: privately printed, 1969.
INDEX SOURCES: None known.
LOCATION SOURCES: Private collectors.

Publication History

MAGAZINE TITLE: *Detective Shorts.*
TITLE CHANGES: None.
VOLUME AND ISSUE DATA: No. 1 (1945) through no. 4 (1946); 4 issues.
PUBLISHER: Gerald Swan, London.
EDITOR: Not known.
PRICE PER ISSUE: Not known.
SIZE AND PAGINATION: 5-3/8'' X 7''; 64 pages.
CURRENT STATUS: Discontinued.

DETECTIVE SHORT STORIES

The girls on the covers, in torn clothes, were tied up and always in fearful danger. Most were blonds, showing a great deal of skin. Guns crashed, and fearful fellows menaced, snarled, and sneered.

Inside the magazine, guns seemed to go off at least once per paragraph. Blood ran down from holes in the forehead or in the chest—mayhem was constant as automatics were emptied into brutal faces. The hero was always suspected. Often he was down on his luck, a has-been, a bum, finding manhood again, a smoking pistol in each hand and the evil scattered about him like so many dead carpets.

"Ten Thrilling Murder Stories."

"All Stories Brand New Written Especially for This Magazine."

Ten stories an issue, 1937 to 1943, the action unflagging, unsubtle, ferocious. The lovely girl shot down. Blood on white velvet. The woman all ashimmer with passion, a woman whose kiss is death. The brutal thug. Knuckles in the face. Cars race, crash, explode; orange flames flare in a shatter of glass.

The story quality varies wildly. Short stories with half the pages being explanation and novelettes where the prose doesn't slow long enough to explain anything.

"Keep the Cadavers Coming"—"The Corpse Was Beautiful"—"The Girl the Ghoul Chose"—"All-Out Homicide."

There were occasional stories by Lawrence Treat, Roger Torrey, Robert Turner, Frederick C. Davis, Stewart Sterling, and Bruno Fischer; Fischer wrote as Russell Gray. And there were shoals of less-familiar names, house names, and names forgotten now.

"Get sex into the story from the first paragraph," advised editor Robert Erisman.[1] Thereafter, the girl was manhandled and the hero beaten (but recovered to shoot with wonderful effect). Men died, and the violent, passionless, empty action rushed on, as one story ended and another began.

Before the end in 1943, the covers deteriorated into undetailed drawings in which all the figures were flat and even the girls' enormous chests lack dimension. The interior illustrations were cut back so that some stories were headed only by a spot drawing.

At that, *Detective Short Stories* ran twenty-five issues, from 1937 through most of 1943. What it offered the reader may now be obscure to our eyes, but some quality kept it alive for more than six years. Whatever it was, it is gone now, leaving back issues of the magazine to speak only of the past's simple ferocity.

Note

1. "Writer's Market," column unsigned, *Writer's Digest*, Vol. 18, no. 10 (September 1938), p. 57.

Information Sources

INDEX SOURCES: None known.
LOCATION SOURCES: Private collectors only.

Publication History

MAGAZINE TITLE: *Detective Short Stories*.
TITLE CHANGES: None.
VOLUME AND ISSUE DATA: Vol. 1, no. 1 (July-August 1937) through Vol. 4, no. 5 (October 1943); 25 issues.
PUBLISHER: Manvis Publications, Inc., 4600 Diversey Avenue, Chicago, Illinois.
EDITOR: Robert O. Erisman.
PRICE PER ISSUE: 10 cents.

SIZE AND PAGINATION: 6-7/8" X 9-7/8"; 114 pages.
CURRENT STATUS: Discontinued.
—*Robert Sampson*

DETECTIVE STORY ANNUAL

This oversized, 8-1/2" X 11," 160-page, 150,000-word magazine was the first of a series of annuals issued by Street & Smith between 1940 and 1948.[1] *Detective Story Annual* was published for eight consecutive years, dated from 1941 through 1948. It was primarily a vehicle for reprinting fiction from Street & Smith's *Detective Story Magazine.**

The first issue of *Detective Story Annual* was released for sale in December 1940 (dated 1941). It contained four "book-length" novels (meaning novelettes) and four novelettes (meaning short stories). Writers included Cornell Woolrich, Steve Fisher, Cleve Adams, and Emile Tepperman—names to sell magazines. The cover was in the same style as was used for the fantasy magazine, *Unknown*—somewhat of a table of contents with story titles and teasing comments about them, lined down a yellow-stock cover. It was a tidy arrangement, with a pedantic scholarly look about it.

The combination of reprinted detective fiction and popular writers was continued in 1942. The cover, now illustrated, showed a pair of hands grasping for the reader's throat. The fiction was selected from *Clues Detective Stories (Clues**), *Crime Busters,** and *Detective Story Magazine.* Eight stories were offered—novels by Theodore Tinsley, Paul Ernst, William Bogart, J. J. des Ormeaux, and Carroll John Daly (a Race Williams adventure). The three shorter pieces were by Lester Dent, Alan Hathway, and Charles Spain Verral.

The later *Detective Story Annuals* were composed of stories from Street & Smith's *Detective Story Magazine,* the remaining all-fiction detective magazine published by the house. The quality of the writing grew rather thin toward the last, and the writers, if they were real, were not widely known beyond the confines of *Detective Story.* The fiction told of contemporary people coping uncertainly with intrusion of crime into their familiar worlds. They were smooth, bland, forgettable pieces. The last issue, in 1948, was digest size.

Note

1. Subject matter of the oversized annuals included reprints of *The Shadow Magazine,* sea stories, football and baseball yearbooks, love stories, western stories, sport stories, and picture books of the latest aircraft. The large format was also briefly adopted for *Unknown Worlds* (1941–1943) and *Astounding Science Fiction* (1942–1943).

Information Sources

BIBLIOGRAPHY:
Reynolds, Quentin. *The Fiction Factory.* New York: Random House, 1955.
INDEX SOURCES: None known.

LOCATION SOURCES: University of California–Los Angeles Library (1941, 1942, 1944); private collectors.

Publication History

MAGAZINE TITLE: *Detective Story Annual.*
TITLE CHANGES: None.
VOLUME AND ISSUE DATA: 1941–1948 (no issue or volume designation); 8 issues.
PUBLISHER: Street & Smith Publications, Inc., 79 Seventh Avenue, New York, New York.
EDITOR: Daisy Bacon (1944–1948).
PRICE PER ISSUE: 25 cents.
SIZE AND PAGINATION: 8-1/2" X 11"; 160 pages (last issue was digest-size and 224 pages). 1943 issue was 8-1/2" X 11-1/2."
CURRENT STATUS: Discontinued.
—*Robert Sampson*

DETECTIVE STORY MAGAZINE (British)

See DETECTIVE STORY MAGAZINE (Street & Smith)

DETECTIVE STORY MAGAZINE (Popular Publications)

See DETECTIVE STORY MAGAZINE (Street & Smith)

DETECTIVE STORY MAGAZINE (Street & Smith)

The first pulp magazine devoted to detective fiction, *Detective Story Magazine* was perhaps the most traditional in content of all the pulp detective magazines. Its mainstay was the classic "clued" detective story, but it served as the vehicle for the transition between the dime novel of the nineteenth century and the "hero pulp" of the twentieth century. It ran for thirty-four years (October 5, 1915, to Summer 1949) for a total of 1,057 issues.

Detective Story Magazine could have included the phrase "formerly *Nick Carter Stories*"* on its masthead. The lead story in the final issue (number 160) of that "nickel weekly" was serialized so that the second part was published in the first issue of *Detective Story Magazine*. The intent was to transfer the reading public of Nick Carter's adventures over to a more adult and sophisticated fiction magazine.

The editorial policy from the start appears to have included capitalizing on currently popular themes in fiction by turning them into a series of stories about a recurring central character. The style of the early issues was still that of the dime novel, but it was gradually refined and sophisticated by the newer writers attracted to the Street & Smith industry.

In the years before the hard-boiled detective emanated from the pages of *The Black Mask*,* there appear to have been two categories of crime story represented by *Detective Story Magazine*. One was the formal English detective story with its country house or urban mansion setting. The other was the "rogue/hero" theme, which developed a number of subcategories and led to the single-character or hero pulp magazine of the 1930s.

The famous, once-famous, and forgotten wrote for the magazine. Nick Carter, Carolyn Wells, Ernest M. Poate, Arthur B. Reeve, Isabel Ostrander, Agatha Christie, Dorothy L. Sayers, Ellery Queen, and Helen Reilly all wrote stories in the classic tradition. J. S. Fletcher and Edgar Wallace were frequent contributors. Wallace's stories fit both of the major categories—some were manor house mysteries while others belonged to the rogue/hero tradition.

Johnston McCulley, the creator of Zorro, was the major producer of rogue/hero stories. He paraded a host of masked, hooded, costumed heroes or hero-villains for the readers who found that type of story more appealing. Black Star, The Spider (not to be confused with the Popular Publications magazine hero), Terry Trimble, the Crimson Clown, and Thubway Tham were only a few of his memorable creations.

Other writers contributed to this strain as well: Charles W. Tyler, Scott Campbell (Frederick W. Davis), Christoper B. Booth, Maxwell Sanderson, Roy W. Hinds, A. E. Apple, Herman Landon, Anna Alice Chapin, and Paul Ellsworth Triem were among the more imaginative ones. By the 1920s, the variations on the theme could be broken down into six groups: humorous crooks, con men, rotten crooks, master crooks, "bent" (or crooked) heroes, and lady crooks. Triem's stories about Dale Worthington, alias "John Doe," lead directly into the high-action pulp narratives of the 1930s. Spiritually close to The Shadow, John Doe was also one of the more realistic characters in an era dominated by the hard-boiled tradition.

While the stories became more realistic in the 1930s and 1940s, *Detective Story Magazine* never succumbed completely to the *Black Mask* school as did *Flynn's Detective Fiction Weekly (Detective Fiction Weekly*)*. The writers who had been prominent and frequent contributors dropped away and were replaced by Roger Torrey, Knight Rhoades, M. V. Heberden, Brett Halliday, Fredric Brown, Carroll John Daly, Margaret Manners, and Cornell Woolrich. In 1943, the magazine became a digest-sized publication and the John Coughlin covers were replaced with photographic ilustrations. The magazine seemed to be emulating *Ellery Queen's Mystery Magazine** in some ways.

In the summer of 1949, the magazine ceased publication along with the rest of Street & Smith's fiction line *(Astounding Science-Fiction* excepted). The final three issues (now quarterly in publishing schedule) were restored to the old pulp size, almost as a nostalgic ending. The rights to the titles of many of the Street & Smith magazines were bought by Popular Publications, who published six issues (November 1952–September 1953) of a second series of *Detective Story Magazine*, beginning once again with volume 1, number 1. Craig Rice was among the writers who appeared in this short-lived effort.

Five issues of a British reprint series were published, March 1953 to March 1954.

Information Sources

BIBLIOGRAPHY:
Cox, J. Randolph. "More Mystery for a Dime: Street & Smith and the First Detective Story Magazine." *Clues: A Journal of Detection*, Vol. 2, no. 2 (Fall/Winter 1981):52–57.
Reynolds, Quentin. *The Fiction Factory*. New York: Random House, 1955.
INDEX SOURCES: None known.
LOCATION SOURCES: University of California–Los Angeles Library (1916–1948, 297 issues); private collectors.

Publication History

MAGAZINE TITLE: *Detective Story Magazine*.
TITLE CHANGES: *Street & Smith's Detective Story Magazine* (with the issue of February 28, 1931).
VOLUME AND ISSUE DATA: Vol. 1, no. 1 (October 5, 1915) through Vol. 177, no. 1 (Summer 1949); 1,057 issues. Second series: Vol. 1, no. 1 (November 1952) through Vol. 2, no. 2 (September 1953); 6 issues.
PUBLISHERS: Street & Smith Publications, Inc., 79–89 Seventh Avenue, New York, New York, later 122 East 42nd Street, New York, New York; Second Series: Popular Publications, Inc., 2256 Grove Street, Chicago, Ilinois, with editorial offices at 205 East 42nd Street, New York, New York.
EDITORS: Frank E. Blackwell (1915–1938); Anthony Rud (1938); Hazlett Kessler (1939–1940); R. B. Miller (1941); Ronald Oliphant (1942); Daisy Bacon (May 1942–Summer 1949); dates approximate.
PRICE PER ISSUE: 10 cents (1915–February 5, 1917); 15 cents (February 20, 1917–January 1947); 25 cents (February 1947–Summer 1949).
SIZE AND PAGINATION: Average 6-3/4'' X 9-3/4''; 128–160 pages.
CURRENT STATUS: Discontinued.
—*J. Randolph Cox*

DETECTIVE TALES (Aldine Publishing) (British)

The Aldine Publishing Company was interested in detective fiction and published as one of their very first ventures in 1889 *The Aldine Celebrated Detective Tales*, incorporating with it their *Half-Holiday Library* in 1902. This weekly publication existed until 1905, a total of 348 issues, with improbable adventures of fearless and crafty detectives rescuing maidens, besting cruel landlords, and bringing swindlers to justice. At times, the masthead proclaimed it as "The Great Detective Weekly."

A second series was commenced in 1922, as *Detective Tales* or *Aldine Detective Tales*, incorporated with *The Diamond Library* (which had begun its second series in 1913). This series was published for 28 issues, terminating in 1923.

The pocket-size, 24- to 48-page magazines had enjoyed great popularity. But, following the trend of the change for "new" reading matter, they were dropped. *Aldine Mystery Novels** soon followed, however, in 1925.

Information Sources

BIBLIOGRAPHY:
Lofts, W.O.G., and Derek J. Adley. *Old Boys Books, A Complete Catalogue*. London: privately printed, 1969.
Rogers, Denis R. "The Early Publications of the Aldine Publishing Co." *Dime Novel Roundup*, Vol. 47, no. 4 (August 1978).
INDEX SOURCES: None known.
LOCATION SOURCES: Private collectors only.

Publication History

MAGAZINE TITLE: *Detective Tales*.
TITLE CHANGES: Also, at various times, *Celebrated Detective Tales* during First Series.
VOLUME AND ISSUE DATA: First Series: 1889–1905; 348 issues. Second Series: 1922–1923; 28 issues.
PUBLISHER: Aldine Publishing Company, London
EDITOR: Not known.
PRICE PER ISSUE: 2 pence.
SIZE AND PAGINATION: 5-3/8" X 7"; 24–48 pages.
CURRENT STATUS: Discontinued.

DETECTIVE TALES (Atlas) (British)

This British reprint magazine began publication in England at full pulp size (7" X 10") in 1952, made one slight reduction in size in mid-life, and then changed to digest size in 1957. The appearance, nevertheless, remained entirely pulpish until 1960 when a nearly slick and conventional digest format was used. This *Detective Tales* contained reprints of the stories from *Detective Tales* (Popular Publications)* of the United States.

For British reprint magazines, this title enjoyed a remarkably long life: 109 issues over approximately a ten-year span, published on a regular monthly schedule. It was the most successful of the several magazines reprinting American stories that was published by Atlas Publishing & Distributing Co., Ltd.; other titles included *Phantom Mystery Magazine* (British),* *The Saint Mystery Magazine (Saint Detective Magazine, The*), Texas Rangers, Western Story, Analog Science Fact & Fiction, Fantasy & Science Fiction*, and *Horoscope*.

The success of the Atlas Company's *Detective Tales* can, perhaps, be explained by the fact that the publisher had a great variety of American stories on which to draw. There was everything from suspense to atmospheric terror, from classic mystery deduction to wild gun melodramas; and with a good crop of contemporary, hard-boiled stories that talked and moved fast, there was mystery and detective fiction of every variety.

The John D. MacDonald stories reprinted here included "Fall Guy" (November 1957), "Dateline—Death" (September 1958), "Death Is My Comrade" (April 1958), "Miranda" (January 1959); and William Campbell Gault was well represented with "Death Is My Shadow" (November 1957), "See No Murder" (February 1958), "Dead-End Road" (November 1960), and "Satan's Children" (January 1961), for example.

The list of stories by other popular American authors was almost endless. Some representative examples would include "Murder—Do Not Disturb" (November 1957) by Day Keene, "Body in Waiting" (October 1957) by John Lawrence, "Till the Noose Do Us Part" by Frederick C. Davis and "Murder Is Simple" by Bruno Fischer (both in April 1958), and "The Black Dahlia" (August 1960) by Philip Ketchum. And there was Frederick Nebel, T. T. Flynn, Talmage Powell, Charles Beckman, Jr., Merle Constiner, Bryce Walton, and G. T. Fleming-Roberts, to name a few more, and a host of other refugees from the pulp magazines.

In some of the late issues of this British *Detective Tales* were short review sections, never more than a page in length.

Information Sources

INDEX SOURCES: Cook, Michael L. *Monthly Murders*. Westport, Conn.: Greenwood Press, 1982.
LOCATION SOURCES: Private collectors.

Publication History

MAGAZINE TITLE: *Detective Tales*.
TITLE CHANGES: None.
VOLUME AND ISSUE DATA: Vol. 1, no. 1 (1952) through Vol. 10, no. 1 (March 1962); 109 issues.
PUBLISHER: Atlas Publishing and Distributing Co., Ltd., 18 Bride Lane, London, E.C. 4, England.
EDITOR: Not known.
PRICE PER ISSUE: 1 shilling (October 1957 to January 1959); 2 shillings (from August 1960).
SIZE AND PAGINATION: Average 7" X 9" until 1957; average 5-1/2" X 7-1/2"; 64–128 pages.
CURRENT STATUS: Discontinued.
—*Robert Adey*

DETECTIVE TALES (Boardman) (British)

See NEW DETECTIVE TALES

DETECTIVE TALES (Popular Publications)

Twelve Stories! Ten cents! Plus other features.

The cover, from a painting by Walter Baumhofer, shows a grim fellow axing the wall of a Chinese den. In the foreground, the rescued girl pistols at an off-cover menace; unseen behind them both, a knife-gripping Oriental leers and prepares to strike.

"Gripping Human Stories of Crime and Mystery—by R.T.M. Scott—Norvell Page—Paul Ernst—Frederick C. Davis—Franklin Martin—Wyatt Blassingame—George Shaftel."

It was the first, August 1935, issue of *Detective Tales*, a new Popular Publications detective magazine.

Detective Tales has been consistently overshadowed by the more vigorously acclaimed *Dime Detective*.* Fads in magazines come and go, but somehow *Detective Tales* has never received its proper measure of renown. The second most successful of Popular Publications detective magazines (again, *Dime Detective* was the first), *Detective Tales* ran for eighteen years, 1935 to 1953, with 202 issues.

It began with wild action-melodrama an ended in modernized hard-boiled stories of relentless movement. Between these two points, the magazine published mystery-action fiction in all its variety, from suspense to atmospheric terror, from deduction to wild, gun, free-for-alls. It was a running showcase for Popular Publications' best-known writers and some writers known in other fields such as John Dickson Carr and Ray Bradbury. It was a colorful, urgent, vigorous periodical, foaming with cheerful excesses; it was one of the classic pulp magazines.

For the initial issues, all of Popular Publications' professional skill was applied to lure readership to the new title. The rose was polished and gilded. Covers were by Baumhofer, John Coughlin, and Tom Lovell. Many showed Oriental menace. Most pictured the start of the wild melee—just as, or just before, the first gun was fired. On each cover, a man and woman were pitted against a horde of maddened killers raging just past the cover's edge, while at their backs, deadly menace glided forward, preparing to strike.

The interior illustrations were provided by a small and ever-changing army of artists. A breathless wonderland was presented, in black and white, of gun fights by Paul Orban; stranglings and girls gripped by thugs by Amos Sewell; one-man attacks on gangsters by Dave Berger; fist fights by John Meola; and guns, guns, and guns by Monroe Eisenberg and Ralph Carlson and everybody else involved.

Those first issues featured not only excellent art but also superlative writers—men of high popularity and golden skill. Their names studded the front covers in blinding glory. Frederick C. Davis and Norvell Page seemed to be in every issue (Page appeared twice in the April 1936 issue, once being bylined as "N. Wooten Poge"). John Dickson Carr appeared in the October 1935 issue; his story, "Terror's Dark Tower," told of crime with horrific, supernatural trappings. And *Black Mask** writer Theodore Tinsley contributed a violent piece about a reporter protecting his girl and his professional honor. Popular Publications' regulars Arthur Leo Zagat, J. Arthur Burks, and George Shaftel were all featured. And, almost at once, Franklin H. Martin began a series about Malachi Gunn, a hard-bitten adventurer who juggled while thinking and slamming the opposition. He was assisted by a Chinese servant, Mac Beth, the series humor being at that level.

At first, *Detective Tales* rigidly limited the use of series characters. The emphasis was on writers and quantity of fiction. Twelve stories an issue promised "High Tension Dramatic Stories of Red Blooded Man Hunters" and "Human, Thrill Packed Tales of the Drama that Lies in Crime Detection."[1]

The magazine's contents also included two departments. One of these, a page-long essay on the evil of crime, was by The Inspector; this quickly made its way to the front of the magazine. The second department, "The Crime Clinic," remained with the magazine to the end; for some years its place was at the rear among the ads. Until about 1939, it was illustrated by a drawing of a man and woman caught in a flashlight's glare. For the first issues, "The Crime Clinic" was an essay-type department. It was later modified to a letters column, with much space devoted to the wonders of the next issue.

Until about August 1936, the magazine continued the twelve-story and two-department format. Then the contents were reduced to perhaps seven items—a 15,000-word novel, one or two 10,000-word novelettes, three short stories, a serial ("M.D.—Doctor of Murder," in five parts, November 1936 through March 1937, by Fred MacIssac), and the department, "The Crime Clinic."

As the contents shrank, those writers so prominently featured in earlier issues melted softly away. More often featured now were Zagat, Joseph Cox, and MacIssac. The Malachi Gunn series was joined by a group of stories by George Bruce. These told the adventures of Information, Incorporated, a crime-fighting organization founded by Ivy Lane (male) and fronted by the suave Senator Greer.

By mid-1937, editorial policy again reversed itself. *Detective Tales* reverted to twelve stories for ten cents—and flaunted the fact across the top of its covers. To quell your doubts, the table of contents numbered each one, and only a person distorted by cynicism might remark that items eleven and twelve were departments. As in *Dime Detective,* some of the lead fiction toyed with grisly menace and bizarre adventures; and the titles, although promising more than was really delivered, were designed to grip the reader with anticipation: "Trail of the Thirteenth Brain" by Frederick C. Davis; "The Butcher Leaves Bouquets" by Wyatt Blassingame; "Roadhouse on the Styx" by John Hawkins; "The Witness and the Seven Corpses" by Philip Ketchum.

The bulk of the magazine, however, featured hard-punching stories with innumerable corpses and fists to the jaw. The merry sound of gun shots excited the pages, and the grate of hard-boiled fiction rasped from the paragraphs.

But nothing remained for long. Change simmered the magazine. The Lovell covers were long gone. The number of pages shrank from 128 to 112. Increasingly, the magazine resembled *Dime Detective* as its fiction leaned evermore toward urban violence, gamblers, gangsters, newspapermen, private investigators, police detectives, and harsh-natured ex-cons. These conventional figures were drawn larger than life, their simple characteristics inflated to towering character traits, their scowls expanded to Alps of passion, and their progress toward their destinies recorded in prose stripped of everything but brevity.

New departments made their appearance. The single-page, illustrated feature began, a combination of line drawings and prose, usually concerning famous crimes and criminals. "Oddities in Crime" started during 1938 and was joined, in 1939, by the "History of the New York Underworld." Around mid-1942, the "History" was replaced by a similar feature, "When Gangdom Ruled," by Cedric W. Windas, about crime in the 1920s.

Across the front cover moved a slowly changing roster of names. Over a two- or three- year period, they would change almost completely. Most of them were Popular Publications regulars, among them Robert Sidney Bowen and Stewart Sterling. But other names appeared with increasing frequency: Richard Sale, Norbert Davis, and John D. MacDonald.

As the magazine aged, an increasing number of series characters moved through its pages. In late 1938, A. L. Zagat had introduced a series about escaped convict Peter Corbin, framed into the penitentiary and now, precariously free, waging a secret war against criminals in hiding behind the law. Stewart Sterling's long series about Fire Marshall Ben Pedley began in 1939, and Carroll John Daly added several stories to the saga of that hit man of the police department, Satan Hall ("Securities Exchanged for Profit," August 1940, and "The Hand of Satan," May 1941).

Among other series which appeared were F. Orlin Tremaine's stories about E. Z. Bart, eccentric criminologist; the Tom Doyle, private detective stories by Day Keene, who also wrote about Silent Smith, gambler, philanthropist, and man-around-Broadway. There was Sherry Lane, R.N., by Cyril Plunkett. And William Cox recounted the violent adventures of Dumb Dan Trout, a hard-drinking, hard-headed private eye.

During 1943–1945, the magazine published a number of off-beat stories by Ray Bradbury, several of them under the pseudonym of Dane Gregory. These included such titles as "One Lucky Corpse" (February 1943, signed Gregory), "Killer Come Back to Me" (July 1944), "Save a Grave for Me" (October 1944, signed Gregory, although the magazine cover said Bradbury), "Half-Pint Homicide" (November 1944), and "Four Way Funeral" (December 1944). The last was "I'm Not So Dumb" (February 1945). To at least three of these, editorial changes were made to cheer up the grim endings. (After 1944, Bradbury's stories began appearing in *Dime Mystery Magazine* [*Dime Mystery Book**] and continued in that publication until at least 1947.)

In 1943, wartime paper restrictions violently impacted *Detective Tales*. The number of pages changed first to ninety-eight, then eighty-two, although returning to ninety-eight pages in the latter part of 1944. It would take four or five years for the magazine to again contain 128 pages.

Even at its leanest, *Detective Tales* still printed superior short stories by Robert Turner, Roy Vickers, D. L. Champion, and Richard Deming. And, in almost every issue, there seemed to be one of John D. MacDonald's clipped, crisp narratives, taut with desperation and suspense.

Across the 1949 covers, the words "Fifteen Stories" was blazoned. It was a familiar number at Popular Publications, which also offered *Fifteen Love Stories, Fifteen Sports Stories,* and *Fifteen Western Tales*. In the case of *Detective Tales,* this advertisement was not precisely true—that number contained four features among the fiction. At this time, none of the stories was a reprint.

But in 1950, very quietly, each issue included one or more republished stories. (For example, the April 1952 issue included Bradbury's "Killer Come Back to Me," bearing the new title of "Murder Is My Business.")

Time was running out in the early 1950s for all pulp magazines. In 1951, *Detective Tales* absorbed *F.B.I. Detective Stories** (whose last issue was May 1951). Instead of expanding, *Detective Tales* was cut to 114 pages and became a bimonthly. It was still, however, a handsome magazine, trim, slender, and crisp, the bright covers featuring endangered girls, the interior illustrations crackling with violence, the fiction concentrating excitement as intense as it could be.

But with the market contracting, distribution problems compounded. In 1953, Popular Publications severely pruned back their detective titles. *Detective Story Magazine (Detective Story Magazine* [Street & Smith]*), and *Detective Tales* were all terminated and encompassed into a new title, *Fifteen Detective Stories.** The eighteen-year run was over after 202 issues, the final one dated August 1953.

Note

1. Text of advertisement for the November 1935 issue, in *Detective Tales,* Vol. 1, no. 3 (October 1935), p. 112.

Information Sources

BIBLIOGRAPHY:
Albright, Donn. "Ray Bradbury, An Index." *Xenophile,* no. 13 (May 1975):20.
Hardin, Nils, and George Hocutt. "A Checklist of Popular Publications Titles 1930–1955." *Xenophile,* no. 33 (July 1977):21–24.
Writer's Digest, Vol. 16, no. 9 (August 1936):19.
INDEX SOURCES: None known.
LOCATION SOURCES: University of California–Los Angeles Library (1935–1948, 105 issues); private collectors.

Publication History

MAGAZINE TITLE: *Detective Tales.*

TITLE CHANGES: None.
VOLUME AND ISSUE DATA: Vol. 1, no. 1 (August 1935) through Vol. 51, no. 2
(August 1953); 202 issues.
PUBLISHER: Popular Publications, Inc., 2256 Grove Street, Chicago, Illinois, later 1125
East Vaile Avenue, Kokomo, Indiana.
EDITORS: Rogers Terrill (1935); Henry Sperry (1936); Loring Dowst (1939); Ryerson
Johnson (1944).
PRICE PER ISSUE: 10 cents (1935–1944); 15 cents (1944–1949); 25 cents (1949–1953).
SIZE AND PAGINATION: Various sizes, average 6-7/8'' X 9-1/2''; 82–128 pages.
CURRENT STATUS: Discontinued.
—*Robert Sampson*

DETECTIVE TALES (Rural Publications)

At the beginning of the 1920s, Jacob C. Henneberg was publisher of the
struggling *The Collegiate World,* a magazine directed to the undergraduate.
Henneberg had noticed a growing interest in magazines of detective stories.
Detective Story Magazine (Street & Smith)* had been published twice a week
since 1915. *The Black Mask** had begun publication in 1920, and *Mystery
Magazine** had begun a long, twice-a-month run in 1917.

Accordingly, Henneberg entered the mystery magazine field with his own
twice-a-month publication. It was titled *Detective Tales*, a standard-sized pulp
of indifferent mystery and detective fiction. The first issue was dated October
1, 1922.

Detective Tales began slowly, taking about a year to establish itself. During
that time, *The Collegiate World* was revamped to *College Humor* (1923). This
magazine quickly became a success and provided funds that sustained *Detective
Tales* and also permitted publication of a new magazine specializing in stories
fantastic and bizarre, the famous *Weird Tales.**

Both *Weird Tales* and *Detective Tales* were edited by Edwin Baird, a writer
of minor detective stories. In addition to the editor, the magazines seem to have
shared many of the same writers and artists, and their physical format was
identical, clearly off the same printing press. The first issue of *Weird Tales*
(March 1923) was the same standard pulp size as *Detective Tales*. And later,
when the May 1923 *Weird Tales* was issued in the large size, so was *Detective
Tales*.

By 1924, *Detective Tales* was stabilized as a large, flat issue with columns
of closely set type and a penchant toward inept fiction of the Florence Mae Pettee
variety. It was produced monthly, six issues to a volume.

At this point, the large *Weird Tales* anniversary issue (May–July 1924) was
issued. The magazine had not been selling enough to recover its costs, and the
special issue threw Henneberg's Rural Publishing Corporation into near disaster.
He elected to sell both *College Humor* and *Detective Tales*—which had just been
retitled as *Real Detective Tales*—and pump the money back into *Weird Tales*.

From that point, the magazines went their separate ways. Edwin Baird had been replaced by Farnsworth Wright for *Weird Tales*. Baird continued with *Real Detective Tales,* eventually becoming a vice-president of the firm, Real Detective Tales, Inc., Publishers.

The magazine developed an interesting group of writers, including Vincent Starrett and Seabury Quinn, both of whom contributed extensively. Other *Real Detective Tales* authors included George Allan England, Miriam Allen De Ford, Eric Howard, A. J. Burks, Paul Ausburg, R.T.M. Scott, and Edward S. Hoag. The stories emphasized amateur investigators of remarkable mental abilities and adventures among the gangsters of the Prohibition era. The action was brisk, the scene contemporary.

By 1927, the magazine title had expanded to *Real Detective Tales & Mystery Stories*. It was now a large (8-1/2" X 11-1/2") magazine containing ninety-six pages, the text set in double columns on soft pulp paper. Contents usually included four novelettes, eight short stories, and four departments. The departments reflected interests of the times: codes and ciphers, fingerprints, handwriting analysis, and a letters-previews-book review section titled "A Chat With the Chief." Baird contributed a signed editorial.

The magazine as such continued into the early 1930s, then was gradually transformed into a true-detective magazine, issued monthly in the same large format. By 1931, only a single piece of fiction was used each issue, occasional stories by MacKinlay Kantor, Eric Howard, and others.

Information Sources

BIBLIOGRAPHY:
Ashley, Michael. *The History of the Science Fiction Magazine, Vol. 1, 1926–35*. Chicago: Henry Regnery Company, 1974.
Weinberg, Robert. *The Weird Tales Story*. West Linn, Ore.: Fax Collector's Editions, 1977.
INDEX SOURCES: None known.
LOCATION SOURCES: Private collectors.

Publication History

MAGAZINE TITLE: *Detective Tales*.
TITLE CHANGES: *Real Detective Tales* (1924); *Real Detective Tales & Mystery Stories* (by 1927); *Real Detective* (by 1931).
VOLUME AND ISSUE DATA: Vol. 1, no. 1 (October 1, 1922) through at least Vol. 24, no. 2 (December 1931); total issues not known.
PUBLISHER: Rural Publishing Corporation, Chicago, Illinois (until April 1924); Real Detective Tales, Inc., 1050 North LaSalle Street, Chicago, Illinois.
EDITOR: Edwin Baird.
PRICE PER ISSUE: 25 cents (*Real Detective Tales; Real Detective*).
SIZE AND PAGINATION: 8-1/2" X 11-1/2"; 96 pages (*Real Detective Tales; Real Detective*).
CURRENT STATUS: Discontinued.
—*Robert Sampson*

DETECTIVE TALES–POCKET (British)

Detective Tales–Pocket would have to be considered an odd little magazine in all respects. It was one of a number of titles published by the enterprising T. V. Boardman & Company and was published circa 1948. The magazines themselves bear no dates.

The numbering system was shared with two companion series, *Western Stories* and *Romance Stories,* which makes for interesting bibliographical work. At least eight issues can be identified under the title *Detective Tales,* but these are without consecutive numbering.

The contents are obviously reprints from American magazines, possibly from the U.S. *Detective Tales* (Popular Publications).* The stories would have to be called routine crime adventure, though occasionally enlivened by such authors as Carroll John Daly with "Cash for a Killer" (issue number 113), Norbert Davis with "No Miracles in Murder" (issue number 107), and John D. MacDonald's "My Husband Dies Slowly!" (issue number 123). Other pulp magazine veterans appearing in *Detective Tales–Pocket* were Philip Ketchum, Fred MacIsaac, Stewart Sterling, Costa Carousso, Wyatt Blassingame, and Talmage Powell. From three to five stories appeared in each issue.

The size of the magazine is rather unique, a scant 4 X 5-1/2 inches. Highly colorful covers, by Denis McLoughlin, helped to keep the magazine from being lost on the newsstands.

Information Sources

INDEX SOURCES: Cook, Michael L. *Monthly Murders.* Westport, Conn.: Greenwood Press, 1982.
LOCATION SOURCES: Private collectors.

Publication History

MAGAZINE TITLE: *Detective Tales–Pocket.*
TITLE CHANGES: None.
VOLUME AND ISSUE DATA: Designated by numbers shared with two other series, *Western Stories* and *Romance Stories*; numbers identifiable as *Detective Tales* are nos. 101, 104, 107, 110, 113, 116, 119, and 123; at least 8 issues, circa 1948.
PUBLISHER: T. V. Boardman & Company Ltd., 14 Cockspur Street, London W.1, England.
EDITOR: Not known.
PRICE PER ISSUE: 6 pence.
SIZE AND PAGINATION: 4" X 5-1/2" (to issue number 110); 4-3/4" X 6-3/4"; 96–113 pages.
CURRENT STATUS: Discontinued.
—*Robert Adey*

DETECTIVE THRILLERS

Detective Thrillers was an early pulp detective magazine by the Clayton magazine group, circa 1930.[1] No other information is available.

Note

1. This title appears in "Tentative Pulp Checklist" from the San Francisco Academy of Comic Art (unpublished manuscript, n.d.).

Information Sources

BIBLIOGRAPHY:
Clayton, W. M. "The Clayton Corral." *Dime Novel Roundup,* no. 15 (March 1932): 7; no. 16 (April 1932):7–8; no. 17 (May 1932):7–8; no. 18 (June 1932):7–8; no. 19 (July/August 1932):9–10.
INDEX SOURCES: None known.
LOCATION SOURCES: Private collectors.

Publication History

MAGAZINE TITLE: *Detective Thrillers.*
TITLE CHANGES: None known.
VOLUME AND ISSUE DATA: Circa 1930; number of issues and extent unknown.
PUBLISHER: W. M. Clayton as The Clayton Magazines, Inc., 155 East 44th Street, New York, New York.
EDITOR: Not known.
PRICE PER ISSUE: Not known.
SIZE AND PAGINATION: Not known.
CURRENT STATUS: Discontinued.

DETECTIVE TRAILS

A pulp magazine publication of the Good Story Magazine Company, *Detective Trails* commenced with the November 1929 issue. The covers featured weird scene-of-the crime situations. No other information is available.

Information Sources

BIBLIOGRAPHY:
Hersey, Harold B. *Pulpwood Editor.* New York: Frederick A. Stokes Co., 1937.
INDEX SOURCES: None known.
LOCATION SOURCES: Private collectors.

Publication History

MAGAZINE TITLE: *Detective Trails.*
TITLE CHANGES: None known.
VOLUME AND ISSUE DATA: Vol. 1, no. 1 (November 1929); number of issues and extent unknown.
PUBLISHER: Good Story Magazine Co., Inc., New York, New York.
EDITOR: W. M. Clayton.
PRICE PER ISSUE: Not known.
SIZE AND PAGINATION: Not known.
CURRENT STATUS: Discontinued.

DETECTIVE WEEKLY (British)

The pink-covered *Union Jack* was published for nearly forty years and over 1,500 issues, from 1894 to 1933, with stories of Indians, explorers, pirates, prospectors, sailors, and a few detectives of note. With the introduction of Sexton Blake, Detective, the detective category was strengthened and became more frequent. During its last years, it was devoted almost exclusively to the detective genre. The final issue of *Union Jack* contained an experiment in a Blake serial The First Part of "The Next Move," written in four parts by different authors— Robert Murray, Anthony Skene, G. H. Teed, and Gwyn Evans. Each author left an insurmountable problem for the next author to solve. Thus, Robert Murray left Roxane locked in an air-tight safe for which only she knew the combination. Skene left Blake drowning in an underground catacomb (and Roxane still in the safe). Readers were invited to comment and give their opinion but must have bought the first issues of the *Detective Weekly* magazine to follow the story.

With the change to the title of *Detective Weekly* on February 25, 1933, the magazine was most modest in its claims. Announcing "The Phantom Dwarf" in the second issue, the editor promised it would be "in the approved Rider Haggard style and written by the celebrated author Maxwell Scott. Do not imagine, however, that we would compare our series with the work of that great writer whose every new book causes its readers to go into raptures."[1]

With belief supported by many of his followers, Sexton Blake was promoted as a real person. Stating "Sexton Blake is not merely a name or a puppet figure of fiction," it was announced that "From our stories, phase by phase, will emerge the real and rounded portrait of a living man—and one who has already won and held the attention of a world-wide audience. Sexton Blake is not a detective; he is THE detective."[2] And like Sherlock Holmes, Blake was credited with a number of monographs which had "added much to the foundations of criminology laid down by such pioneers as Lombroso and Charles Goring, M.D."[3] These included, it was said, works on the use of methylene blue as an antitoxin, single-print classification, fingerprint forgery by the chromicized gelatine method, and speculations on ballistic stigmata in fire-guns. It was thus hard to believe that in the first issue of *Detective Weekly* a skeleton was dragged from the Blake family closet.

A brother, Nigel, who had brought "the grey hairs of his old father in sorrow to the grave," had appeared in London after living in the Cameroons as a wastrel and wife beater. Blake, in looking through his collection of fingerprints (in his study in Baker Street) discovered that the print of Nigel matched that of a mysterious forger. "He could picture the stories, the publicity and scandal of it. 'A brother of the world-famous private detective.' How one or two at the Yard would relish it. . . . "[4] With the aid of Nigel's son, a showdown was accomplished, and Nigel was spirited away to a fortresslike house in Buckinghamshire.

With issue number 131, an identity crisis resulted in the final dropping of the Blake stories after they had for some time been relegated to the inner pages.

The wider world of crime and mystery was emphasized, Scotland Yard in particular. The subtitle at times promoted mystery rather than detective stories.

The type of story, in general, in the Detective Weekly speaks for itself: such titles as "The Clue of the Split Bullet" and "The Gold Comfit Box" (which featured Dr. Grundt, the clubfoot man). Illustrations depicted distressing but thrilling situations in which it could be surmised that the detective could not possibly escape or survive.

The first complete serial published in Detective Weekly was "The White Rider" by Leslie Charteris (Charteris was never a Sexton Blake author); this appeared in numbers 1 through 24. Agatha Christie appeared in issues numbers 124 through 129 with "Murder on the Orient Express." A Charlie Chan serial, "Behind That Curtain," was also published, written, of course, by Earl Derr Biggers.

One of the features was a "roundtable" in which readers were invited to participate. There was intense personal interest in the stories, especially those starring Sexton Blake. Readers expressed desires to see him married, killed off (both of which aroused vigorous rebuttals), and with World War II there were many who wanted Blake to take an active part in fighting the Nazis.

Many factual, or supposedly factual, stories on crime and detection appeared throughout the life of the magazine. With issue number 162, a crime cartoon was introduced and became a regular feature.

However, because of the paper shortage, after 379 issues, the May 25, 1940, issue included an annoucement that the magazine would be discontinued. Thus Detective Weekly became nostalgic history.

Notes

1. E. S. Turner, *Boys Will Be Boys* (London: Michael Joseph Ltd., 1948), p. 107.
2. Ibid., pp. 136–37.
3. Ibid., p. 137.
4. Ibid., p. 138.

Information Sources

BIBLIOGRAPHY:
Lofts, W.O.G., and Derek J. Adley. *Old Boys Books, A Complete Catalogue*. London: privately printed, 1969.
Turner, E. S. *Boys Will Be Boys*. London: Michael Joseph Ltd., 1948.
INDEX SOURCES: None known.
LOCATION SOURCES: Private collectors.

Publication History

MAGAZINE TITLE: *Detective Weekly*.
TITLE CHANGES: Changed from *Union Jack*.
VOLUME AND ISSUE DATA: No. 1 (February 25, 1933) through no. 379, (May 25, 1940); 379 issues.
PUBLISHER: Amalgamated Press Ltd., London, E.C.4, England.
EDITOR: Not known.

SIZE AND PAGINATION: 24-1/2 cm. X 32 cm.; average 32 pages.
CURRENT STATUS: Discontinued.

DETECTIVE YARNS

"A Dozen Stories for a Dime," said the legend on the cover. And on the table of contents was promised "More Words on Every Page!" What *Detective Yarns* offered was quantity, volume, and a lot of reading material for your money from 1938 to 1941.

If quality was of no particular consideration, action was. It began on the front cover, where a man and woman together faced deadly action. He shot and bled; she looked on, aghast, clothing ripped artistically from her limbs. The interior illustrations, concealed from the public eye, generally contrived to show girls with most of their clothing gone. Whether dead, furious, or frightened, they were decidedly bare.

As with the illustrations, so were the stories. No sooner did the girl appear, her creamy flesh gleaming, than she was beat up, tied up, her dress ripped away, and some sadistic thug began to torture her. The descriptions dealt lovingly with torture, carefully detailing the blood trickle, so that no reader would feel his ten cents to have been unwisely invested.

Apart from these touches of sadistic sex, the magazine featured conventional tough-guy stories. Dim-witted but homicidal thugs; dim-witted but homicidal heroes. Fast-action openings. Story endings with an occasional sharp twist, more often with a kiss and the promise that the nice couple would find joy together forever. Between opening and closing, the reader found the usual murder, chase, fist fights, sluggings, framings, beatings up, and trackings down. The heroes plunged into each mystery with the apparent intention of getting tied up as quickly as possible and were prepared for an agonizing death. Shallow, mindless violence is what was offered, twelve times an issue, for ten cents.

Occasionally, a writer appeared who was known to the reader: Wyatt Blassingame, Wilbur S. Peacock, Robert Leslie Bellem, Ray Cummings all drift in and out of the issues. Other names are less familiar and seem to be stirred in with many pseudonyms.

Issues of *Detective Yarns* in the late 1930s contained one or two fact articles, heavily fictionalized, and signed by such authorities as "Convict 12627" and "Undercover Dix." Later articles, during late 1939 and 1940, are signed by "The Editor." You can sympathize with his desire for anonymity.

The last issue known is April 1941, designated as volume 2, number 5. Later that same year, *Black Hood Detective* (*Hooded Detective**) appeared, the first issue labeled volume 2, number 6, so it is highly probable that this was a continuation, at least in numbering, of *Detective Yarns*. In April of that year, most, if not all, of Louis H. Silberkleit's Blue Ribbon magazines were put under the banner of Columbia Publications, the publisher shown for *Black Hood Detective*.

Information Sources

INDEX SOURCES: None known.
LOCATION SOURCES: University of California–Los Angeles Library (1938, 2 issues); private collectors.

Publication History

MAGAZINE TITLE: *Detective Yarns*.
TITLE CHANGES: None confirmed; possibly changed to *Black Hood Detective* (see *Hooded Detective*) with Vol. 2, no. 6.
VOLUME AND ISSUE DATA: Vol. 1, no. 1 (June 1938) through Vol. 2, no. 5 (April 1941); 11 issues.
PUBLISHER: Blue Ribbon Magazines, Inc., 1 Appleton Street, Holyoke, Massachusetts (1938–1939); Double-Action Magazines, Inc., 2256 Grove Street, Chicago, Illinois (1940–1941).
EDITOR: Not known.
PRICE PER ISSUE: 10 cents.
SIZE AND PAGINATION: 7" X 9-7/8"; 98–114 pages.
CURRENT STATUS: Discontinued.
—*Robert Sampson*

DICK DOBBS DETECTIVE WEEKLY

The last dime novel detective series to be established, the *Dick Dobbs Detective Weekly*, was also the shortest lived. It ceased publication with the seventh number. An eighth number was advertised but never published.

Dobbs was a gentleman-detective and a millionaire. Not having to worry about earning a living, he used his "marvelous abilities" as a detective for the sheer joy of the chase. Dobbs was not his real name, nor was his biographer–assistant really named "Shadow Steve," but the publisher's advertisements refused to reveal the real name of either. It has been suggested they were the work of William Perry Brown.

The publisher promised these stories would be unlike the "old-style blood-and-thunder" stories, that they would be "the best, most clever, exciting, thrilling and realistic masterpieces ever penned. It will be BRAINS vs. CRIME. You will be taken through the slum, the palace, the gambler's den, the offices of high financiers—everywhere that crime and dishonesty breeds."[1] They must be read to be believed, so imaginatively bizarre are the dangers and hair-breadth escapes. It is possible they were not intended to be taken seriously.

A recurring menace in the *Dick Dobbs Detective Weekly* was the group called the Red Dagger, a society associated with the Black Hand. Members of the defeated Red Dagger banded together to form a new group called the Brown Thumb. Dobbs had numerous wonderful abilities, including the ability to charm poisonous snakes with a violin while singing instructions for rounding up the gang.

Two or three short stories, mostly anonymous, were used to fill out the pages which followed the Dobbs adventures.

The publisher was George Marsh, just two blocks up the street from Street & Smith, according to the address. A decade earlier, the Marsh experiment with a millionaire detective might have worked and provided some real competition for the famous detective (Nick Carter) from the other company.

Note

1. Editorial announcement, *Dick Dobbs Detective Weekly*, no. 1 (March 20, 1909), p. 2.

Information Sources

BIBLIOGRAPHY:
French, George. "Dick Dobbs Detective Weekly." *Dime Novel Roundup*, no. 42, (June 1935):1–2.
INDEX SOURCES: None known.
LOCATION SOURCES: Private collectors.

Publication History

MAGAZINE TITLE: *Dick Dobbs Detective Weekly*.
TITLE CHANGES: None.
VOLUME AND ISSUE DATA: No. 1 (March 20, 1909) through no. 7 (May 1, 1909); 7 issues.
PUBLISHER: George Marsh Company, 257 William Street, New York, New York.
EDITOR: Not known.
PRICE PER ISSUE: 5 cents.
SIZE AND PAGINATION: 8'' X 11''; 32 pages.
CURRENT STATUS: Discontinued.
—J. Randolph Cox

DICK TURPIN LIBRARY (Aldine Publishing) (British)

Dick Turpin. A name to stir the imaginations and revive nostalgic memories of adults as well as thousands of schoolboys! And although scores of highwaymen were romanticized in the Victorian "penny dreadfuls," there was none as dashing and exciting as Dick Turpin. Historians today portray him as an illiterate, blustering coward, a sheep stealer and cattle rustler and a murderous villain of the lowest order who was eventually hung on the scaffolds, begging for mercy. True, he was a criminal, but literate and compassionate, and he did have mercy on his intended victims to the extent that he would not only pass some by but would contribute money to them if they were needy.

The thousands of stories penned about Dick Turpin, however, without question, make him a tall, dark, handsome man who robbed the rich to feed the poor; and he and his famous horse, Black Bess, were superman and beast to all who read about his adventures and exploits.

The *Dick Turpin Library* published by the Aldine Publishing Company, commencing in 1902, recounted 182 of these adventures in as many issues and was the first periodical to be named for the hero.

Information Sources

BIBLIOGRAPHY:
Lofts, W.O.G. "Dick Turpin, The Famous Highwayman." *Dime Novel Roundup*, Vol. 38, no. 6 (June 15, 1969).
————, and Derek J. Adley. *Old Boys Books, A Complete Catalogue*. London: privately printed, 1969.
Turner, E. S. *Boys Will Be Boys*. London: Michael Joseph, 1948.
INDEX SOURCES: None known.
LOCATION SOURCES: Private collectors only.

Publication History

MAGAZINE TITLE: *Dick Turpin Library*.
TITLE CHANGES: None.
VOLUME AND ISSUE DATA: No. 1 (April 5, 1902) through no. 182 (1909); 182 issues.
PUBLISHER: Aldine Publishing Company, London.
EDITOR: Not known.
PRICE PER ISSUE: Not known.
SIZE AND PAGINATION: 5-3/8'' X 7''; pages not known.
CURRENT STATUS: Discontinued.

DICK TURPIN LIBRARY (Newnes) (British)

Although Dick Turpin, highwayman and Robin Hood to the poor, according to legend, was a swashbuckling figure in his own right, his chroniclers felt no compulsion to limit their tales to the facts of his life. In fact, any similarity was purely coincidental! He and Black Bess, his horse, were led through more than a thousand adventures with the result that although he was in essence a villain, he became a hero whose every exploit was closely followed. As a dashing, handsomely portrayed robber who took from the rich to give to the poor, Dick Turpin had become a legendary figure in England by the time that George Newnes commenced publishing his *Dick Turpin Library*, the second periodical by that name, in 1922. As such, it met with immediate success and existed for 138 issues, until 1930.

Information Sources

BIBLIOGRAPHY:
Lofts, W.O.G. "Dick Turpin, The Famous Highwayman." *Dime Novel Roundup*, Vol. 38, no. 6 (June 15, 1969).
————, and Derek J. Adley. *Old Boys Books, A Complete Catalogue*. London: privately printed, 1969.
Turner, E. S. *Boys Will Be Boys*. London: Michael Joseph, 1948.

INDEX SOURCES: None known.
LOCATION SOURCES: Private collectors only.

Publication History

MAGAZINE TITLE: *Dick Turpin Library.*
TITLE CHANGES: None.
VOLUME AND ISSUE DATA: 1922–1930; 138 issues.
PUBLISHER: George Newnes, London.
EDITOR: Not known.
PRICE PER ISSUE: Not known.
SIZE AND PAGINATION: Not known.
CURRENT STATUS: Discontinued.

DICK TURPIN NOVELS (British)

Dick Turpin Novels was a short run of a thin, pocket-size periodical reprinting the exploits of Dick Turpin, highwayman, robber of the rich who gave to the poor. Six issues were published in 1935 by C. Arthur Pearson. No other information is available.

Information Sources

BIBLIOGRAPHY:
Lofts, W.O.G., and Derek J. Adley. *Old Boys Books, A Complete Catalogue.* London: privately printed, 1969.
INDEX SOURCES: None known.
LOCATION SOURCES: Private collectors.

Publication History

MAGAZINE TITLE: *Dick Turpin Novels.*
TITLE CHANGES: None.
VOLUME AND ISSUE DATA: No. 1 (1935) through no. 6 (1935); 6 issues.
PUBLISHER: C. Arthur Pearson, London.
EDITOR: Not known.
PRICE PER ISSUE: Not known.
SIZE AND PAGINATION: 5-3/8'' X 7''; 32 pages.
CURRENT STATUS: Discontinued.

DIMEBOOKS DETECTIVE STORIES (Canadian)

Virtually unknown today, this abortive experiment by a Canadian publisher lasted only one issue. The sole issue of *Dimebooks Detective Stories* was published in August 1952, along with three nonmystery companion magazines (one was *Brief Fantastic Tales*, a magazine of weird horror stories). The publisher was The Dimebooks Corporation.

Unique in the mystery field, *Dimebooks Detective* was issued in purse or vest-pocket size, being much smaller than today's paperbacks, and was saddle-stitched so that it had no spine. The physical dimensions make it most unusual: 5-3/4'' X 4''; it was only one-sixteenth of an inch thick, with sixty-four numbered pages. As the title implies, it sold for a dime. The back cover had an advertisement for Bromoseltzer.

Four stories were included in the issue: "The Fourth Knife" by Hayward Coleman ("First of four knives dealt her death; Suspected College Girls got two more, in their bodies"); "Snare for Murder" by Nathan Stern ("The trap was to backfire, catch the stalking detective, but Grady had guts, and an idea"); "Suicide Suspect" by Peter Dempson ("Detective Cronin called by man soon to die discards suicide—starts to prove murder"); and "Paroled to Die" by G. J. Blaine ("Joe Langley was innocent. That's not reason D.A. released him from safety of his cell").

This magazine is extremely scarce today, even in Canada where it was printed. However, this scarcity does not imply any quality to the fiction which was published in its sole issue.

Information Sources

INDEX SOURCES: None known.
LOCATION SOURCES: Private collectors.

Publication History

MAGAZINE TITLE: *Dimebooks Detective Stories*.
TITLE CHANGES: None.
VOLUME AND ISSUE DATA: Vol. 1, no. 1 (August 1952); 1 issue.
PUBLISHER: The Dimebooks Corporation, Suite 205, 95 King Street East, Toronto, Canada.
EDITOR: Not known.
PRICE PER ISSUE: 10 cents (Canadian).
SIZE AND PAGINATION: 4'' X 5-3/4''; 64 pages.
CURRENT STATUS: Discontinued.
—*J. Grant Thiessen*

DIME DETECTIVE

Dime Detective, the most popular of Popular Publications' fine array of detective pulp magazines (which included *Dime Mystery Book** and *Detective Tales,** among others) made its debut with the November 1931 issue. It would be one of the company's longest surviving titles.

While emphasizing conventional persons who found themselves unaccountably in bizarre crime situations, there were nevertheless many fine series characters, albeit many eccentric; and an endless array of private investigators, police detectives, gangsters, ex-cons, and gamblers paraded through the pages. Raymond Chandler stories were published in the 1930s, as well as some by Erle Stanley Gardner, Carroll John Daly, Oscar Schisgall, Arthur Leo Zagat, J. Arthur Burks, and Frederick C. Davis, a veritable who's who in detective fiction.

However, *Dime Detective* had made its appearance at a time when the public did not want to read about ordinary detective work. There was a demand for grotesque situations and weird menace. Foul fiends should distress fair maidens but then must be bested by a hero in a fast-moving, blood-curdling format. *Dime Detective* filled the order, although it did not reach, perhaps, quite the heights of depravity as Popular Publications' *Dime Mystery* (which *Dime Detective* announced in a 1932 issue with the publisher's promise: "If you can lay one aside before the last clue's been followed up—the last shot fired—we'll eat the back cover!"[1]

As Robert Kenneth Jones aptly describes it in *The Shudder Pulps,* "These and others excelled in crisp action and bizarre situations such as Ralph Oppenheim's super criminal who delights in sadistically branding his victims, or Frederick C. Davis' phantom killer that stalks a pleasure yacht (both in the September 15, 1933 issue). Writers indulged in some horror but generally stuck to lurid crimes. The contents followed (Harry) Steeger's dictum: 'A murder mysteriously committed before the eyes of the reader.' "[2]

During the early 1940s, perhaps as a result of the war years changing the public's demand for relief from horrendous situations, *Dime Detective* changed its direction from the incredibly fearful and malign backgrounds to a predominance of merely crazily absurd, eccentric, and unusual, and gradually by the early fifties to allowing the crime itself to be the menace. All this, mind you, was within the framework of a detective story!

Thus, surviving the war years and the paper shortage, the magazine was able to continue into the midst of the digest-magazine period before it finally succumbed to its inevitable fate in 1953.

At least three issues of a British reprint series were also published.

Notes

1. Advertisement, *Dime Detective,* November 1932, p. 4.
2. Robert Kenneth Jones, *The Shudder Pulps* (West Linn, Ore.: Fax Collector's Editions, 1975), pp. 4–5.

Information Sources

BIBLIOGRAPHY:
Jones, Robert Kenneth. *The Shudder Pulps.* West Linn, Ore.: Fax Collector's Editions, 1975.
Lewis, Steve. "Speaking of Pulp: Dime Detective." *The Not So Private Eye,* no. 5 (April–June 1979): 27–28.
INDEX SOURCES: None known.
LOCATION SOURCES: University of California–Los Angeles Library (1931–1951, 201 issues); private collectors.

Publication History

MAGAZINE TITLE: *Dime Detective.*
TITLE CHANGES: None

VOLUME AND ISSUE DATA: Vol. 1, no. 1 (November 1931) through Vol. 69, no.
    5 (August 1953); 274 issues.
PUBLISHER: Popular Publications, Inc., 2256 Grove Street, Chicago, Illinois, later 1125
    East Vaile Avenue, Kokomo, Indiana, with editorial offices at 205 East 42nd
    Street, New York, New York.
EDITORS: Rogers Terrill (1934); others not known.
PRICE PER ISSUE: 10 cents; 15 cents; 25 cents.
SIZE AND PAGINATION: Average 6-7/8'' X 9-1/2''; 82–130 pages.
CURRENT STATUS: Discontinued.

DIME DETECTIVE (British)

See DIME DETECTIVE

DIME MYSTERY BOOK

Thomas Jefferson's dictum that institutions must change with the times would
have been stretched to the limit if applied to *Dime Mystery*. The many shifts in
direction taken by that magazine during its two decades on the newsstands, each
accompanied by breathless ballyhoo in the respective issues, seemingly defied
explanation. Yet today, the magazine can be seen as a pace setter and innovator—
a standard bearer, if you will, during the golden age of the pulps.

In 1932, Henry Steeger, publisher, and Harold Goldsmith, treasurer, of Popular Publications added *Dime Mystery Book* to their new company's growing
list of titles. But the public did not take to it as in the case of Popular's *Dime
Detective*.* So after only ten issues, a change took place. The October 1933
issue was revamped, complete with name change to *Dime Mystery Magazine*.
The earlier contents featured a "two-dollar novel," plus a few short stories, for
ten cents. Now, the "novel" was shortened to about 18,000 words, and several
mystery-terror novelettes and short stories were included. Detectives were out,
and purple prose was in.

"My inspiration was the Grand Guignol theater in Paris," Steeger has noted.[1]
He explained that he wanted to reproduce the tortures and depravities depicted
three dimensionally on the stage in the two-dimensional theater of his pulp. This
led to a Gothic style with overtones of sex-sadism—a combination of horror and
sex that pulps had never exploited before.

Following the new look issue, *Dime Mystery* covers showed a succession of
harried heroines seen fleeing from deformed creatures down dank dungeons or
cowering cravenly at the mercy of leering madmen. The weird-menace story
had arrived: an apparent supernatural nemesis menaces the hero and heroine;
some mild sex and sadism is thrown in; and finally, a logical resolution clears
up the mystifying goings-on. As one of the fast-selling pulpsters of the period,
Norvell Page, put it, "I was looking for some clipping that might suggest horror,
that would give me a menace to make the reader's blood run cold."[2]

That he and other authors were successful can be shown in the long line of monsters and villains whose grotesqueness was exceeded only by the bizarre forms of destruction they dealt. There was the hairless creature with scaly skin and lidless eyes, one with a torso and no legs, another with razor-sharp claws, a fourth with gray-green face and leathery skin. Never in literature were so many afflicted so horribly. The deaths they perpetrated took forms such as a fungus that ate away the skin and a rotting affliction that aged the victim a hundred years in a few minutes, not to mention such mundane occurrences as mutilations and skeletons found on street corners.

These evil-doers and their inexplicable deeds nearly always turned out prosaically. The offenders were unmasked as relatives, business partners, and rejected suitors who had disguised themselves to scare everyone. Editor Rogers Terrill's admonition was that no matter how grotesque, there must be a logical explanation. Author Richard Tooker summed it up as follows: "A fearful menace, apparently due to supernatural agencies, must terrify the characters (and reader, but not the writer) at the start, but the climax must demonstrate convincingly that the menace was natural after all."[3]

During the weird-menace period, when *Dime Mystery* added the subtitle, "The Weirdest Stories Ever Told," several authors rose above the purple-prose conventions to produce stories of a high caliber. John H. Knox, for one, proved versatile in the medium. His themes ranged from the touching and frightening diary of a little girl, to a psychological study of a hallucinatory aberration; from a short account of a weird revenge to an ambitious epic blending detective fiction and science fiction overtones with weird mystery.

Another noteworthy "fear merchant" was Hugh B. Cave, whose stories probably exemplified the Gothic weird-menace expression better than any other author. Present-day readers of supernatural fiction met him a few years ago when a collection of his early efforts was published. The most consistently satisfying purveyor of weird-menace chills was probably Wyatt Blassingame. He covered a wide spectrum, from fantasy to character study, from lurid melodrama to trenchant suspense. The majority of his stories in this vein rates as anthology caliber—something that can be said of few authors, pulp or otherwise.

Serials were not used in this magazine. But on one occasion, in 1935, a series of connected stories in six installments appeared, the only time an extended treatment of this type took place. It was a tightly strung saga in the supernatural genre, of a self-sustaining curse that spanned nine hundred years, five countries, and three continents. Chandler H. Whipple, an editor at Popular Publications soon to leave for *Argosy*, chronicled the curse of the Harcourts. The only other continuing series was John Kobler's factual accounts, over ten issues starting in 1937, titled "History's Gallery of Monsters."

Until the beginning of 1936, Walter M. Baumhofer painted the covers. He also worked for Street & Smith on their *Doc Savage** magazine. Then Tom Lovell took over the *Dime Mystery* covers for a year and one-half, bringing the flair that presaged his present-day pioneer patriot that symbolized Continental

Insurance Company in its television ads. Interior illustrations for the first few years were all the work of Amos Sewell, who was later to go on to more ambitious (and better-paying) commitments with the *Saturday Evening Post* and other slick-paper magazines. By the time Lovell came on the scene, interiors were being rendered by Paul Orban, David Berger, and Ralph Carlson.

At the same time, the writing style was changing. Earlier circumlocutions were giving way to a racier prose. Gone were such livid phrases as "agony-mist," "corpse-creature," and "shrieking heap." Soon, "fearful fate" became good old plain "rape" or "ravished."

For the next three years, *Dime Mystery* emphasized sex-sadism. Gothicism was gone. The former shrinking maidens depicted on the covers became pro-vocative females divested of clothing and suffering various forms of torture. Some of the authors couldn't accept the more blatant approach and did not contribute stories during this exploitive period. Others, such as Nat Schachner and Arthur Leo Zagat, who had wallowed in stilted situations, swept away the cobwebs for a more erotic exploitation. New authors came on the scene, like Russell Gray and Ralston Shields, who presented a clean, economical style. So while man's inhumanity to woman became more blatant, the narration became more sophisticated.

Needless to say, other publications of a similar nature soon followed *Dime Mystery's* lead. Popular Publications itself produced companion magazines in the long-running *Horror Stories** and *Terror Tales* (see *Horror Stories*) and in a few shorter-life publications. *Thrilling Mystery,** a Ned L. Pines publication, appeared early, and later on the scene came *Ace Mystery** and *Mystery Tales* (*Uncanny Tales**).

Then, in 1938, as competing weird-menace pulps hit the stands, *Dime Mystery* underwent another transformation, one which was unaccountable. In the October issue, readers would look in vain for the alluring femmes fatales they had grown to love. Instead, a new type of protagonist had taken over, often sans female companion—the defective detective. Signaling the change was this bit of editorial blarney: "All the eerie menace and weirdly terrifying atmosphere, plus speed, dramatic punch, plot complication and breathless tempo of the best detective mysteries." This new breed of hero actually received its start at Popular's *Strange Detective Mysteries,** which, as early as the first issue in 1937, had featured several odd detective heroes.

Each of *Dime Mystery's* detectives was peculiarly afflicted. One was deaf, from a bullet, and had to read lips; another never slept while on a case; one had hemophilia, with the slightest scratch being fatal. Nothing came out of this desultory period other than a few enjoyable Ben Byrn stories by Russell Gray. Byrn was a five-footer, with "tremendous power in his arms and iron in his soul." Gray later went on to hard-boiled hardbound books under his real name, Bruno Fischer.

Within another two years, *Dime Mystery* reverted back briefly to its earlier sex-sadistic phase. This period was the beginning of the decline of the pulps.

Cost savings could be seen in the reprint covers used. For the rest of the 1940s and into the early fifties, the magazine appeared on a bimonthly schedule, featuring detective action with an occasional fantasy. It gave way to further economy measures by raising its price to fifteen cents.

At least three issues of a British reprint series were published.

Notes

1. Robert Kenneth Jones, *The Shudder Pulps* (West Linn, Ore.: Fax Collector's Editions, 1975), p. 6.
2. Ibid., p. 10.
3. Ibid., p. 8.

Information Sources

BIBLIOGRAPHY:
Hardin, Nils. "An Interview with Henry Steeger." *Xenophile,* no. 33 (July 1977): 3–18.
————, and George Hocutt. "A Checklist of Popular Publications Titles 1930–1955." *Xenophile,* no. 33 (July 1977): 21–24.
Jones, Robert Kenneth. "The Defective Detectives." *The Pulp Era,* no. 68 (November/December 1967): 21–23.
————. *The Shudder Pulps.* West Linn, Ore.: Fax Collector's Editions, 1975.
————. "The Weird Menace Magazines." *Bronze Shadows,* no. 10 (June 1967): 3–8; no. 11 (August 1967): 7–13; no. 12 (October 1967): 7–10; no. 13 (January 1968): 7–12; no. 14 (March 1968): 13–17; no. 15 (November 1968): 4–8.
INDEX SOURCES: None known.
LOCATION SOURCES: University of California–Los Angeles Library (Vol. 1, no. 1; Vol. 33, no. 4; Vol. 34, no. 3, only); private collectors.

Publication History

MAGAZINE TITLE: *Dime Mystery Book.*
TITLE CHANGES: *Dime Mystery Magazine* (with Vol. 3, no. 1 [August 1933]); combined with *Ten-Story Mystery* in mid-1940s; became *15 Mystery Stories* (with Vol. 39, no. 3 [February 1950]).
VOLUME AND ISSUE DATA: Vol. 1, no. 1 (December 1932) through Vol. 39, no. 2 (December 1949); 153 issues. As *15 Mystery Stories*: Vol. 39, no. 3 (February 1950) through Vol. 40, no. 3 (October 1950); 5 issues.
PUBLISHER: American Fiction Magazines (subsidiary of Popular Publications, Inc.), 2256 Grove Street, Chicago, Illinois, with editorial offices at 205 East 42nd Street, New York, New York; as of Vol. 4, no. 4 (March 1934), publisher listed as Popular Publications, Inc.
EDITORS: Rogers Terrill (ca. 1933–41), Chandler H. Whipple (ca. 1941–43), Loring Dowst (ca. 1943–).
PRICE PER ISSUE: 10 cents; 15 cents.
SIZE AND PAGINATION: 7" X 9-3/4"; 98–128 pages.
CURRENT STATUS: Discontinued.
—*Robert Kenneth Jones*

DIME MYSTERY MAGAZINE (British)

See DIME MYSTERY BOOK

DIME MYSTERY MAGAZINE (U.S.)

See DIME MYSTERY BOOK

DIME NOVEL ROUNDUP

The *Dime Novel Roundup*, although aimed as a whole at readers and collectors of dime novels, story-papers, and all older forms of popular literature, does include among its wealth of information much on the earliest forms of detective literature. Interviews, articles, bibliographic listings and checklists, and reminiscences present information that can be found in no other publication and is unequaled in its scope.

The *Dime Novel Roundup* is unique, also, for its long span of publication. The first issue was January 1931, and even this was the successor to a previous, similar publication, the *Happy Hours Magazine* (named so as being the journal of the Happy Hours Brotherhood, an association of readers and collectors dating back to January 1925). Through the end of 1981, there have been 552 issues published with but very few gaps in its regular schedule of monthly publication to October 1975 and bimonthly since. It was founded, edited, and published by Ralph F. Cummings for over twenty-one years, until July 1952. The present editor-publisher, Edward T. LeBlanc, has devoted an even longer span to the magazine, from 1952 to the present.

Among the hundreds of fine articles, of particular interest to the detective fiction coterie are: "The Detective-Hero in the American Dime Novel" by J. Randolph Cox (issue number 547); "The Anatomy of Dime Novels, No. 11: Bootblack Detectives" by J. Edward Leithead (issue number 431); "This 'Sleuth' Business" by Leithead (issues numbers 369, 370); and "The Two King Bradys and Their Girl Detective," also by Leithead (issues numbers 372, 373).

Information Sources

BIBLIOGRAPHY:

Cummings, Ralph F. "History of the Happy Hours Brotherhood and the Dime Novel Roundup." *Dime Novel Roundup*, no. 430 (July 15, 1968): 74–75; no. 432 (September 15, 1968): 93–94.

———. "The Life of Happy Hours Magazine and Dime Novel Roundup." *Dime Novel Roundup*, no. 300 (September 15, 1957): 81–82.

———. "Newsy News," (new editor, Edward T. LeBlanc introduction). *Dime Novel Roundup*. no. 238 (July 1952): 52–55.

Duprez, Charles. "Ye Brotherhood, the Roundup, and Its Editor." *Dime Novel Roundup*, no. 274 (July 15, 1955): 53–56.

INDEX SOURCES: LeBlanc, Edward T. "Index of Major Subjects, January 1976–December 1978." *Dime Novel Roundup*, no. 535 (February 1979):10a–c.

————. "Index to Major Subjects, Issues Nos. 1–516." *Dime Novel Roundup*, no. 529 (Special Supplement, February 1978).

LOCATION SOURCES: Akron Public Library, Akron, Ohio: American Antiquarian Society, Worcester, Mass.; Athenaeum of Philadelphia; Boston Public Library; Brandeis University, Waltham, Mass.; British Museum, London; Brooklyn Public Library; Denver Public Library; Florida State University, Tallahassee; University of Illinois, Urbana; Iowa University Libraries, Iowa City; University of Kentucky, Lexington; University of Maryland, College Park; Milwaukee Public Library; Saint Olaf College, Northfield, Minn.; San Francisco Public Library; University of Tulsa Library; University of Wyoming, Laramie.

Publication History

MAGAZINE TITLE: *Dime Novel Roundup (Dime Novel Round-Up)*.

TITLE CHANGES: None.

VOLUME AND ISSUE DATA: Vol. 1, no. 1 (January 1931) through Vol. 50, no. 6 (Whole 552; to date, December 1981) 552 issues.

PUBLISHER: Ralph F. Cummings (until July 1952); Edward T. LeBlanc, 87 School Street, Fall River, Massachusetts 02720.

EDITORS: Ralph F. Cummings (1931–1952); Edward T. LeBlanc (1952 to date).

PRICE PER ISSUE: By subscription only, currently (1982) $10.00.

SIZE AND PAGINATION: 6" X 9"; 4–20 pages average.

CURRENT STATUS: Active.

DIXON BRETT DETECTIVE LIBRARY (British)

Although the *Dixon Brett Detective Library* was a comparatively short-lived magazine and unprepossessing in appearance, the hero character of the tales made a lasting impression on the British reading public, and Dixon Brett today may be considered as a predecessor to Nick Carter.

This scientific sleuth owned one of the first Mercedes race cars, the "Night Hawk," which, despite the heartless way in which the detective set it in motion, played an important role in many of his cases. Two assistants, Pat Malone (often a liability) and Bill Slook (rescued from an opium den), provided some comic relief. An evil Fan Chu Fang was the archenemy, supposedly an agent of the Chinese government.

Perhaps borrowing from Sherlock Holmes, Dixon Brett was often to be found in a deep chair, clad in a loose-fitting dressing gown, smoking an "evil-smelling briar" or "igniting a choice weed." As a scientific sleuth, he had, of course, his own laboratory, although his experiments today would seem trivial.

The characters in the Dixon Brett stories often suffered bizarre, violent deaths, giving each story an unexpected twist and atmosphere.

Information Sources

BIBLIOGRAPHY:

Lofts, W.O.G., and Derek J. Adley. *Old Boys Books, A Complete Catalogue*. London: privately printed, 1969.

Turner, E. S. *Boys Will Be Boys*. London: Michael Joseph, 1948.
INDEX SOURCES: None known.
LOCATION SOURCES: Private collectors only.

Publication History

MAGAZINE TITLE: *Dixon Brett Detective Library*.
TITLE CHANGES: None.
VOLUME AND ISSUE DATA: 1926–1928; no. 1–28; 28 issues.
PUBLISHER: Aldine Publishing Company, London.
EDITOR: Not known.
PRICE PER ISSUE: 2 pence.
SIZE AND PAGINATION: 5-3/8'' X 7''; pages not known.
CURRENT STATUS: Discontinued.

DIXON HAWKE LIBRARY (British)

The tall detective with an aquiline nose wore a dressing gown and smoked a blackened briar; he had a landlady and an assistant. In one case, he left a dummy figure in front of the window to draw the fire of an assailant. Sherlock Holmes? No, Dixon Hawke!

Dixon Hawke and his assistant, Tommy Burke, entertained the British public with 576 cases over some twenty-two years and is still being chronicled today but with somewhat less recognition. A Mrs. Benvie presided over his rooms on Dover Street, and from there, with a minimum of deduction and a maximum of action, he sallied forth to confront a wide variety of crooks.

Published in pocket-size, thin magazines by the D. C. Thomson & Company of Dundee, Scotland, Dixon Hawke is a little-known detective in the United States and deserves better recognition.

Information Sources

BIBLIOGRAPHY:
Lofts, W.O.G., and Derek J. Adley. *Old Boys Books, A Complete Catalogue*. London: privately printed, 1969.
Turner, E. S. *Boys Will Be Boys*. London: Michael Joseph, 1948.
INDEX SOURCES: None known.
LOCATION SOURCES: Private collectors only.

Publication History

MAGAZINE TITLE: *Dixon Hawke Library*.
TITLE CHANGES: None.
VOLUME AND ISSUE DATA: 1919 to December 27, 1941; no. 1–576; 576 issues.
PUBLISHER: D. C. Thomson & Company, Dundee, Scotland.
EDITOR: Not known.
PRICE PER ISSUE: Not known.
SIZE AND PAGINATION: 5-3/8'' X 7''; pages not known.
CURRENT STATUS: Discontinued.

DOC SAVAGE

The character of Doc Savage was the joint creation of Henry W. Ralston and John L. Nanovic of Street & Smith and of Lester Dent, the writer hired to author Savage's adventures under the house name of Kenneth Robeson. Although The Shadow preceded him as the first character to have a magazine built around him, (*The Shadow Magazine**), The Shadow belonged to an older tradition of mystery characters. Doc Savage was intended to be an adventure character, but under Lester Dent's imaginative manipulations he became something more—the first superhero and an inspiration for countless pulp, comic-book, and television characters.

Doc Savage—Clark Savage, Jr.—was created by Henry W. Ralston, who based him largely upon Street & Smith's earlier dime novel hero, Nick Carter, and on a soldier of fortune, Major Richard Henry Savage. Ralston turned the concept over to John L. Nanovic, an editor, who refined it somewhat over a period of months until Lester Dent was picked to write the series. Dent further modified the original concept, turning Doc Savage into, as he often put it, "a combination of Tarzan, Sherlock Holmes, Craig Kennedy, and Jesus Christ."[1] A superman, in other words. A superhero, in retrospect. Pulp artists Walter M. Baumhofer, Robert G. Harris, and Paul Orban provided the visual interpretations of the character that helped make him so memorable to several generations.

The first novel, "The Man of Bronze," introduced a bronzed adventurer with gold-flaked eyes, Clark Savage, Jr. He was a surgeon, scientist, and philanthropist, a man of incredible accomplishments, as well as with impressive physical development. His abilities were the results of his background. At an early age, his father had placed him in the hands of a succession of scientists, physical culture experts, and other unusual tutors (just as Nick Carter's father had done in an earlier generation) in order to prepare Savage for his life's work—to right wrongs and punish evil-doers. During World War I, he met the five men who would later accompany him on his adventures. These were: Andrew Blodgett "Monk" Mayfair, the amiable apelike industrial chemist; Monk's archrival, dapper Brigadier General Theodore Marley "Ham" Brooks, noted lawyer; Colonel John "Renny" Renwick, civil engineer; Major Thomas J. Roberts, a slight electrical expert also called "Long Tom"; and William Harper Littlejohn, archaeologist and geologist, who was nicknamed "Johnny." All experts in their own fields, they were nevertheless eclipsed by Doc Savage's abilities. In actual practice, these men were a group of comic misfits whose primary purpose was acting as foils for the hero and getting into trouble for plot purposes. They were, nevertheless, a major component of the success of the *Doc Savage* magazine.

In the first novel, Doc and his men get together to investigate the death of Clark Savage, Sr.—a trail which leads to a remote valley of Mayan Indians and a hoard of gold. This, Doc uses to finance his career, but only after saving the Mayans from disaster and winning the love of a beautiful Mayan princess (a love which he is unable to return because of his noble work).

The early novels are typical gutsy pulp adventure, relieved only by the humor of Doc's aides and the emerging flair of Dent's unique prose. Doc chased after vicious supercriminals (such as the Gray Spider in "Quest of the Spider"), discovered lost civilizations (in "The Thousand-headed Man" and other novels), and rescued foreign nations from war and ruin (as in "The King Maker"). Originally, Doc was a grim avenger in The Shadow tradition, with a trilling sound comparable to The Shadow's laugh. But all of this changed within the first year. Doc foreswore killing his enemies; his men carried supermachine-pistols which shot nonlethal bullets; and Doc established his Crime College, an institution in upstate New York where criminals were rehabilitated through corrective brain surgery.

By the second year of *Doc Savage*, most of the many main elements had been established (Doc's obsession with nonlethal weapons and his innumerable gadgets, for example). Doc's tough personality metamorphosed into an emotionless but noble demeanor. His grammar improved. He spent more time engaged in philanthropic and surgical pursuits. In "Brand of the Werewolf," the last of the major characters was introduced in the person of Patricia Savage, Doc's attractive and feisty cousin.

Lester Dent established a unique background for his series, the likes of which the world of popular literature would not see again until the comic-strip characters of The Phantom and Superman. Doc Savage operated out of his scientific headquarters on the eighty-sixth floor of an unnamed New York skyscraper (obviously the Empire State Building). He maintained a phony warehouse on the Hudson River which housed many aircraft, including dirigibles and a submarine. His Crime College was a secret from the world, as was the source of his Mayan gold. His Fortress of Solitude was a tantilizing retreat at the North Pole which was often mentioned, but readers were not brought in on its secrets until five years later with the story, "Fortress of Solitude."

Dent's breezy, economical, and often peculiar style was constantly changing, aided by the frequent use of a dictaphone on which he dictated many of the 1930s novels. His characters often wrote themselves—or seemed to—due to the fact that Dent had established them (in other guises) in his pre-*Doc Savage* work. He knew them well. Ultimately, Dent's "Depression Doc" novels were larger than life and struck a balance between frenetic action and tongue-in-cheekiness. He seldom descended into melodrama.

This was not true of the other writers who wrote some of the Doc Savage novels. The first of these was Harold A. Davis, Dent's most prolific and capable ghostwriter. While Davis's earliest novels ("The King Maker" and "Dust of Death," for example) were co-written with Dent, many later stories were his sole efforts. Davis's "The Living Fire Menace" and "The Purple Dragon" were outstanding, as was "The Golden Peril," a sequel to the first Doc Savage novel.

Ryerson Johnson was less prolific, but his "Land of Always-Night" is considered by many to be among the best in the series. William G. Bogart also wrote many of the novels. While somewhat pedestrian, he did not commit any of the lapses in logic to which Davis was prone. His "World's Fair Goblin" and "Hex" are interesting, but none of his novels is outstanding.

On its own, Street & Smith hired two writers for backup purposes. Laurence Donovan wrote nine novels. He was possessed of a wild and bloody imagination. His most memorable works were "Mad Eyes," "Haunted Ocean," and "He Could Stop the World." Donovan had been brought into the series when the firm considered going twice-monthly with *Doc Savage*. It is not known under what circumstances Alan Hathway wrote four stories, but he was very similar to Davis in his approach. "The Devil's Playground" and "The Mindless Monsters" are his best.

All of the Doc Savage novels followed the pattern Dent laid down in the first year. Dent wrote by formula, but he often accentuated character and invention over plot. He was a master at both. His characters, as outrageous as they were, come to life in the mind's eye—especially Doc and Monk Mayfair. Although supposedly emotionless, Doc was not. He was merely trained not to show his feelings. Yet Dent was able to communicate Doc's feelings through deft use of mannerisms, such as his trilling and animation of his eyes. Each novel focused on what Dent called "the treasure." It was a plot device over which all of the characters were in conflict. It could be a real treasure—or a kidnapped person, a lost city, or a scientific device. The treasure could double as the menace, as did the metal-destroying ray in "The Metal Master."

Many were the fantastic villains Doc fought during the 1930s—the Inca in Gray, the Sea Angel, Ark, the Squeaking Goblin. The greatest was John Sunlight, a sort of evil reflection of Doc Savage who appeared in "Fortress of Solitude" and "The Devil Genghis."

By the 1940s, however, Dent toned down some of the most bizarre elements of the series in keeping with the less slam-bang trend in pulp fiction The plots remained much the same, but the novels were shorter, more concise, and more mature in tone. Fewer of Doc's aides appeared, usually just Monk and Ham; Monk because he was a reader favorite who played well against Doc, and Ham because he played well off Monk.

Dent stopped using ghostwriters in 1941, and the series picked up after a brief slump in 1939–1940. But World War II put a crimp in Doc's ability to roam the world at will; more of his adventures took place on the homefront. Likewise, the editors were uncertain as to how to handle Doc's wartime status. They settled initially on portraying the Man of Bronze as eager to get into the fighting but persuaded by the government to work on defense-related assignments. At this time, the emotionless personality was modified to give Doc a greater range of reactions. The year 1943 saw a number of novels which were either noteworthy or harkened back to past glories. These included "The Talking Devil," "The Time Terror," and "They Died Twice," another sequel to "The Man of Bronze," in which Doc discovers that the Mayan princess, Monja, is still holding a torch for him.

The war caused *Doc Savage* to be reduced to digest size in 1944, a change which was accompanied by the ouster of John L. Nanovic as editor in favor of Charles Moran, the first of a string of short-term editors. The character of the magazine changed in more than just size. Doc's adventures became increasingly concerned with the war as the government began sending him on crucial war missions. This led to a new type of Doc Savage novel, beginning with "The Derelict of Skull Shoal." These were intensely realistic and suspenseful war/espionage stories. The best of them were "Jiu San," "Cargo Unknown," "The Lost Giant," and "Violent Night" (in the latter, Doc is assigned to capture Adolf Hitler). At this time, the short stories in the rear of the magazine were most often war fiction, also.

By 1945, the war was close enough to a conclusion that the war stories and themes had to be dropped so that news headlines would not outdate them before publication. Beginning with the novel "The Terrible Stork," the novels revert to a kind of early forties detective format, combined with the realism that had replaced the old pulp action formula. In these efforts, Lester Dent accentuated the detective aspect of Doc Savage, and by 1946, Doc was really little more than a high-powered detective whose cases might take him out of the country on occasion. Unfortunately, he was also but a mere shadow of his former adventurous self.

After an absolute nadir in 1946 in which Dent unsuccessfully recycled his older Doc Savage plots and recast unpublished novels as Doc Savage stories, he brought back both William G. Bogart and Harold A. Davis as ghostwriters. Sweeping changes were instituted by Babette Rosmond, the editor. Beginning in 1947, the magazine went bimonthly and not long after was retitled as *Doc Savage, Science Detective*. The filler stories were drastically improved in quality, as were Dent's novels. Cover space was shared with major mystery novels by quality writers.

These new Doc novels blended a crisp, fine writing with mystery/adventure plots and Cold War backgrounds. The best of them included "Danger Lies East," "The Angry Canary," "Terror Wears No Shoes," and "I Died Yesterday," which was one of five experimental stories written in the first person.

In 1949, the magazine reverted to the past. As a pulp-sized quarterly, it was retitled *Doc Savage*, and the stories reverted to the thirties pulp style, but with little success. The final novel, "Up From Earth's Center," however, was a fitting ending to the series, in which Doc Savage discovers that Hell actually exists under the earth. His journey into the netherworld is right out of mythology, and it ends ambiguously. It was a perfect capstone to the career of a larger-than-life hero—although Dent was working on another novel when the magazine was cancelled, and so it was a fluke that the series ended as it did.

Doc Savage was not the only continuing character to run in the magazine. Others included The Skipper, who was displaced from his own magazine in 1937 (and ran in *Doc Savage* to 1943), Harold A. Davis's Duke Grant during 1936-1939, Bill Barnes during 1939-1943, and Thorne Lee's Rennard and

Bannister stories, 1945-1946. Frequent contributors were Edwin V. Burkholder, Norman A. Daniels, Stuart Friedman, and, under a host of pen names, John D. MacDonald, who learned much of his craft while writing for *Doc Savage* in the late forties.

The success of *Doc Savage* cannot be pinned down to any single element; rather, it was a combination of a well-conceived character, an exceptionally ingenious writer, and the broad scope an adventure series could have. Often imitated, *Doc Savage* never had a serious rival, but the character has influenced popular literature from Superman to The Man from U.N.C.L.E. to The Destroyer. Successfully reprinted by Bantam Books, a previously unpublished Doc Savage novel (''The Red Spider'') was published in 1979. Odyssey Publications brought the noteworthy prototypal *Doc Savage, Supreme Adventurer* into print in 1980, and Lester Dent's 1934 Doc Savage radio scripts are to be published soon.

Note

1. Robert Weinberg, *The Man Behind Doc Savage* (Oak Lawn, Ill.: privately published, 1974), p. 6.

Information Sources

BIBLIOGRAPHY:

Carr, Wooda Nicholas, and Herman S. McGregor. ''Contemplating Seven of the Pulp Heroes.''*Bronze Shadows*, no. 12 (October 1967):3-7.

Farmer, Philip Jose. *Doc Savage: His Apocalyptic Life*. Garden City. N.Y.: Doubleday & Co., 1973.

McGregor, Herman S. ''A Critical Analysis of the Doc Savage Novels.'' *Bronze Shadows*, no. 2 (December 1965):10-14; no. 3 (February 1966):8-11; no. 4 (May 1966):8-11; no. 5 (July 1966):6-15; no. 6 (September 1966):15-19; no. 7 (November 1966):13-18; no. 8 (January 1967):11-17; no. 9 (March 1967):8-13; no. 10 (June 1967):9-13; no. 11 (August 1967):14-18; no. 12 (October 1967): 11-14; no. 13 (January 1968):13-19; no. 14 (March 1968):5-11; no. 15 (November 1968):9-14.

Murray, Will. ''Dent's Detectives.'' *Duende*, no. 1 (1975):8-24.

————. *Doc Savage: Reflections in Bronze*. Greenwood, Mass.: Odyssey Press, 1978.

————. *Doc Savage, Supreme Adventurer*. Greenwood, Mass.: Odyssey Press, 1980.

————. ''The Secret Kenneth Robesons.'' *Duende*, no. 2 (1977):3-25.

————. *Secrets of Doc Savage*. Greenwood, Mass.: Odyssey Press, 1981.

————. ''The Top Ten Doc Savage Novels and One Stinker.'' *The Age of the Unicorn*, Vol. 2, no. 2 (June 1980):22-29.

Weinberg, Robert. *The Man Behind Doc Savage: A Tribute to Lester Dent*. Oak Lawn, Ill.: privately printed, 1974.

INDEX SOURCES: Murray, Will. ''The Duende Doc Savage Index.'' *Duende*, no. 2 (1977):28-32.

Cook, Michael L. *Monthly Murders*. Westport, Conn.: Greenwood Press, 1982.
LOCATION SOURCES: Private collectors.

Publication History

MAGAZINE TITLE: *Doc Savage*.
TITLE CHANGES: *Doc Savage, Science Detective* (with Vol. 29, no. 4 [September/
    October 1947]); reverted to *Doc Savage* (with Vol. 30, no. 5 [Winter 1949]).
VOLUME AND ISSUE DATA: Vol. 1, no. 1 (March 1933) through Vol. 31, no. 1
    (Summer 1949); 181 issues.
PUBLISHER: Street & Smith Publications, Inc., 79 Seventh Avenue, New York, New
    York, later 122 East 42nd Street, New York, New York.
EDITORS: John L. Nanovic (1933-43), Charles Moran (1943-44), Babette Rosmond
    (1944-48), William DeGrouchy (1948-49).
PRICE PER ISSUE: 10 cents; 15 cents; 25 cents.
SIZE AND PAGINATION: 7″ × 9″ (until Vol. 22, no 5 [January 1944]); 5½″ × 7½″
    (until Vol. 29, no. 1 [March-April 1944]); 6″ × 7″ (until Vol. 30, no. 5 [Winter
    1949]); 7″ × 9″ (subsequent three issues).
CURRENT STATUS: Discontinued.
—*Will Murray*

DOC SAVAGE CLUB READER, THE

The Doc Savage Club Reader began in 1978 as an outgrowth of Jim Steranko's authorized Doc Savage fan club, The Brotherhood of Bronze. Steranko's club called upon fans to organize their own local chapters, much in the manner of the Baker Street Irregulars (see *Baker Street Journal, The*), and Chicago fan Frank Lewandowski responded by forming two clubs, The King Makers of Chicago and The Men of Bronze of Berwyn. This led to the publication of *The Doc Savage Club Reader*, a quarterly Lewandowski had intended to publish only for the first four issues. However, fan interest beseeched him to continue, and he has, to date, published at least two issues per year.

One of the strengths of *The Doc Savage Club Reader* is its consistent quality and the fact that it became and has remained one of the major focal points of Doc Savage fan interest, stimulating lively letter columns and informative articles, as well as a healthy variety of artwork. When Bantam Books suspended its reprinting of the Doc Savage novels in 1977, Lewandowski started a mail campaign which was largely responsible for the reinstitution of the series a year later.

Since its inception, *The Doc Savage Club Reader* has attracted a significant body of contributors, including Nick Carr, Tom Johnson, Bob Sampson, Frank Hamilton, Will Murray, and a significant number of new contributors, the most capable and prolific of which appears to be Dafydd N. Dyar. Editor Lewandowski contributes an occasional article but appears more willing to provide artwork (including several interesting collage covers) when the need arises. It was largely due to the diversity of writers' material that the magazine has outgrown its original title and theme and has metamorphosed into *Nemesis, Inc.* While retaining its Doc Savage orientation, the new title will permit the publication to expand its horizons to include articles on most of the important pulp characters and authors and selected pulp reprints. *The Doc Savage Club Reader* has become, in all senses, a fan's fanzine, and an excellent one.

Information Sources

INDEX SOURCES: None known.
LOCATION SOURCES: Private collectors.

Publication History

MAGAZINE TITLE: *The Doc Savage Club Reader*.
TITLE CHANGES: Announced change to *Nemesis, Inc*.
VOLUME AND ISSUE DATA: No. 1 (undated; 1977) through no. 12 (to date February 1981); 12 issues.
PUBLISHER: Frank Lewandowski, 2438 South Highland Avenue, Berwyn, Illinois 60402.
EDITOR: Frank Lewandowski.
PRICE PER ISSUE: $2.00.
SIZE AND PAGINATION: 8-1/2'' X 11''; 20-32 pages.
CURRENT STATUS: Discontinued under old title; continued publication under new title.
—*Will Murray*

DOC SAVAGE QUARTERLY

Like *The Doc Savage Reader** and *The Doc Savage Club Reader,** the *Doc Savage Quarterly* is an amateur publication devoted to the pulp hero, Doc Savage. The first issue of the *Quarterly* appeared in January 1980, three months after the Doc Savage paperback reprint series by Bantam Books was again cancelled (the Bantam series was not revived again until the summer of 1980).

This first issue included a news review, a Star Trek movie review, a first aid article, a Doc Savage pulp appearance chronology, a seven-page short story featuring Doc Savage in a 1979 setting, and a two-hundred-year calendar. Like many one-man projects, the *Doc Savage Quarterly* abounded with enthusiasm. Yet although its path was charted, it seemed to suffer from a wandering format. Succeeding issues improved, offering articles on a 1930s athlete known as the Man of Mystery; the World War I German Ace, Red Baron; the pulp hero Richard Benson (The Avenger); and the 1923 Terror of the Navy.

The first three issues, January, March, and September 1980, were offered to Doc Savage fans that were known to the editor. The first advertisement soliciting a wider audience appeared in the *Buyers Guide for Comic Fandom* in January 1981, and since then the *Quarterly* has strived for more subscribers as well as additional contributors. Recent articles have been by Will Murray, Dafydd Neal Dyar, Nick Carr, Link Hullar, Tom Johnson, Samuel Joyner, and Frank Hamilton. Featured also have been letters from Paul Bonner, Jr., of Street & Smith/Conde Nast Publications, and "Clark Savage, Jr." of New York.

By April 1981, the magazine found itself the last remaining amateur publication devoted primarily to Doc Savage. It remains so, as a quarterly.

Information Sources

INDEX SOURCES: None known.
LOCATION SOURCES: Private collectors.

Publication History

MAGAZINE TITLE: *Doc Savage Quarterly*.
TITLE CHANGES: None.
VOLUME AND ISSUE DATA: Vol. 1, no. 1 (January 1980) through Vol. 1, no. 7 (to date, October 1981); 7 issues.
PUBLISHER: Bill Laidlaw, P. O. Box 301, San Luis Obispo, California 93406.
EDITOR: Bill Laidlaw.
PRICE PER ISSUE: $2.00.
SIZE AND PAGINATION: 8-1/2" X 11"; 14–23 pages.
CURRENT STATUS: Active.
—*Bill Laidlaw*

DOC SAVAGE READER, THE

Although *The Doc Savage Reader* was a modest, mimeographed publication with a circulation of only about 125 copies per issue, it stands as one of the first (only the short-lived *Doc Savage Journal* preceded it) of the fanzines to devote itself exclusively to Doc Savage.

The Doc Savage Reader was edited by John Cosgriff and Mark J. Golden, whose enthusiasm more than overcame the limitations of budget and format. For its short run (three actual issues, despite its numbering) it ran articles, features, and commentary covering Doc Savage in all of his aspects—pulp novels, comics, and related appearances. Contributors included Bob Sampson, Al Grossman, and Dave McDonnell (whose satire, "The Demon of Dayton," featuring "Doc Garbage," ran in all three issues but remained unfinished). Will Murray, writing as Bill Murray, is here with his first two in-print appearances, "Reflections in a Flake-gold Eye" and "The Girl Who Loved Doc Savage."

It is regrettable that outside commitments forced Cosgriff and Golden to suspend the magazine before it could grow past its formative stage.

Information Sources

INDEX SOURCES: None known.
LOCATION SOURCES: Private collectors.

Publication History

MAGAZINE TITLE : *The Doc Savage Reader.*
TITLE CHANGES: None.
VOLUME AND ISSUE DATA: No. 1 (January 1973) through no. 4 (October 1973). Second issue was numbered as a double issue, nos. 2/3; 3 issues.
PUBLISHER: First issue by John Cosgriff, 1198 Cheltenham Road, Elk Grove, Illinois, and Mark J. Golden, 2791 North Quebec Street, Arlington, Virginia 22207; subsequent issues published by Mark J. Golden.
EDITORS: First issue, John Cosgriff and Mark J. Golden; subsequent issues, Mark J. Golden.
PRICE PER ISSUE: Not stated.
SIZE AND PAGINATION: 8-1/2" X 11"; 12–24 pages.
CURRENT STATUS: Discontinued.
—*Will Murray*

DOC SAVAGE, SCIENCE DETECTIVE

See DOC SAVAGE

DOCTOR DEATH

The character of Doctor Death first appeared in four stories in *All-Story Detective** between August 1934 and January 1935. Here, authorship was attributed to Edward P. Norris. In February 1935, the three issues of the pulp magazine, *Doctor Death,* began publication, each issue containing a novel-length story featuring the character. The three published stories were "12 Must Due" (February 1935), "The Gray Creatures" (March 1935), and "The Shriveling Murders" (April 1935).

A fourth issue was announced but never published. Not until decades later, after the pulps had died, were two additional Doctor Death novels, in typed manuscript form, made available to collectors. One of these was the story that was to have appeared as the fourth novel. The author's original title for this story, "Waves of Madness," was changed to "Murder Music" in the blurb announcing it at the end of the third issue of the magazine. The fifth novel bears the title of "The Red Mist of Death," with the alternate suggestion of "The Eye of Wisdom." In the *Doctor Death* magazine, the author is Harold Ward.

It is unfortunate that these two novels were not published, as they are the best of the quintet. A distinct change in the tenor of the series is evident—the supernatural elements are drastically muted and the weird-menace aspects emphasized. In many respects, these stories resemble the more fantastic of the Doc Savage novels of this period. Additionally, the plotting is more tightly executed, new twists are introduced, and more attention is paid to small details.

Of the five stories, the fourth is by far the best. The opening chapter is particularly well done and extremely effective in setting the mood for the balance of the tale. In this respect, it compares very well with what Walter Gibson was doing along these lines with his Shadow stories.

The first issue of the *Doctor Death* magazine announced that each issue would contain a "100-page novel featuring this master mind of menace," yet the first novel ran but eighty-four pages; the second ran ninety-four pages, as did the third.

The best of the three full-length novels is the first, which is able to capitalize on the use of the outre, supernatural character of the menace and death agencies to a far greater degree than the two following stories; these were marred by the use of poorly thought-out plot devices and evidence of hasty writing.

As an example of this deficiency, in the first and second novels, the hero, Detective Jimmy Holm, is described as being considerably smaller than his superior, Detective Inspector Ricks, a huge and burly man. Yet, in the third story, Ricks is disguised as Holm successfully enough to fool Doctor Death, even though the archcriminal has his well-known foe in close custody.

Other instances abound. Much is made of the fact that Doctor Death employs his mental powers to use advanced hypnotism to bring death to his enemies and to control not only his subordinates and agents but also his death devices. Upon numerous occasions, he is mentally strong enough not only to superimpose his will upon both Nina Ferrara and Holm but also upon assorted other characters and minions at the same time. Yet, when the plot demands it, either Holm or Nina is able to exert enough will power to thwart the evil genius.

All in all, these flaws result, at the best, in uneven reading and, at the worst, in stories that lack that most necessary of pulp-reading ingredients: the ability to convince the reader to suspend his powers of independent judgment as to what is believable and what is not. More than any other factor, this is, I believe, the reason why the series failed and was cancelled after such a short life.

This is not to imply that, by pulp standards, the novels were entirely poorly written. To the contrary—Harold Ward was a past master at evoking a mood with but a few sentences of prose, and stories employing supernatural elements depend, primarily, on the author's ability to create an atmosphere wherein the reader is convinced that anything that happens is reasonable. At creating the requisite atmosphere, Ward is eminently successful. His failure lies in not being meticulous enough in his attention to detail of plot and characterization to sustain the suspension of belief.

As examples of his ability to evoke atmosphere and create the proper mood, consider the following passages:

> Over the stagnant waters rose a thin vapor as the heat of the day decreased; it formed a curtain which hid from view the feculent horrors of the fetid morass. . . . But the swamp was quiet—ominously so. It was the silence that comes with the death of day, unbroken save for the mysterious, sucking noises of the quicksand and the occasional, almost indistinguishable, splash of the alligators as they slid into the tepid water.[1]

Also consider:

> The sinister scientist was a nocturnal animal—habitue of caves and underground places, a human fungus—a dweller in the dark, unfrequented corners far below the surface. . . . Like the vampires and other creatures of foulness, he was at his best after the sun had set. Even moonlight jarred against his sensitive nerve centers.[2]

In the first novel, Doctor Death is, at the beginning, described as being thin, gaunt, and cadaverous, with weirdly glaring, deep-set, cavernous eyes which have a sad and weary expression. Later he appears as a tall, shrouded, masked figure, clad from head to foot in somber black, with eyes that gleam sinisterly through the slits of the mask—a calm, cold figure garbed in the habiliments of the grave. Still later, he is described as a tall man, gaunt almost to the point of emaciation, clad in a white surgical coat. Over a thatch of snow-white hair is a knitted cap of white wool such as surgeons wear. Below this, the long straggling locks hang in disorderly array. A hard, crafty, ruthless face belies the sad, sunken, green eyes. His voice is high-pitched and rasping, and he is able to kill by hypnotic suggestion and to impress on a dying brain a posthypnotic command that the body, though dead, will rise to fulfill.

Eventually, he is identified as Doctor Rance Mandarin, who had several years earlier lectured on "The Ceremonies and Mysteries of Conjuration."

He smoked a pipe, and chemistry was his one hobby and relaxation. He referred to himself as the greatest scientist the world had ever known, master of the occult. His ruling passion was to have the world give up scientific progress and technical advancement so that it might return to a simpler way of life. In his own words:

> God's plan has gone amuck. Satan and I have formed an alliance. Together we will rule the world. With the devil's power, I will go forth and destroy, using my brain to tear down what man, using his God-given brain, has accomplished. . . . Through my efforts, the earth will be restored to its

original state. Man will dwell upon it again in primitive simplicity. And I . . . will be hailed as the savior of mankind.[3]

In spite of his hatred for Doctor Death—and he loathed him to the very depths of his soul—Jimmy Holm was awed by the scientist's powers. The Doctor did things in such a vast way. He was colossal—a superman gone wrong, a devil out of hell who, in spite of his sins, invoked respect for his immensity.

Detective Jimmy Holm, newest member of the police force at the start of the first novel, is described as being a tall, slender, dark, keen-faced young man, light in weight, who enjoyed either a pipe or a cigar. Orphaned by an automobile accident at an early age, he was raised by the family attorney. From earliest boyhood, Jimmy had exhibited an inclination toward the occult, the bizarre, and the scientific. By the second novel, he is no longer just a detective, but a captain, and unquestioned national leader in the struggle against Doctor Death.

The most intriguing observation that results from any study of the five novels is probably the change that takes place in the character of Doctor Death. In his first big scene, where he cold-bloodedly kills an old friend, is an element of pathos in action. The reader is left with a feeling of (possibly reluctant) sympathy for the person of Death and almost an admiration for the way he prevents the elementals from gorging on the freshly dead body.

Through the first three novels, there is a definite change in the personality and outlook of the Doctor. The reader is slowly led from the character's original reluctance to kill at all, through a resigned acceptance of a few deaths as necessary to achieve his goal, to a grim determination to do whatever is necessary for his goal's accomplishment—even if it means killing thousands of innocent people. By the fifth novel, the change is complete. Doctor Death not only enjoys killing, he is able to contemplate torture—both psychological and physical—of the leaders of the fight against him and, indeed, even seems to gain a strange sort of relaxation and satisfaction from doing so.

Thus we see how the series would have changed from one oriented primarily to the occult and supernatural to one that was primarily weird-menace adventure, with overtones of the supernatural. It is indeed a pity that a few more issues were not published so that reader reaction might be tested.

Notes

1. Harold Ward, "12 Must Die" *Doctor Death*, Vol. 1, no. 1 (February 1935), p. 7.
2. Ibid., p. 9.
3. Ibid., p. 5.

Information Sources

BIBLIOGRAPHY:
Cervon, Bruce. "Reader's Guide to Doctor Death." *Collecting Paperbacks?* Vol. 3, no. 3 (July 1981): 30.
DeWitt, Jack. "The Return of Doctor Death." *Bronze Shadows*, no. 5 (July 1966): 8.

Johnson, Tom. "Jimmy Holm, Supernatural Detective vs. Dr. Death." *Doc Savage Club Reader*, no. 10 (1981): 8.
INDEX SOURCES: Weinberg, Robert, and Lohr McKinstry. *The Hero Pulp Index*. Evergreen, Colorado: Opar Press, 1971.
LOCATION SOURCES: University of California–Los Angeles Library (Vol. 1, no. 1, only); private collectors.

Publication History

MAGAZINE TITLE: *Doctor Death*.
TITLE CHANGES: None.
VOLUME AND ISSUE DATA: Vol. 1, no. 1 (February 1935) through Vol. 1, no. 3 (April 1935); 3 issues.
PUBLISHER: Dell Publishing Co., Inc., 149 Madison Avenue, New York, New York.
EDITOR: Not known.
PRICE PER ISSUE: 15 cents.
SIZE AND PAGINATION: 7'' X 10''; 128 pages.
CURRENT STATUS: Discontinued.
—*Joseph Lewandowski*

DON PENDLETON'S THE EXECUTIONER MYSTERY MAGAZINE

See EXECUTIONER MYSTERY MAGAZINE, THE

DOSSIER, THE

Despite a considerable and continuing interest on the part of readers for many years in the world of spies and espionage, both real and fictional, there has been no magazine devoted exclusively to this subject, although numerous articles have appeared in various mystery magazines and other publications. A chance meeting of Richard L. Knudson and David A. Reinhardt at the First Annual International James Bond Collectors' Show in Lyndhurst, New Jersey, led to the founding of a journal to fill this void.

The first issue of *The Dossier: The Official Journal of the International Spy Society* appeared in January 1982. Cleverly designed to simulate a dossier, or file, in both appearance and size, the magazine carried the words "TOP SE-CRET" stenciled across its cover in addition to the title and issue number. Published quarterly, the magazine is (in the words of its founders):

> dedicated to a serious look at espionage... fictional as well as real spies will be treated in these pages. Novels and films dealing with spies will be fair subjects for future articles. The tools of the trade will be discussed; guns, cameras, codes, and communications will all be subjects of future articles. Significant missions of real spies will be carefully examined. In short, *The Dossier* will cover the world of espionage; if spies interest you, then *The Dossier* is for you.[1]

The initial thirty-two page issue featured illustrated articles on the Carl Walther Company (manufacturers of fine firearms since 1886 and designers of the famous "PP" series of semiautomatic pistols); the latest James Bond film, "For Your Eyes Only" (including brief profiles of Roger Moore and Joyce Bartle); cryptography (with examples of artificial alphabets and ciphers); Colonel Rudolph Ivanovich Abel; and an interview with John Gardner, author of the newest Bond books, *License Renewed* and *For Special Services*. In addition, there was a section of brief news notes from the world of espionage and an espionage bibliography of over four hundred titles.

The second issue, expanded to forty-eight pages, featured articles on the James Bond cars, the Beretta (Bond's weapon of first choice), the Minox spy camera, and agent Gary Powers. This issue also marked the beginning of a regular and extensive book and film review section.

In addition to articles, reviews and news notes, the magazine also carried advertising.

Note

1. Editorial, *The Dossier*, no. 1 (undated), p. 2.

Information Sources

INDEX SOURCES: None known.
LOCATION SOURCES: Private collectors.

Publication History

MAGAZINE TITLE: *The Dossier, The Official Journal of the International Spy Society*.
TITLE CHANGES: None.
VOLUME AND ISSUE DATA: Issue no. 1 (undated, but appearing in January 1982) through issue no. 2 (to date; undated, but appearing in 1982); 2 issues.
PUBLISHER: The International Spy Society (I.S.S.), Department of English, State University of New York, Oneonta, New York 13820.
EDITOR: Richard L. Knudson.
PRICE PER ISSUE: $4.00 ($12.00 annual subscription; quarterly).
SIZE AND PAGINATION: 11" X 8-1/2"; 30–48 pages.
CURRENT STATUS: Active.
—*David H. Doerrer*

DOUBLE-ACTION DETECTIVE

Double-Action Magazines, Inc. (later to be known as Blue Ribbon Magazines, Inc.) introduced a detective pulp in October 1938 which promised "Double-action thrills in the world of crime." While the earliest issues featured both femmes fatales and good girls in distressing and often weirdly menacing situations, the trend soon changed to tough detective and crime-adventure tableaus. Spotlighting the hard-boiled school of the private eye, this type of material was further developed with fast action and frequently few morals. Yet, surprisingly good stories did appear, as evidenced by authors such as Edward S. Ronns and William G. Bogart.

A typical list of contents was that included in the July 1939 issue: "Hell's Hot Bed of Sin" (by Mat Rand), "Bullets Will Tell" (by Foster Drake), "Hot From a Kill" (by Walter C. Scott), and "That Dame is Dead" (by William G. Bogart). These were accompanied by three "spine-tingling short stories," titled "No Quarter for Killers" (Edward S. Ronns), "It Strikes in the Dark" (Milton L. Marks), and "Ten Grand for a Wop" (Harold Ward).

Blue Ribbon Magazines published a long list of pulp titles, including the *Double Action Western* and *Double Action Gang Magazine*.* Later, under the name of Columbia Publications, Inc., there was a similar-content magazine, *Double-Action Detective Stories*.*

Information Sources

INDEX SOURCES: None known.
LOCATION SOURCES: University of California–Los Angeles Library (Vol. 1, no. 1, only); private collectors.

Publication History

MAGAZINE TITLE: *Double-Action Detective*.
TITLE CHANGES: None.
VOLUME AND ISSUE DATA: Vol. 1, no. 1 (October 1938) through Vol. 2, no. 2 (October 1940); 8 issues.
PUBLISHER: Double-Action Magazines, Inc., 2256 Grove Street, Chicago, Illinois, with editorial offices at 60 Hudson Street, New York, New York: later under name of Blue Ribbon Magazines, Inc., South Canal Street, Holyoke, Massachusetts.
EDITOR: Not known.
PRICE PER ISSUE: 10 cents.
SIZE AND PAGINATION: 6-3/8" X 9-3/4"; 98 pages.
CURRENT STATUS: Discontinued.

DOUBLE-ACTION DETECTIVE AND MYSTERY STORIES

See DOUBLE-ACTION DETECTIVE STORIES

DOUBLE-ACTION DETECTIVE STORIES

Double-Action Detective Stories was a pulp magazine in every way except that of size. It was a small, square magazine, advertised in the columns of other Columbia Publications as "The Newest and Best in Pocket-Size Mystery."

This claim was an exaggeration, perhaps. *Double-Action Detective Stories* found itself pitted against giants such as *Ellery Queen's Mystery Magazine*,* *Manhunt*,* *The Saint Mystery Magazine (Saint Detective Magazine, The*),* and *Nero Wolfe Mystery Mgazine*.* And there were others. The competition was intense, as some of the finest digest mystery-fiction magazines published in America swept, all at one time, a tidal wave of issues, across the newsstands.

The severity of the competition may explain the minimal publication schedule of *Double-Action Detective Stories*. It appeared twice a year in April and October and was identified by "whole number," rather than date. The first issue, undated and unnumbered on the cover, appeared in October 1954. The cover pictured a woman in a phone booth, firing through the side wall into the back of a sorely pained man. This had been the cover also for the August 1952 *Famous Detective (Crack Detective*)*. Inside was a novel ("Hook Up Murder" by Richard Deming), two novelettes ("Trial By Fire" by Margaret Manners and "Play-And-Slay Girl," a Johnny Liddell story by Frank Kane), and a few short stories.

The writers were those familiar to readers of *Famous Detective* and *Smashing Detective;** the stories and illustrations were what you expected to find in either of those magazines; and Robert W. Lowndes, as you might suspect, edited both publications and *Double-Action Detective Stories* as well.

The second issue, released in April 1955, used the March 1953 cover of *Smashing Detective* and continued the same format. Subsequent issues featured authors Craig Rice ("The Headless Hatbox," a John J. Malone story), Randall Garrett, Frederick C. Davis, Richard Deming, and Louis Tremble. The stories were consistently interesting, and a special feature often was worked into the short story selection, such as the Solar Pons adventure, "The Devil's Footprint" by August Derleth, in the number 5 (October 1956) issue. And in the number 6 issue (April 1957) appeared crime and mystery fiction by Margaret St. Clair, Robert Silverberg, and Sam Merwin, Jr., solid names all in science fiction circles.

With issue number 7, the magazine changed its title to *Double-Action Detective and Mystery Stories*. That change affected the cover and spine only since the table of contents, in blissful unawareness, omitted "*and Mystery Stories*" from the title. In that issue, you found two novelettes, six short stories (including one by A. Bertram Chandler and one by Robert Silverberg, using the pseudonym Calvin Knox), and three fact articles. Interior illustrations were either omitted or borrowed from those published in earlier editions of *Famous Detective* or *Smashing Detective*.

A total of twenty-four issues of *Double-Action Detective Stories* were published before lagging sales forced its demise.

Information Sources

BIBLIOGRAPHY:
Rock, James A. *Who Goes There?* Bloomington, Ind.: James A. Rock & Co., 1979.
INDEX SOURCES: Cook, Michael L. *Monthly Murders*. Westport, Conn.: Greenwood Press, 1982.
LOCATION SOURCES: Private collectors.

Publication History

MAGAZINE TITLE: *Double-Action Detective Stories*.

TITLE CHANGES: *Double-Action Detective and Mystery Stories* (with issue number 7 [Summer 1957]).
VOLUME AND ISSUE DATA: No. 1 (undated, but appearing in April 1954) through no. 24 (September 1960); 24 issues.
PUBLISHER: Columbia Publications, Inc., 241 Church Street, New York 13, New York, later 1 Appleton Street, Holyoke, Massachusetts, with editorial offices listed at the New York address.
EDITOR: Robert W. Lowndes.
PRICE PER ISSUE: 35 cents.
SIZE AND PAGINATION: 5-1/4'' X 7-3/8''; 130 pages.
CURRENT STATUS: Discontinued.
—*Robert Sampson*

DOUBLE-ACTION GANG MAGAZINE

A short-lived member of the "Double Action" magazine group, *Double-Action Gang Magazine*—oriented to guns, gangsters, gun molls, and "stories of true gang life"—made its appearance with the May 1936 issue. Some true fact features were used, such as "I Was Hanged by Jesse James," which appeared in the February 1937 issue. Puzzles, fact articles, fillers, and "The Vigilante Club" helped to fill out the magazine. Though its masthead claimed it to be a bimonthly, the magazine appears to have been published on more of an annual basis since the June 1938 issue was volume 1, number 4. It is known to have been published as late as 1939.

Information Sources

INDEX SOURCES: None known.
LOCATION SOURCES: University of California–Los Angeles Library (Vol. 1, no. 4, only); private collectors.

Publication History

MAGAZINE TITLE: *Double-Action Gang Magazine*.
TITLE CHANGES: None.
VOLUME AND ISSUE DATA: Vol. 1, no. 1 (May 1936) through at least into 1939. (Note: The possibility exists that there were two magazines of this title, or perhaps two series. There has been noted a Vol. 1, no. 1, issue, also dated December 1937 [as well as May 1936]).
PUBLISHER: Winford Publications, Inc., 2256 Grove Street, Chicago, Illinois, with editorial office at 165 Franklin Street, later 60 Hudson Street, New York, New York. The company was later known as Double-Action Magazines, Inc., Blue Ribbon Magazines, Inc., and Columbia Publications, Inc., at various times.
EDITOR: Not known.
PRICE PER ISSUE: 15 cents.
SIZE AND PAGINATION: 7'' X 10''; average 112 pages.
CURRENT STATUS: Discontinued.

DOUBLE DETECTIVE

The *Double Detective* ("a Red Star Magazine"), published by the Frank A. Munsey Company in New York, commenced in November 1937 and is distinguished primarily for the stories featuring the pulp-hero character known as the Green Lama. This series first appeared in April 1940, and thirteen additional stories were to follow.

At the time of the *Double Detective's* publication, William T. Dewart served as president and treasurer and William T. Dewart, Jr. was secretary of the Munsey Company. The cost of the magazine in the United States was ten cents and in Canada was twelve cents. *Double Detective* was but one in a long line under the Red Star banner, a group that included *Argosy, Fantastic Novels, Crack Shot Western,* and *Railraod Magazine,* among others.

Double Detective was first scheduled as a monthly, changing to a bimonthly with the February 1941 issue; and the final issue, dated March 1943, was published by Popular Publications (their only issue of this magazine).

Each issue contained, in addition to "a complete full-length detective novel," various short stories and features. Authors included Robert Leslie Bellem, Hugh B. Cave, and Philip Ketchum. The covers and interior illustrations were excellent and possibly among the finest to be found in the pulp magazines.

The author of the Green Lama stories was a very gifted individual, Kendell Foster Crossen (writing here as Richard Foster). He wrote also under other pseudonyms: Kent Richards, Bennett Barlay, Christopher Monig, and M. E. Chaber.

The basis for the Green Lama tales was seeded when Crossen read a nonfiction book review in the *New York Times* about an American who became a lama. Crossen then picked a name that was somewhat similar in sound to that of Lamont Cranston (Cranston was one of the names used by The Shadow). Stories were formulated after Crossen became editor of *Detective Fiction Weekly,** another Munsey publication; in a discussion as to how to compete with *The Shadow Magazine,** the answer arrived at was a character named Green Lama. Originally called the Gray Lama (because it would be hard to see him in the dark), this name was changed so that paintings of the hero would provide better pictorial contrast on the covers. Crossen began research on lamanism and Tibet and later felt that "The real success of the lama was because of mysticism."[1] Each of the stories required two days to write and were always accompanied by numerous footnotes, all authentic and most informative.

Crossen was fully responsible for all of the Green Lama adventures. No manuscripts are unpublished. "If I did another one," he told me, "it would be [set] in the thirties. It would be difficult today because of the time period."[2] In reflecting back on the demise of his hero, Crossen remarked, "Munsey Publications sold all its magazines to Popular [Publications, Inc.]. They dropped several of them. No reason was even given."[3] Oddly enough, when Crossen met with his friend, Walter B. Gibson (creator of The Shadow), no discussion of the pulp heroes ever came up because their chief mutual interest was magic. They would (in the company of other pulp writers) attend any magic show within a fifty-to seventy-mile radius of New York City. This group of men often included Orson Welles, Steve Fisher, Lester Dent, Max Brand, Cornell Woolrich, Borden Chase, Frank Gruber, and the famous mentalist, Dunninger.

The Green Lama was in reality Jethro Dumont, a scholar who had attended Harvard, Oxford, and the Sorbonne in Paris. After going to Drepung University in Tibet, he became a lama and authored numerous books. Upon his return to America, he intended to spread the basic doctrine ("to remove ignorance and relieve suffering") but realized he could accomplish more by fighting crimes of violence. With a rich inheritance, he maintained two homes; he became a member of the Association of American Magicians, studying under well-known makeup artists and escape artists. He demonstrated acute knowledge of various pressure points and nerve centers of the human anatomy. At times, he would drink a vial of radioactive salt, which produced an electrical shock from his fingers—touching someone to produce a paralysis of certain nerve centers. This he called "a form of electrical ju-jitsu." As the Green Lama, his true identity was hidden under a spectacular disguise of robe and cowl, but he often appeared in an alternate identity of Dr. Charles Pali.

"The Green Lama," according to Weinberg and McKinstry in *The Hero Pulp Index,* "was one of the strangest of all crime fighters."[4] The issues of the magazine containing the Green Lama stories are prime collectors' items today and are very scarce. (See also *Love-Crime Detective,* which was intended to be a replacement publication for *Double Detective.*

Notes

1. Interview by Wooda Nicholas Carr (as Dickson Thorpe) with Kendell Foster Crossen as the basis for an article, "Will The Real Ken Crossen Please Stand Up," *The Mystery Fancier,* Vol. 1, no. 2 (March 1977), pps. 5–10.

2. Ibid.

3. Ibid.

4. Robert Weinberg and Lohr McKinstry, *The Hero Pulp Index* (Evergreen, Colo.: Opar Press, 1971), p. 36.

Information Sources

BIBLIOGRAPHY:

Lewis, Steve. "Interview with Kendell Foster Crossen." *The Mystery Nook,* no. 12 (June 1979): 1–4.

Miller, Don. "Kendell F. Crossen: Excerpts from Crossen's Letters." *The Mystery Nook,* no. 12 (June 1979): 17.

Thorpe, Dickson. "Will The Real Ken Crossen Please Stand Up." *The Mystery Fancier,* Vol. 1, no. 2 (March 1977): 5–10.

INDEX SOURCES: None known.

LOCATION SOURCES: University of California–Los Angeles Library (Vol. 1, no. 1, and Vol. 3, no. 5, only); private collectors.

Publication History

MAGAZINE TITLE: *Double Detective.*

TITLE CHANGES: None.
VOLUME AND ISSUE DATA: Vol. 1, no. 1 (November 1937) through Vol. 7, no. 6
     (March 1943).
PUBLISHER: Frank A. Munsey Co., 280 Broadway, New York, New York; last issue
     by Popular Publications, Inc., 2256 Grove Street, Chicago, Illinois.
EDITOR: Not known.
PRICE PER ISSUE: 10 cents (12 cents in Canada).
SIZE AND PAGINATION: 7'' X 10''; average 112 pages.
CURRENT STATUS: Discontinued.
—*Wooda Nicholas Carr*

DRACULA JOURNALS, THE (British)

"For many years," writes Bruce Wightman, former actor and chairman of
The Dracula Society, "my fellow thespian Bernard Davies and I talked of the
possibility of forming a society to respect the Gothic literary originals and to
lead lost souls back to the true path."[1] Thus in October 1973, Wightman and
Davies founded The Dracula Society, aimed at rekindling this wonder and excitement in the writers they called the Gothic Romantics.

With the third anniversary of The Dracula Society came a realization of a
long-held ambition in the Society. With members now all over the world, the
regular newsletter compiled and printed by Society Honorary Secretary, actor-
turned-art-dealer, Davies, was not able to fulfill the needs of an expanding
organization. The Society decided to move out of newsletters and issue its own
magazine, *The Dracula Journals,* beginning with volume 1, number 1, of Winter
1976–1977. Editorship was placed in the hands of freelance journalist and music
critic Angela Errigo and freelance journalist and travel writer Toni Hubeman.

"We hope to meet those needs with *The Dracula Journals,*" wrote the editors
in the first issue, "providing a vehicle for members' news and viewpoints as
well as features on Draculeana and other aspects of gothic horror. We hope that
The Dracula Journals will enable members to participate by sharing their opinions, suggestions and criticisms with us."[2]

Selections in the first issue included "Vampire Lovers" by Lynn Picknett, a
study of the sexual aspects of *Dracula*; "Mountain Greenery" by Bernard Davies, an in-depth examination of the symbolic significance of the various plants
mentioned in *Dracula*; and "In Search of the Castle" by Victor Langley, an
attempt to locate the actual site of Castle Dracula.

The journal has shown itself to be a high-quality magazine—very scholarly,
but at the same time very readable. Regular features have been letters from
members, news and reviews items, updates on the Society's archive collection,
and articles on Dracula and subjects related to the Gothic.

Since we named it [the Society and the journal] after the most evocative
title in the genre," writes Davies, "the most enduring and influential novel
in all macabre literature, the Society naturally devotes a good deal of

attention to the life and works of Bram Stoker, himself surprisingly little known and honoured in Britain and even less so in his native Ireland. However, vampirism in general, werewolves, monsters and many other horrors fall within our field of interest. This interest is confined to literature, the theatre and the cinema, and there are no occult rites or physical research.[3]

Publication of the journal, like most new literary ventures, has been very irregular. Two members of the Society who were professional editors took over from Davies and assured that a minimum of two issues a year was no problem. They produced one. After much badgering and overseeing by Davies, issue number 2 emerged in the winter of 1977–1978. After eighteen months' delay, a sorry effort, quite unprintable, was physically collected for issue number 3. After a complete retyping by Davies, it appeared in Winter 1979.

Founders Wightman and Davies are presently endeavoring to establish a new editorship for the obvious reasons that they are overworked and are devoting all of their spare time to the magazine, leaving nothing for their own researches in the field.

Issue number 4, planned for release in Autumn 1981, will mark the end of volume 1 of *The Dracula Journals*. Volume 2 is being designed to provide an expanded format and to appear at least twice a year. The journal's circulation (and Society's membership) now numbers over two hundred, mainly in England but also scattered over a dozen countries among a wide range of ages and many different walks of life.

Notes

1. Bernard Davies in editorial announcement, *The Dracula Journals*, Vol. 1, no. 1 (Winter 1976–1977), p. 1.
2. Ibid.
3. Ibid.

Information Sources

INDEX SOURCES: None known.
LOCATION SOURCES: Private collectors.

Publication History

MAGAZINE TITLE: *The Dracula Journals*.
TITLE CHANGES: None.
VOLUME AND ISSUE DATA: Vol. 1, no. 1 (Winter 1976–1977) through Vol. 1, no. 3 (to date, Winter 1979); 3 issues.
PUBLISHER: The Dracula Journals, Waterside Cottage, 36 High Street, Upper Upnor, Rochester, Kent ME2 4XC, England.
EDITORS: Angela Errigo and Toni Huberman.
PRICE PER ISSUE: By subscription only, $15.00 per year.
SIZE AND PAGINATION: Average 8'' X 5-3/4''; 30–41 pages.
CURRENT STATUS: Active.
—*Dana Martin Batory*

DRAGNET, THE

In 1928, Publisher and Editor Harold Hersey, who would later become known for creating more short-lived and commercially unsuccessful magazines both within and outside of the pulp field, created perhaps the only magazine of his own devising that could be called successful. By doing so, he inadvertently spawned one of the longest-running detective pulps ever published.

The magazine was *The Dragnet*. It was to exist, through three titles, for twenty-one years and actually did not become lucrative until after it had passed from Hersey's hands. The first issue, dated November 1928, was not a detective magazine at all but featured stories about modern gangsters and organized crime. The Prohibition gangster was a glamorous figure during the twenties and the subject of numerous motion pictures. Public interest led to a number of pulp magazines that more or less celebrated these urban Robin Hoods, of which *The Underworld** (1927) was probably the first and *The Dragnet* only one of the many which followed.

Most of these magazines were short-lived and often met with significant public criticism. By the time Hersey and most of the other pulp publishers had jumped on the bandwagon, the gangster parade was beginning to fade (although many such magazines continued in one form or another well into the thirties). The later versions, however, featured stories where the gangsters usually met with bad ends in the individual stories. This was not always the case in the earlier magazines, and this was what the public most objected to.

By 1930, *The Dragnet* became *Detective–Dragnet Magazine*, and the gangster stories were slowly phased out. Not only was interest and tolerance for these stories on the wane, but Hersey had sold the magazine, along with several others, to A. A. Wyn's new venture called Magazine Publishers, Inc. Sensing the public's change, Wyn, as editor, emphasized stories of detectives and law officers fighting and winning. Contributors remained about the same at this time, including James W. Poling, Horace McCoy, Joe Archibald, John Compton, and others. For the most part, the magazine was undistinguished and its contents entirely forgettable.

However, under Editor Harry Widmer, who assumed increasing control over the magazine's direction in 1931, *Detective–Dragnet* veered away from the said detective tales into sheer melodrama of a type that both harkened back to the days of the dime novel and looked forward to the single-character magazines. Paul Chadwick began the first of his Wade Hammond stories about a New York criminologist who fought weird or seemingly supernatural menaces. These stories, beginning with "A Murder Masterpiece" in July 1931, became progressively more bizarre until Hammond was battling the likes of "Doctor Zero" and "The Grinning Ghoul" in stories of those titles.

After Hammond, James W. Poling's Duke Ayres stories appeared. These were less fantastic but lasted a shorter period. The changes in the magazine's contents were gradual, and the editorial in the January 1932 issue pointed to Donald E.

Keyhoe's "The Capitol Crimes," a novelette of Washington espionage, as the first of a new type of story running in the magazine—even though this story appeared months after Wade Hammond's first appearance.

At this time, a new group of younger writers were attracted to the magazines and began to appear frequently. Among these were W. T. Ballard, Frederick C. Davis, Carl McK. Saunders (whose series character, Captain John Murdock, ran for several years), Norvell Page, and Lester Dent. Dent appeared in each issue in 1932, beginning with the debut of his Lynn Lash character in "The Sinister Ray" (March 1932). Lester Dent, perhaps, was the star of the magazine that year. Lynn Lash, Mel Cross, and other scientific detectives he created appeared in stories like "Terror, Inc." and "The Mummy Murders." These were nothing less than science fiction in mystery format. It was Dent's work for this magazine that led to his writing of the Doc Savage novels for Street & Smith.

Detective–Dragnet was an exciting magazine in 1932, but its evolution was not complete. With the March 1933 issue, it was retitled *Ten Detective Aces,* a title reflecting its new policy of featuring ten detective stories in each issue. The emphasis quickly became series characters. Wade Hammond and Captain John Murdock were carried over from the old magazine, but many more characters, even stranger than before, were born in its pages.

Probably the best known was Frederick C. Davis's eerie Moon Man, who fought crime and distributed criminal wealth to the poor while wearing a moonlike helmet of two-way glass and a long cloak. He first appeared in "The Sinister Sphere" (June 1933). That same issue saw the beginning of Norvell Page's Ken Carter series with "Hell's Music." Lester Dent's Lee Nace, the Blond Adder, started in July with "The Death Blast."

Strange sleuths and weird avengers, along with more prosaic detectives, had proliferated by 1934, inspired, perhaps, by the first wave of single-character pulps in 1933. There was Emile C. Tepperman's Marty McQuade. Alexis Rossoff's Whisperer, and Richard B. Sale's Cobra. Frederick C. Davis, after doing his Moon Man for three years, began to alternate that character with an undercover cop, Peter Kirk. Norman A. Daniels's Russian detective, Renouf, was also popular. Characters were often short-lived, subject to public acceptance and author willingness to keep a series going. The interesting phenomenon, however, was the number of authors—Dent, Page, Tepperman, and Davis—who swiftly graduated to writing whole magazines built around a single-character theme. By the time Magazine Publishers decided to do their own version, *Secret Agent X,** by Paul Chadwick, most of the better writers had departed.

From 1933 to 1936, *Ten Detective Aces* was a dynamic magazine. But trends changed, and by the closing months of 1936, receptivity to these masked and hooded crime busters had evaporated. They were gradually supplanted by more traditional hard-boiled private detectives, just as the gangsters had been replaced by the staid detectives only a few years before. The lineup of writers changed, too. Names like Talmage Powell, Hal Masur, Robert Turner, G. T. Fleming-Roberts, Peter Gunn, and scores of others began to contribute and stayed with the magazine for years. The public was relentlessly fed an unending stream of hard-nosed, two-fisted detectives through a succession of editors; and somehow the magazine managed, from about 1937 to its demise in 1949, to remain with this fixed editorial profile. It survived even through World War II, which had killed off many of the better pulps.

It is ironic that in its most successful years, *Ten Detective Aces* was an uninteresting, run-of-the-mill detective magazine. It sported a repetitive array of Norman Saunders covers, all of which had a garish red-and-yellow border, a trademark going back to its *Detective–Dragnet* days. A final assessment of this many-titled magazine might be that it was an excellent training ground for pulp writers throughout its long run, even if its best years—from a collector's standpoint—were roughly between 1932 and 1936.

There were at least five issues of *Ten Detective Aces* published in a British reprint edition, titled *Detective Aces*.

Information Sources

BIBLIOGRAPHY:
Hersey, Harold B. *Pulpwood Editor*. New York: Frederick A. Stokes Co., 1937.
INDEX SOURCES: None known.
LOCATION SOURCES: University of California–Los Angeles Library (1938–1942, 9 issues); private collectors.

Publication History

MAGAZINE TITLE: *The Dragnet*.
TITLE CHANGES: *Detective-Dragnet Magazine* (in 1930); *Ten Detective Aces* (with March 1933 issue).
VOLUME AND ISSUE DATA: Vol. 1, no. 1 (October 1928) through Vol. 57, no. 2 (September 1949); 226 issues.
PUBLISHER: Harold B. Hersey; in 1930, A. A. Wyn as Magazine Publishers, Inc. (name changed to Ace Periodicals, Inc., in 1947), 29 Worthington Street, Springfield, Massachusetts, with editorial offices at 67 West 44th Street and later 23 West 47th Street, New York, New York.
EDITORS: Harold B. Hersey; Harold Goldsmith; Harry Widmer; Maurice J. Phillips; A. A. Wyn, with Donald A. Wollheim as associate editor.
PRICE PER ISSUE: 10 cents, 20 cents, 15 cents, 25 cents.
SIZE AND PAGINATION: Average 6-5/8'' X 9-7/8''; average 114 pages.
CURRENT STATUS: Discontinued.
—*Will Murray*

DR. YEN SIN

In the slant of his cheekbones and by his height (for he was taller than most Chinese) might be traced the Manchurian blood coursing through his veins.

Picture a suavely courteous yellow face like a living picture of Satan, with a terrible smile and mocking expression. Etch in pitiless lines of power about the eyes and mouth, a mandarin mustache, and black, slanting eyebrows. For the final facial touch, put in yellow eyes that turn to emerald-flecked black orbs in moments of stress: eyes that become horrible, malignant, black pools with the power to transfix a victim as into a bottomless pit where minutes seem to pass like seconds. Add unnaturally long fingers, with nails of such exceptional length that his hands resemble talons, and a soft, penetrating voice that speaks English with a very slight, almost unnoticeable, guttural accent.

To the typical mystery reader, such a description would call to mind Sax Rohmer's Fu Manchu, but the pulp reader of the 1930s would have two other villains to whom this description might apply: Wu Fang and Dr. Yen Sin. Actually, the personage limned above is the latter of these and appeared in three novels in three issues of a magazine aptly named *Dr. Yen Sin*.

The novels, by Donald E. Keyhoe, were accompanied by two or three short stories in the same vein, by authors such as Arden X. Pangborn, Don Cameron, and Frank Gruber.

Dr. Yen Sin is described as "The most dangerous man alive! A super-scientist, an evil genius, with the ruthless will of a dictator—and an Oriental hatred for the white race that amounts to a mania."[1] As depicted in these stories, he is after power and he dreams of heading a yellow rebellion against the white race. To this end, he has recruited thousands of agents who are located throughout the world. Collectively, they are referred to as "The Invisible Empire," and Yen Sin is thus "The Invisible Emperor." This empire is made up not only of criminals but also of their victims, the unwilling members caught in his web. Once a person becomes a citizen of this empire, there is but one way out: death. Both agents and victims are in such terror of Yen Sin that they are afraid to talk.

Michael Traile, the man who leads the fight against these evil machinations, is, in at least one way, even stranger than Dr. Yen Sin. He cannot sleep. As a child of two years of age, he was in India with his parents and suffered a skull fracture in an accident. A Hindu surgeon performed a hasty operation, but the lobe of the brain controlling sleep had been irreparably damaged, so never again had Traile lost consciousness. His mind would always be awake until it was finally put to sleep in death.

Only the flexibility of his young brain and the training of a yogi had saved him from death through utter exhaustion. The miracle man had taught him to relax his body completely for short periods, resting it as though in deepest sleep. To protect the child's sanity, he was educated along unique lines. He had two tutors, one for day and one for night, as well as a physical instructor. By the time he entered his teen years, he was fluent in several languages and adept at such sports as wrestling, boxing, and archery. By the time he entered his twenties, he was a restless seeker of ways to fill the long hours when others were sleeping, and he was so desolately alone.

His Achilles' heel was the need for frequent periods of relaxation to restore the energy he was constantly using; without such rest periods he would approach a point of absolute exhaustion and near paralysis. To recuperate, all that was necessary was for him to sit or recline, stretch out his long arms, and will his tired muscles to relax.

In appearance, he was at least six feet tall, with black hair, lean face, and restless dark brown eyes. His face and arms were deep-burned to the color of bronze. At the time of the incidents related in the first novel, he was twenty-nine years old. A scant three months earlier he had first discovered the existence of The Invisible Empire. From that time on, the Emperor's agents were constantly after him, and there were attempts to assassinate him. He was able to convince officials in Washington, D.C., of the danger posed by Dr. Yen Sin and was given the task of foiling him.

Since Traile was the only one who knew much about Yen Sin, a peculiar scheme was hatched to provide him with what little protection can be given: the Q-Group was formed. Ostensibly, this was a highly select group of five men who knew the face of Dr. Yen Sin, but in reality Traile was the only member. The idea was to force Yen Sin to search for five men instead of being able to concentrate on just one.

In the second story, Traile's New York apartment is referred to as The Q-Station. A special switchboard puts him in direct contact with the FBI in Washington, the Brooklyn Navy Yard, and other strategic offices.

In addition to the assistance Traile gets from official agencies, he drafts Eric Gordon as his aide. Gordon is a teletype expert for World Radio and Cable. Traile also gets occasional help from a source where he would least expect it: Iris Vaughn and Sonya Damatri, two of the minions of The Yellow Doctor.

The first novel, "The Mystery of the Dragon's Shadow," has Yen Sin plotting to steal secret codes and other documents from the vault in the Japanese embassy in Washington, leaving behind incontrovertible evidence that the theft was the work of American agents. In the second novel, "The Mystery of the Golden Skull," an old and dreaded secret society, believed to have become extinct, is revived by Yen Sin to further his nefarious schemes. The third melodrama, "The Mystery of the Singing Mummies," involves a secret means for mass murder.

A fourth novel, "The Mystery of the Faceless Men," was announced, but publication of the magazine ceased before the story could see print. Whether the manuscript was revised and used elsewhere is not known. *Dr. Yen Sin* was terminated in Autumn 1936; and though not confirmed, the volume and issue numbers of this title may have been continued in *The Octopus.**

Note

1. Donald E. Keyhoe, *Dr. Yen Sin*, Vol. 1, no. 2 (July–August 1936), p. 44.

Information Sources

BIBLIOGRAPHY:
Carr, Nick. "Introducing the Yellow Peril." *Megavore*, no. 12 (December 1980); 39–41.

Hardin, Nils. "An Interview with Henry Steeger." *Xenophile*, no. 33 (July 1977): 3–18.
————, and George Hocutt. "A Checklist of Popular Publications Titles 1930–1955." *Xenophile*, no. 33 (July 1977): 21–24.
Hickman, Lynn. "Checklist." *The Pulp Era*, no. 75 (Spring 1971): 11.
INDEX SOURCES: Lewandowski, Joseph. "An Index to Dr. Yen Sin Magazine." *The Age of the Unicorn*, Vol. 1, no. 4 (October 1979): 32–33.
Weinberg, Robert, and Lohr McKinstry. *The Hero Pulp Index*. Evergreen, Colo.: Opar Press, 1971.
LOCATION SOURCES: University of California-Los Angeles Library (Vol. 1, no. 1, only); private collectors.

Publication History

MAGAZINE TITLE: *Dr. Yen Sin*.
TITLE CHANGES: None; numbering probably continued as *The Octopus*.
VOLUME AND ISSUE DATA: Vol. 1, no. 1 (May–June 1936) through Vol. 1, no. 3 (September–October 1936); 3 issues.
PUBLISHER: Popular Publications, Inc., 2256 Grove Street, Chicago, Illinois, with editorial offices at 205 East 42nd Street, New York, New York.
EDITOR: Kenneth White.
PRICE PER ISSUE: 10 cents.
SIZE AND PAGINATION: 7" X 10"; 112 pages.
CURRENT STATUS: Discontinued.
—*Joseph Lewandowski*

DUENDE

Duende is an irregularly published, well-edited and produced, quality journal established for the purpose of preserving and furthering a mutual interest in the pulps. Although emphasis is on The Shadow, the pulp character created and made famous by Walter B. Gibson, articles have also appeared on the various writers of the Doc Savage stories. Bibliographical data, reviews, letters columns, and other material of interest primarily to the pulp-hero fan are included. Although only two issues of *Duende* have been published, the last in 1977, the magazine has promise of future issues.

Information Sources

INDEX SOURCES: None known.
LOCATION SOURCES: Private collectors.

Publication History

MAGAZINE TITLE: *Duende*.
TITLE CHANGES: None.
VOLUME AND ISSUE DATA: No. 1 (April 1975) through no. 2 (to date, Winter 1976–1977); 2 issues.
PUBLISHER: Odyssey Publications, Inc., P.O. Box G–148, Greenwood, Massachusetts, 01880.

EDITOR: Will Murray.
PRICE PER ISSUE: $2.00.
SIZE AND PAGINATION: 8-1/2'' X 11''; 32–48 pages.
CURRENT STATUS: Active, irregular.

DUSTY AYRES AND HIS BATTLE BIRDS

Harry Steeger, president of Popular Publications, was seeking another character in the mold of the highly successful *G-8 and His Battle Aces** to attract the adventure/espionage-conscious reading public, and he found a concept while discussing this with Robert Sidney Bowen. Bowen was one of Steeger's most popular air-war story writers. It was decided to retitle a then-current magazine, *Battle Birds*, changing it to *Dusty Ayres and His Battle Birds*, and altering the format to a series-type, single-character, hero pulp. Plans were made to try the new series for twelve months and to continue *Dusty Ayres* only if it became a hit. However, the title did not survive beyond the original agreement for twelve stories. *G–8 and His Battle Aces,* exclusively written by Robert J. Hogan, was number one in the field at Popular Publications, and *Dusty Ayres* did not meet the same success in the competition.

While G–8 fought in the skies of World War I, Captain Dusty Ayres fought the enemy in a future war in America. The series was billed as "an amazing account of the next great war"; the theme was the invasion of America by an European power. The leader of the invaders was a giant who stood well over seven feet tall and wore a mask to hide his identity. Known only as "Fire Eyes," he came to power in Central Asia and then conquered Europe. From there he turned his eyes toward America. The "invasion of America" theme was a fascinating concept. The adventure stories and plots were thought out very carefully, and the series was written exclusively by Robert Sidney Bowen. Bowen even scripted all of the short stories within the magazine. He was a fine writer, even though he used a somewhat juvenile approach to the stories, which may have been responsible for the discontinuance of the magazine.

With "The Telsa Raiders," the last novel in the series, the enemy had been beaten. Bowen told his readers that this last story would end the magazine. It did. Bowen even apologized to the readers for making war seem "exciting and fun."

This theme of invasion of America did not end, however, with the passing of Dusty Ayres. Steeger liked the concept and adopted it for another of his magazines, *Operator #5*.* The theme had previously been touched upon in this magazine, but not until the June 1936 issue of *Operator #5*, and after the demise of the Dusty Ayres stories, did the "Purple Invasion" commence. America's "Secret Service Ace," Operator #5, was best suited for this theme. There was no juvenile approach this time, and the stories were filled with horrible atrocities. This latter magazine has become known as the "war and peace" of the pulps, furthering the invasion of America idea first commenced in the little-known *Dusty Ayres and His Battle Birds*.

Information Sources

BIBLIOGRAPHY:

Carr, Wooda Nicholas. *America's Secret Service Ace*. Pulp Classics Series. Oak Lawn, Ill.: Robert Weinberg, 1974.

———. "Checklist, Dusty Ayres Series." *Megavore,* no. 10 (August 1980): 45–46.

———. "The Emperor of the World." *Megavore,* no. 10 (August 1980): 42–45.

———. G–8, *The Master Spy*. Pulp Classics Series. Oak Lawn, Ill.: Robert Weinberg, 1975.

Cervon, Bruce. "Dusty Ayres." *Collecting Paperbacks?* Vol. 3, no. 2 (May 1981): 18–19.

Weinberg, "Dusty Ayres." *Pulp*, no. 1 (Fall 1970): 22–24.

INDEX SOURCES: Weinberg, Robert, and Lohr McKinstry. *The Hero Pulp Index*. Evergreen, Colo.: Opar Press, 1971.

LOCATION SOURCES: Private collectors.

Publication History

MAGAZINE TITLE: *Dusty Ayres and His Battle Birds*.

TITLE CHANGES: Changed from *Battle Birds* with Vol. 5, no. 4 (July 1934).

VOLUME AND ISSUE DATA: Vol. 5, no. 4 (July 1934) through Vol. 8, no. 3 (July–August 1935); 12 issues.

PUBLISHER: Popular Publications, Inc., 2256 Grove Street, Chicago, Illinois, with editorial offices at 205 East 42nd Street, New York, New York.

EDITOR: Harry Steeger.

PRICE PER ISSUE: 15 cents.

SIZE AND PAGINATION: 7" X 10"; 128 pages.

CURRENT STATUS: Discontinued.

—*Tom Johnson*

E

ECHOES FROM THE PULPS

This magazine, a pulpzine, featured material almost exclusively devoted to the hero pulps and has made effort to fill in material omitted from the pages of the old pulps: background material on the agents, heroes, and villains, and the unwritten adventures.

The first two issues of *Echoes from the Pulps* were produced on an ordinary Xerox copier and printed on only one side of the page. The third and fourth issues were printed both sides to the page and featured color-Xerox front and back covers related to the contents. The magazine appears on an annual basis.

Information Sources

INDEX SOURCES: None known.
LOCATION SOURCES: Private collectors.

Publication History

MAGAZINE TITLE: *Echoes from the Pulps.*
TITLE CHANGES: None.
VOLUME AND ISSUE DATA: No. 1 (1978) through no. 4 (to date, 1981); 4 issues.
PUBLISHER: Joseph Lewandowski, 26502 Calle San Francisco, San Juan Capistrano, California 92675.
EDITOR: Joseph Lewandowski.
PRICE PER ISSUE: Nos. 1 and 2, $1.50; no. 3, $3.50; no. 4, $4.50.
SIZE AND PAGINATION: 8-1/2'' X 11''; 11–40 pages.
CURRENT STATUS: Active.
—*Joseph Lewandowski*

EDGAR WALLACE CLUB NEWSLETTER

See EDGAR WALLACE SOCIETY NEWSLETTER

EDGAR WALLACE MYSTERY MAGAZINE (British)

Shortly after the demise of *The Sexton Blake Library* (British),* the *Edgar Wallace Mystery Magazine* was born, the birth attended in the early issues by a number of the old Sexton Blake writers. After these first few issues, which were interesting in their own right, the publication's style and content changed to that of the classic magazine of mystery and detection it became.

The first issue, August 1964, featured as the lead novelette a story by Edgar Wallace first published in a Reader's Library edition in 1929. The story, vintage Wallace and in the finest traditions of the British thriller, involves the macabre spectre of a ghost, a figure in the somber habit of a monk. It was titled "The Ghost of Down Hill." This was accompanied by Arthur Kent's "Night of the Hi-Jack," a macabre thriller; "Savage Death" by Vern Hansen; "The Phantom Guest" by Rex Dolphin; and a tale where justice is meted out privately, "Harvest of Homicide," by Martin Thomas. A true-crime story, "The Man Who Paid to Die," was told by Arthur Kent.

A feature of the first, and all succeeding issues, was a photo of Edgar Wallace, smoking a cigarette in a very long holder, on the inside front cover; back covers pictured a scene from a Wallace movie.

An Edgar Wallace story appeared in nearly every issue (all except May 1965), and some of these tales were being published in Britain for the first time. And there were stories, both originals and reprints, by other noted writers, almost all of whom were British. These included Roy Vickers, Margery Allingham, Michael Gilbert, Bill Knox, Penelope Wallace (daughter of Edgar Wallace), Nigel Morland, Herbert Harris, Peter Fraser, and Agatha Christie, as well as many others. However, it was not each author on his or her own, but their combination with other regular features that raised the magazine to its position as one of Britain's best.

One feature was a "period piece," usually of great antiquity and interest. Included were "Murders at the Moorcock" by Geoffrey Whiteley, "The Cloud of Poison" by Charles Franklin, "The Richmond Atrocity" by Franklin, and "The Killing of Christopher Marlowe" by Joel Casavantes. Crossword puzzles, a series of cartoons by Ralph Sallon depicting many of the popular mystery writers of the day, book reviews, and a letters section added to the interest and value.

However, the magazine ceased publication after thirty-five issues, in June 1967. A thirty-sixth issue is believed to have been compiled but was never published.

The blame can be attributed to poor distribution and, unfortunately, lack of support, which resulted in financial difficulty and lack of funds by the publisher.

The *Edgar Wallace Mystery Magazine* was attractively produced and is still one of the most collectable of periodicals.

Information Sources

INDEX SOURCES: Cook, Michael L. *Monthly Murders*. Westport, Conn.: Greenwood Press, 1982.
LOCATION SOURCES: Private collectors.

Publication History

MAGAZINE TITLE: *Edgar Wallace Mystery Magazine*.
TITLE CHANGES: None.
VOLUME AND ISSUE DATA: Vol. 1, no. 1 (August 1964) through Vol. 4, no. 35 (June 1967); 35 issues.
PUBLISHER: Micron Publications Ltd., Micron House, Gorringe Park Avenue, Mitcham, Surrey, England; with the fifth issue, Edgar Wallace Magazines Ltd., 4 Bradmore Road, Oxford, England.
EDITOR: Keith Chapman; commencing fifth issue, Nigel Morland.
PRICE PER ISSUE: 2 shillings 6 pence; with issue no. 5, 3 shillings.
SIZE AND PAGINATION: 4-3/4'' X 7''; 128–144 pages.
CURRENT STATUS: Discontinued.
—*Robert Adey*

EDGAR WALLACE MYSTERY MAGAZINE (U.S.)

A reprint program of the successful British magazine of the same name was attempted by Classic Mystery Publications, Inc., with one issue dated March 1966. The U.S. *Edgar Wallace Mystery Magazine* featured "Murder on the Rocks" by Edgar Wallace and an impressive lineup of other authors which included Richard Deming, Craig Rice, Henry Kane, Frank Kane, C. B. Gilford, and Fredric Brown, among others. Some stories were originals.

No further issues have been noted.

Information Sources

INDEX SOURCES: Cook, Michael L. *Monthly Murders*. Westport, Conn.: Greenwood Press, 1982.
LOCATION SOURCES: Private collectors.

Publication History

MAGAZINE TITLE: *Edgar Wallace Mystery Magazine*.
TITLE CHANGES: None.
VOLUME AND ISSUE DATA: Vol. 1, no. 1 (March 1966); 1 issue.
PUBLISHER: Classic Mystery Publications, Inc., 315 West 70th Street, New York, New York.
EDITOR: Not known.
PRICE PER ISSUE: 50 cents.
SIZE AND PAGINATION: 5-3/8'' X 7-1/4''; pages not known.

CURRENT STATUS: Discontinued.

EDGAR WALLACE SOCIETY NEWSLETTER, THE (British)

Edgar Wallace was a larger-than-life character who would not have been out of place in one of his own books. Such was the audience he commanded that even now, fifty years after his death, the society founded in 1969 by his daughter to commemorate and honor the man and his works is still going strong.

Each broadsheet of the Society's newsletter contains a number of articles by Wallace readers and collectors, a short "books in print" and book-exchange section (solely for Wallace books), and a separate insert that can be anything from a Wallace poem to a "lost" short story rediscovered in the pages of some obscure magazine. The articles are generally well researched and much to the taste of those who fancy themselves in any way interested in the life, books, history, and bibliography of Wallace.

The cost of *The Edgar Wallace Society Newsletter* is far more modest than its achievements.

Information Sources

INDEX SOURCES: None known.
LOCATION SOURCES: Private collectors.

Publication History

MAGAZINE TITLE: *Edgar Wallace Society Newsletter.*
TITLE CHANGES: Changed from *Edgar Wallace Club Newsletter* (with the ninth issue).
VOLUME AND ISSUE DATA: No. 1 (January 1969) through no. 53, (to date, February 1982); 53 issues.
PUBLISHER: Edgar Wallace Society, 4 Bradmore Road, Oxford OX2 6QW, England.
EDITOR: Penelope Wallace.
PRICE PER ISSUE: By membership, currently 3 pounds per year.
SIZE AND PAGINATION: 8'' X 10''; with 7th issue, 8'' X 11-1/2''; 4–8 pages plus insert.
CURRENT STATUS: Active.
—*Robert Adey*

ED McBAIN'S 87th PRECINCT MYSTERY MAGAZINE

With an inauspicious appearance in April 1975, marred only by the misspelling of the magazine title ("Ed McBaines. . .") and built upon an effort to capitalize on the popularity of the police procedural novels of Ed McBain (Evan Hunter), *Ed McBain's 87th Precinct Mystery Magazine* should have been a candidate for a fairly long life. An earlier magazine carried a similar title *(Ed McBain's Mystery Book*)* from another publisher but had been discontinued in 1961.

A story by Ed McBain was featured in each of the four issues published. "Roundelay" appeared in the first issue, "Now Die in It" in the May 1975 issue, "Good and Dead" in the June issue, and "The Death of Me" in the last (August 1975) issue.

A well-known list of authors contributed a better-than-average lineup of detective tales in each issue. Noteworthy are "The Mannequin Murder" by Irwin Porges and "Pit of Despair" by Arthur Porges, both in the first issue. Theodore Mathieson's "Three for the Hounds" (April 1975) was of interest. "Dead Ringer" (May 1975) by Gary Brandner presented a twist-ending; there was "Up River" by Gil Brewer in the June issue, and "The Big Score" by M. G. Ogan in the August magazine. Other authors, most well known to contemporary readers, included Richard O. Lewis, Gerald Tomlinson, John Masters, John Lutz, Nedra Tyre, and Edward D. Hoch.

There were light-hearted crime-adventure vignettes of the type found in *Alfred Hitchcock's Mystery Magazine,** filled with dialogue that moved the story rapidly ahead and usually ending with a wry twist to the situation. This entertaining crime fiction, dominated by police procedural and private investigator stories, was never antagonistic or off-color.

Attractive, low-key, full-color, pictorial covers were used on all four issues. There were no editorials, announcements, or filler material. The magazine was neatly packaged, well printed, and seemingly well distributed.

It should be noted that *Ed McBain's* commenced with issue number 4 of volume 1, so numbered due to its appearance in the fourth month of the year. Consequently, no issues were designated as volume 1, numbers 1, 2, or 3.

It is unfortunate that this title was discontinued since there were few other mystery/detective magazines on the stands at the time, and *Ed McBain's* promising beginning indicated a brighter future.

Information Sources

INDEX SOURCES: Cook, Michael L. *Monthly Murders*. Westport, Conn.: Greenwood Press, 1982.
LOCATION SOURCES: Private collectors.

Publication History

MAGAZINE TITLE: *Ed McBain's 87th Precinct Mystery Magazine*.
TITLE CHANGES: None.
VOLUME AND ISSUE DATA: Vol. 1, no. 4 (April 1975) through Vol. 1, no. 7 (August 1975); 4 issues.
PUBLISHER: Leonard J. Ackerman as Leonard J. Ackerman Productions, Inc., 8730 Sunset Boulevard, Los Angeles, California 90069.
EDITORS: Leonard J. Ackerman and John H. Burrows.
PRICE PER ISSUE: 95 cents.
SIZE AND PAGINATION: 5-3/8" X 7-1/2"; 126–128 pages.
CURRENT STATUS: Discontinued.

ED McBAIN'S MYSTERY BOOK

Ed McBain was and still is the byline under which best-selling novelist Evan Hunter has written a long and hugely popular series of police procedurals about the 87th Precinct in the vividly described metropolis of Isola. The series began in 1956, and its early novels were published as paperback originals by Perma-books, an imprint of the pioneer softcover firm, Pocket Books, Inc. But with the eighth exploit of the Precinct cops, *Killer's Wedge* (1959), the series moved to the more prestigious, hardcover house of Simon & Schuster, with Pocket Books (which in fact was owned by S & S) reprinting each new title in due course. In 1960, with the series selling like wildfire, Pocket decided to enter the mystery magazine market by capitalizing on the McBain name and success.

Ed McBain's Mystery Book, a digest-sized bimonthly retailing for thirty-five cents, was nominally edited by McBain himself, although the actual work was done by Managing Editor Robert Goodney and Associate Editor Demi Marciano. Goodney knew what he wanted and went all out to get it. He would call up well-known mystery writers whose work he admired (many, but by no means all, of them veterans of *Manhunt** magazine), invite them to submit stories or novelettes about their famous characters, and keep repeating the invitations until their resistance was worn down. The tactic worked wonders. Readers of the magazine's first issue were treated to a Shell Scott novelette by Richard S. Prather, a Lew Archer novelette by Ross Macdonald, short stories by Craig Rice and Richard Matheson, and an excellent true-crime essay by the dean of mystery critics, Anthony Boucher. All this was in addition to the main attraction, "The Empty Hours," a new 87th Precinct novelette by McBain himself.

Issue number 2 featured a condensation of the J. J. Marric (John Creasey) Scotland Yard novel, *Gideon's Fire*, which in book form was to win the M.W.A. Edgar Award as best mystery novel of 1961. Also in the second issue were a Peter Chambers novelette by Henry Kane, an Inspector Schmidt short story (the only one there is) by Aaron Marc Stein writing as George Bagby, a short exploit of Father Shanley and Lieutenant Sammy Golden by Jack Webb, a Scott Jordan short by Harold Q. Masur (whose name was spelled on the cover with a *z*), a Chester Drum short by Stephen Marlowe, plus nonseries tales by Robert Bloch and Kenneth Fearing.

The third issue headlined Fredric Brown's "Before She Kills," the first short adventure of Ed and Am Hunter, and "The Mourners at the Bedside," the single short-story case of Hampton Stone's (Aaron Marc Stein's) Gibson and Mac. The contributors of shorter fiction included Irving Shulman, Frank Kane, Bruno Fischer, and Lawrence Block, and there was nonfiction by Donald E. Westlake and Stuart Palmer. All in all, a stellar lineup, not only of bylines but high-quality whodunits to boot.

But *Ed McBain's Mystery Book* quickly proved to be a case of the good dying young. Its fourth issue was scheduled to include the Ed McBain novelette "J," another Shell Scott caper by Prather, another Chester Drum adventure by Mar-lowe, and an article about narcotics by America's most famous junkie, William S. Burroughs of *Naked Lunch* fame. That number never saw print. *Ed McBain's Mystery Book* was born in 1960 and died in 1960, but during its brief life it furnished first-rate reading for those fans who had the good fortune to hunt it out.

Information Sources

INDEX SOURCES: Cook, Michael L. *Monthly Murders*. Westport, Conn.: Greenwood Press, 1982.
LOCATION SOURCES: Private collectors.

Publication History

MAGAZINE TITLE: *Ed McBain's Mystery Book*.
TITLE CHANGES: None.
VOLUME AND ISSUE DATA: No. 1 (undated, but appearing in 1960) through no. 3 (undated, but appearing in 1961); 3 issues.
PUBLISHER: Pocket Books, Inc., 630 Fifth Avenue, New York 20, New York.
EDITOR: Ed McBain; managing editor, Robert Goodney; associate editor, Demi Marciano.
PRICE PER ISSUE: 35 cents.
SIZE AND PAGINATION: 5-1/4" X 7-1/2"; 128 pages.
CURRENT STATUS: Discontinued.
—*Francis M. Nevins, Jr.*

EERIE MYSTERIES

Eerie Mysteries, like its companion magazine, *Eerie Stories*,* both creations of A. A. Wyn's Magazine Publishers, Inc., is somewhat borderline to the mystery and detective field. It did, however, contain some detective stories (including some from other Wyn titles) if there was an element of violence and horror attendant in the unfolding of the tales. Some stories were even retitled to give more of a shock effect.

Authors' house names were used as a rule, rather than as the exception. The magazine blazoned the contents as "10 Complete Horror-Thrillers," and the first issue in August 1938 included such promises as "City of the Corpses" (by Ralph Powers), "Tomb Treachery" (Ronald Flagg), "Brotherhood of the Damned" (Harris Clivesey), "Scourge of the Death Master" (Charles Q. Evans), "Satan's Fire" (Robert A. Gustin), and "Curse of a Thousand Cats" (Leon Dupont).

Information Sources

BIBLIOGRAPHY:
Jones, Robert Kenneth. *The Shudder Pulps*. West Linn, Ore.: Fax Collector's Editions, 1975.
———. "The Weird Menace Magazines." *Bronze Shadows*, no. 10 (June 1967): 3–8; no. 11 (August 1967): 7–13; no. 12 (October 1967): 7–10; no. 13: (January 1968): 7–12; no. 14 (March 1968): 13–17; no. 15 (November 1968): 4–8.
INDEX SOURCES: None known.

LOCATION SOURCES: University of California–Los Angeles Library (Vol. 1, no. 1, only); private collectors.

Publication History

MAGAZINE TITLE: *Eerie Mysteries*.
TITLE CHANGES: None.
VOLUME AND ISSUE DATA: Vol. 1, no. 1 (August 1938) through Vol. 1, no. 4 (April–May 1939); 4 issues.
PUBLISHER: A. A. Wyn as Magazine Publishers, Inc., 29 Worthington Street, Springfield, Massachusetts, with editorial offices at 67 West 44th Street, New York, New York.
EDITOR: Not known.
PRICE PER ISSUE: 10 cents.
SIZE AND PAGINATION: 7" X 10"; pages not known.
CURRENT STATUS: Discontinued.

EERIE STORIES

Eerie Stories, an Ace Magazine produced by A. A. Wyn and his Magazine Publishers, Inc., appeared in August 1937. No further issues were published, but Wyn tried again a year later with *Eerie Mysteries*,* which had little more success. *Eerie Stories* promised "Startling Adventures in Chilling Horror" but promised more than the magazine delivered with stories that really had no redeeming value and were even poor entertainment. It was borderline mystery, at best.

Information Sources

BIBLIOGRAPHY:
Jones, Robert Kenneth. *The Shudder Pulps*. West Linn, Ore.: Fax Collector's Editions, 1975.
———. "The Weird Menace Magazines." *Bronze Shadows*, no. 10 (June 1967): 3–8; no. 11 (August 1967): 7–13; no. 12 (October 1967): 7–10; no. 13 (January 1968): 7–12; no. 14 (March 1968): 13–17; no. 15 (November 1968): 4–8.
INDEX SOURCES: None known.
LOCATION SOURCES: Private collectors.

Publication History

MAGAZINE TITLE: *Eerie Stories*.
TITLE CHANGES: None.
VOLUME AND ISSUE DATA: Vol. 1, no. 1 (August 1937); 1 issue.
PUBLISHER: A. A. Wyn as Magazine Publishers, Inc., 29 Worthington Street, Springfield, Massachusetts, with editorial offices at 67 West 44th Street, New York, New York.
EDITOR: Not known.
PRICE PER ISSUE: 10 cents.
SIZE AND PAGINATION: 7" X 10"; 112 pages.
CURRENT STATUS: Discontinued.

ELEMENTARY, MY DEAR APA

The amateur press association ("apa" for short) has long been a popular vehicle for would-be fan publishers to express themselves in print without having to go through the difficulties and costs attendant on producing a general circulation fanzine. Briefly, apas are limited membership societies for which the members produce and print a defined number of copies of their publication for distribution to the membership via an offical editor, who collates the various fanzines into a periodically issued volume known as a "mailing." Apas have a long history as a central feature of science-fiction fandom, and the vast majority of the scores of apas currently in operation is concerned with that field and related genres such as fantasy literature and comic books.

One apa, however, has concentrated on the mystery field, that being *Elementary, My Dear APA (DAPA-EM* for short). The apa was founded by Donna Balopole of New York in late 1973 with six charter members. Most of the early joiners were science-fiction fans who also had a strong interest in mystery fiction and who were familiar with the unique format and style peculiar to apas. Eventually, word reached the "hard-core" mystery fans, and the group reached its full complement (and limit) of thirty-five members in 1980. The size of the mailings has likewise grown—from 27 pages in the first issue to an average of 350 pages in 1981.

With thirty-five fanzine publishers each producing his or her own publication to taste, the contents of each mailing are extraordinarily diverse; but each mailing will likely contain numerous reviews of current and past mysteries, requests for information on books and authors (and prior queries answered), much news and gossip of the mystery publishing and fan scenes, checklists and author surveys, and much on collecting and book-hunting anecdotes. The membership also spans a broad gamut: from hard-boiled dick fanciers to English body-in-the-library aficionados, from housewives to university professors, from library readers to fanatic collectors. As is the way with apas, there is much cross-commentary on each other's fanzines and a good bit of personal news and chatter. Atypically for apas in general, though, the members rarely stray too far from the central subject, mystery fiction.

Many of the members of longest term are either publishers of or substantial contributors to the general circulation mystery fanzines, such as Jeff Meyerson, Guy Townsend, Bob Briney, Marv Lachman, Steve Lewis, and John Nieminski, to name a few. In some instances, *DAPA-EM* served as a place to float the trial balloons for publications (for example, *The Poisoned Pen,* The Mystery Fancier*),* giving the neophyte publishers a chance to work out publishing procedures and to round up future contributors.

DAPA-EM provides a relaxed, informal, and enjoyable medium for exchange of opinion and information for mystery fans of every sort, and most of its members count the day of arrival of each mailing as a singularly special one.

As an example of the publications included in a mailing, that of July 1981 consisted of the following:

Leaves from a Browser's Notebook #13 (Steve Stilwell)
Mazes #23 (George Kelley)
The Woman in White #10 (Judy Koutek)
I Am Not a Number, I Am a Free APA #11 (Leslie Schaechter)
Zappa Dappa Doo #12 (Liam O'Connor)
The Mummy Speaks #11 (Mary Ann Grochowski)
Deadly Prose #22 (Jeff Meyerson)
Defunct #3 (Dave Lewis)
The Apron String Affair #18 (Ellen Nehr)
Under the Gun #4 (David Grothe)
Macavity #24 (Bill Crider)
Who Was That Masked Pregnant Donut Lady #27 (Stan Burns)
Idle Chatter #23 (Dorothy Nathan)
Doc Vollmer's Neighbor #10 (Jud Sapp)
The French Connection #25 (Walter Albert)
Sergeant Chough #7 (Frank Denton)
Just in Crime #6 (Marv Lachman)
Distaff Dispatch #15 (Terri Krause)
Contact Is Not a Verb #9 (Bob Briney)
The Mysterious Mike #14 (Don Cole)
Mystery Loves Company #17 (Jim McCahery)
Homicide Hussy #11 (Kathi Maio)
Fatal Kiss #18 (Steve Lewis)
Shot Scott's Rap Sheet #26 (Art Scott)
Red Herring #31 (Jeff Smith)
For Your Eyes Only #81 (David Doerrer)
Tales of Adventurers #17 (Martin Wooster)
Sean Walbeck's Mystery APAzine #1 (Sean Walbeck)
Lapsee's Lament #1 (Guy Townsend)
Pfui #13 (Bob Napier)
The On-Looker #3 (Mike Horvat)
(Covers by John Nieminski and Frank Denton)

Information Sources

INDEX SOURCES: None known.
LOCATION SOURCES: Private collectors.

Publication History

MAGAZINE TITLE: *Elementary, My Dear APA (DAPA-EM)*.
TITLE CHANGES: None.
VOLUME AND ISSUE DATA: Vol. 1, no. 1 (December 1973) through Vol. 3, no. 4
    (whole no. 12), quarterly; from November 1976 to present, bimonthly.
PUBLISHER: DAPA-EM, from location of official editor, Binghamton, New York; Floral
    Park, New York; Palo Alto, California; Cupertino, California; Livermore, California.
EDITORS: Donna Balopole (issues 1–12); Art Scott (issues 13 to present).
PRICE PER ISSUE: Members pay dues to cover costs of production and postage; sample
    copy to prospective members, $2.50.

SIZE AND PAGINATION: 8-1/2'' X 11''; 27-350 pages.
CURRENT STATUS: Active.
—*Art Scott*

ELLERY QUEEN REVIEW, THE

See QUEEN CANON BIBLIOPHILE, THE

ELLERY QUEEN'S MYSTERY MAGAZINE

Over forty-one years ago, Ellery Queen (the pseudonym adopted by Frederic Dannay and the late Manfred B. Lee) published the first issue of *Ellery Queen's Mystery Magazine*. Queen's purpose (as stated in an editorial introduction) was to remedy the "lack of quality publications devoted exclusively to the printing of the best in detective-crime short story literature."[1] Today, with a total of 465 issues published, the magazine remains dedicated to that same goal. In an era of overused superlatives and when advertising excesses are commonplace, *Ellery Queen's Mystery Magazine (EQMM)* continues to provide its readers with superior tales of crime, mystery, and detection. There are probably few critics, and fewer readers, who would dispute its claim to be "The World's Leading Mystery Magazine"; a claim which is more a matter of factual record than a mere advertising slogan.

Today, its digest size is so familiar that it is hard to imagine *EQMM* in any other format, yet its small size was a novelty in the early 1940s, as was the quality of its printing and paper. The latter, unfortunately, soon succumbed to the paper shortages of World War II. A far more important innovation was Queen's decision to break out of the mold set by the existing crime fiction magazines, which almost exclusively published "tough" stories of action and violence. *EQMM* was to offer a far broader range of mystery story types, from authors as diverse as Margery Allingham and Dashiell Hammett. By so doing, the magazine became a bridge between the mystery-crime short story and the mystery-crime novel.

What began as a break in an existing pattern soon became a pattern in itself, one firmly established during *EQMM's* first five years. Although Queen began to publish new stories with the fourth issue in May 1942 (the same issue with which the magazine went from quarterly to bimonthly publication), the early years were dominated by the reprinting of many fine but forgotten stories by such notable, and diverse, authors as Frederick Irving Anderson, Nick Carter, G. K. Chesterton, R. Austin Freeman, Carolyn Wells, Ernest Bramah, Marten Cumberland, H. C. NcNeile, Vincent Starrett (who also wrote one of the first new stories to appear in the magazine), Samuel Hopkins Adams, G.D.H. and M. I. Cole, Arthur Sherburne Hardy, C. Daly King, Christopher Morley, P. C. Wren, and numerous others. The quality and variety of stories thus offered were further enhanced by Queen's conviction—a conviction which soon developed into an editorial policy—that virtually every noteworthy writer, past and present, had written at least one story which would fit within the detective-crime category. This led to seeking out and publishing stories by famous mainstream writers such as Arnold Bennett, Irvin S. Cobb, Theodore Dreiser, S. J. Perelman, Damon Runyon, Ben Hecht, and T. S. Stribling. In time, Queen's selections were to include stories from twenty-seven Pulitzer and eight Nobel prize winners. Always entertaining, some of these nevertheless stretched the definition of the field to its limits. In this way, however, *Ellery Queen's Mystery Magazine* gained a reputation for publishing outstanding short fiction as well as outstanding short detective-crime fiction. Yet no matter how far afield Queen's conviction and enthusiasm carried him, he never lost sight of his original goal, and the magazine remained first and foremost a purveyor of quality detective, crime, and mystery short stories.

In November 1945, Queen took another step which would both change and improve the magazine. This issue announced the first of what was to become a series of short story contests. A two-thousand-dollar first prize was offered for the winning story, and the six next best would each receive five-hundred-dollar prizes. The stories would be judged by Christopher Morley, Howard Haycraft, and Ellery Queen.

These contests were held annually from 1945 to 1957, and the keen competition which they engendered produced a tremendous number of excellent original stories, including some which could be tallied among the best short stories ever written. Winners of the first prize "Best Story of the Year" awards were Manley W. Wellman, H. F. Heard, Alfredo Segre, Georges Simenon, John Dickson Carr, Charlotte Armstrong, Thomas Flanagan, Steve Frazee, Roy Vickers, Stanley Ellin, A.H.Z. Carr, and Avram Davidson. Not only prize winners, but many of the other entries were published as well. In addition, the "best of the best" were reprinted in a series of annual hardcover anthologies.

There is no doubt that this addition of outstanding new stories, which complemented the continuing flow of unknown, forgotten, and simply old, unavailable reprints, added immeasurably to the magazine's stature. In 1949, Ellery Queen, as editor of *EQMM*, was awarded the Mystery Writers of America's "Edgar" for "the year's outstanding contribution to the mystery short story." The best short story awards given by the MWA from 1954 through 1956 were won by stories which first appeared in *EQMM*.

An important by-product of the contests was the beginning of the publication of "first" stories by new writers. This practice soon became a regular feature of the magazine and one which endured long after the contests themselves ceased. Continuing to the present, *EQMM* has published a total of 591 "first" stories through the May 1982 issue. In addition, numerous "second" stories by the same authors have also been published, occasionally in the same issue.

The early years of 1941–1957, with their outstanding blending of old and new, have been called the "golden age" of *Ellery Queen's Mystery Magazine,* and it would be difficult indeed to dispute this accolade. Not only was the magazine distinguished by the quality of the stories printed but also by the quality and variety of mystery fiction criticism which appeared.

Much of this was to be found in Queen's own informative and entertaining introductions to the stories. These introductions were often miniature essays in the history and art of the mystery story, frequently containing biographical information on the authors concerned or bibliographical details on related stories or novels. These were supplemented by other "Leaves from the Editors' Notebook," most notably the reprinting (between June 1949 and July 1950) of the "Queen's Quorum," an annotated listing of the most historically important (in Queen's judgment) books of short mystery fiction. The list had first appeared in *20th Century Detective Stories* in 1948.

In addition to Queen's own critical work, the first of a continuing series of columns containing detective-mystery criticism and book reviews began with Howard Haycraft's "Speaking of Crime" in the February 1946 issue. Haycraft continued the column until February 1949, when it was taken on by Anthony Boucher until May 1950. From June 1951 until October 1957, Robert P. Mills, *EQMM*'s managing editor, edited a column entitled "Detective Directory," which was comprised of brief quotes embodying the judgments of various reviewers of crime and mystery fiction throughout the country.

The years from 1946 to 1957 were marked not only by the increasing number of new stories and the inception of the criticism/book review columns but by other changes as well. In January 1946, *EQMM* changed from bimonthly to monthly publication, a schedule which it was to maintain without a break for over thirty years. By February 1948, the number of pages had increased from 128 to 144 and the price from twenty-five cents to thirty-five cents. The number of pages was to remain the same for eight years, the price for fifteen, except for the "special anniversary" issues published in March during the years 1959 through 1963.

Another innovation of *EQMM* had been its covers, which were far less luridly illustrated than those of its contemporaries in the early 1940s. From the first issue through that of February 1949, all cover illustrations were original drawings by George Salter. The March 1949 issue had a photograph as the illustration, and the covers for the next ten years varied from drawings to photographs to no illustrations at all. George Salter continued to do some of those drawings which were used, with his last appearing on the March 1958 issue cover.

An interesting variation during these years occurred during the period from October 1955 to September 1959, when different covers were used for the subscriber and newsstand issues. This experiment was apparently in response to some subscriber complaints about the occasionally lurid covers of the early fifties. The newsstand issues continued to carry illustrated covers—some rather lurid and/or graphic—while the subscriber issues had covers carrying only the titles and authors of the stories contained therein, plus one or two small spot drawings. By mid-1958, the experiment was apparently drawing to an end, with the issues of July and November 1958 and January, March, June, and July of 1959 carrying the same unillustrated cover on both the newsstand and subscriber copies. The September 1959 issue was the last to use two covers.

A second period of change began in the late fifties. The September 1956 issue announced the twelfth, and last, of the annual *EQMM* short story contests. (There was a single attempt to revive these in 1961.) With the same issue, the number of pages was reduced to 138. In January 1957, this was further reduced to 130. In the fall of 1957, Bernard G. Davis resigned as president of Ziff-Davis to take over Mercury Publications, Inc., which shortly thereafter became Davis Publications, Inc. In many ways, then, 1957 did mark the end of an era for *Ellery Queen's*. Few, however, could seriously contend that there was any real decline in the magazine's quality or in the appeal to its readership, which steadily increased. (Total paid circulation was 135,102 in 1960; by the end of the decade it had climbed to 204,109.)

Nevertheless, a major shift in emphasis was becoming clear in the magazine's contents. The well of "unknown" and "forgotten" stories, a well into which Queen had hitherto dipped so frequently and successfully, was obviously running dry, as was that of even the simply old and unavailable. Reprints did not cease to appear, but more and more stories by famous authors in the field were selected. Some forty of Agatha Christie's short stories alone were reprinted between 1960 and 1969. A number of stories which had appeared earlier in *EQMM* itself, including the *EQMM* contests' first prize winners, were printed for a second time.

More important, the number of new stories continued to grow and new types of stories to appear. In many ways, the stories Queen selected for publication during the 1960s reflected new trends in the mystery story itself; in other ways, they continued to reflect his enduring search for the best. As its listing in *The Writer* in 1957 put it, *EQMM* posed "no taboos as to subject matter or style" but always demanded stories of "high quality."

Thus, while the magazine continued to publish both new and old "tough" stories a la *The Black Mask** (and used that prestigious title as a characterization for this kind of story until the early 1970s), as well as detective-mystery tales with themes familiar from the early years, other types made their presence increasingly evident throughout the sixties. Among these was the "police procedural," represented by writers such as Lawrence Treat, Joe Gores (though his protagonists were not strictly law officers), Nicolas Freeling, and John Creasey. Humor, especially "the black humor of the absurd" as Anthony Boucher called it, could be found in the stories of James Powell, Robert McNear, James Cross, and John F. Campbell. Humor, though of a gentler type, also played a dominant role in a renewal of interest in the parody/pastiche story, as exemplified by the writings of Robert L. Fish, Ron Goulart, Jon L. Breen, and others. During the decade of the sixties, Sherlock Holmes parody/pastiches alone accounted for nearly three dozen stories. Another hallmark of the sixties was the spy story, a label often misapplied to any tale however remotely connected to foreign or domestic intrigue. Here again, Queen's concern for quality was manifest in the superior offerings of Michael Gilbert, Edward D. Hoch, Jacob Hay, and Brian Garfield.

Throughout the 1960s, *EQMM* also continued to provide its readers with quality mystery criticism and reviews, as well as quality fiction. In November 1957, Anthony Boucher began the review column, "Best Mysteries of the Month." Boucher continued these columns until February 1968. He was folllowed in January 1969 by John Dickson Carr, who wrote the column under the same heading until May 1970, when the title was changed to "The Jury Box." Carr continued under the new heading until his last column in October 1976. Anthony Boucher and John Dickson Carr were two exceptional mustery critics, reviewers, and authors, and the readers of *Ellery Queen's* were indeed fortunate in the enjoyment of their respective expertise for nearly twenty years. If one were to find fault with the magazine in the years after 1957, it would be to lament the virtual disappearance of those "Leaves from the Editors' Notebooks" as well as Queen's lengthy, erudite, and entertaining introductions to the stories. Queen did bring "The Queen's Quorum" up to date in the November and December 1968 issues, but no further installments have appeared as of the date of this writing.

In addition to those in content, changes occurred in size and price during the sixties as well. Beginning with the eighteenth anniversary issue in March 1959, the annual special anniversary issues through March 1963 were extra-length issues of 162 pages, selling for fifty cents. In March 1963, the regular issue paginations were raised to 162 and the cover price to fifty cents. Although the price has inevitably continued to rise (it went to sixty cents in March 1968), the number of pages has remained the same now for nearly twenty years. The illustrated covers, whether original drawings or photographs, virtually disappeared, with only three covers that could be called "illustrated" appearing between 1964 and the end of the decade.

By the early 1970s, *EQMM's* emphasis had clearly shifted toward a preponderance of new stories over old. Not only had two of the magazine's earlier mottoes—one from its cover, "An Anthology of the Best Detective Stories, New and Old," the other from later contents pages, "The best of the new and the best of the old"—long since disappeared, but virtually every issue now drew attention to the currency of its contents by large-print cover captions such as "16 Stories—12 New," "All-American Issue, 14 Stories—11 New," "All New Issue—13 Stories," "15 Stories—All New," and so forth. This aggressively promoted predominance of new over old was, however, at least in part an indication of something more positive than a mere making of a virtue out of a necessity. It was a reflection of Queen's determination to maintain, in the light of a depleted market for the mystery short story, a viable publishing medium for not only the known, established writers in the genre but for aspiring new writers as well. That this was a matter of policy rather than simple happenstance is clearly indicated by the increasingly frequent appearance of "first" stories. Between the first issue of *Ellery Queen's* and the last of 1969, some 338 "first" stories were published. Between January 1970 and May 1982, 253 appeared, as well as an uncounted number of "second" stories. Several of these writers whose first stories appeared in *EQMM*—Robert L. Fish, James Powell, Francis M. Nevins, Jr., and Joyce Harrington, to name only a few—have gone on to produce both additional short stories, as well as novels of both popular appeal and critical acclaim. While more of the stories were new, many of the trends and themes of the sixties continued into the seventies. Stories of humor (often grim and sardonic), parody, pastiche, procedural, espionage, detection, and those which could chill the reader's blood regularly made their appearance.

Some trends of the seventies were not, however, reflected in the magazine's pages. Despite Queen's expressed willingness to consider any topic and any style, *EQMM* has published no stories of explicit, graphic sex, violence, or language. This is not to say that these elements are lacking, for they are not, but their treatment has never been predominant. *EQMM's* stories may thrill or chill its readers, or give them cause to think, and they will always entertain, but it is almost a certainty that they have never, and never will, offend. The magazine's continuously increasing popularity (circulation was approximately 280,000 at the beginning of the 1980s) has amply demonstrated that while sex and violence are essential elements in many stories of mystery and detection, their graphic or explicit depictions are not.

Along with the steady publication of outstanding fiction, *Ellery Queen's Mystery Magazine* continued through the seventies to provide the best in mystery criticism and reviews. As noted above, John Dickson Carr continued to write the column, "The Jury Box," until October 1976. In January 1977, Jon L. Breen assumed its authorship and has continued it to this date. The December 1975 issue saw another major change in the increased space devoted to criticism and reviews with the appearance of "Ellery Queen's Mystery Newsletter," written by Otto Penzler and Chris Steinbrunner. This was accompanied by the announcement that *EQMM* would "expand the regular book-review section to include publishers' own reviews of their upcoming key mystery and suspense titles; John Dickson Carr will continue 'The Jury Box', augmented by new and interesting material covering personal interviews with authors and the latest developments in films, television and radio." In conjunction with the publishers' reviews, a "new service," the "Ellery Queen Book Department," was added, offering those books mentioned in the "Mystery Newsletter" to the magazine's readers at discounts of "at least 20%." This feature continued on a regular basis until December 1979, when it quietly disappeared.

The sections of the "Mystery Newsletter" written by Penzler and Steinbrunner were, respectively, "Crime Dossier," a column of book reviews and notes of publications in the mystery field, and "Bloody Visions," a review column of film and television mystery offerings. "Crime Dossier" continued until July 1980, when it was replaced by a column of similar content entitled "Crime Beat" by "R. E. Porter" (a pseudonym for Edward D. Hoch). "Bloody Visions" continues as of this date.

The author interviews, promised in the December 1975 issue, began in January 1976 with an interview with Ross Macdonald. As of May 1982, some fifty-two authors have been interviewed, ranging from such venerable names as Hugh Pentecost, Julian Symons, Isaac Asimov, Stanley Ellin, and "Ellery Queen" himself to relative newcomers such as James Grady, William DeAndrea, and William X. Kienzle. Generally quite short, a page to a page and one-half, with an occasional longer one divided between two successive issues, they are clearly tailored to fit the space allotted. Their brevity has been mitigated in many instances by structuring them around only a portion or single aspect of the author's career or work. That they have obviously been welcomed by *EQMM*'s readers is evident by their continuance for over six years.

While the magazine's pagination had long been stabilized (at 162 pages since March 1963), its price has inevitably continued to rise. In March 1968 it was sixty cents; seventy-five cents in March 1971; ninety-five cents in March 1974; one dollar in December 1975 (attributed to the "increased cost of additional pages and the extra editorial charges" occasioned by the addition of the "Mystery Newsletter" and the publishers' reviews), and $1.25 in August 1978. In December 1979, for the first time in over thirty years, the frequency of publication changed, and *EQMM* began to appear thirteen times a year, or once every twenty-eight days. This produced two issues in one month during the year and resulted in the day of the month being added to each issue's date. Volume and "whole numbers" remained unchanged, although every other volume now contained seven rather than six numbers.

The covers of the first half of the 1970s, like those of the last half of the 1960s, were "all type," devoid even of the spot drawings that had enlivened the subscriber issues of the mid-fifties. In October 1974, illustrated covers reappeared and continued somewhat irregularly through March 1978. In April 1978, the first of a series of twelve cover portrayals of famous detectives appeared. These were followed by a series featuring mystery fiction authors. Between May 1979 and March 1981, a total of twenty-six authors were depicted.

For many years, *Ellery Queen's Mystery Magazine* had published semiannual author-title indexes to its stories. In 1974, these were cumulated in John Nieminski's monumental *EQMM 350: An Author/Title Index to Ellery Queen's Mystery Magazine, Fall 1941 through January 1973*, published by the Armchair Detective Press. Nieminski's work went far beyond its modest subtitle in providing complete author and title indexes to not only the stories but to articles as well. In addition, it identified series characters, reprints, and title changes. Several appendices listed true-crime selections, book reviews, poems and verse, Sherlockiana and non-Sherlockiana parodies and pastiches. A chronological listing of the contents of the magazine, with author index, also is included in Michael L. Cook's *Monthly Murders* (Greenwood Press, 1982), which covers the period from 1941 to June 1981.

In March 1982, *EQMM* published its forty-first anniversary issue and its 464th consecutive—issue no small achievement for a magazine exclusively dedicated to a genre too often casually dismissed as "the literature of escape." What is equally, if not more, remarkable is that Ellery Queen (now only Frederic Dannay) continues actively to direct its progress as editor-in-chief. As Anthony Boucher had noted some twenty years ago, Queen was seldom willing simply to reject a story with potential but would instead work actively and personally with its author to achieve the best possible result.

Thus far, *EQMM* in the 1980s appears to be continuing the pattern set in the sixties and seventies, presenting a seemingly endless supply of new, high-quality stories supplemented by excellent book reviews and perceptive criticism. While new material, by established authors as well as first-story writers, continues to dominate the magazine's pages, there is some evidence that Queen is seeking to return to the older themes as well, including the reprinting of "forgotten" stories and tales of mystery and detection by mainstream authors. The April 1981 issue included the first reprinting of Raoul Whitfield's 1931 story, "Mistral," accompanied by this editorial request: "If you too have a favorite story you haven't reread in years, or if there is a story that has persisted in your memory, let us know the author's name, the title of the story, where and when it first appeared, and we will be happy to pay you a modest finder's fee should we be able to clear the reprint rights. . . ." "Mistral" was followed in June 1981 by Nedra Tyre's "Mr. Smith and Myrtle" (from her book, *Red Wine First*, published in 1947); in February 1982 by "They Shouldn't Uv Hung Willie" (also from *Red Wine First*), and in March 1982 by Somerset Maugham's 1925 tale, "A Friend in Need."

The magazine's critical/review columns all continue to date, and its price, unfortunately, has continued to rise: to $1.35 in February 1980 and to $1.50 in December 1981. Even at this price, however, its 162 pages continue to offer as good, or better, a value than many current paperbacks at twice the cost. Following the last mystery author cover, illustrated covers featuring a sort of "still life" selection of items associated with a crime scene have continued.

During the past forty-one years, *Ellery Queen's* has published over 5,000 stories by more than 1,400 authors, and it is not possible here to do justice to an examination of these contributions. While many are represented by only a single story, others have regularly appeared for many years. To mention only four, Stanley Ellin has written a story every year (except 1974) from 1948 to 1980; Hugh Pentecost at least one (except in 1950) from 1947 through 1981 (and never less than two since 1958). James Holding has furnished at least one since 1960 (missing only 1969); and the incredibly prolific Edward D. Hoch has been a steady contributor since 1962, with a story appearing in every issue from January 1973 through May 1982.

Not only has the magazine been a major vehicle in keeping the mystery short story alive in the United States, but it has long appeared abroad as well. As early as 1948, *EQMM* was being published in Australian and French editions, and British editions were first published by Mellifont Press, Ltd., and later by Atlas Publishing & Distributing Co, Ltd. The British issues were all composed of reprints from the U.S. edition. By early 1958, *EQMM* was published in Australia, Brazil, the Caribbean, Britain, France, Italy, and Japan. Currently, the magazine is published in French (Editions D'Iena), German (Wilhelm Heyne Verlag), Greek (Chrissoula Tatari & Co.), Italian (Arnoldo Mondadori Editore), and Japanese (Suedit Corporation) editions.

Note

1. Editorial announcement, *Ellery Queen's Mystery Magazine*, Vol. 1 (Fall 1941), inside front cover.

Information Sources

BIBLIOGRAPHY:
The Armchair Detective, special Ellery Queen issue, Vol. 12, no. 3 (Summer 1979).
Blau, Peter E. "The Sherlockian EQMM." *The Queen Canon Bibliophile,* Vol. 2, no. 1 (February 1970): 15–17.
Boucher, Anthony. "There Was No Mystery in What the Crime Editor Was After." *New York Times Book Review* (February 26, 1961):14.
Lachman, Marvin. "The Magazine." *The Queen Canon Bibliophile,* Vol. 2, no. 1 (February 1970): 6–8.
Miller, Don. "Rex Stout in Ellery Queen's Mystery Magazine." *The Mystery Nook,* no. 9 (August 1976): A24–25.
Mr. Mystery (John D. MacDonald). "Writing for Ellery Queen's Mystery Magazine." *The John D. MacDonald Bibliophile,* no. 27 (January 1981): 12–15.
Nevins, Francis M. Jr. *Royal Bloodline: Ellery Queen, Author and Detective.* Bowling Green, Ohio: Bowling Green University Popular Press, 1974.
Sullivan, Eleanor. "Fred Dannay and EQMM." *The Armchair Detective,* Vol. 12, no. 3 (Summer 1979): 201.
INDEX SOURCES: Cook, Michael L. *Monthly Murders.* Westport, Conn.: Greenwood Press, 1982.
Miller, Don. "Ellery Queen's Mystery Magazine: 1975 Index." *The Mystery Nook,* no. 8 (December 1975): 45.
Nieminski, John. *EQMM 350: An Author/Title Index to Ellery Queen's Mystery Magazine, Fall 1941 through January 1973.* White Bear Lake, Minn.: The Armchair Detective Press, 1974.
LOCATION SOURCES: Private collectors.

Publication History

MAGAZINE TITLE: *Ellery Queen's Mystery Magazine.*
TITLE CHANGES: None.
VOLUME AND ISSUE DATA: Vol. 1 (first issues designated by only "volume"; Fall 1941) through Vol. 79, no. 5 (to date, May 1982); 465 issues.
PUBLISHER: American Mercury, Inc., 570 Lexington Avenue, New York, New York; then by its predecessors, Mercury Publications, Inc., and Davis Publications, Inc.; current address: 380 Lexington Avenue, New York, New York 10017.
EDITOR: "Ellery Queen" (Frederic Dannay and Manfred B. Lee; since 1971, Fredric Dannay).

PRICE PER ISSUE: 20 cents; 25 cents; 35 cents; 50 cents; 60 cents; 75 cents; 95 cents;
     $1.00; $1.25; $1.35; $1.50 (see text).
SIZE AND PAGINATION: Average 5-1/8'' X 7-5/8''; 128–162 pages.
CURRENT STATUS: Active.

British edition

MAGAZINE TITLE: *Ellery Queen's Mystery Magazine.*
TITLE CHANGES: None.
VOLUME AND ISSUE DATA: Vol. 1, no. 1 (February 1953) through whole no. 140
     (September 1964). Identified by volume and issue number through Vol. 5, no. 4
     (September 1954) and thereafter only by whole number commencing with no. 21;
     140 issues.
PUBLISHER: Mellifont Press, Ltd., 1 Furnival Street, London E.C. 4, England; comm-
     encing with issue no. 112, by Atlas Publishing & Distributing Co., Ltd., 18 Bride
     Lane, London, E.C. 4, England.
EDITOR: Ellery Queen.
PRICE PER ISSUE: 1 shilling; 1 shilling 6 pence (August 1954); 2 shillings (August
     1968); 2 shillings 6 pence (April 1962); 3 shillings (January 1964).
SIZE AND PAGINATION: 5-3/8'' X 7-3/8''; average 96 pages.
CURRENT STATUS: Discontinued (British edition).
—*David H. Doerrer*

ELLERY QUEEN'S MYSTERY MAGAZINE (British)

See ELLERY QUEEN'S MYSTERY MAGAZINE

EXCITING DETECTIVE

Exciting Detective offered excitement, action, violence, and constant movement with a minimum of exhausting thought.

It had (from the Fall 1940 issue) ''. . . fast-moving, dynamite-packed, up-
to-the-minute novels, novelettes, and stories that carry a high-powered punch!
Featuring the world's greatest sleuths in thrill-a-minute fiction by the world's
most popular detective writers.''[1]

The scene was the city. Through those deadly streets raced private detectives,
police detectives, and infrequent adventurers. They blazed with zeal and gripped
the handles of their pistols, their eyes cold slits. Most of them had a tendency
to get knocked out and tied up toward the end of a story, waking to the strutting
sneers of human beasts gripping machine guns. In spite of which, good triumphed,
issue after issue.

Story titles snarled with action: ''The Secret of the Tong,'' ''Murder Limited,''
''Live by the Rod,'' ''Killer's Lunch Hour,'' ''Murder for a Million,'' ''The
Murder Necklace,'' ''Death's Bargain Day''. . . .

Many familiar names contributed this fiction, including Johnston McCulley,
Laurence Donovan, Nelson Bond, F. C. Painton, and G. T. Fleming-Roberts.

And, as usual, the contents page bulged with pseudonyms: Owen Fox Jerome (Oscar J. Friend), Harl Vincent (H. V. Schoepflin), and Dale Clark (Ronal Kayser) among them. To each issue, these writers contributed a novel, a novelette, and four or five short stories. The department, "The Desk Sergeant," provided delighted comments about this issue's fiction and foretold coming wonders.

Covers were cluttered with type and figures in violent action, a girl in danger being the focus of attention. Interior illustrations were by half a dozen artists in as many styles, with frequent appropriations of *The Phantom Detective** illustrations from the late 1930s issues.

The first *Exciting Detective* issue was dated Fall 1940. Except for a short period as a bimonthly at the beginning of 1941, it was a quarterly through 1943 and was terminated when the wartime paper shortage became oppressive.

Note

1. Contents page, *Exciting Detective*, Vol. 1, no. 1 (Fall 1940), p. 4.

Information Sources

INDEX SOURCES: None known.
LOCATION SOURCES: University of California–Los Angeles Library (Vol. 1, no. 1, only); private collectors.

Publication History

MAGAZINE TITLE: *Exciting Detective*.
TITLE CHANGES: None.
VOLUME AND ISSUE DATA: Vol. 1, no. 1 (Fall 1940) through Winter 1943.
PUBLISHER: Better Publications, Inc., 22 West 48th Street, New York, New York; later 10 East 40th Street, New York, New York.
EDITOR: Not known.
PRICE PER ISSUE: 10 cents.
SIZE AND PAGINATION: 6-5/8" X 9-3/4"; 114 pages.
CURRENT STATUS: Discontinued.
—*Robert Sampson*

EXCITING MYSTERY

Exciting Mystery appeared on the newsstands with the October 1942 issue, a ten-cent magazine obviously lost in the flood of similar detective pulps available at the time. The first issue featured a Fredric Brown novel, "Legacy of Fear," and a featured novelette, "The Corpse Died Twice." Its cover prominently portrayed a girl in distress, with a low-cut dress and skirt hoisted, menaced by a leering, evil-eyed, mustached, villain with gun.

Published by Nedor Publishing Company, the magazine apparently expired with the third issue, Spring 1943.

Information Sources

INDEX SOURCES: None known.
LOCATION SOURCES: University of California–Los Angeles Library (Vol. 1, no. 1, only); private collectors.

Publication History

MAGAZINE TITLE: *Exciting Mystery*.
TITLE CHANGES: None.
VOLUME AND ISSUE DATA: Vol. 1, no. 1 (October 1942) through at least Vol. 1, no. 3 (Spring 1943); 3 issues.
PUBLISHER: Nedor Publishing Company, Inc.
EDITOR: Not known.
PRICE PER ISSUE: 10 cents.
SIZE AND PAGINATION: Not known.
CURRENT STATUS: Discontinued.

EXECUTIONER MYSTERY MAGAZINE, THE

Although without reference to the character created and made popular by Don Pendleton in his series of paperback books on "The Executioner," this magazine carried the title *Don Pendleton's The Executioner Mystery Magazine* for the first three issues. The fourth issue appeared as just *The Executioner Mystery Magazine*.

Presenting all new stories in a more or less standard crime-adventure fare, the first issue in April 1975 included short stories by Richard O. Lewis, John Lutz, Irwin Porges, Gil Brewer, Edward D. Hoch, Frank Sisk, and Theodore Mathieson among others, all well known to contemporary mystery fans. Many of these same authors also appeared in the subsequent issues.

Consisting of all fiction, with no editorials, announcements, or columns, and no advertising except on the back cover, the magazine existed for four issues. Somewhat puzzling to collectors is the fact that the magazine commenced with volume 1, number 4, as did a companion magazine (*Ed McBain's 87th Precinct Mystery Magazine**), but this is explained in noting that the first issue of *The Executioner* appeared in the fourth month of the year.

Information Sources

INDEX SOURCES: Cook, Michael L. *Monthly Murders*. Westport, Conn.: Greenwood Press, 1982.
LOCATION SOURCES: Private collectors.

Publication History

MAGAZINE TITLE: *The Executioner Mystery Magazine*.
TITLE CHANGES: *Don Pendleton's The Executioner Mystery Magazine* (first three issues).

VOLUME AND ISSUE DATA: Vol. 1, no. 4 (April 1975) through Vol. 1, no. 7 (August
    1975); 4 issues.
PUBLISHER: Leonard J. Ackerman as Leonard J. Ackerman Productions, Inc., 8730
    Sunset Boulevard, Los Angeles, California 90069.
EDITOR: Jack Matcha, editorial director; John H. Burrows, executive editor.
PRICE PER ISSUE: 95 cents.
SIZE AND PAGINATION: 5-1/4'' X 7-1/2''; 126–128 pages.
CURRENT STATUS: Discontinued.

F

FAMOUS DETECTIVE (British)

See CRACK DETECTIVE

FAMOUS DETECTIVE (U.S.)

See CRACK DETECTIVE

FAMOUS SPY STORIES

The first issue of *Famous Spy Stories* reprinted four Anthony Hamilton novelettes that had appeared a few years earlier in *Detective Fiction Weekly.** On the front cover, as part of the title of the magazine, was emblazoned a banner proclaiming ''All by Max Brand.'' The contents page announced that the next issue would contain four more novelettes in the series, but this was not to be.

The first four Anthony Hamilton stories filled the entire initial issue of the magazine except for the six or seven pages of advertisements and the contents page. The next quartet of stories was slightly longer. Even set in a size of type that represented a one-eighth reduction from that used for the original printing, the second quartet required over 130 pages for the stories and illustrations alone. Had these four tales been published in one issue, there would have been no space for the advertisements (five full pages in the second issue), the contents page, and several of the illustrations. And to use a still smaller size was not practical—that actually used was the smallest the pulp-reading public would accept at this time. Thus the second issue reprinted but two of the stories and filled in the remaining pages with other stories and articles that had appeared in magazines previously published by The Frank A. Munsey Company. The other pair of novelettes appeared in the third (and final) issue of the magazine, which again used as fillers items from the Munsey files. For these two issues, the banner was worded "by Famous Authors."

The three issues are unusual in one other aspect: the first two had trimmed edges, while the third was not trimmed. Usually, pulp magazines of this era were not trimmed, to save costs in producing the magazine. However, the outbreak of World War II in September 1939 caused some interference in the supply of pulp paper, and many of the publishers began trimming their magazines and returning the excess to the mills for reprocessing into more paper. It was atypical for a publisher to start trimming magazines, however, and then stop a few months later. No explanation is known for this occurrence in *Famous Spy Stories*.

Thus the three issues of *Famous Spy Stories* reprinted the eight novelettes in the Anthony Hamilton saga, leaving only the previously serialized novel, "The Bamboo Whistle," unreprinted in magazine format. Between the appearances, in *Detective Fiction Weekly* and *Famous Spy Stories,* the entire saga had been reprinted in three books, first by Macrae-Smith Company in the mid-1930s and then by Triangle Books a few years later. In the publishing explosion following the war, all three of these hardback novelizations were also reprinted as paperbacks.

Max Brand, acclaimed as "The King of the Pulps" in the thirties, created many memorable characters. Assuredly, Anthony Hamilton has a place in this pantheon.

The eight novelettes (and the concluding novel) recount Hamilton's efforts to bring to naught the machinations of the number-one Japanese secret agent. To this end, Hamilton adopts the role of a spooning, witless dandy, head over heels in love with a girl in the enemy camp. In one of the many ironies of the series, he is actually in love with her. She puts him off in the beginning, believing him to be no more than the vacuous fop he portrays, but eventually begins to return his love.

When the series opens, Hamilton is the head of the American Secret Service: his word could set in operation all the myriad cogged and interacting wheels of the Service, with millions of dollars at his unquestioned disposal and thousands of trained men at his beck. This constituted the solid head of the axe to which the wits of Hamilton supplied the cutting edge.

When Hamilton permitted himself to laugh with vacuous joy, it was one of the major triumphs of his characterization. He had worked for months perfecting the production of the laugh until it could, at will, sweep every semblance of intelligence out of his face and sponge all record of thought from his brain. On such occasions, even trained observers found it impossible to believe he had ever had a thought more serious than which tailor to patronize or which music hall revue to attend. To top off his performance of the complete ass, he wore a monocle, explaining to a fellow agent that it was a real convenience, as he could drop it out of his face at an embarrassing moment and thereby gain an extra second to compose himself.

The first novelette opens with Hamilton flying to Monte Carlo. The American network has learned that the chief Japanese agent is living in a villa there, but his identity is not known. Hamilton's task is threefold: he must determine the identity of the Japanese agent, foil his nefarious machinations, and keep his own identity secret. Not only does Hamilton determine the identity of the agent, but he also discovers how to break the code being used. The number-one agent is identified as the Viscomte Henri de Graulchier, son of a French nobleman and a Japanese woman.

In the succeeding three stories, de Graulchier plots to foment revolution in Russia, believing that by promoting internal strife in the recently Sovietized country he can embroil all Europe in another war and thus gain an open hand in China for Japan.

The fifth novelette starts a new series of schemes by de Graulchier, who has shifted his headquarters to Lithonia. Now the aim is to embroil Russia in a war with her neighbors, again so that Japan will have a free hand in the Far East.

This ended the Anthony Hamilton saga as reprinted in *Famous Spy Stories*. In contrast to the first two issues, which carried announcements that the next issue would feature more Anthony Hamilton stories, the third issue simply announced that the next issue would feature a very fine selection of favorite spy fiction stories. No such issue ever appeared.

Max Brand was a consummate story teller, and these tales sweep the reader along rapidly. There are remarkably few loose ends left dangling and even fewer inconsistencies. Beyond these considerations are the deft little touches that Brand brings to his characters to make them seem convincingly real. He was an accomplished student of the human condition, with a camera in his brain recording all the foibles and proclivities he observed in the people around him so that he might later use them to flesh out his stock characters. He had a wonderful way of describing the characters in an oblique fashion without interrupting the flow of the narrative. With a pithy phrase here and a casual, but trenchant, clause there, he would gradually build up a character until, in the end, the reader could identify with the character and believe in the reality of the creation—a character with vices as well as virtues, faults as well as excellences. In the pulp world, such writing was rare, indeed, and it made Brand one of the most eagerly sought-after authors.

Information Sources

BIBLIOGRAPHY:
Easton, Robert. *Max Brand: The Big Westerner*. Norman, Okla.: University of Oklahoma Press, 1970.
INDEX SOURCES: None known.
LOCATION SOURCES: University of California–Los Angeles Library (Vol. 1, no. 1, only); private collectors.

Publication History

MAGAZINE TITLE: *Famous Spy Stories*.

TITLE CHANGES: None.
VOLUME AND ISSUE DATA: Vol. 1, no. 1 (January/February 1940) through Vol. 1, no. 3 (May/June 1940); 3 issues.
PUBLISHER: The Frank A. Munsey Co., 280 Broadway, New York, New York.
EDITOR: Not known.
PRICE PER ISSUE: 15 cents.
SIZE AND PAGINATION: 6-1/2'' X 9-1/2''; no. 3, 7'' X 10''; number of pages not known.
CURRENT STATUS: Discontinued.
—*Joseph Lewandowski*

FAST ACTION DETECTIVE AND MYSTERY STORIES

See SMASHING DETECTIVE

FATAL KISS

While nowhere near so prolific as those in the field of science fiction, fans of mystery and detective fiction have produced numerous amateur magazines over the past thirty-five years. Several of these have concentrated on either a single author—Sax Rohmer, Ellery Queen, John D. MacDonald—or a single character—Sherlock Holmes, James Bond, Nero Wolfe. Others have covered the whole spectrum of mystery, detective, suspense, and espionage fiction. Some are far more personal in content and less formalized in frequency of appearance and distribution. Often these amateur publications are the work of one or two individuals who have served as editors, writers, typists, illustrators, printers, publishers, and distributors, and many such magazines do not survive beyond the first few issues.

One of the more enduring is *Fatal Kiss*, which premiered in November 1976 as the successor to *Mystery*File.* Begun as a member contribution to the mystery amateur press association, DAPA-EM (see *Elementary, My Dear APA*), it was also sent to a small, selected number of nonmembers in return for "letters of comment or other worthwhile endeavors."

Throughout its life, the pages of *Fatal Kiss* have included primarily letters of comment to the editor and mailing comments by him on other DAPA-EM members' contributions. Short articles and book reviews have also been occasionally featured. The relatively infrequent appearance of articles is highly deceptive for those who would attempt to evaluate the magazine's content. The many letters, and often the mailing comments as well, are replete with informative, entertaining, and sometimes provocative comments on individual authors and titles, as well as on general matters of interest to mystery fiction fans and scholars.

One long-running feature of particular note in *Fatal Kiss* was a readers' poll of mystery authors, begun in March 1980 and continuing to January 1982. Participants were asked to rank the authors listed on a scale of 1 to 10. Those authors not ranked could be designated as "I don't ever intend to read this person,'' ''I'd like to read this author but I haven't yet,'' or ''I've never heard of this guy.''

Recent issues have featured a list of the titles, dates, and times of the NBC-radio productions of ''The Adventures of Philip Marlowe'' from 1947 to 1951 and a checklist of the first sixty Raven House mysteries, including series characters (where applicable), as well as the authors and titles.

Information Sources

INDEX SOURCES: None known.
LOCATION SOURCES: Private collectors.

Publication History

MAGAZINE TITLE: *Fatal Kiss*.
TITLE CHANGES: *Burnt Gumshoe* (issue no. 6 only).
VOLUME AND ISSUE DATA: No. 1 (November 1976) through no. 19 (to date, January 1982); 19 issues.
PUBLISHER: Steve Lewis, 62 Chestnut Road, Newington, Connecticut 06111.
EDITOR: Steve Lewis.
PRICE PER ISSUE: None stated.
SIZE AND PAGINATION: 8-1/2'' X 11''; 3–34 pages.
CURRENT STATUS: Active.
—*David H. Doerrer*

FAUST COLLECTOR, THE

While Frederick S. Faust is perhaps more noted for his western fiction using the pseudonym of Max Brand, his mystery stories are also of considerable value and interest to readers (*The Secret of Dr. Kildare,* for example). These include the Anthony Hamilton series of espionage stories (as by Frederick Frost) and those written under the name of Walter C. Butler.

The noted bibliographer, William J. Clark, commenced a fan magazine in 1969 featuring articles, commentary, reviews, letters, and bibliographical material relating to Faust. Also printed in *The Faust Collector* were many items of poetry and fiction written by Faust, particularly during his high-school period.

The periodical was billed as a quarterly but suffered irregular appearance. It must be considered as a valuable contribution to the genre and recognized as including much material not available elsewhere.

Information Sources

INDEX SOURCES: None known.
LOCATION SOURCES: University of California–Los Angeles Library; private collectors.

Publication History

MAGAZINE TITLE: *The Faust Collector*.
TITLE CHANGES: None.

VOLUME AND ISSUE DATA: Vol. 1, no. 1 (February 1969) through Vol. 3, no. 2
    (January 1973); 10 issues and one supplement.
PUBLISHER: William J. Clark, 11744-1/2 Gateway Boulevard, Los Angeles, California
    90064.
EDITOR: William J. Clark.
PRICE PER ISSUE: Not stated.
SIZE AND PAGINATION: First issue 5-1/2'' X 8-1/2''; others 8-1/2'' X 11''; 8-12
    pages.
CURRENT STATUS: Discontinued (publisher deceased).

F.B.I. DETECTIVE STORIES (British)

See F.B.I. DETECTIVE STORIES

F.B.I. DETECTIVE STORIES

A fairly long-lived magazine for this category, *F.B.I. Detective Stories* was
introduced with the February 1949 issue and managed to survive, although
somewhat of an anachronism, for fourteen bimonthly issues until May 1951.

Stories portrayed the FBI in action, with emphasis on espionage, spies, and
other areas in which the federal government authorities were prominent. In this
period, the agents were heroes, with a supercop image, and always "got their
man." True-fact fillers and similar features carried the same theme.

At least six issues of a British reprint series by the title of *F.B.I. Detective
Stories* were published.

Information Sources

BIBLIOGRAPHY:
Hardin, Nils. "An Interview with Henry Steeger." *Xenophile,* no. 33 (July 1977):3–18.
———, and George Hocutt. "A Checklist of Popular Publications Titles 1930–1955."
    Xenophile, no. 33 (July 1977): 21–24.
INDEX SOURCES: None known.
LOCATION SOURCES: University of California–Los Angeles Library (1949–1950, 3
    issues); private collectors.

Publication History

MAGAZINE TITLE: *F.B.I. Detective Stories*.
TITLE CHANGES: None.
VOLUME AND ISSUE DATA: Vol. 1, no. 1 (February 1949) through Vol. 4, no. 2
    (May 1951); 14 issues.
PUBLISHER: All-Fiction Field, Inc., a subsidiary of Popular Publications, Inc., 1125
    East Vaile Avenue, Kokomo, Indiana, with editorial offices at 205 East 42nd
    Street, New York, New York.
EDITOR: Henry Steeger.
PRICE PER ISSUE: 25 cents.
SIZE AND PAGINATION: 7'' X 10''; 114 pages.

CURRENT STATUS: Discontinued.

FEAR!

While definitely borderline to the mystery and detective field, *Fear!* presented a combination of macabre mystery and horror stories. Several of the better-known mystery fiction authors, including Hal Ellson, John Jakes, and Wilkie Collins, were represented.

Information Sources

INDEX SOURCES: Cook, Michael L. *Monthly Murders*. Westport, Conn.: Greenwood Press, 1982.
LOCATION SOURCES: Private collectors.

Publication History

MAGAZINE TITLE: *Fear!*
TITLE CHANGES: None.
VOLUME AND ISSUE DATA: Vol. 1, no. 1 (May 1960) through Vol. 1, no. 2 (July 1960); 2 issues.
PUBLISHER: Henry Scharf as Great American Publications, Inc., 10 Ferry Street, Concord, New Hampshire, with editorial offices at 270 Madison Avenue, New York 16, New York.
EDITOR: Joseph L. Marx; editorial director, Sheldon Wax; associate editor, Jack Bernard.
PRICE PER ISSUE: 35 cents.
SIZE AND PAGINATION: 5-3/8'' X 7-5/8''; 130 pages.
CURRENT STATUS: Discontinued.

FEDERAL AGENT

See PUBLIC ENEMY

FEDS, THE

Trends were important to pulp magazine publishers. They were like canoes in the rapids of popular appeal and, as such, were pounced upon and ridden as far as they would go. There were trends toward detective pulps, love pulps, even western love pulps, and finally there was a trend toward no pulps, and they died. The Street & Smith company, although in many ways conservative, was the major trend setter. It virtually initiated the trend toward specialized pulps with its formative *Detective Story Magazine,* * *Love Story,* and *Western Story* magazines, but it was seldom successful when it attempted to follow the trends begun by other publishers.

This was the case with *The Feds*. In late 1935, inspired by a Jimmy Cagney movie, *Public Enemy,* a wave of G-Man fever rippled across America. The FBI's early successes against organized crime fired the country's collective imagination, and the entertainment media responded. In the pulps, it began with Standard Magazine's *G-Men Detective** (featuring the novel-length exploits of FBI agent Dan Fowler); *Public Enemy,** later changed to *Federal Agent,** appeared at the same time. Popular Publications brought out *Ace G-Man Stories** in 1936.

By mid-1936, Street & Smith decided to enter the field with its modestly titled *The Feds*. It was a timid offering at first, a quarterly whose first issue, dated July–September 1936, was composed of stories reprinted from the back pages of *The Shadow Magazine** and *Nick Carter Magazine** for the most part, some barely two months old. The stories were published under various governmental subheadings: FBI Men, Secret Service, T-Men, Postal Inspector, and Customs Inspector. The editor was John L. Nanovic, who handled most of Street & Smith's character pulp magazines (notably *Doc Savage** and *The Shadow*).

The Feds featured no single lead character, however. Its contents consisted of short stories by some of the lesser of Nanovic's writers—Alan Hathway, Laurence Donovan, Steve Fisher, and others. This was an unusual magazine for Nanovic to edit, his first short story magazine. The first issue, which may have been a one-shot effort designed to test the waters, suffered from the fact that the fiction read exactly as if the stories were fillers from *The Shadow*, as they were.

Sales, however, must have been encouraging; the magazine became a monthly with the second issue. New stories were written by many of the same writers. Steve Fisher created a naval intelligence agent, Big Red Brennan. An ex-Navy man himself, Fisher was billed as the Navy's foremost writer. Jean Francis Webb wrote about a Coast Guard officer, Bat Hayward. Laurence Donovan told about postal inspectors and was hailed as a writer who had written more stories about the Postal Service than any other writer. One writer, Ned O'Doherty, was a moonlighting U.S. customs inspector and wrote, of course, about customs inspectors.

Nanovic mobilized virtually all of the writers who were then writing back-of-the-book material for his other magazines, including Harold A. Davis, Ben Conlon, Edwin Burkholder, Theodore Tinsley, William G. Bogart, Norman A. Daniels, and many others. Significantly, neither Lester Dent nor Walter B. Gibson appeared in *The Feds*. Nanovic himself wrote factual articles under a pseudonym, Henry Lysing.

Unfortunately, *The Feds* remained a magazine of filler stories. No attempt was made to introduce a dynamic G-Man agent of the likes of Dan Fowler. Instead, issue after issue featured colorless tales of the less-dramatic government services. It's unlikely that Great Depression readers really cared to read about the heroes of the Bureau of Fisheries or the Bureau of Mines. But that was the type of fiction *The Feds* featured.

In all, *The Feds* lasted through fifteen issues, skipping the August 1937 issue, until it ceased publication in December 1937 when Street & Smith purged many of its weaker titles. It was, on all accounts, an abysmal failure. Most of the other G-Man pulps ran for several years, supported by their strong lead character novels. *The Feds* had none; it expired, a curiously little-read magazine then and unremembered today.

Information Sources

BIBLIOGRAPHY:
Reynolds, Quentin. *The Fiction Factory*. New York: Random House, 1955.
INDEX SOURCES: None known.
LOCATION SOURCES: University of California–Los Angeles Library (Vol. 1, no. 2, only); private collectors.

Publication History

MAGAZINE TITLE: *The Feds*.
TITLE CHANGES: None.
VOLUME AND ISSUE DATA: Vol. 1, no. 1 (September 1936) through Vol. 3, no. 3 (December 1937); 15 issues.
PUBLISHER: Street & Smith Publications, Inc., 79 Seventh Avenue, New York, New York.
EDITOR: John L. Nanovic.
PRICE PER ISSUE: 10 cents.
SIZE AND PAGINATION: 7'' X 10''; number of pages not known.
CURRENT STATUS: Discontinued.
—*Will Murray*

FIFTEEN DETECTIVE STORIES

Fifteen Detective Stories was a continuation of Popular Publications' *New Detective Magazine** under a changed title, the volume and issue numbers remaining the same. The Hardin/Hocutt "Checklist of Popular Publications Titles" indicates that both *Detective Tales* (Popular Publications)* and *Detective Story Magazine (Detective Story Magazine* [Street & Smith]*) were also combined with *Fifteen Detective Stories,* although they left no traces.[1]

The legacy from *New Detective* was, however, quite clear. In addition to the volume numbering, three features carried directly over into *Fifteen Detective Stories*. One of these, M.E. Ohaver's "Solving Cipher Secrets," had been published since 1926 and first appeared in *Flynn's Weekly (Detective Fiction Weekly*)*. Of the remaining departments, "The Witness Chair" was a fact article on aspects of crime, and "Strange Trails to Murder" was a double-page of text and illustrations about interesting, classical murder cases. Usually, three other features were included, ranging from single paragraphs to single pages of smoothly fictionalized true anecdotes and stories.

Each issue of *Fifteen Detective Stories* contained one or two novelettes and from seven to nine short stories. These were slickly done, high-suspense pieces, filled with authentically tough people and dialogue that had the sound of life in them. It was smooth, skillful, contemporary fiction, restrained for the subject matter and glinting with exactly observed description. The hard-boiled tradition was still alive in this magazine, more smoothly done and with more human emotion showing but still hot and exciting and close to the pulse of danger just under reality's skin.

Note

1. Nils Hardin and George Hocutt, "A Checklist of Popular Publications Titles 1930–1955," *Xenophile,* no. 33 (July 1977): 21–24.

Information Sources

BIBLIOGRAPHY:
Hardin, Nils, and George Hocutt. "A Checklist of Popular Publications Titles 1930–1955." *Xenophile,* no. 33 (July 1977): 21–24.
INDEX SOURCES: None known.
LOCATION SOURCES: Private collectors only.

Publication History

MAGAZINE TITLE: *Fifteen Detective Stories.*
TITLE CHANGES: A continuation of *New Detective Magazine*; volume numbering was later continued in *True Adventures.*
VOLUME AND ISSUE DATA: Vol. 19, no. 3 (August 1953) through Vol. 22, no. 2 (June 1955); 12 issues.
PUBLISHER: Popular Publications, Inc., 1125 East Vaile Avenue, Kokomo, Indiana.
EDITOR: Not known.
PRICE PER ISSUE: 25 cents.
SIZE AND PAGINATION: 6-3/4" X 9-3/8"; 114 pages.
CURRENT STATUS: Discontinued.
—*Robert Sampson*

15 MYSTERY STORIES

See DIME MYSTERY BOOK

15 STORY DETECTIVE

See ALL–STORY DETECTIVE

FIFTH COLUMN STORIES

Fifth Column Stories was a "Red Star" publication of the Frank A. Munsey Company. No other information is available.

Information Sources

INDEX SOURCES: None known.
LOCATION SOURCES: Private collectors.

Publication History

MAGAZINE TITLE: *Fifth Column Stories*.
TITLE CHANGES: None known.
VOLUME AND ISSUE DATA: Vol. 1, no. 1 (August 1940); number of issues and
    extent unknown.
PUBLISHER: Frank A. Munsey Company, 280 Broadway, New York, New York.
EDITOR: Not known.
PRICE PER ISSUE: Not known.
SIZE AND PAGINATION: Not known.
CURRENT STATUS: Discontinued.

FINGERPRINTS DETECTIVE

A partially silhouetted policeman approaching the outstretched hand of a corpse, with a smoking gun nearby, highlights the cover of the only issue of *Fingerprints Detective* that was published. There is no date nor volume designation, and no clue even among the advertisements as to when this rare magazine appeared, but the style places it in the late 1940s. A publisher's footnote indicates that the ten stories are from *Scientific Detective,** another title published by the same firm.

The lead story, "The Question Mark," by Margery Allingham, tells of a girl who was too interested in crime for her own good, and Richard Sale's "Three Wise Men of Babylon" recounted the adventures of a reporter who found murder at every turn. Other stories were by less known authors, several of whom utilized the Alfred Hitchcock style ending in a wry twist. A quiz for "super sleuths" posed such questions as "Is It True: that a gun-shot wound is larger at point of entrance than of exit?"[1]

The one issue was a well-produced, appropriately illustrated magazine that deserved a longer life.

Note

1. *Fingerprints Detective*, n.d. (only issue), p. 30.

Information Sources

INDEX SOURCES: None known.

LOCATION SOURCES: University of California–Los Angeles Library; private collectors.

Publication History

MAGAZINE TITLE: *Fingerprints Detective*.
TITLE CHANGES: None known.
VOLUME AND ISSUE DATA: (No. 1), no date nor volume designation; 1 issue.
PUBLISHER: R. and J. Publishing Company, 1745 Broadway, New York 19, New York.
EDITOR: Not known.
PRICE PER ISSUE: 25 cents.
SIZE AND PAGINATION: 5-1/4'' X 7-5/8''; 130 pages.
CURRENT STATUS: Discontinued.

FIRESIDE DETECTIVE CASEBOOK (British)

At least one issue of *Fireside Detective Casebook* was published. No other information is available.

Information Sources

INDEX SOURCES: None known.
LOCATION SOURCES: Private collectors.

Publication History

MAGAZINE TITLE: *Fireside Detective Casebook*.
TITLE CHANGES: None known.
VOLUME AND ISSUE DATA: No. 1; number of issues, date, and extent unknown.
PUBLISHER: Not known.
EDITOR: Not known.
PRICE PER ISSUE: Not known.
SIZE AND PAGINATION: Not known.
CURRENT STATUS: Discontinued.

FIVE-CENT DETECTIVE

One of the "Nickel Series" magazines—along with *Five-Cent Adventures, Five-Cent Flying Stories,* and *Five-Cent Western—Five-Cent Detective* was first published with the June 1932 issue. No other information is available.

Information Sources

INDEX SOURCES: None known.
LOCATION SOURCES: Private collectors.

Publication History

MAGAZINE TITLE: *Five-Cent Detective*.
TITLE CHANGES: None known.
VOLUME AND ISSUE DATA: Vol. 1, no. 1 (June 1932); number of issues and extent unknown.

PUBLISHER: Not known.
EDITOR: Not known.
PRICE PER ISSUE: 5 cents.
SIZE AND PAGINATION: Not known.
CURRENT STATUS: Discontinued.

FIVE-DETECTIVE MYSTERIES

A Dell publication, *Five-Detective Mysteries* was first published with the October–November 1942 issue. No other informmation is available.

Information Sources

INDEX SOURCES: None known.
LOCATION SOURCES: University of California–Los Angeles Library (Vol. 1, nos. 1 and 2); private collectors.

Publication History

MAGAZINE TITLE: *Five-Detective Mysteries.*
TITLE CHANGES: None known.
VOLUME AND ISSUE DATA: Vol. 1, no. 1 (October/November 1942) through at least Vol. 1, no. 2 (December 1943); 2 issues.
PUBLISHER: Dell Publishing Co., Inc., 149 Madison Avenue, New York, New York.
EDITOR: Not known.
PRICE PER ISSUE: Not known.
SIZE AND PAGINATION: Not known.
CURRENT STATUS: Discontinued.

FIVE DETECTIVE NOVELS

Five Detective Novels was a superior reprint (1949–1952) magazine published quarterly by Standard Publications. Each issue contained five novelettes of more than usual quality and interest. At first, these were selected from the Thrilling line of titles, including *Thrilling Detective** (issues from about 1938 to 1945), *Popular Detective** (1937 to 1942), *Thrilling Mystery** (1943 to 1944), and *Exciting Detective** (1941). Later issues of *Five Detective Novels* reprinted novelettes from the *American Magazine* (1935, 1939), a decidedly slick-paper publication which featured a long detective story in each issue. And four stories were also reprinted from *The Black Mask** (1938–1941).

Over the life of this magazine, eighty novelettes were published. They provide an unusual cross-section of what the longer pulp mystery story was like during the 1930s and 1940s. The quality is high. Among the authors represented are William Irish, Craig Rice, Fredric Brown, Philip Wylie, William Gault, W. T. Ballard, and H. H. Stinson. Of the other writers, many had written extensively for the single-character pulps, as well as producing large volumes of shorter fiction. They included Paul Chadwick, Frederick C. Davis, Norman A. Daniels,

Stewart Sterling, and G. T. Fleming-Roberts. The house names of Robert Wallace and C.K.M. Scanlon are also represented.

Early issues of *Five Detective Novels* include G. T. Fleming-Roberts's fine novelettes of The Ghost, a particularly interesting magician-detective. At least four stories were reprinted in 1950 and 1951 issues.

In addition to the usual five novelettes, the magazine customarily published two or three short stories. Most of these do not seem to have been published before, and the authors were not usually as well known as the novelette authors. Seabury Quinn, however, whose work had appeared extensively in *Weird Tales,* * contributed one short story, "Dead Man's Shoes," in the Winter 1951 issue.

Five Detective Novels also used an occasional true-crime article written into short story form. And a department, "On the Docket," appeared through the Winter 1951 issue. After that, the department was renamed "The Lowdown." Under either title, it was mainly concerned with previews of the coming issue and frequent, enthusiastic mentions of the fiction offered in other Standard detective magazines. A "Cryptogram Corner" was added in the Fall 1951 issue, with answers to the puzzle given on the final page. Various brief paragraphs of anecdotes, jokes, and miscellaneous filler material were included, each formally listed on the contents page. The cryptogram was finally dropped with the Winter 1953 issue.

The first six issues of *Five Detective Novels*, through Winter 1951, are splendid examples of the art of producing a full-sized pulp magazine. The issues have a comfortable, thick feel about them (they contain 144 pages). The covers are tasteful, showing attractive young ladies in danger, and the fiction is continuously interesting. With the Spring 1951 issue, the magazine was slimmed and shortened, but it remained equally attractive, and the cover girls stayed beautiful. Few reprint magazines reached the level of professional excellence of *Five Detective Novels,* and it remains an outstanding example of its type.

Information Sources

INDEX SOURCES: None known.

LOCATION SOURCES: University of California–Los Angeles Library 1942–1943 (2 issues); private collectors.

Publication History

MAGAZINE TITLE: *Five Detective Novels.*

TITLE CHANGES: None.

VOLUME AND ISSUE DATA: Vol. 1, no. 1 (December 1949) through Vol. 6, no. 3 (Winter 1954); 18 issues.

PUBLISHER: Standard Magazines, Inc., 29 Worthington Street, Springfield, Massachusetts, later 1125 East Vaile Avenue, Kokomo, Indiana.

EDITORS: Harvey Burns; David X. Manners (commencing Fall 1951); Morris Ogden Jones (commencing Winter 1953).

PRICE PER ISSUE: 25 cents.

SIZE AND PAGINATION: 7" X 9-3/4"; 6-7/8" X 9-1/4"; 130–146 pages.

CURRENT STATUS: Discontinued.
—*Robert Sampson*

FLYNN'S

See DETECTIVE FICTION WEEKLY

FLYNN'S DETECTIVE FICTION MAGAZINE

See DETECTIVE FICTION WEEKLY

FLYNN'S DETECTIVE FICTION WEEKLY

See DETECTIVE FICTION WEEKLY

FLYNN'S WEEKLY

See DETECTIVE FICTION WEEKLY

FLYNN'S WEEKLY DETECTIVE FICTION

See DETECTIVE FICTION WEEKLY

FOREIGN SERVICE

A pulp magazine, *Foreign Service* was published for at least one issue in the late 1920s or early 1930s. No other information is available.

Information Sources

INDEX SOURCES: None known.
LOCATION SOURCES: Private collectors.

Publication History

MAGAZINE TITLE: *Foreign Service*.
TITLE CHANGES: None known.
VOLUME AND ISSUE DATA: Not known.
PUBLISHER: Not known.
EDITOR: Not known.
PRICE PER ISSUE: Not known.
SIZE AND PAGINATION: Not known.
CURRENT STATUS: Discontinued.

G

GANGLAND DETECTIVE STORIES

In this magazine of gangster stories and gang life, Double-Action Magazines promised "10 All New Stories published in the interest of proving that CRIME DOES NOT PAY!"[1] One issue of *Gangland Detective Stories* has been noted, volume 2, number 2, dated April 1940. No other information is available.

Note

1. Contents page slogan, *Gangland Detective Stories,* Vol. 2, no. 2 (April 1940), p. 3.

Information Sources

INDEX SOURCES: None known.
LOCATION SOURCES: Private collectors.

Publication History

MAGAZINE TITLE: *Gangland Detective Stories.*
TITLE CHANGES: None known.
VOLUME AND ISSUE DATA: Only issue noted is Vol. 2, no. 2 (April 1940); number of issues and extent unknown.
PUBLISHER: Double-Action Magazines, Inc., New York, New York.
EDITOR: Not known.
PRICE PER ISSUE: Not known.
SIZE AND PAGINATION: Not known.
CURRENT STATUS: Discontinued.

GANGLAND-RACKETEER STORIES

A pulp magazine published in the early 1930s by Blue Band Publications, *Gangland-Racketeer Stories* was edited by Harold B. Hersey. No other information is available.

Information Sources

BIBLIOGRAPHY:
Hersey, Harold B. *Pulpwood Editor*. New York: Frederick A. Stokes Co., 1937.
INDEX SOURCES: None known.
LOCATION SOURCES: Private collectors.

Publication History

MAGAZINE TITLE: *Gangland-Racketeer Stories*.
TITLE CHANGES: None known.
VOLUME AND ISSUE DATA: Early 1930s; number of issues, date, and extent unknown.
PUBLISHER: Blue Band Publications, Inc. (Harold B. Hersey), New York, New York.
EDITOR: Harold B. Hersey.
PRICE PER ISSUE: Not known.
SIZE AND PAGINATION: Not known.
CURRENT STATUS: Discontinued.

GANGLAND STORIES

Gangland Stories was another of Harold B. Hersey's unsuccessful pulp magazines, one which was charted to follow the trend of the glamorous background of the romanticized gangsters versus detectives. Two issues have been noted, February and April 1932. No other information is available.

Information Sources

INDEX SOURCES: None known.
LOCATION SOURCES: Private collectors.

Publication History

MAGAZINE TITLE: *Gangland Stories*.
TITLE CHANGES: None known.
VOLUME AND ISSUE DATA: Two issues noted, February and April 1932; number of issues and extent unknown.
PUBLISHER: Harold B. Hersey, New York, New York.
EDITOR: Not known.
PRICE PER ISSUE: Not known.
SIZE AND PAGINATION: Not known.
CURRENT STATUS: Discontinued.

GANG MAGAZINE, THE

One of the innumerable magazines introduced to capitalize on the reading public's fascination with gangsters and gun molls, *The Gang Magazine* was first published in May 1935. Featuring a complete novel, two novelettes, and usually four short stories, it was populated with tales penned by William L. Bird, Bill Cook, Steve Fisher, Paul Ernst, H. M. Appel, and other writers who quickly changed to fit the mold.

No issues have been noted beyond number 3, in September 1935.

Information Sources

INDEX SOURCES: None known.
LOCATION SOURCES: Private collectors.

Publication History

MAGAZINE TITLE: *The Gang Magazine*.
TITLE CHANGES: None.
VOLUME AND ISSUE DATA: No. 1 (May 1935) through no. 3 (September 1935); 3 issues.
PUBLISHER: Lincoln Hoffman, 220 West 42nd Street, New York, New York.
EDITOR: Jack Phillips.
PRICE PER ISSUE: 15 cents.
SIZE AND PAGINATION: 7'' X 10''; 128 pages.
CURRENT STATUS: Discontinued.

GANG SHORTS (British)

At least three issues of *Gang Shorts* were published by Gerald Swan during 1944–1946. No other information is available.

Information Sources

BIBLIOGRAPHY:
Lofts, W.O.G., and Derek J. Adley. *Old Boys Books, A Complete Catalogue*. London: privately printed, 1969.
INDEX SOURCES: None known.
LOCATION SOURCES: Private collectors.

Publication History

MAGAZINE TITLE: *Gang Shorts*.
TITLE CHANGES: None.
VOLUME AND ISSUE DATA: No. 1 (1944) through at least no. 3 (1946); 3 issues.
PUBLISHER: Gerald Swan.
EDITOR: Not known.
PRICE PER ISSUE: Not known.
SIZE AND PAGINATION: 5-3/8'' X 7''; 64 pages.
CURRENT STATUS: Discontinued.

GANGSTER STORIES

After serving as Supervising Editor for a number of the Macfadden publications (*True Story Magazine, True Romances, Dream World*, and *True Detective Mysteries*, among others) and as editor for a group of the Clayton Magazines,[1] Harold B. Hersey, with associates, launched his own stable of pulp magazines in 1928. The original four titles were *Flying Aces, The Dragnet,* Western Trails*, and *Under Fire Stories*. At about the same time, Tom Carwood asked Hersey to take over as editor of *The Underworld Magazine (Underworld, The*)*, which had been on the newsstands for some time. It was under Hersey that the romanticized gangster type of story was pushed to its peak. His own titles, during the next several years, included *Gangster Stories, Racketeer Stories,* Mobs,* Gangland Stories,* Gangland-Racketeer Stories,* and *Speakeasy Stories.** With racketeers enjoying prosperity and nearly everyone else suffering from the Great Depression, it was an easy step to make heroes out of hoodlums.

Gangster Stories commenced in October 1929 and, although priced at twenty-five cents, was avidly purchased by the reading public. In many of the stories, the hero was associated with a gang against his will, to right a wrong, to avenge a friend's death, or to rescue a fair damsel by infiltrating the mob. Although the villain accomplished wonders, he was never allowed to win in the end. Justice always triumphed!

"The hottest fight ever carried on its own momentum in any periodical of mine was one that started after Anatole Feldman's serial, 'Gangsters vs. Gobs,' began running in *Gangster Stories*," Hersey recalled.[2] The story involved the theft of a battleship by an underworld mob, boarding it while moored, imprisoning the skeleton crew on board, and actually stealing it from under the eyes of the admiralty. Some of the gangsters had been sailors and officers who understood navigation, and the ship sailed away. This immediately prompted a hot barrage of letters to the magazine's reader department, "The Eavesdropper." Ex-Navy readers were indignant that anyone could even attempt to steal a battleship, much less get away with it. And when a member of the Marine Corps wrote a letter of sympathy for the Navy, tinged with sarcasm, a feud erupted in the letters column between these two branches of the armed forces!

By 1932, a concerted drive was being made by some against magazines that made the underworld glamorous. These self-appointed supervisors against the reading matter enjoyed by the majority were preparing to file suit against Hersey; and rather than face a legal battle, he discontinued *Gangster Stories*. However, similar magazines continued to be circulated by various publishers into the 1940s, and, as Hersey comments, "I have yet to hear of an instance where a reader turned to a criminal career after buying this or any other pulpwood magazine."[3]

Notes

1. W. M. Clayton published *Telling Tales Magazine, Ace-High Magazine, Cowboy Stories, Ranch Romances, Clues,* The Danger Trail*, and *Five-Novels Monthly*, for which Hersey was head editor.
2. Harold B. Hersey, *Pulpwood Editor* (New York: Frederick A. Stokes Co., 1937), p. 99.

3. Ibid., p. 199.

Information Sources

BIBLIOGRAPHY:
Hersey, Harold B. *Pulpwood Editor*. New York; Frederick A. Stokes Co., 1937.
INDEX SOURCES: None known.
LOCATION SOURCES: Private collectors.

Publication History

MAGAZINE TITLE: *Gangster Stories*.
TITLE CHANGES: None.
VOLUME AND ISSUE DATA: Vol. 1, no. 1 (October 1929) through at least March
    1932; number of issues and extent unknown.
PUBLISHER: Harold B. Hersey as Blue Band Publications, Inc., New York, New York.
EDITOR: Harold B. Hersey.
PRICE PER ISSUE: 25 cents.
SIZE AND PAGINATION: 7" X 10"; number of pages not known.
CURRENT STATUS: Discontinued.

GANG WORLD

One of Popular Publications' first detective pulp magazines, *Gang World* was
either a companion to, or was supplanted by *Blue Steel Magazine*.* At least one
issue of *Gang World* was prepared as such and then retitled *Blue Steel*. It is
possible that sales increased sufficiently so that both titles were used for a short
period. In December 1933 the title was assumed by Spencer Publications, Inc.,
who published at least one issue.

The magazine promised "all stories complete, all stories new," which was
exemplified by tales such as "The Blast" by Carl B. Ogilvie ("Mike Foreni
said: 'An' get this, punk. Try to leave town an' you'll leave a corpse. Let him
go, boys, he'll see a light'. . . . Dudley stood on the threshold of the open steel
door. . . . His answer was, with a strange smile on his set face: 'I see a light,
Mike—and it's shinin' on you with a lily in your mitt. S'long, punk!' ") and
"Rough Justice" by Raoul Du Priest ("What would you do if a dame you never
met came up to you from another table in a cabaret—and handed you a wallet
she lifted from a Big Time Rod?").

Information Sources

BIBLIOGRAPHY:
Hardin, Nils. "An Interview with Henry Steeger." *Xenophile*, no. 33 (July 1977): 3–
    18.
———, and George Hocutt. "A Checklist of Popular Publications Titles 1930–1955."
    Xenophile, no. 33 (July 1977): 21–24.
INDEX SOURCES: None known.

LOCATION SOURCES: Private collectors.

Publication History

MAGAZINE TITLE: *Gang World.*
TITLE CHANGES: None.
VOLUME AND ISSUE DATA: Vol. 1, no. 1 (October 1930) through November 1932;
  one issue by Spencer Publications designated as Vol. 1, no. 1 (December 1933);
  number of issues not known.
PUBLISHERS: Popular Publications, Inc., 2256 Grove Street, Chicago, Illinois; 1933,
  Spencer Publications, Inc., 4500 Diversey Avenue, Chicago, Illinois.
EDITOR: Not known.
PRICE PER ISSUE: 20 cents; 15 cents.
SIZE AND PAGINATION: 7'' X 10''; 128 pages.
CURRENT STATUS: Discontinued.

GAZETTE, THE (THE JOURNAL OF THE WOLFE PACK)

The Wolfe Pack, organized in 1978 at the instigation of Murder Ink's Carol
Brener to create a common meeting ground for admirers of Rex Stout's Nero
Wolfe corpus, provides each enrolled member with a free subscription to the
Pack's official journal, *The Gazette*, a quarterly which began publication in
Winter 1979. From its inception, interest in the Wolfe Pack was great. More
than one thousand members signed up in the first year of its existence and deluged
The Gazette with publishable submissions. Thus far, five issues have gone to
press. Under the recently installed editor-in-chief, Sue Dahlinger, who replaced
Patricia Dreyfus (coeditor of the first issue with Lawrence F. Brooks), copy
already gathered for further issues was edited with plans to span, during 1982,
the gap between the Winter 1980 issue and the present.

In addition to reporting on the Pack's annual Black Orchid dinner (held in
New York City annually on the first weekend in December), the Annual Nero
Wolfe Assembly (held in New York City the same weekend), and the Pack's
Annual Nero Wolfe Award for a Mystery Novel Meeting Stout's Criteria for
Excellence, *The Gazette* publishes numerous scholarly articles examining the
Wolfe corpus from many points of view but, usually, without the tongue-in-
cheek drollery that characterizes Holmesian scholarship (as in *The Baker Street
Journal**). These articles have assessed Wolfe's reading habits; his parentage,
birth, and early life; his role as an orchid grower; the architectonics of *Fer-de-
Lance*; the fate of the first made-for-T.V. Nero Wolfe movie; the William Conrad
Nero Wolfe T.V. series; Archie's writing habits; the true location of the brownstone; Rex Stout's correspondence with the father of cybernetics, Norbert Wiener;
and transcripts of hitherto unpublished Stout interviews.

Future issues of *The Gazette* will contain reviews of books and articles relating
to Stout and the Wolfe stories which have been brought out under other auspices,
such as Ken Darby's *The Brownstone House of Nero Wolfe* (Little, Brown,
1982).

Several regional chapters of the Wolfe Pack, for example, in Houston, Texas, and in Massachusetts, have been formed, and chapters are in the process of organizing in other locales. These active chapters promise to funnel materials to *The Gazette*, guaranteeing that it will continue to maintain the high standards with which it began.

The annual Nero Wolfe Assembly, co-chaired by novelists Marvin Kaye and John McAleer, at which scholars and admirers of Rex Stout who have specialized knowledge read papers before an audience of two hundred Wolfe Pack members, provides additional assurance that the Pack's highly literate outlet will continue to render a valuable service to admirers of the world that Rex Stout created. In each of the three years that the Assembly has been held, several of the best papers read have gone at once to the desk of the editor and, in one instance, led to the author of the paper signing a contract with Ungar to do a book-length biocritique of Stout and the Wolfe corpus.

Information Sources

INDEX SOURCES: None known.
LOCATION SOURCES: Private collectors.

Publication History

MAGAZINE TITLE: *The Gazette (The Journal of the Wolfe Pack).*
TITLE CHANGES: None.
VOLUME AND ISSUE DATA: Vol. 1, no. 1 (Winter 1979) through Vol. 2, no. 1 (Winter 1980); 5 issues.
PUBLISHER: The Wolfe Pack, P.O. Box 822, Ansonia Station, New York, New York 10023.
EDITORS: Patricia Dreyfus and Lawrence F. Brooks, first issue; Sue Dahlinger, editor-in-chief; Lawrence F. Brooks, managing editor; John McAleer, consulting editor.
PRICE PER ISSUE: By membership only, $12.50 per year.
SIZE AND PAGINATION: 6-1/2'' X 9-1/2''; 40–78 pages.
CURRENT STATUS: Active, irregular.
—*John J. McAleer*

G-8 AND HIS BATTLE ACES

The 1930s was a time of magic for those who had the good fortune to grow up with the magazines of the period fondly called "the bloody pulps." Devoted fans usually rate among the very top *G-8 and His Battle Aces,* on the same level as *Doc Savage,* The Shadow Magazine,* The Spider,* Operator #5,** and *The Phantom Detective.**

G-8 and His Battle Aces first appeared on the newsstands in October 1933 and survived until June 1944, with a total of 110 issues, a long-running series by any standard. It was published on a monthly basis by Popular Publications, Inc., under the direction of Henry Steeger and Harold S. Goldsmith.

The magazine was priced first at fifteen cents, which, due to the economic climate as well as competition, was reduced to ten cents in March 1936. *G-8 and His Battle Aces* became one of the most popular magazines on the stands because the lead character, G-8, became one individual in that long line of brave men, heroes of our generation, who withstood the test of literary time. The flyers in the stories became real persons to the readers, and their adventures were followed with passion. They still live today in the memories of many avid readers, and mention of the magazine is found in such publications as Jim Harmon's *Nostalgia Catalogue,* Jim Steranko's *History of Comics,* and Arthur Prager's *Rascals at Large.* Ron Goulart speaks fondly of G-8 in *Cheap Thrills,* and Philip Jose Farmer discussed him in *Tarzan Alive.*

As a central character, G-8 was not tall and not short but seemed of medium build, young, rather good looking, and had gray, steel-hard eyes that gave forth magneticlike power. He had broad shoulders and an easy rolling gait that gave hint of having every muscle at his command. He dominated the center stage. Holding the rank of captain in the American Air Service, he was headquartered at Le Bourget Field, near Paris, during World War I. He was a master spy, crack pilot, and expert in disguises.

He was aided particularly by three stalwart companions: Nippy Weston, a first lieutenant, known as "the terrior ace"; Bull Martin, of the same rank; and Battle, manservant, chief cook, and master of makeup.

G-8's foes were not only diabolical villains but an assortment of weapons and machines designed for the eventual destruction of Allied armies along the western front. These included batlike planes, panther-men, giant spiders, monster apes, titanic birds, a liquid that turned men into mummies, and wolf-men!

The author of the G-8 stories was Robert Jasper Hogan, who wrote every story himself and under his own name. A versatile and prolific man at the typewriter (and author also of The Mysterious Wu Fang and The Secret Six stories), Hogan was a voracious worker. He would keep two secretaries busy with G-8, dictating in the mornings and planning novel outlines in the evenings. He would meet with the artist of the series, Frederick Blakeslee, to discuss the covers and was allowed to inspect the final work before acceptance. The interior artwork was usually by John Fleming Gould, though toward the end of the series by Leo Morey and H. W Kimle.

However, the stories lost some of their luster after the 1930s and became shorter, and the later stories never regained the quality of the first ones. The villains were still superb, though, and made the stories worth reading. Month after month, an evil genius always came back to plague the master spy, much to the readers' delight.

Information Sources

BIBLIOGRAPHY:
Bradd, Sidney H. "G-8, Flying Spy of the Pulps." *Xenophile*, no. 11 (March 1975): 11–16.

Carr, Wooda Nicholas. "G-8 Versus Chu Ling." *Pulp*, no. 4 (Spring 1972): 3–8.
———. "G-8 Versus Stahlmaske." *Pulp*, no. 6 (Summer 1974): 10–15.
———. "Quoth the Raven, 'Nevermore.' " *Xenophile*, no. 6 (August/September 1974): 29–30.
———. "The Devil You Say." *Xenophile*, no. 3 (May 1974): (n.p.).
———. *The Flying Spy*. Oak Lawn, Ill.: Robert Weinberg, 1978.
———. "The Flying Spy." *Doc Savage Club Reader*, no. 6 (Spring 1979): 15–17.
———. "The Two Faces of Herr Matzu." *Xenophile*, no. 5 (July 1974): 4–5.
———, and Herman S. McGregor. "Contemplating Seven of the Pulp Heroes." *Bronze Shadows*, no. 12 (October 1967): 3–6.
Cervon, Bruce. "G-8 and His Battle Aces." *Collecting Paperbacks?* Vol. 3, no. 5 (November 1981): 24.
Hardin, Nils. "An Interview with Henry Steeger." *Xenophile*, no. 33 (July 1977): 3–18.
———, and George Hocutt. "A Checklist of Popular Publications Titles 1930–1955." *Xenophile*, no. 33 (July 1977): 21–24.
Overn, Bud. "The Strange Case of Philip Strange, or Will the Real G-8 Please Stand Up." *Bronze Shadows*, no. 5 (July 1966): 16–17; *Pulp*, no. 2 (Spring 1971): 15–18.
INDEX SOURCES: Weinberg, Robert, and Lohr McKinstry. *The Hero Pulp Index*. Evergreen, Colo.: Opar Press, 1971.
LOCATION SOURCES: Private collectors.

Publication History

MAGAZINE TITLE: *G-8 and His Battle Aces*.
TITLE CHANGES: None (replaced *Battle Aces*).
VOLUME AND ISSUE DATA: Vol. 1, no. 1 (October 1933) through Vol. 28, no. 2 (June 1944); 110 issues.
PUBLISHER: Popular Publications, Inc., 2256 Grove Street, Chicago, Illinois, with editorial offices at 205 East 42nd Street, New York, New York.
EDITOR: Henry Steeger.
PRICE PER ISSUE: 15 cents (until March 1936); 10 cents.
SIZE AND PAGINATION: 7" X 10"; 112–114 pages.
CURRENT STATUS: Discontinued.
—*Wooda Nicholas Carr*

GHOST DETECTIVE, THE

See GHOST, SUPER-DETECTIVE, THE

GHOST, SUPER-DETECTIVE, THE

He is a peculiar hero. His face is bloodless white, the eyes sunk deep in blotched hollows. The nostrils gape wide. Yellow teeth fill a distended mouth. In short, he looks like a dead man, a staring corpse. These features appear by night, glowing with dim luminescence, to the confusion of the underworld.

"What are you?" gasps a crook to whom this spectacle has revealed itself.

It is The Ghost Detective. At less dramatic moments, his name is George Chance, a personable young man and professional magician. What he is doing is what they all did in 1940 pulp magazines—he is a disguised crime fighter.

It isn't clear why Mr. Chance elects to glide through nighttime New York City, looking like a ghoul and running the risk of getting his head shot off. Call it a strange hobby. Nor does he seem well protected. Like most of us, Mr. Chance is a hopeless dub with a pistol. His main protection is a throwing knife—and very proficient he is with that—and a huge number of magic sleights, tricks, and illusions applied as needed to save his neck and disconcert the ungodly.

George Chance was of a distinguished line of magician detectives in the pulps. The first noted seems to have been Balbane, Conjurer Detective, in the 1921–1922 *Detective Story Magazine* (Street & Smith)* (later reprints appeared in *Best Detective Magazine,* 1930–1931). Then followed a number of heroes whose magic was real, not just stage illusions. These included Semi-Dual, an occult detective *(Everybody's Favorite Magazine* and *Argosy All-Story)*; Jules de-Grandin *(Weird Tales*)*; and Dr. Satan *(Weird Tales)* and Dr. Death *(in Dr. Death*)*, the last two being fiends.

In many single-character magazines, the skills of the professional stage magician and escape artist augment the hero's ability with a gun. The Shadow, The Phantom Detective, and The Spider were skilled in escape techniques and slight of hand. The Great Merlini *(Detective Fiction Weekly*)* and *Ellery Queen's Mystery Magazine*)* was a professional magician and owner of a magic store. In *Ace G-Man Stories,* Brian O'Reilly (who was also known as The Ghost) practiced as a magician before becoming a G-Man. And Norgil the Magician *(Crime Busters*)* was given to solving mysteries while on tour with a magical road show. About five months after publication of *The Ghost, Super-Detective*, there appeared Don Diavolo, "The Scarlet Wizard" *(Red Star Mystery*)*, another stage professional. At roughly the same time, the Green Lama *(Double Detective*)* used his knowledge of real and stage magic to combat a succession of the Mad Magi, the Invisible Killers, and other ravening menaces.

George Chance used his magical skills to solve violent crime through seven issues of his own magazine, 1940–1941, and six short stories published in *Thrilling Mystery.* Only the seven novels will be considered here.

From the outset, *The Ghost, Super-Detective*, seems to have been a low-budget effort. After the first issue, none of the covers have much to do with the novel. All feature a scene of wild action, blithely irrelevant to the story. Above and behind this activity floats The Ghost's head, a semiskull, peering coldly down.

The magazine offered a slender amount of fiction for a dime. Each issue contained the novel and two short stories. These latter tales were at first written by lesser names—John Endicott, Owen Fox Jerome, Carroll B. Mayers. Then more prominent writers began slipping in: Robert Leslie Bellem, Ray Cummings, and Laurence Donovan, plus a pair of Popular Publications' big-name authors, Hugh B. Cave and Arthur J. Burks.

The first five issues of the magazine also devoted a page each time to recapping George Chance's earlier life; it was hardly required since his life was invariably recapitulated within the novel.

With the second issue, a readers' department was opened; "Calling the Ghost" uttered editorial homilies and published enthusiastic letters from George Chance fans. Later, the department was quietly retitled "Calling the Green Ghost" when the title of the magazine was changed with the Winter 1941 issue.

The Ghost's career was pleasing but short. It was chopped off by the World War II paper shortage, not underworld gunfire. But then, nobody ever killed a pulp hero, no matter how zany his behavior.

Mr. Chance did not go ghosting unassisted. Like other heroes, he was aided by a small staff, themselves an odd crew. The first of these, an old friend from Chance's circus days, was a midget named Tiny Tim Terry who smoked huge cigars, was slangy and irritable, and spent much time disguised as a baby. Joe Harper, a pitchman, con man, and general parasite, shamelessly freeloaded on Chance. He lounged about Chance's home, his pockets full of Chance's cigars and money, but earned his keep by providing The Ghost with a direct pipeline into the seamy side of city life.

Merry White, a lovely little dark-haired sweetie, was going to marry George and he was going to marry her. Someday. Meanwhile, she assisted him on the stage and when he was The Ghost during investigations, and she was efficient and clever, rarely getting trapped more than once per story.

Glenn Saunders was an amiable young man who looked exactly like George Chance—this being partly natural and partly plastic surgery. In return for his dedicated service, Chance was teaching him the art of professional magic.

Two others shared The Ghost's secret. New York Police Commissioner Edward Standish was responsible for introducing Chance to the delights of criminal investigation. He encouraged The Ghost in his little forays—normally including breaking and entering, assault, intimidation, kidnapping, and practicing magic without a license.

The final person to know The Ghost's identity was Police Medical Examiner Robert Standish, a fine, sardonic fellow of biting wit. He did not seem to realize that he was in a pulp magazine, for he felt that ghosting was a peculiar way for an adult to amuse himself.

These interesting people could be found loafing around Chance's New York apartment, at least until an investigation began. Then they all appeared (secretly, in the dead of night) in the basement of a crumbling rectory, battered and ignored, leaning beside a mid-city church. Behind double-locked doors in the rectory basement was a modern apartment, and from this center The Ghost's investigations proceeded.

These were recorded in a jaunty pulp magazine that never quite decided what its title was or what its editorial policy would be. The first issue, dated January 1940, was titled *The Ghost, Super-Detective*. The cover showed a handsome Mr. Chance (hair black instead of the correct shade of red-gold), dressed in formal black tie, looming gigantically among skyscrapers, his hands filled with little writhing crooks. The novel, "Calling the Ghost," was told in the first person by George Chance himself.

The story is about a rather nutty insurance swindle. Criminals kill off slightly larcenous citizens by defenestration and other ways, leaving behind a myriad of clues—a bag of teeth, a bit of coiled wire. (In *The Ghost*, clues are always bizarre, and there are more of them scattered around than any two men could carry off.) The Ghost investigates. With usual luck, he finds lots of clues and several homicidal crooks. Escapes by use of the Dual Head Illusion. Sends out his assistants to investigate. They get trapped. The Ghost rescues them with the Disappearing Aide Illusion. Dead bodies punctuate the prose. Now, Chance disguises himself as Detective-Sergeant Hammell and gets hit on the head. More clues. Disguised as a Dr. Stacy (how Demarest needles him about these disguises), Chance saves Tiny Tim Terry, finds more clues among several bodies, and announces that the mystery is solved. The Ghost makes a personal appearance on a small private stage and uses The Pointing Finger Illusion to identify the guilty.

In the second story, "The Ghost Strikes Back" (Spring 1940), Chance is framed for murder. Glenn Saunders sits in jail while The Ghost frantically investigates the secret of the sinister leper and why murder follows murder. At the end, The Floating Light Bulb Illusion glows upon the secret criminal, and The Ghost explains all.

"Murder Makes a Ghost" (Summer 1940) explains why electrocuted people, smoking slightly and wearing steel hats, are scattered all over the city. With this issue, the magazine goes through the first of many changes: it is retitled *The Ghost Detective*.

Fall 1940: "The Case of the Laughing Corpse." A really rotten fellow is found dead and smiling broadly. There are six keys that everyone wants, and it's nothing but murder, murder, murder. The Ghost and Joe Harper end in a dynamite trap, listening to a dead man tell them how they are to die. They don't.

They escape unscathed, but more change grips the magazine. George Chance's first-person narration is dropped. The author is now revealed as G. T. Fleming-Roberts, a long-experienced pulp writer, whose style is exactly the same as George Chance's.

With the next novel, the title is another "The Case of . . ." as all titles will be. In Winter 1941, it is "The Case of the Flaming Fist," the fist in question being a floating hand named Simon. It is blazing red, attached to no visible body, and holds a .45 which remains red-hot in service of the crooks. As if this were not wonder enough, The Ghost has become The Green Ghost and the magazine title has changed to *The Green Ghost Detective*.

"The Case of the Walking Skeleton" (Spring 1941) and "The Case of the Black Magician" (Summer 1941) continue Mr. Chance's adventures. Both are packed with peculiar situations. In the first novel, nice fresh skeletons sit about, fully clothed. In the second, a magician murders, disappears, reappears to kill again. In both stories, The Ghost (now greenly glowing in the gloom) performs numerous sleights and vanishes when he is not being caught and hurled into death traps. If he isn't caught, his friends are. At the end, the mysterious killer is trapped by magic arts while The Green Ghost chortles chillingly.

On this high point, the magazine itself vanishes. The dematerialization is total; it never reappears. For completeness of the record, however, Mr. Chance and friends suddenly return in the September 1942 issue of *Thrilling Mystery* to begin a superior series of short stories: "The Case of the Murderous Mermaid" (September 1942); "The Case of the Astral Assassin" (November 1942); "The Case of the Clumsy Cat" (March 1943); "The Case of the Bachelor's Bones" (June 1943); "The Case of the Broken Broom" (Fall 1943); and, finally, "The Case of the Evil Eye" (Winter 1944).

These interesting and fast-moving trifles contain twice the character drawing and action of the big, loose, sprawling novels and are the cream of The Ghost's adventures. Most of them were reprinted, about five years later, in the 1951–1952 issues of *Five Detective Novels.**

Information Sources

BIBLIOGRAPHY:
Johnson, Tom. "The Story of G. T. Fleming-Roberts." *The Age of the Unicorn,* Vol. 1, no. 2 (June 1979): 14–15.
INDEX SOURCES: Weinberg, Robert, and Lohr McKinstry. *The Hero Pulp Index.* Evergreen, Colo.: Opar Press, 1971.
LOCATION SOURCES: University of California–Los Angeles Library (Vol. 1, no. 1 only); private collectors.

Publication History

MAGAZINE TITLE: *The Ghost, Super-Detective.*
TITLE CHANGES: *The Ghost Detective* (with Vol. 2, no. 1 [Summer 1940]); *The Green Ghost Detective* (with Vol. 2, no. 2 [Winter 1941]).
VOLUME AND ISSUE DATA: Vol. 1, no. 1 (January 1940) through Vol. 3, no. 1 (Summer 1941); 7 issues.
PUBLISHER: Better Publications, Inc., 22 West 48th Street, New York, New York, later 10 East 40th Street, New York, New York.
EDITOR: Leo Margulies, editorial director.
PRICE PER ISSUE: 10 cents.
SIZE AND PAGINATION: 6-3/4" X 9-3/4"; 114 pages.
CURRENT STATUS: Discontinued.
—*Robert Sampson*

GIANT DETECTIVE

See MYSTERY BOOK MAGAZINE

GIANT DETECTIVE ANNUAL

There was but one issue of *Giant Detective Annual,* in 1950, reprinting the work of an astonishing cross-section of popular detective story writers. Included was a short novel by Jean Francis Webb and short stories by Steve Fisher, Frank Gruber, George Harmon Coxe, George Bruce, Paul Ernst, Richard Sale, and Lawrence Treat. All of these authors had appeared in earlier issues of *Thrilling Detective** and *Popular Detective,** from which the contents of *Giant Detective Annual* seem primarily drawn.

No further issues of this publication have been noted.

Information Sources

INDEX SOURCES: None known.
LOCATION SOURCES: Private collectors only.

Publication History

MAGAZINE TITLE: *Giant Detective Annual.*
TITLE CHANGES: None.
VOLUME AND ISSUE DATA: Vol. 1, no. 1 (1950); 1 issue.
PUBLISHER: Standard Publications, Inc., 10 East 40th Street, New York, New York.
EDITOR: Not known.
PRICE PER ISSUE: 25 cents.
SIZE AND PAGINATION: 6-3/4'' X 9-3/4''; 196 pages.
CURRENT STATUS: Discontinued.
—*Robert Sampson*

GIANT MANHUNT

See MANHUNT

GIRL FROM U.N.C.L.E. MAGAZINE, THE

''The Girl from U.N.C.L.E.'' was a television show that was a spinoff from ''The Man from U.N.C.L.E.'' It was shown during the third season of the latter, the first episode presented on the NBC network at 7:30 P.M. on Tuesday, September 13, 1966.

MGM, who owned the rights to the ''U.N.C.L.E.'' T.V. stories,[1] wanted a magazine based on the female version of the show, just as there was a magazine based on the male version. The Leo Margulies Corporation was publishing *The Man from U.N.C.L.E. Magazine,** and MGM contacted Margulies to see if he was interested or if they should contact another publisher. Margulies was reluctant since the *Man* magazine was barely paying for itself, but he felt he had to protect his interest and so agreed to do the *Girl* magazine as well. The contract was signed in July 1966, just in time to insert a notice into the September issue of *The Man from U.N.C.L.E. Magazine.*

Margulies asked the Scott Meredith Literary Agency in New York to obtain writers for the *Girl* magazine, and the first such writer obtained was Richard

Deming. MGM demanded that all *U.N.C.L.E.* stories be original—they could not be based on the television episodes as MGM did not wish to have to pay royalties to the television scriptwriter. And MGM had to approve every story before it was published. The procedure began with MGM receiving an outline. If the outline was approved, then the author wrote the manuscript and submitted it for approval, also. MGM then had the option of deciding whether any scenes had to be changed before the story could be printed.

Richard Deming's first manuscript was approved by MGM at the beginning of August 1966, as well as the original outline. On August 31, Cylvia Margulies paid Deming $525 for this. The October issue (which was on the newsstands in September) of *The Man from U.N.C.L.E. Magazine* included an announcement that the new *Girl from U.N.C.L.E. Magazine* would appear on the stands on October 1, but the November issue stated that the date was Thursday, October 6. The first issue of the *Girl* bore the date of December 1966.

Each issue of the magazine featured a novel about the exploits of the U.N.C.L.E. agents, April Dancer and Mark Slate. Supposedly, these stories were written by Robert Hart Davis, the same house name used for the stories in the *Man* magazine. The novels in the *Girl* version were supposed to be of 40,000 words, slightly longer than the similar stories in the companion *Man* magazine, and were an average length of ninety pages. The remainder of the 144-page magazine was filled with about a half-dozen short stories.

The magazine lasted for only seven issues, but among the short stories ran several secondary series. There were three stories about U.N. Security Agent Casimiro Lowry, by V.A. Levine, and two stories featuring Desiree Fleming, an agent for the United States, written by Max Van Derveer.

The Girl from U.N.C.L.E. Magazine was never profitable for the Leo Margulies Corporation. In September 1967, the re-runs of the corresponding television show had ceased, and the last issue of the magazine was dated December. A February 1968 issue was promised but never appeared.

In addition to Richard Deming, the actual authors were I. G. Edmonds (three stories), and Charles Ventura (one story).

The magazine was digest-size and appeared every two months during its short life. The front cover had a background color that engulfed either the whole page or just the top portion; a different color was used for each issue. The first five issues portrayed a line drawing of April Dancer and Mark Slate; the last two used an action photograph from the television series with Stefanie Powers and Noel Harrison. Usually, the back cover showed a still photo from the television show.

Note

1. All stories were copyrighted by MGM.

Information Sources

INDEX SOURCES: Cook, Michael L. *Monthly Murders*, Westport, Conn.: Greenwood Press, 1982.

LOCATION SOURCES: Leo Margulies Collection, University of Oregon Library, Eugene, Ore.; Legal Department, MGM Studios, Culver City, Calif.; private collectors.

Publication History

MAGAZINE TITLE: *The Girl from U.N.C.L.E. Magazine.*
TITLE CHANGES: None
.VOLUME AND ISSUE DATA: Vol. 1, no. 1 (December 1966) through Vol. 2, no. 2 (December 1967); 7 issues.
PUBLISHER: Leo Margulies Corporation, 56 West 45th Street, New York, New York.
EDITOR: Cylvia Kleinman Margulies.
PRICE PER ISSUE: 50 cents.
SIZE AND PAGINATION: 5-3/8″ X 7-5/8″; 144 pages.
CURRENT STATUS: Discontinued.
—*Albert Tonik*

GIRL'S DETECTIVE MYSTERIES

Girl's Detective Mysteries, a pulp magazine, has been noted with a date of October 1936.[1] This may have been the only issue published. No other information is available.

Notes

1. The title is listed in the "Tentative Pulp Checklist" from the San Francisco Academy of Comic Art (unpublished manuscripts, n.d.).

Information Sources

INDEX SOURCES: None known.
LOCATION SOURCES: Private collectors.

Publication History

MAGAZINE TITLE: *Girl's Detective Mysteries.*
TITLE CHANGES: None known.
VOLUME AND ISSUE DATA: At least one issue, October 1936; number of issues and extent unknown.
PUBLISHER: Layne Publishing Corp., New York, New York.
EDITOR: Not known.
PRICE PER ISSUE: Not known.
SIZE AND PAGINATION: Not known.
CURRENT STATUS: Discontinued.

G-MEN

See G-MEN DETECTIVE

G-MEN DETECTIVE

Ned Pines, the publisher of the Standard Magazines pulp line, created several top character pulps during the 1930s. Following the success of his competitors with single-character magazines and his own success with *The Phantom Detective*,* he introduced *G-Men*, a title devoted to stories of the FBI and Secret Service agents.

The new *G-Men* magazine was probably the most popular pulp of those featuring federal agent crime stories and enjoyed a large following of devoted readers. Dan Fowler, "Ace" of the FBI, was featured in the lead story, although his name was never featured as part of the magazine title, unlike most of the hero pulps of that period. Fowler began as a young recruit and worked his way to position of inspector.

The first story of his exploits was written under the house name of C.K.M. Scanlon. "C.K.M." were the initials of Cylvia Kleinman Margulies, the wife of Editorial Director Leo Margulies. G. F. Eliot is credited with writing the majority of the Fowler stories as Scanlon, but not all, as many writers found the Standard Magazine group an easy outlet for their work. Several of the authors writing the Phantom Detective tales, for example, contributed to the Dan Fowler episodes.

During the early 1940s, the magazine broke its tradition of series characters appearing under a house name and began giving the actual writers credit for their stories. The name C.K.M. Scanlon was seldom used after that. These credited authors included D. Tracy, J. F. Webb, Stewart Sterling, Norman Daniels, Sam Merwin, Jr., C. Strong, M. W. Wellman, W. Ellsworth, Laurence Donovan, G. T. Fleming-Roberts, E. Churchill, William O'Sullivan, Robert Sidney Bowen, and Richard Foster. Many of these same writers had been, were, or would be involved in many other hero pulp magazines.

The *G-Men* magazine was commenced in October 1935 under the publishing aegis of Beacon Magazines, Inc., and ran for a total of 112 issues, ending with the Winter 1953 issue. Each volume contained three numbers, though there were several errors during the 1941-1942 period which threw off the numbering system. In July 1937, Beacon Magazines became Better Publications, Inc., though still published by Ned Pines.

The publication history, page count, and date system of *G-Men* were very uneven. The magazine was published on a monthly basis from October 1935 until March 1940, at which time it became a bimonthly. In March 1943, it became a quarterly, then in 1946 reverted to a bimonthly for a short period. With the Summer 1949 issue, it was again on a quarterly schedule, and remained so until its termination in 1953. The page count began at 130 pages but by 1938 had been reduced to 114 pages, dropped to 98 pages in 1943, and 82 pages in 1944. It was severely affected by the paper shortage, as were many of the popular magazines during the war years. In 1946 there were 98 pages and by 1947 it was again at 114 pages. One issue, November 1948, even contained 148 pages, counting both sides of the back cover. The Spring 1949 issue had decreased to 130 pages. After the magazine was on a quarterly basis, it would at times date the issue by the season rather than the month, but not always.

There was only one real title change, from *G-Men* to *G-Men Detective* with the March 1940 issue. However, the sole title of *G-Men* was last used on the December 1939 issue; both the January and February 1940 issues contained the subtitle "Detective Stories," printed in smaller type below the actual title. The March 1940 issue dropped the subtitle and elevated "Detective" to be part of the new title.

A British reprint series was responsible for sixteen issues, October 1941 to July 1951.

Information Sources

INDEX SOURCES: None known
LOCATION SOURCES: University of California-Los Angeles Library (1935-1953, 97 issues); private collectors.

Publication History

MAGAZINE TITLE: *G-Men Detective*.
TITLE CHANGES: *G-Men* until March 1940 issue.
VOLUME AND ISSUE DATA: Vol. 1, no. 1 (October 1935) through Vol. 38, no. 3, (Winter 1953); 112 issues.
PUBLISHERS: Beacon Magazines, Inc., then Better Publications, Inc., 22 West 48th Street, New York, New York, and 10 East 40th Street, New York, New York.
EDITOR: Leo Margulies, editorial director.
PRICE PER ISSUE: 10 cents; 15 cents (November 1947); 20 cents (November 1948); 25 cents (Spring 1951).
SIZE AND PAGINATION: 7" X 10"; 82–148 pages (see text).
CURRENT STATUS: Discontinued.
—*Tom Johnson*

G-MEN DETECTIVE (British)

See G-MEN DETECTIVE

GOLDEN LIBRARY OF INDIAN AND DETECTIVE ADVENTURES, THE (British)

The Golden Library of Indian and Detective Adventures was published by the General Publishing Company in 1888 for twelve issues. No information is available, but it is possible the contents were reprints from the U.S. dime novel, *Golden Library* (published by Albert Sibley & Co., New York, in the 1880s).

Information Sources

BIBLIOGRAPHY:

Lofts, W.O.G., and Derek J. Adley. *Old Boys Books, A Complete Catalogue*. London: privately printed, 1969.

INDEX SOURCES: None known.

LOCATION SOURCES: Private collectors.

Publication History

MAGAZINE TITLE: *The Golden Library of Indian and Detective Adventures*.
TITLE CHANGES: None.
VOLUME AND ISSUE DATA: No. 1 (1888) through no. 12 (1888); 12 issues.
PUBLISHER: General Publishing Co., Ltd., London.
EDITOR: Not known.
PRICE PER ISSUE: Not known.
SIZE AND PAGINATION: 5-3/8'' X 7''; 32 pages.
CURRENT STATUS: Discontinued.

GOLD SEAL DETECTIVE

Gold Seal Detective, published from December 1935 through May 1936, was about cops and robbers. For cops, read police of all sorts: police detectives, police lieutenants, police chiefs, G-Men, parole officers. For robbers, read brutal thugs, killers, and underworld gunmen with an insatiable hunger for murder.

It was harsh, rough, unrelenting action. The fiction smashed along, raw, carelessly improbable, throbbing with coarse vigor. Fists slugged, bloody mouths sagged, cars crashed, bodies sprawled, machine guns blasted men apart, hard faces tightened and flaming pistols slammed them down, all was colored by gold badges, scarlet sidewalks, black fury, and purple prose.

Well-known writers ground out these raging fantasies: Norman Daniels, James Perley Hughes, Theodore Tinsley, Frederick C. Painton, and Frederick C. Davis among them. Every other story featured a series character. There was Parole Officer Dan Clark (by David Norman), and two headquarters detectives known as The Crime Busters (by Norman Daniels). James Perley Hughes offered The Ghost, a deadly secret service undercover man, and Clark Aiken (a Frederick C. Davis pseudonym) presented Rough-'em-up-Radigan, a brutal police chief.

Rafael M. DeSoto's March 1936 cover showed a bleeding officer being swooped down upon by two armed thugs. Such was the essence of *Gold Seal Detective*— official determination in the face of peril and .38-caliber justice.

It is a curious testimony to the flexibility of the pulps that this violent magazine, after six issues of masculine bloodshed, seems to have changed its title and editorial policy in a single issue. The final issue of *Gold Seal Detective* (volume 1, number 6 [May 1936]) was followed by *Ace Detective*,* which began with volume 2 and a strong emphasis on "woman interest."[1] That *Gold Seal Detective* was retitled to *Ace Detective* is probable, although not positively confirmed, and the volume 2 continuation certainly suggests that a retitling occurred.

Notes

1. Harriet A. Bradfield, "Markets for Your Stories, Articles, and Novels," *Writers Digest* (August 1936), p. 20. This market article states that "*Ace Detective* is the new title at Magazine Publishers...and seems to succeed *Gold Seal Detective*." The story requirements cited for *Ace Detective* strongly emphasized the need to include women in the fiction.

Information Sources

BIBLIOGRAPHY:
Bradfield, Harriet A. "Markets for Your Stories, Articles, and Novels." *Writers Digest*,
    Vol. 16, no. 9 (August 1936): 20.
INDEX SOURCES: None known.
LOCATION SOURCES: University of California–Los Angeles Library (Vol. 1, no. 1,
    only); private collectors.

Publication History

MAGAZINE TITLE: *Gold Seal Detective*.
TITLE CHANGES: None.
VOLUME AND ISSUE DATA: Vol. 1, no. 1, (December 1935) through Vol. 1, no. 6,
    (May 1936); 6 issues; numbering continued with *Ace Detective*.
PUBLISHER: Magazine Publishers, Inc., 29 Worthington Street, Springfield,
    Massachusetts.
EDITOR: Not known.
PRICE PER ISSUE: 10 cents.
SIZE AND PAGINATION: 7″ X 10″; 128 pages.
CURRENT STATUS: Discontinued.
—*Robert Sampson*

GRAMOL THRILLERS (British)

Gramol Thrillers was published in 1931 for four issues. No other information is available.

Information Sources

BIBLIOGRAPHY:
Lofts, W.O.G., and Derek J.Adley. *Old Boys Books, A Complete Catalogue*. London:
    privately printed, 1969.
INDEX SOURCES: None known.
LOCATION SOURCES: Private collectors.

Publication History

MAGAZINE TITLE: *Gramol Thrillers*.
TITLE CHANGES: None.
VOLUME AND ISSUE DATA: No. 1 (1931) through no. 4 (1931); 4 issues.
PUBLISHERS: Gramol Publishing Co., Ltd., London.
EDITOR: Not known.
PRICE PER ISSUE: Not known.

SIZE AND PAGINATION: Not known.
CURRENT STATUS: Discontinued.

GREAT DETECTIVE

The self-imposed task of *Great Detective* was to publish the best detective-mystery fiction available. And if the word "reprint" was never used, that is what was meant. For nine issues, *Great Detective* carried its standards of quality bravely onward, and, if it failed at last, it was because it bore those standards against the main trend of pulp magazines in 1933.

The detective-mystery pulps of that period were featuring tough, fast-action adventures in contemporary America. *Great Detective* ignored that trend. The 1920s still dominated its pages, and the English mystery was the arbiter of quality.

The first issue, March 1933, presented a concentrated dose of English excellence: a condensed version of Edgar Wallace's 1926 novel, *The Yellow Snake*; a Lord Peter Wimsey short story by Dorothy Sayers; a short story by E. W. Hornung about Tim Erichsen, an Australian bushranger (bandit), this from the 1905 book of short stories, *Stingaree*; and a story by G. K. Chesterton but not a Father Brown mystery. Finally, there was the first of a series about Anna Stuart, a lady pirate, by Mary Edginton; and a story by Sax Rohmer, first of a series titled "The Sins of Severac Bablon," originally published in 1914. The Rohmer series was announced as seven stories long but was gone by the May issue.

Later issues of *Great Detective* moderated the strong English flavor. During the life of the magazine, an interesting and often excellent mix of short stories appeared. Melville Davisson Post had a story in almost every issue. Ellery Queen appeared in the April 1933 issue with "The One Penny Black." There was a Luther Trant story, "The Eleventh Hour," in the May issue; this had previously been reprinted in the March 1930 *Scientific Detective Monthly*.* Agatha Christie's Miss Marple appeared in three stories from "The Tuesday Club Murders" in September, October, and November 1933; all stories had appeared in *Detective Story Magazine* (Street & Smith)* in 1928. The prolific pulp writer J. Allan Dunn was represented. And so was Edgar Allan Poe, whose "Masque of the Red Death" was used in the final issue, November 1933.

As a concession to more modern material, an article series, "Murder Mysteries of New York," by Frank O'Brien, ran in most issues of the magazine.

A serial, "Murder in the Brownstone House," by Wilson Collison, was presented in three parts between April and June. This was followed by Nicolet's "Death of a Bridge Expert," in two parts, August and September; and "The Strange Adventures of the Twelve Coins of Confucius," by Harry Stephen Keeler, in two parts, October and November.

Each issue of *Great Detective* offered these writers and others more obscure. Usually, there was a serial part, seven or eight short stories, and one or two articles. In the final issue, seven "featurettes" were added, these being brief, humorous paragraphs about crime. A department of readers' comment, "With the Reader," was added toward the end of the magazine's existence.

Few magazines were ever published with a plainer cover. It was essentially one color—black, red, or yellow. The title was placed at the top of the cover and again in a vertical strip along the left side. For almost the entire run, the only illustration was that of an oriental-type head in a spiked headdress in the upper-left corner. R. R. Kappel was credited with this design and with the interior illustrations; these were small and square (2" X 3") and were vaguely symbolic— at best, nonrepresentational. The cover for the November 1933 issue was by Boris Chezard and is surrealistic in design.

No issues of *Great Detective* have been noted after November 1933. The magazine was an interesting anthology, superior to most mystery collections of the period, hardcover or otherwise; but the fiction quality did not manage to sustain it.

Information Sources

INDEX SOURCES: None known.
LOCATION SOURCES: University of California–Los Angeles Library (Vol. 1, no. 1); private collectors.

Publication History

MAGAZINE TITLE: *Great Detective*.
TITLE CHANGES: None.
VOLUME AND ISSUE DATA: Vol. 1, no. 1 (March 1933) through Vol. 3, no. 1 (November 1933); 9 issues.
PUBLISHER: L. M. Publishing Company, Inc., 80 Layfette Street, New York, New York, later 545 Fifth Avenue, New York, New York and 4600 Diversey Street, Chicago, Illinois (with editorial offices remaining at 545 Fifth Avenue, New York).
EDITOR: Will Levinrew.
PRICE PER ISSUE: 15 cents.
SIZE AND PAGINATION: 6-7/8" X 9-3/4"; 128 pages.
CURRENT STATUS: Discontinued.
—*Robert Sampson*

GREATER GANGSTER STORIES

Greater Gangster Stories was published at least by December 1933 and as late as the March 1934 issue. No other information is available.

Information Sources

INDEX SOURCES: None known.
LOCATION SOURCES: Private collectors.

Publication History

MAGAZINE TITLE: *Greater Gangster Stories*.
TITLE CHANGES: None known.

VOLUME AND ISSUE DATA: December 1933 and March 1934 issues noted; number
    of issues and extent unknown.
PUBLISHER: Not known.
EDITOR: Not known.
PRICE PER ISSUE: Not known.
SIZE AND PAGINATION: Not known.
CURRENT STATUS: Discontinued.

GREEN GHOST DETECTIVE, THE

See GHOST, SUPER-DETECTIVE, THE

GUILTY

See GUILTY DETECTIVE STORY MAGAZINE

GUILTY DETECTIVE STORY MAGAZINE

Guilty Detective Story Magazine first appeared on the newsstands in July 1956,
a neatly packaged, digest-size magazine that carried every promise on its cover
that the pulp traditions were alive and well. The first issue pictured a partly-clad
blonde, interrupted from a phone call by a suave young buck who was muffling
her screams with one hand and firing a .45 with the other.

It was but one of a large number of digest-size magazines that were only one
step removed from the direct and violent action chronicled in the pulp magazines
of the 1940s. A sense of morality still pervading the times kept the involved
women loose but not erotic, though the brutal strength and sometimes coarse
action could still be found. Everyday people were there, but updated characters
and a more polished presentation provided a level of difference and a possibility
of survival. These magazines have a distinct place in detective literature, having
dominated the detective magazine field for some ten years, peopled with contemporary characters in murder and crime-adventure stories by both veteran and
new authors. Fast action was still the required pace.

"Something about her drove a man to lust and to violence."[1]

"A man must fight for the girl he loves—or live as a coward."[2]

"Augie was marked for death. Even the walls of a prison could bring him
no safety."[3]

"For kids, there's nothing like expensive wheels."[4]

"Killers from the street jungle sent the murder threat."[5]

Damsels in distress graced both the stories and the covers. The content was a cacophony of street people, gang quarrels, and domestic intrigue.

Guilty Detective Story Magazine, published by Feature Publications, was a companion to *Trapped Detective Story Magazine** (introduced a month earlier), published under the trade name of Headline Publications. Both were nearly identical in design and content and were edited by W. W. Scott.

The fiction content normally featured two novelettes and a number of short stories, with no discernible change in the direction of the fiction during its existence. Occasional columns of fact material, such as "What's the Law on That?" by Jose Schorr, the "Police Blotter" (oddities from the underworld) by Harold Helfer, and a number of "strange true cases from police files" by various authors, appeared.

The last two issues were changed: the title was shortened to just *Guilty*, and the title logo was minimized to headline the feature story and give the magazine the appearance of a full-length paperbound book. One or two short stories still were used to fill out the 128 pages. W. W. Scott remained the editor for the entire life of the magazine.

Notes

1. Michael Zuroy, "Man-Trap," *Guilty Detective Story Magazine,* Vol. 6, no. 2 (December 1961), p. 7.

2. Dan Sontup, "No Guts," *Guilty Detective Story Magazine,* Vol. 1, no. 1 (July 1956), p. 54.

3. Warren Shanahan, "The Big Fear," *Guilty Detective Story Magazine,* Vol. 1, no. 2 (November 1956), p. 60.

4. Ron Garret, "Kid Killers in Cadillacs," *Guilty Detective Story Magazine,* Vol. 4, no. 5 (March 1960), p. 82.

5. Ray McKensie, "An Ace of Spades for Death," *Guilty Detective Story Magazine,* Vol. 3, no. 3 (November 1958), p. 75.

Information Sources

INDEX SOURCES: Cook, Michael L. *Monthly Murders*. Westport, Conn.: Greenwood Press, 1982.

LOCATION SOURCES: Private collectors.

Publication History

MAGAZINE TITLE: *Guilty Detective Story Magazine*.

TITLE CHANGES: *Guilty* (last two issues).

VOLUME AND ISSUE DATA: Vol. 1, no. 1 (July 1956) through Vol. 6, no. 4 (June 1962); 32 issues.

PUBLISHER: Feature Publications, Inc., 1 Appleton Street, Holyoke, Massachusetts, with editorial offices at 1790 Broadway, New York 19, New York and later 32 West 22nd Street, New York, New York.

EDITOR: W. W. Scott.

PRICE PER ISSUE: 35 cents.

SIZE AND PAGINATION: 5-3/8'' X 7-3/8''; 128 pages.
CURRENT STATUS: Discontinued.

GUN MOLLS

A publication featuring stories of the underworld, *Gun Molls* was published in the late 1920s by Real Detective Tales, Inc. No other information is available.

Information Sources

INDEX SOURCES: None known.
LOCATION SOURCES: Private collectors.

Publication History

MAGAZINE TITLE: *Gun Molls*.
TITLE CHANGES: None known.
VOLUME AND ISSUE DATA: Number and extent of issues unknown.
PUBLISHER: Real Detective Tales, Inc., New York, New York.
EDITOR: Not known.
PRICE PER ISSUE: Not known.
SIZE AND PAGINATION: Not known.
CURRENT STATUS: Discontinued.

H

HAMILTON T. CAINE'S SHORT STORY NEWSLETTER

Hamilton T. Caine is the creator of Ace Carpenter, a Los Angeles private investigator who appeared in *Mystery* (Mystery Magazine, Inc.)* and several paperback novels, including *Hollywood Heroes* and *Carpenter, Detective*. The first issue of *Hamilton T. Caine's Short Story Newsletter* was announced in the April 1982 issue of *Mystery* but had not been published at the time of this writing. It was slated to be somewhat different from most mystery magazines in that it would contain a short story in each issue and would be published and distributed directly by the author. This has not heretofore been attempted in the mystery field and seldom in other fields.

Information Sources

INDEX SOURCES: None known.
LOCATION SOURCES: Private collectors.

Publication History

MAGAZINE TITLE: *Hamilton T. Caine's Short Story Newsletter*.
TITLE CHANGES: None.
VOLUME AND iSSUE DATA: Announced but not yet published at time of this writing.
PUBLISHER: Hamilton T. Caine, c/o Mystery Magazine, Box 26251, Los Angeles, California 90026.
EDITOR: Hamilton T. Caine.
PRICE PER ISSUE: By subscription only, $10.00 per 12 issues.
SIZE AND PAGINATION: Uninspected; none published to date.
CURRENT STATUS: Active.

HAPPY HOURS MAGAZINE

See DIME NOVEL ROUNDUP

HARDBOILED

Hardboiled was a very early attempt to publish a digest-sized magazine. The first issue appeared in October 1936, on slick paper, and was published by Street & Smith Publications, Inc. No other information is available.

Information Sources

BIBLIOGRAPHY:
Reynolds, Quentin. *The Fiction Factory*. New York: Random House, 1955.
INDEX SOURCES: None known.
LOCATION SOURCES: Private collectors.

Publication History

MAGAZINE TITLE: *Hardboiled*.
TITLE CHANGES: None known.
VOLUME AND ISSUE DATA: No. 1 (October 1936); extent of issues unknown.
PUBLISHER: Street & Smith Publications, Inc., 79 Seventh Avenue, New York, New
     York.
EDITOR: Not known.
PRICE PER ISSUE: Not known.
SIZE AND PAGINATION: Not known.
CURRENT STATUS: Discontinued.

HAUNT OF HORROR, THE

Although the two issues published of *The Haunt of Horror* are borderline to the mystery genre, the inclusion of some stories of mystery content warrants consideration here.

Appearing in June 1973 with a striking cover reminiscent of some of the pulp magazines, the first issue of *The Haunt of Horror* included stories by Robert E. Howard, Harlan Ellison, and Ramsey Campbell, and the first part of "Conjure Wife" by Fritz Leiber, as well as other stories and features. With the second issue, the type style was changed to permit more wordage per page, and there was considerably more illustration, including a cover by Kelly Freas. Len Wein had replaced George Alec Effinger as associate editor, and the promise for succeeding issues was for all new fiction.

Special features included a general article on Atlantis by Lin Carter, an "Author's Page" with biographical information, and announcements of the next issue's contents. The featured story in the second and final issue was "Devil Night" by Dennis O'Neil.

Announcement was made also of a companion magazine, *Vampire Tales*, but it has not been possible to ascertain whether this magazine was actually published or not.

Information Sources

INDEX SOURCES: Schlobin, Roger C. "An Index to the Haunt of Horror." *The Age of the Unicorn*, Vol. 1, no. 1 (April 1979): 5.
Cook, Michael L. *Monthly Murders*. Westport, Conn.: Greenwood Press, 1982.
LOCATION SOURCES: Private collectors.

Publication History

MAGAZINE TITLE: *The Haunt of Horror*.
TITLE CHANGES: None.
VOLUME AND ISSUE DATA: Vol. 1, no. 1 (June 1973) through Vol. 1, no. 2 (August 1973); 2 issues.
PUBLISHER: Stan Lee as Marvel Comics Group, a Division of Cadence Industries Corporation, 575 Madison Avenue, New York, New York 10022.
EDITOR: Gerard Conway; George Alec Effinger, associate editor (no. 1); Len Wein, associate editor (no. 2).
PRICE PER ISSUE: 75 cents.
SIZE AND PAGINATION: 5-1/4" X 7-5/8"; 160 pages.
CURRENT STATUS: Discontinued.

HEADQUARTERS DETECTIVE

Published at least by the early 1930s, *Headquarters Detective* was an A. A. Wyn publication, first under the name of Periodical House, Inc., and later as Magazine Publishers, Inc. (an Ace Fiction group magazine). Authors included G. T. Fleming-Roberts, Donald G. Cooley, H. Frederic Young, Don Cameron, Grant Lane, and many others.

The last issue noted was volume 21, number 1 (March 1937), but the magazine may have been continued beyond that date.

Information Sources

INDEX SOURCES: None known.
LOCATION SOURCES: Private collectors.

Publication History

MAGAZINE TITLE: *Headquarters Detective*.
TITLE CHANGE: None known.
VOLUME AND ISSUE DATA: From circa 1930 to at least Vol. 21, no. 1 (March 1937); number of issues and extent unknown.
PUBLISHER: Periodical House, Inc., 29 Worthington Street, Springfield, Massachusetts, with editorial offices at 23 West 47th Street, New York, New York; later, from same addresses, as Magazine Publishers, Inc.
EDITOR: Not known.

PRICE PER ISSUE: Not known.
SIZE AND PAGINATION: Not known.
CURRENT STATUS: Discontinued.

HEADQUARTERS STORIES

A Hersey magazine, published by the Complete Novel Magazine Company, *Headquarters Stories* was edited by W. M. Clayton in the 1930s. No other information is available.

Information Sources

BIBLIOGRAPHY:
Hersey, Harold B. *Pulpwood Editor*. New York: Frederick A. Stokes Co., 1937.
INDEX SOURCES: None known.
LOCATION SOURCES: Private collectors.

Publication History

MAGAZINE TITLE: *Headquarters Stories*.
TITLE CHANGES: None known.
VOLUME AND ISSUE DATA: 1930s; number of issues and extent unknown.
PUBLISHER: Complete Novel Magazine Co., Inc., New York, New York.
EDITOR: W. M. Clayton.
PRICE PER ISSUE: Not known.
SIZE AND PAGINATION: Not known.
CURRENT STATUS: Discontinued.

HOLLYWOOD DETECTIVE

See DAN TURNER, HOLLYWOOD DETECTIVE

HOLLYWOOD DETECTIVE (British)

See DAN TURNER, HOLLYWOOD DETECTIVE

HOLLYWOOD DETECTIVE MAGAZINE

See DAN TURNER, HOLLYWOOD DETECTIVE

HOLLYWOOD MYSTERY

Hollywood Mystery was a detective pulp title published in 1932. No other information is available.

Information Sources

INDEX SOURCES: None known.

LOCATION SOURCES: Private collectors.

Publication History

MAGAZINE TITLE: *Hollywood Mystery*.
TITLE CHANGES: None known.
VOLUME AND ISSUE DATA: 1932; number of issues, specific date, and extent unknown.
PUBLISHER: Not known.
EDITOR: Not known.
PRICE PER ISSUE: Not known.
SIZE AND PAGINATION: Not known.
CURRENT STATUS: Discontinued.

HOLMESIAN FEDERATION, THE

Signe Landon announced the creation of *The Holmesian Federation* by means of a flyer in January 1978. "This is a 'zine," she wrote, "dedicated to the proposition that Mixing Myths Is an Important Part of Living. (Never let it be said that I discriminated on the basis of a deerstalker cap. . .or a pair of pointed ears. . . .)"[1]

The Holmesian Federation has gone where no magazine has gone before by daring to combine the universes of Sherlock Holmes and "Star Trek" through articles, stories, poetry, and artwork, humorous and serious. It holds the unofficial most irregularly published fanzine award, appearing roughly every two years.

The idea had its conception in the early summer of 1977. Signe planned on bringing out the first issue in March 1978 but by April of that year realized she would not be able to meet her self-imposed deadline. The delay was caused by a number of unexpected problems. The trials and tribulations of her involvement with another publication, *The Other Side of Paradise* (number 3), coedited by Amy Falkowitz and Signe Landon, was one of these. Other problems were her getting a full-time job early in 1978, "general laziness," and the fact that the authors of what were meant to be the main stories were considerably behind schedule.

For example, "The Adventure of the Master Thief" by Melanie Rawn, planned for inclusion in the first issuee of *The Holmesian Federation*, was a superbly intricate Holmes story, which for a year had been a few pages short of completion. Rawn, for various reasons, was unable to finish it. The other intended story, "The Adventure of the Snatch in Time," was a collaboration between Landon and Frankie Jemison which almost made it. After taking a good look at the tale, they realized it would need rewriting; it was shelved. The loss of these two stories considerably lessened the planned size of the magazine; and if there had not been unexpected submissions from two other authors, there would not have been a magazine at all.

The offset-printed, digest-sized first issue eventually appeared in November 1978, nine months late. Due to the decreaed size and, hence, decreased printing costs, Landon refunded one dollar to everyone who ordered first-class mailing and mailed out all copies by that mode.

The Holmesian Federation, number 1, contained among other items "A Study in Harlots" by Frankie Jemison, a shocking account of the real circumstances surrounding the meeting of Holmes and Dr. Watson. The study by Priscilla Pollner, "Holmes Was a Vulcan," and several excellent illustrations by Editor Landon were also included.

Landon was unsure there would ever be a second issue. "When I first started this project, over 18 months ago," she wrote in her editorial in the first issue, "it was because people were practically leaping out of the woodwork with fascinating ideas for stories combining two of my favorite universes, Star Trek and Holmes. But one by one, the writers discovered that, if Holmes himself is difficult to write convincingly, writing Holmes and the ST characters convincingly, in the same story, is well-nigh impossible. So—the existence of *HF #2* will depend solely on the number of acceptable submissions I receive within the next year or so."[2]

Letters received were quite favorable, and there were many enthusiastic responses to the announcement of a second issue. In May 1980 Landon had once again announced by flyer that an issue was in the works. This second issue finally appeared in October 1980, almost two years after the first issue. Partial contents included "The Mysterious Lodger" by R. Merrill Bollerud and "The Adventure of the Missing Monolith" by Eileen Ray.

Surprisingly, this magazine has been ignored by *The Baker Street Journal** and the *Baker Street Miscellanea,** never having been mentioned in the latter two publications' respective review columns. Landon accounted for this in personal correspondence: "It could just be that they have a large number of publications to review, and so concentrate mostly on the professional ones. Or it could be a bit of prejudice—it is not, after all, straight Holmes, but an admittedly weird hybrid, with a small (but very loyal!) audience."[3]

Most of the authors to date in *The Holmesian Federation* have sought to combine Sherlock Holmes and the "Star Trek" characters by transferring the latter group, by ingenious means, into the Victorian past. A notable exception has been the series begun by Dana Martin Batory in the first issue with "A Nostalgic Country of the Mind," followed by "Everything Comes in Circles," "Xenolith," and "Quadrumvirate" in the second issue. These stories place Holmes and Watson as active detectives in the far future.

The Holmesian Federation issue numbers 3 and 4 have been announced.

Notes

1. Flyer, advertising the forthcoming publication of *The Holmesian Federation* (January 1978).
2. Editorial comment, *The Holmesian Federation,* no. 1 (1978), p. 2.
3. Correspondence between Dana Martin Batory and Signe Landon (1981).

Information Sources

INDEX SOURCES: None known.

LOCATION SOURCES: Private collectors.

Publication History

MAGAZINE TITLE: *The Holmesian Federation.*
TITLE CHANGE: None.
VOLUME AND ISSUE DATA: No. 1 (November 1978) through no. 2 (to date, October 1980); 2 issues.
PUBLISHER: Signe Landon, 591 Northwest Witham, Corvallis, Oregon 97330.
EDITOR: Signe Landon.
PRICE PER ISSUE: $3.00.
SIZE AND PAGINATION: 5-1/4'' X 8-1/2''; 63–86 pages.
CURRENT STATUS: Active, irregular.
—*Dana Martin Batory*

HOMICIDE DETECTIVE STORY MAGAZINE

Homicide Detective Story Magazine, and its change of title, *Killers Mystery Story Magazine*, represent the transitional period between the pulp-style detective fiction of the 1940s and early 1950s, and the more polished and sophisticated crime fiction of the 1960s. Stories published in these two magazines seem reluctant to give up the conniving citizen or hoodlum with equally conniving female characters, but they do present more contemporary prose describing law officers and detectives with a more favorable approach and with a more complex, yet natural, environment. Yet at the same time, one cannot help but notice that the fast action, attitudes, and slang of the pulps is just over one's shoulder. While still espousing fast action, violence, murder, and mayhem both on the street and at home, the short fiction here is more entertaining and believable.

While many of the contributing authors are also found in the pulps, *Homicide Detective Story Magazine* was a showcase for new and developing writers. Stories may be found here by such as W. T. Ballard, John D. MacDonald, William Campbell Gault, Charles Beckman, Jr., H. A. DeRosso, Talmage Powell, Henry Slesar, Edward D. Hoch, Joseph Commings, and others.

The first two issues of *Homicide Detective Story Magazine* featured a new story by John D. MacDonald, "Stop, Look and Die," about Rufe Donall, chief of homicide, who "has brought in his last four suspects thoroughly dead."[1] A.W.T. Ballard story, "Don't Turn Me In," is a story of havoc caused by both blondes and horses; and the temptation of a million dollars is the basis for "A Time to Kill" by William Campbell Gault, among the other stories.

As is compatible with other magazines published by Everett M. Arnold (Arnold Magazines, Inc.), *Homicide Detective* had no articles, editorials, announcements, or filler material, and no advertising except on the back covers. The front covers graphically depicted damsels in extreme danger.

After two issues, in an attempt to gain more newsstand attention, the title was changed to *Killers Mystery Story Magazine* in January 1957. The format and content remained without change. The first issue of *Killers* featured "Tooth of the Dragon" by George Wallace Sayre; and three of the short stories should be noted: "Corpse for a Day" by Talmage Powell, "All in the Mind" by Norman Struber, and "The Second Jury" by Henry Slesar. The last two issues of the magazine, under the *Killers* title, included an exceptional story by Edward D. Hoch, "The Naked Corpse," and Carl Milton's "The Death Driver."

No further issues were published, indicating that sales did not justify continuation. The late 1950s was a time when only the well-established titles were surviving.

Note

1. John D. MacDonald, "Stop, Look and Die," *Homicide Detective Story Magazine,* no. 1 (September 1956), p. 31.

Information Sources

INDEX SOURCES: Cook, Michael L. *Monthly Murders*. Westport, Conn.: Greenwood Press, 1982.
LOCATION SOURCES: Private collectors.

Publication History

MAGAZINE TITLE: *Homicide Detective Story Magazine*.
TITLE CHANGE: *Killers Mystery Story Magazine* (with issue no. 3).
VOLUME AND ISSUE DATA: No. 1 (September 1956) through no. 4 (March 1957); 4 issues.
PUBLISHER: Everett M. Arnold as Arnold Magazines, Inc., 1 Appleton Street, Holyoke, Massachusetts, with editorial offices at 303 Lexington Avenue, New York, New York; associate publisher; Marilyn Mayes.
EDITOR: Alfred Grenet.
PRICE PER ISSUE: 35 cents.
SIZE AND PAGINATION: 5-3/8" X 7-3/8"; 130 pages.
CURRENT STATUS: Discontinued.

HOODED DETECTIVE

Although this was a single-character, pulp-hero magazine, at a time when such were popular, it was never a success. The magazine first appeared late in 1941 under the title *Black Hood Detective*, with the first (and only) issue under that title designated as volume 2, number 6. It is believed, but not confirmed, that the numbering was a continuation of *Detective Yarns,** which had been discontinued in April 1941 with volume 2, number 5. Research in the other Blue Ribbon/Columbia Publications detective pulps reveals no other magazines that would meet the date and discontinuance pattern.

The second issue was published under a slightly different title, *Hooded Detective*. The magazine was terminated after a total of three issues under the two titles.

The Black Hood, a creation of G. T. Fleming-Roberts, was a policeman who despaired of the orthodox means of law enforcement and was determined to solve crimes by whatever means was necessary—including breaking and entering, assault, extortion, and kidnapping. But the lack of supernatural or eccentric shading in these stories doomed them to be second-rate, at best, and they failed to meet the competition.

Each issue contained from four to six short stories in addition to the featured novel of The Black Hood.

There was at least one issue of this title published by Gerald Swan as a British reprint.

Information Sources

INDEX SOURCES: Weinberg, Robert, and Lohr McKinstry. *The Hero Pulp Index.* Evergreen, Colo.: Opar Press, 1971.
LOCATION SOURCES: Private collectors.

Publication History

MAGAZINE TITLE: *Hooded Detective.*
TITLE CHANGES: *Black Hood Detective* (first issue), probably a continuation from *Detective Yarns* but not confirmed.
VOLUME AND ISSUE DATA: Vol. 2, no. 6 (September [?] 1941) through Vol. 3, no. 2 (January 1942); 3 issues.
PUBLISHER: Columbia Publications, Inc., 1 Appleton Street, Holyoke, Massachusetts, with editorial offices at 60 Hudson Street, New York, New York.
EDITOR: Not known.
PRICE PER ISSUE: 10 cents.
SIZE AND PAGINATION: 7'' X 10''; 96 pages.
CURRENT STATUS: Discontinued.

HOODED DETECTIVE (British)

See HOODED DETECTIVE

HORROR STORIES

Within a year of the new look of *Dime Mystery Book,** the weird-menace number dated October 1933, Popular Publications issued a companion magazine, *Terror Tales.* Its first issue was September 1934. Four months later, a third Popular entry, *Horror Stories*, hit the newsstands. Both *Terror Tales* and *Horror Stories* carried a fifteen-cent price tag, although, essentially, they were little different from *Dime Mystery.* At first monthlies, they soon became bimonthly; and since they were published on alternate months, to all intent, they were one magazine with two titles–but with many different editors.

Rogers Terrill, who had come to Popular Publications from Fiction House, served as editorial director of *Terror Tales, Horror Stories,* and several other titles. Under him, various editors had the responsibility for individual titles, not necessarily in editorial rapport. In fact, it sometimes seemed that the right hand did not know what the left one was doing. Thus *Horror Stories*, which was a relatively late arrival as far as weird-menace material went, blurbed in its inaugural issue that it was the answer to "the thousands who have long asked for and awaited such a magazine." To paraphrase George Orwell: "Every one is unique, only some are more unique than others."[1]

In the trade press at the time, the stories appearing in the three publications became known as "Terrill Tales." As a counterpart to *Dime Mystery*'s legend, "The Weirdest Stories Ever Told," *Terror Tales* billed itself as "The Magazine of Eerie Fiction," while *Horror Stories* presented "Stories That Thrill and Chill."

These, as well as other magazines published by the company, featured an arresting design on covers and spines: a "PP" with the first "P" reversed. Henry Steeger, publisher, has noted that he had it adapted from the insignia of the Plaza Hotel in New York City. As a symbol for the weird-menace covers, it was especially appropriate. From a short distance, the two *P*'s resembled a skull, although, apparently, the company did not realize this and has not commented on it.

Not only was the fiction in the three magazines similar, but the editors' page in each had a familiar ring. Apparently, a concomitant of the job, no matter who was involved with the magazine at the time, was to point out that fiction was no stranger than truth. Repeatedly, the editors passed along brief reports on some particular outlandish crime gleaned from the newspapers—to support the thesis that Popular's authors were only reflecting the real world in an imaginative way.

What the authors were really doing was conforming to the Gothic style set by *Dime Mystery*, featuring a hero and heroine menaced by a particularly revolting creature who is unmasked at the end, with some sexual titillation thrown in along the way. This type of presentation became known as "weird menace." Some of the successful authors found in the early issues were Arthur Leo Zagat, Hugh B. Cave, Wyatt Blassingame, Frances Bragg Middleton, and Wayne Rogers.

Blassingame was one of the few authors in this group who took time out from writing fiction to write about it. He had worked out a pattern for his plot complications, which he explained in a trade journal. Essentially, what he devised as a guide could be applied to much of the weird-menace fiction then appearing. It took the form of two main themes, with variations (not necessarily used together in the same story): (1) a character flees from a menace, is finally overtaken, then overcomes his adversary, and (2) the hero and heroine are trapped in a room at night, with the walls closing in, or a dire menace approaching, and the hero frantically searches for a way out.

The same settings from the stories in *Dime Mystery* appeared in *Horror Stories* and *Terror Tales*: secret passages, hidden dungeons, mysterious caves, and that oldest and most abused of standbys, the apparently deserted house that in reality is a haven for all sorts of foul fiends. An outstanding example of utilizing these props to advantage is found in Arthur J. Burks's "Six Doors to Horror" *(Terror*

Tales, March 1935). Here are: a mysterious, shuttered house; doors that close by themselves; a crypt with a corpse; and an evil entity eager for a spectral mating with the heroine. Burks, incidentally, was one of the most prolific pulpsters of the period, ranking with H. Bedford-Jones (who would keep two or three stories going at the same time on different typewriters) and Max Brand, all million-words-a-year producers.

Terrill defined horror as what a girl would feel if she watched a diabolical rite from a safe distance. Terror is what she would feel if she knew she was to be the next victim. The definitions are interesting and apt but not necessarily appropriate to each of the publications since the material in each was interchangeable. Most of the stories hewed to Terrill's earlier admonition that there must be a logical resolution—a conformance he had set for *Dime Mystery*'s contents. But there are many examples in all three magazines of out-and-out supernatural stories. Burks's effort was one. And authors such as Blassingame and Paul Ernst, among others, frequently turned to fantasy. Some fine efforts were produced. Unfortunately, few have seen the light of day since.

Popular's most prolific cover artist in the weird-menace line was John Newton Howitt. Older than most of his contemporaries, Howitt was in his fifties when he was rendering covers for *Horror Stories, Terror Tales, Operator #5,** and *The Spider*.* Interestingly, Popular spelled his last name "Howitt" on early covers and "Howett" on the later ones. Yet an announcement years later for a showing of his landscapes spelled it "Howitt." William Papalia's appreciation of the artist, in *Xenophile*'s* Pulpcon 6 dedication issue, praises the subtlety he used in his terrifying conceptions and his ability to make the viewer cringe. By the time both *Horror Stories* and *Terror Tales* began more fully exploiting sex-sadism, in the 1937 period, Howitt's covers reflected the "nude" look. His depiction of a helpless female submerged in an icy bath, ready to be frozen by a leering scientist *(Horror Stories*, August-September 1937), is typical of the cover style prevailing then.

With the focus on a more provocative presentation, "hell-spawned abominations" did not provide the menace any longer. Instead, a more direct exploitation of women took place, women under the sway of strange forces, driven by dark yearnings. Two examples by Wayne Rogers reflect this trend. In "The Mummy Pack Prowls Again," a horrible affliction turns healthy women into shriveled creatures. In "Beast-Women Stalk at Night," nude, ravening women lope after their victims with the ferociousness of wolves. Many of the stories during this period gave graphic descriptions of victims being tortured—usually women. In this setting, an author such as Donald Graham could fashion a literally vicious bacchanal of circus freaks revolting, to wreak havoc on fair maidens, and thus reinforce the weird-menace assumption that the more misshapen and misanthropic a creature is, the more evil he would be.

Several themes either emerged during this period or were given greater attention. One of the more appealing (if you were a male reader, and most were) was the femme fatale, perhaps best exemplified by the urbane Ralston Shields.

He developed what might be termed a miniseries: stories of a similar nature in which the temptress ensnares the hero by seemingly occult means and is finally unmasked as a schemer after money. Another unusual presentation was the science fiction story with sexual overtones—certainly a refreshing departure from some of the stodgy treatises.

As the 1930s drew to a close, Popular Publications phased out sex-sadism. With the likes of the "Little Flower," (Mayor LaGuardia of New York), comstocking about in search of newsstand "filth," the heat was on, and publishers began cleaning up their products. *Horror Stories* and *Terror Tales* prudently put the clothes back on their ladies and took the sex out of their stories. Except for a few examples, the emasculated result had little to recommend it. One author who stands out in this final purgative period is W. Wayne Robbins, whose real name was Ormond Gregory and whose brother, Dane Gregory, also wrote for Popular Publications. He can be contrasted to Wayne Rogers as a delineator of the male obsessed, rather than the female. He penned several stories, told in the first person, by a man apparently deranged and committing all sorts of atrocities. With no letup in intensity, these Freudian nightmares were unlike anything before or since.

Popular Publications, with Henry Steeger at the helm, continued to produce pulps through the forties and fifties, at the same address on East 42nd Street in New York City it had occupied during the thirties—surely a longevity record among pulp publishers. In all, the company published sixty-one original titles, twenty-six titles under imprints other than Popular, and fourteen titles bought from other publishers during its thirty-plus years in the business.

At least two issues of *Terror Tales* were published in a British reprint series.

Note

1. George Orwell, *Animal Farm* (New York: Harcourt Brace Jovanovich, 1974), p. 197.

Information Sources

BIBLIOGRAPHY:

Day, Bradford M., ed. *The Complete Checklist of Science-Fiction Magazines*. New York: Science-Fiction & Fantasy Publishers, 1961.
Hardin, Nils. "An Interview with Henry Steeger." *Xenophile*, no. 33 (July 1977): 3–18.
————, and George Hocutt. "A Checklist of Popular Publications Titles 1930–1955." *Xenophile*, no. 33, (July 1977): 21–24.
Hersey, Harold. *Pulpwood Editor*. New York: Frederick A. Stokes Co., 1937.
Jones, Robert Kenneth. *The Shudder Pulps*. West Linn, Ore.: Fax Collector's Editions, 1975.
————. "The Weird Menace Magazines." *Bronze Shadows*, no. 10 (June 1967): 3–8; no. 11 (August 1967): 7–13; no. 12 (October 1967): 7–10; no. 13 (January 1968): 7–12; no. 14 (March 1968): 13–17; no. 15 (November 1968): 4–8.
Papalia, William. "John Newton Howitt, American Artist/Illustrator." *Xenophile*, no. 33 (July 1977): 87–88.

INDEX SOURCES: None known.
LOCATION SOURCES: University of California–Los Angeles Library (*Terror Tales,* Vol. 1, no. 2 only); private collectors.

Publication History

MAGAZINE TITLE: (1) *Horror Stories,* (2) *Terror Tales.*
TITLE CHANGES: None.
VOLUME AND ISSUE DATA: (1) *Horror Stories,* Vol. 1, no. 1 (January 1935) through Vol. 11, no. 1 (April 1941); 41 issues. (2) *Terror Tales,* Vol. 1, no. 1 (September 1934) through Vol. 13, no. 3 (March 1941); 51 issues.
PUBLISHER: Popular Publications, Inc., 2256 Grove Street, Chicago, Illinois, with editorial offices at 205 East 42nd Street, New York, New York.
EDITORS: Rogers Terrill (1935–1939); Loring Dowst (1939); Steve Farrell (1940–1941).
PRICE PER ISSUE: 15 cents.
SIZE AND PAGINATION: 7" X 9-3/4"; 112–128 pages.
CURRENT STATUS: Discontinued.
—*Robert Kenneth Jones*

HUNTED DETECTIVE STORY MAGAZINE

The pulp magazines, in their last dying throes of the 1950s, spawned a number of digest-size magazines that carried on the same tradition as those of the 1940s— fast-action episodes of murder and mayhem, usually centering on women caught in the snare of unsavory characters. *Hunted Detective Story Magazine* and *Pursuit Detective Story Magazine,** (*Hunted's* companion, published in alternate months by Star Publications) were two of these magazines. *Pursuit* came first in September 1953, and was joined by *Hunted* in December 1954. They were, in essence, the same magazine with two titles.

The first issue of *Hunted*—behind a cover picturing an apprehensive maiden in a trenchcoat being followed by a threatening hatted character down a foggy, mean, factory street—promised "all-new stories by best mystery writers."[1] The featured story was "The Wife-Swap Murder" by Elston Barrett. Robert Turner ("Violent Night") and Richard Deming ("Summer Boarder") contributed novelettes, and four short stories and three true-crime articles filled in the rest of the magazine.

In tough, contemporary prose, the stories told of exploding trouble, domestic situations, love triangles, greed, and avarice, peopled with coarse characters somewhat less than realistic. Sex, although present, was muted. In short, these were fast-moving, sometimes rough, episodes of crime adventure in which a detective was not usually the main character. Unforeseen events and cupidity was the normal ending.

No change was apparent in the style or type of story throughout the run of *Hunted Detective Story Magazine,* twelve issues. The titles of some of the featured novelettes illustrate this: "The Blond Eye" by Michael Morgan (June 1955), "Final Terror" by Bryce Walton (August 1955), "Hang Me High" by

L. J. Gearhart (December 1955), "The Naked Terror" by Bryce Walton (June 1956), and "Cold Blood" by Ray Fulbright (August 1956). The central theme running through a majority of the stories seemed to be based on the adage, "deadlier than the male," and although many of the females were polished predecators, they were still unrealistic.

Hunted Detective Story Magazine ceased publication with the October 1956 issue; *Pursuit* became past history with the November 1956 issue. Pulp-style fiction, even in digest-size magazines, was hard-pressed for readers, and the wheel was slowly turning to the mystery/detective story where plot and characterization were the required factors.

Note

1. Cover slogan, *Hunted Detective Story Magazine*, no. 1 (December 1954).

Information Sources

INDEX SOURCES: Cook, Michael L., *Monthly Murders*. Westport, Conn.: Greenwood Press, 1982.
LOCATION SOURCES: Private collectors.

Publication History

MAGAZINE TITLE: *Hunted Detective Story Magazine*.
TITLE CHANGES: None.
VOLUME AND ISSUE DATA: No. 1 (December 1954) through no. 12 (October 1956); 12 issues.
PUBLISHER: Star Publications, Inc., 1 Appleton Street, Holyoke, Massachusetts, with editorial offices at 545 Fifth Avenue, New York 17, New York; publisher, J. A. Kramer for first 9 issues, Leonard B. Cole for last 3 issues.
EDITORS: Leonard B. Cole, editor, and Phyllis Faren, associate editor, for first 9 issues; George Peltz, editor, and Kit Carroll, associate editor, for last 3 issues.
PRICE PER ISSUE: 35 cents.
SIZE AND PAGINATION: 5⅜" X 7¼"; 128 pages.
CURRENT STATUS: Discontinued.

I

ILLUSTRATED DETECTIVE MAGAZINE, THE

Late in 1929, as paper profits melted and a sickly cold sensation gripped those who had bought on margin, the counters of Woolworth's 5 & 10¢ Store overflowed with stacks of a new magazine. Titled *The Illustrated Detective Magazine*, it was a big, smooth, bright-covered, slick-paper publication devoted to mystery fiction.

The magazine was densely illustrated. Fiction and departments were enlivened by water colors, pencil sketches, cartoons, pen-and-ink renderings, and, mixed with these, large photographs—often spreading across two pages—showing professional models posed in reenactment of story scenes. Artwork saturated *Illustrated Detective* as art saturated other slick paper magazines such as *Saturday Evening Post, Colliers, Ladies' Home Journal,* and *Woman's Home Companion*. With these last two magazines, *Illustrated Detective* had a deep affinity. For not only was it a slick-paper mystery magazine, it was also a magazine directed to the tastes and interests of women.

The fiction emphasized the woman's point of view, was often narrated by a woman, and featured as many feminine as masculine detectives. In the rear of the magazine flowered all the usual departments of a more conventional woman's publication. These offered instruction in makeup, clever meal menus, techniques of sewing and canning, and other such essential arts. Advertisements praised mascara, lipstick, face powders, Paris garters, Tintex and Linit, and that superb children's magazine, *Tiny Tower*.

That this magazine would publish much fiction of interest seems improbable. But without effort, it contrived to be superb. *Illustrated Detective* selected outstanding writers who had made their mark in the 1920s and mingled these with rising writers of the 1930s. Over the years, the magazine would publish work by top names in the mystery field, including Ellery Queen, Stuart Palmer, Sax Rohmer, Arnold Kummer, Hulbert Footner, Vincent Starrett, and H. Bedford-Jones. The fiction was polished, often strongly compressed, and good enough for a large amount of it to appear later between book covers.

The magazine appeared monthly for almost six years, sixty-nine issues, at ten cents a copy. After three years, the title was changed to *The Mystery Magazine*, the name formally appearing on the table of contents. On the cover, however, it declared itself simply *Mystery* in large colored type, with the old subtitle, "The Illustrated Mystery Magazine," shrunk to tiny letters. Facts concerning its distribution are few, but, in addition to being offered through Woolworth's, it was made available on the newsstands from 1934 to the final issue.

Covers were tasteful, bright, and uneventful, relying heavily on the faces of self-confident women. Inside was an astonishing amount of material: eight to ten pieces of fiction, four or more crime-fact articles, and up to ten continuing departments (about half of these slanted directly toward women). When the magazine was at its peak in the early 1930s, it offered material carefully calculated to appeal to most tastes and both sexes.

A typical 1933 issue opened with a classic mystery novel told in pictures and intensely summarized prose. Books of three hundred to four hundred pages were routinely dealt with in five pages of large type and pictures. The titles selected were awesome: *Monsieur Lecoq* by Emile Gaboriau (June 1933), *The Mysteries of Paris* by Eugene Sue (September 1933), *Barnaby Ridge* by Charles Dickens (November 1933), *Black Tulip* by Alexander Dumas (April 1934), and *The Big Bow Mystery* by Israel Zangwell (May 1934).

In addition to these illustrated condensations, each issue of *Mystery* contained a short novel ("A New $2.00 Book-Length Novel") by writers such as Stuart Palmer, Walter Ripperger, Charles Dutton, William Garrett, or Mignon Eberhart. The novel was often accompanied by a serial part, although serials seemed to disappear as the magazine moved into 1934.

The chief glory of *The Mystery Magazine* was its short fiction. Sax Rohmer, H. Bedford-Jones, Albert Payson Terhune, William Corcoran, and Henry LaCossitt frequently appeared. The line between short fiction and serials was not well drawn, and stories featuring series characters had a tendency to develop into episodic novels. There were many series characters. A few had previously appeared in other magazines. Several of the others were first featured in a novel, then returned in at least one short story.

Thus Simeon Graves (a private investigator much consulted by the police) was featured in "The Weird Murder of Mr. Carn" (July 1933), a novel by Walter Ripperger, and returned in "Murder Men of Molokai" (November 1933), a short story. The July 1933 issue also featured the first part of a four-installment serial, "The Adventure of the Queen Bee," which introduced no less a personage than Shirley Holmes, daughter of Sherlock Holmes. Shirley was helped by her charming friend, Joan Watson, daughter of the famous doctor. Both Sherlock and Dr. Watson drifted through the proceedings, which were adapted by Frederic

Arnold Kummer from a London play. Shirley Holmes swiftly reappeared in a December 1933 short story, "The Canterbury Cathedral Murder."

Precisely the same thing happened to Hildegarde Withers, the extraordinary schoolteacher and investigative genius. After the novel, "Murder on the Blackboard" (September 1933), by Stuart Palmer, she returned in a series of short stories that included "The Riddle of the Dangling Pearl" (November 1933), "The Riddle of the Flea Circus" (December 1933), and "The Riddle of the Yellow Canary" (April 1934).

Numerous other series characters brightened the short fiction. Hulbert Footner brought over his dazzling Madame Storey from *Argosy* (where she had detected since 1932, "specializing in the feminine"). In *Mystery Magazine,* she starred in a short story series that ran from July 1933 to May of the following year. During part of that time, Jacques Futrelle's classic detective, The Thinking Machine, was revived in some new short stories: "The Man Who Was Lost" (September 1933) and "The Knife" (October 1933). These seem actually to have been written by Donald Rush since Futrelle had died years before in the 1912 Titanic disaster.

Ellery Queen began a series of stories in April 1934. These were later included in his first short story collection, *The Adventures of Ellery Queen.* The initial story was "The Lame Men" (April 1934), followed by five others through October 1934. (An earlier Queen adventure had appeared in *Mystery* in May 1933, "The Adventure of the Teakwood Case.")

Both the April and May 1934 issues also contained Vincent Starrett's stories of the elegant Chicago investigator, Jimmie Lavender ("The Phantom Flute Player" and "The Body in the Ostrich Cage"). But of series characters, there was no end. Only a few can be squeezed in at this point: John Cabot, The Man with the Rubber Face, by H. Bedford-Jones (early 1933); the modern Raffles, Riley Dillon, whose exploits, by Rodney Blake, continued through 1933 and 1934. You also found The Collegiate Detectives, Judy and Jerry (in late 1933), by Arnold Fredericks (that is, F. A. Kummer). And there were Mark Harrell, the Taxi Detective, by William Corcoran, and Nurse Keate by Mignon G. Eberhart. Each of these characters appeared, adventured a few issues, and was replaced by others.

Mystery was as rich in continuing departments as continuing series characters. Each month, "The Line-Up" offered multiple pages of readers' letters. "I Go Sleuthing" related the detective experiences of other readers and offered one hundred dollars monthly for the best contribution published. The "Rogue's Almanac" gave important dates in the history of crime. And the "Crime Puzzle" laid out a mysterious case in photographs and text and paid twenty-five dollars for the best solution. By 1935, most of these departments had been replaced by special features and true-crime articles.

In January 1935, the size of the magazine was increased to an astonishing 10-5/8" X 13-1/2." Pages were reduced to eighty-eight. The covers, by John Atherton, depicted apprehensive girls' faces set against stylized backgrounds, such as old houses, wharfs, and other eerie places. Inside the magazine, even more photographs were used in layouts often cluttered and confused. Each issue introduced more true articles, up to six of them, including an article series by Theodore Dreiser titled "I Find the Real American Tragedy." Five to eight short stories and a novel were still provided. Serials were dropped. Almost a completely new cadre of writers provided the fiction. They included some names familiar from the slick magazines: Norman Matson, Octavus Roy Cohen, Carl Clausen, Elisabeth Sanxay Holding, Edward Hale Bierstadt, C. Daly King. . . . always, their work was technically finished and smoothly directed toward the feminine reader. Although an October issue was announced, it is believed that the final issue of *The Mystery Magazine* was dated September 1935; however, this has not been verified.

Mystery was as meticulously planned as an orchestral score. Its careful variations played upon every shade of reader interest. It was consciously polished, self-consciously feminine. A curious pared sound rang in its fiction, as if the stories had been edited with a chain saw, but the prose flashed with a bright nickel glitter. Slick the magazine may have been, and often overillustrated, but it was also considerably interesting and, for years, excellent.

Information Sources

BIBLIOGRAPHY:
Nevins, Francis M., Jr. *Royal Bloodline: Ellery Queen, Author and Detective.* Bowling Green, Ohio: Bowling Green University Popular Press, 1974.
INDEX SOURCES: None known.
LOCATION SOURCES: The Library of Congress (complete run); private collectors.

Publication History

MAGAZINE TITLE: *The Illustrated Detective Magazine.*
TITLE CHANGES: *The Mystery Magazine* (with Vol. 6, no. 6 [December 1932]).
VOLUME AND ISSUE DATA: Vol. 1, no. 1 (1929) through Vol. 12, no. 3 (September 1935); believed 69 issues.
PUBLISHER: Tower Magazines, Inc., Washington & South Avenues, Dunellen, New Jersey, later 4600 Diversey Avenue, Chicago, Ilinois.
EDITORS: Hugh Weir, editorial director (1933–1934); Durbin Lee Horner, managing editor (1935); K. W. Hutchinson.
PRICE PER ISSUE: 10 cents.
SIZE AND PAGINATION: 8-3/8" X 11-5/8" (1933–1934); 10-5/8" X 13-1/2" (1935); 88–138 pages.
CURRENT STATUS: Discontinued.
—*Robert Sampson*

INSPECTOR MALONE'S MYSTERY MAGAZINE

Inspector Malone's Mystery Magazine, with its first issue, announced it would carry detective and mystery stories "carefully selected and edited by Inspector

Malone, of Homicide, to cater to the readers seeking relaxation with well-written and unusual fiction."[1]

The first issue was dated September–October 1945 and featured a cover illustrating the principal story, "The Streamliner Mystery," by Mindret Lord. "Inspector Malone" introduced this story with the comment that Mindret Lord was "one of the handiest men I knew with a typewriter. . .a few of the magazines which have used his stories [are] *The New Yorker, Saturday Evening Post, American Magazine, Liberty, This Week, American Home, Mademoiselle,* and many others. . . . [S]ome of his motion picture stories [are] 'The Glass Alibi' and 'You'll Remember Me'. . .and radio plots have been used in such outstanding programs as 'Suspense,' 'F.B.I. in Peace and War,' 'The Saint,' 'Michael Shayne'. . .and many others."[2] Lord collaborated with Isabel Garland for another story, "The Terrible Detective" (as by "Garland Lord") in this issue. Other stories in this first issue were by Dennis Rohlfing, Walter Gerling, Walt Knight, and Philip Shaw.

Although announced as a quarterly, the first issue was the only one published.

Notes

1. Masthead, title page, *Inspector Malone's Mystery Magazine*, no. 1 (September/October 1945), p. 3.

2. Introduction to featured story, "The Streamliner Mystery," *Inspector Malone's Mystery Magazine,* no. 1 (September/October 1945), p. 48.

Information Sources

INDEX SOURCES: Cook, Michael L. *Monthly Murders*. Westport, Conn.: Greenwood
 Press, 1982.
LOCATION SOURCES. Private collectors.

Publication History

MAGAZINE TITLE: *Inspector Malone's Mystery Magazine.*
TITLE CHANGES: None.
VOLUME AND ISSUE DATA: No. 1 (September–October 1945); 1 issue.
PUBLISHER: James H. Wood as Ver Halen Publications, 6960 Sunset Boulevard, Hol-
 lywood 28, California.
EDITOR: "Inspector Malone."
PRICE PER ISSUE: 25 cents.
SIZE AND PAGINATION: 5-1/4" X 8"; 98 pages.
CURRENT STATUS: Discontinued.

INTRIGUE

The editor announced *Intrigue* with this comment: "This is the age of the spy—in fact and fiction. The same day that Americans queue up to see the latest James Bond movie, the F.B.I. announces the apprehension of a former U.S. soldier who admits spying for the Russians. Of the two, we think you'll agree that the fictional espionage agent is more interesting. And that's what this magazine will devote itself to in the months to come, publishing the finest, most interesting, most exciting stories of spying and international intrigue we can find.''[1]

While each issue of *Intrigue* included a story of Peter Baron, secret agent, by Bruce Cassiday, other major authors of espionage fiction were also included, many in new stories. Erle Stanley Gardner appeared in the first issue with one of his rare spy stories, ''Flight into Disaster.'' Ian Fleming was represented with 007 James Bond in ''Berlin Escape.'' And Mickey Spillane's ''The Seven Year Kill'' was featured in the third issue. Other authors included John Jakes, Lawrence G. Blochman, and Richard Deming, all well recognized and known to mystery readers.

Intrigue's subtitle was changed from ''International Espionage & Suspense Stories'' after two issues to ''Spy and Suspense Stories.'' Announcements were made of forthcoming stories, although this information is lacking in the third and final issue.

Intrigue was one of the few espionage fiction magazines in the digest-size format.

Note

1. Introductory editorial announcement, *Intrigue*, Vol. 1, no. 1 (October 1965), reverse front cover.

Information Sources

INDEX SOURCES: Cook, Michael L. *Monthly Murders*. Westport, Conn.: Greenwood Press, 1982.
LOCATION SOURCES: Private collectors.

Publication History

MAGAZINE TITLE: *Intrigue*.
TITLE CHANGES: *Intrigue Magazine* (no. 2); *Intrigue Mystery Magazine* (no. 3).
VOLUME AND ISSUE DATA: Vol. 1, no. 1 (October 1965) through Vol. 1, no. 3 (January 1966); 3 issues.
PUBLISHER: Gerald Levine as Pamar Enterprises, Inc., 10 Ferry Street, Concord, New Hampshire, with editorial offices at 122 East 42nd Street, New York, New York 10017.
EDITOR: John Poe; associate editor, Sean Kelly.
PRICE PER ISSUE: 50 cents.
SIZE AND PAGINATION: 5-3/8'' X 7-1/2''; 144 pages.
CURRENT STATUS: Discontinued.

INTRIGUE MAGAZINE

See INTRIGUE

INTRIGUE MYSTERY MAGAZINE

See INTRIGUE

J

JD–ARGASSY

See PULP ERA, THE

JDM BIBLIOPHILE

The *JDM Bibliophile* is identified in its masthead as a "non-profit amateur journal devoted to the works and readers of John D. MacDonald and related matters." The quality and longevity of this magazine are attributable primarily to the devotion and efforts of Len and June Moffatt, founding editors; Walter and Jean Shine, long-time contributors; and Ed Hirshberg, present editor. Begun as a brief, basic bibliography of MacDonald's novels then current, reproduced in "dittography" and distributed personally by the Moffatts, the *JDM Bibliophile* has become a print journal published under the sponsorship of the University of South Florida.

Almost from the outset, John D. MacDonald himself has supplied information and material to the *JDM Bibliophile*, and Walter and Jean Shine have provided a regular column of notes and comments, "The Shine Section." The Moffatts, of course, originally wrote much of the copy and presently, serving as West Coast editors, offer a regular feature, "& Everything." Ed Hirshberg's "From the Editor's Dreadful Grey Typewriter" now opens each issue. All three regular columns alert subscribers to new developments on the MacDonald and crime fiction scenes. Much of the remaining material has always consisted of original contributions by *JDM Bibliophile* readers, though some articles are reprints from other publications. And, as in the case of almost every "fanzine," the letters section, "Please Write for Details," allows for further exchange of information, suggestions to the editor, and commentary about earlier issues.

Though the stated scope of the *JDM Bibliophile* includes material outside the MacDonald canon, most of the subject matter focuses upon the author, his life, and his work. Individual articles in the journal range from sheer entertainment (some parody, for example) through reviews to analyses of JDM's stories, novels, and characters; and, naturally, a great deal of attention is paid to Travis McGee, the protagonist of MacDonald's famous series. The tone of the *JDM Bibliophile* is relaxed, informal, and assured. Most contributors' grasp of MacDonald's fiction and of the various genres in which he writes is impressively sound, and, as a rule, academese and the format of formal literary criticism are avoided.

Issue number 24, however, capitalizes on the interaction between author and scholars. "John D. and the Critics" (pp. 4–12; see also *Clues**) is based on papers that had been presented at the John D. MacDonald Conference on Mystery and Detective Fiction (held at the University of South Florida in November 1978). Brief abstracts of six papers examining various sources and aspects of MacDonald's fiction are followed by the author's responses to the critics' analyses. Though scholar and author are not always in complete agreement, the exchange is civil and good humored and represents one of *JDM Bibliophile*'s unique features—interplay between a major writer and his informed, attentive readers.

Fans and scholars alike find interest and value in John D. MacDonald's other contributions, which have included personal reminiscences (an encounter with Richard and Pat Nixon: "Flight 54—Not Quite First Class," no. 25, pp. 7–9); social commentary ("Economic Despair Fueled Miami Riots," no. 26, pp. 10–12); travel impressions ("Fragments of the Indian Scene," written in 1943, no. 25, pp. 9–11; "Reflections on China," based on a 1949 visit, no. 24, pp. 13–21); and "Commencement Address," delivered June 13, 1981, at the University of South Florida (no. 25, pp. 6–9).

Two works fostered by the *JDM Bibliophile (JDMB)* must be noted here because of their importance. By 1969, the Moffatts, with great help from the Shines and the late William J. Clark, as well as with contributions from other readers, published a substantial bibliography, *The JDM Master Checklist*. In 1981, the University of Florida Libraries published *A Bibliography of the Published Works of John D. MacDonald, with Selected Biographical Materials and Critical Essays,* by Walter and Jean Shine. This volume, characterized by the *JDMB* as "definitive," is an updated and much expanded outgrowth of the *Checklist* that had been regularly augmented through a column in the *JDMB*.

Also by Jean and Walter Shine was the *Special Confidential Report, a Private Investigators' File on Travis McGee,* which appeared in conjunction with *JDMB* number 25. The *Report* documents McGee's background, cases, skills, associates, clients, habits, and possessions, drawing upon all of the McGee novels published through 1978.

The *JDM Bibliophile*, like the publications associated with it, presents the pleasurable union of careful research, candid opinion, and cheerful admiration.

Publishing some of the best efforts of both amateur and professional contributors, it is a useful companion to the works of its subject-author.

Information Sources

INDEX SOURCES: None known.
LOCATION SOURCES: University of Florida, Gainesville; private collectors.

Publication History

MAGAZINE TITLE: *JDM Bibliophile*.
TITLE CHANGES: None.
VOLUME AND ISSUE DATA: No. 1 (March 1965) through no. 28 (to date, July 1981); 28 issues.
PUBLISHER: Len and June Moffatt, Box 4456, Downey, California 90214 (issue nos. 1–22); Dr. Ed Hirshberg, Department of English, University of South Florida, Tampa, Florida 33620.
EDITOR: Len and June Moffatt (nos. 1–22); Dr. Ed Hirshberg.
PRICE PER ISSUE: No formal price for first 22 issues; thereafter $1.50 ($5.00 annual).
SIZE AND PAGINATION: 8-1/2" X 11"; 2–52 pages.
CURRENT STATUS: Active.
—*Jane S. Bakerman*

JOHN CREASEY MYSTERY MAGAZINE (British)

The *John Creasey Mystery Magazine* started quietly enough, with an undated (August 1956) regular digest-size format and with mainly good-quality reprint material. In the very first issue, Creasey himself stated that he had jumped at the chance to help select stories, and certainly, throughout the magazine's life, the level achieved was consistently high.

The first issue led off with Agatha Christie's "The Arcadian Deer." Dennis Wheatley had "Orchids on Monday," Louis Golding had "Foolproof Murder," and Julian Symons contributed "The Case of the Frightened Promoter." And there was Dashiell Hammett with "The Farewell Murder" and Victor Canning with "The Key." And, of course, John Creasey was present, with "The Toff and the Terrified Lady."

There was almost always a Creasey story or serial. "Find Inspector West" was serialized in four installments, July to October 1957; "Strike for Death" was in three parts, January to March 1958. "Gideon's Week" (as by "J. J. Marric") appeared in two installments, April and May 1959. "Kill My Love" (as by "Kyle Hunt") was published from July through November 1959. And as Michael Halliday, Creasey's "Thicker Than Water" was broken into four segments, February through April 1960. Other Creasey novels serialized included "Mountain of the Blind" (May–August 1960), "Murder on the Line" (September–December 1960), "Scene of the Crime" (January–April 1961), "Death in Cold Print" (June–September 1961), "The Hollywood Hoax"—as by "Robert Caine Frazer"—(October–December 1961), "Policeman's Dread" (May–August 1962), "Mark Kilby Takes a Risk"—by "Frazer"—(September–December 1962), "Guilt of Innocence" (April–July 1964), and "The Sleep" (August–November 1964). And there were many short stories from this prolific author's busy pen.

Creasey did the book reviews, also, which ran through volume 5, number 5 (February 1962). James Dillan White, the author, did an occasional book review column in the early issues.

The authors represented made up a veritable who's who among mystery writers: Ellery Queen, Peter Cheyney, Agatha Christie, Dennis Wheatley, Michael Innes, Dorothy L. Sayers, Nigel Morland, Herbert Harris, Josephine Bell, Michael Underwood, John Dickson Carr, Lawrence G. Blochman, and many others.

From the beginning, Creasey's hand was much in evidence; but from the time that he assumed publication himself, there were obvious changes in editorial policy. The number of true-crime articles greatly increased. And, although the reprints continued to appear, there was a fair sprinkling of new stories both by old favorites and by new authors.

The magazine lasted almost ten years, but there is evidence throughout of the struggle Creasey faced to keep it going. No other digest magazine went through so many changes of format in such a short space of time, changes including the covers, from full-color ilustrations to a series of eye-catching patterns.

Two issues in 1959 were lost to a printing dispute; and in 1963, "rising costs" forced it, for a year or so, to a quarterly schedule. Then in 1965, it faltered again, and the last issue carried brief greetings from Creasey in New York. One can only assume that the absence of his driving force was one of the factors that finally finished the magazine.

In retrospect, the magazine must be counted as one of the comparatively few top-class mystery and detective publications.

Information Sources

INDEX SOURCES: Cook, Michael L. *Monthly Murders*. Westport, Conn.: Greenwood Press, 1982.
LOCATION SOURCES: Private collectors.

Publication History

MAGAZINE TITLE: *John Creasey Mystery Magazine*.
TITLE CHANGES: Originally *The Creasey Mystery Magazine*, until October 1957; after this date, both titles were used for various issues on spine, contents page, and statement of ownership.
VOLUME AND ISSUE DATA: Vol. 1, no. 1 (August 1956) through Vol. 8, no. 12 (April 1965); 90 issues.
PUBLISHER: Dalrow Publishing Company, 55 Knowsley Street, Bolton, Lancaster, England, later from Dalrow House, Church Bank, Bolton, Lancaster; from Vol. 1, no. 13 (September 1957), by The Creasey Mystery Magazine, Granville House, Arundel Street, Strand, London W.C.2, England.

EDITORS: John Creasey (later named as executive editor); Leslie Syddall (from Vol. 1, no. 10); Connie George as associate editor in later issues.
PRICE PER ISSUE: 1 shilling 6 pence (to Vol. 1, no. 3); 2 shillings (to Vol. 2, no. 11); 2 shillings 6 pence (to Vol. 8, no. 6); 3 shillings (to final issue).
SIZE AND PAGINATION: Average 5-1/4" X 8-1/2"; from Vol. 2, no. 11, 4-3/4" X 7-1/4"; 112-128 pages.
CURRENT STATUS: Discontinued.
—*Robert Adey*

JUSTICE

The pulp magazines were not yet cold in their graves when *Justice* was launched in a digest-size format (May 1955) by Martin Goodman under the publishing name of Non-Pareil Publishing Corporation. Goodman was a veteran of the pulp magazine business, having been associated with his brother, Abraham, in starting the Red Circle line (including *Mystery Tales* and *Real Mystery [Uncanny Tales*]) as early as 1932, and he was known for the publications under the name Manvis Publications and its subsidary, the Western Fiction Publishing Company.

Justice was, indeed, a pulp magazine in all but its format. It carried the subtitle of "Amazing Detective Mysteries," but there was little in the form of detective puzzle plots; concentration was, instead, on crime-adventure. The first issue included a novelette, "Husband's Best Friend," by Robert Martin (infidelity involving new neighbors and, of all things, their pets); a novel by David Karp, "Why, Killer, Why?" (unorthodox solving of a crime wave); and eight short stories by authors such as Tom Roan, John Bender, William R. Cox, George C. Appell, and others.

The second issue (July 1955) blossomed forth with a much better-known roster of writers, including John D. MacDonald with "In a Small Motel" (two suitors plan to kill a young widow for her money) and a novel (long novelette) by Richard S. Prather, "Lie Down, Killer" (a life-or-death alibi was an armful of cheating woman). Dorothy Dunn, Charles Beckman, Jr., and Edward A. Herron were among the short story contributors.

John D. MacDonald appeared again in the October 1955 issue with "Scared Money." Although Travis McGee was not to appear by MacDonald's pen until 1964, MacDonald was a veteran of the pulp magazines and several paperback books by this time. Richard Matheson and William R. Cox wrote the longer pieces in this issue, accompanied by Bryce Walton, Gil Brewer, John Bender, and Philip Weck.

And when in the fourth issue there was a new novelette by Cornell Woolrich ("The Black Bargain") and more stories by the same lineup of good writers as in the past issues, one would have thought that the magazine could have continued. The pulplike covers and well-printed interiors were among the better of the many similar magazines appearing at the time, but the fourth issue was the last. While the first three issues had included announcements of forthcoming stories, the last issue omitted this and thus forecast its demise.

Information Sources

INDEX SOURCES: Cook, Michael L. *Monthly Murders*. Westport, Conn.: Greenwood Press, 1982.
LOCATION SOURCES: Private collectors.

Publication History

MAGAZINE TITLE: *Justice*.
TITLE CHANGES: None.
VOLUME AND ISSUE DATA: Vol. 1, no. 1 (May 1955) through Vol. 2, no. 1 (January 1956); 4 issues.
PUBLISHER: Martin Goodman as Non-Pareil Publishing Corporation, 655 Madison Avenue, New York 21, New York.
EDITOR: Harry Widmer.
PRICE PER ISSUE: 35 cents.
SIZE AND PAGINATION: 5-1/4'' X 7-5/8''; 160 pages.
CURRENT STATUS: Discontinued.

K

KEYHOLE DETECTIVE STORY MAGAZINE

See KEYHOLE MYSTERY MAGAZINE

KEYHOLE MYSTERY MAGAZINE

For the first three issues, at least, this was one of the better-conceived mystery magazines. *Keyhole Mystery Magazine*, digest-sized, made its inital debut with the April 1960 issue and "an assortment of villains and villainy to tempt the palate of the most bloodthirsty among you."[1]

Despite this description, the magazine presented a good array of the more standard mystery and detection short stories by many of the better-known mystery fiction authors. Anthony Boucher's "Mr. Lupescu" was featured in the first issue, along with "Full Circle" by Miriam Allen deFord and "The North Star Caper" by Norman Katkov, as well as others.

The second issue, June 1960, contained "I.O.U." by Cornell Woolrich, a classic story of a father-teenage daughter relationship and the necessity to choose between gratitude and duty. "Night Ride" by Theodore Sturgeon was a harrowing tale of a corpse (and thirty-two live passengers) on a runaway bus. And Norman Daniels's "The Trap" was suspenseful, detailing two young people who were watched night after night—until fate gave them a chance to strike back. John Collier explored whether some people are more likely to be murdered than others in "Born for Murder." And Lawrence G. Blochman was present with Dr. Coffee and his forensic solution to "A Kiss for Belinda," in which beautiful, blonde, kissable Belinda was found drowned in a bathtub that contained no water. Other stories included were by Melville Davisson Post, Frank Atterholz, Rog Phillips, Joseph Whitehill, Rod Reed, Robert Bloch, Avram Davidson, and Mary Thayer Muller.

Lawrence G. Blochman returned in the third (August 1960) issue with one of his favorite stories, "Zarapore Beat." Here, a New York cop who has never been farther from home than Asbury Park is, by circumstances, transported to India and there continues to function as if he were home in Manhattan. Blochman (who worked for a newspaper in Calcutta in 1922–1923) presents a vivid background setting which enhances the tale. In an unusual handling, Bill Boltin's "The Hit-Run Homicide" presents Fabian, the real-life teenage singing idol, as the detective. Other outstanding stories included "Broker's Special" by Stanley Ellin, "Fat Chance" by Robert Bloch, and "Case of the Clumsy Cadaver" by Will Folke, as well as stories by Roald Dahl, Charles Beckman, George Kauffman, R. A. Lafferty, Miriam Allen deFord, John Collier, and William T. Harrel.

A letters column commenced in the second issue with the usual assortment of bouquets and brickbats. Semiprovocative, full-color covers were appropriate, several of which gave the impression of peering through a giant keyhole.

However, without a well-established title, and at a time when other digest-sized magazines were experiencing sales difficulties, the policy of plot over action could not be maintained. The original publisher discontinued publication after three issues, the last being August 1960.

With the fourth issue, January 1962, after a lapse of more than a year, the magazine appeared from a new publisher. Although the numbering was continued (the first "new" magazine being designated as volume 2, number 1), the title was slightly changed, to *Keyhole Detective Story Magazine*. But this was not the major change. It was a completely different magazine under the successor, the Pontiac Publishing Corporation.

Emphasis was now directed to a more violent, fast-action clip, heavily laced with tough and coarse characters and, above all, sex. This was a complete reversal of the policy existing under the original publisher, Winston Publications.

Heavily contemporary—seeded with street-tough gangs, hoodlums, petty gangsters, and connivers of both sexes—the prose raced at an improbable pace using every cliche possible. There were only two excuses for it all: sex and greed. The story titles, behind covers of lurid action by Carl Pfeufer, illustrate amply the shallowness and degradation portrayed:

"Her Kind Die Hard!" by Norman Struber ("She changed her name and thought she was safe.")[2]

"Die in My Embrace, Darling!" by William H. Duhart ("He was unable to control the urge.")[3]

"Striptease for the Damned!" by Jim Arthur ("She was forced to give them all they wanted.")[4]

"Rogue Bull!" by Gordon Burns ("Cindy's body brushed him gently, and he followed her inside. It was working as we'd planned.")[5]

"I Like to See Them Squirm!" by Flip Lyons ("Her delicate flesh was warm, like the water. Soon she would breathe her last.")[6]

"Thrill Babe!" by Grover Brinkman ("She cuddled closer to him in the car. 'Bring me here again,' she cooed.")[7]

For the last four issues, all published by the "new" publisher, every story title carried an exclamation mark. Every story was intended to arouse vehemently the reader's excitement or passion.

Fortunately, the demand for this type of detective fiction was short-lived, and the magazine perished with the September 1962 issue.

Notes

1. Editorial announcement, *Keyhole Mystery Magazine*, Vol. 1, no. 1 (April 1960), reverse front cover.
2. *Keyhole Detective Story Magazine*, Vol. 2, no. 1 (January 1962), p. 3.
3. Ibid., p. 23.
4. Ibid., p. 98.
5. *Keyhole Detective Story Magazine*, Vol. 2, no. 2 (April 1962), p. 83.
6. *Keyhole Detective Story Magazine*, Vol. 2, no. 4, (September 1962), p. 38.
7. Ibid., p. 96.

Information Sources

INDEX SOURCES: Cook, Michael L. *Monthly Murders*. Westport, Conn.: Greenwood Press, 1982.
LOCATION SOURCES: Private collectors.

Publication History

MAGAZINE TITLE: *Keyhole Mystery Magazine*.
TITLE CHANGES: *Keyhole Detective Story Magazine* (with Vol. 2, no. 1 [January 1962]).
VOLUME AND ISSUE DATA: Vol. 1, no. 1 (April 1960) through Vol. 2, no. 4 (September 1962); 7 issues.
PUBLISHER: William Woolfolk as Winston Publications, Inc., 157 West 57th Street, New York 19, New York (first three issues); Pontiac Publishing Corp., 1546 Broadway, New York, New York (last 4 issues).
EDITOR: Dan Roberts (first 3 issues); not known for subsequent issues.
PRICE PER ISSUE: 35 cents.
SIZE AND PAGINATION: 5-3/8" X 7-5/8"; 114–130 pages.
CURRENT STATUS: Discontinued.

KILLERS MYSTERY STORY MAGAZINE

See HOMICIDE DETECTIVE STORY MAGAZINE

L

LLOYDS DETECTIVE SERIES (British)

A weekly series of "penny dreadfuls," *Lloyds Detective Series* was published for thirty-two issues during 1921–1922 in a thin, pocket-size format, cheaply produced. Companion magazines were *Lloyds Boys' Adventure Series, Lloyds School Yarns,* and *Lloyds Sports' Library*, all oriented to the youth market. No other information is available.

Information Sources

BIBLIOGRAPHY:
Lofts, W.O.G., and Derek J. Adley. *Old Boys Books, A Complete Catalogue.* London: privately printed, 1969.
INDEX SOURCES: None known.
LOCATION SOURCES: Private collectors.

Publication History

MAGAZINE TITLE: *Lloyds Detective Series.*
TITLE CHANGES: None.
VOLUME AND ISSUE DATA: No. 1 (1921) through no. 32 (1922).
PUBLISHER: United Newspapers Syndicate Ltd., London.
EDITOR: Not known.
PRICE PER ISSUE: Not known.
SIZE AND PAGINATION: 5-3/8" X 7"; 32 pages.
CURRENT STATUS: Discontinued.

LONDON MYSTERY MAGAZINE (British)

See LONDON MYSTERY SELECTION (British)

LONDON MYSTERY SELECTION (British)

Of the many mystery magazines begun in Britain over the years, only one remains, and it now faces death for the second time.

In December 1949, the Hulton Press Ltd. (43–44 Shoe Lane, London E.C.4) began to publish the *London Mystery Magazine* for The Proprietors, The London Mystery Magazine Ltd., whose address was 221b Baker Street. But after only twelve issues, Hulton announced in *The Times* its intention to cease publication. Paper was scarce and expensive in the postwar years, and all publishers were feeling the pinch. Norman Kark read the notice and, being an adventurous man, took on the task practically single-handedly of keeping the magazine alive for an uninterrupted span of some thirty-three years.

In March 1958, the magazine changed its name to the *London Mystery Selection*. This quarterly anthology has published stories and poems by nearly two thousand authors, and many a bright new writer—such as Anthony Schaffer and Kenneth Tynan—found subsequent fame after having his first work printed in its pages.

The stories throughout the years have been in the best possible taste, directed at "connoisseurs of original crime and mystery fiction," continuing to uphold the admirably high standard of abstinence from lewdness, foul language, and excessive violence. Kark never succumbed to the suggestion that he could double his circulation with a half-naked blonde dripping blood from a dagger displayed on the cover; instead, an illustration of a London Bobby and the Houses of Parliament suggest a sense of law and order. Mingled with detective stories are tales of ghosts and the supernatural.

A limited American edition was brought out briefly in the United States, but these proved to be mostly copies of the British edition with a different price tag. The publisher was Ziff-Davis Publishing Co., 366 Madison Avenue, New York 17, New York.

In each issue of the *London Mystery Selection*, there were about eight pages of advertising, a number of which were devoted to charitable organizations. "Crooks in Books" was the title of its quarterly review of "worthwhile mystery reading," and there was, of course, an editorial page written by Norman Kark.

Many editorials have been written about Norman Kark: how he ran away from school in Johannesburg at the age of sixteen and became a dispatch rider under General Smuts during the First World War; how he went to England in 1920 and fought a twenty-year battle with the Westminster City Council, who objected to his illuminating Trafalgar Square—Kark lost, but not before he had directed the first naval spotlight on Lord Nelson atop the column. He did, however, manage to illuminate the Pavilion corner of Piccadilly Circus instead. He again served in the army during World War II, attaining the rank of major. One can't begin to chronicle here all the colorful events in this remarkable man's life or the tremendous amount of work he has done for the disabled. It took a man of such daring and determination to sustain a magazine for so long when other magazines failed.

Now, sadly, the *London Mystery Selection* has announced in its 131st issue that the March 1982 (the 132nd issue) will be the last. Norman Kark, now in his eighties, feels he can no longer keep it going. This may be the last of the British mystery magazines unless there is another Norman Kark ready to step in and rescue it again, just in the nick of time.

(Editor's Note: The last issue of the magazine includes the following from Norman Kark:
". . . I intend putting myself out to graze in the fertile fields of South Africa and try to read just for the pleasure of reading."[1] *Many of us wish him an additional long life back in his native land.)*

Note

1. Editorial announcement, *London Mystery Selection*, no. 132, (March 1982), p. 5.

Information Sources

BIBLIOGRAPHY:
"London Mystery Selection, a Tribute." *The Times* (London), no. 118 (September 1978): 32.
"London Mystery Selection." Article. *The Times* (London) (September 30, 1980): 38.
INDEX SOURCES: Cook, Michael L. *Monthly Murders*. Westport, Conn.: Greenwood Press, 1982.
LOCATION SOURCES: Private collectors.

Publication History

MAGAZINE TITLE: *London Mystery Selection*.
TITLE CHANGES: *London Mystery Magazine* (until issue no. 36 [March 1958]).
VOLUME AND ISSUE DATA: No. 1 (December 1949) through no. 132 (March 1982): 132 issues.
PUBLISHERS: Hulton Press Ltd., for The Proprietors, The London Mystery Magazine Ltd., 221b Baker Street, London (Hulton Press: 43–44 Shoe Lane, London E.C.4) for first 12 issues; thereafter, Norman Kark Publications, 268–270 Vauxhall Bridge Road, London S.W.1, England.
EDITOR: Norman Kark (commencing with no. 13).
PRICE PER ISSUE: 2 shillings 6 pence (until no. 66); 3 shillings 6 pence (until December 1970); 25 pence (until September 1975); 35 pence (until December 1977); 50 pence; 75 pence; ($2.00 in U.S., 1982).
SIZE AND PAGINATION: First issues 5-3/8" X 7-3/8," later issues 4" X 7"; 128 pages.
CURRENT STATUS: Discontinued.
—*Faith Clare-Joynt*

LONDON MYSTERY SELECTION (U.S.)

See LONDON MYSTERY SELECTION (British)

LONE WOLF DETECTIVE

Lone Wolf Detective was published by Ace Magazines, Inc. (A. A. Wyn) commencing in 1938 and existing through at least April 1941 (volume 4, number 4). The illustration on the front cover on this last issue noted was the same as used on the December 1935 issue of *Secret Agent X**, another Wyn publication. A typical issue of *Lone Wolf Detective*, containing five novels, was "Merchant of Menace" by Robert Turner, "One Escort, Missing or Dead" by Roger Torrey, "Homicide Ledger" by Clifton T. Holmes, "The Corpse Maker" by Eric Lennox, and "Bullet Banknight" by Paul Adams.

Information Sources

INDEX SOURCES: None known.
LOCATION SOURCES: University of California–Los Angeles Library (1940, 1 issue); private collectors.

Publication History

MAGAZINE TITLE: *Lone Wolf Detective*.
TITLE CHANGES: None known.
VOLUME AND ISSUE DATA: Vol. 1, no. 1 (1938) through at least Vol. 4, no. 4 (April 1941); number of issues and extent unknown.
PUBLISHER: Ace Magazines, Inc., 29 Worthington Street, Springfield, Massachusetts, with editorial offices at 67 West 46th Street, New York, New York.
EDITOR: A. A. Wyn.
PRICE PER ISSUE: Not known.
SIZE AND PAGINATION: Not known.
CURRENT STATUS: Discontinued.

LONE WOLFE

Lee E. Poleske had been reading the Nero Wolfe stories of Rex Stout for eight years when he decided to publish his "Nero Wolfe fanzine," as he referred to it, confidently using a word Nero Wolfe would never tolerate. In a letter to Stout's authorized biographer, John J. McAleer, Poleske said: "I have read all the Nero Wolfe stories, and re-read most of them several times. I have tried some of the other Stout books, but have never liked them. Wolfe is such a tremendous characterization, others seem pale in comparison. I have never found any other detective stories or series of much interest. The character of Nero Wolfe has to be one of the great ones of fiction."

Poleske was determined that *Lone Wolfe*, which during the first half of its existence was called *Nero Wolfe and Archie Goodwin Fans Newsletter*, would be neither pretentious nor corny. He invited his subscribers to determine what the content would be and hoped that they themselves would supply 99 percent of it.

Lone Wolfe published brief Wolfe quizzes; Neronian aphorisms; bibliographical information; letters from readers; queries on the Nero Wolfe radio shows;

informational excerpts on orchids; excerpts from books alluding to the Wolfe corpus; a review of the film *Meet Nero Wolfe* taken from the *New York Times* (July 16, 1936); and the *Times* review (July 2, 1937) of *The League of Frightened Men,* also made into a film. It published, as well, thumbnail biographies of Escoffier and Brillat-Savarin; Poleske's own impressions of *A Family Affair,* the final novel of the Wolfe corpus; and a synopsis of David McReynolds's review of the same book from *WIN* magazine; and a diagram showing the structure of a cattleya orchid plant.

Information Sources

INDEX SOURCES: None known.
LOCATION SOURCES: Private collectors.

Publication History

MAGAZINE TITLE: *Lone Wolfe*.
TITLE CHANGES: Originally (3 issues) *Nero Wolfe and Archie Goodwin Fans Newsletter*.
VOLUME AND ISSUE DATA: Vol. 1, no. 1 (January 1975) through Vol. 1, no. 6 (January 1976).
PUBLISHER: Lee E. Poleske, Box 871, Seward, Alaska 99664.
EDITOR: Lee E. Poleske.
PRICE PER ISSUE: By subscription, $1.50 per year.
SIZE AND PAGINATION: 8-1/2'' X 11'' (except no. 3, 8–1/2'' X 14''); 1–4 pages.
CURRENT STATUS: Discontinued.
—John J. McAleer

LOVE-CRIME DETECTIVE

Love-Crime Detective was published for one issue in August 1942 by the Frank A. Munsey Company and was possibly the last new title inaugurated by that company before it was sold to Popular Publications.

The magazine was intended as a replacement for *Double Detective,** which experienced declining sales. The Munsey firm at the time was under the direction of Colonel William T. Dewart, Sr., as president and treasurer, and William T. Dewart, Jr., as secretary. Their policy seemed to be cutting the circulation of declining magazines until they showed a profit, and this is what had happened to *Double Detective*—until the magazine was virtually nonexistent. When it was discontinued, in 1942, a new title, *Love-Crime Detective*, took its place. However, at about the same time, other titles were purchased by Popular Publications.

The love field was of little interest to Popular Publications, although it did venture into this area with several magazines with frequently changing titles. *Love-Crime Detective* was not continued, but *Double Detective* was revived for one issue under its banner.

Information Sources

BIBLIOGRAPHY:

Hardin, Nils. "An Interview with Henry Steeger." *Xenophile*, no. 33 (July 1977): 3–18.

————, and George Hocutt. "A Checklist of Popular Publications Titles 1930–1955." *Xenophile*, no 33 (July 1977): 21–24.

INDEX SOURCES: None known.

LOCATION SOURCES: University of California-Los Angeles Library; private collectors.

Publication History

MAGAZINE TITLE: *Love-Crime Detective*.

TITLE CHANGES: None.

VOLUME AND ISSUE DATA: Vol. 1, no. 1 (August 1942); 1 issue.

PUBLISHER: Frank A. Munsey Co., 280 Broadway, New York, New York.

EDITOR: Not known.

PRICE PER ISSUE: 10 cents.

SIZE AND PAGINATION: 7'' X 10''; 112 pages.

CURRENT STATUS: Discontinued.

M

MACABRE

Although designed to be a medium for both established and new writers in the weird, supernatural, and bizarre genres, considerable mystery element exists in the material published in *Macabre*. Joseph Payne Brennan, the editor and publisher, was known and recognized as one of the old *Weird Tales** school of writers, and his name alone brought many manuscripts for consideration. It was hoped that a semiannual publication schedule could be maintained, but this was not possible due to the workload of the editor and his severe heart attack in 1968. The last issue published, in 1973, advised that "the [previous] issue of *Macabre*, number twenty-one, appeared in 1970. Continued illness, coupled with financial crises, made it impossible for us to publish the magazine on schedule."[1] Although no further issues have appeared, there is still intent to do so: "Rumors have had *Macabre* dead and buried—and your editor along with it. We hope these rumors continue to prove unfounded. . . ."[2]

Joseph Payne Brennan is perhaps best known to mystery fans for his Lucius Leffing stories, some of which have appeared in *Macabre*, along with top-quality stories and poetry by many other authors.

Notes

1. Editorial announcement, *Macabre*, no. 22 (1973), p. 3.
2. Ibid.

Information Sources

INDEX SOURCES: None known.
LOCATION SOURCES: Private collectors.

Publication History

MAGAZINE TITLE: *Macabre*.

TITLE CHANGES: None.

VOLUME AND ISSUE DATA: No. 1 (Spring 1957) through no. 22 (undated, 1973); 22 issues.

PUBLISHER: Joseph Payne Brennan, 91 Westerleigh Road, New Haven, Connecticut 06515, later 26 Fowler Street, New Haven, Connecticut 06515.

EDITOR: Joseph Payne Brennan.

PRICE PER ISSUE: 40 cents (1957–1963); 50 cents (1964–1970); 75 cents (1973).

SIZE AND PAGINATION: Average 6-1/4'' X 9-1/4''; 16–30 pages.

CURRENT STATUS: Inactive, though not officially discontinued.

MacKILL'S MYSTERY MAGAZINE (British)

Although *MacKill's Mystery Magazine* was principally a reprint magazine, its appearance was welcomed by British mystery fans in September 1952. The publishers, Todd Publishing Group, Ltd., had produced at the end of World War II a series of very thin paperbacks (as well as some hardbacks) containing one or more short stories by popular crime fiction authors. These writers had included Michael Innes, Anthony Gilbert, Mignon G. Eberhart, Margery Allingham, John Dickson Carr (writing at times under the pen name Carter Dickson), Agatha Christie, Peter Cheyney, and Nigel Morland, among others. The trade name of the book series included Polybooks, Bantam, Todd, and Valency Press.

It was not surprising, therefore, when *MacKill's Mystery Magazine* reprinted some of these stories and, indeed, concentrated on this good-quality reprint material. Thus, although the contents are largely not original short stories, one could constantly expect to find good authors and their best creations.

The editor promised in the first issue that one of Roy Vickers's famous "Department of Dead Ends" stories[1] would appear in each issue, and in this first issue was "The Case of the Respectful Murders." Subsequent issues included "The Case of the Perpetual Sneer," "Murder in the Cowshed," "The Cosy Nook Murder," "The Nine Pound Murder," and others of this series.

In addition to the Vickers tale in the first issue, other authors represented made for *MacKill's* a very auspicious beginning. Agatha Christie's "The Sign in the Sky" and Ellery Queen's "The Adventure of the Seven Black Cats" shared honors with a short book-length novel by Mignon G. Eberhart, "Bermuda Grapevine," and there were also stories by Michael Innes, Edmund Crispin, E.C.R. Lorac, Anthony Gilbert, and J. Jefferson Farjeon. The first issue carried a full-color back cover depicting a scene from the Eberhart story, but the back cover color paintings were not continued for subsequent issues.

The second (October 1952) issue was also a banner release. Carter Dickson's story, "The House in Goblin Wood," had won a special award in the annual contest conducted by *Ellery Queen's Mystery Magazine** in America. An unusual Saint adventure, "The Arrow of God," was by Leslie Charteris, and the featured book-length tale was "Murder on Tuesday" by Rex Stout, a Nero Wolfe epic. Innes, Crispin, and Lorac returned with short stories, as well as Margery Allingham, Q. Patrick, and E. R. Punshon.

Another *Ellery Queen's* contest-winning story by John Dickson Carr, "The Gentleman from Paris," appeared in the third (November 1952) issue of *MacKill's*, along with "Deadlock" by Edmund Crispin and Raymond Chandler's "The King in Yellow," as well as five other stories.

Succeeding issues continued the publishing of outstanding authors and stories: "The Case of the Runaway Blonde" by Erle Stanley Gardner, Hercule Poirot in Agatha Christie's "The Under Dog," John Dickson Carr's "The Third Bullet," Erle Stanley Gardner's "The Clue of the Hungry Horse," Rex Stout's "Before I Die," and Georges Simenon's "A Matter of Life and Death," along with seven or eight outstanding short stories in each issue.

A standard yellow, nonpictorial front cover, quite attractive, was used for all but the last several issues, and these were drawings depicting a scene from the book-length feature. The quality of the paper was quite poor but commensurate with other magazines of the time.

MacKill's Mystery Magazine was discontinued after twenty-two top-grade issues, the last one being dated August 1954. It was one of the best.

Note

1. "The Department of Dead Ends," wrote Roy Vickers, "came into existence in the first decade of this century. It took everything rejected by other departments—it noted and filed all those clues that had the exasperating effect of proving a palpably guilty man innocent. To this Department, too, were taken all those members of the public who insisted on helping the police with obviously irrelevant information and preposterous theories. Its files were mines of misinformation; it proceeded largely by guess-work and its main function was to connect persons and things that had no logical connection. It played always for the lucky fluke. In short it stood for the antithesis of scientific detection." *MacKill's Mystery Magazine*, Vol. 1, no. 1 (September 1952), p. 41.

Information Sources

INDEX SOURCES: Cook, Michael L. *Monthly Murders*. Westport, Conn.: Greenwood Press, 1982.
LOCATION SOURCES: Private collectors.

Publication History

MAGAZINE TITLE: *MacKill's Mystery Magazine*.
TITLE CHANGES: None.
VOLUME AND ISSUE DATA: Vol. 1, no. 1 (September 1952) through Vol. 4, no. 4 (August 1954); 22 issues.
PUBLISHER: Todd Publishing Group, Ltd., 132–134 Fleet Street, London E.C.4, England.
EDITOR: Not known.
PRICE PER ISSUE: 1 shilling.
SIZE AND PAGINATION: 5-1/2" X 7-1/2"; 128 pages.
CURRENT STATUS: Discontinued.
—*Robert Adey*

MAGAZINE OF HORROR

Largely oriented toward reprints of pulp stories from the thirties and largely from *Weird Tales,** and edited by Robert W. Lowndes with fine informative and insightful introductions, *Magazine of Horror* was almost a twin of its younger, shorter-lived sister magazine, *Startling Mystery Stories.** *Magazine of Horror*, however, ran few detective-crime stories.

"MOH," Lowndes said, "has a broad policy, covering a wide range of stories. . .bizarre, gruesome, frightening. . .[but unlike *Startling Mystery Stories,* which] requires some mystery element in all that appears there."[1]

The *Magazine of Horror* had a few exceptions: Seabury Quinn's novel, "The Devil's Bride," ran in three, fat installments; here occult detective Dr. Jules de Grandin searched through Africa for a bride stolen by the devil-worshipping cult of Yezidees. Ambrose Bierce's "My Favorite Murders" and several stories featuring psychic investigators such as William Hope Hodgson's Carnacki the Ghost-Finder and Algernon Blackwood's Dr. John Silence also appeared, as well as a few more.

Generally, however, the *Magazine of Horror* featured the supernatural and has little in its thirty-five issues to be of interest to the hard-core detective story reader.

Note

1. Editorial announcement, *Weird Terror Tales,* Vol. 1, no. 1 (Winter 1969–1970), p. 3.

Information Sources

BIBLIOGRAPHY:
Bates, Dave and Su. "Health Knowledge Publications." *Collecting Paperbacks?*, Vol. 2, no. 3 (July 1980): 28.
INDEX SOURCES: Cook, Michael, L. *Monthly Murders.* Westport, Conn.: Greenwood Press, 1982.
Marshall, Gene, and Carl F. Waedt. "An Index to the Health Knowledge Magazines." *The Science-Fiction Collector*, no. 3 (1977): 3–42.
LOCATION SOURCES: Private collectors.

Publication History

MAGAZINE TITLE: *Magazine of Horror*.
TITLE CHANGES: Originally *Magazine of Horror and Strange Stories* (Vol. 1, no. 1, through Vol. 1, no. 5); *Magazine of Horror, Strange Tales and Science Fiction* (Vol. 1, no. 6, through Vol. 2, no. 1).
VOLUME AND ISSUE DATA: Vol. 1, no. 1 (August 1963) through Vol. 6, no. 5 (February 1971); 35 issues.
PUBLISHER: Health Knowledge, Inc., 140 Fifth Avenue, New York, New York.
EDITOR: Robert A. W. Lowndes.
PRICE PER ISSUE: 50 cents (through Vol. 6, no. 1); 60 cents.

SIZE AND PAGINATION: Average 5-1/2'' X 7-1/2''; 130 pages.
CURRENT STATUS: Discontinued.
—*Frank D. McSherry, Jr.*

MAGAZINE OF HORROR AND STRANGE STORIES

See MAGAZINE OF HORROR

MAGAZINE OF HORROR, STRANGE TALES AND SCIENCE FICTION

See MAGAZINE OF HORROR

MALCOLM'S

"*Malcolm's* is the mystery fiction magazine you would publish if you were publishing one."[1] With this statement, the magazine was launched with the January 1954 issue, a well-designed and printed detective and crime-adventure periodical. Authors represented were among both the well-known and the lesser-known. "Symbolism, impressionism, realism, and just plain, ordinary commercial art"[2] were all utilized in the many illustrations, most of which were by Constance Koch, the daughter of the publisher. It was promised that covers would be both appropriate and unoffensive. A number of mild crime cartoons were included and continued with the succeeding issues. With the second issue, a letters column was commenced.

The feature stories in the three issues published included "The Prophetic Portrait Painter" by Charles Beckman, Jr., "Blonde XX" by Octavus Roy Cohen, and "The Little Knife That Wasn't There" by Craig Rice.

An unusual offer made by the publisher was a "guarantee" that you would like the magazine; if not, the front cover could be returned with a brief note stating the reason, and the cover price would be refunded.

Malcolm's was published by R. Malcolm Koch, president of George Koch Sons, Inc., an industrial firm in Evansville, Indiana, and was commenced because Mr. Koch was a mystery fan. According to his advice, the magazine folded due to inadequate newsstand distribution and display. A fourth issue was prepared but apparently never published.[3]

Notes

1. Editorial announcement, *Malcolm's*, Vol. 1, no. 1 (January 1954), reverse front cover.
2. Ibid.
3. Information from Logan Miller, *Malcolm's* production manager, personal conversation (1981).

Information Sources

INDEX SOURCES: Cook, Michael L. *Monthly Murders*. Westport, Conn.: Greenwood Press, 1982.

LOCATION SOURCES: Private collectors.

Publication History

MAGAZINE TITLE: *Malcolm's*.
TITLE CHANGES: None.
VOLUME AND ISSUE DATA: Vol. 1, no. 1 (January 1954) through Vol. 1, no. 3
 (May 1954); 3 issues.
PUBLISHER: R. Malcolm Koch as R. Malcolm & Associates, 421 Hudson Street, New
 York, New York, with editorial offices at P.O. Box 304, Evansville, Indiana.
EDITOR: Ruth Maness; assistant editor, Dorothy Dailey.
PRICE PER ISSUE: 35 cents.
SIZE AND PAGINATION: 5-1/2'' X 7-1/2''; 128 pages.
CURRENT STATUS: Discontinued.

MAMMOTH DETECTIVE

Mammoth Detective is the older of the two mystery-detective pulp magazines in the Ziff-Davis Fiction Group, the other being *Mammoth Mystery*.* The first issue of *Mammoth Detective* appeared in May 1942 under B. G. Davis, editor, and Raymond A. Palmer, managing editor. Howard Browne (aka John Evans) joined the staff with volume 2 as assistant editor and in March 1947 moved up to the post of managing editor when Palmer replaced Davis as editor. Davis himself had been appointed president. From all indications, however, it was Howard Browne who held the editorial reins at both publications, with Palmer admittedly not even a reader of detective fiction (see editorial, "Off the Blotter," *Mammoth Detective*, Vol. 6, no. 7 [July 1947]). Browne even took his editorial colleague to task in the final issue of *Mammoth Mystery* for his uninformed attack on the so-called abuses of the hard-boiled genre.

Supposedly started as a monthly, *Mammoth Detective* soon became bimonthly with volume 2, finally going quarterly at the end of the same volume in 1943. It reverted again to a bimonthly with volume 5, number 2 (March 1946) and became a monthly two issues later (August 1946), which it remained until the final issue in September 1947 (volume 6, number 9). Likewise, there were changes in pagination, the 300-plus pages dwindling to a standard 276 when the magazine became quarterly. With volume 4, number 3 (August 1945), it was reduced to 178 pages due to the wartime paper shortage. Advertising contracts at this time were also cancelled to allow more room for the fiction contents.

Each issue contained short stories, novelettes, and, whenever possible, a full-length novel. The latter, in most cases, was published in the magazine prior to hardcover publication. Some, judging from the fact that they do not appear in Allen J. Hubin's *The Bibliography of Crime Fiction*, may not have made it to hardcover, at least not under the same title. Those not listed in Hubin are Wyndham Martyn's "Death by the Lake" and "Enemy Agent," John Wiley and Willis March's "With This Gun," John Evans's "Murder Wears a Halo" and "Halo 'Round My Dead," William G. Bogart's "The Cincinnati Murders" (later published as "The Queen City Murder Case"), John Evans's "Halo in Blood," Wade Miller's "This Deadly Weapon," and others by Stewart Sterling, Bruno Fischer, Frank Gruber, Harold Q. Masur, and Brett Halliday.

Among the shorter fiction should be noted Carroll John Daly's "You'll Remember Me," William P. McGivern's first detective story, "Secret of the Goldfish Bowl," followed by "Death Lays the Odds," and Robert Leslie Bellem's "Hot Skins," as well as stories by Howard Browne, W. T. Ballard, Robert Bloch, Vincent Starrett, and others.

A picture crime puzzle graced the back cover until volume 5, number 6 (September 1946), and other nonfiction features included autobiographical sketches of many contributing authors, a "Personals" column and "Correspndence Corner," and even an early column devoted to missing heirs and other persons. Howard Browne took over the "Off the Blotter" editorial from Raymond A. Palmer beginning with volume 4, number 4 (November 1945) and did a far superior job. Especially humorous today are his comments about newly discovered author John Evans, who, of course, is Browne himself. This is a plot not unheard of even today.

There was no mention in the editorial column in September 1947 of things to come, as was usually the case. *Mammoth Mystery* had vanished after the August 1947 issue, so perhaps the axe was expected for *Mammoth Detective* even as the final issue went to press.

Information Sources

INDEX SOURCES: None known.
LOCATION SOURCES: Private collectors.

Publication History

MAGAZINE TITLE:*Mammoth Detective*.
TITLE CHANGES: None.
VOLUME AND ISSUE DATA: Vol. 1, no. 1 (May 1942) through Vol. 6, no. 9 (September 1947); number of issues not ascertained.
PUBLISHER: William B. Ziff as Ziff-Davis Publishing Co., 540 North Michigan Avenue, Chicago 1, Illinois, later 185 North Wabash Avenue, Chicago, Illinois.
EDITORS: B. G. Davis (through Vol. 6, no. 2 [February 1947]) as editor; Raymond A. Palmer, managing editor; Howard Browne, assistant editor and later managing editor (commencing with Vol. 2 [1943]).
PRICE PER ISSUE: 25 cents.
SIZE AND PAGINATION: 6-3/4" X 9-3/4"; 178–322 pages.
CURRENT STATUS: Discontinued.
—*James R. McCahery*

MAMMOTH MYSTERY

Mammoth Mystery was the fourth member of the Ziff-Davis Fiction Group, along with sister magazines *Amazing Stories, Fantastic Adventures,* and *Mam-*

moth Detective.* It appeared for the first time in a 274-page edition in February 1945 when *Mammoth Detective* was ending its third year. Both magazines were run by the same group of editors: B. G. Davis, editor; Raymond A. Palmer, managing editor; and Howard Browne (aka John Evans), assistant editor. In the case of *Mammoth Mystery*, Davis became president with the appearance in February 1947 of volume 3, number 1. He was replaced as editor by Palmer, with Browne moving up to the post of managing editor.

Strictly speaking, Browne seems to have done most of the editorial work for both detective magazines, writing the editorial "The Call Box" for *Mammoth Mystery* from the outset and replacing Palmer as writer of "Off the Blotter" for *Mammoth Detective* in November 1945 (volume 4, number 4). The strangest fact of all in this whole editorial hierarchy was the admitted fact that Raymond A. Palmer did not even read detective fiction (see "Off the Blotter" in *Mammoth Detective*, Vol. 6, no. 7 [July 1947]). Browne, in fact, even took Palmer to task in the October 1947 issue of *Mammoth Mystery* for a guest editorial Palmer had written for the previous issue, during Browne's absence, in which he criticized the overdone, hard-boiled school of writing. Strangely enough, this also happened to be the final issue of *Mammoth Mystery* (volume 3, number 4 [August 1947]). He also referred to the same guest editorial when writing for *Mammoth Detective* the same month (volume 6, number 8).

The second issue of *Mammoth Mystery* did not appear until almost a year later (January 1946), by which time it was billed as a bimonthly which, in fact, it remained until its demise after the eleventh issue. While it remained priced at twenty-five cents, it was also cut to 178 pages, a fate that befell its sister magazine as a result of the wartime paper shortage.

Each issue of *Mammoth Mystery* contained either a full-length novel or one or more "short novels," as well as novelettes and short stories. The novels, for the most part, preceded their hardcover publication. These included Bruno Fischer's "The Spider Lady," Roy Huggin's "The Double Take," and William P. McGivern's "Heaven Ran Last," among others. The latter-mentioned novel by McGivern was published in hardcover in 1949.

The shorter fiction that appeared was by writers such as Bruno Fischer, Robert Bloch, William G. Bogart, John D. MacDonald (of whom Browne says,"...a newcomer who shows a world of promise. . . ."), Alexander Blade, and others. The MacDonald short was "Get Dressed for Death" (volume 2, number 5 [October 1946]).

Also included were a number of nonfiction articles and fillers, as well as a back-cover pictorial puzzle initiated by Alexander Blade along the lines of the one made popular in *Mammoth Detective*. It disappeared, however, after August 1946.

The double-column-a-page pulp with its fine color-art covers, the best of which were by Arnold Kohn, was destined to be short-lived, however. An October 1947 issue was envisioned featuring Paul W. Fairman's "The Glass Ladder" (eventually published by Handi-Books in 1950), but that issue never made it to the newsstands.

Information Sources

INDEX SOURCES: None known.
LOCATION SOURCES: University of California–Los Angeles (Vol. 1, no. 1, only); private collectors.

Publication History

MAGAZINE TITLE: *Mammoth Mystery*.
TITLE CHANGES: None.
VOLUME AND ISSUE DATA: Vol. 1, no. 1 (February 1945) through Vol. 3, no. 4 (August 1947); 11 issues.
PUBLISHER: William B. Ziff as Ziff-Davis Publishing Co., 540 North Michigan Avenue, Chicago, Illinois, later 185 North Wabash Avenue, Chicago, Illinois.
EDITORS: B. G. Davis (1945); Raymond A. Palmer (1945–1947); Howard Browne (1947).
PRICE PER ISSUE: 25 cents.
SIZE AND PAGINATION: 6-3/4" X 9-3/4"; 178–274 pages.
CURRENT STATUS: Discontinued.
—*James R. McCahery*

MAN FROM U.N.C.L.E. MAGAZINE, THE

This magazine was a spinoff from a very popular television show. The first episode of "The Man from U.N.C.L.E." was shown on the NBC network on the Tuesday evening of September 22, 1964. The show was not an instant success; in mid-season it was switched to Monday evening, where it began to pick up a following and by the end of the season was one of the most popular T.V. shows. MGM held the rights to "U.N.C.L.E." property and began to sell off those rights for various spinoffs. One of the derivatives of this move was this magazine.[1]

The right to publish the magazine was won by Renown Publications, a small publishing house in New York City. At the time, they were publishing only one other magazine, the *Mike Shayne Mystery Magazine*.* The publisher, Leo Margulies, had published about fifty different pulp magazines (all proclaiming it was "A Thrilling Publication") for Better Publications, Inc., and had gained considerable fame in doing so.

Renown was a two-person operation. Margulies was assisted by his wife, Cylvia Kleinman (Margulies) as editor. Often, she would use her maiden name. For *The Man from U.N.C.L.E. Magazine*, a new company was instituted, the Leo Margulies Corp., with financial assistance from Publishers Distributing Corporation.

Each issue of the magazine was to have a 30,000-word story about the adventures of U.N.C.L.E. agents, Napoleon Solo and Illya Kuryakin. MGM specified that the stories would have to be originals (no adaptations from the television scripts was permitted, to avoid payment of royalties to scriptwriters).

An author was sought for the magazine series, and Dennis Lynds (who was writing the Mike Shayne stories for Renown under the usual pseudonym of Brett Halliday) agreed to write six stories. The Scott Meredith Literary Agency proposed two writers: Harry Whittington, a prolific writer of paperback novels and author of the second U.N.C.L.E. story published by Ace Books; and John Jakes, a science fiction writer who was a fan of the television series and who would later become a famous novelist.

Lynds was paid $450 for the first story, which appeared on the newsstands the second week of January 1966, dated February. In February, the second issue was on sale, and it was reported that sales of the first issue were considerable. The final sales report, made in April, revealed that the first issue sold well on the East and West Coasts but not so well elsewhere. Since sales overall were marginal, the print run was reduced.

Every issue featured an U.N.C.L.E. story under the pseudonym Robert Hart Davis, a name chosen for reader identification when Margulies realized he would be using different actual authors. Robert Davis was the name of an editor at the Frank A. Munsey Company who had given Margulies his first job. Why "Hart" was used as a part of the house name is not known now. During the first year of the U.N.C.L.E. magazine, Dennis Lynds wrote five stories, Harry Whittington four, and John Jakes three stories.

The history of the second issue has interesting sidelights. The March 1966 issue had an U.N.C.L.E. story titled "The Beauty and Beast Affair." Margulies received a manuscript from Harry Whittington during the first week in October 1965, and this was sent on to MGM for their approval, as was required. It was rejected by Frederick Houghton, and the suggestion was made that an outline be submitted prior to a completed story. The reason given for the rejection— that inoculating animals with a deadly disease resembled too closely the premise in Ian Fleming's *On Her Majesty's Secret Service*. Undaunted by the rapidly approaching deadline, Whittington turned in a new story in less than two weeks; and fighting a delay in approval which was finally obtained, Margulies had the issue on the stands on schedule. The original, rejected manuscript was then changed, as to characters and organizations, and printed in the February 1968 issue of *Mike Shayne Mystery Magazine* as "The Ship of Horror" by Harry Whittington.

The Man from U.N.C.L.E. Magazine was not a long-running one; the first issue was February 1966, the last, January 1968, for a total of twenty-four issues. Covers had a solid-color background; a different color was used for each issue. There was always a picture of Robert Vaughn and David McCallum, the two actors who played the parts of Napoleon Solo and Illya Kuryakin in the television series, in an action scene from the television show. On the back cover was another scene, in black and white.

In addition to the featured U.N.C.L.E. story, there were about a half-dozen short stories in each issue, including a number of secondary series. Five stories were about John Pond, an American agent of the State Department. Each of these was very short, about two pages, and was written by Daniel French. There were four stories about Joe Rodriquez of Army Counter-Intelligence in Vietnam, by Tom H. Moriarty, and four stories by Stuart M. Kaminsky about Pete Breedlove, an eleven-year-old who helped his chief of police solve murders. Another series was by Dan Ross, in which Mei Wong, an Indian art dealer, was an amateur criminologist. Several other series were of two stories each.

The strangest series began in the October 1966 issue, debuted by "The Perfect Host" by Theordore Sturgeon. This was a reprint from the old *Weird Tales** magazine, and within the next fifteen issues, nine more reprints from *Weird Tales* appeared. Whether these stories were included for lack of filler material or in the hope they would boost circulation, they did give class to the magazine. Some were advertised on the cover as a "lost story masterpiece."

Of the stories of the U.N.C.L.E. agents, seven were written by Dennis Lynds, seven by John Jakes, four by Harry Whittington, and two by I. G. Edmonds. Single stories were written by Talmage Powell, Frank Belknap Long, Richard Curtis, and Bill Pronzini.

A February 1968 issue was announced but was never published due to poor sales. And the last television episode aired on January 15, 1968, which coincided with the demise of the magazine.

Note

1. All stories were copyrighted by MGM Studios.

Information Sources

INDEX SOURCES: Cook, Michael L. *Monthly Murders*. Westport, Conn.: Greenwood Press, 1982.
LOCATION SOURCES: Leo Margulies Collection, Library of the University of Oregon, Eugene, Ore.; Legal Department, MGM Studios, Culver City, Calif.; private collectors.

Publication History

MAGAZINE TITLE: *The Man from U.N.C.L.E. Magazine*.
TITLE CHANGES: None.
VOLUME AND ISSUE DATA: Vol. 1, no. 1 (February 1966) through Vol. 4, no. 6 (January 1968); 24 issues.
PUBLISHER: Leo Margulies as Leo Margulies Corporation, 160 West 46th Street, New York, New York, later 56 West 45th Street, New York, New York.
EDITOR: Cylvia Kleinman (Margulies).
PRICE PER ISSUE: 50 cents.
SIZE AND PAGINATION: 5-3/8" X 7-5/8"; 144 pages.
CURRENT STATUS: Discontinued.
—*Albert Tonik*

MANHUNT

Manhunt, once boasting that it was the world's best-selling crime fiction magazine, was off to an auspicious beginning with its first issue in January 1953. An outstanding selection of stories was headed by the first installment of Mickey Spillane's "Everybody's Watching Me," the only story ever serialized in *Manhunt*. This continued through the first four issues. (It is of interest to note that the entire story was reprinted again in June 1955 in one unusually thick issue of the magazine and again in January 1964 as "I Came to Kill You," the only time that a story has been printed three times by one magazine. The British edition of *Manhunt* also carried the story in its first four issues, and it appeared again in three installments in the *Bloodhound Detective Story Magazine* [British].*)

Manhunt encouraged tough-minded crime fiction, without taboos, and in the fifties was one of the most important hard-boiled detective magazines published. Not only were significant novelists included, such as Erskine Caldwell, Nelson Algren, James M. Cain, James T. Farrell, and Evan Hunter (including under his pseudonyms of Ed McBain, Hunt Collins, and Richard Marsten), but many of the top-name mystery writers also appeared. Here are found short stories by Rex Stout, William Irish, Leslie Charteris, Raymond Chandler, Robert Bloch, John D. MacDonald, Erle Stanley Gardner, Donald Hamilton, Fredric Brown, Fletcher Flora, Richard E. Prather, Frank Kane, and others—a veritable who's who of mystery fiction. Anthony Boucher contributed a review column under the name of H. H. Holmes, and there were occasional true-crime and fact-article columns. As well as contributing many stories, Robert Turner wrote a memorable "Requiem for a Magazine," describing *Manhunt*'s demise, published in the August 1968 issue of *The Mystery Lovers Newsletter (Mystery Reader's Newsletter*)*.

In an experiment to gain better newsstand display, the March 1957 issue of *Manhunt* was published in an 8-1/2" X 11" format; this continued for twelve issues, but with the May 1958 issue, *Manhunt* reverted to digest size.

The British firm of Monthly Magazines, Ltd., contracted with Flying Eagle Publications, Inc., to publish *Manhunt* in England, using strictly reprints of the U.S. magazine. The first of thirteen such issues appeared there in August 1953.

In late 1953 and early 1954, on a quarterly basis, Flying Eagle Publications produced an omnibus volume of the magazine titled *Giant Manhunt*. Four such issues were produced, being four monthly issues bound together with a new cover for seventy-five cents.

Information Sources

BIBLIOGRAPHY:

Breen, Jon L. "On the Passing of Manhunt," *The Armchair Detective*, Vol. 1, no. 3 (April 1968): 89–93.

Turner, Robert. "Requiem for a Magazine." *The Mystery Lovers' Newsletter*, Vol. 1, no. 6 (August 1968): 5–6.

INDEX SOURCES: Cook, Michael L. *Monthly Murders*. Westport, Conn.: Greenwood Press, 1982.
LOCATION SOURCES: University of California–Los Angeles Library (Vol. 1, nos. 1–4, 6, 7, only); private collectors.

Publication History

MAGAZINE TITLE: *Manhunt*.
TITLE CHANGES: First three issues titled *Manhunt Detective Story Monthly*.
VOLUME AND ISSUE DATA: Vol. 1, no. 1 (January 1953) through Vol. 15, no. 2 (April–May 1967); 113 issues.
PUBLISHER: Eagle Publications, Inc., affiliate of [Michael St. John's] St. John Publishing Company; later as Flying Eagle Publications, Inc., 545 Fifth Avenue, New York, New York.
EDITORS: 1953: John McCloud, editor; E. A. Tulman, managing editor. 1955: Hal Walker, managing editor. 1956: Walter R. Schmidt, editorial director; N. F. King, managing editor, G. F. St. John, associate editor. 1957: William Manners, managing editor; N. F. King, associate editor. 1958: Francis X. Lewis, editor; Jeff Cooke, managing editor. 1960: John Underwood, editor; J. Proske, associate editor.
PRICE PER ISSUE: 35 cents (through December 1963); 50 cents.
SIZE AND PAGINATION: 5-1/2" X 7-5/8" (except for 12 issues, March 1957 through April 1958, which were 8-1/2" X 11"); average 128 pages (oversize, 64 pages).
CURRENT STATUS: Discontinued.

British edition

MAGAZINE TITLE: *Manhunt*.
TITLE CHANGES: None.
VOLUME AND ISSUE DATA: Vol. 1, no. 1 (August 1953) through Vol. 2, no. 2 (September 1954); 13 issues.
PUBLISHER: Monthly Magazines, Ltd., 109 Great Russell Street, London W.C.1, England.
EDITOR: Not stated.
PRICE PER ISSUE: 1 shilling 6 pence (until March 1954); 2 shillings.
SIZE AND PAGINATION: 5-1/2" X 7-1/2"; average 128 pages.
CURRENT STATUS: Discontinued.

Omnibus edition (U.S.)

MAGAZINE TITLE: *Giant Manhunt*.
TITLE CHANGES: None.
VOLUME AND ISSUE DATA: 1953–1954; 4 issues (each issue consisting of four monthly issues of U.S. edition bound together with a new cover).
PUBLISHER: Same as magazine.
EDITOR: Same as magazine.
PRICE PER ISSUE: 75 cents.
SIZE AND PAGINATION: 5-1/2" X 7-5/8"; 512 pages.
CURRENT STATUS: Discontinued.

MANHUNT (British)

See MANHUNT

MANHUNT DETECTIVE STORY MONTHLY

See MANHUNT

MAN-HUNTERS

First published in January 1934,[1] there is the possibility this was a true-crime magazine. No other information is available.

Note

1. As listed in the "Tentative Pulp Checklist," San Francisco Academy of Comic Art (unpublished manuscript, n.d.).

Information Sources

INDEX SOURCES: None known.
LOCATION SOURCES: Private collectors.

Publication History

MAGAZINE TITLE: *Man-Hunters*.
TITLE CHANGES: None known.
VOLUME AND ISSUE DATA: Vol. 1, no. 1 (January 1934); number of issues and
        extent unknown.
PUBLISHER: Not known.
EDITOR: Not known.
PRICE PER ISSUE: Not known.
SIZE AND PAGINATION: Not known.
CURRENT STATUS: Discontinued.

MANTRAP

There is a striking similarity of *Mantrap* to one of its contemporary magazines, *Manhunt,** and this can perhaps be understood by knowing that both were by the same publisher. *Mantrap*, however, failed to achieve the success of *Manhunt* and was limited to only two issues. It is difficult to understand why. Both magazines featured the same type of hard-boiled crime-adventure stories, with many of the same authors, and with the same type of one-color story illustrations. Covers of *Mantrap* were from color photographs of a staged crime scene.

The first issue offered two short novels, "Body in Blue Jeans" by Allen Lang and "The Glass Alibi" by Harry Whittington, plus thirteen short stories. The second issue featured a full-length novel, "Death in the Mirror," by Helen Nielsen, and eleven short stories. Authors included Richard Hardwick, Dan

Sontup, Robert Turner, Richard Deming, Norman Struber, Philip Ketchum, and others equally familiar to the reading public. Short crime fillers were judiciously used. There were no announcements, editorials, or columns. Advertisements appeared only on the back cover.

Information Sources

INDEX SOURCES: Cook, Michael L. *Monthly Murders*. Westport, Conn.: Greenwood Press, 1982.
LOCATION SOURCES: Private collectors.

Publication History

MAGAZINE TITLE: *Mantrap*.
TITLE CHANGES: None.
VOLUME AND ISSUE DATA: Vol. 1, no. 1 (July 1956) through Vol. 1, no. 2 (October 1956); 2 issues.
PUBLISHER: Secret Life Publications, Inc., later as Flying Eagle Publications, Inc., both at 545 Fifth Avenue, New York 17, New York. Publisher, Michael St. John.
EDITOR: Walter R. Schmidt, editorial director. First issue, N. F. King, managing editor; William Manners, associate editor. Second issue: William Manners; managing editor, N. F. King, associate editor.
PRICE PER ISSUE: 35 cents.
SIZE AND PAGINATION: 5-3/8'' X 7-5/8''; 128 pages.
CURRENT STATUS: Discontinued.

MARCH OF CRIME

See THIRD DEGREE, THE

MARTIN SPEED, DETECTIVE (British)

Ten issues of *Martin Speed, Detective,* were published during 1943–1947. No other information is available.

Information Sources

BIBLIOGRAPHY:
Lofts, W.O.G., and Derek J. Adley, *Old Boys Books, A Complete Catalogue*. London: privately printed, 1969.
INDEX SOURCES: None known.
LOCATION SOURCES: Private collectors.

Publication History

MAGAZINE TITLE: *Martin Speed, Detective*.
TITLE CHANGES: None.
VOLUME AND ISSUE DATA: No. 1 (1943) through No. 10 (1947); 10 issues.
PUBLISHER: Gerald Swan, London.
EDITOR: Not known.

PRICE PER ISSUE: Not known.
SIZE AND PAGINATION: 5-3/8'' X 7''; 64 pages.
CURRENT STATUS: Discontinued.

MASKED DETECTIVE, THE

As a companion magazine to the *Phantom Detective,* The Ghost, Super-Detective,* The Lone Eagle,* and the *Black Book Detective Magazine,** there was *The Masked Detective*. This title carried what were by far among the most unusual and rather intriguing epics in all of pulp fiction, and The Masked Detective was sometimes referred to as "the world's greatest crime sleuth" by his admirers.

The Masked Detective, published by Better Publications, Inc., featured three "exciting short stories" and a department for readers labeled "Under the Domino" in addition to the lead novel. The department concerned itself with the next adventure to be offered but also contained letters from readers. Covers and interior art were extremely well executed, although artists and illustrators were not identified.

A total of twelve book-length novels featured The Masked Detective—"Daring Exploits of a Mysterious Crime Avenger"—and another was later published in *Thrilling Mystery** ("Monarchs of Murder," Fall 1944).

The first issue of *The Masked Detective* appeared in the fall of 1940 and was so labeled; the last was the Spring 1943 issue. With the United States being eventually involved in World War II, the covers included the slogan "Buy War Bonds and Stamps for Victory," and inside were advertisements that proclaimed "And industrial warfare has its 'commandos' too; men, whether you are 16 or 50, you are vitally needed in our national victory program." One ad, especially appealing, said: "Let's go. Help fire that last shot with the Marines." Probably the one that many recall most was a sketch of a white-haired lady embracing a soldier; below the picture were these words: "You give to someone you know when you give to the USO."

The author of The Masked Detective series was C.K.M. Scanlon, a house name. There were actually several writers involved, believed to include G. F. Eliot and Norman A. Daniels.

In the stories, the man behind that black velvet mask was really Rex Parker, newshawk crime reporter for the *New York Comet*. He was seen as a rather genial, long-legged, lazy cuss, a bit taller than average, wearing loose-fitting clothing and a battered hat. He was a student of *La Savate,* the French art of fighting with the feet. His alter ego, The Masked Detective, worked independently of all law enforcement agencies, slashing through red tape whenever it suited his purpose. In this guise, he wore a neat black suit, gray shirt, dark bow tie, black hat, and a black mask covering his eyes, forehead, and nose. He wore specially built shoes with square, hard toes. He was also a master of ju-jitsu, a good shot, a trained boxer, a makeup artist, and a ventriloquist.

Only two individuals were aware of his double identity. One, a detective-sergeant of homicide, was Dan Gleason, a bulky, gruff man who never minced words. The other, a columnist for New York papers, Winnie Bligh, supplied the female interest.

The Masked Detective's adventures, often of a violent nature, included stories with the then-current war as background, such as "The League of the Iron Cross," "The Fifth Column Murders," and "The Canal Zone Murders." The novels were action-packed and fast moving. Rex Parker was a worthy hero in every sense of the word and found a rightful place in the pulps.

Information Sources

BIBLIOGRAPHY:
Carr, Wooda Nicholas. "The Masked Detective." *Pulp*, no. 8 (Spring 1976): 3–8.
INDEX SOURCES: None known.
LOCATION SOURCES: University of California–Los Angeles Library (Vol. 1, no. 1 only); private collectors.

Publication History

MAGAZINE TITLE: *The Masked Detective*.
TITLE CHANGES: None.
VOLUME AND ISSUE DATA: Vol. 1, no. 1 (Fall 1940) through Vol. 4, no. 3 (Spring 1943); 12 issues.
PUBLISHER: Better Publications, Inc., 10 East 40th Street, New York, New York; Ned L. Pines, president.
EDITOR: Not known.
PRICE PER ISSUE: 10 cents.
SIZE AND PAGINATION: 7" X 10"; 128 pages.
CURRENT STATUS: Discontinued.
—*Wooda Nicholas Carr*

MEGAVORE (Canadian)

Megavore was a well-produced and edited magazine covering all phases of popular fiction, with considerable emphasis on mystery and detective fiction commencing with the ninth (June 1980) issue. The first eight issues were titled *The Science Fiction Collector* and included numerous articles and bibliographical material on science fiction and fantasy, particularly in the paperback format. With issue number 9, the periodical *The Age of the Unicorn** was incorporated into the magazine, and information on pulp magazines, as well as mystery and detective data, began to appear. With the ninth issue, the title was changed to *Megavore*, but with the fourteenth issue the title reverted to *The Science Fiction Collector*. Contents continued to feature articles on collecting, reviews, commentary, and bibliographical data.

With the fifteenth issue, the magazine changed to tabloid, newspaper format, and it was discontinued with issue number 15-1/2,'' which was entirely advertisements.

Information Sources

INDEX SOURCES: None known.
LOCATION SOURCES: Private collectors.

Publication History

MAGAZINE TITLE: *Megavore*.
TITLE CHANGES: Originally *The Science Fiction Collector* (nos. 1–8), which was also title of the last three issues (nos. 14–15-1/2).
VOLUME AND ISSUE DATA: No. 1, undated (1976), through No. 15-1/2 (September 1981); 16 issues.
PUBLISHER: J. Grant Thiessen as Pandora's Books Ltd., Box 1298, Altona, Manitoba ROG OBO, Canada; U.S. address: Box 86, Neche, North Dakota 58265.
DITOR: J. Grant Thiessen.
PRICE PER ISSUE: $1.00.
SIZE AND PAGINATION: First 14 issues 8-1/2'' X 11''; last two issues in tabloid, newspaper format; average 48 pages.
CURRENT STATUS: Discontinued.

MENACE

Menace, like *Murder**, was a short-lived attempt to please the reading public with contemporary crime-adventure stories that were but one step removed from the pulp magazines. The first issue of *Menace*, in November 1954, presented a Shell Scott Novel by Richard S. Prather (''Blood Ballot''), novelettes by Frank Ward and Fletcher Flora, and four short stories, accompanied by crime feature articles (''It's a Racket,'' ''Scene of the Crime,'' ''Tricks of the Trade,'' and ''On the Blotter''). These features were also present in the second issue, January 1955, which headlined ''The Dike Breakers'' by Samuel A. Krasney as the complete novel.

Although not lacking better-known writers, the competition was such that many magazines were crowded from the racks or displayed poorly, and distribution seemed to be a widespread problem. And after two issues, *Menace* disappeared from the scene.

Information Sources

INDEX SOURCES: Cook, Michael L. *Monthly Murders*. Westport, Conn.: Greenwood Press, 1982.
LOCATION SOURCES: Private collectors.

Publication History

MAGAZINE TITLE: *Menace*.
TITLE CHANGES: None.

VOLUME AND ISSUE DATA: Vol. 1, no. 1 (November 1954) through Vol. 2, no. 1 (January 1955); 2 issues.
PUBLISHER: Michael St. John as St. John Publishing Corp., 545 Fifth Avenue, New York 17, New York.
EDITOR: John McCloud; Hal Walker, managing editor.
PRICE PER ISSUE: 35 cents.
SIZE AND PAGINATION: 5-1/2'' X 7-3/4''; 130–148 pages.
CURRENT STATUS: Discontinued.

MERCURY MYSTERY-BOOK MAGAZINE

The American Mercury, Inc./Mercury Publications, Inc., published a long-running series of full-length and condensed mystery novels in digest-size, paperback format titled *Mercury Mystery*. The first of these, interestingly, was James M. Cain's *The Postman Always Rings Twice,* which was so titled because it was rejected by so many publishers that some days the postman rang twice in returning copies of the manuscript.

With the 210th book in the series, the digest was changed to *Mercury Mystery-Book Magazine,* continuing for a total of twenty-three issues. This magazine, along with its companion, the *Bestseller Mystery Magazine,** must be considered a pioneer of the digest-size mystery magazine as we know it today. Following the tradition of *Ellery Queen's Mystery Magazine,** here were to be found mystery stories, rather than detective tales, and by some of the authors that we have come today to recognize as some of the best in the genre. The content is unsurprising since Mercury was also the originating publisher of *Ellery Queen's Mystery Magazine*.

Among the eight stories in the first ''magazine'' issue were three very short stories by Damon Runyon: ''False Identification,'' ''Grunt Guy,'' and ''The Dutchman.'' A prophetic story, ''Is Your Phone Tapped?'' by Jack Kerhoff, is strangely appropriate today. The time was, however, September 1955.

The second monthly issue brought Frank Gruber's ''Falcon City Frame-Up,'' Lawrence G. Blochman's ''The Case of the Greedy Groom,'' and ''The Murdered Magdalen'' by Craig Rice, among others; Craig Rice returned with ''The House of Missing Girls'' in November 1955, ''The Air-Tight Alibi'' in February 1956, and ''Sixty Cents Worth of Murder'' in July 1957. Erle Stanley Gardner had ''The Lingering Doubt'' in July 1956, the first of eight stories to appear by this master. Among other writers were Gil Brewer, Edward Ronns, Miriam Allen deFord, George Bagby, Thomas B. Dewey, Ed Lacy, Stuart Palmer, and many others.

As the magazine progressed, the number of stories gradually decreased, although the quality overall was well above average. The last four issues contained but four or five stories each.

The last issue was numbered as 232 and dated April 1959; after termination, the masthead of *Bestseller Mystery Magazine* stated that it included *Mercury Mystery Magazine*.

Information Sources

INDEX SOURCES: Cook, Michael L. *Monthly Murders*. Westport, Conn.: Greenwood Press, 1982.
LOCATION SOURCES: Private collectors.

Publication History

MAGAZINE TITLE: *Mercury Mystery-Book Magazine*.
TITLE CHANGES: *Mercury Mystery Magazine,* with the October 1958 issue (whole no. 229). Upon discontinuation in 1959, this title was included on the masthead of a companion magazine, *Bestseller Mystery Magazine*..
VOLUME AND ISSUE DATA: Vol. 1, no. 1 (September 1955, whole no. 210) through Vol. 5, no. 2 (April 1959, whole no. 232); 23 issues.
PUBLISHER: Mercury Publications (Press), Inc., 527 Madison Avenue, New York 22, New York; Joseph W. Ferman, publisher.
EDITORS: Joseph W. Ferman, editor; Robert P. Mills, managing editor; Charles Angoff and Gloria Levitas, associate editors; later, Edward Ferman, editorial assistant.
PRICE PER ISSUE: 35 cents.
SIZE AND PAGINATION: 5-3/8'' X 7-5/8''; 130 pages.
CURRENT STATUS: Discontinued.

MERCURY MYSTERY MAGAZINE (British)

Mercury Mystery Magazine, like so many others in Britain, relied on reprints from an American edition, (*Mercury Mystery-Book Magazine**). At least two-thirds of each issue was taken up with a full-length novel; among the earlier issues the featured authors included Ed Lacy and Thomas B. Dewey.

This was a well-produced and brightly covered magazine. Judging from its comparative scarcity now, one can only assume that it never gained the mystery fans' approval.

Information Sources

INDEX SOURCES: Cook, Michael L. *Monthly Murders*. Westport, Conn.: Greenwood Press, 1982.
LOCATION SOURCES: Private collectors.

Publication History

MAGAZINE TITLE: *Mercury Mystery Magazine*.
TITLE CHANGES: None.
VOLUME AND ISSUE DATA : No. 1 (March 1963) through No. 12 (February 1964); later issues, if any, not noted; 12 issues.
PUBLISHER: Atlas Publishing & Distributing Co., Ltd., 18 Bride Lane, London E.C.4, England.

EDITOR: Not known.
PRICE PER ISSUE: 2 shillings 6 pence.
SIZE AND PAGINATION: 5-1/4'' X 7-1/2''; 128 pages.
CURRENT STATUS: Discontinued.
—*Robert Adey*

MERCURY MYSTERY MAGAZINE (U.S.)

See MERCURY MYSTERY-BOOK MAGAZINE

MICHAEL SHAYNE MYSTERY MAGAZINE

See MIKE SHAYNE MYSTERY MAGAZINE

MIKE SHAYNE MYSTERY MAGAZINE

Leo Margulies was the editorial director for Ned Pines's "Thrilling" line of pulp magazines during the 1930s and 1940s. After the demise of the pulps, in 1956, he founded Renown Publications and began his own line of magazines, maintaining the pulp tradition that he knew so well. Approaching Davis Dresser, an old friend and creator of the fictional detective character, Mike Shayne, an arrangement was made whereby Shayne could be used by Margulies, along with the Brett Halliday name, for a new magazine. Shayne was to be named in the title and was to be the featured character in a lead story in each issue; short stories by other writers were to be used for the remainder of the magazine.

The publication, titled *Michael Shayne Mystery Magazine,* first appeared in September 1956. It was digest size and 160 pages. The format was very similar to the many pulp magazines with which Margulies had gained his experience (*The Masked Detective,** *The Phantom Detective,** *G-Men Detective,** and so forth), but Margulies brought in his own writers to script the lead Mike Shayne stories. An unconfirmed report credits Sam Merwin, Jr., then editor for the magazine, as the actual author of the first four Mike Shayne stories in the new magazine. Then the authorship reads like a who's who in mystery fiction: Robert Arthur, Richard Deming, Michael Avallone, Ryerson Johnson, Dennis Lynds, Frank Belknap Long, Clayton Matthews, Gary Brandner, David Mazroff, Edward Breese, L. M. Van Derveer, Bill Pronzini, Jeff Wallmann, James and Livia Reasoner, and others.

The series began as a monthly publication but, for a period in 1957 and 1958, was bimonthly before it reverted to the monthly schedule. The magazine ran for six issues per volume until 1977, at which time volume 41 contained only five issues; then in 1978, with volume 42, numbering placed twelve issues in a volume. The magazine changed title only once, with the April 1957 issue, to *Mike Shayne Mystery Magazine.*

The magazine has had a number of associate editors during its long run, beginning with Sam Merwin, Jr., to the present Charles Fritch. Margulies's wife,

Cylvia Kleinman Margulies, was listed as managing editor and remained in this position, or that of editor, until after her husband's death. At that time, she became the publisher and served in this position until early 1978, when Renown Publications was sold. She had been an editor for Standard Magazines, Inc., during the thirties and forties; her initials were used for the once-popular house name, C.K.M. Scanlon.

Beginning with 160 pages, this count was reduced to 144 pages with the June 1957 issue, further reduced to 128 pages in August 1957, and was increased to 144 pages again in February 1964. It remained that size until March 1968, when it reverted to 128 pages. By January 1973, the page count was again 160, but by September 1974, it was only 128 pages. In April 1980, it boasted 162 pages, but this was in conjunction with a price increase. In June 1980, the pages dropped back to 130.

Cylvia Margulies sold Renown Publications and the *Mike Shayne Mystery Magazine* in April 1978; the files and records during the Margulies's ownership are now located at the University of Oregon. The purchasers were Edward and Anita Goldstein.

Margulies published several companion magazines, all in the early pulp tradition, as well as the Shayne series; these included *Satellite Science Fiction, The Man from U.N.C.L.E. Magazine,* * *The Girl from U.N.C.L.E. Magazine,* * *Shell Scott Mystery Magazine,* * and *Charlie Chan Mystery Magazine.* *

Three annuals were published, in 1971, 1972, and 1973. Each of these was 192 pages and sold for one dollar. The Mike Shayne stories were new, but the majority of the other fiction was reprinted from other Renown magazines.

Only three times during its long run has the monthly publication schedule been disrupted: the 1957–1958 period when the magazine was bimonthly, and when two months were missed, November 1974 and November 1977.

The character of Mike Shayne was created in 1938 by pulp writer Davis Dresser. Dresser had been a western fiction writer but turned to mystery fiction, partly inspired by his admiration of Dashiell Hammett. His first Shayne story was submitted to over twenty New York publishers—who all told him that the hard-boiled detective was out—before Brett Stokes (son of Frederick Stokes), editor at Henry Holt Company, thought differently. He published the first Shayne book, *Dividend on Death*, in 1939. The "Brett" half of Dresser's pen name was his compliment to Stokes.

The second book, *The Private Practice of Michael Shayne,* was a hit. Twentieth Century Fox Studio bought it and made a total of seven Shayne movies, starring Lloyd Nolan, in 1946–1947. A radio show featured Jeff Chandler from 1945 to 1947. In 1960, a television series, with Richard Denning as the star, was made under the auspices of Four Star Productions.

There have been sixty-nine novels of Mike Shayne, printed in hardback and paperback editions. Three of the novels were adapted for a comic book in the 1960s by Gold Key Publications.

But it was the digest magazine from Renown Publications that captured the majority of the Shayne fans. The magazine celebrated its twenty-fifth year of publication with the release of the September 1981 issue; and as of December 1981, a total of 293 issues had been published, plus the three annuals.

One story in novel length, "Weep for a Blonde Corpse," was serialized in February, April, and June 1957. Another, "The Body That Came Back," was serialized in the December 1963 and January and February 1964 issues, though the latter two issues also contained a Shayne short story.

There have been two British series of the *Mike Shayne Mystery Magazine*. The first series, from 1957 to 1958, was published by Frew Publications Pty. Ltd. in Australia and distributed in England. These issues are identified with volume and issue number; twelve issues were published, priced at one shilling, six pence; the last issue of this series was dated May–June 1958. The second series, by Atlas Distributing & Publishing Co., Ltd., was identified by issue number only, commencing with number 101 in March 1964 and ending with number 108 in October 1964.

All of the British magazines' stories were reprints from the U.S. edition but did not exactly match the U.S. issues. In general, the first series started with reprinting volume 1, number 1, of the U.S. edition, and the second series began with reprinting volume 13, number 5, of the U.S. edition. In some cases, the British editions published an occasional story prior to its appearance in the United States and, in several instances, omitted stories that were in the U.S. issues.

Information Sources

INDEX SOURCES: Cook, Michael L. *Monthly Murders*. Westport, Conn.: Greenwood Press, 1982.

LOCATION SOURCES: Leo Margulies Collection, University of Oregon, Eugene, Ore.; private collectors.

Publication History

MAGAZINE TITLE: *Mike Shayne Mystery Magazine*.

TITLE CHANGES: Originally *Michael Shayne Mystery Magazine* (until April 1957).

VOLUME AND ISSUE DATA: Vol. 1, no. 1 (September 1956) through Vol. 45, no. 12 (to date, December 1981); 293 issues.

PUBLISHER: Renown Publications, Inc., 16 East 84th Street, New York, New York, later 501 Fifth Avenue, 160 West 46th Street, and 56 West 45th Street, New York, New York; also 8230 Beverly Boulevard and P.O. Box 69150, Los Angeles, California, and P.O. Box 1084 and P.O. Box 178, Reseda, California.

EDITORS: Sam Merwin, Jr.; Frank Belknap Long (March 1960); William Scott (May 1963); Frank B. Long (August 1963); H. N. Alden (November 1965); Holmes Taylor (or Taylor Holmes; names were shown both ways) (December 1966); Thom Montgomery (April 1974); Sam Merwin, Jr. (July 1976); Charles E. Fritch (November 1979).

PRICE PER ISSUE: 35 cents; 50 cents (February 1964); 60 cents (August 1971); 75 cents (January 1973); $1.00 (January 1978); $1.25 (March 1979); $1.50 (April 1980).

SIZE AND PAGINATION: 5-1/2'' X 7-1/2''; 128–162 pages.
CURRENT STATUS: Active.

British editions

MAGAZINE TITLE: *Mike Shayne Mystery Magazine*.
TITLE CHANGES: None.
VOLUME AND ISSUE DATA: First Series: Vol. 1, no. 1 (May 1957) through Vol. 1,
     no. 12 (May–June 1958). Second Series: No. 101 (March 1964) through no. 108
     (October 1964); 12 issues (First Series); 8 issues (Second Series).
PUBLISHER: First Series: Frew Publications Pty., Ltd., 70 Bathurst Street, Sydney,
     Australia. Second Series: Atlas Publishing & Distributing Co. Ltd., 18 Bride
     Lane, London, E.C.4, England.
EDITOR: Not known.
PRICE PER ISSUE: First Series, 1 shilling 6 pence; Second Series, 2 shillings 6 pence,
     except final issue, 3 shillings.
SIZE AND PAGINATION: 5-3/8'' X 7-1/2''; average 112 pages.
CURRENT STATUS: Discontinued (British editions).
—*Tom Johnson*

MIKE SHAYNE MYSTERY MAGAZINE (British)

See MIKE SHAYNE MYSTERY MAGAZINE

MOBS

Mobs was one of several pulp magazines published by Harold B. Hersey and
associates in the late 1920s and early 1930s.

"It was not a sudden brainstorm that led me to create *Gangster Stories,** and
other magazines such as *Racketeer Stories,** *Mobs,* and *Gangland Stories,**"
wrote Hersey. "When we launched *Flying Aces* and the other titles I was asked
to take over *Underworld Magazine [Underworld, The*],* a periodical that had
been on the newsstands for some time. Having been aware (weren't we all?)
that the public fancy was engrossed with the amazing spectacle of racketeers
enjoying a fabulous prosperity in the period of The Noble Experiment, when
the newspapers made heroes out of the great gangsters, I decided to concentrate
on this theme. . . ."[1]

Mobs existed for a short time, under the editorship of W. M. Clayton, a "Blue
Band" publication.

Note

1. Harold Hersey, *Pulpwood Editor* (New York: Frederick A. Stokes Co., 1938), p. 198.

Information Sources

BIBLIOGRAPHY:
Hersey, Harold B. *Pulpwood Editor*. New York: Frederick A. Stokes Co., 1938.
INDEX SOURCES: None known.
LOCATION SOURCES: Private collectors.

Publication History

MAGAZINE TITLE: *Mobs*.
TITLE CHANGES: None.
VOLUME AND ISSUE DATA: Number of issues, date, and extent unknown.
PUBLISHER: Harold B. Hersey as Blue Band Publications, Inc., New York, New York.
EDITOR: W. M. Clayton.
PRICE PER ISSUE: Not known.
SIZE AND PAGINATION: Not known.
CURRENT STATUS: Discontinued.

MOBSTERS

Although published for only three issues, from December 1952 to April 1953, *Mobsters* was an important traditional pulp magazine with "Stories of the fight against the Underworld." It featured a complete novel, several short stories, an editorial ("The Gang's All Here!"), and filler features such as crime facts, quizzes, and "Crime Clinic." The covers were similar to the paperback books that began in this period to crowd out the magazines. *Mobsters* was published by Standard Magazines, Inc. (a "Thrilling" publication).

Information Sources

INDEX SOURCES: None known.
LOCATION SOURCES: University of California–Los Angeles Library (Vol. 1, no. 1, only); private collectors.

Publication History

MAGAZINE TITLE: *Mobsters*.
TITLE CHANGE: None.
VOLUME AND ISSUE DATA: Vol. 1, no. 1 (December 1952) through Vol. 1, no. 3 (April 1953); 3 issues.
PUBLISHER: Standard Magazines, Inc., 1125 East Vaile Avenue, Kokomo, Indiana, with editorial offices at 10 East 40th Street, New York, New York.
EDITOR: Not known.
PRICE PER ISSUE: 25 cents.
SIZE AND PAGINATION: 6-5/8" X 9-3/8"; pages not known.
CURRENT STATUS: Discontinued.

MODERN ADVENTURES

See SCARLET ADVENTURES

MOVIE DETECTIVE

Movie Detective, published for just two issues, December 1942 and January 1943, capitalized on the popularity of the Hollywood screen magazines. A typical cover showed James Cagney in a gangster pose, a revolver in each hand (January 1943). In this issue, the lead story was "Maori Murder Case" in which the "Man in the Red Mask Outwits Headhunters in America"—the Red Mask's final appearance in the pulps after being the hero of his own magazine (*Red Mask Detective Stories**). In this issue also was a story by Ellery Queen ("Ellery Queen and the Perfect Crime") which had been filmed starring Ralph Bellamy and Margaret Lindsay.

Information Sources

INDEX SOURCES: None known.
LOCATION SOURCES: Private collectors.

Publication History

MAGAZINE TITLE: *Movie Detective*.
TITLE CHANGES: None.
VOLUME AND ISSUE DATA: Vol. 1, no. 1 (December 1942) through Vol. 1, no. 2
    (January 1943); 2 issues.
PUBLISHER: Not known.
EDITOR: Not known.
PRICE PER ISSUE: Not known.
SIZE AND PAGINATION: Not known.
CURRENT STATUS: Discontinued.

MOVIE MYSTERY MAGAZINE

Movie Mystery Magazine was a digest-sized magazine issued by Anson Bond Publications of Hollywood. Printed on the rough paper of the day's paperback books, this short-lived publication bore little similarity in appearance to the slick, large, movie magazines with which it (unwisely) had to compete. Debuting in 1946 with an adaptation of the Orson Welles and Edward G. Robinson film, "The Stranger" (novelized by Cameron Blake), *Movie Mystery Magazine* was edited by Anson Bond and Eddie Koblitz. Issue number 1, July–August, starred Loretta Young, Welles, and Robinson on the cover. Reviews and cartoons complemented the photos from the movie, representing the bulk of the issue. The second issue, September–October, featured an adaptation of "Home Sweet Homicide" from Craig Rice's novel, which, when filmed, starred Randolph Scott. Rice was one of Bond's honorary "star" editors, undoubtedly a major factor in choosing this relatively obscure film to adapt.

The third and apparently final issue (December–January 1947) contained a novelization of the United Artists' film, "The Chase," derived from a Cornell Woolrich novel (probably *The Black Path of Fear*), starring Robert Cummings, Peter Lorre, and Michele Morgan. Again, the cover painting featured the stars of the film, with just two photos from the production gracing the book's interior. The novelization, typically uncredited, was broken into fifteen chapters, accounting for seventy of the issue's 128 pages. The rest of the magazine was devoted to departments and features, such as "Stop, You're Killing Me" (cartoons by Sam Gorley), "Reel Crime" (a photo-story depicting a crime with the reader left to deduce the clues from the twelve pictures); book, radio, and movie reviews and news; and a short story by Charles G. Booth titled "Orchid Lady." Most of the issue's photographs were attached to a lengthy essay on horror and suspense film classics.

The factors that defeated *Movie Mystery Magazine* are not that much of a mystery. The magazine was too large to fit into the paperback racks on which most books after World War II were displayed, and its side-stapled spine couldn't bear lettering for flat display. Its West Coast point of origin was no help in a business dominated by East Coast publishers and distributors. The choice of films was less than overwhelming. And the publishing situation for paperbacks and magazines was extremely unfavorable—there were so many newcomers, once the paper quotas were lifted, that there literally was no space on the newsstands for all the material being printed. It was not a bad idea, but its hybrid format and unfortunate timing doomed it to a premature demise.

Information Sources

INDEX SOURCES: Cook, Michael L. *Monthly Murders*. Westport, Conn.: Greenwood Press, 1982.
LOCATION SOURCES: Private collectors.

Publication History

MAGAZINE TITLE: *Movie Mystery Magazine*.
TITLE CHANGES: None.
VOLUME AND ISSUE DATA: No. 1 (July–August 1946) through no. 3 (December–January 1947); 3 issues.
PUBLISHER: Anson Bond Publications, Inc., 913 La Cienega Boulevard, Hollywood 46, California.
EDITORS: Anson Bond and Eddie Koblitz.
PRICE PER ISSUE: 25 cents.
SIZE AND PAGINATION: 5-1/2" X 7-1/2"; 128 pages.
CURRENT STATUS: Discontinued.
—*Michael S. Barson*

MURDER

With the great success experienced in the publishing of *Manhunt*,* Flying Eagle Publications launched a similar publication in September 1956 under the title of *Murder*. This featured the identical style of murder and crime-adventure as their other publications, very contemporary in nature, often raw and violent, but mirroring the real-life crime scene.

The magazine was announced as a quarterly and maintained this schedule for three issues—and possibly would have been a success with a more frequent appearance—but was discontinued in the face of fierce competition while still trying to establish its identity with the mystery reading public.

Information Sources

INDEX SOURCES: Cook, Michael L. *Monthly Murders*. Westport, Conn.: Greenwood Press, 1982.
LOCATION SOURCES: Private collectors.

Publication History

MAGAZINE TITLE: *Murder*.
TITLE CHANGES: None.
VOLUME AND ISSUE DATA: Vol. 1, no. 1 (September 1956) through Vol. 2, no. 1 (March 1957); 3 issues.
PUBLISHER: Michael St. John as Flying Eagle Publications, Inc., 545 Fifth Avenue, New York 17, New York.
EDITOR: Not known.
PRICE PER ISSUE: 35 cents.
SIZE AND PAGINATION: 5-1/4'' X 7-5/8''; 128 pages.
CURRENT STATUS: Discontinued.

MURDER MYSTERIES MAGAZINE (1929)

One of the short-lived titles of the Good Story Magazine Company, *Murder Mysteries Magazine* was published for at least two issues. No other information is available.

Information Sources

BIBLIOGRAPHY:
Hersey, Harold B. *Pulpwood Editor*. New York: Frederick A. Stokes Co., 1937.
INDEX SOURCES: None known.
LOCATION SOURCES: Private collectors.

Publication History

MAGAZINE TITLE: *Murder Mysteries Magazine*.
TITLE CHANGES: None known.
VOLUME AND ISSUE DATA: Vol. 1, no. 1 (April 1929) through at least Vol. 1, no. 2 (date unknown); 2 issues.
PUBLISHER: Good Story Magazine Co., Inc., New York, New York (Harold B. Hersey).
EDITOR: Not known.
PRICE PER ISSUE: Not known.
SIZE AND PAGINATION: Not known.
CURRENT STATUS: Discontinued.

MURDER MYSTERIES MAGAZINE (1935)

Although bearing the same title as a magazine published by Hersey (Good Story Magazine Company) in 1929, this *Murder Mysteries Magazine* was apparently a different publication, commencing in 1935. No other information is available.

Information Sources

INDEX SOURCES: None known.
LOCATION SOURCES: University of California–Los Angeles Library (Vol. 1, no. 1); private collectors.

Publication History

MAGAZINE TITLE: *Murder Mysteries Magazine*.
TITLE CHANGES: None known.
VOLUME AND ISSUE DATA: Vol. 1, no. 1 (October 1935); number of issues and extent unknown.
PUBLISHER: Not known.
EDITOR: Not known.
PRICE PER ISSUE: Not known.
SIZE AND PAGINATION: Not known.
CURRENT STATUS: Discontinued.

MURDER STORIES

Murder Stories was a short-lived attempt by Harold B. Hersey's Good Story Magazine Company, with at least one issue, the first, dated July–August 1931. This was edited by Hersey. No other information is available.

Information Sources

INDEX SOURCES: None known.
LOCATION SOURCES: Private collectors.

Publciation History

MAGAZINE TITLE: *Murder Stories*.
TITLE CHANGES: None known.
VOLUME AND ISSUE DATA: Vol. 1, no. 1 (July–August 1931); number of issues and extent unknown.
PUBLISHER: Harold B. Hersey as Good Story Magazine Co., Inc., New York, New York.
EDITOR: Harold B. Hersey.
PRICE PER ISSUE: Not known.
SIZE AND PAGINATION: Not known.
CURRENT STATUS: Discontinued.

MY POCKET DETECTIVE STORIES LIBRARY (British)

Two issues of *My Pocket Detective Stories Library* were published in 1924 by Hornsey Journal, Ltd. No other information is available.

Information Sources

BIBLIOGRAPHY:
Lofts, W.O.G., and Derek J. Adley. *Old Boys Books, A Complete Catalogue*. London: privately printed, 1969.
INDEX SOURCES: None known.
LOCATION SOURCES: Private collectors.

Publication History

MAGAZINE TITLE: *My Pocket Detective Stories Library*.
TITLE CHANGES: None.
VOLUME AND ISSUE DATA: No. 1 (1924) through no. 2 (1924): 2 issues.
PUBLISHER: Hornsey Journal, Ltd., London.
EDITOR: Not known.
PRICE PER ISSUE: Not known.
SIZE AND PAGINATION: 5-3/8'' X 7''; number of pages unknown.
CURRENT STATUS: Discontinued.

MY POCKET MYSTERY STORIES LIBRARY (British)

One issue of *My Pocket Mystery Stories Library* was published in 1924 by Hornsey Journal, Ltd. No other information is available.

Information Sources

BIBLIOGRAPHY:
Lofts, W.O.G., and Derek J. Adley. *Old Boys Books, A Complete Catalogue*. London: privately printed, 1969.
INDEX SOURCES: None known.
LOCATION SOURCES: Private collectors.

Publication History

MAGAZINE TITLE: *My Pocket Mystery Stories Library*.
TITLE CHANGES: None.
VOLUME AND ISSUE DATA: No. 1 (1924); 1 issue.
PUBLISHER: Hornsey Journal, Ltd., London.
EDITOR: Not known.
PRICE PER ISSUE: Not known.
SIZE AND PAGINATION: 5-3/8'' X 7''; number of pages unknown.
CURRENT STATUS: Discontinued.

MYSTERIOUS TIMES

Originating as the brainstorm and ambitious dream of an energetic but naive fifteen-year-old mystery fan, *Mysterious Times* made its first unheralded and inauspicious appearance as a national mystery fanzine in April 1977. William Karpowicz, Jr., editor-in-chief, had intended to produce a fanzine that would represent the total scope of the mystery genre by containing news, opinions, reviews, stories, and articles. In fact, the fanzine was subtitled "A compendium of news, opinions, reviews, stories, and articles in the world of mystery fiction."[1]

Unfortunately, Mr. Karpowicz assumed that reader support and contributions would pour in as soon as *Mysterious Times* arrived in the hands of the knowledgeable fans. The first issue, however, consisted almost entirely of an amateurish short story by an unknown, John McNamara (suspected by some to be a pseudonym of the editor), which instead of inspiring contributions, turned many fans away.

Subsequent issues did indeed include some reviews of mystery literature and movies, a few letters from subscribers, and an occasional article, but nowhere near the landslide response the editor, in his naivety, had expected. The dearth of reader response, along with the mounting monetary loss, proved the fanzine's undoing.

Of the four issues, the last is definitely the best, containing book reviews, a short story, a creative Sherlockian article, an interview with Otto Penzler, and information about a variety of new items in the field of mystery fiction. Even as the last issue was published and the editors faced a back debt of close to eight hundred dollars, Karpowicz was still optimistic about the future of the fanzine, hoping to pay his debts by working part-time as "a Polish busboy in a German restaurant."[2]

The editor's initial fascination with mystery-detective novels may partially stem from his father's occupation as a police officer in Grand Rapids, Michigan. The printing for the fanzine was done by the father and son in their own part-time printing shop.

As late as 1981, Karpowicz was still seriously contemplating another issue of *Mysterious Times*, but, to date, further issues have not been forthcoming.

Critics of the magazine have cited its juvenile, amateurish literary style, its lack of pithy content, and its irregular appearance as reasons for the ultimate demise. Other reasons may be the editor's lack of foresight in not stockpiling articles in advance of the initial publication of the fanzine, the youth and inexperience of the editors, and the paucity of the editor's acquaintances in the realm of mystery fandom.

Still, some credit and acknowledgment must be given to the ambitious undertaking of a fifteen-year-old high school boy in Grand Rapids, who was able to compile, edit, print, and distribute four issues of a national mystery fanzine.

Notes

1. Cover slogan, first three issues, *Mysterious Times*.
2. William Karpowicz, Jr., correspondence to Mary Ann Gottschalk.

Information Sources

INDEX SOURCES: None known.

LOCATION SOURCES: Private collectors.

Publication History

MAGAZINE TITLE: *Mysterious Times*.
TITLE CHANGES: None.
VOLUME AND ISSUE DATA: Vol. 1, no. 1 (April–May 1977) through Vol. 1, no. 4 (March 1978); 4 issues.
PUBLISHER: William A. Karpowicz, Jr., 1013 Short Northeast, Grand Rapids, Michigan 49503.
EDITOR: William A. Karpowicz, Jr.
PRICE PER ISSUE: $1.00.
SIZE AND PAGINATION: 8-1/2'' X 11'' (no. 1); 5-1/2'' x 8-1/2'' (nos. 2–4); 48 pages.
CURRENT STATUS: Discontinued.
—*Mary Ann Grochowski*

MYSTERIOUS TRAVELER MAGAZINE, THE

Based on Mutual Broadcasting System's radio program of the same name, *The Mysterious Traveler* first saw print in November 1951.

While basically a reprint magazine, there were a few original stories—in all, thirteen originals out of sixty-one stories published. The majority of these were in the third issue; the last issue was of all reprint material.

Each issue featured a story as by the "Mysterious Traveler." The fifth issue had two so designated. In issue number 1, The Mysterious Traveler story was credited "as by Andrew Fell," but others were credited just to the "Traveler." According to the first issue's introduction, some of "his" stories were adapted to print from the radio shows.

The lead stories usually dealt with the macabre and suspense, but the cover listings of the contents read like a mystery authors' convention roster. Reprinting such authors as John Dickson Carr, Agatha Christie, Ray Bradbury, Cornell Woolrich, Dorothy Sayers, and Sax Rohmer, just to name a few, there was a wide variety, with emphasis on stories with a surprise ending. Each issue usually contained a dozen stories; the last contained thirteen.

Vividly painted scenes of the "good girl" type of art graced the covers, usually an attractive girl in skimpy clothes being done in by an unseen assailant. But even with the lurid covers, and the "Mysterious Traveler's" endorsement, the magazine expired after five issues.

Information Sources

INDEX SOURCES: Cook, Michael L. *Monthly Murders*. Westport, Conn.: Greenwood Press, 1982.
LOCATION SOURCES: Private collectors.

Publication History

MAGAZINE TITLE: *The Mysterious Traveler Magazine*.

TITLE CHANGES: *Mysterious Traveler Mystery Reader* (with issue no. 5).
VOLUME AND ISSUE DATA: No. 1 (November 1951) through no. 5 (August 1952);
     5 issues.
PUBLISHER: Grace Publishing Co., Inc., 100 Fifth Avenue, New York 11, New York.
EDITOR: Robert Arthur.
PRICE PER ISSUE: 35 cents.
SIZE AND PAGINATION: 5-3/8'' X 7-3/8''; 130–160 pages.
CURRENT STATUS: Discontinued.
—*Paul Palmer*

MYSTERIOUS WU FANG, THE

The seven-issue run of *The Mysterious Wu Fang* was an obvious attempt on the part of Popular Publications to capitalize on the popularity of Sax Rohmer's Fu Manchu character.

It is one thing, however, for the reading public to accept a novel or two every year on such a character. The author has had time to meticulously construct his basic plot and the complications thereto and to concoct all manner of ingenious murder devices and death-dealing agencies; he has had time to garnish his story with richly embroidered action and profusely embellished descriptions of places, minor characters, "things that go bump in the night," and details of agonizing deaths. It is another matter to produce these on a monthly basis and to be able to satisfy the 1935 pulp-buying public.

To produce such a monthly novel, Popular Publications turned to Robert J. Hogan, a writer who had been responsible for a score of hero yarns featuring the beloved spy pilot, G–8 (in *G–8 and His Battle Aces**). That Hogan managed to turn out seven such novels under the pressures of time, demands, and requirements is quite an accolade to him. Despite this, one must recognize the faults in these stories inherent from hasty writing.

According to Val Kildare, who led the fight against the Dragon Lord for whom this series is named, Wu Fang was the most dangerous man in the world as well as the most unscrupulous. He was invariably pictured with a thin Fu Manchu mustache and slanting eyes with pupils of jade green. In garb he favored a mandarin robe of yellow silk, highly ornamented with embroidery, and a tasseled cap of Chinese design.

The basic plot of the first novel was a familiar Hogan concept. An inventor concocts a poison so powerful that when a small vial of it is dropped from an airplane on a small English village, it wipes out the entire population. Naturally, Wu Fang wants the secret of this poison.

In the second novel, a chemist rediscovers a poison once used to execute people in ancient Egypt. It is distilled from an insect once common and is so powerful that ten drops could wipe out a town of 100,000—and the five bottles that Wu Fang steals is enough to kill every person in the world.

The first two novels drag interminably, but the third yarn really rolls. This is Hogan at his pulp-writing best. Wu Fang is seeking the Yellow Mask of Unga, a ruler of ancient Peru before the time of the Incas. Though the mask is made of gold, its value is far more than that of the precious metal it contains. According to legend, a small gland of a certain Peruvian beetle produces a secretion which, if rubbed around the eyes of a human being, would give that person irresistible hypnotic power over all other humans. And this mask would have traces of this substance.

Through succeeding novels, Hogan deals with an ancient Hopi legend of a great plague among the Aztecs, an inventor who is working on a new way to commit mass murder with a death ray machine, a Wu Fang plot to kill every person in the United States unless the country is surrendered to him, and Nebuchadnezzar's ancient use of a strange form of electricity.

The seventh issue contains an announcement that the next story will be "The Case of the Living Poison." The short blurb that accompanies this states, "Once again, the Dragon Lord of Crime laughs at all the forces of white man's justice to weave his web of crime and murder in the most hideous, appalling adventure of death. . ."[1] But this issue never appeared, and it is not known what happened to the story. It may have been reworked by Hogan into one of his G–8 spy novels that featured an oriental villain. There has even been some speculation that it may have been given to Donald E. Keyhoe for revision into a *Dr. Yen Sin** story, but there is no evidence to account for it.

It is strange, though, that the final *Wu Fang* issue is dated March 1936, while the first *Dr. Yen Sin* issue is that of May 1936. The decision to suspend the one oriental menace magazine must have been made at about the same time as the decision to start the other. According to one rumor that has persisted for years, the major reason for halting *Wu Fang* and starting *Dr. Yen Sin* was that the former was written at too juvenile a level, and the latter was to be designed for a mature audience. Whatever, the new magazine lasted for but three issues.

As weird-menace stories go, the Wu Fang novels fall short of the mark. Several of them make rattling, good adventure novels, but they are mispackaged with the heavy stress on the Yellow Peril theme. For the reader who can disregard this emphasis and read them merely as stories of stange adventure, they are a pleasant way to spend a few idle hours.

NOTE

1. *The Mysterious Wu Fang*, Vol. 2, no. 3 (March 1936), p. 110.

Information Sources

BIBLIOGRAPHY:
Carr, Wooda Nicholas. "The Mysterious Wu Fang." *Doc Savage Club Reader*, no. 8 (1979): 5–8.
INDEX SOURCES: Weinberg, Robert, and Lohr McKinstry. *The Hero Pulp Index*. Evergreen, Colo.: Opar Press, 1971.

LOCATION SOURCES: University of California–Los Angeles Library (Vol. 1, no. 1, only); private collectors.

Publication History

MAGAZINE TITLE: *The Mysterious Wu Fang.*
TITLE CHANGES: None.
VOLUME AND ISSUE DATA: Vol. 1, no. 1 (September 1935) through Vol. 2, no. 3 (March 1936); 7 issues.
PUBLISHER: Popular Publications, Inc., 2256 Grove Street, Chicago, Illinois, with editorial offices at 205 East 42nd Street, New York, New York.
EDITOR: Edith Seims.
PRICE PER ISSUE: 10 cents.
SIZE AND PAGINATION: 7" X 10"; 112–128 pages.
CURRENT STATUS: Discontinued.
—*Joseph Lewandowski*

MYSTERY (Mystery Magazine, Inc.)

With the first issue dated November–December 1979, *Mystery* magazine indicated that it would not only cover "works of fiction concerned with the identification and capture of criminals" but would include the field of "international spying and intrigue" and also works of nonfiction which related. The editor promised that "adherents of the traditional forms of mystery need not despair, for the hardboiled detective, Sherlock Holmes, Miss Marple, et al., will be covered regularly and thoroughly. . . . The detective novel is alive and well, and, hopefully, *Mystery* will play a role in helping this type of novel reach a larger audience and consequently, receive the recognition it has long been denied."[1] Thus, with this noble intent, the magazine was launched.

The first issue included an interview with Ross Macdonald; a glossary of terms and quotes from the hard-boiled category; television, film, and book reviews and news; an article on mystery-book clubs; reports; and two items of fiction. These were "Ace Carpenter, Detective" by Hamilton T. Caine and "Eight Ball" by Joseph Allen.

The magazine was published in an 8-1/2" X 11" format on slick paper, was well illustrated, and was available only by subscription; with the January 1981 issue, the magazine began to appear on newsstands.

Subsequent issues included much on Raymond Chandler, John Ball, and other West Coast authors, while also featuring frequent interviews and articles of commentary, film and television features, book reviews, and special columns. The March 1981 issue included a special commemorative section marking Holmes and Watson's one hundredth anniversary, with a new Holmes pastiche. The mystery scene in different parts of the country was explored as a regular feature. Fiction continued to appear but not as the major content of the magazine.

With the April 1982 issue, the magazine changed to digest size.

Note

1. Editorial announcement, *Mystery*, Vol. 1, no. 1 (November/December 1979), p. 2.

Information Sources

INDEX SOURCES: None known.
LOCATION SOURCES: Private collectors.

Publication History

MAGAZINE TITLE: *Mystery*.
TITLE CHANGES: None.
VOLUME AND ISSUE DATA: Vol. 1, no. 1 (November/December 1979) through Vol. 4, no. 1 (to date, April 1982); 10 issues.
PUBLISHER: Stephen L. Smoke as Mystery Magazine, Inc., 411 North Central, Suite 203, Glendale, California 91203.
EDITORS: Stephen L. Smoke (first four issues); Thomas Godfrey.
PRICE PER ISSUE $1.00.
SIZE AND PAGINATION: 8-1/2'' X 11'' (until Vol. 4, no. 1); 5-3/8'' X 7-5/8''; 48–64 pages.
CURRENT STATUS: Discontinued.

MYSTERY (Street & Smith)

See CRIME BUSTERS

MYSTERY ADVENTURE

See NEW MYSTERY ADVENTURE

MYSTERY ADVENTURE MAGAZINE

See NEW MYSTERY ADVENTURE

MYSTERY ADVENTURES MAGAZINE

See NEW MYSTERY ADVENTURE

MYSTERY AND ADVENTURE SERIES REVIEW, THE

The Mystery and Adventure Series Review was the child of a long gestation period. Publisher and Editor Fred Woodworth's interest in juvenile mystery series books sprang from his boyhood in the 1950s. Although throughout the late 1960s and early 1970s he had entertained the thought of publishing a magazine which focused on these books, it was not until the summer of 1980 that issue number 1 appeared.

Woodworth was a teacher of Spanish when, in 1969, he began writing for a newspaper in Tuscon, Arizona, gradually moving into a full-time career of writing, publishing, and printing. The paper, called *The Match*, was, as he said, "going along pretty well,"[1] with Woodworth at the helm, but in 1976 the unexpected loss of his building's lease necessitated a move in which a number of important pieces of machinery were damaged. This loss of equipment resulted in the eventual demise of the paper in 1977.

"I always had hopes of reviving my paper," Woodworth said, "but as time passed it began to look like a remote possibility."

Finally one day I was talking with the proprietor of a local comic book store, and I mentioned that I collected boys' series books. He reacted to this with the information that he knew another fellow in town who did also, and mentioned the name of my now close friend, Cliff Erickson. Cliff, it turned out, was primarily interested at that point only in the Ken Holt series which had always been a favorite of mine. He didn't have all the books, but I did, and we started getting together to talk about them. Back in 1967 I had started corresponding with Sam Epstein, author (as "Bruce Campbell") of the Ken Holt series, and now I dug out the letters, and we discussed all this, as well as other series.

Through all these conversations, my interest in the series began to really flare up again, and it seemed like perhaps it was time to reconsider that old idea of publishing a book on the subject, or perhaps a magazine. Then we saw an ad for Jennings' *Boys Book Buff*. Once it developed that there was already a magazine in existence, I shelved the idea of publishing one of my own, since I figured there wouldn't be enough readership to sustain two in the same area of interest. Well, then, Jennings started getting irregular, and by the latter part of 1979 I was getting very anxious to get into some form of publishing again, even if only on a hobby basis. I finally decided to go ahead with a magazine, as it looked as though Bob Jennings had quit, so I spent some time in the fall and winter of 1979 and early 1980 re-reading all the Striker books I had and preparing notes for articles. In February the general idea of the *Review* had become pretty clear, and I began actually doing some typesetting, design of the cover page, and so on, working around the limitations of the old machinery, repairing things whenever I could.[2]

Issue number 1 was a twenty-eight-page magazine (including covers, which carried text) measuring slightly less than 6" X 9." It focused on the writings of Frank Striker and included Kent Winslow's "Hunting for Hidden Books," which was to become a continuing feature. Originally priced at fifty cents, the magazine was forced to meet the rising costs of production, with a subsequent increase in the subscription rate to $1.25 per issue.

A quarterly magazine, *The Mystery and Adventure Series Review* established a quality format at an early stage. Woodworth's interest in typography, design, and the art of printing has resulted in two- and three-color covers, stunning center spreads, and an appealing blend of text and illustrations. Page count has increased to as high as thirty-six per issue, double-column.

The *Review*, in the course of its publication, has covered the Ken Holt, Hardy Boys, and Nancy Drew mystery series, as well as the mystery books of Capwell Wyckoff and adventure series such as Rick Brant, Tom Quest, and various western heroes. The detective work of Fred Woodworth and his writers in tracking down the authors, editions, and artists of these series has provided its readers with a great deal of information previously unavailable.

The *Review* has moved from Woodworth's home to an office area which he has rented from a friend. As with most small publishing ventures, the magazine is an operation in which the typesetting, printing, and production are done on a limited budget by dedicated people who are more concerned with a good product than they are with profit. "Series books and their collecting is a field that has grown a lot in the last several years," Woodworth declares,

> and no area of literature could deserve it more. I feel that those of us who are publishing about these books are doing something that is surely appreciated by our readers, so even if we don't become millionaires at it, it is worthwhile.[3]

Notes

1. Fred Woodworth, correspondence to Gil O'Gara, January 25, 1982.
2. Ibid.
3. Ibid.

Information Sources

INDEX SOURCES: None known.
LOCATION SOURCES: Private collectors.

Publication History

MAGAZINE TITLE: *The Mystery and Adventure Series Review*.
TITLE CHANGES: None.
VOLUME AND ISSUE DATA: No. 1 (Summer 1980) through no. 8 (to date, Spring 1982); 8 issues.
PUBLISHER: Fred Woodworth, P.O. Box 3488, Tucson, Arizona 85722.
EDITOR: Fred Woodworth.
PRICE PER ISSUE: 50 cents (no. 1); 75 cents (nos 2–4); $1.25.
SIZE AND PAGINATION: 6" X 9"; 28–36 pages.
CURRENT STATUS: Active.
—*Gil O'Gara*

MYSTERY BOOK MAGAZINE

Mystery Book Magazine was one of the most interesting of the digest magazines to compete with *Ellery Queen's Mystery Magazine.** It was in every respect a tasteful, high-quality production. *Mystery Book* advertised "the best in new crime fiction—no reprints,"[1] and it specialized in the longer forms—novels and novelettes—rarely used by *Ellery Queen's*. Each issue also had short stories as well as a book review column by humorist Will Cuppy. Perhaps the most unusual feature was a regular mystery crossword puzzle by Margaret Petherbridge that had the clues written into a brief story about Inspector Cross and had the puzzle squares arranged into the shape of a gun, skull, or other appropriate object. Covers were mostly type, with only small illustrations, but the interiors were generously illustrated by H. Laurence Hoffman (for the first four issues) and Lawrence Sterne Stevens. Frank McSherry, writing about the crossword puzzles, observed that "the entire magazine had that indefinable touch of class for which there is no easy formula."[2]

The stories printed in *Mystery Book Magazine* were of consistently high quality. The authors who appeared most frequently were Fredric Brown (nine times), Patrick Quentin (eight times, including appearances as Q. Patrick and Jonathan Stagge), Brett Halliday (eight times), and Wiliam Irish (as Cornell Woolrich, six times). Other notable authors included Margery Allingham, Anthony Boucher, Leslie Charteris, George Harmon Coxe, Carroll John Daly, Mignon Eberhart, Bruno Fischer, Dorothy B. Hughes, Jonathan Latimer, John D. MacDonald, William MacHarg, Wade Miller, Max Murray, Hugh Pentecost, Lawrence Treat, and Roy Vickers, among others. This is quite an impressive list, considering the "no reprint" policy.

Unfortunately, *Mystery Book Magazine* never achieved the degree of success it deserved. It lasted for only six years (1945–1951) and, during that time, suffered continual tinkering with the format, frequency, and even the title. The greatest change came in the fall of 1947 when, after nineteen issues, it was converted to the old pulp format. While the fiction remained much the same, many of the distinctive touches were lost. The covers became more typically pulpish, with art by Rudolph Belarski, and Paul Orban took over the interior illustrations. Advertising, previously limited to the covers, ran riot through the magazine. The crosswords were dropped, and the book reviews were replaced by plugs for new Popular Library paperbacks (also published by Ned Pines's Popular/Standard/Thrilling group). This format change was caused by the easing of the paper shortage, according to veteran editor Leo Margulies, though this does not seem entirely logical, especially since the frequency was reduced from monthly to quarterly at the same time.

Leo Margulies edited *Mystery Book Magazine* in both formats (though two final issues were published under the title of *Giant Detective* after he left Standard Publications), and he considered it one of his favorite magazines. "I had suggested we do a digest-sized detective magazine featuring full-length novels, with the idea of eventual use in Popular Library. We saw tremendous possibilities in paperbacks. We saw them replacing the pulps. . . . That's why *Mystery Book* was born."[3] This does not seem to have succeeded too well, however. While at least twenty-four of the magazine's featured novels had subsequent book editions, only one (Jonathan Latimer's *The Fifth Grave*) ever appeared in a Popular Library paperback.

"In surveying the 34-issue run of *Mystery Book*, one is struck by the evidence of consistently intelligent editorship. . . , the tasteful appearance of the digest-sized issues, and the sheer quality of top-level stories," notes Robert Briney. "It takes no more than a cursory glance at the index of stories from *Mystery Book* for us to realize the great contribution which this magazine made to the mystery field."[4]

Notes

1. Masthead slogan on contents pages, *Mystery Book Magazine*.
2. Frank D. McSherry, Jr., "Lady in a Straightjacket," *The Armchair Detective*, Vol. 9, no. 3 (June 1976), p. 201.
3. Robert E. Briney, "Mystery Book Magazines: An Appreciation and Index," *The Armchair Detective*, Vol. 8, no. 4, (August 1974), p. 246.
4. Ibid., p. 245.

Information Sources

BIBLIOGRAPHY:

Briney, Robert E. "Mystery Book Magazines: An Appreciation and Index." *The Armchair Detective*, Vol. 8, no. 4 (August 1974): 245–50.

McSherry, Frank D., Jr. "Lady in a Straightjacket." *The Armchair Detective,* Vol. 9, no. 3 (June 1976): 201–2.

INDEX SOURCES: Briney, Robert E. "Mystery Book Magazines: An Appreciation and Index." *The Armchair Detective,* Vol. 8, no. 4 (August 1974): 245–50.

Cook, Michael, L. *Monthly Murders.* Westport, Conn.: Greenwood Press, 1982.

LOCATION SOURCES: University of California–Los Angeles Library (Vol. 1, no. 1; Vol. 6, no. 1, only); private collectors.

Publication History

MAGAZINE TITLE: *Mystery Book Magazine.*
TITLE CHANGES: *Giant Detective* (last two issues).
VOLUME AND ISSUE DATA: Vol. 1, no. 1 (July 1945) through Vol. 10, no. 3 (Winter 1951); 34 issues.
PUBLISHERS: William Wise & Company (nos. 1–7), Mystery Club, Inc. (nos. 8–19), Best Publications, Inc. (all imprints of Ned Pines), 4600 Diversey Avenue, Chicago, Illinois.
EDITOR: Leo Margulies.
PRICE PER ISSUE: 25 cents.
SIZE AND PAGINATION: 5-1/4'' X 7-1/4'' (through Vol. 5, no. 3); 6-3/4'' X 9-3/4'' (subsequent issues); 130–194 pages.
CURRENT STATUS: Discontinued.
—*Brian KenKnight*

MYSTERY DIGEST

One of the more successful digest-sized mystery magazines, *Mystery Digest* first appeared in May 1957 with an impressive array of stories and authors. The first issue included "Such Interesting Neighbors" by Jack Finney; "The Strange Case of Washington Irving Bishop" by the author of The Shadow stories, Walter B. Gibson; "I'll Cut Your Throat Again, Kathleen," by Fredric Brown; 'The Man with Two Faces" by Henry Slesar; and other stories by William Fryer Harvey, Harlan Ellison, William P. McGivern, and Bill Peters. The quality and style, a refreshing relief from the force-fed diet of hard-boiled stories, continued throughout the life of the magazine.

With its first anniversary, the publisher noted thus:

> When the *Mystery Digest* was created, the policy was to publish only stories of the highest literary standards, because we believed that any reader of mystery stories is usually an avid reader of mystery books—and thus is an authority on the subject. Up until ten years ago, a squeaking door that opened mysteriously or a scream in the dark was satisfying for the readers, but try it today. . .the readers will laugh you off the newstand.[1]

Perhaps one reason for the quality was that this magazine was primarily edited by mystery fiction writers. Through forty-one issues, until May 1963, the magazine found and published discriminating mystery fiction by, among the impressive lineup of authors, Joseph Commings, Stuart Palmer, Jonathan Craig, Harold Q. Masur, Q. Patrick, Octavus Roy Cohen, and Margaret Manners. Many of these were also very successful and popular mystery book writers.

Later issues included letter columns and book, television, and stage reviews.

Note

1. Editorial comment, *Mystery Digest*, Vol. 2, no. 3 (May 1958), reverse front cover.

Information Sources

INDEX SOURCES: Cook, Michael L. *Monthly Murders*. Westport, Conn.: Greenwood Press, 1982.

LOCATION SOURCES: University of California–Los Angeles Library (Vol. 1, no. 1, only); private collectors.

Publication History

MAGAZINE TITLE: *Mystery Digest*.

TITLE CHANGES: None.

VOLUME AND ISSUE DATA: Vol. 1, no. 1 (May 1957) through Vol. 7, no. 3 (May/June 1963); 41 issues.

PUBLISHER: First issue by Passer Press Company, a subsidiary of Filosa Publications, Inc., 527 Lexington Avenue, New York 17, New York; second issue as Grenville Press, Inc., same address; subsequent issues by Shelton Publishing Corporation, same address and later P.O. Box 164, Cathedral Station, New York 25, New

York. Publisher was Gary Fairmont Filosa, first two issues; subsequent issues, Rolfe Passer.

EDITORS: Rolfe Passer (first two issues); Joseph Commings (until Vol. 2, no. 2); William Mcfarlane (until Vol. 3, no. 3); Donald E. Westlake (March–December 1959); Jon A. Tetra (for January/February 1960 issue). After January 1960, Tetra was executive editor, and the editor was Rolfe Passer.

PRICE PER ISSUE: 35 cents.

SIZE AND PAGINATION: 5-3/8'' X 7-1/2''; 96–128 pages.

CURRENT STATUS: Discontinued.

MYSTERY FANCIER, THE

In November 1976, Guy M. Townsend, founder, editor, and publisher of *The Mystery Fancier*—"a balance of articles, reviews, and letters"[1]—inaugurated his journal by paying tribute to two of its most important predecessors, *The Armchair Detective** and *The Mystery Nook,** and suggesting that there was ample room for another magazine devoted to crime fiction. Subsequent issues have proved him correct. For the most part, Townsend has been faithful to his announced aim, and *The Mystery Fancier* is a pleasing combination of both formal and informal criticism, its contents contributed primarily by its readers and subscribers. Most material is original, written especially for *The Mystery Fancier*, but there are occasional reprints. The tones of the various articles range from chatty to scholarly, and Townsend's editorial policy of mixing these approaches to mystery writing is the subject of hot debate in the magazine's letter columns.

Indeed, "The Documents in the Case," the letters section, is one of the most vivid features of almost every issue. Here, readers comment on the quality and subject matter of previous issues, commend or condemn earlier articles, suggest new topics of interest, ask and answer questions. Some discussions/debates/quarrels become fairly intense and continue through several months, and for many readers, "Documents" is priority reading.

The Mystery Fancier also carries other regular columns. The editorial, "Mysteriously Speaking," as in most magazines, opens each issue and provides, in retrospect, a running history of the fanzine. Events and new publications of interest to mystery buffs are also discussed here; Townsend, for instance, gives generous space to the Bouchercons (the major annual crime fiction conventions), publishing "reviews" and reminiscences of each meeting as well as publicizing them beforehand.

There are also book reviews aplenty. "The Mystery*File," short reviews by Steve Lewis (who also edits a magazine called *Mystery*File**, appears in most issues; these comments are succinct and reliable, and Lewis assigns each reviewed book a letter grade. Marvin Lachman's "It's About Crime" is a highly personal, conversational column which calls attention to writers Lachman admires, presents his "Notes on Recent Reading," and covers news of interest to the readership. Dozens of contributors keep "Verdicts," more reviews (both current and retrospective), lively and useful. These submissions vary in length from one paragraph to several hundred words, just as they vary in focus: some are plot summaries; some are analyses; almost all reveal a sound knowledge and understanding of the genre. The year's budget of reviews is generally indexed in the subsequent volume, a handy aid.

The articles published in *The Mystery Fancier* during its initial five years of life have ranged over almost all forms of mystery writing. Guy Townsend himself wrote "The Nero Wolfe Saga," which continued through nineteen issues (volume 1, number 3 through volume 4, number 3). This commentary surveys Rex Stout's plots, throws light on life in the brownstone, points up relationships between characters, and reveals the personalities of Wolfe and Archie Goodwin especially. Other pieces have covered other very famous authors, such as John Dickson Carr (volume 1, number 6, pp. 13–14); pointed out crossovers between popular and "high" culture ("Freedom and Mystery in John Fowles' *The Enigma,*" volume 3, number 5, pp. 14–19); and called attention to the less well-known writers ("Law, Lawyers and Justice in the Novels of Joe L. Hensley," volume 4, number 1, pp. 3–7), to cite a very small sampling. None of the other articles or series is as detailed as the "Saga," but most give sound introductions to their subjects.

The Mystery Fancier's covers for the first four volumes were often drawings, some brilliant, all of interest. Portraits of the Maltese falcon, Nero Wolfe, and Joe Friday have alternated with sketches of brownstones, depictions of scenes of the crime, cartoons, and a tribute to a loyal contributor. With volume 6, the journal opted for the same cover throughout. Varied or settled, the cover pictures are an attractive feature.

Mystery novels, stories, magazines, films, television programs, anc critical works about crime writing are all good copy for *The Mystery Fancier*, which has ably demonstrated its worth as a source of information and pleasure. *The Mystery Fancier* is valued by fans who want to stay current in the field.

Note

. 1. Editorial announcement, *The Mystery Fancier* preview issue (November 1976), p. 1.

Information Sources

INDEX SOURCES: None known.
LOCATION SOURCES: Private collectors.

Publication History

MAGAZINE TITLE: *The Mystery Fancier (THE MYSTERY FANcier)*.
TITLE CHANGES: None.
VOLUME AND ISSUE DATA: Vol. 1, no. 1 (January 1977) through Vol. 6,, no. 2 (to date, March–April 1982); preceded by a preview issue (November 1976); 33 issues.
PUBLISHER: Guy M. Townsend, 1711 Clifty Drive, Madison, Indiana 47250.

EDITOR: Guy M. Townsend.
PRICE PER ISSUE: $1.50 (through Vol. 4, no. 6); $2.00.
SIZE AND PAGINATION: Preview issue 8-1/2" X 11" (and through Vol. 1, no. 3);
      thereafter 5-1/2" X 8-1/2"; 42–58 pages.
CURRENT STATUS: Active.
—*Jane S. Bakerman*

MYSTERY*FILE

Begun as a mailing list of books for sale, the *Mystery*File* gradually expanded
to include miscellaneous items of interest to the collector of mystery and detective
fiction. Steve Lewis, sole perpetrator of the *Mystery*File* and long-time science
fiction fan, knew that much interest can be generated in a fanzine and that the
mystery-detective readers had long been without any means of communication
with others of similar interests. *The Armchair Detective,** at the time one of two
or three general fanzines for mystery readers and collectors, was flourishing.
There were people throughout the country with little or no access to used bookstores, Salvation Army outlets, and house sales where used books could be
purchased for relatively little money. The *Mystery*File* always included a list
of books for sale and editorial comments by Lewis.

*Mystery*File* expanded to include brief articles on books and/or authors, bibliographies, and information about the mystery-detective genre, short commentaries, and excerpts from letters. For example, by issue number 4, the "Mystery
Dial" was added as a regular feature, consisting of listings of monaural reel and
cassette tapes of old mystery, detective, and adventure fiction from the radio
and scattered lectures and panel discussions about mystery and detective fiction.

Issue number 4 also saw the addition of short articles by people other than
the editor. Tim Dumont supplied "Fifty Years of Mysteries." Issue number 5
included Michael L. Cook's partial compilation of the titles published by the
Unicorn Mystery Book Club, which was revised and expanded for later publication in *The Armchair Detective*. "Nuggets (and Otherwise) from the Golden
Age" by Jay Jeffries was in issue number 6, and *Mystery*File* number 7 contained illustrations by Frank Hamilton. These were to be the only illustrations
ever printed in its pages. Also included were "Remembering Avon Murder
Mystery Monthly" by Francis M. Nevins, Jr.; "Ruth Rendell—A Bibliography"
by J. Clyde Stevens; Jay Jeffries's "Nuggets from the Golden Age" as well as
"Mystery Views," a sampling of letters received by the editor.

With issue no. 7, the *Mystery*File* ceased to exist as a separate publication.
Steve Lewis became associate editor of *The Mystery Nook,** a fanzine published
by Don Miller, and *Mystery*File* was incorporated into it. Lewis used "Son of
Mystery*File" in volume 1, numbers 1, 3, and 4 of *The Mystery Nook* as the
heading for an annotated editorial and letter column. Letters received and answered by Miller came under the heading of "Daughter of Mystery*File," but
in later issues the headings were dropped. In 1976, all reference to *Mystery*File*

was deleted from *The Mystery Nook*, and Lewis was no longer shown as associate editor. Currently, Lewis uses the title as the name of his fine column of short reviews appearing in *The Mystery Fancier,** a fanzine edited and published by Guy Townsend, since its first issue.

Information Sources

BIBLIOGRAPHY:
Albert, Walter. "A Bibliography of Secondary Sources for 1974." *The Armchair Detective,* Vol. 8, no. 4 (August 1975): 290–93.
Banks, R. Jeff. "Letter." *The Armchair Detective,* Vol. 9, no. 1 (November 1975): 82–83.
Lewis, Steve. "Letter." *The Armchair Detective,* Vol. 8, no. 4 (August 1975): 322.
Townsend, Guy. "Mysteriously Speaking. . . ." *The Mystery Fancier,* preview issue (November 1976): 1–2.
INDEX SOURCES: None known.
LOCATION SOURCES: Private collectors.

Publication History

MAGAZINE TITLE: *Mystery*File*.
TITLE CHANGES: None.
VOLUME AND ISSUE DATA: No. 1 (Spring 1974) through no. 7 (May 1975) (no. 1 was sales list only and was unnumbered); 7 issues (one issued numbered "5-1/2").
PUBLISHER: Steve Lewis, Newington, Connecticut.
EDITOR: Steve Lewis.
PRICE PER ISSUE: 25 cents.
SIZE AND PAGINATION: 5-1/2" X 8-1/2"; 15–23 pages.
CURRENT STATUS: Discontinued.
—*Jo Ann Vicarel*

MYSTERY LEAGUE MAGAZINE, THE

In 1932, just three years after the first successful book (*The Roman Hat Mystery*) was published by the then still very young writing partners and cousins, Frederic Dannay and Manfred B. Lee, ambition spawned the idea of a mystery magazine. Writing under the pen name of "Ellery Queen," the authors had become well known, and the League Publishers, Inc., of Chicago, when approached with the suggestion, agreed. The League Publishers had been producing full-length, hardcover mystery and detective novels for several years, using the "Mystery League" name as identification. Since sales were difficult during the depression years, the books, selling at fifty cents, were not doing as well as hoped, and the publisher may have thought that an item selling at a lower price would do better. *The Mystery League Magazine* was thus born, with the first issue dated October 1933.

Manfred B. Lee, writing in 1969, stated:

Mystery League Magazine was the child of the Queen imagination and early ambition. . . . It was published on the proverbial shoelace under the publishing aegis of a gentleman into whose finances we didn't delve too deeply, and we [Frederic Dannay and Manfred B. Lee] were its entire staff—you read me—*entire*; we did not even have a secretary. We selected the stories, prepared copy, read proofs, dummied, sweated, etc., and almost literally swept out the office as well. The magazine disseminated four or five issues and died of insufficient wherewithal. All this was some thirty-five years or so ago, and the pain is only just beginning to ebb.[1]

The Mystery League Magazine, launched when every nickel counted, was nevertheless priced at twenty-five cents per copy, thus facing stiff opposition when other mystery and detective pulp magazines were a dime. With the desire for a quality magazine both in appearance and content, the first issue was larger than the usual pulp (8-1/2" X 11") and 160 pages. The quality of the stories cannot be denied. The first issue featured a story by Dannay and Lee under the name Barnaby Ross ("Drury Lane's Last Case"), a short story as by Ellery Queen ("The Glass-Domed Clock"), and included, among others, stories by Dashiell Hammett and Dorothy Sayers. The editorial in this and all succeeding issues borrowed a title from Lewis Carroll, "Through the Looking Glass," with Ellery Queen shown as editor. The editorial policy was such that Dannay and Lee believed the "public's tastes have been under-rated," and it was revealed that this was confirmed by the "hundreds of letters we are receiving weekly." Queen advised authors that "if you have good stories, *Mystery League* is definitely in the market for them."[2]

However, despite the ambitious intentions of Ellery Queen and the determination to produce a magazine that would publish only quality fiction, the economy was such that it was doomed to failure from the beginning. By January 1934, when the fourth and final issue was published, the size had diminished to 128 pages. Although there was nothing in the fourth issue to indicate this was the last, no further issues were published. A fifth issue was assembled but never printed.

Notes

1. Manfred B. Lee, letter, *The Armchair Detective*, Vol. 2, no. 3 (April 1969), p. 202.
2. Nils Hardin, "Mystery League—A Summary," *Xenophile,* No. 14 (June 1975), p. 10.

Information Sources

BIBLIOGRAPHY:

Hardin, Nils. "Mystery League—A Summary." *Xenophile*, no. 14 (June 1975): 8–10.
Lee, Manfred B. "Letter." *The Armchair Detective,* Vol. 2, no. 3 (April 1969): 202.
Nevins, Francis M., Jr. *Royal Bloodline: Ellery Queen, Author and Detective*. Bowling Green, Ohio: Bowling Green University Popular Press, 1974.
INDEX SOURCES: Cook, Michael L. *Monthly Murders*. Westport, Conn.: Greenwood Press, 1982.

Hardin, Nils, "Mystery League—A Summary." *Xenophile*, no. 14 (June 1975): 8–10.
LOCATION SOURCES: University of California–Los Angeles Library (Vol. 1, no. 1,
    only); private collectors.

Publication History

MAGAZINE TITLE: *The Mystery League Magazine.*
TITLE CHANGES: None.
VOLUME AND ISSUE DATA: Vol. 1, no. 1 (October 1933) through Vol. 1, no. 4
    (January 1934); 4 issues.
PUBLISHER: League Publishers, Inc., 4600 Diversey Avenue, Chicago, Illinois.
EDITOR: Ellery Queen (Frederic Dannay and Manfred B. Lee).
PRICE PER ISSUE: 25 cents.
SIZE AND PAGINATION: 8-1/2" X 11"; 128–160 pages.
CURRENT STATUS: Discontinued.

MYSTERY LOVERS' NEWSLETTER, THE

See MYSTERY READER'S NEWSLETTER, THE

MYSTERY MAGAZINE

Mystery Magazine was one of the truly senior detective story publications.
As far as is known, only Street & Smith's *Detective Story Magazine** appeared
earlier, its first issue being dated October 5, 1915.

The first issue of *Mystery Magazine* was dated slightly more than two years
later—November 15, 1917. Appearing twice a month, it contained a novelette,
short stories, and articles about crime and law enforcement. All these were
scrambled together, fiction and nonfiction thoroughly mixed and all of them
looking the same, so that the reader who did not refer to the contents page had
no idea what he was reading until getting deep into each piece.

This suggests that *Mystery Magazine* fiction was slow to start and ill-defined
as to type, and it was. But remember that styles have changed, and the magazine
obviously suited the audience of the period. Still, to contemporary eyes, the
stories drag miserably. They begin in leisure and crawl somnolently forward.
They feature improbable policemen and incredible crooks and dialogue arch and
literary. Dim-witted police suspect fumble-fingered heroes. It's a wonder the
girl is ever rescued. Other stories feature criminals deep in crime—con folk and
safe crackers and such ilk—none of them seeming competent to cross the street
without being run over by a circus parade.

The writers of these sluggish entertainments were often (according to Sam
Moskowitz [see Bibliography]) writers of dime novels. (The editor, himself,
Luis P. Senarens, had written Frank Reade dime novels, a primitive sort of
science fiction featuring marvelous inventions and daring deeds.) Few of the
Mystery Magazine writers show the narrative skill that made the dime novels

blaze and rage, although admittedly, the earliest issues of this magazine have not been reviewed, and those may blaze and rage with great power.

Many of the novelette writers appeared in the various Munsey and Street & Smith titles, and there is an occasional name that survived the years, such as Octavus Roy Cohen, Jack Bechdolt, and George Bronson-Howard. Around the mid-1920s appears a thin salting of more familiar names: Frederick C. Davis, Arthur B. Reeve, and Nels Leroy Jorgensen (May 1, 1924: "Laughing Death's Trail"). These were exceptions.

Most of *Mystery Magazine*'s remaining writers have long since vanished from sight and their works lost. Even then, their novelettes bore old-fashioned titles, half dime novel, half early 1920s: "The Eel Man" (issue number 1); "The Mystic Emblem" (number 7); "A Masked Mystery" (number 40); "The Inspector's Strange Case" (number 55); "A Keyless Mystery" (number 80); "Trailed by a Private Detective" (number 119).

The magazines were identified both by date and whole numbers, as well as a volume number which (at least in the early 1920s) seems to have included twenty-four yearly issues, from May 1 to the following year's April 15. The whole numbers were discontinued by 1926.

The *Mystery Magazine* of the early 1920s was a slender pamphlet, sixty-four pages long, essentially unillustrated inside with the exception of three or four pencil sketches that headed major stories. The covers contained the words "Mystery Magazine" in red, with a red circle enclosing the black price. Cover backgrounds were white, the illustrations being done in black and various red tints. This drawing was usually skillfully done (by Hap Hadley during 1923-1924), although often as static as a stone wall. Above the magazine title appeared the words "Detective Stories" in black, and beneath the title appeared the date and issue number.

Those magazines inspected contained a novelette, a serial part, five or six short stories, and perhaps ten articles. These ranged from long paragraphs to two-and-one-half-page essays. Typical topic titles were "Loses $1,000 Trying to Obtain a Job," "The Crime Without a Clue," "Police Radio Service," and "A Bomb Explodes in Auto." To these miscellaneous features was added the department "What Handwriting Reveals" by Louise Rice. This began during May 1924.

During 1926, more contemporary writers appeared, among them Agatha Christie ("The Under Dog," April 1, 1926) and Charles G. Booth ("Sinister House," four-part serial, March 15 to May 1, 1926). A small amount of fantasy appeared, perhaps a story an issue, tucked in without fuss among the shrewd detectives and gallant crooks. Series characters had appeared, and Dale Collin's adventures of Peter Lamb continued through early 1926. In February began a feature signed by famous people (Ethel Barrymore and others) revealing "true" mysterious happenings they had experienced. Most or all the experiences appear to have been ghostwritten, which seems proper given the subject matter.

In mid-1926, the smooth pulse of *Mystery Magazine* was interrupted when publication dates skipped from July 15 to September, the magazine became a monthly, and it was acquired by a new publisher, The Priscilla Company. *Mystery Magazine* continued monthly for another ten issues and was then retitled *Mystery Stories*. The initial issue of the new title, dated August 1927,, continued the volume and issue numbers of *Mystery Magazine*.

Mystery Stories became a standard-sized pulp magazine that featured detective and mystery-suspense fiction. Almost every issue also contained a single science fiction or fantasy story (including at least one by Henry S. Whitehead). The magazine continued publication at least through July 1929. By that date, pressures of the marketplace had altered the magazine almost beyond recognition, and, at the end, it was featuring not only mystery stories but equal amounts of adventure, western, and flying fiction.

Information Sources

BIBLIOGRAPHY:
Moskowitz, Sam. *Under the Moons of Mars: A History of the Scientific Romance in the Munsey Magazines 1912–1920.* New York: Holt, Rinehart and Winston, 1970.
The Writer, Vol. 39, no. 10 (December 1927): 330.
INDEX SOURCES: None known.
LOCATION SOURCES: University of California–Los Angeles Library (Vol. 11, no. 4, only); private collectors.

Publication History

MAGAZINE TITLE: *Mystery Magazine.*
TITLE CHANGES: *Mystery Stories* (with Vol. 11, no. 5, [August 1927]).
VOLUME AND ISSUE DATA: Vol. 1, no. 1 (November 15, 1917) through Vol. 11, no. 4 (July 1927) as *Mystery Magazine; Vol. 11, no. 5 (August 1927) through Vol. 19, no. 1 (July 1929) as Mystery Stories.*
PUBLISHER: Harry E. Wolff, Publisher, Inc., 166 West 23rd Street, New York, New York (until 1926); Mystery Magazine Co., 1133 Broadway, New York, New York (from 1926 to 1927); The Priscilla Company, 55 West 42nd Street, New York, New York (August 1927 through July 1929).
EDITORS: Luis P. Senarens (through 1924); Robert Simpson (1926).
PRICE PER ISSUE: 10 cents (1923–1924); 15 cents (1924); 25 cents.
SIZE AND PAGINATION: 7'' X 10''; 64–160 pages.
CURRENT STATUS: Discontinued.
—*Robert Sampson*

MYSTERY MAGAZINE, THE

See ILLUSTRATED DETECTIVE MAGAZINE, THE

MYSTERY MONITOR, THE

The Mystery Monitor, one of a number of similar publications on various aspects of popular literature, was aptly described by its name. The publication attempted, and with a good measure of success, to monitor what was being written in other media about the mystery fiction scene. One of the most important features was the regular appearance of review extracts from a wide range of magazines and newspapers. The publication also presented news, information, announcemments, and a number of reviews and minireviews of books contributed by a number of readers.

Information Sources

INDEX SOURCES: None known.
LOCATION SOURCES: Private collectors.

Publication History

MAGAZINE TITLE: *The Mystery Monitor*.
TITLE CHANGES: None.
VOLUME AND ISSUE DATA: Vol. 1, no. 1 (February 7, 1976) through Vol. 2, no. 5 (April 28, 1978); 16 issues.
PUBLISHER: M Press, 12315 Judson Road, Wheaton, Maryland 20906.
EDITOR: Don Miller.
PRICE PER ISSUE: Not stated.
SIZE AND PAGINATION: 8-1/2'' X 11''; 10–22 pages.
CURRENT STATUS: Discontinued.

MYSTERY MONTHLY

The month of June 1976 witnessed the appearance of one of the finest and most promising new digests in the mystery-detective field, *Mystery Monthly*, published simultaneously in the United States and Canada by Looking Glass Publications, Inc. During the course of its short existence, it more than managed to live up to its initial promise to cover, in a comprehensive manner, all mystery-related entertainment—movies, books, television, the stage, and interviews with prominent personalities in the field. All this was in addtion to some of the finest new short fiction to date, by authors such as Edward D. Hoch, Gil Brewer, Jack Ritchie, Ed McBain, Barbara Paul, Robert J. Randisi, Richard Forrest, Ron Goulart, Nedra Tyre, Michael Avallone, Jon A. Jackson, George C. Chesbro, and Joseph Hansen.

Unlike its competitors, *Mystery Monthly* did not shy away from controversial topics or language. More freedom was given its writers than ever before in the short form. Joseph Hansen's short story ''Murder on the Surf,'' featuring homosexual insurance investigator Dave Brandstetter, for example, appeared in volume 1, number 7 (December 1976).

The entertainment sections outside the fiction area were covered in reviews of movies (by Steven Vail), books (by Tom Seligson), theater and television (by Mike Madrid). Each issue also contained an interview with either a writer (Harlan Ellison, Derek Marlowe) or a figure otherwise known in or related to the mystery-detection field (Dilys Winn, Willie Sutton, a private investigator, a former narcotics agent, a debugging company, a New York City medical examiner, or the head of the Insurance Crime Prevention Institute, for example).

Highlighting each issue in the nonfiction area was the continuing feature "The Crime Lab" by George O'Toole, author and former head of the CIA's Problem Analysis Branch. The topics his column covered were: mistaken identification, psychic detectives, false identity, hypnosis and crime detection, bugging Agnew's office, the deaths of President Kennedy and Officer Tippitt, real private eyes, Richard III, and dental detectives.

For those so inclined the editors included various puzzles and a regular cash-awards contest with fifty dollars going to each of the first three winners each month.

With volume 1, number 9 (February 1977) came a letter to subscribers stating, "This is to inform you that we are postponing the publication of issue number 10 of *Mystery Monthly*. We are in the process of reorganizing and at this time plan to be back on the stands in May. . . ." Unfortunately for mystery fans everywhere, the digest was never seen or heard from again.

Information Sources

INDEX SOURCES: Cook, Michael L. *Monthly Murders*. Westport, Conn.: Greenwood
    Press, 1982.
LOCATION SOURCES: Private collectors.

PUBLICATION HISTORY

MAGAZINE TITLE: *Mystery Monthly*.
TITLE CHANGES: None.
VOLUME AND ISSUE DATA: Vol. 1, no. 1 (June 1976) through Vol. 1, no.9 (February
    1977); 9 issues.
PUBLISHER: Lionel Chetwynd as Looking Glass Publications, Inc., 119 West 57th
    Street, New York, New York 10019.
EDITOR: Eric Protter; F. Joseph Spieler, executive editor.
PRICE PER ISSUE: $1.00.
SIZE AND PAGINATION: 5-1/4" X 7-3/8"; 128 pages.
CURRENT STATUS: Discontinued.
—*James R. McCahery*

MYSTERY NEWS

Mystery News was introduced by Editor-Publisher Patricia Shnell with the January–February 1982 issue. With the primary aim of informing "about as many new mystery books, those recently published and those about to be published, as possible," the publication also plans to include interviews with authors, dates and locations of autograph parties and appearances of authors, and letters from authors commenting on their latest books. "There will be reviews, too, by people who enjoy the kind of mystery they are reading, and are knowledgeable about the mechanics of writing."[1]

Note

1. Notice to Guy Townsend by Patricia Shnell, quoted in "Mysteriously Speaking" (editorial), *The Mystery Fancier*, Vol. 6, no. 2 (March/April 1982), p. 4.

Information Sources

BIBLIOGRAPHY:
Townsend, Guy. "Mysteriously Speaking," *The Mystery Fancier*, Vol. 6, no. 2 (March/April 1982): 4.
INDEX SOURCES: None known.
LOCATION SOURCES: Private collectors.

Publcation History

MAGAZINE TITLE: *Mystery News*.
TITLE CHANGES: None.
VOLUME AND ISSUE DATA: Vol. 1, no. 1 (to date, January/February 1982); 1 issue.
PUBLISHER: Mystery News, P.O. Box 3750, Sparks, Nevada 89431.
EDITOR: Patricia Shnell.
PRICE PER ISSUE: $1.95.
SIZE AND PAGINATION: Tabloid; 16 pages.
CURRENT STATUS: Active.

MYSTERY NOOK, THE

Fanzines are special in that they provide a place for the fan to communicate with others of like interest, share information which may not be available elsewhere, expound on favorite authors, review books, write articles that may not otherwise see print, and meet and/or correspond with people whose taste in literature is basically the same as their own. Fanzines are indispensible outlets for many who read mystery and detective fiction, yet in 1975 *The Armchair Detective** and *The Mystery Trader* (British)* were the only general mystery fanzines available.

The Mystery Nook began as a combined effort by Don Miller and Steve Lewis after Lewis's *Mystery*File** ceased publication. The editors, both science fiction fans of long standing, wanted to interest mystery-detective readers in sharing their thoughts, opinions, and knowledge with other fans, just as science fiction fans had been doing for many years. *The Mystery Nook* made its first appearance on July 1, 1975, and consisted of ten pages of editorial comments, odds and ends, book reviews, and an extra two-page book sale list. The second issue was much the same. But by the third and fourth issues, articles and letters began to appear.

In the meantime, Don Miller published *The Mystery Monitor** (first appearing March 7, 1976), originally designed as a monthly "news/info/advertising" supplement to be mailed with *The Mystery Nook*. The numbering system used for *The Mystery Nook* is somewhat confusing by the fact that it ran in tandem with that of *The Monitor*. Some issues were published as double-issues, using a double-number.

Volume 1, number 5–6 (October 10, 1975) was much larger than the preceding issues. Cover artwork was a plus; "Things That Go Bump in the Mailbox" became the heading for the letters column; and a new, regular feature titled "The Amateur Press" covered reviews of other fanzines in the field. Whole issue number 8 (volume 2, number 2) was the first double-issue worthy of the name. The number of pages increased from twenty to sixty, and it contained many book reviews, letters, much publishing news, and an index of *Ellery Queen's Mystery Magazine** for the year 1975.

The ninth issue (August 1976) was a Rex Stout memorial issue, with marvelous black-and-white cover art by Frank D. McSherry, Jr., and Mary Groff, plus thirty-three articles on Stout's works. Three supplements accompanied this issue, containing letters, reviews, and a list of books for sale. It was the first issue edited solely by Miller.

In the tenth issue of *The Mystery Nook* (May 1977) a section on Ruth Rendell was featured; the eleventh issue, a general issue, highlighted John Nieminski's "EQA 30; An Author/Title Index to Ellery Queen's Anthology, 1960–1975" and Barbara A. Buhrer's "Checklist of Mystery Awards." Kendall Foster Crossen was featured in the next issue (June 1979), as was Georgette Heyer in the thirteenth issue (July 1981). Each special author-issue contained numerous articles plus an exhaustive bibliography, compiled by Don Miller.

Throughout its history, *The Mystery Nook* has been distinguished by the variety of subject matter treated, the number of individuals contributing articles, and the wide scope of the information.

Information Sources

INDEX SOURCES: None known.
LOCATION SOURCES: Private collectors.

Publication History

MAGAZINE TITLE: *The Mystery Nook*.
TITLE CHANGES: None.
VOLUME AND ISSUE DATA: Vol. 1, no. 1 (July 1, 1975) through whole no. 13 (July 1981); 13 issues.
PUBLISHER: Don Miller, 12315 Judson Road, Wheaton, Maryland 20906.
EDITOR: Don Miller; Steve Lewis, associate editor (nos. 1–8).
PRICE PER ISSUE: 30 cents (issues nos. 1–8); $2.25.
SIZE AND PAGINATION: 8-1/2" X 11"; 10–60 pages.
CURRENT STATUS: Active; irregular.
—*Jo Ann Vicarel*

MYSTERY NOVELS AND SHORT STORIES

Possibly a derivative from *Mystery Novels Magazine* (Doubleday,Doran),*
this bimonthly was published as a "Double-Action Group" magazine by Columbia Publications, Inc. It began in 1939 and soon gained a reputation as one
of the better weird-menace magazines, stressing the luscious female in most
distressing situations. No other information is available.

Information Sources

INDEX SOURCES: None known.
LOCATION SOURCES: Private collectors.

Publication History

MAGAZINE TITLE: *Mystery Novels and Short Stories*.
TITLE CHANGES: None.
VOLUME AND ISSUE DATA: 1939; number of issues and extent unknown.
PUBLISHER: Columbia Publications, Inc., 1 Appleton Street, Holyoke, Massachusetts,
    with editorial offices at 241 Church Street, New York, New York.
EDITOR: Not known.
PRICE PER ISSUE: Not known.
SIZE AND PAGINATION: Not known.
CURRENT STATUS: Discontinued.

MYSTERY NOVELS MAGAZINE (Doubleday, Doran)

One of the few detective pulp magazines attempted by the book publishing
firm of Doubleday, Doran & Company, *Mystery Novels Magazine* was a giant-
sized, 256-page quarterly which commenced with the Summer 1932 issue. No
other information is available.

Information Sources

INDEX SOURCES: None known.
LOCATION SOURCES: University of California–Los Angeles Library (Vol. 1, no. 1,
    only); private collectors.

Publication History

MAGAZINE TITLE: *Mystery Novels Magazine*.
TITLE CHANGES: None.
VOLUME AND ISSUE DATA: Vol. 1, no. 1 (Summer 1932); number of issues and
    extent unknown.
PUBLISHER: Doubleday, Doran & Company, New York, New York.
EDITOR: Not known.
PRICE PER ISSUE: Not known.
SIZE AND PAGINATION: 7'' X 10''; 256 pages.
CURRENT STATUS: Discontinued.

MYSTERY NOVELS MAGAZINE (Winford Publications)

With emphasis on weird crime situations, *Mystery Novels Magazine* first appeared in 1934. Despite the same name, Louis H. Silberkleit's Winford Publications denied that it was a continuation of the earlier magazine published by Doubleday, Doran & Company.[1] No other information is available.

Note

1. Robert Kenneth Jones, *The Shudder Pulps* (West Linn, Ore.: Fax Collector's Editions, 1975), p. 145.

Information Sources

BIBLIOGRAPHY:
Jones, Robert Kenneth. *The Shudder Pulps.* West Linn, Ore.: Fax Collector's Editions, 1975.
INDEX SOURCES: None known.
LOCATION SOURCES: Private collectors.

Publication History

MAGAZINE TITLE: *Mystery Novels Magazine.*
TITLE CHANGES: None known.
VOLUME AND ISSUE DATA: 1934; number of issues and extent unknown.
PUBLISHER: Winford Publications, Inc., New York, New York.
EDITOR: Not known.
PRICE PER ISSUE: Not known.
SIZE AND PAGINATION: Not known.
CURRENT STATUS: Discontinued.

MYSTERY READER'S NEWSLETTER, THE

Thirty-seven years after the first amateur magazine had appeared in the science fiction field *(The Comet, 1930)*, the first such publication in the mystery field which was not devoted to a single author or character was introduced with a prospectus issue in August 1967. This was sent without charge to a number of persons known to be interested in mystery-detective fiction, inviting subscriptions at two dollars per year. Titled *The Mystery Lover's Newsletter*, the publication promised both to "entertain and inform those who cherish the art of the mystery story," while hoping to "enlighten the reader concerning the many facets of the mystery story."[1] The magazine, to be published bimonthly, would include information about authors and new books, articles of special interest to the mystery fan, letters from readers, questions, a search service, and free listings for subscribers who had books to trade, buy, or sell. There was to be no fiction. The prospectus issue included a listing of recently published books and a reprint of the first part of an article, "Detective Fiction," by W. B. Stevenson, originally published in London *(The National Book League, 1949)*.

The first regular issue appeared in October 1967 with the comment that the response had been gratifying and that the editor's opinion that "a magazine of this sort is sorely needed by those who are devoted to mystery and detective fiction"[2] had been verified. Note should be made that October 1967 also saw the birth of the other pioneer mystery amateur magazine, *The Armchair Detective*.*

A new title for *The Mystery Lover's Newsletter* was announced in August 1969 with the comment that this would better "encompass the casual fan, as well as those who are more serious about their detective fiction,"[3] and with the October 1969 issue (volume 3, number 1), the name was changed to *The Mystery Reader's Newsletter*. The name *Newsletter* perhaps was misleading since much of the content of the issues was of more permanent value than this term would imply. Its size was also more substantial, for the bimonthly issues never fell below twenty-one pages after the first year and averaged thirty-eight pages during the third through fifth years. In March 1973 (volume 5, number 6), it was announced that the magazine would change from bimonthly to quarterly publication. The two quarterly issues published were each fifty pages.

The magazine included well-researched articles of comment, comparison, criticism, and controversy presented in such a way as to appeal to both the reader and the researcher. Bibliographical listings and author checklists frequently appeared. Also featured were articles on authors' backgrounds; mystery on film, radio, and television (notably the many contributions by Jack Edmund Nolan and Charles Shibuk); interviews with authors (some reprinted, some done especially for the magazine); and news notes of happenings in the mystery field. The letters and reviews sections were popular with the readers as evidenced from the well-written responses which often amplified or corrected previous contributions. These, together with listings of new books (both in hardcover and paperback) and notices of books wanted or for sale by readers, soon became regular features in each issue. With the October 1969 issue (volume 3, number 2), a collector's directory was added in which collectors could list their interests. Also appearing fairly frequently were book dealers' advertisements. An index for each completed volume appeared in the last issue of that volume.

With the exception of the six issues of volume 4, the covers all featured original designs by Stanley A. Carlin and John E. Withee (volumes 1–2), John Wilmunen (volume 3), Dany Frolich (volume 5), and Terry Witmer (volume 6). The covers for volume 4 were illustrated with reproductions of dust-jacket photographs from J & S Graphics' Catalogue No. 6, "First Editions of Mysteries, Rogueries and Detective Fiction." Interior illustrations were usually reproductions of photographs.

Almost from its beginning, the magazine attracted a number of regular and semiregular contributors who were responsible for several particularly noteworthy series of articles. Perhaps the most monumental of these was Marvin Lachman's "The American Regional Mystery." This was a "guided tour" of the United States, in ten regions, as the locales of mystery fiction and how the locations were a part of the story. Ten installments, beginning in February 1970 (volume 3, number 3), appeared during the remaining life of the magazine. Subsequent installments appeared in *The Armchair Detective*. Less lengthy, but no less informative and entertaining with regard to their respective subjects, were Lachman's "Quotations from the Mysteries" and the various series by Francis M. Nevins, Jr. ("Department of Unreprinted Masterpieces," "Department of Unrelated Miscellanea"), and Robert C.S. Adey ("My Favourite Detective"). Frank D. McSherry, Jr., contributed "A Study in Black," a series which began in volume 5, number 5, introduced as "the first part of a long article that will run continuously in future issues until it is completed."[4] This was an exploration of the continuing thread of the supernatural in mystery and detective fiction, but this article was unfortunately still uncompleted when the magazine ceased with the November 1973 issue.

Notes

1. Editorial, *The Mystery Lover's Newsletter*, prospectus issue (August 1967), p. 1.
2. *Mystery Lover's Newsletter*, Vol. 1, no. 1 (October 1967), p. 1.
3. *Mystery Lover's Newsletter*, Vol. 2, no. 6 (August 1969), p. 9.
4. Frank D. McSherry, "A Study in Black," *The Mystery Reader's Newsletter*, Vol. 5, no. 5 (n.d. [1972]), p. 23.

Information Sources

INDEX SOURCES: None known.
LOCATION SOURCES: Private collectors.

Publication History

MAGAZINE TITLE: *The Mystery Reader's Newsletter*.
TITLE CHANGES: Originally *The Mystery Lover's Newsletter* (until Vol. 3, no. 1 [October 1969]).
VOLUME AND ISSUE DATA: Prospectus issue, August 1967; Vol. 1, no. 1 (October 1967) through Vol. 6, no. 2 (November 1973); 33 issues.
PUBLISHER: Mrs. Lianne Carlin, 30 Florence Avenue (P.O. Box 107), Revere, Massachusetts 02151, and later P.O. Box 113, Melrose, Massachusetts 02176.
EDITOR: Mrs. Lianne Carlin; associate editor, Stanley A. Carlin.
PRICE PER ISSUE: By subscription only, originally $2.00 for 6 issues; $2.50 (commencing August 1968); $3.00 (commencing August 1969); $4.00 (commencing March 1973).
SIZE AND PAGINATION: 8-1/" X 11"; 12–50 pages.
CURRENT STATUS: Discontinued.
—*David H. Doerrer*

MYSTERY STORIES

See MYSTERY MAGAZINE

MYSTERY TALES (Atlas Magazines)

Mystery Tales magazine appeared in December 1958 with an assortment of well-known and lesser-known authors writing crime-adventure stories. Although oriented more to fast action and swinging locales than to mystery, many were well written and, while reminiscent of the pulp plots, depicted contemporary situations involving female victims, small-time hoodlums, and domestic mayhem. Rough-and-ready action alternated with intrigue, and many tales had surprise endings. An example of the story titles demonstrates what was thought to be appealing to the reader: "Nymph in the Keyhole," "Lady in the Swamp," "Die Now, Lover," and "Let's All Go Kill the Scared Old Man."

Published bimonthly, the magazine lasted for six issues.

Information Sources

INDEX SOURCES: Cook, Michael L. *Monthly Murders*. Westport, Conn.: Greenwood Press, 1982.
LOCATION SOURCES: Private collectors.

Publication History

MAGAZINE TITLE: *Mystery Tales*.
TITLE CHANGES: None.
VOLUME AND ISSUE DATA: Vol. 1, no. 1 (December 1958) through Vol. 1, no. 6 (October 1959); 6 issues.
PUBLISHER: Martin Goodman as Atlas Magazines, Inc., 655 Madison Avenue, New York 21, New York.
EDITOR: Evan Lee Heyman; Kenneth Markel as assistant editor on first issues.
PRICE PER ISSUE: 35 cents.
SIZE AND PAGINATION: 5-3/8" X 7-1/4"; 128 pages.
CURRENT STATUS: Discontinued.

MYSTERY TALES (Western Fiction Publishing)

See UNCANNY TALES

MYSTERY THRILLERS (British)

Two issues of *Mystery Thrillers*, a pocket-size, thin (sixty-four pages) magazine, were published in 1942 by Gerald Swan. No other information is available.

Information Sources

BIBLIOGRAPHY:
Lofts, W.O.G., and Derek J. Adley, *Old Boys Books, A Complete Catalogue*. London: privately printed, 1969.
INDEX SOURCES: None known.

LOCATION SOURCES: Private collectors.

Publication History

MAGAZINE TITLE: *Mystery Thrillers*.
TITLE CHANGES: None.
VOLUME AND ISSUE DATA: No. 1 (1942) through no. 2 (1942); 2 issues.
PUBLISHER: Gerald Swan, London.
EDITOR: Not known.
PRICE PER ISSUE: Not known.
SIZE AND PAGINATION: 5-3/8'' X 7''; 64 pages.
CURRENT STATUS: Discontinued.

MYSTERY TRADER, THE (British)

Although mystery and detective fiction finds ready acceptance in the British isles and as a result forms a staple ingredient in the overall publishing picture, amateur magazines in this category are rarely attempted.

In recent years, the only such general news and commentary magazine, modeled after the American counterparts, has been the work of a retired nursing officer in Scotland. Ethel Lindsay, an avid fan of both mystery and science fiction and realizing the need for such an outlet, commenced *The Mystery Trader* in 1971. The first two issues were concerned only with selling books and also included "want-lists" from a number of mystery and detective readers. But by the third issue, *The Mystery Trader* became a fanzine for the genre, and its subscribers extended beyond the United Kingdom.

This third issue, undated but published in 1972, included "Locked Room Mania" by Robert Adey and "Elemental My Dear Watson" by George Locke, both of interest and value. John A. Hogan's "Edgar Wallace: This Was a Man" appeared in the fourth issue, and Francis M. Nevins, Jr., contributed "Four Retrospective Reviews from the Thirties" in the fifth issue and followed with "American Retrospectives from the Forties" in the next issue. D. J. Morris added to the "locked room" detection literature with "To Produce a Locked Room Effect" in the same issue, dated March 1973. An interesting "Victorian Book Production" by N. C. Ravenscroft and the third in a series of "Impossible Crime Review" pieces by Robert Adey were in the June 1973 magazine.

Other important articles published in subsequent issues included "The Three Gentleman Adventures of James Hadley Chase" and "On the Run: The Books of Francis Ryck" by T. P. Dukeshire; "The Date? The Name?" and "Ghost Hunting as a Way of Life" by Mary Groff; "A Survey of the Unusual" by Derek J. Adley; and "A Quite Abnormal Talent for Suspense: Dick Francis" by John Boyles. Francis M. Nevins, Jr., added a commentary on thrillers in the sixties, and Robert Adey continued his "Impossible Crime Review" commentaries. Throughout all twenty-one issues published one would find well-researched and conceived articles on crime fiction and its authors.

Book reviews, various news items, and a letters department added to the interest of each issue. Mary Groff contributed artwork for the covers. But with increasing costs and the retirement of the editor, the sole mystery fanzine from Britain ceased publication in July 1980, sadly ending a ten-year span.

Information Sources

INDEX SOURCES: None known.
LOCATION SOURCES: Private collectors.

Publication History

MAGAZINE TITLE: *The Mystery Trader*.
TITLE CHANGES: None.
VOLUME AND ISSUE DATA: No. 1 (June 1971) through no. 21 (July 1980); 21 issues.
PUBLISHER: Ethel Lindsay, 69 Barry Road, Carnoustie, Angus, DD7 7QQ, Scotland.
EDITOR: Ethel Lindsay.
PRICE PER ISSUE: Varied from four issues for 50 pence to 50 pence each.
SIZE AND PAGINATION: 8" X 11-1/2"; average 12 pages.
CURRENT STATUS: Discontinued.
—*Ethel Lindsay*

MYSTERY WRITERS ANNUAL

See THIRD DEGREE, THE

MYSTIC AGENT DOUBLE X

This fifty-page, well-illustrated magazine was published for distribution through the Pulp Heroes Amateur Press Association (PHAPA) and had a limited distribution to other interested persons. The one issue published to date contains pages of editorial comments, news and notes, and a discussion of the fact that few pulp heroes in the magazines fought in World War II. This is followed by a lengthy, illustrated article on Eugene Thomas's "Lady from Hell" series originally published in *Detective Fiction Weekly** in 1935 and 1936. The article included a complete, chronological list of these stories with dates and story synopses. Some mailing comments and notes on the 1979 Boston convention of the PHAPA were included, as well as a serious, in-depth review of the "Great Marvel" series by Roy Rockwood (a boys' series of nine titles from 1906 through 1935).

The announced second issue was to feature an article on "The Griffin," but this issue has not appeared to date.

Information Sources

INDEX SOURCES: None known.

LOCATION SOURCES: Private collectors.

Publication History

MAGAZINE TITLE: *Mystic Agent Double X.*
TITLE CHANGES: None.
VOLUME AND ISSUE DATA: No. 1 (undated [1981]); 1 issue.
PUBLISHER: Robert Jennings, R.F.D. 2, Whiting Road, Dudley, Massachusetts, 01570.
EDITOR: Robert Jennings.
PRICE PER ISSUE: Not specified.
SIZE AND PAGINATION: 8-1/2'' X 11''; 50 pages.
CURRENT STATUS: Inactive, though not officially discontinued.
—*David A. Bates*

N

NEMESIS, INC.

See DOC SAVAGE CLUB READER, THE

NERO WOLFE AND ARCHIE GOODWIN FANS NEWSLETTER

See LONE WOLFE

NERO WOLFE MYSTERY MAGAZINE

When the first issue appeared in January 1954, the *Nero Wolfe Mystery Magazine* was announced as a bimonthly. The second issue was on schedule, in March, but the third, and final, issue was not published until June 1954, an indication that publication plans had already gone awry.

Each issue of the *Nero Wolfe Mystery Magazine* reprinted ten reputable short stories, a Wolfe novella, and a "Criminal Crossword Puzzle." The crossword was prepared for the magazine by Margaret Farrar, since the 1920s the crossword editor of the *New York Times* and, in a very real sense, the person who created the vogue of the crossword puzzle. Margaret Farrar was the wife of John Farrar, the publisher who persuaded Rex Stout, in 1933, to create a detective hero and then, once he had done this, to launch the Nero Wolfe series. She and her husband were Wolfe's first fans. During more than forty years as crossword editor, Mrs. Farrar often gave Nero Wolfe a boost by introducing him into a *Times* crossword. At age eighty-four, she actively continues as one of the judges of the Wolfe Pack's annual Nero Wolfe Award (see *Gazette, The; The Journal of the Wolfe Pack*). Because of the special relationship, her crosswords in *Nero Wolfe Mystery Magazine* are coveted items for collectors of Stoutiana.

Stories by Wilbur Daniel Steele and Elisabeth Sanxay Holding first achieved publication in the January issue. The March issue published a story of Julian Symons, at that time a newcomer to the scene of crime fiction. New stories by Dave Grubb appeared in both the March and June magazines. And a new Solar Pons story, "The Swedenborg Signatures," by August Derleth, saw print in the June issue. Others whose short stories were published in the *Nero Wolfe Mystery Magazine* include Mary Roberts Rinehart, Ellery Queen, Agatha Christie, James Thurber, Dorothy Sayers, Edmund Crispin, Alexander Woollcott, Erle Stanley Gardner, August Derleth, Craig Rice, and Anthony Boucher, among others. The June issue included a bonus feature, a "Conscience Quiz," and a minimystery.

As supervising editor, Rex Stout wrote an introduction to each issue, touching on topics such as "the preposterous in fiction" and on the one characteristic—inscrutability—that all detective heroes share in common. These conversational pieces usually are bantering in tone and seem touched with Archie Goodwin's brio.

Information Sources

BIBLIOGRAPHY:
McAleer, John. *Rex Stout, A Biography*. Boston: Little, Brown, 1977.
INDEX SOURCES: Cook, Michael L. *Monthly Murders*. Westport, Conn.: Greenwood Press, 1982.
McSherry, Frank D., Jr. "Index." *The Mystery Nook,* no. 9 (August 1976): A25.
LOCATION SOURCES: Private collectors.

Publication History

MAGAZINE TITLE: *Nero Wolfe Mystery Magazine*.
TITLE CHANGES: None.
VOLUME AND ISSUE DATA: Vol. 1, no. 1 (January 1954) through Vol. 1, no. 3 (June 1954); 3 issues.
PUBLISHER: Hillman Periodicals, Inc., 4600 Diversey Avenue, Chicago, Illinois.
EDITOR: Rex Stout, supervising editor.
PRICE PER ISSUE: 35 cents.
SIZE AND PAGINATION: 5-3/8" X 7-3/8"; 144 pages.
CURRENT STATUS: Discontinued.
—*John J. McAleer*

NEW DETECTIVE

New Detective, the first of two magazines of a similar name, was published by Two-Books Magazine Publishers commencing with the November 1934 issue. No other information is available.

Information Sources

INDEX SOURCES: None known.

LOCATION SOURCES: Private collectors.

Publication History

MAGAZINE TITLE: *New Detective*.
TITLE CHANGES: None.
VOLUME AND ISSUE DATA: Vol. 1, no. 1 (November 1934) through Vol. 3, no. 1 (November 1935); 7 issues.
PUBLISHER: Two-Books Magazine Publishers, Inc., New York, New York.
EDITOR: Not known.
PRICE PER ISSUE: Not known.
SIZE AND PAGINATION: Not known.
CURRENT STATUS: Discontinued.

NEW DETECTIVE MAGAZINE

Promising "the NEWest in Crime Fiction," *New Detective Magazine* carried the standard fare of crime stories, with emphasis on police detectives, by some of the most popular authors. These included Richard Deming, Day Keene, Charles Beckman, Jr., Hugh Pentecost, Larry Holden, Fletcher Flora, Donald Barr Chidsey, G. T. Fleming-Roberts, John MacDonald, and others who were to continue on into the digest-size mystery magazine market. Each issue of *New Detective Magazine* included an editor's column, "The Witness Chair," along with cipher puzzles, true-fact items, and crime fillers. Published by Fictioneers, a subsidiary of Popular Publications, Inc., the magazine enjoyed a comparatively long life, from March 1941 through June 1953, a total of seventy-three issues. In August 1953, *New Detective Magazine*'s legacy was evident in a new Popular Publications magazine, *Fifteen Detective Stories,** which continued *New Detective*'s volume and issue numbering and several regular features.

A British reprint series of at least eleven issues has been noted.

Information Sources

BIBLIOGRAPHY:
Hardin, Nils. "An Interview with Henry Steeger." *Xenophile*, no. 33 (July 1977): 3–18.
————, and George Hocutt. "A Checklist of Popular Publications Titles 1930–1955." *Xenophile*, no. 33 (July 1977): 21–24.
INDEX SOURCES: None known.
LOCATION SOURCES: University of California–Los Angeles Library (1941–1952, 6 issues); private collectors.

Publication History

MAGAZINE TITLE: *New Detective Magazine*.
TITLE CHANGES: Continued as *Fifteen Detective Stories* (August 1953).
VOLUME AND ISSUE DATA: Vol. 1, no. 1 (March 1941) through Vol. 19, no. 2 (June 1953); 73 issues.

PUBLISHER: Fictioneers, Inc., a subsidiary of Popular Publications, Inc., 1125 East
     Vaile Avenue, Kokomo, Indiana.
EDITOR: Not known.
PRICE PER ISSUE: 10 cents; 15 cents; 20 cents; 25 cents.
SIZE AND PAGINATION: 6-3/4'' X 9-3/8''; 114 pages.
CURRENT STATUS: Discontinued.

NEW DETECTIVE TALES (British)

A series of pocket-size, thin (sixty-four-page), cheaply produced magazines,
this publication was undistinguished but met the postwar public's appetite for
crime fiction. The first two issues in 1949 were titled *New Detective Tales,* but
the name was then changed to *Detective Tales,* under which the magazine continued for another 117 issues.

Information Sources

INDEX SOURCES: None known.
LOCATION SOURCES: Private collectors only.

Publication History

MAGAZINE TITLE: *New Detective Tales.*
TITLE CHANGES: *Detective Tales* (with issue no. 3).
VOLUME AND ISSUE DATA: 2 issues as *New Detective Tales;* 117 issues as *Detective
     Tales,* Nos. 1–119, 1949–1951.
PUBLISHER: T. V. Boardman & Company, London.
EDITOR: Not known.
PRICE PER ISSUE: 9 pence.
SIZE AND PAGINATION: 5-3/8'' X 7''; 64 pages.
CURRENT STATUS: Discontinued.

NEW MYSTERY ADVENTURE

Harold B. Hersey, erstwhile but often unsuccessful publisher, tried a wide
variety of stories in this pulp magazine, which debuted in 1935, and he even
changed its title three times. But although there was claimed circulation of
600,000 at one point, *New Mystery Adventure* did not seem to catch the public's
fancy.

The magazine was somewhat of a weird-menace type, implying sex in the
illustrations (some, as interior art, pictured nearly nude ladies), but this was
never quite delivered in the story lines. A reader would more often find straight
mystery adventures. One of the phantom female crime fighters, the Domino
Lady, did appear briefly but was then dropped. Many house names were credited
with the bylines, along with Octavus Roy Cohen, Steve Fisher, L. Ron Hubbard,
and others recognizable by mystery fans of the period.

The magazine commenced in March 1935 as *New Mystery Adventure*, an issue
that made an auspicious beginning with a Mary Roberts Rinehart story, ''The

Sabine Woman.'' An assortment of mystery, mystery-adventure, and oriental stories filled the rest of the magazine. By May 1936, the title had been changed to *Mystery Adventure Magazine*. It became *Mystery Adventure* with the December 1936 issue and *Mystery Adventures Magazine* in January 1937. With but few exceptions, a monthly publication schedule was maintained. The last issue was May 1937, at which time it was being published under the Fiction Magazines, Inc., imprint.

Information Sources

BIBLIOGRAPHY:
Goulart, Ron. *Cheap Thrills*. New Rochelle, N.Y.: Arlington House, 1972.
Jones, Robert Kenneth. *The Shudder Pulps*. West Linn, Ore.: Fax Collector's Editions, 1975.
INDEX SOURCES: Cook, Fred, and Gordon Huber. ''Index to New Mystery Adventures Magazine.'' *Xenophile*, no. 22 (March/April 1976): 47, and no. 30 (March 1977): 146.
LOCATION SOURCES: Private collectors.

Publication History

MAGAZINE TITLE: *New Mystery Adventure*.
TITLE CHANGES: *Mystery Adventure Magazine* (with Vol. 3, no. 3 [May 1936]); *Mystery Adventure* (with Vol. 4, no. 4 [December 1936]); *Mystery Adventures Magazine* (with Vol. 5, no. 1 [January 1937]).
VOLUME AND ISSUE DATA: Vol. 1, no. 1 (March 1935) through Vol. 5, no. 4 (May 1937); 25 issues.
PUBLISHERS: Harold B. Hersey; Fiction Magazines, Inc.
EDITOR: Not known.
PRICE PER ISSUE: 20 cents; 15 cents (with sixth issue).
SIZE AND PAGINATION: 7'' X 10''; 112 pages.
CURRENT STATUS: Discontinued.

NEWNES' "NICK CARTER" SERIES (British)

See NICK CARTER WEEKLY

NEW NICK CARTER LIBRARY

See NICK CARTER WEEKLY

NEW NICK CARTER WEEKLY

See NICK CARTER WEEKLY

NEW YORK DETECTIVE LIBRARY

Two months after the *Old Cap. Collier Library* proved there was a market for a periodical devoted to detective stories, Frank Tousey launched his *New York Detective Library*. Like *Old Cap. Collier, New York Detective* was an anthology series which drew on the talents of the regular contributors to Tousey's story-papers. T ᷦ ᷣe were occasional reprints of serials from the *Boys of New York*, as well as original material. The year was 1883.

An elaborate logo depicted the title against a background of columns on an impressive building, perhaps the Hall of Justice. On either side of the words "Detective Library" were shadowy figures, perhaps a thief and his quarry. In the center was a dark lantern. This was replaced starting with issue number 157 with the title alone and no accompanying illustrations. When in 1894 the title becamme merely the *Detective Library*, the portraits of Old King Brady, the James and Ford Boys, and Carl Greene were used on each issue.

The authors were largely pseudonymous; some names, like Police Captain Howard, were also found in the *Old Cap. Collier Library*. Allan Arnold, A. F. Hill, K. F. Hill (his brother or a misprint?), a U.S. Detective, a N.Y. Journalist, Tom Fox (Philadelphia Detective), Old Cap Lee, Gus Williams (a real figure in the annals of the theater) were some of the other names used. Occasionally, only initials were signed; some can be identified (G.G.S., T.W.H., for example, were George G. Small and Thomas W. Hanshew), others cannot.

Two themes appear dominant in the early numbers: the influence of Emile Gaboriau and the French school, and the pretense that these are true stories written by and about the great manhunters of the world. Among the earliest figures to appear in a series of stories in the *Library* was "Young Sleuth" no relationship to George Munro's "Old Sleuth"). The character was also found in the pages of the *Boys of New York* and later became the title figure in the *Young Sleuth Library*.*

The most popular character in the *New York Detective Library* was James (Old King) Brady, the creation of Francis W. Doughty, writing as "A New York Detective." He first appeared in issue number 154, November 14, 1885, in a story called "Old King Brady, the Sleuth-Hound." His adventures appeared with increasing frequency for the next thirteen years, eventually alternating with D. W. Stevens's stories of the James Boys. Some of the Brady stories had originally appeared as serials in the *Boys of New York*.

As with other dime-novel series, later numbers of the *New York Detective Library* were reprints of earlier numbers. There were 104 numbers which featured Old King Brady (occasionally with two stories in one number). Of these, eighty-two contained material original to the *Library*, and twenty-two reprinted selected early stories. Old King Brady was later the central figure in the colored-cover series, *Secret Service: Old and Young King Brady, Detectives*.*

Information Sources

BIBLIOGRAPHY:
Bleiler, E. F., ed. *Eight Dime Novels*. New York: Dover Publications, 1974.

Bragin, Charles. *Dime Novels Bibliography 1860-1928*. Brooklyn, New York: privately printed, 1938.

Holmes, Harold C. "New York Detective Library No. 171." *Dime Novel Roundup*, no. 122 (November 1942): 1–8.

LeBlanc, Edward T. "Dime Novel Sketches No. 85." *Dime Novel Roundup*, no. 412 (January 15, 1967): 1.

Leithead, J. Edward. "The Great Detective Team: Old and Young King Brady." *American Book Collector* 20 (November/December 1969): 25–31.

O'Gara, Gil. "Old King Brady: His Rise and Decline." *The Age of the Unicorn*, no. 2 (April 1980): 19–22; and *Yellowback Library*, no. 1 (January/February 1982): 5–7.

Pearson, Edmund. *Dime Novels, or Following an Old Trail in Popular Literature*. Boston: Little, Brown, 1929.

INDEX SOURCES: None known.

LOCATION SOURCES: Hess Collection, University of Minnesota; private collectors.

Publication History

MAGAZINE TITLE: *New York Detective Library*.

TITLE CHANGES: *Detective Library* (with no. 543, [April 22, 1892]).

VOLUME AND ISSUE DATA: No. 1 (June 7, 1883) through no. 801 (April 1, 1898); 801 issues.

PUBLISHER: Frank Tousey, Publisher, 34 and 36 North Moore Street, New York, New York.

EDITOR: Not known.

PRICE PER ISSUE: 10 cents.

SIZE AND PAGINATION: 8-1/2" X 11-3/4"; 9" X 12-1/2" (with no. 157); 32 pages.

CURRENT STATUS: Discontinued.

—*J. Randolph Cox*

NICK CARTER DETECTIVE LIBRARY

See NICK CARTER LIBRARY

NICK CARTER DETECTIVE MAGAZINE

See NICK CARTER MAGAZINE

NICK CARTER LIBRARY

Nick Carter had been the hero of only three novels (1886–1889) when the first number of *Nick Carter Detective Library* was published in August 1891. That first number contained only one story, "Nick Carter, Detective," by "A Celebrated Author." The anonymity of the "Celebrated Author" would not be broken for many years. The rest of the stories in the *Library* were signed "by the Author of 'Nick Carter.' "

If the *Old Cap. Collier Library** (an anthology series) may be called the first regularly published "magazine" of detective fiction, the *Nick Carter Library* (the word "Detective" was dropped from the title after the third number) may be called the first regularly published "magazine" devoted to the adventures of a single detective hero.

Much of the content of the *Nick Carter Library* may seem to be common to the genre: tales of fraud and forgery, murder and revenge, "policy" and "green goods" and "peter players" (one sometimes needs a dictionary of nineteenth-century criminal argot to read the early stories), as well as twin siblings (one good, the other evil), all with events that are improbable, almost impossible, to swallow.

What the *Nick Carter Library* had to distinguish it from its competitors was the hero. Nick Carter was a young, handsome, and brave character. Occasionally witty, he was also well read in the works of his authors' favorite writers. Contrary to popular myth, he smoked cigars on occasion and even drank beer and wine, but never to excess. His name must certainly be among the most successful combinations of syllables in American fiction.

In the early stories, Nick has a quasi-official position with the New York police and was called upon by Superintendent Thomas Byrnes when the officials were at their wits' end. Gradually the stories added more supporting characters: Nick's wife, Ethel; his chief assistants, Chick and Patsy; as well as a girl detective named Nellie; another girl detective named Ida Jones; and yet another assistant named Warwick Carter. Nick's archenemy, Dr. Jack Quartz, was the earliest example of a recurring criminal foe in detective fiction, three years prior to Professor Moriarty.

Master of disguise, adept with picklocks, twin revolvers held up his sleeves by springs—there is something appealing about the great New York detective which outweighs the dime novel prose in which he appears. He could, and did, go everywhere to solve mysteries: out West chasing the Daltons, to Chinatown rooting out opium dens, to London or Paris tracking international crooks. If the mysteries were not profound or difficult for the reader to solve, the adventures made up for it.

In 282 weekly issues, there were 240 original stories of between 20,000 and 33,000 words. For years, it was assumed that all had been the work of Frederic Van Rensselaer Dey, but the publisher's records indicate that there were eleven writers contributing to the *Nick Carter Library*. Besides Dey (the chief writer), there were stories by George Waldo Browne, Frederick R. Burton, O. P. Caylor, Wiliam Wallace Cook, E. C. Derby, Charles W. Hooke, Eugene T. Sawyer, Edward L. Stratemeyer, Alfred B. Tozer, and R. F. Walsh. When Dey was unable to deliver a story, another writer was used, or an earlier story was reprinted. Frederick R. Burton, for example, wrote stories in which only Patsy Murphy was featured as the hero, excluding Nick Carter almost entirely. From September 21, 1895, to the end of 1896, these were alternated with Nick Carter adventures which were almost entirely reprints of earlier numbers.

Most of the stories in the *Library* were reprinted in its successor, the *Nick Carter Weekly*,* and, in combinations of two or three, in the paper-covered novel series, the *Magnet Library*.

Information Sources

BIBLIOGRAPHY:

Bragin, Charles. *Dime Novels Bibliography 1860–1928*. Brooklyn, N.Y.: privately printed, 1938.

Cox, J. Randolph. "Nick Carter: The Man and the Myth." *The Mystery Lover's Newsletter,* Vol. 2, no. 3 (February 1969): 15–18.

LeBlanc, Edward T. "Dime Novel Sketches, No. 30." *Dime Novel Roundup*, no. 353 (February 15, 1962): 11.

Leithead, J. Edward. "The Greatest Sleuth That Ever Lived." *Dime Novel Roundup*, no. 272 (May 15, 1955): 37–43.

Noel, Mary. *Villains Galore*. New York: Macmillan, 1954.

Pearson, Edmund. *Dime Novels, or Following an Old Trail in Popular Literature*. Boston: Little, Brown, 1929.

Reynolds, Quentin. *The Fiction Factory*. New York: Random House, 1955.

Turner, E. S. *Boys Will Be Boys*. London: Michael Joseph Ltd., 1948.

INDEX SOURCES: Cox, J. Randolph. *Nick Carter Library*. Fall River, Mass.: Edward T. LeBlanc, 1974.

LOCATION SOURCES: Hess Collection, University of Minnesota; private collectors.

Publication History

MAGAZINE TITLE: *Nick Carter Library*.

TITLE CHANGES: *Nick Carter Detective Library* (first three issues, until August 29, 1891).

VOLUME AND ISSUE DATA: No. 1 (August 8, 1891) through no. 282 (December 26, 1896); 282 issues.

PUBLISHER: Street & Smith, Publishers, 31 Rose Street, New York, New York; later 29 Rose Street, New York, New York.

EDITOR: Not known.

PRICE PER ISSUE: 5 cents.

SIZE AND PAGINATION: 8-1/2" X 10-3/4"; 16 pages (no. 16 was 32 pages).

CURRENT STATUS: Discontinued.

—*J. Randolph Cox*

NICK CARTER LIBRARY (British)

See NICK CARTER WEEKLY

NICK CARTER MAGAZINE

The character of Nick Carter had been literally coasting on his reputation by the time Street & Smith put him into a pulp magazine of his own. The last original novel had been published in the *New Magnet Library*, a paper-covered novel series, in 1918, just about the time the character disappeared from the pages of *Detective Story Magazine* (Street & Smith).* Between 1924 and 1927, eleven new Nick Carter stories were added to that magazine, ending with a novelette called "Nick Carter Dies" (May 14, 1927). This was, of course, death in a metaphorical sense, for no hero ever died in a Street & Smith series.

In 1933, the publisher discontinued the *New Magnet Library*, which had only issued reprints for the past 15 years. Even by early twentieth-century standards, the material was beginning to seem dated. At the same time began publication of a hero pulp magazine with Nick Carter as the central figure in the lead novel. The author hired to write the stories on a schedule of one every two weeks was Richard Wormser.

Wormser kept little of the traditional Nick Carter. This was a magazine for a new generation. It was not a hard-boiled detective publication, but some of the toughness and flavor of the gangster years may be found there. Chick Carter and Patsy Garvan (originally Patsy Murphy until sometime in the *Nick Carter Weekly** series when his creator decided to change the name) were retained, but a Filipino valet replaced Nick's old butler, Joseph. A government agent named Con Connors made semiregular appearances as well.

Wormser wrote only the first seventeen novels. He was replaced by Thomas Calvert McClary, John Chambliss, and T. Henderson. Chambliss and Philip Clark were also responsible for the novelettes about Nick Carter that appeared occasionally as backup features between 1934 and 1936. Using two stories about the title character in a hero pulp wasn't the usual practice. The signature used on these stories, Harrison Keith, was an insider's joke. Keith had been the central figure in an earlier series published in the *Magnet* and *New Magnet Libraries*. Those stories had been signed by Nicholas Carter. The lead novels in the *Nick Carter Magazine* still used that name as a signature, continuing the illusion that Nick Carter was a real person.

When the *Nick Carter Magazine* was discontinued in June 1936, the character was transferred to a new series in *Clues Detective Stories (Clues*)*, but only one story appeared there ("Murder in a Black Frame," by "Harrison Keith"— probably Philip Clark, July 1936).

At the suggestion of Walter B. Gibson, six of the lead novels were reissued as digest-sized paperbacks by Vital Publications between 1945 and 1948. Gibson did some of the editing on these to remove some of Wormser's inconsistencies or to tighten up the endings.

The authors of the short stories (two to four per issue) included George Allan Moffatt, Paul Ernst, Paul Ellsworth Triem, Jean Francis Webb, John L. Chambliss, Arthur J. Burks, Laurence Donovan, Theodore Tinsley, and Steve Fisher. Tinsley contributed two stories to what may have been intended as a series, with Detective Terry "Bulldog" Black as the central character.

Information Sources

BIBLIOGRAPHY:
Reynolds, Quentin. *The Fiction Factory*. New York: Random House, 1955.

Turner, E. S. *Boys Will Be Boys*. London: Michael Joseph Ltd., 1948.
INDEX SOURCES: Cox, J. Randolph. *Nick Carter Stories and Other Series Containing Stories about Nick Carter*. Fall River, Mass.: Edward T. LeBlanc, 1980.
LOCATION SOURCES: University of California–Los Angeles Library (Vol. 1, no. 1, only); private collectors.

Publication History

MAGAZINE TITLE: *Nick Carter Magazine*.
TITLE CHANGES: *Nick Carter Detective Magazine* (with Vol. 6, no. 1 [January 1936]).
VOLUME AND ISSUE DATA: Vol. 1, no. 1 (March 1933) through Vol. 7, no. 4 (June 1936); 40 issues.
PUBLISHER: Street & Smith Publications, Inc., 79 Seventh Avenue, New York, New York.
EDITOR: John L. Nanovic.
PRICE PER ISSUE: 10 cents.
SIZE AND PAGINATION: 6-3/4" X 10"; 128 pages.
CURRENT STATUS: Discontinued.
—*J. Randolph Cox*

NICK CARTER STORIES

The third series of nickel weeklies devotd to Nick Carter's adventures presented no startling differences from its predecessor, the *New Nick Carter Weekly (Nick Carter Weekly*)*. It was the same format and the same formula. Each story was twenty to twenty-six pages in length, followed by fillers, short stories, and episodes of serials made up of the contents of the twenty-two issues of the *Shield Weekly** of a decade earlier.

Three numbers containing original stories alternated with three numbers which reprinted stories from the *Nick Carter Weekly* for at least the first year. The remaining numbers contained new stories or ones based on the Sexton Blake tales then appearing in the British weekly, *Union Jack (Detective Weekly* [British]*). Street & Smith had arranged to use this material in exchange for allowing the British publication to use some of its contents.

In the 160 numbers of *Nick Carter Stories*, there were 118 original stories and 42 reprints. The final number, "The Yellow Yabel; or, Nick Carter and The Society Looters," was the first episode of a serial which was continued in *Detective Story Magazine* (Street & Smith)*. *Nick Carter Stories* was the first stage in the transition between dime novel detective fiction and pulp magazine detective fiction. Five titles were projected beyond issue number 160, but were never published.

Only eight writers contributed material to the publications: Frederick R. Burton, William Wallace Cook, Frederick W. Davis, Frederic Van Rensselaer Dey (mostly reprints, but a few original stories which had not been used in the *Nick Carter Weekly*), George C. Jenks, Charles Agnew MacLean, Rich (first name not recorded), and Samuel C. Spalding. As with the contributors to the *Nick Carter Weekly*, some of these names were contributors to *Nick Carter Stories* only by virtue of having had older material reprinted in its pages.

The practice of planning stories in groups of three which could be reprinted in the paper-covered novel series, the *Magnet Library*, was continued in the *Nick Carter Stories* publication. Along with Nick Carter serials from the pages of *Detective Story Magazine*, these were among the last of the series to be collected and reissued in that manner.

Information Sources

BIBLIOGRAPHY:

Bragin, Charles. *Dime Novels Bibliography 1860-1928*. Brooklyn, N.Y.: privately printed, 1938.

LeBlanc, Edward T. "Dime Novel Sketches No. 18." *Dime Novel Roundup,* no. 338 (November 15, 1960): 91.

Noel, Mary. *Villains Galore*. New York: Macmillan Co., 1954.

Pearson, Edmund. *Dime Novels, or Following an Old Trail in Popular Literature*. Boston: Little, Brown, 1929.

Reynolds, Quentin. *The Fiction Factory*. New York: Random House, 1955.

Turner, E. S. *Boys Will Be Boys*. London: Michael Joseph Ltd., 1948.

INDEX SOURCES: Cox, J. Randolph. *Nick Carter Stories*. Fall River, Mass.: Edward T. LeBlanc, 1977.

LOCATION SOURCES: Private collectors.

Publication History

MAGAZINE TITLE: *Nick Carter Stories*.

TITLE CHANGES: None (replaced by *Detective Story Magazine*).

VOLUME AND ISSUE DATA: No. 1 (September 13, 1912) through no. 160 (October 2, 1915); 160 issues.

PUBLISHER: Street & Smith, Publishers, 79–89 Seventh Avenue, New York, New York.

EDITOR: Not known.

PRICE PER ISSUE: 5 cents.

SIZE AND PAGINATION: 8-1/2" X 10-3/4"; 32 pages.

CURRENT STATUS: Discontinued.

—*J. Randolph Cox*

NICK CARTER WEEKLY

The successor to the *Nick Carter Library** went through a number of changes in format and title during its sixteen-year run. For the first two years, (1897–1898), reprints of stories from the *Nick Carter Library* alternated with original stories in three subseries: Trimble Carter's Adventures, the Tales of the Detective School, and the Riverdale Academy stories. Nick Carter himself made few appearances in the new stories.

From 1899 to April 11, 1903, the *Nick Carter Weekly* republished a great number of older stories as well as some new adventures with Nick Carter as hero. The majority of these were by Frederick R. Burton. Beginning with the issue of April 18 and continuing for almost a year, the publishers used plots and texts of stories originally published in the *Old Cap. Collier Library,** to which they had purchased the rights. All were altered to some extent to fit the Nick Carter formula.

Early in 1904, Frederick Van Rensselaer Dey began writing for the series again. The difference in style and the degree of imagination was immediately apparent. He reintroduced Dr. Quartz and many of the other characters from the early 1890s. He added new supporting characters; killed off Nick's wife, Ethel; allowed Patsy to mature and marry; and sent Nick on special assignments for President Theodore Roosevelt. These stories are considered to constitute the golden age in the Nick Carter series.

Toward the end of the long run of the *Nick Carter Weekly*, the main story no longer filled the entire publication, followed by only a few pages of advertisements for other titles in the Street & Smith line. The title story was accompanied by fillers, short stories, anecdotes, news notes, even chapters of serials. The days of the nickel weekly were numbered when Dey stopped contributing to the Nick Carter series in 1911 or 1912. The series itself would continue under different hands in the successor to the *Weekly*, which was called *Nick Carter Stories.**

Twenty-six writers contributed to the *Nick Carter Weekly*: A. L. Armagnac, Babcock (his first name was not recorded), George Waldo Browne, Buchanan (again, no first name recorded), Frederick R. Burton, O. P. Caylor, Weldon J. Cobb, William Wallace Cook, Frederick W. Davis, E. C. Derby, Frederic Van Rensselaer Dey, Ferguson (no first name recorded), W. Bert Foster, Charles W. Hooke, Howard (no first name recorded), William C. Hudson, George C. Jenks, W. L. or Joseph Larned (the first name is not certain), Charles Agnew MacLean, Makee (no first name recorded), Eugene T. Sawyer, Vincent E. Scott, Edward L. Stratemeyer, Alfred B. Tozer, R. F. Walsh, and Willard (no first name recorded). Some were contributors because the stories they had written for the *Nick Carter Library* were reprinted in the *Nick Carter Weekly*.

Of the 819 issues, there were 644 original novelettes (including those rewritten from other sources). Of these, 175 were reprinted from the *Nick Carter Library* or appeared more than once in the *Weekly*. Sooner or later, most dime novel series began reprinting earlier numbers from the same series. Beginning with its first number in September 1897, the *Magnet Library* (a paper-covered novel series) began collecting the stories from the *Nick Carter Weekly*, two or three to a volume.

Many of the stories in the *Nick Carter Weekly* were translated into other languages and published under the original, gaudy covers, with only the series title altered. In England, there were two magazine series which reissued stories from the later years of the American series. The stories were slightly altered so that Nick was no longer so obviously American.

One British version, *Nick Carter Weekly*, numbers 1 through 7 (November 22, 1911, to January 3, 1912) was in the same size and format as its American version, 7-3/4" X 11-1/8" and thirty pages. It was published by George Newnes.

Another British edition, *Newnes' "Nick Carter" Series*, numbers 1 through 118 (1918–1920) appeared in a smaller format, 4-3/4" X 6" (after number 100, 5" X 7"), with thirty-two pages. It was also published by George Newnes. The correct title of this series is difficult to determine. *Newnes Series* and *Nick Carter* appear on all covers followed by the story title; page one sometimes had *"Nick Carter and. . ."* followed by the appropriate title, sometimes just the title without Nick Carter's name. Lofts and Adley (see Bibliography) list it as the *Nick Carter Library*, but advertisements within the publication use *Newnes' "Nick Carter" Series* as the title.

Information Sources

BIBLIOGRAPHY:
Bragin, Charles. *Dime Novels Bibliography 1860-1928*. Brooklyn, N.Y.: privately printed, 1938.
Holmes, Harold C. "Nick Carter Weekly Nos. 91 and 92." *Dime Novel Roundup*, no. 55 (October 1936): 1–11.
Larmon, L. H. "Nick Carter." *Dime Novel Roundup*, no. 59 (February 1937): 1–2.
LeBlanc, Edward T. "Dime Novel Sketches No. 34." *Dime Novel Roundup*, no. 357 (June 15, 1962): 59.
Lofts, W.O.G., and Derek J. Adley. *Old Boys Books, A Complete Catalogue*. London: privately printed, 1969.
Noel, Mary. *Villains Galore*. New York: Macmillan Co., 1954.
Pearson, Edmund. *Dime Novels, or Following an Old Trail in Popular Literature*. Boston: Little, Brown, 1929.
Reynolds, Quentin. *The Fiction Factory*. New York: Random House, 1955.
Turner, E. S. *Boys Will Be Boys*. London: Michael Joseph Ltd., 1948.
INDEX SOURCES: Cox, J. Randolph. *New Nick Carter Weekly*. Fall River, Mass.: Edward T. LeBlanc, 1975.
LOCATION SOURCES: Hess Collection, University of Minnesota; private collectors.

Publication History

MAGAZINE TITLE: *Nick Carter Weekly*.
TITLE CHANGES: *New Nick Carter Library* (nos. 1–7); *New Nick Carter Weekly* (nos. 8–42); *Nick Carter Weekly* (nos. 43–320); *New Nick Carter Weekly* (nos. 321–819).
VOLUME AND ISSUE DATA: No. 1 (January 2, 1897) through no. 819 (September 7, 1912).
PUBLISHER: Street & Smith, publishers, 29 Rose Street, New York, New York, later 238 William Street and 79–89 Seventh Avenue, New York, New York.
EDITOR: Not known.
PRICE PER ISSUE: 5 cents.

SIZE AND PAGINATION: 7'' X 10-1/4'' (nos. 1–90, 95–227); 8-1/2'' X 10-3/4'' (nos. 91–94, 228–819); 32 pages.
CURRENT STATUS: Discontinued.
—*J. Randolph Cox*

NICK CARTER WEEKLY (British)

See NICK CARTER WEEKLY

NICKEL DETECTIVE

It was a slender, sixty-four page publication, slightly narrower than the usual pulp magazine. The spine was white with the words *Nickel Detective* in red; and on the front cover, beneath the title in yellow type, appeared the statement ''The Nickel Series.''

This cryptic statement was explained inside the front cover, where an advertisement frequently appeared for *Nickel Western*. The five-cent price of these magazines seems to have been a ploy to develop sales, although the immutable laws governing publication of pulp magazines establishes that a five-cent, sixty-four page magazine costs half as much, and offers half the pages, of a ten-cent, 128-page magazine (the usual format).

For five cents, *Nickel Detective* offered a novel (a long short story) and four short stories, plus two or three ''Special Features.'' The features included one or two ''Minute Mysteries''—a short crime problem with all clues given for the reader to unravel; the answer was concealed ''elsewhere in the issue.'' An occasional true-crime article was used, and, in February 1933, an ambitious series began that was to inform readers of the science of criminology.

The fiction was by unfamiliar names such as S. Gordon Gurwit, who signed many of the magazine's novels, Fred Scott, and George Meeter. More familiar names included Norman Daniels, Roy Somerville, and Ernest M. Poate. The fiction was divided almost equally between cop and crook stories. In one, policemen and detectives, unfettered by organizational discipline, struggled to save their honor and win the girl. In the other stories, greatly improbable crooks and gangsters connived and murdered, talked dialect, and sometimes reformed.

Each story was illustrated by a single pencil sketch. These were provided by four or five artists, their work ranging from good to excellent; they were pleasing evocations of the fashions and people at the turn of the 1930s.

The magazine has not been fully traced. First issued in late 1931, it continued into 1933. Final issues have not been examined. Reputedly, *Nickel Detective* was continued with *Strange Detective Stories** by the same publisher.

Information Sources

INDEX SOURCES: None known.

LOCATION SOURCES: Private collectors.

Publication History

MAGAZINE TITLE: *Nickel Detective*.
TITLE CHANGES: None known.
VOLUME AND ISSUE DATA: Vol. 1, no. 1 (October 1931[?] through Vol. 4, no. 5
    (October 1933); 23 issues.
PUBLISHER: Nickel Publications, Inc., 537 Dearborn Street, Chicago, Illinois.
EDITORS: Samuel Bierman; associate editor, Henry W. Schuettauff.
PRICE PER ISSUE: 5 cents.
SIZE AND PAGINATION: 6-3/4'' X 8-7/8''; 64 pages.
CURRENT STATUS: Discontinued.
—*Robert Sampson*

19 TALES OF INTRIGUE, MYSTERY AND ADVENTURE

First issued in 1950, it is probable there was only one issue of *19 Tales of
Intrigue, Mystery and Adventure*. No other information is available.

Information Sources

INDEX SOURCES: None known.
LOCATION SOURCES: University of California–Los Angeles Library (Vol. 1, no. 1);
    private collectors.

Publication History

MAGAZINE TITLE: *19 Tales of Intrigue, Mystery and Adventure*.
TITLE CHANGES: None known.
VOLUME AND ISSUE DATA: Vol. 1, no. 1 (1950); number of issues and extent
    unknown.
PUBLISHER: Not known.
EDITOR: Not known.
PRICE PER ISSUE: Not known.
SIZE AND PAGINATION: Not known.
CURRENT STATUS: Discontinued.

NOTES FOR THE CURIOUS

The subtitle, "A John Dickson Carr Memorial Journal," is the best short
description of this small magazine. *Notes for the Curious* was conceived and
edited by Larry L. French, an attorney for Southern Ilinois University and an
avid John Dickson Carr fan. The "Memorial Journal" was a form of prelude
for a book-length biography and critical evaluation of Carr. When the first issue
was complete, French intended to continue *Notes for the Curious,* printing his
own on-going research and other articles on Carr and his work. He was also
attempting to establish a John Dickson Carr Memorial Library in St. Louis in
his efforts to draw attention and acclaim for the master of the locked-room and

impossible-crimes stories. Unfortunately, French's death in an auto accident in December 1978 brought an end to his projects.

The only issue of *Notes* is primarily a series of noncritical eulogies. Carr had died only a year earlier. French accumulated a few tributes and commentaries by detective fiction critics and enthusiasts, added biographies of Carr's detectives, and provided a bibliography of Carr's work to make up the Memorial Journal. The "Commentaries for the Curious" are primarily personal reminiscences of Carr by reviewers, critics, editors, and other writers. The tone and manner of some of these item lead to the suspicion that excerpts or quotes were taken from previous writings about Carr rather than getting fresh or updated material for the Journal. Jon Breen's comments are among the longest and least unabashed idolatry. He makes some valid critical assessments of Carr that hopefully would have been pursued in later issues of the magazine.

One of the high points of *Notes* is the bibliography of Carr's work, compiled by French. It is categorized by detective hero and includes short stories. In addition to the listings for Dr. Gideon Fell and Sir Henry Merrivale, French lists the Henri Bencolin series and gives the Colonel March stories a category of their own. Also listed are the detectives of several nonseries books and Carr's historical novels. Not itemized, however, are the radio plays Carr wrote in the 1940s.

The title, *Notes for the Curious*, is taken from a postscript that Carr added to several of his historical novels, giving the basis of certain events, people, and locations that occur in the novels.

Information Sources

INDEX SOURCES: None known.
LOCATION SOURCES: Private collectors.

Publication History

MAGAZINE TITLE: *Notes for the Curious*.
TITLE CHANGES: None.
VOLUME AND ISSUE DATA: No. 1 (undated, [1978]); 1 issue.
PUBLISHER: Carrian Press (no address given).
EDITOR: Larry L. French.
PRICE PER ISSUE: $5.00.
SIZE AND PAGINATION: 5-1/2" X 8-1/2"; 32 pages.
CURRENT STATUS: Discontinued (editor deceased).
—*Fred Dueren*

NOT SO PRIVATE EYE, THE

It all started back in fall 1978 when film-noir, private-eye, and Naked-City enthusiast Andy Jaysnovitch decided he should do his part to help the private eye, who, in his opinion, had fallen on hard times. A reading of his initial "Eye Opener" editorial in the first issue (August–September 1978) of *The Not So Private Eye* is essential for complete enjoyment of his explanation.

Originally intended to extol the private eye in fiction and film, the first eight issues were typed, photocopied, stapled, and mailed by the indomitable editor himself. Issues number 1 and number 2 (August–September and October–November 1978) were in a unique 7'' X 8-1/2'' format, twenty-eight and forty-eight pages respectively. Those through issue number 8 (not dated, late 1980) were in the more standard 8-1/2'' X 11'' size, with issues numbers 3 through 6 displaying specially printed covers by such diverse artists as Frank Hamilton, Brad W. Foster, Lari Davidson, and Tom Fisher.

Articles, reviews, and letters comprised the bulk of each issue. A continuing feature, titled "Series Spotlight," by Jim McCahery focused on fictional private eyes of the past (Jonathan Latimer's William Crane, Bart Spicer's Carney Wilde, and M. Scott Michel's Wood Jaxon), with Paul Bishop's "The Trenchcoat Files" doing much the same for more contemporary investigators (George Chesbro's Mongo, J. J. Lamb's Zach Rolfe, P. B. Yuill's James Hazell, and Charles Alverson's Joe Goodey). Also appearing were Steve Lewis's column, "Speaking of Pulp"; articles on radio and television private eyes; the real-life investigator; "Sex and the Single Sleuth"; and full-length articles on authors such as William Campbell Gault, Frank Kane, Peter Israel, Robert Leslie Bellem, James Hadley Chase, Mickey Spillane, and many others. Also included were television logs and an interview with Mike Avallone.

The first four issues of this labor of love were bimonthly, with the fifth intended to initiate a quarterly sequence. After that, however, the issues appeared sporadically, and the magazine's demise was announced in the seventh issue, April 1980. Surprisingly, an issue number 8 appeared later the same year, announcing that the fan magazine would be revived as a ten-page, bimonthly newsletter. These plans, too, eventually fell through and *EYE*, as it was often referred to, seemed definitely to have gone the way of its acclaimed heroes. But, like the phoenix, *The Not So Private Eye* arose anew in January 1982 in a slightly new format and with many plans for the future, the main difference being that a regular schedule would no longer be offered. Digest-sized (5-1/2'' X 8-1/2''), in reduced-print offset, issue number 9 contained twenty pages. Editor Jaysnovitch said of the newly revived magazine:

The main focus will still be on the private detective and other hardboiled characters in fiction and film, but there will also be coverage of some other areas of the "adventure" field. One of the new features will be "Kolchak Country," an excursion into the field of weird menace fiction and film. For lack of a better title, there may also be something called "Ten Paces from the Old Oak Tree," about the search for elusive treasures. And there may be a column called "The Collector," about all those sick souls who create their own personal archives at the expense of money, family, friends, and a normal life. . . . "Stakeout" will be a regular column devoted to news and citations of hardboiled material appearing in offbeat places such as science-fiction magazines, general circulation magazines, men's magazines, etc.[1]

In addition, there are plans for reprinting the "Best of *EYE*" for the many who seek back issues. Issue number 10 was scheduled to go to the printer in mid-April 1982, which was certainly good news for the growing number of private-eye fans.

NOTE

1. *The Not So Private Eye*, no. 9 (January 1982), p. 2.

Information Sources

INDEX SOURCES: None known.
LOCATION SOURCES: Private collectors.

Publication History

MAGAZINE TITLE: *The Not So Private Eye*.
TITLE CHANGES: None.
VOLUME AND ISSUE DATA: No. 1 (August–September 1978) through no. 9 (to date, January 1982); 9 issues.
PUBLISHER: Andy Jaysnovitch, 6 Dana Estates Drive, Parlin, New Jersey 08859.
EDITOR: Andy Jaysnovitch.
PRICE PER ISSUE: Varies from 75 cents to $1.25.
SIZE AND PAGINATION: 7'' X 8-1/2'' (nos. 1–2), 8-1/2'' X 11'' (nos. 3–8), 5-1/2'' X 8-1/2'' (no. 9); 10–48 pages.
CURRENT STATUS: Active.
—*James R. McCahery*

O

OCTOPUS, THE

The Octopus and *The Scorpion* are sequential issues of the same magazine. Both dated in 1939, they are linked by identical characters, similar backgrounds, similar themes, and closely related plots. They differ only in title and depiction of the villain.

It is curious that these magazine titles reflect the evil genius of each. Most single-character mmagazines bore the name of the lead character or his professional *nom de plume*. Thus, The Shadow, The Spider, Secret Agent X, Operator 5. It might be expected, then, that the magazines titled *The Octopus* and *The Scorpion* might better have been titled ''The Skull Killer,'' the deadly hero of this brief series.

Upon The Skull Killer, variously disguised and undisguised, the narrative glares continuously. It focuses upon him from the first chapter. With only momentary intermissions, it remains fixed upon him. Straining, agonizing, slaying, emotionalizing, The Skull Killer dominates the stories. The Octopus and The Scorpion appear briefly in their respective magazines. But for all their sadistic malignity, they are bit players in their own publications. The Skull Killer is the featured player.

Twice before, Popular Publications had attempted series magazines featuring strong villains—*The Mysterious Wu Fang** (1935–1936) and *Dr. Yen Sin** (1936). Both were quickly terminated. In mid-1938, however, Popular Publications once more began work on a magazine which was to feature a continuing villain, The Octopus.

The facile Norvell Page, author of most of The Spider novels and a diligent contributor to the Popular Publications magazine line, was selected to write the series. Using the house name, Randolph Craig, Page produced two violent novels. These may be regarded as variant Spider adventures; the differences are essentially cosmetic.

The initial novel, "The City Condemned to Hell" *(The Octopus*, February–March 1939), describes The Skull Killer's battle against The Octopus and his legions of purple-eyed killers. (Much is made of purple eyes; according to the text, every major historical disaster is accompanied by the abrupt appearance of purple eyes.)

The Octopus has created a gigantic extortion plot. By mysterious gases and ultraviolet beams, he creates a reign of terror in New York City. Innocent men and women are converted to deformed, purple-eyed monsters, shambling awfully about, swilling blood from living flesh.

Behind these disorders weaves the vague form of The Octopus, a sea-green thing of weaving tenacles and malformed legs. He wears a small mask over luminous, purple eyes. Whether he is a man, or a deformed thing, or an undying eddy from hell is left unclear.

On the other hand, the figure of The Skull Killer is quite clear. He is that traditional pulp magazine hero, the wealthy young man, engaged in the usual activity of defending his city against crime monsters. His name is Jeffery Fairchild. A master of disguise, he has established an alternate identity as Dr. Skull, an apparently aged physician who labors in the slums, doing good. Fairchild's second identity is that of The Skull Killer, a deadly justice figure who battles crime with blazing guns. The foreheads of those he kills he stamps with a steel tool that drives a needle into their brains; at the same time, it leaves an acid-seared outline of a skull. The Skull Killer slaughters from thirty to sixty criminals a novel and is tolerated by the police because he is so effective against crime.

The heroine of these adventure, Carol Endicott, is Dr. Skull's nurse, a freckled-face sweetie with gleaming dark hair. She spends much of her time being captured and menaced picturesquely. Other continuing characters include Fairchild's brother, Robert, an embittered cripple; and Tom Wiley, the commissioner of police, who is exceedingly supportive of Fairchild.

The story rages wildly along, the pace vivace, the guns never cool—a succession of plots, death traps, horrible fatality, hurtling automobiles, and hideous hordes. Occasionally, the unrelenting blood chant is freshened by scenes of girls, beautiful and helpless, being tortured by inhuman fiends in the grand tradition of weird-menace fiction. The story peaks in a violent slaughter in which The Octopus is perhaps killed, perhaps not.

The Octopus was identified as volume 1, number 4. From information presently available, it is probable (although not confirmed) that the magazine was a continuation of an earlier title, possibly *Dr. Yen Sin*.[1] It was a frequent practice among pulp magazine publishers to continue the volume numbering of a terminated magazine with a new title. In that way, the second-class mailing permit of the defunct magazine could be used, eliminating the need for a new application.

In addition to the main novel, *The Octopus* contained a short story by Russell Gray (pseudonym of Bruno Fischer[2]) and two long novelettes by Donald G.

Cormack and Arthur Leo Zagat. All were mystery-terror stories, strongly seasoned by sadism and weird menace. Also included were a pseudo-historical essay, "The Purple Eye"; a single-page, illustrated feature, "Horrors of History"; and a department, "The Horror-Scope," which spoke in general terms of the next Dr. Skull adventure to be issued May 1.

The next number, however, was issued on March 1, 1939, with a date of April–May 1939. No longer was it titled *The Octopus*; it had now become *The Scorpion*.

Concerning the title, Publisher Henry Steeger wrote:

I arrived at the title *The Scorpion* because I sat on one once, fortunately with no paticular damage, and I felt this might be a possible entry in the field of *The Shadow,* * *The Spider,* * *The Octopus*, etc., i.e., the name that connoted fear and terror and would lend a frightening image to a character even before a single word had been written about him. . . . *The Scorpion* was a re-titled and revision of a second "Octopus" novel. As you can see, I didn't hold out much hope for it and it didn't do too well, either.[3]

Norvell Page's second Octopus manuscript was rewritten by Ejlar Jacobson, removing the Octopus and substituting The Scorpion.[4] Instead of a sea-green thing with twisting arms, we are presented with a lean figure in black robe and hood; across his face twists a black birthmark in the form of a scorpion. His henchmen, murderous monsters all, wear black robes, and their brows are branded with small scorpion emblems. The purple-eyed theme from *The Octopus* is continued in this novel, all aides and victims of The Scorpion showing a change of eye color.

Once again, the premise of the novel is that a crime master creates a reign of terror to extort untold millions. New York City businesses are the victims, being forced to raise prices enormously and pay The Scorpion. If they do not, they face destruction at the hands of fiends, and loved ones become homicidal maniacs, shrieking and rending.

The city government has been penetrated by The Scorpion's men. Madmen rush about, decency reels, and Dr. Skull/Jeffery Fairchild and his associates have a dangerous time of it—right to the ending, in a cavern beneath the city incinerator. There, nude maidens are exposed as living pictures, and The Scorpion purrs taunts at the trapped Fairchild, revealed as The Skull Killer. How soon tables are turned. The henchmen are destroyed, and The Scorpion. . . . But who knows what happened to The Scorpion, that evil genius?

The Scorpion magazine, however, was cancelled. Norvell Page returned to The Spider, and further adventures of The Skull Killer do not seem to have been written.

Notes

1. Only two other Popular Publications magazines were terminated on the third issue and appeared prior to December 1938, the month *The Octopus* was published. The probability that this magazine was a continuation of the *Dr. Yen Sin* volume/issue numbers was first pointed out by collector Charles Cockey. Refer to "A Checklist of Popular Publications Titles 1930–1955," compiled by Nils Hardin and George Hocutt, *Xenophile*, no. 33 (July 1977), pp. 21–24.

2. Robert Kenneth Jones, *The Shudder Pulps* (West Linn, Ore: Fax Collector's Editions, 1975), pp. 125–27, gives a discussion of Fischer's writing style for the weird-menace pulps and his use of the Gray pseudonym.

3. Nils Hardin, "An Interview with Henry Steeger," *Xenophile*, no. 33 (July 1977), p. 10. This article contains a detailed discussion by mail with Henry Steeger concerning the history of Popular Publications and its magazines.

4. That Ejlar Jacobson rewrote the second Page manuscript to a Scorpion tale was discovered by Robert Weinberg during examination of the Popular Publications' check files. (Weinberg purchased files of checks.) (Robert Weinberg, *The Octopus*, Pulp Classics no. 11 [Oak Lawn, Illinois, 1975].)

Information Sources

BIBLIOGRAPHY:

Hardin, Nils. "An Interview with Henry Steeger." *Xenophile*. no. 33 (July 1977): 3–20.

Hardin, Nils, and George Hocutt. "A Checklist of Popular Publications Titles 1930–1955." *Xenophile*, no. 33 (July 1977): 21–24.

Hickman, Lynn. "The Pulp Collector." *The Pulp Era*, no. 75 (Spring 1971): 6–11.

Jones, Robert Kenneth. *The Shudder Pulps*. West Linn, Ore.: Fax Collector's Editions, 1975.

Weinberg, Robert. *The Octopus*, Pulp Classics No. 11. Oak Lawn, Ill.: Robert Weinberg Publications, 1975.

INDEX SOURCES: Weinberg, Robert. *The Hero Pulp Index*. Evergreen, Colo.: Opar Press, 1971.

LOCATION SOURCES: Private collectors.

Publication History

MAGAZINE TITLE: *The Octopus*.

TITLE CHANGES: *The Scorpion* (with second issue).

VOLUME AND ISSUE DATA: Vol.1, no. 4 (February/March 1939, as *The Octopus*; possibly, though, unconfirmed, a continuation of *Dr. Yen Sin*); Vol. 1, no. 1 (April/May 1939, as *The Scorpion*); 1 issue of each title.

PUBLISHER: Popular Publications, Inc., 2256 Grove Street, Chicago, Illinois.

EDITOR: Not known.

PRICE PER ISSUE: 10 cents.

SIZE AND PAGINATION: 6-3/4" X 9-3/4"; 112 pages.

CURRENT STATUS: Discontinued.

—*Robert Sampson*

OFF BEAT DETECTIVE STORIES

Off Beat Detective Stories is probably a change of title from *Sure Fire Detective Stories*,* published by Pontiac Publishing Corporation; but in the absence of confirmation, *Sure Fire Detective Stories* is listed as a separate entry in this volume. The last issue found of *Sure Fire Detective Stories* was dated February 1958, volume 2, number 1. Issues of *Off Beat Detective Stories* have not been noted prior to September 1958, volume 2, number 4. It is thus possible that two additional issues of *Sure Fire* or two earlier issues of *Off Beat* were published.

Regardless, *Off Beat Detective Stories* was a mirror image of *Sure Fire Detective Stories,* both in appearance and content. The pattern of rough, tough, raw, crime adventure, liberally studded with sex, was the mainstay of both magazines. Lust was an overpowering matter in many of the stories: "The Lust Patrol" by Gil Grayson (November 1959), "Lust Leaves Ugly Scars" by Edward L. Stacey (January 1960), "Little Darling of Lust" by Art Riordan (May 1960), "Lust of the Damned" by Christopher Mace (July 1960), and "Bribe Me With Lust" by Bob Shields (November 1960), among many others. And lust was joined by flagellation, incest, homosexuality, and other daring acts that were normally taboo in fiction and particularly uncalled for in detective fiction. There were no plots in these tales; they were primarily crime adventure of the rawest sort, in situations where sex could be exploited for the sake of sex. They were definitely, as the title indicated, off-beat.

But it was not all sex. Rage, greed, and arguments all resulted in murder, without compassion or ample reason. It was the seamy side of the tracks in the worst possible way. The antagonist was as often a woman as a man. But there was no question as to who killed whom. It was graphically described in glowing, descriptive text.

The titles of stories are indicative of the general trend: "One Brutal Night" by Bill Rank (September 1958), "Play With Me, Sucker" by Jay Richards (January 1963), "Bikini Babe" by Jackson Queens (July 1962), "Horror Rides the Night" by Alan Lance (April 1962), "Sweet Night of Revenge" by Flip Lyons (November 1962), and "Her Corpse Needs Loving" by Grover Brinkman (July 1961), for example.

The covers, by Carl Pfeufer, exemplified the contents, with half-clad girls in violent poses, threatened with a knife, led off in bondage, or being the aggressor with various weapons.

However, the magazine had found a market since there were at least twenty-five issues published. Then, it, too, was a victim and disappeared from the stands.

Information Sources

INDEX SOURCES: Cook, Michael L. *Monthly Murders*. Westport, Conn.: Greenwood Press, 1982.
LOCATION SOURCES: Private collectors.

Publication History

MAGAZINE TITLE: *Off Beat Detective Stories*.
TITLE CHANGES: Possibly a title change from *Sure Fire Detective Stories*.

VOLUME AND ISSUE DATA: Vol. 2, no. 4 (September 1958) through Vol. 6, no. 4 (January 1963) (last issue is labeled Vol. 7, no. 4, in publisher's error); 25 issues. Possibility of one or two earlier issues, see text.
PUBLISHER: Pontiac Publishing Corporation, 1 Appleton Street, Holyoke, Massachusetts, with editorial offices at 1776 Broadway, later 1546 Broadway, New York, New York.
EDITOR: Not known.
PRICE PER ISSUE: 35 cents.
SIZE AND PAGINATION: 5-1/2" X 7-1/4"; 112 pages.
CURRENT STATUS: Discontinued.

OFFICIAL JOURNAL OF THE INTERNATIONAL SPY SOCIETY

See DOSSIER, THE

OLD BROADBRIM WEEKLY

When, in 1902, Street & Smith purchased the rights to over half of the stories published by Norman L. Munro in the *Old Cap. Collier Library,** the buyer was not slow to reprint them. Some were used in existing series *(New Nick Carter Weekly [Nick Carter Weekly*]*, for example), while other series were created expressly for them. One of these was the *Old Broadbrim Weekly*.

The first forty-five numbers of this "new" *Weekly* were reprinted from the *Old Cap. Collier Library*. In some instances, the titles were altered, but in many there was enough similarity to make comparisons a simple matter for one familiar with both series. The hero of *Old Broadbrim Weekly* was a Quaker named Josiah Broadbrim. Fictional Quakers were once given the name "broadbrim" after the type of broad-brimmed hat with which they were popularly associated. The character had its origin in a series of stories (five in number) from the *Old Cap. Collier Library*, but only one of the original series was actually used in the new publication. Instead, the stories of Old Search, Gideon Gault, Dave Dotson, Larry Murtaugh, Jack Sharp, and Old Cap. himself (among others) were used. Character delineation was not strong enough in either publication to make this alteration difficult.

With issue number 46 (August 15, 1903), original stories, written for the *Weekly*, began to appear. Numbers 46 through 50 also boasted a co-star for Old Broadbrim, in the person of Nick Carter. Charles Agnew MacLean, Frederick R. Burton, Stephen Chalmers, A. L. Armagnac, and Vincent Scott contributed to the rest of the series. With number 52, the publication changed its focus as well as its title when Burton, author of the Trim Carter and Detective School stories in *Nick Carter Weekly*, introduced Harry Wilson, alias Young Broadbrim, as protégé for the older sleuth. Very few of these stories had some basis in material from the older Norman L. Munro publication, but they were substantially rewritten.

The stories went through yet another metamorphosis as most of them became Nick Carter stories when two or three would be collected and reissued in the paper-covered novel series, the *Magnet Library*.

Information Sources

BIBLIOGRAPHY:

Reynolds, Quentin. *The Fiction Factory*. New York: Random House, 1955.

Bragin, Charles. *Dime Novels Bibliography, 1860–1928*. Brooklyn, N.Y.: privately printed, 1938.

LeBlanc, Edward T. "Dime Novel Sketches No. 64." *Dime Novel Roundup*, no. 391 (April 15, 1965): 33.

INDEX SOURCES: Cox, J. Randolph. *Nick Carter Stories and Other Series Containing Stories about Nick Carter*. Fall River, Mass.: Edward T. LeBlanc, 1980.

LOCATION SOURCES: Private collectors.

Publication History

MAGAZINE TITLE: *Old Broadbrim Weekly*.

TITLE CHANGES: *Young Broadbrim Weekly* (with no. 52).

VOLUME AND ISSUE DATA: No. 1 (October 4, 1902) through no. 81 (April 16, 1904); 81 issues.

PUBLISHER: Street & Smith, Publishers, 238 William Street, New York, New York.

EDITOR: Not known.

PRICE PER ISSUE: 5 cents.

SIZE AND PAGINATION: 8-1/2'' X 10-3/4''; 32 pages.

CURRENT STATUS: Discontinued.

—*J. Randolph Cox*

OLD CAP. COLLIER LIBRARY

The oldest dime novel publication devoted specifically to detective fiction, the *Old Cap. Collier Library* was almost the longest-lived. Only *Secret Service: Old and Young King Brady, Detective,** of this "nickel weekly" format published more issues, but nearly half of those were reprinted from the earlier numbers. Named for the central hero of some of the titles in the *Library* and the pseudonym used on other titles, the *Old Cap. Collier Library* was basically an anthology series like its competition from Frank Tousey, the *New York Detective Library*.* Both were established the same year, 1883, but *Old Cap.* was first; it quickly proved the popularity of detective fiction with a mass audience.

The early numbers actually appeared in two editions. Those early numbers had nonpictorial covers in one color, buff or brick-red, with an elaborate title logo. This alone made the series distinctive and even distinguished in appearance. Eventually, these were replaced by pictorial covers, and the earlier numbers were reissued to match.

While the majority of the stories were written for the *Library* itself, several numbers reprinted stories by European writers. The first American editions of

Emile Gaboriau's detective stories appeared here, as did James McGovan's "Edinburgh detective" stories. The first fictional treatment of the crimes of Jack the Ripper were published here also.

There were at least a score of series heroes within the *Old Cap. Collier Library*, some of which survived only a few weeks while others were still popular at the end in 1899. Old Cap. himself appeared only in a few stories in this collection which bore his name. He was largely replaced in later years by his assistant and protégé, Dave Dotson.

Other detectives in series included Clear Grit, Larry Murtaugh, Gideon Gault, Old Search, Calvert Cole, Rody Regan, and V-Spot. The most recurrent authors were W. I. James, Old Cap. Maori, Bernard Wayde, Mark Merrick, Maro O. Rolfe, F. Lusk Broughton, Jack Howard, Gilbert Jerome, Warne Miller, Will Winch, Anthony P. Morris, and Major A. F. Grant. Some of them may not have been pseudonyms.

Toward the end of the run, many of the numbers reprinted serials from the story-paper, *Golden Hours*. Beginning with number 765, the *Library* alternated humorous stories with the detective stories. The last eight numbers did not contain detective stories at all. With number 822, the *Old Cap. Collier Library* ceased publication but resumed under the more generic title of *Up-to-Date Boys' Library*.*

Three years after it ceased publication, over four hundred stories from the *Library* were purchased by Street & Smith, who gave them a new lease on life in their *Magnet Library, Nick Carter Weekly,* * *Old Broadbrim Weekly,* * and *New Secret Service Series*.

The *Old Cap. Collier Library* was granted immortality of a sort when humorist Irvin S. Cobb included it in his "defense" of sensational literature, "A Plea for Old Cap. Collier, " in the *Saturday Evening Post* (July 5, 1920). The first novel, "Old Cap. Collier; or, 'Piping' the New Haven Mystery," was given lengthy synopsis and discussion by Edmund Pearson in his *Dime Novels* (1929).

Information Sources

BIBLIOGRAPHY:

Cobb, Irvin, S. *Irvin Cobb at His Best*. Garden City, N.Y.: Sun Dial Press, 1940.

Lahmon, L. H. "Old Cap Collier and Norman L. Munro." *Dime Novel Roundup,*. no. 64 (July 1937): 3.

LeBlanc, Edward T. "Dime Novel Sketches No. 36." *Dime Novel Roundup*, no. 359 (August 15, 1962): 75.

Leithead, J. Edward. "Boy Detectives." *Dime Novel Roundup*, no. 240 (September 1952): 66–71.

———. "This 'Sleuth' Business." *Dime Novel Roundup*, no. 369 (June 15, 1963): 50–54; no. 370 (July 15, 1963): 62–65; no. 371 (August 15, 1963): 70–75.

Pearson, Edmund. *Dime Novels, or Following an Old Path in Popular Literature*. Boston: Little, Brown, 1929.

INDEX SOURCES: Cox, J. Randolph. *Nick Carter Stories and Other Series Containing Nick Carter Stories*. Fall River, Mass.: Edward T. LeBlanc, 1980.

LOCATION SOURCES: Private collectors.

Publication History

MAGAZINE TITLE: *Old Cap. Collier Library*.
TITLE CHANGES: None.
VOLUME AND ISSUE DATA: No. 1 (April 9, 1883) through no. 822 (September 9, 1899); 822 issues.
PUBLISHER: Norman L. Munro, 24 & 26 Vandewater Street, New York, New York.
EDITOR: Not known.
PRICE PER ISSUE: 10 cents (nonpictorial covers); 5 cents.
SIZE AND PAGINATION: 6-3/4" X 9-1/2" (nos. 1–330); 8-1/2" X 12" (nos. 331-394); 6-3/4" X 9-1/2" (nos. 395–822); 32-48 pages.
CURRENT STATUS: Discontinued.
—*J. Randolph Cox.*

OLD SLEUTH LIBRARY

Old Sleuth, the first dime novel detective to appear in a series of stories, made his debut in 1872 in the pages of the story-paper, *New York Fireside Companion*. It was thirteen years before his name was used on the title of a detective periodical, yet that name, "Old Sleuth" was nearly synonymous with the word "detective."

The original printing of the *Old Sleuth Library* was a quality publication printed on good paper with a black-and-white cover illustration. Some of the titles were published in two parts, each with the same issue number.

The stories were all signed by "Old Sleuth" and are considered to have been the work of Harlan Page Halsey. Some of them were signed by other names when they appeared as serials. As with its immediate predecessors, the *Old Cap. Collier Library** and the *New York Detective Library,** *Old Sleuth* was an anthology series. Within that framework, there were a few subseries, including six novels about the title character: "Old Sleuth, the Detective," "Old Sleuth's Triumph," "Old Sleuth in Harness Again," "Old Sleuth's Luck," "Old Sleuth, Badger & Co.," and "Old Sleuth in Philadelphia."

Halsey took the word "sleuth-hound," shortened it and made of it a proper name which became famous. Old Sleuth, in his original adventure, was not even an old man at all but was young Harry Loveland, one of those masters of disguise who once populated the pages of detective literature.

The prevailing theme throughout the *Old Sleuth Library* is the concept of the Great Detective (a different one in each number) whose "wonderful exploits and hair-breadth escapes. . .are all described in brilliant style" (from the advertisement for number 7: "The Shadow Detective"). There is a Lightning Detective, a River Detective, a Ventriloquist Detective, a French Detective, a St. Louis Detective, an Irish Detective, a Yankee Detective, several other ethnic detectives, and three women detectives. The most delightfully named of the latter is Lady Kate, the Dashing Female Detective (number 30, September 1, 1886). The ingenuity of the variety is startling.

The stories from this magazine were later reissued by Arthur Westbrook in the colored-cover *Old Sleuth Weekly** and (along with numerous other tales) was retitled for paperback publication by J. S. Ogilvie.

Information Sources

BIBLIOGRAPHY:

Bragin, Charles. *Dime Novels Bibliography 1860–1928.* Brooklyn, N.Y.: privately printed, 1938.

Godfrey, Lydia. "Old Sleuth, Nineteenth Century 'Nipper,' America's First Serialized Detective and His World." *Clues: A Journal of Detection,* Vol. 1, no. 1 (Spring 1980): 53–56.

LeBlanc, Edward T. "Dime Novel Sketches No. 90." *Dime Novel Roundup,* no. 417 (June 15, 1967): 53.

Leithead, J. Edward. "Boy Detectives." *Dime Novel Roundup,* no. 240 (September 1952): 66–71.

————. "This 'Sleuth' Business." *Dime Novel Roundup,* no. 369 (June 15, 1963): 50–54; no. 370 (July 15, 1963): 62–65; no. 371 (August 15, 1963): 70–75.

Pearson, Edmund. *Dime Novels, or Following an Old Trail in Popular Literature.* Boston: Little, Brown, 1929.

Smeltzer, Bob. "Old Sleuth Library." *Dime Novel Roundup,* no. 167 (August 1946): 2–3.

INDEX SOURCES: None known.

LOCATION SOURCES: Hess Collection, University of Minnesota; private collectors.

Publication History

MAGAZINE TITLE: *Old Sleuth Library.*

TITLE CHANGES: None.

VOLUME AND ISSUE DATA: No. 1 (March 3, 1885) through no. 101 (1905, no month and day given); 101 issues.

PUBLISHER: George Munro, Publisher, nos. 17 and 27 Vandewater Street, New York, New York.

EDITOR: Not known.

PRICE PER ISSUE: 10 cents (nos. 1–56); 5 cents (nos. 57–101).

SIZE AND PAGINATION: 9" X 12-3/4"; 32–48 pages.

CURRENT STATUS: Discontinued.

—*J. Randolph Cox.*

OLD SLEUTH WEEKLY

If a dime novel was worth being published at all, it was worth being reprinted, often with a complete change of title, cover, author, and even publisher. Between 1908 and 1912, the Arthur Westbrook Company of Cleveland began reissuing the venerable Old Sleuth stories with colored covers. It was advertised as "A Series of the Most Thrilling Detective Stories Ever Published. Everyone [*sic*] Written by Old Sleuth Himself." The editor was also "Old Sleuth."

The first issue contained "The Return of Old Sleuth, the Detective," which, on examination, turns out to be a new title for "Old Sleuth in Philadelphia," the last Old Sleuth story from the *Old Sleuth Library*.* It seemed fitting to begin by taking up where the other series ended.

Many of the issues contained a sort of editorial page with fillers, facts, trivial information, and anecdotes. Short stories, serials, and other features accompanied the lead novel, which itself was often carried over into a succeeding number. The size of the print varied from time to time, depending on the source from which the stories were reprinted. With number 114, each story was prefaced by a boxed insert, "Principal Characters in This Story," which continued through the final number with only two exceptions, numbers 167 and 168.

Sources for the lead novels included Beadle & Adams, as well as George Munro's *Old Sleuth Library*. Each story was copyrighted by the original publisher, and that indication was printed on the first page, so that tracing the original appearances would be possible.

Numbers 93 through 104 serialized "Jeff Clayton's Strange Quest" and advertised the regular appearance of complete Jeff Clayton novels in the *Adventure Series*, a paper-covered novel series. The Clayton stories were intended as a regular series; but in spite of the advertising, the serial vanished from the back pages after number 104 and did not reappear until number 185 when the new story was "Foiling the Slave Traders."

As with the *Old Sleuth Library,* the *Old Sleuth Weekly* anthology series printed only a few stories in which Old Sleuth was the central character. Westbrook, however, managed to add a number of titles to the original six which had appeared in Munro's earlier series. They also included some Old Sleuth novels in the *Adventure Series*. It is probable that these were rewritten from some older stories which had featured other detectives. By keeping these stories in print, Westbrook prolonged the life and name of the first dime novel series detective of all.

Information Sources

BIBLIOGRAPHY:

Bragin, Charles. *Dime Novels Bibliography 1860–1928*. Brooklyn, N.Y.: privately printed, 1938.

Godfrey, Lydia. "Old Sleuth, Nineteenth Century 'Nipper,' America's First Serialized Detective and His World." *Clues: A Journal of Detection,* Vol. 1, no. 1 (Spring 1980): 53–56.

LeBlanc, Edward T. "Dime Novel Sketches No. 48." *Dime Novel Roundup*, no. 372 (September 15, 1963): 79.

Leithead, J. Edward. "Boy Detectives." *Dime Novel Roundup*, no. 240 (September 1952): 66–71.

———. "This 'Sleuth' Business." *Dime Novel Roundup*, no. 369 (June 15, 1963): 50–54; no. 370 (July 15, 1963): 62–65; no. 371 (August 15, 1963): 70–75.

Pearson, Edmund. *Dime Novels, or Following an Old Trail in Popular Literature*. Boston: Little, Brown, 1929.

INDEX SOURCES: None known.

LOCATION SOURCES: Hess Collection, University of Minnesota; private collectors.

Publication History

MAGAZINE TITLE: *Old Sleuth Weekly.*
TITLE CHANGES: None.
VOLUME AND ISSUE DATA: No. 1 (April 17, 1908) through no. 203 (May 17, 1912);
    203 issues.
PUBLISHER: Arthur Westbrook Company, Cleveland, Ohio.
EDITOR: "Old Sleuth."
PRICE PER ISSUE: 5 cents; three issues bound together, 10 cents.
SIZE AND PAGINATION: 8-1/2" X 11-3/4"; 32 pages.
CURRENT STATUS: Discontinued.
—*J. Randolph Cox*

OPERATOR #5

Operator #5 was a magic name in the thirties and even today stirs the imagination and resurrects a scarlet glow of the past. There it was on the newsstands, with the title in bold yellow letters grabbing your attention. Directly under the title was "America's Undercover Ace." It was a favorite of many, priced at ten cents, leaving just enough of your weekly allowance for the Saturday matinee with maybe Buck Jones or Hopalong Cassidy. There were forty-eight issues between April 1934 and November 1939, probably the greatest period of all for the hero pulp magazines.

From April 1934 to April 1936, *Operator #5* appeared monthly and then, for the rest of 1936, every other month. In January 1937, it returned to a monthly basis through March, then became bimonthly again through November 1939. Of the forty-eight issues, thirty-seven were titled "America's Undercover Ace," ten were blazoned "America's Secret Service Ace," and only one extolled "America's G-Man Ace."

Harry Steeger told this writer:

> Operator 5 came to mind because of the success of the Spider and other one-man series. This idea for Operator 5 had been boiling around in my head for quite some time and there seemed to be a good opening for this type of hero. The climate nationally was also such that we believed it would be well received. Frederick C. Davis was selected to write the series because he was one of the most competent writers we had. Also he had enough of an opening in his schedule to be able to devote the necessary time to the project. In giving the story in the series to Fred to do we knew they would be extremely well done and well received by the public.[1]

The stories, according to Davis, ran from about 50,000 to 60,000 words each. "As you know," he wrote in a letter to me in 1974, "Operator 5 must single-handedly, or almost, save the nation from complete destruction regularly every month. This was the basic idea given to me by Mr. Steeger and Rogers Terrill, the editor."[2] Davis was indeed a workhorse, spending from nine in the morning to four in the afternoon, six days a week, at the typewriter. He produced about thirty, double-spaced pages a day.

The published story length varied from 67 to 113 pages; the longest episodes were written between 1934 and 1935. The magazine, in addition to the lead story, usually included two short stories, a column titled "The Secret Sentinel" (or "Secret Sentinel Reports"), and, with the June 1936 issue, an editorial feature. In May 1937, "Things That Made America Great" was instituted.

Curtis Steele, shown as author of the Operator 5 stories, was a house name. In reality, stories were by Frederick C. Davis, the original author of the series, followed by Emile C. Tepperman (who did the Purple Invasion episodes, thirteen stories) and Wayne Rogers (who finished the series with the Yellow Vulture stories). It was the research work of Robert Weinberg and Joel Freeman that uncovered the name of Wayne Rogers.

The first cover was by Jerome Rosen. Interior art was by Rudolph Belarski and Amos Sewell. The majority of covers, however, were by John Howitt, with interior illustrations by John Fleming Gould and Ralph Carlson. The covers were exceptional paintings, particularly those for the magazines containing the Operator 5 stories "Cavern of the Damned," "Legions of Starvation," and "Legions of the Death Master."

The hero, Operator 5, was Jimmy Christopher, a true red-blooded American to the very core, fully dedicated to God, country, and flag, and willing to die, if necessary, for all three. Above all, he was the top agent of American intelligence, carrying in a flat, silver case a credential signed by the president of the United States.

He was aided by a young lady, Diane Elliot, who spent much of her time in mortal danger. Also on hand was a young Irish lad, Tim Donovan, unofficial assistant. And there was John Christopher, Operator 5's father, a former intelligence agent himself ("Q–6"), and Nan Christopher, Jimmy's twin sister. The last major character was Z–7, chief of intelligence.

Operator 5 carried a watch charm in the form of a tiny gold skull (and within the top was a tiny sphere of deadly gas); in 1973, in reply to questions about the series' characters, Frederick C. Davis wrote: "I can tell you nothing now about the origin of the skull ornament, except that it was one of the many embellishments I dreamed up for the series. It's the same way with Z–7. Today I haven't the foggiest idea whether that's the designation of a secret agent or a submarine."[3]

The villains from *Operator #5* have stood well the test of time. Notable was Ursus Young, the prophet of violence from "Blood Reign of the Dictator," and Emperor Rudolph, a man dedicated to evil (in the Purple Invasion subseries). Moto Taronago, the Yellow Vulture, is also unforgettable. He swore to deliver all of America into the hands of the Mikado of Japan. Jengis Dhak, described by Christopher as "one of the most dangerous men to walk the globe," possessed a deadly electronic ray generator that removed oxygen from the air.

Operator 5 was, and continues to be, regarded as one of the greatest pulp heroes found in the pages behind the gaudy covers that attracted so many. As one fan has remarked, "As we become more involved in the novels they tend to take on a fresh, new interest and we can observe our respective heroes and their women turning into real personalities."[4] Even Harry Steeger had his own answer for this idiosyncratic quirk: "I think one should regard the pulp heroes as real. After all, we all regarded them as real and it would be difficult to think of them as otherwise. Naturally, we know that they are fictional characters, but it enhances our enjoyment to think of them as flesh and blood characters, so why not? It adds to the pleasure and doesn't hurt anyone."[5]

In the final analysis, the one factor that made *Operator #5* outstanding was the overpowering element of patriotism, something badly needed then as now. Charles Beaumont, writing in *Playboy*, said that "in the days of our youth they [the pulps] were not deemed good reading and to us at the time they weren't good, *they were great!* [6]

Notes

1. Henry (Harry) Steeger, correspondence to Wooda, Nicholas Carr, 1975.
2. Frederick C. Davis, correspondence to Wooda, Nicholas Carr, 1974.
3. Ibid., 1973.
4. Herman S. McGregor, *Bronze Shadows*, no. 12 (October 1967), p. 3.
5. Henry (Harry) Steeger, correspondence to Wooda Nicholas Carr.
6. Charles Beaumont, "The Bloody Pulps," *Playboy* (September 1962), p. 66.

Information Sources

BIBLIOGRAPHY:

Carr, Wooda Nicholas, "Deadlier Than the Male." *Pulp*, no. 11 (Fall 1978): 3–16.

———. "Emperor Rudolph." *Pulp*, no. 10 (Winter 1978): 22–27.

———. "Let's Face It!"—A Look at the Disguises of Operator 5 During the Purple Invasion." *The Age of the Unicorn*, Vol. 1, no. 3 (August 1979): 3–8.

———. "Operator 5." *Pulp*, no. 1 (Fall 1970): 3–11.

———. "Operator 5 Bounds Out of the Thirties." *Bronze Shadows*, no. 6 (September 1966): 9–14; no. 7 (November 1966): 7–12.

———. "Operator 5 Speaks." *Pulp*, no. 5A (special issue, 1973 Pulpcon): 8–12.

———. "The Subject Was Death." *The Science-Fiction Collector*, no. 15 (1981): 9–14.

———, and Herman S. McGregor. "Contemplating Seven of the Pulp Heroes." *Bronze Shadows*, no. 12 (October 1967): 3–6.

Grennel, Dean A. "Jumping Jimmy Christopher." *Xenophile*, no. 30 (March 1977): 17–19.

INDEX SOURCES: Weinberg, Robert, and Lohr McKinstry. *The Hero Pulp Index*. Evergreen, Colo.: Opar Press, 1971.

LOCATION SOURCES: Private collectors.

Publication History

MAGAZINE TITLE: *Operator #5*.

TITLE CHANGES: None (prefixed *Secret Service,* September 1935).

VOLUME AND ISSUE DATA: Vol. 1, no. 1 (April 1934) through Vol. 12, no. 4 (November–December 1939); 48 issues.

PUBLISHER: Popular Publications, Inc., 2256 Grove Street, Chicago, Illinois, with editorial offices at 205 East 42nd Street, New York, New York.

EDITOR: Rogers Terrill.

PRICE PER ISSUE: 10 cents.

SIZE AND PAGINATION: 7'' X 10''; 112 pages.

CURRENT STATUS: Discontinued.

—*Wooda Nicholas Carr*

P

PHANTOM (British)

Of some interest to mystery fans, *Phantom* was a brave attempt to produce a magazine that concentrated almost entirely on stories of the occult. The early issues included both fictional stories and factual articles; as the magazine progressed, the nonfiction soon disappeared except for the regular feature, "Phantom Forum."

The contributors were mainly British, and only in the last few issues did a number of well-known names appear, including Robert Bloch, Seabury Quinn (with Jules de Grandin, detective investigator), and Russell Wakefield.

The magazine was well produced, with attractive, full-color covers, but it managed to survive for only sixteen issues, departing with a sad little poem lamenting its own demise.

Information Sources

INDEX SOURCES: Cook, Michael L. *Monthly Murders*. Westport, Conn.: Greenwood Press, 1982.
LOCATION SOURCES: Private collectors.

Publication History

MAGAZINE TITLE: *Phantom*.
TITLE CHANGES: None.
VOLUME AND ISSUE DATA: Vol. 1, no. 1 (April 1957) through Vol. 1, no. 16 (July 1958); 16 issues.
PUBLISHER: Vernon Publications (Bolton) Ltd.; from no. 4: Dalrow Publications, Ltd., Dalrow House, Church Bank, Bolton, Lancaster, England; from no. 13: Pennine Publications, Ltd., Stewart Street, Bolton, Lancaster, England.
EDITOR: Leslie Syddall (from at least no. 10).

PRICE PER ISSUE: 2 shillings.
SIZE AND PAGINATION: 5-1/2'' X 8-3/8''; 104–112 pages.
CURRENT STATUS: Discontinued.
—*Robert Adey*

PHANTOM DETECTIVE, THE

Ned L. Pines, only recently out of college, had founded Standard Magazines, Inc., in 1931, thereby releasing upon the world such agreeable pulp titles as *Thrilling Detective,* *Thrilling Love,* and *Thrilling Adventure.* But now another magazine form beckoned.

During September 1932, Street & Smith's *The Shadow Magazine* had burst into a twice-a-month publication, with the issues dated October 1 and October 15 of that year. *The Shadow* was the first single-character magazine in years, and its obvious success demonstrated an active market for fiction about gun-using justice figures with mysterious identities.

Accordingly, Pines took steps to add a single-character publication to his line of titles. About September 1932, he began planning for *The Phantom Detective.* Its lead character, The Phantom, would owe something to The Shadow, a great deal to Edgar Wallace, and a lot more to the tradition of the disguise master and the face changer who never looked the same twice.

The first issue of *The Phantom Detective* was offered for sale in December 1932 (bearing a February 1933 date). The magazine contained a long novel, "The Emperor of Death," signed by G. Wayman Jones, a pseudonym devised to show uniformity of authorship, no matter how many writers participated. Through this novel, Richard Curtis Van Loan, The Phantom Detective, battled the Mad Red, a sinister, murdering figure bent on subversion and doom. Three short stories were also included, plus a pair of double-page thrillers, "Introducing the Phantom" and "True Phantom Facts." This latter was two pages of illustrated crime facts, after the manner of Ripley's "Believe It or Not."

Thus began the longest chronological run of all single-character magazines: 170 issues spread across twenty years. *The Shadow* and *Doc Savage* runs were of more issues, but *The Phantom* out-endured them both.

You wonder why. Through the novels, from 1933 to 1953, pours a tidal wave of blood. It is murder, serial murder, freak murder, mass murder—slaughter continuous and mindless, perpetrated by underworld thugs and their gloating masters, decoratively costumed. Character development was nil, and inconsistency was usual. Plots and narrative incidents were brazenly repeated, issue after issue. But the action was continuous and compelling. It raced hotly past robberies, killings, beatings, captures, chases, and hand-to-hand struggles. The hammer of machine guns never ceased, and the narrative pressure never slackened.

Through these scarlet pages ranged the chameleon figure of The Phantom, his features altering as fluidly as mist. His life was hard. He was battered, stomped, knifed, clubbed, strangled, beaten, and shot. No matter, for up he rose, dripping gore, and in the next paragraph all wounds were forgotten. He was tied up, locked in, blown up, buried under, and trapped, trapped, trapped. No other hero was ensnared as easily or escaped so glibly, five to seven times an issue. And rarely was his disguise disturbed.

Beneath the disguise, The Phantom Detective was a big, physically powerful, quick-witted, impressively informed fellow, who was also prodigiously wealthy. He was that traditional figure of popular fiction, the bored rich young man.

Early orphaned, heir to an immense fortune, Van Loan was a frivolous playboy until the First World War. Then he commanded an air squadron, tasting the joys of combat. After the war's excitement, he found hopeless boredom in peace. He ached for action, for a sense of purpose, finding his social set only brainless pleasure seekers. At that moment, his life-long friend, Frank Havens (head of a national newspaper chain and publisher of the New York *Clarion*) suggested that Van Loan attempt solution of a crime which had the police baffled. Van Loan did so, and from that success developed the figure of The Phantom.

The Phantom's disguises were, at first, simply devices to protect Van Loan from the underworld's vengeance. You can't kill a man you cannot identify. Later, disguise became a technique for investigating, for penetrating close-knit criminal gangs or for confusing the opposition by a constant stream of identities.

Since his face constantly changed, The Phantom identified himself with a small platinum shield upon which tiny diamonds shaped a mask. Or he tugged inconspicuously on his left ear lobe. Or he merely said, "Hello, Frank," in Van Loan's voice. Since he was, for all practical purposes, a wraith, he could be contacted only through Frank Havens—unless he happened to be standing where a particularly horrible outrage took place. At first, Havens called The Phantom by phone. But in the July 1936 "Dealers in Death," red lights mounted at the top of Havens's Clarion Building flickered a coded message in Morse Code: "Calling The Phantom." And sooner or later, a stranger appeared to show his badge, tug his ear, or speak in Van Loan's voice.

No one knew The Phantom's identity but Havens. Not until the final issues of the series. Then everybody seemed to learn, all at once. To begin with, Muriel Havens (the publisher's daughter) finally connected Van Loan and The Phantom, and then only because she loved both; this happened in the Winter 1952 issue, "The Silent Killer." Thereafter, Van Loan shamelessly blew the long-held secret to Steve Huston (Spring 1952, "The Doomed Millions"). Then Inspector Gregg somehow knew all in "Odds On Death," Spring 1953. All this compromising did no harm since the series terminated almost at once.

Gregg wouldn't have told anyhow. He and the police admired The Phantom hugely. He could do no wrong. They forgave his killings and excused his wrecks, fights, and destruction of property. They doted on his words and quivered with ecstacy at his praise. Wonderfully submissive, the police were. They obeyed him as a superior. In early issues, such blind respect was unfortunate, for The Phantom was often ineffectual and bungled rather frequently. But the police never lost faith. Unlike the reader.

The 1933 Phantom Detective was the latest figure in a line of face changers extending back to the dime novels of the 1880s and probably earlier. The disguise masters of that period included Nick Carter, Young Sleuth, and even Buffalo Bill. All could alter their appearances with ease and did so, years before Sherlock Holmes amazed Watson with disguise artistry.

By the early 1900s, disguise had become a convention of popular fiction. During those years, the face changer was most often a criminal; those ranks included such famous names as Colonel Clay (1896), Romney Pringle (1902), Arsene Lupin (1907), Fantomas (1915), and The Gray Phantom (1919). The disguise master might be as harmless as The Benevolent Picaroon (1922) or as lethal as The Ringer (1925). In all cases, the face changers concealed their true identities by art and traveled unsuspected through the world.

The Shadow (1931) continued this long tradition. The Phantom followed immediately behind, and then the single-character pulps foamed up with other notable disguise artists, including The Spider, Secret Agent X, and The Avenger. Disguise was an accepted practice—and a convenient device to keep the story pulsing and the hero deep in action.

For a long-run magazine, *The Phantom Detective* used few continuing characters. Four were introduced in the first issue: Frank Havens (called Elmer then); his daughter, Muriel (loved by Van Loan, but he couldn't tell her because of his dangerous life); and Police Inspector Iverness. By 1936, Iverness had been replaced by Captain Brady, and a new character was added, the tough little reporter, Steve Huston (July 1936). His hair began black and turned red but otherwise did not change much. A second new character appeared in the September and October 1936 issues. Named Jerry Lannigan, he had been Van Loan's chief mechanic during the war. Lannigan was a promising character, but a change in authorship eliminated him.

In 1939, the young, helpful boy, Chip Dorlan, arrived. With astounding speed he matured, became an adult, and entered military intelligence. And, finally, Police Inspector Gregg appeared in the late 1930s and remained through most of the following years.

Of The Phantom's many disguises, only one reached the status of a continuing identity. This was Professor (or Doctor) Paul Bendix, a walking cliché, old, gray-headed, and bearded. He puttered about a laboratory located in a warehouse on the East River docks. The lab was one of those supertechnical facilities, glittering with special equipment, that requires a hundred people to install and operate. The Phantom did it single-handedly. Bendix and laboratory both appear in the July 1936 "Dealers In Death," and thereafter The Phantom could perform miracles of scientific criminology at will.

The Phantom Detective was an excessively uneven magazine. It was monthly, bimonthly, and quarterly, thick and thin. The paper was occasionally good and usually terrible. Its columns were pocked by ads for scurrilous booklets, potency enhancements, and cures for menstrual irregularities. The covers ranged from superb portraits and action scenes by Rudolph Belarski to ill-drawn fumblings by unknown hands. The novels themselves quickly plunged into formula, revived in 1936 for a few years, then blundered along, dull and improbable, until a sudden flare in the mid-1940s when the series peaked in an interesting sequence of novels that were strongly realistic and hard-boiled in tone.

The quality of the fiction varied so because a swarm of authors wrote Phantom novels. The man credited with creating The Phantom was Jack D'Arcy, better known by his pseudonym, D. L. Champion. As far as is known, D'Arcy wrote the series from 1933 to about mid-1935. Then other writers began contributing. Their novels were intermixed with D'Arcy's work, thoroughly scrambling the tenous narrative continuity and indifferently changing character traits and background details.

It is known that some Phantom novels were written by Ryerson Johnson, Charles Green, Laurence Donovan, Norman Daniels, Robert Sidney Bowen, and George McDonald. In only a few cases is authorship of a specific novel known.[1] (Other authors are believed to include Emile Tepperman, Wayne Rogers, George F. Eliot, G. T. Fleming-Roberts, and Stewart Sterling; as was once remarked, everybody wrote at least one Phantom.)

Most of these writers also published short fiction in the magazine, as did such well-known names as Arthur J. Burks, George Allan Moffett, George H. Coxe, Ray Cummings, Oscar Schisgall, and Norvell Page. At first, each issue contained three short stories; later, four appeared.

During 1933–1934, *The Phantom Detective* briskly evolved. The second issue (April 1933) added the department "The Phantom Speaks," containing editorial comment and, eventually, readers' letters. In that issue, the front cover adopted the device of showing The Phantom's masked, transparent head peering down upon an action scene, his lips set. With rare exceptions, that cover style persisted until the Winter 1952 issue.

The December 1933 issue used small illustrations to decorate the beginning of each chapter. These evolved into an elaborate illustrated alphabet, a separate illustration for each letter starting a chapter. During the life of the magazine, these illustrations were changed several times and were finally displaced in the Fall 1952 issue by three standardized pieces of art which were alternated at the beginning of each new chapter.

The January 1934 issue introduced that staple feature of all single-character magazines, the readers' club. This one was called "The Friends of The Phantom" and was organized "to arouse public opinion against the evils of kidnapping, racketeering, and organized crime." The Friends also favored purity and good health. At first, only a membership card was offered. Eventually, in May 1935, a bronze pin stamped with a likeness of The Phantom was offered for ten cents and a title strip from the magazine cover.

About the time that The Friends of the Phantom began pouring out their hearts in letters to the editor, a new, unidentified artist began illustrating the novel. His work was lightly cartoonistic. His straining, struggling figures, locked in deadly violence, appeared until the July 1940 issue. The initial Phantom interiors

(1933–1934) had been drawn by Mel Graff, Will Gilbert, and perhaps one other artist. Their work was remarkably stylized, art deco for the mass market, and usually pictured the moment just before the shooting started. Much later, from August 1940 through Summer 1953, the well-known illustrator, Paul Orban, took up the interior drawings.

Numerous artists painted *The Phantom* covers, and most of their identities are not known. The 1933 covers were done by Emmett Watson, and other artists identified only as "B.G." or "L" or "O." Most often they used cartoonlike characters leering against flat backgrounds. The mid-1934 covers featured high-action scenes, engagingly showing a savage man attacking a scared one. The colors were bright. The effect was of a painted drawing.

Rudolph Belarski's brilliant 1935–1936 covers also pictured violent action. He painted in realistic detail, the faces anguished, the straining bodies in proportion, and two or three figures balanced in frantic struggle. Belarski's work ranks with the finest pulp cover art. The covers that appeared during 1937–1943 are by a mixed bag of artists, some of them skilled at their craft. Many covers have so little to do with the lead novel that they seem to have been taken from the reject pile at press time. But beautifully composed works return in 1943, the artist unidentified. Then Belarski resurfaced once again, painting self-possessed women facing a man with a gun. Finally, Kirk Wilson began doing covers around 1951. His technically polished work shows sleek girls reacting to assorted menaces, all male.

While artists came and went, the format and contents of *The Phantom Detective* altered relatively little from 1934 to 1942. In October 1935, the spine changed from yellow to blue. Then in March 1937, it added white edges and the words "World's Most Famous Detective." Thereafter, the spine could be any color, each gaudier than the last.

Changes in the magazine's contents came more slowly. During 1938, the short stories were reduced from three to two. By 1942, wartime paper restrictions violently affected the magazine. Standard Magazines elected to continue their publications as full-sized pulps, rather than digest size (as Street & Smith had done). Paper was conserved by issuing smaller magazines less frequently, and *The Phantom* spent the final war years and postwar period as a ninety-eight-page bimonthly. After that, a slow increase in number of pages began, and the number of short stories was increased to three or four. A novelette was added to the contents of the September 1948 issue and also a "Feature," the first of a series of illustrated articles about real detectives.

In spite of these editorial changes, *The Phantom Detective* was unable to return to monthly publication. With the Spring 1949 issue, it was changed to a quarterly. Four departments were added, then six, mostly filler material. The novel shrank in size. The prose tightened, was streamlined, and addressed contemporary problems: drugs and war mongering. The characters showed every sign of developing emotional lives.

With a new price of twenty-five cents, it was a neat magazine and smoothly professional. But dual-identity face changers no longer had their former appeal. In the Summer 1953 issue, The Phantom himself announced that his next adventure was titled "The Merry Widow Murders," but that issue was never published. The pulps' last face changer had solved his final case.

Note

1. The following writers have confirmed specific novels: Ryerson Johnson (December 1936); Charles Green (January and March 1937); May and July 1938; January, May, and August 1939; September 1940). The Norman Daniels files, while incomplete, show that he wrote at least the novels of January, April, June, July, August, September, October 1935; January annd June 1936; December 1939; April 1943; April, August, and October 1944; February 1945; September 1948; Spring 1949; Winter, Spring, Summer 1950; Winter, Summer, Fall 1951; Winter, Spring, Summer 1952; and Summer 1953. Style indications suggest that Emile Tepperman wrote the stories of at least August 1936 and January 1937; Wayne Rogers those of December 1935, and July, September, and October 1936; and Laurence Donovan, August 1938, among others. G. T. Fleming-Roberts's work seems to appear intermittently from 1945 to 1949, and Stewart Sterling may have contributed some of the last novels. All these attributions are speculative and are neither confirmed nor complete.

Information Sources

BIBLIOGRAPHY:
Goulart, Ron. *Cheap Thrills*. New Rochelle, New York: Arlington House, 1972.
Gruber, Frank. *The Pulp Jungle*. Los Angeles: Sherbourne Press, 1967.
Jones, Robert Kenneth. *The Shudder Pulps*. West Linn, Ore.: Fax Collector's Editions, 1975.
Sampson, Robert. "Blood Chronicle." *The Mystery Readers Newsletter*, Vol. 3, no. 3 (February 1970): 3–8.
Turner, Robert. *Some of My Best Friends Are Writers, But I Wouldn't Want My Daughter to Marry One*. Los Angeles: Sherbourne Press, 1970.
INDEX SOURCES: Sampson, Robert. "Blood Chronicle." *The Mystery Reader's Newsletter*. Vol. 3, no. 3 (February 1970): 8–10.
Wermers, Bernie. "The Phantom Detective Magazine." *Bronze Shadows*, no. 11 (August 1967): 4–6.
LOCATION SOURCES: University of California–Los Angeles Library (1933–1952, 5 issues); private collectors.

Publication History

MAGAZINE TITLE: *The Phantom Detective*.
TITLE CHANGES: None.
VOLUME AND ISSUE DATA: Vol. 1, no. 1 (February 1933) through Vol. 59, no. 1 (Summer 1953); 170 issues.
PUBLISHERS: Phantom Detective, Inc., 570 Seventh Avenue and 22 West 48th Street, New York, New York (until February 1941); Standard Magazines, Inc., 10 East 40th Street and 570 Seventh Avenue, New York, New York.
EDITORS: Ned L. Pines, managing editor 1933–1934; Harvey Burns (house name) 1935–1950; Alexander Samalman, 1951–1953. Note: "Burns" is believed to be Leo Margulies.

PRICE PER ISSUE: 10 cents (through November 1946); 15 cents (through September 1948); 20 cents (through Winter 1951); 25 cents.
SIZE AND PAGINATION: Much variation,. from 6-3/4'' X 9-1/4'' to 7'' X 10''; 98–146 pages.
CURRENT STATUS: Discontinued.
—*Robert Sampson*

PHANTOM DETECTIVE CASES (British)

At least three issues of *Phantom Detective Cases* were published by John Spencer & Co. (Publishers) Ltd., London. No other information is available.

Information Sources

BIBLIOGRAPHY:
Lofts, W.O.G., and Derek J. Adley. *Old Boys Books, A Complete Catalogue*. London: privately printed, 1969.
INDEX SOURCES: None known.
LOCATION SOURCES: Private collectors.

Publication History

MAGAZINE TITLE: *Phantom Detective Cases*.
TITLE CHANGES: None.
VOLUME AND ISSUE DATA: No. 1 through no. 3; number of issues and extent unknown; circa 1960.
PUBLISHER: John Spencer & Co. (Publishers), Ltd., London.
EDITOR: Not known.
PRICE PER ISSUE: Not known.
SIZE AND PAGINATION: Not known.
CURRENT STATUS: Discontinued.

PHANTOM MYSTERY MAGAZINE (British)

In America, the vehicle was *The Phantom Detective,** a pulp magazine which expired in 1953 after 170 issues; in England, it was *Phantom Mystery Magazine*, a digest-sized periodical that enjoyed a run of only nine issues. But the main attraction was the same: the amazing man of a thousand disguises, the superhero detective, Richard Curtis Van Loan, better known as The Phantom.

The *Phantom Mystery Magazine*, commencing with the August 1961 issue, was from Atlas Publishing & Distributing Co. Ltd., a publisher that specialized in offering reprints of American magazines. On the title page, a domino-masked Phantom, in evening clothes and with top hat, peered pensively at the reader. Each issue included a full-length Phantom novel by ''Robert Wallace,'' a house name.[1] The first issue introduced the hero to the British public with ''The Staring Killer,'' a waterfront epic, and was accompanied by short stories from popular American authors: ''Homicide'' by Carroll John Daly, ''A Lethal Bit of Heaven'' by Gene Austin, ''The Man Who Killed a Hundred Men'' by Thomas Thursday,

"Thubway Tham's Crisis" by Johnston McCulley, and "A Hand for Murder" by Morris Cooper—all crime adventure tales.

But The Phantom was the main attraction, and he reappeared in each issue, starring in "Odds on Death," "Candidate for Death" (Senator John Midworth, presidential candidate, killed by bomb), "The Diamond Killers," "The Listening Eyes," "Murder Acres," "The City of Dreadful Night," and "Billion-Dollar Blitz," among others.

Short stories continued to fill out the magazine, although by the fifth issue these had been reduced to two in number. A British flavor was added by the inclusion in some of the issues of a brief book review column, "Crime Corner," in which British publications received comment.

This was a well-produced magazine with attractive color covers which amazingly never depicted The Phantom but, like most American character magazines in Britain, had a short life. Perhaps 1961 was too sophisticated for the likes of The Phantom.

Note

1. In the early 1960s, Regency Press as Corinth paperbacks, published twenty-two Phantom novels, also using the house name.

Information Sources

INDEX SOURCES: Cook, Michael L. *Monthly Murders*. Westport, Conn.: Greenwood Press, 1982.
LOCATION SOURCES: Private collectors.

Publication History

MAGAZINE TITLE: *Phantom Mystery Magazine*.
TITLE CHANGES: None.
VOLUME AND ISSUE DATA: Vol. 1, no. 1 (August 1961) through at least Vol. 1, no. 9 (April 1962); 9 issues.
PUBLISHER: Atlas Publishing & Distributing Co., Ltd., 18 Bride Lane, London E.C.4, England.
EDITOR: Not known.
PRICE PER ISSUE: 2 shillings.
SIZE AND PAGINATION: 5-3/8" X 7-3/8"; 112–128 pages.
CURRENT STATUS: Discontinued.
—*Robert Adey*

PHOENIX MYSTERY NOVELS (British)

Phoenix Press Ltd., London, published two issues of *Phoenix Mystery Novels* in 1946, thin, pocket-size, and on cheap paper. No other information is available.

Information Sources

BIBLIIOGRAPHY:
Lofts, W.O.G., and Derek J. Adley, *Old Boys Books, A Complete Catalogue*. London: privately printed, 1969.
INDEX SOURCES: None known.
LOCATION SOURCES: Private collectors.

Publication History

MAGAZINE TITLE: *Phoenix Mystery Novels*.
TITLE CHANGES: None.
VOLUME AND ISSUE DATA: No. 1 (1946) through no. 2 (1946); 2 issues.
PUBLISHER: Phoenix Press, Ltd., London.
EDITOR: Not known.
PRICE PER ISSUE: Not known.
SIZE AND PAGINATION: 5-3/8" X 7"; 64 pages.
CURRENT STATUS: Discontinued.

POCKET DETECTIVE MAGAZINE (Street & Smith)

Street & Smith Publications managed to become one of the few magazine publishers to last more than a century, possibly because of the guiding principle of diversity. The two seemingly indestructible brothers, Ormond Smith and George Campbell Smith, who had weathered cut-throat competition and changes in reading and publishing styles, had both died in 1933; but the remainder of the old employees—and the new management—were determined to carry on as before. While reaching for the few cents that the public, still struggling to recover from the depression, had, the "pocket" size magazine, *Pocket Detective*, was introduced in December 1936.

The year had also seen the introduction of *The Whisperer,** *The Feds,** *The Skipper,** and *Hardboiled** by Street & Smith. In 1937, the pocket format was further probed with *Pocket Love*.

Pocket Detective Magazine featured many of the same authors as were appearing in the firm's other magazines, including Judson P. Philips, Carroll John Daly, Hugh B. Cave, Cornell Woolrich, Norbert Davis, Frank Gruber, Arden X. Pangborn, and others. Also included were a number of feature articles and fact departments, such as announcements of stories in the forthcoming issue.

It was hoped that the small size and ease with which it could be carried would attract possible readers and persuade them to part with fifteen cents. Too, this size magazine could be printed more economically than the larger, bulkier, pulp-size magazines. But sales did not result in the anticipated success, and *Pocket Detective Magazine* was discontinued after eleven issues.

It should be noted that another magazine of the same title was published in 1950, for two issues, by Trojan Publications, Inc. (*Pocket Detective Magazine* [Trojan]*).

Information Sources

BIBLIOGRAPHY:
Reynolds, Quentin. *The Fiction Factory*. New York: Random House, 1955.
INDEX SOURCES: Cook, Michael L. *Monthly Murders*. Westport, Conn.: Greenwood Press, 1982.
LOCATION SOURCES: George Arents Research Collection, Syracuse (New York) University; University of California–Los Angeles (Vol. 1, no. 1, only); private collectors.

Publication History

MAGAZINE TITLE: *Pocket Detective Magazine*.
TITLE CHANGES: None.
VOLUME AND ISSUE DATA: Vol. 1, no. 1 (December 1936) through Vol. 2, no. 5 (October 1937); 11 issues.
PUBLISHER: Street & Smith Publications, Inc., 79 Seventh Avenue, New York, New York.
EDITOR: Robert Arthur.
PRICE PER ISSUE: 15 cents.
SIZE AND PAGINATION: 4-1/2" X 7-1/4"; 130–160 pages.
CURRENT STATUS: Discontinued.

POCKET DETECTIVE MAGAZINE (Trojan)

The first issue of this *Pocket Detective Magazine* appeared in September 1950 and was slated to be issued bimonthly. It should not be confused with the magazine of the same title published in 1936–1937 by Street & Smith Publications (*Pocket Detective Magazine* [Street & Smith]*).

The format was smaller than the digest-size magazines then prevalent, and it was designed in a size that could be accommodated in a man's hip-pocket, presumably. The first issue included seven "Bullet-Packet Stories—All Complete," and the second issue contained nine stories. Publication ceased after two issues. "The Case of the Beheaded Dowager" by Walt Grey was featured in the first issue; "Dressed to Kill" by Ed Barcelo highlighted the second issue. Stories were of the fast-action, crime-adventure category, each one preceded by a pulplike illustration and printed on cheap paper.

Information Sources

INDEX SOURCES: Cook, Michael L. *Monthly Murders*. Westport, Conn.: Greenwood Press, 1982.
LOCATION SOURCES: Private collectors.

Publication History

MAGAZINE TITLE: *Pocket Detective Magazine*.
TITLE CHANGES: None.
VOLUME AND ISSUE DATA: Vol. 1, no. 1 (September 1950 through Vol. 1, no. 2 (November 1950); 2 issues.

PUBLISHER: Frank Armor as Trojan Magazines, Inc., 125 East 46th Street, New York 17, New York.
EDITOR: Adolphe Barreaux.
PRICE PER ISSUE: 15 cents.
SIZE AND PAGINATION: 4-1/2'' X 6-5/8''; 98 pages.
CURRENT STATUS: Discontinued.

POISONED PEN, THE

Chance may have been partly the catalyst for *The Poisoned Pen,* but the encouragement of others and solid work produced the first issue of this bimonthly publication in January 1978. When its editor, Jeffrey Meyerson, discovered the Hardy Boys at the age of eleven, he became a mystery buff; when, in 1977, he somehow—by chance—found a copy of Don Miller's *The Mystery Nook*,* a mystery fanzine, he discovered DAPA–EM (*Elementary, My Dear APA**) because Miller was in it. Meyerson began contributing and soon after had his own DAPA-EM (mystery amateur press association) issue at the same time that he was sending material to the then-new *The Mystery Fancier.**

In an interview at the Bouchercon XII conference on October 9, 1981, Meyerson spoke of the decisions that seem to make his the best of all possible worlds. For several years, he had worked as a statistician for the Modern Language Association at its headquarters, but books had a stronger appeal than figures. As that job was being phased out, he thought of opening a bookstore and decided on a mail-order book business about the time he started association with DAPA-EM. He sent his first DAPA-EM issue to a few people, and they responded with reviews and comments; the issues got bigger and bigger. With the encouragement of Steve Lewis and others, including his wife, Jackie, Meyerson began his independent publication, *The Poisoned Pen.*

In volume 1, number 1, in "The Pen Rambles," his regular editorial, he wrote: "My priorities were mainly to have an interesting, informative zine, keep it on a regular bimonthly schedule, and mail it via first class to speed delivery and response."[1] Additional initial encouragement for response included a subscription extension of one issue for anyone who contributed an article, a review, or a letter. Response was good. Meyerson has never had to reprint any material from DAPA-EM as he thought he might.

If subscriber-fans knew that *The Poisoned Pen* was produced from a brownstone, they might whimsically associate it with a more famous brownstone on West 35th Street in Manhattan. Not so. The great detective solved mysteries, and the editor aids and abets elucidation of mystery information, but there the association ends. Jeffrey Meyerson has none of the girth or petulance of the created Nero Wolfe; he modestly claims a top floor only, and he is a gentle man who ventures into the world outside for contact with those who have helped to make *The Poisoned Pen* a fanzine of the fans, by the fans, and for the fans.

Why has this fanzine continued to be a success, even with two other established publications going? Regular features, frequent contributors, reviews, informative checklists, and "Pen Letters" (usually the first part that most subscribers read) are likely reasons.

One of the regular features is Mary Groff's "All Too True," wherein she recounts the facts of true crime and lists the books that imaginatively use the facts. Marvin Lachman has a "Department of Unknown Mystery Writers," in which he discusses those who have written at least one good mystery but who are not in the current limelight. R. Jeff Banks writes "Mystery Plus," which calls attention to the pleasures of mysteries in works not labeled as mysteries. Don Cole in "Conversations" puts to print tape-recorded interviews of U.S. mystery writers: Barry Pike handles "Pen Profiles" on authors and their works. Steve Lewis in "The Mystery Dial" discusses radio shows, and Maryell Cleary in "First Appearances" records in depth the debut of series detectives. A new feature begun recently is "Mainstream Mysteries and Novels of Crime" by Gary Warren Niebuhr. These all comprise a wide and steady range of features that are both interesting and informative.

There are other frequent contributors who write on a variety of topics; among them are Jim McCahery, Mary Ann Grochowski, and Neville Wood. In addition, the featured and frequent contributors also write book reviews, joining the ranks of reviewers Bob Adey, Philip Asdell, Bill Crider, Dave Doerrer, Winston Graham, Douglas Green, George Kelley, Edward S. Lauterbach, Steven Miller, and Martin Morse Wooster.

It would be misleading to withhold comment on other contributors. Even just skimming the pages of *The Poisoned Pen,* one notes several score of more occasional writers. The editorial doors are wide open with welcome.

Covers for the white-paged text are pleasantly colored and have pen illustrations by Bob Napier, Jackie Meyerson, and Mary Groff. And each volume of *The Poisoned Pen* is indexed by enthusiastic volunteers for ready reference for those doing research and for those who remember a "fact," a title, a review, or a letter but cannot remember in what issue.

Subscribers and contributors have increased not only from personal and postal grapevines but from reviews in professional publications. Jon Breen in the *Wilson Library Bulletin* encouraged libraries to subscribe to "still another good fanzine."[2] In *The Library Journal*, Bill Katz called *The Poisoned Pen* a "winning mimeo approach to an appreciation of mystery books and films. . . . The fine reviews alone make it a useful item for libraries."[3] Libraries were not the only targets for encouraged subscriptions, however. In *Ellery Queen's Mystery Magazine,** R. E. Porter acknowledged a news item in "The Crime Beat" taken from *The Poisoned Pen,* praised the contents, and concluded: "It's well worth the $9.00 a year subscription for six issues."[4]

Alas, rising costs and larger issues have increased the subscription rate to ten dollars as of June 1981, although this is still a modest price. Cost has also forced withdrawal of the offer of a free issue for a letter, but the offer holds for those who write an article. Beginning at five dollars a year, the rate has gradually inched to its present state, but subscribers think the price is right. Subscriptions have increased from a moderate 75 to a list of 350.

Meyerson finds personal gratification for all the writing, typing, mimeographing, collating, and mailing. After returning from a buying trip to England in the summer of 1981 for his book business, he was pleased to find a whole pile of subscriptions, new and renewals, and ten to fifteen contributions: letters, reviews, and articles.

With its "something for every fan" *The Poisoned Pen* has a rosy future, the color of a few of the covers in the single-spaced typed issues that keep fandom alive and well.

Notes

1. Editorial, *The Poisoned Pen*, Vol. 1, no. 1 (January 1978), p. 2.
2. Jon Breen, "Murder in Print," *Wilson Library Journal* (April 1979).
3. Bill Katz, "Magazines," *The Library Journal* (April 15, 1981).
4. R. E. Porter, "Crime Beat," *Ellery Queen's Mystery Magazine* (April 22, 1981), p. 91.

Information Sources

INDEX SOURCES: None known.
LOCATION SOURCES: Private collectors.

Publication History

MAGAZINE TITLE: *The Poisoned Pen.*
TITLE CHANGES: None.
VOLUME AND ISSUE DATA: Vol. 1, no. 1 (January 1978) through Vol. 4, no. 5/6 (double issue), (to date, December 1981); 23 issues.
PUBLISHER: Jeffrey Meyerson, 50 First Place, Brooklyn, New York 11231.
EDITOR: Jeffrey Meyerson.
PRICE PER ISSUE: By subscription only; currently $10.00 per year.
SIZE AND PAGINATION: 8-1/2" X 11"; 32–50 pages.
CURRENT STATUS: Active.
—*Jane Gottschalk*

PONTINE DOSSIER, THE

Edited and published by Luther Norris, *The Pontine Dossier* first appeared as the official newsletter of the Praed Street Irregulars, the society founded by Norris in June 1966 to pay tribute to the great detective, Solar Pons; to Pons's loyal friend and chronicler, Dr. Lyndon Parker; and their creator, August Derleth.

The first Solar Pons story was written in 1928 as an enthusiastic pastiche after Sir Arthur Conan Doyle responded to a query from Derleth with confirmation that there would indeed be no more stories about Sherlock Holmes. And from that modest beginning, Solar Pons became the hero of a long series of stories, longer, in fact, than the "Sacred Writings" so beloved by Sherlockians and full of echoes of the world of Sherlock Holmes. Solar Pons lived in London in the 1920s and 1930s, rather than the 1890s and 1900s; his address was 7B Praed

Street rather than 221B Baker Street; and his street-urchin assistants were the Praed Street Irregulars rather than the Baker Street Irregulars.

Just as the latter-day admirers of Sherlock Holmes decided to call themselves the Baker Street Irregulars, Norris and his fellow admirers of Solar Pons chose to be the Praed Street Irregulars. Styling himself the Lord Warden of the Pontine Marshes, Norris filled his society's newsletter with contributions from his friends: illustrations by Henry Lauritzen, Roy Hunt, and Frank Utpatel, and letters and articles by Alvin F. Germeshausen, Nathan L. Bengis, A. E. Van Vogt, Michael Harrison, Philip Jose Farmer, Fritz Leiber, and many others.

Published irregularly for nine issues and with circulation climbing rapidly past five hundred copies, *The Pontine Dossier* was converted in 1970 to a forty-page annual, filled with scholarly and pseudo-scholarly essays and articles about Solar Pons, his contemporaries (such as Mr. J. G. Reeder and Craig Kennedy), and about August Derleth. Luther Norris published six issues of *The Pontine Dossier Annual*; and when he died in January 1978, the pages of his magazine were left as a splendid example of how contagious his enthusiasm was.

Information Sources

INDEX SOURCES: None known.
LOCATION SOURCES: Private collectors.

Publication History

MAGAZINE TITLE: *The Pontine Dossier*.
TITLE CHANGES: *The Pontine Dossier Annual* (1970).
VOLUME AND ISSUE DATA: Vol. 1, no. 1 (February 1967) through Vol. 2, no. 5 (March 1970); 9 issues. New Series: Vol. 1, no. 1 (1970, annual) through Vol. 3, no. 2 (1977, annual); 6 issues.
PUBLISHER: Luther Norris, 3844 Watseka Avenue, Culver City, California 90230.
EDITOR: Luther Norris.
PRICE PER ISSUE: *The Pontine Dossier* was distributed without charge for the 4 issues in Vol. 1; a contribution of $1.00 was requested to cover part of the expenses of Vol. 2. *The Pontine Dossier Annual*: $3.00 per year (1970–1971), $4.00 per year (1973–1974), and $5.00 per year (1975–1977).
SIZE AND PAGINATION: *The Pontine Dossier*: 8-1/2'' X 11''; 4 pages. *The Pontine Dossier Annual*: 5-3/8'' X 8-1/4''; 40 pages.
CURRENT STATUS: Discontinued.
—*Peter E. Blau*

PONTINE DOSSIER ANNUAL, THE

See PONTINE DOSSIER, THE

POPULAR DETECTIVE

Popular Detective must be considered as one of the basic detective pulp magazines, both for its longevity and for its class of material that was more or less consistent over approximately a twenty-year publishing history.

The magazine normally included one complete novel, two novelettes, and three to five short stories. Many authors with whom readers today are familiar had frequent appearances in *Popular Detective* including Richard Deming, Robert Leslie Bellem, Robert Sidney Bowen, Johnston McCulley, M. E. Chaber, Philip Weck, Wayland Rice, G. T. Fleming-Roberts, Stewart Sterling, and Fredric Brown. Others included Edward S. Ronns, Norman A. Daniels, Craig Rice, Bruno Fischer, Leslie Charteris, Brett Halliday, and Carroll John Daly—a veritable encyclopedia of authors.

Here, one would find stories featuring The Saint, Mike Shayne, Race Williams, Chet Lacey, and Keene Madden, among the better-known detective characters. Tantalizing covers motivated the sale from newsstands, and the magazine was one that could look forward to continued loyalty and support.

In "Official Business," a regular editorial and letters column described as "a friendly department where our readers and the editor meet," one would find such a typical letter as "I certainly think you are doing a swell job with your *Popular Detective Magazine.* I like all your authors because very seldom do I see a story in your magazine that is not good. For pasttime and complete mental relaxation, your publication is tops."[1] Other letters included inquiries, and minor complaints, the usual for the period.

The later issues included a variety of special features, departments, fact fillers, movie news, true-crime articles, and cartoons. At least seven issues were published of a British reprint edition.

Note

1. Letters column, *Popular Detective*, 25, no. 3 (October 1943), p. 7.

Information Sources

INDEX SOURCES: None known.
LOCATION SOURCES: University of California–Los Angeles Library (1939–1947, 7 issues); private collectors.

Publication History

MAGAZINE TITLE: *Popular Detective*.
TITLE CHANGES: None.
VOLUME AND ISSUE DATA: Vol. 1, no. 1 (November 1934 [?]) through Vol. 45, no. 1 (Fall 1953); 136 issues.
PUBLISHER: Beacon Publications, Inc., later as Better Publications, Inc., 144 West 48th Street, later 29 Worthington Street, Springfield, Massachusetts, and 10 East 40th Street, New York, New York (Ned L. Pines, president).
EDITOR: Not known.
PRICE PER ISSUE: 10 cents; 15 cents; 20 cents.

SIZE AND PAGINATION: 6-5/8'' X 9-5/8''; 114–128 pages.
CURRENT STATUS: Discontinued.

POPULAR DETECTIVE (British)

See POPULAR DETECTIVE

PRISON LIFE STORIES

At least three issues of *Prison Life Stories*—a large (8-3/4'' X 11-1/2''), thin, pulp magazine—were published in 1935, filled with wild stories about things that happen behind prison bars. No other information is available.

Information Sources

INDEX SOURCES: None known.
LOCATION SOURCES: Private collectors.

Publication History

MAGAZINE TITLE: *Prison Life Stories*.
TITLE CHANGES: None known.
VOLUME AND ISSUE DATA: 1935; at least 3 issues; number of issues and extent
    unknown.
PUBLISHER: Not known.
EDITOR: Not known.
PRICE PER ISSUE: Not known.
SIZE AND PAGINATION: 8-3/4'' X 11-1/2''; number of pages unknown.
CURRENT STATUS: Discontinued.

PRISON STORIES

Prison Stories (1930–1931), a Harold Hersey title, was a highly specialized magazine that focused on the world of convicts, ex-convicts, and those about to become convicts. The magazine was one long dirge to lost freedom—gray stone walls and barred cells, the innocent framed and disgraced, sullen cons in striped suits, and corrupt prison officials and sadistic guards.

"The guard, his gross face purple with anger, had rushed [forward]. Again and again the lash fell, but Larry Dexter was game. Through a mask of blood his grey eyes glared scornfully at the guard."[1]

Since the reader might find it difficult to empathize with the garden variety of crooks populating the prisons, the magazine tended to celebrate some pretty nice people framed by a bitter enemy and sent up the river. In the magazine, about 93 percent of those sent up had been framed. Most of these remained decent, of self-evident excellence: "Say, baby," I cried. "You've got some class. You'll never burn."[2] But a few of these framed innocents were corrupted by their fate and the need for a dramatic story: "Bess Robbins discarded every remnant of the lady about her and became once more the hardboiled, calloused gun moll that two stirs had made of her."[3]

Whether innocent or guilty, the convicts' misfortunes are told in a degenerate prose, rancid with fake argot, clumsy, inept self-conscious: "Gangland and its unsolved mysteries—the roar of guns blasting into the night. The roads stained with red—the hi-jacking and the beer running in order that those who frequented the Great White Way might find everything there conducive to joy."[4]

The situations are contrived, events unmotivated, and the characters barely rise to cartoon levels: "Keep your hand on your gat. We're not going to get caught now."[5]

"Opportunity 'Raps' Twice": A good girl, framed into the stir, goes down the path of crime. She redeems herself by spoiling the plot of the leering, cruel, heartless criminal who wrecked her life, then commits suicide.

"A Square Deal": Cons escape in a freight car, only to be routed, by a trick of fate, back again into the stir.

"Stone Walls": Framed by a sneaking coward, the imprisoned war hero is tormented unmercifully until an accident proves his innocence and a prison fire destroys the wicked.

"Molly O'Hare": The beautiful girl, framed to the chair, is rescued at the last possible second when her pals stage a full-scale massacre of the corrupt warden, the sadistic shrew, the murderous guards, the sneering commissioner's gang. All this slaughter is later lightly excused because they deserved it, every one.

The mechanism of inversion is in full force here. To intensify the dramatic possibilities of the stories, prison authorities are given the role of the devil. Their bodies are bloated, their eyes glare with lunatic malice. By contrast, the prisoners are often admirable, occasionally heroic, representing flawed good opposed to the corrosive evil of officialdom. The contrast is pounded home by sledgehammers; however, the fifteenth stereotype is no more believable than the first.

Prison Stories' usual offering was a novel, about four short stories, and a department of semihumorous paragraphs about crime and criminals. In the first issues, one of the short stories turned out to be a serial in disguise: "Ace In the Hole" by John Gerand. Other writers included Edwin Vernon Burkholder, Henry Leverage (whose series about the convict, Big Scar, had run for several years in *Flynn's [Detective Fiction Weekly*]*), E. Parke Levy, Edward Lancelot, Elwood Pierce, Carl Henry. . . . A few of these names may not be pseudonyms.

Covers were painted by C. Wren, who had a way with stripes and bars and raging convicts. Interior drawings, as far as noted, were done by the accomplished Tom Lovell, soon to begin his superb work for *The Shadow Magazine.** Lovell's line drawings, composed and dramatically presented, showing character in every bodily attitude, are easily the best thing in *Prison Stories*. The magazine had little else to be proud of.

Notes

1. John Gerard, "Ace in the Hole," *Prison Stories,* Vol. 1, no. 1 (November 1930), p. 72.
2. E. V. Burkholder, "Molly O'Hare," *Prison Stories,* Vol. 1, no. 1 (November 1930), p. 24.
3. E. Parke Levy, "Opportunity 'Raps' Twice," *Prison Stories,* Vol. 1, no. 1 (November 1930), p. 105.
4. Ibid., pp. 106–107.
5. Elwood Pierce, "A Square Deal," *Prison Stories*, Vol. 1, no. 1 (November 1930), p. 72.

Information Sources

INDEX SOURCES: None known.
LOCATION SOURCES: Private collectors only.

Publication History

MAGAZINE TITLE: *Prison Stories*.
TITLE CHANGES: None.
VOLUME AND ISSUE DATA: Vol. 1, no. 1 (November 1930) through Vol. 2, no. 2 (May–June 1931); 6 issues.
PUBLISHER: Good Story Magazine Co., Inc., Myrick Building, Springfield, Massachusetts.
EDITOR: Not known.
PRICE PER ISSUE: 10 cents.
SIZE AND PAGINATION: 6-3/4'' X 9-7/8''; 160 pages.
CURRENT STATUS: Discontinued.

PRIVATE DETECTIVE (British)

See PRIVATE DETECTIVE STORIES

PRIVATE DETECTIVE (Canadian)

Although bearing the same title in essence as the *Private Detective Stories** of the United States published by Trojan Magazines, Inc. (which was also distributed in Canada), this *Private Detective* was an entirely different magazine, published by Duchess Printing & Publishing Co., Ltd. Under the banner of a "Superior Magazine," emphasis was focused on the fact that it was not a reprint vehicle and that it was all Canadian stories, by Canadian authors, and published in Canada. However, the contents were the standard fare of period detective and crime-adventure stories in pulp format.

There was no identification on copies inspected as to year published, but the Canadian *Private Detective* was apparently produced in the late 1940s or early 1950s. The last issue noted was labeled volume 2, number 2.

Information Sources

INDEX SOURCES: None known.

LOCATION SOURCES: Private collectors.

Publication History

MAGAZINE TITLE: *Private Detective*.

TITLE CHANGES: None.

VOLUME AND ISSUE DATA: Vol. 1, no. 1 (n.d.) through at least Vol. 2, no. 2 (n.d.); number of issues and extent unknown.

PUBLISHER: Duchess Printing & Publishing Co., Ltd., 104 Sherbourne Street, Toronto, Ontario, Canada.

EDITOR: Not known.

PRICE PER ISSUE: 10 cents.

SIZE AND PAGINATION: 7'' X 10''; 98 pages.

CURRENT STATUS: Discontinued.

PRIVATE DETECTIVE (U.S.)

See PRIVATE DETECTIVE STORIES

PRIVATE DETECTIVE STORIES

Private Detective Stories appeared in mid-1937, about three years after the first of the Spicy magazine line—*Spicy Detective** (April 1934)—had breathed fire at the reader.

The magazines were much the same. *Private Detective Stories* was *Spicy Detective* with less-decorative covers and some of the psychopathology left out, but not much. Both were part of publisher Frank Armor's sex-drenched list of magazine titles, and both were written by a small number of men using large numbers of pseudonyms.

Robert Leslie Bellem was one of the housewriters. A prolific, rapid writer, he had developed a style of brief declarative sentences that bristled with slang and casual violence. It was the hard-boiled technique with all the poetry and ethical structure boiled away. Only the action skeleton was left. And the action was continuous. It never let up and was one long sequence of slugging, shooting, being hit on the head, swallowing glasses of rye, rushing up, and storming down.

Through all the hubbub slithered the women. Described in terms of scarlet lips, lush bosoms, warm white flesh, and perfumed tresses, they were not human beings but collections of attributes to make the boys sit up bug-eyed and slap their knees. The point was not to characterize women but to linger over their existence. And, incidentally, to show them malicious, drunk, raging, or pliable, and murdered or beaten up.

There are no women in *Private Detective Stories*. Only collections of sex characteristics against which the male protagonist acts with greater or less brutality. Sometimes he kisses her, sometimes he slugs her in the face. It's all the same. In *Private Detective Stories*, nobody likes women much.

Bellem specialized in these concupiscent adventures, as did four or five others who contributed to the magazine over the next six years. Those signing their names were E. Hoffman Price and Roger Torrey in addition to Bellem. More usually, the table of contents was solid with pseudonyms, and who was really responsible for the aphrodisiac prose isn't accurately known.

The magazine published six to eight pieces of fiction per issue. A novel (a long short story) started things off, and the rest were short stories. There were no departments. Illustrations concentrated on the theme of undressed girls or girls mainly undressed except for scraps of silk dangling about them. Even when the illustrations showed one bruiser hitting or shooting another, a stripped girl decorated the immediate area, helpless, covered with nothing but perfumed white skin.

At the beginning of 1943, the magazine's contents included what were called "Special Articles" but which were filler material worked up to a single-page size and topped with a large-print title. From that point on, most issues included at least one article or filler paragraph.

By late 1943, a distinct format change gripped the magazine. Pages were reduced to 112. Only four pieces of fiction and three filler items were offered. And new names, names of real people, began appearing in the table of contents. From 1943 to about 1947, the magazine featured Dale Clark, Henry Norton, Harold de Polo, Wyatt Blassingame, Ray Cummings, Day Keene, Laurence Donovan, and Talmage Powell. Bellem was still present, with his pseudonyms scattered among the pages. But now a new style of story-telling moved through the magazine, one that was a distinct improvement.

Slowly the stories moved away from the tough, hard-drinking private eye. Heroes were now sheriffs, framed citizens, or servicemen back from the war. A few stories featured criminals. By 1947, a portion of the fiction had reentered the literary world. Characters were motivated and often skillfully drawn; the writing flowed more smoothly, with a sense of place, narrative bridges, and touches of descriptive color.

Even the covers showed change. George Rozen and Modest Stein painted frightened girls who were fully dressed. The interior illustrations showed little change, but then the interiors were not the best part of the magazine even after the improvements. A few cartoons had crept into the pages, and occasionally the magazine featured a true-fact article that was more than just filler material.

The renaissance of quality did not last long. By 1948, the tough private investigators had again taken over, and the girls were being pounded on again, as in the good old days. Something seems to have gone wrong with the formula about then. The magazine begins to oscillate, seeking new ways to appeal to the readership.

Stories were shortened and their number increased to eight or nine. Once more, the names on the contents page were primarily pseudonyms. At the end of the 1940s, "The Criminologist's Corner" was added; this answered letters about crime and cautioned against evil ways. In 1949, a pair of black-and-white comic-book sections were inserted into the magazine. One of these featured Jerry Jasper, the usual wealthy young socialite and criminologist; the other, "Sally The Sleuth" (by Charles Barr), was about a beautiful private investigatoress with a long and notorious history. A mainstay in *Spicy Detective* for years, Sally's adventures had been continued in *Speed Detective* (a retitling of *Spicy Detective*) until mid–1943. Her revival in *Private Detective* lasted until the mid-1950s, when both comics were eliminated.

Shortly after this, the magazine itself ended. The final issue is believed to be October 1950, although a next issue was advertised. The October 1950 magazine contained 132 pages—a novel, seven stories, and the "Criminologist's" department. On rear pages were ads for *Pocket Western Magazine* and *Pocket Detective Magazine* (Trojan).* At least six issues of a British reprint edition were published.

Information Sources

BIBLIOGRAPHY:
Carr, Wooda Nicholas. "Dan Turner." *Xenophile*, Vol. 2, no. 8 (February 1976): 51–53.
Jones, Robert Kenneth. *The Shudder Pulps*. West Linn, Ore.: Fax Collector's Editions, 1975.
Mertz, Stephen. "Robert Leslie Bellem: The Great Unknown." *Xenophile*, Vol. 2, no. 8 (February 1976): 49–51.
INDEX SOURCES: None known.
LOCATION SOURCES: University of California–Los Angeles Library (1937–1949, 39 issues); private collectors.

Publication History

MAGAZINE TITLE: *Private Detective Stories*.
TITLE CHANGES: *Private Detective* (with June 1949 issue).
VOLUME AND ISSUE DATA: Vol. 1, no. 1 (June 1937) through Vol. 23, no. 1 (October 1950); 139 issues.
PUBLISHER: Trojan Publishing Corporation, 2242 Grove Street, Chicago, Illinois, later 125 East 46th Street, New York, New York.
EDITORS: M. R. Bindamin (1948); Adolphe Barreaux (1950).
PRICE PER ISSUE: 15 cents (1937–1947); 20 cents (1948–1949); 25 cents.
SIZE AND PAGINATION: 7" X 10" (1937–1944), 6-3/4" X 9-1/2" (1944–1950); 80–132 pages.
CURRENT STATUS: Discontinued.
—*Robert Sampson*

PRIVATE EYE

The editor, Stephen Bond, described the intent of *Private Eye* in its first issues as:

something new—something different—something challenging in the way of escape reading that at the same time is not offensive and a distortion of the life you and I know. . .stories that reflect the tempo and the excitement of our times, stories of murder, suspense and adventure that could happen to you and your neighbors if you crossed that invisible line that separates the lives of most of us from the lives of those grim men, the hunted and the hunters.[1]

In a fairly successful attempt to follow this ambitious program, *Private Eye* featured stories of hoodlums and small-time crooks, private investigators and the police, and some stories with surprise endings. It was a good selection of contemporary crime-adventure and mystery stories by well-known authors such as Michael Avallone, Harold Q. Masur, Bryce Walton, Frank Kane, Richard Deming, Jonathan Craig, and others.

Promised as a quarterly, the magazine folded after but two issues, publishing material that was too little different from so many others.

Note

1. Announcement, *Private Eye*, Vol. 1, no. 1 (July 1953), reverse front cover.

Information Sources

INDEX SOURCES: Cook, Michael L. *Monthly Murders*. Westport, Conn.: Greenwood Press, 1982.
LOCATION SOURCES: Private collectors.

Publication History

MAGAZINE TITLE: *Private Eye*.
TITLE CHANGES: None.
VOLUME AND ISSUE DATA: Vol. 1, no. 1 (July 1953) through Vol. 1, no. 2 (December 1953); 2 issues.
PUBLISHER: John Vincent (first issue) and John Raymond (second issue) as Future Publications, Inc., 80 Fifth Avenue, New York 11, New York.
EDITORS: Stephen Bond (first issue); John Vincent (second issue).
PRICE PER ISSUE: 35 cents.
SIZE AND PAGINATION: 5-1/4" X 7-1/2"; 152 pages.
CURRENT STATUS: Discontinued.

PRIVATE INVESTIGATOR DETECTIVE MAGAZINE

Private Investigator Detective Magazine, published first in 1956 by Republic Features Syndicate, debuted at the same time as their *American Agent** and *Tales of the Frightened** and had an equally short life of but two issues.

The magazine, with covers by Freeman Elliott, featured Michael Avallone's well-known detective, Ed Noon,[1] in the lead story in each issue, "The Bouncing Betty" (Winter 1956) and "The Alarming Clock" (Spring 1957). Avallone was actually the behind-the-scenes editor but was not credited as such to avoid conflict with the fact that he would be writing the featured story in each issue. The magazine was originally to be called "Ed Noon's Mystery Magazine," but Avallone "thought it far too early in my career for that sort of thing. . . ."[2]

Distribution problems arising with a strike by American News Company precipitated the demise of the magazine.

Notes

1. Ed Noon, a detective character created by Avallone, had debuted in 1951 with the mystery novel, *The Tall Dolores* (New York: Henry Holt).
2. Michael Avallone, correspondence to Michael L. Cook (April 1982).

Information Sources

INDEX SOURCES: None known.
LOCATION SOURCES: Private collectors.

Publication History

MAGAZINE TITLE: *Private Investigator Detective Magazine.*
TITLE CHANGES: None.
VOLUME AND ISSUE DATA: Vol. 1, no. 1 (Winter 1956) through Vol. 1, no. 2 (Spring 1957); 2 issues.
PUBLISHER: Republic Features Syndicate, Inc., 39 West 55th Street, New York, New York.
EDITOR: Lyle Kenyon Engel.
PRICE PER ISSUE: 35 cents.
SIZE AND PAGINATION: 8-1/2" X 11"; 96 pages.
CURRENT STATUS: Discontinued.

PUBLIC ENEMY

In 1934, following the investigation of the Lindbergh baby kidnapping and the dramatic ends of John Dillinger and Baby Face Nelson, the Federal Bureau of Investigation was cheered and ballyhooed. A G–Man fad gripped the country. And this, like every major fad, found its way into the pulp magazines.

About mid–1935, the Dell Publishing Company began preparation of a magazine depicting G–Men at war with the underworld. A modified single-character magazine format was selected, the lead novel featuring an FBI hero.

The central idea was that this agent would spend each issue battling a sinister national menace identified as Public Enemy No. 1. J. Edgar Hoover had popularized these words when he had designated various criminals Public Enemies No. 1, No. 2, and so forth, grading each as to a degree of menace.

Few of the fiends stamping through *Public Enemy* resembled Dillinger or Nelson. They did, however, closely resemble the ferocious masterminds who stalked the pages of *The Phantom Detective** and the early *Operator #5.** Most enjoyed a respectable public life as professors and businessmen and such solid types; only in private, wearing decorative masks, did their eyes blaze and their minds sweat doom.

Facing these blood-thirsty geniuses was Lynn Vickers, Agent G–77. His identification number was drawn from the football-uniform number he had once made famous. Like any respectable single-character hero, Vickers was tall, thin, tough, gun-quick, and hotly admired by all characters. Criminals had framed his father, who then committed suicide in protest, causing Vickers to swear a mighty oath of vengeance on crime, and in consequence of which he could not marry or love because he was entirely dedicated to the eradication of one criminal or another.

Although the FBI, even then, was tautly disciplined, Vickers was subject to no discernible organizational control. J. Edgar Hoover (identified only as The Chief) gave Vickers an entirely free hand. "You have full authority." Go forth and get them. Like The Phantom Detective, Vickers spent much time in disguise and an equal amount of time tied up, waiting to be obliterated. But sooner or later, he surfaces, holding out his leather identification-card holder, and draws the instant cooperation from local law enforcement agencies. These are always glad to assist him, fiction being fiction.

The stories rage through a chaos of super crime, high-technology weapons in criminal hands, gun fights, fist fights, machine-gun fights, knocks on the head, daring disguises, maniacal auto chases, national peril, and deadly traps in subterranean lairs. It is familiar fare.

The first issue of *Public Enemy*, December 1935, contained an eighty-four page novel (including much internal artwork). This was signed by Bryan James Kelley. The issue included one short story and what purported to be a fact article. With the second issue, February 1936, *Public Enemy* had become a monthly; and with the third issue, March 1936, it was announced that readers could join the G–77 Club, an obligatory feature in single-character magazines.

With the fourth issue, April 1936, the magazine was expanded to 128 pages. The novel was slightly shortened, three short stories were used, plus two comic-strip features about the FBI, and the G–77 Club department, "With the G–Men," was added. The last quarter of the novel was moved to the rear of the magazine where it could be invisibly extended by columns of advertisements.

This set the pattern for the magazine. With each succeeding issue, the novel shrank and shrank again. Various G–Men fillers—"features"—used up available space. A "Secret Codes and Ciphers" department was added in the June 1936 issue, but this vanished two issues later.

No matter what was stirred into the magazine's contents, *Public Enemy* did not seem to ignite readers. In a major shakeup, the title of the seventh issue, August 1936, was changed to *Federal Agent*, with the added sub-title of "G–Men Action Stories." The novel, now sixty pages long (or fifty-one pages after art and ads have been deducted), was accompanied by four short stories. Of these, three were by Theodore Tinsley, Jack D'Arcy, and "Tom Champion" (likely, D'Arcy). In the following issues, ever more short stories were added.

By the January 1937 issue, change had had its way. The magazine contained five short stories (two of them by Paul Ernst and Theodore Tinsley), a novelette (actually a short story) by A. L. Zagat, and what were called two novels (both of them long short stories). As usual, the lead G–77 novel was signed by Bryan James Kelley, although the style strongly suggests Paul Ernst.

The entire original concept of the magazine had collapsed by March 1937. Agent G–77 was gone; his club was no more. In his place appeared Agent K–67 (a deadly millionaire named Emory Craig), assisted by his big, fat, tough pal, Gaffney. The novel, now twenty-two pages long, was written by Franklin H. Martin.

No longer did the magazine attempt the single-character format. Its emphasis was now on short stories by prominent detective-action writers, among them Hugh B. Cave, A. L. Zagat, Steve Fisher, and Wyatt Blassingame. No less than eight short stories cram the May 1937 issue, nine if you include the novel.

The magazine continued thus for two more issues, July and September but, without notice, was then discontinued.

Information Sources

BIBLIOGRAPHY:
Kelley, Bryan J. "G–77 in Public Enemy #1." *Pulp*, no. 2 (Spring 1971): 14–17.
INDEX SOURCES: None known.
LOCATION SOURCES: University of California–Los Angeles (Vol. 1, nos. 1–2); private
      collectors.

Publication History

MAGAZINE TITLE: *Public Enemy*.
TITLE CHANGES: *Federal Agent* (with Vol. 2, no. 1 [August 1936]).
VOLUME AND ISSUE DATA: Vol. 1, no. 1 (December 1935) through Vol. 4, no. 1
      (September 1937); 13 issues.
PUBLISHER: Dell Publishing Co., Inc., 149 Madison Avenue, New York, New York.
EDITORS: West F. Peterson (through January 1937); Arthur Lawson.
PRICE PER ISSUE: 10 cents.
SIZE AND PAGINATION: 6-3/4" X 10"; 114–130 pages.
CURRENT STATUS: Discontinued.
—*Robert Sampson*

PULP

Pulp, a fanzine for pulp magazine collectors, represents an important link between the early pulp-oriented fanzines of the 1960s and the magazines of like nature in the seventies. With the demise of *Bronze Shadows** and *The Pulp Era,** both edited by old-time pulp collectors, there were no fanzines devoted to the pulp field overall until the first issue of *Pulp*, dated Fall 1970. Robert Weinberg, the first of the new generation of pulp enthusiasts who had not experienced those magazines when younger, deserves considerable credit for picking up the fallen torch. His numerous articles for various nonpulp fanzines were designed to introduce the subject to an audience broader than just nostalgic members of an older generation. In publishing *Pulp*, he kept interest alive in fan circles and more. Past contributors to *Bronze Shadows* and *The Pulp Era* were recruited and new ones discovered.

Weinberg himself has generally taken a passive role in shaping *Pulp*, preferring instead to let his contributors—most notably Robert Sampson, Nick Carr, Frank Eisgruber, Jr., and Will Murray—write on subjects of their own choosing. Surprisingly, Weinberg's contributions to his own magazine usually take the form of short, unsigned articles and checklist material, despite his ability to write pointed assessments of authors and magazines as he has for other publications. Graphically, *Pulp* is not ambitious. The text is everything; artwork is often mere decoration. Cover reproductions are the rule. However, *Pulp*'s premier cover artist, Franklyn Hamilton, whose work has appeared regularly since 1973, was a Weinberg discovery, and Hamilton's work has appeared in virtually every pulp-interest publication since then.

The character of *Pulp*'s articles were an important step forward. Instead of the nostalgic reminiscences of past fanzines, its pages have contained well-researched, probing analyses—with little unfounded conjecture. Important interviews with writers like Walter B. Gibson and Frederick C. Davis have appeared with regularity. If its focus seems limited only to the single-character magazines (the so-called hero pulps), *Pulp* has covered those magazines with single-minded relentlessness.

In its more than a decade of erratic publication, *Pulp* has managed to achieve several coups. The most valuable of these was probably "An Inside Look at Captain Future," in which that character's creator provided an important look at the genesis of *Captain Future* magazine, including a review of unpublished original writings. *Pulp* number 5-1/2, a special issue, carried Philip Jose Farmer's "Writing Doc's Biography," an exclusive article on Farmer's book, *Doc Savage: His Apocalyptic Life*. Beginning with issue number 13, the magazine began a series of bibliographic articles based on the actual files of Popular Publications. These promise to clear up a number of authorship questions pertaining to long-running series such as The Spider and Operator #5. The magazine has also reprinted occasional short stories, including all of the unreprinted Avenger novelettes.

Under the name of "Pulp Classics," Weinberg has also spun off a series of reprints of magazines such as *The Octopus,* Secret Agent X,* The Phantom Detective,** and several anthology titles. Most importantly, several of these booklets have been original studies of major pulp magazine characters, written by *Pulp* contributors, all exhaustive assessments.

Weinberg is also known for his 1971 *Hero Pulp Index* (compiled with Lohr McKinstry), in which all the major series were first indexed.

Information Sources

INDEX SOURCES: None known.

LOCATION SOURCES: Private collectors.

Publication History

MAGAZINE TITLE: *Pulp*.
TITLE CHANGES: None.
VOLUME AND ISSUE DATA: No. 1 (Fall 1970) through no. 13 (to date, Fall 1981); 14 issues (one issue number "5-1/2").
PUBLISHER: Robert Weinberg, 15145 Oxford Drive, Oak Forest, Illinois 60452.
EDITOR: Robert Weinberg.
PRICE PER ISSUE: $2.00; as of issue no. 13, $2.50.
SIZE AND PAGINATION: 8-1/2" X 11" (nos. 1-5-1/2); 5-1/2" X 8-1/2"; average 32 pages.
CURRENT STATUS: Active, irregular.
—*Will Murray*

PULP ERA, THE

One of the outstanding periodicals devoted to the pulp magazines, this was published for sixteen issues, commencing with one titled *JD-Argassy (The Pulp Era)*. The editor and publisher had previously produced fifty-nine issues of a "fannish" type of magazine under several different titles, the last of which was *JD-Argassy*, which carried the subtitle of "The Pulp Era"; announcement was made that "if you are a faaaanish fan and not interested in science fiction and the old pulp magazines, *The Pulp Era* will not be the zine for you. . . . *The Pulp Era* will be a serious fanzine devoted to the old pulp magazines and the new books of science fiction and fantasy."[1]

The contents of succeeding issues featured many articles, commentaries, reminiscences, bibliographies, and checklists of the pulp magazines in the mystery and detective field, as well as some in science fiction, espionage, war and hero pulps, and general short story pulp magazines.

Although discontinued in the spring of 1971, there is some thought, the editor advises, of reviving the publication.

Note

1. Editorial, *JD-Argassy*, no. 60 (Winter 1963), p. 4.

Information Sources

INDEX SOURCES: None known.
LOCATION SOURCES: Private collectors.

Publication History

MAGAZINE TITLE: *The Pulp Era*.
TITLE CHANGES: *JD-Argassy (The Pulp Era)* (issue no. 60 only; previous issues under various titles consisted of more personalized fan-related material).
VOLUME AND ISSUE DATA: No. 60 (Winter 1963) through no. 75 (Spring 1971); 16 issues.

PUBLISHER: Lynn Hickman, present address 413 Ottokee Street, Wauseon, Ohio 43567.
EDITOR: Lynn Hickman.
PRICE PER ISSUE: 50 cents.
SIZE AND PAGINATION: 8-1/2'' X 11''; 22–130 pages.
CURRENT STATUS: Discontinued.

PULPETTE

The first, and only, issue of *Pulpette* to date featured a short detective novelette written in what the author thought might be the style and format if the pulps were still being published today. It was illustrated with many reproductions from the old magazines; front and back covers were produced by the color-Xerox process.

Information Sources

INDEX SOURCES: None known.
LOCATION SOURCES: Private collectors.

Publication History

MAGAZINE TITLE: *Pulpette.*
TITLE CHANGES: None.
VOLUME AND ISSUE DATA: No. 1, (to date, 1981); 1 issue.
PUBLISHER: Joseph Lewandowski, 26502 Calle San Francisco, San Juan Capistrano, California 92675.
EDITOR: Joseph Lewandowski.
PRICE PER ISSUE: $4.00.
SIZE AND PAGINATION: 8-1/2'' X 11''; 30 pages.
CURRENT STATUS: Active.
—*Joseph Lewandowski*

PURSUIT DETECTIVE STORY MAGAZINE

Take eight or nine unvarnished, no-nonsense tales of tough, uninhibited characters on the wrong side of the law, add unscrupulous females, stir in a good variety of veteran pulp magazine authors, blend behind garish, lurid, violence-dominated covers, squeeze to digest-size, and print on rough, pulp paper. Then simmer while the public decides that this is still what they desire.

This is what Star Publications did in 1953, refusing to recognize that not only was the pulp-size magazine an anachronism but that the style of story prevalent in them in the 1940s was also past its prime. But, apparently, so did the reading public, since *Pursuit Detective Story Magazine* survived for three years and eighteen issues, as did a companion magazine *(Hunted Detective Story Magazine,** commencing December 1954) published on alternate months.

Pursuit and *Hunted* were, in essence, the same magazine, with two titles. The style, logo, and intent was the same.

The editor commented in the first issue of *Pursuit* that "*Pursuit* is not for the squeamish, and it definitely is not designed for those readers who are looking for 'just another detective story magazine.' While we hope never to be guilty of bad taste, we have thrown most of the editorial taboos out the window, and, thus unfettered, we are able to present the devotee of superior crime fiction with a truly different kind of magazine."[1]

Promising to present "stand-out examples of adult detective fiction at its top-level best," with balance attained by "accenting variety—variety in plot and mood and setting, in writing styles and length and pace,"[2] the editor hoped for word-of-mouth advertising to make the magazine a success.

If *Pursuit* was different from much of what had preceded it, in other magazines, it was different only as to its contemporary setting. This was crime adventure in the raw, peopled with characters of questionable conscience and less ethics, scrambling with avarice for money, power, and women. Or domestic situations exploding into hell. It was what good people imagaine bad people do. It was fast-moving murder and mayhem set in mean streets and grubby motel rooms, the littered bedrooms and the smoke-filled hideouts.

Despite the style and subject matter, a long list of experienced authors gave it their best. The first issue led with Craig Rice's "The Last Man Alive," and Evan Hunter contributed "The Reluctant Hostess." Jonathan Craig was there with "The Corpse That Came Back," as well as Charles Beckman, Jr., Tedd Thomey, Elston Barrett, John C. Fleming, and others.

The pattern continued. Frank Kane's "It's A Murder" and William Vance's "Occupational Hazard" were very good in the second issue (November 1953). Bryce Walton's "End of Night" and "I Killed Jeannie" by Evan Hunter should also be noted. Robert Turner, Dan Sontup, Fletcher Flora, Johnston McCulley, Robert Carlton, Stephen Marlowe, Grover Brinkman, Mel Colton, Norman Struber, and many others who had been prominent names in the pulp magazines were present in *Pursuit*.

There was little change in the direction of the magazine during its existence. Commencing with the sixth issue, articles were included on aspects of crime and the underworld, and an occasional true-crime story appeared.

Pursuit was itself caught, however, in its unwillingness to change, and both it and its sister magazine, *Hunted*, were laid to rest in 1956. The last issue of *Pursuit* was dated November of that year.

Notes

1. Editorial announcement, *Pursuit Detective Story Magazine*, no. 1 (September 1953), reverse front cover.
2. Ibid.

Information Sources

INDEX SOURCES: Cook, Michael L. *Monthly Murders*. Westport, Conn.: Greenwood Press, 1982.

LOCATION SOURCES: Private collectors.

Publication History

MAGAZINE TITLE: *Pursuit Detective Story Magazine.*

TITLE CHANGES: None.

VOLUME AND ISSUE DATA: No. 1 (September 1953) through no. 18 (November 1956); 18 issues.

PUBLISHER: Star Publications (Editions), Inc., 1 Appleton Street, Holyoke, Massachusetts, with editorial offices at 545 Fifth Avenue, New York 17, New York; J. A. Kramer, publisher, for first 15 issues; Leonard B. Cole, 2 issues; Robert Sproul, 1 issue.

EDITORS: Leonard B. Cole, with Phyllis Faren, associate editor, for first 15 issues; last three issues, George Peltz, editor, and Kit Carroll, associate editor.

PRICE PER ISSUE: 35 cents.

SIZE AND PAGINATION: 5-3/8'' X 7-3/8''; 128 pages.

CURRENT STATUS: Discontinued.

Q

QUEEN CANON BIBLIOPHILE, THE

One of the earliest amateur mystery magazines was *The Queen Canon Bibliophile* published by Reverend Robert E. Washer. Reverend Washer, a "compulsive lover of the mystery/suspense field, Ellery Queen in particular," is an American Baptist clergyman graduated from Colgate University where he was a major in English ("primarily literature"), and he obtained his B.D. degree from Colgate Rochester Divinity School. He studied at the Institute of Pastoral Care, Gowanda State Hospital (Buffalo, New York), Union Theological Seminary (New York, New York), the Divinity School of Yale University, and the Rochester Center of Theological Studies. A teaching associate at the American Baptist convention, he was also president of the Oneida Council of Churches and director of the Baptist New York State Youth Conference at Keuka College, as well as an active participant in other educational work.

The Queen Canon Bibliophile was dedicated "to the critical appreciation of Ellery Queen. . .as novelist. . .editor. . .scholar."[1] The first issue in November 1968 promised the "publication of articulate attitudes, reactions, reviews and comments with reference to our highly regarded subject matter."[2] The wish was expressed that the readers would keep in touch and share their comments.

Under Reverend Washer's devoted interest, the journal published well-written and researched articles on aspects of the Queen stories and background; the author(s), Frederic Dannay and Manfred B. Lee; pastiches; news and reviews of pertinent books; bibliographical articles, including on *Ellery Queen's Mystery Magazine**; and letters from the readers. One of the most important contributions was a serialized presentation of what was apparently an early draft of *Royal Bloodline: Ellery Queen, Author and Detective* (published in 1974 by Bowling

Green University Popular Press, Bowling Green, Ohio), by Francis M. Nevins, Jr.

Although commencing as a quarterly, the magazine became somewhat irregular as the schedule changed to but two issues a year. With the eighth issue, the title was changed to *The Ellery Queen Review* (October 1971), but only the last issue appeared with this name.

Notes

1. Editorial announcement, *The Queen Canon Bibliophile*, Vol. 1, no. 1 (n.d. [1968]), p. 1.
2. Ibid.

Information Sources

BIBLIOGRAPHY:

Nevins, Francis M., Jr. *Royal Bloodline: Ellery Queen, Author and Detective*. Bowling Green, Ohio: Bowling Green University Popular Press, 1974.

INDEX SOURCES: None known.

LOCATION SOURCES: Private collectors.

Publication History

MAGAZINE TITLE: *The Queen Canon Bibliophile*.

TITLE CHANGES: *The Ellery Queen Review* (with Vol. 3, no. 2 [October 1971]).

VOLUME AND ISSUE DATA: Vol. 1, no. 1 (November 1968) through Vol. 3, no. 2 (October 1971); 8 issues.

PUBLISHER: Rev. Robert E. Washer. 82 East Eighth Street, Oneida Castle, New York 13421.

EDITOR: Rev. Robert E. Washer.

PRICE PER ISSUE: Originally designed as complimentary in return for contributions; by subscription commencing July 1970, $2.00 per year.

SIZE AND PAGINATION: 8-1/2'' X 11''; 14–28 pages.

CURRENT STATUS: Discontinued.

R

RACKETEER AND GANGLAND STORIES

At least one issue of *Racketeer and Gangland Stories*, a pulp magazine, was published in May 1932.[1] No other information is available.

Notes

1. Title listed in "Tentative Pulp Checklist" from the San Francisco Academy of Comic Art, (unpublished manuscript, n.d.).

Information Sources

INDEX SOURCES: None known.
LOCATION SOURCES: Private collectors.

Publication History

MAGAZINE TITLE: *Racketeer and Gangland Stories*.
TITLE CHANGES: None known.
VOLUME AND ISSUE DATA: At least one issue (May 1932); number of issues and extent unknown.
PUBLISHER: Not known.
EDITOR: Not known.
PRICE PER ISSUE: Not known.
SIZE AND PAGINATION: Not known.
CURRENT STATUS: Discontinued.

RACKETEER STORIES

All the Federal Bureau of Investigation and the other government undercover agencies had to contend with in the '30s's were John Dillinger,

Machine Gun Kelly, Ma Barker, Baby Face Nelson and the spies Hitler
sent over. In real life anyway. In the pulps it was a much harder life and
the occupational hazards were monumental. Next to the masked mystery
men, nobody in the Depression years' pulp magazines had more troubles
than the spies and secret agents.[1]

The late 1920s and early 1930s had produced a fictional crop of romanticized
gangsters that enjoyed a remarkable amount of success in perpetrating their
sometimes flamboyant deeds. This is certainly understandable when gangs were
able to amass wealth while everyone else was struggling even to keep a job,
and such follows the glamour that is often attributed, albeit mistakenly, to those
who break the law and get away with it.

A flurry of magazines, always quick to recognize and pursue a trend, appeared
with tales of underworld life. Harold B. Hersey, who, with associates, had
published his first group of four magazines (*Flying Aces, The Dragnet,* * *Western
Trails,* and *Under Fire Stories*) and who had taken over *Underworld Magazine
(Underworld, The* *)* soon after, promptly added more titles of similar nature as
soon as financial considerations could be met.

Racketeer Stories commenced in a bad month,[2] December 1929, and was
continued at least through August 1930. Hersey was careful in all of his gangster
magazines that the good hero always won out over the bad hero. The good hero
was usually epitomized as an innocent party who had been involved—perhaps
even joining the gang—to revenge a friend's death, regain lost savings, and
always rescue the beautiful maiden who had become snared by the gangsters.

Racketeer Stories was published as a "Blue Band Publication," along with
a lengthy group of other titles carrying this identification.

Notes

1. Ron Goulart, *Cheap Thrills* (New Rochelle, N.Y.: Arlington House, 1972), p. 85.
2. "The average pulp is launched in the late summer so as to benefit by a running start when
cold weather comes. Sales rise toward November, lapse in December, increase again after the New
Year festivities are over, reaching their peak just before the spring breaks...." Harold B. Hersey,
Pulpwood Editor (New York: Frederick A. Stokes Co., 1937).

Information Sources

BIBLIOGRAPHY:
Hersey, Harold B. *Pulpwood Editor*. New York: Frederick A. Stokes Co., 1937.
INDEX SOURCES: None known.
LOCATION SOURCES: Private collectors.

Publication History

MAGAZINE TITLE: *Racketeer Stories*.

TITLE CHANGES: None known.
VOLUME AND ISSUE DATA: Vol. 1, no. 1 (December 1929) through at least August
    1930; number of issues and extent unknown.
PUBLISHER: Blue Band Publications, Inc., New York, New York.
EDITOR: Not known.
PRICE PER ISSUE: Not known.
SIZE AND PAGINATION: 7" × 10"; number of pages unknown.
CURRENT STATUS: Discontinued.

RACKET STORIES

Racket Stories is a pulp magazine title on which no information is available.[1]
It was possibly published in the 1930s.

Notes

1. Title listed in "Tentative Pulp Checklist" from the San Francisco Academy of Comic Art
(unpublished manuscript, n.d.).

Information Sources

INDEX SOURCES: None known.
LOCATION SOURCES: Private collectors.

Publication History

MAGAZINE TITLE: *Racket Stories*.
TITLE CHANGES: None known.
VOLUME AND ISSUE DATA: Not known.
PUBLISHER: Not known.
EDITOR: Not known.
PRICE PER ISSUE: Not known.
SIZE AND PAGINATION: Not known.
CURRENT STATUS: Discontinued.

RAILROAD DETECTIVE STORIES

Pulp magazines were generated as the popular culture demanded, and writers
were quickly put to work to churn out stories utilizing whatever was current.
Railroad Detective Stories[1] was obviously such a venture. No information is
available, however, on this title. It is probable there was but one issue.

Notes

1. Title listed in "Tentative Pulp Checklist" from the San Francisco Academy of Comic Art
(unpublished manuscript, n.d.).

Information Sources

INDEX SOURCES: None known.

LOCATION SOURCES: Private collectors.

Publication History

MAGAZINE TITLE: *Railroad Detective Stories*.
TITLE CHANGES: None known.
VOLUME AND ISSUE DATA: Not known.
PUBLISHER: Not known.
EDITOR: Not known.
PRICE PER ISSUE: Not known.
SIZE AND PAGINATION: Not known.
CURRENT STATUS: Discontinued.

RAPID-FIRE DETECTIVE STORIES

Rapid-Fire Detective Stories, a pulp detective magazine, commenced with the October 1932 issue and continued at least through May 1933, a companion to *Rapid-Fire Western Stories* published by the same company. No other information is available.

Information Sources

INDEX SOURCES: None known.
LOCATION SOURCES: University of California-Los Angeles Library (Vol. 1, no. 1, only); private collectors.

Publication History

MAGAZINE TITLE: *Rapid-Fire Detective Stories*.
TITLE CHANGES: None known.
VOLUME AND ISSUE DATA: Vol. 1, no. 1 (October 1932) through at least May 1933; number of issues and extent unknown.
PUBLISHER: Rapid-Fire Publishers, Inc., New York, New York.
EDITOR: Not known.
PRICE PER ISSUE: Not known.
SIZE AND PAGINATION: Not known.
CURRENT STATUS: Discontinued.

REAL DETECTIVE

See DETECTIVE TALES (RURAL PUBLICATIONS)

REAL DETECTIVE TALES

See DETECTIVE TALES (RURAL PUBLICATIONS)

REAL DETECTIVE TALES AND MYSTERY STORIES

See DETECTIVE TALES (RURAL PUBLICATIONS)

REAL MYSTERY

See UNCANNY TALES

REAL WESTERN MYSTERY NOVELS

Real Western Mystery Novels was a short-lived title from Doubleday, Doran & Company.[1] No other information is available.

Notes

1. Title listed in "Tentative Pulp Checklist" from San Francisco Academy of Comic Art (unpublished manuscript, n.d.).

Information Sources

INDEX SOURCES: None known.
LOCATION SOURCES: Private collectors.

Publication History

MAGAZINE TITLE: *Real Western Mystery Novels*.
TITLE CHANGES: None known.
VOLUME AND ISSUE DATA: Number of issues, date, and extent unknown.
PUBLISHER: Doubleday, Doran & Co., New York, New York.
EDITOR: Not known.
PRICE PER ISSUE: Not known.
SIZE AND PAGINATION: Not known.
CURRENT STATUS: Discontinued.

RED HERRINGS (BRITISH)

Red Herrings, the news-bulletin of the Crime Writers' Association (CWA) of Great Britain, is at the time of this writing in its twenty-sixty year of publication. It is produced monthly, and no issue has ever been missed in all its years of existence; it acheived its three hundredth issue in August 1981.

Red Herrings was launched in July 1956 by crime writer and CWA member Herbert Harris, who remained its honorary editor for nearly nine years and served as such at additional various times. Other honorary editors (and CWA members) throughout its life have included Anne Britton, H. L. Lawrence, Martin Russell, and, jointly, the current editors, Alex Auswaks and Leo Harris.

For their long service as *Red Herrings* honorary editors, both Herbert Harris and Anne Britton received the Association's "Gold Dagger" (Special Merit) Awards in 1964 and 1975 respectively. In 1967, a further Gold Dagger Award was made to Charles Franklin for his honorary editorship of the *Crime Writer* (a series of bulletins covering the CWA's Annual Awards and distributed at the Annual Awards Dinners), a publication which ran in conjunction with *Red Herrings* from 1956 but which was abandoned after ten years' annual publication.

Since the inception of *Red Herrings*, it has mirrored the development over the past quarter-century of the British crime writing scene, providing the news and views of leading British crime writers, together with those of American and other overseas members of the CWA. It has played a leading role in furthering the growth of the Crime Writers' Association, one of the U.K.'s most lively literary coteries, having achieved a membership of more than four hundred.

The Association came into being on November 5, 1953, when John Creasey called together fourteen crime writers for a preliminary meeting. The fourteen founders were: John Creasey (chairman), Josephine Bell, John Bude, Ernest Dudley, Elizabeth Ferrars, Andrew Garve, Michael Gilbert, Bruce Graeme, Leonard Gribble, T.C.H. Jacobs, Frank King, Nigel Morland, Colin Robertson, and Julian Symons.

The founder, John Creasey, remained chairman from 1953 to 1956, followed in the chair by Bruce Graeme, Julian Symons, Josephine Bell, T.C.H. Jacobs, Van Gielgud, Charles Franklin, John Boland, Michael Underwood, Philip McCutchan, Berkely Mather, Gavin Lyall, Miles Tripp, Herbert Harris, H.R.F. Keating, John Bingham, Christianna Brand, Dick Francis, Kenneth Benton, Jean Bowden, Duncan Kyle, Elizabeth Ferrars, Donald Rumbelow, Margaret Yorke, Penelope Wallace, and Basil Copper (chairman until May 1982).

Since its foundation in 1953, the Crime Writers' Association has sponsored the publication of twenty collections of short stories by its members. The first five appeared between 1956 and 1964, the earliest being *Butcher's Dozen* (Heinemann), edited by Josephine Bell, Michael Gilbert, and Julian Symons. Then came, all from Hodder & Stoughton: *Planned Departure*, edited by Elizabeth Ferrars; *Choice of Weapons*, edited by Michael Gilbert; and *Some Like Them Dead* and *Crime Writers' Choice*, both edited by Roy Vickers, who had assumed the mantle of the CWA's honorary anthology editor.

In 1965, three events happened to affect the future of CWA anthologies. Roy Vickers died, and Herbert Harris succeeded him as honorary anthology editor. Then John Creasey, the Association's founder, went over to the CWA *John Creasey's Mystery Bedside Book*, which had been published annually by Hodder & Stoughton for the six years of 1960 to 1965.

In 1966, *John Creasey's Mystery Bedside Book* became the Association's anthology, and Hodder & Stoughton published ten volumes under that title, all edited by Herbert Harris, between 1966 and 1976. In 1977, under the new title of *John Creasey's Crime Collection*, the anthology joined the list of Victor Gollancz (already publishers of the CWA's transatlantic sister organization's anthologies, those of the Mystery Writers of America).

Gollancz published *John Creasey's Crime Collections* in 1978, 1979, 1980, and 1981, all sponsored by the CWA and all edited by Herbert Harris, who compiled a further collection for 1982.

Another excellent publication to appear under the banner of the Crime Writers' Association was *Crime in Good Company*, a collection of essays on criminals and crime writing collected by Michael Gilbert and published on behalf of the CWA by Constable.

Finally, one must not forget the brilliant series of "Crime Background" pamphlets, compiled and edited on behalf of CWA members by Gavin Lyall, which won him the CWA's Gold Dagger Award in 1970. The nine pamphlets provided detailed information on police procedure, pistols, prosecutions, forensic medicine, fakes and forgeries, intelligence, drugs and drug traffic, industrial espionage, and what the human body can stand.

Information Sources

INDEX SOURCES: None known.
LOCATION SOURCES: Private collectors and authors.

Publication History

MAGAZINE TITLE: *Red Herrings*.
TITLE CHANGES: None
VOLUME AND ISSUE DATA: No. 1 (July 1956) through no. 304 (to date, December 1981); 304 issues.
PUBLISHER: Crime Writer's Association, c/o Marian Babson, Secretary, 42 Trinity Court, Gray's Inn Road, London WC1 8JZ, England.
EDITORS: Herbert Harris, Anne Britton, H. L. Lawrence, Martin Russell, Alex Auswaks, and Leo Harris.
PRICE PER ISSUE: Distributed to members of CWA only.
CURRENT STATUS: Active.
—*Herbert Harris*

RED HOOD DETECTIVE STORIES

See RED MASK DETECTIVE STORIES

RED MASK DETECTIVE STORIES

In spite of the title's promise, *Red Mask Detective Stories* was not a single-character publication but a bimonthly collection of short detective fiction. Of eight stories, two were fractionally longer than the others and so were acclaimed as a short novel and a novelette. Most were by obscure writers, and most were sluggish trivialities.

The lead novel, about twenty-six pages long, was written by Stanley Richards and featured the Red Mask, a tall, mysterious being with jagged teeth, glaring eyes, and some sort of a mask. The inept cover drawing shows the Mask wearing a loose bag pulled over the head; the narrative merely says that he wore a mask.

With the red mask/hood/bag removed, the man disguised was Perry Morgan, a bright young fellow with a taste for unofficial investigation. Sole owner of the famous Hotel Jefferson, his pleasure was to slip about ineptly, with a pistol in his pocket and good will for mankind in his heart. In no way was Morgan a superhero. Indeed, he was barely competent.

The Red Mask stories are slight, ambling entertainments, full of realistic dialogue spiced by occasional, not-so-realistic action scenes. The action takes quite a while to get off the ground, and the suspense generated is hardly enough to stir the most excitable reader.

Perhaps for this reason, *Red Mask Detective Stories* changed its title with the third issue, becoming *Red Hood Detective Stories* (July 1941). That issue featured the usual stories, the department called "The Handwriting Sleuth," and a full-page message from the editor, assuring readers that the title change had not changed the magazine while predicting innovations in magazine presentation.

Part of the innovations were in the July issue—the first page of each story was set single column, straight across the page, just like a book. Another part of the innovations was to come: the magazine's pages would be numbered consecutively for six issues, so that they would be in sequence if bound into a volume.

However, *Red Hood Detective Stories* never saw a second issue, and all of the editor's intricate plans were for naught. According to the Weinberg *The Hero Pulp Index* (1971), Perry Morgan put on the red mask once more. His final appearance is in still another magazine, *Movie Detective*,* "The Maori Murder Case" (January 1943).

Information Sources

INDEX SOURCES: Weinberg, Robert, and Lohr McKinstry. *The Hero Pulp Index.* Evergreen, Colo.: Opar Press, 1971.
LOCATION SOURCES: University of California*Los Angeles (*Red Mask*, Vol. 1, no. 1; *Red Hood,* Vol. 1, no. 1); private collectors.

Publication History

MAGAZINE TITLE: *Red Mask Detective Stories.*
TITLE CHANGES: *Red Hood Detective Stories* (with third issue; numbering not continued).
VOLUME AND ISSUE DATA: *Red Mask Detective Stories,* Vol. 1, no. 1 (March 1941) through Vol. 1, no. 2 (May 1941); 2 issues. *Red Hood Detective Stories,* Vol. 1, no. 1 (July 1941); 1 issue.
PUBLISHER: Albing Publications, 1 Appleton Street, Holyoke, Massachusetts.
EDITOR: Jerry Albert.
PRICE PER ISSUE: 15 cents.
SIZE AND PAGINATION: 7" X 9-7/8"; 114 pages.
CURRENT STATUS: Discontinued.
—*Robert Sampson*

RED SEAL DETECTIVE STORIES

Red Seal Detective Stories, a pulp magazine title, was published by Periodical House, Inc. No other information is available.

Information Sources

INDEX SOURCES: None known.
LOCATION SOURCES: Private collectors.

Publication History

MAGAZINE TITLE: *Red Seal Detective Stories*.
TITLE CHANGES: None known.
VOLUME AND ISSUE DATA: Not known.
PUBLISHER: Periodical House, Inc., 29 Worthington Street, Springfield, Massachusetts, with editorial offices at 23 West 47th Street, New York, New York.
EDITOR: Not known.
PRICE PER ISSUE: Not known.
SIZE AND PAGINATION: Not known.
CURRENT STATUS: Discontinued.

RED SEAL MYSTERY

RED SEAL MYSTERY commenced publication in June 1940, by Periodical House, Inc. Other magazines utilizing the "Red Seal" in their titles, by the same company, were the *Red Seal Detective Stories* and *Red Seal Western*. No other information is available.

Information Sources

INDEX SOURCES: None known.
LOCATION SOURCES: Private collectors.

Publication History

MAGAZINE TITLE: *Red Seal Mystery*.
TITLE CHANGES: None known.
VOLUME AND ISSUE DATA: Vol. 1, no. 1 (June 1940); number of issues and extent unknown.
PUBLISHER: Periodical House, Inc., 29 Worthington Street, Springfield, Massachusetts, with editorial offices at 23 West 47th Street, New York, New York.
EDITOR: Not known.
PRICE PER ISSUE: Not known.

SIZE AND PAGINATION: Not known.
CURRENT STATUS: Discontinued.

RED STAR DETECTIVE

See DETECTIVE DIME NOVELS

RED STAR MYSTERY

One of a swarm of Red Star (Munsey) titles unleashed in 1940, *Red Star Mystery* featured the novel-length mystery adventures of Don Diavolo, the Scarlet Wizard. The tales were by Stuart Towne, a pseudonym of Clayton Rawson, author of four books and many short stories about another magician character, The Great Merlini.

Don Diavolo's four adventures were, in order: "Ghost of the Undead," "Death Out of Thin Air," "The Claws of Satan," and "The Enchanted Dagger." Announced but never published was "Murder from the Grave." Diavolo was also an off-stage character mentioned in Rawson's 1942 Merlini novel, "No Coffin for the Corpse." In fact, Rawson enjoyed sprinkling clues about his characters and pen name in his work; Stuart Towne was mentioned in another Rawson novel, "The Headless Lady," and Merlini's Magic Shop was named in one Diavolo tale.

Don Diavolo was a professional stage magician on the order of Blackstone. He often appeared on Broadway, astounding audiences with his vanishing princess and elephant and other grand illusions, and maintained a workshop in Greenwich Village, where he worked with his technical assistant, Karl Hartz.

Others in the Diavolo company included the twin sisters, Pat and Mickey Collins, who were under orders never to appear together in public lest the secret of some of his illusions be given away. One twin or another usually wore a dark wig—which one was anybody's guess. Rounding out the cast were The Horseshoe Kid, a friendly gambler; Chan the Eurasian boy; "Woody" Haines, a Broadway columnist; and Inspector Church of homicide.

Clayton Rawson, who worked at various times in the editorial departments of *True Detective, Master Detective,* and *Ellery Queen's Mystery Magazine,** wrote the Diavolo stories soon after Merlini was published in hardcover, hence the frequent cross-references.

All four Diavolo novels were reportedly reprinted: the first two as *Death Out of Thin Air* (Coward-McCann, 1941) and the second two as *Death From Nowhere* (Wiegers Publishing Company, n.d.).

Each issue of *Red Star Mystery* also featured a novelette by G. T. Fleming-Roberts, who later wrote the Captain Zero stories for Popular Publications and several short stories. The magazine's covers had distinctive white borders, red-and-blue lettering, and, adding Diavolo's brazen red costume, were quite striking.

Information Sources

BIBLIOGRAPHY:

Briney, Robert E. "Don Diavolo (The Scarlet Wizard)," *The Pulp Era*, no. 64 (July/August 1968): 14–15.

Nevins, Francis M., Jr. "The Diavolo Quartet." *The Armchair Detective*, Vol. 3, no. 4 (July 1970): 243–44; and *Xenophile*, no. 3 (May 1974): n.p.

INDEX SOURCES: Briney, Robert E. "Red Star Mystery Index." *The Pulp Era*. no. 64 (July/August 1968): 16.

LOCATION SOURCES: University of California–Los Angeles Library (Vol. 1, no. 1, only); private collectors.

Publication History

MAGAZINE TITLE: *Red Star Mystery*.
TITLE CHANGES: None.
VOLUME AND ISSUE DATA: Vol. 1, no. 1 (June 1940) through Vol. 1, no. 4 (December 1940); 4 issues.
PUBLISHER: The Frank A. Munsey Co., 280 Broadway, New York, New York.
EDITOR: Not known.
PRICE PER ISSUE: 10 cents.
SIZE AND PAGINATION: 7" X 10"; 112 pages.
CURRENT STATUS: Discontinued.
—*Bernard A. Drew*

REX STOUT MYSTERY MAGAZINE

See REX STOUT'S MYSTERY MONTHLY

REX STOUT MYSTERY QUARTERLY

See REX STOUT'S MYSTERY MONTHLY

REX STOUT'S MYSTERY MONTHLY

In June 1943, several months after Avon Book Company acquired paperback rights to three early Nero Wolfe novels and found that they sold well, Avon told Rex Stout that they would like to publish a digest-size mystery magazine to be called *Rex Stout's Mystery Monthly*. In addition to allowing the magazine to bear his name, Stout would write an introduction for each issue and be carried as editor-in-chief. Louis Greenfield, whom Stout knew as a fellow member of the Baker Street Irregulars (see *Baker Street Journal*, The*), was named managing editor of the new magazine and given the responsibility of choosing the contents of each issue. Recommendations from Stout about what to include or exclude would weigh heavily when the final selection was made.

The magazine's publication did not occur until 1945, in May and August, making its first two appearances as a quarterly, a factor that necessitated a change in title from that chosen originally (to *Rex Stout Mystery Quarterly*). During 1946, its most regular year, the magazine was published in February, March, June, October, and December. With issue number 3 that year, reflecting its greater frequency of appearance, the magazine acquired a new title, now becoming *Rex Stout Mystery Magazine*. Yet with the fifth issue, it reverted to the originally chosen but never used title, *Rex Stout's Mystery Monthly*. This remained its title through the remaining period of its existence. Only two issues appeared in 1947. The eighth issue was released in May, and the ninth issue, assigned no designation by month, also was dated 1947; with that issue, publication ceased.

Although, with his duties as chairman of the Writers' War Board in 1945, and, after that, with his duties as chairman of the Writers' Board for World Government, Rex Stout was too busy to concern himself much with the magazine that bore his name, he did use his editorial post as a forum where he could discuss matters of concern for him. Thus, in the February 1946 issue, he rebuked Edmund Wilson for his ranting onslaughts against detective fiction. In October 1946, he offered some shrewd comments on the merits of Hercule Poirot. In the same issue, he emphasized that characterization, as well as plot and method of narration, is important in a detective story.

Only two of Stout's own stories, "Black Orchids" and "Help Wanted, Male," were published in this run of magazines. At that time, Stout had written few Nero Wolfe novellas. He was successful, however, in persuading his friend, Christopher LaFarge, to write an original detective story for the eighth issue. The sixth issue, October 1946, featured "Operation Luella," a new Saint story by Leslie Charteris. A few other stories by writers of lesser reputation also appeared first in this series of magazines. Most of the reprinted stories were the work of authors of established reputation, among them, Steinbeck, Fitzgerald, Cain, Lardner, Crofts, R. Austin Freeman, Lovecraft, Hammett, Chandler, Carr, Irish, Blackwood, Christie, Ambler, Orczy, and Sayers.

Information Sources

BIBLIOGRAPHY:
McAleer, John. *Rex Stout, A Biography*. Boston: Little, Brown, 1977.
INDEX SOURCES: Cook, Michael L. *Monthly Murders*. Westport, Conn.: Greenwood Press, 1982.
LOCATION SOURCES: University of California–Los Angeles Library (1945–1947, 2 issues); private collectors.

Publication History

MAGAZINE TITLE: *Rex Stout's Mystery Monthly*.
TITLE CHANGES: *Rex Stout's Mystery Quarterly* (Vol. 1, nos. 1 and 2); *Rex Stout Mystery Magazine* (Vol. 1, nos. 3 and 4).

VOLUME AND ISSUE DATA: Vol. 1, no. 1 (Spring 1945) through Vol. 1, no. 9 (no date [1947]); 9 issues.
PUBLISHER: Avon Book Company, 119 West 57th Street, New York, New York.
EDITOR: Rex Stout, editor-in-chief; Louis Greenfield, managing editor.
PRICE PER ISSUE: 25 cents.
SIZE AND PAGINATION: 5-3/8'' X 7-5/8''; 130–166 pages.
CURRENT STATUS: Discontinued.
—*John J. McAleer*

ROHMER REVIEW, THE

The Rohmer Review was founded in 1968 by Dr. Douglas A. Rossman, an associate professor of zoology at the Louisiana State University. The first four issues were published and edited by Dr. Rossman between July 1968 and March 1970. With issue number 5, published in August 1970, Robert E. Briney became the *Review's* editor and publisher. *The Rohmer Review* appeared regularly, twice a year, between 1968 and December 1973. Issues number 12 through number 17 appeared less regularly, and there was a lapse of four years between numbers 17 and 18.

The Rohmer Reivew, for all of its recent irregular appearance in print, is a highly professional effort to provide information about the writings of Sax Rohmer, best known for his Dr. Fu Manchu stories. Rohmer, a prolific writer, also wrote detective stories, novels of the occult, science fiction and fantasy, mysteries and adventure tales. While countless readers devoured his books, hardly a word of literary criticism or commentary appeared in print. The *Review* has endeavored to fill this void by including detailed bibliographic listings of Rohmer's works, radio adaptations of his stories, foreign translations, miscellany, plus an occasional attempt at humor. Thus it has become an invaluable source of information and data for the serious scholar as well as the Rohmer aficionado.

Articles on all aspects of Sax Rohmer's life and writings are printed, as well as reprints of interviews with Rohmer, occasional reprints of his short stories, reminiscences of people who knew him, and book news. Letters from readers and contributors are included, as are occasional photographs and illustrations. A random sampling of articles from *The Rohmer Review* shows the depth and variety of material that a fanzine focusing on one author and his works can provide. For example, issue number 2 provided "How Fu Manchu Was Born" by Sax Rohmer; number 5 had "Were Houdini's Feats Supernatural?" by Rohmer; and his "Live Instruments of Villainy" was in number 6. Issue number 9 printed the first U.S. edition of Rohmer's short story, "The Haunted Temple" and the text of one of his radio talks, "Meet Dr. Fu Manchu," was in number 10.

Articles from contributors range from Anice Page Cooper's "Sax Rohmer and the Art of Making Villains" in issue number 5; "The Politics of Fu Manchu" by Jim Pobst in number 10; number 12 provided both "Radio Fu Manchu," an article on the U.S. Fu Manchu radio series, by Ray Stanich, and a checklist of French editions of Rohmer's works. W.O.G. Lofts and R. E. Briney in number 11 wrote "Shhh! Dr. Fu Manchu Is On The Air!," this being an article and checklist on the British radio dramatizations of the Fu Manchu series, and "Musette, Max and Sumuru" in number 15, which included more information on British radio adaptations of Rohmer's work. Cay Van Ash, Rohmer's biographer, wrote "Seals Of The Si-Fan" for issue number 11, plus "Outselves and Gaston Max" and "A Question of Time" for numbers 15 and 17. There have been a few attempts at humor, such as "Fu Chin Chow," a humorous comic strip by Jack Gaughan, and Ron Goulart's "The Hand of Dr. Insidious."

The Rohmer Review is beautifully put together, using ancient Egyptian designs to mark the end of an article or to add balance and aesthetic appeal to its pages. As fanzines go, it is second only to *The Armchair Detective** in layout design and attractiveness. Furthermore, a fanzine is only as good as its editor and its contributors, and this one has provided a standard of excellence throughout its history in both respects.

Information Sources

BIBLIOGRAPHY:
Katz, Bill, and Barry G. Richards. *Magazines for Libraries*. 3d ed. New York: R. R. Bowker Co., 1978.
McSherry, Frank D., Jr. "Letter." *The Armchair Detective*, Vol. 7, no. 3 (May 1974): 230–31.
Townsend, Guy. "Mysteriously Speaking." *The Mystery Fancier*, Vol. 5, no. 6 (November/December 1981): 2.
INDEX SOURCES: None known.
LOCATION SOURCES: Private collectors.

Publication History

MAGAZINE TITLE: *The Rohmer Review*.
TITLE CHANGES: None.
VOLUME AND ISSUE DATA: No. 1 (July 1968) through no. 18 (to date, Spring/Summer 1981); 18 issues.
PUBLISHERS: Dr. Douglas A. Rossman, Louisiana State University (nos. 1–4); Robert E. Briney, 4 Forest Avenue, Salem, Massachusetts 01970.
EDITORS: Dr. Douglas A. Rossman (nos. 1–4); Robert E. Briney.
PRICE PER ISSUE: Currently $1.50.
SIZE AND PAGINATION: 5-1/2" X 8-1/2"; average 30 pages.
CURRENT STATUS: Active.
—*Jo Ann Vicarel*

ROMANTIC DETECTIVE

Despite the name, this Trojan Magazines title, which appeared on the newsstands with the February 1938 issue, presented stories that were perhaps more in the detective vein than the romance. A full-length novel was accompanied by several featured novelettes and one or two shorts stories. A typical issue of *Romantic Detective* included "Family Affair" (Roger Torrey), "The Cop Hates Murder" (Dale Clark), "Immodest Corpse" (James S. Moynahan), "Murder—Double or Nothing" (Laurence Donovan), and "Double Kick Back" (Robert Leslie Bellem). It was published at least into 1939 on a bimonthly schedule.

Information Sources

INDEX SOURCES: None known.

LOCATION SOURCES: University of California–Los Angeles Library (Vol. 1, no. 1, only); private collectors.

Publication History

MAGAZINE TITLE: *Romantic Detective*.

TITLE CHANGES: None known.

VOLUME AND ISSUE DATA: Vol. 1, no. 1 (February 1938) to at least in 1939; number of issues and extent unknown.

PUBLISHER: Frank Armor as Trojan Magazines, Inc., 125 East 46th Street, New York 17, New York.

EDITOR: Not known.

PRICE PER ISSUE: Not known.

SIZE AND PAGINATION: Not known.

CURRENT STATUS: Discontinued.

S

SAINT DETECTIVE MAGAZINE, THE

The Saint Detective Magazine was launched with the Spring 1953 issue as a quarterly, becoming bimonthly with the second issue and monthly with the September 1954 issue. It was named after the character created by Leslie Charteris and immediately found success with mystery fans by utilizing the program of publishing a Saint story in each issue, plus an offering of other short stories by recognized writers. Charteris, featured with a newsy column appearing on the inside-front cover of each issue, was shown as the supervising editor.

Simon Templar, as The Saint, first appeared from the pen of Charteris in 1928 in book form in *Meet the Tiger*. Here, The Saint is living in a converted pillbox in North Devon, near Baycombe, twenty-seven years old, tall, dark, keen-faced, deeply tanned, and with blue eyes. His athletic ability is developed here. The character of The Saint was shown as a gentleman crook who often took the law into his own hands to help those who had been victimized, swindled, or robbed— a modern day Robin Hood. He was portrayed as a romantic bachelor and adventurer. A number of The Saint stories appeared in the British weekly paper, *The Thriller* (British),* comencing in 1929.

Despite the crowded newsstands, the magazine continued to enjoy moderate success with the attraction of both old and new Saint stories; but with so many different magazines for the public to choose from, the popularity began to wane. With only a limited number of Saint stories to offer, including the new stories, features such as "Instead of the Saint" (Charteris's "mental meanderings"), "The Saint in Modern Art," and "As Others See Us" (comments by Charteris) began to appear. The name was changed to *The Saint Mystery Magazine* as of November 1958 and to *The Saint Magazine* as of May 1966. Hans Stefan Santesson was added as editor in May 1956, and his book review columns brought renewed interest. Some of The Saint stories were printed for the second time in the magazine. A change in publishers gave some spark of life in November 1959 and again in 1961; but with inadequate sales, the magazine was discontinued with the October 1967 issue. It remains, however, one of the more valuable runs of digest-size mystery magazines, and its contribution to the genre is of major importance.

Information Sources

BIBLIOGRAPHY:
Alexandersson, Jan, and Iwan Hedman. "Leslie Charteris and The Saint." Translated and edited by Carl Larsen, *The Mystery Fancier*, Vol. 4, no. 4 (July/August 1980): 21–27.
Hubin, Allen J. "Death of a Magazine." *The Armchair Detective*, Vol. 1, no. 2 (January 1968): 47.
Lofts, W.O.G., and Derek J. Adley. *The Saint and Leslie Charteris*. Bowling Green, Ohio: Bowling Green University Popular Press, 1972.
INDEX SOURCES: Cook, Michael L. *Monthly Murders*. Westport, Conn.: Greenwood Press, 1982.
LOCATION SOURCES: University of California–Los Angeles Library (1953–1964, 72 issues); private collectors.

Publication History

MAGAZINE TITLE: *The Saint Detective Magazine*.
TITLE CHANGES: *The Saint Mystery Magazine* (with November 1958 issue); *The Saint Magazine* (with May 1966 issue).
VOLUME AND ISSUE DATA: Vol. 1, no. 1 (Spring 1953) through Vol. 25, no. 6 (October 1967); 141 issues.
PUBLISHERS: Leo Margulies as King-Size Publications, Inc., 11 West 42nd Street, New York 36, New York, and later 320 Fifth Avenue, New York 1, New York. As of November 1959, Great American Publications, Inc., 270 Madison Avenue, New York 16, New York, and later 41 East 42nd Street, New York, New York. As of September 1961, Sales Publications, Inc., 320 Fifth Avenue, New York 1, New York, by arrangement with Saint Magazine, Inc. As of December 1961, Fiction Publishing Co., 331 Madison Avenue, New York 17, New York, and later 155 East 50th Street, New York, New York, by arrangement with Saint Magazine, Inc.
EDITORS: Sam Merwin, Jr., (1953-1959); Hans Stefan Santesson (1959–1967). (Leslie Charteris throughout credited as "supervising editor").
PRICE PER ISSUE: 50 cents (first 4 issues); 35 cents (until November 1963); 50 cents.
SIZE AND PAGINATION: 5-1/8" X 7-5/8"; 128–192 pages.
CURRENT STATUS: Discontinued.

British edition

MAGAZINE TITLE: *The Saint Detective Magazine*.
TITLE CHANGES: *The Saint Mystery Magazine* (with Vol. 6, no. 2); *The Saint Magazine* (with Vol. 12, no. 2).

VOLUME AND ISSUE DATA: Vol. 1, no. 1 (November 1954) through no. 153 (November 1966; with June 1966 issue, the volume and issue designation was replaced
with a "whole number" designation); 153 issues.
PUBLISHERS: Magazine Enterprises, 39 Martin Place, Sydney, Australia, and later 70
Bathurst Street and 149 Castlemeagh Street, Sydney, and distributed in England
by Atlas Publishing & Distributing Company Ltd., 18 Bride Lane, Fleet Street,
London E.C.4, England. With Vol. 6, no. 2, Atlas became the publisher by
arrangement with Great American Publications, Inc., of New York. Later issues
were licensed by Saint Magazines, Inc., Nassau, Bahamas. The British edition
suspended publication briefly in November 1960 and recommenced with Vol. 7,
no. 1, edited in the United States by Hans Stefan Santesson.
EDITOR: James Grant; Hans Stefan Santesson. (Throughout, the "supervising editor"
was listed as Leslie Charteris).
PRICE PER ISSUE: 1 shilling 6 pence (until January 1960); 2 shillings (until November
1961); 2 shillings 6 pence (until August 1964); 3 shillings (until February 1966);
3 shillings 6 pence thereafter.
SIZE AND PAGINATION: 5-3/8" X 7-1/2"; average 112 pages.
CURRENT STATUS: Discontinued.
Note: Some stories appeared first in the British edition, and some were published exclu-
sively in the British edition.

Other editions

French; Dutch.

SAINT DETECTIVE MAGAZINE, THE (British)

See SAINT DETECTIVE MAGAZINE, THE

SAINT MAGAZINE, THE

See SAINT DETECTIVE MAGAZINE, THE

SAINT MAGAZINE, THE (British)

See SAINT DETECTIVE MAGAZINE, THE

SAINT MYSTERY LIBRARY

The *Saint Mystery Library*, a hybrid, may be termed either a magazine or a
paperback book by some. With the editorial policy of *The Saint Mystery Magazine
(Saint Detective Magazine, The*)* changing the emphasis to new stories, the
Saint Mystery Library came into existence in August 1959; having no articles,
and produced in paperback format, it was actually an anthology series. It com-

bined stories from its parent magazine with original stories and stories from other sources. The series ran for fourteen issues. Strangely enough, the first is number 118, with the rest following in sequence. While numbered, each had an individual title, usually the featured story or novel.

The front cover featured the *Saint Mystery Library* imprint, number, and a stick figure of The Saint, with the phrase, "edited by Leslie Charteris," across the top. The remainder was either a painted picture or photograph with the title and author imposed over it. Other stories were listed at the bottom. Eight numbers had painted covers, the rest had photographs; the artwork was by Sussman (four covers), Frank Kalin (two covers), and Leonard Goldberg and Ted Coconis (one each).

The first two numbers were stories reprinted from *The Saint Mystery Magazine*. The third had an original story by John Jakes. He was the major contributor during the *Library*'s lifespan, with six stories, all featuring the same mysterious character, "Roger." Edward D. Hoch contributed two original Simon Ark stories. Talmage Powell, Lawrence Blackman, Harlan Ellison, and others made additional contributions of stories. Oddly enough, the Ellison story, "Find One Cuckaboo" (number 128), had been rejected by *The Saint Mystery Magazine*.

In all, *The Saint Mystery Library* printed fifty-one stories and novels consisting of twenty-five stories from its parent magazine and seventeen original stories, including one novel ("The Rum and Coca-Cola Murders" by Wenzell Brown). There were six stories from other sources (*Private Eye*,* three; *Black Mask*,* one; and *Double-Action Western*, two and three reprint novels. All were of the same high quality as the *Library*'s parent magazine.

Information Sources

BIBLIOGRAPHY:
Hill, M. C. "The Saint Mystery Library." *Paperback Quarterly*, Vol. 2, no. 4 (Winter 1979): 4–6.
INDEX SOURCES: Cook, Michael L. *Monthly Murders*. Westport, Conn.: Greenwood Press, 1982.
Hill, M. C. "The Saint Mystery Library." *Paperback Quarterly*, Vol. 2, no. 4 (Winter 1979): 4–6.
LOCATION SOURCES: Private collectors.

Publication History

MAGAZINE TITLE: *The Saint Mystery Library*.
VOLUME AND ISSUE DATA: Nos. 118–131, August 1959–March 1960; 14 issues.
TITLE CHANGES: None (each issue featured title of lead story).
PUBLISHER: Great American Publications, 270 Madison Avenue, New York 16, New York.
EDITOR: Leslie Charteris (actual editor unknown).
PRICE PER ISSUE: 35 cents.

SIZE AND PAGINATION: 4-1/4'' X 6-3/8'' (nos. 118–123); 4-1/4'' X 7-1/4'' (nos. 124–131); 160 pages.
CURRENT STATUS: Discontinued.
—*Paul Palmer*

SAINT MYSTERY MAGAZINE, THE

See SAINT DETECTIVE MAGAZINE, THE

SAINT MYSTERY MAGAZINE, THE (British)

See SAINT DETECTIVE MAGAZINE, THE

SAINT'S CHOICE, THE

This title may very well be considered either a magazine or a paperbound book; and *The Saint's Choice*, being a series within two series and having four publishers, is somewhat of a mystery itself. The original series, "Bonded Books," was a series of mystery digests, with *The Saint's Choice*, a series of mystery anthologies, a part of it.

All that actually seems clear is that Anson Bond split off from his partnership with Leslie Charteris (creator of The Saint character) and began his own series of "Bonded Mysteries" in 1946, while Charteris continued the old series as "Chartered Books" under the Saint Enterprises imprint. How the other publishers fit into all this is still a mystery. Added to this confusion is the fact that the numbering system had no continuity, with some titles having two numbers and some having no numbers at all.

The Saint's Choice lasted for seven numbers, each with a different theme. In order, they were: "The Saint's Choice of. . .:" English Mystery, American Mystery, True Crime, Humorous Crime, Impossible Crime (science fiction), Hollywood Crime, and Radio-Thrillers. They were all edited by Leslie Charteris and were of the same basic format, the only difference being that "Impossible Crime" was staple-bound instead of square spined and was unnumbered. All had the same cover design, a white rectangle on which was listed the contents, the title, and the "Saint's Choice" imprint, with the familiar stick figure of The Saint at the left. The term, "A Bonded Collection," appeared on all, with Hollywood Crime and Radio-Thrillers being exceptions and appearing as "Chartered Collections." The interior format was the same throughout the numbers. All had an introduction on the inside-front cover, an introduction to each story, and an editorial on the back cover, all written by Leslie Charteris. There was usually a Saint story in each (with the exception of "True Crime," which had a story which was the basis for a Saint story, "The Case of the Sizzling Saboteur." [1]

The stories, while thematic to its own volume, were reprints, with the exception of "Death Whispers" by Phillip Wylie in number 2, and included a wide variety of authors from Mark Twain to Edgar Allan Poe, from O. Henry to Robert Leslie Bellem, and all points between.

But even The Saint's endorsement could not stop the wartime paper shortage, and the series came to an end two years after it began.

Note

1. Charteris used a story in "True Crime" as the basis for a story he wrote later, "The Case of the Sizzling Saboteur," which was published only in the British edition of *The Saint Detective Magazine*, no. 148 (June 1966).

Information Sources

INDEX SOURCES: Cook, Michael L. *Monthly Murders*. Westport, Conn.: Greenwood Press, 1982.
LOCATION SOURCES: Private collectors.

Publication History

MAGAZINE TITLE: *The Saint's Choice*.
TITLE CHANGES: None.
VOLUME AND ISSUE DATA: No. 1 (1945) through no. 7 (1946);7 issues.
PUBLISHERS: No. 1: Bond-Charteris Enterprises; nos. 2–3: Jacobs Publishing Company; no. 4: The Shaw Press; no. 5: Bond-Charteris Enterprises; nos. 6–7: Saint Enterprises, 314 North Robertson Boulevard, Hollywood 34, California.
EDITOR: Leslie Charteris.
SIZE AND PAGINATION: 4-3/8" X 6-3/4"; 120–144 pages.
CURRENT STATUS: Discontinued.
—*Paul Palmer*

SATURN WEB

See SATURN WEB MAGAZINE OF DETECTIVE STORIES

SATURN WEB DETECTIVE STORIES

See SATURN WEB MAGAZINE OF DETECTIVE STORIES

SATURN WEB MAGAZINE OF DETECTIVE STORIES

This magazine well illustrates the intense competition in the late 1950s and early 1960s in that it underwent so many drastic changes in an attempt to become established. The magazine commenced in March 1957 using the title *Saturn Web*, and the first five issues contained all science fiction stories. With the sixth issue, the science fiction was abruptly discontinued, the name was changed to *Saturn Web Magazine of Detective Stories*, and fast-action, contemporary, raw crime-adventure was substituted. Titles of the tales in this issue amply show the type: "Night of Discovery," "Too Hot to Handle," "Jealous Husband," "Rumble Bait," and others.

The seventh issue, October 1958, carried the same type of material, but the title was shortened to *Saturn Web Detective Stories*. By February 1960, the "Saturn" part of the title had been gradually phased out, and the magazine became *Web Detective Stories*. With still unsatisfactory sales results, the direction of the magazine was again changed. The August 1962 issue became *Web Terror Stories*, and the reader was entertained, hopefully, with crime stories against exotic backgrounds: "Orbit of the Pain-Masters," "The Girl in the Iron Collar," "Terror Slaves of the Nile," "The Fanatic Justice of Satan's Cult," and similar titles. With cults, oriental tortures, and just plain mean people, the magazine populated its stories until it ceased publication in June 1965.

Information Sources

INDEX SOURCES: Cook, Michael L. *Monthly Murders*. Westport, Conn.: Greenwood Press, 1982.
LOCATION SOURCES: Private collectors.

Publication History

MAGAZINE TITLE: *Saturn Web Magazine of Detective Stories*.
TITLE CHANGES: *Saturn Web* (original title, first five issues, all science fiction); *Saturn Web Magazine of Detective Stories* (commencing Vol. 1, no. 6); *Saturn Web Detective Stories* (with Vol. 2, no. 1); *Web Detective Stories* (with Vol. 2, no. 6); *Web Terror Stories* (with Vol. 4, no. 1).
VOLUME AND ISSUE DATA: Vol. 1, no. 1 (March 1957) through Vol. 5, no. 2 (June 1965); 26 issues.
PUBLISHER: Candar Publishing Co., Inc., 1 Appleton Street, Holyoke, Massachusetts, with editorial offices at 218 West 48th Street, New York, New York.
EDITOR: Not known.
PRICE PER ISSUE: 35 cents (until Vol. 5, no. 1 [February 1965]); 50 cents.
SIZE AND PAGINATION: 5-3/8" X 7-1/4"; 112 pages.
CURRENT STATUS: Discontinued.

SAUCY DETECTIVE

Published first in 1930 by Movie Digest Company, *Saucy Detective* was a companion magazine to *Saucy Stories* and *Saucy Movie Tales*. No other information is available.

Information Sources

INDEX SOURCES: None known.
LOCATION SOURCES: Private collectors.

Publication History

MAGAZINE TITLE: *Saucy Detective*.
TITLE CHANGES: None known.
VOLUME AND ISSUE DATA: Mid-1930s; number of issues, date, and extent unknown.
PUBLISHER: Movie Digest Co., New York, New York.

EDITOR: Not known.
PRICE PER ISSUE: Not known.
SIZE AND PAGINATION: Not known.
CURRENT STATUS: Discontinued.

SCARAB MYSTERY MAGAZINE

With a somewhat different approach to attract the readers, *Scarab Mystery Magazine* appeared on the newsstands, with rather poor distribution, with the November 1950 issue. It presented a rather modest, saddle-stapled format, the cover featuring a stylized Egyptian scarab as the central part of the design.

The magazine offered what it termed "three complete new novels," albeit they were more of the novelette length. Beneath the red, black, and white cover of the first issue were listed "The Uncertain Corpse" (a Johnny Liddell novel) by Frank Kane, "Brainstorm" by Paul Marcus, and "Noose Around My Neck" by Edward Ronns.

The second issue, January 1951, presented "The Career Girl and the Corpse" by Anne Wormser, "The Clay Pigeons" by Edward Ronns, and "Terror for Two" by Marty Holland. The cover of the second issue was identical to that of the first except that green had replaced the red in the design.

The magazine carried no advertisements; the back cover gave a synopsis of the three novels included within. There were no further issues published.

Information Sources

INDEX SOURCES: Cook, Michael L. *Monthly Murders*. Westport, Conn.: Greenwood
  Press, 1982.
LOCATION SOURCES: Private collectors.

Publication History

MAGAZINE TITLE: *Scarab Mystery Magazine*.
TITLE CHANGES: None.
VOLUME AND ISSUE DATA: Vol. 1, no. 1 (November 1950) through Vol. 1, no. 2
  (January 1951); 2 issues.
PUBLISHER: Black Horse Press, Inc., Chicago, Illinois, with editorial offices at 104
  Fifth Avenue, New York, New York.
EDITOR: Not known.
PRICE PER ISSUE: 25 cents.
SIZE AND PAGINATION: 5-1/4" X 7-1/4"; 128 pages.
CURRENT STATUS: Discontinued.

SCARLET ADVENTURESS

The annals of unrepentant trash contain few examples more sleazy than *Scarlet Adventuress*. According to its editorial requirements:

> . . . the woman adventuress must be sophisticated, charming, and quick-witted. . . . The story must be told from the woman's angle and she must be of the sort who has a definite goal—love, money, power, or revenge—toward which she steadily forges, using the allure of her body and her ready wit to carry her through perilous situations, but never actually losing her virtue. The sex angle can be played up. . . . We want the glamorous type of woman who takes all and gives nothing.[1]

Or that's what the editor claimed he wanted. In practice, other material was included which he forgot to mention.

The magazine seems to have begun about 1935. There is a great lack of volume and issue numbers, and the title-page information is uncommonly reticent about frequency of publication. The magazine appears to have been quarterly for at least part of its life. In late 1937, the title was changed to *Modern Adventuress*. That watering down brought forth mildly reduced editorial requirements—they wanted "Sophisticated short stories of female adventuresses, involving sex without licentiousness."[2]

Presumably, the magazine melted into a perfumed haze soon afterward. Final issues have not been traced. The magazine had a rather short life, but it certainly threw up gaudy sparks.

Scarlet Adventuress was not quite a confessions magazine and not quite a pulp. It was large, about 8" X 11", and flat. It looked as if the editors had ripped out about one-third of the pages of a standard pulp magazine, then squeezed the rest very hard in a press. The residue was juiced up by ads for black lace underthings and virility improvers.

Just how many authors wrote the contents is unknown. There were two or three, at least, although up to ten names appeared on the table of contents. Among these were Thelma Ellis, Edmund O. Kyle, Franz LeBaron, Roberta Dean, and Robert Leslie Bellem. At least Bellem was not a pseudonym.

The story was usually told from what passed for the woman's point of view. The prose is unbelievable. The word *exotic* appears about six times per page, never correctly used. *Alluring* is used once per paragraph. The story lines, such as they are, support descriptions of feminine undressing and sly mention of other various mysteries.

Through all the literary raptures about silk underwear and warm flesh, the adventuresses came and went, all about the same—all with the identical, dehumanized air of scented bait about them. Many returned in a series of exploits in which the main variable was the country in which they took off their clothing. Among these casual women was Lady Nora O'Neil, an iron-willed Irish fighter for liberty. She wore a pistol holstered in the top of her silk stockings, and demoralized various Colonel Blimps, her virtue trembling in the balance.

Kara Vania—Secret Agent XW9, the Lady of Doom, the Tiger Woman, the World's Most Glamorous Spy—was red-headed and had a terribly hard time staying dressed. But the chief cream puff among these feminine pastries was

Nila Rand, "that strange exotic creature who turned the blood of all men into molten fire. . . ."[3]

In addition to these series characters, six to eight other adventuresses appeared in each issue, their warm flesh clad only in a spraying of exotic perfume, their stories seasoned liberally with lesbianism, voyeurism, symbolic castration, aggravated assault, pornography, rape, near-rape, and similar activities.

Sensation was the guideline to this magazine, clad in lust and passion at any cost, but even this failed to survive. Other titles published by this group included *Scarlet Confessions, Scarlet Murderess* (announced but may not have been published), *True Gang Life,* and *Detective and Murder Mysteries.**

Notes

1. "Writer's Market," *Writers Digest,* Vol. 16, no. 12 (November 1936), p. 60.
2. *The Author and Journalist,* Vol. 22, no. 2 (February 1937), p. 20.
3. *Scarlet Adventuress* (January 1936), p. 4.

Information Sources

INDEX SOURCES: None known.
LOCATION SOURCES: Private collectors only.
Publication History
MAGAZINE TITLE: *Scarlet Adventuress.*
TITLE CHANGES: *Modern Adventuress* (late 1937).
VOLUME AND ISSUE DATA: None designated by publisher; published 1935–1937.
PUBLISHER: Associated Authors, Inc., 1008 West York Street, Philadelphia, Pennsylvania.
EDITOR: M. T. Pattie.
PRICE PER ISSUE: 25 cents.
SIZE AND PAGINATION: 8-1/2" X 10-3/4"; 96 pages.
CURRENT STATUS: Discontinued.
—*Robert Sampson*

SCIENCE FICTION COLLECTOR, THE

See MEGAVORE (Canadian)

SCIENTIFIC DETECTIVE

A saddle-stitched, digest-size magazine of standard crime-adventure fare, *Scientific Detective* belied its name and had several fact articles and an occasional quiz about its fiction, which appears to be primarily reprint material. Its commencement is not known; the earliest issue noted has been February 1947, labeled volume 6, number 12; the latest issue inspected was dated May 1948. It sold for twenty-five cents and was published by ERB Book Company. At least one issue has been noted with title *Scientific Detective Annual*, bearing no date or volume/issue identification.

Information Sources

INDEX SOURCES: None known.
LOCATION SOURCES: Private collectors.

Publication History

MAGAZINE TITLE: *Scientific Detective*.
TITLE CHANGES: *Scientific Detective Annual* (at least one issue, n.d.).
VOLUME AND ISSUE DATA: Earliest noted, Vol. 6, no. 12, (February 1947) to at
    least May 1948; number of issues and extent unknown.
PUBLISHER: ERB Book Company, 1745 Broadway, New York 19, New York.
EDITOR: Not known.
PRICE PER ISSUE: 25 cents.
SIZE AND PAGINATION: 5-3/8'' X 7-3/8''; 148 pages.
CURRENT STATUS: Discontinued.

SCIENTIFIC DETECTIVE ANNUAL

See SCIENTIFIC DETECTIVE

SCIENTIFIC DETECTIVE MONTHLY

Nearly all the fiction magazines published by Hugo Gernsback in the 1920s and 1930s were designed to be educational as well as entertaining, and *Scientific Detective Monthly* was not an exception. The other educational magazines were science fiction; this magazine did run some stories which could qualify as science fiction, but the bulk of the material was straight detection or mystery wherein scientific principles and/or devices were used either in the commission or detection of crime (usually the latter).

The rationale of the magazine is explained in Gernsback's editorial in the first issue, which went on sale in December 1929, dated January 1930.

In the firm belief that science in its various applications will become one of the greatest deterrents to crime, *Scientific Detective Monthly* has been launched. . . .

Chemistry, photography, electricity, microscopy, and many other branches of science are called upon continuously in the solving of crime. Slowly but steadily the police departments are adding research laboratories to their regular equipment for the general detection of crime.[1]

As with all his magazines in that period, Hugo Gernsback is listed as editor; nothing appeared that he had not read and approved. There was also (as in the science fiction magazines) an impressive-looking list of consultants and associates. Arthur B. Reeve, creator of the popular "scientific" detective, Craig Kennedy, was editorial commissioner; Hector G. Grey, an expert on criminology, was the editorial deputy (he actually did the bulk of the editorial work), and there were a couple of noted academicians in the field, as well as expert police contacts in France and Germany.

Each issue contained factual articles dealing with scientific crime detection, as well as crime news of the month (not the sensations; rather, reports of scientific work), book reviews of both new detective novels and books on crime and criminology, a questionnaire for the readers testing their observational and deductive talents after examining a line drawing for two minutes, and a readers' department.

Each of the ten issues contained a story by Reeve, but only the first was new; all the others were reprints from his collection of Craig Kennedy short stories, *The Silent Bullet* (1912). All but the final issue also contained a reprint of one of the short stories by Edwin Balmer and William MacHarg, dealing with their "scientific" detective, Luther Trant; those stories were even older, and some had been reprinted earlier in Gernsback's *Amazing Stories* (1926–1927).

The first three issues reprinted S. S. Van Dine's popular Philo Vance novel, *The Bishop Murder Case*. After the March 1930 issue, all serials and short stories were new, except for the two series mentioned above.

While a number of stories were contributed by authors who had appeared and were appearing in Gernsback's and others' science fiction magazines, not all of them were science fiction writers. Among the exceptions were two stories in Captain S. P. Meek's "Dr. Bird" series (also running in *Amazing Stories, Astounding Stories,* and *Wonder Stories*): "The Perfect Counterfeit" (January 1930), which deals with a duplication machine, and "The Gland Murders" (June 1930), which deals with a gland-extract poison that makes the victim a homicidal maniac. Dr. David H. Keller contributed three adventures of his tongue-in-cheek detective, Taine of San Francisco: "A Scientific Widowhood" (February 1930), "Burning Water" (June 1930), and "Menacing Claws" (September 1930). Only the second might be considered science fiction; the culprit seems to have unlocked atomic energy, but the ending is ambiguous. (Taine adventures were also running in *Amazing Stories*.)

The Craig Kennedy and Luther Trant tales nearly all deal with detection through the use of electronic devices which, in one way or another, display the subject's concealed emotions. Some may have introduced new uses for the instruments, as in Reeve's "The Seismograph Adventure" (March 1930), where Kennedy uses a seismograph to detect the unheard footfall of a phoney "ghost" outside a cabinet.

The magazine's career falls into two distinct parts: January to May 1930 and June to October 1930, the latter five issues appearing under a different title: *Amazing Detective Tales*. Other outstanding stories in the first group were two ingenious tales by the popular science fiction author, Edmond Hamilton: "The Invisible Master" (April 1930), which seems to be about the scientific achievement of invisibility but proves to be a masterly criminal hoax, and "The Murder in the Clinic" (May 1930), wherein the dying man's words provide the essential clue to a different kind of scientific criminality.

The most popular story in the first five issues, however, was "The Electrical Man," by Neil R. Jones (May 1930), wherein the protagonist has developed a novel means of protecting himself against assault (including bullets): an electrified suit, powered by remote control. It was not a detection story; it was crime adventure. The results of Gernsback's request to readers to write and tell him whether they preferred that type of story to the more cerebral detection tales showed that the former was more desired.

Obviously, *Scientific Detective Monthly* was not a selling title. The five issues of *Amazing Detective Tales* have somewhat more sensational covers, but the inside of the magazine looked exactly the same as before, except that Hector Grey had gone and David Lasser (Gernsback's managing editor for his science fiction titles) had replaced him. Apparently, it was not easy to find detection stories that really fitted Gernsback's approach; more and more proved to be rather commonplace in their "science" aspects. An example would be "The Mystery of the Phantom Shot" by Amelia Reynolds Long (July 1930); Miss Long was better known for science fiction. An old powder-and-ball pistol hanging on the wall is made to go off by reflecting sunlight upon it; the ball breaks a glass paperweight in the next room. The paperweight has been tampered with, too, and filled with lethal gas. Clever, but it could as well have appeared in one of the other detective magazines on the market.

Aside from Luther Trant and Craig Kennedy, clever plots involving a minimal use of science and more-or-less scientific crime adventures were predominant in *Amazing Detective Tales*. Had the magazine lasted longer, it is very possible that crime adventure, relating to some manner of scientific devices but with little mystery and no real detection, would have predominated. There were, however, two real scientific detective mysteries by Eugene De Reske that were excellently written: "The Painted Murder" (August 1930), based on little-known aspects of anatomy, and "The Clasp of Doom" (October 1930), rooted in chemistry.

Only two serials were published after the Van Dine novel: "Rays of Death" by Tom Curry (April and May 1930) and "The Carewe Murder Mystery" by Ed Earl Repp. Both of those authors were known in the science fiction magazines, but neither serial was science fiction—and neither memorable.

The October 1930 issue carried an announcement that the magazine would appear in regular pulp size, starting with the next issue, just as was being done at the same time with Gernsback's *Wonder Stories*. However, that plan was not carried through; Gernsback sold the title, and while a November pulp-size *Amazing Detective Tales* did appear, there was not a shred of resemblance to Gernsback's magazine.

In the first issue, Arthur B. Reeve had had an article, "What Are the Great Detective Stories and Why?," wherein he notes that he had stopped writing "scientific" adventures for Craig Kennedy because he felt that the time for that type of story had passed. Hugo Gernsback hoped to prove him wrong, but Reeve proved to be right. There had never been a detective magazine like *Scientific Detective Monthly/Amazing Detective Tales* before, and there never would be again. It remains unique.

Note

1. Editorial, *Scientific Detective Monthly*, Vol. 1, no. 1 (January 1930), p. 4.

Information Sources

BIBLIOGRAPHY:

Lowndes, Robert A. W. "The Unique Magazine: Hugo Gernsback's Scientific Detective Monthly." *The Armchair Detective*, Vol. 14, no. 1 (Winter 1981): 24–30; Vol. 14, no. 2 (Spring 1981): 157–62; Vol. 14, no. 3 (Summer 1981): 243–46; Vol. 14, no. 4 (n.d. [1981]): 367–71; Vol. 15, no. 1 (n.d. [1982]): 18–22.

Nichols, Peter, ed. *The Science Fiction Encyclopedia*. Garden City, N.Y.: Doubleday & Co., 1979, pp. 252–53.

INDEX SOURCES: None known.

LOCATION SOURCES: University of California–Los Angeles Library (complete run); private collectors.

Publication History

MAGAZINE TITLE: *Scientific Detective Monthly*.

TITLE CHANGES: *Amazing Detective Tales* (with Vol. 1, no. 6 [June 1930]).

VOLUME AND ISSUE DATA: Vol. 1, no. 1 (January 1930) through Vol. 1, no. 10 (October 1930); 10 issues.

PUBLISHER: Techni-Craft Publishing Co., 404 North Wesley Avenue, Mount Morris, Illinois, with editorial offices at 96–98 Park Place, New York, New York.

EDITOR: Hugo Gernsback.

PRICE PER ISSUE: 25 cents.

SIZE AND PAGINATION: 8-1/2" X 11"; 96 pages.

CURRENT STATUS: Discontinued.

—*Robert A.W. Lowndes*

SCORPION, THE

See OCTOPUS, THE

SCOTLAND YARD

"*Scotland Yard*. . .insists that its stories be true and told by a participant in the arrest. It takes you to strange places in the world, paints a picture of the crime and how it was solved, detail by detail; how police officers and scientists matched their wits against the cunning of criminals all over the world."[1] Thus was the promise made by this magazine, but the promise was itself an elaborate fiction.

Truth or fiction or both, *Scotland Yard* is a fine example of a magazine making that delicate transition from the 1920s to the 1930s. In his book, *Pulps,* Tony Goodstone remarked that the publisher of *Scotland Yard* bought English pulp stories cheaply, then rewrote them for the magazine. That would explain much. In first issues, the stories brim with lovable crooks and heroes of rich sentiment but no instinct for self-preservation. Womanhood is sacred, as is honor, and gentlemen have codes. And police officers, gruff Irishmen with soft hearts, instinctively know that good breeding equates innocence, regardless of the evidence.

The first issue (March 1930) features the novel "A Modern Robin Hood." It is written in self-conscious, 1920s prose and tells how a crooked young disguise artist outwits the Paris police. The lead serial, "Charity Sheen, Gentlemen," features another dashing crook who robs from the rich to give to the poor; this serial wallowed tediously along for six issues, verbose, stale, and improbable.

Slightly more vigor is to be found in the short stories. Their titles reflect contemporary usage: "The Rat Killer" and "The Shake Down." As fiction, they are blighted by sentimentality. The first issue also contains the first of a series of fact articles, "Tales of a Prison Doctor," later retitled "Leave It To The Doctor," a series full of "inside stuff," some of it possibly true. "The Laboratory" was the obligatory editorial department, by "The Inspector." Neither this nor the stories were illustrated. At this time the magazine was 126 pages long, including fourteen pages of ads in the front of the magazine and sixteen in the rear.

The second issue, May 1930, continues the adventures of The Modern Robin Hood, plus the serial, the doctor article, and the department. There are three short stories, all written in what seems like first-draft haste. Neither wit nor artistry brightens the dilapidated prose, the characters were stereotypes in 1900, and no human emotion interrupts endless pages of attitudizing.

The magazine became a monthly with the third (July 1930) issue. This featured a "Smashing Gangland Novel," which was an improbable short story, and several lesser stories—"As the Clock Strikes," or how the convict's revenge was foiled; in "Peril's Pause," the hero was a double, and there are bad girls and pistol shots and shabby excitement.

The next issue (August 1930) continues as before. "Crystals of Fire" is offered as a "Smashing Mystery of New York Life": "Into the whirlpool of night club life came a strange figure to weave one of the greatest mysteries that ever blackened the Great White Way."[2] Short stories tell about a clever dog, a soulless killer trapped by a mirror, and a pickpocket.

With the September 1930 issue, there are some improvements. Interior illustrations appear; they are by Frank Tinsley, who also provides a masthead drawing showing an English bobby peering across the type toward a policeman. The front cover now reads *Scotland Yard Detective Stories* and lists "The Voice of Nemesis," but this will not appear until the next issue. Inside, the stories are as feeble as ever. "Behind the Bars" tells how a convict escapes from prison, dislikes life outside, and escapes back into custody. "Tomb of Dread" is a sort of 1920s Gothic with floor traps, secret doors, a black-cowled monk creeping through a grim old house, and malignant secrets. In "Traitor's Claws," a shrewd young attorney outfoxes a crazy crime master and his killers. As in the other stories, the sentences are short, the crooks unreal, and the hero a fumbler.

A new department, "Bafflegram," is added in the October 1930 magazine: read this two-page mystery, then submit your solution for cash prizes. There are now 128 pages, twenty of which are advertisements; the spine is decorated with pictures of a yellow revolver and a yellow mask, each in a blue box. With the next issue, the spine turns scarlet, and the pistol and mask are white. On the cover, a flapper wearing a blue cloche blasts an automatic with her right hand and steers a coupe with her left, her escort slumped over the wheel, and a bullet hole in the windshield. Of the fiction, "Blood on Broadway" is the first piece to have a distinctly modern tang, its flavor being close to that of *Dime Detective** five years later. Internal evidence suggests that it was written by Hugh Austin, an early specialist in the police procedural mystery.

The January issue was skipped, although the "whole number" count (in this case, number 9) remained correct, and the magazine continued to call itself a monthly. With the February 1931 issue, the magazine spine has again changed color, once more scarlet—a color it remained until the end.

There are now several innovations on the title page. The locale of each story is specified—Australia, London, Chicago, and such. Each story is identified as written by a newspaperman, an ex-secretary, a county coroner. Beneath these names lurk the same authors whose intellectual effusions have stimulated and regaled readers through past issues. The illusion that all is true and factual is further advanced by the use of photographs illustrating the "true-crime" articles, plus a double-page drawing. The Bafflegram is omitted from the February issue, apparently from lack of space.

The March 1931 magazine features a sneering masked punk, splendid in top hat, who menaces the reader with a pair of uncocked automatics. Across the top of the cover, white script proclaims "Man-Hunts in All Nations!" Below the words "*Scotland Yard*" is a line of red type that shouts "International Detective Stories!" The interior art is divided between Reussing and a newcomer, Hewitt, and a third, unidentified artist. This issue is packed with odd material. Light verse by John H. Thompson. Three true articles. "Leave It To the Doctor," the fourth article, is signed by Dr. Edward Podolsky, and there are short stories by "G. Wayman Jones" under various pseudonyms—a house name under a *nom de plume*. But there is also the lead novel, "Wildcat," by "A Tulsa Newspaperman." As best is known, this is the first appearance of private detective Curt Flagg; the writer is Lester Dent, who would begin the *Doc Savage** series in about two years. Dent again writes the lead novel in the June 1931 issue, "One Billion—Gold," and he likely was the contributor of "Out China Way," a story about a tough hero who blackjacks his enemies and is mad at everybody.

On the cover of the fourteenth issue, August 1931, after again missing a monthly issue, appears a green-eyed terror, wearing a black hood and choking a fat-cheeked young lady. At the bottom is an announcement in small print that the magazine is now bimonthly. In much larger type, the table of contents announces "Three Full-Length Action Novelets, Four Vivid International Tales, Five Absorbing Features." Despite this all-out effort, the magazine expired.

Into fourteen issues, *Scotland Yard* managed to concentrate about thirty years of popular fiction styles. It was a cross-section of detective fiction as it evolved from 1915 pseudo gentility to the 1930s blood and action—although the hardboiled realism of *The Black Mask** is not represented.

The magazine was consistently inconsistent. That must surely reflect the editor's efforts to earn some sort of profit while the Great Depression savaged magazine sales. The fact that *Scotland Yard* survived fourteen issues is a tribute to the improvisional brilliance of the editorial effort.

Overall, the magazine was so extremely erratic that it is best taken as a complete set so that one can trace the disparate literary conventions melting one into the other, creating a unique artifact—a sort of fossilized history of early mystery fiction. It is especially fascinating to those who relish the oddities of change.

Notes

1. Editorial, *Scotland Yard*, Vol. 1, no. 1 (March 1930), p. 4.
2. (No Author Given), "Crystals of Fire," *Scotland Yard*, Vol. 2, no. 4 (August 1930), p. 2.

Information Sources

BIBLIOGRAPHY:
Goodstone, Tony. *The Pulps*. New York: Chelsea House, 1970.
Sampson, Robert. "Fourteen Issues." *Xenophile*, no. 22 (March–April 1976): 4–11.
INDEX SOURCES: Sampson, Robert. "Fourteen Issues." *Xenophile*, no. 22 (March–April 1976): 10–11.
LOCATION SOURCES: Private collectors only.

Publication History

MAGAZINE TITLE: *Scotland Yard*.
TITLE CHANGES: None; however, subtitles were used in various issues: *Detective Stories, International Detective Stories*.
VOLUME AND ISSUE DATA: Vol. 1, no. 1 (March 1930) through Vol. 5, no. 14 (August 1931); 14 issues.
PUBLISHER: Dell Publishing Co., Inc., 100 Fifth Avenue, New York, New York.
EDITOR: Richard A. Martinsen.
PRICE PER ISSUE: 20 cents.
SIZE AND PAGINATION: 7" X 10"; 126–128 pages.
CURRENT STATUS: Discontinued.
—*Robert Sampson*

SCOTLAND YARD DETECTIVE STORIES.

See SCOTLAND YARD

SCOTLAND YARD SERIES OF DETECTIVE NOVELS (British)

Although "penny dreadfuls" were published as early as 1866 in England, the *Scotland Yard Series of Detective Novels* was one of the earliest to use the detective theme in its title. This periodical was published in 1888 for twelve issues. No other information is available.

Information Sources

BIBLIOGRAPHY:
Lofts, W.O.G., and Derek J. Adley, *Old Boys Books, A Complete Catalogue*. London: privately printed, 1969.
INDEX SOURCES: None known.
LOCATION SOURCES: Private collectors.

Publication History

MAGAZINE TITLE: *Scotland Yard Series of Detective Novels*.
TITLE CHANGES: None.
VOLUME AND ISSUE DATA: No. 1 (1888) through no. 12 (1888); 12 issues.
PUBLISHER: General Publishing Co., Ltd., London.
EDITOR: Not known.
PRICE PER ISSUE: Not known.
SIZE AND PAGINATION: Not known.
CURRENT STATUS: Discontinued.

SECRET AGENT SERIES (British)

Fleetway Publications published twenty-six issues of *Secret Agent Series*—a pocket-size, sixty-four page, cheaply produced espionage series—from January 16, 1967, to January 1968. No other information is available.

Information Sources

BIBLIOGRAPHY:
Lofts, W.O.G., and Derek J. Adley. *Old Boys Books, A Complete Catalogue*. London: privately printed, 1969.
INDEX SOURCES: None known.
LOCATION SOURCES: Private collectors.

Publication History

MAGAZINE TITLE: *Secret Agent Series*.
TITLE CHANGES: None.
VOLUME AND ISSUE DATA: No. 1 (January 16, 1967) through no. 26 (January 1968); 26 issues.

PUBLISHER: Fleetway Publications, Ltd., London.
EDITOR: Not known.
PRICE PER ISSUE: Not known.
SIZE AND PAGINATION: 5-3/8'' X 7''; 64 pages.
CURRENT STATUS: Discontinued.

SECRET AGENT X

During the 1920s, Harold Hersey was responsible for a number of pulp magazines that used the current fads and movies for titles and stories. When he sold out, about 1930, pulp writer and editor A. A. Wyn bought *The Dragnet**, one of Hersey's gangster pulp titles, and retitled it, in 1931, to *Detective Dragnet Magazine* (see *Dragnet, The*). The gangster stories were discontinued and replaced with the mystery-detective story. In 1933, this magazine was again retitled, to *Ten Detective Aces* (see *Dragnet, The*), and published under Wyn's "Ace Publications" imprint, an imprint that included detective, romance, western, and air-story magazines.

By 1934, the hero, or single-character, magazine was doing exceptionally well at other publishing houses, and Wyn decided to create his own: *Secret Agent X*. He used many of his *Ten Detective Aces'* writers to fill in the new magazine with short stories of mystery fiction. It was to be published as by Periodical House, Inc., with Wyn's wife, Rose, as editor/president. Paul Chadwick, author of the Wade Hammond stories for *Ten Detective Aces*, was drafted to write the lead stories of Secret Agent X using the house name of Brant House.

Secret Agent X was never given an identity, and he lived constantly in disguise. In the beginning, he fought crime in New York City, seldom venturing far afield; but as interest in the magazine and its hero character grew, Secret Agent X began to travel to Washington, Chicago, California, Hawaii, and even to a mysterious island. During the early part of the series, he usually fought alone, although he did have a girl friend, Miss Betty Dale, who aided him at times. Later, he recruited Harvey Bates and Jim Hobart to act as investigators for his far-flung, crime-fighting organization. These agents, along with Betty Dale, were dropped before the end of the series, and Secret Agent X again fought alone. He worked for an official in Washington but was thought to be a criminal by local police departments.

Paul Chadwick left the series after a number of stories, and new writers began to contribute material, including Emile C. Tepperman, R.T.M. Scott, G. T. Fleming-Roberts, and others. All wrote under the house name of Brant House.

The magazine had fascinating subtitles, which would change with the trends. With the February 1934 issue (the first), the subtitle read "The Man of a Thousand Faces." By November 1935, this was changed to "Detective Mysteries," reflecting the story contents of the magazine as well. The December 1936 issue proclaimed "G-Man Action Adventures," and federal agents were thrown into the stories. The June 1937 issue juggled the above subtitles and suddenly became

"G–Man Action Mysteries" but with the February 1938 issue reverted to "Detective Mysteries" and remained thus until the magazine's demise in March 1939.

Beginning as a monthly publication, *Secret Agent X* missed July 1934 and May 1935 and became a bimonthly from June 1936 to June 1938. At this point, the schedule was reduced to quarterly. The page count was also erratic, beginning with 128 pages, dropping to 112 with the April 1937 issue, returning to 128 pages in October 1937, and falling again to 112 in February 1938. With the April 1938 issue, it presented only 96 pages and remained at that size until December 1938, when it returned to 112 pages.

A. A. Wyn published only one other character magazine. This was *Captain Hazzard** (1938), of which only one issue was published. It was also written by Paul Chadwick but under the house name of Chester Hawks. When this title was cancelled, a second story intended for *Captain Hazzard* was rewritten into a Secret Agent X adventure.

Information Sources

BIBLIOGRAPHY:
Cervon, Bruce. "Secret Agent X." *Collecting Paperbacks?* Vol. 3, no. 1 (n.d. [March 1981]): 14–16.
Johnson, Tom. "Destroy Secret Agent X." *Pulp* (Summer 1976): 3–9.
————. "Fading Shadows: Erlika, Daughter of Satan." *Doc Savage Club Reader*, no. 11 (n.d. [August 1980]): 24–27.
————. "Fading Shadows: Lady X." *The Age of the Unicorn*, Vol. 1, no. 6 (February 1980): 24–25.
————. "Fading Shadows: Madame Death." *Doc Savage Club Reader*, no. 11 (n.d. [August 1980]): 12–14.
"These Ven." "Solution for 'X'," with chronology of issues. *Xenophile*, no. 42 (September/October 1979): 138–45.
INDEX SOURCES: Weinberg, Robert, and Lohr McKinstry. *The Hero Pulp Index.* Evergreen, Colo.: Opar Press, 1971.
LOCATION SOURCES: Private collectors.

Publication History

MAGAZINE TITLE: *Secret Agent X.*
TITLE CHANGES: None (various subtitles; see text).
VOLUME AND ISSUE DATA: Vol. 1, no. 1 (February 1934) through Vol. 14, no. 3 (March 1939); 41 issues.
PUBLISHER: Periodical House, Inc., 29 Worthington Street, Springfield, Massachusetts.
EDITOR: Rose Wyn.
PRICE PER ISSUE: 10 cents.
SIZE AND PAGINATION: 7" X 10"; 96–128 pages.
CURRENT STATUS: Discontinued.
—*Tom Johnson*

SECRET SERVICE DETECTIVE STORIES

A short-lived title, *Secret Service Detective Stories* was published in 1927 by Carwood Publications. No other information is available.

Information Sources

INDEX SOURCES: None known.
LOCATION SOURCES: Private collectors.

Publication History

MAGAZINE TITLE: *Secret Service Detective Stories.*
TITLE CHANGES: None known.
VOLUME AND ISSUE DATA: 1927; number of issues and extent unknown.
PUBLISHER: Tom Wood as Carwood Publications (Fiction Unit).
EDITOR: Tom Wood (unconfirmed).
PRICE PER ISSUE: Not known.
SIZE AND PAGINATION: Not known.
CURRENT STATUS: Discontinued.

SECRET SERVICE: OLD AND YOUNG KING BRADY, DETECTIVES

It was nearly one year after Frank Tousey's *Detective Library* (originally the *New York Detective Library**) had ceased publication before Old King Brady returned in a regular series. In keeping with newer trends in the field, *Secret Service: Old and Young King Brady, Detectives*, was a colored-cover weekly and was devoted to the Brady stories. The stories were shorter than those in the earlier publication (these averaging 30,000 words) but were cut from the same pattern.

The new series did introduce a partner for the old detective in Harry Brady, who became known as Young King Brady. While no relation to James (Old King) Brady, the similarity in names was not unique in the dime novel. For example, Tousey's chief competition in the detective field was Street & Smith's Nick Carter, whose chief assistant was named Chick Carter (but who was not otherwise related to his mentor).

The office of the Brady Detective Bureau was at an unspecified address in New York City. The agency appears to have worked on nearly every kind of case known to the dime novel. Occasionally, the detectives reported to the chief of the secret service. The Bradys were equally at home in New York, San Francisco, Chicago, and out West. To many readers, however, their most interesting cases took them to Chinatown, where they were involved with the usual opium dens of iniquity. During one of these adventures, they met and added Alice Montgomery to the Brady Bureau.

There were 725 stories published over a thirteen-year period before the weekly began to reprint the early numbers. Number 726 reprinted the second number from February 3, 1899; and by the time the publication ceased in 1925 with number 1,374, nearly every story had been reissued, a total of 679.

Students of the Brady series have contended that the early numbers were not written by Francis W. Doughty, who had created the character for the *New York Detective Library*. Doughty's "trademark" was the working of the title of the story into the final paragraph, so that stories without this stylistic device are not considered to be his work. An examination of the early issues of *Secret Service*, however, indicates that this was done on occasion, even from the start.

Doughty's work is considered to be the best in the series and the reason for the greater popularity of some stories over others. Walter F. Mott and Luis P. Senarens have been credited with substantial contributions to the series. One of the most prolific of dime novelists, Senarens was the author of most of the Frank Reade, Jr., science fiction stories.

With the death of Frank Tousey on September 7, 1902, the publishing company passed first to his brother, Sinclair, and then to Harry E. Wolff, who had married into the family. When Wolff discontinued *Secret Service*, the rights to the other Tousey publications were sold to Westbury Publishing, an imprint of Street & Smith. Before that time, however, the quality of production had greatly deteriorated, and even the colored covers were being printed on cheap newsprint.

Information Sources

BIBLIOGRAPHY:
Bleiler, E.F., ed. *Eight Dime Novels*. New York: Dover Publications, 1974.
Bragin, Charles. *Dime Novels Bibliography 1860–1928*. Brooklyn, N.Y.: privately printed, 1938.
Leithead, J. Edward. "The Great Detective Team: Old and Young King Brady." *American Book Collector*, Vol. 20 (November/December 1969): 25–31.
O'Gara, Gil. "Old King Brady: His Rise and Decline." *The Age of the Unicorn*, no. 2 (April 1980): 19–22; and *Yellowback Library*, no. 1 (January/February 1981): 5–7.
Pearson, Edmund. *Dime Novels, or Following an Old Trail in Popular Literature*. Boston: Little, Brown, 1929.
Turner, E. S. *Boys Will Be Boys*. London: Michael Joseph Ltd., 1948.
INDEX SOURCES: None known.
LOCATION SOURCES: Hess Collection, University of Minnesota; private collectors.

Publication History

MAGAZINE TITLE: *Secret Service: Old and Young King Brady, Detectives*.
TITLE CHANGES: None.
VOLUME AND ISSUE DATA: No. 1 (January 28, 1899) through no. 1,374 (May 22, 1925); 1,374 issues.
PUBLISHERS: Frank Tousey, Publisher, 29 West 26th Street, New York, New York, later 24 Union Square and 168 West 23rd Street, New York, New York; Harry E. Wolff, 166 West 23rd Street, New York, New York.
EDITOR: Not known.

PRICE PER ISSUE: 5 cents (1899–1916); 6 cents (1917–1919); 7 cents (1920–1923); 8
    cents (1923–August 1924); 10 cents (August 22, 1924–May 22, 1925).
SIZE AND PAGINATION: 8'' X 11'' (nos. 1–1112); 7'' X 9-1/2'' (nos. 1,113–1,374).
CURRENT STATUS: Discontinued.
—*J. Randolph Cox*

SECRET 6, THE

The four novels recounting the exploits of The Secret 6 have to rank among Robert J. Hogan's best adventure yarns. Though they were originally presented as detective stories, there is little "detecting" in them, so the dyed-in-the-wool detective story buff should not seriously expect much along these lines. If, instead, they are read purely as straight adventure stories with a thin veneer of the eerie, the reader can expect lots of exciting, fast-paced action. On the other hand, the devotee of the weird or supernatural should not anticipate much from the overlay of the uncanny in the stories, for in typical Hogan style these elements are treated as minutiae that need slight explanation.

Of the four stories in *The Secret 6*, the first suffers somewhat from being the first: Hogan has to slow down his slap-dash action to introduce all the continuing characters and give a reason for them to come together as a team of crime fighters. Even though Hogan was never noted for devoting much verbage to descriptions of characters or settings, still there is a minimum that must be observed so the reader can fill in his own mental picture of the person or scene.

Once past this perfunctory requirement, Hogan delivers thrills, hazards, and perils galore, all in his best quick-paced, slam-bang, pulp style. And, once past the first story, Hogan wastes little more than an occasional adjective in describing his sextet of protagonists. He saves his words for conversations and actions that move the story along at such a rapid clip that the reader has great difficulty putting aside the story once it is started. Even the passage of a third of a centruy cannot diminish the fascination of these tales.

The opening scene of the first story has King, who emerges as the leader of The Secret 6, on death row, awaiting imminent execution. Not that King was guilty of the crime for which he was convicted, but he did face execution. He was a young man, almost six feet tall, with a straight, unwavering look in his cold, blue eyes. Both his father and his uncle had been lawmen killed by criminals. He is rescued from his death row cell by The Bishop and The Key, who are convinced he is innocent.

The Bishop is short and stout, ruddy-faced, and clean-shaven, with a soft, kindly voice and bright, dancing eyes. Despite his exterior, he possesses more than average strength. The Key, so named because he has a way with locks and safes, is a dapper little man: young, slender, and wiry. He walks with a quick, light step and has a thin face with a prominent nose bent slightly to one side.

The other members of the sextet are Luga, a chief of the Amakozi tribe of Zulus and a former side-show attraction, with wild hair growing straight out in every direction; The Professor, who, before losing his job when the depression became acute, was a scholar of applied science bearing on criminology; Shakespeare, a retired actor and a master of makeup and mimicry; and The Doctor, experienced in chemistry, surgery, and medicine and a student of strange superstitions and unusual tribal practices.

The accomplished pulp reader will have already noted (and wondered at) the fact that there were seven members in The Secret 6; thus he will not be surprised at the denouement of the first novel.

In all four of the novels presented in this magazine, The Secret 6 are considered by the authorities to be outlaws and criminals. The 6 depend on information from a motley band of agents, each of whom has an improbable name: The Dummy, Legs Larkin, Flo the Fleecer, The Worm, and The Whistler.

The plots are rather low-key for Hogan—there is no threat to the continued existence of humanity or the world or even of the nation. Instead, the threat is limited in scope to either one family or to a small group. For this reason, perhaps, the plots strike closer to home and become that much more believable, even though the threats are explained away so prosaically and with so little attention to convincing detail that they are almost an embarrassment. There is a "death ray" in one story, zombies in a second, a gland beneath the pituitary that actually controls growth in a third, and an oversize alligator that swallows people whole in the fourth.

The writing is so smooth, the pacing so nicely done, and the wrap-up so glib that the reader is not even aware of so many loose ends left dangling. It is almost as if Hogan either did not know how the story was going to be resolved or had forgotten the threads he had so neatly woven into the yarn. But it doesn't really matter: the telling of the tale is the thing, and this is well done. For the fifteen cents the magazine originally cost, what more could anyone want—even when that sum represented a full hour's work.

A close reading leads one to believe that the cancellation of the magazine was not anticipated by Hogan. The groundwork was laid for future stories throughout the four published issues.

Each of the four stories was over one hundred pages, including illustrations, and they represent some of the best efforts of one of the major pulp authors of the thirties. Hogan had his faults, but he was a consummate story teller, and in this short-lived series he provided rapidly paced, vivid action and smooth writing.

Information Sources

BIBLIOGRAPHY:
Hardin, Nils. "An Interview with Henry Steeger." *Xenophile*, no. 33 (July 1977): 3–18.
———, and George Hocutt. "A Checklist of Popular Publications Titles 1930–1955." *Xenophile*, no. 33 (July 1977): 21–24.
Hickman, Lynn. "Checklist of Issues: Secret Six." *The Pulp Era*, no. 75 (Spring 1971): 11.

Weinberg, Robert. "The Not-So-Secret–Six." *Pulp*, no. 4 (Spring 1972): 18–25.
INDEX SOURCES: Weinberg, Robert, and Lohr McKinstry. *The Hero Pulp Index*.
     Evergreen, Colo.: Opar Press, 1971.
LOCATION SOURCES: University of California–Los Angeles Library (Vol. 1, no. 1,
     only); private collectors.

Publication History

MAGAZINE TITLE: *The Secret 6*.
TITLE CHANGES: None.
VOLUME AND ISSUE DATA: Vol. 1, no. 1 (October 1934) through Vol. 1, no. 4
     (December 1935); 4 issues.
PUBLISHER: Popular Publications, Inc., 2256 Grove Street, Chicago, Illinois, with
     editorial offices at 205 East 42nd Street, New York, New York.
EDITOR: Robert J. Hogan (unconfirmed).
PRICE PER ISSUE: 15 cents.
SIZE AND PAGINATION: 7" X 10"; 128 pages.
CURRENT STATUS: Discontinued.
—*Joseph Lewandowski*

SECRETS OF THE SECRET SERVICE

A Clayton Magazines title, *Secrets of the Secret Service* was first published
in November 1930; it was probably very short-lived. No other information is
available.

Information Sources

INDEX SOURCES: None known.
LOCATION SOURCES: University of California–Los Angeles Library (Vol. 1, no. 1;
     note that UCLA Library indexes this as *Secret Service Detective Stories*, not to
     be confused with another publication of this title by Carwood Publications); private
     collectors.

Publication History

MAGAZINE TITLE: *Secrets of the Secret Service*.
TITLE CHANGES: None known.
VOLUME AND ISSUE DATA: Vol. 1, no. 1 (November 1930); number of issues and
     extent unknown.
PUBLISHER: The Clayton Magazines, Inc., 155 East 44th Street, New York, New York.
EDITOR: Not known.
PRICE PER ISSUE: Not known.
SIZE AND PAGINATION: Not known.
CURRENT STATUS: Discontinued.

77 SUNSET STRIP

Appearing promptly after the demise of a very similar magazine, *Tightrope*,*
from the same publisher, *77 Sunset Strip* was also hoping to gain from the

publicity of a popular television series by the same name. The magazine's first issue, however, in July 1960, was the only one published.

The lead story featured the television characters, Bailey and Spencer, in a "new 77 Sunset Strip mystery" titled "Elephant Blues" written by Ben Christopher. Other short stories were by Charlotte & Dan Ross, C. B. Gilford, Tom Stevenson, Robert Andrea, Al James, Talmage Powell, John Jakes, and Lois Eby.

The pulp size and format used was an anachronism that could not be successfully revived, however, and despite the better-than-average run of contemporary crime-adventure stories, the bimonthly schedule was not continued.

Information Sources

INDEX SOURCES: Cook, Michael L. *Monthly Murders*. Westport, Conn.: Greenwood Press, 1982.
LOCATION SOURCES: Private collectors.

Publication History

MAGAZINE TITLE: *77 Sunset Strip*.
TITLE CHANGES: None.
VOLUME AND ISSUE DATA: Vol. 1, no. 1 (July 1960); 1 issue.
PUBLISHER: Henry Scharf as Great American Publications, Inc., 270 Madison Avenue, New York 16, New York.
EDITOR: Jonas Carter; Sheldon Wax, editorial director.
PRICE PER ISSUE: 35 cents.
SIZE AND PAGINATION: 6-1/2" X 9-1/4"; 92 pages.
CURRENT STATUS: Discontinued.

SEXTON BLAKE LIBRARY, THE (British)

With the phenomenal success of Conan Doyle's creation, Sherlock Holmes, it was inevitable that others in his mold would follow. Editors of boys' magazines were swift to rise to the occasion and produce a host of detectives for the juvenile market. These included characters such as Sexton Blake, Nelson Lee, Kenyon Ford, Dixon Brett, Panther Grayle, Colwyn Dane, and Dixon Hawke. All, to suit the market, had boy assistants; many also had bloodhounds with names such as Pedro and Solomon, who were almost human. Boys especially could identify themselves in the leading role. It was quite obvious that juvenile readers would want a little more from their heroes than a man who, in the midst of meditation, would suddenly arrive at the solutions to the crimes or talk them through with his Doctor Watson. With this in mind, therefore, they were created as primarily men of action, and they were thrown into all manner of incredible and bizarre situations.

But most of these detectives were stereocopies of each other, each having two-syllable, Christian names; and with masses of manuscripts being churned out, it was necessary to change the names from one detective to another only to suit any publication or publisher. But of all the detectives created, it was Sexton Blake who was to have the biggest impact—and why Blake did is a mystery that has been debated many times. Perhaps it was simply due to the constant exposure of the character that had the effect. Maybe even the name of Sexton for the Baker Street sleuth, with its suggestion of sombre and graveyard tones, was responsible.

After an early beginning in the weekly *Halfpenny Marvel*, Sexton Blake settled down in a similar paper of his own entitled *Union Jack*, where his run was assured for nearly forty years. In 1933, the paper was remodeled as *Detective Weekly* (British),* and Blake continued to fight crime within its pages until the outbreak of the Second World War. Created in 1893, it was not until 1915 that the Amalgamated Press launched *The Sexton Blake Library*, a handy pocket-sized publication that contained a 60,000-word, novel-length story in each issue.

Sexton Blake had appeared previously in many other publications, such as *Boys Friend Library, Answers,* and *Penny Pictorial*, and such was his popularity that the publishers felt assured that the new publication would be a success. How right they were, for in this form it ran for about fifty years.

For most of its time, *The Sexton Blake Library* catered to an undeterminate market of readers from age nine to ninety. Advertisements for the publication would appear in boys' weeklies of a far more juvenile type, yet again the stories themselves would be written to attract older readers. With the coming of a new editor, W. Howard Baker, in the middle 1950s, also came a new look (like Nick Carter) for the detective with his newly formed organization, and glamorous secretaries moved with him from Baker Street to larger premises in Berkeley Square. From this point on, a definite move to an adult readership was made, and this revealed itself in not only the stories but the illustrations also.

During its successful run, over one hundred authors wrote stories of Sexton Blake (but certainly not Edgar Wallace, Leslie Charteris, or Sax Rohmer, as widely reported), many of whom were successful in other spheres of writing. These included John Creasey, Donald Stuart, Gwyn Evans, Berkeley Gray, Jack Trevor Story, and Hank Janson, among others.

Information Sources

BIBLIOGRAPHY:
Hertzberg, Francis. "Sexton Blake the Office Boys Sherlock Holmes." *Xenophile*, no. 7 (October 1974): 5.
Lofts, W.O.G. "Sexton Blake." *Dime Novel Roundup*, no. 273 (June 15, 1955): 48–50.
———. "Sexton Blake." *Dime Novel Roundup*, no. 439 (April 15, 1969): 40–43.
———, and Derek J. Adley. *The Men Behind Boys' Fiction*. London: Howard Baker Publishers Ltd., 1970.
———. *Old Boys Books, A Complete Catalogue*. London: privately printed, 1969.
Turner, E. S. *Boys Will Be Boys*. London: Michael Joseph Ltd., 1948.
INDEX SOURCES: None known.

LOCATION SOURCES: Private collectors.

Publication History

MAGAZINE TITLE: *The Sexton Blake Library*.
TITLE CHANGES: None.
VOLUME AND ISSUE DATA: First Series: September 1915 through May 1925, nos.
    1–382; 382 issues. Second Series: June 1925 through May 1941, nos. 1–744; 744
    issues. Third Series: June 1941 through June 1963, nos. 1–526; 526 issues. (Note:
    From W. Howard Baker's editorship, commencing with no. 359 of the Third
    Series in 1956, it was unofficially known as the Fourth Series because of the
    startling change of format). Fifth Series: February 1965 through November 1968,
    nos. 1–45; 45 issues. From Fifth Series, No. 34, publication became irregular.
PUBLISHERS: Amalgamated Press, Ltd., London; Fleetway Publications circa 1960;
    Fifth Series published by Mayflower Press, London.
EDITOR: W. Howard Baker, 1956.
PRICE PER ISSUE: Various, 2 pence to 9 pence.
SIZE AND PAGINATION: 5-1/2" X 7"; average 64 pages.
CURRENT STATUS: Discontinued.
—*W.O.G. Lofts and Derek J. Adley*

SHADOW ANNUAL, THE

The Shadow Annual was part of a series of large-size, "bedsheet" format of
magazines, issued by Street & Smith in the early 1940s, usually annually. Each
consisted of stories reprinted from one of their genre magazines, such as *Detective
Story Magazine* (Street & Smith),* *Western Story*, and *Sea Story*. At 160 pages
for twenty-five cents, the three *Shadow Annuals*, containing three novels each,
were definite bargains.

The first (1942) *Shadow Annual* featured a portrait of The Shadow as Lamont
Cranston, a revised version of one of George Rozen's better cover paintings for
*The Shadow Magazine** (January 1, 1939, issue) and led off with "The Living
Shadow," the first story featuring that sinister, black-cloaked crime fighter.
Slightly abridged and with chapters rearranged from its first appearance in the
April 1931 magazine, it has The Shadow emerging from a foggy night to save
a young man from suicide, recruiting him as an agent, and solving jewel robberies
and murders in New York City. "The Ghost Makers" (October 15, 1932) is a
flawed novel about a ring of murderous mediums, interesting for the expert
knowledge of magic tricks shown by author Maxwell Grant, himself a professional magician. "The Black Hush" (August 1, 1933), very popular with Shadow
fans, is borderline science fiction in which criminals strike throughout the city
in a power blackout created by a searchlight throwing beams of darkness instead
of light.

The 1943 *Annual* led off with another popular novel, "The Voodoo Master"
(March 1, 1936), a melodrama in which Dr. Moxquino, master hypnotist and
creator of zombies, lures The Shadow at the climax into a red room, where the

latter's black-cloaked form will be a perfect target. In "Hidden Death" (September 1932), an eccentric inventor is found shot to death in a locked room, the first of several seemingly perfect murders announced ahead of time through the mail. An interesting but flawed story, its cool, analytical tone is jarred in its middle by a long account of a violent gun battle between The Shadow and a horde of mobsters. "The Gray Ghost" (May 1, 1936), a well-liked novel, featured one of the trickiest plot devices of Gibson's tricky career. Who is the hooded, grey-clad Ghost who pillages and kills the rich? Though suspects are few, the problem is remarkably difficult and the solution a real surprise.

The World War II paper shortage cancelled many annuals and delayed others. Not until 1947 did the third, and last, *Shadow Annual* appear.

All the novels in the third *Annual* are chosen from *The Shadow's* digest period, from late 1942 (when all Street & Smith pulp magazines were converted to the smaller size to save paper) to late 1948. Few novels from this period have rated highly with Shadow fans. Good ideas are poorly developed; the novels are too short for the plot complications Gibson loved; and the writing seems tired. War-induced editorial restrictions—"I couldn't have any of those fantastic spy rings or anything," Gibson said, "because they were in reality"[1]—turned the tone of the tales "from melodrama to whodunit."[2]

Perhaps the real problem is that these are not Shadow novels at all except by courtesy. The crimes are those that any good private detective agency could handle. There is no real need for The Shadow's underground network of agents, his icy genius, and hot guns. More and more in this period, the action is carried by one of his alter egos, Lamont Cranston.

Still, "Toll of Death" (March 1944) has suspense and some fine atmospheric touches as people die in Long Valley, apparently from a supernatural curse, their passing marked by the tolling of giant phantom bells. In "No Time for Murder" (December 1944), aged Colonel Tolland finds that his dreams correctly foretell the death by violence of his old friends and associates. Despite this intriguing premise, the novel is weak and confused. By contrast, "Murder By Magic" (August 1945) is a bright and sprightly tale of murderous magicians seeking the stolen fabulous horde of the jewels of Malkara, hidden somewhere by a dead magician's magic tricks. Sparkling with Gibson's first-hand experience with stage illusions such as the Chinese Pagoda, the Water Into Wine, and the Linking Rings, it is easily the best of the three novels in this *Annual*. But basically, it's a Norgil novel about Gibson's suave magician-detective, not a Shadow story at all.

The novels in each *Annual* seem chosen for variety (the first, for example, includes a New York murder story, a science fiction story, and a tale of crooked stage magicians). There is no common atmosphere to them. Though many of the best Shadow stories were ignored and there were no stories from the most important period of the magazine (1937–1943), these *Annuals* unintentionally provide a fair short course and history of the Shadow novel as written by the remarkable Walter B. Gibson.

Notes

1. Walter B. Gibson, "Out of the Shadows," *Duende*, Vol. 1, no. 2 (Winter 1977), p. 35.
2. Will Murray, *The Duende History of The Shadow Magazine*, (Greenwood, Mass.: Odyssey Publications, 1980), p. 116.

Information Sources

BIBLIOGRAPHY:
Gibson, Walter B. "Out of the Shadows." *Duende,* Vol. 1, no. 2 (Winter 1977): 33–46.
Murray, Will. *The Duende History of The Shadow Magazine*. Greenwood, Mass.: Odyssey Press, 1980.
Reynolds, Quentin. *The Fiction Factory*. New York: Random House, 1955.
Sampson, Robert. *The Night Master*. Chicago: The Pulp Press, 1982.
INDEX SOURCES: None known.
LOCATION SOURCES: Private collectors.

Publication History

MAGAZINE TITLE: *The Shadow Annual.*
TITLE CHANGES: None.
VOLUME AND ISSUE DATA: 1942; 1943; 1947; no volume or issue designation; 3 issues.
PUBLISHER: Street & Smith Publications, Inc., 79–89 Seventh Avenue, New York, New York.
EDITOR: Not known.
PRICE PER ISSUE: 25 cents.
SIZE AND PAGINATION: 8-1/2" X 11-1/2"; 160 pages.
CURRENT STATUS: Discontinued.
—*Frank D. McSherry, Jr.*

SHADOW MAGAZINE, THE

When *The Shadow Magazine* debuted with the April 1931 issue, it marked the beginning of a major revolution in the pulp magazine industry. Pulp magazines had always traded on the hero as their chief staple, and often a successful character could run for years in the same magazine. But he could never dominate it. That had been done in the days of the dime novel, which was defunct in 1931. Street & Smith had been a pioneer in the dime novel, with Nick Carter and Frank Merriwell, but a consequence of depending on a single character to carry a publication was the inevitable decline of the publication when that character's adventures grew stale. In the pulp magazine, stale characters could be dropped or replaced in time to salvage the publication.

But Street & Smith's business manager, Henry W. Ralston, who had joined the firm in its dime novel days and firmly believed in the viability of the series character, felt that such characters could be revived successfully. He may or may not have been influenced in his opinion by the Great Depression climate, and it was not because of Ralston's faith that The Shadow was created. At that time, the "Detective Story Hour," a radio program which consisted of readings from *Detective Story Magazine* (Street & Smith),* enjoyed an unprecedented popularity due to the sinister voice of its narrator (who had been dubbed "The Shadow"). Fearful of having that characteristic stolen by other publishers, Ralston deputized Editor Frank Blackwell to assemble a Shadow magazine, to protect the copyright. He evidently also felt the new venture could test the waters for a new kind of pulp magazine in the tradition of the Nick Carter dime novel.

Blackwell fortuitously happened upon a newspaperman-turned-fiction-writer named Walter B. Gibson while he was looking for someone to write a novel featuring the nebulous Shadow. Gibson readily accepted and produced "The Living Shadow," a loose, mysterioso forerunner of The Shadow novels to come. Gibson fleshed out the radio voice into a tall, black-cloaked, slouch-hatted apparition, who operated as a detective yet was often more sinister than the criminals he stalked.

The first issue of *The Shadow Magazine* (April 1931) sold well, by which time Gibson was at work on a third novel. The Shadow was swiftly inaugurated as a bimonthly, and by late 1932, it was being published twice a month. Gibson was writing a 60,000-word novel every two weeks in order to meet the demand.

The accelerated schedule, which might have intimidated a lesser writer, merely accelerated Gibson's inventiveness. By this time, John L. Nanovic had been hired to edit the new *wunderkind* of the pulps, and he, with Ralston and Gibson, developed a method of plotting the stories in conference and then having them written from straight outlines. This enabled Gibson to produce regularly yet still be able to keep the stories fresh and full of variety—thanks to the input of the other two men, as well as to Gibson's own fertile imagination.

It was decided that The Shadow should remain a figure of mystery, the better to retain reader interest, as well as to allow for the greatest range of future development. Despite the fact that Gibson had identified The Shadow as millionaire Lamont Cranston in the second novel, with the third it was established that The Shadow was merely impersonating the real Cranston. Cranston was only the first of the many long-term alternate egos to which The Shadow resorted in order to infiltrate various segments of society as a secret detective by day, leaving the violent work of the night to The Shadow.

The Shadow, thus an enigma, his true identity unknown even to his creator, built an ever-growing network of secret agents, drawn from all walks of life, who owed their lives and allegiance to their master, The Shadow, and who acted on his behalf. These included Harry Vincent, underworld tough Cliff Marsland, Burbank investment-broker Rutledge Mann, reporter Clyde Burke, and many others. The law was represented by Police Commissioner Ralph Weston and Detective Joe Cardona.

But these supporting characters were stiffly drawn. Only The Shadow was given a strong personality. He was no less than a master detective, sharing an identical hawk-nosed profile with Sherlock Holmes (with whom he had many things in common), possessing burning eyes and a singular fire-opal ring. Hints dropped in early novels tantalized readers with The Shadow's past as a World War I spy and of his various contacts throughout the world, but ultimately, Gibson raised more questions than he answered.

By far, however, it was Walter Gibson's genius for plotting and writing the atmospheric detective story on a regular basis, with frequent changes in story type, which kept *The Shadow Magazine* going. Gibson's mysterious character attracted the readers, but only his superior writing could keep them coming back twice a month over the years.

Within the first year or so, Gibson had worked out his basic approaches to the characters, and he concentrated upon expanding his formulas. He never worked from an established pattern; rather, his individual outlines became his formulas. The first novel contained some strong scenes laid in Chinatown, so the Chinatown story became a regular event. The best of these included "The Fate Joss" and "The Grove of Doom." The Shadow often battled the dregs of the underworld on their own terms. He carried for this purpose two automatics and did not hesitate to use them in carefully choreographed scenes of gunplay. "The Condor," "Lingo," and "The Red Blot" show Gibson's rather stylized New York underworld at its seedy best.

But it was the supercrooks who were The Shadow's meat. These were criminals far beyond the law's reach, often possessed of vast and fantastic resources, not to mention hordes of trigger-happy gunmen. Their names were as fantastic as their schemes—The Death Giver, The Python, Gray Fist, Cyro, The Plot Master, and scores of others. Not restricted to stories of mere crime, Gibson at intervals introduced science fiction elements to the stories. "Atoms of Death," "The Dark Death," and "Charg, Monster" are among the best of these.

Gibson's range was amazing. Against a backdrop of The Shadow versus Crime, he took time to tell the stories of people caught in personal dilemmas ("Road of Crime" and "Battle of Greed"), send The Shadow abroad ("The London Crime" and "'The North Woods Mystery"'), and create a kind of Gothic Shadow novel set in a gloomy mansion ("The Ghost of the Manor" and "House of Silence").

Where Gibson excelled was in those novels in which he employed the magician's trick of misdirection in the course of a story's denouement. Classic Shadows for this reason include "Zemba," "The Green Box," and "The Fifth Face." A constant experimenter, Gibson was not satisfied with falling into comfortable formulas; he continually struggled to outguess his readers even as they were trying to second-guess him.

But even Walter Gibson could not be expected to maintain a twenty-four-novels-a-year pace unassisted. In 1935, Ralston and Nanovic, fearful of *The Shadow Magazine* falling into a rut, had Gibson write some experimental novels with emphasis more on action than plot. "The Salamanders" was one of these, but concern that Gibson might be thrown off stride impelled the firm to hire a new writer to share the Maxwell Grant house name with Gibson. This was Theodore Tinsley, who, beginning in 1936 with "Partners of Peril," would write four novels per year, each filled with sometimes sadistic violence and a kind of sexy *femme fatale*, the likes of which The Shadow seldom encountered under Gibson.

Tinsley's efforts brought a mild sexiness into the series, which also crept into Gibson's own work in the late thirties, but it also increased the variety in the series once Tinsley shook off the imitation Gibson style of his earliest Shadows. His best work is striking and includes "The Fifth Napoleon" and "Death's Harlequin." Tinsley produced nearly thirty novels in all, one of which was such a taboo breaker that the firm felt compelled to kill the story and run it in *Clues** under Tinsley's name—but only after The Shadow had been revised out of the story. This was "Satan's Signature" in the November 1941 issue of *Clues*.

Another consequence of the new directions taken in *The Shadow Magazine* was the introduction of recurring villains, all of them supercrooks. The first was the Voodoo Master, in the novel of that name in 1936, who appeared erratically until 1938. Five loosely connected novels, beginning with "The Hand," brought The Shadow into conflict with a gang of criminals. Between 1939 and 1941, there was a concentration of such recurring villains. Shiwan Khan, the evil descendant of Genghis Khan (probably The Shadow's greatest foe), appeared in four excellent novels. At the same time, starting with "The Prince of Evil," Benedict Stark harried the Master of Darkness through an equal number of stories written by Tinsley. Finally, there was The Wasp, who returned only once.

After 1941, Gibson's novels seemed to close in on themselves, becoming repetitious, sometimes lifeless, and even becoming inadvertent parodies of their former selves. Still, his inventiveness seldom flagged, and there were interesting novels even after this, but The Shadow had lost his mystery. In a 1937 revelation ("The Shadow Unmasks"), he was portrayed as really the aviator-spy, Kent Allard. At first, Allard supplanted Lamont Cranston in the novels, but a combination of a new radio show starring Cranston as The Shadow and the lack of strength in Gibson's portrayal of Allard caused the latter to be gradually (but not totally) phased out of the series. Cranston, aided by Margo Lane, who had been created for the radio version, became the stars of the pulp from 1941 on. This dilution of the characters hampered Gibson's creativity.

By 1943, the war caused *The Shadow Magazine* to convert to digest format and to lose editor Nanovic and writer Tinsley. Gibson, cramped for space and forced by recent trends to eschew melodrama for standard mystery stories, produced several year's worth of unexciting novels. Only two, "Malmordo" and "Jade Dragon," are notable. Between these two novels, interestingly enough, Gibson stopped writing the stories due to a contract dispute. He was replaced by Bruce Elliott, a protégé who eradicated much of Gibson's carefully laid background and began writing short, crisp, often experimental mystery novelettes in which The Shadow was all but absent and Cranston (without Margo Lane) was the star. It could be argued that Elliott was the superior writer in that his stories were contemporary with their times, while Gibson tended to write from an older mystery tradition, but Elliott's work did not sit well with *The Shadow's* readers. In early 1947, the magazine was retitled *The Shadow Mystery Magazine*, and The Shadow shared the pages with mystery novels by significant authors. But even as a bimonthly, sales continued to slip. In an attempt to salvage the magazine, Elliott was instructed to follow the old Gibson pattern; his only effort in this direction, "Reign of Terror," was quite good.

With a reappearance of the old title, *The Shadow Magazine*, Gibson returned in 1948 with "Jade Dragon," after which the magazine reverted to the old pulp format with covers by George Rozen (who was responsible for most of the covers of the thirties and early forties). But the move was to no avail, and *The Shadow* was cancelled with the Summer 1949 issue, along with most of the firm's other pulp magazines. The final novel, "The Whispering Eyes," was a standard, old-style Shadow adventure.

Even after 1949, The Shadow continued on radio and in numerous reprints. In 1963, the character was revived briefly in paperback with Gibson's *Return of The Shadow*, followed by a group of modernized stories by Dennis Lynds. Two Shadow novelettes, "Riddle of the Rangoon Ruby" (*The Shadow Scrapbook*, Harcourt Brace Jovanovich, 1979) and "Blackmail Bay," (*The Duende History of The Shadow Magazine*, Odyssey Publications, 1980) remain the most recent of Gibson's Shadow stories.

The magazine in its day ran a number of other series, including Grace Culver stories by Roswell Brown (Jean Francis Webb), Steve Fisher's Sheridan Doome and Danny Garrett stories (which were continued by William G. Bogart as "Grant Lane"), The Whisperer, and Nick Carter. Frequent contributors included Alan Hathway, Frank Gruber, Talmage Powell, Edwin Burkholder, D. A. Hoover, and John D. MacDonald, whose early writings appeared here in the late forties.

The success of *The Shadow* was due largely to the striking personality of the character as reinforced by the incredible talents of chief author Walter B. Gibson. It could be argued that *The Shadow*—because it was the first magazine of its kind and because it was reinforced by a nearly continuous radio program which firmly fixed the character and his famous phrase, "The Shadow knows," in the public consciousness—was destined to be successful. It is also undeniable that Gibson kept the magazine going. And some credit must go to the striking covers by George Rozen and Graves Gladney and to interior artists Tom Lovell, Edd Cartier, and Earl Mayan. But it was Gibson who single-handedly modified the eerie radio voice into a compelling mystery figure and an immortal of popular fiction.

A British reprint series published at least eight issues under the title of *The Shadow Mystery Magazine*.

Information Sources

BIBLIOGRAPHY:
Carr, Wooda Nicholas. "The Shadow Speaks" (interview with Walter B. Gibson). *Pulp*, no. 5 (Winter 1973): 3–8.

Carr, Wooda Nicholas, and Herman S. McGregor. "Contemplating Seven of the Pulp Heroes." *Bronze Shadows*, no. 12 (October 1967): 3–6.

Cook, Fred. "A Full-Length Shadow Novel as Told to. . . ." *Bronze Shadows*, no. 3 (February 1966): 12–13.

———. "The Shadow Magazine—Checklist by Dates Issued." *Bronze Shadows*, no. 1 (n.d. [October 1965]):5–6.

Cox, Ed. "Early J. D." (John D. MacDonald in *The Shadow Magazine*). *JDM Bibliophile*, no. 2 (May 1966): 3–4.

Cox, J. Randolph. "That Mysterious Aide to the Forces of Law and Order." *The Armchair Detective*, Vol. 4, no. 4 (July 1971): 221–29.

Edwards, John. "From Shadow to Superman." *The Age of the Unicorn*, Vol. 2, no. 1 (April 1980): 10–18.

Eisgruber, Frank, Jr. *Gangland's Doom: The Shadow of the Pulps*. Oak Lawn, Ill.: Robert Weinberg, 1974.

Gibson, Walter B. "Out of the Shadows." *Duende*, Vol. 1, no. 2 (Winter 1977): 33–46.

———. *The Shadow Scrapbook*. New York: Harcourt Brace Jovanovich, 1979.

Grennell, Dean A. "The Shadow." *The Pulp Era*, no. 61 (July 1964): 13–24.

Murray, Will. "Graves Gladney Speaks." *Duende*, no. 1 (April 1975): 23–30.

———. *The Duende History of The Shadow Magazine*. Greenwood, Mass.: Odyssey Press, 1980.

———. "The Top 25 Shadow Novels—and One Stinker." *The Age of the Unicorn*, Vol. 1, no. 4 (October 1979): 3–17.

Myers, Dick. "The Case of the Elusive Author." *Bronze Shadows*, no. 10 (June 1967): 14–15.

Nevins, Francis M., Jr. "Notes on Two Shadows of JDM." *JDM Bibliophile*, no. 13 (January 1970): 10.

Sampson, Robert. "Just a Little Matter of Doom." *Xenophile*, no. 4 (June 1974): 7–8.

———. *The Night Master*. Chicago: The Pulp Press, 1982.

Warren, James. "The Shadow Knows. . .and Tells His Secrets." *Doc Savage Club Reader*, no. 6 (n.d. [Spring 1979]): 12.

INDEX SOURCES: Cook, Michael L. *Monthly Murders* (digest size). Westport, Conn.: Greenwood Press, 1982.

LOCATION SOURCES: Private collectors.

Publication History

MAGAZINE TITLE: *The Shadow Magazine*.

TITLE CHANGES: *The Shadow Mystery Magazine* (with February–March 1947 issue); reverted to *The Shadow Magazine* (1948).

VOLUME AND ISSUE DATA: Vol. 1, no. 1 (April 1931) through Vol. 55, no. 1 (Summer 1949); 326 issues.

PUBLISHER: Street & Smith Publications, Inc., 79 Seventh Avenue, New York, New York, later 122 East 42nd Street, New York, New York.

EDITOR: John L. Nanovic.

PRICE PER ISSUE: 10 cents; 15 cents; 25 cents.

SIZE AND PAGINATION: Average 7" X 10" (through Vol. 46, no. 3); 5-3/8" X 7-5/8" (through Vol. 54, no. 3); thereafter pulp size again for remaining issues.

CURRENT STATUS: Discontinued.

—*Will Murray*

SHADOW MYSTERY MAGAZINE, THE (British)

See SHADOW MAGAZINE, THE

SHADOW MYSTERY MAGAZINE, THE (U.S.)

See SHADOW MAGAZINE, THE

SHELL SCOTT MYSTERY MAGAZINE

Leo Margulies, the founder of Renown Publications in 1956, was a magazine publisher of some stature. He had been editorial director on Ned Pine's line of magazines (Standard Magazines, Inc.) in the 1930s and 1940s and left that position only at the time of the demise of the pulps. There, he had been in control of such series as the Phantom Detective, G–Men Detective, The Masked Detective, plus many others, all of which were character magazines, featuring a popular detective.

While many magazine publishers had continued the old pulp format in their own publications, it was Margulies with his new (in 1956) *Michael Shayne Mystery Magazine (Mike Shayne Mystery Magazine*)* that actually captured the old style of the hero character magazines from the thirties.

Margulies, in February 1966, added *The Man From U.N.C.L.E. Magazine** and the *Shell Scott Mystery Magazine* as companions to the then-titled *Mike Shayne Mystery Magazine*. These, too, were patterned after the hero pulp examples.

The *Shell Scott Mystery Magazine* was published under the imprint of the LeMarg Publishing Corporation, the name being somewhat of an anagram of Margulies's name. The principal feature of the new magazine was a short novel by Richard S. Prather (a "Shell Scott" story) and was accompanied by a number of short stories by some of the leading mystery fiction writers of that period, such as Michael Avallone, Harry Whittington, Evan Hunter, Jonathan Craig, and Dennis Lynds. Other frequent contributors were Talmage Powell, John Jakes, Bill Pronzini, and John D. MacDonald. The stories were of top quality.

Beginning as a monthly publication in February 1966, it survived in the face of fierce competition only through its ninth issue, in November of that same year. The last issue indicated a change to a bimonthly schedule, but no further issues appeared.

Information Sources

INDEX SOURCES: Cook, Michael L. *Monthly Murders*. Westport, Conn.: Greenwood
    Press, 1982.
LOCATION SOURCES: Private collectors.

Publication History

MAGAZINE TITLE: *Shell Scott Mystery Magazine*.
TITLE CHANGES: None.
VOLUME AND ISSUE DATA: Vol. 1, no. 1 (February 1966) through Vol. 2, no. 3 (November 1966); 9 issues.
PUBLISHER: The LeMarg Publishing Corporation, 160 West 46th Street, later 56 West 45th Street, New York, New York.
EDITORS: Cylvia K. Margulies, editorial director; H. N. Alden, associate editor.
PRICE PER ISSUE: 50 cents.
SIZE AND PAGINATION: 5-1/2'' X 7-1/2''; 144 pages.
CURRENT STATUS: Discontinued.
—*Tom Johnson*

SHERLOCK HOLMES JOURNAL, THE (British)

British admirers of the world's greatest detective first joined forces as a formal organization in 1934, as the Sherlock Holmes Society, but the group dissolved only a few years later with the approach of World War II. It was not until 1951 that some members of the prewar society joined with others attracted by the well-publicized Sherlock Holmes Exhibition at 221B Baker Street during the Festival of Britain to resurrect the organization, renamed the Sherlock Holmes Society of London.

Acting quickly to achieve one of the goals set out in their constitution, "to publish the transactions of the Society and communications dealing with the Sherlock Holmes canon," the members launched *The Sherlock Holmes Journal* as a semiannual that over the years has far surpassed those modest objectives.

The first eight issues were mimeographed from typewritten masters, but a larger membership and stronger finances then allowed printing (Baskerville, of course) on slick paper and plentiful use of photographs and other illustrations to accompany the literary contributions of the society's members. The members rallied from Europe and the United States, as well as Great Britain, offering current news, reviews, pastiches, articles, limericks, competitions, and letters that have allowed publication of a thoroughly professional magazine.

One of its greatest strengths is its sense of place. With their ability to carry out on-the-spot investigations, its British authors have devoted considerable attention to the London and England of Sherlock Holmes, identifying many of the locales, both city and country, presented in the Sherlock Holmes stories in greater or lesser disguise. *The Sherlock Holmes Journal* also pays frequent tribute to Sir Arthur Conan Doyle, honored by the society's members as the author of the stories rather than, as in the United States, as Dr. Watson's literary agent. Many articles over the years have discussed Doyle's other works, and the magazine commemorated his birth with a centenary issue in 1959.

Another aspect worthy of mention is the sense of continuity in *The Sherlock Holmes Journal*. Its first issue included a collection of short items by James Edward Holroyd under the title "The Egg-Spoon," and the column continued almost without interruption for fifty-five issues, ending in 1980. Colin Prestige, whose article in the first issue described the press coverage of the 1951 Sherlock Holmes Exhibition, now contributes "The Jack-Knife" as a successor to Holroyd's column. And Anthony Howlett, reviewing various film versions of "The Hound of the Baskervilles" in the first issue, still arranges the society's annual film evenings and wrote on Doyle's life and career in the magazine's Summer 1980 issue.

The Sherlock Holmes Journal has always provided thorough coverage of the society's activities, which included a spectacular pilgrimage to Switzerland that culminated in a reenactment of the battle between Sherlock Holmes and Professor Moriarty at the Reichenbach Falls. A special thirty-six-page pictorial supplement was published to describe the "Tour of Switzerland in the Footsteps of Sherlock Holmes," with dozens of photographs of the society's members in full costume as Sherlockian characters and detailed accounts of the tour's many events by the participants and the accompanying press.

Information Sources

INDEX SOURCES: None known.
LOCATION SOURCES: Private collectors.

Publication History

MAGAZINE TITLE: *The Sherlock Holmes Journal*.
TITLE CHANGES: None.
VOLUME AND ISSUE DATA: Vol. 1,, no. 1 (May 1952) through Vol. 15, no. 3 (to date, Winter 1981); 58 issues (plus pictorial supplement—see text).
PUBLISHER: Sherlock Holmes Society of London, 8 Queen Anne Street, London W.1, England; other subsequent addresses: 12 St. James Place, London S.W.1; 46 Charles Street, London W.1; 3 Deanery Street, London W.1; The Studio, 39 Clabon Mews, London S.W.1. Present: 8 Southern Road, Fortis Green, London N2 9LE, England.
EDITORS: James Edward Holroyd and Philip Dalton (through Vol. 2, no. 4); the Marquis of Donegall (through Vol. 11, no. 4); James Edward Holroyd and Philip Dalton (through Vol. 12, no. 3/4); Nicholas Utechin and Philip Dalton (through Vol. 13, no. 3); Philip Dalton and Nicholas Utechin (present).
PRICE PER ISSUE: By membership only; currently $20.00 annually U.S.
SIZE AND PAGINATION: 8" X 10" (through Vol. 2, no. 4); 7-1/4" X 9-3/4" (subsequent); 44 pages (first 8 issues), 32 pages (subsequent).
CURRENT STATUS: Active.
—*Peter E. Blau*

SHIELD WEEKLY

One of the more short-lived publications in the Street & Smith line, the *Shield Weekly* lasted only twenty-two weeks. Named after the paper-covered novel series of the 1890s, the *Shield Series*, all twenty-two numbers were probably written by Frederick W. Davis using the pen name Alden F. Bradshaw.

The first eight numbers had the subtitle of "True Detective Stores—Stranger Than Fiction" below a policeman's shield, from which scowled a mustached police chief. With issue number 9, the subtitle became "True Stories from the Note-Books of Famous Chiefs of Police," and the shield was replaced with the standing figure of a policeman.

Numbers 1 through 16 had, as hero, Sheridan Keene, a detective assigned to the Boston Detective Service under Chief Inspector William B. Watts. Inspector Watts's portrait was used as a frontispiece in many numbers, and his likeness appeared on two covers as well.

With number 17, the scene shifted to Pittsburgh for several adventures with Steve Manley, who worked for Chief of Detectives Roger O'Mara of that city. In Chicago, for the final number, Kit Keen solved one case for "the chief of Chicago's detective corps," who was not named.

In spite of being advertised as "true detective stories," the contents of *Shield Weekly* were standard narratives with no attempt to present them in a documentary style. All of the stories were later incorporated into the paper-covered novels about Nick Carter published in the *Magnet Library*, with Nick Carter's name substituted for that of the original detective. A decade later, they were serialized, one story divided into three episodes, in the issues of *Nick Carter Stories.**

Information Sources

BIBLIOGRAPHY:
Bragin, Charles. *Dime Novel Bibliography 1860–1928*. Brooklyn, N. Y.: privately printed, 1938.
Holmes, Harold C. "Shield Weekly." *Dime Novel Roundup*, no. 138 (March 1944): 1–3.
LeBlanc, Edward T. "Dime Novel Sketches No. 51." *Dime Novel Roundup*, no. 375 (December 15, 1963): p. 107.
INDEX SOURCES: Cox, J. Randolph. *Nick Carter Stories and Other Series Containing Stories of Nick Carter*. Fall River, Mass.: Edward T. LeBlanc, 1980.
LOCATION SOURCES: Private collectors.

Publication History

MAGAZINE TITLE: *Shield Weekly*.
TITLE CHANGES: None.
VOLUME AND ISSUE DATA: No. 1 (December 8, 1900) through no. 22 (May 4, 1901); 22 issues.
PUBLISHER: Street & Smith, Publishers, 238 William Street, New York, New York.
EDITOR: Not known.
PRICE PER ISSUE: 5 cents.
SIZE AND PAGINATION: 6-7/8'' X 10-1/4''; 32 pages.
CURRENT STATUS: Discontinued.
—*J. Randolph Cox*

SHOCK

"The NEW MYSTERY Magazine," shouted the cover, and the editorial page amplified eagerly:

> Every story in *Shock* is written especially for us by a leading author in the crime-mystery field. . . . It is an adventure in violence. . . .
> The best tales of crime and violence have never been published, for fear of wounding sensitive minds. We feel that in this day and age of enlightenment, a realistic approach to the fascinating subject of crimes of pathological violence is no longer taboo. We are blowing off the lid. We are permitting our writers to pull out all stops and present their stories of men and women caught in the entangling web of crime and all its ramifications as it really happens. . . .
> It is our intention to give you stories that are ordinarily considered too strong for the average reader. . . .The accent is on the bizarre and shocking in crime adventures happening to believable, recognizable people.[1]

In general, it was true. *Shock* did present ordinary characters who wandered into an appalling maze of crime, experienced emotional conflicts, and met murder grinning from familiar eyes. The stories began in tension, proceeded through complexity, and ended in shrieks and spouting gore; most stories contained a violent surprise at the very end. The fiction was often contrived and the melodrama a shade overripe—but not always.

Those "leading authors" were excellent, among them being Bruno Fischer, D. L. Champion, and Theodore Sturgeon (one story each during *Shock's* three-issue run); Frederick C. Davis, Robert Turner, and Bruce Cassidy (two stories each); John Bender (three stories); and John D. MacDonald (six stories, including two under the name Scott O'Hara and, it is assumed, one under the name Marian O'Hearn).

The magazine, itself, was rough-edged, with a pulp-paper smell and an air of vivacious sleaziness. From the covers stared shocked girls, eyes glassy, their shining mouths gaping, their cleavages remarkable. On the first cover, a redhead stares down at a skeleton bedded among gold coins in a coffin, the finger bones clamped about a knife hilt. On the second cover, a blond glares wildly as a gloved male hand extends a smoking pistol, butt first. And on the final cover, another blond clings to the outside of a balastrade, wide-eyed as a male hand slashes at her with a pink slipper's heel. No cover is signed, although the first one is possibly by Rafael DeSoto.

Inside, the text is illustrated by pencil sketches. These range from smudgy, atmospheric drawings to magnificent action scenes, crisp, freshly realized, intensely satisfying. Again, no illustrator's name was given.

For whatever economic reason, *Shock* was a miserly thin magazine. It contained ninety-eight numbered pages, and within this narrow compass was found a novel (seventeen pages long), two novelettes (varying from twelve to twenty-five pages) and from four to six short stories. Each issue also included a one-page preview of a coming story, as a special department, titled either "Without Warning" or "Shockers Ahead." In the first and second issues appeared a two-page picture essay about a spooky subject, "Adventures In the Unknown," by Frederick Blakeslee.

In one way or another, the stories are about perverted love, love gone sour and malignant. In the course of three issues, *Shock* published twenty-five pieces of fiction. Through most of these, the sexes devour each other with their eyes, glower at chosen spouses, and slaughter each other with relentless joy.

The favorite character was a neat, modest, attractive individual knotted with concealed homicidal rage. These aberrations drive the stories and contribute to the violent, last-paragraph twists that wrench into horror. It is true horror, the worst kind, that closes on you while you stand in a sunny place on a familiar street among friends.

Some twists are merely mechanical. A gold digger, expecting a necklace, gets a strangler's noose instead. Or a killer, knocked unconscious, is given the poisoned brandy he intended for another. Or a hemophiliac mobster discovers that the man he killed had the only blood compatible with his own—and proceeds to bleed to death. Other stories, more artfully constructed, drive violently to their conclusion, then twist effectively.

The initial story in the first issue sets the tone of the magazine ("Death is a Dame," March 1948, Frederick C. Davis.) Zelda, the twin sister of the hero's wife, is dead. Or is Zelda posing as his wife, waiting, watching, planning to slaughter him? In the same issue, Robert Turner's "Hell's Belle" tells how Roxy has this little quirk about collecting mementos of murder. She wants the lipstick of a murdered girl—and so do other lethal people, including a girl with a pet rattlesnake.

Many stories ride the eternal triangle, varying the end wonderfully. Other stories strongly emphasize the woman's angle. In MacDonald's "Satan's Angel" (July), the heroine describes her adventures when she goes to skid row, all tarted up, to select a bum she can lead away into a murder trap. Still other stories are tricky excursions into pure violence.

The final issue of *Shock* announced still another MacDonald story coming in the next issue. "No Grave Has My Love" will tell (it promised) how the unconscious girl lies bound on the surgeon's table. She has witnessed his crime—but he loves her. So he will make only a little incision and slice the memory from her brain—not to hurt—just a very small incision. . . . Like most of the other stories in *Shock*, this, too, would have been a sort of love story. Of a most specialized type.

Note

1. Editorial, "Blowing Off the Lid," *Shock*, Vol. 1, no. 2 (May 1948), p. 6.

Information Sources

BIBLIOGRAPHY:
Hardin, Nils, and George Hocutt. "A Checklist of Popular Publications Titles 1930–1955." *Xenophile*, no. 33 (July 1977): 21–24.
Rock, James A. *Who Goes There, A Bibliographic Dictionary*. Bloomington, Ind.: James A. Rock & Co., 1979.
INDEX SOURCES: None known.
LOCATION SOURCES: University of California–Los Angeles Library (Vol. 1, nos. 1, 3); private collectors.

Publication History

MAGAZINE TITLE: *Shock*.
TITLE CHANGES: None.
VOLUME AND ISSUE DATA: Vol. 1, no. 1 (March 1948) through Vol. 1, no. 3 (July 1948); 3 issues.
PUBLISHER: New Publications, Inc., subsidiary of Popular Publications, Inc., 2256 Grove Street, Chicago 16, Illinois, with editorial offices at 210 East 43rd Street, New York 17, New York.
EDITOR: Not known.
PRICE PER ISSUE: 15 cents.
SIZE AND PAGINATION: 6-7/8" X 9-1/2"; 98 pages.
CURRENT STATUS: Discontinued.
—*Robert Sampson*

SHOCK MYSTERY TALES

Although the numbering was presumably continued from *Shock—The Magazine of Terrifying Tales,** issued by another publisher, *Shock Mystery Tales* was a completely different type of magazine. While being billed as "sensational tales of terror," it actually presented much of the same type of violent, raw crime-adventure stories as were appearing in other Pontiac publications. Macabre backgrounds, cults, and weird characters highlighted these stories, however, as is evidenced by examples of story titles: "Brides for the Devil's Cauldron," "Lust of the Vampire Queen," "Curse of the Undead," and "Satan's Mistress." Art Crockett, Don Unatin, Bill Ryder, and Larry Dickson were among the authors.

Covers were straight from the pulp tradition, with scantily clad, shapely young women menaced by hooded or horned cult members.

There were no departments, columns, articles, or announcements of forthcoming stories. And in 1961–1962, this magazine led a very short life, as could be expected.

Information Sources

INDEX SOURCES: Cook, Michael L. *Monthly Murders*. Westport, Conn.: Greenwood
    Press, 1982.
LOCATION SOURCES: Private collectors.

Publication History

MAGAZINE TITLE: *Shock Mystery Tales*.
TITLE CHANGES: None.
VOLUME AND ISSUE DATA: Vol. 2, no. 1 (December 1961) through Vol. 2, no. 4
    (July 1962), 4 issues. (The numbering was possibly continued from *Shock—The
    Magazine of Terrifying Tales*.)
PUBLISHER: Pontiac Publishing Corporation, 1546 Broadway, New York 36, New
    York.
EDITOR: Not known.
PRICE PER ISSUE: 35 cents.
SIZE AND PAGINATION: 5" X 7-1/4" and 5-3/8" X 7-1/4"; 128 pages.
CURRENT STATUS: Discontinued.

SHOCK—THE MAGAZINE OF TERRIFYING TALES

Bugs, rats, spiders, and dismembered monkey's paws frequent the stories of *Shock—The Magazine of Terrifying Tales* in an effort to provide an atmosphere of terror. Shock endings are represented by Stanley Ellin's classic short story,

"The Specialty of the House." Jack the Ripper is present in Robert Bloch's "Yours Truly, Jack the Ripper."

A mixture of both new and reprint stories gave a satisfying representation of macabre tales, including mystery and detective stories hopefully cloaked in terror. Some of the best-known authors contributed, including Ray Bradbury, Theodore Sturgeon, John Collier, Anthony Boucher, Edward D. Hoch, and Miriam Allen deFord. These names lent a prestigious air to the magazine; but after three issues, it gave up the ghost.

Information Sources

INDEX SOURCES: Cook, Michael L. *Monthly Murders*. Westport, Conn.: Greenwood Press, 1982.
LOCATION SOURCES: University of California–Los Angeles; private collectors.

Publication History

MAGAZINE TITLE: *Shock—The Magazine of Terrifying Tales*.
TITLE CHANGES: None.
VOLUME AND ISSUE DATA: Vol. 1, no. 1 (May 1960) through Vol. 1, no. 3 (September 1960) (The numbering was possibly continued in 1961 with *Shock Mystery Tales*.); 3 issues.
PUBLISHER: Winston Publications, Inc., 157 West 57th Street, New York 19, New York.
EDITOR: Not known.
PRICE PER ISSUE: 35 cents.
SIZE AND PAGINATION: 5-1/2" X 7-5/8"; 130 pages.
CURRENT STATUS: Discontinued.

SHOT RANG OUT, A

A mimeographed publication, *A Shot Rang Out* is primarily distributed through the Pulp Heroes Amateur Press Association (PHAPA), but the piece has some general circulation. The first issue, Spring 1981, featured a complete survey of Hugo Gernsback's *Scientific Detective Monthly** (later changed to *Amazing Detective*), including the test sample issue of November 1929. All series were identified, and information was given on the stories written and purchased but never published when the magazine folded. The second issue, Fall 1981 and entitled *Two Shots Rang Out*, contained book and movie reviews but no in-depth research articles such as in the first issue. A third issue was announced, to contain a survey and review of the late David H. Keller's "Taine of San Francisco" series (now very rare); this issue was not published. The magazine had wide acceptance but was handicapped by poor reproduction.

Information Sources

INDEX SOURCES: None known.

LOCATION SOURCES: Private collectors.

Publication History

MAGAZINE TITLE: *A Shot Rang Out.*
TITLE CHANGES: Second issue as *Two Shots Rang Out.*
VOLUME AND ISSUE DATA: No. 1 (Spring 1981) through no. 2 (Fall 1981); 2 issues.
PUBLISHER AND PLACE OF PUBLICATION: Blue Star Book Store, 355 Kennedy
    Drive, Putnam, Connecticut 06260.
EDITORS: David and Susannah Bates.
SIZE AND PAGINATION: 8-1/2" X 11"; 8 pages.
CURRENT STATUS: Inactive.
—*David A. Bates*

SINISTER STORIES

Popular Publications, having had good reader acceptance of its weird-menace magazines (*Dime Mystery Magazine [Dime Mystery Book*], Horror Stories,** and *Terror Tales* [see *Horror Stories*)] and its weird-detective pulp, *Strange Detective Mysteries,** decided to augment its "shudder" group. *Sinister Stories* appeared in January 1940 but ran for only three issues. It was published on alternating months with *Startling Mystery** (commenced February 1940).

That Popular Publications employed economies in publishing *Sinister Stories* is evident. Covers and interior illustrations were taken from earlier issues of the other weird-menace Popular publications, and the rate of payment for stories was one-half cent a word rather than the customary one cent. Some of the stories may have been left over from other publications, as well. Such was one by Hugh B. Cave, "School Mistress for the Mad" (May 1940), with its backwoodsy setting and distraught schoolmarm menaced by loutish, overgrown students—straight out of the 1934 *Terror Tales* era. Few of the stories published in *Sinister Stories* are still effective today.

Information Sources

BIBLIOGRAPHY:
Hardin, Nils. "An Interview with Henry Steeger." *Xenophile*, no. 33 (July 1977): 3–
    18.
————, and George Hocutt. "A Checklist of Popular Publications Titles 1930–1955."
    Xenophile, no. 33 (July 1977): 21–24.
Hersey, Harold. *Pulpwood Editor*. New York: Frederick A. Stokes Co., 1937.
Jones, Robert Kenneth. *The Shudder Pulps*. West Linn, Ore.: Fax Collector's Editions,
    1975.
————. "The Weird Menace Magazines." *Bronze Shadows*, no. 10 (June 1967): 3–8;
    no. 11 (August 1967): 7–13; no. 12 (October 1967): 7–10; no. 13 (January 1968):
    7–12; no. 14 (March 1968): 13–17; no. 15 (November 1968): 4–8.
INDEX SOURCES: None known.

LOCATION SOURCES: Private collectors.

Publication History

MAGAZINE TITLE: *Sinister Stories*.

TITLE CHANGES: None.

VOLUME AND ISSUE DATA: Vol. 1, no. 1 (January 1940) through Vol. 1, no. 3 (May 1940); 3 issues.

PUBLISHER: Popular Publications, Inc., 2256 Grove Street, Chicago, Illinois, with editorial offices at 210 East 43rd Street, New York, New York.

EDITOR: Costa Carousso.

PRICE PER ISSUE: 15 cents.

SIZE AND PAGINATION: 7'' X 9-3/4''; 112 pages.

CURRENT STATUS: Discontinued.

—*Robert Kenneth Jones*

SKIPPER, THE

In 1936, Street & Smith, anxious to duplicate the entrenched successes of their *Doc Savage** and *The Shadow Magazines** publications and finding it economically unfeasible to issue *Doc Savage* twice a month, hired author Laurence Donovan, then writing Doc Savage novels for the unrealized increase in frequency, to write the lead novels for two new magazines, *The Skipper* and *The Whisperer*,* meant to be *Doc Savage* and *Shadow* take-offs, respectively.

The Skipper was created by Business Manager Henry W. Ralston and edited by John L. Nanovic, both of whom had originated the firm's formative single-character magazines. The Skipper was, in essence, a sea-going Doc Savage but on a much less juvenile level. The covers, by Lawrence Toney, featured close-ups of The Skipper's exuberant face set off by colorful quotes such as "When I'm right—I fight!" It was only on the later covers that Toney depicted the expected pulp action scenes.

The Skipper was better known as Captain John Fury—"Cap" for short—the stern and uncompromising master of the freighter *Whirlwind*. Cap Fury is red-headed, quick-tempered, and on the short side—quite a difference from the tall, self-possessed Doc Savage, or any other typical pulp hero, for that matter. Neither is Fury his own man. He works for Grump Rollin, who owns the fleet of which the *Whirlwind* is a part. In the first novel, "The Red Heart Pearls," the *Whirlwind* is sent into the South Seas to locate her sister ship, the *Half Moon*, which is skippered by Fury's brother, Tom. When Fury discovers his brother has been killed by criminals, he goes after those responsible and thereafter swears to eradicate pirates and criminals on the high seas—where presumably his work will not intrude upon that of Doc Savage or any other Street & Smith hero.

Cap Fury's ship looks like a tramp steamer but is outfitted for war. There are numerous concealed guns, cannon, a plane catapult, and a small submarine. Homely without, its staterooms are luxurious, and the ship contains a floating scientific laboratory, among other wonders. Its crew consists of pugnacious James

Jonathan "Marlin Spike" Briggs, the first mate; "Hurricane" Dan Belmont, the giant second mate; "Cock-eye" Sammons, the third mate; and the rest of the crew, who are nameless. "Bumps" McCarthy, a newsreel cameraman, often joins in The Skipper's adventures.

In the first novel, discredited New York Police Inspector Peter Doom joins the crew. Doom is a two-gun cop of the old school, bitter over the politicians who maneuvered his ouster and whose black clothes and mournful expression fit his name.

The last addition to the cast was Mara, the Black Leopard Princess. She is something of a female Tarzan. Fury discovered her in the jungles of Indo-China. She first appears in "The Black Leopard Princess" but thereafter infrequently.

Unlike Doc Savage, The Skipper did not believe in tempering justice with mercy. The harsh law of the sea prevailed aboard the *Whirlwind*. Fury carried an assortment of lethal weapons in his hip-deep seaboots and did not hesitate to kill transgressors. There was the *Whirlwind*'s scourging post for lesser criminals, those who did not meet death at his hands. Because Fury in his own law beyond the twelve-mile limit, he sentences the major criminals who fall into his hands to various unsavory fates—usually life at hard labor on an Arctic or Asian island.

Donovan's novels, written under the house name of Wallace Brooker, were often fantastic. In "Devils of the River," a South American dictator, wielding a magnetic force, kidnaps the president of the United States. Mexico is the scene in "Black Daylight," where a scientific genius has harnessed a power to plunge large areas into darkness even in the daytime. "Breathless Island" is set in the Bahamas, where a meteorite containing an element which robs the air of oxygen has fallen into the evil hands of the Choker.

Other novels are more prosaic. "The Clipper Menace" concerns the disappearance of clipper planes in mid-Pacific. When plague-ridden rats are unleashed upon Chicago, the *Whirlwind* sails into the Great Lakes to combat them. In the final published novel, "The Green Plague," the action centers upon the Great Cypress Swamp of Mississippi where voodoo has not been forgotten.

In keeping with the more adult nature of the magazine, Donovan's novels had a harsher tone than is usually found in single-character magazines. Fury and his blood-thirsty crew were less altruists than they were avengers of the seas. Consequently, their appeal was considerably less than it might have been, and the cast of *The Skipper* is not nearly as memorable as the cast of its inspiration, *Doc Savage*.

During its twelve-issue run, the Skipper novels were poorly illustrated by Kirchner, and occasionally by Werl. Numerous maritime illustrations by various artists, having nothing to do with the novels and obviously culled from older Street & Smith magazines (probably from *Sea Stories*), gave the magazine a piecemeal look. The short stories in the back of the magazine,, all of a seafaring nature, were by Carl Jacobi, Steve Fisher, and George Allan Moffatt (really Edwin V. Burkholder). Of particular interest were two series. Harold A. Davis contributed several stories about a poetry-spouting business scout named Bill

Wheeler, who was virtually identical to Davis's Duke Grant, another business scout who appeared frequently in *Doc Savage*. More interesting were Kenneth MacNichol's novelettes featuring Deacon, Swede, and Jellybean, whose adventures in various exotic seas on the schooner *Boolawaru* were continued in *Doc Savage* after *The Skipper* ceased publication.

The Skipper was cancelled with the December 1937 issue when several titles were purged in a reorganization of Street & Smith. Two complete novels, "The Murder Maker" and "The Diamond Devil," were left over. "The Murder Maker" was later published in *Mystery (Crime Busters,** May 1941) under the house name of Jack Storm, but the novel was shortened and revised into an ordinary mystery novelette with the entire *Skipper* cast altered beyond recognition. "The Diamond Devil" met a similar fate. It appeared in *Mystery* (July 1942) under the Wallace Brooker byline as "The Devil of Diamonds."

Cap Fury and his crew continued well past their short-lived magazine, however. Beginning in the November 1937 issue of *Doc Savage*, Donovan did a series of monthly Skipper novelettes whose flavor was only a little diluted from the longer novels. The first of these was "Black Ivory Death." Donovan wrote eleven of these in all, ending with "Death's Pay-off Man." This run was broken by a single story, "Quest of Death," which was the work of William G. Bogart.

Thereafter, the series was continued by Harold A. Davis, who did "It Pays to Fight," "Submarine Strategy," "Cap Fury Goes to War," and "The Fourth Money," and Norman A. Daniels, who wrote the remainder of the series beginning with "The Sea Vulture." The Davis and Daniels efforts were short stories, of very limited scope, and often concerned with unnamed foreign belligerents on the high seas (World War II having already begun in Europe). One Skipper story by Daniels, "Voodoo Bullets," appeared in *Crime Busters* (September 1939). For these short stories, most of the regular characters were dropped. Daniels, who wrote several single-character tales such as The Phantom Detective and The Black Bat, put little effort into his Skipper stories, and they are uniformly unimpressive.

After Pearl Harbor, the series became a war series. For eleven stories, from "The Skipper Goes to War" (*Doc Savage*, September 1942), to "The Grim Pilot" (*Doc Savage*, December 1943), the crew of the *Whirlwind*, now a converted Q-ship, battled the Nazis and the Japanese all over the globe. The series finally expired when *Doc Savage* was reduced in size due to the wartime paper shortage, and all supporting series were dropped.

By that time, the original characters were long past their prime. Laurence Donovan had joined Norman Daniels in writing The Phantom Detective and The Black Bat stories for a competitor, and the original *Skipper* magazine was long-forgotten. It was an interesting but not exceptional example of the variety of the single-character pulps during their heyday.

Information Sources

BIBLIOGRAPHY:

Goulart, Ron. *Cheap Thrills*. New Rochelle, N.Y.: Arlington House, 1972.

Hullar, Link, and Will Murray. "The Fighting Fury." *Megavore*, no. 12 (December 1980): 3–12.

Murray, Will. "The Secret Kenneth Robesons." *Duende*, Vol. 1, no. 2 (Winter 1977): 3–27.

Reynolds, Quentin. *The Fiction Factory*. New York: Random House, 1955.

INDEX SOURCES: None known.

LOCATION SOURCES: University of California–Los Angeles Library (Vol. 2, no. 5, only); George Arents Research Library, Syracuse (N.Y.) University (complete run).

Publication History

MAGAZINE TITLE: *The Skipper*.

TITLE CHANGES: None.

VOLUME AND ISSUE DATA: Vol. 1, no. 1 (October 1936) through Vol. 2, no. 6 (December 1937); 12 issues.

PUBLISHER: Street & Smith Publications, Inc., 79 Seventh Avenue, New York, New York.

EDITOR: John L. Nanovic.

PRICE PER ISSUE: 10 cents.

SIZE AND PAGINATION: 7" X 10"; 128 pages.

CURRENT STATUS: Discontinued.

—*Will Murray*

SKULLDUGGERY

Skullduggery was a short-lived mystery magazine which enjoyed two separte small-press incarnations. The magazine was founded in 1979 by Michael L. Cook, then also editing a magazine for pulp magazine and mystery collectors called *The Age of the Unicorn*.* Seeing a need for a new mystery magazine not bound by the selectiveness of *Ellery Queen's Mystery Magazine*,* *Alfred Hitchcock's Mystery Magazine*,* and *Mike Shayne Mystery Magazine*,* Cook created *Skullduggery*. It was both an alternative to the three extant newsstands mystery magazines and a training ground for new and upcoming writers.

Skullduggery was initially published by Cook-McDowell Publications, a partnership between Cook and Sam McDowell which also produced genealogical publications. Cook, a long-time mystery reader and fan, edited the quarterly from its first issue (dated January 1980). Under Cook, *Skullduggery* was distinctly a writer's magazine. Acceptances were based upon story quality, not story type or author's reputation. As a result, *Skullduggery* attracted a broad spectrum of story types and authors.

Professional authors such as Bill Pronzini and Barry N. Malzberg, writing in collaboration, and Basil Wells, Michael Avallone, and Jon L. Breen appeared in various issues. From Cook's own *Age of the Unicorn* came writers such as Joe Lewandowski, Wooda N. Carr, and Will Murray (who would later play a larger role in the magazine). In addition, *Skullduggery* attracted quite a number of new writers, many of whom were published for the first time in its pages.

A brief survey of the highlights of *Skullduggery's* first year indicates the variety of its fiction. Pronzini and Malzberg's "Strikes" was a suspenseful murder tale with a grimly ironic finish. James M. Reasoner, then writing the Mike Shayne magazine novelettes as Brett Halliday, did "The Golden Bear." Joe R. Lansdale's "Huitzilopochtli" was a grim horror story, and "Melisande's Ghosts" was Melanie Livengood-Tem's atmospheric ghost story. "The Ropes," by Paul Harwitz, was a police procedural. "The Long and Short of It" offered Will Murray's humorous dwarf detective, Don Hull. "The Bird" was a poignant fantasy by Wooda N. Carr featuring Martin Gort, an undertaker-sleuth.

After two regularly published issues, various personal and business reasons impelled Cook to announce suspension of publication, which he did after producing two more issues published simultaneously and available only to subscribers. However, within a few months, *Skullduggery* was revived when pulp historian and author Will Murray acquired title to the magazine. Going into partnership with William A. Desmond, past editor of the ill-fated *Science Fiction Times*, and Karen Shapiro, a technical writer, Murray instituted sweeping changes in the magazine.

When *Skullduggery* reappeared in January 1981, exactly a year from the date of its first issue, it was still a quarterly available by mail, and it retained the original logo; but gone was the horrific Frank Hamilton cover which had been repeated on each issue of the original *Skullduggery*. New covers were by Hamilton, Doreen Greeley, and others. Now subtitled "the Magazine of Fiction Noir," *Skullduggery*, under Murray's editorial guidance, focused on gritty crime stories in the traditions of *The Black Mask** and the *film noir* movies of the 1940s. At the same time, the magazine remained open to a wide range of story types, although somewhat more restricted than Cook's *Skullduggery*. In addition, various features were inaugurated, including book reviews and author interviews by Murray writing as Carl Shaner and as police reporter Jack Butterworth, doing a regular column.

The new *Skullduggery* attracted some of the contributors to the old, including James M. Reasoner and Hal Charles (really Hal Blythe and Charles Sweet in collaboration), as well as new writers, of whom the best were Carl Hoffman and Robert Sampson. Of the various contributions, it might be argued that Sampson's "Liar's Night" and "Blue Legs" were superior. Richard Grant's "Denver" was a traditional, hard-boiled detective tale. Carl Hoffman's 'Bad Guys" was also noteworthy.

Humor was not absent from the magazine, despite its new direction. Will Murray continued his burlesque of the private eye with his Mike Brunt character, who had appeared in the first Cook issue in "The Big Nothing." He returned in "The Zeppelin Tattoo," but the stories were now bylined Preston Danger. A series of special reprints was also inaugurated, the first of which was Richard Sale's funny "Mellow Drama," an inside look at the pulp magazine industry, which was followed by the equally off-beat story, "The Cats," written for *Unknown Worlds* but never published when that magazine folded in 1943. Other notable contributors included Dan J. Marlowe and W. S. Doxey.

While the new version of *Skullduggery* was promising, it was ill-fated. After two issues, Will Murray stepped down as editor in a dispute over the direction and professionalism of the magazine. With the third issue, the magazine acquired a new look, and the subtitle was dropped as Karen Shapiro sat in the editors' chair and began a new book review column under the name Annie Sebastion. The magazine retained much of the same tone it had under Murray, inasmuch as he had already accepted a sizable manuscript inventory, and other than packaging differences, the only significant changes were in a lack of focus in the editorial matter. Whatever new directions Shapiro may have intended, they were never realized, for after two more issues, the three partners (Murray had remained a silent partner) found the magazine could not be continued. *Skullduggery* was again suspended, in a curious repetition of history, after four issues.

In all, eight issues were published of this experimental magazine, under three editors. Its failure should not signify that a viable small-press mystery magazine cannot be published.

Information Sources

INDEX SOURCES: Cook, Michael L. *Monthly Murders*. Westport, Conn.: Greenwood
 Press, 1981.
LOCATION SOURCES: Private collectors.

Publication History

MAGAZINE TITLE: *Skullduggery*.
TITLE CHANGES: None.
VOLUME AND ISSUE DATA: Vol. 1, no. 1 (January 1980) through Vol. 2, no. 4 (Fall
 1981); 8 issues.
PUBLISHERS: Cook-McDowell Publications, 3318 Wimberg Avenue, Evansville, In-
 diana 47712 (first four issues); Skullduggery, P. O. Box 191, M.I.T. Branch
 Station, Cambridge, Massachusetts 02139 (second four issues).
EDITORS: Michael L. Cook (Vol. 1, nos. 1–4); Will Murray (Vol. 2, nos. 1–2); Karen
 Shapiro and Bill Desmond (Vol. 2, nos. 3–4).
PRICE PER ISSUE: $2.00 (Vol. 1); $2.50 (Vol. 2).
SIZE AND PAGINATION: 5-1/2'' X 8-1/2''; 52–68 pages.
CURRENT STATUS: Discontinued.
—*Will Murray*

SLEUTH MYSTERY MAGAZINE

Mystery writers are always seeking new markets for their stories and are ever-conscious that since the heyday of the pulp magazines there has been a dwindling number of magazines to consider their efforts. Thus when the opportunity arose in 1958 for the Mystery Writers of America (MWA), the published mystery writers' national association, to work in conjunction with a publisher, it seemed a wonderful idea. The MWA's slogan, "Crime Does Not Pay—Enough," was to find a way to accomplish the end result of every author, to see more work in print. The result was the *Sleuth Mystery Magazine*, published "in cooperation with the Mystery Writers of America, Inc."[1] by Richard E. Decker as Fosdeck Publications, making its initial appearance in October 1958.

An introduction by Rex Stout, then president of the MWA, stated:

"In *Sleuth*, the readers of mysteries have a magazine published in cooperation with the Mystery Writers of America. . . . Certainly we do not expect you, the customer-readers, to buy *Sleuth* and keep on buying it because you love mystery writers, either individually or collectively; we know we can get you and keep you only by giving you your money's worth in entertainment. But what of the writers? Will having a share in a magazine give a fillip to their ingenuity and felicity? Will A's plots be a little more adroit, or B's characterizations a little sharper, or C's atmosphere a little more electric? I really think they may be. . . ."[2]

William Manners was editor, who was also editing *Alfred Hitchcock's Mystery Magazine*,* and the finished product was almost identical to that magazine. From a lineup of distinct, quality, well-known writers came a crop of above-average, light-hearted, nonantagonizing, crime-adventure vignettes that were entertaining and satisfying. Many had surprise twists and endings. The style of detective fiction in *Alfred Hitchcock's Mystery Magazine*, duplicated here in *Sleuth Mystery Magazine*, has come to be recognized as a distinct school of crime fiction. It does not have the puzzle plot of the classic detective story; it does not have the hard-boiled or tough mien developed in the 1930s and 1940s. And it is not characterized by sex or gore. But it is definitely entertaining.

There do not seem to be any outstanding stories in either of the two issues published. This is not to say that the stories were mediocre, however. From the pens of Stanley Ellin, Bill S. Ballinger, Lawrence Treat, Henry Slesar, Baynard Kendrick, Ed Lacy, Oscar Schisgall, Nedra Tyre, and Margaret Manners, among others, came a wide variety of short stories that were a credit to each author. The illustrations were also the same as in *Alfred Hitchcock's Mystery Magazine*, pen-and-ink sketches highlighted in monochrome, by several artists. The graphic covers by Reese Brandt were not appealing.

Distribution and display problems were rampant in this period and may have contributed to the demise of the magazine after such a short trial run. But, whatever, without further ado, and with no prior indication, the magazine was discontinued, and readers looked in vain for the sharper, adroit, and electric tales promised.

Notes

1. Cover slogan, *Sleuth Mystery Magazine*, both issues.
2. Editorial announcement and introduction, *Sleuth Mystery Magazine,* Vol. 1, no. 1 (October 1958), reverse front cover.

Information Sources

INDEX SOURCES: Cook, Michael L. *Monthly Murders*. Westport, Conn.: Greenwood Press, 1982.
LOCATION SOURCES: University of California–Los Angeles Library (complete); private collectors.

Publication History

MAGAZINE TITLE: *Sleuth Mystery Magazine*.
TITLE CHANGES: None.
VOLUME AND ISSUE DATA: Vol. 1, no. 1 (October 1958) through Vol. 1, no. 2 (December 1958); 2 issues.
PUBLISHER: Fosdeck Publications, Inc., 122 East 42nd Street, New York 17, New York.
EDITOR: William Manners, editorial director; Marguerite Bostwick, managing editor; Nadine King, associate editor.
PRICE PER ISSUE: 35 cents.
SIZE AND PAGINATION: 5-3/8'' X 7-5/8''; 128 pages.
CURRENT STATUS: Discontinued.

SLICK DETECTIVE YARNS (British)

Ten issues of *Slick Detective Yarns*, a pocket-size, thin periodical, were published by Gerald Swan in 1951. No other information is available.

Information Sources

BIBLIOGRAPHY:
Lofts, W.O.G., and Derek J. Adley. *Old Boys Books, A Complete Catalogue*. London: privately printed, 1969.
INDEX SOURCES: None known.
LOCATION SOURCES: Private collectors.

Publication History

MAGAZINE TITLE: *Slick Detective Yarns*.
TITLE CHANGES: None.
VOLUME AND ISSUE DATA: No. 1 (1951) through no. 10, (1951); 10 issues.
PUBLISHER: Gerald Swan, London.
EDITOR: Not known.
PRICE PER ISSUE: Not known.
SIZE AND PAGINATION: 5-3/8'' X 7''; 64 pages.
CURRENT STATUS: Discontinued.

SMASHING DETECTIVE

The early 1950s were the final years for the big, old-fashioned pulps with ragged page edges and an air of sleazy good nature. In 1950, recovery from the war had plunged the pulp market into violent competition and even more violent duplication. Similar magazines struggled for shelf space as prices slowly inched from fifteen cents to twenty cents and soon higher.

In the midst of this fever, Columbia Publications introduced several new magazines, among them *Romantic Love Stories, Action Packed Western,* and *Smashing Detective.* The latter ws to complement its companion magazine, *Famous Detective,* which had changed its name from *Crack Detective Stories (Crack Detective*)* in late 1949.

As the name implies, *Smashing Detective* featured hard-action stories of mystery and detection. There were a few puzzle stories and a number of the once-popular private investigator adventures. These had been the staple of tough detective fiction in dozens of pulps through the late 1930s and 1940s, and the vein was becoming thin and mannered. The private investigators of *Smashing Detective* echoed the pretty ways of Mike Shayne and Dan Turner. They met a stream of stunning girls, were slugged unconscious at inconvenient times, and were framed more often than not. It is a tribute to Editor Robert Lowndes's ability that he was able to find viable fiction from these weary lines. Not only did he keep *Smashing Detective* alive as a quarterly, but he managed to promote it to a bimonthly, despite a minimum of best-selling names among the writers.

There were a few famous writers and some soon to be famous. Carroll John Daly, then in the twilight of his career, contributed a story, although it did not feature any of his more prominent series characters. Thomas Thursday and Richard Deming appeared, as did Norman Daniels, and T. S. Stribling (whose Dr. Poggioli has been anthologized to the point of becoming one of the old masters). The Poggioli short story published in *Smashing Detective* lends little luster to the master's name, involving a corpse on public display as an advertising gimmick ("Dead Wrong," March 1953).

Large numbers of the other authors were either pseudonyms or just not well known. In any case, Editor Lowndes selected the stories that he personally liked, whether or not a well-known name was in evidence.

The magazine normally published five or six short stories, a novelette, and a very short novel that was indistinguishable from a short story. A fact feature, "Spotlight on Crime," appeared irregularly. This was replaced by Thomas Thursday's "Annuals of Crime," which began in mid-1955. In the March 1954 issue, the magazine was reduced to ninety-six pages. At that time, the short stories increased to seven or nine, depending on whether a novel or novelette was used.

Various special features were tried: short-short suspense stories, a brief narrative mystery that the reader could try to solve, and an occasional poem. And, in late 1956, began "According to the Books," a department discussing new crime and mystery hardbacks.

By then, *Smashing Detective* had bowed to the forces of modernization. The magazine shrank and had trimmed edges. Those rude old covers were discontinued—the ones that showed scared ladies with large chests shrinking from guns held by tough types. That theme was reversed by the 1954–1955 covers which persisted in depicting crafty ladies pointing or firing guns at scared tough guys.

In 1956, the cover title was moved to a neat red block at cover top. From this, the words "Smashing Detective" glared in yellow type. On those covers, the girls were endangered, sometimes dead, and always painted with high competence. At the very last—after *Smashing Detective* became *Fast Action and Mystery Stories*—Norman Saunders handled the covers. He caught the action at its height, full of screams, pants, and gasps as girls battled beefy thugs. There were few Saunders covers, for *Fast Action Detective and Mystery Stories* lasted only three issues in pulp size. About the only thing that was changed was the title; it continued *Smashing Detective's* volume numbers, departments, and story types. There were three bimonthly issues, January through May 1957, after which the magazine became digest size. At least five issues were also published in a British reprint edition.

Information Sources

BIBLIOGRAPHY:
Lowndes, Robert, A.W. "The Columbia Pulps." *The Pulp Era*, no. 67 (May/June 1967): 5–20.
INDEX SOURCES: None known.
LOCATION SOURCES: University of California–Los Angeles Library (1951–1954, 3 issues); private collectors.

Publication History

MAGAZINE TITLE: *Smashing Detective*.
TITLE CHANGES: *Fast Action Detective and Mystery Stories* (with Vol. 5, no. 4 [January 1957]).
VOLUME AND ISSUE DATA: Vol. 1, no. 1 (March 1951) through Vol. 6, no. 3 (February 1958); 32 issues.
PUBLISHER: Columbia Publications, Inc., 1 Appleton Street, Holyoke, Massachusetts, with editorial offices at 241 Church Street, New York 13, New York.
EDITOR: Robert A.W. Lowndes; associate editor, Marie Antoinette Park.
PRICE PER ISSUE: 20 cents (1951–1952); 25 cents (1953–1957); 35 cents (1957–1958).
SIZE AND PAGINATION: 6-7/8" X 9-3/4" (through Vol. 3, no. 2); 6-1/2" X 9-3/8" (through Vol. 5, no. 6); digest-size,, 5-1/4" X 7-1/2" (with Vol. 6, no. 1 [August 1957]); 100–132 pages.
CURRENT STATUS: Discontinued.
—*Robert Sampson*

SMASHING DETECTIVE (British)

See SMASHING DETECTIVE

SNAPPY DETECTIVE MYSTERIES

Snappy Detective Mysteries was a large-size ("bedsheet") magazine published by Edmar Publications. At least two issues were published in 1935. No other information is available.

Information Sources

INDEX SOURCES: None known.
LOCATION SOURCES: Private collectors.

Publication History

MAGAZINE TITLE: *Snappy Detective Mysteries.*
TITLE CHANGES: None known.
VOLUME AND ISSUE DATA: Vol. 1, no. 1 (May 1935) through at least Vol. 1, no. 2 (June 1935); number of issues and extent unknown.
PUBLISHER: Edmar Publications, New York, New York.
EDITOR: Not known.
PRICE PER ISSUE: Not known.
SIZE AND PAGINATION: 8-1/2" X 11-1/2"; number of pages unknown.
CURRENT STATUS: Discontinued.

SNAPPY DETECTIVE STORIES

Culture Publications was established in Chicago in 1933 and gained instant notoriety and remembrance in April 1934 when it launched *Spicy Detective*,* espousing fast-moving stories with an obsession for sex that bordered on pornography. Nothing like it had been seen before, and, with the style of writing changed since, nothing has appeared to duplicate it. Not, of course, unless you want to include the other pulp titles that poured forth in ecstasy from this publisher. *Spicy Mystery Stories** supposedly appeared in July 1934 (although this issue, if published then, has disappeared from the scope of collectors); the same month, the newsstands groaned under four other new Culture Publications titles: *Snappy Detective Stories, Snappy Mystery Stories,* Snappy Adventures,* and *Spicy Adventures*. All followed the same formula. Another, *Spicy Western,* did not blossom forth until November 1936. Apparently, this was too much, though, since only *Spicy Detective* and *Spicy Mystery Stories* lasted any appreciable time.

In all, the stories were heavily laden with beautifully, bubbly women who almost went too far. The detective story was secondary, providing just the reason for being there. The villains had all the fun, it seemed, but the heroes were not far behind. Or the heroines. If the girl instigated a sexual encounter, it was because she was threatened by impending doom to her hero. If the hero provoked the sexual desire, it was because of the girl's appearance, which was described in very graphic terms, or his desire to protect her. The more sadistic erotic feelings, of course, came from the villains. Everything was described in vivid terms but the pelvic area. But at the last moment, as in the earlier, tame by comparison, *Snappy Stories* (a Clayton magazine commencing in 1912), *The Parisienne, Silk Stocking Stories*, and others, the reader was left to his imagination.

Information Sources

INDEX SOURCES: None known.
LOCATION SOURCES: Private collectors.

Publication History

MAGAZINE TITLE: *Snappy Detective Stories*.
TITLE CHANGES: None known.
VOLUME AND ISSUE DATA: Vol. 1, no. 1 (July 1934); number of issues and extent unknown.
PUBLISHER: Culture Publications, Inc., 2242 Grove Street, Chicago, Illinois.
EDITOR: Not known.
PRICE PER ISSUE: 25 cents.
SIZE AND PAGINATION: 6-7/8'' X 9-7/8''; 128 pages.
CURRENT STATUS: Discontinued.

SNAPPY MYSTERY STORIES

When Frank Armor's Culture Publications began publishing in 1934 what became their staple product, stories of blatant sex disguised as mystery and detective stories, little did they know that they would create a magazines that today command prices of one hundred times their cover price from collectors. At the time, the publisher was just interested in introducing magazines that had no competition, magazines that were "daring" and provocative, and the likes of which had not been seen before. The magazines were a success—there can be no doubt of that—successful even to the extent that they had to be toned down and the titles changed later.

When Armor sought to outdo the competition, however, he provided his own by publishing too many of the same type of magazine. The first was *Spicy Detective** in April 1934; when this was a success, the floodgates opened, and by July there was *Spicy Mystery Stories** (although the first issue of this magazine has not been seen by collectors), *Snappy Detective Stories,** Snappy Adventures, Spicy Adventures,* and, two years later, *Spicy Western.*

Snappy Mystery Stories presented to the wide-eyed reader a fare of thinly disguised, almost pornographic, stories of sex. The mystery-detective element was there, and the stories were fast moving (and probably even faster read). But the always beautifully dressed and coiffured lady was subjected to all manner of fear and abuse, left in but a scrap of clothing and reduced to emotional distresses before finally being rescued. Even so, the writers of these tales could go only so far. The imagination, however, stoked the sales, despite the fact that virtue was always the winner.

The number of issues published is not known to this writer; but in all probability, Culture Publications provided too much "culture" with the group of magazines and *Snappy Mystery Stories* was not a title that survived for any appreciable time.

Information Sources

INDEX SOURCES: None known.
LOCATION SOURCES: Private collectors.

Publication History

MAGAZINE TITLE: *Snappy Mystery Stories*.
TITLE CHANGES: None known.
VOLUME AND ISSUE DATA: Vol. 1, no. 1 (July 1934); number of issues and extent unknown.
PUBLISHER: Culture Publications, Inc., 2242 Grove Street, Chicago, Illinois.
EDITOR: Not known.
PRICE PER ISSUE: 25 cents.
SIZE AND PAGINATION: 6-7/8" X 9-7/8"; 128 pages.
CURRENT STATUS: Discontinued.

SPEAKEASY STORIES

In the midst of the Prohibition era, when unparalleled drinking gained at least a tacit seal of approval and speakeasies were investitured with a degree of glamour, Harold B. Hersey introduced another title in his gangster/underworld series of pulp magazines. *Speakeasy Stories* was launched with the April/May 1931 issue and was published for at least three issues. No other information is available.

Information Sources

BIBLIOGRAPHY:
Hersey, Harold B. *Pulpwood Editor*. New York: Frederick A. Stokes Co., 1937.
INDEX SOURCES: None known.
LOCATION SOURCES: Private collectors.

Publication History

MAGAZINE TITLE: *Speakeasy Stories*.
TITLE CHANGES: None known.
VOLUME AND ISSUE DATA: Vol. 1, no. 1 (April/May 1931) through at least Vol. 1, no. 3 (August/September 1931); 3 issues.
PUBLISHER: Good Story Magazine Co., Inc., New York, New York.
EDITOR: Not known.
PRICE PER ISSUE: Not known.
SIZE AND PAGINATION: Not known.
CURRENT STATUS: Discontinued.

SPEED DETECTIVE

See SPICY DETECTIVE

SPEED MYSTERY

See SPICY MYSTERY STORIES

SPICY DETECTIVE

Spicy Detective was the first magazine issued by Culture Publications, Inc., a Chicago publishing house established in 1933 by Frank Armor. Like later *Spicy* titles, *Spicy Detective* achieved wide notoriety by simple means—it laced fast-action stories with high concentrations of sex. It exploited women joyously, with no outer signs of remorse.

The formula had been tried before, although never so blatantly. For almost twenty years, a small number of pulp magazines featured "daring" stories about women, from *Snappy Stories, Breezy Stories, Pep* to *Silk Stocking Stories* and *Paris Nights*. These magazines published frothy tales of young women who almost went too far, almost got compromised. Almost, not quite. The fiction was suggestive and faintly erotic, although it customarily faded to four-square virtue in the final paragraphs.

Spicy Detective went well beyond these timid efforts. It reveled in partially clothed girls, proud bosoms, gleaming flesh, and topics such as justified the price of twenty-five cents an issue.

The formula worked. The magazine was published monthly for eight years, April 1934 through December 1942. At that time, the forces of reform forced the magazine into a less provocative form; it became *Speed Detective*, published from January 1943 to December 1946, most of the issues bimonthly.

During its *Spicy* phase, the magazine glowed with sex interest, sex activities, and various pathological distortions of sex, inserted like hypodermic injections into high-action private detective stories.

Customarily, these injections were descriptions of women in various stages of undress and in various emotional states, from fear, homicidal rage, and drunkenness to arousal or voluptuous yielding. The more sexually enticing the description, the more certain it was that the woman would be slugged or whipped or murdered during the story. And, willingly or not, she would lose most of her clothing. At this point, descriptive material burst out all over the prose.

Fiction of *Spicy Detective* was provided by a small cadre of house writers; Robert Leslie Bellem, E. Hoffman Price, and Roger Torrey were prominent among these. Using a gigantic selection of pseudonyms, these writers filled the pages of most of the *Spicy* titles. Of them all, Bellem seems to have been the most prolific. He appeared two or three or more times an issue, his identity concealed under such suggestive names as Justin Case. At the same time, he

poured out equal volumes of fiction for the other *Spicy* titles, as he would later
do for *Private Detective Stories** and *Dan Turner, Hollywood Detective.**

Bellem's main character, Dan Turner, was intensely popular and long enduring. Introduced in the second, June 1934, issue of *Spicy Detective*, he appeared
in every issue and on through *Speed Detective*. Turner was a hard-case private
investigator who freelanced in Hollywood and was, in a way, a detective to the
stars, as well as starlets, agents, leading men, technical crews, and others in
and out of the movie industry. Fortified by endless cigarettes ("I lit another
gasper") and Vat 69, his favorite Scotch, he charged head first through the
endless murders, assaults, and ripped-off clothing which constituted social life
as interpreted by *Spicy Detective*. His stories were told in the first person, in a
wonderful mixture of slang and allusion, seemingly written in a language remotely based on English. Dan was a profound student of feminine breasts and
divided his time between describing these in flaming language and slugging those
who annoyed him. He slugged them all, men and women. And he was slugged
in return. In every Dan Turner story, he is knocked cold at least once. But then
he rises, fortified with Vat 69, and smashes enthusiastically about to the end of
the case.

Unlike most of the hard-headed, hard-drinking, hard-living private investigators, Turner does not go in for much gun play. He usually carries a small-
calibre pistol in a shoulder holster. But his forte is punching and observing, not
shooting.

The second most popular character in *Spicy Detective* was Sally The Sleuth.
She appeared not in the stories but in a short, black-and-white comic-book feature
inserted among the pages. Sally's real ability was in losing her clothing; she
managed this in every story, overcoming dire perils and concluding each burst
of action while stripped down to the underwear.

The fiction's intense concentration on seminudes was reflected in both covers
and interior art. The covers featured a single theme, variously arranged: a young
lady in scraps of pink silk struggling with a great burly fellow, clearly intent
upon more than housebreaking. The interior illustrations, by several artists,
shared the common theme. These shameless wenches sprawled artistically about
scenes of bitter action. Their physical development was extraordinary, their
danger dire, their scraps of silk barely sufficient.

Toward the end of the 1930s, the girl-exploitive elements of the *Spicy* titles
brought the magazines to wide disrepute. They were lumped with other, far less
savory magazines and were attacked by reformers as being immoral, indecent,
lewd, and dangerous to spiritual life. In New York City, Mayor Fiorella La-
Guardia led the attack, and powerful civic groups pressed hard in Chicago. The
threat of a distribution ban and cancellation of business permits eventually forced
Culture Publications to discontinue the *Spicy* titles. By editorial legerdemain,
the magazines changed their wicked ways, their cover style, their editorial policy,
and their titles. It happened almost overnight. The December 1942 *Spicy De-*

tective was followed by the January 1943 *Speed Detective*. Not an issue was skipped.

Change, however, was radical and deep.

To begin with, the seminude girl vanished from the illustrations. From shrieking cover beauty to Sally The Sleuth, all girls were now primly dressed from neck to knees. And in the text, those descriptive paragraphs, cataloging beauty's every curve, also vanished. In *Speed Detective*, the girls still got slugged and murdered. But the distinctive essence of *Spicy Detective* had evaporated.

What was left was a solid, 128–page, fifteen-cent, fast-action detective magazine that contained, most usually, a novelette and five short stories. After four or five issues, Sally The Sleuth was discontinued, her fascination evidently smothered by clothing. The magazine's contents were topped off by two or more brief crime fact articles that were added in sufficient numbers to fill up blank space at the end of stories.

Almost at once, new names appeared on the contents page. To the works of Bellem (whose Dan Turner continued, mildly bowdlerized), Torrey, and Price were added signed fiction by Wyatt Blassingame, Ray Cummings, Laurence Donovan, Ellery Calder, Harold de Polo, and George A. McDonald. The magazine now began a definite swing to the fast-action, mainstream detective adventure. Fiction concentrated on movement, doom, and tough confusion, and, if extramarital activities were occasionally implied, they were couched in prose as neutral as possible.

Before *Speed Detective* had quite adjusted to its new self, the wartime paper shortage got it. The April 1943 issue dropped from 128 to 112 pages, still remaining at fifteen cents. Then the frequency of publication skipped to bimonthly, beginning with the November 1943 issue.

During 1944, the number of pages was again reduced, this time to ninety-six. Contents shrank; a single novelette, four short stories, and a brief crime article were offered. The fiction was undistinguished. Even Dan Turner sounded tired.

For a short period in 1946, an attempt was made to revitalize the magazine. For several issues, seven pieces of fiction were published, though the stories shortened as the number increased. But nothing really worked now. The December 1946 issue contained only five titles, including a Dan Turner adventure, and the magazine was quietly terminated with this issue.

Information Sources

BIBLIOGRAPHY:
Jones, Robert Kenneth. *The Shudder Pulps*. West Linn, Ore.: Fax Collector's Editions, 1975.
Mertz, Stephen. "Robert Leslie Bellem: The Great Unknown." *Xenophile*, no. 21 (February 1976): 71–73.
INDEX SOURCES: None known.
LOCATION SOURCES: Private collectors.

Publication History

MAGAZINE TITLE: *Spicy Detective*.

TITLE CHANGES: *Speed Detective* (with January 1943 issue).
VOLUME AND ISSUE DATA: *Spicy Detective*: Vol. 1, no. 1 (April 1934) through Vol.
        18, no. 2 (December 1942); 104 issues. *Speed Detective*: Vol. 1, no. 1 (January
        1943) through Vol. 5, no. 3 (December 1946); 27 issues.
PUBLISHER: *Spicy Detective*: Culture Publications, Inc., 2242 Grove Street, Chicago,
        Illinois. *Speed Detective*, as Trojan Publishing Corp., 2242 Grove Street, Chicago,
        Illinois, later 29 Worthington Street, Springfield, Massachusetts.
EDITOR: Not known.
PRICE PER ISSUE: 25 cents *(Spicy Detective)*; 15 cents *(Speed Detective)*.
SIZE AND PAGINATION: 6-7/8'' X 9-7/8''; 6-7/8'' X 9-5/8''; 96–128 pages.
CURRENT STATUS: Discontinued.
—*Robert Sampson*

SPICY MYSTERY STORIES

Spicy Mystery Stories was one of the notorious *Spicy* titles. Published in
Chicago by Culture Publications, Inc., a magazine house established in 1933 by
publisher Frank Armor. The following year, 1934, the house began issuing its
sex-laced titles.

Just when *Spicy Mystery Stories* appeared is an unsolved problem. Its first
issue has widely been assumed to be dated July 1934; however, no issue of that
date has ever been found or examined. The initial issue that is available is volume
1, number 2, dated June 1935. The lead story is "Fangs of the Bat" by Robert
Leslie Bellem, and this more-than-rare-magazine reposes in a private collection.

From its first issue (whenever that appeared), *Spicy Mystery* was an enigma.
It was also a hybrid. It combined elements of *Weird Tales,* Dime Mystery
Magazine (Dime Mystery Book*),* and *Snappy Stories,* an incredible and, you
would assume, indigestible mixture. To this was added the concentrated essence
of sex that was characteristic of the *Spicy* line.

Spicy Mystery was issued to exploit that new twist to pulp literature introduced
by Popular Publications near the end of 1933. Popular had overhauled the faltering *Dime Mystery Magazine,* transforming it, with the October 1933 issue,
into a vehicle for stories soon to be known as "weird menace." This fiction, in
oversimplification, concentrated upon the experiences of beautiful young girls
whose sanity, life, and, perhaps, virginity were threatened by what seemed to
be supernatural forces.

The weird-menace story experienced a highly compressed evolution. In less
than two years, it picked up an awe-inspiring load of sadism, unnatural horror,
blood lust, insanity, and fear ripened to nightmare. Magazines such as *Terror
Tales* (Horror Stories*) (first dated September 1934), *Horror Stories* (first dated
January 1935), and *Ace Mystery** (May 1936) gleefully expanded on these characteristics. The lesser, later magazines at the decade's end, following the example
of their seniors, featured ever larger doses of pain, anguish, and sexual threat.

Spicy Mystery Stories came early to this field. Because of the elusive volume
1, number 1 issue, we don't know whether it was the second or fourth weird-

menace magazine. We do know that it carefully hedged its editorial bets. Each issue contained about nine short stories and novelettes. Of these, two or three were weird menace. The others addressed more conventional forms and concentrated heavily on the supernatural: pacts with the devil, werewolves, psychic possession, witchcraft, return from the dead, and the exchange of souls. However, for every story using the supernatural, there was another story in which these elements turned out to be faked.

Inside the magazine raved bright orange titles: "Hands of the Undead," "Hell's Tryst," "Pact of the Wine God," "Ghoul's Nightmare," "Lobster Girl," and "The Cat Tastes Blood." Around 1937, these rantings were supplemented by a black-and-white comic-book story featuring Olga Mesmer, who had weird adventures and a lot of difficulty staying dressed.

Of the more formal fiction, at least half was provided by the Culture Publications house writers, including Robert Leslie Bellem, E. Hoffman Price, Wyatt Blassingame, Roger Torrey, and others unidentified, and innumerable pseudonyms of each. Many other writers contributed less frequently, among them A. L. Zagat, Henry Kuttner, William B. Rainey, Ray Cummings, and others disguised almost permanently by pseudonyms.

Common to all stories were the sexual elements. The subject was female flesh—the subject, the point, the main interest. It is correct to say female flesh, not women. Rarely did the magazine feature a woman as a character, that is, in the sense that a character has some tenuous connection with human life. In *Spicy Mystery*, women were not characters but decorative objects that happened to move around and talk. All descriptions were confined to the feminine exterior: the lips, the eyes, the bosom, the perfumed tresses. The narrative action stopped dead while inventories of these charms swelled into paragraphs.

It was required that the girls constantly find themselves nude or reduced to underthings or in wonderfully ragged states that revealed much skin. Once in this situation, the girls could be described all over again, the charged adjectives flaring.

The magazine's illustrations made the most of this material. Interior drawings featured underdressed, overdeveloped young ladies in the grip of lustful brutes or deformed horrors, while a protector, the fine young man, struggled ineffectually. On the covers, horrified maidens in pink underwear shrieked in the clutchs of skeletons (a favorite terror), gigantic hands, scaled awfuls, and subhuman men, depraved and bestial:

Walk the chalk line between sanity and madness as the powers of evil do battle with those of good. As beautiful, exotic, alluring women and real he-men wage relentless warfare against the eerie denizens of the world of darkness.[1]

But the days of girl and ghoul fiction were numbered. During the mid-1930s, ever louder, ever stronger protests rose against "indecent" magazines—those containing nudity, suggestive poses, searing prose. The excesses of the *Spicys*, weird-menace magazines, and other girl-exploitive pulps caused them to be lumped with much less savory publications. In New York City, Mayor Fiorella LaGuardia led the attack; in 1940, he convened a meeting of publishers and distributors and blistered them for their sins. Similar pressures were exerted in Chicago, a city not usually known for tender sensibilities.

After some years of escalating pressure, Culture Publications finally bent. The *Spicy* titles were discontinued after release of the December 1942 issues. However, the sequence of publication continued without interruption. The following month, the magazines appeared as usual, dated January 1943, but were now identified as *Speed* rather than *Spicy*.

As *Speed Mystery*, the magazine changed considerably. Gone were the tantalizing covers and peek-a-boo interiors. The girls were fully clothed now, and their erotic adventures among the sadists were severely muted. The magazine's contents continued to mix fantasy and fast-action adventure. The price lowered from twenty-five cents to fifteen cents. The stories shortened. After a few issues, the comic feature ("Vera Ray") was cancelled, and the magazine's page count dropped from 128 to 112.

On the whole, the transition from *Spicy* to *Speed* blighted the magazine. After the third issue (March 1943), it became a bimonthly, and slow degeneration set in. The September 1943 issue contained eight stories and five filler paragraphs (grandly identified on the contents page as "Special Articles"). In the following issue, November 1943, the contents were reduced to a short novel and three other stories, plus two fillers. During 1944, stories of fantasy and the supernatural were pared back to one per issue. Many more detective-action pieces were used, and the magazine took on the look and content of a standard detective pulp.

By March 1945, *Speed Mystery* offered six short stories (one of them a fantasy), a true-crime article, and a filler paragraph. Then came total change.

With the June 1945 issue, the magazine became a quarterly and radically changed its format. The December 1945 issue was a ninety-six page publication, devoted almost entirely to an abridgment of Edward Anderson's previously published hardback novel, "Thieves Like Us." Two unillustrated short-short stories were tucked into the rear pages. The final issue, March 1946, featured "Emergency Exit" by that most sedate of novelists, Anthony Wynne. The white fire of *Spicy Mystery Stories* had been effectively extinguished.

Note

1. Advertisement for *Spicy Mystery Stories* reproduced in Odyssey Publications, number 1, reprint of *Spicy Adventure Stories* (February 1941), p. 109.

Information Sources

BIBLIOGRAPHY:
Heckscher, August. *When LaGuardia Was Mayor*. New York: W. W. Norton & Co., 1978.

Jones, Robert Kenneth. *The Shudder Pulps*. New York: New American Library, 1978.

Mertz, Stephen. "Robert Leslie Bellem: The Great Unknown." *Xenophile,* Vol. 2, no. 8 (February 1976): 71–73.

Murray, Will. Introduction. Odyssey reprint edition of *Spicy Mystery Stories*. Melrose Highlands, Mass.: Odyssey Publications,, 1976.

Weinberg, Robert, ed. "Death Orchids & Other Bizarre Tales," (selections from *Spicy Mystery Stories*). Pulp Classics No. 13 (1976), Robert Weinberg Publications, Oak Lawn, Illinois.

INDEX SOURCES: None known.
LOCATION SOURCES: Private collectors only.

Publication History

MAGAZINE TITLE: *Spicy Mystery Stories*.
TITLE CHANGES: *Speed Mystery* (with January 1943 issue).
VOLUME AND ISSUE DATA: *Spicy Mystery Stories*: Vol. 1, no. 1 (June or July [?] 1934) through Vol. 13, no. 1 (December 1942); 73 issues. *Speed Mystery*: Vol. 1, no. 1 (January 1943) through Vol. 4, no. 1 (March 1946); 19 issues.
PUBLISHER: *Spicy Mystery Stories*: Culture Publications, Inc., 2242 Grove Street, Chicago, Illinois. As *Speed Mystery:* Trojan Publishing Corp., 2242 Grove Street, Chicago, Illinois, and later 29 Worthington Street, Springfield, Massachusetts.
EDITORS: Lawrence Cadman (*Spicy Mystery Stories*).
PRICE PER ISSUE: 25 cents (*Spicy Mystery Stories*); 15 cents (*Speed Mystery*).
SIZE AND PAGINATION: Average 6-7/8" X 9-5/8"; 96–128 pages.
CURRENT STATUS: Discontinued.
—*Robert Sampson*

SPIDER, THE

The Spider was Popular Publications' first and most important entry in the single-character mystery magazine field. Created in response to the sweeping successes of Street & Smith's *The Shadow Magazine** and Standard Magazine's *The Phantom Detective,** publisher Henry Steeger conceived the idea one day in 1933 when, while playing tennis, a scuttling spider caught his attention.

The first issue of *The Spider* was dated October 1933 and appeared simultaneously with Popular's *G–8 and His Battle Aces,** the firm's only other long-running character magazine. *The Spider's* first issue featured the lead novel "The Spider Strikes" by R.T.M. Scott, whose earlier prototype of The Spider, Secret Service Smith, enjoyed great success in pre-Great Depression hardcover books, even though Smith was originally a magazine character. The Spider was really wealthy New Yorker Richard Wentworth, a cool eradicator of criminals somewhat in the manner of The Saint, who was not adverse to shooting his enemies and leaving the vermillion seal of The Spider on their foreheads as proof of his work. Because he worked outside the law, the police—especially Police Com-

missioner Stanley Kirkpatrick (who all but knew Wentworth was The Spider)—
hunted The Spider as actively as any felon.

The first two novels were bylined R.T.M. Scott and are presumed to be the
work of the author of the Secret Service Smith novels. But Scott had a son,
R.T.M. Scott II, who happened to work at Popular at the time *The Spider* began;
and that fact, coupled with the sudden and mysterious disappearance of the Scott
byline from the series, along with the recollections of some of those who worked
at Popular that it was Scott's son who started the series, casts some doubt on
the true authorship of the original novels.

Without question, the series owes a great debt to Scott's Aurelius Smith, who,
like Richard Wentworth, was accompanied by a Hindu servant. Wentworth's
Sikh assistant, Ram Singh, was a more ferocious version of Smith's Langa
Doonh. Wentworth's love interest was his fiancée, socialite Nita Van Sloan,
who was not adverse to taking on The Spider's identity herself when Wentworth
was unable to do so. Most of the time, however, she suffered unbelievably at
the hands of Wentworth's satanic enemies and for one stretch of issues remained
a hopeless cripple.

Beginning with the third novel, "Wings of the Black Death," the Spider
novels were the work of ex-newspaperman Norvell W. Page, writing under a
house name as Grant Stockbridge. Under the direction of Editor Rogers Terrill,
Page abruptly recreated the series, infusing it with the violence and bizarre
situations which would give the pulp magazine its most notorious appellation—
"bloody." Although an excellent craftsman, Page's Spider novels are often
irrationally plotted and depend more on effect than substance. This was dia-
metrically opposed to the strengths of The Shadow and seems to have been
deliberately calculated by Editor Terrill, who demanded one thing of his writers
above all others—that they provided readers with what he called "emotional
urgency," placing the lead characters in situations of intense peril or conflict.
Thus, character was everything in *The Spider*, and the stories invariably grew
out of character and situation—often sensationalized, emotionally hysterical,
even absurd, but always compelling, even down to the creepy editorial touch
by which The Spider's name was always italicized.

Page's first effort, "Wings of the Black Death," was a clear foreshadowing
of the many nightmarish Spider novels to come. A master criminal known as
the Black Death was extorting ransom from Manhattan under threat of unleashing
a mutated strain of black plague through infected pigeons. While this was a big
jump ahead from the Scott novels, both of which pitted Wentworth against
comparatively ordinary underworld figures, Page's Wentworth was not much
different from Scott's version. This changed with the sixth novel, "The Citadel
of Hell," in which The Spider suddenly became a distorted *doppelganger* for
The Shadow. But in addition to the black cloak, slouch hat, twin automatics,
and blood-curdling laughter borrowed directly from Lamont Cranston, The Spider
wore a lanky wig, vampire fangs, and an appliance under his cloak which gave
him the appearance of a sinister hunchback. Originally, this weird figure was

an alias of Wentworth known as Tito Caliepi, a sidewalk violinist. Unlike The Shadow, The Spider did not operate under a host of aliases, although in later years Wentworth often prowled the underworld in the guise of Blinky McQuade, a small-time crook.

Subsequent Page novels became increasingly horrific. "The Mad Horde" is an early watershed novel wherein the master criminal (and there is always a master criminal) employed rabid animals as part of a terror campaign. This was an idea that Page used many times throughout his career and was not limited to *The Spider*. For the first three years of the series, Norvell Page's imagination reached farther and farther into unreality. "The Red Death Rain" was the first of many Spider novels pitting Wentworth against a sinister Chinese archvillain in the Fu Manchu tradition. Here, the Red Mandarin plotted to poison Manhattan's cigarettes, liquor, and coffee. "The City Destroyer" was more gargantuan; the city's skyscrapers fell victim to a destroying influence. "Hordes of the Red Butcher" concerned a rampage by surviving Neanderthal men. The "Dragon Lord of the Underworld" was Ssu Hsi Tze, a self-styled "Emperor of Vermin" who first released venomous creatures, then stole at will from corpse-strewn banks. The villain of "The Flame Master" was Aronk Dong, supposedly a Martian who resembled a lion, but the actual culprit was a pulp writer.

As lurid as these novels sound, and were, Page's imagination usually ran away with the story to the detriment of logic. The villains in two consecutive novels, "Overlord of the Damned" and "Death Reign of the Vampire King," were both revealed to be minor characters not directly involved in the story. Often, these lapses in logic were major, as in the unusual and somewhat metaphysical "Master of the Death Madness" in which none of the events surrounding the depradations of a Cult of Anubis were plausibly explained. Page often was carried away in the heat of his work in other ways, as well. In "The Pain Emperor," he killed off Wentworth's aide, Ronald Jackson. Professor Ezra Brownlee, who inspired Wentworth to become The Spider, died in "Dragon Lord of the Underworld," and the faithful Great Dane, Apollo, was poisoned in "Laboratory of the Damned." All but Brownlee were resurrected in later novels, but not convincingly.

Page also created a number of recurring antagonists for The Spider. The first of these was the appropriately named Fly, who dueled with Wentworth in "Prince of the Red Looters" and "Green Globes of Death." "The Mayor of Hell" and "Slaves of the Murder Syndicate" was a two-part story about a criminal ring that had taken over New York City. A few years later, a similar group would take over New York State in the three-part epic which comprised "The City That Paid to Die," "The Spider at Bay," and "Scourge of the Black Legions." Perhaps The Spider's most notorious foe was Tang-Akhmut, the Living Pharaoh, who plagued Wentworth through four consecutive novels: "The Coming of the Terror," "The Devil's Death Dwarfs," "City of Dreadful Night," and "Reign of the Snake Men."

In the middle of the Living Pharaoh stories, Norvell Page stopped writing the novels for eight issues. Beginning with "City of Dreadful Night," Emile C. Tepperman, who was simultaneously writing Popular's *Operator #5** series and who had earlier worked on the rival *Secret Agent X,** carried the series. His third novel, "Dictator of the Damned," began another multinovel subseries in which Count Calypsa was the villain. But Calypsa never returned. Tepperman's Spider novels are substantially similar to Page's but contain less-authentic characterizations of Wentworth, Ram Singh, and Nita Van Sloan.

When Page returned to the series in 1937, with the excellent but gruesome novel, "The Man Who Ruled in Hell," he began to alternate with Wayne Rogers, each writing approximately every other novel for about two years. Rogers was a frequent contributor to Popular's *Terror Tales (*see *Horror Stories)* and *Horror Stories* magazines. Although Rogers would later inherit the Operator #5 stories from Tepperman, his horror fiction background came through in his Spider novels quite clearly and made them as distinctly different from Page's, as were those by Tepperman (whose inclinations tended toward the underworld and detective story). Rogers's work was best exemplified by "The City That Dared Not Eat." This concerned a criminal organization which had poisoned food supplies and, to further its extortions, was preparing to flood the marketplace with human flesh disguised as animal meat. The cover illustration for this tale, which might be called the quintessential Spider cover, showed The Spider charging a group of masked butchers, behind whom helpless people hung from meat hooks.

Many of the Wayne Rogers novels recycled Page's original ideas. But, by then (1937), Page himself was actively doing the same, as he did when he wrote "The Spider and the Eyeless Legions," whose premise was identical to that of his earlier "Satan's Sightless Legion." At this point, Rogers Terrill was editor-in-chief, and a succession of editors actually handled *The Spider* magazine.

Wayne Rogers bowed out of the series in 1939 with "The Corpse Broker," a novel whose idea was borrowed from his own 1937 Secret Agent X novel, "Plague of the Golden Death." For most of 1940, Norvell Page and a returned Emile C. Tepperman shared the Grant Stockbridge house name. In keeping with the then-current pulp trend, the novels were toned down to some degree, and many of them made use of Fifth Column activity in the United States as springboards, including Page's "The Spider and the War Emperor" and Tepperman's "Dictator's Death Merchants." For several months, John Howitt's busy, lurid covers featured a fanged and evil-visaged Spider instead of the sanitized version who wore a simple domino mask. At this point, Page introduced The Spider's final recurring enemy, the master of disguise known only as Munro, who made his debut in "The Spider and the Faceless One" and who returned in "Slaves of the Laughing Death" and "The Spider and the Deathless One." Despite being the unmistakable work of Norvell Page, these later novels were less satisfactory when compared to the formative Spider adventures, as were most of the rest of the series. Page seems to have resumed full control in writing all the stories after 1940.

The last classic Spider novels were probably the group of five beginning with "Rule of the Monster Men" in 1939, in which Nita Van Sloan is surgically crippled, and extending through "The Spider and the Slaves of Hell," "The Spider and the Fire God," Rogers's "The Corpse Broker," and "The Spider and the Eyeless Legions." These followed Wentworth as a fugitive as he tried to put his life back together. But even this subplot had been used before.

The Spider novels of the 1940s were characterized primarily by a renewed interest in the personal lives of the supporting cast. Police Commissioner Kirkpatrick, who had had a brief tenure as governor before he resumed his old post, met a mysterious woman named Lona Deeping in "Murder's Black Prince." Her past created a moral dilemma for him until their marriage in the horrific and jingoistic "Volunteer Corpse Brigade," in which Fifth Columnists brought a fast-acting leprosy strain to America. Earlier, in "The Devil's Paymaster," Ronald Jackson met Marianne Harcourt, whom he later married.

The final two years of *The Spider* magazine, 1942 and 1943, were especially weak but out of which came two outstanding novels by Page. "Death and the Spider" was the one hundredth novel in the series, and, although the end is a cheat, it was a compelling example of Page's emotion-charged handling of his beloved character (Page was known to dress in imitation of The Spider) as Wentworth ventured out in fulfillment of a Tibetan abbott's prediction of The Spider's death. His goal was to stop a supernatural figure dressed as the classic image of Death, whose random killing of ordinary citizens culminated in an attack on America's top leaders. Less metaphysical was "Recruit for the Spider Legion," in which Wentworth convinced his old friend, Kirkpatrick, that The Spider's extralegal methods had their place in the fight against criminal monsters, in this case, the unexplained human cyclops whose Kali cult had recruited Manhattan's worst criminals.

Throughout its run, *The Spider* magazine presented a view of the world which was identical to its brother *Operator #5* magazine, in which the greatest fears of the average American—loss of life, loss of liberty, loss of loved ones, loss of civilization—were exploited mercilessly. No one could consider himself safe when criminals like the Butcher, the Red Hand, and Judge Torture were free to slaughter for gain or even without purpose, as was often the case. The only hope lay in one man, a savior, but a very human savior who could be hurt and who might not be able to protect all of the innocents from danger. In *The Spider*, that savior was Richard Wentworth, appropriately known also as the Master of Men, who fought evil on its own terms and with its own deadly weapons.

The Spider, with its lurid John Howitt and Raphael De Soto covers and lavish John Fleming-Gould illustrations, may have superficially resembled *The Shadow Magazine* but in reality was designed for an audience that wanted a less-neat explanation for the turmoil of the day and that believed its heroes had to struggle to be heroes.

The final issue of *The Spider* was dated December 1943 and contained the first and only novel by Prentice Winchell, the undistinguished "When Satan

Came to Town." The paper shortage caused by the Second World War had killed *The Spider* when countless bullets could not. An unpublished Spider novel, "Slaughter, Inc.," by Donald G. Cormack, appeared in a 1979 paperback book bylined Spider Page and titled *Legend in Blue Steel* (in which all the characters' names were changed for copyright reasons). Of greater interest is a short story featuring The Spider, written by Norvell Page, which appeared in *Xenophile** magazine.[1]

At least one British reprint issue was published.

Note

1. Untitled story by Norvell Page in form of letter dated May 16, 1942, to Virginia Combs (Nanek) Anderson, *Xenophile*, no. 40 (July 1978), pp. 32–38.

Information Sources

BIBLIOGRAPHY:
Anderson, Virginia Combs, and William Papilia. "A Remembrance of Early Pulp Collecting and Fandom: 1938–1943." *Xenophile*, no. 40 (July 1978): 3–25.
Carr, Wooda Nicholas. "The Pulp Villains: Tang-Akhmut, The Man from the East." *Doc Savage Club Reader*, no. 5 (n.d. [December 1978]): 10–12.
———, and Herman S. McGregor. "Contemplating Seven of the Pulp Heroes." *Bronze Shadows*, no. 12 (October 1967): 3–6.
Hardin, Nils. "An Interview with Henry Steeger." *Xenophile*, no. 33 (July 1977): 3–18.
———, and George Hocutt. "A Checklist of Popular Publications Titles 1930–1955." *Xenophile*, no. 33 (July 1977): 21–24.
McGregor, Herman S. "Comprehensive Survey of The Spider Novels." *The Pulp Era*, no. 66 (March/April 1967): 41–48; no. 67 (May/June 1967): 77–82; no. 68 (November/December 1967): 29–31; no. 70 (n.d. [1969]): 13–24; no. 71 (n.d. [1969]): 15–17.
Murray, Will. "The Top Ten Spider Novels–and One Stinker." *Megavore*, no. 13, (March 1981): 5–16.
Myers, Dick. "The Case of the Elusive Author." *Bronze Shadows*, no. 9 (March 1967): 5–7.
Steinkuhl, John. "The Spider Magazine Checklist." *The Age of the Unicorn*, Vol. 1, no. 1 (April 1979): 17–19.
Weinberg, Robert. "The Man from the East." *Pulp*, no. 10 (Winter 1978): 32–38.
———. "The Spider vs. Munro." *Pulp*, no. 10 (Winter 1978): 25–31.
INDEX SOURCES: Weinberg, Robert, and Lohr McKinstry. *The Hero Pulp Index*. Evergreen, Colo.: Opar Press, 1971.
LOCATION SOURCES: University of California–Los Angeles Library (1933–1942, 5 issues); private collectors.

Publication History

MAGAZINE TITLE: *The Spider*.
TITLE CHANGES: None.
VOLUME AND ISSUE DATA: Vol. 1, no. 1 (October 1933) through Vol. 30, no. 2 (December 1943); 118 issues.

PUBLISHER: Popular Publications, Inc., 2256 Grove Street, Chicago, Illinois, with
     editorial offices at 205 East 42nd Street, New York 17, New York.
EDITOR: Rogers Terrill.
SIZE AND PAGINATION: 6-5/8'' X 9-7/8''; 112–128 pages.
CURRENT STATUS: Discontinued.
—*Will Murray*

SPIDER, THE (British)

See THE SPIDER

SPIDERWEB

While in essence this is a continuation of a similar publication, *Skullduggery,**
it is a different magazine and published by a different publisher. Internal difficulties forced the dissolution of *Skullduggery*, and two of the three partners
publishing that magazine then formed a new company, Corsair Press, to continue
with the same intent.

The first issue, Winter 1982, presented a thoroughly professional magazine,
with fiction by Janwillem Van de Wetering (author of seven mystery novels
featuring the Dutch detectives, Grijpstra and Sergeant de Gier), Robert Sampson,
Dan Marlowe, Hal Charles, W. S. Doxey, and Ray Jay Wagner. An interview
with Max Collins gave an in-depth look at his work, what he's doing, and why,
and ''Verdicts'' by Annie Sebastian (Karen Shapiro) commented on new but
obscure mystery books.

Frank Hamilton's cover art, picturing a thoroughly evil fellow wielding a
butcher knife, was a sure invitation to sample the contents.

Information Sources

INDEX SOURCES: None known.
LOCATION SOURCES: Private collectors.

Publication History

MAGAZINE TITLE: *Spiderweb*.
TITLE CHANGES: None.
VOLUME AND ISSUE DATA: Vol. 1, no. 1 (to date, Winter 1982); 1 issue.
PUBLISHER: Corsair Press, Drawer F, M.I.T. Branch Station, Cambridge, Massachu-
     setts 02139.
EDITORS: Karen Shapiro and William Desmond.
PRICE PER ISSUE: $2.50.
CURRENT STATUS: Active.

SPRINGHEELED JACK (British)

Although the highwayman-hero of this Victorian ''penny dreadful'' arises
from a legend, there are several accounts of his origin. One said that Springheeled

Jack had been active in the Midlands in the 1850s. Another attributed the legend to a coal merchant's son who had terrorized country folk in Warwickshire. Among other beliefs was that he was an eccentric Marquess of Waterford. But, regardless of his identity, Springheeled Jack supposedly had powerful springs in the heels of his boots, enabling him to jump or leap amazing distances and heights with ease.

The stories in the "penny dreadfuls" in the 1870s had described Jack as wearing a skin-tight, glossy crimson suit, with bat-style wings, lion's mane, devil's horns, talon hands, cloven hoofs, and a sulphurous-breathing mouth! Later stories made him the friend of the weak and downtrodden but still Mephistophelian in appearance so that all fled from his approach. Many tales gave him a decided mischievous aspect.

The Springheeled Jack in the turn-of-the-century magazine bearing his name was a cashiered officer with a grievance. These tales were written by Charlton Lea, an author who had penned many various highwaymen stories.

The colored covers of *Springheeled Jack* were luridly magnificent. But perhaps the sophistication of the readers in 1904 made Jack an unfit subject for a long-running series, and the magazine existed for only twelve issues.

Information Sources

BIBLIOGRAPHY:

Lofts, W.O.G. "Spring-Heeled Jack." *Dime Novel Roundup*, Vol. 42, no. 6 (June 15, 1973): 59–62.

————, and Derek J. Adley. *Old Boys Books, A Complete Catalogue*. London: privately printed, 1969.

Turner, E. S. *Boys Will Be Boys*. London: Michael Joseph, 1948.

INDEX SOURCES: None known.

LOCATION SOURCES: Private collectors only.

Publication History

MAGAZINE TITLE: *Springheeled Jack*.
TITLE CHANGES: None.
VOLUME AND ISSUE DATA: March 19, 1904, to (later) 1904; 12 issues.
PUBLISHER: Aldine Publishing Company, London.
EDITOR: Not known.
PRICE PER ISSUE: 2 pence.
SIZE AND PAGINATION: Not known.
CURRENT STATUS: Discontinued.

SPY NOVELS MAGAZINE

In December 1934, A. A. Wyn's Magazine Publishers introduced *Spy Novels Magazine*. The intent, it would seem, was to provide to eager readers of *Spy Stories* (Magazine Publishers)* a second fountain to ease their thirst for action spy fiction. *Spy Stories* and *Spy Novels*, issued on alternate months, were identical sisters. They shared the same format and editorial policy, tne same artists, and most of the same writers. The difference was essentially that of title.

The "novels" referred to in the *Spy Novels Magazine* title were (as customary) four short stories ranging in length from about twenty-two to twenty-eight pages, illustrations included. The rest of the magazine was filled either by a single short story or what was euphemistically called a "True Spy Story"—in other terms, a short story.

If these contents were minimal, they were packaged with high skill. The first two (of three) issues of *Spy Novels* are beautiful examples of the pulp magazine as an art form. Along the crimson spine, the title appears in blocky yellow letters. On the front cover, the word "Spy" rises in enormous yellow letters, outlined in red, the other portion of the title appearing in much smaller letters immediately below.

All covers were painted by Rafael M. DeSoto. The first two feature decorative women in peril. They are foreign spies; you can tell in an instant, noting their foreign hairdos and dangling foreign earrings and bare shoulders. They are nice girls, though. The third cover, less successful, shows a naval officer struggling with a slick-haired no-good for possession of a detonator, while a hard-boiled female spy glares at the action; the painting is flat, precise, and unsubtle; and the magazine title, black outlined in red, appears against a broad yellow band across the top.

The interior illustrations were drawn by a variety of artists, including Jayem Wilcox, A. Leslie Ross, and G. L. McMann. Most illustrations are curiously static, even when showing scenes of violent action.

Of the twelve stories published in *Spy Novels Magazine* during its brief life, three were written by E. Hoffman Price, three by James Perley Hughes, and three by Frederick C. Painton. Of the remaining, two were by Major George Fielding Eliot and one by William E. Barrett.

The general tone of these stories is more than a little jingoistic: true Americans against arrogant foreign plotters. But the stories move along, neatly plotted, full of atmosphere and calculated suspense. They are ingratiatingly handled.

The premise is that a young American spy must face the deadly action of foreign agents. These latter seek the formula, the plans, or they prepare the act of terrorism. Less often, they plot complexly to cripple U.S. military power or to set friendly nations upon each other. Fortunately for the peace of the world, the young American agent consistently manages to beat the enemy. It is always a near thing; he is drugged, beaten, tricked, tied up, tortured, and otherwise treated badly. But not badly enough to interfere with his accurate shooting as the story rages from one hot incident to the next.

Since even spirited American spies might find the odds difficult, they are aided by a succession of beautiful girls, whose loyalties are ambiguous. In a few instances, romance blooms, occasionally it does not; there is no fixed pattern. The girl is certainly more competent than the usual pulp magazine heroine.

In addition to the stories, each issue also contained at least one "fact" article. This was an intensely fictionalized account of an American spy's activities during the First World War, a different spy in each issue. Dana R. Marsh contributed an article in the first and second issues of the magazine. For the third issue, both Vaughn Ellis and Arch Whitehouse published articles. Whitehouse's piece was solidly factual; all others were mostly fiction, and all were nearly the best part of the magazine.

Spy Novels Magazine began as a bimonthly and continued so. It was cancelled without notice, victim of a low interest in spy adventures.

Information Sources

INDEX SOURCES: None known.
LOCATION SOURCES: Private collectors.

Publication History

MAGAZINE TITLE: *Spy Novels Magazine*.
TITLE CHANGES: None.
VOLUME AND ISSUE DATA: Vol. 1, no. 1 (February 1935) through Vol. 1, no. 3 (June 1935); 3 issues.
PUBLISHER: Magazine Publishers, Inc., 67 West 44th Street, New York, New York.
EDITOR: A. A. Wyn; associate editor, H. M. Wismer.
PRICE PER ISSUE: 15 cents.
SIZE AND PAGINATION: 7" X 10"; 128 pages.
CURRENT STATUS: Discontinued.
—*Robert Sampson*

SPY STORIES (Albert Publishing)

Albert Publishing Company's *Spy Stories* was the first of four magazines with the same title, this one commencing February 1929. One issue was published. It is not known if subsequent issues of *Spy Stories* (Monthly Magazine Publishers)* was by the same company under a different publishing name. No other information is available.

Information Sources

INDEX SOURCES: None known.
LOCATION SOURCES: University of California–Los Angeles Library (Vol. 1, no. 1); private collectors.

Publication History

MAGAZINE TITLE: *Spy Stories*.
TITLE CHANGES: None.
VOLUME AND ISSUE DATA: Vol. 1, no. 1 (February 1929); 1 issue.
PUBLISHER: Albert Publishing Company, New York, New York.
EDITOR: Not known.
PRICE PER ISSUE: Not known.

SIZE AND PAGINATION: Not known.
CURRENT STATUS: Discontinued.

SPY STORIES (Magazine Publishers)

Magazine Publisher's *Spy Stories*, commencing in November 1934, was the last of four magazines with this title. Its first issue was identified as volume 2, number 1, and it was the continuation of a terminated magazine of the same appellation. (The two earlier publications using this title were *Spy Stories* [Albert Publishing]* and *Spy Stories* [Monthly Magazine Publishers].*)

Under A. A. Wyn's editorship, the 1934–1935 *Spy Stories* was the elder of identical twin sisters, the other being *Spy Novels Magazine*.* These magazines alternated months of issue, *Spy Stories* being the first published. Both magazines shared format, artists, and writers. Both featured "novels" (short stories), plus massively fictionalized "fact" articles and one or more short stories. *Spy Stories*, however, also included an editorial department, "The Black Chamber," for readers' letters and general comment. Throughout its life, it was dated bimonthly, although there is a break in its dating in mid-1935 (no July issue).

Since *Spy Stories* and *Spy Novels* were essentially two separate titlings of the same publication, refer to the discussion of *Spy Novels Magazine* elsewhere in this volume.

Information Sources

INDEX SOURCES: None known.
LOCATION SOURCES: Private collectors.

Publication History

MAGAZINE TITLE: *Spy Stories*.
TITLE CHANGES: None.
VOLUME AND ISSUE DATA: Vol. 2, no. 1 (November 1934) through Vol. 3, no. 2 (October 1935); 6 issues.
PUBLISHER: Magazine Publishers, Inc., 67 West 44th Street, New York, New York.
EDITOR: A. A. Wyn; associate editor, H. M. Wismer.
PRICE PER ISSUE: 15 cents.
SIZE AND PAGINATION: 7'' X 10''; 128 pages.
CURRENT STATUS: Discontinued.
—*Robert Sampson*

SPY STORIES (Monthly Magazine Publishers)

Monthly Magazine's *Spy Stories* was the second of four magazines with the same title, this one commencing March 1929 and continuing the volume and issue numbering from *Spy Stories* (Albert Publishing).* The connection, if any, between Albert Publishing Company and Monthly Magazine Publishers is not known. Note that the title was again used in 1934 by yet another publisher (*Spy Stories* [Magazine Publishers]*). No other information is available.

Information Sources

INDEX SOURCES: None known.
LOCATION SOURCES: Private collectors.

Publication History

MAGAZINE TITLE: *Spy Stories*.
TITLE CHANGES: None.
VOLUME AND ISSUE DATA: Vol. 1, no. 2 (March 1929) through Vol. 1, no. 4 (July 1929); 3 issues.
PUBLISHER: Monthly Magazine Publishers, Inc., New York, New York.
EDITOR: Harold B. Hersey.
PRICE PER ISSUE: Not known.
SIZE AND PAGINATION: Not known.
CURRENT STATUS: Discontinued.

STAR DETECTIVE

Western Fiction Publishing Company introduced *Star Detective* in May 1935. This thick pulp magazine, while known for its weird-menace stories, is also noted as featuring what are now recognized as some of the most popular detective characters, such as Ellery Queen and The Saint. Issues have been noted as late as mid-1938, but its discontinuance date is not known. A companion magazine from the same publisher was commenced in October 1936, *Star Sports Magazine*.

Information Sources

INDEX SOURCES: None known.
LOCATION SOURCES: Private collectors.

Publication History

MAGAZINE TITLE: *Star Detective*.
TITLE CHANGES: None known.
VOLUME AND ISSUE DATA: Vol. 1, no. 1 (May 1935) through at least mid-1938; number of issues and extent unknown.
PUBLISHER: Western Fiction Publishing Co., Inc., New York, New York.
EDITOR: Not known.
PRICE PER ISSUE: 25 cents.
SIZE AND PAGINATION: 6-7/8'' X 9-7/8''; 196 pages.
CURRENT STATUS: Discontinued.

STARTLING DETECTIVE ADVENTURES

Startling Detective Adventures, a pulp magazine, is believed to have commenced in November 1929. No other information is available.

Information Sources

INDEX SOURCES: None known.
LOCATION SOURCES: Private collectors.

Publication History

MAGAZINE TITLE: *Startling Detective Adventures*.
TITLE CHANGES: None known.
VOLUME AND ISSUE DATA: Vol. 1, no. 1 (November 1929); number of issues and
    extent unknown.
PUBLISHER: Not known.
EDITOR: Not known.
PRICE PER ISSUE: Not known.
SIZE AND PAGINATION: Not known.
CURRENT STATUS: Discontinued.

STARTLING MYSTERY

With wide reader acceptance of its "shudder" group of pulp magazines, Popular Publications added two more titles in that many months early in 1940. *Sinister Stories** was commenced in January and *Startling Mystery* in February; the two titles continued to be published on alternate months, although both had short lives. Perhaps they never had a decent chance. Employing reprint covers and interior illustrations from earlier issues of the other weird-menace Popular magazines, and paying authors only half of the then-going rate of one cent a word, there was a handicap from the beginning. Story quality suffered, and, in retrospect, the stories are quite ineffective. In addition, Popular had already phased out its Gothic-type presentation and, in fact, was moving away from its sex-sadistic phase (both *Horror Stories** and *Terror Tales* [see *Horror Stories]* were nearing their ends. Only two issues were published.[1] The eight stories in the first issue and the seven in the second were accompanied by several departments.

As the leading circulation publisher of pulps during the thirties and into the forties, Popular Publications proved ready and able to try out new titles—and canny enough to drop them when they were unprofitable.[2]

Notes

1. Popular Publications (no longer in business) made available to *Xenophile* magazine (no. 33 [July 1977], pp. 21–24) a checklist of its titles. There may be a discrepancy. The company listed three issues. It is possible that the third and final issue, to be dated June 1940, was prepared and scheduled but never published. It has not been noted in existence.

2. The cost of an average pulp was $5,000 on a print run of 125,000 copies. Thus, a ten-cent magazine which grossed the publisher six cents had to sell 85,000 copies to break even.

Information Sources

BIBLIOGRAPHY:

Hardin, Nils. "An Interview with Henry Steeger." *Xenophile*, no. 33 (July 1977) 3–18.

————, and George Hocutt. "A Checklist of Popular Publications Titles 1930–1955." *Xenophile*, no. 33 (July 1977): 21–24.

Hersey, Harold. *Pulpwood Editor*. New York: Frederick A. Stokes Co., 1937.

Jones, Robert Kenneth. *The Shudder Pulps*. West Linn, Ore.: Fax Collector's Editions, 1975.

————. "The Weird Menace Magazines." *Bronze Shadows*, no. 10 (June 1967): 3–8; no. 11 (August 1967): 7–13; no. 12 (October 1967): 7–10; no. 13 (January 1968): 7–12; no. 14 (March 1968): 13–17; no. 15 (November 1968): 4–8.

INDEX SOURCES: None known.

LOCATION SOURCES: Private collectors.

Publication History

MAGAZINE TITLE: *Startling Mystery*.

TITLE CHANGES: None.

VOLUME AND ISSUE DATA: Vol. 1, no. 1 (February 1940) through Vol. 1, no. 2 (April 1940); 2 issues.

PUBLISHER: Fictioneers, Inc., subsidiary of Popular Publications, Inc., 2256 Grove Street, Chicago, Illinois, with editorial offices at 210 East 43rd Street, New York, New York.

EDITOR: Costa Carousso.

PRICE PER ISSUE: 15 cents.

SIZE AND PAGINATION: 7" X 9-3/4"; 112 pages.

CURRENT STATUS: Discontinued.

—*Robert Kenneth Jones*

STARTLING MYSTERY STORIES

Of borderline interest to most detective-crime fans, *Startling Mystery Stories* specialized in stories where either the detective or the villain had supernatural powers or their scientific equivalent. Here, ghost breakers and psychic investigators faced vampires, werewolves, and alien things from other dimensions: "strange and eerie mysteries," said editor Robert W. Lowndes, "beyond the scope of the mundane."[1] This met the public's fancy in 1966.

Not all the stories in its eighteen, frequently handsome, quarterly issues were like this. In some, the crimes only seemed supernatural, and some of the stories were not mysteries at all.

Nearly all reprints, nearly all from *Weird Tales** (but some from *Argosy, Strange Tales of Mystery and Terror,** Science Wonder Stories,* and *The Witch's Tales*), and nearly all from the 1930s, the stories ranged from gloriously awful to powerfully effective. Authors included H. P. Lovecraft, Charles Dickens, and a then-new writer named Stephen King.

A glance at some of the typical tales will illustrate the tone. The most popular author was Seabury Quinn (fourteen stories, all but one featuring phantom fighter Dr. Jules de Grandin, a dapper, French, occult detective and his American friend, Dr. Trowbridge). When a party of tourists are found savagely beaten to death, their bodies oddly drained of blood, Dr. de Grandin and friend are invited to Pine Lake for hunting. On arrival, they learn what they are to hunt—when their hurtling car is pursued and overtaken by a tall white thing of incredible strength and speed. Revived by sorcery, mummies of ancient Egypt walk the earth again in this flawed but interesting novelette ("The Mansion of Unholy Magic," issue number 1).

Paul Ernst had five novelettes about sinister, red-masked Dr. Satan. In "Hollywood Horror" (number 9), huge, secretly altered, studio lights turn on, and a glamorous movie star screams as she sees the flesh of her face slowly become invisible, leaving only a horrifying skull. Psychic detective Ascott Keane investigates in an undated but poorly written tale.

In "The Adventure of the Tottenham Werewolf," one of the better of August Derleth's many pastiches in the style of Sherlock Holmes, two girls and a man have been found murdered, their throats torn out as if by a giant wolf. Young Septimus Grayle, heir to a huge family fortune, believes he might be guilty of the murders. Someone is a maniac; but is it young Grayle, afflicted with a neurosis that makes him howl at the moon? Private enquiry agent Solar Pons and his assistant, Dr. Parker, investigate and find a shocking answer in the garden on the night of the next full moon, in issue number 4.

Edward D. Hoch has five stories about Simon Ark, who may be two thousand years old and seeking to personally destroy Satan. In "The Man from Nowhere," a short story based on the Kaspar Hauser case, Ark investigates the strange death of Douglas Zadig, leader of a worldwide cult, who is knifed in the center of a field of snow. But the only tracks are Zadig's own, and there is no trace of the knife. . . .

In effect, *Startling Mystery Stories* was a mystery companion to the old *Weird Tales*, an effect heightened by its reprinting of a story's original illustrations. The covers, often reprints of black-and-white illustrations by famed fantasy artist Virgil Finlay, on paper stock that showed his intricate detail to advantage against a full-color background, were frequently striking.

Circulation had been rising steadily; and with the last issue published, a bimonthly schedule had been established. But costs and distribution problems were greater, and in 1971 *Startling Mystery Stories* and all its sister titles folded.

The magazine is avidly collected today since many of its stories are unavailable in any other form. And Editor Lowndes's introductions were gems of insightful information about the authors, works, and magazines of the period.

Note

1. Editorial, *Startling Mystery Stories*, Vol. 1, no. 1 (Summer 1966), p. 4.

Information Sources

INDEX SOURCES: Cook, Michael L. *Monthly Murders*, Westport, Conn.: Greenwood
    Press, 1982.
Marshall, Gene, and Carl F. Waedt. "An Index to the Health Knowledge Magazines."
    The Science-Fiction Collector, no. 3 (n.d. [1977]): 3–42.
LOCATION SOURCES: Private collectors.

Publication History

MAGAZINE TITLE: *Startling Mystery Stories*.
TITLE CHANGES: None.
VOLUME AND ISSUE DATA: Vol. 1, no. 1 (Summer 1966) through Vol. 3, no. 6
    (March 1971); 18 issues.
PUBLISHER: Health Knowledge, Inc., 140 Fifth Avenue, New York, New York 10011.
EDITOR: Robert A. W. Lowndes.
PRICE PER ISSUE: 50 cents (through Vol. 3, no. 3); 60 cents (through Vol. 3, no. 5);
    75 cents (subsequent issues).
SIZE AND PAGINATION: Average 5-1/2" X 7"; 130 pages.
CURRENT STATUS: Discontinued.
—*Frank D. McSherry, Jr.*

STIRRING DETECTIVE AND WESTERN STORIES

A hybrid pulp magazine *Stirring Detective and Western Stories* featured both
western fiction and detective stories. At least one issue was published in November 1940.[1] No other information is available.

Note

1. Title listed in "Tentative Pulp Checklist" from San Francisco Academy of Comic Art, (unpublished manuscript, n.d.).

Information Sources

INDEX SOURCES: None known.
LOCATION SOURCES: Private collectors.

Publication History

MAGAZINE TITLE: *Stirring Detective and Western Stories*.
TITLE CHANGES: None known.
VOLUME AND ISSUE DATA: Vol. 1, no. 1 (November 1940); number of issues and
    extent unknown.
PUBLISHER: Albing Publishing Co., Inc., 1 Appleton Street, Holyoke, Massachusetts.
EDITOR: Not known.
PRICE PER ISSUE: Not known.
SIZE AND PAGINATION: Not known.
CURRENT STATUS: Discontinued.

STIRRING DETECTIVE STORIES (British)

No information is available.

Information Sources

INDEX SOURCES: None known.
LOCATION SOURCES: Private collectors.

Publication History

MAGAZINE TITLE: *Stirring Detective Stories.*
TITLE CHANGES: None known.
VOLUME AND ISSUE DATA: Not known.
PUBLISHER: Not known.
EDITOR: Not known.
PRICE PER ISSUE: Not known.
SIZE AND PAGINATION: Not known.
CURRENT STATUS: Discontinued.

STORY DIGEST MAGAZINE

The *Story Digest Magazine,* a "Gold Key" series, published at least one mystery issue. This was subtitled "Boris Karloff—Tales of Mystery" and contained eleven short stories, all written by Dick Wood and illustrated by Luis Dominguez. While somewhat on a juvenile level, this magazine does bear mention. Other issues of this periodical featured Tarzan, Dark Shadows (based on the television series), and a "Believe It or Not" ghost story collection. These were not numbered, but the mystery issue described was dated June 1970.

Information Sources

INDEX SOURCES: None known.
LOCATION SOURCES: Private collectors.

Publication History

MAGAZINE TITLE: *Story Digest Magazine* (June 1970 issue subtitled "Boris Karloff—
  Tales of Mystery").
TITLE CHANGES: None.
VOLUME AND ISSUE DATA: Not designated. Published circa 1970–1971.
PUBLISHER: Periodicals Department of Golden Press, Western Publishing Co., Inc.,
  New York, New York; Richard W. Eiger, publisher.
EDITOR: Wallace I. Green, managing editor; Paul Kuhn, associate editor.
PRICE PER ISSUE: 60 cents.
SIZE AND PAGINATION: 4-3/4" X 6-3/8"; 144 pages.
CURRENT STATUS: Discontinued.

STRANGE

A beautiful young woman, nearly undressed, is lying in a flower-strewn field, one hand suggestively cupped around her breast—while menacing green hands reached toward her. . . .[1]

A wraith of a beautiful lady, draped in a red, revealing cloth, her body bone-white, is at the rail of a ship. . . .[2]

An evening-clad brunette, with hand on hip and breasts nearly revealed, looks suggestively out the door where a typical hood is posed. . . .[3]

These were the cover scenes of the three issues of *Strange*. Was this a pulp magazine at the height of the lurid-cover phase? Are the contents filled with weird characters and gangster episodes? Not at all. *Strange* was a digest-size magazine published in 1952 with the subtitle "The Magazine of True Mystery." It was a hybrid, or attempted to be. Proposing to publish accounts of true happenings, not all of them explainable, in fictional mode, it was, to all effect, an attempt to capitalize both on crime fiction and on true-crime stories. And if there was a supernatural twist, so much the better.

Crime was not always the criteria for a selection. Some were based on social crimes, such as prostitution; others on historical or legendary events.

Among the classic mystery situations explored were "Mystery of the Bell Witch" by William T. Brannon (March 1952); "Mystery of the Mary Celeste" by Tony Field (March 1952), "The Tichbourne Mystery" by Dwight Manners (March 1952), "The Elusive Oak Island Treasure" by Bruce Parker (May 1952), and "The Tragic Fate of Starr Faithful" by Tony Field (May 1952). Each issue had between eleven and fourteen "stories" plus filler material. Unless written under pseudonyms, none of the stories was by an author recognizable to crime fiction fans.

Notes

1. Cover painting, *Strange*, Vol. 1, no. 1 (March 1952).
2. Cover painting,*Strange*, Vol. 1, no. 2 (May 1952).
3. Cover painting, *Strange*, Vol. 1, no. 3 (July 1952).

Information Sources

INDEX SOURCES: Cook, Michael L. *Monthly Murders*. Westport, Conn.: Greenwood Press, 1982.
LOCATION SOURCES: Private collectors.

Publication History

MAGAZINE TITLE: *Strange*.
TITLE CHANGES: None.
VOLUME AND ISSUE DATA: Vol. 1, no. 1 (March 1952) through Vol. 1, no. 3 (July 1952); 3 issues.
PUBLISHER: Quinn Publishing Co., Inc., 8 Lord Street, Buffalo, New York.
EDITOR: James L. Quinn.
PRICE PER ISSUE: 35 cents.

SIZE AND PAGINATION: 5-1/4'' X 7-5/8''; 128 pages.
CURRENT STATUS: Discontinued.

STRANGE DETECTIVE MYSTERIES

With perhaps an envious side-glance at the weird-menace magazines, *Strange Detective Mysteries* appeared in October 1937 with this introduction: "Remember the time you read that one perfect knockout detective story—bizarre, mysterious, thrill-packed, different?. . .We give you. . .not only one bizarre, thrilling, eerie-laden mystery story such as you've searched for, but a whole magazine full of them!. . .Here is detective mystery, strange, extraordinary—bizarre!"[1]

And, indeed, a host of bizarre crime fighters appeared in its pages, from the pens of such as Norvell Page (Dunne, ju-jitsu expert), Arthur Leo Zagat (Dr. John Bain), Wyatt Blassingame (The Thin Man, a circus performer), and Donald G. Cormack (Schuyler Montgomery as "The Hand" and the "Parson").

The weird-crime approach was fairly successful, and the magazine survived for nearly six years with but one interruption, when it was temporarily replaced by *Captain Satan.**

Note

1. Introductory editorial, *Strange Detective Mysteries*, Vol. 1, no. 1 (October 1937), p. 4.

Information Sources

BIBLIOGRAPHY:
Hardin, Nils. "An Interview with Henry Steeger." *Xenophile*, no. 33 (July 1977): 3–18.
———, and George Hocutt. "A Checklist of Popular Publications Titles 1930–1955." *Xenophile*, no. 33 (July 1977):21–24.
INDEX SOURCES: None known.
LOCATION SOURCES: University of California–Los Angeles Library (Vol. 1, no. 1; Vol. 5, no. 2, only); private collectors.

Publication History

MAGAZINE TITLE: *Strange Detective Mysteries*.
TITLE CHANGES: Replaced by *Captain Satan* (see separate entry) with Vol. 1, no. 3 (March 1938) through Vol. 2, no. 3 (July 1938), then continued as *Strange Detective Mysteries* again.
VOLUME AND ISSUE DATA: Vol. 1, no. 1 (October 1937) through Vol. 1, no. 2 (November 1937); Vol. 2, no. 4 (November 1938) through Vol. 9, no. 1 (May 1943); 28 issues.
PUBLISHER: Popular Publications, Inc., 2256 Grove Street, Chicago, Illinois, with editorial offices at 205 East 42nd Street, New York, New York.
EDITORS: Willard Crosby; Ejler Jacobson; John Bender.
PRICE PER ISSUE: 15 cents.
SIZE AND PAGINATION: 7'' X 9-3/4''; 112 pages.
CURRENT STATUS: Discontinued.

STRANGE DETECTIVE STORIES

The highlights of this short-lived magazine were the stories by Robert E. Howard, which also categorized the magazine. The February issue of *Strange Detective Stories* included "Fangs of Gold," featuring Steve Harrison, detective. Another Howard story in the same issue was written under the pseudonym of Patrick Ervin; "The Tomb's Secret" had the detective changed to Brock Rollins. This issue carried an announcement that the forthcoming issue would include "Dead Man's Doom" (by Howard), but no further issues were published. "Dead Man's Doom" did appear much later in the paperback book of Howard stories, *Skull-Face,* edited by Glenn A. Lord (Berkeley Medallion Books, 1978).

Information Sources

INDEX SOURCES: None known.
LOCATION SOURCES: Private collectors.

Publication History

MAGAZINE TITLE: *Strange Detective Stories.*
TITLE CHANGES: None.
VOLUME AND ISSUE DATA: Vol. 4, no. 6 (November 1933) through Vol. 5, no. 3 (February 1934); 4 issues.
Note: Numbering reputed to be a continuation from the firm's *Nickel Detective* (see separate entry).
PUBLISHER: Nickel Publications, Inc., 537 Dearborn Street, Chicago, Illinois.
EDITOR: Not known.
PRICE PER ISSUE: 15 cents.
SIZE AND PAGINATION: 7" X 10"; 160 pages.
CURRENT STATUS: Discontinued.

STRANGE STORIES

Although *Strange Stories* could be classified as a "true weird tales" type of pulp magazine, there was some mystery element included, and it should be mentioned. It was published by Ned Pines's Better Publications as a "Thrilling Publication" from February 1939 through February 1941. The magazine is, however, peripheral to the mystery genre.

Information Sources

INDEX SOURCES: Cockcroft, T.G.L. *Index to the Weird Fiction Magazines.* 2 vols. Wellington, New Zealand: John Milne Ltd., 1962, 1964.
LOCATION SOURCES: University of California–Los Angeles Library (complete run); private collectors.

Publication History

MAGAZINE TITLE: *Strange Stories.*
TITLE CHANGES: None.

VOLUME AND ISSUE DATA: Vol. 1, no. 1 (February 1939) through Vol. 5, no. 1
　　(February 1941); 13 issues.
PUBLISHER: Better Publications, Inc., 11 East 39th Street, New York, New York.
EDITOR: Mortimer Weisinger.
PRICE PER ISSUE: 15 cents (through June 1940); 10 cents (subsequent issues).
SIZE AND PAGINATION: 6-7/8'' X 9-7/8''; 128 pages (through June 1940); 96 pages
　　(subsequent issues).
CURRENT STATUS: Discontinued.

STRANGE TALES OF MYSTERY AND TERROR

This pulp magazine, despite its title indicating an equal mystery element, was
predominantly weird-terror fiction. *Strange Tales of Mystery and Terror* should
be mentioned, however, for the few stories that would interest the mystery reader.
Seven issues were published between 1931 and 1933.

Information Sources

INDEX SOURCES: Cockcroft, T.G.L. *Index to the Weird Fiction Magazines*. 2 vols.
　　Wellington, New Zealand: John Milne Ltd., 1962, 1964.
LOCATION SOURCES: University of California–Los Angeles Library (complete run);
　　private collectors.

Publication History

MAGAZINE TITLE: *Strange Tales of Mystery and Terror*.
TITLE CHANGES: None.
VOLUME AND ISSUE DATA: Vol. 1, no. 1 (September 1931) through Vol. 3, no. 1
　　(January 1933); 7 issues.
PUBLISHER: The Clayton Magazines, Inc., 155 East 44th Street, New York, New York.
EDITOR: Harry Bates.
PRICE PER ISSUE: 25 cents.
SIZE AND PAGINATION: 6-5/8'' X 9-3/4''; 144 pages.
CURRENT STATUS: Discontinued.

STREET & SMITH'S DETECTIVE MONTHLY (British)

One of the longest-surviving British reprint magazines, commencing late in
1939, was *Street & Smith's Detective Monthly,* known briefly at the beginning
as *Street & Smith's Detective Stories*. Its contents were reprints from the American *Detective Story Magazine* (Street & Smith).* For most of its life, it was
published in a pulp format, changing to digest-size only with the January 1958
issue.

The stories were in the traditional detective story vein, tempered by contemporary settings, language, and atmosphere, and laced with hard-boiled characters.
It seemed to retain a ''pulp flavor'' throughout its life, as did the parent American
magazine. With some humor, and some pathos, the stories were realistic and
well done.

Many of the authors had become veterans while writing for earlier pulp magazines; others were newcomers who would soon become known to mystery fans. The stories were satisfying and carefully nonantagonistic; the protagonists, as well as the lesser characters, were, for the most part, believable. It was one of the classic crime fiction magazines of the period.

Featuring usually one long short story, termed a "novelette," and a number of shorter tales, there were title-tempting pieces such as "Death Paces the Widow's Walk" by Bruce Elliott (January 1958), "Death in Dirty Dishes" by Talmage Powell (January 1958), "Scalp Treatment" by Ted Stratton (February 1958), "The Green Vest" by Bruno Fischer (August 1958), and "Design in Red" by William Brandon (March 1958), as well as good stories by John D. MacDonald, Emile C. Tepperman, John L. Nanovic, Norman A. Daniels, and others.

After eighty-eight issues, the last rites were administered to this magazine in August 1958.

Information Sources

INDEX SOURCES: None known.
LOCATION SOURCES: Private collectors.

Publication History

MAGAZINE TITLE: *Street & Smith's Detective Monthly*.
TITLE CHANGES: First seven issues as *Street & Smith's Detective Stories*.
VOLUME AND ISSUE DATA: Vol. 1, no. 1 (November 1939) through Vol. 4, no. 9 (August 1958); 88 issues.
PUBLISHER: Atlas Publishing & Distributing Co., Ltd., 18 Bride Lane, London E.C.4, England.
EDITOR: Not known.
PRICE PER ISSUE: 1 shilling.
SIZE AND PAGINATION: 6-1/2" X 9-1/2"; 5-3/8" X 7-1/2" (with Vol. 4, no. 2 [January 1958]); 64 pages.
CURRENT STATUS: Discontinued.
—*Robert Adey*

STREET & SMITH'S DETECTIVE STORIES (British)

See STREET & SMITH'S DETECTIVE MONTHLY (British)

STREET & SMITH'S DETECTIVE STORY MAGAZINE

See DETECTIVE STORY MAGAZINE (STREET & SMITH)

STREET & SMITH'S MYSTERY DETECTIVE (British)

Street & Smith's Mystery Detective was a British reprint series of material from the U.S. publication, *Detective Story Magazine* (Street & Smith),* and should not be confused with a similar British reprint series called *Street & Smith's Detective Monthly* (British).*

Information Sources

INDEX SOURCES: None known.
LOCATION SOURCES: Private collectors.

Publication History

MAGAZINE TITLE: *Street & Smith's Mystery Detective*.
TITLE CHANGES: None.
VOLUME AND ISSUE DATA: No. 1 (August 1955) through no. 12 (September 1957); 12 issues.
PUBLISHER: Not known.
EDITOR: Not known.
PRICE PER ISSUE: Not known.
SIZE AND PAGINATION: Not known.
CURRENT STATUS: Discontinued.

SUPER-DETECTIVE

Two U.S. magazines were published under similar names. The first was the short-lived *Super-Detective Stories,** published in 1934, which may have been edited by Frank Armor, later connected with Culture Publications, producers of *Spicy Detective** and the other infamous *Spicy* titles.

In October 1940, Trojan Publications, an affiliate of Culture, began *Super-Detective*, which may or may not have been a revival of the older title. In any case, the new periodical, despite its name, was not a detective magazine as much as it was a single-character adventure magazine. The character was a Doc Savage imitation, Jim Anthony, who made his debut in the premier issue in the novel titled "Dealer in Death." The author was John Grange, a house name masking the work of Robert Leslie Bellem and W. T. Ballard. The nature of their collaboration is not known.

Jim Anthony was a scientist, businessman, and adventurer, the son of an Irish explorer and a Comanche princess, and was described by the editors as "half-Irish, half-Indian and all-American." Anthony was a black-haired giant, often clad only in yellow trunks of Indian design (according to the early covers by *Spicy* artist H. J. Ward). His financial empire included his New York-penthouse headquarters in the Waldorf-Anthony and his underground hideaway, the Teepee, where he went to "get away from civilization."

Anthony was assisted by his best friend, Tom Gentry; his fiancée, Dolores Cloquitt; Dawkins, his butler; and his ancient Indian grandfather, Mephito, whose shaman's powers included the ability to read the future. Because *Super-Detective* was a brother to the *Spicy* pulps, many subplots involved romantic entanglements among the regular cast and other characters. The supporting characters were sometimes more realistic than others of their type because they were definitely ruled by their passions and, for that reason, often at odds with each other.

In "Dealer of Death," Anthony met a radical revolutionary, Rado Ruric, who orchestrated an unsuccessful attempt to subvert the U.S. government. Ruric returned in "Legion of Robots" and again in the third novel, "Madame Murder," in which he was finally vanquished.

"Bloated Death" was a peculiar novel in which Anthony reverted to the primitive, in the North Woods, but this Tarzan-like behavior was not entirely convincing. "Killer in Yellow" and "Murder in Paradise" comprised a two-part story focusing on a supercity at the North Pole ruled by a mad genius who had harnessed atomic power.

Up to and including "Spies of Destiny," the novels were adventures with some scientific background. Only a few, such as "Murder Syndicate," were solely crime stories, despite the predominance of titles with the words *death* and *murder*. In "Spies of Destiny," Anthony grappled with the Red Dragon Organization, as well as with an antagonistic New York homicide policeman named Trotter. After this novel, Trotter became a regular character, and the series metamorphosed into a detective series without the adventure trappings. Jim Anthony's trunks were replaced by an ordinary business suit on the magazine's covers and interior illustrations (the latter largely the work of Joseph Sokoli).

The first of these new, shorter Anthony novels was "I.O.U. Murder," which appeared in the December 1942 issue, an undistinguished story, as many of them were despite enticing titles ("Cold Turkey," "Needle's Eye"). "The Caribbean Cask," about the discovery of a floating cask reputedly containing Christopher Columbus's papers, was interesting. But "Murder Between Shifts," with its war-economy background, was more typical of the later novels. Not a few of these, "Mrs. Big" and "Mark of the Spider" among them, pitted Anthony against distaff killers.

The final Anthony novel, "Pipeline to Murder," was published in the October 1943 issue. This, ironically, found Anthony investigating crime among oil-rich Indians in Oklahoma.

Although *Super-Detective* featured twenty-five Jim Anthony novels, the magazine continued well beyond the life of the series. During its first three years, the magazine fluctuated wildly between monthly and bimonthly publication, just as the series underwent frequent changes. In the early issues, Anthony's resemblance to Doc Savage was augmented by other devices: a pair of bat wings allowed him to glide like a bird and a skin-tight black outfit enabled him to blend with darkness, just like The Shadow. But the fact that the stories changed abruptly into the traditional hard-boiled detective type was certain indication that these gimmicks were unsuccessful.

All told, *Super-Detective* was a shakily conceived magazine. Originally somewhat of an adventure magazine, in its first year it was more of a science fiction periodical. The Jim Anthony novels aside, the early backup stories—by Henry Kuttner, Don Cameron, and others—were distinctly futuristic and of the type which often ran in *Spicy Mystery Stories*.* One redeeming feature was a series about a supposed psychic, Abba the Absolute, which Dale Boyd wrote until 1941.

The short stories had proliferated by 1941, all hard-boiled, with a touch of sex. After Jim Anthony had been phased out, these stories—by Laurence Donovan, Paul Hanna, and Robert Leslie Bellem (under a plethora of pennames)—took over entirely, and this remained the case until the magazine ceased publication in 1951.

Information Sources

INDEX SOURCES: None known.
LOCATION SOURCES: University of California–Los Angeles Library (1940–1950, 4 issues); private collectors.

Publication History

MAGAZINE TITLE: *Super-Detective*.
TITLE CHANGES: None.
VOLUME AND ISSUE DATA: Vol. 1, no. 1 (October 1940) to 1951; number of issues unknown.
PUBLISHER: Trojan Publications, Inc., 29 Worthington Street, Springfield, Massachusetts, later 125 East 46th Street, New York, New York, as editorial office.
EDITOR: Not known.
PRICE PER ISSUE: 15 cents.
SIZE AND PAGINATION: 6-5/8'' X 9-7/8''; 128 pages.
CURRENT STATUS: Discontinued.
—*Will Murray*

SUPER DETECTIVE LIBRARY (British)

Published, for the most part, every two weeks from March 1953 to December 1960, *Super Detective Library* was a thin, pocket-size, cheaply produced magazine. It was published by Amalgamated Press, Ltd. No other information is available.

Information Sources

BIBLIOGRAPHY:
Lofts, W.O.G., and Derek J. Adley. *Old Boys Books, A Complete Catalogue*. London: privately printed, 1969.
INDEX SOURCES: None known.
LOCATION SOURCES: Private collectors.

Publication History

MAGAZINE TITLE: *Super Detective Library*.
TITLE CHANGES: None.
VOLUME AND ISSUE DATA: No. 1 (March 1953) through no. 188 (December 1960); 188 issues.

PUBLISHER: Amalgamated Press, Ltd., London.
EDITOR: Not known.
PRICE PER ISSUE: 9 pence.
SIZE AND PAGINATION: 5-3/8'' X 7''; 64 pages.
CURRENT STATUS: Discontinued.

SUPER-DETECTIVE STORIES

In what may have been the forerunner of Trojan Publications'*Super-Detective** (1940), *Super-Detective Stories* was first published in March 1934 and survived for three issues. One of the notable stories included was Robert E. Howard's ''Names in the Black Book'' (May 1934).

Information Sources

INDEX SOURCES: None known.
LOCATION SOURCES: University of California–Los Angeles (Vol. 1, nos. 1, 3); private
    collectors.

Publication History

MAGAZINE TITLE: *Super-Detective Stories*.
TITLE CHANGES: None.
VOLUME AND ISSUE DATA: Vol. 1, no. 1 (March 1934) through Vol. 1, no. 3 (May
    1934); 3 issues.
PUBLISHER: D. M. Publishing Co., Chicago, Illinois.
EDITOR: Frank Armer.
PRICE PER ISSUE: 10 cents.
SIZE AND PAGINATION: 7'' X 10''; 112 pages.
CURRENT STATUS: Discontinued.

SURE-FIRE DETECTIVE MAGAZINE

Aaron Wyn's Magazine Publishers, Inc., was responsible for a great number of pulp titles and crowded the newsstands with *Ten Detective Aces,* Secret Agent X,* Detective Romances,* Headquarters Detective,* Ace Detective,** and others. In February 1937, another title was introduced, *Sure-Fire Detective Magazine*, but apparently only one issue was published.

This was rather standard fare for the era, with four ''drama-packed'' novelettes: ''The Cartoon Crimes'' by Donald G. Cooley, ''Died in Red'' by Hal Murray Bonnett, ''Bullets for a Big Shot'' by Alexis Rossoff, and ''Ring Around the Hot-Seat'' by S. J. Bailey. Other frequent contributors to the stable of Wyn's magazines presented four ''Ace Short Stories'' to round out the magazine: ''Honors for a Thief'' by Barnard James, ''Hell's Scoop'' by Steve Fisher, ''No Match for Murder'' by Cleve F. Adams, and ''The Visiting Corpse'' by Thomas Walsh. The cover was by Rafael M. DeSoto.

It should be noted that twenty years later, another magazine with almost the same title, *Sure-Fire Detective Stories*,* was published for a short run by the Pontiac Publishing Corporation.

Information Sources

INDEX SOURCES: None known.
LOCATION SOURCES: University of California–Los Angeles Library; private collectors.

Publication History

MAGAZINE TITLE: *Sure-Fire Detective Magazine.*
TITLE CHANGES: None.
VOLUME AND ISSUE DATA: Vol. 1, no. 1 (February 1937); 1 issue.
PUBLISHER: Aaron A. Wyn as Magazine Publishers, Inc., 29 Worthington Street, Springfield, Massachusetts, with editorial offices at 67 West 44th Street, New York, New York.
EDITOR: Harry Widmer.
PRICE PER ISSUE: 10 cents.
SIZE AND PAGINATION: 6-1/4'' X 9-5/8''; 112 pages.
CURRENT STATUS: Discontinued.

SURE FIRE DETECTIVE STORIES

Typical of the action-packed, violent, crime-adventure fiction of the mid-1950s, *Sure Fire Detective Stories* not only continued the tradition of the pulp magazines but added to it by inserting a healthy measure of sex. There was no excuse for the sex except lust; it was unlike the stories that had been the mainstay of such magazines as *Spicy Detective** and *Spicy Mystery Stories*,* among others, in the mid-1930s, where frothy sex was the result of a hero's passion to protect a wriggling, passionate woman or where the villain attempted to consummate his desires. This was, instead, brutal sex, completely stripped of sensuousness:

> Suddenly he grabbed her. She struggled but her strength was gone. Will jerked the jacket down from her shoulders and ripped her blouse to the waist. Her bra was torn from her breasts and flung aside. 'Oh God!' she groaned as he forced her submission and began devouring her with brutal lust.[1]

> Laughing wildly, Charlie walked around the bed. In a matter of seconds her other arm was fettered above her head. Then her ankles were securely bound. She was spread-eagled to the bed unable to do more than move her head and eyes.[2]

The titles of the stories were designed to instill prurient interest as well: "Bursting Passions" by Jim Barnett ("Cindy was one doll headed for trouble.'').[3] ''It's Your Turn to Die'' byu Randall Chaffin (''She excited him. So now she had to die!'').[4] ''Shakedown Girl'' by Al James (''He knew something was wrong, but he didn't want to stop.'').[5]

There was little of redeeming interest, other than sex and violence. The pages resounded with gun fire; the characters were uninhibited, greedy, and rotten. There were no heroes. Each story emphasized what was hoped to shock the reader in one way or another. Even the detectives were apt to display their weaknesses or be masochistically hard-boiled.

Sure Fire Detective Stories survived for at least five issues; the last identified was dated February 1958. The publisher introduced *Off Beat Detective Stories** by at least September 1958, with numbering apparently continued from *Sure Fire Detective Stories*. Whether this was a change in title or a replacement is not known.

Notes

1. James W. Lumpp, ''Win With Murder,'' *Sure Fire Detective Story Magazine*, Vol. 1, no. 2 (February 1957), p. 92.
2. Bill Ryder, ''Tickled to Death,'' *Sure Fire Detective Stories*, Vol. 1, no. 2 (February 1957), p. 23.
3. Contents page, *Sure Fire Detective Magazine*, Vol. 1, no. 2 (February 1957).
4. Contents Page, *Sure Fire Detective Story Magazine*, Vol. 2, no. 1 (February 1958).
5. Ibid.

Information Sources

INDEX SOURCES: Cook, Michael L. *Monthly Murders*. Westport, Conn.: Greenwood Press, 1982.
LOCATION SOURCES: Private collectors.

Publication History

MAGAZINE TITLE: *Sure Fire Detective Story Magazine*.
TITLE CHANGES: Possible change to *Off Beat Detective Stories* with September 1958 issue.
VOLUME AND ISSUE DATA: Vol. 1, no. 1 (January 1957) through at least Vol. 2, no. 1 (February 1958); possibly 2 additional issues; at least 5 total issues.
PUBLISHER: Pontiac Publishing Corporation, 1 Appleton Street, Holyoke, Massachusetts, with editorial offices at 1776 Broadway, New York, New York.
EDITOR: Not known.
PRICE PER ISSUE: 35 cents.
SIZE AND PAGINATION: 5-1/2'' X 7-1/4''; 128 pages.
CURRENT STATUS: Discontinued.

SUSPECT DETECTIVE STORIES

Suspect Detective Stories appeared on the crowded newsstands in November 1955 and had little to recommend it over a number of similar magazines struggling for the reader's thirty-five cents. It was adequate but not outstanding; it provided the same fare, from the same authors, as was already available.

"The World is full of crime and every man's a Suspect,"[1] proclaimed the third issue profoundly, and although this perhaps described the philosophy in selecting the fast-action, contemporary, crime adventures, it was not enough. Sex was present but muted. Violence was nothing new. The crimes were as to be expected, and the characters were stereotyped. Yet these were not poor stories. Just more of the same.

The first issue was filled with nine short stories and a column titled "Bullets and Bulletins" by "The Prowler," which presented odd facts in the crime world. The stories included "Angelica Is Still Alive" by Walter Snow (warped passions led to sour-searing fates), "Death is Where You Find It" by Larry Holden (torture and death was the result of double-cross), "Anything for a Friend" by Jerome Bixby (Big Joe's sadistic goons stalked a jittery compatriot), "The Naked and the Deadly" by Robert Turner (crazed emotions promised death tonight!), "Specialty Kill" by Fletcher Flora (the dame used men, then discarded them, until. . . .), and "Dead Men Never Die" by Roy Lopez (Johnny was ready for Las Vegas but not for Sharleen), as well as stories by Matt Christopher, Lorenz Heller, and William Tenn.

Succeeding issues highlighted a down-on-his-luck reporter as killers closed in ("Fall Guy—Exclusive" by Walter Snow, June 1956), misunderstandings with fellow gangsters, those on the run, and a plethora of tangled emotions.

The "Bullets and Bulletins" was continued in each issue. Appearances in the author's lineup were made by Bruno Fischer, Bryce Walton, James T. Farrell, Robert Bloch, Harlan Ellison, Craig Rice, and Joseph Commings, to name a few, all with frequent bylines in similar magazines.

The covers, in full color, were par for the course: static violence between a man and a woman. One notable cover was that for the June 1956 issue, picturing a man wearing a horrible Halloween mask, ready to tear the sweater from a terrified red-head and to stab her with a gleaming, long-bladed knife.

After five issues, the magazine quietly disappeared and was no more.

Note

1. Editorial announcement, *Suspect Detective Stories*, Vol. 1, no. 3 (June 1956), reverse front cover.

Information Sources

INDEX SOURCES: Cook, Michael L. *Monthly Murders*, Westport, Conn.: Greenwood Press, 1982.
LOCATION SOURCES: Private collectors.

Publication History

MAGAZINE TITLE: *Suspect Detective Stories*.
TITLE CHANGES: None.
VOLUME AND ISSUE DATA: Vol. 1, no. 1 (November 1955) through Vol. 1, no. 5 (October 1956); 5 issues.

PUBLISHER: Irwin Stein as Royal Publications, Inc., 47 East 44th Street, New York, New York.
EDITOR: Larry T. Shaw; associate editors, John C. Johnson and Leonore Hailparn.
PRICE PER ISSUE: 35 cents.
SIZE AND PAGINATION: 5-3/8'' X 7-1/2''; 130 pages.
CURRENT STATUS: Discontinued.

SUSPENSE

Suspense (1951–1952) was the second of two tries by magazine publishers to tie in with the popular CBS radio mystery show of the same name (the other attempt was made with *Suspense—The Mystery Magazine**).

Oddly, for a magazine whose cover design—a nude woman face down on a bed with her throat cut—was clearly meant to attract detective-crime story readers, more than half of that first issue (seven of twelve stories) were science fiction. This may have launched the magazine with a bad start, for mystery readers would have been disappointed at finding so much science fiction. At any rate, succeeding issues had less, and the fourth and last issue had only one fantastic story.

John Dickson Carr's "Honeymoon Terror" is an unusual feature, but superb—a play selected from the radio show "Suspense," retitled (from "Cabin B–13") and reprinted from *Ellery Queen's Mystery Magazine.** A bride boards a fog-enshrouded liner with her groom, returns after a walk on deck to find their cabin, B–13, has disappeared, and that everyone insists she came aboard alone. "Faces Turned Against Him," by John Gearon, is a fine novelette about an unfriendly man whose wife vanished one mild October night, wearing a formal dress and leaving the house lit up. Why has no one seen her? James A. Kerch has a good human-interest short, a story about a man who doesn't want to talk about a mob killing and his girl, who will. The other mysteries are only of average quality.

The next quarterly issue has three fantastics and a slight drop in quality among the mysteries. The radio show feature this time is a Gothic, "Maiden Beware," by Richard Lewis, predictable but exciting, about an innocent girl who becomes a companion to an old lady whose background she should have checked more thoroughly. Georges Simenon has a solid tale, "Elusive Witness," about Inspector Maigret and a choirboy who claims to see a corpse that isn't there. Other stories are competent but not remarkable, somewhat like stories that didn't quite make it into *Alfred Hitchcock's Mystery Magazine.**

The third issue has six fantastic stories and no radio script. With several exceptions, the mysteries, all shorts, again are less than outstanding. Philip Weck's "You Can't Run Away" tells with some power about murder resulting when a G.I. returns home and his girl has married someone else. Russell Branch's "Riptide," about passion and killing among California surfers, is told in an unusual, almost avant-garde, style that is surprisingly effective.

With the fourth issue, *Suspense* hit its stride at last. The stories are nearly all detective-crime (only one fantasy) and original (only two reprints); *Suspense* was standing on its own feet now. The stories are all strong, emotional, varied in style and type, and having one thing in common: suspense.

For the women, there's a fine story of the type Alfred Hitchcock loved to film, Dorothy Marie Davis's "And Never Come Back," about what happens to a divorced woman who boards a transcontinental express with her small daughter and finds her former husband's new, insanely jealous wife is aboard—waiting. For men, there's a tense prize-fight yarn, Duane Yarnell's "Ask No Quarter," a neat variation on the theme of "throw the fight, champ, or your kid gets it." Charles Lenart has a *Black Mask** type of story called "The Third Degree." Ray Bradbury's reprinted short, "The Screaming Woman," shows a group of children trying desperately to get adults to believe their story about a woman buried alive. Brett Halliday's "You Killed Elizabeth" is a quiet, interesting study of how murder results when two men who have been friends for years fall in love with the same girl. In "Murder Town," when a pretty girl operative of his detective agency disappears on a seemingly routine task, Jim Brady tears apart the wide-open town of Jordanville with tommyguns and gasoline bombs, in Raymond Drennan's Hammett-like novelette of Prohibition-style, gangland warfare set in today's times. The tone, atmosphere, and quality of this issue is roughly that of an excellent, somewhat more pulp-oriented, issue of *Ellery Queen's Mystery Magazine*.

But that was the last issue.

If the fourth issue was all that good, why was it the final one? The two-color covers and the fact that the first three issues, best stories by the big-name, buyer-getting authors, are nearly all reprints suggests an all-too-familiar answer: inadequate financing. The money may have run out just as the 1950's *Suspense* was on the verge of success. If only the fourth issue could have been the first.

Information Sources

INDEX SOURCES: Cook, Michael L. *Monthly Murders*. Westport, Conn.: Greenwood Press, 1982.

LOCATION SOURCES: University of California–Los Angeles (complete run); private collectors.

Publication History

MAGAZINE TITLE: *Suspense*.

TITLE CHANGES: None.

VOLUME AND ISSUE DATA: Vol. 1, no. 1 (Spring 1951) through Vol. 1, no. 4 (Winter 1952); 4 issues.

PUBLISHER: Farrell Publishing Corp., 350 East 22nd Street, Chicago, Illinois, with editorial offices at 420 Lexington Avenue, New York 17, New York.

EDITOR: Theodore Irwin.

PRICE PER ISSUE: 35 cents.

SIZE AND PAGINATION: 5-1/2" X 7-3/4" (Vol. 1, no. 3: 5-1/2" X 7-1/2"); 144
   pages.
CURRENT STATUS: Discontinued.
—*Frank D. McSherry, Jr.*

SUSPENSE (British)

In 1940, a short fiction magazine titled *Argosy* began in Great Britain; it had
nothing whatever to do with the American magazine of the same name. For a
number of years, its contents were mainly literary in direction and reprints. But
in the 1950s, the bias of the magazine began to move toward crime stories, and
by 1958, the publishers decided that *Argosy* should bear offspring; *Suspense*, a
magazine totally concerned with crime fiction, was born.

As a magazine production, it was frankly uninspiring, with its somewhat
dowdy card-stock covers. This, and its small size (4-3/4" X 7-3/8"), however,
were more than offset by the richness of its contents and the generous number
of pages, 160 pages at the beginning and never less than 144 pages.

It featured many original stories by writers of the first rank. The first issue in
August 1958 led off with "Murderer's Eye" by Gerald Kersh, and this was
followed by Berkely Mather's "Red for Danger" in which the James Sheldon
character was introduced for the first time, in a tale set in the Orient. Michael
Gilbert had a "followed" story, titled "Safe," and Agatha Christie contributed
"Double Alibi," a Hercule Poirot story. "The Stranger From Dying Boys' Reef"
was by Adrian Conan Doyle, son of the creator of Sherlock Holmes. Georgette
Heyer was present with one of her usual, witty, short murder mysteries, and
Wilson Tucker appeared with a bookish "MCMLIX." David C. Cooke, Mark
Derby, and Charles McCormac presented short crime adventures, and the first
installment of Margery Allingham's "Hide My Eyes" was included. "Wagon
Train: The Wallace Carey Story" was the first of a number of tales based on
the British ITV television series.

The second issue had the first of seven savory stories to be published by
Dashiell Hammett, "Fly Paper." Other issues included "The Creeping Siamese"
(January 1959), "Too Many Have Lived" (May 1959), "The Man Who Killed
Dan Odams" (July 1959), "The Hairy One" (October 1959), "The Judge
Laughed Last" (December 1959), and "The House in Turk Street" (March
1960). Raymond Chandler's "Playback" was serialized in the October and
November 1958 issues.

There seemed no end to the top-grade crime fiction. There was Leslie Charteris,
Fredric Brown, John Dickson Carr (and as Carter Dickson), Charlotte Armstrong,
Cyril Hare, Michael Gilbert, Christianna Brand, Julian Symons, Manning Coles,
Edgar Wallace, and Georges Simenon, to name but a few.

The longer stories were presented in installments; these included "The Case
Against Carell" by Ellery Queen, "World in My Pocket" by James Hadley
Chase, "Down Among the Dead Men" by James Lake, "The Happy Travellers"

by Manning Coles, "This Bride is Dangerous" by Victor Canning, "See Naples and Die!" by John Davies, and "The Kingdom of Death" by Hugh Pentecost.

There was even "The Vine" by Tennessee Williams, in the October 1960 issue and "Murder Begins at Home" by Alfred Hitchcock in the December 1960 issue.

There were occasional competitions and challenges for the reader, but in the main, *Suspense* was all fiction, of the kind one would have thought might guarantee the life of the magazine forever. Apparently this was not enough, for in May 1961 it was absorbed back into the British *Argosy*, and *Argosy* itself died in February 1974.

Information Sources

INDEX SOURCES: Cook, Michael L. *Monthly Murders*. Westport, Conn.: Greenwood Press, 1982.
LOCATION SOURCES: Private collectors.

Publication History

MAGAZINE TITLE: *Suspense*.
TITLE CHANGES: None.
VOLUME AND ISSUE DATA: Vol. 1, no. 1 (August 1958) through Vol. 4, no. 1 (April 1961); 32 issues.
PUBLISHERS: The Amalgamated Press, Ltd., The Fleetway House, Farringdon Street, London E.C.4, England; from September 1959, Fleetway Publications, Ltd., same address.
EDITOR: Not known.
PRICE PER ISSUE: 2 shillings (through May 1959); 2 shillings 6 pence (subsequent issues).
SIZE AND PAGINATION: 4-3/4" X 7-2/5"; 144–160 pages.
CURRENT STATUS: Discontinued.
—*Robert Adey*

SUSPENSE NOVELS

A nicely produced series launched by Farrell Publishing Company as a quarterly in 1951, *Suspense Novels* lasted for only three issues. The cover art was unimpressive, but the contents of each issue were definitely of high quality.

Suspense Novels was published as a companion to *Suspense,** which, as a parent magazine, from first to last was a hodge-podge of material, very similar to the long-lasting radio show on which it was patterned. *Suspense Novels*, however, concentrated on novel-length mysteries, well plotted and well developed. There were no interior illustrations in any of the issues, and editorial features consisted of advertisements for *Suspense*, plus a terse breakdown of each novel, along with the listing of the chief characters, in order of importance. The novels were all listed as "original suspense novels....Never Before Published....the Best in High-Tension Fiction" and included "Strange Pursuit" by N. R. DeMexico, "The Case of the Lonely Lovers" by Will Daemer, and "Naked Villainry" by Carl G. Hodges.

Despite the high quality, the great wonder is that *Suspense Novels* lasted for even three issues when the strikes against it are counted: poor circulation, unattractive cover art, and the nearly identical titles of two other digest-size magazines. A thirty-five cent price tag in 1951 was probably the *coup de grace*.

Information Sources

INDEX SOURCES: Cook, Michael L. *Monthly Murders*. Westport, Conn.: Greenwood
    Press, 1982.
LOCATION SOURCES: Private collectors.

Publication History

MAGAZINE TITLE: *Suspense Novels*.
TITLE CHANGES: None.
VOLUME AND ISSUE DATA: No. 1 (1951) through no. 3 (1951); 3 issues.
PUBLISHER: Farrell Publishing Corp., 420 Lexington Avenue, New York 17, New
    York.
EDITOR: Not known (possibly N. R. DeMexico).
PRICE PER ISSUE: 35 cents.
SIZE AND PAGINATION: 5-1/2" X 8"; 132 pages.
CURRENT STATUS: Discontinued.
—*David A. Bates*

SUSPENSE STORIES (British)

Suspense Stories was one of the many short-run British magazines that flared to life briefly in the early fifties but one of the few that was of digest size. It seems that, unlike so many of its contemporaries, it did not rely on reprints of American stories but turned instead to its publishers' own in-house writers to provide, under a bewildering variety of most unlikely sounding pseudonyms, stories that ranged from gangster yarns to conventional tales of detection. The emphasis, if any, was on mystery with a science fictional or supernatural touch, much in keeping with Curtis Warren's own publishing policy. Otherwise, the setting was almost always English, and there were no nonfiction articles in the magazine at all.

With attractive full-color covers, it is sad to think that the magazine appears to have made no impact on readers. The print runs were apparently small since although Curtis Warren paperback books turn up regularly (and the publisher did not outlast the decade), this little magazine is scarce and hard to find.

Information Sources

INDEX SOURCES: None known.

LOCATION SOURCES: Private collectors.

Publication History

MAGAZINE TITLE: *Suspense Stories*.
TITLE CHANGES: None.
VOLUME AND ISSUE DATA: Three unnumbered issues circa 1954.
PUBLISHER: Curtis Warren, Ltd., Holbex House, 81 Lambs Conduit Street, London
    W.C.1, England.
EDITOR: Not known.
PRICE PER ISSUE: 1 shilling.
SIZE AND PAGINATION: 5-1/2'' X 8-1/2''; 96 pages.
CURRENT STATUS: Discontinued.
—Robert Adey

SUSPENSE—THE MYSTERY MAGAZINE

Suspense—The Mystery Magazine was one of many magazines published under
the aegis of Leslie Charteris and was the first of two magazines based on the
Columbia Broadcasting System's radio show "Suspense" (the later one was
Suspense*). Charteris's magazine was first published in November 1946 and
survived for four issues.

As a whole, the stories were rather shallow and, it is hoped, were more
effective when heard on the air. They were by authors largely unknown to the
mystery-reading public—Cleve Cartmill, Eugene King, Roby Wentz, Valerie
Kurtz, Carmen Morrison, Stanley Sprague, and others, Even the titles were
uninspired, such as "Fury and Sound" (November 1946), "The Bet" (November
1946), "Sneak Preview" (December 1946) and "Death at Miss Plim's" (March
1947).

Each issue included a preview of two pages from a story to appear in the next
issue. The covers were vignettes of the radio show participants.

Information Sources

INDEX SOURCES: Cook, Michael L. *Monthly Murders*. Westport, Conn.: Greenwood
    Press, 1982.
LOCATION SOURCES: Private collectors.

Publication History

MAGAZINE TITLE: *Suspense—The Mystery Magazine*.
TITLE CHANGES: None.
VOLUME AND ISSUE DATA: Vol. 1, no. 1 (November 1946) through Vol. 1, no. 4
    (March 1947); 4 issues.
PUBLISHER: Suspense Magazine, Inc., 314 North Robertson Boulevard, Los Angeles
    36, California.

EDITOR: Leslie Charteris.
PRICE PER ISSUE: 25 cents.
SIZE AND PAGINATION: 5-1/4'' X 8''; 112 pages.
CURRENT STATUS: Discontinued.

T

TALES OF MAGIC AND MYSTERY

There were but five issues of this Romance Publications title. *Tales of Magic and Mystery*, from December 1927 to April 1928. No other information is available.

Information Sources

INDEX SOURCES: None known.
LOCATION SOURCES: Private collectors.

Publication History

MAGAZINE TITLE: *Tales of Magic and Mystery*.
TITLE CHANGES: None known.
VOLUME AND ISSUE DATA: Vol. 1, no. 1 (December 1927) through Vol. 1, no. 5 (April 1928); 5 issues.
PUBLISHER: Romance Publications, New York, New York.
EDITOR: Not known.
PRICE PER ISSUE: Not known.
SIZE AND PAGINATION: Not known.
CURRENT STATUS: Discontinued.

TALES OF THE FRIGHTENED

In the winter of 1956, this digest-sized anthology of stories in the weird, horror, and fantasy motif was clearly the very magazine that a nation of *Weird Tales**-denied readers had been waiting for. The premier issue, dated Spring 1957, featured a glorious cover by Rudy Nappi showing a Cleopatra-like beauty looking over her shoulder as a skeletal hand beckoned, and behind that cover were sixteen of the finest terror tales ever written, concocted by such diversely gifted talents as John Jakes, John Wyndham, Hal Ellson, and others, Following in the second issue were stories by Poul Anderson, Mack Reynolds, A. Bertram Chandler, Mark Mallory, and Boris Karloff.

The sales and fan mail were most gratifying, but the looming strike at the American News Company was to throw the entire Lyle Kenyon Engel magazine group into discard, as promising as it was.

Tales of the Frightened, in particular, was designed by loving hands. Engel was a horror film and book buff, and his behind-the-scenes editor, Michael Avallone, was laboring in vineyards he also loved. Both issues published of this magazine included Avallone stories: "The Curse of Cleopatra," "The Man Who Thought He Was Poe," "The Stop at Nothing," and "White Legs" (the last two under an Avallone pseudonym, Mark Dane).

The original intent had been to call the magazine *Boris Karloff's Tales of the Frightened*, but just prior to publication Karloff declined, not wanting to be associated with a magazine venture.

In any case, *Tales of the Frightened*, a grand experiment and lauded by many, ran but two issues.

Information Sources

INDEX SOURCES: None known.
LOCATION SOURCES: University of California–Los Angeles Library (Vol. 1, no. 1); private collectors.

Publication History

MAGAZINE TITLE: *Tales of the Frightened*.
TITLE CHANGES: None.
VOLUME AND ISSUE DATA: Vol. 1, no. 1 (Spring 1957) through Vol. 1, no. 2 (August 1957); 2 issues.
PUBLISHER: Republic Features Syndicate, Inc., New York, New York.
EDITOR: Lyle Kenyon Engel.
PRICE PER ISSUE: 35 cents.
SIZE AND PAGINATION: 5-1/4" X 7-1/2"; 128 pages.
CURRENT STATUS: Discontinued.
—*Michael Avallone*

TEN DETECTIVE ACES

See DRAGNET, THE

10 DETECTIVE MYSTERIES

No information is available on *10 Detective Mysteries*, a Red Circle pulp magazine.[1]

Note

1. Title listed in "Tentative Pulp Checklist" from San Francisco Academy of Comic Art (unpublished manuscript, n.d.).

Information Sources

INDEX SOURCES: None known.
LOCATION SOURCES: Private collectors only.

Publication History

MAGAZINE TITLE: *10 Detective Mysteries.*
TITLE CHANGES: None known.
VOLUME AND ISSUE DATA: Not known.
PUBLISHER: Western Fiction Publishing Co., 4600 Diversey Avenue, Chicago, Illinois, with editorial offices at RKO Building, New York, New York, later 330 West 42nd Street, New York, New York.
EDITOR: Not known.
PRICE PER ISSUE: Not known.
SIZE AND PAGINATION: Not known.
CURRENT STATUS: Discontinued.

10-STORY DETECTIVE

10-Story Detective was the youngest brother of *Ten Detective Aces (Dragnet, The*)* and a close relation of the short-lived *Gold Seal Detective** and *Ace Detective** magazines. It shared a penchant with these latter publications for police and detective action stories; so close were the ties that at least one *10-Story Detective* cover, January 1939, was a scarcely changed cover from the March 1936 *Gold Seal Detective*. Rafael DeSoto was credited with both.

For that eleven-year period between 1938 and 1949, the similarities to *Ten Detective Aces* are even more striking. Similar cover artists, similar format, and a few of the same writers. Or perhaps more than a few, for *10-Story Detective* was packed by names that leave the impression that someone had donned false whiskers.

But these are unprovable speculations. *10-Story Detective* was a bimonthly vehicle for a novelette and nine short stories. Very rarely, an eleventh story was added as a bonus.

For the first year or so, the fiction followed that pattern formerly laid down by *Gold Seal Detective*: law enforcement officers wre the heroes, racing, battling, and blasting through unsubtle stories of high energy and vividly described bloodshed. Early issues contain a thin dusting of popular writers, such as William Cox, Robert C. Blackmon, Emile Tepperman, and Harold Sorensen. Titles reflect hard doings by very hard people: "Free Fare to a Coffin," "Murder Memento," "The Iron Corpse," and "Four and Twenty Blackjacks."

Then stories featuring reporters, medical students, crooks, and interested men on the street began to appear. The names of Norman Daniels, Bruno Fischer, and Joe Archibald appeared more frequently. Although it seemed hardly possible, the prose simplified and became more violent. Heroes, constantly framed, constantly slammed about violently, proved their innocence by shattering a law in each paragraph. Gallons of rye were swallowed, and thousands of cigarettes were lighted; dozens of highly sexed women, brightly decorated and deadly, met their match; and the pages thudded with tumbling corpses. It was simple, glittering, busy narrative, rarely touched by human emotion; but its sheer pace gripped, and the excitement rarely flagged long enough to allow thought.

Only a few series intruded upon these homicidal doings. Around 1946, Joe Archibald introduced Alvin Hinkley and Hambone, a pair of big-city detectives in mildly humorous stories done loosely after the fashion of Damon Runyon. And Harold Gluck began contributing a true-crime feature about a year later.

The 1949 issues contain almost enough well-known writers to confirm *10-Story Detective's* motto, "All Star, All Different." G. T. Fleming-Roberts and Philip Ketchum were present, together with Robert Turner, Ray Cummings, and at least one story by M. E. Counselman (February 1949), better known for her fantasy than detective fiction.

Final issues of *10-Story Detective* seem better than earlier ones. The action swirls and leaps. The characters are slangy, casual, studiedly tough, all fitting nicely into stories where reality, in all its statling complexity, is expressed in the simple terms of a bunched fist and a crooked trigger-finger.

At least three issues of a British reprint edition were also published.

Information Sources

INDEX SOURCES: None known.
LOCATION SOURCES: University of California–Los Angeles Library (1938–1946, 7 issues); private collectors.

Publication History

MAGAZINE TITLE: *10-Story Detective*.
TITLE CHANGES: None.
VOLUME AND ISSUE DATA: Vol. 1, no. 1 (January 1938) through Vol. 17, no. 3 (August 1949); 67 issues.
PUBLISHER: Periodical House, Inc., 29 Worthington Street, Springfield, Massachusetts.
EDITOR: Not known.
PRICE PER ISSUE: 10 cents (through July 1947); 15 cents.
SIZE AND PAGINATION: 7" X 10" (1938–1939); 6-7/8" X 9-3/4" (1940–1949); 80-112 pages.
CURRENT STATUS: Discontinued.
—*Robert Sampson*

10-STORY DETECTIVE (British)

See 10-STORY DETECTIVE

TEN STORY GANG

A late entry into the gangster-story pulp field, *Ten Story Gang* commenced August 1938. No other information is available.

Information Sources

INDEX SOURCES: None known.
LOCATION SOURCES: Private collectors.

Publication History

MAGAZINE TITLE: *Ten Story Gang*.
TITLE CHANGES: None known.
VOLUME AND ISSUE DATA: Vol. 1, no. 1 (August 1938); number of issues and extent unknown.
PUBLISHER: Winford Publications, Inc., 2256 Grove Street, Chicago, Illinois (last issues probably published under company name change to Double-Action Magazines, Inc.).
EDITOR: Not known.
PRICE PER ISSUE: Not known.
SIZE AND PAGINATION: Not known.
CURRENT STATUS: Discontinued.

TEN STORY MYSTERY

Although titled as featuring ten stories, one or more consisted of true-crime stories or fact articles in *Ten Story Mystery* by Popular Publications. Stories included weird menace, "daring mystery," and stories of the "sinister and strange" as a rule. Many of the better-known authors contributed, including Stewart Sterling, Francis K. Allan, and G. T. Fleming-Roberts. The magazine promised all new stories and no reprints, but with the misfortune to be born in December 1941, it lasted but nine issues into the war years before it was apparently dealt the death blow by the paper shortage.

Information Sources

BIBLIOGRAPHY:
Hardin, Nils. "An Interview with Henry Steeger." *Xenophile*, no. 33 (July 1977): 3–18.
———, and George Hocutt. "A Checklist of Popular Publications Titles 1930–1955." *Xenophile*, no. 33 (July 1977): 21–24.
INDEX SOURCES: None known.
LOCATION SOURCES: University of California–Los Angeles Library (Vol. 1, no. 1, only); private collectors.

Publication History

MAGAZINE TITLE: *Ten Story Mystery*.
TITLE CHANGES: None.

VOLUME AND ISSUE DATA: Vol. 1, no. 1 (December 1941) through Vol. 3, no. 1
     (April 1943); 9 issues.
PUBLISHER: Fictioneers, Inc., subsidiary of Popular Publications, Inc., 2256 Grove
     Street, Chicago, Illinois, with editorial offices at 210 East 43rd Street, New York,
     New York.
EDITOR: Not known.
PRICE PER ISSUE: 10 cents.
SIZE AND PAGINATION: 6-5/8'' X 9-7/8''; 128 pages.
CURRENT STATUS: Discontinued.

TERROR DETECTIVE STORY MAGAZINE

Sex, as the usual basis for the eternal triangle, is a motivating force underlying
many crime situations. In most crime fiction, however, it is indirectly treated
and secondary to the theme or plot of the story. The mid-1930s brought a rash
of detective fiction that was little more than thinly disguised pink pornography
(*Spicy Detective**   and *Spicy Mystery Stories**   as examples) with the passion
included and the consummation excluded, but the public furor, coupled with a
limited market, decimated the ranks of such magazines.

The mid-1950s saw a revival of sex as a major ingredient in detective fiction;
but the froth and fantasy had disappeared into the women's romance stories, and
the new breed was coarse and direct. This was exploited in a small group of
magazines with varying degrees of licentiousness. With *Terror Detective Story
Magazine*, introduced in October 1956 by Everett Arnold as Arnold Magazines,
Inc., blatant sex seems to have been the prevailing vehicle on which the story
revolved. The title of the magazine itself is a misnomer. Any terror felt was not
in the usual definition but was directed toward what one character felt was going
to happen as a result of his own wrongdoing. Detective? Perhaps in a loose
sense. The characters were cardboard, the situations seamy and sordid, and the
reader's emotional involvement was nil. Whether the stories were teenage hood-
lumism or gang stories or bedroom fracases, sex was the motivating force. If
the reader expected frightening stories of intense dread, he was disappointed.

> She put her hand behind my head, and pulled me to her. Her mouth crushed
> against mine. I felt the warm swells of her breasts against me, and my
> hands began roving. . . .[1]

While some stories were less explicit, others left little to the imagination:

> Harker turned down the covers and climbed into the bed while she finished
> undressing. She reached behind her neck and unsnapped her bra. The twin
> cups fell away from her breasts and she wriggled out of the bra. Then she
> pulled off her panties. . . . ''The stockings don't matter,'' she said, half
> to herself. ''And it's too much of a nuisance taking them on and off.''[2]

The stories without sex so blatantly displayed were people with mobsters with names such as "The Gorilla" and "The Fat Man." And violence that never ceased.

Terror Detective Story Magazine did have some material by the better-known writers—Fredric Brown ("See No Murder," October 1956), Jonathan Craig ("Execution at Eleven," April 1957), Robert Turner ("Touchdown for Murder," April 1957), and Henry Slesar ("Handcuffed Slayer," February 1957)—but these were not their best efforts.

The covers were the to-be-expected, with scenes of a lovely lady (aren't plain women ever threatened?) in a soon-to-be distressful situation. There was no advertising except on the back cover; and, apparently, in accordance with the policy of the publisher, there were no columns, announcements, editorials, or filler material.

With little to recommend this magazine over the flood of others on the newsstands, it did manage to survive for four issues.

Notes

1. Matt Christopher, "Death's Lovely Mistress," *Terror Detective Story Magazine*, no. 4 (April 1957), p. 32.
2. Robert Silverberg, "Bedroom Blonde," *Terror Detective Story Magazine*, no. 4 (April 1957), p. 27.

Information Sources

INDEX SOURCES: Cook, Michael L. *Monthly Murders*. Westport, Conn.: Greenwood Press, 1982.
LOCATION SOURCES: Private collectors.

Publication History

MAGAZINE TITLE: *Terror Detective Story Magazine*.
TITLE CHANGES: None.
VOLUME AND ISSUE DATA: No. 1 (October 1956) through no. 4 (April 1957); 4 issues.
PUBLISHER: Everett M. Arnold as Arnold Magazines, Inc., 1 Appleton Street, Holyoke, Massachusetts, with editorial offices at 303 Lexington Avenue, New York 16, New York; associate publisher, Marilyn Mayes.
EDITOR: Alfred Grenet.
PRICE PER ISSUE: 35 cents.
SIZE AND PAGINATION: 5-1/4" X 7-1/4"; 130 pages.
CURRENT STATUS: Discontinued.

TERROR TALES (British)

See HORROR STORIES

TERROR TALES (U.S.)

See HORROR STORIES

THIRD DEGREE, THE

The Third Degree is the house organ of the Mystery Writers of America, Inc., an organization of published mystery writers founded in 1945, and *The Third Degree* is, in fact, a newsletter designed for the benefit of members only. Published monthly (with July and August issues combined) and edited presently by Chris Steinbrunner, the newsletter has been a forum in which the problems of authors have been aired and discussed, as well as a report of trade news, new markets, contract wording, and general news of special interest to mystery writers. Earlier issues included a wide range of articles and inspirational material. A regular feature is "MWA in Print," a listing of all new stories by members appearing in book or magazine form.

The combined July-August issue is titled *Mystery Writers Annual* and is a much larger, magazine-format issue printed on coated paper. This issue inncludes a good range of articles, slanted to appeal primarily to an author, as well as news and other announcements of interest. The 1980 *Annual*, for example, by Edward D. Hoch and Robert W. Douty, included a complete listing of the MWA Anthologies (books) and the contents of each.

Regional chapters of the Mystery Writers of America also publish their own newsletters; these, again, pertain primarily to the interests of the members. The Southern California chapter publishes the *March of Crime,* and the Midwest chapter publishes *Clues*, each being from two to six pages in length.

Information Sources

INDEX SOURCES: None known.
LOCATION SOURCES: Private collectors and authors.

Publication History

MAGAZINE TITLE: *The Third Degree*.
TITLE CHANGES: None (July-August issue of each year is titled *Mystery Writers Annual*).
VOLUME AND ISSUE DATA: Published monthly; commenced 1945 to present. Designated by date only.
PUBLISHER: Mystery Writers of America, Inc., 150 Fifth Avenue, New York, New York 10011.
EDITORS: Currently Chris Steinbruner; associate editor, H. Edward Hunsburger. Past editors include Clayton Rawson, Lawrence G. Blochman, Michael Avallone, and others.
PRICE PER ISSUE: Obtainable only through membership in the Mystery Writers of America, Inc.
SIZE AND PAGINATION: 8-1/2" X 11"; 6–20 pages; *Annual*: 40 pages.
CURRENT STATUS: Active.

THORNDYKE FILE, THE

In his introduction to the first issue of *The Thorndyke File,* in Spring 1976, its original editor-publisher identified himself as a long-time admirer of the works of R. Austin Freeman, creator of Dr. John Evelyn Thorndyke, detective fiction's foremost medico-legal expert. For a time, Philip T. Asdell said, having read all the Thorndyke stories, he assuaged his hunger for more with Norman Donaldson's dual biography of Freeman and Thorndyke (*In Search of Dr. Thorndyke*, Bowling Green University Press, 1971); but, at last, in consultation with other Thorndyke enthusiasts, he concluded that a subscribership existed for a journal devoted to Freeman annd his works, most especially the Thorndyke stories. *The Thorndyke File*, accordingly, was begun and soon showed its worth.

From the first issue of the *File*, it carried articles of permanent interest to Freeman's readers. Here, for example, first appeared Dr. Oliver Mayo's observations on Freeman's work as an eugenicist. The reception gave Mayo, an Australian scientist, the encouragement needed to complete *R. Austin Freeman: The Anthropologist at Large* (Investigator Press, Adelaide, Australia) (1980), a biography of Freeman which contains much information new to his following. Other admirable articles by John Dirckx, M.D., R. Narasimhan, Michael Heenan, Donaldson, Asdell, and John Mayo, M.D., added steadily to the *File's* value. In addition, fugitive pieces by Freeman and his great admirer, P. M. Stone, to whom all Freeman addicts are indebted because of his timely inquiries into the early days of Freeman scholarship, were reprinted. Particularly laudable was the campaign conducted by *The Thorndyke File*, among Freeman's friends on five continents, to place a suitable stone on his grave, left unmarked since his death in 1943. Under the energetic leadership of Frank Archibald of Needham, Massachusetts, their efforts prospered, and on September 23, 1979, at Gravesend, England, Archibald, accompanied by the Mayor and Mayoress of Gravesend, by Michael Heenan, and by novelists H.R.F. Keating and Catherine Aird, saw the stone set in place.

In 1980, drawn into other commitments, Asdell relinquished *The Thorndyke File* to John McAleer, who, as Rex Stout's authorized biographer (*Rex Stout: A Biography*, Little, Brown, 1977; winner of the Mystery Writers of America's Edgar Award, 1978), had discovered Freeman when he found many of Freeman's books on Stout's bookshelves. A vigorous recruitment drive by McAleer more than doubled the number of *File* subscribers in the first year of his editorship, bringing the total to 156. Half of these are doctors of medicine.

McAleer has also been successful in finding a score of new contributors to the *File*, several of them physicians and medico-legal experts. Their inquiries are shedding much new light on Freeman's achievements and explain why his books are recommended reading in many law schools. McAleer has procured also hitherto unpublished Freeman materials and interviews with people who knew Freeman personally, as well as original Freeman drawings and photographs and fugitive Freeman vignettes which will appear in forthcoming issues of the magazine. Thus McAleer is enabled to increase the number of pages in each issue.

The Thorndyke File, McAleer concludes, will never be a best seller, but it will consistently have a quality readership—bishops, jurists, writers, editors, pulishers, professors, as well as doctors—which attests to the superior merit of Freeman's work. Raymond Chandler, Dorothy Sayers, and June Thomson, as well as H.R.F. Keating, Catherine Aird, and Rex Stout, have, at various times, commented with favor on Freeman's accomplishments. To his two sons, Freeman was "the Emperor." He inspires the same kind of homage from the admirers of the Thorndyke saga.

Information Sources

INDEX SOURCES: None known.
LOCATION SOURCES: Private collectors.

Publication History

MAGAZINE TITLE: *The Thorndyke File*.
TITLE CHANGES: None.
VOLUME AND ISSUE DATA: No. 1 (Spring 1976) through no. 13, (to date, Spring 1982); 13 issues.
PUBLISHER: Philip T. Asdell and John McAleer, Mount Independence, 121 Follen Road, Lexington, Massachusetts 02173.
EDITORS: Philip T. Asdell (nos. 1–12); John McAleer.
PRICE PER ISSUE: $5.00 per year, by subscription only; includes membership fee in R. Austin Freeman Society.
SIZE AND PAGINATION: 5" X 8-1/2"; 36–52 pages.
CURRENT STATUS: Active.
—John J. McAleer

THRILLER, THE (British)

"A 7/6 Novel for 2d!" [A seven shilling, sixpence novel for two pence.]
"The New Paper With a Thousand Thrills!"
So ran the publicity blurbs for *The Thriller*, a 1930s paper that lived up to its name and promises and yet, as a tuppenny book, was still destined to be sold on the boys' papers rack alongside *Hotspur, Wizard,* and the like.

The Thriller is a publication that has always been difficult to classify, for although accepted generally to be in the juvenile category, probably because it contained advertisements of current boys' publications and adolescent card games, it would appear to have been intended for an adult market or at least aimed at a higher age group than those who normally read boys' weeklies. Certainly, Leslie Charteris, famous for his Saint stories and himself a regular contributor to *The Thriller's* pages, was of the opinion that it catered to the teenage-upward market more so than to those who read the *Magnet, Gem, Pilot,* and *Startler* range. Perhaps that tuppenny status prevented the city gent from reading this in the train, lest he be thought a little unusual to be seen with such a trifling paper. The late Frank Vernon Lay, a well-known dealer and collector of juvenilia and detective fiction, was always of the firm opinion that it was an adult publication. But whatever the publishers' intentions were, *The Thriller* definitely had its fans in all age groups (even if it was sometimes hidden between the pages of the *Times*).

Percy Montague Haydon could not have been described as an ordinary editor. Through the eyes of an ambitious office boy, he was seen as a majestic figure, a controlling editor with a large group of weekly and monthly papers under his control and only one step away from becoming a director (a position he did attain in later years). In late 1928, the Amalgamated Press was riding on the crest of a wave. Dozens of their magazines of all descriptions were selling in the millions, and it could be claimed that they were one of the largest publishers of popular fiction in the world.

"Monty," as Haydon was affectionately called, had worked his way up to the position of editor from that of an office boy. During the First World War, he had served with great distinction as an officer, winning the Medal of Courage. He was a born leader, the ideal man for the job, always showing great enthusiasm, initiative, and shrewd judgment; in short, as a creative editor, he was a genius. Someone—and in all probability it was "Monty" himself—had suggested having a new weekly paper, to be called *The Thriller*; this was to feature a seven-shilling-and-sixpence-value, top-class, mystery/crime/thriller detective story for the modest sum of twopence, a price likely to appeal greatly to the less-affluent members of the reading public. Monty, who had the task of submitting the "dummy" to the board of directors, persuaded them it would be a commercial proposition, and they gave the go-ahead for the paper to be launched. To start this new venture with a flourish, he had commissioned Edgar Wallace, the undisputed king of thriller writers, to pen the opening story, and this was entitled "Red Aces." It appeared in the first issue, of February 9, 1929. To say that Edgar Wallace had been obtained at enormous expense was to put it mildly— he was paid the staggering figure of twenty-five pounds per one thousand words! As the average author received only two guineas per thousand words, one can gather the fame and pulling power of Edgar Wallace in those days. News soon spread down Fleet Street (via the taverns, haunts, clubs, and other popular meeting places of authors) of this new paper, and soon *The Thriller* office was bombarded with manuscripts of both established and unknown authors.

The actual editor (under Monty Haydon) was Leonard Pratt, assisted by "Jackie" Hunt, a very pleasant and likable man and later a group editor. Leonard Pratt, or "Pratty," as he was called, was also editor of the famous *The Sexton Blake Library* (British)* and was a rather stolid man of the old-fashioned school. Indeed, he was much older than Monty and was senior in length of service at the Amalgamated Press. In general, he was the solid type of editor and certainly proficient at his job; but he was the kind of man who was quite content with his present position in the firm and wanted no more than to have his regular pint of beer at the same Fleet Street tavern, smoke his Woodbines, and catch the same train to and from work each day, year in and year out. In fact, Leslie Charteris dealt directly with Monty in all his stories for *The Thriller* and completely bypassed Leonard Pratt, the editor, who became little more than a nodding acquaintance.

The illustrations for the full-length *Thriller* stories were entirely original and were never used again, even though many of the stories were subsequently reprinted. Certain artists were featured more prominently than others, such as Nat Long; Arthur Jones, artist of many Nelson Lee covers; and Eric Parker, famous for his illustrations of Sexton Blake. Of the artists mentioned, it was Arthur Jones who seemed to create the greatest air of mystery. His sombre and grim characters that seemed forever lurking in the shadows were most fitting for this paper, and, indeed, his work added a lot to the stories themselves.

Apart from its fictional contents, there were also a considerable number of articles covering various aspects of crime, its detection, sciences involved, and of real-life criminals.

One interesting feature was "Bafflers," which was a detective story-game in which the reader had to solve the mystery, an idea that has been used many times and one that will always interest the avid crime reader. There were other crime puzzles, and space was allotted also to the football league, with the fixture list for forthcoming matches, form, and a forecast of results.

With issue number 525, *Wild West*, a short-lived cowboy story-paper, was incorporated with *The Thriller*. The only effect this had was to continue to a conclusion two unfinished serials, one of which was a Sexton Blake story.

Toward the end of its run, with issue number 579, the paper was retitled *War Thriller*, and as such it remained to the last issue, number 589 (May 18, 1940).

Consistently of a high quality, *The Thriller's* pages contained work from the highest in their field, for apart from Wallace and Charteris, its contributors included such notables as Margery Allingham, Max Brand, Peter Cheyney, Agatha Christie, Hugh Clevely, John Creasey, Gerard Fairlie, J. Jefferson Farjeon, Francis Gerard, Maxwell Grant, Dashiell Hammett, Captain W. E. Johns, E. Phillips Oppenheim, and Sax Rohmer. But even though this is a short list, it seems an injustice to leave out all those other great writers included in its pages. A true appreciation for *The Thriller* began to grow after its eventual demise, and indeed, today, issues containing prime stories of authors such as Edgar Wallace and Leslie Charteris are eagerly sought after. But it is not just these authors that attract collectors, for a whole wealth of superb detective stories were included in its modest run.

Information Sources

BIBLIOGRPAHY:
Lofts, W.O.G., and Derek J. Adley. *Old Boys Books, A Complete Catalogue*. London: privately printed, 1969.
INDEX SOURCES: None known.
LOCATION SOURCES: Private collectors.

Publication History

MAGAZINE TITLE: *The Thriller*.

TITLE CHANGES: *War Thriller* (with no. 579).
VOLUME AND ISSUE DATA: No. 1 (February 9, 1929) through no. 589 (May 18, 1940); 589 issues.
PUBLISHER: The Amalgamated Press, Ltd., London E.C.4, England.
EDITORS: Percy Montague Haydon, supervising editor; Leonard Pratt, managing editor; Jackie Hunt, associate.
PRICE PER ISSUE: 2 pence (1929), to 4 pence (1940).
SIZE AND PAGINATION: 7-1/2'' X 10''; 24 pages.
CURRENT STATUS: Discontinued.
—*Derek J. Adley*

THRILLING DETECTIVE

Thrilling Detective was the first of Ned Pines's long line of pulp magazines, which were published with M. A. Goldsmith under a number of imprints, including Standard Magazines, Beacon Publications, and Better Publications. The group was generally known as the "Thrilling" Group because so many of the titles contained that key word. *Thrilling Detective* debuted in the same month, November 1931, as its companion, *Thrilling Love Stories*. These magazines got their start when Street & Smith dropped their main distributor, the American News Company, and American News went to Pines and asked him to start a pulp chain which they could distribute in place of the Street & Smith magazines.

The editorial director of the Thrilling Group was Leo Margulies, the so-called Little Giant of the Pulps, although the earliest issues listed Harvey Burns as editor. Burns was a house name.

Unlike its later companions, *Popular Detective,* Exciting Detective,** and *Thrilling Mystery,* Thrilling Detective* did not play up long-running series characters or the mysterious masked detectives who seemed to be prerequisites for all of Margulies's other mystery pulps. Instead, the magazine ran fast-action tales of suitably hard-nosed and hard-boiled detectives and police characters. Margulies liked to say that his line was "probably the fastest bunch of all the pulps." This meant, quite simply, nonstop action, and action was what *Thrilling Detective* delivered—even if it was sometimes at the expense of characterization and, in keeping with the Great Depression trends, no continued stories.

The early years of the magazine featured a good number of regular contributors, of whom Paul Ernst, Ed Lybeck Fredrick C. Painton, Edmund Hamilton, and Preston Grady were often seen. Grady was a discovery of Margulies, made when the latter, annoyed by competitors' boasts of new writing discoveries, picked Grady's first submission out of the slush pile, read the first paragraph, and announced Grady as his first "discovery." Grady later became an editor. Many of Margulies's writers wrote for him exclusively, but he attracted many from other publications, including two *The Black Mask** standards, George Harmon Coxe, creator of "Flashgun Casey," and James H.S. Moynahan. Frank Gruber, later to write extensively for *Black Mask*, created the popular series about Oliver Quade, the Human Encyclopedia, for *Thrilling Detective* in 1936. The character came to be when Gruber complained to Margulies that he couldn't think up plots, and the latter handed him an encyclopedia with the comment that plots could be had from it.

Another series character to appear in the magazine's pages was George Bruce's Red Lacey, private detective, but such characters were more the exception than the rule. British writer Barry Perowne, better known for his continuation of F. W. Hornung's character, A. J. Raffles, was an early contributor as well. And the famous creator of Zorro, Johnston McCulley, sent his character, the Green Ghost, through a series of stories in those early days, too.

Despite a rigorous acceptance policy—no story was accepted unless it was unanimously approved by the three-man team who handled the slush pile—the fiction published in this magazine was not of such a high standard that it was memorable, and today *Thrilling Detective* is not popular among collectors. This may be due, in part, to the "action-over-all-else" editorial policy and, in part, because Margulies would sometimes accept substandard stories, which were revised for publication by his editors.

During the forties, *Thrilling Detective* underwent a shift in emphasis away from all-out action. This was no isolated event but a major turning point in all of the pulp field. Action was still important, but action for action's sake was now passe. Instead, characterization, plausibility, motivation, and plot became important in magazines where they had not been heretofore and more important in those magazines where they had previously been given priority. This was as true for such titles as *Doc Savage** and *The Spider** as it was for *Thrilling Detective*.

With this shift, new writers entered *Thrilling Detective's* pages. Among them were Robert Leslie Bellem, whose Dan Turner ran in *Spicy Detective** and *Dan Turner, Hollywood Detective*.* For this title, however, he wrote about another Hollywood detective, Nick Ransom, whose adventures were not confined to *Thrilling Detective* or even to the Thrilling Group. Louis L'Amour, J. Lane Linklater, Wayland Rice, and William Campbell Gault were some of the other late contributors. Carroll John Daly, who created the whole hard-boiled detective genre with his two-gun dick, Race Williams (in *Black Mask* in the early twenties), wrote some of the final—if not the absolute last—of that tired but important character's exploits in the later issues.

Two long-time pulp writers, Arthur Leo Zagat and C. S. Montayne, were steady contributors until their untimely deaths in or about 1949. Other significant contributors included Ed Churchill, Jean Francis Webb, Westmoreland Gray, Carl G. Hodges, George A. MacDonald, Steve Fisher, Edward Parrish Ware, Frederick C. Davis (usually under his pen name, Clark Aiken), and one of the few women pulp writers, Margie Harris. For all the hundreds of stories which were run in *Thrilling Detective*, none can be singled out as exemplary or outstanding in any way. The only possible exception might be Frank Gruber's Human Encyclopedia stories, which were later adapted to film. Had this not been done, however, even these might not be remembered today.

There is, however, one writer who stand out in the *Thrilling Detective* stable, and that is Norman A. Danberg, who wrote primarily as Norman A. Daniels and John L. Benton. Daniels (as he is best known) has the distinction of being perhaps the most regular contributor the magazine ever had inasmuch as he was in the earliest issues as well as the latest and was seldom missing for any great length of time. This, in spite of his incredible prolificness as an author of short stories, novelettes, and lead novels for an incredible array of titles and publishers. However, on the whole, Daniels's work is not outstanding; he was a swift, competent, writing machine whose regularity far surpassed his creativity. In many respects, Daniels's output is emblematic of the entire run of the magazine.

In its latter days, *Thrilling Detective* came under the editorial control of a number of editors, of whom David X. Manners may have been the last. While the melodramatic covers of the issues of the thirties were by a host of artists, by the late forties, at least, Rudolph Belarski contributed most of the covers in his highly recognizable and stylized fashion. Interior art was largely anonymous, but the work of Amos Sewell, Pete Costanza, S. Strather, Leo Morey, V. E. Pyles, and Paul Orban are recognizable.

The magazine finally expired as a quarterly with the Summer 1953 issue— one of the last of the pulps to give up the ghost. The day of the pulp had passed with a certainty, and Leo Margulies, in a sweeping move, killed the last of his line. At the time, he claimed they were merely "dormant," but no one could have been fooled. Better magazines than *Thrilling Detective* had succumbed to changing trends and shifting reader tastes.

There was a British reprint edition of forty-seven issues, September 1940 to November 1954.

Information Sources

INDEX SOURCES: None known.
LOCATION SOURCES: University of California–Los Angeles (1931–1953, 81 issues); private collectors.

Publication History

MAGAZINE TITLE: *Thrilling Detective*.
TITLE CHANGES: None.
VOLUME AND ISSUE DATA: Vol. 1, no. 1 (November 1931) through Vol. 71, no. 3 (Summer 1953); 213 issues.
PUBLISHER: Better Publications, Inc., 22 West 48th Street, New York, New York (also as Metropolitan Magazines, Inc.).
EDITOR: Leo Margulies, supervising editor; various subeditors, including David X. Manners.
PRICE PER ISSUE: 10 cents.
SIZE AND PAGINATION: 7'' X 10''; 128 pages.
CURRENT STATUS: Discontinued.
—*Will Murray*

THRILLING DETECTIVE (British)

See THRILLING DETECTIVE

THRILLING MYSTERIES

Because its three weird-menace titles (*Dime Mystery Magazine [Dime Mystery Book*], Horror Stories,*￼ and *Terror Tales* [see *Horror Stories*]) were finding reader acceptance, Popular Publications launched a fourth entry in April 1935. This was *Thrilling Mysteries.*

Arthur Leo Zagat, one of the more prolific pulpsters of the thirties, led off with a novel, and other familiar names such as Hugh B. Cave and Arthur J. Burks also appeared. The stories in this publication were of the Gothic tradition.

However, this magazine ran into title trouble with the word "Thrilling," which Ned Pines felt belonged to him (since so many of his titles included that word). The two companies settled out of court, with the "Thrilling" name conceded to Pines's company (Better Publications, Inc.), and Pines used it once again, six months later, to introduce *Thrilling Mystery.*￼

Thus, there was but one issue published by Popular Publications of *Thrilling Mysteries*, a standard-sized pulp magazine.

Information Sources

BIBLIOGRAPHY:

Hardin, Nils. "An Interview with Henry Steeger." *Xenophile*, no. 33 (July 1977): 3–18.

———, and George Hocutt. "A Checklist of Popular Publications Titles 1930–1955." *Xenophile*, no. 33 (July 1977): 21–24.

Hersey, Harold. *Pulpwood Editor*. New York: Frederick A. Stokes Co., 1937.

Jones, Robert Kenneth. *The Shudder Pulps*. West Linn, Ore.: Fax Collector's Editions, 1975.

———. "The Weird Menace Magazines." *Bronze Shadows*, no. 10 (June 1967): 3–8; no. 11 (August 1967): 7–13; no. 12 (October 1967): 7–10; no. 13 (January 1968): 7–12; no. 14 (March 1968)- 13–17; no. 15 (November 1968): 4–8.

INDEX SOURCES: None known.

LOCATION SOURCES: Private collectors.

Publication History

MAGAZINE TITLE: *Thrilling Mysteries*.

TITLE CHANGES: None.

VOLUME AND ISSUE DATA: Vol. 1, no. 1 (April 1935); 1 issue.

PUBLISHER: Popular Publications, Inc., 2256 Grove Street, Chicago, Illinois, with editorial offices at 210 East 43rd Street, New York, New York.

EDITOR: Rogers Terrill.

PRICE PER ISSUE: 15 cents.

SIZE AND PAGINATION: 7'' X 9-3/4''; 112 pages.
CURRENT STATUS: Discontinued.
—*Robert Kenneth Jones*

THRILLING MYSTERY

If there was one thing pulp publishers kept their eye on, besides the pulse of the reading public (to mix metaphors), it was what the opposition was doing. After all, the pulps were a $25 million business, catering to 10 million readers. When Popular Publications found modest success with its three weird-menace titles (*Dime Mystery Magazine [Dime Mystery Book*], Horror Stories,* and *Terror Tales* [see *Horror Stories*]), rival publisher Ned L. Pines decided to try the same tack. So his Thrilling Group added a new title in October 1935, *Thrilling Mystery*. According to Leo Margulies, editorial director, "We had seen the success of some other magazines, like *Horror Stories* and *Terror Tales*. It was the only type we didn't have at the time." Harvey Burns was listed as editor, but that was a house name. "In those days, we had a fiction factory," Margulies explains. "I grouped the magazines and gave them to the guys who worked for me."[1]

Margulies was an indefatigable individual, referred to by Earl Wilson as "The Little Giant of the Pulps."[2] He was one of the few well-paid editors, earning $25,000 a year. This was in an era when the average editor earned about $2,000 a year, rarely more than $5,000, and usually was in danger of losing his job. The "little giant" remained in editing to the time of his death in 1975.

A description by author Steve Fisher, of Margulies attending an American Fiction Guild luncheon, is interesting. On hand were pulp luminaries such as Lester Dent (Doc Savage), Robert J. Hogan (G-8 and His Battle Aces), Norvell W. Page (The Spider), Arthur J. Burks, Richard B. Sale, and Arthur Leo Zagat. "But in the middle of the luncheon, there was a sudden silence. Fifty people stopped eating and looked up. Leo Margulies made his usual dramatic entrance. Behind him came the stalwarts of his staff. . . . I thought for a moment President Art Burks was going to leap to his feet and salute."[3]

As reported by the trade journals of the time, Margulies wanted stories for his new title, *Thrilling Mystery*, centering on vampires, witches, ghouls, werewolves, strange cults, horrible monsters, and villains employing horror methods against their victims. In light of this emphasis on the occult, it is surprising that the magazine actually utilized few of these themes. Most of the stories were concerned with a villain working his nefarious ways—the usual *modus operandi* of the other weird-menace publications. In contrast to what Popular Publications had been emphasizing, however, *Thrilling* did not parade an army of revolting creatures (later unmasked as evil perpetrators) or pique the reader's prurient interest. In the main, the evil nemeses kept their identities a secret until the end, using horror methods to achieve their results. The editor expressed a preference for women's interest in the magazine's material, but often the heroine filled only a subordinate role and often was not even the focus of the villain's evil machinations.

Many of the stories were strong on abhorrent details, as for instance: "He forced the blade of his knife between dead, blue lips."[4] "The head was only a quarter of its actual size, but Horton identified it without a single doubt."[5] "It was a grey and bony hand with long prehensile fingers. Tightly, they grasped the edge of the coffin lid and thrust it upwards."[6] Typical of this type of story was Wayne Rogers's "Hell's Brew" (January 1936), with its mutilated corpses, a big, black beast (ostensibly a werewolf), and fantastic rituals. But *Thrilling Mystery* stayed with the weird-menace stylization so that there should be a logical denouement. Thus, when a kidnapped group of bus passengers finds itself deep in the bowels of the earth, at the mercy of Satan and his devils, and when the mystification is at its height, things soon start unraveling, and they learn that the whole charade was staged by someone who wanted the property for its natural oil and gas.

On occasion, a fantasy appeared. One of the most effective in that or any other similar pulp of the period was Arthur J. Burks's "Devils in the Dust" (December 1935), a stark, bitter account of man in search of his bride. The mood is as bleak as an arctic blizzard as he searches through a storm, overcoming adversaries who resemble the lay preacher who married them.

Many of the authors already appearing in Popular Publications' weird-menace magazines found a ready market at Thrilling. In fact, the two companies practically operated a writers' exchange. Names like Arthur J. Burks, John H. Knox, Wyatt Blassingame, Ray Cummings, Hugh B. Cave, G. T. Fleming-Roberts, and Wayne Rogers appeared under one company's imprint one month and under the other the next or often under both at the same time.

Several authors well versed in science fiction appeared in *Thrilling Mystery*, names like Jack Williams, Frank Belknap Long, and Henry Kuttner. What they wrote was promoted as science fiction and began that way but ended as the usual unmasking of a villain. In one, a robot leaves a trail of corpses, but when finally brought to bay, a murderer is discovered hiding within. There were other science fiction situations, such as giant spiders running amok and an ethereal young lady brought to Earth from a frigid drifting mass, and in all cases, these, too, turned out to be people in disguise.

Just as the stories in *Thrilling Mystery* made no attempt to exploit sex, the covers did not arouse lecherous feelings. The women were modestly attired with just a rent here or there in their clothing. But the *mise en scenes* went beyond what other publishers were showing in gruesomeness, with mutilated bodies and considerable bloodshed. Rudolph Belarski, busy on covers for *Argosy*, and Rafael de Soto (*Operator #5* and *The Spider**), who has been called the dean of pulp cover artists, rendered many of the scenes. De Soto notes that he was making about $75 a cover for Street & Smith before going to Pines's Thrilling publications, where he earned in the neighborhood of $125. Interior illustrations were by Monroe Eisenberg, Leo Morey, Alex Schomberg, Parkhurst, Jayem Wilcox, and Belarski.

In the forties, the magazine adopted a crime-fighting format. By the November 1941 issue, it was carrying the legend "Best Action Detective Stories" and featuring the likes of Colonel Fabian Crum, John Knox's diminuitive detective. In 1942, G. T. Fleming-Roberts's Green Ghost appeared there. The magazine had been bimonthly since 1937; in 1943 it went quarterly, brought in more investigator types, but then succumbed to the war and the competition of comic books.

Notes

1. Robert Kenneth Jones, *The Shudder Pulps*, (West Linn, Ore.: Fax Collector's Editions, 1975), p. 25, quoting Leo Margulies in *The Writer*, March 1939.
2. Robert Kenneth Jones, *The Shudder Pulps*, p. 25.
3. Ibid., p. 89.
4. Ibid., p. 36.
5. Ibid., p. 37.
6. Ibid., p. 39.

Information Sources

BIBLIOGRAPHY:
Jones, Robert Kenneth. *The Shudder Pulps*. West Linn, Ore.: Fax Collector's Editions, 1975.
INDEX SOURCES: None known.
LOCATION SOURCES: University of California–Los Angeles (Vol. 11, no. 3, only); private collectors.

Publication History

MAGAZINE TITLE: *Thrilling Mystery*.
TITLE CHANGES: None.
VOLUME AND ISSUE DATA: Vol. 1, no. 1 (October 1935) through Vol. 16, no. 2; 50 issues.
PUBLISHER: Better Publications, Inc., 22 West 48th Street, New York, New York.
EDITOR: Leo Margulies (with various subeditors).
PRICE PER ISSUE: 10 cents.
SIZE AND PAGINATION: 7" X 10"; 128 pages.
CURRENT STATUS: Discontinued.
—*Robert Kenneth Jones*

THRILLING MYSTERY NOVEL

Thrilling Mystery Novel, published by Ned L. Pines's Better Publications, was commenced in 1935 and featured one book-length mystery novel, several short stories, and an editorial department previewing the stories of the next issue and containing letters from readers. It was published to at least March 1946. No other information is available.

Information Sources

INDEX SOURCES: None known.
LOCATION SOURCES: Private collectors.

Publication History

MAGAZINE TITLE: *Thrilling Mystery Novel.*
TITLE CHANGES: None.
VOLUME AND ISSUE DATA: From 1935 to at least Vol. 23, no. 4 (March 1946);
    number of issues unknown.
PUBLISHER: Better Publications, Inc., 22 West 48th Street, New York, New York.
EDITOR: Not known.
PRICE PER ISSUE: 10 cents.
SIZE AND PAGINATION: 7'' X 10''; number of pages unknown.
CURRENT STATUS: Discontinued.

THRILLING SPY STORIES

Each of the four issues of *Thrilling Spy Stories* contained a very short novel (more properly termed a novelette) featuring Jeff Shannon, The Eagle. To bolster the contents, short fiction was included by some of the leading pulp writers of the period: E. Hoffman Price, Robert Leslie Bellem, G. T. Fleming-Roberts, C.K.M. Scanlon (house name), Major George Fielding Eliot, and Dale DeV. Kier.

The first issue of *Thrilling Spy Stories* appeared on the newsstands in early August 1939. Less than a month later, Germany invaded Poland. It would appear that a pulp magazine oriented to counterespionage, casting the Nazis as villains, would have been an instant success. But such was not the case.

Science fiction and western pulps proliferated in this period, and even the mystery story magazine enjoyed somewhat of a boom but to a more limited extent. Mystery fiction is more closely geared to the real world than either science fiction or westerns, thus reflecting the political madness of a world at war or a nation trying to maintain neutrality.

Jeff Shannon, the counterespionage agent known as The Eagle, was known from Tokyo to Berlin—known and hated and feared. He was a skilled boxer, a master of the art of shadowing, and a master of codes. He could intercept an enemy message and decode it mentally, without reference to a code book. Fortunately for him (and the stories), for the more difficult codes he seemed to have no difficulty in procuring enemy code books.

The editorial column of the first issue added several paragraphs of additional aptitudes:

But The Eagle, wise in the ways of spies and trained to detect the
hundred and one subterfuges to which spies resort, fights the enemy with

its own undercover weapons, and handles those weapons with a skill brought to perfection by a tireless body, an agile brain, and a fighting heart imbued with the love of his country and her democratic institutions.

Counter espionage is unusual and taxing work. A first-rate counter-spy like The Eagle isn't turned out overnight. He is a combination of brains, breeding, and fearlessness. He must wear a full dress suit as though poured into one, but he must be equally at home in a pair of longshoreman's brogans.

The world of officialdom, diplomacy and government intrigue must be as familiar to him as his own home—although he never lives long enough in one spot to call it that. He must move from one hazardous experience to the next. . .ever increasing his effectiveness as a sentinel guarding his country's liberties, in peace and in war.[1]

In the first novel, the Nazis had established an entirely secret manufacturing plant in the Venezuelan highlands, near Lake Maracaibo. Here, munitions, pursuit planes, and a newly invented stratosphere bomber were being mass-produced and stockpiled against the eventuality that the United States might go to war with Germany.

The locale of the second novel is North Africa and the Sahara. Hereditary enemies among the desert tribes have been united in an effort to drive the French from North Africa. Behind all the cunning and duplicity is the sinister Nazi spy, Erich, Graf von Drakenfels, who seemed to know every move made by the Foreign Legion almost before it was made.

The third and fourth novels brought The Eagle back to the United States to foil the nefarious schemes hatched by still other Nazi spies. In number three, the spies have managed to set secret explosives in munitions plants against the day when America would be in the war against the Axis powers. Probably the most prosaic plot of the quartet was presented in the fourth novel. An inventor had devised a poison gas that could be loaded in a bullet and fired in a rifle. The gas was so potent that it would kill any living thing in a radius of six feet from point of impact. Once the inventor was killed, the chase was on to discover where the formula had been hidden.

Of a certainty, the stories were not in a class with those featuring The Shadow, The Spider, or Operator #5, but they were presented with a verve and elan that allowed them to fulfill their intended function: to grip the reader's interest and hold his attention.

This was not, however, an auspicious period for launching new pulp publications. The pulps, though few realized it at the time, were on the way out. Comics and paperbacks were taking over the readers who, in previous decades, had had no other choice but the pulps. The comics took the younger readers and deprived the pulps of the constant influx of new adherents, while the paperbacks attracted and ensnared the older pulp readers. This was not the leading reason, however, for the short life of this particular pulp magazine. In spite of the solicitude and attention lavished on the new magazine, the publishers hedged in two vital areas. They limited the lead novel to under forty pages, and it was published on an infrequent basis, quarterly. Together, these ensured that no pulp-hero following would develop around the character of The Eagle—it was another case of too little and too late. Beyond this, times led the readers to prefer stories that would take their minds off the realities of the world situation. They just did not want to meet the war and world politics in their attempts to escape from reality.

Note

1. Editorial, *Thrilling Spy Stories,* Vol. 1, no. 1 (Fall 1939), p. 4.

Information Sources

INDEX SOURCES: None known.
LOCATION SOURCES: Private collectors.

Publication History

MAGAZINE TITLE: *Thrilling Spy Stories.*
TITLE CHANGES: None.
VOLUME AND ISSUE DATA: Vol. 1, no. 1 (Fall 1939) through Vol. 2, no. 1 (Summer 1940); 4 issues.
PUBLISHER: Better Publications, Inc., 22 West 48th Street, New York, New York.
EDITOR: Not known.
PRICE PER ISSUE: 10 cents.
SIZE AND PAGINATION: 7'' X 10''; 114 pages.
CURRENT STATUS: Discontinued.
—*Joseph Lewandowski*

TIGHTROPE!

Although long after the demise of the pulp magazines was apparent and digest-size magazines crowded the newsstands, Henry Scharf hoped for support for a new pulp which traded upon the publicity of a then popular television series. *Tightrope!* was introduced in April 1960, featuring stories in each issue by Robert H. Brown of the "Undercover Man 'Nick'," along with a good selection of other mystery and crime-adventure stories.

Among the authors included in the three issues were Edward D. Hoch, Al James, Donald Westlake, Arthur Porges, Talmage Powell, John Jakes, Norman Struber, and others; but despite the better-than-average fiction, the pulp format apparently contributed to an early demise.

It should be noted that the publisher, undaunted, followed with another magazine with the same idea—77 *Sunset Strip**—but this, too, was unsuccessful.

Information Sources

INDEX SOURCES: Cook, Michael L. *Monthly Murders*. Westport, Conn.: Greenwood Press, 1982.
LOCATION SOURCES: Private collectors.

Publication History

MAGAZINE TITLE: *Tightrope!*
TITLE CHANGES: None.
VOLUME AND ISSUE DATA: Vol. 1, no. 1 (April 1960) through Vol. 1, no. 3 (June 1960); 3 issues.
PUBLISHER: Henry Scharf as Great American Publications, Inc., 270 Madison Avenue, New York 16, New York.
EDITOR: Jonas Carter; Sheldon Wax, editorial director.
PRICE PER ISSUE: 35 cents.
SIZE AND PAGINATION: 6-1/2" X 9-1/4"; 98 pages.
CURRENT STATUS: Discontinued.

TIP TOP DETECTIVE TALES (British)

A series of boys' papers, *Tip Top Detective Tales* featured material oriented to younger readers. Thirty-six issues were published by the Aldine Publishing Company during 1910–1914, similar to its several series of a publication titled *Tip Top Tales*. No other information is available.

Information Sources

BIBLIOGRAPHY:
Lofts, W.O.G., and Derek J. Adley. *Old Boys Books, A Complete Catalogue*. London: privately printed, 1969.
INDEX SOURCES: None known.
LOCATION SOURCES: Private collectors.

Publication History

MAGAZINE TITLE: *Tip Top Detective Tales*.
TITLE CHANGES: None.
VOLUME AND ISSUE DATA: No. 1 (1910) through no. 36 (1914), 36 issues.
PUBLISHER: Aldine Publishing Co., Ltd., London.
EDITOR: Not known.
PRICE PER ISSUE: Not known.
SIZE AND PAGINATION: Not known.
CURRENT STATUS: Discontinued.

TOP DETECTIVE ANNUAL

Four issues of *Top Detective Annual*, a mystery anthology, have been noted: 1950, 1951, 1952, and 1953. Customarily, it reprinted mystery fiction from the Standard Publications magazines, mainly selections of material from the 1940s but occasionally dipping as far back as the mid-1930s for an especially effective story. The *Annual* emphasized the work of well-known writers, and the relatively high standard of fiction in the *Annual* is but occasionally marred by reprinting a lesser story in order to use a glittering name.

Among authors represented are Carroll John Daly, Robert Leslie Bellem, Ray Cummings, Wyatt Blassingame, Joe Archibald, and Fredrick Brown. Magazines from which the fiction was selected included *Thrilling Detective,* Thrilling Mystery,* Popular Detective,* Exciting Detective,* G-Men Detective,** and *Detective Mystery Novel Magazine.**

Top Detective Annual contents were typically stretched by the inclusion of filler materials—brief articles; small, mildly humorous paragraphs; and the like. The 1953 *Annual* is a particularly nice example of the later pulps, being sleekly covered, trimmed smooth, and tastefully laid out, an altogether agreeable magazine.

Information Sources

INDEX SOURCES: None known.
LOCATION SOURCES: University of California–Los Angeles (1953 only); private collectors.

Publication History

MAGAZINE TITLE: *Top Detective Annual*.
TITLE CHANGES: None.
VOLUME AND ISSUE DATA: Vol. 1, no. 1 (1950) through Vol. 1, no 4 (labeled, in error, as Vol. 2, no. 4; 1953); 4 issues.
PUBLISHER: Best Books, Inc., 10 East 40th Street, New York 16, New York.
EDITORS: David X. Manners (1952); Everett H. Ortner (1953).
PRICE PER ISSUE: 25 cents.
SIZE AND PAGINATION: 6-1/2" X 8-3/4"; 162 pages.
CURRENT STATUS: Discontinued.
—*Robert Sampson*

TOP-NOTCH DETECTIVE

Only one issue of *Top-Notch Detective*, a Red Circle magazine, has been noted, but this (March 1939) was designed as volume 3, number 1, indicating perhaps that the magazine was published over at least a two- or three-year span.

Information Sources

INDEX SOURCES: None known.

LOCATION SOURCES: University of California–Los Angeles Library (Vol. 3, no. 1); private collectors.

Publication History

MAGAZINE TITLE: *Top-Notch Detective*.
TITLE CHANGES: None known.
VOLUME AND ISSSUE DATA: Number of issues and extent unknown (Vol. 3, no. 1, dated March 1939).
PUBLISHER: Western Fiction Publishing Co., Inc., New York, New York.
EDITOR: Not known.
PRICE PER ISSUE: Not known.
SIZE AND PAGINATION: Not known.
CURRENT STATUS: Discontinued.

TRAPPED

See TRAPPED DETECTIVE STORY MAGAZINE

TRAPPED DETECTIVE STORY MAGAZINE

Trapped Detective Story Magazine was a bona fide companion to *Guilty Detective Story Magazine,** the two appearing in an uneven schedule on alternate months. They were, in fact, the same magazine appearing under two different titles. *Trapped* was published by Headline Publications and *Guilty* by Feature Publications, but these were two names for the same company, and all issues of both magazines were edited by W. W. Scott. *Trapped Detective Story Magazine* was first published with the June 1956 issue (*Guilty* commenced July 1956).

This was an attractively packaged digest magazine, with a neat, clean appearance; and behind the pulplike covers, the contents were but one blink of the eye removed from the pulps of the 1940s. Contemporary private investigators, black-jacketed hoods, prison characters, and small-time crooks populated the stories with direct and sometimes violent action. And ladies, as we should call them, were present. There were some that did not deserve the title, but nonetheless, all were products of a bountiful nature and whether good or bad, were good either way.

The titles were perhaps the worst part of the magazine; the stories certainly deserved better. "I'll Dance at Your Funeral" (by Milton K. Ozaki, June 1956), "Naked on the Highway" (by James Finnegan, August 1956), "Killer in the Can" (by Harlan Ellison, August 1956), "Don't Say I'm Crazy" (Herbert D. Kastle, May 1961), and "A Kiss for the Dead" (by Norman Struber, June 1957) all seem to play for shock attention.

Although the stories were reminiscent of the pulp magazines, they were, in fact, transitional stories that bridged the gap to a more polished type of story that would appear in the 1960s. Here were to be found John Jakes, Norman

Struber, Carroll Mayers, Henry Slesar, Gil Brewer, Dan Sontup, as well as Talmage Powell, Francis Battle, Charles Beckman, and others—capable writers producing adequate stories.

While most issues of this magazine included twelve or more short stories, the last issues were devoted to one major story with two filler short stories. With these issues, the name of the magazine was relegated to very small print and the feature story headlined, to the extent that the magazine's issues very much resembled full-length paperbound books. It was the paperbound books that were posing the most competition for the digest-size magazines, and *Trapped Detective Story Magazine* was an attempt to meet that competition and even join it. However, sales continued to lag, and the November 1962 issue was the last.

Information Sources

INDEX SOURCES: Cook, Michael L. *Monthly Murders*. Westport, Conn.: Greenwood Press, 1982.
LOCATION SOURCES: Private collectors.

Publication History

MAGAZINE TITLE: *Trapped Detective Story Magazine*.
TITLE CHANGES: *Trapped* (and title de-emphasized, last two issues).
VOLUME AND ISSUE DATA: Vol. 1, no. 1 (June 1956) through Vol. 7, No. 2 (November 1962); 34 issues.
PUBLISHER: Headline Publications, IOnc., 1 Appleton Street, Holyoke, Massachusetts, with editorial offices at 1790 Boradway, New York 19, New York, and later 32 West 22nd Street, New York, New York.
EDITOR: W. W. Scott.
PRICE EPR ISSUE: 35 cents.
SIZE AND PAGINATION: 5-3/8" X 7-1/4"; last two issues 5" X 7-1/4"; 128 pages.
CURRENT STATUS: Discontinued.

TRIPLE DETECTIVE

Taking its name from the practice of presenting three "complete detective novels" in each issue, this was a Thrilling Group publication under Ned L. Pines's aegis as Best Publications, Inc. This was but one of the many imprints used by Pines in his years of pulp magazine publishing; others included Standard Magazines, Beacon Publications, and Better Publications.

Some of the best-quality mystery fiction, by the most popular authors, including many of the earlier best-sellers, are to be found here. Notable examples are "The Dogs Do Bark" by Jonathan Stagge, "Lady to Kill" by Lester Dent, Dent's "The Endless Night," "Some Buried Caesar" by Rex Stout, "3 Kills for 1" by Cornell Woolrich, "The Diamond Feather" by Helen Reilly, and "Death of a Countess" by Georges Simenon. Among other outstanding authors are Phoebe Atwood Taylor, Octavus Roy Cohen, John D. MacDonald, Hugh Pentecost, and Peter Cheyney.

The full-length novels were accompanied by a lengthy list of departments, true stories, short fiction, verse, quizzes, and fact articles. In "The Reader's Jury" were letters from readers, for the most part complimentary.

At least six issues of a British reprint edition were also published.

Information Sources

INDEX SOURCES: None known.
LOCATION SOURCES: University of California-Los Angeles (1947-1955, 6 issues); private collectors.

Publication History

MAGAZINE TITLE: *Triple Dectective*.
TITLE CHANGES: None.
VOLUME AND ISSUE DATA: Vol. 1, no. 1 (Spring 1947) through at least Vol. 12, no. 1 (Summer 1955); 34 issues (?).
PUBLISHER: Ned L. Pines as Best Publications, Inc., 1125 East Vaile Avenue, Kokomo, Indiana, with editorial offices at 10 East 40th Street, New York, New York.
EDITORS: David X. Manners (1952-1953); Samuel Mines (1954); Morris Ogden Jones (1953-1954); Jim Hendryx, Jr. (1955).
PRICE PER ISSUE: 25 cents.
SIZE AND PAGINATION: 6 5/8'' X 9 7/8''; average 160 pages.
CURRENT STATUS: Discontinued.

TRIPLE DETECTIVE (British)

See TRIPLE DETECTIVE

TUTTER BUGLE, THE

With a warm glow, and perhaps a chuckle, a large part of the over-age-forty male population living today will unhesitatingly nominate the Jerry Todd boy's series books as one of their fondest memories of boyhood reading. Despite the efforts of the Stratemeyer syndicate in promoting Tom Swift and the Hardy Boys, none could compare to the antics of Jerry Todd and his gang in extricating themselves from the hilarious predicaments they found themselves in while being detectives.

The sixteen Jerry Todd books were written by Edward Edson Lee, using the pen name of Leo Edwards. He was also responsible for eleven Poppy Ott books, which generated almost—but not quite—as much interest as those starring Jerry Todd, as well as several other series involving Andy Blake, Trigger Berg, and Tuffy Bean. The last Leo Edwards book (*Jerry Todd's Cuckoo Camp*, Grosset & Dunlap) was published in 1940, and he died four years later.

The Jerry Todd series centered around "Tutter, Illinois," which boasted a newspaper called *The Tutter Bugle*. It is from this that the delightful publication devoted to the books and stories of Leo Edwards takes its name, fittingly enough.

The Tutter Bugle was originated in 1967 by Robert L. Johnson and Julius R. (''Bob'') Chenu and was published, in its early issues, by the Leo Edwards Juvenile Jupiter Detective Association.

An astounding variety of enjoyable data and reminiscences were to be found among its pages. Articles, including many on the author, his home, and visits made there, appeared in every issue. There was commentary on the books and short stories of the author. A wealth of bibliographical data was included. Frequent publication of letters from the readers showed the intense interest, and even the advertisements were fascinating, many being from collectors of the books. And, by no means of least importance, many of the short stories that had appeared in obscure boy's and church papers were reprinted, along with installments of a ''new'' Jerry Todd story (''Jerry Todd, Detective''), written by Bob Chenu.

The issues of *The Tutter Bugle* themselves were in an amazing variety, in all colors (of paper) and of every imaginable size, lending frustration to any who wished to bind them. But the contents more than made up for this as, through the original editor-publishers and later through Jack Tornquist, the issues appeared. But, as with all good things, the publication came to an end in February 1975, leaving a real vacuum among its many boosters.

Information Sources

INDEX SOURCES: None known.
LOCATION SOURCES: Private collectors.

Publication History

MAGAZINE TITLE: *The Tutter Bugle*.
TITLE CHANGES: None.
VOLUME AND ISSUE DATA: Old Series: Vol. 1, no. 1 (December 1, 1967) through Vol. 4, no. 2 (December 1971); 16 issues. New Series: Vol. 1,, no. 1 (April 1, 1973) through Vol. 2, no. 6 (February 1, 1975); 10 issues.
PUBLISHERS: Leo Edwards Juvenile Jupiter Detective Association, P. O. Box 1732, Bisbee, Arizona 85603; later, Jack Tornquist, 4645 Vincent Avenue, South Minneapolis, Minnesota 55410.
EDITORS: Robert L. Johnson and Julius R. Chenu.
PRICE PER ISSUE: $1.00 per year (1967); $1.50 per year (1969); $3.00 per year (1970). New Series: $2.00 per year (1973); $3.00 per year (1974–1975).
SIZE AND PAGINATION: 4-3/4'' X 9'' to 8-1/2'' X 14''; 4–18 pages.
CURRENT STATUS: Discontinued.

TWELVE STORIES DETECTIVE TALES

Twelve Stories Detective Tales, a pulp magazine, commenced March 1942.[1] No other information is available.

Note

1. Title listed as *Twelve Detective Tales* in "Tentative Pulp Checklist" from San Francisco Academy of Comic Art (unpublished manuscript, n.d.).

Information Sources

INDEX SOURCES: None known.
LOCATION SOURCES: Private collectors.

Publication History

MAGAZINE TITLE: *Twelve Stories Detective Tales*.
TITLE CHANGES: None known.
VOLUME AND ISSUE DATA: Vol. 1, no. 1 (March 1942); number of issues and extent unknown.
PUBLISHER: Not known.
EDITOR: Not known.
PRICE PER ISSUE: Not known.
SIZE AND PAGINATION: Not known.
CURRENT STATUS: Discontinued.

TWO-BOOK DETECTIVE MAGAZINE

Two-Book Detective Magazine, a pulp magazine, commenced with the Summer 1933 issue and terminated in 1935. No other information is available.

Information Sources

INDEX SOURCES: None known.
LOCATION SOURCES: University of Califoria–Los Angeles Library (Vol. 1, no. 1, only); private collectors.

Publication History

MAGAZINE TITLE: *Two-Book Detective Magazine*.
TITLE CHANGES: None known.
VOLUME AND ISSUE DATA: Vol. 1, no. 1 (Summer 1933) through Vol. 1, no. 9 (Jannuary 1935); 9 issues.
PUBLISHER: Two-Books Magazine Company, New York, New York.
EDITOR: Not known.
PRICE PER ISSUE: Not known.
SIZE AND PAGINATION: Not known.
CURRENT STATUS: Discontinued.

2-BOOK MYSTERY MAGAZINE

Two issues of a digest-sized magazine titled *2-Book Mystery Magazine* were published in 1946 by Golden Willow Press in attempted competition with others offering full-length novels in magazine form. While emphasizing that two "complete novels" were included, the magazine also included several short stories.

With pulplike illustrations and less than top-name mystery writers, the magazine perished in the flood of similar publications on the newsstands.

Information Sources

INDEX SOURCES: Cook, Michael L. *Monthly Murders*. Westport, Conn.: Greenwood Press, 1982.
LOCATION SOURCES: Private collectors.

Publication History

MAGAZINE TITLE: *2-Book Mystery Magazine*.
TITLE CHANGES: None.
VOLUME AND ISUE DATA: Vol. 1, no. 1 (March 1946) through Vol. 1, no. 2 (June 1946); 2 issues.
PUBLISHER: Frank Armor as Golden Willow Press, Inc., 125 East 46th Street, New York 17, New York.
EDITOR: William Jeffers; Wilton Matthews, managing editor.
PRICE PER ISSUE: 25 cents.
SIZE AND PAGINATION: 5-1/4'' X 7-3/8''; 128 pages.
CURRENT STATUS: Discontinued.

TWO COMPLETE DETECTIVE BOOKS

The first sixteen issues of *Two Complete Detective Books* appeared quarterly between Winter 1939 and Winter 1942. The magazine turned bimonthly in January 1943 with issue number 17 (the editors ceased using the term "volume" after volume 1, number 12) and maintained this regular schedule until issue number 68 (Summer 1951). At that time, it began to be published only three times a year, a schedule maintained until the publication finally folded in Spring 1954 with issue number 76.

The magazine's bimonthly production coincided roughly with the editorship of Jack Byrne (issue numbers 18 through 67), who had replaced Malcolm Reiss. Reiss returned as general manager in November 1944. The editor for the last nine issues, after the departure of Byrne, was Jack O'Sullivan. T. T. Scott remained president throughout the entire life of the magazine. He had also been the earlier general manager.

Two Complete Detective Books magazine is one of the precursors of book clubs like The Detective Book Club (April 1942) in that it afforded the general public current, full-length fiction in the mystery/detective field at a low price. Available by subscription or at the corner newsstand, it included two complete novels in double-column-to-a-page pulp format. The magazine was twenty-five cents per copy from the outset in 1939 through the seventy-first issue and then was increased to thirty-five cents. The original quarterly subscription rate was eighty cents per year and later, when bimonthly, was $1.50, raised to $1.75 with issue number 58.

The avowed purpose of the editors can be found in the first issue:

The task *Two Complete Detective Books* sets for itself is simply this: out of brilliantly jacketed mountains of current detective novels—some excellent, some good, some not-so-good—*Two Complete Detective Books* magazine aims to unearth two gems. It aspires to select a pair of standout books, the two most thrilling, unique, colorful detective-mysteries available. In magazine form these two great books can be had by thousands of detective novel readers who otherwise might never even have heard of them.[1]

The cover of each issue advertised the magazine as a "$4.00 value for 25¢" (later 35¢), referring to the then price of hardcovers. The usual policy was to present books the year following their appearance in hardcover, with acknowledgment to the original publishers. Occasionally, books were reprinted that had appeared two or more years earlier. In one case, at least, a title was printed twice: Robert George Dean's "Murder Makes a Merry Widow" (issues number 1 and number 73). There were also a few cases of novels that were printed in the magazine "in advance of publication in book form." Examples are John Godey's "The Blue Hour" (number 52), Day Keene's "If the Coffin Fits" (number 63), and Wade Miller's Max Thursday novel, "The Corpse Walked Away" (later published in hardcover as *Murder Charge*. Three other novels also fall into this category. They are mentioned separately because they do not appear in Allen J. Hubin's *The Bibliography of Crime Fiction* under these titles: J. F. Hutton's "Seller of Souls" (number 55), Richard Wormser's "The Dead Tycoon" (number 60), and Charlotte Armstrong's "Fatal Lady" (number 61).

Examination, where possible, seems to indicate that the "Complete Novels" were just that—complete and unabridged. There are two notable exceptions, mentioned in the magazine proper: Frederick Davis's "The Cocktail Murders" (number 71) is an abridged version of his novel, *From Lilies in Her Garden Grew,* and "Thursday's Blade" by the same author is also in abridged form (number 76).

The magazine retained the same color cover format for all seventy-six issues, advertising both novels with artwork below the magazine's heading. There had been good interior artwork for each novel, which altered drastically in 1947 when it became cheapened and the interior illustrations seemed almost an afterthought.

Novelists whose work was represented included M. V. Heberden, John Dickson Carr, the Lockridges, George Bagby, Kelley Roos, Cornell Woolrich, Craig Rice, Rex Stout, and Dorothy B. Hughes, among scores of others.

Note

1. Editorial, *Two Complete Detective Books*, Vol. 1, no. 1 (Winter 1939), p. 4.

Information Sources

INDEX SOURCES: None known.
LOCATION SOURCES: University of California–Los Angeles (Vol. 1, no. 1; no. 70, only); private collectors.

Publication History

MAGAZINE TITLE: *Two Complete Detective Books*.
TITLE CHANGES: None.
VOLUME AND ISSUE DATA: Vol. 1, no. 1 (Winter 1939) through no. 76 (no volume designation; Spring 1953; 76 issues.
PUBLISHER: Real Adventures Publishing Co., Inc., 670 Fifth Avenue, New York 19, New York, and later 130 West 42nd Street, New York, New York, and 1658 Summer Street, Stamford, Connecticut.
EDITORS: Malcom Reiss (nos. 1–17); Jack Byrne (nos. 18–67); Jack O'Sullivan (nos. 68–76).
PRICE PER ISSUE: 25 cents (through no. 71); 35 cents (subsequent).
SIZE AND PAGINATION: 6-3/4'' X 9-3/4''; 112–176 pages.
CURRENT STATUS: Discontinued.
—*James R. McCahery*

2 DETECTIVE MYSTERY NOVELS

This publication was a continuation of *Detective Mystery Novel Magazine,** the last issue of which was volume 29, number 3. The title was changed with the next quarterly issue to *2 Detective Mystery Novels* (Winter 1950).[1] As far as is known, five quarterly issues were released under this title, the last issue noted being in 1951. Contents included two long novelettes (the ''novels'' of the title), plus filler material.

The fiction was fast-paced and contemporary, featuring private investigators, police, gangsters, and citizens accidentally involved in criminal violence. The tone was unsentimental and tough-minded, with intense physical movement regularly punctuated by murder.

Writers included familiar names from *Thrilling Detective** and *Popular Detective,** including Fredric Brown, W. T. Ballard, Rufus King, and August Muir.

Note

1. The title was given as *2 Detective Mystery Novels* on the cover and contents page; on the spine, however, it was cited as *Two Detective Mystery Novels*.

Information Sources

INDEX SOURCES: None known.
LOCATION SOURCES: Private collectors.

Publication History

MAGAZINE TITLE: *2 Detective Mystery Novels*.
TITLE CHANGES: Continuation of *Detective Mystery Novel Magazine*.
VOLUME AND ISSUE DATA: Vol. 30, no. 1 (Winter 1950) through Vol. 31, no. 2 (Winter 1951); 5 issues.
PUBLISHER: Standard Magazines, Inc., 10 East 40th Street, New York, New York.
EDITOR: Not known.
PRICE PER ISSUE: 25 cents.
SIZE AND PAGINATION: 6-3/4'' X 9-1/2''; 146 pages.
CURRENT STATUS: Discontinued.
—*Robert Sampson*

TWO-FISTED DETECTIVE STORIES

Tough but luscious females, in situations of greed, brutality, and lust, littered the pages of *Two-Fisted Detective Stories* from its beginning in June 1959; and for a small (digest-size) magazine, it delivered tale after tale, many with surprise endings, of murder and mayhem. They were rough and ruthless, and all were highlighted with episodes of gals having the clothes ripped from them with absolutely no finesse. Sexual contact was intimated, but the final act was never graphically described. Nevertheless, the suggestion was enough for red-blooded readers of the era to keep reading and to keep buying so that the magazine survived for at least eight issues. There were no plots for the reader to unravel; there was never any doubt as to who did it. In most stories, it was done before the reader's eyes. There were no heroes; it was dog eat dog until one came out the winner. And scantily clad females, after having been threatened, beaten, and sometimes subjected to rape or worse, managed to get the upper hand without any help from a good guy. The enticed male, regardless of his motives, was the loser.

In between, however. . . .

With malicious viciousness he grabbed the collar of her dress. The shimmering silken material parted in his hands and ripped downward over her writhing body. Her pointed breasts pushed against her net bra. Her supple hips wriggled under the shining transparency of her brief panties. Big tears oozed out of her eyes and rolled down her cheeks. . . .[1]

She moved closer to him, clad only in panties and brassiere, shaking her hips and flinging her long blonde hair across her face, her blue eyes feverish. Then she had torn the brassiere away and her full milky breasts were bouncing before his eyes .... In a few moments she was naked, twisting before him...in another instant she was flinging her belly toward him repeatedly in a jerky suggestive movement.[2]

Sheila's big breasts strained against her pink net bra. Her firm thigh muscles rippled under the sheen of her tight pink panties. She was built like the proverbial you know what.[3]

The titles, spread all over the covers (which still managed to show a copious amount of unclad flesh), were intended to entrap: "Lust Be My Destiny" (by AmCrockett, November 1959), "Tease of Death" (by Leslie G. Sabo, November 1959), "Drive Her to Hell" (by Bill Ryder, September 1959), and "As Hot as Hell" (by Vic Heston, December 1960), for examples.

The later issues carried advertisements for "male-order" readers, promising to provide "a way with women,"[4] as well as books on how to have sexual fulfillment and how to learn karate. There were no editorials, announcements, columns, or departments.

Notes

1. Bill Ryder, "Drive Her to Hell," *Two-Fisted Detective Stories,* Vol. 1, no. 3 (September 1959), p. 118.
2. Leslie G. Sabo, "The Lusting Ones," *Two-Fisted Detective Stories,* Vol. 2, no. 4 (December 1960), p. 23.
3. Don Unatin, "The Devil is a Dame," *Two-Fisted Detective Stories,* Vol. 2, no. 4 (December 1960), p. 80.
4. Advertisement, *Two-Fisted Detective Stories,* Vol. 2, no. 4 (December 1960), p. 3.

Information Sources

INDEX SOURCES: Cook, Michael L. *Monthly Murders.* Westport, Conn.: Greenwood Press, 1982.
LOCATION SOURCES: Private collectors.

Publication History

MAGAZINE TITLE: *Two-Fisted Detective Stories.*
TITLE CHANGES: None.
VOLUME AND ISSUE DATA: Vol. 1, no. 1 (June 1959) through Vol. 2, no. 4 (December 1960); 8 issues (possibility of two additional issues published).
PUBLISHER: Reese Publishing Co., Inc., 1776 Broadway, New York 19, New York.
EDITOR: Not known.
SIZE AND PAGINATION: 5-1/4" X 7-1/4"; 112–128 pages.
CURRENT STATUS: Discontinued.

U

UNCANNY TALES

If women's lib had flourished in the thirties, one of its prime targets might well have been the Red Circle pulps. Distinguished by the distinctive cover symbol of a red bullet, with the legend, "A Red Circle Magazine," the three weird-menace-type titles under the imprint of Manvis Publications (*Uncanny Tales, Mystery Tales,* and *Real Mystery*) existed, apparently, only to exploit the weaker sex. Going a gasp further than anything similar then on the market, they featured blatant sex-sadism with eroticism spread thick.

In essence, the Red Circle magazines were one magazine with three titles. *Mystery Tales,* appearing first in March 1938, was followed a year later by *Uncanny Tales,* the two of which were published on alternate months. They may as well have been the same title published monthly. When both ceased publication in May 1940, *Real Mystery* had been introduced the previous month to continue with reprints of material from *Mystery Tales* and *Uncanny Tales.*

Martin Goodman, described as having started from a hole in the wall in 1932, was the publisher. Unlike his fellow producers who hinted at the sex issue but actually skirted it, Goodman promoted it heavily, beginning with the first of his terror-mystery publications in 1938, *Mystery Tales.* The style that emerged, and at which his authors became quite adept, was a seemingly fast-developing, compromising situation, overlaid with a heady, intoxicating passion and generally sadistic overtones—but never reaching the consummation stage, naturally.

The following issues of *Mystery Tales,* as well as the alternate-month title commencing in 1939, *Uncanny Tales,* featured scantily clad women on the covers and hinted at lascivious and extramarital relationships with story titles such as "Satan Is My Lover," "Debutantes for the Damned," "Lovely Daughters of Madness," and "Dead Mates for the Devil's Devotees." Further story promotion within the issues continued in this vein: "A Girl Debased, A Girl Who Has Learned the Lure of Things Unspeakable." Naturally, these pulps, with the limitations and restrictions of that particular form of publication, stopped short of fulfilling their promise, but not before they had worked the reader up to a veritable fever pitch of anticipation. Even today, with our more jaded outlook toward shock in fiction, we can recognize the effectiveness of the Red Circle blandishments.

A typical decription by the author for getting things started would go like this: "Her small round breasts, standing pertly upright, seemed to tremble with her emotion." Soon, the hero was trembling himself, his hot, surging ardor ready to explode. But everything quickly boiled away when it was explained that (1) the protagonist had been hypnotized or under the influence of aphrodisiacs (devices used frequently), or (2) drugs and narcotics gave an illusory reality, and nothing really happened after all (a *deus ex machina* found in nearly half the stories in some issues).

But if the passion often was false, the sex-sadism was real. If the intention was to make the reader cringe, and at the same time thrill to the lurid descriptions of female exploitation, then the Red Circles succeeded better than any of their competitors. Definitely, they were not for the squeamish.

Donald Graham best exemplified this approach. He plotted as well (in shorter form) as Norvell Page, another thrill merchant who was the delineator of *The Spider,** perhaps the most believable of the superheroes. Graham's breathless pace, like Page's, left little room for genuine motivation. Yet he generated an acrid, pervasive emotionalism, always on the verge of erupting, whether describing the protagonist caught up in a sexual fantasy or deluded, driven women whipping defenseless members of their own sex.

A high (or low, as the case may be) point in this type of presentation is found in one of Russell Gray's stories ("Fresh Fiancés for the Devil's Daughter"). Gray, whose real name was Bruno Fischer, later went into hardbacked publication and finally into the administrative end of book publishing. His story of the beautiful woman who traps and then tortures the men—and their wives—who spurned her, avidly selecting a lover from her victims to cool off her passions before continuing her cruelties, is one of the raciest stories to be found in the pulps of that era.

While Graham led the charge of the Red Circle shock troops, Ray Cummings and his wife, Gabrielle, brought to full flowering the same publisher's hothouse of erotica. Cummings was one of the deans of science fiction, turning to story telling after serving as a secretary to Thomas A. Edison. So by the late thirties, it seemed he had been around a lifetime, although he was actually in his early fifties at the time. Under the Gabriel Wilson byline, he and his wife turned out several stories of lush young women, actually teenage girls, caught up in the throes of sexual compulsions. They wrote these for the Red Circles, as well as other publications. One of them, from *Mystery Tales*, is typical: a hooded creature creeps into the girl's room at night. "With the touch of his hands, an incomprehensible submission seemed to come over her. . . . She was awake physically. Awake with a woman's desires, although she was only sixteen."[1] And so it went in the Red Circles. Propinquity always turned to lust. . .but the final denouement turned to dust.

A fashion then prevalent with some of the mystery-terror magazines in the use of pseudonyms was also adopted by *Real Mystery, Uncanny Tales,* and *Mystery Tales*: good Anglo-Saxon bylines, such as Paul Howard, Taylor Ward, Alan Blake, and John Trask. Among the more familiar names appearing in the magazines were Arthur J. Burks, Frederick C. Davis, Wayne Rogers, Donald Dale (whose real name, when it was revealed in another publication, Mary Dale Buckner, shocked many readers who considered the weird-menace profession fit only for males), Henry Kuttner, John H. Knox, and Robert Leslie Bellem (the author appearing in the Spicy line who created the popular *Dan Turner, Hollywood Detective**).

On occasion, these authors gave their readers an off-beat story of some substance. But little of any worth emerged from the two-plus years of the three Red Circle publications.

While the contents promoted sadism, interestingly enough, the Red Circle covers took a different tack, for the most part. This is in contrast to Popular Publications, when it went into a similar phase and emphasized sadism on the covers as well. Other than a few flogging-burning oil scenes, the Red Circle covers tended more toward such situations as a ritualistic stabbing of a fair damsel, other-worldly creatures menacing another charmer, and a chained woman watching her deliverer fight the nemesis—with the femininity suitably exposed. Some of the most seductive creatures to grace pulp covers appeared on the Red Circles, thanks in part to Norman Saunders, who was very successful at depicting alluring and full-fleshed heroines.

Among the interior illustrators, Alex Schomberg effectively captured the anguish annd fear of the fair sex facing torture and "a fate worse than death."

It is puzzling why Goodman pushed the sex-sadistic type of story so vigorously in the late thirties, even to including it in two issues of *Marvel Tales*, his science fiction magazine. The timing was wrong. Considerable pressure, in those days, was put on the pulps to change their image. One critic even went so far as to charge that pulp magazines contained "enough illustrated sex perversion to give Kraft-Ebbing the unholy jitters." *Reader's Digest* grew indignant over the "smutty" magazines and their salacious material. Bruno Fischer later commented that as clean-up organizations started throwing their weight, "the artists and writers were instructed to put panties and brassieres on the girls."[2]

The Goodmans, Martin and his brother Abraham, also ran into trouble with the Federal Trade Commission after the first issue of *Real Mystery* appeared in April 1940, containing mostly reprints from *Uncanny Tales* and *Mystery Tales*, retitled to sound like new stories. They and other publishers had to promise to desist from reprinting material unless it was so designated.

With the passing of *Real Mystery* (July 1940), sex-sadism in the pulps came to an end. It flickered briefly again in the early sixties, in *Shock Mystery Tales** and *Web Terror Tales (Saturn Web Magazines of Detective Stories*)*, pale reincarnations that tried to whip up support through suggestive story titles and covers of unclad females being tortured. But the two titles did not last long. In the forties, Goodman had concentrated on comic books, in keeping with other pulp publishers, and developed the popular Marvel line. Later he published men's magazines and finally sold his company.

Notes

1. Gabriel Wilson, "Betrothal of the Thing," *Mystery Tales,* Vol. 3, no. 5 (May 1940), p. 78.

2. Robert Kenneth Jones, *The Shudder Pulps* (West Linn, Oregon: Fax Collectors Editions, 1975), p. 194.

Information Sources

BIBLIOGRAPHY:
Jones, Robert Kenneth. *The Shudder Pulps*. West Linn, Ore.: Fax Collector's Editions, 1975.
————. "The Weird Menace Magazines." *Bronze Shadows*, no. 10 (June 1967): 3–8; no. 11 (August 1967): 7–13; no. 12 (October 1967): 7–10; no. 13 (January 1968): 7–12; no. 14 (March 1968): 13–17; no. 15 (November 1968): 4–8.
INDEX SOURCES: None known.
LOCATION SOURCES: University of California–Los Angeles Library (*Real Mystery*, Vol. 1, no. 1, only); private collectors.

Publication History

MAGAZINE TITLES: (1) *Uncanny Tales,* (2) *Mystery Tales*, (3) *Real Mystery*.
TITLE CHANGES: None.
VOLUME AND ISSUE DATA: (1) *Uncanny Tales*: Vol. 2, no. 6 (first issue, April–May 1939) through Vol. 3, no. 4 (May 1940); 5 issues. (2) *Mystery Tales*: Vol. 2, no. 3 (first issue, March 1938) through Vol. 3, no. 5 (May 1940); 9 issues. (3) *Real Mystery*: Vol. 1, no. 1 (April 1940) through Vol. 1, no. 2 (July 1940); 2 issues.
PUBLISHER: Western Fiction Publishing Co., Inc., 4600 Diversey Avenue, Chicago, Illinois, with editorial offices at RKO Building, New York, New York, and later 330 West 42nd Street, New York, New York.
EDITOR: Robert O. Erisman.
PRICE PER ISSUE: 15 cents.
SIZE AND PAGINATION: 7'' X 10''; 112 pages.
CURRENT STATUS: Discontinued.
—*Robert Kenneth Jones*

UNDERCOVER DETECTIVE

A "Double-Action" group magazine, *Undercover Detective* was published for at least two issues, December 1938 and February 1939. No other information is available.

Information Sources

INDEX SOURCES: None known.
LOCATION SOURCES: University of California–Los Angeles Library (Vol. 1, no. 1, only); private collectors.

Publication History

MAGAZINE TITLE: *Undercover Detective*.
TITLE CHANGES: None known.
VOLUME AND ISSUE DATA: Vol. 1, no. 1 (December 1938) through at least Vol. 1, no. 2 (February 1939); 2 issues.
PUBLISHER: Winford Publications, Inc., 2256 Grove Street, Chicago, Illinois.
EDITOR: Not known.
PRICE PER ISSUE: Not known.
SIZE AND PAGINATION: Not known.
CURRENT STATUS: Discontinued.

UNDERWORLD, THE

The Underworld commenced with the May 1927 issue, which offered "The World's Best Writers—The World's Best Detective and Mystery Stories" and announced "Here's a new magazine built for the lover of thrilling detective and mystery stories. Its contents will include the best stories ever written by the world's most famous authors on actual and imaginative episodes of mystery and crime detection, within and without the law."[1]

Published by J. Thomas Wood, and later as Carwood Publishing Company, Tom Wood was listed as publisher (and later also as editor), but Frank Gruber in *The Pulp Jungle* commented that "He did not really own the magazine. It was owned by a printer in Boston who paid him a monthly pittance for editing it."[2] At one time it was also edited by Harold B. Hersey.[3]

Despite the title, the magazine featured better-than-average, dynamic action-crime stories by authors largely unknown today, although by the end of the magazine's run in 1935, such as Westmoreland Gray and W. T. Ballard were appearing. The title was changed several times, including to *The Underworld Detective* at some point to better reflect the contents. At least one issue of a British reprint edition was also published.

Notes

1. Editorial announcement, *The Underworld*, Vol. 1, no. 1 (May 1927), p. 2.
2. Frank Gruber, *The Pulp Jungle* (Los Angeles: Sherbourne Press, 1967), p. 39.

3. Harold B. Hersey states ". . .I was asked to take over *Underworld Magazine*, a periodical that had been on the newsstands for some time," (circa 1928), *Pulpwood Editor* (New York: Frederick A. Stokes Co., 1937), p. 198.

Information Sources

BIBLIOGRAPHY:
Gruber, Frank. *The Pulp Jungle*. Los Angeles: Sherbourne Press, 1967.
Hersey, Harold B. *Pulpwood Editor*. New York: Frederick A. Stokes Co., 1937.
INDEX SOURCES: None known.
LOCATION SOURCES: University of California–Los Angeles Library (1927–1931, 20 issues); private collectors.

Publication History

MAGAZINE TITLE: *The Underworld*.
TITLE CHANGES: *The Underworld Magazine; The Underworld Detective Magazine; The Underworld Detective*.
VOLUME AND ISSUE DATA: Vol.1, no. 1 (May 1927) through at least Vol. 22, no. 1 (July 1935); 85 issues.
PUBLISHER: J. Thomas Wood as Carwood Publishing Co., Lyon Block, Albany, New York, with editorial offices at 236 West 55th Street, New York, New York; later 29 Worthington Street, Springfield, Massachusetts, with editorial offices at Suite 622, 551 Fifth Avenue, New York, New York.
EDITORS: Tom Chadburn; Harold B. Hersey; Tom Wood.
PRICE PER ISSUE: 25 cents; 15 cents.
SIZE AND PAGINATION: 7'' X 10''; 138–142 pages.
CURRENT STATUS: Discontinued.

UNDERWORLD, THE (British)

See UNDERWORLD, THE

UNDERWORLD DETECTIVE, THE

See UNDERWORLD, THE

UNDERWORLD DETECTIVE MAGAZINE, THE

See UNDERWORLD, THE

UNDERWORLD MAGAZINE, THE

See UNDERWORLD, THE

UNION JACK

See DETECTIVE WEEKLY (British)

UP-TO-DATE BOYS' LIBRARY

This short-lived publication of the turn of the century was a continuation of the *Old Cap. Collier Library*.* The earlier publication had lost its peculiar identity as a series publishing only detective fiction when it began to reprint some of the humor and boys adventure serials from the story-paper, *Golden Hours* (Norman L. Munro, 1888-1904), so the title and format were altered to fit the new purpose. The adventure serials were published in alternating numbers, the second half designated as a sequel to the first half.

Included in the forty numbers of the *Up-To-Date-Boys' Library* were eight stories about Dave Dotson, the name used for both the narrator-detective and the author. The Dave Dotson stories published in the *Old Cap. Collier Library* had been signed by Old Cap. himself, which was only fitting since the character served as an assistant and protégé to that venerable sleuth. All material in the *Up-To-Date-Boys' Library* has been considered to have been reprinted from earlier Norman Munro publications, but prior appearances for the Dave Dotson stories have not been established definitely.

Numbers 41 through 44 of the *Up-To-Date-Boys' Library* were advertised but never published. Number 43 would have been "The Virginia Bond Swindler," a Dave Dotson story. When the *Library* ceased publication, "stories by Dave Dotson. . .and other popular authors" were promised for future issues of *Golden Hours*, but no Dotson stories have been traced to that story-paper.

Information Sources

BIBLIOGRAPHY:

Bragin, Charles. *Dime Novel Bibliography 1860-1928*. Brooklyn, N.Y.: privately printed, 1938.

LeBlanc, Edward T. "Dime Novel Sketches No. 5." *Dime Novel Roundup*, no. 323 (August 15, 1959): 65.

Rogers, Denis R. *Bibliographic Listing of Golden Hours—English Edition*. Fall River, Mass.: Edward T. LeBlanc, 1963.

Steinhauer, Donald R. *Bibliographic Listing of Golden Hours*. Fall River, Mass.: Edward T. LeBlanc, 1962.

INDEX SOURCES: None known.

LOCATION SOURCES: Private collectors.

Publication History

MAGAZINE TITLE: *Up-To-Date Boys' Library*.

TITLE CHANGES: Formerly *Old Cap. Collier Library*.

VOLUME AND ISSUE DATA: No. 1 (September 23, 1898) through no. 40 (June 23, 1900); 40 issues.

PUBLISHER: (Norman L.) Munro's Publishing House, 24 & 26 Vandewater Street, New York, New York.

EDITOR: Not known.

PRICE PER ISSUE: 5 cents.
SIZE AND PAGINATION: 7'' X 10-1/2''; 32 pages.
CURRENT STATUS: Discontinued.
—*J. Randolph Cox*

V

VAMPIRE TALES

See HAUNT OF HORROR, THE

VARIETY DETECTIVE MAGAZINE

Variety Detective Magazine was published by A. A. Wyn as Ace Magazines, Inc., and commenced publication with the August 1938 issue. It ran to at least August 1939 (volume 2, number 2). No other information is available.

Information Sources

INDEX SOURCES: None known.
LOCATION SOURCES: University of California–Los Angeles Library (Vol. 1, nos. 1, 3, 4; Vol. 2, no. 2); private collectors.

Publication History

MAGAZINE TITLE: *Variety Detective Magazine.*
TITLE CHANGES: None known.
VOLUME AND ISSUE DATA: Vol. 1, no. 1 (August 1938) through at least Vol. 2, no. 2 (August 1939); 6 issues.
PUBLISHER: Ace Magazines, Inc., 29 Worthington Street, Springfield, Massachusetts.
EDITOR: Not known.
PRICE PER ISSUE: Not known.
SIZE AND PAGINATION: Not known.
CURRENT STATUS: Discontinued.

VERDICT

With the success of the still-young *Manhunt** promised, Michael St. John launched a similar magazine in June 1953 titled *Verdict*. It was off to an auspicious beginning with the first installment of a Rex Stout story, "Fer-de-Lance," which continued in each issue of the total four issues published. Other well-known writers appearing in *Verdict* were Raymond Chandler, Henry Kane, Craig Rice, Fredric Brown, Cornell Woolrich, Bruno Fischer, Dorothy Hughes, Frank Kane, Damon Runyon, Anthony Boucher, William Irish, Evan Hunter, James M. Cain, and George Harmon Coxe, among others, all comprising what had to be an all-star lineup of talent.

The great number of competing magazines on the newsstands appears to have been the only reason that the magazine did not survive. St. John made another attempt in 1956, reviving the magazine under a slightly different title (*Verdict Crime Detective Magazine**), but this also suffered a short run.

A British edition using the same original title was commenced in August 1953, publishing in its early issues reprints from the U.S. edition and in its later issues publishing reprints from another U.S. magazine, *Pursuit.**

Information Sources

INDEX SOURCES: Cook, Michael L. *Monthly Murders*. (including British editions). Westport, Conn.: Greenwood Press, 1982.
LOCATION SOURCES: Private collectors.

Publication History

MAGAZINE TITLE: *Verdict*.
TITLE CHANGES: None.
VOLUME AND ISSUE DATA: Vol. 1, no. 1 (June 1953) through Vol. 1, no. 4 (September 1953); 4 issues.
PUBLISHER: Michael St. John as Flying Eagle Publications, Inc., an affiliate of St. John Publishing Co., 545 Fifth Avenue, New York 17, New York.
EDITOR: Not known.
PRICE PER ISSUE: 35 cents.
SIZE AND PAGINATION: 5-1/4" X 7-5/8"; 128 pages.
CURRENT STATUS: Discontinued.

British edition

MAGAZINE TITLE: *Verdict*.
TITLE CHANGES: None.
VOLUME AND ISSUE DATA: Vol. 1, no. 1 (August 1953) through Vol. 1, no. 7 (June–July 1954); 7 issues.
PUBLISHER: Monthly Magazines, Ltd., 109 Great Russell Street, London, W.C.1, England.
EDITOR: Not known.

PRICE PER ISSUE: 1 shilling 6 pence (until May 1954); 2 shillings.
SIZE AND PAGINATION: 5-1/4'' X 7-1/2''; 128 pages.
CURRENT STATUS: Discontinued.

VERDICT (British)

See VERDICT

VERDICT CRIME DETECTION MAGAZINE

Verdict Crime Detection Magazine was one of the better-quality crime-sus-pense-adventure magazines of the 1950s, but it was also one of the shortest-lived titles, seeing but two issues.

Michael St. John, under Flying Eagle Publications, had found great success in his *Manhunt,* * which had been started in 1953. *Verdict Crime Detection Magazine* was nearly a twin sister, published by St. John under a different firm name, Secret Life Publications. An earlier version had been tried under the name of *Verdict** in 1953 and had survived four issues.

Verdict Crime Detection Magazine was commenced with the August 1956 issue. While featuring rough, tough, hard-boiled fiction, the majority of the stories were reprinted, some from earlier mainstream publications. The featured story in the first issue was by Evan Hunter, "Get Out of Town!" Hunter was well known, including for stories in *Manhunt*; this was a story of a sailor on liberty in a nightclub in Panama City. A novelette, "Two Kinds of Murder," by Richard Deming, had earlier been published by the McCall Corporation as "Two Tins of Murder." Craig Rice's "Hanged Him in the Mornin'" was a reprint of a 1943 story, "His Heart Could Break." And the other eight stories, by writers such as Hunt Collins, Lawrence G. Blochman, Q. Patrick, and Allan Vaughan Elston, were all reprinted from other sources.

The second issue of *Verdict Crime Detection Magazine* did not appear until five months later, January 1957. The cover featured a James M. Cain story, "Tiger in the Kitchen" (original title, "The Baby in the Icebox"). This was accompanied by a novelette, "The Restless Corpse," by Norman Matson (orig-inal title, "Remains to be Found"), with short stories by William H. McMasters, Henry Slesar, C. S. Forester, David X. Manners, and others.

With realistic, fast-moving fiction by top writers, many in the hard-boiled tradition, there seems to be no clear reason why this magazine was discontinued. That there were sales difficulties from the first is evident by the lapse of time between the first and second issue. This did not lend credence to the firm trying to sell subscriptions on a twelve-issue basis. And the covers were most unat-tractive. The same cover design was used for both issues, but with different color background—a rather plain cover dominated by the list of contents, relieved only by a black-and-white caricature of a man with a rifle, his back turned and head lowered. Distribution and display problems are sure to have plagued this magazine, and this, coupled with the lack of a more pictorial cover, and perhaps the heavy reprint schedule, hastened its demise.

There were no editorials, announcements, or filler material, and no advertising except on the back cover. *Verdict Crime Detection Magazine* died quietly, without fanfare.

Information Sources

INDEX SOURCES: Cook, Michael L. *Monthly Murders*. Westport, Conn.: Greenwood Press, 1982.
LOCATION SOURCES: Private collectors.

Publication History

MAGAZINE TITLE: *Verdict Crime Detection Magazine*.
TITLE CHANGES: None.
VOLUME AND ISSUE DATA: Vol. 1, no. 1 (August 1956) through Vol. 2, no. 1 (January 1957); 2 issues.
PUBLISHER: Michael St. John as Secret Life Publications, Inc. (first issue) and Flying Eagle Publications (second issue), 545 Fifth Avenue, New York 17, New York.
EDITORS: Walter R. Schmidt, editorial director; William Manners, managing editor; N. F. King, associate editor.
PRICE PER ISSUE: 35 cents.
SIZE AND PAGINATION: 5-1/2'' X 7-5/8''; 128 pages.
CURRENT STATUS: Discontinued.

VICE SQUAD DETECTIVE

One issue of *Vice Squad Detective*, a pulp magazine, was published in 1934. No other information is available.

Information Sources

INDEX SOURCES: None known.
LOCATION SOURCES: Private collectors.

Publication History

MAGAZINE TITLE: *Vice Squad Detective*.
TITLE CHANGES: None known.
VOLUME AND ISSUE DATA: One issue, 1934; month unknown.
PUBLISHER: Not known.
EDITOR: Not known.
PRICE PER ISSUE: Not known.
SIZE AND PAGINATION: Not known.
CURRENT STATUS: Discontinued.

W

WAR THRILLER

See THRILLER, THE (BRITISH)

WEB DETECTIVE STORIES

See SATURN WEB MAGAZINE OF DETECTIVE STORIES

WEB TERROR STORIES

See SATURN WEB MAGAZINE OF DETECTIVE STORIES

WEIRD MYSTERY

In possibly an attempt to emulate the nostalgic success of *Weird Tales,** a quarterly digest-size magazine was introduced in Fall 1970 by Ultimate Publishing Company offering tales that will take you to your wildest dreams. Featuring a mixture of macabre mystery and the supernatural, the magazine existed for four issues and included such well-known authors as Arthur Porges, Robert Bloch, Marion Zimmer Bradley, Richard O. Lewis, and William P. McGivern. The last two issues included filler items of like genre.

Information Sources

INDEX SOURCES: Cook, Michael L. *Monthly Murders*. Westport, Conn.: Greenwood Press, 1982.

LOCATION SOURCES: Private collectors.

Publication History

MAGAZINE TITLE: *Weird Mystery*.
TITLE CHANGES: None.
VOLUME AND ISSUE DATA: No. 1 (Fall 1970) through no. 4 (Summer 1971); 4
    issues.
PUBLISHER: Ultimate Publishing Co., Box 7, Oakland Gardens, Flushing, New York
    11364.
EDITOR: Not known.
PRICE PER ISSUE: 50 cents (nos. 1–3); 60 cents.
SIZE AND PAGINATION: 5-1/4'' X 7-5/8''; 130 pages.
CURRENT STATUS: Discontinued.

WEIRD TALES

Although this is not properly a mystery, detective, or espionage-oriented magazine, there is at least a thin line of distinction between some mystery fiction and that in the field of the macabre and supernatural. It would be remiss to discard entirely at least a brief mention of what was perhaps the most important magazine published in the latter field.

The first issue of *Weird Tales*, published by Rural Publications, Inc., appeared on the newsstands in March 1923 at twenty-five cents a copy, then a high price for a pulp magazine. Beginning with this issue, the magazine introduced a serial story by Otis Adelbert Kline, and this practice of continuing stories from one issue to the next became a standard feature until approximately 1940. The third issue, May 1923, was published in "bedsheet" format, 8-1/2'' X 11'', with a decreased number of pages. Despite plunging into debt by the end of the first year, the magazine continued to survive and became the longest running of all such magazines, publishing a total of 279 issues before finally being discontinued in 1954.

Several attempts to revive it did not succeed beyond a few issues.

And although the mystery-detective element was almost completely lacking, and so it cannot be properly classified as such, *Weird Tales* remains *the* classic magazine in the pulp field and for its peripheral interest must be noted.

Information Sources

BIBLIOGRAPHY:
Weinberg, Robert. *The Weird Tales Story*. West Linn, Ore.: Fax Collector's Editions,
    1977.
INDEX SOURCES: Cockcroft, T.G.L. *Index to the Weird Fiction Magazines*. 2 vols.
    Wellington, New Zealand: John Milne Ltd., 1962, 1964.

LOCATION SOURCES: University of California–Los Angeles Library (1923–1949 complete); private collectors.

Publication History

MAGAZINE TITLE: *Weird Tales*.

TITLE CHANGES: None.

VOLUME AND ISSUE DATA: Vol. 1, no. 1 (March 1923) through Vol. 46, no. 4 (September 1954); 279 issues. (*Note*: Several revival attempts not included in this data.)

PUBLISHERS: Rural Publications, Inc., Chicago, Illinois (until April 1924); Popular Fiction Co., Baldwin Building, Indianapolis, Indiana, later Holliday Building, Indianapolis, Indiana, 3810 North Broadway, Chicago, Illinois, and 840 North Michigan Avenue, Chicago, Illinois (until 1938); Weird Tales, Inc., 9 Rockefeller Plaza, New York, New York.

EDITORS: Edwin Baird (through May-July 1924 issue); Farnsworth Wright (through March 1940); Dorothy McIlwaite (to last issue, September 1954). Associate editors: Henry Aveline Perkins (1940–1942); Lamont Buchanan (1942–1949).

PRICE PER ISSUE: 25 cents (first 12 issues); 50 cents (May–July 1924); 25 cents (through August 1939); 15 cents (through July 1947); 20 cents (through March 1949); 25 cents (through July 1953); 35 cents (subsequent issues).

SIZE AND PAGINATION: 6-1/2" X 9-1/2" (through April 1923); 8-1/2" X 11-1/2" (through September 1925); 6-1/2" X 9-1/2" (through August 1930); 6-5/8" X 9-3/4" (through July 1953); 5-3/8" X 7-5/8" (subsequent issues); 192 pages; 144 pages (commencing October 1925); 160 pages (commencing January 1939); 128 pages (commencing September 1939); 112 pages (commencing May 1943); 96 pages (commencing May 1944); 128 pages (commencing September 1953).

CURRENT STATUS: Discontinued.

WEIRD TERROR TALES

Between 1963 and early 1971, a number of low-budget, mostly reprint, digest-size magazines were published by Health Knowledge, Inc., a subsidiary of the Acme News Company. These titles were bimonthlies, two titles appearing each month; but toward the middle of 1969, the distribution problem had aggravated to the point where all were changed to quarterlies in order to give them a better chance of newsstand life. That left holes in the schedule, which were filled with new titles, *Weird Terror Tales* being among them.

While *Magazine of Horror** included a broad spectrum of weird, horror, science fiction, and strange stories, and *Startling Mystery Stories** (both Health Knowledge titles) concentrated on mystery, both natural and supernatural, *Weird Terror Tales* was designed to the terror type of story in weird, supernatural, or occult form. It was therefore marginal as a mystery or crime magazine, but such stories did appear. Because of its short life, it is possible to examine the contents of each of the three issues.

The first issue was dated Winter 1969–1970 inside; on the cover, you saw only "Winter no. 1." The cover was a reprinted, black-and-white drawing on a black background, by Virgil Findlay. Any inside artwork was a reprint of the art that had appeared when the story was first published.

Many, if not most, of the stories in the old issues of *Weird Tales** (between 1925 and 1938) and the Clayton *Strange Tales of Mystery and Terror** (early 1930s) were in the public domain. A letter to the Library of Congress certified whether copyright had been renewed. If the authors were still alive and findable, or had an agent, then we at Health Knowledge, Inc., made a token payment; otherwise, the stories were free. We were open to new short-short stories and short stories, but my editor's budget rarely allowed me to purchase new novelettes at one cent per word, the going rate for all new material.

The first issue contained "Dead Legs" (a weird-crime story) by Edmond Hamilton; "The House and the Brain" (weird-mystery classic) by Edward Bulwer-Lytton; "Ms. Found in a Bottle" by Edgar Allan Poe; "The Beast of Averoigne" (weird mystery) by Clark Ashton Smith; "The Whispering Thing" (new weird mystery) by Eddy C. Bertin; and "The Dead-Alive" (science fiction mystery) by Nat Schachner and Arthur L. Zagat. The Bertin story was translated from the original Dutch by the author; the Hamilton piece was a reprint from *Strange Tales*; and the Lovecraft, Smith, and Schachner-Zagat stories came from *Weird Tales*. All of the magazine reprints came from issues earlier than 1940.

A printer's strike, after the cover had been rolled, delayed the first issue so long that the publisher had to date the second issue as Summer 1970. It, too, had a reprinted, black-and-white, Virgil Finlay drawing on the cover, this time with a green background. There were no "classic" reprints in number 2, "The Dead Walk Softly" (weird mystery) by Sewell Peaseless Wright from *Strange Tales*; "The Shadow on the Sky" by August Derleth, also from *Strange Tales*; "The Laundromat" (new weird mystery) by Dick Donley; "The Man Who Never Came Back" (a weird African mystery) by Pearl Norton Swet; and "The Web of Living Death" by Seabury Quinn. The last two stories were from *Weird Tales*, 1932 and 1935.

The third, and final, issue was dated Fall 1970, and the cover had a new black-and-white drawing by Richard Schmand on an orange background. Contents were: "Stragella" (vampire mystery) by Hugh B. Cave; "The Girdle" (werewolf tale) by Joseph McCord; "The Trap" (weird mystery-mirror tale) by Henry S. Whitehead; "The Church Stove at Raebrudafisk" (crime; weird but not supernatural) by G. Appleby Terrill; "The Cellar Room" (new weird mystery) by Steffan B. Aletti; and "The Wheel" (torture-revenge tale) by H. Warner Munn. Again, *Strange Tales* and *Weird Tales* were the sources for reprints, all from issues of the 1920s and 1930s.

The second and third issues ran letters (both of praise and fault-finding) from the readers, and all three had editorials designed to arouse comment. There were also book and fan-magazine reviews in the second and third issues.

A fourth issue was prepared and made ready for printing but then was cancelled. Acme News went into the kind of bankruptcy in 1970 that left the owner in possession; Country Wide Publications took over the magazines. Since Country Wide had a large comics line that included the titles *Weird* and *Terror*, they decided that a magazine with the title *Weird Terror Tales* would cause too much confusion in record keeping. The other reprint titles were continued for a time, though.

Information Sources

INDEX SOURCES: Cook, Michael L. *Monthly Murders*. Westport, Conn.: Greenwood Press, 1982.
Marshall, Gene, and Carl F. Waedt. "An Index to the Health Knowledge Magazines." *The Science-Fiction Collector*, no. 3 (1977): 3–42.
LOCATION SOURCES: Private collectors.

Publication History

MAGAZINE TITLE: *Weird Terror Tales*.
TITLE CHANGES: None.
VOLUME AND ISSUE DATA: Vol. 1, no. 1 (Winter 1969–1970) through Vol. 1, no. 3 (Fall 1970); 3 issues.
PUBLISHER: Health Knowledge, Inc., 140 Fifth Avenue, New York, New York.
EDITOR: Robert A. W. Lowndes.
PRICE PER ISSUE: 50 cents (no. 1); 60 cents (nos. 2–3).
SIZE AND PAGINATION: 7-1/4" X 5-1/2"; 130 pages.
CURRENT STATUS: Discontinued.
—*Robert A. W. Lowndes*

WHISPERER, THE

In 1936, Street & Smith, anxious to duplicate the entrenched successes of their *Doc Savage** and *The Shadow Magazine** publications, and finding it economically unfeasible to issue *Doc Savage* twice a month, hired author Laurence Donovan, then writing Doc Savage novels for the unrealized increase in frequency, Donovan would write the lead novels for two new magazines, *The Skipper** and *The Whisperer*, meant to be *Doc Savage* and *Shadow* take-offs, respectively.

The Whisperer was created by Business Manager Henry W. Ralston, who was responsible for Street & Smith's formative single-character magazines, and edited by John L. Nanovic, who edited the bulk of those same magazines for the firm. Not content with simply doing another *Shadow, The Whisperer* was created as a more adult entry into the character magazine field, much like a rival, *The Spider,** and to this end, *Spider* cover artist John Newton Howitt was commissioned to do *The Whisperer* covers, most of which showed the grim gray face of The Whisperer looking down upon a crime scene.

The Whisperer was really James "Wildcat" Gordon, the tough, brutal police commissioner of an unnamed city. Gordon was not cast in the traditional heroic mold. He was a short, stocky veteran of World War I who wore his red hair cropped short under a battered army campaign hat. His clothes were outrageously colorful, as was his no-nonsense personality. Gordon was a firm believer in law and order and in cutting through political red tape, which he did. As The Whisperer, however, he was a personality who was the opposite of himself—a small, wispy man in gray who spoke in a hissing whisper caused by special dental plates which changed the shape of his jaw and disguised both his face and voice. The Whisperer was also known as D. Smith, an underworld character. He carried two silenced automatics and, like The Shadow, shot to kill. He wore a strange round hat. He chuckled eerily. Most of The Shadow borrowings, however, were muted.

In the first novel, "The Dead Who Talked," The Whisperer had been operating for some time, inspired by political corruption and the death of his policeman father. He was aided by Deputy Commissioner Richard "Quick Trigger" Traeger, who had invented the dental plates and spent most of the series regretting it. His daughter, Tiny Traeger, was interested in Gordon, but Gordon considered her too young for him. She was forever getting into trouble to prove him wrong.

Conflict was provided by liberal Mayor Van Royston and obnoxious Deputy Commissioner Henry Bolton, neither of whom had any use for Wildcat's hard-fisted ways and less use for The Whisperer (considered by many to be a crook). Detective Sergeant Tom Thorson and Judge Patrick Kyley were unofficial supporters of Wildcat's policies. The last cast member was a scotch-terrier named Brian Boru, owned by The Whisperer.

Laurence Donovan's novels, written under the house name of Clifford Goodrich, eschew the more fantastic elements of The Shadow and The Spider. No mysterious masterminds challenge The Whisperer. No masked criminals going by colorful aliases. Instead, The Whisperer deals with underworld thugs, racketeers, and dishonest politicians. The world of organized crime, with its seedy dens and swank nightclubs, was played up. For pulp fiction of this type, these were brutal, uncompromising stories of a type for which Laurence Donovan's gritty style was particularly suited. In a departure from Street & Smith taboos, criminals could be of either sex, and Donovan was not adverse to portraying the underworld moll or female killer, as he did in "Murder Queens."

If there was a theme to The Whisperer novels, it was the inroads that crime made into daily life. "The Football Racketeers" was about crime in professional sports. "Murders in Crazyland" dealt with criminality in an amusement park. "Murder on the Line" focused on the trucking industry, and "The Lost Face Murders" concentrated on the medical profession. In a nod to a Shadow tradition, there were occasional novels set in Chinatown, where The Whisperer was respected as a force for good (among them, "The Red Hatchets" and "Murder Brotherhood"). Throughout these novels, The Whisperer's attitude toward criminals remained constant and unswerving, as exemplified in, and by the title of, "Kill Them First!"

Donovan wrote fifteen Whisperer novels before the magazine was cancelled with the December 1937 issue, leaving one novel, "The Crime Prophet," unpublished. The magazine was suspended in a purge of titles initiated when the company was reorganized and not necessarily because of lagging sales. "The Crime Prophet" was revised and published in novelette form under the Jack Storm house name in the January 1941 issue of *Clues Detective (Clues*)*, with all Whisperer characters deleted or altered unrecognizably. In 1942, Donovan revised the same novel as a Black Bat story entitled "The Murder Prophet," and it appeared in the September issue of *Black Book Detective Magazine.**

Between 1937 and 1940, The Whisperer ran as a series of short stories in *The Shadow*. Only two of these, "Bullet Bait" and "Boulevard of Death," were by Donovan. The remainder were the work of a newspaperman, Alan Hathway, later to gain fame as the editor of *Newsday*. Hathway's Whisperer was outwardly no different than Donovan's, but the stories tended to be more juvenile. They were not uninteresting, however. Among the better were "The Vampire Murders," "Arrowhead," and "Ex-Cop" (in which The Whisperer battles The Black Beetle). One Whisperer novelette, "The White Mandarins," appeared in *Crime Busters,** June 1939, as a test. A Chinatown adventure, it is one of the best of the shorter stories.

Reader interest was evidently strong because within a few months the character dropped out of *The Shadow,* and *The Whisperer* magazine was revived (the only character magazine to have that honor) with the October 1940 issue. Initial response to *The Avenger** may have had something to do with the revival. In any case, the magazine began again with issue number 1, with no mention of the earlier incarnation. Alan Hathway contributed the character but with significant changes, perhaps prompted by the general similarity between The Avenger and The Whisperer. Both were gray-clad, white-haired crime fighters with colorless eyes.

But, without explanation, The Whisperer was changed. He now wore black, and he taped his eyes to give them an Oriental slant. Green contact lenses and black powder changed his eye and hair colors. The dental plates and silenced automatics were still in evidence, though he now carried scientific gadgets very much out of *Doc Savage*. In fact, hedging bets, Editor John Nanovic appears to have infused quite a number of Doc Savage elements into the series (among them a new character, Slug Minor, a colorful giant of a man who talked like a dictionary). Missing from the series were Mayor Van Royston, Thorsen, Judge Kyley, and Brian Boru, as well as Donovan's gritty concern with the underside of society. Hathway's novels are more fantastic and improbable.

The first, "The Trail of Death," is an undistinguished murder mystery set in New York, now firmly established as the locale of the series. Inasmuch as Hathway had been writing Doc Savage novels just prior to doing the new Whisperer novels, it is not surprising that his characters were colorfully unlikely, in the Lester Dent mold. The Whisperer took on a new alias, that of Winky Withers, and maintained his D. Smith alter ego, going by the name Dunk Smith now. Wildcat Gordon was inexplicably younger, dressed better, and his World War I background was replaced by a past stint with the FBI.

Of the various new novels, the more interesting were "The Chariot of Fire," "The Secret Menace," and "The Dyak Murders." Evil cults and organizations, as well as Fifth Column activities, fuel many plots. The Chinatown adventure tradition continues in "Brotherhood of Death." An occasional criminal master-mind surfaces, as in "Nihil," "Doctor of Retribution," and The Jackal in "Killer From Nowhere."

On the whole, Hathway's Whisperer, while more interesting than that of Donovan, suffered from the more juvenile approach and the striking softening of the character's toughness. However, both writers found to their dismay that the chuckling, soft-voiced Whisperer was a difficult character to portray as a figure of vengeance, and Wildcat Gordon invariably eclipsed him. This was a problem neither cover artist could quite handle, either, and Hubert Rogers's covers for the second series are as weak as Howitt's. The Donovan novels, in the final analysis, are vastly superior, if only because of their mature tone.

The short stories in the back of both series of *The Whisperer* were the work of the same pool of writers. These included Edward V. Burkholder, Norman A. Daniels, William G. Bogart, and others. Two series characters ran in the back of the first version: Theodore Tinsley's Bulldog Black novelettes and Frank Gruber's Jim Strong, Racket Man.

The final postscript to the series was the novel "Heritage of Death," which was scheduled for the June 1942 issue but not published. It was revised and shortened, like Donovan's "Crime Prophet," and published in *The Shadow*, August 1943, as "Murder at Flood Tide." All Whisperer characters were altered beyond recognition. However, the complete original version survived and will be published by Odyssey Publications in the near future.

Information Sources

BIBLIOGRAPHY:
McConnell, Arn. "The Case of Commissioner James Gordon." *The World Atlas,* Vol. 1, no. 3 (Fall 1977): 14–18.
Murray, Will. "The Many Faces of The Whisperer." *Pulp*, no. 7 (Spring 1975): 3–18.
———. "The Secret Kenneth Robesons." *Duende*, Vol. 1, no. 2 (Winter 1977): 3–27.
INDEX SOURCES: None known.
LOCATION SOURCES: University of California–Los Angeles Library (Vol. 1, no. 1, only); private collectors.

Publication History

MAGAZINE TITLE: *The Whisperer*.
TITLE CHANGES: None.
VOLUME AND ISSUE DATA: First series: Vol. 1, no. 1 (October 1936) through Vol. 3, no. 2 (December 1937); 14 issues. Second Series: Vol. 1, no. 1 (October 1940) through Vol. 2, no. 4 (April 1942); 10 issues.
PUBLISHER: Street & Smith Publications, Inc., 79 Seventh Avenue, New York, New York.
EDITOR: John L. Nanovic.

PRICE PER ISSUE: 10 cents.
SIZE AND PAGINATION: 6-5/8'' X 9-7/8''; 6-3/8'' X 9-5/8''; 112 pages.
CURRENT STATUS: Discontinued.
—*Will Murray*

WHODUNIT?

Whodunit? was an unusual, indeed, unique magazine because of its stated policy of using only stories with surprise endings. "Every story in these pages," said Editor Douglas Stapleton, "will have one aim: to fool and trick you."[1]

The promise was kept in the first and only issue (October 1967). In Phelps Goodhue's "Assassin," for example, an unnamed, strutting actor plots with a general and a politician to assassinate President Lincoln; as the actor pauses that night at Ford's Theater to gloat over his coming fame, John Wilkes Booth rushes past him and shoots the president. In Carol Sturmond's "The Man Who Cheated the Devil," a man who has just sold his soul for youth and happiness as long as the world exists, looks out the window to see the sun going nova. . . .

Also unusual and (at the time) unique was the featured story, "Ransom for a Rogue!", a novelette by Douglas and Dorothy Stapleton. While Ellery Queen would stop his early novels near the end to challenge the reader to identify the murderer from the clues given, the Stapletons stopped their story for every major clue and issued a challenge: Which ransom note is the genuine one? The one instructing that the ransom be sent to the mission or the one directing the ransom to the housing development? If you think it's the former, turn to page so-and-so; if the latter, to page thus-and-thus. Remember, if your deduction from the clues you have seen are wrong, a child may die. The story is tricky and ingeniously plotted. And the story has another Ellery Queen touch: its detective hero is Douglas Stapleton himself.

Despite the magazine's title, only one of its ten stories (and one more in comic-book form, also featuring Stapleton as the hero) are whodunits. Of the rest, two are mainstream, one fantasy, and the others crime stories. There are no major authors, but all the stories are at least good; the general level of quality is comparable to an issue of *Alfred Hitchcock's Mystery Magazine** of this period. The production values are only adequate; the cover, consisting largely of the title repeated five times, is cluttered; and the art, despite many two-color interiors, is weak.

Nevertheless, the magazine's editorial policy of surprise endings makes it worth reading. Though the stories vary in tone (some are grim, such as Mary Linn Roby's "The Practical Way," in which a farm woman in the midst of canning preserves has to dispose somehow of a dead body), the editor's policy of "let's outwit the reader" gives the magazine a gamelike, enjoyable appeal that its stories would not have if published elsewhere. It deserved a better fate.

Note

1. Editorial announcement, *Whodunit?*, Vol. 1, no. 1 (October 1967), reverse front cover.

Information Sources

INDEX SOURCES: Cook, Michael L. *Monthly Murders*. Westport, Conn.: Greenwood Press, 1982.
LOCATION SOURCES: Private collectors.

Publication History

MAGAZINE TITLE: *Whodunit?*
TITLE CHANGES: None.
VOLUME AND ISSUE DATA: Vol. 1, no. 1 (October 1967; on contents page, "September–October 1976"); 1 issue.
PUBLISHER: I.D. Publications, Inc., 8383 Sunset Boulevard, Hollywood, California.
EDITOR: Douglas Stapleton.
PRICE PER ISSUE: 50 cents.
SIZE AND PAGINATION: 5-1/4" X 7-1/2"; 112 pages.
CURRENT STATUS: Discontinued.
—*Frank D. McSherry, Jr.*

WITCHCRAFT & SORCERY

With the purchase of *Coven 13** by Fantasy Publishing Company, Inc., a continuation of the magazine was effected but with some changes. The last issue of *Coven 13* was dated March 1970; under the new ownership, the numbering was continued, and the first "new" magazine appeared dated January-February 1971 in an 8-1/2" X 11" format. The title carried the name "Coven 13" in the upper left corner, as a subtitle, for two issues, but the new title was prominently displayed in two colors, green and red.

The new editor, Gerald W. Page, informed the readers that the issue had been prepared in the old digest-size format but that the distributor suggested the larger size. The only major change predicted was that where formerly some stories were "light tongue in cheek fantasy," now stories would be more oriented to the weird and the supernatural. The editor advised that he preferred to think of this now as a "great new magazine."

In essence, there was little change. A letters column, verse, and nonfiction features continued to appear. Succeeding issues did include a predominance of witchcraft and weird fiction, but some fantasy tales were provided. Except in the peripheral sense, there is little to recommend here for the crime-mystery buff.

Information Sources

INDEX SOURCES: None known.

LOCATION SOURCES: Private collectors.

Publication History

MAGAZINE TITLE: *Witchcraft & Sorcery*.
TITLE CHANGES: None (though a continuation of *Coven 13*.
VOLUME AND ISSUE DATA: Vol. 1, no. 5 (first issue, January-February 1971) through
    Vol. 1, no. 10 (n.d. [1974]); 6 issues.
PUBLISHER: William L. Crawford as Fantasy Publishing Co., Inc., 1855 West Main
    Street, Alhambra, California 91801.
EDITOR: Gerald W. Page; Susan Burke, assistant editor.
PRICE PER ISSUE: 60 cents (nos. 5–8); 75 cents (no. 9); $1.00 (no. 10).
SIZE AND PAGINATION: 8-1/2'' X 11''; 32–64 pages.
CURRENT STATUS: Discontinued.

WIZARD, THE

For adventures stressing chicanery, cunning, cozening, fraud, mendacity, misrepresentation, perfidy, and trickery (not to mention duplicity, dissembling, dissimulation, and deceit), the sextet of novels featuring The Wizard/Cash Gorman are unparalleled.

The line of print below the magazine's title on the cover of the first issue (October 1940) reads ''Adventures in Money Making,'' while the opening blurb billed the first novel as an adventure of ''a musketeer with weapons more formidable than guns; a quick wit and the courage to use it daringly.''[1] The editor's page of this issue amplified this by adding that Cash Gorman has ''an unscrupulous conscience where the forces of lawlessness and dishonor are concerned.''[2]

The same editorial column further stated that Cash Gorman was no modern Robin Hood taking pelf from the plundered to spread among the oppressed. ''Cash is in there pitching for and against the odds for the sake of the odds themselves. . . . He does not rise to the bait of money for the sake of turning a pretty profit on anything which happens along. . . .''[3] He does not go in ''for conservative, well-heeled investments. He likes excitement for his dollars, especially if the opposition appears anxious to push him around as well as to fleece him.'' As Cash, himself, put it, ''Oh, I'm just a kind of financial freebooter. I go around disguised as a sheep, the better to put the bite on wolves.''[4]

If there was one thing Cash Gorman relished more than life itself, it was his reputation for being a smooth operator to whom the angles were as obvious as they were to the designer. People always seemed to live up to his worst expectations, and to him, swindling swindlers was one of the most entertaining methods imaginable for turning a dishonest penny into an honest dollar.

As always in the character pulps, he had assistants. Jimmy Ranger was the house detective at the hotel where most of the action in the first novel took place. Before the end of the story, he had entered the employment of Thomas Jefferson ''Cash'' Gorman. Bobbie Lane, rescued from a job with a swindler, had a major part in the first novel and a minor one in the second. Martin Rossi was another, mainly off-scene, personage in the series. He was a San Francisco banker-friend. Phineas T. Gardiner was a New York financier who filled the role of "friendly rival" to Gorman.

By the end of the thirties and the beginning of the forties, the censors were in full cry against the pulps. In defense, publishers began looking for stories that would be less offensive to the censors while still having sufficient mass appeal to be profitable. The weird-menace and Spicy (for example, *Spicy Detective**) magazines were the first to go, but all pulps felt the hot breath of the reformers, who were convinced that all were instruments of depravity that doomed readers to perdition.

The Wizard, later titled *Cash Gorman*, seems to have been a knee-jerk reflex to this situation, but it failed to attract sufficient audience approval to sustain itself. This is not to say that the fault was with the stories. It was simply that the pulp readership was changing. The comics were beginning to infiltrate the newsstands and take over the readers. In less than a decade, they and the paperbacks would have administered the *coup de grace* to the pulps.

The Cash Gorman stories certainly deemphasized violence, even if they did not entirely eliminate it. Instead of violence, they stressed the risks and perils of high finance, corporate maneuvers, and monetary manipulations, with all the attendant attractions of beautiful (but chaste) women, plentiful (though elusive) dollars, fluent (although not always entirely desirable) characters, and plots that were vastly different from the other gun-toting, shoot-em-down-in-droves hero pulps.

Though the tone was light, the action was fast-paced and the writing smooth and full of wry humor. In many ways, the stories are the direct antecedents of the "Maverick" television shows that appeared some fifteen years later.

There is no denying the stories were unique, just as there is no way to disparage the fascination they have for the discriminating pulp reader. They are delightful, captivating, and refreshing. With their emphasis on the intricacies and previously unexplored labyrinths of financial manipulations, they have an appeal to the more mature reader. By all previous standards, they should have attracted a large and loyal following, but the times had changed—and so had the taste of the pulp buying public when they were published. Thus, there were but six Cash Gorman novels.

Notes

1. Editorial, *The Wizard,* Vol. 1, no. 1 (October 1940), p. 3.
2. Ibid., p. 4.
3. Ibid., p. 4,
4. Ibid., p. 5.

Information Sources

INDEX SOURCES: Weinberg, Robert, and Lohr McKinstry. *The Hero Pulp Index.* Evergreen, Colo.: Opar Press, 1971.

LOCATION SOURCES: University of California–Los Angeles Library (Vol. 1, no. 1, only); private collectors.

Publication History

MAGAZINE TITLE: *The Wizard.*

TITLE CHANGES: *Cash Gorman* (nos. 5 and 6).

VOLUME AND ISSUE DATA: Vol. 1, no. 1 (October 1940) through Vol. 1, no. 6 (August 1941); 6 issues.

PUBLISHER: Street & Smith Publications, Inc., 79 Seventh Avenue, New York, New York.

EDITOR: Charles Moran.

PRICE PER ISSUE: 10 cents.

SIZE AND PAGINATION: 6-3/4'' X 9-1/4''; 114 pages.

CURRENT STATUS: Discontinued.

—*Joseph Lewandowski*

X

XENOPHILE

Xenophile was "a monthly advertiser and journal devoted to fantastic and imaginative literature" edited by Nils Hardin. It was primarily an advertising vehicle. But while some issues did contain only advertising, others had up to seventy-six pages of articles, indexes, and illustrations. Particularly notable were special anniversary issues and issues focusing on themes, such as hard-boiled detectives, Ellery Queen, and Popular Publications.

Xenophile was aimed mainly at serious collectors. It did print some worthwhile material on well-known authors such as Queen, Raymond Chandler, Dashiell Hammett, and a number of fantasy and science fiction writers. However, what remains most valuable in the magazine are the many articles, indexes, and checklists devoted to relatively obscure and neglected authors and publications that have rarely ever been covered elsewhere. Of course, *Xenophile* also had less-elevated moments. Three issues devoted to Ray Bradbury contained little of significance, and some other issues were also rather slight.

The only continuing features in *Xenophile* were "The Pulp Information Center," a question-and-answer column that began in issue number 15, and, of course, the editorials in every issue by editor Nils Hardin. These editorials sometimes became almost a soap opera as they chronicled Hardin's ill health, lack of money, dissatisfaction with printers and the postal service, and weariness from long nights of typing. For example, in issue number 38, Hardin wrote, "The ads are what make this publication possible. And since I made a total profit of $324 last year, and since I have no other source of income, and since subscribers have come to expect certain other material in *Xenophile*, I need all the ads I can get."[1] Two issues later, he wrote, "I MUST lessen my workload. I need a rest. I need it badly. And I need to do something other than work on this magazine, which

I have been doing at the expense of a lot of things, for most of the day, seven days a week, for over four years.''[2]

Xenophile was originally a monthly publication, and it followed that schedule, skipping only a few months, until issue number 36, November 1977. The last eight issues appeared irregularly over the next two and one-half years. In issue number 44, Hardin wrote that he was preparing a ''very special'' issue devoted to one author, which would tie in with the release of a major motion picture and would have newsstand distribution. ''There's no doubt that it will be the best issue of *Xenophile* ever published. The problem in the meantime is to keep the magazine viable!''[3] Unfortunately, this was not to be, and no further issues appeared.

Much of the best material in *Xenophile* appeared in a few special issues which are worth examining in some detail. The first mystery theme issue, number 14, June 1975, was devoted to Ellery Queen. The most notable articles concerned Queen as a magazine editor: a profile, with index of Queen's *The Mystery League Magazine** (by Hardin) and memoirs of Queen as editor of *Ellery Queen's Mystery Magazine** (by Stanley Ellin and Francis M. Nevins, Jr.). Several items were reprinted from *The Queen Canon Bibliophile** fanzine.

Issue number 21, February 1976, was devoted to hard-boiled detectives. The major topics included John Lawrence and his ''Marquis of Broadway'' series in *The Black Mask** and *Dime Detective** (by Nevins), Robert Leslie Bellem (by Stephen Mertz) and his character Dan Turner (by Nick Carr), Judson Philip's ''Park Avenue Hunt Club'' series (by William J. Clark), as well as the inevitable pieces on Dashiell Hammett, Raymond Chandler, Robert B. Parker, and Michael Avallone.

Issue number 38, March–April 1978, was the fourth anniversary issue and the second issue on hard-boiled detectives. This one featured articles on Street & Smith's *Crime Busters** magazine (by Bob Sampson and Will Murray, with index); Bellem-Cleve Adams collaborations (by Mertz); Mark Sadler, actually Dennis Lynds (by Nevins); and the best private eye novels (by Avallone). There were also memoirs of *Manhunt** (by Robert Turner) and of *The Black Mask* (by Hal Murray Bonnett), as well as pieces on Hammett (by Joe Gores and Peter Wolfe) and Chandler (by William F. Nolan). Illustrations included seven *Black Mask* covers reproduced in full-page size and many smaller book and magazine cover photos.

Issue number 33, July 1977, was devoted to Popular Publications, which published many mystery magazines, including *Dime Detective, Detective Tales* (Popular Publications),* and *Black Mask*. Contents included a checklist of magazine titles (1930–1955); pictures of one hundred covers, usually of first issues; a lengthy interview with founder Henry Steeger; and an article on cover artist John Newton Howitt, with fifteen full-page illustrations.

Other theme issues included ones on The Shadow (number 17), Lovecraft (number 18), Ray Bradbury (numbers 13, 26, 36), westerns (number 32), and pulp collecting and prices (number 24).

Among the notable series were "Foreshadowings" by Bill Blackbeard on precursors of The Shadow (numbers 17, 22); "How Are the Mighty Fallen" by Dean A. Grennell, which consisted of satirical pieces on The Shadow (number 22), Operator #5 (number 30), and Captain Satan (number 42) reprinted from his fanzine *Grue*; and "The Pulp Library" by Bob Sampson, comprised of descriptions of single issues of *The Black Mask, The Spider,* * *Sea Stories,* and *Crime Busters* (numbers 30, 33, 38, 42).

Notable magazine profiles included those of *Scotland Yard** (by Sampson, with index in *Xenophile's* number 22), *Unknown* (by Will Murray, with index, no. 42), *Thrill Book* (by Bob Jones, with index, number 30), *Strange Tales of Mystery and Terror** (by Jones, no. 42), and *Fantastic Novels* (by James Ellis, number 20, indexed earlier in number 7). Magazine indexes included *Planet Stories* (numbers 20, 21, 22, 26), *New Mystery Adventure** (no. 22), *Avon Fantasy & SF Reader* (numbers 9, 10), *Star Magazine* (number 7), and *Masked Rider* (number 42).

Indexed characters included Grace Culver in *The Shadow Magazine** (number 17), Nick Carter in *Detective Story Magazine* (Street & Smith)* (number 22), The Shadowers in *Argosy* and *All-Story* (number 28), and The Occult Detector in various magazines (number 17). In addition to many articles on The Shadow, Operator #5, and other hero pulps, a piece on Frank L. Packard's Jimmie Dale series (in issue number 22) is worth noting. Authors indexed included Bedford-Jones in *Blue Book* and *People's* (number 22), F. R. Buckley and Harold Lamb in *Adventure* (number 28), and Hal Dunning in *Complete Story* (number 24).

Notes

1. Editorial, *Xenophile*, no. 38 (March/April 1978), p. 1.
2. Editorial, *Xenophile*, no. 40 (July 1978), p. 1.
3. Editorial, *Xenophile*, no. 44 (March 1980), p. 1.

Information Sources

INDEX SOURCES: None known.
LOCATION SOURCES: Private collectors.

Publication History

MAGAZINE TITLE: *Xenophile*.
TITLE CHANGES: None.
VOLUME AND ISSUE DATA: No. 1 (March 1974) through no. 44 (March 1980); 45 issues (one numbered "10-1/2").
PUBLISHER: Nils Hardin, P.O. Box 9660, St. Louis, Missouri, and later 26 Chapala, #5, Santa Barbara, California.
EDITOR: Nils Hardin.
PRICE PER ISSUE: Various, $1.00–$2.00.
SIZE AND PAGINATION: 5-1/2" X 8-1/2" (nos. 1–10-1/2); 8-1/2" X 11" (subsequent issues); 24–152 pages.
CURRENT STATUS: Inactive.
—*Brian KenKnight*

Y

YANKEE GANG SHORTS (British)

At least three issues of *Yankee Gang Shorts* were published. No other information is available.

Information Sources

INDEX SOURCES: None known.
LOCATION SOURCES: Private collectors.

Publication History

MAGAZINE TITLE: *Yankee Gang Shorts*.
TITLE CHANGES: None known.
VOLUME AND ISSUE DATA: Number of issues, date, and extent unknown; at least three issues published.
PUBLISHER: Not known.
EDITOR: Not known.
PRICE PER ISSUE: Not known.
SIZE AND PAGINATION: Not known.
CURRENT STATUS: Discontinued.

YANKEE MYSTERY SHORTS (British)

At least one issue of *Yankee Mystery Shorts* was published. No other information is available.

Information Sources

INDEX SOURCES: None known.

LOCATION SOURCES: Private collectors.

Publication History

MAGAZINE TITLE: *Yankee Mystery Shorts*.
TITLE CHANGES: None known.
VOLUME AND ISSUE DATA: Number of issues, date, and extent unknown.
PUBLISHER: Not known.
EDITOR: Not known.
PRICE PER ISSUE: Not known.
SIZE AND PAGINATION: Not known.
CURRENT STATUS: Discontinued.

YELLOWBACK LIBRARY

As an avid fan of the Hardy Boys mystery stories, Gil O'Gara had been collecting series books from the age of twelve. "I was fortunate enough to live in eastern Nebraska where the nearest library was a one-room creation built by the WPA during the Depression," he recalled years later. "Consequently, lack of funds had made 'cheap' literature a necessity and the children's section of the library was stocked primarily with shelf after shelf of series books. I imagine the educators and the librarians must have sighed with regret at this situation, but decided that any book was better than no book at all. In my opinion, it was the greatest thing that ever happened."[1]

As time passed and his collection of juvenile series books increased, O'Gara toyed with the idea of publishing a magazine for others with similar interests. He had begun researching the subject of series books, and the information he had garnered formed the basis of a number of articles which appeared in hobby publications such as *The Antique Trader, Collectors News* and *The Book-Mart*. After the discovery of *Dime Novel Roundup,** he began contributing to that magazine, also. Encouraged by response to his efforts, plans to issue a new publication in the field began to grow.

It wasn't until he landed a job with a West Des Moines printing firm that O'Gara decided to go ahead with the magazine. Through an agreement with the owner and manager, he was free to use the shop's various equipment in producing the magazine and in addition was given a generous discount off the cost of printing.

Thus *Yellowback Library* appeared in January 1981, borrowing its name from the derisive label critics attached to the cheap, mass-produced literature of by-gone days. It was a twenty-eight-page publication measuring 5-1/2" X 8-1/2", professionally typeset, printed on twenty-pound bond with a seventy-pound prime yellow cover. Several experts in the field of series book collecting agreed to contribute articles. Series authority Bob Chenu began a regular column of miscellaneous information, and Harry K. Hudson, compiler of the *Bibliography of Hard-Cover Series Type Boys' Books* (privately published, Tampa, 1977) began running additions to this well-known reference work in the pages of the *Yellow-back Library*.

"Like most people with a hobby, I enjoy telling people about it," O'Gara said in an editorial which appeared in the first issue. "I also enjoy learning as much as I can. Juvenile series collecting is a relatively new field, and there is much information to be turned up concerning series, authors, publishers, editions, illustrators, etc. Most of us, despite the size of our collections, feel we need to know more, and one of the ways to get that information is through a fanzine or other publication devoted to this hobby."[2]

Although *Yellowback Library* is primarily, as its masthead proclaims, "a magazine devoted to the collector and enthusiast of juvenile series, dime novels, and related literature," it frequently includes subject matter related to mystery and detective tales. Articles on the Judy Bolton series by Margaret Sutton; Graham M. Dean's G–Man series, Agent Nine; and an examination of the dime novel detectives, Old and Young King Brady, have appeared in its pages.

Dave Farah's piece on Cameo Edition Nancy Drews, which was published in the September–October issue of *Yellowback Library*, led to a series of articles on the popular female detective beginning with the following issue. Entitled "Basic Nancy Drew," Farah believes the column could run for an indefinite number of issues as he explores the myriad aspects of the girl-sleuth's career.

In October 1981, O'Gara left the printing business to attempt a career of free-lance writing. No longer eligible for a discount at the shop and unable to make use of the company's equipment, he dropped photo-typesetting, purchased an IBM Selectric typewriter, and continued to turn out issues of *Yellowback Library* from his home. In March 1982, yearly subscription rates were raised to meet increases in printing and postage costs, but otherwise the magazine continues to be published in its yellow-covered format on a regular bimonthly schedule.

Notes

1 Editorial, *Yellowback Library*, Vol. 1, no. 1 (January/February 1981), reverse front cover.
2. Ibid.

Information Sources

INDEX SOURCES: None known.
LOCATION SOURCES: Private collectors.

Publication History

MAGAZINE TITLE: *Yellowback Library*.
TITLE CHANGES: None.
VOLUME AND ISSUE DATA: Vol. 1, no. 1 (January-February 1981) through Vol. 2, no. 2 (to date, March-April 1982); 8 issues.
PUBLISHER: Gil O'Gara, 2019 Southeast 8th Street, Des Moines, Iowa 50315.
EDITOR: Gil O'Gara.
PRICE PER ISSUE: $1.00 (through Vol. 2, no. 1); $1.50.
SIZE AND PAGINATION: 5-1/2" X 8-1/2"; 28 pages.

CURRENT STATUS: Active.
—*Gil O'Gara*

YOUNG BROADBRIM WEEKLY

See OLD BROADBRIM WEEKLY

YOUNG SLEUTH LIBRARY

With Frank Tousey's emphasis on the juvenile market for dime novels, it is not surprising that he should have countered the popularity of Old Sleuth by introducing a boy detective of a similar name. Young Sleuth (which appears to have been his real name) had appeared in the story-paper, *Boys of New York*, as well as in the *New York Detective Library** (in four appearances there) before he achieved his own publication.

He is referred to as the New York police inspector's youngest and most successful officer, but he appears never to have had the following that Old King Brady or Nick Carter enjoyed. The most distinctive feature of the stories is the Young Sleuth's assistant. A French valet named Jean Guillaume St. Croix Jenkeau, formerly in the service of a "celebrated French detective," he adds necessary comic relief. Though he claims he is a French count and a nobleman in hard luck, he is always in search of champagne (his solution to the problems of transporting a few bottles of wine is to drink it) and suffers from gout. Young Sleuth refers to him as Jenkins, The Count of No Account.

The author signed to the stories in the *New York Detective Library* was "Police Captain Howard," a stock house name used by a number of Tousey writers, including the prolific Luis P. Senarens. In the *Young Sleuth Library*, the stories are signed "by the Author of 'Young Sleuth'."

Information Sources

BIBLIOGRAPHY:
Bragin, Charles. *Dime Novel Bibliography 1860–1928*. Brooklyn, N.Y.: privately printed, 1938.
LeBlanc, Edward T. "Dime Novel Sketches No. 110." *Dime Novel Roundup,* no. 437 (February 15, 1969): 17.
Leithead, J. Edward. "Boy Detectives." *Dime Novel Roundup*, no. 240 (September 1952): 65–71.
INDEX SOURCES: None known.
LOCATION SOURCES: Private collectors.

Publication History

MAGAZINE TITLE: *Young Sleuth Library*.
TITLE CHANGES: None.
VOLUME AND ISSUE DATA: Vol. 1, no. 1 (October 1, 1892) through Vol. 6, no. 143 (December 4, 1896); 143 issues.

PUBLISHER: Frank Tousey, 34 and 36 North Moore Street, New York, New York.
EDITOR: Not known.
PRICE PER ISSUE: 5 cents.
SIZE AND PAGINATION: 8-1/2'' X 11-1/2''; 16 pages (no. 39 was 32 pages).
CURRENT STATUS: Discontinued.
—*J. Randolph Cox*

Z

ZEPPELIN STORIES

In an effort to combine the then-popular trends toward aviation fiction and espionage fiction, *Zeppelin Stories* was published for four issues in 1929. Stories featured spies using the exotic zeppelins as a means of accomplishing their ends. With very artificial backgrounds, spies were dropped from zeppelins, escaped with zeppelins, conducted counterespionage in zeppelins, and routinely traveled in zeppelins.

The covers were even more fanciful, highlighted by one in which a gorilla is shown being lowered from, what else, a zeppelin.

Information Sources

INDEX SOURCES:None known.
LOCATION SOURCES: Private collectors.

Publication History

MAGAZINE TITLE: *Zeppelin Stories*.
TITLE CHANGES: None known.
VOLUME AND ISSUE DATA: Vol. 1, no. 1 (April 1929) through Vol. 1, no.4, August (?) 1929; 4 issues.
PUBLISHER: Ramer Reviews, Inc., New York, New York.
EDITOR: Not known.
PRICE PER ISSUE: Not known.
SIZE AND PAGINATION: Not known.
CURRENT STATUS: Discontinued.

OVERVIEWS OF FOREIGN MAGAZINES

There is interest in crime fiction in all parts of the world, but, while crime itself is universal, the predominant interest in crime fiction is centered particularly in the United States, the British Isles, and Scandinavia.

This is not to imply that it is not produced in other areas. There are well-known crime fiction authors throughout Europe and in Japan, India, and even Russia, for example, and crime fiction is a valuable import commodity in almost every country. However, for home-produced mystery and detective stories, in quantity at least, it is the English-speaking countries and the Scandinavian countries that take the lead.

Crime fiction interest is increasing in Europe. French authors have produced many famous detective characters known worldwide, and while true-crime episodes have had at least equal billing with crime fiction in the past, crime fiction is now taking an edge. German authors, likewise, have a staunch foundation, originally imitating other styles but now developing their own, despite the thought that for many readers in Germany, the entertainment possibly derived from such fiction is looked on as being a little suspicious. The Soviet Bloc writers, although producing mystery fiction, follow for the most part the "official view," which is less entertaining to Western readers.

While not every country can be portrayed in this overview, the selection of the Scandinavian countries will provide a detailed picture of the activity there in the mystery magazine field. France has been included, not only because of the historical importance of a number of French mystery authors, but in order to include an European view through mystery magazines. And Australia has been selected in order to show the importance of imported materials to the reading public of a country that has produced little itself.

AUSTRALIA

Overview

One of the truly great mysteries, and one which is likely to remain well-nigh unsolved, is the extent to which mystery and detective fiction has been published in Australia. Even the Australian National Library, which purports to be a repository for all books and magazines published in Australia, can boast a collection which includes only one example of an indigenous detective magazine.

Granted, Australia can hardly lay claim to having a rich heritage of mystery literature (Arthur Upfield, Peter Carter Brown, and Don Haring's "Larry Kent" series notwithstanding), but the fact is that mystery and detective fiction, both the imported and domestic varieties, have been published extensively in this country.

Unfortunately, it is not always easy to distinguish between local and overseas products, as many Australian authors, particularly during the 1950s, which seems to have been *the* decade for mystery fiction, chose to set their writings in San Francisco, New York, or other American locations. Presumably, such locations were seen by Australian mystery fans as more glamorous and certainly more sinister and crime ridden than either Sydney or Melbourne.

It would seem that publishers of mystery and detective fiction in Australia have regarded Australians primarily as readers of novels rather than of short fiction, as a great many Australian publications in the genre have concentrated on novel-length stories. Leading this style of publication was the *Phantom Books* series, which ran well in excess of three hundred issues between 1951 and 1961. Initially published in a digest-sized magazine format, it switched to regular paperback-book format for a handful of issues in 1958 before reverting to the original style for the remainder of its life (as "Phantom Classics"). The series featured novels primarily, if not exclusively, by American writers, including Edward S. Aarons (who wrote also under the pseudonym Edward Ronns), Richard S. Prather, Robert Wade and Bill Miller (under pseudonyms Wade Miller and Dale Wilmer), Robert Bloch, Lester Dent, and Frank Gruber.

A similar series featuring British, American, and Australian writers was published by Invincible Press in the late 1940s and early 1950s, while other series of American novels appeared as the *Lovely Lady* series, *Front Page Mysteries, Detective Library, Cleveland Detective,* and *Red-Back Mysteries*.

I have been able to track down only a small number of indigenous mystery and detective fiction magazines. The earliest of these was *Famous Detective Stories*, which should not, perhaps, be classified as "fiction." This commenced publication in December 1946 and ran for at least fifty-seven pulp-sized monthly issues (and later in a digest-sized, undated edition). It featured fictionalized accounts of famous (or so they said) Australian and New Zealand adventures of crime and detection. Stories appeared generally to have been written under pseudonyms, including "H. Mycroft"!

From the same publisher as *Famous Detective Stories* came *Detective Fiction*. This ran for only four issues between December 1948 and March 1949 and included the first four parts of a five-part serialization of Arthur Upfield's "The Mountains Have A Secret," along with a variety of short stories.

Detective Monthly was a slight (thirty-six page) digest-sized magazine that ran for an indeterminate number of issues (I have seen only the first two) during the early 1950s.

The early 1950s also saw the publication of a variety of small (again, often not more than thirty-six pages) magazines that featured both original fiction by Australian writers, including Kevin M. Slattery, Peter Williams, and G. C. Bleeck, and material reprinted from American mystery and detective magazines. These magazines went under such titles as *Action Detective, American Crime, American Detective Magazine, Downtown Detective, Leisure Detective, Popular Detective, and Westend Detective*. Other titles, including *Detective Stories* and *Invincible Detective Magazine*, seem to have utilized only material by American writers.

Another magazine which featured fictionalized accounts of so-called true-crime stories was *Master Detective*, which was published by the publishers of *Man*, an Australian "girlie" magazine, during 1953 and 1954. This included stories of American crimes as well as those which took place in this part of the world.

It has not been the indigenous magazines that have provided serious mystery and detective fans in Australia with the most reading enjoyment over the years, but rather the imported variety. This category includes both magazines that originated in either England or the United States and simply distributed in this country and also those magazines that existed in locally published editions.

The oldest magazine in the first category of which I am aware is *Detective Weekly* (British),* which was published in Britain during the 1930s and available on newsstands throughout Australia.

This practice was to become common during the 1960s but was preceded by a period during which various magazines actually had editions printed in Australia. The most important and certainly the longest-running of these was *Ellery Queen's Mystery Magazine*,* which existed in an Australian edition between 1947 and 1962 for a total of over 175 issues. These editions did not necessarily correspond exactly with the original U.S. issues but generally included the majority of stories from the U.S. edition of some two months previous. Also published in Australia, but in far less impressive numbers, were editions of *Alfred Hitchcock's Suspense Magazine (Alfred Hitchcock's Mystery Magazine*), The Saint Detective Magazine,* and *Verdict Detective Story Monthly (Verdict*)*.

Even though *Ellery Queen's Mystery Magazine* ceased to be published in Australia in 1962, it continued to be available for at least another two years in an edition printed in England but with the inscription "Australian Edition" printed on the front cover. Both *Mercury Mystery Magazine* (British) and *Mike Shayne Mystery Magazine** were also available in joint British/Australian editions, while other British magazines, such as *MacKill's Mystery Magazine* (British)* (in the 1950s), *Suspense* (British)* (in the 1950s and 1960s), and *Edgar*

Wallace Mystery Magazine (British)* (in the 1960s), were widely distributed in this country.

The last mystery and detective fiction magazine published in Australia of which I am aware is *Crime Story Magazine*, which ran for at least eight issues during the mid-sixties. This featured undistinguished stories by authors unknown to me which could just as easily been written by Australian writers as reprinted from some of the lesser American detective pulps.

The immediate future of the mystery and detective magazine in Australia appears somewhat bleak, with the U.S. editions of *Ellery Queen's Mystery Magazine* and *Alfred Hitchcock's Mystery Magazine* being the only available fiction magazines and only a variety of lurid "true-crime" titles such as *Front Page Detective, Crime File Stories, Headline Police Stories, New Detective Stories,* and *Amazing Police Stories* actually published in this country.

Checklist

Action Detective
Alfred Hitchcock's Mystery Magazine
American Crime
American Detective Magazine
Crime Story Magazine
Detective Fiction
Detective Monthly
Detective Stories
Downtown Detective
Ellery Queen's Mystery Magazine
Invincible Detective
Leisure Detective
Master Detective
Phantom Books/Magazine
Popular Detective
Saint Detective
Verdict Detective Story Monthly
Westend Detective
—*Graeme K. Flanagan*

DENMARK

Overview

In Denmark, as in all of the Scandinavian countries, there is a high degree of interest in mystery and detective literature.[†] Detective magazines have been

---

†The information on Danish magazines, authors, and publishers was generously provided from the files of Bjarne Nielsen, of Copenhagen.

immensely popular and widely read, but the life of most has been short. This is due in part to the fact that short stories of any kind have never been particularly popular.

The first real detective magazine in Denmark was *Nick Carter* (reprints from *Nick Carter Library** in 1908, unique in that it was the first magazine of detective stories that were complete in one issue; several earlier publications had included some detective serials which were concluded only after a number of issues. This led to a number of other series, most of the magazines imported from Germany or France, such as *Nat Pinkerton, Lord Percy of the Excentric* (sic) *Club,* and *Lord Lister The Gentleman Thief,* as well as the same type that featured western stories *(Texas Jack, Buffalo Bill).*

One of the most prolific of Danish writers had his start in translating the Lord Lister stories from the German, Niels Meyn. He found he could write the stories himself, both better and quicker, and is known today not only for detective and crime stories but also in the adventure, science fiction, historical, and animal genres, including juvenile books. Many of his works were written under as many as forty-seven different pseudonyms, as well as his own name. One of the most professional of Danish writers, he wrote rapidly, using stock cliches, unhampered by social messages or significance; but his stories were filled with action, excitement, surprise, brave heroes and pretty heroines, and evil villains (usually an Oriental or mad scientist) without sex or profane language.

As in the United States, such magazines were considered to be a bad influence for the youth of the country, and teachers and educators made a concerted effort to have them prohibited. By 1925, these magazines had all but disappeared, with only a few series reprinted.

The brothers Christtreu, inheriting a printing company in the late 1930s, are responsible for a revival in the magazines at that time. *Record* and *Popular* were started in 1936, with Niels Meyn as the top contributor of stories; these "book" series, soon popular, were mostly crime stories with a few adventure tales. In 1937, one of the brothers visited the United States to study publishing and evidently became familiar with the U.S. magazine, *The Black Mask.**

Upon his return to Denmark, the brothers in 1938 launched a short story magazine called *Record Magasinet* (same title as the earlier "book" series); and although only eleven issues were published, they were almost identical to the U.S. *Black Mask* for the same year. When this was not a success, two more short story magazines were commenced in 1939. One was *Den Bla Serie (The Blue Series),* which contained almost exclusively the hard-boiled American crime fiction by writers one would associate with *Black Mask*: Theodore Tinsley, Roger Torrey, Frederick C. Davis, Norbert Davis, William Irish, W. T. Ballard, and, in his first Danish appearance, Raymond Chandler. Unfortunately, this short story format ceased after ten issues, and it was changed to featuring one novelette and one or two short stories; with the change in format, though Mickey Spillane, John Creasey, Fredric Brown, and Clayton Rawson still appeared.

The other magazine begun by the Christtreu brothers in 1939 was *Den Sorte Maske (The Black Mask)*, commencing with Berkeley Grey's Norman Conquest stories (first thirty-two issues). Unlike *Record,* the Christtreus's earlier attempt at a *Black Mask*-type of magazine, *Den Sorte Maske* soon established itself as the most popular, and since 1939, these stories have been reprinted at least six times and never out of print for long. Other authors were added, many today as unknown as they were then. These included Carroll John Daly (unreprinted in Denmark in any other periodical), Erle Stanley Gardner, Roy Vickers, Frank Gruber, and Dwight V. Babcock.

Other magazines commenced by the Christtreus during this period were *Browning* and *Charming* (both begun in 1938) and *Den Gule Serie (The Yellow Series,* 1940). These were usually sixty-six-page magazines, with one long story and one or more short stories or a serial.

World War II brought changes. The Christtreu firm had by now changed its name to Ark. Foreign literature was not welcomed. Danish authors used Anglo-Saxon pseudonyms now (Sven Aage Bremer wrote as Clark Harrigan, Else Faber as Waldo Armstrong, and Børge Madsen used several pen names). But this was not acceptable to Danish crime writers and was largely responsible for the formation of Kriminalist Klubben De Tretten (The Crime Writer's Club "The Thirteen") and under the aegis of Carl Aller's Publishing Firm published a series of stories written mostly by the members. When the books had some success, a magazine was commenced, *Detektiv-Serien K-13 (The Detective Series K-13)*. Published by Valentin & Lund, containing short stories and a serial, the magazine was intended as a counterweight to all the foreign magazines (in which many of the same authors had written under pseudonyms). However, some of the authors still hid behind pen names, and most of the stories seemed to be set in London, Paris, or New York. Mogens Linck wrote as Jørgen Jelling (which still had a Danish sound), but Knud Meister's Kay Masters pen name, as well as Børge Madsen's "Tony Borg" were more continental. And Jens Anker (which was a pseudonym for Robert Hansen) even changed to Gert Kassow—a pen name for a pen name. When the twenty-third issue, *Døden I Badekarret (Death in the Bath Tub)* had a photographic cover showing a young girl in a bath tub— in the nude—and the issue was seized by the censors, this spelled the end for the magazine. One additional issue, already printed, did appear.

In 1948, the first serious attempt was made to publish a magazine in which the stories were carefully chosen for their quality. *Det Grønne Magasin (The Green Magazine)* was commenced with this philosophy in 1948. Despite top-quality authors such as Dashiell Hammett (the first Hammett short stories published in Denmark), Dorothy Sayers, Ellery Queen, Craig Rice, H. C. Bailey, Damon Runyon, Cornell Woolrich, and Freeman Wills Crofts, the magazine did not catch the favor of the mystery fans and survived only for six issues. Detective stories were still not "good literature."

Tage la Cour, in 1955, was coeditor of the first attempt at a Danish version of

Ellery Queen's Mystery Magazine* (in Danish, *Ellery Queen Q-Magasinet*). Only three issues were published of *Q-Magasinet*, but it is still fondly remembered as publishing one memorable story, Stanley Ellin's "Husets Specialittet" (The Specialty of the House).

La Cour's second attempt to publish a Danish version of *Ellery Queen's Mystery Magazine*, under the title of *Ellery Queens Kriminalmagasin*, fared somewhat better. Ten issues were published, from June 1968 to March 1969. Detective literature was by then considered more seriously, a change partly engineered by La Cour himself with his many published articles in newspapers and books. A third attempt, by Spektrum, to publish a Danish edition (under the same title as La Cour's) was successful for twenty-six issues in 1969-1971; edited by Miss Bitten Söderberg, the stories selected for the Danish edition seem to have been the least interesting ones from the U.S. editions.

The last two attempts for a Danish mystery magazine were also the work of Tage la Cour. La Cour and Frits Remar (a Danish crime writer) founded *Tage La Cours Kriminal Magasin (Tage la Cour's Crime Magazine)* in 1977. This featured a mix of old and new stories, both Danish and foreign—some good, some bad, but all interesting. However, it was limited to twelve issues before it met its demise. La Cour and Remar tried again, in 1979, with *Det Ny Kriminal Magasin (The New Crime Magazine)*, similar to their first attempt, but this, too, had a short life—eight issues.

The most promising indication that crime fiction is still alive and well in Denmark, however, is the commencement in 1981 of the first amateur, or semi-professional, mystery fan magazine. Bjarne Nielsen has published five issues to date of what he terms is "a small and modest attempt at a Danish *The Armchair Detective.**" Although he advised that the interest and subscription numbers are still minimal, there is still hope, and at least, it is a beginning opportunity for the Danish mystery fans to participate and unite for self-preservation.

Checklist

Bedste Detektivroman, Den

(The Best Detective Story). Translated short stories. Published by Skandinavisk Romanforlag, 1950, 5 issues.

Betjent Ole Ny

(Constable Ole Ny). A series about a young police constable and his adventures in the Copenhagen underworld. After the liberation from German occupation in May 1945, many of the adventures involved Ole Nye as a member of the resistance. Written by several authors under the pseudonym of Peter Anker. Published by Kay Nielsens Forlag, 1943-1949, 252 issues, 64 pages.

Bla Serie, Den

(The Blue Series). Commenced as a short story magazine, but after 10 issues featured novels or novelettes; continued in book form. Included hard-boiled American authors such as Vickers, Creasey, and Frederick C. Davis. Published by Arks Forlag, 1939-1955, about 201 issues; 66 pages.

Bob Harder

Written by H. Wayne (pseudonym for Z. Zinglersen?) and R. Patrick (also a pseudonym?). Published by Forlagt Heffez, 1943-1944, 56 issues, 32 pages.

Browning

Primarily translated novelettes and short stories. A few Danish writers contributed their work pseudonymously, including Børge Madsen (first 10 issues) and Erik B. Volmer Jensen writing as Martin South. Among the British and American writers were Ladbroke Black, Berkeley Grey, and Roy Vickers. Published by Christtreu's Forlag (later Ark's Forlag), 1938-1943; 173 issues; 66 pages.

Charming

Translated stories. Published by Christtreu's Forlag, 1938-1941, 88 issues; 64 pages.

Detectiven

(The Detective). Articles about "sensational" crimes and a few short stories. Edited and probably also written by Marius Wulff, 1938, 3 issues; 8 pages.

Detektivkongen Sherlock Holmes

(Sherlock Holmes, The King of Detectives). From the Portuguese series. Published by Forlaget for Folkelitteratur, 1915, about 20 issues; 32 pages.

Detektiv-Magasinet

(Detective Magazine). Translated stories. Published by Det Ny Forlag, 1930, 24 issues; about 40 pages.

Detektivmagasinet, John MacCarty

(The John McCarty Detective Magazine). Origin unknown. Perhaps written by Niels Meyn. Published by Centraltrykkeriet i Haderslev with two stories in each issue, no date; 1 or 2 issues; 32 pages.

Detektivmysterier

(Detective Mysteries). Translated stories. Published by Skandinavisk Blad-forlag, 1943, 23 issues.

Detektiv-Serien K-13

(The Detective Series, K-13). Published by Valentin & Lund's Bogtryk for the Kriminalist Klubben "De Tretten" (The Crime Writers Club "The Thirteen"), in an attempt to publish better magazines featuring Danish writers exclusively. Published 1943-1944, 24 issues; 66 pages.

Dr. Carson

Most likely of Danish origin. Published by Bogforlaget Urania, 1926, 7 issues; 32 pages.

Dr. Morrison

Written anonymously by Robert Hansen. Published by Kommissionsforlaget, 1913-1914, 11 issues, and by Nyt Dansk Forlag, 1915, 11 issues; 24 pages. Reissued by J. G. Pedersen, 1942, 6 issues, comprised of reprints from the second series.

Dr. Zigomar

Written anonymously by Louis Møller, with covers from *The Black Mask.** Published by Bogforlaget, 1936, 4 issues, and Kioskernes Faellesindkøb, 1936, 4 issues; 20 pages.

Ellery Queen Q-Magasinet

The First Danish edition of *Ellery Queen's Mystery Magazine.** Edited by Bendix Bech-Thostrup and Tage la Cour. Published by Jørgen Nørredam's Forlag, 1955, 3 issues; 128 pages.

Ellery Queens Kriminalmagasin

The second attempt to push a Danish edition of *Ellery Queen's Mystery Magazine.** Edited by Bitten Söderberg, published by Egmont H. Petersens Fond, June 1968-March 1969, 10 issues; 98 pages.

Ellery Queens Kriminalmagasin

The third and last attempt to publish a Danish version of *Ellery Queen's Mystery Magazine.** Edited by Bitten Søderberg, published by Spektrum, 1969-1971, 26 issues; 126 pages.

Fred Parker, Den Store Ubekendtes Oplevelser

(Fred Parker, Exploits of the Great Unknown). Translated stories, probably of German origin. Published by Litteraturselskabet, 1923, 16 issues; 24 pages.

Fyrst Basil: De Tusind Maskers Mester

(Count Basil: Man of a Thousand Faces). Probably written by Harry Hansen and Niels Meyn. Published by Det Ny Forlag, 1927, 44 issues; by Forlaget Kodan, 1928, 2 issues; and by Forlaget Kora, 1928, 2 issues; 24 pages.

Gadefulde Dr. X, Den

(The Mysterious Dr. X). This series was claimed to have been written by Niels Meyn, but none is available in The Royal Library, and no private collector seems to have seen issues. There is a possibility this is identical to Meyn's *Den Mystiske Mr. X* (The Mysterious Mr. X). Supposedly published by Centraltrykkeriet Haderslev; 32 pages.

Gentlemandetektiven–Storstadmysterier

(Gentleman Detective–Metropolitan Mysteries). Written anonymously by Niels Meyn. Published by Forlaget Lille Kongensgade, 1917, 6 issues; reissued in 1920; 32 pages.

Grønne Magasin, Det

(The Green Magazine). Short stories of quality, including some by American authors Hammett, Sayers, Queen, Woolrich, Bailey, Rice, and Runyon. Edited by Sverkel Biering. Published by A/S Halvor Schleisner, 1948–1949, 6 issues; 80 pages.

Gule Serie, Den

(The Yellow Series). Translated novelettes. Published by Christtreu's Forlag, 1940–1943, 66 issues; 65 pages.

Illustreret Kriminal-Revue

(Illustrated Crime Review). Edited and published by E. Wikstrom, 1934, 5 issues; 8 pages.

Illustreret Kriminal-Tidende

(Illustrated Crime Magazine). From Vol. 6, edited by Marius Wulff. Title change to K.T.–SMART, becoming just a "sensational" magazine with no short stories. Published in Copenhagen, 1921–1926, weekly, about 150 issues; 23 pages.

Jack Franklin, Verdensdetektiven

(Jack Franklin, World Detective). Possibly of German origin. Published by Litteraturselskabet, 1918–1919, 41 issues; 24 pages.

Journalisten Bob Strong's Oplevelser–Ugens Gyser

(Adventures of Bob Strong, Journalist–The Weekly Thriller). Published by Forlaget Norden u.a., circa 1945, 4 issues.

KKK-Magasinet (Kriminalassisten Kristian Kraft)

Written by Niels Meyn under the pseudonym of Rex Nelson. Published by Avis-og Forlagscentralen, 1946, 12 issues; 42 pages.

Københavnerdetektiven Nicton

(Nicton, The Copenhagen Detective). Published by William Larsen's Forlag, 1921, 2 issues; 24 pages

Kriminal-Bøgerne

(The Crime Books). A Danish series published by Nordjydsk Forlag, Alborg, 1930, 3 issues; 32 pages.

Kriminal-Magasinet

(The Crime Magazine). Short stories, edited by Niels Meyn and written by him under various pseudonyms. Published in Copenhagen, 1942, 3 issues; 36 pages.

Kriminal Serien

(The Crime Series). Written by Kaj G. Lauritzen. Published by Detektivforlaget, no date, 5 issues.

Kurt Danner's Bedrifter

(Exploits of Kurt Danner). Kurt Danner is more of an adventurer, traveling worldwide and getting involved with spies, smugglers, pirates, and, after 1945, Nazi resistance. Written by several authors under the joint pseudonym of Peter Anker. Among the authors: Neils Meyn and Søren A. Dahl. Published by Kay Nielsen's Forlag, 1942–1947, for 280 issues; 60 pages.

Lord Kingsley–Gentlemantyven, ell. Nat Pinkertons Skygge

(Lord Kingsley, Gentlemen Thief, or The Shadow of Nat Pinkerton). Probably written by Niels Meyn and Harry Hansen. Published by Centraltrykkeriet in Haderslev, 1925, 133 issues; 32 pages.

Lord Lister Alias Mestertyven Raffles

(Lord Lister alias Raffles, The Master Thief). Translated from the German by Niels Meyn, later written by Meyn. First Series: published by Anderson & Westi,

1909–1910, 12 issues; 96 pages. Second Series: published by Litteraturselskabet, 1913–1914, 254 issues; 32 pages. Third Series: (reprints) published by Litterselskabet, 1926–1927, 60 issues; 32 pages. Fourth Series: (reprints) published by Chr. Nielsens Forlag, 1938–1939, 17 issues; 32 pages.

Lord Percy Fra den Excentriske Klub

(Lord Percy from the Eccentric Club). Possibly of German origin. Published by Litterselskabet, 1915, 247 issues; 24 pages. Later reprinted.

Mesterdetektiven Dick Donald, Forbrydernes Overmand

(Dick Donald, Master Detective). Most probably of Danish origin. Published as Dynamit-Serien nos. 1–8 by Forlaget Havis, 1942–1943; 32 pages.

Mesterdetektiven Leon Pitaval

(Leon Pitaval, the Master Detective). Possibly of French or German origin. published by Litteraturselskabet, 1919–1921, 85 issues; 32 pages.

Mesterdetektiven Pat Connor

(Pat Connor, Master Detective). The first two issues were labeled "Pat Corner." Published by Chr. Flor's Boghandel, no date (circa 1915); 12 issues.

Mesterdetektiven Robert Sterling

(Robert Sterling, The Master Detective). Written anonymously by Niels Meyn. Published by Centraltrykkeriet in Haderslev, 1925, 17 issues; 20 pages.

Moderne Gentlemantyv, Den

(The Modern Gentleman Thief). Stories written anonymously by Niels Meyn. Published by H. Hansens Bogtryk, Arhus, 1936, 4 issues; 24 pages.

Mr. Fox Bedrifter

(Exploits of Mr. Fox). Published by Henningsen's Tryk, 1910, 10 issues; 16 pages.

Mystiske Mr. X, Den

(The Mysterious Mr. X). Written by Niels Meyn; from Vol. 72, under the pseudonym of Jan Dorph. Published by Kaj Nielsen's Forlag, 1943–1944, 76 issues; 64 pages.

Nat Pinkerton, Opdagernes Konge

(Nat Pinkerton, King of Detectives). Probably translated from the German. Published by Litteraturselskabet, 1924, 419 issues; 32 pages.

Nick Carter

Translated from the U.S. edition; published by Litteraturselskabet, no date (circa 1908), 69 issues; 32 pages.

Ny Kriminalmagasin, Det

(The New Crime Magazine). Short stories. Danish and foreign, edited by Tage la Cour and Frits Remar. Published by Winthers Forlag, no date (1979), 8 issues; 66 pages.

Opdageren Jack White, New York Mysterier

(Jack White, The Detective, New York Mysteries). Origin unknown. Published by Ebeltoft Bogtrykkeri, no date, 7 issues.

Opdagernes Konge Sherlock Holmes

(Sherlock Holmes, King of Detectives). Only one issue known. Published by Nationaltrykkeriet, no date (circa 1910); 32 pages.

Pikante Kriminanoveller

(Spicy Crime Stories). Short stories. Published by Forlaget Cameron, 1941, 1 issue; 54 pages.

Pinkerton

The Danish version of *The Armchair Detective*.* Started as a series of monographs on authors; no. 1 covered Raymond Chandler, and no. 2 discussed Dashiell Hammett. From no. 3 on, a general magazine on detective fiction. Edited by Bjarne Nielsen. Published by Antikvariat Pinkerton, commenced 1981, 5 issues to date; 40 pages.

Protea, Den Kvindelige Forbryderchef

(Protea, The Female Gangster Boss). Probably of German origin. Published by Frederiksberg Bibliotek's Forlag, 1917, 1 issue; 24 pages.

Record Magasinet

(The Record Magazine). Actually a Danish version of *The Black Mask*. Published by Christtreu's Forlag, 1938, 11 issues; 130 pages.

Robert Watt, KKK-Klubben

(Robert Watt, the Ku-Klux-Klan Club). Written by Jack MacCarter (pseudonym). Published by Forlaget Skandia, 1943, 10 issues; 48 pages.

Sherlockiana

Articles, essays, news, and book reviews pertaining to Sherlock Holmes. Edited by A. D. Hendriksen (1956–1970) and Henry Lauritzen (1971–). Published by Sherlock Holmes Klubben i Danmark since 1956, quarterly, about 100 issues; 6–8 pages per issue.

Sorte Hand, Den–Camorraen

(The Black Hand–The Camorra). Probably of German origin. Published by Forlaget Lille Kongensgade, no date (circa 1915), 4 issues.

Sorte Maske, Den

(The Black Mask). Mostly translated stories. A few Danish authors contributed under Anglo-Saxon pseudonyms. Series commenced with Berkeley Grey's ''Conquest'' series, most of which has been reprinted a number of times. Published by Christtreu's Forlag, 1939–1946, 237 issues; 65 pages.

Spaending: Alexander-Serien

(Suspense: The Alexander Series). A Danish series inspired by the Norman Conquest stories. Written by Erik B. Volmer Jensen and Else Faber under the joint pseudonym of Jørgen Rastholt; illustrated by Palle Wennerwald. Published by Ark's Forlag, 1943–1950, 211 issues; 34 pages.

Styrmand Rasmussen

(Rasmussen, First Mate). Often stories of spies, smugglers, and pirates. Also provided an almost complete history of the Second World War after the liberation in 1945. Written by several authors under one pseudonym, Peter Anker. Published by Kay Nielsen's Forlag, 1943–1948, 240 issues; 40 pages.

Tage La Cour's Kriminal Magasin

(Tage la Cour's Crime Magazine). Danish and foreign short stories. Edited by Tage la Cour and Frits Remar. Published by Schroder Publications, 1977–1978, 12 issues; 66 pages.

Ugens Kriminalovelle

(Crime Stories of the Week). Short stories edited by H. Almind. Published 1921–1922, for 55 issues; 12 pages.

Will Morton's Oplevelser

(Adventures of Will Morton). Probably of German origin. Published by Litteraturselskabet, 1923, 46 issues; 32 pages.

FRANCE

Overview

Since 1929, there have been one or more commercial French detective magazines, except for the period between July 1934 and January 1948.[†] There have also been countless weeklies and monthlies which included some detective fiction and newspapers specializing in judicial current events.

Checklist

Anthologie du Suspense

(Anthology of Suspence). Supplements to the French *Hitchcock Magazine* (anthologies of short stories). Published by Opta, 1964–1970, 8 issues.

Choc

(Shock). An attempt to continue the French magazine *Suspense* with anthologies of stories taken from the U.S. *Manhunt*.* Published by Opta, April 1967–March 1968; 4 issues.

Contre-Enquete

(Counter-Investigation). An essentially journalistic magazine with the slogan, "All aspects of the struggle against crime." Included investigations into the different professional activities of worldwide detectives and fictionalized stories of famous cases. Published by La Librairie Parisienne, March 1952–December 1952, 10 issues.

Enigmatika

See full profile following checklist.

Hebdo-Police (and *ICI Police*)

(Detective Weekly/Police Calling). A weekly publication that changed title and publisher with the fifth issue. This magazine featured short stories, serial

---

[†]The article on French mystery and detective magazines was translated form the French by Walter Albert, Department of French and Italian Languages and Literature, University of Pittsburgh.

novels (including Peter Cheyney and Mickey Spillane), articles, comic strips, and games. Published November 8, 1951 – January 24, 1952, 11 issues.

Hitchcock Magazine

The French edition of U.S. *Alfred Hitchcock's Mystery Magazine** was edited by Alain Dorémieux (editor-in-chief), then Luc Geslin. In addition to the short stories, this magazine included a literary column bringing together two well-known writers of detective novels, Michel Lebrun and Maurice Bernard Endrebe, plus a column on the cinema and western novels. Published by Opta (Maurice Renault), May 1961–March 1975, 166 issues.

La Revue des Études Lupiennes

See full profile following checklist.

La Revue du Mystere

(The Mystery Review). As the French edition of *London Mystery Magazine (London Mystery Selection* [British]*), British stories were emphasized. Although announced as a bimonthly, there was but one issue published, April–May 1951, by Editions Le Dragon.

Le Club des Masques

(The Masks' Club). The first series was published monthly for 29 issues, from February 15, 1932 to June 15, 1934, and included interviews with important crime writers (as Agatha Christie), a short story, columns on current theater, cinema, and literature, and some games. There was a second series, nos. 30 to 38, published from July 15, 1934 to March 15, 1935, in a smaller format. A previously unpublished story appeared in each issue, along with problems in bridge, checkers, chess, cryptography, deduction, and logic. Also featured were charades, a rebus, and scientific oddities. These series were both directed by Albert Pigasse, founder of the collection "Le Masque" (The Mask). Published by Librairie des Champs Elysees.

La Masque Magazine

(The Mask Magazine). Complemented the oldest French collection of detective novels by introducing authors such as Agatha Christie, Patricia Wentworth, and Stanislas-André Steeman. Each issue included a long story (Steeman; Robert Louis Stevenson), one or two shorter titles, and columns on the tourist industry, films, radio, crossword puzzles, and other features. Published monthly by the Librairie des Champs Elyssés, January–May 1929, 5 issues.

Le Saint Detective Magazine

The French edition of the English-language *The Saint Detective Magazine** was essentially composed of short stories with columns by Pierre Boileau on books and Pierre Nord on films. Published monthly by Arthème Fayard, March 1955–December 1967; 154 issues.

Les Amis du Crime

See full profile following checklist.

Magazine du Mystere

(Magazine of Mystery). After the disappearance of *Mystere Magazine*, Luc Geslin founded (and edited) this magazine to free himself, he said, from the obligation to publish American stories. The greater part of the stories were by French authors; columnists from the former *Mystere Magazine* also appeared. Published bimonthly by Elyssés Promotions, November 1976 to approximately March 1978, 12 issues. At the same time, Opta Editions tried, with a new team, to continue the publication of anthologies in the manner of *Mystere Magazine Bis*. Two issues were published: *L'Affaire de la Lapine Blanche* (The Case of the White Bunny) in 1977, and *Cellule Insonorisee* (The Soundproof Cell) in 1978.

Minuit

(Midnight). As the French edition of *Mike Shayne Mystery Magazine,* Minuit* featured American short stories, plus columns by Francis Didelot and Jacqueline Barde. Published monthly by Arthème Fayard, April 1959–March 1960, 12 issues. When this magazine ceased, Didelot and Barde joined the team of *Le Saint Detective Magazine* which was also published by Fayard.

Mystere Magazine

(Mystery Magazine). Becoming the most important French detective magazine, this was founded by Maurice Renault, who was the most active person in postwar detective fiction and science fiction. As the French edition of *Ellery Queen's Mystery Magazine,** emphasis was on American and English authors at first, but these were soon joined by French and Belgian writers. The critical material varied but included reports on current books and films and author profiles. The magazine collapsed after the retirement of Maurice Renault (circa 1968). Published Monthly by Opta, January 1948–October 1976, 343 issues.

Mystere Magazine

(Mystery Magazine). Edited by Luc Geslin, this new magazine (note one by same title published previously), using the format of *Time* magazine, featured some stories, current detective fiction, and articles on various subjects (for example "La navette spaciale"—"The Space Shuttle"). Published by Editions d'Iéna, December 1981–January 1982 (then suspended); 2 issues.

Mystere Magazine Bis

(Mystery Magazine Supplement). Seventeen issues are titled *Anthologie du Mystere* (Mystery Anthology); two are titled *Les Grands Detectives* (The Great Detectives); and three are titled, respectively: *Violences; A Tue et a Toi* (To the Murdered Woman and You); and *Neuf Dames Sans Merci* (Nine Ladies without Pity). The Supplements were anthologies taken for the most part from the monthly Opta *Mystere Magazine*, with some unpublished stories added. Published by Opta semimonthly and every three weeks, 1961–1976, 23 issues.

Noir Magazine

The editor-in-chief was Albert Simonin, author of the best-seller, *Touchez-Pas au Grisbi* (Don't Touch the Loot). This magazine featured French authors; and articles and stories of Leo Malet, Albert Simonin, Pierre Boileau, and Catherine Arley were featured. Published for two issues, by Charles Frémanger, April and May–June 1954.

Polar

('Tec Fiction). Edited by Franqis Guérif, each issue focuses on a dossier of an author (William Irish, Jim Thompson, Léo Malet, James Cain, W. R. Burnett, and others), including an interview, an unpublished story, a filmography, a bibliography, and an in-depth article on the writer's work. In addition, regular columns appear on the current *polar* (films, books, television, comic strips), as well as one or two stories. Published by Les jarres d'or, on a monthly basis, April 1979–October 1981, 21 issues.

Police et Contre-Espionnage

(Detectives and Counter-Espionage). Each issue featured a long story and several columns. Published monthly by Presses-Éditions Parisiennes, September 1949–February 1950, 6 issues.

Super Policier Magazine

(Super Detective Magazine). Edited by Georges H. Gallet, who was a science fiction specialist; this may explain the presence of a science fiction story (by Richard Matheson) in the midst of detective stories. Included articles on criminal cases, police work, and judicial columns. Published monthly by André Jaeger, December 1953–June 1954, 6 issues.

Suspense

The French edition of the U.S. *Manhunt.** With stories of David Goodis, Evan Hunter, Mickey Spillane, and others, this magazine was the victim of censorship—the illustrated covers, in the style of the pulps, were made the object of an edict banning them for public sale and for sale to minors, in May 1957. Without this "advertising," the magazine was unable to continue and ceased publication soon thereafter. Published by Opta (founded by Maurice Renault) on a monthly schedule, April 1956–April 1958, 25 issues.

Thriller

One issue to date, January 1982, published by Campus Editions, and slated to be bimonthly. Featured short stories (by William Irish, Robert Bloch, Avram Davidson), comic strips, and a very short report on the current mystery scene.

"22"

This was the French edition of *Best Detective Stories of the Year* with short stories by Ellery Queen, Evan Hunter, Ray Bradbury, and others. No French authors were represented. Published monthly by Arthègme Fayard, January–June 1958, 6 issues.

—*François Guèrif*

Enigmatika (French)

After publishing a preliminary series of studies on detective fiction in the magazine *Subsidia Patapysica,* a group known acronymically as OULIPOPO (*Ouvroir de littérature policière potentielle* or the Workroom of Potential Detective Literature) decided to collaborate on a bulletin in which material of interest to the reader and scholar would be published on a regular basis. Jacques Baudou agreed to serve as managing editor, with other members of the team as editorial consultants. The first issue, a *varia,* appeared in February 1976 and consisted of fifty-six mimeographed pages with a cover by artist Alain Margotton. The magazine is usually divided into two sections: a main body with articles, interviews, and critical texts; and an appendix with reviews, letters, indexes to titles published in book series, and events of note in France and non-French-speaking countries. Of particular interest in this appendix is a "Dictionary of Authors," compiled by Michel Lebrun, which is an international bio-bibliographical listing of authors and works which aspires to an inclusiveness that distinguishes it from the *Encyclopedia of Mystery and Detection* and from the *Dictionary of 20th Century Mystery Writers.* In *Enigmatika 19* (June 1981), the index has reached only the letter *B*, and it is obvious that unless the dictionary is published separately, it may not be completed in the pages of the magazine in this century. This is unfortunate given the scope and importance of this project, but attempts to find a publisher willing to underwrite it have been unsuccessful.

The first issue was, as I have noted, a *varia*, with the only focus that of the subject matter. There have been, however, a number of special issues devoted to a single writer or topic:

No. 2. *"Dossier Arsène Lupin."* An issue conceived as a hommage to the senior Lupinian scholar, Jean-Claude Dinguirard. Bibliography.

No. 6. *"Spécial Stanislaw Andrè Steeman."* Essays and a bibliography.

No. 8. *"Dossier Arsène Lupin II."*

No. 10. *"Dossier Chesterton."* Focuses on Gilbert K. Chesterton as an author of detective fiction. Includes a compilation of the complete notes of Borges on Chesterton.

No. 12–13. *"Spécial Série Noire."* Hommage to the American writers of the 1970s as fathers of the new *série noire*.

No. 15. *"Dossier Pierre Véry."* The first comprehensive series of studies devoted to the writer many critics consider the most important modern French creator of detective fiction.

No. 18. Léo Malet and Nestor Burma. The writer and his fictional detective.

No. 19. Maurice Bernard Endrebe. A salute to the influential novelist, editor, translator, and critic.

Although the articles are often unsigned, many of the leading French critics of detective fiction have contributed to *Enigmatika*. Among them are François Rivière, François Le Lionnais, Maurice Bernard Endrebe, Yves Ollivier Martin, and Jean-Jacques Schleret, in addition to Editor Baudou. The team has also published a series, *Bibliothèque Enigmatique*, devoted to contemporary authors or to the reprinting of little-known works.

One of the features that distinguishes *Engimtika* from its closest American counterpart, *The Armchair Detective*,* is its sense of humor. The Oulipopians are critical progeny of the influential satirist Alfred Jarry, the first "pataphysician," and while their research is substantial and serious, the writings are sometimes marked by an ironic playfulness. It is, however, a refusal to accept themselves as promoters of a holy canon that is at work here, so that their writings are always informed by a sense of the "potential" rather than the fully realized or entombed. There is a recognition that theirs is very much work-in-progress, and there is always the sense of a team engaged in a common enterprise of great purpose. And it is also, one might say, a team characterized by its collective intelligence and wit.

Information Sources

INDEX SOURCES: None known.
LOCATION SOURCES: Private collectors only.

Publication History

MAGAZINE TITLE: *Enigmatika*.
TITLE CHANGES: None.

VOLUME AND ISSUE DATA: No. 1 (February 1976) through no. 19 (to date, June 1981); 19 issues.

PUBLISHER: OULIPOPO, under the direction of Jacques Baudou, 4 rue de l'Avenir, Les Mesneux 51500, Rilly La Montagne, France.

EDITOR: Jacques Baudou.

PRICE PER ISSUE: By subscription only, 4 issues for 50 francs.

SIZE AND PAGINATION: 8-1/2" X 11"; varied pagination.

CURRENT STATUS: Active.

—*Walter Albert*

La Revue des Études Lupiennes (French)

Arsène Lupin, a French detective who captured the imagination and hearts of countless French, English, and American readers, first appeared in 1906 in a story titled "The Arrest of Arsène Lupin." His creator, Maurice Leblanc, was persuaded to then produce a series of tales involving what he himself described as a combination of the "two most extraordinary detectives that the imagination of man has hitherto conceived, the Dupin of Edgar Allan Poe, and the Lecoq of Emile Gaboriau" (*Arsene Lupin vs. Herlock Sholmes,* 1908).

One of the early stories brought Sherlock Holmes (as "Herlock Sholmes") into the plot, although in this and succeeding tales, it was Lupin, and not Holmes, who was able to solve the crime.

Interest in Lupin was solidified in 1965 when F. Anqueti-Turet founded, in France, the Society of Lupinian Studies (La Societé des Études Lupiniennes) for the purpose of studying and perpetuating the works and exploits of this famous fictional detective. Four issues of a newsletter-journal, the *Gazette of Lupinian Studies,* were published during 1965 and 1966 and in 1967 was succeeded by *La Revue des Etudes Lupiniennes* under the editorship of Jean-Claude Dinguirard, who was the sole editor, typist, proofreader, and publisher during the next five years of the *Revue's* existence. Numbering was continued from its predecessor.

The *Revue* was strictly limited in the number of copies printed, never having more than sixty-four subscribers, to avoid taxation, and it has been estimated that there are less than twenty complete runs now still in existence. In fact, the *Revue* was discontinued when the demand for it increased to the point where it was not practical to continue it as a free publication.

The *Revue* was published on cheap, pastel-shaded, varicolored paper, with six issues between 1967 and 1971. Emphasis was more on Arsène Lupin than his author, Maurice Leblanc, and could be compared in content with the early issues of *The Baker Street Journal.** Articles and commentary treated Lupin as a real-life person, with serious literary study, a la Sherlock Holmes.

Information Sources

BIBLIOGRAPHY:

Dinguirard, Jean-Claude. "Five Years of Lupinian Studies," trans. by Ann Byerly. *Baker Street Miscellany,* no. 20 (December 1979): 3–11.

Leblanc, Maurice. *Arsène Lupin contre Sherlock Holmes*. Paris: Pierre Lafitte, 1908.
INDEX SOURCES: None known.
LOCATION SOURCES: Private collectors only.

Publication History

MAGAZINE TITLE: *La Revue des Études Lupiniennes* (The Revue of Lupinian Studies).
TITLE CHANGES: Continuation of *The Gazette of Lupinian Studies*, with no. 5 as a
   continuation of numbering also.
VOLUME AND ISSUE DATA: No. 1 (1965) through no. 7/8 (1971); 10 total issues
   (irregular numbering).
PUBLISHERS: F. Anqueti-Turet (1965–1966); Jean-Claude Dinguirard, University of
   Toulouse (1967–1971).
EDITORS: F. Anqueti-Turet (1965–1966); Jean-Claude Dinguirard (1967–1971).
PRICE PER ISSUE: Complimentary.
SIZE AND PAGINATION: 21 X 27 cm; 24–80 pages.
CURRENT STATUS: Discontinued.

Les Amis du Crime (French)

Since its first issue in January 1977, this offset bibliographical magazine has
been published by Jean-François Naudon, owner of a specialty bookstore in
Paris, Au Troisieme Oeil (At the Third Eye). The first issue of *Les Amis du
Crime* established the format which has generally been followed through eleven
successive issues: a bibliography of the works of a single author ("the most
exhaustive possible"), with a short biography, an interview where feasible, a
filmography, and "especially a telefilmography, which is becoming increasingly
important." The titles are arranged chronologically with information on publication in the original language in both hardback and paperback editions and,
where appropriate, bibliographical information on the French edition(s). Both
original book and magazine publications are noted, and there is often a listing
of short story publications. The first issue on John Dickson Carr/Carter Dickson
was exhausted in its initial printing of 150 copies, and a revised and expanded
edition (1 *bis* or supplement) was published in May 1979. However, the other
issues have had the print run increased to three hundred and even when the
printing was sold out have not been reprinted.

Although Naudon is both the general editor and publisher of the series, individual issues have been edited by various specialists who have followed the
basic format, with some variations as noted in the following summary index:

No. 1 and 1 *bis*. Carr/Dickson as described above. Compiled by J. F. Naudon and
François Guérif.
No. 2. Patrick Quentin (Richard Wilson Webb and Hugh Callingham Wheeler),
a.k.a. Q. Patrick and Jonathan Stagge. Compiled by J. F. Naudon. Also includes
a Carr/Dickson supplement with corrections for no. 1.
No. 3. Fredric Brown.

No. 4. *Catalogue français des oeuvres de John Dickson Carr*. Compiled by Roland Lacourbe, this "French catalogue of JDC's work" consists of an "inventory" of 36 novels with brief summaries and critical comments.

No. 5. Harry Whittington. Conceived and produced by Jean-Jacques Schleret. Interview, critical essay by J. P Schweig, bibliography and filmography. Also: a tribute to Frederick C. Davis by Whittington and a bibliography.

No. 6. William Irish/Cornell Woolrich.

No. 7. "The Adventures of Ellery Queen in France." A catalog compiled by Jean-Louis Touchant. An annotated, chronologically ordered bibliography of the works of Ellery Queen available in French translation. Each of the items has a short critical note with cursory analysis of characters and thematic material.

No. 8. Michael Avallone. Interview (first published in *The Not So Private Eye*,* no. 8), bibliography, essay by Francis M. Nevins, Jr., and two articles by Avallone.

No. 9. Peter Cheyney. Compiled by J. P. Schweig, J. J. Schleret and F. Guerif. Illustrated.

No. 10. Day Keene. Also includes a substantial essay on Keene's work by J. P. Schweig. The bibliography was compiled under the direction of Schleret and is, as he admits, incomplete. Illustrated.

No. 11. Edgar Wallace 1. A bibliography with a descriptive and critical narrative on Wallace's work by Jean-Louis Touchant. Touchant is principally concerned with novels by Wallace that can be considered crime or detective fiction and only those that have been translated into French. Illustrated.

No. 12. Edgar Wallace 2. Announced for publication.

Naudon has said that he initiated the series as a result of interest shown by customers of his bookstore in obtaining information on important authors. Material has been gathered from a variety of sources, and the listing are, as in the case with most bibliographies, incomplete. But the work of this bibliographic team has produced a valuable source of information not only for French readers and scholars but for foreign scholars. The bibliographies of texts published in French given as a corollary to the original publication provide accurate detail of a kind often difficult to come by. Although the works of Brown, Carr, Queen, and Irish have been indexed by English-language bibliographers, these texts are useful supplements, and the remaining bibliographies do not, to my knowledge, duplicate work done elsewhere. The sympathetic and informative narrative on Edgar Wallace is of particular interest and will come as a surprise to readers who may have thought of him only as a thriller writer of limited importance.

Naudon has recently, in collaboration with H. Y. Mermet, begun to publish catalogs listing, by author, stories appearing in French detective magazines or anthologies. Two sections have been published (A–B and C), and this appears to be a project of major interest to the field.

Information Sources

INDEX SOURCES: None known.

LOCATION SOURCES: Private collectors only.

Publication History

MAGAZINE TITLE: *Les Amis du Crime* (Friends of Crime).
TITLE CHANGES: None.
VOLUME AND ISSUE DATA: No. 1 (January 1977) through no. 11 (to date, November 1981); 11 issues.
PUBLISHER: Jean-François Naudon, 7 rue de l'abbé Gregoiré, 92130 Issy Les Mouli-neaux, France.
EDITOR: J. F. Naudon.
PRICE PER ISSUE: 15 francs (plus foreign postage to U.S.)
SIZE AND PAGINATION: 8-1/2" X 11"; paging variable.
CURRENT STATUS: Active, irregular.
—*Walter Albert*

NORWAY

Overview

The first mystery magazine in Norway—not counting novels published in weekly or monthly parts of sixteen to thirty-two pages—appeared in the first decade of the twentieth century. Dime detective series such as *Nick Carter* were printed and published in Denmark and sold in both countries since written languages at the time were similar. The first domestically produced mystery magazine seems to be the dime novel series *Lys og Skygge* (1908–1910, q.v.), which featured, fittingly, a Norwegian rival of Nick Carter, Police Inspector Knut Gribb. In 1909, a series of translations from the German dime magazine *Aus den Geheimakten des Weltdetektivs* was produced by a Kristiania publisher under the title *Verdensdetektiven*, the "World Detective" in question being Sherlock Holmes. Another fifty-two issues from this series, and this time named for the hero, were published in Norway in about 1915. Indeed, during and shortly after World War I, dime novel heroes seemed to be crowding in on the Norwegian public—from America (Nick Carter), from France (Ethel King, Lady Detective), and notably from Germany (Lord Percy Stuart of the Eccentric Club, Nat Pinkerton, Lord Lister, and others)—most of them under the aegis of Publisher K. Lundberg of Kristiania.

The only local competition after the demise of *Lys og Skygge* seems to have been *Eventyrernes Gentleman: Normanden Willums Kriminal-Politiets Gaade* (The Gentleman Adventurer: Willums the Norseman Riddle of the Detective Police), also published by Lundberg, in 1917 and totaling at least eight issues. Since there was no byline, the authorship of this series is in doubt. In fact, much too little is known about the numerous dime novel series that appeared in Norway at this time; there are no complete records or archives, and enthusiasts are only slowly filling in the gaps.

During the early twenties, however, most of the dime novel heroes disappeared and few periodicals specialized in mystery and crime fiction, although stories of this kind were offered by many popular magazines as part of their fare. (This is still quite common.) In 1924, there was the oddly named *Detektiv- og Sjø-Magasinet* (The Detective and Sea Magazine), but special mention should rather be made of *Rivertons Magasin* (1925–1927), named for its editor-in-chief, Stein Riverton, aka Sven Elvestad, the most prolific and popular Norwegian mystery writer of all time and for a while famous over all of continental Europe. As an editor he was, however, conspicuous by his absence; the magazine was in fact edited by friends and colleagues. It can best be described as a literary periodical leaning toward mystery, crime and detection, printing stories by Guy de Maupassant and Dostoevsky as well as Poe, Conan Doyle, and the editor himself.

Then, in 1928, came *Detektiv-Magasinet* (q.v.), bringing the return of Knut Gribb, the longest running mystery magazine in Norway (thirty-eight years) and for most of its run primarily based on material provided by domestic writers. It did not reign alone for long, for the next year saw the appearance of *Mystikk, Magasin for Detektivhistorier og Fantastiske Hendelser* (Mystery: Magazine of Detective Stories and Fantastic Events). It deserves some words in passing. *Mystikk*, thirty-six pages and roughly pulp-sized, increasing to forty-four pages and dime-novel-size in 1940, was at first published biweekly but went weekly after several years. For most of its run, it presented in each issue a long lead story (or rather, a short novel of approximately 20,000 words) and a serial. Eventually, short stories, true-crime articles, regular columns, and other matter were added. Up to World War II, *Mystikk* printed almost exclusively stories translated from the English, its main source being Amalgamated Press' *The Thriller* (British),* with *Union Jack (Detective Weekly* [British]*) as a close second (although with the name of Sexton Blake often changed to Silas Ward or George Kennedy, perhaps to avoid having to pay for copyright). Thus, it introduced to the Norwegian public most of the British magazine heroes of the day: in addition to Blake/Ward/Kennedy, others included The Saint, The Toff, The Baron, Norman Conquest, and even, in his slightly changed British persona, Maxwell Grant's The Shadow. (One of these Shadow novels presents an interesting variation of the origin of The Shadow: he was in reality Joe Harverson, a lawyer who had been innocently jailed, was released from prison to find that his son had disappeared into the underworld, and became the mysterious crime fighter in order to trace him.) Even the covers and the interior illustrations of *Mystikk* were taken from the British magazines.

From 1940 onward, as supplies from abroad dwindled due to the Nazi German occupation of Norway, the stories in *Mystikk* were increasingly written by Norwegian authors such as Øyulv Gran, king of domestic pulp fiction; husband-and-wife team Fridtjof and Lalli Knutsen (aka ''Peter Pan''); and pioneering police proceduralist Lorentz N. Kvam. Paper rationing forced the magazine off the stands for a year and one-half, and when it reappeared in 1945, it quickly changed its name to *Alle Menns Blad* (Magazine for All Men) and considerably broadened its range of subject matter. Well into the sixties, however, it usually featured a long mystery lead story but by American rather than English writers, such as Cornell Woolrich/Wiliam Irish, Erle Stanley Gardner, Frank Gruber, Rex Stout, and Ellery Queen. *Alle Menns Blad* still exists; but after changing publishers several times and making equally as many transitions, it emerged some years ago as a soft-porn magazine. Bodies are still, after more than fifty years, its main attraction, but the emphasis has been changed.

The original publisher of *Mystikk/Alle Menns Blad,* Forlagshuset, was for some twenty-five years the leading firm in the field of mystery and detection, both in regard to magazines and to books. In 1939, it took over *Kriminal-Magasinet,* which had been originated in 1935 by Publisher Johs. Dahl and under his editorship printed primarily short stories by Norwegian writers. Forlagshuset turned *Kriminal-Magasinet* into a companion of *Mystikk*, though with greater emphasis on Norwegian writers such as Gran and Riverton, but due to the wartime shortage of paper, it was discontinued in 1940.

Although the afterwar years saw a change in taste toward westerns, true-crime, and war stories, and a flood of cheap paperback books made it harder to complete, a few new mystery magazines were launched. None of them managed to survive for long. Forlagshuset's effort to produce a Norwegian edition of *Ellery Queen's Mystery Magazine,* * titled *Verdens Beste Detektivfortellinger* (1952–1954), lasted for sixteen issues. A later similar effort, *Ellery Queens Kriminalmagasin* (1968, six issues) proved even more short-lived. A brief but interesting experiment was the *Black Mask*-type *Garbels Magasin* (1951–1953, four issues). Quite successful was the digest-sized, sixty-four page *Krim-Eliten* (1950–1958, ninety-two issues), but it was a series of short novels rather than a magazine. For most of its run, it was devoted to the adventures of Kaj Henning, Scandinavian private detective based in Buenos Aires, Argentina, written by Swedish author Kurt Hördahl under the alias of Frank Waldor. Other contributors to *Krim-Eliten* were Niels Meyn (from Denmark) and the Norwegian Ove Fedde, a prolific contributor to *Detektiv-Magasinet*.

Then, except for the *Ellery Queen* effort mentioned above, nothing happened until 1979 and the advent of *Alibi*—the official magazine of Rivertonklubben, the Norwegian association of mystery writers. Pulp-sized, sixty-eight pages, published quarterly, it was an ambitious attempt to create a periodical for the connoisseur of crime fiction, presenting stories by the best domestic and foreign writers, as well as features and articles on various aspects of the genre. Judging from the immense increase in the popularity of mystery fiction in the seventies, the timing seemed just right. Unfortunately, it proved to be a success as to quality but otherwise a commercial failure; it folded with its fifth issue in 1980. Plans to revive it have not matured.

In 1981, the present publishers of *Alle Menns Blad* introduced *Krim*, another pulp-sized, sixty-eight page magazine, somewhat patterned after *Alibi* but with a greater emphasis on true-crime articles and more commercial in style, Its second issue, published in 1982, seems to point to its going in the wrong direction—which may be the right one as far as sales are concerned: towards sex and gore.

An overall survey must arrive at the pessimistic conclusion that the died-in-the-blood quality mystery magazine cannot at present survive in the small albeit enthusiastic Norwegian market due to the harsh conditions brought on by printing and paper costs. The writer would love to be proved wrong.

Checklist

Alibi: Rivertonklubbens Magasin

See profile following checklist.

Detektive-Magasinet

See profile following checklist.

Detektiv Og Sjø-Magasinet

(The Detective and Sea Magazine). A short-lived series published in 1924.

Ellery Queens Kriminalmagasin

This was a second attempt to publish a reprint of the U.S. magazine, *Ellery Queen's Mystery Magazine.** Commencing in 1968, 6 issues were published.

Eventyrernes Gentleman: Normanden Willums Kriminal Politiets Gaade

(The Gentleman Adventurer: Willums the Norseman Riddle of the Detective Police). A dime novel-type publication. Published by K. Lundberg of Kristiania, in 1917.

Garbels Magasin

(Garbels Magazine). A Norwegian attempt to publish a magazine of *The Black Mask** (U.S.) type, lasting for four issues during 1951–1953.

Krim

(Crime). Pulp-sized, 68-page magazine first published in 1981, with emphasis on true-crime articles, sex and gore. Two issues published to date.

Krim-Eliten

(New Crime). Featured a series of short novels of the adventures of Kaj Henning, a Scandinavian private detective based in Buenos Aires. There were 92 issues of this digest-sized, 64-page magazine published from 1950 to 1958.

Kriminal-Magasinet

(Criminal Magazine). Published by Forlagshuset of Kristiania from 1935 to 1940 in an attempt to emphasize Norwegian authors, but it was discontinued due to the wartime paper shortage.

Lys og Skygge

See profile following checklist.

Mystikk, Magasin for Detektivhistorier og Fantastiske Hendelser

(Mystery: Magazine of Detective Stories and Fantastic Events). Commencing in 1929, this pulp-sized magazine was published at first on a biweekly, and then a weekly schedule, with at first almost all stories translated from the English language. During the war years, by necessity, the emphasis changed to Norwegian and other Scandinavian authors. In 1943, the magazine was discontinued for a brief period, recommencing again in 1945 and changing its title to *Alle Menns Blad* (Magazine for All Men). Under this title, it is still published, but with less emphasis on detective fiction.

Rivertons Magasin

(Riverton's Magazine). Published 1925–27, this magazine was named for its editor, Stein Riverton, the most popular and prolific Norwegian mystery and adventure author.

Verdens Beste Detektivfortellinger

(World's Best Detective Stories). The first Norwegian attempt to publish a reprint edition of *Ellery Queen's Mystery Magazine*. There were 16 issues published from 1952 to 1954.

Verdensdetektiven

(World Detective). Two series of dime-novel-like publications published in 1908 and 1912, with contents translated from a German magazine: *Aus den Geheimakten des Weltdetektivs*.
—*Nils Nordberg*

Alibi: Rivertonklubbens Magasin (Norwegian)

In the Scandinavian countries, more people read than in almost any other place in the world. More newspapers and books are sold per capita than anywhere else. In Norway alone, there are almost four hundred book stores. Crime fiction is a very popular form of entertainment, and the number of native Norwegian writers of detective and crime fiction is proportionately high. The equivalent to the Mystery Writers of America is the Riverton Club (Rivertonklubben) named for Stein Riverton, (his real name was Sven Elvestad: 1884–1934), the founding father of Norwegian detective fiction.

Alibi: The Riverton Club Magazine, lasted only five issues. A high-quality publication in both production value and content, it published fact and fiction in a pleasing combination. Not only new stories by Norwegian writers but rediscovered classics and translations from English writers were featured in every issue. Interviews with contemporary writers and editors on the state of Norwegian crime fiction, on freedom of the press, and other topics, along with book reviews, a contest for the best new story written for the magazine, and true-crime articles were regular features. Each story was lavishly illustrated.

Among the more significant of the nonfiction aspects was Bjørn Carling's "Norsk Kriminalbiografisk Leksikon," a biographical dictionary of Norwegian crime writers, past and present. It had reached only the "H's" when the magazine ceased publication, but there were already 225 entries, including cross-references from pseudonyms.

One of the discoveries was a reconstruction of the story which introduced Stein Riverton's detective hero, Asbjørn Krag, "Mordet i D-gaten 83" ("The Murder at 83 D-Street"), originally published in 1904 in *Ørebladet*. The original text having disappeared, a Swedish translation published in 1915 was retranslated back into Norwegian.

English and American writers whose stories or articles were translated for *Alibi* included Mary Higgins Clark, Bill Pronzini, Ruth Rendell, Thomas Walsh, Patricia Highsmith, Barbara Owens, Dashiell Hammett, Julian Symons, Colin Wilson, and John Dickson Carr. Norwegian authors included Marit Hoem Kvam, Ejlert Bjerke, Jon Barak, Knut Holt, Michael Grundt Spang, Bernhard Borge (Andre Bjerke), Tone Maagerø, Benny Brechmann, Pio Larsen, Egil Silvertssen, Ella Griffiths, Carlos Wiggen and Terje Nordberg. Other contributors, especially in interviews, included Gerd Nyquist and Nils Nordberg.

Information Sources

INDEX SOURCES: None known.
LOCATION SOURCES: Private collectors only.

Publication History

MAGAZINE TITLE: *Alibi: Rivertonklubbens Magasin.*
TITLE CHANGES: None.
VOLUME AND ISSUE DATA: No. 1 (April 2, 1979) through no. 5 (June 17, 1980); quarterly; 5 issues.
PUBLISHER: Ernst G. Mortensens Forlag, Sørkedalsveien 10 A, Oslo, Norway.
EDITOR: Olav Ottersen.
PRICE PER ISSUE: 12.50 krone (nos. 1–3); 19.50 krone. (nos. 4–5).
SIZE AND PAGINATION: 8" X 10-1/2"; 66 pages.
CURRENT STATUS: Discontinued.
—*J. Randolph Cox*

Lys og Skygge (Norwegian)

This curiously titled dime novel series (Light and Shadow) was the first completely domestic mystery magazine in Norway, and it sparked off the career of a detective hero who is still very much around.

In 1908, H. Schjønneberg, publisher of the comic weekly *Humoristen*, an optimist as well as a humorist, asked journalist-author Sven Elvestad to make competition for Nick Carter and other imported dime novel heroes. Elvestad, of whom there is more to be said later, proved more than equal to the task. The first issue of *Lys og Skygge* appeared in the autumn of the same year and introduced stalwart Police Inspector Knut Gribb of the Kristiania C.I.D. and his deadly archenemy, gentleman-crook Thomas Ryer. The original plan was probably to have those two fight a duel in every issue (the original subtitle of the series was *Den hemmelighedsfulde Thomas Ryer Norges farligste Forbryder*— The Mysterious Thomas Ryer Most Dangerous Criminal of Norway); but after the first fifteen issues, Elvestad found difficulty in ringing constant variations on this theme and Ryer was featured less regularly. Sometimes he had to bow out to real-life criminals like the Russian *agent provocateur* Azew and to Elias Tønnesen, cracksman, thief and escape artist.

In some seven or eight months Elvestad, under the byline of Kristian F. Biller, wrote twenty-eight novels for *Lys og Skygge*, each about 25,000 words. Then he abandoned the chore and went on to greater, even international, fame under his other alias, Stein Riverton. Born in 1884, and living to be a scant fifty, he managed to write some eighty detective novels, three-fourths of which were published during his twenties, as well as thousands of newspaper articles and features and even a number of mainstream novels and stories. In the years 1910 to 1925, he completely dominated Scandinavian detective fiction, and his fame reached most of continental Europe. The hero of most of the novels was Detective Asbjørn Krag, including of "Jernvognen" ("The Iron Chariot"), Elvestad's greatest effort, in which he anticipated by seventeen years the trick that was "invented" by Agatha Christie in *The Murder of Roger Ackroyd*.

When Elvestad abandoned *Lys og Skygge*, he was succeeded by "Oscar Jaerven" (Engebret Amundsen) and "Finn Bratt" (Torvald Bogsrud), who wrote respectively twenty-three and four novels.

The stories of *Lys og Skygge*, particularly—and as might be expected—those written by Elvestad, were rather ingeniously plotted and well written as dime novels go. They usually concerned some spectacular form of fraud, confidence trick, burglary, or swindle, but no murders. Although death was used as a threat often enough, the bodies that invariably turned up were dead from natural causes. These self-imposed restrictions were no doubt due to the criticism raised some years before against the "excessive violence" of the Nick Carter stories.

Of the main characters, Ryer was decidedly the most intriguing. He had an international background, used a number of aliases, and was a connoisseur of food, drink, women, and art; and was the perfect gentleman in appearance, dress, and manners. His name may have been inspired by that of a notorious German axe murderer, Thomas Ruckert, but he is best described as a darker, more dangerous version of Raffles and Arsène Lupin, on whom he was obviously patterned. He was a master of disguise, as was Knut Gribb. Ryer was called upon to do some extraordinary stunts. On one occasion, he stole an entire house; on another, he turned up as a mystery boxer in a black mask; or, as a circus clown. He jumped the famous Holmenkollen ski jump in top hat, tails, and, of course, skis. One story had him taking the entire town of Ostend hostage. Like a certain great detective, he cannot resist a touch of the dramatic, like forcing— in the disguise of a madman—his adversary Gribb to play a chess game of life and death or making use of an old family curse to further his plans.

All this inventiveness is mostly to be found in Elvestad's stories, no doubt necessitated by the ban on murder; and unavoidably his successors had a hard time matching it, which accounts for the eventual demise of *Lys og Skygge*. But although Knut Gribb was a down-to-earth, surprisingly uneccentric character for a master detective, his popularity survived the passing of the series. He appeared sporadically in the weekly family magazine *Tidsfordriv* during World War I, and he made a triumphant return in *Detektiv-Magasinet* in 1928.

Information Sources

BIBLIOGRAPHY:

Carling, Bjørn. *Norsk Kriminallitteratur Gjennom 150 AR*. Oslo: Gyldendal Norsk forlag, 1976.

Dahl, Willy. *Bla Briller og Løsskjegg I Kristiania*. Oslo: Gyldendal Norsk forlag, 1975.

Nordberg, Nils. *Mesterdetektiven Knut Gribb*. Oslo: Bladkompaniet, 1968.

Syversen, Odd Magnar. "Sven Elvestads Kriminalfortellinger." *DAST Magazine*, nos. 3–5 (1978) and no. 1 (1979).

INDEX SOURCES: None known.

LOCATION SOURCES: Private collectors only.

Publication History

MAGAZINE TITLE: *Lys og Skygge*.
TITLE CHANGES: None.
VOLUME AND ISSUE DATA: No. 1 (1908) through no. 55 (1910); 55 issues. PUBLISHER: "Humoristens" Forlag, Kristiania, Norway.
EDITOR: H. Schjønneberg.
PRICE PER ISSUE: 25 øre.
SIZE AND PAGINATION: 210 X 290 mm.; 32 pages.
CURRENT STATUS: Discontinued.

—Nils Nordberg

Detektiv-Magasinet (Norwegian)

When the dime novel series *Lys og Skygge* (q.v.) disappeared from the stands in 1910, Printer and Publisher Albert Johansen of Johansen & Nielsen acquired character rights to detective hero Knut Gribb, probably in lieu of payment for debts. Johansen wrote a handful of Gribb stories for his own family weekly, *Tidsfordriv*, during World War I. To make matters confusing, the original creator of Gribb, Sven Elvestad, at the same time put out his *Lys og Skygge* novels in book form under his "Stein Riverton" byline, the hero was renamed Asbjørn Krag, but the stories retained such regulars of the Knut Gribb entourage as Detectives Harald Brede and Jaerven and gentleman-crook Thomas Ryer.

In the end, Johansen, realizing that he had a commodity on hand that warranted a return on a regular basis, created a new magazine for Knut Gribb. Edited by the publisher's son, Arne Ramn Johansen, *Detektiv-Magasinet* started in 1928 by reprinting stories from *Lys og Skygge*. Soon, however, new writers appeared, and the reprints were discontinued.

During its first three or four years, the average issue of *Detektiv-Magasinet* contained a 20,000- to 25,000-word Knut Gribb novel and little else. Eventually, the Gribb story was shortened to novella length, and other features appeared: short stories, true-crime articles, crossword puzzles, a serial ("The Count of Monte Crisco" leading off), and notably "Detektivklubben" (The Detective Club). This venerable institution was founded in 1940 and lasted until the end of the magazine. It occupied three to five pages in every issue, containing a special column signed by Gribb (the handwritten signature of later years was the work of yours truly), puzzles, problems, and information of interest to would-be detectives. By sending in the correct solutions to ten problems, you became a member of the club and received a special lapel pin as a sign thereof.

By 1940, the magazine's general appearance and content were pretty well established and saw few changes for the rest of its run. The cover would have a color painting showing a scene from the lead story, rather like the American pulp magazines, though emphasizing mystery rather than action. (The only exceptions to this rule were to be found in the middle and late 1930s when the covers had two-tone paintings or black-and-white line drawings on a red background.) Inside you would find a Gribb novella, a mystery or adventure serial, and "The Detective Club." There were no interior illustrations until the last years when the title of the lead story was graced by a pen-and-ink drawing. Thus there are surprisingly few artistic depictions of Knut Gribb; for many years, however, his portrait appeared on the cover, inside a six-pointed star next to the name logo. Also, for the sake of completion, it should be added that from 1945 onward, the magazine intermittently printed comic strips. The first two, "Lyn-detektiven" and "Jon Varg," were of Norwegian origin, featuring Gribb-like detectives; later strips were Dean Miller's "Vic Flint" and, rather out of character with the rest, Mac Raboy's "Flash Gordon."

Published fortnightly at the outset, *Detektiv-Magasinet* went monthly for a brief period in the middle thirties, then weekly until wartime paper rationing forced it back to biweekly and even, in late 1943, off the stand. It was back in the spring of 1945; but peace did not bring an end to paper rationing, so for the next ten years, it continued on a biweekly schedule, along with all other popular magazines. In 1954, magazines were allowed by the authorities to resume weekly schedules.

Until this point, Knut Gribb had remained the constant, undisputed star of *Detektiv-Magasinet*. He had been in all but a handful of its more than 650 issues. Due to lack of sufficent original material for a weekly schedule and a wish to introduce more variation in subject matter, Gribb novellas were from then on alternated with mystery and western stories translated from the American pulps (among the writers represented were Dashiell Hammett and Erle Stanley Gardner). This was the first serious sign that Gribb's position was crumbling. Three years later, he once more came into sole possession of the magazine for some months, during which he acquired an adopted son, a reformed juvenile delinquent who went by the alias of Rotta (The Rat). Rotta then quickly usurped the seat of glory and banished his mentor to the status of subsidiary character.

To diehard Knut Gribb fans of long standing, this was nothing short of sacrilege, and the addition of a Gribb short story in the back pages did little to appease their frustration. This revolution was carried out, of course, in order to boost the magazine's flagging sales, by making a more direct appeal to its main reader group, boys of ten to fifteen years of age, after efforts to catch more readers among adolescents and adults had proved unsuccessful. Its success was transitory; by the early 1960s, readers, writers, and publishers alike had tired of Rotta, and he faded away, reportedly to some U.S. campus, leaving the arena once more to the indestructible shamus of Oslo C.I.D. Indestructible, indeed, he managed to survive also the demise of *Detektiv-Magasinet*, and is now starring in his own series of paperback novels.

Over the years, more than sixty writers (the exact number is hard to ascertain) have chronicled the exploits of Knut Gribb. Øyulv Gran and Sverre Vegenor wrote between them most of the first 150 issues of *Detektiv-Magasinet*. Their styles of writing, different though they were, influenced most of the later writers of the magazine. Their fame also went abroad; the Swedish *Detektiv-Magasinet* and *Alibi-Magasinet* published their stories. Indeed, Gran's popularity was at one time such that he reigned as the undisputed king of pulp fiction in the Scandinavian peninsula. His stories had all the trappings of the blood-and-thunder thriller and were written in a no-clichés-missed, damn-probability style that bowled the readers over at the time but seems hopelessly dated now. More so than Vegenor's, who also threw probability to the wolves from time to time but who did have, all the same, a nice sense of realistic detail and a mischievous tongue in his cheek. Vegenor published 187 Gribb stories altogether, Gran close to 140 and in addition another forty or fifty novellas for other Swedish and Norwegian mystery magazines about Detective Harald Ask, who was none other than Gribb under an assumed name.

Among the lesser luminaries of the Knut Gribb pantheon, some certainly deserve mention, such as John Korsell ("John Stark," "Omar Storm," and so forth) who published 197 stories, a record yet unbeaten; Ove Fedde ("Walter Gun," "Max Maister") who, at 184, including two novels, is still going strong;

Lalli Knutsen, who, aided by her crime reporter husband Fridtjof, produced 107 stories under several bylines, notably "Peter Pan" and "Stein Welle," the creator of "Rotta"; and Alf Halvor Kalmoe, whose various noms-de-plume ("Stein Wang," and so on) are to be found on ninety stories and two novels.

What with so many biographers, Gribb is a do-it-yourself character. In one story he is presented as moody and eccentric, in another as quiet and charming, or grim and unrelenting almost to hard-boiledness, or sometimes simply as the realistic, patient cop. The color of his hair shifts between dark and fair. The only points that his writers seem agreed upon regarding his looks are his sharp grey eyes and firm mouth.

Still, some facts about his life and career may be gleaned from bits and pieces of information scattered around in the stories. It seems certain that he was born some time in the late 1850s, took a law degree at the University of Kristiania in the early 1880s, and spent the next years in the United States working for the Pinkerton Detective Agency. On his return, he set up as a private detective but around 1890 joined the detective force of the Kristiania police in a semiofficial capacity. Eventually, his private detective practice dwindled, and he became a full-time (or rather over-time) chief inspector, rising to superintendent ("full-mektig") during the first year of *Detektiv-Magasinet*. Today, he is the leader of the Oslo C.I.D. Special Investigation Group.

His age remains a constant forty, the only signs of age being his greying temples mentioned by some writers. He lives in comfortable bachelor quarters with his German shepherd, Nero, for companionship and the proverbial elderly housekeeper to look after him. Apart from cigarettes, he has very few vices, women being the least of them.

His constant companions over the years have been detective inspectors Harald Brede, a big, thick-set investigator of solid peasant stock, plodding but sure-footed; and Finn Jerven, young, slight of frame, a ladies' man, and expert "tail."

Like Sexton Blake, whom he in many ways resembles, Gribb has a number of regular adversaries. Thomas Ryer stepped over from the old *Lys og Skygge* in his typical flamboyant fashion, though over the years his relationship with Gribb has rather mellowed and they may sometimes be found on the same side. Øyulv Gran introduced Russian-exiled countess Olga Barcowa, whose chief asset is her remarkable command of the art of hypnosis (her nickname, "The Green Terror," is due to the fact that when she puts her occult powers into operation, her usually dark eyes are lit by green flames). There are also Simon Farr, "the Man With a Thousand Faces," able to masquerade as any person; Stern, "the Man Without a Country," a cold-blooded organizer of gangster crimes; and Dr. Geyser, elderly, respectable-looking, a plastic surgeon of extraordinary ability employed by criminals on the run.

All these followed Gribb from the pages of *Detektiv-Magasinet* into the present series of paperback novels, which came about as follows. During the sixties, the sales of the magazine sank steadily. Going from weekly to monthly and increasing the number of pages in order to include two Gribb novellas in each issue was to no avail, and the magazine was discontinued in 1966. A five-year hiatus followed for Knut Gribb, during which former Gribb writers and others banded together into a "Gribbological Society." This, and the rising interest in popular fiction and nostalgia, made the copyright holders of the Gribb character, Bladkompaniet, decide to give him a new lease on life. Thus, in 1971, a series of small paperback novels was started and is still going strong at four volumes a year, partly new stories and others reprinted, supported by a small but loyal group of followers.

Knut Gribb has by now appeared in more than 1,200 adventures, and to the Norwegian public at large, his name remains eponymous with the great detective, Sherlock Holmes, as in the rest of the world.

Information Sources

BIBLIOGRAPHY:
Arnesen, Finn. *Fra Rudolf Muus Til Morgan Kane*. Oslo: Bladkompaniet, 1975.
Nordberg, Nils. *Mesterdetektiven Knut Gribb*. Oslo: Bladkompaniet, 1968.
Syversen, Odd Magnar. "Knut Gribb." *DAST Magazine*, no. 6 (1981) and nos. 2 and 2 (1982).
INDEX SOURCES: None known.
LOCATION SOURCES: Private collectors only.

Publication History

MAGAZINE TITLE : *Detektiv-Magasinet*.
TITLE CHANGES: None.
VOLUME AND ISSUE DATA: Vol. 1, no. 1 (1928) through Vol. 38, no. 11 (whole no. 1108, (October 26, 1966); 1,107 regular issues, plus two specials, no. 90B and Christmas 1938. There was no issue numbered 236.
PUBLISHERS: Johansen & Nielsens Boktrykkeri, Oslo, Norway (1928–1935); Bladkompaniet A/S, Storgaten 31, Oslo, Norway (1935–1966).
EDITORS: Arne Ramn Johansen (1928–1935); Herlof Hauger (1935–1956); Hans Faye-Lund (1956–1960); Erling Nordahl (1960–1962); Claus Huitfeldt (1962–1966).
PRICE PER ISSUE: 25 øre (through no. 282); 30 øre (through no. 591); 35 øre (through no. 637); 40 øre (through no. 768); 50 øre (through no. 902); 60 øre (through no. 993); 75 øre (through no. 1046); 1.00 krone (through no. 1089); 1.15 krone (through no. 1108).
SIZE AND PAGINATION: 140 X 190 mm.; 36–68 pages.
PRESENT STATUS: Discontinued.
—*Nils Nordberg*

SWEDEN

Overview

If there were mystery and detective magazines in Sweden before 1900, I am unaware of them, so this survey will commence at that time.

The first half-dozen magazines of this type were called "Nick Carter Magazines"—and that at the worst meaning! The magazines were banned; furious parents burned them in huge magazine fires on schoolyards. Many speeches were made condemning these as a bad influence on the young generation. It was a bad beginning for magazines of this kind in Sweden, but perhaps because of this, they were popular, and the few copies remaining today are most valuable. The only hero from that time who has survived is Nick Carter, now in modern surroundings, and more popular than ever.

It was many years until anyone dared to publish such a magazine again in Sweden. In 1933, Harry Molin started *Alibi Veckans Kriminalroman* (Alibi, The Mystery Novel of the Week), containing a complete novel by a good American, English, or Scandinavian (and sometimes German) author. The magazine was very simple and printed on pulp paper, but it was inexpensive (twenty-five öre, which is today about five cents). The success is shown by the fact that it ran 319 issues, until 1941, under several titles but maintaining the same type of format and style. During one period, it published good short stories only. Frank Heller was a frequent contributor; he is among Sweden's best mystery writers, and some of his novels have been translated into English.

At about the same time, two other good detective magazines were being published: *Detektivmagasinet* (Detective Magazine), and *Nyckelböckerna* (Key-Books). The former, a weekly, and the latter, twice a month, contained some of the best authors from all parts of the world, and both were very popular.

Detektivjournalen was another very popular magazine with good authors and is now published in Norway. Övre Richter-Frich was the Ian Fleming of the time and wrote exciting thrillers about his hero, Jonas Fjeld, a Norwegian doctor, and his friend, Ilmaro Erko, a dwarf. Many of his excellent thrillers—some of which were science fiction of high class—can easily be compared with the best James Bond stories by Fleming. One of Fjeld's friends from America was named Felix Leiter (of Pinkerton's) and had lost one arm and one leg—a similar circumstance being found in the James Bond adventures. Some of the best American authors also contributed to this magazine.

During the 1940s, the mystery magazine scene was uneventful. *Äventyrsmagasinet* (Adventure Magazine) was popular among the very young boys, but had no class. *Blixtmagasinet* contained a few good authors: S. S. Van Dine, Edgar Allan Poe, Austin Freeman, and Earl Derr Biggers. The best magazine during that time was *Alibi-Magasinet*, which had a good start with many very good Scandinavian authors, including Øyulv Gran, Stein Riverton Niels Meyn, and Frank Waldor. Although the best of the magazines were readable and enjoyable, none compared with the better British and American magazines of the period.

Many small magazines were born in the 1950s. There was the *Sexton Blake Magasinet*, entirely a reprint magazine from the British edition published by Amalgamated Press in London, most of which was poor quality. The *Trio* and *Thriller Piller* were good attempts but suffered from the fact that most of the authors were unknown to the public. Again, it was a good try, but with poor material.

Världsdeckaren was the best magazine in the 1950s, but suffered from the fact that it is almost impossible to publish short stories successfully in Sweden. (This was the same story with my attempt to publish a Swedish version of *Ellery Queen's Mystery Magazine.** I had met with Mr. Davis [Davis Publications, Inc.] in New York, and arrangements were made, but the Swedish reluctance to read short stories made the results negative.)

There was hope for *Thriller-Magasinet,* with excellent material by Peter Cheyney, Agatha Christie, Victor Canning, Quentin Patrick, Geroges Simenon, and Leslie Charteris. This was puiblished by the brothers Kindvall, in Jönköping, commencing in 1959, but survived only for sixteen issues.

Another attempt to publish stories from *Ellery Queen's Mystery Magazine* was made in 1968, but *Ellery Queen's Kriminal Pocket* perished after ten issues.

There has been more success, however, in magazines about the mystery and detective field than the magazines of fiction themselves. The former type are magazines of articles, reviews, interviews, and news for the fans, collectors, and readers.

I founded *DAST-Magazine* in 1969 without knowing that there was a similar-purpose magazine in the United States, *The Armchair Detective,** which had been started in 1967. *DAST* commenced as a very small fanzine, with only thirty-four member-subscribers in Stockholm and Strangnäs (my home). When it increased to over one hundred subscribers during the first year, it was decided to publish it on a larger scale. It now can boast over one thousand subscribers worldwide and is a professionally established magazine. With my retirement and pension at age fifty, in 1982, I will be devoting full time to the publication of this magazine.

Another similar magazine was born in 1972, *Jury,* with many of the best contributors in Scandinavia, and the two magazines provide a complete coverage of virtually worldwide information on the mystery-thriller genre today.

Also worthy of mention is a special type of magazine, those distributed by the Swedish book clubs. The first of these in Sweden was *Gebers Kriminal-Nyheter* (Gebers Criminal-News), published from March 1950 to March 1955. It was edited by Vic Suneson, one of the best mystery writers in Sweden at the time, and Borje Alm, a keen reader and collector of mystery novels. Here were introduced many of the best British and American authors.

In 1969, Bra Böcker, a publisher in the south of Sweden, started a new book club called "Bra Deckare" (Good Mysteries). Under the title *Bra Deckare,* their magazine gave a long presentation of the forthcoming packages of books offered (two books to a parcel) and the authors. It was often illustrated in color and is still published. Some years ago, the same company founded a companion book club, "Bra Spänning" (Good Thrillers), which also has a similar little magazine.

In 1975, the Lindqvist Publishing Company founded a book club which offered two types of mystery novels, one being regular mystery novels, the other, thrillers. Editors were Iwan Hedman for "Hedman-Thrillers" and the author, K. Arne Blom, for "Bulldog-Serien." The magazine was titled *Fyrklövern* (Fourleaf Clover) and was published until the end of 1977.

Checklist

Alfred Hitchcock's Mystery Magazine

Commenced 1964 but short-lived due to the unpopularity of short stories in Sweden. Edited by S. Nilsson. Published by Journalförlaget AB, Stockholm, 1.75 krona per issue; 80 pages.

Alibi-Magasinet

(Alibi Magazine). A popular weekly magazine, with primarily Scandinavian authors. Each issue had a short novel featuring almost the same hero, despite different authors. Covers compared to the American pulps. Edited by John Lorén. Published by AB Romantidning, Stockholm, 1945–1957, 13 issues; price, 30 öre (1945) to 65 öre (1955–1957); 64 pages.

Alibi Mästarserien

(Alibi Master Series). Reprint magazine of two to four stories that had been previously printed in *Alibi-Magasinet*. Published by AB Romantidning, Stockholm, 1939, for possibly just 8 issues; price, 1.25 krona; 100–200 pages (21 cm X 27 cm).

Alibi Veckans Detektivroman

Commenced in 1933 as *Alibi Veckans Kriminalroman* and was so titled for the first thirteen issues. With no. 219 the title became *Alibi Veckans Detektivnoveller;* with no. 247, *Detektivjournalen Alibi;* and in its last year, *Alibi Svensk Herrtidning*. A popular magazine in which many well-known authors appeared, including Arno Alexander, Wyndham Martin, Georges Simenon (1934), Mignon G. Eberhart, Frank L. Packard, Carolyn Wells, Edgar Wallace, and Sweden's Frank Heller. Edited by Harry Molin. Published by AB Romantidning, Stockholm, 1933–1941, 319 issues; at first 16–20 pages and later 48.

Äventyrsmagasinet

First featuring Swedish and foreign authors, the magazine changed in 1944 to stories under a house name (Jörgen Rastholt). Edited by Douglas Elander. Published annually by Pingvinförlaget, in Gothenburg, 1940–1957, 18 issues; priced from 25–40 öre; 64 pages.

Blixtmagasinet

A rare magazine today, it featured mostly lesser-known authors with but a few exceptions (S. S. Van Dine, Edgar Allan Poe, Austin Freeman, and Earl Derr Biggers. Published by Bokförlaget Suecia, Stockholm, 1940–1941; 57 issues; priced at 25 öre; 24–64 pages.

DAST-Magazine

See profile following checklist.

Detektiven

(Detective). Published both fiction and true criminal stories. Published by Detektiven, Göteborg, 1930–1933, 30 issues; priced at 30 öre; 32 pages.

Detektivjournalen

(Detective Journal). This magazine was published every other Friday with stories by Scandinavian, British, and American authors. Notable were Stein Riverton and Ovre Richter-Frich from Norway; Edgar Wallace and John Goodland from England; and Frank L. Packard, Carolyn Wells, R. Austin Freeman, and Sax Roher from America. Published by AB Romantidning, Stockholm, 1939–1942; 88 issues; first 42 issues priced 25 öre, in 1941 price increased to 35 öre.

Detektivmagasinet

Probably the best magazine of its kind published in Sweden, with many good American and British authors (Leslie Charteris, Cornell Woolrich, G. Wayman Jones, Erle Stanley Gardner, Dashiell Hammett, L. Ron Hubbard, and others). The early issues used the best Scandinavian authors, such as Oyulv Gran, Stein Riverton, Sverre Vegenor, and Kaj Renertz. Many stories from abroad were possibly used without permission, under pseudonyms; these are still unidentified, although a DAST member (see *DAST–Magasinet*), Kjell Hjalmarsson, has done much research on this. Edited by John Loren. Published by Romanforlaget, Göteborg, 1934–1956, 23 volumes; priced at 25–65 öre; 64 pages.

Ellery Queen's Kriminal Pocket

A quality magazine, the Swedish version of the American *Ellery Queen's Mystery Magazine,** with seven or eight short stories in each issue. Hugh Pentecost, Julian Symons, Donald E. Westlake, and John Dickson Carr were among the authors included. Published by Hemmets Journal, Helsingborg, 1968–1969, 10 issues; priced at 3.95 krona; 98 pages.

Jury–Tidskrift for Deckarvänner

As the translation of the Swedish title implies, *Jury* is a magazine for crime-novel and thriller addicts. It contains the usual fanzine material, reviews, author sketches, a Sherlock Holmes column, and an international sweep over at least the English and American crime and thriller field (with intent to expand into other areas). Articles delve into the somewhat deeper levels of the crime and thriller novel, with analysis. One of the purposes is to cope with "double standards" found and to see the novels both as light entertainment and serious literature. Often the issues of *Jury* are concentrated on a specific theme, for example, T.V. and crime, woman and crime, the crime short story, book covers, and other artistic elements. Contributors include most of Sweden's top mystery authors and critics as well as fans. *Jury* has also published three books through February 1982: a book on scientific research on the crime novel, a history of the Swedish crime novel (published by the Crime Writers Congress 1981), and a book about the Swedish crime writer, Stieg Trenter. *Jury*, primarily nonfiction, is published by Bertil R. Widerberg, Stockholm, 1972–to date; price is 75 krona per year; 100 pages.

Knock Out

Among the authors were Richard S. Prather, Peter Cheyney, Henry Kane, Richard Deming, and Mickey Spillane ("Everybody's Watching Me"). Published by AB Parrot, Stockholm, 1958–1959, 8 issues; 2 krona per issue; 145 pages.

Masken

A semiprofessional magazine; some suspect most of the stories were written by the editor, L. H. Landen. Published in Göteborg, 1934–1937, 59 issues.

Mysterie Magasinet

A short-lived magazine of juvenile short mystery stories, cartoons, quizzes, and short articles. Edited by Rolf Lindberg. Published by Serieförlaget, 1954–1955, probably 7 issues; 50 öre.

Nat Pinkerton

Translated from the U.S. edition. Published by A. Eichler, circa 1909, 15 issues; at 10 öre per copy; 32 pages.

Nick Carter

All issues had full-color covers taken from the American original, as well as the text. Subtitled "*Amerikas Största Detektiv.*" Edited by E. Jonsson. Published by Nick Carters Förlag of Malmö, 1909–1910, 32 issues; priced at 25 öre; 32 pages.

Novellmagasinet

Commenced as a romantic magazine for women, but later issues included much mystery and thriller fiction, including one story by Cornell Woolrich. Covers continued in the romance vein. Edited and published by John Lorèn, Göteborg, Vol. 2, no. 1 (1935) to Vol. 23, no. 24; 25 öre.

Nyckel-Böckerneä

One of the best Swedish mystery magazines. The first 500 issues (1937–1958) published mystery stories but after that changed to western-type fiction. The magazine was dominated by British authors in the beginning, but later issues included Earl Derr Biggers, Rex Stout (a very popular author in Sweden), Erle Stanley Gardner, Patrick Quentin, and many others. British authors included Edmund Snell, J. G. Brandon, Sydney Horler, John Creasey, and Berkeley Grey, as examples. Edited by John Loren. Published by Romanförlaget, Göteborg; 50 öre per issue; 96 pages.

Öyulv Gran-Magasinet

Discontinued after one issue (1956) due to poor sales. Edited by John Loren. Published by Öyulv Gran-Magasinet, Göteborg; 95 öre; 96 pages.

Pat Conner

Possibly reprinted from a foreign original. Published by Skanska Förlaget, of Malmö, 1908–1909, 20 issues; 10 öre per copy; 32 pages.

Sexton Blake Magasinet

Popular among young boys, this was a reprint of the British magazine published by Amalgamated Press Ltd. of London. The Swedish version was published by Elanders, Göteborg, 1951– , 162 issues; 95 öre per issue; 96 pages.

Sherlock Holmes Detektiv-Historier

A rare magazine today for collectors, the stories were badly written and hardly readable. They were not by A. Conan Doyle. Published by Skandias Bokförlag, Stockholm, 1909, 32 issues; selling for 25 öre each; 32 pages.

Stjärndeckaren

All stories were taken from *The Sexton Blake Library* (British)* and were by lesser-known authors. Edited by Erik Lindqvist, who also published it in Stockholm, 1958, 12 issues; 75 öre each; 48 pages.

Thriller Magasinet

A very good mystery magazine with mostly translated English and American stories (by authors such as Agatha Christie, Leslie Charteris, Peter Cheyney, Quentin Patrick, Georges Simenon, Victor Canning). An anthology was chosen and published by Iwan Hedman called *Villa Näktergalen* (after the lead story by Christie). Edited by Kjell Ekstrom. Published by Grafiska Förlaget, of Jönköping, 1959–1960, 16 issues; 1.75 krona per issue; 98 pages.

Thriller Piller

Stories ranged from mysteries and thrillers to jungle adventures and tales of the Royal Canadian Mounted Police. American authors such as Norman A. Daniels, Richard Deming, T. T. Flynn, and Jerome Owen Fox were represented. Articles also appeared. Edited by Per Åke Gillberg. Published by Thriller-piller of Stockholm, 1953–1954; 1.85 krona per issue; 130 pages.

Trio

A magazine which never became popular, featuring short stories by American and British authors. Nineteen issues were published during 1952–1953 before the title was changed to *Thriller Piller*. Edited by Per Åke Gillberg. Sold for 85 öre; 130 pages.

Världsdeckaren

Taking most of its short stories from *Ellery Queen's Mystery Magazine* but with some by Swedish authors, the magazine had some popularity. R. Jansson was the editor. Published by Serieförlaget of Stockholm, 1952–1954, 1.50 krona each; 29 issues; 96 pages.

Veckans Äventyr

Primarily a science fiction magazine, the only such issued weekly anywhere in the world, the title was originally *Jules Verne Magasinet*. After the title change, it featured westerns and thrillers and is still published. Originally published by AB Nordpress, 1940–1947, it was revived in 1969, and is now published by Sam J. Lundwall.

Vecko-Deckaren

The ten issues of this magazine published in 1972 by Rotopress of Stockholm were an attempt to revive a famous Norwegian detective, Knut Gribb, who was popular during the 1930s and 1940s. The magazine was 66 pages and sold for 1.50 krona. It was edited by S. Soneryd.
—*Iwan Hedman*

DAST-Magazine (Swedish)

The year 1967 was the start of a new era in the mystery world with the birth in the United States of *The Armchair Detective*. Soon after, in 1968, Iwan Hedman founded *DAST-Magazine* in Sweden, a magazine of commentary devoted to the mystery and thriller genre. It was at first a mimeographed magazine, sent to thirty-four persons who received it without cost. At the end of the first year, there were one hundred subscribers and the avalanche had begun. At present, there are over one thousand subscribers in all parts of the world.

The magazine has reviews, articles, interviews, and extensive news of publications and events relating to the field. It is considered, along with *Jury*, as one of the two such leading magazines in Europe.

The editor, Iwan Hedman, travels extensively to meet with authors, publishers, and collectors as far away as the United States. Although most of the material comes from Swedish contributors, including the best critics and mystery writers, there are also contributors from Norway, Denmark, England, and the United States.

A regular film column is written by the leading film critic in Sweden, Roland Adlerberth.

The name "DAST" stems for "Detective–Agents–Science fiction–Thriller," and "DAST" is also used as the name of a book publishing company. The company has published books in the mystery genre, including a bio-bibliography of Leslie Charteris, the same on Dennis Wheatley, one about Cornell Woolrich, one featuring "Detectives on Stamps," and a complete bibliography of all such books in the Swedish language. All books are maintained in print.

Information Sources

BIBLIOGRAPHY:
Hedman, Iwan. "The History and Activities of Mystery Fans in Sweden (and Scandinavia)." *The Mystery Fancier*, July–August 1979, Vol. 3, no. 4: 12.
Lewis, Caleb A. "Iwan Hedman: An Interview." *The Armchair Detective*, Spring 1980, Vol. 13, no. 2: 166.
INDEX SOURCES: None known.
LOCATION SOURCES: Private collectors only.

Publication History

MAGAZINE TITLE: *DAST-Magazine*.
TITLE CHANGES: None
VOLUME AND ISSUE DATA: Vol. 1, no. 1 (1968) through Vol. 14, no. 6 (to date, 1981); 90 issues (published six issues per year).
PUBLISHER: Dast Forlag AB, Iwan Hedman, Flodins vag 5, S 152 00 Strangnäs, Sweden.
EDITOR: Iwan Hedman.
PRICE PER ISSUE: By subscription only, 75 krona per year.
SIZE AND PAGINATION: 15.5 cm X 22 cm; 56–64 pages.
CURRENT STATUS: Active.
—*Iwan Hedman*

BOOK CLUBS IN PROFILE

The concept of book clubs is not new. There have been, and still are, many offering books either of a specialized nature or books of general interest. There are few clubs, however, which have specialized in the mystery and detective (and the related espionage) genre.

The Detective Book Club* was the first in this country, releasing their announcement on February 15, 1942. This club is still active and features "3 in 1" volumes, although single-title volumes have been published at various times for introductory offers and in series of books of one author.

The Unicorn Mystery Book Club* was soon to enter the field, in September 1945, but did not prevail and discontinued with their November 1952 selection. The Unicorn volumes contained (with but one exception) four mystery novels in one volume and during the life of the club did include several science fiction titles.

The Mystery Guild,* a subsidiary of The Literary Guild, Inc. (Doubleday & Company), commenced in late 1949 and offered for the most part single-title volumes, two each month, with some of the monthly selections being omnibus volumes. The Mystery Guild is still active.

The book clubs in the United States operate on the advance-notice principle. After an introductory "free" gift of a number of books, usually past club selections, in return for an agreement to purchase a specified number of books in the future (usually within a specified time), the member is sent periodically a club magazine. In essence, the magazine is a preview of the forthcoming club selections and usually includes past selections that may still be purchased. Forthcoming books, if not rejected by the member within a specified time, will be sent automatically, with invoice. The member may cancel his membership at any time after meeting the required number of purchases.

There have also been several instances of a "club" operating on the subscription basis. With this method, and usually after an introductory "free" number of books, the member is sent automatically the forthcoming book(s) with invoice. There is no advance rejection, but books may be returned after received.

The British Isles are the home of a great many book clubs also, but there have been only two in the mystery field: the British version of The Mystery Guild,* which operates on the same basis as the U.S. club, and the Thriller Book Club.*

In England, the Publishers Association regulates the operation of book clubs, defining the clubs as selling book-club editions to registered book-club members at less than the price of the original publishers' edition. (Otherwise, under the Net Book Agreement between the Publishers Association and the Booksellers Association, most books cannot be sold at less than the price fixed by the publisher. An exception is during the National Book Sale, which is the sale of remainders.)

There are two major categories for British book clubs: (1) "simultaneous book clubs," which offer a book-club edition of a published title within nine months of the original edition, and (2) those who offer reprint editions more than nine months after the original edition at a substantially reduced price. The former type will offer books that look the same as the original edition but with the club's name or logo on the title page and dust-jacket; the books of the latter type of club are unlikely to be of the same quality of production and will have a different appearance.

As in the United States, British book clubs operate on several different patterns: (1) Advance notice of forthcoming books allowing advance rejection, and you are billed for books when shipped but have to purchase a specific number to complete membership obligations. (2) Selections are sent automatically with billing but may be returned. (3) You are required to purchase every book offered for a specific period, such as six months. (4) Advance subscription payment required, entitling member to a specific number of books during the year. (5) Advance deposit required, which prepays for a specific number of books to be chosen at the members discretion, without a time element.

Although book-club editions are frowned upon by many U.S. and British collectors as being "later," "inferior" editions, the collecting of such toward a complete collection has seen renewed interest in recent years. Many readers and collectors are now attempting to form a collection of all volumes published by one or more book clubs.

DETECTIVE BOOK CLUB

The Detective Book Club was launched with a full-page advertisement in the *New York Times* on February 15, 1942, offering charter memberships with the right to obtain monthly, triple-volume selections for $1,89 plus postage. There was no free offer or special introductory price. The first volume offered included *The Case of the Empty Tin*, a Perry Mason story by Erle Stanley Gardner; *Evil Under the Sun*, a Hercule Poirot book by Agatha Christie; and *A Pinch of Poison*, a Mr. and Mrs. North novel by Frances and Richard Lockridge. With the exception of minor changes in binding, and the original dust-jacket design becoming the cover design (*sans* jacket), the triple volumes have continued unchanged for over forty years Inflation has caused changes in price, to the present $7.49 plus postage (as of April 1982); but new-membership offers have become more liberal, now providing a number of complete mystery and detective novels for a token charge.

With the firm conviction that "good literature could and should be made available at reasonable prices which people of moderate means could afford to pay," Walter J. Black, later the founder of the Detective Book Club, started his first publishing venture in 1923. This was a limp-leather, one-volume edition of Shakespeare, offered in a New York *Herald* advertisement on Sunday, November 11, 1923, for $4.95. With only $600 saved from his salary by his wife, Elsie J. Black, and the belief that a one-volume Shakespeare could be sold by mail, Walter J. Black rented a small office at 7 West 42nd Street, in Manhattan, using the name "Plymouth Publishing Company." This was named after Mrs. Black's father's Brooklyn butcher shop, the Plymouth Market.

The company's name was changed to Walter J. Black Company in 1926 and was incorporated in 1927, moving to larger quarters at 171 Madison Avenue. During the depression, Walter J. Black, Inc., moved into department-store sales, with Mr. Black himself traveling to sell low-priced classics to the stores. The company moved to Two Park Avenue in 1934, then to the McGraw-Hill Building at 330 West 42nd Street in 1938 as a serious, prolonged illness prostrated Mr. Black and brought the firm to the brink of failure.

With the introduction of the Book Coupon Exchange, the firm recovered. Under this plan, books were sold at low prices to newspaper readers who clipped coupons and presented them at neighborhood stationery stores. With the change to handling the coupons by mail again, in 1941, the operation became America's first specialized book club, The Classics Club. Shortly after this, with the country at war, the Detective Book Club was formed to broaden the operation.

A move to One Park Avenue, an address still familiar to many of the club's present members, followed in 1944. Theodore M. Black, the only child of Walter J. Black, joined the company on October 3, 1945, while on terminal leave as a captain in the U.S. Army after combat service in Europe.

In 1948, Black's Reader Service was formed to sell the firm's early classics in a series form; this affiliate became a partnership of father and son in 1949. In 1950, the firm began promoting the complete works of Zane Grey in a sixty-four volume set.

The thirtieth anniversary in 1953, found the company occupying more than 14,000 square feet at the Park Avenue address, renting for $42,000 a year—a far cry from the humble office in 1923 that rented for $480 a year—and it was in this anniversary year that the company decided to move to Long Island. Ground was broken in May at a new site on Flower Hill, Roslyn, New York, and the move was completed on January 28, 1954, into 23,000 square feet on two floors.

In 1956, the company began inserting card-advertisements in paperback books, and this continues today, along with extensive advertising on the back covers of all of the major digest-size mystery magazines. The works of Max Brand, in a series, were published first in 1957 and added to the company's list of products.

Theodore Black became president and treasurer in 1958 when his father died as a result of a serious operation, and, in the family tradition, the younger Black has continued to search for new ways to sell books. The Erle Stanley Gardner Mystery Library, a series of individual, hardbound volumes of the Perry Mason and other Gardner mystery novels, was published in 1963 in sixty-four volumes. And in 1971, the Inner Circle was formed, a club-within-a-club, offering one or two triple volumes in addition to the club's regular selections, available only to club members.

Since only new mysteries are usually offered as selections by the club, books are selected after only a few months of over-the-counter sales by the trade publisher. Mr. Black had felt that by limiting output to just three titles per month, some of the good titles could not be included. The Inner Circle, of course, expands the club's operation by as much as 100 percent, as has the formation of another club in 1979, the Ellery Queen's Mystery Book Club.*

Material which would be offensive to a family readership is rejected, and books not already published by a trade publisher are not considered. Mr. Black advised in a letter in 1974 that "We like whodunits, suspense stories, police procedurals, tales of espionage and intrigue, 'capers,' Gothic mysteries—in short, those kind of mystery/detective novels which a family audience prefers and which do not capitalize on explicit sex, excessive violence, and the like."

That this formula has been succcessful cannot be denied. To date, April 1982, the club has published 478 triple-volumes, plus 81 "Inner Circle" triple-volumes, a total of 1,677 first-rate mystery-detective-espionage novels in forty years, and the club is still agressively active.

ELLERY QUEEN'S MYSTERY BOOK CLUB

In late 1979, the Detective Book Club announced the formation of another book club, Ellery Queen's Mystery Book Club, designed to offer short stories in quality, hardbound volumes. A new member was offered the choice of one of three volumes as a free gift for joining: *Ellery Queen's Wings of Mystery, Alfred Hitchcock's Tales to Send Chills Down Your Spine,* or *Alfred Hitchcock's Tales To Scare You Stiff.* There was to be no obligation to purchase a specific number of books. Advance description of the forthcoming volumes was contained in the club's semimonthly announcements titled "The Ellery Queen Mystery Club Previews," and one or both of the announced volumes could be rejected in advance. The club selections were priced at $5.99 plus shipping charges.

While subsequent volumes have included a number of the Ellery Queen anthologies (in hardbound editions), a good selection of other mystery short story collections has also been offered. These have included *Women's Wiles* (edited by Michele Slung), *Who Done It?* (edited by Alice Lawrence and Isaac Asimov), *Some Things Strange and Sinister* (edited by Joan Kahn), *Fen Country* (Edmund Crispin), and *The Door to Doom* (John Dickson Carr).

The club was discontinued as of May 31, 1983.

MASTERPIECES OF MYSTERY LIBRARY

Commencing in April 1977, the Meredith Corporation, in cooperation with the publisher of *Ellery Queen's Mystery Magazine*,* Davis Publications, Inc., offered a limited form of book club known as the Masterpieces of Mystery Library. This was somewhat different than the usual book club in that volumes were limited to a specific series and volumes were to be shipped automatically without an individual volume-rejection option.

An introductory volume, *The Supersleuths*, containing fourteen mystery stories, was offered as an inducement for membership. There was no minimum number of books to be purchased to complete membership obligations, and membership could be cancelled at any time. Each volume was priced at $4.95 plus shipping costs; a deluxe edition, with gilded page edges and a red chiffon ribbon, sewed-in bookmark could be chosen for an additional $2.00 each.

Each volume consisted of a collection of short stories chosen from past issues of *Ellery Queen's Mystery Magazine** and was bound in an attractive, bright red binding with profuse, gold-stamped designs on both front and back cover.

Although it was indicated that volumes were to be shipped each month, there were some monthly intervals without selections; a total of twenty volumes were published.

The club ceased operation early in 1979; and shortly thereafter, a sizable quantity of the various volumes were released to remainder book dealers.

The volumes published were all titled *Masterpieces of Mystery*, with subtitles such as *The Prize-Winners, The Grand Masters, The Golden Age, The Detective Directory, The Forties, The Fifties, The Sixties, The Seventies, Blue Ribbon Specials*, and others.

MYSTERY GUILD

The Mystery Guild is a subsidiary club of The Literary Guild, Inc., and is owned by the publishing firm of Doubleday & Company.

The club dates to 1948 when late that year the introductory books were offered and the membership details made public. As an inducement to membership, the club offered *Ten Days' Wonder* by Ellery Queen and *And Be a Villain* by Rex Stout. Throughout the intervening years since, these two authors were prominently featured, along with hundreds of other best-selling mystery writers.

Howard Haycraft served as editor of the Mystery Guild during its early years. In 1966, he was succeeded by Marie R. Reno, who served until 1973. She was succeeded by Norman O'Connor.

Volumes offered are usually single-title selections, with two being offered each month and with certain additional selections designated as "Fall," "Spring," and so on. At times, omnibus volumes are offered, featuring two or more titles, usually by the same author. The Mystery Guild books are their own special editions and include dust-jackets.

Volumes were originally priced at $1.00 (during the period when the club was known as the Doubleday Dollar Book Club) plus mailing costs and have increased gradually over the years to the present range of from $3.98 to $7.98 (April 1982) plus shipping. An occasional title is offered at a higher price.

The Mystery Guild is one of twenty-three satellite clubs owned by the Literary Guild, Inc.; among the more prominent of these are the Doubleday Book Club, the Science Fiction Book Club, the American Garden Guild, the Cook Book Guild, the Garden Guild, and the Military Book Club.

Although membership figures are not released, the clubs had about 800,000 members in 1972, according to *Publishers Weekly*, March 13, 1972 ("The Booming Book Clubs" by Thomas Weyr).

MYSTERY GUILD (British)

The (British) Mystery Guild is owned, like the U.S. version, by a parent publisher-associated company. In this case, the Mystery Guild is one of twenty book clubs owned by the Book Club Associates (a joint operation of W. H. Smith and the American publisher, Doubleday & Company) and is operated very similarly to the one in the United States. A recent survey revealed that about 1.3 million people belonged to the various clubs of the Book Club Associates, with a wide range of specialized interests. The member clubs include Ancient History, Arts Guild, Aviation, Biography, Book of the Month, British Heritage Guild, History Guild, Home and Garden Guild, Literary Guild, and the Military Book Society, among others.

Members of the Mystery Guild receive a catalog or magazine monthly; this describes the forthcoming selection. Undesired selections may be rejected, but members are obligated to purchase a specified number of books each year. Selections offered range from mystery novels, thrillers, and spy stories, to the supernatural. Volumes offered are new, having been published within the preceding nine months. Members have the opportunity to choose from as many as eighteen previous club selections as alternatives or additional selections, or no books at all, each month.

The Mystery Guild, along with the Thriller Book Club,* are the only two actively operating mystery book clubs in England.

MYSTERY LIBRARY

The October 1976 issue of *The Armchair Detective** contained an announcement that the University of California Extension, San Diego, would be launching the Mystery Library in November. Special, numbered, exclusive memberships were available only to subscribers of this magazine. Charter members were to receive a free volume, *The Mystery Story*, edited by John Ball, and the first fifty members would receive an autographed (by John Ball, who provided the introduction) copy of *The New Shoe,* by Arthur W. Upfield, as the first selection.

The new book club, organized under the auspices of the University of California Extension and in cooperation with Publishers, Inc., of Del Mar, California, included a distinguished editorial board. John Ball was editor-in-chief, and others were Robert E. Briney, E. T. Guyman, Jr., Howard Haycraft, Allen J. Hubin, Francis M. Nevins, Jr., Otto Penzler, Ellery Queen, James Sandoe, Aaron Marc Stein, Hilary Waugh, and Phyllis A. Whitney.

Each club selection was to be a reprint of a detective classic, with a new introduction by an acknowledged expert on the book. Volumes were attractively bound and included new illustrations at a $5.95-plus-shipping-and-handling cost.

Among the volumes published before the club ceased operation were: *The Crooked Hinge* (by John Dickson Carr), *The Circular Staircase* (Mary Roberts Rinehart), *A Coffin for Dimitrios* (Eric Ambler), and *The Tragedy of X* (Ellery Queen).

A total of twelve volumes, plus the introductory volume, were published and offered to members.

RAVEN HOUSE MYSTERIES BOOK CLUB

When early in 1980, Harlequin Romances of Canada decided to introduce a paperback line of mysteries, a need was felt to "test" the market before embarking on a wide range of marketing procedures. This was done by offering to mail subscribers the opportunity to acquire four paperback volumes each month at what became a reduced price. As an inducement to become a subscription member of the Raven House Mysteries Book Club, four free volumes were offered.

The first volume of the new line, known as Raven House Mysteries, was published in March 1980. This was *Crimes Past* by Mary Challis. Literature distributed announced that each new book would be by a member of the Mystery Writers of America. Many of the subsequent titles were written, however, under a pseudonym.

Advertising of the club seems to have been somewhat haphazard and limited to direct mail, as well as on the rear pages of the published books.

The cover price of the mass-market paperbacks was $1.75, later increased to $2.25; "members" were offered four books each month at the total price of $7.00 (which included mailing costs), and this did not change when the cover price increased. There was no advance announcement or rejection possibilities offered, although unwanted books could be returned. Resignation could be at any time.

The books were not available on the newsstands until late in 1981, at which time seventy-two volumes had been published. At that point, the books to be sent to the mail membership was changed to those volumes already published but not sent in the usual mailing. Introduction of the line on the newsstands was to be made at the rate of six per month, commencing with the first volume published; but in effect, four volumes per month have been available.

It is not known at this time whether additional volumes will be published and offered by mail after the seventy-two books are available on the stands and in bookstores. Presumably, this will depend upon the success of the series.

THRILLER BOOK CLUB (British)

The Thriller Book Club, one of two British book clubs specializing in mystery, detective, thriller, and espionage books, is owned and operated by W. & G. Foyle, Ltd., "The World's Greatest Bookshop," of London. It is but one of a number of book clubs owned by Foyle, all of which have been in existence since the 1940s. The other clubs specialize in Catholic, Gardening, Romance, Scientific, Travel, and Western books, and there are two that go simply by the names of Quality Book Club and The Book Club.

All of the Foyle clubs publish titles under license from the original publisher, in an exclusive reprint, and normally print titles of the better-known writers. Titles are current, never reprinted more than nine months after original publication, but there are no alternative selections.

The club selections are sent to members at monthly intervals, without prior announcement of the book and without opportunity of rejection. Members are required to accept a book a month for a period of six months to satisfy their membership obligations.

UNICORN MYSTERY BOOK CLUB

The Unicorn Mystery Book Club released its first volume in September 1945, less than four years after Walter J. Black's Detective Book Club* made its debut, and was, no doubt, inspired by the interest that was shown in a club offering mystery selections at a reduced price and on a regular basis.

The announcement of the club, by the Unicorn Press, was made during the summer of 1945, offering four mystery and detective novels in one volume, at a special price of $2.00 plus postage for the regular edition and $3.00 plus postage for the deluxe edition. Most readers are familiar with the deluxe volumes, and these feature a uniform, tan binding with title-and-author-strips in gold on a red-and-black background and no dust-jacket.

The Unicorn Mystery Book Club operated from New York, with Hans Stefan Santesson as editor and Joseph L. Morse as president. Titles, at least from the third volume on, were selected by Santesson.

Quoting from an article by Edward D. Hoch (*The Armchair Detective*, May 1975, p. 186):

> Though its advertising budget was never large, the Unicorn Mystery Book Club did well in those early years. It paid authors less for its selections than did the Detective Book Club, but in those days there were enough good selections each month to go around. It was not until the launching of Doubleday's high-powered Mystery Guild in 1948 that Unicorn began to encounter difficulties. The Mystery Guild paid more, advertised more, and offered the biggest names....Though the field managed to support three mystery book clubs over the next four years, Unicorn finally called it quits late in 1952. By then its membership had dwindled to fewer than 10,000.

The Unicorn Club included a number of science fiction titles during its existence and one well-known volume of pastiches of Sherlock Holmes stories, *The Memoirs of Solar Pons,* by August Derleth. The last club selection was November 1952. A total of eighty-three volumes were published, of which all but one (November 1946) contained four full-length mystery (and related) books.

APPENDIXES

APPENDIX A

MAGAZINES BY CATEGORY

The American, British, and Canadian commercial magazines of the mystery, detective, and espionage genre are normally categorized by the format of "dime novels," "pulps," and so on, and this classification is utilized in this listing. Those produced, however, primarily on a semiprofessional basis, called "fanzines," are best described by subject matter. The latter group is, almost without exception, oriented to nonfictional aspects of the genre.

UNITED STATES

Fiction

Dime Novels

Bob Brooks Library
Detective Library
Detective Library, The
Dick Dobbs Detective Weekly
New Nick Carter Library
New Nick Carter Weekly
New York Detective Library
Nick Carter Detective Library
Nick Carter Detective Magazine
Nick Carter Library
Nick Carter Stories
Nick Carter Weekly
Old Broadbrim Weekly
Old Cap. Collier Library
Old Sleuth Library
Old Sleuth Weekly

Secret Service: Old and Young King Brady, Detectives
Shield Weekly
Up-to-Date Boys' Library
Young Broadbrim Weekly
Young Sleuth Library

Pulp Magazines

Ace Detective
Ace G-Man Stories
Ace-High Detective
Ace Mystery
Alibi
All Detective Magazine
All Fiction Detective Anthology
All Fiction Detective Stories
All Star Detective
All Star Detective Stories
All-Story Detective
Amazing Detective Tales
Angel Detective, The
Avenger, The
Baffling Detective Mysteries
Battle Aces
Battle Birds
Best Detective
Best Detective Magazine
Big-Book Detective Magazine
Black Aces
Black Bat Detective Mysteries
Black Book Detective Magazine
Black Hood Detective
Black Mask, The
Black Mask Detective
Black Mask Detective Magazine
Blue Steel Magazine
Bull's-Eye Detective
Captain Combat
Captain Hazzard
Captain Satan
Captain Zero
Cash Gorman
Clues
Clues: All Star Detective Stories
Clues: A Magazine of Detective Stories
Clues Detective Stories
Complete Detective
Complete Detective Novel Magazine
Complete Gang Novel Magazine

Dragnet, The
Dr. Yen Sin
Dusty Ayres and His Battle Birds
Eerie Mysteries
Eerie Stories
Exciting Detective
Exciting Mystery
F.B.I. Detective Stories
Famous Detective
Famous Spy Stories
Fast Action Detective and Mystery Stories
Federal Agent
Feds, The
Fifteen Detective Stories
15 Mystery Stories
15 Story Detective
Fifth Column Stories
Fingerprints Detective
Five-Cent Detective
Five-Detective Mysteries
Five Detective Novels
Flynn's Detective Fiction Magazine
Flynn's Detective Fiction Weekly
Flynn's Weekly
Flynn's Weekly Detective Fiction
Foreign Service
Gangland Detective Stories
Gangland-Racketeer Stories
Gangland Stories
Gang Magazine, The
Gangster Stories
Gang World
G-8 and His Battle Aces
Ghost Detective, The
Ghost, Super-Detective, The
Giant Detective
Giant Detective Annual
Girl's Detective Mysteries
G-Men
G-Men Detective
Gold Seal Detective
Great Detective
Greater Gangster Stories
Green Ghost Detective, The
Gun Molls
Headquarters Detective
Headquarters Stories
Hollywood Detective

Hollywood Mystery
Hooded Detective
Horror Stories
Lone Wolf Detective
Love-Crime Detective
Mammoth Detective
Mammoth Mystery
Man-Hunters
Masked Detective, The
Mobs
Mobsters
Murder Mysteries Magazine (1929)
Murder Mysteries Magazine (1935)
Murder Stories
Mysterious Wu Fang, The
Mystery (Mystery Magazine, Inc.)
Mystery (Street & Smith)
Mystery Adventure
Mystery Adventure Magazine
Mystery Adventures Magazine
Mystery Book Magazine
Mystery Magazine
Mystery Magazine, The
Mystery Novels and Short Stories
Mystery Novels Magazine (Doubleday, Doran)
Mystery Novels Magazine (Winford Publications)
Mystery Stories
Mystery Tales (Atlas)
Mystery Tales (Western Fiction Publishing)
New Detective
New Detective Magazine
New Mystery Adventure
Nick Carter Magazine
Nickel Detective
19 Tales of Intrigue, Mystery and Adventure
Octopus, The
Operator #5
Phantom Detective, The
Popular Detective
Prison Life Stories
Prison Stories
Private Detective
Private Detective Stories
Public Enemy
Racketeer and Gangland Stories
Racketeer Stories
Racket Stories
Railroad Detective Stories

Rapid-Fire Detective Stories
Real Detective
Real Detective Tales
Real Detective Tales and Mystery Stories
Real Mystery
Real Western Mystery Novels
Red Hood Detective Stories
Red Mask Detective Stories
Red Seal Detective Stories
Red Seal Mystery
Red Star Detective
Red Star Mystery
Romantic Detective
Saucy Detective
Scientific Detective Monthly
Scorpion, The
Scotland Yard
Scotland Yard Detective Stories
Secret Agent X
Secret Service Detective Stories
Secret 6, The
Secrets of the Secret Service
77 Sunset Strip
Shadow Annual, The
Shadow Magazine, The
Shadow Mystery Magazine, The
Shock
Sinister Stories
Skipper, The
Smashing Detective
Snappy Detective Mysteries
Snappy Detective Stories
Snappy Mystery Stories
Speakeasy Stories
Speed Detective
Speed Mystery Stories
Spicy Detective
Spicy Mystery Stories
Spider, The
Spy Novels Magazine
Spy Stories (Albert)
Spy Stories (Magazine Publishers)
Spy Stories (Monthly Magazine Publishers)
Star Detecive
Startling Detective Adventures
Startling Mystery
Stirring Detective and Western Stories
Strange

Strange Detective Mysteries
Strange Detective Stories
Strange Tales of Mystery and Terror
Street & Smith's Detective Story Magazine
Super-Detective
Super-Detective Stories
Sure-Fire Detective Magazine
Tales of Magic and Mystery
Ten Detective Aces
Ten Detective Mysteries
10-Story Detective
Ten-Story Gang
Ten-Story Mystery
Terror Tales
Thrilling Detective
Thrilling Mysteries
Thrilling Mystery
Thrilling Mystery Novel
Thrilling Spy Stories
Tightrope!
Top Detective Annual
Top-Notch Detective
Triple Detective
Twelve Stories Detective Tales
Two-Book Detective Magazine
Two Complete Detective Books
Two Detective Mystery Novels
Uncanny Tales
Undercover Detective
Underworld, The
Underworld Detective, The
Underworld Magazine, The
Vampire Tales
Variety Detective Magazine
Vice-Squad Detective
Weird Tales
Whisperer, The
Wizard, The
Zeppelin Stories

Digest Size Magazines

Accused Detective Story Magazine
Alfred Hitchcock's Mystery Magazine
All Mystery
American Agent
Avon Detective Mysteries
Avon Murder Mystery Monthly
Bestseller Mystery Magazine

Bizarre! Mystery Magazine
Charlie Chan Mystery Magazine
Chase
Conflict
Coven 13
Craig Rice Crime Casebook
Craig Rice Crime Digest
Craig Rice Mystery Digest
Crime and Justice Detective Story Magazine
Crime Digest
Dell Mystery Novels Magazine
Detective Files
Doc Savage Science Detective
Don Pendleton's The Executioner Magazine
Ed McBain's 87th Precinct Mystery Magazine
Ed McBain's Mystery Book
Edgar Wallace Mystery Magazine
Ellery Queen's Mystery Magazine
Executioner Mystery Magazine, The
Fear!
Giant Manhunt
Girl From U.N.C.L.E. Magazine, The
Guilty
Guilty Detective Story Magazine
Hardboiled
Haunt of Horror, The
Homicide Detective Story Magazine
Hunted Detective Story Magazine
Inspector Malone's Mystery Magazine
Intrigue
Intrigue Magazine
Intrigue Mystery Magazine
Justice
Keyhole Detective Story Magazine
Keyhole Mystery Magazine
Killers Mystery Story Magazine
London Mystery Selection
Magazine of Horror
Magazine of Horror and Strange Stories
Magazine of Horror, Strange Tales and Science Fiction
Malcolm's
Man From U.N.C.L.E. Magazine, The
Manhunt
Manhunt Detective Story Monthly
Mantrap
Menace
Mercury Mystery Magazine
Mercury Mystery-Book Magazine

Michael Shayne Mystery Magazine
Movie Mystery Magazine
Murder
Mysterious Traveler, The
Mystery Digest
Mystery Monthly
Nero Wolfe Mystery Magazine
Off Beat Detective Stories
Pocket Detective Magazine (Street & Smith)
Pocket Detective Magazine (Trojan)
Private Eye
Private Investigator Detective Magazine
Pursuit Detective Story Magazine
Rex Stout Mystery Magazine
Rex Stout Mystery Quarterly
Rex Stout's Mystery Monthly
Saint Detective Magazine, The
Saint Magazine, The
Saint Mystery Library
Saint Mystery Magazine, The
Saint's Choice, The
Saturn Web Detective Stories
Saturn Web Magazine of Detective Stories
Scarab Mystery Magazine
Scientific Detective
Scientific Detective Annual
Shell Scott Mystery Magazine
Shock Mystery Tales
Shock—The Magazine of Terrifying Tales
Sleuth Mystery Magazine
Startling Mystery Stories
Story Digest Magazine
Strange
Sure Fire Detective Stories
Suspect Detective Stories
Suspense
Suspense Novels
Suspense—The Mystery Magazine
Tales of the Frightened
Terror Detective Story Magazine
Trapped Detective Story Magazine
Two-Book Detective Magazine
2-Book Mystery Magazine
Two-Fisted Detective Stories
Verdict
Verdict Crime Detection Magazine
Web Detective Stories
Web Terror Stories

Weird Mystery
Weird Terror Tales
Whodunit?
Witchcraft & Sorcery

Other

Hamilton T. Caine's Short Story Newsletter
Illustrated Detective Magazine, The
Macabre
Modern Adventuress
Movie Detective
Mystery (Mystery Magazine, Inc.)
Mystery League Magazine, The
Scarlet Adventuress
Skullduggery
Spiderweb

Nonfiction

Academic

Clues: A Journal of Detection

Detectives in Boys' Books

Mystery and Adventure Series Review, The
Tutter Bugle, The
Yellowback Library

Dime Novels

Dime Novel Roundup
Happy Hours Magazine

Espionage

Bondage
Bondage Quarterly
Dossier, The
Official Journal of the International Spy Society

Mystery/Detective: General

Armchair Detective, The
DAPA-EM
Elementary, My Dear APA
Fatal Kiss
Mysterious Times
Mystery Fancier, The
*Mystery*File*
Mystery Lovers' Newsletter, The
Mystery Monitor, The
Mystery News

Mystery Nook, The
Mystery Reader's Newsletter, The
Mystic Double Agent X
Poisoned Pen, The
Shot Rang Out, A

Popular Literature in General

Age of the Unicorn, The
JD-Argassy
Xenophile

Private Eye-Detective

Burnt Gumshoe
Cloak and Dagger
Not So Private Eye, The

Professional Organization Journals

Clues (Mystery Writers of America)
March of Crime
Mystery Writers Annual
Third Degree, The

Pulp Magazines

Bronze Shadows
Cloak and Pistol
Doc Savage Club Reader, The
Doc Savage Reader, The
Duende
Echoes from the Pulps
Nemesis, Inc.
Pulp
Pulp Era, The
Pulpette

Specific Author/Character

August Derleth Society Newsletter, The
Baker Street Journal, The
Baker Street Miscellanea
Castle Dracula Quarterly
Doc Savage Quarterly
Ellery Queen Review, The
Faust Collector, The
Gazette, The: The Journal of the Wolfe Pack
Holmesian Federation, The
JDM Bibliophile
Lone Wolfe
Nero Wolfe and Archie Goodwin Fans Newsletter
Notes for the Curious

Pontine Dossier, The
Pontine Dossier Annual, The
Queen Canon Bibliophile
Rohmer Review, The
Thorndyke File, The
(See also Appendix F, "Sherlock Holmes Scion Society Periodicals")

GREAT BRITAIN

Fiction

Penny Dreadfuls and related

Aldine Mystery Novels
Aldine Thrillers
Bullseye, The
Bull's Eye, The
Celebrated Detective Tales
Ching Ching Yarns
C.I.D. Library
Detective Library (1895)
Detective Library (1919–1920)
Detective Tales (Aldine)
Detective Weekly
Dick Turpin Library (Aldine)
Dick Turpin Library (Newnes)
Dick Turpin Novels
Dixon Brett Detective Library
Dixon Hawke Library
Golden Library of Indian and Detective Adventures, The
Gramol Thrillers
Lloyds Detective Series
Martin Speed, Detective
New Nick Carter Weekly
Newnes "Nick Carter" Series
Nick Carter Library
Scotland Yard Series of Detective Novels
Springheeled Jack
Thriller, The
Tip Top Detective Tales
Unionjack

Pulp Magazines

All-Story Detective
Amazing Detective Mystery Stories
Crack Detective Stories
Crime Detective

Crime Investigator
Detective Aces
Detective Magazine
Detective Story Magazine
Dime Detective
Dime Mystery Magazine
Famous Detective
F.B.I. Detective
Fireside Detective Casebook
G-Men Detective
Hollywood Detective
Hooded Detective
Popular Detective
Private Detective
Smashing Detective
Spider, The
Stirring Detective Stories
Street & Smith's Detective Monthly
Street & Smith's Detective Stories
Street & Smith's Mystery Detective
10-Story Detective
Terror Tales
Thrilling Detective
Triple Detective
Underworld, The

Pocket-Size Magazines

Creasey Mystery Magazine, The
Detective
Detective Shorts
Detective Tales (Boardman)
Detective Tales-Pocket
Gang Shorts
My Pocket Detective Stories Library
My Pocket Mystery Stories Library
Mystery Thrillers
New Detective Tales
Phantom Detective Cases
Phantom Mystery Magazine
Phoenix Mystery Novels
Secret Agent Series
Sexton Blake Library, The
Shadow Mystery Magazine, The
Slick Detective Yarns
Super Detective Library
War Thriller
Yankee Gang Shorts
Yankee Mystery Shorts

Digest-Size Magazines

Alfred Hitchcock's Mystery Magazine
Bloodhound Detective Story Magazine
Detective Tales (Atlas)
Edgar Wallace Mystery Magazine
Ellery Queen's Mystery Magazine
John Creasey Mystery Magazine
London Mystery Magazine
London Mystery Selection
MacKill's Mystery Magazine
Manhunt
Mercury Mystery Magazine
Mike Shayne Mystery Magazine
Phantom
Saint Detective Magazine, The
Saint Magazine, The
Saint Mystery Magazine, The
Suspense
Suspense Stories
Verdict

Nonfiction

Mystery/Detective: General

Current Crime
Mystery Trader, The

Professional Organization Journals

Crime Writer
Red Herrings

Specific Author/Character

Dracula Journals, The
Edgar Wallace Society Newsletter, The
Sherlock Holmes Journal, The

CANADA

Fiction

Pulp Magazines

Ace G-Man Stories
Big-Book Detective Magazine
Dimebooks Detective Stories
Private Detective

Other

    Black Cat Mystery Magazine
    Black Cat Mystery Quarterly

Nonfiction

Popular Literature in General

    Black Box Mystery Magazine
    Megavore
    Science Fiction Collector, The

KEY WRITERS IN THE GOLDEN AGE

The era of the pulp magazines was the period of development for the detective, mystery, and espionage story. Never before, nor since, has the reader been regaled with such a wide variety of situations, characters, and gimmicks. The fiction was from the mundane to the fantastic. Each development brought forth a mass of related fiction, as was evidenced by the introduction of the private investigator stories, the secret agent tales, and the invincible-hero sagas.

This was, indeed, the golden age of mystery and related fiction, and the names of the contributors are legion. Certain authors, however, have become known as key participants. While this list is by no means complete, either for the authors listed or for the magazines in which they were published, it will serve to identify many of the early markets for these selected writers.

ADAMS, CLEVE F. *Black Mask, Clues Detective Stories, Detective Fiction Weekly, Headquarters Detective, Sure-Fire Detective Magazine, Ten Detective Aces.*

BALLARD, W.T. *Ace G-Man Stories, Black Mask, Captain Satan, Complete Underworld Novelettes, Crime Busters, Detective Short Stories, Detective Tales,* (Popular Publications), *Dime Detective, Feds, Five Detective Novels, Mammoth Detective, Super-Detective, Ten Detective Aces, 10-Story Detective, Thrilling Detective, 2 Detective Mystery Novels, Underworld Detective.*

BATTLE, FRANCIS C. *Crack Detective and Mystery Stories, Famous Detective.*

BECKMAN, CHARLES, Jr. *Detective Tales* (Popular Publications), Famous Detective, Mystery Book Magazine, New Detective, Thrilling Detective.

BEDFORD-JONES, H. *Detective Fiction Weekly.*

BELLEM, ROBERT LESLIE. *Detective Novels Magazine, Detective Yarns, Double Detective, G-Men Detective, Hollywood Detective, Mammoth Detective, Popular Detective, Private Detective, Romantic Detective, Secret Agent X, Speakeasy Stories, Speed Detective, Spicy Detective, Spicy Mystery Stories, Super-Detective, Thrilling Detective, Thrilling Spy Stories, Top Detective Annual.*

BLACKMON, ROBERT C. *Ace Mystery, Avenger, Clues Detective Stories, Crack Detective, Crime Busters, Dime Detective, Mystery Magazine, Secret Agent X, 10-Story Detective, Thrilling Detective, Whisperer.*

BLASSINGAME, WYATT. *Ace G-Man Stories, Ace-High Detective Magazine, Black Mask, Captain Satan, Crime Busters, Detective Fiction Weekly, Detective Short Stories, Detective Tales* (Popular Publications), *Detective Yarns, Dime Mystery Book, Feds, Five Detective Novels, G-Men Detective, Mystery Book Magazine, Popular Detective, Private Detective, Secret Agent X, Speed Detective, Strange Stories, Terror Tales, Thrilling Detective, Thrilling Mystery, Top Detective Annual, Triple Detective.*

BLOCH, ROBERT. *Detective Tales* (Popular Publications), *Dime Mystery Book, Dime Mystery Magazine, Mammoth Detective, Mammoth Mystery.*

BOGART, WILLIAM G. *Clues Detective Stories, Detective Reporter, Dime Mystery Book, Dime Mystery Magazine, Doc Savage, Double-Action Detective, Feds, Mammoth Detective, Mammoth Mystery, Phantom Detective, Secret Agent X, Ten Detective Aces.*

BOWEN, ROBERT SIDNEY. *Black Book Detective Magazine, Captain Satan, Detective Novels Magazine, Detective Tales, Dime Detective, Dusty Ayres and His Battle Aces, G-Men Detective, Mysterious Wu Fang, Popular Detective* (Popular Publications), *Thrilling Mystery.*

BRADBURY, RAY. *Detective Tales* (Popular Publications).

BROWN, FREDRIC. *All Fiction Detective Stories, Black Book Detective Magazine, Clues Detective Stories, Detective Book Magazine, Detective Fiction Weekly, Exciting Mystery, Five Detective Novels, Masked Detective, Mystery Book Magazine, New Detective, Popular Detective, Ten Detective Aces, Thrilling Detective, Thrilling Mystery, Top Detective Annual, Triple Detective, 2 Detective Mystery Novels.*

BURKS, ARTHUR J. *Clues Detective Stories, Detective Tales* (Popular Publications), *Famous Detective, Masked Detective, Phantom Detective, Terror Tales, Thrilling Mysteries, Thrilling Mystery.*

CAVE, HUGH B. *Ace Mystery, All Fiction Detective Anthology, Black Mask, Detective Fiction Weekly, Detective Short Stories, Dime Detective, Dime Mystery Magazine, Double Detective, Feds, Horror Stories, Mystery Adventure, Pocket Detective Magazine* (Street & Smith), *Secret Agent X, Sinister Stories, Strange Detective Stories, Ten Detective Aces, Terror Tales, Thrilling Mysteries, Thrilling Mystery.*

CHAMPION, D. L. *Black Mask, Detective Novels Magazine, Detective Tales* (Popular Publications), *Dime Detective, 15 Story Detective, Mystery Book Magazine, New Detective, Phantom Detective, Popular Detective, Ten Detective Aces, Thrilling Detective.*

CHANDLER, RAYMOND. *Black Mask, Dime Detective*

CHARTERIS, LESLIE. *Black Mask, Detective Mystery Novel Magazine, Detective Novels Magazine, Mystery Book Magazine, Popular Detective, Star Detective.*

CHESTERTON, G. K. *Great Detective.*

CHEYNEY, PETER. *Triple Detective.*

CHIDSEY, DONALD BARR. *Black Mask, Detective Fiction, Dime Detective, Fifteen Detective Stories, Five Detective Novels, New Detective.*

CHRISTIE, AGATHA. *Flynn's Weekly, Great Detective.*

COHEN, OCTAVUS ROY. *Best Detective Magazine, Mystery Adventure, Mystery Magazine, New Mystery Adventure, Triple Detective.*

COLES, MANNING. *Detective Book Magazine.*

CONSTINER, MERLE. *Black Mask, Mammoth Detective, Popular Detective, Ten Detective Aces.*

COX, WILLIAM R. *Ace G-Man Stories, Black Mask, Captain Satan, Detective Book Magazine, Detective Fiction Weekly, Detective Short Stories, Detective Tales* (Popular Publications), *Dime Mystery Magazine, Fifth Column Stories, New Detective, Secret Agent X, Star Detective, Strange Detective Mysteries, Ten Detective Aces, 10-Story Mystery.*

COXE, GEORGE HARMON. *Black Mask, Clues Detective Stories, Detective Fiction Weekly, Dime Detective, Five Detective Novels, Giant Detective Annual, Phantom Detective.*

CREASEY, JOHN. *Phantom Detective.*

CROSSEN, KENDALL FOSTER. *Double Detective, Mystery Book Magazine, Popular Detective, Triple Detective.*

CUMMINGS, RAY. *Ace G-Man Stories, Black Book Detective Magazine, Black Mask, Clues Detective Stories, Detective Fiction Weekly, Detective Mystery Novel Magazine, Detective Novels Magazine, Detective Tales, Detective Yarns, Dime Mystery Magazine, Five Detective Novels, New Detective, Phantom Detective, Popular Detective, Private Detective, Speed Detective, Super-Detective, Ten Detective Aces, 10-Story Detective, Thrilling Detective, Thrilling Mystery, Triple Detective, Top Detective Annual.*

DALY, CARROLL JOHN. *Ace G-Man Stories, Ace-High Detective Magazine, Black Mask, Clues Detective Stories, Crime Busters, Detective Book Magazine, Detective Fiction, Detective Fiction Weekly, Detective Story Magazine* (Street & Smith), *Detective Tales* (Popular Publications), *Dime Mystery Magazine, Famous Detective, Mammoth Detective, New Detective, Phantom Detective, Pocket Detective Magazine* (Street & Smith), *Popular Detective, Thrilling Detective, Top Detective Annual.*

DALY, ELIZABETH. *Detective Book Magazine.*

DANNENBERG, NORMAN A. *Ace Detective, Avenger, Black Book Detective Magazine, Clues Detective Stories, Crack Detective, Crime Busters, Detective Novels Magazine, Doc Savage, Doctor Death, Famous Detective, Feds, Five Detective Novels, G-Men Detective, Gold Seal Detective, Masked Detective, New Detective, Phantom Detective, Popular Detective, Secret Agent X, Smashing Detective, Strange Detective Stories, Strange Stories, Ten Detective Aces, 10-Story Detective, Thrilling Detective, Triple Detective, 2 Detective Mystery Novels.*

DAVIS, FREDERICK C. *Ace Detective, Ace G-Man Stories, Ace Mystery, Best Detective Magazine, Black Mask, Detective Fiction, Detective Fiction Weekly, Detective Short Stories, Detective Tales* (Popular Publications), *Dime Detective, Dime Mystery Magazine, 15 Story Detective, Five Detective Novels, Gold Seal Detective, Mystery Magazine, Operator #5, Secret Agent X, Ten Detective Aces, Triple Detective.*

DAVIS, NORBERT. *Ace-High Detective Magazine, Black Mask, Detective Fiction Weekly, Detective Story Magazine* (Street & Smith), *Detective Tales* (Popular Publications), *Dime Detective, Pocket Detective Magazine* (Street & Smith).

DEMING, RICHARD. *Black Mask, Detective Fiction, Detective Story Magazine* (Popular), *Detective Tales* (Popular Publications), *Famous Detective, F.B.I. Detective, Five Detective Novels, New Detective, Popular Detective, Smashing Detective.*

DENT, LESTER. *Black Mask, Crime Busters, Doc Savage, Triple Detective.*

DERLETH, AUGUST. *Dragnet, Strange Stories.*

EBERHART, MIGNON G. *Dragnet.*

ERNST, PAUL. *Ace G-Man Stories, Ace Mystery, Clues Detective Stories, Crime Busters, Detective Tales* (Popular Publications), *Dime Mystery, Feds, Five Detective Novels, Gang Magazine, Giant Detective Annual, Mysterious Wu Fang, Pocket Detective Magazine* (Street & Smith), *Public Enemy, Thrilling Mystery.*

FAUST, FREDERICK. *Detective Fiction Weekly, Dime Detective, Famous Detective.*

FISCHER, BRUNO. *Black Mask, Clues Detective Stories, Detective Short Stories, Detective Tales* (Popular Publications), *Mammoth Detective, Mammoth Mystery, Mystery Book Magazine, New Detective, Popular Detective, Shadow Magazine, 10-Story Detective, Thrilling Detective.*

FISHER, STEVE. *Ace Detective, All Mystery, Clues Detective Stories, Crime Busters, Detective Fiction Weekly, Detective Tales* (Popular Publications), *Doc Savage, Feds, Five Detective Novels, Gang Magazine, Giant Detective Annual, Headquarters Detective, Mysterious Wu Fang, Mystery Adventure, New Mystery Adventure, Pocket Detective Magazine* (Street & Smith), *Secret Agent X, Sure-Fire Detective Magazine, Ten Detective Aces.*

FLEMING-ROBERTS, G. T. *Ace Mystery, Black Hood Detective, Black Mask, Captain Zero, Clues Detective Stories, Detective Story Magazine* (Street & Smith), *Detective Tales* (Popular Publications), *Dime Mystery Magazine, Double-Action Gang Magazine, Five Detective Novels, G-Men Detective, Gun Molls, Headquarters Detective, Hooded Detective, New Detective, Phantom Detective, Popular Detective, Red Mask Detective Stories, Secret Agent X, Ten Detective Aces, 10-Story Detective, Thrilling Detective, Thrilling Mystery, Thrilling Spy Stories, Top Detective Annual.*

FLORA, FLETCHER. *Detective Story Magazine* (Popular), *Detective Tales* (Popular Publications), *Fifteen Detective Stories, New Detective.*

GARDNER, ERLE STANLEY. *Black Mask, Clues Detective Stories, Detective Fiction Weekly, Detective Story Magazine* (Street & Smith), *Dime Detective, Strange Detective Stories.*

GAULT, WILLIAM CAMPBELL. *All Fiction Detective Anthology, Black Book Detective Magazine, Black Mask, Detective Book Magazine, Detective Novels Magazine, Detective Story Magazine* (Popular), *Detective Tales* (Popular Publications), *Five Detective Novels, New Detective, 10-Story Detective, Top Detective Annual.*

GRUBER, FRANK. *Crime Busters, Detective Fiction Weekly, Detective Story Magazine* (Street & Smith), *Dr. Yen Sin, Feds, Giant Detective Annual, Mammoth Detective, Mysterious Wu Fang, Pocket Detective Magazine* (Street & Smith), *Secret Agent X, Ten Detective Aces.*

HALLIDAY, BRETT. *All Fiction Detective Stories, Mammoth Detective, Popular Detective.*

HAMMETT, DASHIELL. *Black Mask, Mystery League Magazine.*

HOBART, DONALD BAYNE. *Black Book Detective Magazine, Detective Novels Magazine, Famous Detective, G-Men Detective, Popular Detective, Smashing Detective, Triple Detective, 2 Detective Mystery Novels.*

HOCH, EDWARD D. *Crack Detective, Crack Detective and Mystery Stories, Famous Detective, Fast Action Detective and Mystery Stories, Smashing Detective, Tightrope!*

HOLDER, LARRY. *Detective Story Magazine* (Popular), *Detective Tales* (Popular Publications), *Dime Detective, Doc Savage, F.B.I. Detective, Fifteen Detective Stories, Mammoth Detective, Mammoth Mystery, Mystery Book Magazine, New Detective, Private Detective, 10-Story Detective, Thrilling Detective.*

HUGHES, JAMES PERLEY. *Ace Detective, Crime Busters, Gold Seal Detective, Secret Agent X, Spy Novels Magazine.*

KANE, FRANK. *Clues Detective Stories, Crack Detective, Mystery Book Magazine, Smashing Detective.*

KEENE, DAY. *Ace G-Man Stories, Detective Tales* (Popular Publications), *Dime Detective, Famous Detective, 15 Story Detective, Five Detective Novels, New Detective, Private Detective.*

KETCHUM, PHILIP. *Black Mask, Detective Short Stories, Detective Tales* (Popular Publications), *Double Detective, Dime Detective, New Detective, Popular Detective, 10-Story Detective.*

L'AMOUR, LOUIS. *Black Mask, Detective Tales* (Popular Publications), *G-Men Detective, Thrilling Detective.*

LINKLATER, J. LANE. *Angel Detective, Black Book Detective Magazine, Detective Fiction Weekly, Detective Novels Magazine, Popular Detective, Secret Agent X, Ten Detective Aces, Thrilling Detective.*

MacDONALD, JOHN D. *All-Story Detective, Black Mask, Detective Book Magazine, Detective Fiction, Detective Short Stories, Detective Tales* (Popular Publications), *Dime Detective, Mammoth Mystery, Mystery Book Magazine, New Detective, Thrilling Detective, Triple Detective.*

MASUR, HAROLD Q. *Mammoth Detective, Ten Detective Aces, 10-Story Detective.*

McCULLEY, JOHNSTON. *Best Detective Magazine, Black Book Detective Magazine, Clues Detective Stories, Detective Fiction Weekly, Detective Novels Magazine, Detective Story Magazine* (Street & Smith), *G-Men Detective, Mystery Book Magazine, Popular Detective.*

McGIVERN, WILLIAM P. *Dime Detective, Mammoth Detective, Mammoth Mystery.*

MILLAR, MARGARET. *All Fiction Detective Stories.*

PAGE, NORVELL W. *Ace G-Man Stories, Crime Busters, Detective Tales* (Popular Publications), *Detective Yarns, Dime Mystery Magazine, Phantom Detective, Spider, Strange Detective Stories.*

PAINTON, FREDERICK C. *Ace Detective, Ace G-Man Stories, Detective Short Stories, Doctor Death, Five Detective Novels, Gold Seal Detective, Spy Novels Magazine, Strange Detective Stories.*

PEROWNE, BARRY. *Black Book Detective Magazine, Mystery Book Magazine.*

PHILIPS, JUDSON. *Detective Fiction Weekly, Detective Story Magazine* (Street & Smith), *New Detective, Pocket Detective Magazine* (Street & Smith), *Triple Detective.*

PLUNKETT, CYRIL. *Clues Detective Stories, Detective Fiction Weekly, Detective Tales* (Popular Publications), *Detective Yarns, Dime Detective, Dime Mystery Magazine, Five Detective Novels, Mystery Novels and Short Stories, Popular Detective, Spider, Ten Detective Aces, Thrilling Detective, Underworld Detective.*
POST, MELVILLE DAVISSON. *Great Detective.*

POWELL, TALMAGE. *Clues Detective Stories, Detective Story Magazine* (Popular), *Detective Tales* (Popular Publications), *Five Detective Novels, Hollywood Detective, Popular Detective, Private Detective, Smashing Detective, Ten Detective Aces, 10-Story Detective, Thrilling Detective, Tightrope!*

PRICE, E. HOFFMAN. *Ace G-Man Stories, Detective Fiction, Detective Short Stories, Doc Savage, Double-Action Gang, Private Detective, Speakeasy Stories, Speed Detective, Spicy Mystery Stories, Spy Novels Magazine, Strange Detective Stories, Thrilling Spy Stories.*

QUEEN, ELLERY. *Great Detective, Movie Detective, Mystery League Magazine, Star Detective.*

RAWSON, CLAYTON. *Red Star Mystery.*

REEVE, ARTHUR B. *Best Detective Magazine, Complete Detective Novel Magazine.*

RICE, CRAIG. *Detective Story Magazine* (Popular), *Detective Tales* (Popular Publications), *Five Detective Novels, Popular Detective.*

RINEHART, MARY ROBERTS. *Flynn's Weekly, Mystery Adventure, New Mystery Adventure.*

ROGERS, WAYNE. *Detective Tales* (Popular Publications), *Dime Mystery Magazine, Mystery Adventure, Spider.*

ROHMER, SAX. *Best Detective.*

RONNS, EDWARD S. *Angel Detective, Avenger, Clues Detective Stories, Double-Action Detective, Mystery Book Magazine, Phantom Detective, Popular Detective, Thrilling Detective.*

SALE, RICHARD. *Black Mask, Clues Detective Stories, Detective Fiction Weekly, Detective Tales* (Popular Publications) *Dime Mystery Magazine, Five Detective Novels, Giant Detective Annual, Mystery Adventure, Secret Agent X.*

SAYERS, DOROTHY. *Great Detective, Mystery League Magazine.*

SCHISGALL, OSCAR. *Best Detective Magazine, Clues Detective Stories, Complete Mystery Novelettes, Detective Story Magazine* (Street & Smith), *Dime Detective, Dragnet, Phantom Detective, Popular Detective.*

SONTUP, DAN. *Detective Story Magazine* (Popular).

STARRETT, VINCENT. *All Mystery, Black Mask, Mammoth Detective.*

STERLING, STEWART. *Black Book Detective Magazine, Black Mask, Detective Book Magazine, Detective Short Stories, Detective Tales* (Popular Publications), *Dime Detective, Dime Mystery Magazine, Five Detective Novels, G-Men Detective, Mammoth Detective, Phantom Detective, Popular Detective, Strange Detective Stories, 10-Story Detective, Thrilling Detective, Top Detective Annual, Triple Detective.*

STRIBLING, T. S. *Famous Detective, Smashing Detective.*

TAYLOR, PHOEBE ATWOOD. *Detective Mystery Novel Magazine, Mystery League Magazine, Triple Detective.*

TEPPERMAN, EMILE C. *Ace Detective, Ace G-Man Stories, Clues Detective Stories, Operator #5, Secret Agent X, Spider, Ten Detective Aces, 10-Story Detective.*

THURSDAY, THOMAS. *Crack Detective, Detective Fiction, Famous Detective, Masked Detective, Smashing Detective.*

TINSLEY, THEODORE A. *Black Mask, Clues Detective Stories, Crime Busters, Detective Tales* (Popular Publications), *Feds, Gold Seal Detective, Pocket Detective Magazine* (Street & Smith), *Public Enemy.*

TORREY, ROGER. *All Fiction Detective Stories, Black Mask, Detective Short Stories, Dime Detective, G-Men Detective, Hollywood Detective, Lone Wolf Detective, Phantom Detective, Pocket Detective Magazine* (Street & Smith), *Private Detective, Romantic Detective, Speed Detective, Super-Detective.*

TRAIN, ARTHUR. *Best Detective Magazine.*

TREAT, LAWRENCE. *Detective Fiction Weekly, Detective Short Stories, Giant Detective Annual, Ten Detective Aces, Two Complete Detective Books.*

TURNER, ROBERT. *Ace G-Man Stories, Black Mask, Crack Detective, Detective Fiction, Detective Short Stories, Detective Tales* (Popular Publications), *Fifteen Detective Stories, 15 Story Detective, Lone Wolf Detective, Mystery Book Magazine, Ten Detective Aces, 10-Story Detective.*

VAN DINE, S. S. *Scientific Detective Monthly*.

VICKERS, ROY. *Best Detective, Detective Tales* (Popular Publications).

WALLACE, EDGAR. *Best Detective Magazine, Clues Detective Stories, Detective Story Magazine* (Street & Smith), *Great Detective*.

WALLACE, ROBERT. *Black Book Detective Magazine, G-Men Detective, Masked Detective, Mystery Book Magazine, Phantom Detective, Thrilling Detective, Thrilling Spy Stories*.

WALTON, BRYCE. *Famous Detective, Hollywood Detective, Mystery Book Magazine, New Detective*.

WELLS, BASIL. *Famous Detective, Ten Detective Aces*.

WELLS, CAROLYN. *Best Detective, Clues Detective Stories, Complete Detective Novel Magazine, Detective Fiction Weekly, Detective Story Magazine* (Street & Smith).

WOOLRICH, CORNELL. *All Mystery, Detective Fiction, Detective Fiction Weekly, Detective Novels Magazine, Dime Detective, Dime Mystery Magazine, Five Detective Novels, New Detective, Pocket Detective Magazine* (Street & Smith), *Ten Detective Aces, Thrilling Detective, Triple Detective*.

ZAGAT, ARTHUR LEO. *Ace G-Man Stories, Detective Story Magazine* (Street & Smith), *Detective Tales* (Popular Publications), *Detective Novels Magazine, Dime Mystery Magazine, Five Detective Novels, Horror Stories, Mystery Book Magazine, New Detective, Octopus, Popular Detective, Spider, Strange Detective Mysteries, Terror Tales*.

PSEUDONYMS

Since the key writers listed in this section are known also under various pseudonyms, a list of their pseudonyms will be useful to the reader and researcher. This list must not be considered complete, particularly since many pseudonyms are as yet unidentified. Asterisks indicate house names.

Real name	*Pseudonyms*
ADAMS, CLEVE F.	Franklin Charles
	John Spain
BALLARD, W. T.	Brian Agar
	P.D. Ballard
	Willis T. Ballard
	Parker Bonner
	Sam Bowie
	Hunter D'Allard
	Harrison Hunt
	John Hunter
	Neil MacNeil
	John Shepherd

BEDFORD-JONES, H.

Samri Frikell
John Wycliffe

BLASSINGAME, WYATT

William Rainey

BLOCH, ROBERT

Tarleton Fiske
Nathen Hinden
Collier Young

BOGART, WILLIAM G.

Wallace Brooker*
Russ Hale
Grant Lane
Kenneth Robeson*

BOWEN, ROBERT SIDNEY

Lt. Scott Morgan*

BRADBURY, RAY

D. R. Banat
Leonard Douglas
William Elliott
Leonard Spaulding
Brett Sterling*

BROWN, FREDRIC

Felix Grahame

BURKS, ARTHUR J.

Estill Critchie
Burke MacArthur
Spencer Whitney

CAVE, HUGH B.

Allen Beck
Geoffrey Vance

CHAMPION, D. L.

G. Wayman Jones*

CHARTERIS, LESLIE

Harry Harrison

CHRISTIE, AGATHA

Mary Westmacott

CREASEY, JOHN

Gordon Ashe
M. E. Cooke
Norman Deane
Robert Caine Frazer
Patrick Gill
Michael Halliday
Charles Hogarth
Brian Hope
Colin Hughes
Kyle Hunt
Abel Mann
Peter Manton
J. J. Marric
Richard Martin
Anthony Moreton
Ken Ranger
William K. Reilly
Tex Riley
Jeremy York

CROSSEN, KENDALL FOSTER	Bennett Barclay
	M. E. Chaber
	Ken Crossen
	Richard Foster
	Christopher Monig
	Clay Richards
DANNENBERG, NORMAN	John Benton*
	Wallace Brooker*
	Norman Danberg
	Norman A. Daniels
	G. Wayman Jones*
	Lt. Scott Morgan*
	Kenneth Robeson*
	Robert Wallace*
DAVIS, FREDERICK C.	Murdo Coombs
	Stephen Ransome
	Curtis Steele*
DEMING, RICHARD	Max Franklin
DENT, LESTER	John Blaine*
	Harmon Cash
	Maxwell Grant*
	Kenneth Roberts*
	Kenneth Robeson*
	Tim Ryan
FAUST, FREDERICK	Frank Austin
	George Owen Baxter
	Lee Bolt
	Max Brand
	Walter G. Butler
	George Challis
	Martin Dexter
	Evin Evans
	Evan Evans
	John Frederick
	Frederick Frost
	Dennis Lawton
	David Manning
	Peter Henry Moreland
	Hugh Owen
	Arthur Preston
	Nicholas Silver
	Henry Uriel
FISCHER, BRUNO	Russell Gray
	Harrison Storm
FISHER, STEVE	Stephen Gould
	Grant Lane

FLEMING-ROBERTS, G. T.   George Chance*
                                  Brant House*
                                  G. Wayman Jones*
                                  Robert Wallace*
GARDNER, ERLE STANLEY   Kyle Corning
                                  A. A. Fair
                                  Charles M. Green
                                  Carleton Kendrake
                                  Charles J. Kenny
                                  Robert Parr
                                  Les Tillray
GRUBER, FRANK   Stephen Acre
                                  Charles K. Boston
                                  Tom Gunn
                                  C. K. M. Scanlon
                                  John K. Vedder
HALLIDAY, BRETT   Davis Dresser
HOCH, EDWARD D.   Irwin Booth
                                  Anthony Circus
                                  Stephen Dentinger
                                  Pat McMahon
                                  R. E. Porter
                                  R. L. Stephens
                                  Mister X
L'AMOUR, LOUIS   Tex Burns
                                  Jim Mayo
MacDONALD, JOHN D.   John Wade Farrell
                                  Robert Henry
                                  John Lane
                                  Scott O'Hara
                                  Peter Reed
                                  Henry Rieser
McCULLEY, JOHNSTON   Raley Brien
                                  George Drayne
                                  Frederick Phelps
                                  Rowena Raley
                                  Harrington Strong
McGIVERN, WILLIAM P.   Alexander Blade*
                                  Bill Peters
PAGE, NORVELL W.   Randolph Craig*
                                  Grant Stockbridge*
PHILIPS, JUDSON   Hugh Pentecost
POWELL, TALMAGE   Jack McCready
PRICE, E. HOFFMAN   Hamlin Daley
RAWSON, CLAYTON   Stewart Towne
RICE, CRAIG   Ruth Malone
                                  Michael Venning

ROGERS, WAYNE   H. M. Appel
                                 Conrad Kimball
SONTUP, DAN   Topsun Daniels
STERLING, STEWART   G. Wayman Jones*
TAYLOR, PHOEBE ATWOOD   Alice Tilton
TEPPERMAN, EMILE C.   Kenneth Robeson*
                                 Curtis Steele*
TINSLEY, THEODORE A.   Maxwell Grant*
VICKERS, ROY   David Durham
                                 Sefton Kyle
                                 John Spencer
WELLS, BASIL   Gene Ellerman
WOOLRICH, CORNELL   George Hopley
                                 William Irish
ZAGAT, ARTHUR LEO   Brant House*

CHRONOLOGY

The following is a chronological catalog of the founding of U.S., British, and Canadian magazines and standard book clubs, listing the year first commenced and the originating publisher. Note that some entries represent title changes for previously published magazines.

1882

New York Detective Library　Frank A. Tousey, Publisher

1883

Old Cap. Collier Library　Norman L. Munro Co.

1885

Old Sleuth Library　George Munro, Publisher

1888

Golden Library of Indian and Detective Adventures, The (British)　General Publishing Co., Ltd.
Scotland Yard Series of Detective Novels (British)　General Publishing Co., Ltd.

1889

Detective Tales (British)　Aldine Publishing Company

1891

Nick Carter Detective Library　Street & Smith, Publishers
Nick Carter Library　Street & Smith, Publishers

1892

Young Sleuth Library　Frank A. Tousey, Publisher

1893

Bob Brooks Library   Lou H. Ostendorff, Jr.
Ching Ching Yarns (British)   T. Harrison Roberts
Detective Library   Frank A. Tousey, Publisher

1895

Detective Library (British)   Richard Crompton

1897

New Nick Carter Library   Street & Smith, Publishers

1898

Bull's Eye, The   Aldine Publishing Company
Up-to-Date Boys' Library   Munro's Publishing House

1899

Secret Service: Old and Young King Brady, Detectives   Frank A. Tousey, Publisher

1900

Shield Weekly   Street & Smith, Publishers

1902

Dick Turpin Library (British)   Aldine Publishing Company
Old Broadbrim Weekly   Street & Smith, Publishers

1903

Young Broadbrim Weekly   Street & Smith, Publishers

1904

Springheeled Jack (British)   Aldine Publishing Company

1908

Old Sleuth Weekly   Arthur Westbrook Company

1909

Dick Dobbs Detective Weekly   George Marsh Company

1910

Tip Top Detective Tales (British)   Aldine Publishing Company

1911

Nick Carter Weekly (British)   George Newnes

1912

Nick Carter Stories   Street & Smith, Publishers

1915

Detective Story Magazine   Street & Smith Publications, Inc.
Sexton Blake Library, The (British)   Amalgamated Press, Ltd.

1917

Mystery Magazine   Harry E. Wolff, Inc.

1918

Newne's "Nick Carter" Series (British)   George Newnes

1919

Detective Library (British)   Amalgamated Press, Ltd.
Dixon Hawke Library (British)   D. C. Thomson & Company

1920

Black Mask, The   Pro-Distributors, Inc.

1921

Lloyd's Detective Series (British)   United Newspapers Syndicate, Ltd.

1922

Detective Tales   Rural Publishing Corporation
Dick Turpin Library (British)   George Newnes

1923

Weird Tales   Rural Publications, Inc.

1924

Flynn's   Red Star News Co.
My Pocket Detective Stories Library (British)   Hornsey Journal, Ltd.
My Pocket Mystery Stories Library (British)   Hornsey Journal, Ltd.
Real Detective Tales   Rural Publishing Corporation

1925

Aldine Mystery Novels (British)   Aldine Publishing Company

1926

Clues   Clues, Inc.
Dixon Brett Detective Library (British)   Aldine Publishing Co.

1927

Crime Mysteries   Dell Publishing Co.
Flynn's Weekly Detective Fiction   Red Star News Co.
Mystery Stories   The Priscilla Company
Real Detective Tales & Mystery Stories   Real Detective Tales, Inc.
Secret Service Detective Stories   Carwood Publishing
Tales of Magic and Mystery   Romance Publications
Underworld, The   Carwood Publishing Co.

1928

All Star Detective Stories   Clayton Magazines, Inc.
Complete Detective Novel Magazine   Teck Publications, Inc.

Detective Fiction Weekly   Frank A. Munsey Co.
Detective Mystery Novel Magazine   Best Publications, Inc.
Dragnet, The   Harold B. Hersey

1929

Best Detective Magazine   Street & Smith Corporation
Detective Classics   Fiction House, Inc.
Detective Trails   Good Story Magazine Co., Inc.
Gangster Stories   Blue Band Publications, Inc.
Illustrated Detective Magazine, The   Tower Magazines, Inc.
Murder Mysteries Magazine   Good Story Magazine Co., Inc.
Racketeer Stories   Blue Band Publications, Inc.
Spy Stories   Albert Publishing Company
Spy Stories   Monthly Magazine Publishers, Inc.
Startling Detective Adventures   (publisher not known)
Thriller, The (British)   Amalgamated Press, Ltd.
Zepplin Stories   Ramer Reviews, Inc.

1930

Aldine Thrillers (British)   Aldine Publishing Co.
Amazing Detective Tales   Techni-Craft Publishing Co.
Detective Action Stories   Popular Publications, Inc.
Detective Dragnet Magazine   Magazine Publishers, Inc.
Detective Thrillers   Clayton Magazines, Inc.
Gang World   Popular Publications, Inc.
Headquarters Detective   Periodical House, Inc.
Prison Stories   Good Story Magazine Co., Inc.
Saucy Detective   Movie Digest Co.
Scientific Detective Monthly   Techni-Craft Publishing Co.
Scotland Yard   Dell Publishing Co., Inc.
Secrets of the Secret Service   Clayton Magazines, Inc.

1931

Complete Gang Novel Magazine   Hersey Magazines
Complete Mystery Novelettes   Clayton Magazines, Inc.
Courtroom Stories   Good Story Magazine Co.
Dime Detective   Popular Publications, Inc.
Dime Novel Roundup   Ralph F. Cummings
Gramol Thrillers (British)   Gramol Publishers Co., Ltd.
Murder Stories   Good Story Magazine Co., Inc.
Nickel Detective   Nickel Publications, Inc.
Real Detective Tales, Inc.   Real Detective Tales, Inc.
Shadow Magazine, The   Street & Smith Publications, Inc.
Speakeasy Stories   Good Story Magazine Co.
Strange Tales of Mystery and Terror   Clayton Magazines, Inc.
Street & Smith's Detective Story Magazine   Street & Smith Publications, Inc.
Thrilling Detective   Better Publications, Inc.

1932

All Detective Magazine   Dell Publishing Co., Inc.
Black Aces   Fiction House, Inc.
Blue Steel Magazine   Popular Publications, Inc.
Complete Underworld Novelettes   Carwood Publishing Co.
Detective Library, The   Clayton Magazines, Inc.
Dime Mystery Book   American Fiction Magazines
Five-Cent Detective   (publisher not known)
Gangland Stories   Harold B. Hersey
Gang World   Popular Publications, Inc.
Hollywood Mystery   (publisher not known)
Mystery Magazine, The   Tower Publications, Inc.
Mystery Novels Magazine   Doubleday, Doran & Co.
Racketeer and Gangland Stories   (publisher not known)
Rapid-Fire Detective Stories   Rapid-Fire Publishers, Inc.

1933

Black Bat Detective Mysteries   The Berryman Press, Inc.
Black Book Detective Magazine   Better Publications, Inc.
C.I.D. Library (British)   Target Publishing Co., Ltd.
Clues Detective Stories   Clayton Magazines, Inc.
Conflict: Tales of Fighting Adventures   Centaur Publications, Inc.
Detective Book Magazine   Fiction House, Inc.
Detective Weekly (British)   Amalgamated Press Ltd.
Dime Mystery Magazine   American Fiction Magazines
Doc Savage   Street & Smith Publications, Inc.
G-8 and His Battle Aces   Popular Publications, Inc.
Great Detective   L. M. Publishing Company, Inc.
Greater Gangster Stories   (publisher not known)
Mystery League Magazine, The   League Publishers, Inc.
Nick Carter Magazine   Street & Smith Publications, Inc.
Phantom Detective, The   Phantom Detective, Inc.
Spider, The   Popular Publications, Inc.
Strange Detective Stories   Nickel Publications, Inc.
Ten Detective Aces   Magazine Publishers, Inc.
Two-Book Detective Magazine   Two-Book Magazines Company

1934

Alibi   (publisher not known)
Battle Birds   Popular Publications, Inc.
Dusty Ayres & His Battle Birds   Popular Publications, Inc.
Manhunters   (publisher not known)
Mystery Novels Magazine   Winford Publications, Inc.
New Detective   Two-Book Magazines, Inc.
Operator #5   Popular Publications, Inc.
Popular Detective   Beacon Publications, Inc.
Secret Agent X   Periodical House, Inc.

Secret 6, The   Popular Publications, Inc.
Snappy Detective Stories   Culture Publications, Inc.
Snappy Mystery Stories   Culture Publications, Inc.
Spicy Detective   Culture Publications, Inc.
Spicy Mystery Stories   Culture Publications, Inc.
Spy Stories   Magazine Publishers, Inc.
Super-Detective Stories   D. M. Publishing Co.
Terror Tales   Popular Publications, Inc.
Vice Squad Detective   (publisher not known)

1935

Detective Adventures   Lorelei Publishing Company
Detective Tales   Popular Publications, Inc.
Dick Turpin Novels (British)   C. Arthur Pearson
Doctor Death   Dell Publishing Co., Inc.
Gang Magazine, The   Lincoln Hoffman
G-Men   Beacon Magazines, Inc.
Gold Seal Detective   Magazine Publishers, Inc.
Horror Stories   Popular Publications, Inc.
Murder Mysteries Magazine   (publisher not known)
Mysterious Wu Fang, The   Popular Publications, Inc.
New Mystery Adventure   Hersey Magazines
Prison Life Stories   (publisher not known)
Public Enemy   Dell Publishing Co., Inc.
Scarlet Adventuress   Associated Authors, Inc.
Snappy Detective Mysteries   Edmar Publications
Spy Novels Magazine   Magazine Publishers, Inc.
Star Detective   Western Fiction Publishing Co., Inc.
Thrilling Mysteries   Popular Publications, Inc.
Thrilling Mystery   Better Publications, Inc.
Thrilling Mystery Novel   Better Publications, Inc.

1936

Ace Detective   Magazine Publishers, Inc.
Ace G-Man Stories   Popular Publications, Inc.
Ace-High Detective Magazine   Popular Publications, Inc.
Ace Mystery   Periodical House, Inc.
Dan Dunn Detective Magazine   C.J.H. Publications, Inc.
Detective Romances   Ace Magazines, Inc.
Double-Action Gang Magazine   Winford Publications, Inc.
Dr. Yen Sin   Popular Publications, Inc.
Federal Agent   Dell Publishing Co., Inc.
Feds, The   Street & Smith Publications, Inc.
Girl's Detective Mysteries   Layne Publishing Corp.
Hardboiled   Street & Smith Publications, Inc.
Mystery Adventure   Hersey Magazines
Mystery Adventure Magazine   Hersey Magazines

Nick Carter Detective Magazine   Street & Smith Publications, Inc.
Pocket Detective Magazine   Street & Smith Publications, Inc.
Skipper, The   Street & Smith Publications, Inc.
Whisperer, The   Street & Smith Publications, Inc.

1937

Crime Busters   Street & Smith Publications, Inc.
Detective Digest   Ace Magazines, Inc.
Detective Reporter   (publisher not known)
Detective Short Stories   Manvis Publications, Inc.
Double Detective   Frank A. Munsey, Co.
Eerie Stories   Magazine Publishers, Inc.
Modern Adventuress   Associated Authors, Inc.
Private Detective Stories   Trojan Publishing Corporation
Strange Detective Mysteries   Popular Publications, Inc.
Sure-Fire Detective Magazine   Magazine Publishers, Inc.

1938

Bull's-Eye Detective   Love Romance Publishing Co.
Captain Hazzard   Magazine Publishers, Inc.
Captain Satan   Popular Publications, Inc.
Complete Detective   Western Fiction Publishing Co.
Detective Mysteries   (publisher not known)
Detective Novels Magazine   Better Publications, Inc.
Detective Yarns   Blue Ribbon Magazines, Inc.
Double-Action Detective   Double-Action Magazines, Inc.
Eerie Mysteries   Magazine Publishers, Inc.
Lone Wolf Detective   Ace Magazines, Inc.
Mystery Tales   Western Fiction Publishing Co.
Romantic Detective   Trojan Magazines, Inc.
10-Story Detective   Periodical House, Inc.
Ten Story Gang   Winford Publications, Inc.
Undercover Detective   Winford Publications, Inc.
Variety Detective Magazine   Ace Magazines, Inc.

1939

Avenger, The   Street & Smith Publications, Inc.
Detective and Murder Mysteries   Blue Ribbon Magazines, Inc.
Jungle Stories   Glen-Kel Publishing Co.
Mystery   Street & Smith Publications, Inc.
Mystery Novels and Short Stories   Columbia Publications, Inc.
Octopus, The   Popular Publications, Inc.
Scorpion, The   Popular Publications, Inc.
Strange Stories   Better Publications, Inc.
Street & Smith's Detective Stories (British)   Atlas Publishing & Distributing Co., Ltd.
Thrilling Spy Stories   Better Publications, Inc.
Top-Notch Detective   Western Fiction Publishing Co.

Two Complete Detective Books   Real Adventures Publishing Co., Inc.
Uncanny Tales   Western Fiction Publishing Co.

1940

Black Mask (British)   (publisher not known)
Captain Combat   Fictioneers, Inc.
Crack Detective   Columbia Publications, Inc.
Detective Dime Novels   Frank A. Munsey Company
Exciting Detective   Better Publications, Inc.
Famous Spy Stories   Frank A. Munsey Company
Fifth Column Stories   Frank A. Munsey Company
Gangland Detective Stories   Double-Action Magazines
Ghost Detective, The   Better Publications, Inc.
Ghost, Super-Detective, The   Better Publications, Inc.
G-Men Detective   Better Publications, Inc.
Green Ghost Detective, The   Better Publications, Inc.
Masked Detective, The   Better Publications, Inc.
Real Mystery   Western Fiction Publishing Co.
Red Seal Mystery   Periodical House, Inc.
Red Star Detective   Frank A. Munsey Company
Red Star Mystery   Frank A. Munsey Company
Sinister Stories   Popular Publications, Inc.
Startling Mystery   Fictioneers, Inc.
Stirring Detective and Western Stories   Albing Publishing Co., Inc.
Super-Detective   Trojan Publications, Inc.
Thrilling Detective (British)   (publisher not known)
Wizard, The   Street & Smith Publications, Inc.

1941

All Star Detective   Manvis Publications, Inc.
Angel Detective, The   Manvis Publications, Inc.
Big-Book Detective Magazine   Fictioneers, Inc.
Black Hood Detective   Columbia Publications, Inc.
Cash Gorman   Street & Smith Publications, Inc.
Detective and Murder Mysteries   Columbia Publications, Inc.
Detective Story Annual   Street & Smith Publications, Inc.
Ellery Queen's Mystery Magazine (U.S.)   American Mercury, Inc.
G-Men Detective (British)   (publisher not known)
Hooded Detective   Columbia Publications, Inc.
New Detective Magazine   Fictioneers, Inc.
Red Hood Detective Stories   Albing Publications
Red Mask Detective Stories   Albing Publications
Ten Story Mystery   Fictioneers, Inc.

1942

Ace G-Man Stories (Canadian)   Popular Publications, Inc.
All Fiction Detective Stories   Street & Smith Publications, Inc.
Avon Murder Mystery Monthly   Avon Book Company

Dan Turner, Hollywood Detective   Culture Publications
DETECTIVE BOOK CLUB,   Walter J. Black, Inc.
Exciting Mystery   Nedor Publishing Company
Five-Detective Mysteries   Dell Publishing Co., Inc.
Love-Crime Detective   Frank A. Munsey Co.
Mammoth Detective   Ziff-Davis Publishing Co.
Movie Detective   (publisher not known)
Mystery Thrillers (British)   Gerald Swan
Shadow Annual, The   Street & Smith Publications, Inc.
Twelve Stories Detective Tales   (publisher not known)

1943

Baffling Detective Mysteries   Baffling Mysteries, Inc.
Crack Detective Stories   Columbia Publications, Inc.
Flynn's Detective Fiction Weekly   Popular Publications
Hollywood Detective   Culture Publications, Inc.
Martin Speed, Detective (British)   Gerald Swan
Speed Detective   Culture (Trojan) Publications
Speed Mystery   Culture (Trojan) Publications

1944

Detective Novel Magazine   Better Publications, Inc.
Gang Shorts (British)   Gerald Swan

1945

Craig Rice Mystery Digest   Bonded Publications
Detective Shorts (British)   Gerald Swan
Inspector Malone's Mystery Magazine   Ver Halen Publications
Mammoth Mystery   Ziff-Davis Publications
Mystery Book Magazine   William Wise & Company
Rex Stout Mystery Magazine   Avon Book Company
Rex Stout Mystery Quarterly   Avon Book Company
Saint's Choice, The   Bond-Charteris Enterprises
Third Degree, The   Mystery Writers of America
UNICORN MYSTERY BOOK CLUB   Unicorn Press Pub., Inc.

1946

Baker Street Journal, The   Ben Abramson
Craig Rice Crime Digest   Anson Bond Publications, Inc.
Movie Mystery Magazine   Anson Bond Publications, Inc.
Phoenix Mystery Novels (British)   Phoenix Press, Ltd.
Rex Stout's Mystery Monthly   Avon Book Company
Suspense—The Mystery Magazine   Suspense Magazine, Inc.
2-Book Mystery Magazine   Golden Willow Press, Inc.

1947

Avon Detective Mysteries   Avon Book Company
Best Detective   Exclusive Detective Stories, Inc.

Doc Savage, Science Detective   Street & Smith Publications, Inc.
Private Detective (Canada)   Duchess Printing & Publishing Co., Ltd.
Shadow Mystery Magazine, The   Street & Smith Publications, Inc.
Scientific Detective   ERB Book Company
Triple Detective   Best Publications, Inc.

1948

All Fiction Detective Anthology   Street & Smith Publications, Inc.
Detective Tales-Pocket (British)   T.V. Boardman & Company, Ltd.
THE MYSTERY GUILD (BOOK CLUB)   Doubleday & Co.
Shock   New Publications, Inc.

1949

All-Story Detective   Popular Publications, Inc.
Captain Zero   Recreational Reading, Inc.
Detective (British)   Gerald Swan
Detective Tales (British)   T.V. Boardman & Co.
Famous Detective   Columbia Publications, Inc.
F.B.I. Detective Stories   All-Fiction Field, Inc.
Five Detective Novels   Standard Magazines, Inc.
London Mystery Magazine (British)   Hulton Press, Ltd.
New Detective Tales (British)   T.V. Boardman & Co.
Private Detective   Trojan Publishing Corporation

1950

All Mystery   Dell Publishing Co., Inc.
15 Mystery Stories   Popular Publications, Inc.
15 Story Detective   Popular Publications, Inc.
Giant Detective Annual   Standard Publications, Inc.
Hollywood Detective Magazine   Trojan Magazines
19 Tales of Intrigue, Mystery and Adventure   (publisher not known)
Pocket Detective Magazine   Trojan Magazines, Inc.
Scarab Mystery Magazine   Black Horse Press, Inc.
Top Detective Annual   Best Books, Inc.
2 Detective Mystery Novels   Standard Magazines, Inc.

1951

Detective Fiction   Popular Publications, Inc.
Giant Detective   Best Publications, Inc.
Mysterious Traveler Magazine, The   Grace Publishing Co., Inc.
Slick Detective Yarns (British)   Gerald Swan
Smashing Detective   Columbia Publications, Inc.
Suspense (U.S.)   Farrell Publishing Corp.
Suspense Novels   Farrell Publishing Corp.

1952

Detective Tales (British)   Atlas Publishing and Distributing Co., Ltd.
Dimebooks Detective Stories (Canadian)   Dimebooks Corporation

MacKill's Mystery Magazine (British)   Todd Publishing Group, Ltd.
Mobsters   Standard Magazines, Inc.
Mysterious Traveler Mystery Reader   Grace Publishing Co., Inc.
Sherlock Holmes Journal, The (British)   Sherlock Holmes Society
Strange   Quinn Publishing Co., Inc.

1953

Conflict   Ziff-Davis Publishing Co.
Detective Story Magazine (British)   (publisher not known)
Ellery Queen's Mystery Magazine (British)   Mellifont Press, Ltd.
Fifteen Detective Stories   Popular Publications, Inc.
Manhunt (British)   Monthly Magazines, Ltd.
Manhunt (U.S.)   Eagle Publications, Inc.
Private Eye   Future Publications, Inc.
Pursuit Detective Story Magazine   Star Publications, Inc.
Saint Detective Magazine, The   King-Size Publications, Inc.
Super Detective Library (British)   Amalgamated Press, Ltd.
Verdict   Flying Eagle Publications, Inc.
Verdict (British)   Monthly Magazines, Ltd.

1954

Double-Action Detective Stories   Columbia Publications, Inc.
Hunted Detective Story Magazine   Star Publications, Inc.
Malcolm's   R. Malcolm & Associates
Menace   St. John Publishing Corp.
Nero Wolfe Mystery Magazine   Hillman Periodicals, Inc.
Saint Detective Magazine, The (British)   Magazine Enterprises
Suspense Stories (British)   Curtis Warren, Ltd.

1955

Dell Mystery Novels   Dell Publishing Co., Inc.
Justice   Non-Pareil Pub. Corporation
Mercury Mystery-Book Magazine   Mercury Publications, Inc.
Street & Smith Mystery Detective (British)   (publisher not known)
Suspect Detective Stories   Royal Publications, Inc.

1956

Accused Detective Story Magazine   Atlantis Publishing Co., Inc.
Alfred Hitchcock's Mystery Magazine   H.S.D. Publications, Inc.
Crack Detective and Mystery Stories   Columbia Publications, Inc.
Crime and Justice Detective Story Magazine   Arnold Magazines, Inc.
Detective Files   Caravan Books, Inc.
Guilty Detective Story Magazine   Feature Publications, Inc.
Homicide Detective Story Magazine   Arnold Magazines, Inc.
John Creasey Mystery Magazine (British)   Dalrow Publishing Co.
Mantrap   Secret Life Publications, Inc.
Michael Shayne Mystery Magazine (U.S.)   Renown Publications, Inc.
Murder   Flying Eagle Publications, Inc.

Private Investigator Detective Magazine   Republic Features Syndicate, Inc.
Red Herrings (British)   Crime Writer's Association
Terror Detective Story Magazine   Arnold Magazines, Inc.
Trapped Detective Story Magazine   Headline Publications, Inc.
Verdict Crime Detection Magazine   Secret Life Publications, Inc.

1957

Alfred Hitchcock's Mystery Magazine (British)   Strato Publications, Ltd.
American Agent   Republic Features Syndicate, Inc.
Double-Action Detective and Mystery Stories   Columbia Publications, Inc.
Fast Action Detective and Mystery Stories   Columbia Publications, Inc.
Killers Mystery Story Magazine   Arnold Magazines, Inc.
Macabre   Joseph Payne Brennan
Mike Shayne Mystery Magazine (British)   Frew Publications Pty., Ltd.
Mike Shayne Mystery Magazine (U.S.)   Renown Publications, Inc.
Mystery Digest   Passer Press Company
Phantom (British)   Vernon Publications (Bolton) Ltd.
Saturn Web   Candar Publishing Co., Inc.
Sure Fire Detective Story Magazine   Pontiac Publishing Corporation
Tales of the Frightened   Republic Features Syndicate, Inc.

1958

Bestseller Mystery Magazine   Mercury Press, Inc.
Mystery Tales   Atlas Magazines, Inc.
London Mystery Selection   Norman Kark Publications
Off Beat Detective Stories   Pontiac Publishing Corporation
Saint Mystery Magazine, The   King-Size Publications, Inc.
Sleuth Mystery Magazine   Fosdeck Publications, Inc.
Suspense (British)   Amalgamated Press, Ltd.

1959

Saint Mystery Library   Great American Publications, Inc.
Two-Fisted Detective Stories   Reese Publishing Co., Inc.

1960

Ed McBain's Mystery Book   Pocket Books, Inc.
Fear!   Great American Publications
Keyhole Mystery Magazine   Winston Publications, Inc.
77 Sunset Strip   Great American Publications, Inc.
Shock—The Magazine of Terrifying Tales   Winston Publications, Inc.
Tightrope!   Great American Publications, Inc.

1961

Bloodhound Detective Story Magazine (British)   T.V. Boardman & Company, Ltd.
Phantom Mystery Magazine (British)   Atlas Publishing & Distributing Co., Ltd.
Shock Mystery Tales   Pontiac Publishing Corporation

1962

Guilty   Feature Publications, Inc.
Keyhole Detective Story Magazine   Pontiac Publishing Corporation

1963

Magazine of Horror and Strange Stories   Health Knowledge, Inc.
Mercury Mystery Magazine (British)   Atlas Publishing & Distributing Co., Ltd.
Pulp Era, The   Lynn Hickman

1964

Chase   Health Knowledge, Inc.
Edgar Wallace Mystery Magazine (British)   Micron Publications Ltd.

1965

Bizarre! Mystery Magazine   Pamar Enterprises, Inc.
Bronze Shadows   Fred Cook
Intrigue   Pamar Enterprises, Inc.
JDM Bibliophile   Len and June Moffatt

1966

Edgar Wallace Mystery Magazine (U.S.)   Classic Mystery Publications, Inc.
Girl from U.N.C.L.E. Magazine, The   Leo Margulies Corporation
Man from U.N.C.L.E. Magazine, The   Leo Margulies Corporation
Saint Magazine, The   Fiction Publishing Co.
Shell Scott Mystery Magazine   LeMarg Publishing Corporation
Startling Mystery Stories   Health Knowledge, Inc.

1967

Armchair Detective, The   Allen J. Hubin
Mystery Lover's Newsletter, The   Lianne Carlin
Pontine Dossier, The   Luther Norris
Secret Agent Series (British)   Fleetway Publications, Ltd.
Tutter Bugle, The   Juvenile Jupiter Detective Association
Whodunit?   I.D. Publications, Inc.

1968

Queen Canon Bibliophile, The   Rev. Robert E. Washer
Rohmer Review, The   Dr. Douglas A. Rossman

1969

Coven 13   Camelot Publishing Co.
Edgar Wallace Club Newsletter (British)   Penelope Wallace
Faust Collector, The   William J. Clark
Mystery Reader's Newsletter, The   Lianne Carlin
Weird Terror Tales   Health Knowledge, Inc.

1970

Pontine Dossier Annual, The   Luther Norris
Pulp   Robert Weinberg
Weird Mystery   Ultimate Publishing Co.

1971

Ellery Queen Review, The   Rev. Robert E. Washer
Mystery Trader, The (British)   Ethel Lindsay
Witchcraft & Sorcery   Fantasy Publishing Co., Inc.

1973

Charlie Chan Mystery Magazine   Renown Books, Inc.
Current Crime (British)   Nigel Morland
Doc Savage Reader, The   Cosgriff & Golden
Elementary, My Dear APA   DAPA-EM
Haunt of Horror, The   Marvel Comics Group

1974

*Mystery*File*   Steve Lewis
Xenophile   Nils Hardin

1975

Baker Street Miscellanea   Sciolist Press
Duende   Odyssey Publications, Inc.
Ed McBain's 87th Precinct Mystery Magazine   Leonard J. Ackerman Productions, Inc.
Executioner Mystery Magazine, The   Leonard I. Ackerman Productions, Inc.
Lone Wolfe   Lee E. Poleske
Mystery Nook, The   Donald Miller
Nero Wolfe and Archie Goodwin Fans Newsletter   Lee E. Poleske

1976

Dracula Journals, The (British)   The Dracula Journals
Fatal Kiss   Steve Lewis
Mystery Monitor, The   M Press
Mystery Monthly   Looking Glass Publications, Inc.
Science Fiction Collector, The (Canadian)   Pandora's Books Ltd.
Thorndyke File, The   Philip T. Asdell and John McAleer

1977

August Derleth Society Newsletter   Richard Fawcett
Black Box Mystery Magazine (Canadian)   Bakka Book Stores, Ltd.
Cloak and Dagger   Jim Huang
Doc Savage Club Reader, The   Frank Lewandowski
Mysterious Times   William A. Karpowicz, Jr.
Mystery Fancier, The   Guy M. Townsend

1978

Castle Dracula Quarterly   Gordon R. Guy
Echoes From the Pulps   Joseph Lewandowski
Holmesian Federation, The   Signe Landon
Notes for the Curious   Carrian Press
Not So Private Eye, The   Andy Jaysnovitch
Poisoned Pen, The   Jeffrey Meyerson

1979

Age of the Unicorn, The   Cook-McDowell Publications
Gazette, The   The Wolfe Pack
Mystery   Mystery Magazine, Inc.

1980

Clues: A Journal of Detection   Bowling Green University Popular Press
Doc Savage Quarterly   Bill Laidlaw
Mystery and Adventure Series Review, The   Fred Woodworth
Skullduggery   Cook-McDowell Publications

1981

Black Cat Mystery Magazine (Canadian)   March Chase Publishing
Cloak and Pistol   Joseph Lewandowski
Crime Digest   Davis Publications, Inc.
Dossier, The   International Spy Society
Mystic Double Agent X   Robert Jennings
Pulpette   Joseph Lewandowski
Shot Rang Out, A   Blue Star Book Store
Yellowback Library   Gil O'Gara

1982

Hamilton T. Caine's Short Story Newsletter   Hamilton T. Caine
Mystery News   Mystery News
Spiderweb   Corsair Press

AMERICAN TRUE-DETECTIVE MAGAZINES

While true-detective (accounts of actual crimes) periodicals are not the subject of this volume, some note should be made of these if for nothing more than identification, since many bear titles similar to fiction magazines.

These magazines appeared in great number, many with long runs, and some are still being published today. This list does not profess to be complete as there has been no attempt to make it so. Commencement dates, or period of publication, are shown when they are available.

Action Detective
Actual Detective Cases of Women in Crime (November 1937)
Amazing Detective Cases (June 1940)
American Detective Cases (May 1934)
Baffling Detective Fact Cases (1947)
Best True Fact Detective
Candid Detective
Case File Detective (1940)
Chief Detective (Winter 1946)
Confidential Detective
Crime Detective
Daring Detective (1934)
Detective Dragnet
Detective Parade (1945)
Detective World
Dynamic Detective (March 1937)
Exposed (1930s)
Famous Detective Cases
Front Page Detective
Gem Detective (Fall 1946)
Headline Detective (July 1939)

Human Detective
Inside Detective (March 1935)
International Detective (July 1933)
Master Detective (September 1929)
National Detective
Official Detective Stories
Prize Detective
Sizzling Detective
Special Detective (September 1937)
Startling Detective
True Crime Detective Cases
True Cases of Scotland Yard
True Detective
True Detective Cases
True Detective Mysteries
True Gangster Stories (1939–1942)
True Police Cases
Uncensored Detective
Voice of Experience
Women in Crime

Many readers are familiar with the lurid, sensational covers and contents of "true-detective" magazines that fill a sizable section of the newsstand today, but it is not generally known that, in essence, a similar type of story was the beginning of the detective dime novel a century ago and the grandfather of the crime fiction magazines of today.

What is generally recognized as the first detective dime novel was published in 1883 by the N. L. Munro Company, titled "Old Cap. Collier: or 'Piping' the New Haven Mystery," the first issue of the *Old Cap. Collier Library*.* Cap. Collier, of course, was a fictional detective, whose name was later used for a long series (over seven hundred) of novels, written by various authors, and describing the adventures of every kind of detective in all manner of places. Some started with a small percentage of fact, as in the first title noted; this describes the "horror" of "a comely young girl,...discovered in the water, face downward, DEAD!"[1]

Dime novels continued to use some measure of fact in many of the tales chronicled, and it was not until the late 1920s that a number of "true-crime" magazines began to appear, so labeled to differentiate them from fiction. They were, and continue to be, a success, appealing largely to a different readership than crime fiction, a readership that is horrified by the sensationalism which accompanied many of the crimes. The appeal may be likened to the morbid interest shown today when all rush to the scene of a crime or bloody accident, or even drive by later, just "to see."

True-crime magazines, written in fictional prose, were often accompanied by photographs of the principals and scenes of the crime, and such photos today make up a good portion of the magazines.

Historical crimes have had the same fascination as the more contemporary real-life thrillers and have played a prominent part in the true-crime magazines; both are apt to be embroidered with questionable details as well as emphasis on the gore.

Note

1. Edmund Pearson, *Dime Novels* (Boston: Little, Brown and Co., 1929), p. 138, taken from the *Old Cap. Collier Library*, no. 1 (1883).

CANADIAN TRUE-DETECTIVE MAGAZINES

Canada, like the United States, has experienced the "true-detective" magazine in which the truth that forms the bases of the accounts of actual crimes is perhaps heavily embellished by sensationalism. No attempt has been made here to offer a complete compilation. Rather, the following list is comprised of twenty-one Canadian "true-detective" publications that are in a sense all issues of a single multimagazine produced in Toronto between 1941 and 1950 under the editorship of the publisher, Alex Valentine:

American Detective Cases
Best True Fact Detective
Certified Detective Cases
Classic Detective
Confessions
Daring Confessions
Daring Crime Cases
Factual Detective Stories
Feature Detective Cases
Line-Up Detective Cases
Personal Experiences
Private Confessions
Private Love Affairs
Scoop Detective
Sensational Crime Confessions
Sensational Love Experiences
Special Detective Cases
Startling Confessions
Startling Crime Cases
Women in Crime
Worldly Confessions

To study the publishing data of these twenty-one magazines is to follow a multiplicity of companies (though always the same one) through a variety of addresses. There are three principal company names: Norman Book Company, 95 King Street East, from which these magazines were issued between 1941 and 1946; Pastime Publications Limited, of the same address, which produced the magazines for the next two years; and Alval (an obvious version of the publisher's name), the last address of all, at 159 Bay Street. The advertisements in the publications suggest the readership at which Valentine aimed: titles such as "How to Draw the Nude," "Come Into My Parlour," and squibs for marriage manuals, all liberally illustrated with scantily clad women, relevant or irrelevant to what is being sold. A book club offers any four novels for a dollar, "packed with passion," and the description may be used to characterize the stories themselves.

Though many of these stories are proffered as factual, this, too, must be seen as catering to a particular readership, one accustomed to a constant barrage of "fact" during and after the Second World War and continuing to look for verisimilitude. A great many of the stories are certainly more fiction than fact. For example, "I Knew the Heartbreak of Helen Morgan" characteristically allies a well-known actual tragedy with an imaginary incident. Even the covers mix fact with fiction, or alternate the two; they include line drawings of idealized or terrifying figures (mostly, of course, women), as well as photographs of Faye Emerson, Marjorie Reynolds, and even Boris Karloff. Within the stories themselves, the same illustrations appear again and again, further reminding the reader that what passes for fact is, after all, fiction, for the "real life" subjects of these illustrations are given different names in different stories.

The repetition of illustrations and of covers reminds us, too, that publishing these magazines must have been a shoestring operation: one can visualize the publisher moving ever further down King Street East, thence to the suburbs, thence back to the unfashionable end of Bay Street. An article in the Toronto *Globe and Mail* of March 15, 1975, quotes Valentine as saying that he was eventually driven out of business by *True Confessions*, in a court action which prevented his abundant use of the word "confessions" (and perhaps of the word "true" as well!) on his publications. While he lasted, however, he evidently catered (or pandered) to a need in the Toronto reading public. It is said that he habitually used Canadian illustrators, and one of his magazines carries the endearing rubric, "edited and produced in Canada by Trade Union workmen on Canadian paper." But there is little enough of true Canadian content in the stories themselves; the same *Globe and Mail* piece reports that Valentine would travel regularly to New York "to search the used-book stores for old plots safely out of print." And if the report is to be believed, the very facts of his business activities followed the stereotypes of fiction, for his chief writer was a sixty-year-old lady, spectacles perched on the end of her nose, who needed the money to put her two sons through college.

As the price of the magazines moves from fifteen cents to twenty-five, and as Faye Emerson gives way to Jane Wyman, we are following a brief and very minor chapter in Canadian cultural history; but its end is predictable. A giant American conglomerate, glossier but no less vulgar, and no more factual than its victim, usurps the home-grown product.

—*Barrie Hayne*

SHERLOCK HOLMES SCION SOCIETY PERIODICALS

The widespread interest in Sherlockiana is seen, in part, with the great number of local groups and societies formed to study, explore, enlarge, and comment on the stories written by A. Conan Doyle. Many of these groups have published newsletters and journals on a regular basis. While some are of general interest to all who like Sherlock Holmes and Dr. Watson, others are primarily of value only to their own members. These are listed here with the name of the society and location, although it should be noted that some are no longer published.

Note should be made that the four journals intended for wide circulation (*The Baker Street Journal,* * *Baker Street Miscellanea,* * *The Pontine Dossier,* * and *The Sherlock Holmes Journal* *) are surveyed in the profile-article section of this book. Those publications possibly discontinued are marked (X).

Afghanistan Perceivers Dispatch, The. The True Perceiver, Tulsa, Oklahoma.
Afghanistanzas. The Double-Barrelled Tiger Clubs of Champaign-Urbana, Urbana, Illinois.
Baker Street Cab Lantern, The (X). Ted Bergman, editor, Lidingo, Sweden.
Baker Street Collecting (X). The Baker Street Collectors, Hebron, Illinois.
Baker Street Gasogene (X). Publisher not known.
Baker Street Pages (X). The Pageboys, Bronx, New York.
Baker Street Regular, The. Arkansas Valley Investors, Ltd., Little Rock, Arkansas.
Bull Pup, The. The Loungers and Idlers of the Empire, Pomona, California 91767.
Camden House Journal, The. The Occupants of the Empty House, DuQuoin, Illinois.
Canadian Holmes. The Bootmakers of Toronto, Canada.
Commonplace Book, The. A. J. Peck, editor, New York, New York.
Common Scents Journal. The Followers of Toby's Nose, Louisville, Kentucky.
Confederate Canoneer, The. The Confederates of Wisteria Lodge, Atlanta, Georgia.
Cormorant's Ring, The (X). The Trained Cormorants of Long Beach, California.
Covert Notes. An Irish Secret Society in Buffalo (New York).
Devon County Chronicle, The. R. W. Hahn, editor, Lombard, Illinois.
Encyclical Letter (X). The Amateur Mendicant Society, Grosse Point Park, Michigan.

Feathers From the Nest. The Noble and Most Singular Order of the Blue Carbuncle, Portland, Oregon.

Fluffy Ash, The. The Arcadia Mixture of Ann Arbor, Michigan.

From the Mantelpiece. B. R. Beaman, editor, Stevens Point, Wisconsin.

Gamebag, The (X). J. V. Wilmunun, editor, Buhl, Minnesota.

Garroter, The. The Cavendish Squares Ltd., St. Louis, Missouri.

Gaslight. Deutsche Sherlock Holmes Gesellschaft, Braunschweig, West Germany.

General Communications. The Pleasant Pieces of Florida, St. Petersburg, Florida.

Grimpen Mire Gazette, The. Hugo's Companions, Park Forest, Illinois.

Honker, The. Goose Club of the Alpha Inn, Topanga, California.

Hurlstone Papers, The. The Musgrave Ritualists, Suffern, New York.

Hydraulic Press, The (X. The Eyford Engineers of San Diego (California).

Investigations. Atlanta-Area Sherlockians, Atlanta, Georgia.

Journal of the Amateur Mendicant Society. P. Corrick, editor, Madison, Wisconsin.

Kansas City Daily Journal. Great Alkali Plainsmen, Shawnee Mission, Kansas.

Lens, The. The Masters' Class, Philadelphia, Pennsylvania.

Medical Bulletin, The. Dr. Watson's Neglected Patients, Littleton, Colorado.

Montana Times, The. Holmes of the Big Sky, Alberton, Montana.

Morning Post, The. The Noble Bachelors of St. Louis, Kirkwood, Missouri.

Moulton's Sluice-Box. Moulton's Prospectors, Sun City, Arizona.

Mycroft's Messenger. D. S. Kluk, editor, Chicago, Illinois.

Naval Signals. Altamount's Agents, Schenectady, New York.

Northumberland Dispatch, The. Fifth Northumberland Fusiliers, Pittsburgh, Pennsylvania.

Notes From a Notorious Card Club (X). The Notorious Canary-Trainers of Madison, Menomonee Falls, Wisconsin.

Pink 'Un, The. The Hansom Wheels, Lexington, South Carolina.

Poldhu Bay Breeze. The Blustering Gales from the South-West, Torrance, California.

Prescott's Press. Three Garridebs, Eastchester, New York.

Racing Form, The. The Silver Blazers, Anchorage, Kentucky.

Rat's Tale, The. The Giant Rats of Sumatra, Memphis, Tennessee.

Register, The. The Mexborough Lodgers, El Paso, Texas.

Report. The Anderson Murderers of North Carolina, Skyland, North Carolina.

Report Card, The. The Board-School Beacons, Jewett City, Connecticut.

Reuter's Dispatch, The. The Final Problems, Hollis, New Hampshire.

Scandal Sheet, The. The Scandalous Bohemians of New Jersey, Middletown, New Jersey.

Serpentine Muse, The. Adventuresses of Sherlock Holmes, New York, New York.

Shades of Sherlock (X). Three Students Plus, Chappaqua, New York.

Sherlockiana. Sherlock Holmes Klubben i Danmark, Aalborg, Denmark.

Sherlockian Meddler. Non-Canonical Calabashes of Los Angeles, West Hollywood, California.

Sidelights of Holmes. Priory Scholars of Fenwick High School, Oak Park, Illinois.

Spokes from the Cycle. Society of the Solitary Cyclists, South Bend, Indiana.

Studies in Scarlet. Pearl River, New York.

Subjoined Paper, The. The Reigate Squires, Natrona Heights, Pennsylvania.

Three Pipe Problems. Baker Street Irrationals, Rockford, Illinois.

Timetable, The. The Seven Passengers, Anchorage, Kentucky.

Tonga Times. The Mini Tonga Scion Society, North Palm Beach, Florida.

Treaty, The. The Naval Treaty, St. Louis, Missouri.

Underground Jottings (X). Baker Street Underground of Cornell University, New York, New York.

Vermissa Daily Herald. San Francisco, California.

Wheelwritings. Hansoms of John Clayton, Peoria, Illinois.

OTHER PERIODICALS OF INTEREST TO THE COLLECTOR

Arkham Collector, The
A semiannual publication of Arkham House, Publishers, Inc., Sauk City, Wisconsin, *The Arkham Collector* existed from its Summer 1967 issue through Summer 1971 issue. Ten issues were published, and these were later offered hardbound; all are out of print. A quality, professional publication, the *Collector* featured announcements of forthcoming books, short stories, poetry, and related material, particularly on H. P. Lovecraft and August Derleth.

Avengers/Patrick Macnee Newsletter
As the publication of The Avengers/Patrick Macnee Fan Network, the *Newsletter* covers the books of The Avengers series and the different formats of the characters. It is published under the direction of Heather Firth, P. O. Box 1190, Belton, Missouri 64012.

Bony Bulletin
An irregularly published newsletter dedicated to the crime stories of Arthur W. Upfield and particularly those involving Inspector Bonaparte, the *Bony Bulletin* is edited and published by Philip T. Asdell, 5719 Jefferson Boulevard, Frederick, Maryland 21701.

Boy's Book Buff, The
One of the admirable boys'-books magazines, *The Boy's Book Buff* was suspended after seven issues (during 1977 and 1978), but with the promise of continuation. With coverage on the boys' series books in general, there is included those with mystery themes; and whether one collects this type of material or not, the magazine provides a healthy dose of nostalgia. It was edited and published by Robert Jennings, R.F.D. 2, Whiting Road, Dudley, Massachusetts 01570.

Boys' Book Collector, The
Published for thirteen issues, from Fall 1969 to 1973, this digest-size magazine featured articles, commentary, checklists, bibliographical data, reminiscences, letters, and how-

to articles on collecting boys' series books in general, including those with mystery elements. *The Boys' Book Collector* was edited by Alan S. Dikty and published by T. E. Dikty, 1105 Edgewater Drive, Naperville, Illinois 60540.

Chesterton Review

As the journal of The Chesterton Society, the *Chesterton Review* promotes critical interest in the works of G. K. Chesterton and in the author. The journal includes articles of comparison and on style and influence, reprints, foreign publications, new publications, commentary, reminiscences, reviews, bibliographies, and letters. The Chesterton Society has branches in England, Canada, France, Australia, Japan, Poland, and the United States. The *Review* is published by the Department of English, St. Thomas More College, University of Saskatchewan, 1437 College Drive, Saskatoon, Saskatchewan S7N 0W6, Canada, on a semiannual basis.

Collecting Paperbacks?

Collecting Paperbacks? is a quarterly publication of interest to all who collect paperback books and magazines, including those of the mystery, detective, and espionage fields. The magazine included regular columns by contributors, commentary, articles, questions and answers, checklists, bibliographical data, letters, reviews, and advertisements, and it had been published since March 1979 by Lance Casebeer, 934 Southeast 15th Street, Portland, Oregon 97214. It is now discontinued.

Collectors' Digest

Devoted to the collecting of old boys' papers, magazines, and books as published in England, this distinguished periodical was founded in 1946 by the late Herbert Leckenby and is now edited and produced monthly by Eric Fayne, Excelsior House, Crookham Road, Crookham, near Aldershot, Hampshire, England. Subscription to the *Collectors' Digest* is 3 pounds for six months by seal mail or 4.25 pounds by air mail. Subscribers must pay by postal money order.

Collectors' Digest Annual

A special publication by the publisher of *Collectors' Digest*, just before Christmas each year, the *Collectors' Digest Annual* was commenced in 1947. Inquire of the address above for acquisition details, sending international reply coupon for sea mail reply or two for air mail reply.

(*Note*: Several other publications of like nature are now defunct, but attention should be called to the *Old Boys' Journal* (edited by Henry Steele), published in 209 issues from 1929 to 1933; *Vanity Fair* (edited by Joseph Parks), 31 issues, 1917–1927, and its continuation, *Collectors' Miscellany*, published from 1928 to 1932 (24 issues). These were all published in England.

Doc Savage and Associates

Although but one issue of *Doc Savage and Associates* was published in February 1975, this periodical is of note for Doc Savage fans. It contained articles, commentary, and reviews, and it was published by Mark Stucle and George Rock (no address shown).

Huntress, The
A relatively new amateur magazine devoted to "The Avengers" television series, Patrick Macnee, and supporting cast, *The Huntress* is offset printed and published quarterly by Richard Davis, Box 1327, Harlan, Kentucky 40831.

Jack London Newsletter
Devoted to the life and works of Jack London, the *Jack London Newsletter* was edited by Hensley C.Woodbridge, Department of Foreign Languages and Literature, Faner Hall, Southern Illinois University, Carbondale, Illinois 62901. It had been published semiannually since 1967; present status is unknown.

Journal of the H. P. Lovecraft Society
The H. P. Lovecraft Society was formed in 1974 by Raymond H. Ramsey of Berkeley, California, and the *Journal* began in 1976, containing critical, biographical and bibliographical material on Howard Phillips Lovecraft. For various reasons, Ramsey was unable to continue, and the Society management was turned over to Scott Connors, P. O. Box 354, South Heights, Pennsylvania 15801, who published a second *Journal* issue in 1979.

London Collector
The *London Collector* is a journal on Jack London and his books, containing bibliographies, news and commentary, and reviews. It is edited by Richard Weiderman, 1420 Pontiac Road S.E., Grand Rapids, Michigan 49506.

Man of Bronze, The
A publication limited to one issue in 1975 on Doc Savage and related material, *The Man of Bronze* was published and edited by John Boehm, 107 Stoneybrooke Drive, Ashland, Kentucky 41101, and Mark Justice, 1708 Callihan Street, Flatwoods, Kentucky 41139.

Paperback Quarterly
Subtitled "Journal of Mass Market Paperback History," this quality magazine emphasizes all facets of the paperback book, with special attention to bibliographical material including information on publishers. While the *Paperback Quarterly* is not limited to mystery fiction, this genre does comprise a major portion among the interviews, indexes, checklists, bibliographies, commentaries, book reviews, and letters. It was published by The Pecan Valley Press, 1710 Vincent Street, Brownwood,Texas 76801, and edited by Billy C. Lee and Charlotte Laughlin but is now discontinued.

Penguin Collector's Society Newsletter
Of interest to all collectors and students of paperbacks and paperback publishing, this is the semiannual newsletter of the Penguin Collector's Society, c/o Richard Smith, 30 Alexandra Grove, London N.4, England. Penguin has published many books of mystery and espionage. The Society was organized in 1974 and has also published *The King Penguin Series*, an excellent checklist and bibliography of Penguin's King Series paperbacks.

Poe Messenger
The *Poe Messenger* is a journal on the works of Edgar Allan Poe, published on an irregular basis since 1970 by the Poe Foundation, Edgar Allan Poe Museum, 1914–16 East Main Street, Richmond, Virginia 23223.

Poe Studies
Formerly the *Poe Newsletter*, the *Poe Studies* is edited by G. R. Thompson, Department of English, Purdue University, Lafayette, Indiana 47907, and is published semiannually, with scholarly articles on Edgar Allan Poe and his works.

Poe Studies Association Newsletter
Published semiannually since May 1973 and devoted to scholarly studies of Edgar Allan Poe and his works, the *Newsletter* is edited by Eric W. Carlson, John E. Reilly, and Richard P. Benton. The Association address is c/o J. Lasley Dameron, Department of English, Memphis State University, Memphis, Tennessee 38152.

Puck
Puck was an unpredictable journal, now discontinued, devoted to books, collectors, Edgar Rice Burroughs, the West, pulp fiction, and escape literature in general. It was published by R. & J. Kudlay, 4 Concord Street, Gloucester, Massachusetts 01930. The last issue published was in mid-1979, volume 2, number 4.

Pulpwoody
Pulpwoody, a newsletter, was limited to two issues, featuring news, columns of comment, and reviews on pulp fandom and pulp fiction. It was published during 1981 by Link Hullar, 10942 North Freeway, Suite 203, Houston, Texas 77037.

State of Shock
A monthly newsletter concentrating on horror and thriller books and films, *State of Shock* commenced in 1982 and was published by State of Shock, P.O. Box 395, Mattoon, Illinois 61938.

Weird Tales Collector, The
As a journal devoted to all facets of *Weird Tales* magazine, especially its authors and stories, *The Weird Tales Collector* has maintained a high level of quality with the many articles, reminiscences, and other material, and it has published within its six issues to date (since 1977) a complete index to *Weird Tales* magazine, as well as other bibliographical material. It is published by Robert Weinberg, 15145 Oxford Drive, Oak Forest, Illinois 60452.

Wold Atlas, The
A somewhat unique periodical with emphasis on speculative pastiches, especially pertaining to Doc Savage, The Shadow, Sherlock Holmes, and other pulp and detective heroes, *The Wold Atlas* was discontinued in Fall 1978 after five issues.

SELECTED BIBLIOGRAPHY

Bragin, Charles. *Dime Novels Bibliography 1860–1928*. Brooklyn, N.Y.: privately published, 1938.

Breen, Jon L., *What About Murder: A Guide to Books About Mystery and Detective Fiction*. Metuchen, N.J.: The Scarecrow Press, Inc., 1981.

Cockcroft, T.G.L. *Index to the Weird Fiction Magazines*, Vols. 1 and 2. Lower Hutt, New Zealand: privately published, 1962, 1964.

Cook, Michael L. *Monthly Murders*. Westport, Conn.: Greenwood Press, 1982.

———. *Murder by Mail: Inside the Mystery Book Clubs*. Evansville, Ind.: Cook Publications, 1979.

Cox, J. Randolph. *New Nick Carter Weekly*. Fall River, Mass.: Edward T. LeBlanc Publisher, 1974.

———. *Nick Carter Library*, Fall River, Mass.: Edward T. LeBlanc Publisher, 1974.

———. *Nick Carter Stories and Other Series Containing Stories About Nick Carter*, Parts 1 and 2. Fall River, Mass.: Edward T. LeBlanc Publisher, 1977, 1980.

DeWaal, Ronald Burt. *The International Sherlock Holmes*. Hamden, Conn.: Archon Books, 1980.

———. *The World Bibliography of Sherlock Holmes and Dr. Watson*. Boston, Mass.: New York Graphic Society, 1974.

Gibson, Walter B. *The Shadow Scrapbook*. New York, N.Y.: Harcourt Brace Jovanovich, 1979.

Goodstone, Tony, ed. *The Pulps*. New York, N.Y.: Bonanza Books, 1970.

Goulart, Ron. *Cheap Thrills*. New Rochelle, N.Y.: Arlington House, 1972.

Gruber, Frank. *The Pulp Jungle*. Los Angeles, Calif.: Sherbourne Press, Inc., 1967.

Haining, Peter, ed. *The Fantastic Pulps*. New York, N.Y.: Vintage Books, 1975.

———. *Weird Tales*. Jersey, Channel Islands, U.K.: Neville Spearman (Jersey) Limited, 1976.

Hersey, Harold B. *Pulpwood Editor*. New York, N.Y.: Frederick A. Stokes Co., 1937.

Inge, M. Thomas, ed. *Handbook of American Popular Culture*, Vols. 1 and 2. Westport, Conn.: Greenwood Press, 1978.

Johannsen, Albert. *The House of Beadle and Adams and Its Dime and Nickel Novels*, Vols. 1–3. Norman, Okla.: University of Oklahoma Press, 1950, 1962.

Jones, Daryl. *The Dime Novel Western*. Bowling Green, Ohio: The Popular Press, Bowling Green State University, 1978.

Jones, Robert Kenneth. *The Shudder Pulps*. West Linn, Ore.: Fax Collector Editions, 1975.

Lofts, W.O.G., and Derek Adley. *The British Bibliography of Edgar Wallace*. London, England: Howard Baker Publishers Ltd., 1969.

———. *The Men Behind Boys' Fiction*. London, England: Howard Baker Publishers Ltd., 1970.

———. *Old Boys Books: A Complete Catalogue*. London, England: privately printed, 1969.

———. *The Saint and Leslie Charteris, A Biography*. Bowling Green, Ohio: The Popular Press, Bowling Green State University, 1972.

Melvin, David Skene, and Ann Skene. *Crime, Detective, Espionage, Mystery and Thriller Fiction & Film*. Westport, Conn.: Greenwood Press, 1980.

Moskowitz, Sam. *Under the Moons of Mars*. New York, N.Y.: Holt, Rinehart & Winston, 1970.

Mott, Frank Luther. *A History of American Magazines*, Vols. 3 and 4. Cambridge, Mass.: Harvard University Press, 1938.

Murray, Will. *The Duende History of The Shadow Magazine*. Greenwood, Mass.: Odyssey Publications, 1980.

Nevins, Francis M., Jr. *Royal Bloodline: Ellery Queen Author and Detective*. Bowling Green, Ohio: The Popular Press, Bowling Green State University, 1974.

Noel, Mary. *Villains Galore: The Heyday of the Popular Story Weekly*. New York, N.Y.: The Macmillan Company, 1954.

O'Brien, Geoffrey. *Hardboiled America*. New York, N.Y.: Van Nostrand Reinhold Company, 1981.

Pearson, Edmund. *Dime Novels*. New York, N.Y.: Little, Brown and Company, 1929.

Reynolds, Quentin. *The Fiction Factory*. New York, N.Y.: Random House, 1955.

Sampson, Robert. *The Night Master*. Chicago, Ill.: Pulp Press, 1982.

San Francisco Academy of Comic Art. "Pulp Magazines, A Tentative Checklist." Unpublished.

Schreuders, Piet. *Paperbacks, U.S.A*. San Diego, Calif.: Blue Dolphin Enterprises, Inc., 1981.

Smith, Myron J., Jr. *Cloak-and-Dagger Bibliography: An Annotated Guide to Spy Fiction 1937–1975*. Metuchen, N.J.: The Scarecrow Press, 1976.

Stern, Madeleine B., ed. *Publishers for Mass Entertainment in Nineteenth Century America*. Boston, Mass.: G. K. Hall & Company, 1980.

Syracuse University. "Street & Smith Collection, Shelf List." Unpublished.

Titus, Edna Brown, ed. *Union List of Serials in Libraries of the United States and Canada*, Vols. 1–5. New York, N.Y.: H. W. Wilson Company, 1965.

Turner, E. S. *Boys Will Be Boys*. London, England: Michael Joseph Ltd., 1948.

University of California Los Angeles, "Shelf List [card file], Pulp Magazines." Unpublished.

Weinberg, Robert. *The Weird Tales Story*. West Linn, Ore.: Fax Collectors Editions, 1977.

Wertham, Fredric. *The World of Fanzines*. Carbondale, Ill.: Southern Illinois University, 1973.

INDEX

Magazines and descriptive material included in those sections of the appendix pertaining to foreign magazines, and to other lists of material in the appendix, are not included in the index. The fictional characters discussed in this book have likewise been omitted from the index except for those of general interest. Page numbers of magazine profiles are in italics.

CONTRIBUTORS

ROBERT CLIVE SMITH ADEY, Stourbridge, West Midlands, England. Surveyor in Her Majesty's Customs & Excise Service; member of the Crime Writers Association; special interest in "locked room mysteries in short story form"; author of *Locked Room Murders* (1979); articles published in *Antiquarian Book Monthly, The Mystery Fancier, The Poisoned Pen*, and *The Armchair Detective*.

DEREK JOHN ADLEY, South Harrow, Middlesex, England. Author of *The British Bibliography of Edgar Wallace* (1969); *The Saint and Leslie Charteris* (1970); *The Men Behind Boys Fiction* (1970); *The World of Frank Richards* (1972); *William A Bibliography* (1972); *The Rupert Index* (1974); *Old Boys Books, A Complete Catalogue* (1969), and others; has had hundreds of articles appear in various publications.

WALTER ALBERT, Pittsburgh, Pennsylvania. Professor of French, University of Pittsburgh (since 1967); member of the Modern Language Association and the American Association of Teachers of French; special interest in secondary sources bibliography; editor/translator of *Selected Writings of Blaise Cendrars* (1966); author of *A Bibliography of Secondary Sources (Mystery & Related)* (in preparation); articles published in *The Armchair Detective, The Mystery Fancier, Enigmatika*, and others.

MICHAEL ANGELO AVALLONE, JR., East Brunswick, New Jersey. Writer and lecturer; formerly an editor, journalist, cartoonist, film critic; awards include Literary Luminary New Jersey 1977, Writer of the Year 1982; author of 190 books (suspense, science fiction, gothic, horror, children's, romance, mystery, detective, western, how-to, war, and hundreds of short stories and articles); hailed as "The Fastest Typewriter in the East."

JANE SCHNABEL BAKERMAN, Terre Haute, Indiana. Associate Professor of English, West Virginia Wesleyan College (1959-1964), Professor of English, Indiana State University (1964-   ); member of the Mystery Writers of America, Modern Language Association, Society for the Study of Midwestern Literature; special interest in female crime writers and English country houses; over 100 articles, reviews, and interviews published in *The Mystery Fancier; The Armchair Detec-*

tive, American Literature, Clues, Writers Digest, and other publications; adviser and contributor to *Twentieth Century Crime and Mystery Writers* (1980) and to *American Women Writers* (1977).

MICHAEL S. BARSON, Brooklyn, New York. Writer; special interest in hard-boiled detective fiction; articles published in *Publishers Weekly, Heavy Metal, Fanfare, Clues, The Armchair Detective, Paperback Quarterly, The Journal of Poplar Culture*, and other publications.

ALBERT DAVID BATES, Putnam, Connecticut. Proprietor of the Blue Star Book Store (with wife) since 1975; member of the Paperback Collector's Guild, International Wizard of Oz Club; articles published in *Collecting Paperbacks?; Paperback Advertiser; Saddles, Sixguns & Sagebrush; The Poisoned Pen*; and other publications; contributor to *The Conan Companion* (1975).

DANA MARTIN BATORY, Crestline, Ohio. Freelance writer, miniature-cabinet maker; special interest in authors Sir Arthur Conan Doyle, Wilkie Collins, and Sax Rohmer; member of The Count Dracula Society of Great Britain; author of *The Annotated "The Lost World"* (1983), *The Annotated "The War of the Worlds"* (1983), and *The Annotated "A Journey to the Center of the Earth"* (in preparation); articles published in *Baker Street Miscellanea, The Sherlock Holmes Journal, The Riverside Quarterly, The Age of the Unicorn, Megavore, The Journal of Popular Fiction, The Science Fiction Collector, The Holmesian Federation, Rocks and Minerals*, and *The Dracula Journals*; blames interest in Dracula on fact that he is a descendant of Stephen Bathory (1444-1493), who put the historical Dracula back on his throne for the third and last time in 1476, and of Elizabeth Bathory (1570-1614), the "Blood Countess" of Hungary, one of the history's few genuine vampiresses.

LESTER CRYSTAL BELCHER, Saltville, Virginia. Machinist, landscape artist; special interest in pulp heroes The Black Bat, The Shadow, The Spider; pulp magazine researcher.

PETER E. BLAU, Washington, D.C. Correspondent for the Petroleum Information Corp. (1974-   ); editor of *The Baker Street Journal*, Fordham University Press, (1982-   ); special interest in Sir Arthur Conan Doyle and Sherlock Holmes; articles published in *The Baker Street Journal; Baker Street Miscellanea, The Pontine Dossier*, and *Geotimes*.

WOODA NICHOLAS CARR, Mesa, Arizona. U.S. Army (retired); awarded The Lamont Award at Pulpcon 7, 1978; co-founder of Pulpsters Ltd.; special interest in the hero pulp magazines; author of *America's Secret Service Ace* (1974); *The Flying Spy* (1978); articles in *Bronze Shadows, The Pulp Era, The Mystery Reader's Newsletter, The Mystery Fancier, Stan's Weekly Express, Pulp, The Good Old Days, Penny Dreadful, Xenophile, Fantasy Mongers, Bakka Magazine, The Doc Savage Club Reader, The Age of the Unicorn*; fiction in *Skullduggery*; pseudonym: Dickson Thorpe.

FAITH CLARE-JOYNT, Toronto, Ontario, Canada. Editorial and production assistant in London (1949-1954), in R.A.F. Photographic Intelligence in England and Germany, (1954-1958), in advertising and public relations (1959-1967), rights editor for Macmillan of Canada (1967-1974), executive assistant of *Globe & Mail* (1974-1980), president of March Chase Publishing (1980-   ); member of the Canadian Periodical Publishers Association; publisher and editor of the *Black Cat*

Mystery Magazine; author of a book on Lancashire (England) cotton mills (in prepration).

J. RANDOLPH COX, Northfield, Minnesota. Librarian and instructor, St. Olaf College; special interest in boys' literature, the American dime novel and its British equivalent, and mystery fiction; author of *New Nick Carter Weekly* (1975), *Nick Carter Library* (1974), *Nick Carter Stories* (1977), *Nick Carter Stories and Other Series Containing Stories About Nick Carter* (1980); many articles published, including in *The Armchair Detective, The Mystery Reader's Newsletter, The Tutter Bugle, The Pulp Era, Clues, Bronze Shadows, Xenophile*, and *The Poisoned Pen*.

DAVID H. DOERRER, Pensacola, Florida. Librarian, University of West Florida (since 1976); previously librarian, Cornell University (1966-1973) and librarian, Iowa State University (1973-1976); received honorable mention, Woodrow Wilson Fellowship; articles published in *College and Research Libraries News*; special interest in espionage fiction and thrillers.

BERNARD ALGER DREW, Great Barrington, Massachusetts. Freelance writer since 1977; assistant editor (1980-1981) and editor (1981-   ) of *The Berkshire Courier*; author of a regional history, *Berkshire Off the Trail* (1982); has had over 500 articles published in national and regional magazines and newspapers, including in *Gallery, The Canadian Magazine, Sea, Writer's Digest, Camping Journal, The Washingtonian, Arizona*, and others; editor and publisher of *Attic Revivals*, a series of pulp magazine story reprints.

FREDERICK R. DUEREN, Shawnee Mission, Kansas. Wausau Insurance Company claim adjuster (1967), supervisor (1974), compensation claim manager (1980); special interest in series detectives; articles published in *The Armchair Detective, The Mystery Fancier*; adviser and contributor to *Twentieth Century Crime and Mystery Writers* (1980); and narrator, "The Mystery Forum," weekly cable television show.

RICHARD HAROLD FAWCETT, Uncasville, Connecticut. Assistant superintendent, Montville Public Schools, Oakdale, Connecticut (1970-   ); editor and publisher of the *August Derleth Society Newsletter*; co-editor and founder of *Fantasy Macabre*; book on August Derleth in preparation; articles in *The August Derleth Society Newsletter and New England School Development Council*.

GRAEME KENNETH FLANAGAN, Canberra City, Australia. Department of Defense (Finance), Australian government, since 1966; special interest in research on Australian mystery magazines; music critic for *International Record Buyers Guide*; former editor of *Crazy Music* (The Australian Blues Society); member of U.S. amateur press associations for H. P. Lovecraft and Robert E. Howard studies; author of *Robert Bloch: A Bio-Bibliography* (1979).

JANE GOTTSCHALK, Oshkosh, Wisconsin. Instructor of English, Marquette University (1959-1962); assistant professor (1965-1967), associate professor (1967-1970), professor (1970-   ) of English, University of Wisconsin, Oshkosh; articles in *The Armchair Detective, Philological Quarterly, Phylon, Renascence, The Wisconsin Review*, and others.

MARY ANN GROCHOWSKI, West Allis, Wisconsin. Freelance writer; psychotherapist, for the Family Social and Psychotherapy Services West Allis, Wisconsin; speaker for the Mental Health Association of Milwaukee Co.; member of the Mystery Writers of America; special interests in "locked room" murders, female private investigators, British and American authors of the 1940s; adviser and contributor to *Twentieth Century Crime and Mystery Writers* (1980); articles in *The Poisoned Pen, The Armchair Detective; The Mystery Fancier, The Milwaukee Journal, The Therapist.*

FRANÇOIS GUÈRIF, Paris, France. Reporter for *TeleCine Video* editor of *Polar* mystery magazine; member of Les Amis de la Littèrature Policiere; author of *Paul Newman* (1975), *Redford* (1976), *Marlon Brando* (1976, 1979), *Steve McQueen* (1978), *Le Film Noir Americain* (1979), *Le Cinema Policier Français* (1981); articles published in *Polar, TeleCine Video, L'Éxpress, la Revue du Cinema, Mystere Magazine, Pilote.*

E. R. HAGEMANN, Louisville, Kentucky. Professor of English, University of Louisville, (1954-1959, 1964-   ); special interest in hard-boiled, tough-guy, private eye fiction; author of many books in the western and other fields, the latest being *A Comprehensive Index to Black Mask 1920-1951* (1982); some 60 articles on popular culture and American literature, bibliography, art, history, and so forth, plus over 125 book reviews, miscellaneous pieces, and professional papers.

HERBERT HARRIS, Ventnor, Isle of Wight, England. Writer; awarded the "Dagger" special merit award of Crime Writers Association for 1965, member of the Crime Writers Association (CWA) since 1954), founder of CWA's monthly bulletin, *Red Herrings*, chairman of the CWA during 1969-1970, honorary anthology editor of the CWA since 1965; member of the London Press Club since 1946; chairman of the Institute of Journalists, Free Lance Section, 1957; special interest in most short detective, mystery and suspense stories; author of *Who Kill to Live* (1962), *Serpents in Paradise* (1975), *The Angry Battalion* (1976); editor of *John Creasey's Mystery Bedside Book* (ten annual anthologies, 1966-1975), *John Creasey's Crime Collection* (six annual anthologies, 1977-1982), and *A Handful of Errors* (1978); named by the *Guinness Book of Records* since 1969 as the U.K.'s most prolific short-story writer, with some 3,5000 published in thirty countries and twenty languages, reprinted in thirty anthologies, and adapted for T.V. and radio drama (100 stories broadcast).

BARRIE HAYNE, Toronto, Ontario, Canada. Professor of English (teaches courses in popular culture, detective fiction), Innis College, University of Toronto; adviser and contributor to *Twentieth Century Crime and Mystery Writers* (1980).

IWAN SVEN HUGO HEDMAN-MORELIUS, Strängnäs, Sweden. Swedish Army (Medical), captain (retired); publisher of *DAST-Magazine*; book publisher, member of the Swedish Literary Association, The Mystery Writers of America, and Crime Writers Assocation; special interest in collecting mystery books in general (20,000) and has the largest extant collection of James Bond material; author of *Fyra Decennier med Dennis Wheatley* (1973), *Leslie Charteris & Helgonet under 4 Decennier* (1974), *grav i Sand* (1974), *Deckare & Thrillers pa Svenska 1964-1973* (1974), *Vara Popularforfattare* (1976), *Villa Naktergalen* (1978), *Detektiver pa Frimarken* (1978); articles published in *Espionage Actualité, Ellery Queen's Mystery Magazine* (French edition), *DAST-Magazine, The Armchair Detective, The Mystery Fancier,* and *The Mystery Reader's Newsletter.*

THOMAS EDWARD JOHNSON, Knox City, Texas. U.S. Army and U.S. Air Force, law enforcement (1958-1979); managerial (1979-   ); proprietor of a book store; special interest in hero pulp fiction; author of *Secret Agent X: A History* (1981) and *Into the Dawn World* (in preparation); articles published in many newspapers and in *Xenophile, Pulp, The Age of the Unicorn, The Doc Savage Club Reader,*

Doc Savage Quarterly, and other publications; editor and publisher of *Echoes*; pseudonym: John Edwards.

ROBERT KENNETH JONES, Arlington, Virginia. Managing editor of *Air Force Times*; special interest in weird-menace pulp magazines; author of *The Shudder Pulps* (1975); articles published in *Bronze Shadows, The Mystery Reader's Newletter, The Pulp Era*, and *Xenophile*.

BRIAN WAYNE KENKNIGHT, Northfield, Minnesota. Bookstore clerk; editor and publisher of *Small World of Murder* for mystery amateur press association; special interest in mystery fiction in general.

WILLIAM ALLEN LAIDLAW, San Luis Obispo, California. Home health aide and hospital volunteer, proprietor of the Hidalgo Mail Order Company; publisher and editor of the *Doc Savage Quarterly* and *International Dateline News*; special interest in hero pulp fiction; articles published in *The Age of the Unicorn, The Doc Savage Club Reader*, and *Doc Savage Quarterly*.

JOSEPH M. LEWANDOWSKI, San Juan Capistrano, California. Teacher and counselor, weather observer, machine operator, coremaker, quality-control technician, typesetter, perpetual student; Jennings Scholar, 1963-1964; special interest in photographing covers and interior illustrations of pulp magazines and dime novels; member of the Small Press Writers and Artists Organization; lecturer on pulp magazines and interior art illustrations; editor and publisher of *Echoes from the Pulps, Pulpette*, and *Cloak and Pistol*; articles published in *Fantaseer, Xenophile, Skullduggery, The Age of the Unicorn, Film Clippers Journal, Fantasy Mongers*, and *Megavore*.

ETHEL LINDSAY, Carnoustie, Angus, Scotland. Nursing officer (retired), state registered nurse; interest in mystery fiction in general; editor and publisher of *The Mystery Trader* (1971-1980); author of *Here Be Murder and Mystery: Reference Books in the Mystery Genre Excluding Sherlockiana* (1982); articles published in *The Poisoned Pen*.

WILLIAM OLIVER GUILLEMONT LOFTS, London, England. Occupation is classified under Official Secrets Act; writer, bibliographer, literary researcher; special interest in boys' fiction but is a recognized authority on popular fiction in general; co-author of *The British Bibliography of Edgar Wallace* (1969), *The Men Behind Boys Fiction* (1970), *Old Boys Books, A Complete Catalogue* (1969), *The Saint and Leslie Charteris* (1971); articles published in many periodicals, including in *The Saint Detective Magazine, The Armchair Detective, The Rohmer Review, The Mystery Reader's Newsletter, Dime Novel Roundup, Story Paper Collector's Digest,* and nearly 1,000 other articles.

ROBERT AUGUSTINE WARD LOWNDES, Hoboken, New Jersey. Production associate for Radio-Electronics (1948); managing editor of *Sexology* and *LUZ* (1941-1948), editor for Health Knowledge Publications (1960-1971), editor for (science-fiction) Avalon Books (1955-1967), editorial director of Columbia Publications (1941-1960); member of the Science Fiction Writers of America; author of *Mystery of the Third Mine* (1953), *The Duplicated Man* (with James Blish) (1953); *The Puzzle Planet* (1961), *Believers' World* (1961), and *Three Faces of Science Fiction* (1975); articles published in *The Armchair Detective, Famous Science Fiction, Exploring the Universe, Warhoon, Algol, Riverside Quarterly*, and many other publications.

JOHN J. McALEER, Lexington, Massachusetts. Professor of English, Boston University; special interest in Rex Stout and R. Austin Freeman; author of a number of books, both fiction and nonfiction, including *Rex Stout: A Biography* (1977), associate editor of *Rex Stout: An Annotated Primary and Secondary Bibliography* (1980), editor and publisher of *The Thorndyke File*.

JAMES R. McCAHERY, Union, New Jersey. Teacher of French language and literature at Xavier High School in New York (1960–), director of international student exchange at Xavier High School, past teacher of Romanian and Italian languages, Fulbright Scholar (1956–1957); listed in *Who's Who in Romanian America* (1976); editor and publisher of *Mystery Loves Company* for the mystery amateur press association; member of the Mystery Writers of America and the American Association of Teachers of French; adviser and contributor to *Twentieth Century Crime and Mystery Writers* (1980); articles published in *Megavore, The Poisoned Pen, The Not So Private Eye*, and other publications.

FRANK D. McSHERRY, JR., McAlester, Oklahoma. Writer, commercial artist; special interest in cases of vanished persons and in Sherlock Holmes; author of *Baseball 3000* (1981); contributor to *The Mystery Writer's Art* (1971); numerous articles in *The Armchair Detective* and other publications.

WILL MURRAY, North Quincy, Massachusetts. Writer and publisher for Odyssey Press; recipient of the Lamont Award, 1979; special interest in Doc Savage and other single-character pulp magazines; author of *The Man Behind Doc Savage* (1974), *The Duende History of The Shadow Magazine* (1980), *Secret Agent X: A History* (1980), *The Assassin's Handbook* (1981), and *Encounter Group* (in collaboration with Warren Murphy, a Destroyer novel, in preparation); over 200 articles, essays, interviews and stories published in *Ellery Queen's Mystery Magazine, Skullduggery, Pulp, Xenophile, Duende, The Doc Savage Reader, Echoes, The Age of the Unicorn, The Armchair Detective, Paperback Quarterly, Science Fiction Times,* and others; editor and publisher of *Duende*, past editor and co-publisher of *Skullduggery*.

FRANCIS MICHAEL NEVINS, JR., St. Louis, Missouri. Professor, St. Louis University School of Law (1971–); recipient of the Edgar Award from the Mystery Writers of America, 1975; member of the Mystery Writers of America; author of *Royal Bloodline: Ellery Queen, Author and Detective* (1974), *Publish and Perish* (1975), and *Corrupt and Ensnare* (1978); a great number of articles published in *The Armchair Detective, The Poisoned Pen, The Mystery Reader's Newsletter, The Queen Canon Bibliophile, Mystery, Notes for the Curious, Xenophile, JDM Bibliophile, The August Derleth Society Newsletter, The Mystery Fancier, Clues, The New Republic, Films in Review, Book Forum,* and *Journal of Popular Culture,* and other publications.

BJARNE NIELSEN, Copenhagen, Denmark. School teacher (1971–1977); antiquarian bookdealer (1977–); editor and publisher of *Pinkerton* (1981–); member of the Sherlock Holmes Klubben i Danmark and the Poe-Klubben; special interest in Sherlock Holmes; author of *Hvem Begik Hvad? Dansk Kriminallitteratur Indtil 1979: En Bibliografi* (1981), *A Case of Identity* (English translation; 1981), and *Sherlock Holmes I Danmark* (1981); articles published in *Kosmorama* and *Sunset Boulevard*.

NILS NORDBERG, Lorenskog, Norway. Writer; special interest in Scandinavian detective and crime fiction; author of *Mesterdetektiven Knut Gribb* (1968); articles in *DAST-Magazine* and other publications.

GILBERT WILLIAM O'GARA, Des Moines, Iowa. Freelance writer; managing editor of AppaNewspapers, Appanoose County, Iowa, (1979); editor and publisher of the *Yellowback Library*; special interest in boys' literature, dime novels, and story-papers; articles published in *The Antique Trader Weekly, Collectors News, The Book-Mart, The Age of the Unicorn, Dime Novel Roundup, Firehouse, Spinning Wheel, American Collector, Yellowback Library*, and other publications.

PAUL EDWARD PALMER, Tacoma, Washington. Custodian (1972–); special interest in mystery fiction in general, particularly in digest-size magazines; articles published in *Collecting Paperbacks?*

ROBERT DALE SAMPSON, Huntsville, Alabama. Publications editor in Huntsville, Alabama, and Middletown, Pennsylvania (1955–1965), assistant to the Office of the Director of Science and Engineering for the Marshall Space Flight Center (1965–1975), management analyst for the test laboratory of MSFC, (1975–); special interest in pulp magazines and Nick Carter dime novels; author of *The Night Master* (1982); *Yesterday's Faces: Glory Figures*, Vol. 1 (in press); short stories in *Planet Stories, Science Fiction Adventures, Skullduggery, Spiderweb*; articles published in *Xenophile, Dime Novel Roundup,The Mystery Fancier, The Age of the Unicorn, Clues, The Mystery Reader's Newsletter, The Science Fiction Collector, Pulp, The Doc Savage Reader, The Weird Tales Collector*, and other publications.

ARTHUR C. SCOTT, Cupertino, California. Research chemist for SRI International (1970–1981), research engineer for Kaiser Aluminum (1981–); special interest in private eye fiction and in paperback originals of the 1950–1960s; adviser and contributor to *Twentieth Century Crime & Mystery Writers* (1980); editor of *Elementary, My Dear APA* (parent publication, mystery amateur press association); articles published in *The Mystery Fancier, Collecting Paperbacks?, Inside Comics*, and other publications.

JAMES GRANT THIESSEN, Altona, Manitoba, Canada. Comptroller and accountant (1967–1976); proprietor of Pandora's Books Ltd. (1976–); editor and publisher of *The Science Fiction Collector/Megavore* (1976–1981); contributor to *The Weird Tales Story* (1977), author of *Science Fiction and Fantasy Authors* (1979) and *The Science Fiction Magazines* (in preparation); articles published in various publications, including *The Science Fiction Collector, Megavore, Famzine* (Italian); special interest in identifying pseudonyms and in near-future thrillers and private eye stories.

ALBERT BURTON TONIK, Dresher, Pennsylvania. Department head of logic design and a staff consultant for the Univac Division of Sperry Corporation; teacher of computer science courses at Villanova University; member of Phi Beta Kappa; special interest in multistory characters involving scientific gadgets; articles published in *The Age of the Unicorn*.

JO ANN VICAREL, University Heights, Ohio. Librarian for the Cleveland Public Library until 1972, librarian for the Cleveland Heights-University Heights Public Library since 1980; special interest in collecting and lecturing women crime writers in paperbacks; articles published in *The Armchair Detective, The Mystery Nook, The Mystery Fancier*, and other publications.

About the Author

MICHAEL L. COOK's earlier books include the *Genealogical Dictionary, Pioneer History of Washington County, Kentucky* (with Betty Cook), *Murder by Mail*, and *Monthly Murders* (Greenwood Press, 1982).